MARY STEWART MARY STEWART MARY STEWART
MARY STEWART MARY STEWART MARY STEWART
MARY STEWART MARY STEWART MARY STEWART
MARY STEWART MARY STEWART MARY STEWART
MARY STEWART MARY STEWART MARY STEWART
MARY STEWART MARY STEWART MARY STEWART
MARY STEWART MARY STEWART MARY STEWART
MARY STEWART MARY STEWART MARY STEWART
MARY STEWART MARY STEWART MARY STEWART
MARY STEWART MARY STEWART MARY STEWART
MARY STEWART MARY STEWART MARY STEWART
MARY STEWART MARY STEWART MARY STEWART
MARY STEWART MARY STEWART MARY STEWART
MARY STEWART MARY STEWART MARY STEWART
MARY STEWART MARY STEWART MARY STEWART
MARY STEWART MARY STEWART MARY STEWART
MARY STEWART MARY STEWART MARY STEWART
MARY STEWART MARY STEWART MARY STEWART
MARY STEWART MARY STEWART MARY STEWART
MARY STEWART MARY STEWART MARY STEWART
MARY STEWART MARY STEWART MARY STEWART
MARY STEWART MARY STEWART MARY STEWART
MARY STEWART MARY STEWART MARY STEWART
MARY STEWART MARY STEWART MARY STEWART
MARY STEWART MARY STEWART MARY STEWART
MARY STEWART MARY STEWART MARY STEWART
MARY STEWART MARY STEWART MARY STEWART
MARY STEWART MARY STEWART MARY STEWART
MARY STEWART MARY STEWART MARY STEWART

Malorah Ingraham

MARY STEWART

MARY STEWART

The Moonspinners

Nine Coaches Waiting

The Ivy Tree

Madam, Will You Talk?

Octopus/Heinemann

The Moonspinners was first published in the United States by William Morrow
& Co Inc in 1963; in Great Britain by Hodder & Stoughton Ltd in 1962.
Nine Coaches Waiting was first published in the United States by William
Morrow & Co Inc in 1959; in Great Britain by Hodder & Stoughton Ltd in 1958.
The Ivy Tree was first published in the United States by William Morrow
& Co Inc in 1962; in Great Britain by Hodder & Stoughton Ltd in 1961.
Madam, Will you Talk? was first published in the United States by William
Morrow & Co Inc in 1956; in Great Britain by Hodder & Stoughton Ltd in 1955.

This edition first published in the United States of America
in 1979 jointly by

William Heinemann Inc
450 Park Avenue, New York, NY 10022

and

Octopus Books Inc
The Olympic Towers, 645 Fifth Avenue,
New York, NY 10022

ISBN 0 905712 41 2

Printed in the United States of America
by R. R. Donnelley and Sons Company.

CONTENTS

The
Moonspinners

For
Kitty and Gerald Rainbow

The author is indebted to Mr. A.E. Gunther
for permission to quote from his father's
edition of The Greek Herbal of Dioscorides.

CHAPTER ONE

Lightly this little herald flew aloft . . .
Onward it flies . . .
Until it reach'd a splashing fountain's side
That, near a cavern's mouth, for ever pour'd
Unto the temperate air . . .

KEATS: *Endymion*

It was the egret, flying out of the lemon-grove, that started it. I won't pretend I saw it straight away as the conventional herald of adventure, the white stag of the fairy-tale, which, bounding from the enchanted thicket, entices the prince away from his followers, and loses him in the forest where danger threatens with the dusk. But, when the big white bird flew suddenly up among the glossy leaves and the lemon-flowers, and wheeled into the mountain, I followed it. What else is there to do when such a thing happens on a brilliant April noonday at the foot of the White Mountains of Crete; when the road is hot and dusty, but the gorge is green, and full of the sound of water, and the white wings, flying ahead, flicker in and out of deep shadow, and the air is full of the scent of lemon-blossom?

The car from Heraklion had set me down where the track for Agios Georgios leaves the road. I got out, adjusted on my shoulder the big bag of embroidered canvas that did duty as a haversack, then turned to thank the American couple for the lift.

'It was a pleasure, honey.' Mrs. Studebaker peered, rather anxiously, out of the car window. 'But are you sure you're all right? I don't like putting you down like this, in the middle of nowhere. You're sure this is the right place? What does that sign-post say?'

The sign-post, when consulted, said, helpfully, ΑΓ ΓΕΩΡΓΙΟΣ. 'Well, what do you know?' said Mrs. Studebaker. 'Now, look, honey—'

'It's all right,' I said, laughing. 'That *is* "Agios Georgios", and, according to your driver – and the map – the village is about three-quarters of a mile away, down this track. Once round that bit of cliff down there, I'll probably be able to see it.'

'I surely hope so.' Mr. Studebaker had got out of the car when I did, and was now supervising the driver as he lifted my one small case from the boot, and set it beside me at the edge of the road. Mr. Studebaker was large and pink and sweet-tempered, and wore an orange shirt outside his pearl-grey drill trousers, and a wide, floppy linen hat. He thought Mrs. Studebaker the cleverest and most beautiful woman in the world, and said so; in consequence she, too, was sweet-tempered, besides being extremely smart. They were both lavish with that warm, extroverted, and slightly naïve kindliness which seems a specifically American virtue.

13

I had made their acquaintance at my hotel only the evening before, and, as soon as they heard that I was making for the southern coast of Crete, nothing would content them but that I should join them for part of their hired tour of the island. Now, it seemed, nothing would please them better than for me to abandon my foolish project of visiting this village in the middle of nowhere, and go with them for the rest of their trip.

'I don't like it.' Mr. Studebaker was anxiously regarding the stony little track which wound gently downhill from the road, between rocky slopes studded with scrub and dwarf juniper. 'I don't like leaving you here alone. Why—' he turned earnest, kindly blue eyes on me— 'I read a book about Crete, just before Mother and I came over, and believe me, Miss Ferris, they have some customs here, still, that you just wouldn't credit. In some ways, according to this book, Greece is still a very, very primitive country.'

I laughed. 'Maybe. But one of the primitive customs is that the stranger's sacred. Even in Crete, nobody's going to murder a visitor! Don't worry about me, really. It's sweet of you, but I'll be quite all right. I told you, I've lived in Greece for more than a year now, and I get along quite well in Greek – and I've been to Crete before. So you can leave me quite safely. This is certainly the right place, and I'll be down in the village in twenty minutes. The hotel's not expecting me till tomorrow, but I know they've nobody else there, so I'll get a bed.'

'And this cousin of yours that should have come with you? You're sure she'll show up?'

'Of course.' He was looking so anxious that I explained again. 'She was delayed, and missed the flight, but she told me not to wait for her, and I left a message. Even if she misses tomorrow's bus, she'll get a car or something. She's very capable.' I smiled. 'She was anxious for me not to waste any of my holiday hanging around waiting for her, so she'll be as grateful to you as I am, for giving me an extra day.'

'Well, if you're sure . . .'

'I'm quite sure. Now, don't let me keep you any more. It was wonderful to get a lift this far. If I'd waited for the bus tomorrow, it would have taken the whole day to get here.' I smiled, and held out my hand. 'And still I'd have been dumped right here! So you see, you *have* given me a whole extra day's holiday, besides the run, which was marvellous. Thank you again.'

Eventually, reassured, they drove off. The car gathered way slowly up the cement-hard mud of the hill road, bumping and swaying over the ruts which marked the course of winter's overspills of mountain rain. It churned its way up round a steep bend, and bore away inland. The dust of its wake hung thickly, till the breeze slowly dispersed it.

I stood there beside my suitcase, and looked about me.

The White Mountains are a range of great peaks, the backbone of the westerly end of the mountainous island of Crete. To the south-west of the island, the foothills of the range run right down to the shore, which, here, is wild and craggy. Here and there along the coast, where some mountain stream, running down to the sea, has cut a fresh-water inlet in the ramparts of the cliff, are villages, little handfuls of houses each clinging to its crescent of shingle and its runnel of fresh water, backed by the wild mountains where the sheep and goats scratch a precarious living. Some of these villages are approached only by steep tracks through the maze of the foothills, or by caique from the sea. It was in one of them, Agios Georgios, the village of St. George, that I had elected to spend the week of my Easter holiday.

As I had told the Studebakers, I had been in Athens since January of the previous year, working in a very junior capacity as a secretary at the British Embassy. I had counted myself lucky, at twenty-one, to land even a fairly humble job in a country which, as far back as I could remember, I had longed to visit. I had settled happily in Athens, worked hard at the language (being rewarded with a fair fluency), and I had used my holidays and week-ends in exploration of all the famous places within reach.

A month before this Easter holiday was due, I had been delighted to hear from my cousin, Frances Scorby, that she planned to visit Greece in a cruise she was making with friends that spring. Frances is a good deal older than I am, being my parents' contemporary rather than my own. When my mother's death, three years before, had orphaned me (I had never known my father, who was killed in the war), I went to live with Frances in Berkshire, where she is part-owner of a rather famous rock-plant nursery. She also writes and lectures on plants, and takes beautiful colour-photographs which illustrate her books and talks. My ecstatic letters to her about the Greek wildflowers had borne fruit. It seemed that friends of hers were taking a small hired yacht from Brindisi to Piraeus, where they intended to stay for a few days while they explored Athens and its environs, after which they planned a leisurely sail through the islands. Their arrival in Piraeus was to coincide with my own Easter holiday, but (as I had written at some length to Frances) not even for her would I spend my precious few days' holiday among the Easter crowds, and the milling throng of tourists who had been pouring into the city for weeks. I had suggested that she abandon her party for a few days, and join me in Crete, where she could see the countryside – and the legendary flowers of the White Mountains – in peace. We could join the yacht together, when it called at Heraklion the following week, on its way to Rhodes and the Sporades; then later, on the way home, she could stay off in Athens with me, and see the 'sights' unencumbered by the Easter crowds.

Frances was enthusiastic, her hosts were agreeable, and it was left to me to discover, if possible, some quiet place in south-west Crete which combined the simple peace and beauty of 'the real Greece' with some of the standards of comfort and cleanliness which the new tourist age is forcing on it. An almost impossible mixture of virtues – but I believed

I had found it. A café-acquaintance in Athens – a Danish writer of travel-books, who had spent some weeks exploring the less frequented parts of the Greek archipelago – had told me of a small, isolated village on the southern coast of Crete at the foot of the White Mountains.

'If it's the real thing you want, an unspoiled village without even a road leading to it – just a couple of dozen houses, a tiny church, and the sea – Agios Georgios is your place,' he said. 'You'll want to swim, I suppose? Well, I found a perfect place for that, rocks to dive off, sandy bottom, the lot. And if you want the flowers, and the views – well, you can walk in any direction you please, it's all glorious, and as wild as anyone could wish. Oh, and Nicola, if you're interested, there's a tiny, deserted church about five miles eastward along the coast; the weeds are right up to the door, but you can still see the ghost of a rather quaint Byzantine mosaic on the ceiling, and I'll swear one of the door-jambs is a genuine Doric column.'

'Too good to be true,' I had said. 'All right, I'll buy it, what are the snags? Where do we have to sleep? Over the taverna, with the genuine Doric bugs?'

But no. This, it appeared, was the whole point. All the other attractions of Agios Georgios could be found in a score of similar villages, in Crete or elsewhere. But Agios Georgios had a hotel.

This had, in fact, been the village *kafenéion*, or coffee-shop, with a couple of rooms over the bar. But this, with the adjoining cottage, had been recently bought by a new owner, who was making them the nucleus of what promised to be a comfortable little hotel.

'He's only just started; in fact, I was their first guest,' said my informant. 'I understand that the authorities are planning to build a road down to the village some time soon, and meanwhile Alexiakis, the chap who bought the taverna, is going ahead with his plans. The accommodation's very simple, but it's perfectly clean, and – wait for it – the food is excellent.'

I looked at him in some awe. Outside the better hotels and the more expensive restaurants, food in Greece – even the voice of love has to confess it – is seldom excellent. It tends to a certain monotony, and it knows no variation of hot and cold; all is lukewarm. Yet here was a Dane, a well-rounded, well-found Dane (and the Danes have possibly the best food in Europe), recommending the food in a Greek village taverna.

He laughed at my look, and explained the mystery. 'It's quite simple. The man's a Soho Greek, originally a native of Agios Georgios, who emigrated to London twenty years ago, made his pile as a restaurateur, and has now come back, as these folk do, and wants to settle at home. But he's determined to put Agios Georgios on the map, so he's started by buying up the taverna, and he's imported a friend of his from his London restaurant, to help him. They've not seriously started up yet, beyond tidying up the two existing bedrooms, turning a third into a bathroom, and cooking for their own satisfaction. But they'll take you, Nicola, I'm sure of that. Why not try? They've even got a telephone.'

I had telephoned next day. The proprietor had been surprised, but pleased. The hotel was not yet officially opened, he told me; they were still building and painting, I must understand, and there were no other guests there; it was very simple and quiet . . . But, once assured that this was exactly what we wanted, he had seemed pleased to welcome us.

Our plans, however, had not worked out quite smoothly. Frances and I were to have taken Monday evening's flight to Crete, stayed the night in Heraklion, and gone to Agios Georgios next day, by the bi-weekly bus. But on Sunday she had telephoned from Patras, where her friends' boat had been delayed, and had begged me not to waste any of my precious week's holiday waiting for her, but to set off myself for Crete, leaving her to find her own way there as soon as possible. Since Frances was more than capable of finding her way anywhere, with the least possible help from me, I had agreed, swallowed my disappointment, and managed to get straight on to Sunday evening's flight, intending to have an extra day in Heraklion, and take Tuesday's bus as planned. But chance, in the shape of the Studebakers, had offered me a lift on Monday morning, straight to the south-west corner of Crete. So here I was, with a day in hand, set down in the middle of a landscape as savage and deserted as the most determined solitary could have wished for.

Behind me, inland, the land rose sharply, the rocky foothills soaring silver-green, silver-tawny, silver-violet, gashed by ravines, and moving with the scudding shadows of high cirrus which seemed to smoke down from the ghostly ridges beyond. Below the road, towards the sea, the land was greener. The track to Agios Georgios wound its way between high banks of maquis, the scented maquis of Greece. I could smell verbena, and lavender, and a kind of sage. Over the hot white rock and the deep green of the maquis, the judas-trees lifted their clouds of scented flowers the colour of purple daphne, their branches reaching landwards, away from the African winds. In a distant cleft of the land, seemingly far below me, I saw the quick, bright gleam that meant the sea.

Silence. No sound of bird; no bell of sheep. Only the drone of a bee over the blue sage at the road-side. No sign of man's hand anywhere in the world, except the road where I stood, the track before me, and a white vapour-trail, high in the brilliant sky.

I picked my case up from among the dusty salvias, and started down the track.

A breeze was blowing off the sea, and the track led downhill, so I went at a fair speed; nevertheless it was fully fifteen minutes before I reached the bluff which hid the lower part of the track from the road, and saw, a couple of hundred yards further on, the first evidence of man's presence here.

This was a bridge, a small affair with a rough stone parapet, which led the track over a narrow river – the water-supply, I supposed, on which Agios Georgios lived. From here the village was still invisible, though I guessed it could not be far, as the sides of the valley had opened out to show a wide segment of sea, which flashed and glittered beyond the next curve of the track.

I paused on the bridge, set down my case and shoulder-bag, then sat down on the parapet in the shade of a sycamore tree, swinging my legs, and staring thoughtfully down the track towards the village. The sea was – as far as I could judge – still about half a mile away. Below the bridge the river ran smoothly down, pool to pool dropping through glittering shallows, between shrubby banks lit by the judas-trees. Apart from these the valley was treeless, its rocky slopes seeming to trap the heat of the day.

Midday. Not a leaf stirring. No sound, except the cool noise of the water, and the sudden *plop* of a frog diving in the pool under the bridge.

I looked the other way, up-stream, where a path wound along the water-side under willows. Then I slid to my feet, carried my case down below the bridge, and pushed it carefully out of sight, into a thicket of brambles and rock-roses. My canvas bag, containing my lunch, fruit, and a flask of coffee, I swung back on to my shoulder. The hotel was not expecting me; very well, there was no reason why I should not, in fact, take the whole day 'out'; I would find a cool place by the water, eat my meal, and have my fill of the mountain silence and solitude before going down later to the village.

I started up the shady path along the river.

The path soon began to rise, gently at first, and then fairly steeply, with the river beside it rockier, and full of rapids which grew louder as the valley narrowed into a small gorge, and the path to a roughly-trodden way above a green rush of water, where no sun came. Trees closed in overhead; ferns dripped; my steps echoed on the rock. But, for all its apparent seclusion, the little gorge must be a highway for men and beasts: the path was beaten flat with footprints, and there was ample evidence that mules, donkeys, and sheep came this way daily.

In a few moments I saw why. I came up a steepish ramp through thinning pines, and emerged at once from the shade of the gorge, on to an open plateau perhaps half a mile in width, and two or three hundred yards deep, like a wide ledge on the mountain-side.

Here were the fields belonging to the people of Agios Georgios. The plateau was sheltered on three sides by the trees: southwards, towards the sea, the land fell away in shelving rock, and slopes of huge, tumbled boulders. Behind the fertile ground, to the north, soared the mountain-side, silver-tawny in the brilliant light, clouded here and there with olives, and gashed by ravines where trees grew. From the biggest of these ravines flowed the river, to push its way forward across the plateau in a wide meander. Not an inch of the flat land but was dug, hoed and harrowed. Between the vegetable fields were rows of fruit trees: I saw locust-trees, and apricots, as well as the ubiquitous olives, and the lemon-trees. The fields were separated from one another by narrow ditches, or by shallow, stony banks where, haphazard, grew poppies, fennel, parsley, and a hundred herbs which would all be gathered, I knew, for use. Here and there, at the outlying edges of the plateau, the gay little Cretan windmills whirled their white canvas sails, spilling the water into the ditches that threaded the dry soil.

There was nobody about. I passed the last windmill, climbed through the vine-rows that terraced the rising ground, and paused in the shade of a lemon-tree.

Here I hesitated, half inclined to stop. There was a cool breeze from the sea, the lemon-blossom smelt wonderful, the view was glorious – but at my feet flies buzzed over mule-droppings in the dust, and a scarlet cigarette-packet, soggy and disintegrating, lay caught in weeds at the water's edge. Even the fact that the legend on it was *EΘNOΣ*, and not the homely *Woodbine* or *Player's Weights*, didn't make it anything but a nasty piece of wreckage capable of spoiling a square mile of countryside.

I looked the other way, towards the mountains.

The White Mountains of Crete really are white. Even when, in high summer, the snow is gone, their upper ridges are still silver – bare, grey rock, glinting in the sun, showing paler, less substantial, than the deep-blue sky behind them; so that one can well believe that among those remote and floating peaks the king of the gods was born. For Zeus, they said, was born in Dicte, a cave of the White Mountains. They showed you the very place . . .

At that moment, on the thought, the big white bird flew, with slow, unstartled beat of wings, out of the glossy leaves beside me, and sailed over my head. It was a bird I had never seen before, like a small heron, milk-white, with a long black bill. It flew as a heron does, neck tucked back and legs trailing, with a down-curved, powerful wing-beat. An egret? I shaded my eyes to watch it. It soared up into the sun, then turned and flew back over the lemon-grove, and on up the ravine, to be lost to view among the trees.

I am still not quite sure what happened at that moment.

For some reason that I cannot analyse, the sight of the big white bird, strange to me; the smell of the lemon-flowers, the clicking of the mill-sails and the sound of spilling water; the sunlight dappling through the leaves on the white anemones with their lamp-black centres; and, above all, my first real sight of the legendary White Mountains . . . all this seemed to rush together into a point of powerful magic, happiness striking like an arrow, with one of those sudden shocks of joy that are so physical, so precisely marked, that one knows the exact moment at which the world changed. I remembered what I had said to the Americans, that they, by bringing me here, had given me a day. Now I saw that, literally, they had. And it seemed no longer to be chance. Inevitably, here I was, alone under the lemon-trees, with a path ahead of me, food in my bag, a day dropped out of time for me, and a white bird flying ahead.

I gave a last look behind me at the wedge of shimmering sea, then turned my face to the north-east, and walked rapidly through the trees, towards the ravine that twisted up into the flank of the mountain.

CHAPTER TWO

When as she gazed into the watery glass
And through her brown hair's curly tangles scanned
Her own wan face, a shadow seemed to pass
Across the mirror . . .

WILDE: *Charmides*

It was hunger, in the end, that stopped me. Whatever the impulse that had compelled me to this lonely walk, it had driven me up the track at a fair speed, and I had gone some distance before, once again, I began to think about a meal.

The way grew steeper as the gorge widened, the trees thinned, and sunlight came in. Now the path was a ribbon along the face of a cliff, with the water below. The other side of the ravine lay back from it, a slope of rock and scrub studded here and there with trees, but open to the sun. The path was climbing steeply, now, towards the lip of the cliff. It did not seem to be much used; here and there bushes hung across it, and once I stopped to gather a trail of lilac orchids which lay, unbruised, right at my feet. But on the whole I managed to resist the flowers, which grew in every cranny of the rock. I was hungry, and wanted nothing more than to find a level place in the sun, beside water, where I could stop and eat my belated meal.

Ahead of me, now, from the rocks on the right, I could hear water, a rush of it, nearer and louder than the river below. It sounded like a side-stream tumbling from the upper rocks, to join the main water-course beneath.

I came to a corner, and saw it. Here the wall of the gorge was broken, as a small stream came in from above. It fell in an arrowy rush right across the path, where it swirled round the single stepping-stone, to tumble once again, headlong, towards the river. I didn't cross it. I left the path, and clambered, not without difficulty, up the boulders that edged the tributary stream, towards the sunlight of the open ground at the edge of the ravine.

In a few minutes I had found what I was looking for. I climbed a tumble of white stones where poppies grew, and came out on a small, stony alp, a level field of asphodel, all but surrounded by towering rocks. Southwards, it was open, with a dizzying view down towards the now distant sea.

For the rest, I saw only the asphodel, the green of ferns by the water, a tree or so near the cliffs, and, in a cleft of a tall rock, the spring itself, where water splashed out among the green, to lie in a quiet pool open to the sun, before pouring away through the poppies at the lip of the gorge.

I swung the bag off my shoulder, and dropped it among the flowers. I knelt at the edge of the pool, and put my hands and wrists into the water. The sun was hot on my back. The moment of joy had slackened, blurred, and spread itself into a vast physical contentment.

I stooped to drink. The water was ice-cold, pure and hard; the wine of Greece, so precious that, time out of mind, each spring has been guarded by its own deity, the naiad of the stream. No doubt she watched it still, from behind the hanging ferns . . . The odd thing was – I found myself giving a half-glance over my shoulder at these same ferns – that one actually did feel as if one were being watched. Numinous country indeed, where, stooping over a pool, one could feel the eyes on one's back . . .

I smiled at the myth-bred fancies, and bent to drink again.

Deep in the pool, deeper than my own reflection, something pale wavered among the green. A face.

It was so much a part of my thoughts that, for one dreaming moment, I took no notice. Then, with that classic afterthought that is known as the 'double-take', reality caught up with the myth; I stiffened, and looked again.

I had been right. Behind my mirrored shoulder a face swam, watching me from the green depths. But it wasn't the guardian of the spring. It was human, and male, and it was the reflection of someone's head, watching me from above. Someone, a man, was peering down at me from the edge of the rocks high above the spring.

After the first startled moment, I wasn't particularly alarmed. The solitary stranger has, in Greece, no need to fear the chance-met prowler. This was some shepherd-lad, doubtless, curious at the sight of what must obviously be a foreigner. He would probably, unless he was shy, come down to talk to me.

I drank again, then rinsed my hands and wrists. As I dried them on a handkerchief, I saw the face there still, quivering in the disturbed water.

I turned and looked up. Nothing. The head had vanished.

I waited, amused, watching the top of the rock. The head appeared again, stealthily . . . so stealthily that, in spite of my common sense, in spite of what I knew about Greece and the Greeks, a tiny tingle of uneasiness crept up my spine. This was more than shyness: there was something furtive about the way the head inched up from behind the rock. And something more than furtive in the way, when he saw that I was watching, the man ducked back again.

For it was a man, no shepherd boy. A Greek, certainly; it was a dark face, mahogany-tanned, square and tough-looking, with dark eyes, and

that black pelt of hair, thick and close as a ram's fleece, which is one of
the chief beauties of the Greek men.

Only a glimpse I had, then he was gone. I stared at the place where
the head had vanished, troubled now. Then, as if he could still be
watching me, which was unlikely, I got to my feet with somewhat
elaborate unconcern, picked up the bag, and turned to go. I no longer
wanted to settle here, to be spied on, and perhaps approached, by this
dubious stranger.

Then I saw the shepherds' hut.

There was a path which I hadn't noticed before, a narrow sheep-trod
which had beaten a way through the asphodel towards a corner under
the rocks, where a hut stood, backed against the cliff.

It was a small, un-windowed penthouse, of the kind that is commonly
built in Greece, in remote places, to house the boys and men whose job
it is to herd the goats and sheep on the bare hillsides. Sometimes they are
used as milking-places for the sheep, and cheeses are made there on the
spot. Sometimes, in stormy weather, they serve to house the beasts
themselves.

The hut was small and low, roughly built of unshaped stones, the
spaces packed with clay. It was roofed with brushwood and dried scrub,
and would hardly be seen at all from any sort of distance, among the
stones and scrub that surrounded it.

This, then, was the explanation of the watcher of the spring. The man
would be a shepherd, his flock, doubtless, feeding on some other mountain-
meadow above the rocks where he lay. He had heard me, and had come
down to see who it was.

My momentary uneasiness subsided. Feeling a fool, I paused there
among the asphodel, half minded, after all, to stay.

It was well after noon now, and the sun was turning over to the south-
west, full on the little alp. The first warning I had was when a shadow
dropped across the flowers, as sudden as a black cloth falling to stifle me.

I looked up, with a gasp of fright. From the rocks beside the spring
came a rattle of pebbles, the scrape of a foot, and the Greek dropped
neatly into my path.

There was one startled moment in which everything seemed very clear
and still. I thought, but not believing it: the impossible really has
happened; this is danger. I saw his dark eyes, angry and wary at the
same time. His hand – more incredible still – grasped a naked knife.

Impossible to remember my Greek, to cry, 'Who are you? What do
you want?' Impossible to run from him, down the breakneck mountain.
Impossible to summon help from the vast, empty silence.

But of course, I tried it. I screamed, and turned to run.

It was probably the silliest thing I could have done. He jumped at me.
He caught me, pulled me against him, and held me. His free hand
covered my mouth. He was saying something half under his breath,
curses or threats that, in my panic, I didn't understand. I struggled and

fought, as if in a nightmare. I believe I kicked him, and my nails drew blood on his wrists. There was a clatter of kicked stones, and a jingling as he dropped the knife. I got my mouth free for a moment, and screamed again. It was little more than a shrill gasp this time, barely audible. But in any case, there was nobody to help . . .

Impossibly, help came.

From behind me, from the empty mountain-side, a man's voice called out, sharply, in Greek. I didn't hear what it said, but the effect on my attacker was immediate. He froze where he stood. But he still held me, and his hand clamped tightly again over my mouth.

He turned his head and called, in a low, urgent voice: 'It's a girl, a foreigner. Spying around. I think she is English.'

I could hear no movement behind me of anyone approaching. I strained round against the Greek's hand to see who had saved me, but he held me tightly, with a low, 'Keep still, and hold your noise!'

The voice came again, apparently from some way off. 'A girl? English?' A curious pause. 'For pity's sake, leave her alone, and bring her here. Are you mad?'

The Greek hesitated, then said sullenly to me, in strongly accented but reasonably good English: 'Come with me. And do not squeak again. If you make one other sound, I will kill you. Be sure of that. I do not like women, me.'

I managed to nod. He took his hand from my mouth then, and relaxed his hold. But he didn't let go. He merely shifted his grip, keeping hold of my wrist.

He stooped to pick up his knife, and motioned towards the rocks behind us. I turned. There was no one to be seen.

'Inside,' said the Greek, and jerked his head towards the shepherds' hut.

The hut was filthy. As the Greek pushed me in front of him across the trodden dust, the flies rose, buzzing, round our feet. The doorway gaped black and uninviting.

At first I could see nothing. By contrast with the bright light at my back, the interior of the hut seemed quite dark, but then the Greek pushed me further in, and in the flood of light from the doorway, I could see quite clearly even into the furthest corners of the hut.

A man was lying in the far corner, away from the door. He lay on a rough bed of some vegetation, that could have been ferns or dried shrubs. Apart from this, the hut was empty; there was no furniture at all, except some crude-looking lengths of wood in another corner that may have been parts of a primitive cheese-press. The floor was of beaten earth, so thin in places that the rock showed through. What dung the sheep had left was dried, and inoffensive enough, but the place smelt of sickness.

As the Greek pushed me inside, the man on the bed raised his head, his eyes narrowed against the light.

The movement, slight as it was, seemed an effort. He was ill; very ill; it didn't need the roughly swathed cloths, stiff with dried blood, on his left arm and shoulder, to tell me that. His face, under the two-days' growth of beard, was pale, and hollowed under the cheekbones, while the skin round his eyes, with their suspiciously bright glitter, looked bruised with pain and fever. There was a nasty-looking mark on his forehead, where the skin had been scraped raw, and had bled. The hair above it was still matted with the blood, and filthy with dust from the stuff he was lying on.

For the rest, he was young, dark-haired and blue-eyed like a great many Cretans, and would, when washed, shaved, and healthy, be a reasonably personable man, with an aggressive-looking nose and mouth, square, capable hands, and (as I guessed), a fair amount of physical strength. He had on dark-grey trousers, and a shirt that had once been white, both garments now filthy and torn. The only bed-covering was an equally battered windcheater jacket, and an ancient khaki affair which, presumably, belonged to the man who had attacked me. This, the sick man clutched to him as though he was cold.

He narrowed those bright eyes at me, and seemed, with some sort of an effort, to collect his wits.

'I hope Lambis didn't hurt you? You . . . screamed?'

I realized then why he had seemed to be speaking from some distance away. His voice, though steady enough, was held so by a palpable effort, and it was weak. He gave the impression of holding on, precariously, to every ounce of strength he had, and, in so doing, spending it. He spoke in English, and such was my own shaken condition that I thought at first, merely, what good English he speaks; and only afterwards, with a kind of shock, he *is* English.

Of course that was the first thing I said. I was still only just taking in the details of his appearance; the bloody evidence of a wound, the sunken cheeks, the filthy bed. 'You're – you're English!' I said stupidly, staring. I was hardly conscious that the Greek, Lambis, had dropped his hand from my arm. Automatically, I began to rub the place where he had gripped me. Later, there would be a bruise.

I faltered: 'But you're hurt! Has there been an accident? What happened?'

Lambis pushed past me, to stand over the bed, rather like a dog defending a bone. He still had that wary look; no longer dangerous, perhaps, but he was fingering his knife. Before the sick man could speak, he said, quickly and defensively: 'It is nothing. An accident in climbing. When he has rested I shall help him down to the village. There is no need—'

'Shut up, will you?' The sick man snapped it, in Greek. 'And put that knife away. You've scared her silly as it is, poor kid. Can't you see she's nothing to do with this business? You should have kept out of sight, and let her go past.'

'She'd seen me. And she was coming this way. She'd have come in here, as likely as not, and seen you ... She'll blab all over the village.'

'Well, you've made sure of that, haven't you? Now keep quiet, and leave this to me.'

Lambis shot him a look, half defiant, half shamefaced. He dropped his hand from the knife, but he stayed beside the bed.

The exchange between the two men, which had been in Greek, had the effect of reassuring me completely, even if the discovery of the sick man's nationality hadn't already (absurdly enough) begun to do so. But I didn't show it. At some purely instinctive level, it seemed, I had made a decision for my own protection – which was that there was no positive need for me to betray my own knowledge of Greek ... Whatever I had stumbled into, I would prefer to stumble out of again as quickly as possible, and it seemed that the less I knew about 'this business', whatever it was the more likely they were to let me go peaceably on my way.

'I'm sorry.' The Englishman's eyes turned back to me. 'Lambis shouldn't have frightened you like that. I – we've had an accident, as he told you, and he's a bit shaken up. Your arm ... did he hurt you?'

'Not really, it's all right ... But what about you? Are you badly hurt?' It would be a very odd sort of accident, I thought, that would lead a man to attack a stranger as Lambis had attacked me, but it seemed only natural to show some sort of curiosity and concern. 'What happened?'

'I was caught by a fall of stone. Lambis thought it was someone further up the hill who set it away, in carelessness. He swore he heard women's voices. We shouted, but nobody came.'

'I see.' I had also seen Lambis' quick glance of surprise, before the sullen brown eyes went back to the ground. It wasn't a bad lie on the spur of the moment, from a man who plainly wasn't as clear in the head as he would have liked to be. 'Well,' I said, 'it wasn't me. I've only just arrived at Agios Georgios today, and I haven't—'

'Agios Georgios?' The glitter this time wasn't only put there by fever. 'You've walked up from there?'

'From the bridge, yes.'

'Is there a track all the way?'

'Not really, I suppose. I followed it up the ravine, but left it where this spring comes in. I—'

'The track comes straight here? To the hut?' This was Lambis, his voice sharp.

'No,' I said. 'I told you I left the path. But in any case the place is seamed with paths – sheep-tracks. Once you get some way up the ravine, they branch all over the place. I stayed by the water.'

'Then it is not the only way down to the village?'

'I don't know; I'd say almost certainly not. Though it may be the easiest, if you're thinking of going down. I wasn't taking much notice.' I opened my hand, where I still held some crushed shreds of the lilac orchids. 'I was looking at the flowers.'

'Did you ... ?' It was the Englishman this time. He stopped, and waited a moment. I saw he was shivering; he waited with clenched teeth for the fit to pass. He was clutching the khaki jacket to him as if he was cold, but I saw sweat on his face. 'Did you meet anyone, on your ... walk?'

'No.'

'No one at all?'

'Not a soul.'

A pause. He shut his eyes, but almost immediately opened them again. 'Is it far?'

'To the village? Quite a long way, I suppose. It's hard to tell how far, when you're climbing. Which way did you come yourself?'

'Not that way.' The phrase was a full stop. But even through his fever he seemed to feel its rudeness, for he added: 'We came from the road. Further east.'

'But—' I began, then paused. This was perhaps not the moment to tell them that I was quite well aware that there was no road from the east. The only road came in from the west, and then turned northwards over a pass which led it back inland. This spur of the White Mountains was served only by its tracks.

I saw the Greek watching me, and added, quickly: 'I started at about midday, but it wouldn't take so long going back, of course, downhill.'

The man on the bed shifted irritably, as if his arm hurt him. 'The village ... Where are you staying?'

'The hotel. There's only one; the village is very small. But I haven't been there yet. I only arrived at noon; I got a lift out from Heraklion, and I'm not expected, so I – I came up here for a walk, just on impulse. It was so lovely—'

I stopped. He had shut his eyes. The gesture excluded me, but it wasn't this that stopped me in mid-sentence. It was the sharp impression that he had not so much shut me out, as shut himself in, with something that went intolerably far beyond whatever pain he was feeling.

I got my second impulse of the day. Frances had often told me that one day my impulses would land me in serious trouble. Well, people like to be proved right sometimes.

I turned sharply, threw the crushed and wilted orchids out into the sunlight, and went across to the bed. Lambis moved as swiftly, thrusting out an arm to stop me, but when I pushed it aside he gave way. I dropped on one knee beside the wounded man.

'Look—' I spoke crisply – 'you've been hurt, and you're ill. That's plain enough. Now, I've no desire to push my way into what doesn't concern me; it's obvious you don't want questions asked, and you needn't tell me a single thing; I don't want to know. But you're sick, and if you ask me, Lambis is making a rotten job of looking after you, and if you don't watch your step, you're going to be very seriously ill indeed, if not downright dead. For one thing, that bandage is dirty, and for another—'

'It's all right.' He was speaking, still with closed eyes, to the wall. 'Don't worry about me. I've just got a touch of fever . . . be all right soon. You just . . . keep out of it, that's all. Lambis should never have . . . oh well, never mind. But don't worry about me. Get down now to your hotel and forget this . . . please.' He turned then, and peered at me as if painfully, against the light. 'For your own sake. I mean it.' His good hand moved, and I put mine down to meet it. His fingers closed over mine: the skin felt dry and hot, and curiously dead. 'But if you do see anyone on your way down . . . or in the village, who—'

Lambis said roughly, in Greek: 'She says she has not been to the village yet; she has seen no one. What's the use of asking? Let her go, and pray she does keep quiet. Women all have tongues like magpies. Say no more.'

The Englishman hardly seemed to hear him. I thought that the Greek words hadn't penetrated. His eyes never left me, but his mouth had slackened, and he breathed as if he were all at once exhausted beyond control. But the hot fingers held on to mine. 'They may have gone towards the village—' the thick mutter was still in English – 'and if you're going that way—'

'Mark!' Lambis moved forward, crowding me aside. 'You're losing your mind! Hold your tongue and tell her to go! You want sleep.' He added in Greek: 'I'll go and look for him myself, as soon as I can, I promise you. He's probably back at the caique; you torture yourself for nothing.' Then to me, angrily: 'Can't you see he's fainting?'

'All right,' I said. 'But don't shout at me like that. I'm not the one that's killing him.' I tucked the now unresponsive hand back under the coat, and stood up to face the Greek. 'I told you I'm asking no questions, but I am not going away from here and leaving him like this. When did this happen?'

'The day before last,' sullenly.

'He's been here two nights?' I said, horrified.

'Not in here. The first night, he was out on the mountain.' He added, as if defying me to go further: 'Before I find him and bring him here.'

'I see. And you've not tried to get help? All right, don't look like that, I've managed to gather that you're in some sort of trouble. Well, I'll keep quiet about it, I promise you. Do you think I *want* to get mixed up in whatever skulduggery you're up to?'

'*Oriste?*'

'Whatever trouble you're in,' I translated impatiently. 'It's nothing to me. But I told you. I don't intend to walk away and leave him like that. Unless you do something about him – what was his name? Mark?'

'Yes.'

'Well, unless something's done about your Mark, here and now, he will die, and that will be something more to worry about. Have you any food?'

'A little. I had bread, and some cheese—'

'And fine stuff it looks, too.' There was a polythene mug lying in the dirt beside the bed. It had held wine, and there were flies on the rim. I picked it up.

'Go and wash this. Bring my bag, and my cardigan. They're where I dropped them when you jumped on me with your beastly knife. There's food there. It's not sickroom stuff, but there's plenty of it, and it's clean. Oh, look, wait a moment, there's a cooking-pot of a sort over there – I suppose the shepherd use it. We ought to have hot water. If you fill it, I can get some wood and stuff together, and we'll get a fire going—'

'No!' Both men spoke together. Mark's eyes had flown open on the word, and I saw a look flash between them which was, for all Marks' weakness, as electric as a spark jumping across points.

I looked from one to the other in silence. 'As bad as that?' I said at length, 'Skulduggery was the word, then. Fallen stones, what nonsense.' I turned to Lambis. 'What was it, a knife?'

'A bullet,' he said, not without a certain relish.

'A *bullet*?'

'Yes.'

'Oh.'

'So you see,' said Lambis, his surliness giving way to a purely human satisfaction, 'you should have kept away. And when you go, you will say nothing. There is danger, great danger. Where there has been one bullet, there can be another. And if you speak a word in the village of what you have seen today, I shall kill you myself.'

'Yes, all right.' I spoke impatiently; I was scarcely listening. The look in Mark's face was frightening me to death. 'But get my bag first, will you? And here, wash this, *and* make sure it's clean.'

I thrust the mug at him, and he took it, like a man in a dream.

'And hurry up!' I added. He looked from me to the mug, to Mark, to the mug again, then left the hut without a word.

'Greek,' said Mark faintly from his corner, 'meets Greek.' There was the faintest definable gleam of amusement in his face, under the pain and exhaustion. 'You're quite a girl, aren't you? What's your name?'

'Nicola Ferris. I thought you'd fainted again.'

'No. I'm pretty tough, you don't have to worry. Have you really got some food?'

'Yes. Look, is the bullet out? Because if it's not—'

'It is. It's only a flesh wound. And clean. Really.'

'If you're sure—' I said doubtfully. 'Not that I'd know a darned thing about bullet-wounds, so if we can't have hot water, I'd better take your word for it, and leave it alone. But you've a temperature, any fool could see that.'

'Out all night, that's why. Lost a bit of blood . . . and it rained. Be all right soon . . . in a day or two.' Suddenly he moved his head, a movement of the most violent and helpless impatience. I saw the muscles of his face twist, but not – I thought – with pain.

I said feebly: 'Try not to worry, whatever it is. If you can eat something now, you'll be out of here all the sooner, and believe it or not, I've got a flask of hot coffee. Here's Lambis coming now.'

Lambis had brought all my things, and the newly-rinsed mug. I took the cardigan from him, and knelt by the bed again.

'Put this round you.' Mark made no protest when I took the rough jacket away, and tucked the warm, soft folds of wool round his shoulders. I spread the jacket over his legs. 'Lambis, there's a flask in the bag. Pour him some coffee, will you? Thanks. Now, can you lift up a bit? Drink this down.'

His teeth chattered against the edge of the mug, and I had to watch to make sure he didn't scald his mouth, so eagerly did he gulp at the hot stuff. I could almost imagine I felt it running, warming and vital, into his body. When he had drunk half of it he stopped, gasping a little, and the shivering seemed to be less.

'Now, try to eat. That's too thick, Lambis; can you shred the meat up a bit? Break the crust off. Come on, now, can you manage this . . . ?'

Bit by bit he got the food down. He seemed at once ravenously hungry, and reluctant to make the effort to eat. From the former fact I deduced thankfully that he was not yet seriously ill, but that, if he could be got to care and help, he would recover fairly quickly. Lambis stood over us, as if to make sure I didn't slip poison into the coffee.

When Mark had eaten all that could be forced into him, and drunk two mugs of coffee, I helped him lower himself back into the bedding, and tucked the inadequate covers round him once more.

'Now, go to sleep. Try to relax. If you could sleep, you'd be better in no time.'

He seemed drowsy, but I could see him summoning the effort to speak. 'Nicola.'

'What is it?'

'Lambis told you the truth. It's dangerous. I can't explain. But keep out of it . . . don't want you thinking there's anything you can do. Sweet of you, but . . . there's nothing. Nothing at all. You're not to get mixed up with us . . . Can't allow it.'

'If I only understood—'

'I don't understand myself. But . . . my affair. Don't add to it. Please.'

'All right. I'll keep out. If there's really nothing I can do—'

'Nothing. You've done plenty.' An attempt at a smile. 'That coffee saved my life, I'm sure of that. Now go down to the village, and forget us, will you? Not a word to anyone. I mean that. It's vital. I have to trust you.'

'You can.'

'Good girl.' Suddenly I realized what his dishevelment and sickness had disguised before; he was very young, not much older, I thought, than myself. Twenty-two? Twenty-three? The drawn look and painfully tightened mouth had hidden the fact of his youth. It was, oddly enough, as he tried to speak with crisp authority that his youth showed through, like flesh through a gap in armour.

He lay back. 'You'd ... better be on your way. Thanks again. I'm sorry you got such a fright ... Lambis, see her down the hill ... as far as you can ...'

As far as you dare ... Nobody had said it, but he might just as well have shouted it aloud. Suddenly, out of nowhere, fear jumped at me again, like the shadow dropping across the flowers. I said breathlessly: 'I don't need a guide. I'll follow the water. Good-bye.'

'Lambis will see you down.' The edged whisper was still surprisingly authoritative, and Lambis picked up my bag and moved towards me, saying flatly: 'I will go with you. We go now.'

Mark said 'Good-bye,' in a voice whose dying fall made it utterly final. I looked back from the doorway, to see that he had shut his eyes and turned away, pulling my cardigan close with a small nestling movement. Either he had forgotten about it, or he valued its comfort too highly to have any intention of returning it.

Something about the movement, about the way he turned his cheek into the white softness, caught at me. He seemed all at once younger even than his years; younger by far than I.

I turned abruptly and left the hut, with Lambis close behind me.

CHAPTER THREE

When the sun sets, shadows, that showed at noon
But small, appear most long and terrible.

NATHANIEL LEE: *Oedipus*

'I will go first,' said Lambis.

He shouldered past me without ceremony, then led the way through the flowers towards the spring. I noticed how his head turned from side to side as he walked; he went warily, like a nocturnal beast forced to move in daylight. It was not a comforting impression.

Here was the naiad's pool, and, not far from it, the trail of orchids I had dropped. A few steps further, and we were out of sight of the hut.

'Lambis,' I said, 'one moment.'

He turned, reluctantly.

'I want to talk to you.' I spoke softly, though we could certainly not be heard from the hut. 'Also—' this hurriedly, at his movement of protest – 'I'm hungry, and if I don't eat *something* before I set off for Agios Georgios, I shall die in my tracks. You could probably do with a sandwich yourself, if it comes to that?'

'I am okay.'

'Well, I'm not,' I said firmly. 'Let me see that bag. There's tons of stuff here, he's eaten very little. I left the coffee for him, and you'd better keep the oranges and the chocolate, and some of the meat. There: we'll leave those. Surely you can help me eat the rest?'

I thought he hesitated, eyeing the food. I added: 'I'm going to, anyway. You really needn't see me any further, you know. I'll be quite all right on my own.'

He jerked his head sideways. 'We cannot stay here, it is too open. There is a place above, where we can see, and not be seen. You can see the hut from there, and the way up to it. This way.'

He slung my bag over his shoulder, turned aside from the pool, and began to clamber up through the rocks, towards the place where I had first caught sight of him. I saw him pause once, glancing about him with that tense, wary look, and his free hand crept, in the gesture I was beginning to know, towards the hilt of his knife. He was coatless, and the wooden hilt, worn smooth with much handling, stuck piratically up from the leather sheath in his trouser-belt.

He jerked his head again. 'Come.'

I hesitated, then looked determinedly away from that polished knife-hilt, and followed him up the dizzy goat-track that led past the spring.

The place he chose was a wide ledge, some way above the little alp where the hut stood. As a hiding-place and watch-tower combined, it could hardly have been bettered. The ledge was about ten feet wide, sloping a little upwards, out from the cliff face, so that from below we were invisible. An overhang hid us from above, and gave shelter from the weather. Behind, in the cliff, a vertical cleft offered deeper shelter, and a possible hiding-place. A juniper grew half across this cleft, and the ledge itself was deep with the sweet aromatic shrubs that clothed the hillside. The way up to it was concealed by a tangling bank of honeysuckle, and the spread silver boughs of a wild fig-tree.

I found myself a place at the back of the ledge, and sat down. Lambis stretched himself full-length near the edge, his eyes watchful on the rocky stretches below us. From this height I could see a wide reach of the sea. Its bright leagues of water hurt the eyes. It seemed a long way off.

We shared what food there was. Lambis abandoned all pretence, and ate ravenously. He didn't look at me, but lay, propped on one elbow, never taking his eyes off the mountain-side below us. I kept silent, watching him, and when at length I saw him give a sigh, and reach into a pocket for a cigarette, I spoke, gently.

'Lambis. Who shot Mark?'

He jumped, and turned his head sharply. The ready scowl came down.

'Not that I care,' I added, mildly, 'but you've made it obvious that you expect them, whoever they are, to have another bash at him, so you're both in hiding. That's all very well, but you can't stay that way indefinitely . . . I mean, for ever. And you ought to have the sense to see it.'

'Do you think I do not know this?'

'Well, when do you plan to go – if not for help, then for supplies?'

'Is it not obvious that I cannot leave him—?'

'It's obvious he can't be moved, and he ought not to be left, but the way things look now, if someone doesn't get help very soon, he'll get worse. Let's face it, he may even die. If not of the wound, then of exposure. You told me he'd had a night in the open. People die of that – shock, pneumonia, goodness knows what, didn't you know?'

No answer. He was lighting his cigarette, and he didn't look at me, but at least he was making no move to leave me, or hurry me on my way.

I said abruptly: 'You came here by boat, didn't you? Was it your own?'

His head jerked up at that, and the match went fizzing down among the dry juniper-needles. Absently, he put the heel of his hand down on the tiny gyre of blue smoke to crush it out. If it burnt him, he gave no sign. His eyes were on me, unwinking.

'By – boat?'

'Yes, by boat. I heard you say something about "the caique", to Mark.' I smiled. 'Good heavens, everybody knows that much Greek. And then, Mark lied about how you got here. There's no road from the east; in fact, there's only one road through this corner of Crete, and if you'd come by that you'd not have needed to ask me all those questions about the route down to the village. If Mark hadn't been feverish, he'd have known I'd see through such a silly lie. Well? You can't have come by the supply-boat from Chania, because that'd tie up in Agios Georgios, and – again   you'd know the way. *Was* it your own boat?'

A p .use. 'Yes, it is mine.'

'And where is it now?'

A longer pause. Then a reluctant gesture towards a part of the coast out of our sight, some way to the east. 'Down there.'

'Ah. Then I assume you'll have supplies on board – food, blankets, medical things?'

'And if I have?'

'Then they'll have to be fetched,' I said calmly.

'How?' He said it angrily; but at least, I thought, he was listening. His initial mistrust gone, he might even be half-way to accepting me as a possible ally. 'You might not find the boat. The way is not easy. Besides, it is not safe.'

So he had accepted me. I waited for a moment, then said, slowly: 'You know, Lambis, I think you had better tell me about this – affair. No, listen to me. I know you don't really trust me, why should you? But you've had to trust me this far, and you'll have to, again, when I finally do go down to the village. So why not trust me a bit further? Why not take advantage of the fact that I came along? There may not be much I can do, but there may be something, and I promise to be very careful. I won't interfere where I'm not needed, but obviously I'm less likely to make mistakes, if I know what's involved.'

The dark eyes were fixed on my face. They were quite unreadable, but the stony sullenness had gone from his mouth. He seemed to be hesitating.

I said: 'I have understood one thing, I think. It was a man from Agios Georgios who shot Mark?'

'We do not know. We do not know who did it.'

I said sharply: 'If you don't intend to tell me the truth even now—'

'This is the truth. Can you not see? If we knew from where the danger comes, or why, then we would know what to do. But we do not know. This is why I am afraid to go into the village, or to ask there for help from anyone – even the headman. I do not know if this is some affair of family, or who may be concerned in it. You are from England: perhaps you have stayed in Athens, or even in the *Peloponnisos*—' I nodded – 'but still you do not know what it is like in these mountain villages of Crete. It is a wild country, still, and the law does not always reach here. Here, in Crete, they still kill sometimes for affairs of family, you understand? They still have the – I do not know the word, family killings and revenge—'

'Vendettas. Blood-feuds.'

'Yes, "vendetta" I know; killing for blood. Blood will always have blood.'

He pronounced this involuntarily Shakespearian line in a matter-of-fact voice that chilled me. I stared. 'Are you trying to tell me that Mark has injured someone – by mistake, I presume? And was shot at in revenge, or something, by someone he doesn't know? Why, it's absurd! I suppose it *could* have happened, in a country like Crete, but surely they must realize by now—'

'He injured nobody. That was not his mistake. His mistake was that he saw a murder done.'

I heard my breath go out between my teeth. 'I – see. And the *murderer's* mistake was that Mark is still alive to talk about it?'

'That is so. And we do not know even who the people were ... the murderers, and the man they killed; and so we do not know in what direction we can go for help. We only know that they still search for Mark, to kill him.' He nodded at my look. 'Yes, these are wild parts, *thespoinís* – miss. If a man is injured, his whole family, perhaps his whole village, will support him, even in the case of murder and death. Not always, of course, but sometimes, in some places. Often here, in these mountains.'

'Yes, I'd read it, but somehow one doesn't—' I paused, and drew in my breath. 'Are you a Cretan, Lambis?'

'I was born in Crete, yes. But my mother was from Aegina, and when my father was killed, in the war, she returned to her mother's house. I lived in Agia Marina, in Aegina.'

'I know it. Then you don't belong to this part of the world? It couldn't have been anything to do with you, this horrible affair?'

'No, I was not even here. I found him next morning. I told you.'

'Oh yes, so you did. But I still can't think that it literally isn't safe to go down for supplies, and even to see the headman in Agios Georgios. Why, he'd be—'

'No!' He spoke sharply, as if in sudden fear. 'You do not know it all. It is not so simple.'

I said gently: 'Then supposing you tell me.'

'I will do that.' But he waited for a moment, letting his eyes move slowly over the empty reaches of the mountain-side below us. When he was satisfied that there was no movement anywhere, he settled himself more comfortably on his elbow, and took a deep drag at his cigarette.

'I told you I have a caique. I live now in Piraeus. Mark hired me there, to take a voyage to some of the islands. We have been to different places, during two weeks, but no matter of that, two days ago we come round to the south of Crete. We mean to come in to Agios Georgios, perhaps, later that night. I speak of Saturday. Well, Mark he know of an old church, in a hollow of the mountains, not far from the coast, to the east of Agios Georgios. This church is very ancient –' he pronounced it 'auncient' ' – perhaps classical, who knows, and I think it is in the old books.'

'I've heard of it. There was a classical shrine. I think, then later a church was built on the site. Byzantine.'

'So? Well, in the auncient times there was a harbour near by. Still, in calm weather, you can see the old wall under the water, and a small caique can get right in where the old landing-place was. Mark, he tells me to stop there. We had been sailing for two days, and now they were wanting to go on land, to walk—'

'They?'

'Mark and his brother.'

'Oh!' I stared at him, with the beginnings of frightened comprehension. I was remembering the look of agonized helplessness on Mark's face, and something Lambis had said, to quiet him: *"I'll go and look for him myself, as soon as I can."*

'I begin to see,' I said, rather hoarsely. 'Go on.'

'Well, Mark and Colin leave the caique, and go up through the hills. This is Saturday, did I say? They are to be gone all the day. They have food and wine with them. I stay with the caique. There is a small thing wrong with the engine, so I am to go along to Agios Georgios for what I need, then return in the evening to meet Mark and Colin. But I find the engine goes right quite easily, so I just stay and fish, and sleep, and swim, until it is evening, and they have not come. I wait and wait, but not knowing when they will come, or if perhaps I should go and look . . . you know how this is—'

'I know.'

'Then it is night, and they are not coming, and now I am very anxious. These are wild hills. I do not think they can be lost, but I think of accidents. At last, when I can wait no more, I lock the cabin on the caique, and put the key where they will know to find it, then I take a torch, and go up to find the little church. But you will understand that, even with the torch, it is not possible to find a way.'

'I can well believe that.'

'I shout, of course, and I go as far as I can, but I do not even find the church. I do not wish myself to be lost, so I go back where I can hear the sea, and I wait for the moon.'

'It's rising late, isn't it?'

He nodded. He was talking easily now. 'It was a long time to wait. When it rose, it was not a big moon, but I could see the way well enough. I go slowly, very slowly. I find the church, but they are not there. I do not know where to go from there, but then there is cloud, and sharp rain, and it is dark again, very dark. I have to take shelter till first light. I shout, but there is nothing. I do not think they have passed me, back to the boat, so when it is light, I go on. I am lucky. I find a path – not just a goat-path, but a wide one, of stones worn flat, as if men went that way. Perhaps in the old days it was the road from Agios Georgios to the church and the auncient harbour, I do not know. But it was a path. I go along it. Then, on it, I see blood.'

The bare simplicity of Lambis' style, together with the matter-of-fact tone he used, had an absurdly sensational impact. As he paused, with totally unconscious effect, to grind his cigarette out on a stone, I found myself watching him so tensely that when a shadow scudded across the ledge between us, I flinched from it as if it had been a flying knife. It was only a kestrel, sailing in to feed its young in a nest on the rock above us. The air shrilled with the ecstatic hissing with which they greeted the food.

Lambis never even glanced up, his nerves being that much better than mine. 'Now,' he said, 'I am sure there is an accident. This has happened before the rain, because the rain has washed most of it away, but I see blood between the stones. I am afraid. I call, but there is no answer.' He hesitated, and glanced up at me. 'Then – I cannot explain you why – but I do not call any more.'

'You don't have to explain. I understand.'

I did understand, very well. I could picture it as he had told it me: the man alone on the mountain-side; the blood on the stones; the eerie silence, and the echoing rocks; the creeping fear. I had been to Aegina, the idyllic little island in the Saronic Gulf where Lambis had been brought up. There, one solitary hill, sea-girdled, is crowned with a temple which stands among its sunlit pines. From between the pillars, on every side, you can see woods and fields, edged with the calm, blue sea. The road winds through gentle valleys, past slopes where little Christian shrines perch, it seems, every fifty yards or so, among the ferns and wild blue iris . . . But here, in Crete, it is a different world. These cloud-bound crags, with their eagles and ibexes and wheeling vultures, have, time out of mind – it is said – been the haunt of outlawed and violent men. So, Lambis had hunted in silence. And, finally, he had found Mark.

Mark was lying some three hundred yards further on, full in the path. 'He had crawled that way, from where the blood was spilt. How, I do not know. I think at first that he is dead. I see then that he is fainting, and that he has been shot. I do what I can, quickly, then I look for the boy.'

'The boy? You mean that the brother – Colin – is *younger*?'

'He is fifteen.'

'Oh, God. Go on.'

'I do not find him. But now it is light, and I am afraid they – whoever it is who has done this – will come back to look for Mark. I cannot take him back to the boat, it is too far. I carry him away, off the path, up through the rocks and along under the ridge, and then I find this place. It is easy to see that there has been nobody here for many weeks. I look after Mark, and make him warm, then I go back to the place where I find him, to cover the marks with dust, so that they will think he recovered and went away. I will tell you of that later. Now I will tell you what Mark told me, when he could speak.'

'Just a minute. You've not found Colin yet?'

'No. There was no sign.'

'Then – he's probably alive?'

'We do not know.'

The whistling in the cliff had stopped. The kestrel flew out again, rocked in a lovely curve below eye level, then tore away to the right, and vanished.

'What did Mark tell you?'

Lambis had taken out another cigarette. He had rolled over on his stomach, and gazed out over the hot hillside as he talked. Still briefly, unemotionally, he told me Mark's story.

Mark and Colin had walked to the little church (he said), and had their meal there. After they had explored it, they had walked on, up into the hills, intending to spend the whole day out before returning to the caique. Though the day had been fine, clouds had begun to pile up during the latter part of the afternoon, so that twilight came early. The two brothers had gone perhaps a little further than they had intended, and when at length they regained the path with the 'worn stones' that led down towards the church, the dusk was already gathering. They were walking fast, not talking, their rope-soled shoes making very little sound on the path, when suddenly, just ahead of them round a bend in the track, they heard voices speaking Greek, raised as if in some sort of quarrel. Thinking nothing of this, they held on their way, but, just as they came round the bluff of rock that masked the speakers from them, they heard shouts, a scream from a woman, and then a shot. They stopped short by the corner, with a very eloquent little tableau laid out just ahead of them at the edge of a wooded gully.

Three men and a woman stood there. The fourth man lay on his face at the gully's edge, and it didn't need a closer look to know that he was dead. Of the three living men, one stood back, aloof from the rest of the group, smoking – apparently unmoved. He seemed, by the very calmness of his gestures, no less than by his position, to be demonstrating his detachment from what was going on. The other two men both had rifles. It was obvious which one had fired the recent shot; this was a dark man in Cretan costume, whose weapon was still levelled. The woman was clinging to his arm, and screaming something. He shook her off roughly, cursing her for a fool, and struck her aside with his fist. At this the second man shouted at him, and started forward, threatening him with his clubbed rifle. Apart from the woman, whose distress was obvious, none of them seemed very concerned with the fate of the dead man.

As for Mark, his first concern was Colin. Whatever the rights and wrongs of what had happened, this was not a moment to interfere. He dropped an arm across the boy's shoulders to pull him back out of sight, with a muttered, 'Let's get out of this'.

But the third man – he of the unconcerned cigarette – turned, at that unlucky moment, and saw them. He said something, and the faces of the group turned, staring, pale in the dusk. In the moment of startled stillness before any of them moved, Mark thrust Colin behind him. He had opened his mouth to shout – he was never afterwards quite sure what he had been going to say – when the man in Cretan costume threw his rifle to his shoulder, and fired again.

Mark, as the man moved, had flinched back, half-turning to dodge out of sight. It was this movement that had saved him. He was near the gully-edge, and, as he fell, the momentum of his turn, helped by the swing of the haversack on his shoulders pitched him over it.

The next few minutes were a confusion of pain and distorted memory. Dimly, he knew that he was falling, bumping and sprawling down among rocks and bushes, to lodge in a thicket of scrub (as he found later) some way below the path.

He heard, as from a long way off, the woman screaming again, and a man's voice cursing her, and then Colin's voice, reckless with terror: 'You've killed him, you stupid swine! Mark! Let me get down to him! Mark! Let me go, damn you! *Mark!*'

Then the sound of a brief, fierce scuffle at the gulley's edge, a cry from Colin, bitten off short, and after that, no further sound from him. Only the woman sobbing, and calling in thick Greek upon her gods; and the voices of the two Cretans, furiously arguing about something; and then, incongruously – so incongruously that Mark, swimming away now on seas of black pain, could not even be sure it was not a dream – a man's voice saying, in precise and unconcerned English: 'At least take time to think it over, won't you? Three corpses is a lot to get rid of, even here . . .'

And that, said Lambis, was all that Mark remembered. When he awoke to consciousness, it was almost daylight. The thought of Colin got

him, somehow, up out of the gully and on to the path. There he lay
awhile, exhausted and bleeding, before he could summon the strength to
look about him. The dead man had gone, and there was no sign of Colin.
Mark had retained the dim impression that the murderers had gone
inland, so he started to crawl along the path after them. He fainted
several times in his passage of three hundred yards. Twice the rain
revived him. The last time, Lambis found him lying there.

Lambis' voice had stopped. I sat for a few minutes – for ages it seemed
– in silence, with my hands pressed to my cheeks, staring, without seeing
it, at the bright, far-off sea. I had imagined nothing like this. No wonder
Lambis had been afraid. No wonder Mark had tried to keep me out of
it . . .

I said hoarsely: 'I suppose they'd left Mark for dead?'

'Yes. It was dark, you see, and they may not have wanted to go down
the gully after him. It was a very steep place. If he was not then dead,
he would be dead by morning.'

'Then – when the Englishman told them to "think it over", he must
have been meaning Colin? The other two "corpses" being Mark, and
the dead man?'

'It seems so.'

'So Colin *must* have been alive?'

'The last Mark heard of it, yes,' said Lambis.

A pause. I said, uncertainly: 'They would come back, by daylight, for
Mark.'

'Yes.' A glance from those dark eyes. 'This I guessed, even before I
heard his story. When I went back to cover our tracks, I brushed the dust
over them, and went down for the haversack, then I hid above, among
the rocks, and waited. One came.'

Again the breathless impact of that sparse style. 'You saw him?'

'Yes. It was a man of perhaps forty, in Cretan dress. You have seen
this dress?'

'Oh, yes.'

'He had a blue jacket, and dark-blue breeches, the loose kind. The
jacket had some – what is the word for little balls of colour along the
edge?'

'What? Oh – I suppose I'd call them bobbles, if you mean that fancy
braided trimming with sort of tufts on, like a Victorian fringed table-
cloth.'

'Bobbles.' Lambis, I could see, had filed my thoughtless definition
away for future reference. I hadn't the heart to dissuade him. 'He had
red bobbles, and a soft black cap with a red scarf tied round, and hanging,
the way the Cretans wear it. He was very dark of face, with a moustache,
like most Cretans; but I shall know him again.'

'Do you think it was the murderer?'

'Yes. It was very nearly dark when the shooting happened, and Mark did not see faces, but he is certain that the man who did the shooting was in Cretan dress. Not the others.'

'What did he do when you saw him?'

'He looked about him, and went down into the gully, looking for Mark. He took a long time, as if he could not believe that he had gone. When he could find no body, he looked puzzled, and then anxious, and searched further, to see if perhaps Mark had crawled away, and died. He searched all the time below, in the gully, you understand. He did not think that Mark could have climbed up to the path. But when he looked for a long time without finding, then he came back to the path. He was very worried, I could see. He searched the path, then, but I think he saw nothing. After a time he went off, but not towards Agios Georgios. He went up there—' a gesture vaguely north '—where is another village, high up. So we still do not know from where the murderers come.'

'No. I suppose you couldn't—?' I hesitated, picking my words. 'I mean, if he was alone ...?'

For the first time, Lambis smiled, a sour enough smile. 'You think I should have attacked him? Of course. I do not have to tell you that I wait for the chance to force him to tell me the truth, and what they have done to Colin. But there is no chance. He is too far from me, and between us is the slope of open hillside. And he has his rifle, which he carries, so.' A gesture, indicating a gun held at the ready. 'He is too quick with his gun, that one. I have to let him go. If I take a risk, me, then Mark dies also.'

'Of course.'

'And because of Mark, who looks to be dying, I cannot follow this Cretan, to see where he goes ...' Suddenly he sat up, turning briskly towards me. 'So now you understand? You see why I speak of danger, and why I do not dare to leave Mark, even to find where Colin is? Mark wishes me to go, but he is too ill, and when he has the fever, he tries to leave the hut, to look himself for his brother.'

'Oh, yes, I see that all right. Thank you for telling me all this. And now, surely, you'll let me help?'

'What can you do? You cannot go down now to the village, and buy food or blankets, and then come back here. The whole village would know of it within the hour, and there would be a straight path back there, to Mark. And you cannot go to the boat; it will be dark soon, and I have told you, you could not find the way.'

'No, but you could.'

He stared.

I said: 'Well, it's obvious, isn't it? You go, and I'll stay with him.'

You would have thought I had offered to jump straight off the side of the White Mountains. '*You?*'

'What else is there to do? Someone has to stay with him. Someone has to get supplies. I can't get supplies, therefore I stay with him. It's as simple as that.'

'But – I shall be gone a long time, perhaps many hours.'

I smiled. 'That's where the luck comes in. The hotel doesn't expect me until tomorrow. Nobody in Agios Georgios knows I've arrived. Whatever time I get there, nobody's going to ask questions.'

He scooped up a handful of the dry juniper needles, and let them run softly through his fingers. He watched them, not looking at me as he spoke. 'If they come back, these murderers, to look for Mark, you will be alone here.'

I swallowed, and said with what I hoped sounded like resolute calm: 'Well, you'll wait till it gets dusk, won't you, before you go? If they haven't been back and found the hut before dark, they're not likely to find it afterwards.'

'That is true.'

'You know,' I said, 'this isn't silly heroics, or anything. I don't *want* to stay here, believe me. But I simply don't see what else there is to do.'

'You could do what Mark told you, and go down to your hotel and forget us. You will have a comfortable bed, and a safe one.'

'And how well do you think I should sleep?'

He lifted his shoulders, with a little twist of the lips. Then he gave a quick glance at the western sky. 'Very well. At first dark, I shall go.' A look at me. 'We shall not tell Mark, until I have gone.'

'Better not. He'd only worry about me, wouldn't he?'

He smiled. 'He does not like to be helpless, that one. He is the kind that tries to carry the world.'

'He must be half out of his mind about Colin. If he could only sleep, then you might even be able to go, and get back again, without his knowing.'

'That would be best of all.' He got to his feet. 'You will stay up here, then, until I give you a signal? I shall see to him before I leave him. There will be nothing for you to do except see that he does not wake with fever, and try to crawl out of the hut, to look for his brother.'

'I can manage that,' I said.

He stood looking down at me with that unreadable, almost surly expression. 'I think,' he said slowly, 'that you would manage anything.' Then suddenly, he smiled, a genuine smile of friendliness and amusement. 'Even Mark,' he added.

CHAPTER FOUR

Mark how she wreaths each horn with mist,
yon late and labouring moon.

WILDE: *Panthea*

Lambis left at dusk. Soon after the sun had vanished below the sea, darkness fell. I had been watching from the ledge, and, in the two long hours before sunset, I had seen no sign of movement on the mountain-side, except for Lambis' short trips from the hut to get water from the pool.

Now, as the edges of sea and landscape became dim, I saw him again, small below me, appearing at the door of the hut. This time he came out a short way, then stopped, looked up in my direction, and lifted a hand.

I stood up and raised an arm in reply, than made my way carefully down to meet him.

He said, low-voiced: 'He is asleep. I gave him the rest of the coffee, and I have bathed his arm. It looks better, I think; he has been a little feverish, talking stupid things, but no longer fighting to be out. He will be okay with you. I have filled the flask now with water; you will not need to come out again.'

'Very well.'

'I will go now. You are not afraid?'

'I am, a little, but then that's only natural. It doesn't change anything. You'll take great care?'

'Of course.' He hesitated, then there came again that familiar gesture of hand to hip. 'You would like this?'

'This' was his kinfe. It lay across his palm.

I shook my head. 'Keep it. If one of us is going to need it, I hope it'll be you! In any case, it would be wasted on me – I wouldn't quite know how to start using it. Oh, and Lambis—'

'Yes?'

'I've been thinking, sitting up there. Isn't it just possible that Colin may have got away? Or even that they've actually let him go? They know Mark's got away, and may be still alive, so they must know it'd only be running into worse trouble if they kill Colin. I mean, the first murder may be a local affair that they think they can get away with, but it'd be a different matter to involve two British nationals.'

'I have thought this myself.'

'And if he were fee – Colin, I mean – he'd go first of all to look for Mark's body, then, when he didn't find it, he'd go straight to the caique, wouldn't he?'

'I have thought this also. I have been hoping I shall find him there.'

I said doubtfully: 'As long as *they've* not found the caique ... I suppose, if they have, they'd be bound to connect it with Mark? Does the path, the "ancient path", lead straight to the old harbour? Would they assume that was where Mark and Colin were making for? If so, you'd think they'd have followed it up.'

He shook his head. 'The path goes on right over the hills, past the church, then it divides towards the hill village to the north, Anoghia, where the Cretan went, and to another village further along the coast to the east. There, there is a road to Phestos, where the antiquities are, and the tourists go. It is certain that the murderers would think that Mark was going that way. Why should they think of a boat? Mark and Colin had a haversack, and it would seem, perhaps, that they were walking, and sleeping out – going, perhaps, to sleep that night in the old church. People do these strange things, especially the English.'

'Well, let's hope you're right. Let's hope they never think about a boat. Can it be seen easily, from the shore above?'

'No, but I shall hide it better. There was a cave . . . not quite a cave, but a deep place between rocks, which could not be seen from the shore paths. I shall put her in there; she will be safe enough; there will be no wind tonight.'

'But if Colin came back to where you had left her before—'

'He will still find her. If he does go down to the place, and she is not there, you know what he will do, what anyone does. He will think, first, that this is not the same place, and he will search; there are many rocks and little bays, he will search them all, near by. And so he will see her.'

'Yes, of course. It's what one does. If you expect to see something in a certain place, you simply don't believe it can't be there.' I looked at Lambis with a new respect. 'And you? Do you really expect to find him there?'

He gave a quick glance at the door of the hut, as if he were afraid that Mark might hear him. 'I know no more than you, *thespoinís*. It may be that they are now afraid because they have shot at Mark, and that they try only to persuade Colin to be silent – and that Colin is even now searching for his brother. I do not know. It may be that there is no danger at all.'

'But you don't believe that.'

In the pause before he answered, I heard, high overhead in the darkening sky, the call of some late-going gulls. The sound was muted by distance, and very lonely.

'No,' he said at length, 'I do not believe it. There is danger here. The man I saw, he was dangerous, as a wild beast is dangerous. And the men Mark spoke of . . . yes, there is danger, I can feel it. It is in the air of these mountains.'

I smiled, I hope cheerfully. 'Perhaps that's only because you're not used to them. You've become a city-bird, like me. High mountains frighten me now.'

He said seriously: 'The city, the hills, they are all the same, where there are wicked men. When I was a child, in my village, it was the same. We were afraid in our houses, in our own beds . . . only then, for a young boy, the war was also exciting. But this . . . no, not now.'

There was a sound from inside the hut, the rustle of dried leaves and a sighing breath, then silence again.

Lambis lowered his voice. 'I must go. I will bring everything I can carry. Be careful, *thespoinís*.'

'Nicola.'

'Nicola, then.'

'Good-bye, and good luck.' I swallowed. 'You be careful, too. We'll see you soon. And for pity's sake don't fall and break a leg in the dark . . . How long do you think it will take?'

'I shall wait for daylight. Perhaps three hours after that.'

'Right,' I said, as steadily as I could, 'And if you're not back by noon, I'll come and look for *you*.'

'Okay.'

He was soon invisible down the darkening hillside. His steps faded. I heard the crack of a twig, then, more faintly, the rattle of a displaced stone, and then silence.

The sea-birds had gone. To the east, beyond the high towers of rock, the sky looked clouded, but from here to the sea it seemed clear, deepening rapidly towards night. The early stars, king-stars, burned there already, bright and steadfast. I remembered that last night there had been a moon of a kind, a pale quarter, waning, like silver that is polished so thin that it has begun to wear away . . .

Beside me, the entrance to the hut gaped black, like a cave-mouth. The hut itself crouched back against the rock as if huddling there for protection, as indeed it was. I glanced from it again up at the night sky. For Lambis' sake, I hoped there would be a moon, any sort of a moon, rising clear of the clouds, and dealing even a little light. But for my own, and Mark's, no night could be dark enough.

I shook the thought away. It did not do to think about the possibility of our being found. We would not be found. And if we were, the whole thing was a mistake, and there was no danger at all. None.

On this reflection – or bit of mental bluster – I turned and groped my way into the darkness of the hut.

'Lambis?'

So he was awake. I went quietly across towards the voice, and sat down at the edge of the brushwood bed.

'Lambis has gone down to the boat, to get supplies, and to see if Colin's there.'

'*You?*'

'Yes. Now don't worry, please. Someone had to go down. We couldn't either of us get stuff in the village, and I didn't know the way to the boat. He'll be back by morning. Are you hungry?'

'What? No. A bit thirsty. But look, this is nonsense. I thought you'd have been safe in your hotel by this time. You ought to go, they'll ask questions.'

'No, I told you, I'm not expected till tomorrow. My cousin Frances was delayed, and she can't arrive before tomorrow, either, so no one'll be worrying about me, honestly. Now stop thinking about it; I'll get you a drink, there's water in the flask . . . if I can just see to pour it out . . . Here.'

As his hand met mine, gropingly, on the cup, I could feel him searching for words. But he must have been weary, and still fogged with fever, for he accepted my presence without further argument, merely fetching a long sigh when he had drunk, and going back to the first thing I had said. 'He's gone to the boat?'

'Yes.'

'He's told you all about it? About Colin?'

'Yes. We think it's possible Colin may already have made his way to the boat.'

He said nothing. I heard the bedding rustle as he lay back. A dry, sharp scent came from it, not quite strong enough to counteract the smell of dirt and sickness. 'How do you feel now?' I asked.

'Fine.'

I found his pulse. It was light and fast. 'I wish to goodness I dared heat some water. How's the arm?'

'It's sore, but it's not throbbing quite so much.' He answered patiently, like an obedient child. 'It'll be better by morning.'

'If we can keep you warm enough,' I said, 'and you get some sleep. *Are* you warm?'

'Lord, yes, boiled.'

I bit my lip. The night, mercifully, was far from cold, and, as yet, the rock surfaces of the mountain breathed warmth. But there were hours to go, and the chill of dawn to come, and the possibility, at that time of year, of low cloud, or rain.

Under my fingers the light pulse raced. He lay, slack and silent, in his corner.

He said, suddenly: 'I've forgotten your name.'

'Nicola.'

'Oh, yes. I'm sorry.'

'It doesn't matter. You're Mark – Mark what?'

'Langley. When will he get back?'

'He didn't say,' I lied. 'He's going to move the boat out of sight of the coast paths. He'll need daylight for that.'

'But if Colin goes back to the boat—'

'He'll find it. He'll hunt. It'll be quite near, only closer under the cliff. Now stop thinking about it. We can't do anything till daylight, so if you can empty your mind, and rest and sleep, then you might be well enough tomorrow to move down towards the boat.'

'I'll try.' But he moved restlessly, as if the arm hurt him. 'But you?

You should have gone. I'd have been all right alone. You really will go tomorrow? You'll get out of this – whatever it is?'

'Yes,' I said soothingly, 'when Lambis comes back, I'll go. We'll talk about it in the morning. You must be quiet now, and try to sleep.'

'Did Lambis say there was an orange somewhere?'

'Of course. Wait a moment till I peel it.'

He was silent while I dealt with the orange, and took the piece I handed to him, almost greedily, but when I passed him another, he suddenly seemed to lose all interest, pushed my hand aside, and began to shiver.

'Lie down,' I said. 'Come on, pull this up round you.'

'You're cold yourself. You've got no coat.' He sat up, seeming to come to himself. 'Heavens, girl, I've got your woolly thing here. Put it on.'

'No. I'm fine. *No*, Mark, damn it, you've got a temperature. Don't make me fight you every inch of the way.'

'Do as you're told.'

'I'm the nurse, you're only the patient. Put the beastly thing on and shut up and lie down.'

'I'm dashed if I do. With you sitting there with nothing on but that cotton thing—'

'I'm all right.'

'Maybe. But you can't sit there all night.'

'Look,' I said, in some alarm, for his teeth were beginning to chatter, 'lie down, for pity's sake. We'll share the wretched thing. I'm coming in with you, then we'll both be warm. *Lie down.*'

He shivered his way down into the bedding, and I slid down beside him, at his uninjured side. I slipped an arm under his head, and, quite simply, he half turned away from me and curled his back into the curve of my body. Avoiding the bandaged shoulder, I put my arms round him, and held him closely. We lay like this for some time. I felt him slowly begin to relax into warmth.

'There are probably fleas,' he said drowsily.

'Almost certainly, I should think.'

'And the bed smells. I wouldn't be surprised if I smelt a bit myself.'

'I shall wash you tomorrow, cold water or not.'

'You certainly won't.'

'You try stopping me. That Greek of yours'll kill you with his notions of super-hygiene. I'd like to see what you look like, anyway.'

He gave what might even have been called a chuckle. 'It's not worth it. My sisters tell me I'm nice, but plain.'

'Sisters?'

'Charlotte, Ann, and Julia.'

'Good heavens, three?'

'Yes, indeed. And then Colin.'

A little pause. 'You're the eldest?'

'Yes.'

'I suppose that's why you're not used to doing as you're told?'

'My father's away a lot, and I suppose I've rather got into the habit of looking after things. At present he's in Brazil – he's Resident Engineer on Harbour Construction at Manaos, on the Amazon, and he'll be there two years, off and on. Before that he was in Cuba. It's lucky, really, that I've been able to be at home most of the time . . . though of course they're all away now, mostly – Charlotte's at RADA, and Ann's in her first year at Oxford. Julia and Colin are still at school.'

'And you?'

'Oh, I followed in Father's footsteps – I'm a civil engineer . . . just. I did a couple of years in a drawing-office straight after school, then took a degree at Oxford. Passed last year. This trip's a reward, in a way . . . Father stood us three weeks in the Islands, and of course we waited till now, for the best weather . . . '

He talked on, half drowsily, and I let him, hoping that he would talk himself to sleep before he thought again, too closely, about Colin . . .

'What's the time?' He sounded thoroughly drowsy now.

'I can't quite see. You're lying on it. There.'

My arm was under his head. I turned my wrist, and felt him peering at it. The luminous dial was worn, but distinct enough.

''Bout midnight.'

'Is that all? Are you sleepy now?'

'Mm. Nice and warm. You?'

'Yes,' I lied. 'Shoulder comfortable?'

'Marv'llous. Nicola, you're marv'llous girl. Feel quite at home. Feel as if I'd been sleeping with you for years. Nice.' I felt him hear what he had said, then his voice came, sharply, shaken into wakefulness. 'I'm awfully sorry. I can't think what made me say that. I must have been dreaming.'

I laughed. 'Think nothing of it. I feel the same. Shockingly at home, just as if it was a habit. *Go to sleep.*'

'U-huh. Is there a moon?'

'A sort of a one, just up. Waning quarter, all fuzzy at the edges, like wool. There must be a bit of cloud still, but there's enough light; just enough to help Lambis, without floodlighting everything he does.'

He was silent after that, for so long that I hoped he had gone to sleep, but then he moved his head restlessly, stirring up the dust in the bedding.

'If Colin *isn't* at the boat—'

'You can bet your boots he is. He'll come up with Lambis in a few hours' time. Now stop that, it gets us nowhere. Stop thinking, and go to sleep. Did you ever hear the legend of the moon-spinners?'

'The what?'

'Moon-spinners. They're naiads – you know, water-nymphs. Sometimes, when you're deep in the countryside, you meet three girls, walking along the hill tracks in the dusk, spinning. They each have a spindle, and on to these they are spinning their wool, milk-white, like the moonlight.

In fact, it *is* the moonlight, the moon itself, which is why they don't carry a distaff. They're not Fates, or anything terrible; they don't affect the lives of men; all they have to do is to see that the world gets its hours of darkness, and they do this by spinning the moon down out of the sky. Night after night, you can see the moon getting less and less, the ball of light waning, while it grows on the spindles of the maidens. Then, at length, the moon is gone, and the world has darkness, and rest, and the creatures of the hillsides are safe from the hunter and the tides are still . . .'

Mark's body had slackened against me, and his breathing came more deeply. I made my voice as soft and monotonous as I could.

'Then, on the darkest night, the maidens take their spindles down to the sea, to wash their wool. And the wool slips from the spindles, into the water, and unravels in long ripples of light from the shore to the horizon, and there is the moon again, rising from the sea, just a thin curved thread, re-appearing in the sky. Only when all the wool is washed, and wound again into a white ball in the sky, can the moon-spinners start their work once more, to make the night safe for hunted things . . .'

Beyond the entrance of the hut, the moonlight was faint, a mere greyness, a lifting of the dark. Enough to save Lambis a fall or a sprain; enough to steer his boat into hiding without waiting for daylight; but not enough for prying eyes to see the place where Mark and I lay, close together, in the dark little hut. The moon-spinners were there, out on the track, walking the mountains of Crete, making the night safe, spinning the light away.

He was asleep. I turned my cheek on the tickling shrubs. It met his hair, rough, and dusty, but smelling sweetly of the dried verbena in our bed.

'Mark?' It was barely a breath.

No answer. I slipped a hand down under the khaki jacket, and found his wrist. It was clammy, and warm. The pulse was still fast, but regular, and stronger. I tucked the coat round him again.

For no reason, except that it seemed the thing to do, I kissed his hair, very lightly, and settled myself down to sleep.

CHAPTER FIVE

There bathed his honourable wounds, and dressed
His manly members in the immortal vest.

POPE : *The Iliad of Homer*

I got some sleep – enough – though I was stiff when I finally woke. Mark was still sound asleep, curled back against me. His breathing sounded easy and normal, and his skin, where I cautiously felt it, was cool. The fever had gone.

It was still early. The light which came through the doorway was pearled, but without sun. My wrist was somewhere under Mark's cheek, and I dared not move it again to try to see my watch. I wondered whether the cool light were only that of early morning, or if, today, those cirrus clouds were lying lower, across the sun. In some ways, it would be better for us if they were; but they would be cold and damp; and, until we had blankets . . .

The thought brought me fully awake. Lambis. Surely Lambis should have been back by now?

I raised my head cautiously, and tried to turn my wrist where it lay under Mark's head. He stirred, gave a little grunting snore, and woke. He put a hand up to rub his eyes, and then stretched. The movement pushed him against me, and the discovery brought him round with a jerk that must have hurt his arm.

'Why, hullo! Good heavens, I'd forgotten you were there! I must have been half-seas-under last night.'

'That's the sweetest thing a man's ever said to me after a long night together,' I said. I sat up, and began to extricate myself from the bedding, brushing it off me. 'If I could have got out without waking you, I'd have done it, but you were so touchingly curled up—'

He grinned, and I realized it was the first time I had really seen him smile. Even with the two-days' beard and the strained pallor of his face, the effect was to make him look very young. 'Bless you,' he said, as if he meant it. 'I got a good sleep and I feel wonderful. I even feel as if I might be able to make a move today. Heaven knows, I'd better. But you – did you get any sleep at all?'

'Some,' I said, truthfully. 'Enough, anyway. I feel wide awake.'

'What's the time?'

'Just after five.'

I saw the creases of worry settle back between his brows. He shifted the arm as if it had suddenly begun to hurt. 'Lambis isn't back?'

'No.'

'I hope to heaven nothing's happened to him. If I've got *him* into this mess as well—'

'Look,' I said, 'don't for pity's sake take Lambis on to your shoulders, too. He wouldn't thank you, and it's my guess he can look after himself.' I got up, still brushing bits off. 'Now, I've been thinking, while you lay snoring. I think we should get you out of this hut. And the sooner the better.'

He rubbed a hand over his face, as if chasing the last mists of sleep. His eyes still looked blurred with the clogging weariness and worry of the night. 'Yes?'

'If anyone does come looking for you again, and gets up here – and mind you, if they've any sense they'll go hunting where the water is – they're bound to look in the hut first thing. Lambis was right to bring you here in the first place, for shelter. But now that you're a bit better,

I think you should find a place in the open, in the warmth and air, a shady place, where we can see around us. You're much better to be hidden out on the mountain-side, than in the only obvious shelter on the hill.'

'That's true. And I can't say I'll be sorry to get out of this . . . For a start, could you help me outside now?'

'Sure.'

He was heavier than he looked, and also a good deal less able to help himself than he had hoped. It took quite a time before he was at last upright, half-propped against the wall of the hut, half-leaning on me. I saw now that he was not tall, but compactly and toughly built, with broad shoulders and a strong-looking neck.

'Okay.' He was panting as if he had run a race, and there was sweat on his face. 'Keep near the wall. I can make it.'

Slowly, we made it. As we reached the doorway, the sun came up, brilliance streaming from the left between the tall asphodels. Long shadows from the flowers ran along the turf. The corner where the hut stood was still in shadow, and the air was chilly.

I left Mark sitting on the trunk of a fallen olive-tree, and went across to the spring.

The pool, too, was still in shadow, and the water was icy. When I had washed, I went back to the hut for the metal pot that I had noticed there. This was a sort of kettle, or small cauldron, which must have been used by the shepherds. Though the outside of the pot was smoked black, the inside was clean enough, with no speck of rust. I scoured it out as best I could, with coarse sand from the stream, then filled it, and went back to Mark.

He was sitting on the ground now, beside the fallen tree-trunk, slumped back against it, looking exhausted, and so ill, in the cold daylight, that I had to control an exclamation of panic. If only Lambis would come; Lambis, blankets, hot soup . . .

I scooped a mug-full of the icy water out of the pot.

'Here's a drink. And if you want a wash of a sort, I've a clean hankie . . . No, on second thoughts, I think you'd better let me. Keep still.'

He made no objection this time, but allowed me to wash his face for him, and then his hands. I let it go at that. Cleanliness might be next to godliness, but the water was ice-cold. He looked like a rather badly-off tramp. I had a feeling that I probably looked a pretty suitable mate for him. Today, I hadn't had the hardihood to look into the naiad's pool.

Breakfast was rather horrible. The bread was as hard as pumice, and had to be soaked in the icy water before he could eat it. The chocolate was better, but was cloying and unsatisfying. The orange had gone soft, like limp suede, and tasted of nothing in particular.

The effort of will with which he chewed and choked down the unappetizing stuff was palpable. I watched him with anxiety, and a

dawning respect. Stubborn and autocratic he might be, but here was a
kind of courage as definite as any gun-blazing heroics, this grim private
battle with his own weakness, this forcing himself to remain a lay-figure
for long enough to gather effective strength, when every nerve must have
been screaming the necessity of action. To me, it was a new slant on
courage.

When the beastly little meal was finished, I looked àt him uncertainly.
'There was a place where Lambis took me yesterday; it's a sort of ledge,
and there's plenty of cover, and you can see for miles. The only thing is,
it's a bit higher up. Round that bluff and then up, quite a clamber.
There, do you see? If you can't manage it, I can scout round now, and
find something else.'

'I'll manage it.'

How he did, I shall never quite know. It took us the best part of an
hour. By the time he was lying, white-faced and sweating, on the ledge,
I felt as if I had run from Marathon to Athens myself, and with bad
news to tell at the end of it.

After a while I sat up, and looked down at him. His eyes were shut,
and he looked terrible, but the sun was on the ledge, and he was lying
with face turned almost greedily towards its growing warmth.

I got to my knees. 'I'm going back for the haversack now, and to cover
our tracks at the hut. And when I get back, I don't care what you say,
I'm going to light a fire.'

His eyelids flickered. 'Don't be silly.'

'I'm not. But first things first, and the essential thing for you is warmth.
You must have something hot to drink, and if I'm to do your arm, I must
have hot water.' I nodded towards the cleft-like cave behind us. 'If I lit
a small one, deep in there, with very dry stuff that didn't make much
smoke, we could get something heated. Better to do it now, before
anyone's likely to be about.'

He had shut his eyes again. 'As you like,' indifferently.

It didn't take long to cover our traces in the hut. Any shepherd might
have left the bedding, and, while it might still look suspicious, I felt
reluctant to remove it, in case Mark should need it again that night. I
merely ruffled it over, until it showed no signs of having been recently
lain on, then, with a broom of twigs, scattered dust over our recent footprints.

A quick look round, and then I was climbing back to the ledge, a fresh
pot-full of water held carefully in my hands, and the bag and haversack
over my shoulder, filled with as much dry kindling as they would hold.

Mark lay exactly where I had left him, eyes shut. I carried my load
quietly into the cleft. As I had hoped, this ran back fairly deeply into the
cliff, and, some way in, under a smoothed-off overhang for all the world
like a chimney-breast, I built the fire. When it was ready, I made a swift
but cautious survey from the ledge. Nothing, nobody, no movement,

except of the kestrel hunting along the edge of the ravine. I went back and set a match to the fire.

I am not much good at making fires, but with the dry cones, and the verbena scrub I had collected, anyone could have done it. The single match caught hold, fingered the strands of dead stuff with bright threads, then went streaming up in a lovely blaze of ribbon flames. The sudden heat was wonderful, living and intense. The pot crackled as it heated, tilting dangerously as a twig charred and broke under it, and the water hissed at the edges against the burning metal.

I glanced upwards anxiously. What smoke there was, was almost invisible, a transparent sheet of vapour no thicker than pale-grey nylon, sliding up the curved cliff-face, to vanish, before it reached the upper air, in a mere quivering of heat-vapour. Ten minutes of this could do no harm.

The pot hissed and bubbled. I broke the last of the chocolate into the mug, poured boiling water over it, and stirred it with a bone-white twig which was as clean as the weather could scour it. The fire was dying rapidly down in a glow of red ash. I replaced the pot in its still hot bed, then carried the steaming mug out to Mark.

'Can you drink this?'

He turned his head reluctantly, and opened his eyes. 'What is it?' His voice sounded blurred, and I wondered, with a pang of real fear, if I had done wrongly in allowing the dreadful effort of the climb. 'Good lord, it's hot! How did you do it?'

'I told you. I lit a fire.'

I saw the sudden flicker of alarm in his eyes, and realized that he had been too exhausted to take in what had been said earlier. I smiled quickly, and knelt beside him.

'Don't worry, the fire's out. Drink this now, all of it. I've saved some hot water, and I'm going to do your arm when you've had this.'

He took the mug, and sipped the scalding liquid. 'What is it?'

'My own recipe; healing herbs gathered under a waning moon in the White Mountains.'

'It tastes to me like weak cocoa. Where in the world did you get it?' His head jerked up as a thought struck him, and some cocoa spilled. 'Have they – has Lambis come?'

'No, not yet. It's only the chocolate, melted up.'

'There wasn't much left, I saw it. Have you had yours?'

'Not yet. There's only one mug. I'll have mine if you'll get that drunk up. Hurry up.'

He obeyed me, then lay back. 'That was marvellous. I feel better already. You're a good cook, Nicolette.'

'Nicola.'

'I'm sorry.'

'So you should be. Now grit your teeth, hero, I'm going to take a look at your arm.'

I went back to my fire, which had died down to white ash. I drank a mug-full of hot water – which tasted surprisingly good – then went back to Mark, with the steaming pot, and my courage, held carefully in both hands.

I am not sure which of us showed the more resolution during the ensuing process, Mark or myself. I knew very little about wounds and nursing – how should I? – and I had a strong feeling that the sight of anything unpleasant or bloody would upset me shamefully. Besides, I might have to hurt him, and the idea was horrifying. But it had to be done. I tightened my stomach muscles, steadied my hands, and – with what I hoped was an air of calm but sympathetic efficiency – set myself to undo the distinctly nasty wrappings that Lambis had last night put back on Mark's arm.

'Don't look so scared,' said the patient comfortingly. 'It stopped bleeding hours ago.'

'Scared? Me? For pity's sake, where did Lambis *get* this stuff?'

'Part of his shirt, I think.'

'Good heavens. Yes, it looks like it. And what in the world's this? It looks like *leaves!*'

'Oh, it is. More of your healing herbs gathered under a waning moon. It's something Lambis found, I can't remember what he called it, but he swore his grandmother used it for practically everything, from abortions to snake-bite, so you'd think—' He stopped on a sharp intake of breath.

'I'm sorry, but it's stuck a bit. Hang on, this will hurt.'

Mark didn't answer, but lay there with his head turned away, examining the rock above the ledge with apparent interest. I gave him a doubtful look, bit my lips together, and started to sponge the stuff loose from the wound. Eventually, it came.

The first sight of the exposed wound shocked me inexpressibly. It was the first time I had seen any such thing, and the long, jagged scoring where the bullet had ploughed through the flesh looked sickening. Mark had been lucky, of course, several times lucky. Not only had the murderer, aiming at his heart, scored a near miss, hitting nothing that would matter, but the bullet had gone cleanly through, ploughing its way upwards for about four inches through the flesh of the upper arm. To me, on that first shrinking glance, it looked awful enough. The edges were not lying cleanly together, and the jagged scar looked inexpressibly raw and painful.

I blinked hard, braced myself, and looked again. This time, to my surprise, I was able to see the wound without that slight lurching of the stomach. I put the dirty wrappings aside, out of sight, and concentrated.

Find out if the wound was clean; that was the main thing, surely? These dried smears and crusts of blood would have to be washed away, so that I could see . . .

I started gingerly to do this. Once, Mark moved, uncontrollably, and I faltered, cloth in hand, but he said nothing. His eyes seemed to be

following the flight of the kestrel as it swept up to the nest above ↄ⸱⸱ _
went doggedly on with the job.

The wound was washed at last, and I thought it was clean. The flesh
surrounding it looked a normal enough colour, and there was no sign of
swelling anywhere. I pressed gentle fingers here and there, watching
Mark's face. But there was no reaction, except that almost fierce concentration on the kestrel's nest over our heads. I hesitated, then, with a
hazy memory of some adventure novel I had read, bent down and sniffed
at the wound. It smelt faintly of Mark's skin, and the sweat of his recent
climb. I straightened up, to see him smiling.

'What, no gangrene?'

'Well,' I said cautiously, 'hope on, hope ever, it takes some days to set
in ... Oh, Mark, I don't know a darned thing about it, but it honestly
does look clean to me, and I *suppose* it's healing.'

He twisted his head to look down at it. 'It looks all right. Keep it dry
now, and it'll do.'

'All *right!* It looks just *awful!* Does it hurt terribly?'

'That's not the thing to say at all, didn't you know? You should be
bright and bracing. "Well, my lad, this looks wonderful. On your feet
now, and use it all you can." No, really, it does look fair enough, and
it is clean, though heaven knows how. Maybe those herbs did do the
trick; queerer things have happened. Though if I'd been in a fit state to
know that it was Lambis' old shirt, that he'd worn at least since we left
Piraeus—'

'These tough types. It just shows what you can do when you leave it
all to Nature. Who'd want silly little modern things like antiseptics? Lie
still, will you? I'm going to tie it up again.'

'What with? What's that?'

'Nicola's old petticoat, that she's been wearing ever since Athens.'

'But look here—'

'Lie *still*. Don't worry, I washed it this morning. It's been drying like
a flag of truce over that bush just inside the cleft.'

'I didn't mean that, don't be silly. But you can't shed any more clothes,
my goodness. I've got your jersey, and now your petticoat—'

'Don't worry. I won't give you anything else. If it comes to that, I've
nothing else to spare. There, that looks better, and it'll keep dry. How
does it feel?'

'Wonderful. No, honestly, it does feel better. No more throbbing, just
beastly sore, and hurts like blazes if I jar it.'

'Well, there's no need for you to move any more. You stay where you
are, and keep a look-out on the hill. I'm going to bury these rags, and
then I'll bring up a fresh supply of water, so that we can stay up here
if we have to.'

By the time I had got back with the water and fresh kindling, and
relaid my fire in readiness, it was a few minutes short of eight o'clock.
I lay down beside Mark, and propped my chin on my hands.

'I'll watch now. Lie down.'

Without a word, he did as he was told, closing his eyes with that same air of fierce and concentrated patience.

I looked down the long, bare wings of the mountain. Nothing. Eight o'clock of a fine, bright morning.

It was going to be a long day.

CHAPTER SIX

Push off . . .

TENNYSON: *Ulysses*

It was, in fact, barely twenty minutes before the man appeared.

I saw the movement, far down the hillside, south-east of where we lay. My first thought was, naturally, that this might be Lambis returning, but then, as the tiny figure toiled nearer, it struck me that he was making remarkably little effort to conceal himself.

I narrowed my eyes against the sun. At that distance I could make out very little, except that the man was wearing something dark, which could have been Lambis' brown trousers and navy-blue jersey; but he did not seem to be carrying anything except a stick, and not only did he walk openly across the barest stretches of the hillside, but he seemed to be in no hurry, pausing frequently, and turning to stare about him, with his hand up to his eyes as if to shield them from the glare of the sun.

When he had stopped for the fourth time in as many minutes, I had decided – still more in curiosity than apprehension – that it could not be Lambis. Then, as his hand lifted, I caught the flash of the sun on something he held to his eyes. Binoculars. And then, as he moved on, another gleam, this time on the 'stick' that he carried under one arm. A rifle.

I lay flattened against the juniper-needles that strewed the ledge, watching him, now, as I would have watched a rattlesnake. My heart, after the first painful kick of fear, settled down to an erratic, frightened pumping. I took deep breaths, to help control myself, and glanced down at Mark beside me.

He lay motionless, with shut eyes, and that awful look of exhaustion still on his face. I put a hand out, tentatively, then drew it back. Time enough to disturb him when the murderer came closer.

That it was the murderer, there could be no possible doubt. As the small figure, dwarfed by distance, moved nearer across an open stretch of the mountain-side, I caught a glimpse of red – the red head-band of which Lambis had spoken – and the impression of the baggy outline of Cretan dress. Besides, the man was patiently hunting for something. Every minute or so he paused to rake some part of the hillside with his glasses, and once, when he turned aside to beat through a stand of young cypresses, he did so with his rifle at the ready ...

He came out from the shadow of the grove, and paused again. Now the glasses were directed upwards ... they were swinging towards the ledge ... the shepherds' hut ... the way Lambis would come ...

The glasses moved past us, back eastwards, without a pause, and were directed for a long look at the tree-thicketed rocks above the cypress-grove where he stood. Finally he lowered them, gave a hitch to his rifle, and began to make his way slowly uphill, until a jutting crag hid him from view.

I touched Mark gently. 'Are you awake?'

His eyes opened immediately at the whisper, and their expression, as he turned his head, showed that the significance of my stealthy movement and dropped voice hadn't escaped him. 'What it it?'

'There's someone out there, some way below us, and I think he may be your man. He seems to be looking for something, and he's got a gun.'

'In sight of the ledge now?'

'Not at the moment.'

Mark turned awkwardly on to his stomach, and cautiously peered down through the junipers. I put my mouth to his ear. 'Do you see those cypresses away down there? The grove beyond the stunted tree with a dead branch like a stag's horn? He's been making his way uphill from there. You can't see from here, but there are trees above there, away beyond that cliff, and the top of a gorge like this one, only smaller. I think I saw a little waterfall running down to it.' I swallowed, painfully. 'I – I said he'd hunt where the water was.'

Mark was craning his neck to study the rocks above and below our own ledge. 'I wasn't fit to notice, when we were on our way up here. This place really can't be seen from below?'

'No, at least no one would think there was a ledge. All you can see is these shrubs, and they look as if they were in a crack in the face of the cliff.'

'And the way up?'

'That's hidden, too, among those bushes at the bottom, by the fig-tree.'

'Mm. Well, we'll have to chance it. Can you crawl back into that cave without showing yourself or making a single sound?'

'I – I think so.'

'Then get back in there, now, while he's out of sight.'

'But if he comes up here at all, he'll look in there, and there's nowhere we can hide. It's quite bare.' I shifted my shoulders. 'Anyway, I – I'd rather stay out here. If there was a fight, we'd stand a better chance out here—'

'A fight!' Mark's breath was sucked in with sudden, furious exasperation. 'What sort of a fight do you think we could put up against a rifle? Penknives at thirty yards?'

'Yes, I know, but I could surely—'

'Look, there isn't time to argue, just get in there out of sight, for pity's sake! I can't make you do as I say, but will you please, for once, *just do as you're told?*'

I have never seen anyone's jaw drop, but I'm sure mine did then. I felt it. I just sat there gaping at him.

'He's looking for me,' said Mark, with a kind of angry patience. '*For me*. Only. He doesn't even know you exist – or Lambis either, for that matter. You'll be quite safe in the cave. Now, have you got that, dimwit?'

'But . . . he'll kill you,' I stammered, stupidly.

'And just how,' said Mark savagely, 'do you propose to stop him? Get killed yourself as well, and add that to my account? Now get in there and shut up. I haven't the strength to argue.'

I turned, without a word.

But it was too late. Even as I began to slither backwards from my hide between the junipers, Mark's good hand shot out, and gripped and held me still.

For a moment I couldn't see why; then, just a glimpse, nearer through the green, I saw the red head-dress. Immediately afterwards – so close was he now – I heard plainly the grate of his boot-soles in the dust, and the flick of a kicked pebble.

Mark lay like an image. He looked, despite the bandaged arm and the shocking pallor, surprisingly dangerous. Surprisingly, when you saw that all the weapon he had was a clasp-knife, and a pile of stones.

The Cretan came on steadily, along the path by which Lambis had gone. It would lead him past the little field of asphodel, below the shepherds' hut, past the spring which marked the beginning of the climb to our ledge . . .

I could see him clearly now. He was a strongly-built man, not tall, but tough-looking, with mahogany-dark skin. While I could not at that distance make out his features, I could see the squared cheekbones, and full lips under a thick moustache. The sleeves of his dark-blue skirt were pushed up, showing brown knotty forearms. I could even see the scarlet trimming of the sleeveless jacket, and the swathed sash with the knife stuck into it, that completed the Cretan 'heroic' dress.

He lifted the field-glasses again. We lay as still as stones. A long, heart-shaking minute passed. The sun poured on to the rock; the scents of verbena and thyme and sage winnowed up around us in the heat. Encouraged by our stillness, a small brown snake crept out from the rock a few feet away, lay for a moment watching us, his little eyes catching the light like dewdrops; then he poured himself away down a hole. I hardly noticed; there was room for no more fear; this was hardly the moment to worry about a small brown snake, while a murderer stood down there at the edge of the alpine meadow, with his glasses to his eyes . . .

The swing of the glasses checked. The man froze like a pointer. He had seen the shepherds' hut.

If he was a local man, he must already have known of its existence, but it was obvious, I thought, that until this moment he had forgotten it. He dropped the glasses on their cord round his neck, and shifted his rifle forward once more; then, with his eyes fixed unwaveringly on the door of the hut, he moved forward, warily, through the asphodel.

I turned my head, to meet a question in Mark's eyes. I knew what it was. Was I certain I had removed all traces? Feverishly, I cast my mind back: the bedding; the floor; my bag, and its contents; Mark's haversack; the traces of our meal; the dressings from Mark's shoulder; the orange-peel. Yes, I was certain. I gave Mark a jerky little nod of reassurance.

He sketched the ghost of a thumbs-up sign, which meant congratulation, then gestured with his head towards the cleft behind us. This time there was a smile in his eyes. I returned it, after a fashion, then obediently slithered back, rather in the style of the small brown snake, into the shadow of the narrow cave.

The cleft ran back at an angle to the ledge, so that from where I settled myself, well towards the back, I could see only a crack of daylight, with a narrow section of the ledge, and one of Mark's legs, from the knee down.

For all its illusion of shelter, the cave was worse than the ledge, for there, at least, I had been able to see. I sat close, listening to my own heart-beats.

Presently, I heard him. He was walking carefully, but in the tranced stillness of the morning his steps sounded loud. They came nearer, moved from grass to stone, from stone to dust, were lost behind a barrier of rock where the trickle of the spring drowned them . . .

Silence. So long a silence that I could have sworn, watching that narrow section of light, that the sun wheeled, and the shadows moved . . .

Then suddenly, he was here, just below the ledge. The soft steps trod through the stony dust. The bushes by the fig-tree rustled as he parted them. I saw the muscles of Mark's leg tense themselves.

The rustling stopped. The footsteps felt their way through dust again, moved away a little, paused . . .

In my mind's eye I could see him standing, as before, with the glasses to his eyes, raking the crannies and clefts above him for a possible hiding-place. Perhaps even now he was discovering the cave where I crouched, and wondering how to get up to it . . .

A shadow swept across the sector of light. The kestrel. I heard, in that deadly stillness, the small sound it made as it met the edge of the nest: I could swear, to this day, that I heard the whiffling of air in its feathers as it braked, flaps down, for the final approach. The hissing, mewing delight of the young ones shrilled as piercingly in the stillness as a double-sized pipe band on the dead air of a Scottish Sunday.

The flake of shadow swept out again. The young ones fell abruptly silent. A twig cracked under the fig-tree.

Then all at once, it seemed, the watcher had moved away. It was possible that the fearless approach of the bird had convinced him that there was nothing on that section of the cliff; whatever the case, he had certainly gone. The sounds retreated, faded, ceased. As my pulses slowly steadied, I found that I had shut my eyes, the better to hear that reassuring diminuendo.

Once more, at last, silence. I opened my eyes on the wedge of light at the mouth of the cleft, to see that Mark's leg had vanished.

If I had been in a fit state to think at all, I suppose I would have assumed that he had merely inched further along the ledge, the better to watch the Cretan out of sight. But as it was, I stared at the empty gap of light with horror, for two eternal minutes, with my common sense in fragments, and my imagination racing madly through a series of nightmare pictures that would have done credit to a triple-X film . . . Perhaps, after all, the murderer hadn't gone; perhaps, even now, Mark was lying, throat cut, staring at the sky, while the murderer waited for me at the mouth of the cleft, with dripping knife . . .

But here, at last, some sort of courage and common sense asserted itself. For one thing, the man had had a rifle, and for another, disabled though Mark was, the Cretan could hardly have shot, stabbed, or clubbed him to death in perfect silence . . .

I craned forward to see. Nothing but a tuft of salvia, purple-blue, with scented grey leaves, flattened where Mark had lain. Nothing to be heard, either, but a faint rustling . . .

The snake. That was it. He had been bitten by the snake. With hideous promptitude, the new picture presented itself: Mark, dead in (silent) agony, lying with blackened face, staring at the sky . . .

If I didn't stare at the sky pretty soon myself, I should go mad. I crawled forward to the mouth of the cleft, lay flat, then peered out.

Mark wasn't lying dead, and his face wasn't black. It was, on the contrary, very white indeed, and he was on his feet, looking as if he had every intention of climbing down from the ledge in pursuit of the murderer. Of the latter there was no sign. Mark was pulling aside the trails of honeysuckle that masked the entrance to the ledge.

'*Mark!*'

He turned, as sharply as if I had thrown something.

I was across the ledge like an arrow, and had hold of his sound arm. I said furiously: 'And just where do you think you're going?'

He answered with a sort of desperation: 'He's gone back along the hillside. I want to see where he goes. If I could follow, he might lead straight to Colin.'

I had just been very badly frightened, and was still ashamed of my reactions to that fear. It made it difficult, for the moment, to think straight. 'Do you mean to tell me that you were just *going*, and leaving me *alone in there*?'

He looked bewildered, as if the question were irrelevant; as I suppose it was. 'You'd have been quite safe.'

'And you think *that's* all that matters? You think I don't even care whether you—?' I stopped short. Things were coming straight now, rather too straight for speech. In any case, he wasn't listening. I said, still angrily, because I was annoyed with myself: 'And just how far do you think you'd get? Have a grain of common sense, will you? You wouldn't get a hundred yards!'

'I've got to try.'

'You can't!' I swallowed, conscious of the greatest reluctance to say anything more at all. I never wanted to leave the shelter of that ledge as long as I lived. But one must save a rag of pride to dress in. 'I'll go,' I said huskily. 'I can keep out of sight—'

'Are you mad?' It was his turn to be furious; more, I could see, with his own helplessness than with me. That the conversation was conducted in hissed whispers did nothing to detract from its forcefulness. We glared at one another. 'You don't even begin to—' he began, then stopped, and I saw his face change. The relief that swept into it was so vivid that for the moment all exhaustion and worry seemed wiped away, and his smile was almost gay. I swung round, to look where he was looking.

A man had dropped lightly from the tumble of rocks above the little alp, and was making a cautious way between the clumps of asphodel. Brown trousers, dark-blue jersey, bare head: Lambis. Lambis, watching the watcher, following him down to Colin . . .

In a few moments more he, too, skirted the base of the cliff, and vanished.

'He got away,' said Lambis, breathlessly, in Greek. 'There's another gorge further along the hill, where a stream runs down. It's full of trees – plenty of cover. I lost him there.'

It was perhaps an hour later. Mark and I had waited, watching the hillside, until we saw Lambis returning. He approached slowly and wearily, pausing at length at the edge of the flowery plateau to look up towards the rocks where we lay. It was obvious from his bearing that he was alone, so Mark had waved some sort of signal to show him where we were, while I had made a hurried way down, to meet him on the narrow path above the spring. He was empty-handed still. I guessed that he had cached whatever he had been carrying, in order to follow the Cretan.

'Was he heading downhill – down the gorge?' I asked quickly. 'That's probably another way down to Agios Georgios; in fact, I don't see where else it can go. Did you see?'

The Greek shook his head, then rubbed the back of his hand over his forehead. He looked tired, and was sweating profusely. He had spoken in his own language as if too exhausted to attempt English, and I had answered in the same tongue, but he gave no sign that he had noticed this. 'No. I couldn't get too close to him, you understand, so it was not easy to follow him. I lost him among the rocks and bushes. He could have climbed out of the gorge and gone further east, or he may have been making for the village. Look, I must tell Mark. He got up there?'

'Yes, I helped him up. He's much better. What about Colin?'

'Eh? No. Nothing. He wasn't there. He had not been to the boat.' He spoke, I thought, as if his mind was not quite on what he was saying. He had hardly looked at me, but kept his eyes on the upper rocks where Mark lay. He rubbed a hand again across his damp face, and made as if to push past me without further speech.

I caught at his sleeve in a sudden flash of apprehension. 'Lambis! Are you telling me the truth?'

He paused and turned. It seemed to take two or three seconds before his eyes focused on me. 'The truth?'

'About Colin. Have you got bad news for Mark?'

'No, of course I haven't! Of course I'm telling you the truth, why not? I went to the boat last night; he was not there. There was no sign, no sign of him at all. Why should I lie to you?'

'I - it's all right. I just thought . . . Sorry.'

'It is because I have nothing to tell him that I am angry now. If I had found out something from this man—' a quick exasperated shrug - 'but I did not. I have failed, and this is what I have to tell Mark. Now let me go, he will be wondering what's happened.'

'Wait just a moment, he knows you haven't got Colin, we were watching you from the ledge. But the food - did you get the food and stuff?'

'Oh. Yes, of course I did. I brought all I could carry. I should have been here a long time ago, but I had to stop and hide, because of that one.' He jerked his head downhill, a curiously dismissive gesture. 'When I saw him come this way, I hid the things, and came, quickly. It was a good thing you'd left the hut.'

'He saw it, did you know?'

'Yes. I guessed that he had. When I came here, he was just coming along under this ledge, and I knew he must have seen the hut. But he was still hunting . . . and I had heard no shot . . . so I knew that you had gone. I guessed you would be here.'

'Where did you put the food? We ought - never mind, Mark'll want to hear your news first. Come along, then, let's hurry.'

This time it was Lambis who hung back. 'Listen, why don't you go for the food straight away, yourself? Just the food, leave the other things; I can carry them later.'

'Well, all right. If you think I can find the place.'

'It's near the top of the gorge where I lost him. Follow round where you saw me go - see? There's a goat-track of a kind; it takes you along the foot of the ridge to where the stream runs down into the gorge. It's rocky at the top, but there are trees, lower down. You can see their tops.'

'Yes.'

'At the head of the gorge, where the spring leaves the rocks, there is an olive-tree. It is in shelter, and has grown big, and very old, with a hollow body. You must see it, there are no others near. I left the things inside it. I shall come when I have seen Mark.'

Almost before he had finished speaking, he had turned away. I got the sharp impression of preoccupation, almost as if I had been dismissed, and with relief. But the nagging little thought that this brought to me didn't last long. Even if Lambis (having presumably fed on board the caique) could so lightly dismiss the thought of food and drink, I could not. The very thought of what the hollow tree contained drove me towards it at the speed with which a pin approaches a magnet.

I found it easily enough. It was the only olive-tree in sight, but even without that, I felt sure that I should have flown straight to the food by instinct, like a vulture to its kill, even had that been buried in the very middle of Minos' labyrinth.

I rummaged eagerly in the hollow trunk. There were two blankets, wrapped round what appeared to be a sizeable collection of stuff. I untied the blankets, and foraged for what he had brought.

There were medical supplies, bandages, antiseptic, soap, a razor . . . But for the moment I pushed these aside, to concentrate on the food.

The thermos flask, full. Some tins, among them one of Nescafé, and some sweetened milk. Tins of corned beef. Biscuits. A small bottle of whisky. And, final miracle, a tin-opener.

I threw these happily into one blanket, tied the corners up into a bundle, and set off back again.

Lambis met me half-way. He didn't speak, just nodded at me, as he made way for me on the path. I was glad of this, as it is not easy to speak politely with one's mouth full of Abernethy biscuit, and to speak Greek – which contains gutturals – would have been less elegant still.

All the same, I would have been the happier for something to lighten the look he gave me. It wasn't that the distrust had come back; it was something far less positive than that, and slightly more disconcerting. Say, rather, that confidence had been withdrawn. I was back on the outside.

I wondered what he and Mark had been saying.

I found Mark sitting at the back of the ledge, leaning against the rock, staring out over the open hillside. He turned with a start when I spoke.

'Here's the thermos,' I said. 'Lambis says there's soup in it. There, have the mug, I'll use the top of the thermos. Get yours straight away, will you? I'm going to light the fire again, for coffee.'

I waited for his protest, but it didn't come. He took the flask from me without speaking. I added, hesitatingly: 'I – I'm sorry Lambis didn't have better news.'

The thermos top seemed to have stuck. He gave it a wrench with his good hand, and it came. 'Well, it's what I expected.' He glanced up then, but I had the impression that I wasn't fully in focus. 'Don't worry any more, Nicola.' A smile, that looked like something taken out to wear, that one wasn't used to. 'Sufficient unto the day. Let's eat first, shall we?'

I left him carefully pouring soup, and hurried into the cleft to get the fire going.

It was a wonderful meal. We had the soup first, then corned beef, sandwiched between the thick Abernethy biscuits; some cake stiff with fruit; chocolate; and then the coffee, scalding hot, and sweetened with the tinned milk. I ate ravenously; Lambis, who had fed himself on the boat, took very little; Mark, making, after the first few mouthfuls, an obvious effort, did very well. When at last he sat cradling his half-empty cup of coffee between his hand, as if treasuring the last of its warmth, I thought he looked very much better.

When I said so, he seemed to come with a jerk out of his thoughts. 'Well, yes, I'm fine now, thanks to you and Lambis. And now, it's time we thought about what happens next.'

Lambis said nothing. I waited.

Mark blew a cloud of smoke, and watched it feather to nothing in the bright air. 'Lambis says this man was almost certainly making for Agios Georgios, and – since it's the nearest – it does seem only reasonable to suppose that, whoever these blighters are, they come from there. That makes it at once easier, and more complicated. I mean, we know where to start looking, but it's certain, now, that we can't go down there for official help.' He shot a quick glance at me, as if prepared for a protest, but I said nothing. He went on: 'All the same, obviously, the first step is to get down there – somehow – and find out about my brother. I'm not such a fool as to think—' this with a touch of weary hopelessness – 'that I could do very much myself yet, but even if I can't make it, Lambis will go.'

Lambis made no reply; indeed, he hardly seemed to be listening. I realized, suddenly, that between the two men, everything that had to be said had already been said. The council of war had been held already – while I had been sent to get the food – and its first conclusions reached. I thought I knew what they were.

'And so,' Mark was saying smoothly, without looking at me, like someone trying out a delicate tape-recorder set somewhere in the middle distance, 'will Nicola, of course.'

I had been right. First order in council: *Women and camp-followers, out of the way; the campaign's about to start.*

He was addressing me directly now. 'Your cousin's coming today, isn't she? You'll have to be there, or there'll be questions asked. You could be down at the hotel, and checked in . . .' a glance at his wrist . . . 'good heavens, by lunch-time, probably. Then you can – well, forget all this, and get on with that holiday of yours, that Lambis interrupted.'

I regarded him. Here we were again, I thought: the smile, friendly, but worn as a vizard to anxiety; the obstinate mouth; the general wariness of manner which meant 'thank you very much, and now, please go away – and stay away.'

'Of course,' I said. I pulled my canvas bag towards me over the juniper needles, and began putting my things into it, rather at random. He was perfectly right, I knew that; and anyway, there was nothing more I could do. With Frances coming today, I would have to get out, and keep out. Moreover – I was rather sharply honest with myself here – I wasn't exactly eager to run into any more situations such as I had met last night and today, with their tensions, discomforts, and moments of extreme fear. Nor was I prepared to be regarded – as Mark, once on his feet, would obviously regard me – as a responsibility, even a liability.

So I smiled rather tightly at him, and pushed things into my bag.

'Bless you.' The smile he gave me now was one of swift and genuine relief. 'You've been wonderful, I don't have to tell you how wonderful, and I don't want to seem filthily ungrateful now, after all you've done, but – well, you've seen something of what's going on, and it's obvious that if I can keep you out of it, I must.'

'It's all right, you don't have to bother. I'm the world's crawlingest coward anyway, and I've had enough excitement to last me a lifetime. I shan't cramp your style. You won't see me for dust once I get within sight of the hotel.'

'I hope to heaven your luggage is still where you left it. If it's not, you'll have to be thinking up some story to account for it. Let me see . . .'

'I'll dream up something, something they can't disprove till I've left. Good heavens, you don't have to start worrying about that! That's *my* affair.'

If he noticed that one, he let it pass. He was crushing out his cigarette, frowning down at it, withdrawing into those dark thoughts again.

'There's one thing, and its desperately important, Nicola. If you do see Lambis – or even me – around in the village, or anywhere else for that matter, you don't know us.'

'Well, of course not.'

'I had to mention it.'

'That's okay.' I hesitated. 'But you will let me know somehow – sometime – what happens, won't you? I shall worry, who wouldn't?'

'Of course. Will the British Embassy in Athens find you?'

'The British Embassy?' Lambis had looked up sharply.

'Yes.' Mark's eyes met his, in that now-familiar, excluding look. 'It's where she works.' Then, to me, 'I can get you there?'

'Yes.'

'I'll write to you. Another thing . . .'

'What?'

He wasn't looking at me, he was fingering the stones beside him. 'You'll have to promise me something, for the sake of my peace of mind.'

'What is it?'

'You won't go near the police.'

'If I'm getting out of your affairs, I'm not likely to complicate them by doing that. But I still can't see why you don't go at least to the headman in Agios Georgios. Personally, I'm all for doing the simplest thing, and going straight to the authorities, wherever I am. But it's your affair.' I looked from one man to the other. They sat in uncompromising silence. I went on, slowly, feeling more than ever an intruder: 'Mark, you know, you haven't done anything wrong. Surely, now they realize you're just an English tourist—'

'That won't hold water.' He spoke dryly. 'If they didn't realize on Saturday night, they did on Sunday, and this morning. And still our friend's looking for me with a gun.'

Lambis said: 'You're forgetting Colin. He is the reason for this.' His gesture took in the ledge, the scraps of food, all the evidence of our rough-and-ready camp. 'Until we know where Colin is, how can we do anything? If he is still alive, he is their – I do not know the word – *ó ómeros.*'

'Hostage,' said Mark.

'Yes, of course. I – I'm sorry. Well . . .' My voice faded feebly, as I looked from one to the other; Mark wooden, Lambis sullen and withdrawn once more. Suddenly I was conscious of nothing but a longing to escape, to be away down the mountainside, back to yesterday – the lemon-grove in the sunshine, the egret, the point where I came in . . .

I got up, and Lambis rose with me.

I said: 'Are you coming too?'

'I will see you part of the way.'

I didn't demur this time; didn't want to. Besides, I supposed he would want to make his own way into the village, once he had seen me, so to speak, off his pitch. I turned to Mark. 'Don't get up, don't be silly.' I smiled, and put down a hand, which he took. 'Well, I'll say good-bye. And good luck, of course.'

'You got your cardigan?'

'Yes.'

'I'm sorry I couldn't return your petticoat.'

'That's all right. I hope your arm will soon be better. And of course I hope . . . well, that things will turn out right.' I lifted my bag and slung it over my shoulder. 'I'll be going. I expect in a couple of days' time I'll think all this has been a dream.'

He smiled. 'Pretend it has.'

'All right.' But I still hesitated. 'You can trust me not to do anything silly; for one thing, I'd be too scared. But you can't expect me to shut my eyes and ears. You see, if Agios Georgios *is* the guilty village, then I'm bound to see that man with the rifle, and find out who he is, and all about him. And I'm bound to find out who speaks English. I certainly won't bother you, unless I hear something terribly important. But if I do, I – I think I ought to know where to find you. Where's the boat?'

Lambis looked swiftly at Mark. Mark hesitated, then said, across me, in Greek: 'We'd better tell her. It can do no harm. She knows nothing, and—'

'She understands Greek,' said Lambis sharply.

'Eh?' Mark threw a startled, incredulous look at me.

'She speaks it almost as well as you do.'

'*Does* she?' I saw his eyes flicker, as he did a bit of rapid back-thinking, and, for the first time, a trace of colour came up under his skin.

'It's all right,' I said blandly, in Greek. 'You haven't given much away.'

'Oh well,' said Mark, 'it serves me right for being rude. I'm sorry.'

'That's all right. Are you going to tell me about the boat? After all, you never know, *I* might need help. I'd feel better, if I knew where to find you.'

'Well,' said Mark, 'of course,' and he began to give me instructions as to how to reach the caique from the ruined Byzantine church. 'And you could ask anyone the way over to the church itself, that would be quite a normal trip for an English visitor to want to make. I think that's clear enough? Yes? But I hope it won't be necessary for you to come.'

'That,' I said, 'has been made awfully clear. Well, good-bye again. All the best.'

Lambis went first. My last glimpse of Mark was of him sitting stiffly, as if braced against the warm rock, with the empty mug beside him, and that grey look of worry still draining the youth from his face.

CHAPTER SEVEN

Oh mistress, by the gods, do nothing rash!

MATTHEW ARNOLD: *Merope*

Lambis spoke very little on the way down through the ravine. He kept a short way ahead of me, reconnoitring with some caution at the corners, but most of the time we walked as fast as the roughness of the path would allow. We met nobody, and came in good time through the tangle of young oaks above the lemon-groves. Already, through the boughs, I could see the white flanks of a windmill, and the gleam of sunlight on the open water of the stream.

Lambis stopped in a patch of sunlight, and waited for me to catch up with him.

Beside the path where he stood was a little wayside shrine. This was merely a wooden box, wedged somehow back among a pile of rocks, with primitive little oil-lamps burning in front of a brightly coloured plaque of the Panaghia, the Virgin who is at once Mother of God, and the Mother herself, the ancient Goddess of the earth. A beer-bottle, standing to one side, held oil for the lamps. Verbena grew near, and violets.

Lambis gestured towards the lit lamps, and the small bunch of flowers that stood there in a rusty tin.

'I will leave you here. People come this way, and I must not be seen.'

I said good-bye, wished him luck again, and, leaving him there, went down through the lemon-groves towards the open sunlight with, it must be confessed, a definite lightening of the spirits.

It was about noon, and the heat of the day. The breeze had dropped, and even the silky poppy-heads, and the quaker-grass that bordered the path, hung motionless. The white sails of the windmills rested still and slack. A donkey browsed beside a tumbledown wall, in the shade of an ilex. Flies buzzed over the dust.

There was nobody about. People would be at home for the midday meal, or eating it in the fields, somewhere in the shade. I could see no one except a boy, sprawled sleepily in the sun while his goats cropped the vetches, and one man, working a field away, beyond a thick barrier of sugar-cane. Neither looked up as I passed.

I stopped for a moment, gratefully, as I reached the spare shade of the pines at the edge of the lower valley. I looked back.

There it all lay, the hot fields, the lemon-trees, the wooded gorge leading up into the silver wilderness of rock.

From here, there could be seen no sign of life in that empty landscape. Lambis had long since disappeared; the lemon-trees hung without a quiver; above them the mountain-side was dead, empty of all motion. But this time yesterday . . .

There was the movement of wings over the gorge. For a split second I stared, incredulous. But this time the wings weren't white: what had caught my eye was the slow wheel of enormous brown feathers climbing the sky. An eagle? More likely a vulture, I thought; perhaps the lammergeier itself. At any other time I would have watched with excitement. Now, because the big bird had reminded me of the white egret, and of yesterday, I felt the tears rising in my throat.

I turned my back on it, and made my way down to the bridge.

When I reached it, I thought for a moment that my luck had deserted me. Two children were leaning over the parapet, spitting orange-pips into the water; a boy and a girl, thin and dark and burned brown, with huge dark eyes and black hair, and the shy manners of the country children. They were spitting very close to my suitcase.

'How do you do?' I said formally.

They stared in silence, backing a little, like calves. I regarded them. I knew quite well that now they would never let me out of their sight until I reached the hotel, and probably not even then. I, the stranger, was their capture. I was news. Whatever I said or did, as from now, would be all over the village within the hour.

I crooked a finger at the boy. 'What's your name?'

He began to grin, probably at the humour of my speaking Greek. 'Georgi.'

It always was. 'And yours?' I asked the little girl.

'Ariadne.' I could hardly hear the whisper.

'Hullo, then, Georgi and Ariadne. I'm a foreigner, English. I've come from Chania this morning, to stay at the hotel in Agios Georgios.'

Silence. There was no answer to this, so they didn't make one. They stood and stared, the boy with the beginnings of that urchin grin, the girl Ariadne taking in every detail of my frock, sandals, bag, wrist-watch, hair-do . . . Even from a child of eight it was not a comfortable scrutiny: I had done my best, with comb and lipstick, before I finally left the ledge, but I would hardly, I thought, look as if I had just recently left the portals of Chania's best hotel.

'Georgi,' I said, 'do you think you could carry a case down to the hotel for me?'

He nodded, looking round him, then reached for my canvas bag. 'This?'

'No, no, a proper case. It's in the bushes, hidden.' I added, carefully: 'I came with a car from Chania, and carried my case down from the road. I left it here, because I wanted to eat my – have my coffee, that is, in the shade further up the river. So I hid my case and left it here. Can you see it? Down there, under the bridge?'

The little girl ran to the parapet and peered over. The boy went more slowly after her. 'You can't see it? I hid it very well,' I said, laughing.

A shriek from Ariadne. 'There, there, Georgi! See!'

Georgi scrambled over the parapet, hung by his hands, and dropped some ten feet into the bushes. He could easily have gone round by the bank, but, being a boy, and a Cretan at that, he no doubt felt obliged to do it the hard way. His sister and I watched him with suitable expressions of admiration, while he dusted his hands on his seat, dived intrepidly (and quite unnecessarily) through some brambles, and finally dragged my case from its hiding-place. He carried it up to the road – this time by the orthodox route – and the three of us set off for the village.

Ariadne, her shyness gone, skipped along beside me, chattering all the time, in a dialect that was too fast and in places too thick for me to follow. Georgi trudged along more slowly, concerned, I could see, to carry my case with apparent ease. Both children answered my questions readily, supplying a lively commentary of their own which I made no attempt to check.

. . . Yes, the hotel was just at this end of the village. Yes, it faced the sea; the back of it, you understand, looked right on the bay. There was a garden, a beautiful garden, right on the shore, with tables and chairs, where you could eat wonderful food, 'real English food', promised Ariadne, wide-eyed, while Georgi hurried to explain this magnificence. It was due to the new owner – I had heard of Stratos Alexiakis, of course, since I came from England, and so did he? He was very rich, and he came from London, which was in England, and he spoke English so that you could not tell he was a Cretan. Indeed, he—

'How can you tell?' I asked, laughing.

'Tony says so.'

'Tony? Who's he?'

'The bar-man,' said Georgi.

'No, the cook,' amended Ariadne, '*and* he waits at table, and sits at the desk, and – oh, he does everything! Mr. Alexiakis is not always there, you see.'

'A sort of manager?' I said. I remembered what my Danish informant had told me about the new owner's 'friend from London'. 'This Tony—' I hesitated. Somehow I didn't really want to ask the next question. 'Did he come from England, too?'

'He is English,' said Georgi.

A short silence. '*Is* he?' I said.

'Yes, oh yes!' This was Ariadne. 'Mr. Alexiakis had a taverna there, a *huge* taverna, very splendid, and so—'

'Are there any other English people in Agios Georgios just now?' It would have been a natural question to ask, anyway; and the context made it doubly so. I hoped my voice sounded normal.

'No.' Georgi's replies were getting shorter. His face had reddened, and there were beads of sweat on it, but I knew better than to offer to relieve him of the case. His pride as a *pallikári* – a man's man – was involved. 'No,' he said, shifting the case from one hand to the other, 'only Tony, and the English ladies. That is you.' He looked doubtfully at me, and finished on a question. 'They said there would be two ladies?'

'My cousin's coming later today.' I didn't feel like attempting to explain further, and luckily, being children, they took the statement for granted, as they had taken my apparent eccentricity over the suitcase. I was thinking furiously, and not very pleasantly. I had told Mark – had known quite well – that if the *dramatis personae* of his murder-play were in fact from Agios Georgios, I would be bound, in such a tiny place, to come across traces of them almost straight away. But to do so as soon as this, and in the hotel itself . . .

I wetted my lips. I might be wrong. After all, people could come and go. I tried again. 'Do you get many visitors here?'

'You are the first at the new hotel. The first this year.' This was Ariadne, still intent on offering me what honour she could.

'No,' Georgi contradicted her, stolidly. 'There was another, a foreigner.'

'English?' I asked.

'I don't know. I don't think so.'

'He *was* English!' cried Ariadne.

'The fat one who went all the way to see the old church on the mountain? And took the picture that was in the *Athens News*? I'm sure he wasn't!'

'Oh, *that* one! No, I don't know what he was. I wasn't counting him, he wasn't a proper visitor.' By 'visitor', I gathered that Ariadne meant 'tourist'. I had already recognized my Danish friend. 'No, I meant the one who came here the other day. Don't you remember? Tony met him at the harbour, and we heard them talking as they went to the hotel, and you said it was English they spoke.'

'He wasn't a proper visitor either,' said Georgi obstinately. 'He came by caique one afternoon, and stayed only one night, and went away again next morning early. I think he must have gone by the road. There was no boat.'

I said: 'When did he come?'

'Three days ago,' said Ariadne.

'Saturday, it was,' said Georgi.

'What do you come here for, to Agios Georgios?' asked Ariadne.

I must have gazed at her blankly for a moment, before, with an effort as great as any Georgi was making, I heaved myself back out of deep waters into the safe shallows of small-talk.

'Oh, just for a holiday. It's – it's so very pretty here.' I gestured, rather lamely, towards the flower-strewn rocks, and the glittering sea. The children looked at me blankly. It had not occurred to them that scenery could be pretty. I tried another harmless lead. 'The vines are good this year?'

'Yes, they are good. They are the best vines in Crete.'

Stock response; of course they were. 'Really? We don't have vines in England. Or olives, either.'

They looked at me, shocked. 'Then what do you eat?'

'Bread, meat, fish.' I realized too late that bread and meat were a rich man's diet, but the admiration in their eyes showed no trace of envy. If there is one thing a Greek respects above intelligence, it is riches. 'And drink?' asked Ariadne.

'Tea, mostly.'

This time the look in their faces made me laugh. 'Yes, but not Greek tea. It's made differently, and it's *nice*. We make our coffee differently, too.'

This didn't interest them. 'No vines!' said Ariadne. 'Tony at the hotel says that in England everybody has electricity and a wireless and you can have it on all day and all night as loud as you like. But also, he says, it is very cold and full of fog, and the people are silent, and London is not a healthy place to live in. He says it is better here.'

'Does he? Well, you do get the sun, don't you? We do see it sometimes in England, but not like this. That's why we come here for holidays, to sit in the sun, and swim, and walk in your hills, and look at the flowers.'

'The flowers? You like flowers?' Ariadne, darting like a humming-bird, was already pulling up the anemones in handfuls. I had to restrain myself. To me, they were exotics as gorgeous as any I had seen at Kew: to the child, weeds. But I ate meat every day. Riches? Perhaps.

Georgi wasn't interested in flowers. The case changed hands again, as he stumped heroically forward. 'You like swimming?'

'Very much. Do you?'

'Of course. No one bathes here yet; it's still too cold, but later it's very good.'

I laughed. 'It's quite warm enough for me. Where's the best place to swim?'

'Oh, that way is best.' He waved his free hand vaguely towards the west. 'There are bays, with rocks, where you can dive.'

'Oh yes, I remember, a friend told me that was the best way. Does one have to go far?'

'To the Dolphins' Bay? No, not very.'

'It's miles and *miles*!' cried Ariadne.

'You are only small,' said her brother contemptuously, 'and your legs are short. For me, or for the *thespoinís*, it is not far.'

'My legs are not much shorter than yours!' Ariadne bristled, with every intention, I saw, of doing instant battle. I intervened hastily, wondering, with some pity, at what age the Cretan girls are actually taught their place in the masculine scheme of things: 'Why do you call it Dolphins' Bay? Do you really see dolphins there?'

'Oh, yes,' said Georgi.

'Sometimes they come amongst the swimmers!' cried Ariadne, happily diverted. 'There was a boy once, who used to ride on them!'

'Was there?' What ancient story was this, still surviving here among the children? Pliny's boy from Baiae? Arion on the dolphin's back? Telemachus, the son of Odysseus? I smiled down at her. 'Well, I've never even seen a dolphin. Do you suppose they'd come and play with me?'

Truth struggled in her face with the Greek's desire to please the stranger at all costs. 'Perhaps ... but it is a long time since they did this ... I am eight years old, but it was before I was born, *thespoinís*. People tell stories ...'

'But you'll *see* them,' promised Georgi, confidently, 'if the weather stays warm. It's best if you go out in a caique, into deeper water. Sometimes, when I have been out fishing, we have seen them, swimming near the boat, sometimes with their young ones ...'

And, my earlier questions forgotten, he embarked happily on the Cretan version of the fisherman's yarn, until he was interrupted by his sister, who pushed into my arms an enormous bunch of slim, purple-red gladioli, the sort that are called 'Byzantine' in our seedsmen's catalogues, where the corms retail at about fivepence each. In Crete, they grow wild in the corn. The bundle was shaggy with lilac anemones, dragged up anyhow, and scarlet tulips with pointed petals – a variety that rates at least sevenpence apiece in Frances' nurseries.

'For you, *thespoinís*!'

My delighted thanks took us round the last bend in the track, and there was the hotel.

This was, at first sight, hardly deserving of the name.

Originally, there had been two houses, square-built and two storeyed, joined to make one long, lowish building. The one on the right had been an ordinary dwelling-house – large, as village standards went – of perhaps five rooms in all. The other had been the village *kafenéion* or coffee-shop: its big ground-floor room, with shutters pulled back, was open to the street, and played, now, the dual role of village *kafenéion* and hotel dining-room. Across one corner of this room was a curved counter, stacked with crockery and glasses, and with shelves of bottles behind it. Between the coffee-making apparatus, and the stove of *loukoumáthes*, were some sophisticated-looking pyramids of fruit. A door at the back of the room led, presumably, to the kitchen premises. The restaurant still had the scrubbed board floor and white-washed walls of the village coffee-shop, but the white cloths on the tables were of starched linen, and on some of them were flowers.

At the end of the building, against the outer wall of the restaurant, was an outside stairway, built of stone, leading to the rooms above. This was still in use, it appeared; each worn step was whitened at the edge; and on every one stood a flowering plant, blue convolvulus with long belled strands looping down the wall below; scarlet geraniums; and carnations of every shade from deep flame to the mother-of-pearl flush of a Pacific shell. The walls of the building were newly whitewashed, and the paintwork blue.

The effect was simple, fresh, and – with the flowers, and the tamarisk trees at the back, and the glimpse of the sea beyond – delightful.

Georgi dumped my case with a flourish that effectively hid his relief, and was persuaded, without much difficulty, to accept five drachmae. His *pallikarás* dignity concealing his delight, he went staidly off, with Ariadne scampering beside him. But just before he was out of sight past the first cottage wall, I saw him break into a run. The news was on the wing already.

Georgi had abandoned me at the edge of a covered terrace which had been built right along the front of the hotel. In the shade of its trellised roof were set a few little metal tables, where the elders of the village sat. This morning three of them were there, two playing backgammon, the third watching in motionless appraisal. A youth sat on a table near them, swinging his legs and smoking; he looked up, and watched me with some interest, but the old men never even gave me a glance.

As I turned towards the main door – it had been that of the house on the right – the youth turned his head, and called something, and a man who had been busying himself somewhere at the back of the dining-room came hurrying out past the backgammon players.

'You must be Miss Ferris?'

The voice was unmistakably English. This, then, was 'Tony'. I looked at him with sharp interest.

He was young, somewhere under thirty, it was difficult to guess where;

of middle height, slightly-built, but moving with the kind of tough grace that one associates with ballet. His hair was fairish, fine and straight, rather too long, but impeccably brushed. His face was narrow-featured, and clever, with light-blue eyes. He wore close-fitting and very-well-tailored jeans, and a spotlessly white shirt. He was smiling, a rather charming smile; his teeth were small and even, like milk-teeth.

'Yes,' I said. 'How do you do? You're expecting me for tonight, aren't you? I know I'm a little early, but I was hoping for lunch.'

'Early?' He laughed. 'We were just going to put the police on your trail. You've no idea. Miss Scorby thought—'

'*Police?*' I must have sounded startled beyond all reason, and I thought I saw the flicker of surprise in his eyes. My heart jumped painfully, then ground jaggedly into top gear. 'Miss Scorby? What are you talking about? Is my cousin here already?'

'No, no. She rang up last night. She said the boat was still held up in Patras, but that she'd gone by train to Athens, and managed to catch the flight after all.'

'Oh, good for her! Then she'll get today's bus? She'll be here for dinner?'

'For tea. She said she wasn't going to wait for the bus; she thought the vegetable caique might be more fun, and would get her here sooner.' The small teeth showed. 'An enterprising lady. She should be here any time now. The boat's overdue as it is.'

I laughed. 'I might have known Frances would make it! And *before* she was due, at that! That's marvellous!'

'Yes, she did think she'd been rather clever. She thought she'd be catching you up in Heraklion – you were both to have got the bus today, weren't you? – but you'd gone. They told her you'd left yesterday, with a message saying you were coming straight here.'

He finished on a note of perfectly normal inquiry. I managed to say, I hoped naturally: 'I did. I did leave Heraklion yesterday, and I fully intended to come on here, if I could. But I was offered a lift by some sweet Americans, and they decided to stay overnight in Chania, to look at the Turkish quarter. They'd offered to bring me on here today, and there was no hurry, as I didn't think you were expecting me.'

'Ah, well, that explains it. We weren't really worried, you know, dear, we thought you'd have let us know if you were coming sooner, and, to tell you the truth, I doubt if we could have taken you before today.'

'Full up?'

'No, no, nothing like that. But busy, you know, busy. We're still only half in order here. Did you walk down from the road?'

'Yes. I had some coffee near the bridge, and then Georgi carried my case the rest of the way.'

'Well, come and sign the Golden Book, then I'll show you your room.'

The lobby was merely a wide passage running straight through the house. Half-way along it stood an old-fashioned table with a chair behind it, and a rack holding four keys. This was the reception desk. A door beside it was marked 'Private'.

'Not just the Ritz, you know,' remarked Tony cheerfully, 'but all in good time, we're expanding like mad. We've got four whole bedrooms now. Not bad, for Agios Georgios.'

'It's delightful. But how do you come to be here – you're English, aren't you?' The visitors' book was brand new, its blank pages as informative as a shut eye.

'Yes, indeed. My name's Gamble, but you can call me Tony, everybody does. Gamble by name, and gamble by nature, to coin a phrase. There's money to be made over here, you know, with this tourist boom, and hotels going up everywhere like mushrooms; not so much just yet, perhaps, but when they build the road this way – real money. We want to be ready for that. And the climate's nice, too, for someone like me, with a chest.' He paused, perhaps feeling that he had been a shade over-eager with his explanations. Then he smiled, and an eyelid flickered. '*La dame aux camélias*, and all that, you know. That's really what persuaded me to settle so far from the dear old Vicarage.'

'Oh?' I said. 'Bad luck. Ariadne did tell me that you'd found London unhealthy. That must have been what she meant. Well, this seems a lovely place, so I wish you luck. Is this where I write, at the top?'

'Yes, just there.' A beautifully-kept finger indicated the first line of the virgin page. 'Our very first guest, dear, did you know? One thing, you can be certain the sheets are clean.'

'I wouldn't have dreamed of doubting them. But what about my Danish friend, the man who sent me here? You should have collected his signature – it's famous, in a mild way.' I gave his name.

'Oh, yes, but he doesn't count. We weren't officially 'open', and Stratos only put him up for the publicity, and because there was nowhere else. We were still painting.'

I wrote my name with what I hoped was a casual flourish. 'And the Englishman?'

'Englishman?' His stare was blank.

'Yes,' I picked up the blotting-paper and smoothed it over my signature. 'I thought those children said you'd had an Englishman here last week?'

'Oh, him.' There was the tiniest pause. 'I know who they mean.' He smiled. 'He wasn't English; he was a Greek, a friend of Stratos'. I suppose those brats heard him talking to me?'

'Probably, I hardly remember. There.' I pushed the book across to him.

He picked it up, ' "Nicola Ferris". A very pretty start to the page. Thanks. No, dear, he didn't count either; he didn't even stay here, just called on business, and left the same night. Well, come and see your room.' He flicked a key off its hook, picked up my case, and led the way back towards the front door.

'You said the boat was due now?'

'Any minute, but you know how it is. She'll certainly be here by tea-time.' He grinned over his shoulder. 'And that's one of your worries away, let me tell you. I make the tea myself.'

'Oh? Good. She loves her tea. Not me; I've had time to get acclimatized.'

'Acclimatized? You mean you've been over here for a bit?' He sounded genuinely interested.

'Over a year. I work at the British Embassy in Athens.'

I thought his glance was appraising. He swung my case as if it weighed no more than an ounce. 'Then you'll talk the lingo, I suppose? This way, dear. We go up the outside steps; rather primitive, I'm afraid, but it's all part of our simple, unstudied charm.'

I followed him up the flower-bordered steps. The smell of carnations was thick as smoke in the sun.

'I've picked up a bit of Greek.' I had had to decide on this admission when I met the children, and he would certainly find out – in fact, I had already implied – that I had talked to them. I added, apologetically: 'But it's terribly difficult, and of course there's the alphabet. I can ask simple questions, and so on, but as for *talking*—' I laughed. 'In my job we tend to mix, most of the time, with our own people, and I room with an English girl. But one day I really mean to get down to learning the language. What about you?'

'Oh my dear, a little, only a little, and ghastly Greek at that, I do assure you. I mean, one gathers it *works*, but I never speak it unless I have to. Luckily, Stratos' English is quite shatteringly good . . . Here we are. Primitive, but rather nice, don't you think? The décor was my own idea.'

Originally, the room had been plain and square, with roughly plastered walls, a scrubbed wooden floor, and a small window cut in the thick wall facing the sea. Now the rough walls were washed blue-white, some fresh straw matting covered the floor, and the bed, which looked comfortable, was covered with a dazzling white counterpane. The sun, reaching round towards afternoon, already poured a slanting shaft through the window embrasure; the shutters were open, and there were no curtains, but outside there was a vine sifting the sunlight so that the walls of the room were patterned most beautifully with the moving shadows of leaf and tendril.

'A shame to shut it out, don't you think?' said Tony.

'It's lovely. Is *this* your "décor"? I thought you meant you'd designed it.'

'Oh well, you could say I did in a way. I stopped them spoiling it. Stratos was all for Venetian blinds, and two colours of wallpaper, just like home sweet home.'

'Oh? Well, I'm sure you were right. Is, er, "Stratos" your name for Mr. Alexiakis?'

'Yes, he's the owner, you knew that? Did your Danish friend tell you about him? Quite the romantic local-boy-makes-good story, isn't it?

That's what all the emigrants from these poverty-stricken rabbit-hutches dream of doing – coming home after twenty years, buying up the place, and showering money on the family.'

'Oh, he has a family?'

'Well, there's only a sister, Sofia, and between you and me, dear, there's a little bit of difficulty about showering money on her.' Tony dumped my case on a chair, and turned confidingly, with very much the air of one who has been missing the pleasures of a nice, cosy gossip. 'It would mean showering it on her husband, too, and dear Stratos doesn't, but *doesn't* get on with his brother-in-law. But then, who does? I can't say I just fell madly for him myself, and I'm fearfully easy to please, far too easy-going, really. I remember—'

'What's wrong with him?'

'Josef? Oh, first of all, he's a Turk. Not that I mind *that*, but some of these village types think it's just the *last* thing, next to a Bulgarian or a German. And the poor girl was left well off, respected papa and all that, just the job for a nice local Cretan boy, but she had to go and marry this Turkish foreigner from Chania, who's frittered and drunk most of it away – won't lift a finger, *and* rather pushes her around. Oh, the usual, you know, *such* a dreary tale. What's more, he won't let her go to church, and *that*, of course, is the last straw. Quaint, isn't it?'

'Can't the priest help?'

'We haven't one, dear, he only visits.'

'Oh. Poor Sofia.'

'Yes, well, things have looked up for her since brother Stratos got home.'

'He must have done well for himself; he had a restaurant, didn't he? Where was it, Soho somewhere?'

'Oh, you wouldn't know it, it wasn't big – though of course the locals think it was the Dorchester, no less, and give Stratos an income to match. Far be it from him to disillusion them. It was a nice little place, though; I was there myself for six years. That's where I picked up my bit of Greek; most of the boys were Greeks, made Stratos feel at home, he said. Ah well,' he twitched the peach-coloured table-cloth straight, 'it's quite amusing here, tarting the place up a bit, though I don't know that little Tony'd just want to settle here for life. We're going to build, you know, on to the other end. Get a nice long, low block, facing the sea. Take a look at that view.'

'It's wonderful.'

The window faced south-west, over one end of the land-locked bay. To the left, I caught a glimpse of the edge of a roof; that was all; the rest of the village was out of sight. Directly below me, through the masking vine, I could see a flat space of gravel where a few tables and chairs were set – this, no doubt, would be Ariadne's 'beautiful garden'. What flowers there were grew in pots, enormous earthenware *pithoi*, like the old wine-jars from the Cretan palaces. A clump of tamarisk trees stood where the gravel gave way to that flat rock of the foreshore; this, smoothed and fissured by water, burned white in the sun. In every cranny of rock blazed the brilliant pink and crimson sunbursts of ice-daisies, and, just beside them, the sea moved lazily, silky and dark, its faint bars of light and shadow gently lifting and falling against the hot rock. Beyond the stretch of sea, at the outer curve of the bay, tall cliffs towered jaggedly, their feet in the calm summer water, and along their bases curled the narrow golden line of shingle that rings the islands of the tideless Aegean. Even this, if the wind stiffened from the south, would be covered. A small boat, painted orange and cobalt, rocked, empty, at anchor a little way out from the shore.

'Next stop, Africa,' said Tony, behind me.

'It's lovely, oh, it's lovely! I'm glad I came before you've built your new wing, you know.'

'Well, I do see what you mean, not that I think we'll exactly put Billy Butlin out of business,' said Tony cheerfully. 'If it's peace and quiet you want, dear, we've bags of that.'

I laughed. 'Well, that's what we came for. Is it warm enough to swim yet? I asked Georgi, but he has a different sort of built-in thermostat from me, and I don't know if I can take his word for it.'

'Well, heavens, don't take mine, I've not tried it, and I don't suppose I ever shall, not being just a child of Nature. I wouldn't risk the harbour, it's dirty, but there are bound to be plenty of places where it's safe. You'd better ask Stratos; he'll know if there are currents and things. Your cousin'll go with you, I suppose?'

'Oh, she'll probably sit on the shore and watch – though it wasn't safety I was thinking about; there won't be any currents here that could matter. No, Frances isn't a swimmer, she's mainly interested in the flowers. She's a rock garden expert, and works in a big nursery, and she always takes a busman's holiday somewhere where she can see the plants in their natural homes. She's tired of Switzerland and the Tyrol, so, when I told her what I'd seen last spring over here, she just had to come.' I turned away from the window, adding casually: 'Once she sees the place, I probably shan't be allowed time off for swimming. I'll have to spend the whole time tramping the mountainside with her, hunting for flowers to photograph.'

'Flowers?' said Tony, almost as if it were a foreign word he had never heard before. 'Ah, well, I'm sure there are plenty of nice ones around. Now, I'll have to be getting down to the kitchen. Your cousin's room is next door – that one, there. There's only the two in this end of the place, so you'll be lovely and private. That's a bathroom there, no less, and that door goes through to the other side of the house. Now, if there's anything you want, just ask. We don't rise to bells yet, but you don't need to come down; just hang out of the door and yell. I'm never far away. I hear most that goes on.'

'Thanks,' I said, a little hollowly.

'Cheerio for now,' said Tony amiably. His slight figure skated gracefully away down the stairway.

I shut my door, and sat down on the bed. The shadows of the vine moved and curtseyed on the wall. As if they were my own confused and drifting thoughts, I found that I had pressed my hands to my eyes, to shut them out.

Already, from the fragments I had gleaned, one thing showed whole and clear. If the murder which Mark had witnessed had had any connection with Agios Georgios, and if his impression of the Englishness of the fourth man had been correct, then either Tony, or the mysterious 'Englishman' from the sea – whom Tony had denied – must have been present. There were no other candidates. And, in either case, Tony was involved. The thing could be, in fact, centred on this hotel.

I found a wry humour in wondering just what Mark would have said, had he known that he was packing me off, with prudent haste, from the perimeter of the affair into its very centre. He had wanted me safely out of it, and had made this abundantly clear, even to the point of rudeness; and I – who had taken my own responsibilities for long enough – had resented bitterly a rejection that had seemed to imply a sexual superiority. If I had been a man, would Mark have acted in the same way? I thought not.

But at least emotion no longer clouded my judgement. Sitting here quietly, now, seeing things from the outside, I could appreciate his point of view. He wanted to see me safe – and he wanted his own feet clear. Well, fair enough. In the last few minutes, I had realized (even at the risk of conceding him a little of that sexual superiority) that I wanted both those things, quite fervently, myself.

I took my hands from my eyes, and there were the patterned shadows again, quiet now, beautiful, fixed.

Well, it was possible. It was perfectly possible to do as Mark had wished; clear out, forget, pretend it had never happened. It was obvious that no suspicion of any sort could attach itself to me. I had arrived as expected, having successfully dropped the dangerous twenty-four hours out of my life. All I had to do was forget such information as came my way, ask no more questions, and – how had it gone? – 'get on with that holiday of yours, that Lambis interrupted'.

And meanwhile, Colin Langley, aged fifteen?

I bit my lip, and snapped back the lid of the suitcase.

CHAPTER EIGHT

She shall guess, and ask in vain . . .

THOMAS LOVELL BEDDOES: *Song of the Stygian Naiades*

There was a woman in the bathroom, just finishing with a cloth and pail. When I appeared, towel on arm, she seemed flustered, and began picking up her tools with nervous haste.

'It's all right,' I said, 'I'm not in a hurry. I can wait till you've finished.'

But she had already risen, stiffly, to her feet. I saw then that she was not old, as her movements had led me to imagine. She was of medium height, a little shorter than I, and should have been broadly built, but she was shockingly thin, and her body seemed flattened and angular under the thick, concealing peasant clothing. Her face, too, was meant to be full and round, but you could see the skull under the skin – the temporal bone jutting above deep eye-sockets, the sharp cheekbones, and the squared corners of the jaw. She was shabbily dressed, in the inevitable black, with her dress kilted up over her hips to show the black underskirt below, and she wore a black head-covering, wrapped round to hide neck and shoulders. Under this her hair seemed thick, but the few wisps which had escaped the covering were grey. Her hands were square, and must have been stronger than they looked; they seemed to be mere bones held together by sinews and thick, blue veins.

'You speak Greek?' Her voice was soft, but full and rich, and still young. And her eyes were beautiful, with straight black lashes as thick as thatch-eaves. The lids were reddened, as if with recent weeping, but the dark eyes lit straight away with the pleased interest that every Greek takes in a stranger. 'You are the English lady?'

'One of them. My cousin will arrive later. This is a lovely place, *kyria*.'

She smiled. Her mouth was thinned almost to liplessness, but not unpleasantly. In repose it did not seem set, but merely showed a kind of interminable and painful patience, a striving for mindlessness. 'As for that, it is a small village, and a poor one; but my brother says that you know this, and that many people will come, only to be tranquil.'

'Your – brother?'

'He is the patron.' She said this with a kind of pride. 'Stratos Alexiakis is my brother. He was in England, in London, for many years, but last November he came home, and bought the hotel.'

'Yes, I heard about it from Tony. It's certainly very nice, and I hope he does well.'

I hoped the conventional words had concealed my surprise. So this was Sofia. She had the appearance of the poorest peasant in a poor country – but then, I thought, if she was helping her brother start up his hotel, no doubt she would wear her oldest clothes for the rough work.

It occurred to me that if she had fallen heir to Tony's cooking it hadn't
– as yet – done her much good.

'Do you live in the hotel?' I asked.

'Oh, no,' hastily, 'I have a house, down the road a little, on the other
side of the street. The first one.'

'The one with the fig-tree? I saw it. And the oven outside.' I smiled.
'Your garden was so lovely; you must be very proud of it. Your husband's
a fisherman, is he?'

'No. He – we have a little land up the river. We have vines and lemons
and tomatoes. It is hard work.'

I remembered the cottage, spotlessly clean, with its ranked flowers
beside the fig-tree. I thought of the hotel floors, which she had been
scrubbing. Then of the fields, which no doubt she would till. No wonder
she moved as if her body hurt her. 'Have you many children?'

Her face seemed to shut. 'No. Alas, no. God has not seen fit.' A gesture
to her breast, where a tiny silver ornament – a Greek cross, I thought
– had swung loose on its chain while she was scrubbing. Encountering
this, her hand closed over it quickly, an oddly protective movement, with
something of fear in it. She thrust the cross quickly back into the breast
of her frock, and began to gather her things together.

'I must go. My husband will be home soon, and there is a meal to get.'

My own meal was a good one; lamb, which the Cretans call *amnos*
– many of the classical terms still survive in the dialect – and green
beans, and potatoes.

'*Sautées*, my dear, in olive oil,' said Tony, who served me. 'Butter's
too scarce here, but I do assure you I made them go steady on the oil.
Like them?'

'Fine. But I like olive oil. And here, where it's so to speak fresh from
the cow, it's terrific. You were right about the wine, *King Minos, sec*.
I must remember that. It's dryish for a Greek wine, isn't it? – and the
name is wonderfully Cretan!'

'Bottled in Athens, dear, see?'

'Oh, no, you shouldn't have showed me that!' I glanced up. 'I met Mr.
Alexiakis' sister upstairs.'

'Sofia? Oh yes. She helps around,' he said vaguely. 'Now, will you
have fruit for afters, or *fromage*, or what my dear friend Stratos calls
"compost"?'

'It depends rather on what that is.'

'Between you and me, tinned fruit salad, dear. But don't worry, we'll
really let ourselves go at dinner. The caique gets in today – oh, of course
you know all about that.'

'I'm not worrying, why should I? That was excellent. No, *not* an
orange, thank you. May I have cheese?'

'Sure. Here. The white one's goat and the yellow one with holes is
sheep, so take your pick ... Excuse me one moment. Speak of angels.'

He twitched the coffee-percolator aside from its flame, and went out of the dining-room, across the terrace into the sunlight of the street. A woman was waiting there, not beckoning to him, or making any sign, just waiting, with the patience of the poor. I recognized her; it was Stratos' sister, Sofia.

If only one could stop doing those uncomfortable little addition-sums in one's head . . . If only there was some way to switch off the mechanism . . . But the computer ticked on, unwanted, adding it all up, fraction by fraction. Tony and the 'Englishman'. And now, Tony and Sofia. There had been a woman there, Mark had said. Sofia and her brother . . .

I ate my cheese doggedly, trying to ignore the unwanted answers that the computer kept shoving in front of me. Much better concentrate on the cheese, and there was some wine left, and the coffee, which was to follow, smelt delicious; *café français*, no doubt Tony would `call it . . . Here, the computer ticked up a fleeting memory of Mark, dirty, unshaven, hagridden, swallowing indifferent thermos coffee, and choking down dry biscuits. I stamped fiercely on the switch, expunged the memory, and turned my attention back to Tony, graceful and immaculate, standing easily in the sun, listening to Sofia.

She had put one of those flattened claws on his arm, almost as if in pleading. Her coif was drawn up now, shadowing half her face, and at that distance I could not see her expression, but her attitude was one of urgency and distress. Tony seemed to be reassuring her, and he patted the hand on his arm before he· withdrew it. Then he said something cheerfully dismissive, and turned away.

As he turned, I dropped my gaze to the table, pushing my cheese-plate aside. I had seen the look on Sofia's face as Tony turned and left her. It was distress, and she was weeping; but there was also, unmistakably, fear.

'*Café français*, dear?' said Tony.

Not even the computer – aided by two cups of coffee – could have kept me awake after lunch. I carried my second cup out to the garden, and there, alone with the drowsy sound of bees, and the tranquil lapping of the sea, I slept.

It was no more than a cat-nap, a doze of half an hour or so, but it must have been deep and relaxing, for, on waking, I found that I had none of the hangover feeling that one sometimes gets from sleeping in the afternoon. I felt fresh and wide-awake, and full of a sense of pleasant anticipation which resolved itself into the knowledge that Frances would soon be here. Frances, who would know just what to do . . .

I didn't pursue this thought; didn't even acknowledge it. I sat up, drank the glassful of water – tepid now – that had been served with my coffee, and dutifully set about writing a postcard to Jane, my Athens room mate. That Jane would be very surprised to get it was another of the things I didn't acknowledge; I merely told myself that I wanted a walk, and that the card would be a good excuse for a quiet little stroll down as far as the village post office. I certainly did not stop to consider why I should need the excuse, or why, indeed, I should want a walk, after the amount of exercise I had already had that day. Jane (I said to myself, writing busily) would be delighted to hear from me. The message that was to arouse all this astonished delight ran as follows: '*Arrived here today; lovely and peaceful. Frances due here this afternoon. She'll be thrilled when she sees the flowers, and will spend pounds on film. Hotel seems good. Am hoping it will be warm enough to swim. Love, Nicola.*'

I wrote this artless missive very clearly, then took it into the lobby. Tony was there, sitting behind the table, with his feet up, reading *Lady Chatterley's Lover*.

'Don't get up,' I said hastily. 'I just wondered if you had stamps. Just one, for a local postcard; one drach.'

He swung his feet down, and fished below the table to pull open a cluttered drawer.

'Sure. One at one drach, did you say?' The long fingers leafed through three or four sad-looking sheets of postage stamps. 'Here we are. Only two left, you're lucky.'

'Thanks. Oh, are there any at five? I might as well get them now, for air mail to England.'

'I'll see. Five . . . How nice that one's very first tourist knows all the ropes. I can never remember that sort of thing – I'd make the lousiest information-clerk ever. Railway time-tables simply *panic* me, you've no idea.'

'Then you've come to the right place. D'you mean,' I asked innocently, 'that you've never written home once, since you came to Greece?'

'My dear, I couldn't shake the dust of the dear old Vicarage off my feet fast enough. No, I'm sorry, we've no fives, only twos and fours. Are you in a hurry, because I can easily get some for you?'

'Don't trouble, thanks, I'd like to go out anyway, to explore. Oh look, I'm sorry, I can't even pay you for this one now, I've left my purse upstairs. I'll be down in a minute.'

'Don't worry about that. We'll put it on the bill. Double for the trouble, and don't mention it.'

'No, I'll need it anyway, to get the stamps in the village. And I must get my dark specs.'

I left the postcard lying on the desk, and went upstairs to my room. When I got back, I could swear the card had not been moved, not even a millimetre.

I smiled at Tony.

'I suppose this town does have a post office?'

'It does indeed, but I won't insult you by directing you, dear. Agios Georgios isn't exactly complicated. Once down the main street and straight into the sea. Have a lovely walk.' And he subsided into *Lady Chatterley's Lover*.

I picked up my postcard and went out into the street.

'Street,' of course, is a misleading word for the dusty gap between Agios Georgios' straggling houses. Outside the hotel was a wide space of trodden, stony dust where hens scratched, and small, brown, half-naked children played under a pistachio-tree. The two cottages nearest the hotel were pretty in their fresh whitewash, each with a vine for shade, and with a low white wall fencing the tiny yard where the vine grew. Sofia's house stood by itself at the other side of the street. This was a little bigger than the others, and meticulously kept. A fig-tree – that most shapely of trees – grew near the door, its shadow throwing a vivid pattern against the brilliant white wall. The little garden was crammed with flowers; snapdragons, lilies, carnations, mallows – all the spired and scented profusion of the English summer, growing here, as rank as wild-flowers, in the Cretan April. Against the outer wall of the house was a primitive fireplace whose blackened pots stood on trivets of a design so old that it was as familiar as the skin of one's hands. A vine-covered wall at the back did its best to hide a cluttered yard where I saw the beehive shape of a baking oven.

I walked slowly downhill. All seemed innocent and quiet in the afternoon heat. Here was the church, very small, snow-white, with a Reckitt's-blue dome, perched on a little knoll with its back to the cliffs. In front of it some loving hand had made a pavement of sea-pebbles, blue and terracotta and slate-grey, hammered down in patterns into the iron ground. Beyond it, the street sloped more steeply towards the sea, and here, though every house had a pot or two of flowers outside, the place looked barer, and there had been very little use of paint or white-wash. It was as if the richness of the flowery hills had faded and died, dwindling down to starve in the sea-bare poverty of the harbour.

And here was the post office. It was, also, the only shop the village boasted; a dark cave of a place, with double doors open to the street, beaten earth floor, and sacks of produce standing everywhere – beans, maize, and pasta, along with huge square tins swimming with oily-looking pilchards. On the counter were earthenware bowls of black olives, a stack of cheeses, and a big, old-fashioned pair of scales. Shelves, crowded with jars and tins, sported (it seemed incongruously) the familiar labels of everyday advertising. Beside the door, casually supporting a stack of brushes, was the letter-box, painted the dark post-office blue. And, on the wall opposite the doorway, the telephone, in the very middle of the shop. You threaded your way between the sacks to get to it.

The shop was, obviously, the meeting-place of the village women. Four of them were there now, talking over the weighing of some flour. As I entered, a little hesitantly, conversation stopped abruptly, and they stared; then good manners reasserted themselves, and they looked away, talking more quietly, but not, I noticed, about the foreigner; their conversation – about some sick child – was taken up where it had ceased. But all made way for me, and the shop-keeper put down the flour-scoop and said inquiringly: 'Miss?'

'These ladies—' I said, with a gesture meaning that I could not take their turn. But I had to in the end, defeated by their inflexible courtesy: 'I only came for some stamps, please. Six at five drachs, if you will be so good.' Behind me I heard the stir and whisper: 'She speaks Greek! Listen, did you hear? English, and she speaks Greek ... Hush, you ill-mannered one! Silence!'

I smiled at them, and made some remark about their village, and was, on the instant, the centre of a delighted group. Why did I come to such a place? It was so small, so poor, why did I not stay in Heraklion, where there were big hotels, like Athens or London? Did I live in London? Was I married? Ah, but there was a man? No? Ah, well, one could not always be fortunate, but soon, soon, if God willed ...

I laughed, and answered as best I could, and asked, in my turn, as many questions as I dared. Did they not get many strangers, then, in Agios Georgios? Many English? Oh, yes, Tony, of course, but I meant visitors like myself, foreigners ... The Danish gentleman, yes, I had heard of him, but nobody else? No? Ah, well, now that the hotel was getting under way, and so efficiently, no doubt there would soon be many visitors, Americans too, and Agios Georgios would prosper. Mr. Alexiakis was making a good job of it, wasn't he? And his sister was helping him? Yes, Sofia, I had met her; I believed she lived in the pretty house at the top of the village, opposite the hotel ...?

But on Sofia, we stuck. Beyond swiftly-exchanged glances – kindly enough, I thought – and murmurs of 'Ah, yes, poor Sofia, it was lucky for her that such a brother had come home to look after her,' the women said nothing more, and the conversation died, to be ignited again by one of them, young and pretty, with a child clinging to her hand, and an air of assurance, inviting me to her house. The others, who seemed only to have waited for her lead, pressed eagerly forward with similar invitations. How long was I to be in Agios Georgios? I would come and see them, yes, and bring my cousin, too. Which house? The one by the harbour wall – the one above the bakery – behind the church ... it was no matter, (this with laughter), I had only to walk in, there was no house in Agios Georgios where I would not be welcome, so young and pretty, and speaking such good Greek ...

Laughingly promising, but temporarily parrying all the charming invitations, I finally escaped, not much the wiser about Georgi's phantom Englishman, but having learned what I had come for, and more as well.

First, the telephone was out. Even without my promise to Mark, there was no chance, whatever happened, of getting in touch with authority, either the Embassy, or even Heraklion, by telephone. The one in the hotel, impossible. The one in the post office, open to the day in what amounted to the Ladies' Clubroom – in English or in Greek, it couldn't even be tried. We were on our own.

I found that, without conscious direction, I had reached the tiny harbour. A sea-wall, and a little curved pier, held the water clear and still as a tear in the flower-cup. Someone had scrawled CYPRUS FOR GREECE along the harbour wall, and someone else had tried to scratch it out. A man was beating an octopus; some family would eat well tonight. Two boats lay at anchor, one white, with vermilion canvas furled along her beautiful spars, the other blue, with the name *Eros* along her bows. On *Eros* a youth was working, coiling down a rope. He was wiry and quick-moving, and wore a green sweat-shirt and blue denim trousers tucked into short gum-boots. It was the lad who had been watching the backgammon players. He eyed me curiously, but did not interrupt his work.

I stood there a moment or two longer, conscious of eyes watching me from the dark doorway of every house, where the women sat. I thought: if only Lambis' boat would come in now, sailing quietly in from the east, with them all on board; Lambis at the engine, and Mark steering, and Colin in the bows, with a fishing line, laughing . . .

I turned sharply away from the shining stretch of the empty sea, and, the terms of my self-deceit forgotten, brought my mind back with a jerk to my problem, the other thing that I had discovered in the village shop – that there was, in fact, no house in Agios Georgios which could have anything to hide. Colin Langley was not here. Nothing could be served by my prying further in a village where every woman must know all her neighbours' affairs. Any answer to the mystery was only to be found at the hotel.

Or – and here I started to walk slowly back up the street, conscious of the eyes that watched me from the dark doorways – or at Sofia's cottage.

There might, in fact, be one house in Agios Georgios at which I was not welcome.

Well, there was nothing like trying. And if the husband was still at home, over his meal, then I should be quite interested to meet him, too.

I wondered if he favoured Cretan dress.

CHAPTER NINE

She seem'd an ancient maid, well-skill'd to cull
The snowy fleece, and wind the twisted wool

POPE: *The Iliad of Homer*

She was sitting just inside the door of her cottage, spinning. In all my months in Greece, I had never quite got used to the pleasure of watching the peasant women at this primitive task. The soft, furry mass of white wool on the distaff, the brown fingers pulling it out like candy-floss to loop across the front of the black dress, the whirling ball of woollen thread on the spindle – these made a pattern that it would have been hard not to appreciate.

She had not looked up at my approach; the trunk of the fig-tree must have hidden the movement from her. I paused for a moment, just beyond its shade, to watch her. In the deep shadow where she sat, the lines of trouble could no longer be seen: her face showed the smooth planes of youth, while even the ugly hands, caught in the fluid movements of her task, had taken on a kind of beauty.

I thought, then, of the legend I had told Mark, the story of the moonspinners that had been intended to send him to sleep, and to bring me comfort. I looked again at Sofia, a black-clad Cretan woman, spinning in the hot afternoon. An alien, a suspect, an incomprehensible native of this hard, hot country, whose rules I didn't know. Somebody to be questioned.

I walked forward and put my hand on the gate, and she looked up and saw me.

The first reaction was pleasure, of that I was sure. Her face split into a smile, and the dark eyes lighted. Then, though she did not move her head, I got the impression that she had cast a quick glance into the cottage behind her.

I pushed open the gate. 'May I come in and talk to you?' I knew that such a direct query, though perhaps not good manners, could not, by the rules of island hospitality, be refused.

'Of course.' But I thought she looked uneasy.

'Your husband has gone?'

She watched me with what could have been nervousness, though the deft, accustomed movements helped her to an appearance of ease, as a cigarette will sometimes help in a more sophisticated situation. Her glance went to the small fire of twigs outside, where a pot still simmered. 'He did not come.' Then, making as if to rise: 'Be pleased to sit down.'

'Thank you – oh, please don't stop your spinning, I love to watch it.' I entered the tiny yard, and, obedient to her gesture, sat on the bench near the door, under the fig-tree. I began to praise her spinning, admiring the smoothness of the wool, and fingering the piece of woven cloth she showed me, until soon she had forgotten her shyness, and put down her work to fetch more of her weaving and embroidery to show me. Without being asked, I left my seat, and followed her indoors.

The cottage had two rooms, with no door between them, merely an oblong gap in the wall. The living-room, opening straight off the yard, was scrupulously neat, and very poor. The floor was of earth, beaten as hard as a stone, with a drab, balding rug covering half of it. There was a small fireplace in one corner, unused at this time of year, and across the back of the room ran a wide ledge, three feet from the floor, which served apparently as a bed-place, and was covered with a single blanket patterned in red and green. The walls had not yet been freshly white-washed, and were still grimed with winter's smoke. Here and there, high up in the plastered walls, were niches which held ornaments, cheap and bright, and faded photographs. There was one in a place of honour, a child – a boy – of perhaps six; behind this was a fuzzy print, much enlarged, of a young man in what looked like irregular battle-dress. He was handsome in a rather glossy and assured way. The boy was very like him, but stood shyly. The husband, I supposed, and a lost child? I looked for the family ikon, but could see none, and remembered what Tony had told me.

'My little boy,' said Sofia, behind me. She had come out of the inner room with an armful of cloths. She betrayed neither resentment nor surprise that I should have followed her into the house. She was looking sadly at the picture, with – you would have sworn – no other thought in mind. 'He died, *thespoinís*, at seven years old. One day he was well, and at school, and playing. The next – pff – dead. And it was the will of God that there should be no more.'

'I'm sorry. And this is your husband?'

'Yes, that is my husband. See, this cushion that I have made last year . . .'

She began to lay the things out in the sunlight near the door. I bent over them, but turning, so that I could see into the inner room.

This was darkened, with shutters drawn against the sun. It was merely a small oblong box of a room, with a double bed, a wooden chair, and a table by the window covered with a pink cloth with bobbles on. Every corner of the house seemed open to the view . . .

She was putting up her work again.

'And now, if you will sit in here, where it is cool, I will get you a glass of the peppermint drink which I make myself.'

I hesitated, feeling ashamed. I had not wanted to take her meagre hospitality, but, since I had asked myself into her house, I had forced her to offer it. There was nothing to do but thank her, and sit down.

She reached to a shelf near the door where, behind a faded curtain of that same red and green, stood a stock (how pitifully scanty a stock) of food. She took down a small bottle and glass.

'Sofia?'

It was a man's voice calling from outside. I had heard – but without attending – the footsteps coming rapidly down the track from the bridge. They had paused at the gate.

Sofia, near the door, turned quickly, glass in hand. The man was still beyond my range of vision, and he could not have seen me.

'All is well,' he said shortly. 'And as for Josef – what is the matter?'

This, as Sofia made some little hushing gesture, indicating that she was not alone. 'Someone is with you?' he asked sharply.

'It is the English lady from the hotel, and—'

'*The English lady?*' The swiftly-spoken Greek was almost explosive.

'Have you no more sense than to invite her in to show off your work, when at any minute Josef—?'

'It is all right to speak Greek in front of her,' said Sofia. 'She understands it perfectly.'

I heard his breath go in, as if he had shut his mouth hard on whatever he had been going to say. The latch clicked.

I stepped forward. The newcomer had swung open the gate and we met in the sunlit doorway.

He was a powerful-looking man in the late forties, broadly built and swarthy, with the gloss of good living on his skin. His face was square, going to fat a little, with high cheek-bones and the inevitable moustache; a typically Greek face, which could have been the one I had last seen under the red head-dress, but I didn't think it was. In any case, he was not wearing Cretan dress. He had obviously been working, and wore shabby grey trousers covered with dust, and a khaki shirt, with a scarlet kerchief knotted at the neck. A brown linen jacket hung from his shoulders. This last garment looked expensive, and bore, almost visibly, the label of a Knightsbridge 'sports' department. My interest focused and sharpened. This must be my host, Stratos Alexiakis.

'This is my brother,' said Sofia.

I was already giving him my nicest smile, and my hand. 'How do you do? I'm sorry, I know I shouldn't have taken Kyria Sofia's time, when her husband is expected home for his meal. But I was walking through the village, and your sister was the only person I knew, so I invited myself in. I'll go now.'

'No, no, indeed!' He had retained my hand, and now led me, almost forcibly, to the seat under the fig-tree. 'I am sorry, I would never have spoken so, if I had realized you understood me! But my sister's husband is not a man for company, and I thought if he came home to find her gossiping—' a grin and a shrug – 'well, you know how it is if a man is hungry, and a meal not ready. No, no, please sit down! What would my sister think of me if I drive her guest away? You must taste her peppermint drink; it is the best in the village.'

Sofia, her face expressionless, handed me the glass. There was nothing to show that either of them was relieved at the way I had interpreted his remarks. I tasted the drink, and praised it lavishly, while Stratos leaned one powerful shoulder against the door-jamb, and watched me benignly. Sofia, standing stiffly in the doorway, watched him.

'He is late,' she said. The statement sounded tentative, like a question, as if Stratos might have known the reason why.

He shrugged, and grinned. 'Perhaps, for once, he is working.'

'He did not – help you in the field?'

'No.'

He turned back to me, speaking in English.

'You're comfortable at my hotel?' His English was excellent, but still, after twenty years, hadn't lost the accent.

'Very, thank you, and I love my room. You've got a good place here, Mr. Alexiakis.'

'It is very quiet. But you told me on the telephone that this is what you want.'

'Oh, yes. I live in Athens, you see, and it gets a bit crowded and noisy towards summer. I was longing to get away somewhere, where the tourist crowds didn't go . . .'

I talked easily on, explaining yet again about my own and Frances' reasons for choosing Agios Georgios. I didn't even try to conceal from myself, now, that I wanted to establish a very good reason for the time I intended to spend exploring the mountain and shore round about. A movie camera, I thought, as I talked on and on about film (of which I know nothing), is an excellent excuse for a lot of unholy curiosity . . .

'And the boat,' I finished, 'will pick us up on Monday, if all goes well. The party's going on to Rhodes from here, and I'll join them for a couple of days, then I must go back to Athens. They'll go on to the Dodecanese, then my cousin'll come to stay with me in Athens, on her way home.'

'It sounds very nice.' I could see him chalking up the score; a party, a boat, a private tour; money. 'So you work in Athens? That accounts for your excellent Greek. You make mistakes, of course, but you are very fluent, and it is easy to understand what you mean. Do you find that you follow all you hear, as well?'

'Oh, no, not really.' I wondered, as I spoke, how often tact and truth go hand in hand. 'I mean, I couldn't translate word for word, though I get the gist of speech pretty well, except when people talk fast, or with too much of a regional accent. Oh, thank you,' to Sofia, who had taken my empty glass. 'No, no more. It was lovely.'

Stratos was smiling. 'You've done very well, all the same. You'd be surprised how many English people stay over here for quite some time, and never trouble to learn more than a word or two. What is your work in Athens?'

'I'm a rather unimportant junior secretary at the British Embassy.'

This was chalked up, too, and with a shock: I saw it.

'What does she say?' This, almost in a whisper, from Sofia.

He turned his head, translating carelessly: 'She works at the British Embassy.'

'Oh!' It was a tiny exclamation as the glass slipped to the ground, and broke.

'Oh dear!' I exclaimed. 'What a shame! Let me help!'

I knelt down, in spite of her protests, and began to pick up the fragments. Luckily the glass was thick and coarse, and the pieces were large.

Stratos said, without stirring: 'Don't worry, Sofia, I'll give you another.' Then, with a touch of impatience: 'No, no, throw the pieces away, girl, it'll never mend. I'll send Tony across with a new glass for you, a better one than this rubbish.'

I handed Sofia the pieces I had collected, and stood up. 'Well, I've enjoyed myself very much, but, in case your husband does come home soon, *kyria*, and doesn't appreciate a crowd, I think I'll go. In any case, my cousin should be arriving any minute now.'

I repeated my thanks for the drink, and Sofia smiled and nodded and bobbed, while giving the impression that she hardly heard what I was saying; then I went out of the gate, with Stratos beside me.

He walked with his hands dug deep into his pockets, and his shoulders hunched under the expensive jacket. He was scowling at the ground so ferociously that I began to wonder uneasily what he might say. His first words showed, disarmingly enough, that he was deeply chagrined that I had seen the threadbare poverty of his sister's home.

'She won't let me help her.' He spoke abruptly, as if I should have known what he was talking about. 'I've come home with money, enough to buy all she needs, but all she will take is a little payment for work in the hotel. Scrubbing work. My sister!'

'People are proud sometimes.'

'Proud! Yes, I suppose it's that. It's all she has had for twenty years, after all, her pride. Would you believe it, when we were children, my father had his own caique, and when his uncle died, we inherited land, the land up at the head of the plateau, where it is sheltered, the best in Agios Georgios! Then my mother died, and my father had ill-health, and the land was all there was for my sister's dowry. I went to England, and I worked. Oh, yes, I worked!' His teeth showed. 'But I have something to show for those years, while she – every drach she has, she makes herself. Why, even the fields—'

He broke off, and straightened his shoulders. 'Forgive me, I should not throw my family troubles at you like that! Perhaps I needed a European ear to pour them into – did you know that a great many Greeks regard themselves as living east of Europe?'

'That's absurd, when you think what Europe owes them.'

'I dare say.' He laughed. 'Perhaps I should have said an urban and civilized ear. We're a long way from London, are we not – even from Athens? Here, life is simple, and hard, especially for women. I had forgotten, in the time I have been away. One forgets that these women accept it . . . And if one of them is fool enough to marry a Mussulman, who uses his religion as an excuse for . . .' His shoulders lifted, and he laughed again. 'Well, Miss Ferris, and so you're going to hunt flowers and take movies while you're here?'

'Frances will, and I dare say I'll tag along. Does the *Eros* belong to you, Mr. Alexiakis?'

'The *Eros*? Yes, did you see her, then? How did you guess?'

'There was a boy working on her, that I'd seen up at the hotel. Not that that meant anything, but I just wondered. I rather wanted to ask . . .' I hesitated.

'You would like to go out, is that it?'

'I'd love it. I'd always wanted to see this coast from the sea. Some children told me there was a good chance of seeing dolphins; there's a bay a short distance to the west, they said, with rocks running out deep, and sometimes dolphins even come in among the swimmers.'

His laugh was hearty, even a little too hearty. 'I know the place. So that old legend still goes on! There hasn't been a dolphin seen there since the time of Pliny! I ought to know, I fish that way quite often. Not that I go out much with the caique, that's Alkis' job; I'm not used to hard work of that kind any more. But the caique was going cheap, so I bought her; I like a lot of irons in the fire, and some day, when business gets keen, I shall make money with visitors. Meanwhile, I get my fish cheap, and soon, I think, we shall be able to bring our own supplies from Chania.'

We were in front of the hotel now. He stopped.

'But of course you may go out with Alkis, any time. You must go eastwards, the coast is better, and some way along there is a ruin of an old harbour, and if you walk a little way, there is an old church, if these things interest you?'

'Oh, yes. Yes, of course they do.'

'Tomorrow, then?'

'I – well, no, that is, perhaps my cousin'll have some ideas . . . I mean, she's just been cruising, after all, and I expect she'll want a day or so ashore. Later, I – I'd love it. You . . . don't use the caique yourself, you said?'

'Not often. I have little time at present. I only fish for sport, and for that I have a small boat.'

'Oh, yes, that little boat beside the hotel? The orange one? You mean you go light-fishing, with those huge lamps?'

'That's right, with a spear.' Again that grin, friendly, slightly deprecating, claiming – but not offensively – a common bond of knowledge unshared by the villagers. 'Nice and primitive, eh? But terrific sport – like all primitive pastimes. I used to be very good at it when I was a young man, but one gets a little out of practice in twenty years.'

'I watched the light-fishers once, in the bay at Paros. It was fascinating, but one couldn't see much from the shore. Just the lights bobbing, and the man lying with the glass, peering down, and sometimes you could see the one with the spear, striking.'

'Do you want to come out with me?'

'I'd love to!' The words were out, genuinely, thoughtlessly, before it came back to me, with a kick of recollection, that – until I knew a great deal more about him – I quite definitely was not prepared to spend a night with Stratos Alexiakis in a small boat, or anywhere else.

'Well,' he was beginning, while my mind spun uselessly, like a gramophone with a broken spring, when Tony came running down the steps to meet us, as lightly as something out of the chorus of *The Sleeping Beauty*.

'*There* you are, my dears, you've met. Stratos, that wretched get from Chania wants twelve drachs each for the wine, he says he won't send it else. Dire, isn't it? He's on the blower now, could you cope? Did you have a nice walk, dear? Find the post office? Marvellous, isn't it? But you must be *flaked*. Let me bring you a lemon *pressé*, eh? Guaranteed straight off our very own tree. Oh, look, isn't that the caique, just come in? And someone coming up from the harbour as ever was, with Georgi carrying her case. How that child always manages to be in the way of making a couple of drachs ... Just like our Stratos here, madly lucky. It is your cousin? Now, isn't that just ducky? By the time Miss Scorby's unpacked it'll be just nice time for tea.'

CHAPTER TEN

*And, swiftly as a bright Phoebean dart
Strike for the Cretan isle: and here thou art!*

KEATS: *Lamia*

'Well,' said Frances, 'it's very nice to be here. And the tea is excellent. I suppose Little Lord Fauntleroy makes it himself?'

'Hush, for goodness' sake, he'll hear you! He says if you want him, you only have to yell, he's always around. What's more, he's rather sweet. I've fallen for him.'

'I never yet met the male you didn't fall for,' said Frances. 'I'd begin to think you were ill, if you weren't somewhere along the course of a love-affair. I've even learned to know the stages. Well, well, this is really very pleasant, isn't it?'

We were sitting in the hotel 'garden', in the shade of the vine. There was nobody about. Behind us, an open door gave on the empty lobby. Tony was back in the bar: faintly, round the end of the house, came the sound of talk from the café tables on the street.

The sun was slanting rapidly westward. There was a little ripple now, running across the pale silk of the sea, and the breeze stirred the sleepy scent from the carnations in the wine-jars. In full sunlight, at the edge of the gravel, stood a big pot of lilies.

Frances stretched her long legs in front of her, and reached for a cigarette. 'Yes, this was a ve-ery good idea of yours. Athens at Easter could be a bit much. I can see that. I'd forgotten, till you wrote, that the Greek Easter would be later than ours. We had it last week-end when we were in Rome. I imagine the Greek country Easter'll be a bit of a contrast, and I must say I'm looking forward to it. Oh, thanks, I'd love another cup. Now, how long since I saw you? Good heavens, nearly eighteen months! Tell me all about yourself.'

I regarded her with affection.

Frances, though a first cousin, is very much older than I. She was at this time something over forty, and though I know it is a sign of immaturity to think of this as being a vast age, I know that it seemed so to me. From the earliest days I remember, Frances has been there. When I was very small I called her 'Aunt Frances' but she put a stop to that three years ago – at the time when, after my mother's death, I went to live with her. Some people, I know find her formidable; she is tall, dark, rather angular, with a decisive sort of voice and manner, and a charm which she despises, and rarely troubles to use. Her outdoor job has given her the kind of complexion which is called 'healthy'; she is as strong as a horse, and an excellent business woman. She dresses well, if severely. But her formidable exterior is deceiving, for she is the most genuinely tolerant person I know, and sometimes carries 'live and let live' to alarming lengths. The only things she cannot stand are cruelty and pretentiousness. I adore her.

Which is why, on her command to 'tell her all about myself', I did just that – at least, I plunged into a haphazard and pretty truthful account of my job, and my Athens friends. I didn't trouble to edit, though I knew that some of the latter would have fitted a bit oddly into Frances' staid Berkshire home.

She heard me out in amused silence, drinking her third cup of tea, and tapping ash in the nearest *pithos*.

'Well, you seem to be getting a lot of fun out of life, and after all that's what you came for. How's John? You don't mention him.'

'John?'

'Or was it David? I forget their names, though heaven knows why I should, as your letters are spotted with them like a currant-cake, while the fit's on. Wasn't it John, the reporter from the *Athens News*?'

'Oh, him. That was ages ago. Christmas, anyway.'

'So it was. Come to think of it, your last two letters were remarkably blank. Heart-whole and fancy-free?'

'Entirely.' I pulled a pink carnation near to me on its swaying stalk, and sniffed it.

'Well, it makes a change,' said Frances mildly. 'Of course, it's all very well having a heart like warm putty, but one of these days your impulses are going to land you in something you won't easily get out of. Now what are you laughing at?'

'Nothing. Is the *Paolo* calling for us on Monday?'

'Yes, all being well. You are coming with us to Rhodes, then? Good. Though just at the moment I feel I never want to move again. This is what the travel guides call "simple", but it's nice, and terribly restful . . . Listen.'

A bee in the lilies, the soft murmur of the sea on the shingle, the subdued Greek voices . . .

'I told Tony I wished they could keep it like this,' I said. 'It's heaven just as it is.'

'Mmm. And you were right, my love. The flowers I've seen so far, even just along the roadside, are enough to drive a woman to drink.'

'But you came by boat!'

'Oh, yes, but when we were stuck that Sunday night, in Patras, three of us hired a car and went exploring. We didn't have time to go far before dark, but I made the driver stop so often, while I rushed off into the fields, that he thought I was mad – or else that my bladder was permanently diseased. But as soon as he gathered that it was just the flowers I was looking at, do you know what he did?'

I laughed. 'Picked some for you?'

'Yes! I came back to the car, and there he was, six foot two of what *you* would recognize as magnificent Hellenic manhood, waiting for me with a bunch of orchids and anemones, and a kind of violet that sent my temperature up by several degrees. Aren't they sweet?'

'Well, I don't know which violet—'

'Not the violets, ass, the Greeks.' She stretched again, luxuriously. 'My goodness, I'm glad I came! I'm going to enjoy every minute, I can see that. Why, oh *why* do we live in England, when we could live here? And incidentally, why does Tony? Live here, I mean, when he could live in England?'

'He said there was money to be made here when they put up the new wing, which is a polite way of saying when they build a hotel that *is* a hotel. I wondered if he had money in it himself. He *says* he's got a weak chest.'

'Hm. He looks a pretty urban type to settle here, even for a short spell . . . unless the *beaux yeux* of the owner have got something to do with it. He came with him from London, didn't he? What's *he* like?'

'Stratos Alexiakis? How did you – oh, of course, I told you the set-up in my letter, I forgot. He seems very nice. I say, Frances.'

'Mmm?'

'Would you care for a walk along the shore? It gets dark here fairly soon. I – I'd quite like a stroll, myself.'

This was not true, but what I had to say could hardly be said under the listening windows.

'All right,' she said amiably, 'when I've finished this cup of tea. What did you do with yourself in Chania, if that's how you pronounce it?'

'You don't say the "ch" like ours; it's a *chi*, a sort of breathed "k", like in "loch" . . . Chania.'

'Well, what was it like?'

'Oh, it – it was very interesting. There are Turkish mosques.'

Another thing I should have mentioned about Frances: you can't fool her. At least, I can't. She's had too much practice, I suppose, in detecting the little off-white lies of my childhood. She glanced at me, as she shook another cigarette loose from the pack. 'Was it, now? Where did you stay?'

'Oh, it's the biggish hotel in the middle of the town, I forget the name. You're chain-smoking, you'll get cancer.'

'No doubt.' Her voice came muffled through the lighting of her cigarette. She looked at me across the flame, then she got to her feet. 'Come along, then. Why the shore?'

'Because it's lonely.'

She made no comment. We picked our way through the vivid clumps of ice-daisies, to find that a rough path of a sort led along the low, dry rocks that backed the shingle. Further along there was a ridge of hard sand, where we could walk side by side.

I said: 'I've got something I want to talk to you about.'

'Last night's stay in Chania?'

'Clever, aren't you? Yes, more or less.'

'Is that why you laughed when I said that your impulses'd land you in trouble one day?' As I was silent, she glanced at me sideways, quizzically. 'Not that I'm any judge, but Chania seems an odd place to choose to misbehave in.'

'I wasn't even *in* Chania last night! And I haven't—!' I broke off, and suddenly giggled. 'As a matter of fact, I *did* spend the night with a man, now that I come to think about it. I'd forgotten that.'

'He seems,' said Frances tranquilly, 'to have made a great impression. Well, go on.'

'Oh, Frances, darling, I do love you! No, it's not some foully embarrassing love-tangle – when did I ever? It's – I've run into trouble – not my trouble, someone else's, and I wanted to tell you about it, and ask you if there's anything in the world I can do.'

'If it's not your trouble, do you have to do anything?'

'Yes.'

'A heart like warm putty,' said Frances resignedly, 'and sense to match. All right, what's his name?'

'How d'you know it's a he?'

'It always is. Besides, I assume it's the one you spent the night with.'

'Oh. Yes.'

'Who is he?'

'He's a civil engineer. His name's Mark Langley.'

'Ah.'

'It isn't "ah" at all! As a matter of fact,' I said, very clearly, 'I rather detest him.'

'Oh, God,' said Frances, 'I knew this would happen one day. No, don't glare at me, I'm only teasing. Well, go on. You've spent the night with a detestable engineer called Mark. It makes a rousing start. Tell all.'

Her advice, when I had at length told all, was concise and to the point. 'He told you to get out and stay out, and he's got this man Lambis to look after him. They sound a pretty capable pair, and your Mark's

probably fairly well all right by now. The two of them will be back on
their boat, you may be sure, with everything under control. I should stay
out.'

'Y-yes, I suppose so.'

'Besides, what could you do?'

'Well, obviously, I could tell him what I've found out. I mean, I'm
absolutely certain it must be Tony and Stratos Alexiakis and Sofia.'

'Quite probably. Granted that your Mark remembers accurately what
he saw and heard, and that there was an Englishman there on the scene
of the murder, along with a man in Cretan dress and another Greek, and
a woman . . .' She paused a moment. 'Yes, once you've accepted Tony's
involvement, the others follow as the night the day. It's a little closed
circle, Tony, Stratos, Sofia, Josef – and the stranger, whether English
or Greek, whom Tony certainly knew and talked to.'

I stopped in my tracks, staring at her. 'Him? But how? He wasn't
there. There was only the Greek, and the Cretan, and—'

'My dear,' she said gently, 'you've got yourself so involved with Mark's
side of this that you've forgotten how it started.'

'How it started?'

'There was a murdered man,' she said.

Silence, broken only by the crisping of the shingle at the sea's edge.
I stooped, picked up a flat pebble, and skimmed it at the surface of the
water. It sank immediately. I straightened up, dusting my hands.

'I've been awfully stupid,' I said humbly.

'You've been right in the thick of it, honey, and you've been frightened.
It's easy for me, walking calmly in at half-time. I can see things more
clearly. Besides, I'm not emotionally involved.'

'Who said I was?'

'Aren't you?'

I was still watching the place where my pebble had struck. 'Frances,
Colin Langley's only fifteen.'

She said gently: 'Darling, that's the point. That's why I'm telling you
to keep away from it unless you actually do find out what's happened
to him. Otherwise you might only do harm. Look, don't you think we'd
better go back now? The sun's nearly gone, and the going's getting
beastly rough.'

This was true. As I had told my story, we had been making our way
round the bay, and had reached the foot of the big cliffs at the far side.
What had looked from the distance like a line of shingle round their feet,
proved to be a narrow storm-beach of big boulders piled there by the
south wind and the sea. Above this, between the topmost boulders and
the living cliff, ran a narrow path, steep and awkward. It skirted the
headland, then dived steeply down towards the crescent beach of a small,
sandy bay.

'It looks nice along there,' said Frances. 'I wonder if that's your Bay
of the Dolphins?'

'I think that's further along, the water's too shallow here at the edge, and Georgi said you could get right out along the rocks above deep water, and even dive. Look, that must be it, beyond the next headland, I think you can see the rock-stacks running out. With the sun going down behind them, they look just like shadows.'

We stood for a few minutes in silence, shading our eyes against the glitter of the brilliant sea. Then Frances turned away.

'Come along, you're tired. And you could do with a good stiff drink before dinner, by the look of you.'

'It's an idea.' But my voice sounded dreary, even to myself. I turned to follow her back the way we had come.

'Don't think I don't know how you feel.' Her tone was matter-of-fact and curiously soothing. 'It isn't just to keep you out of trouble that I'm telling you to keep away from Mark. I can give you good reasons. If you went trailing up there looking for him, you might be seen, followed, anything: you might lead them to him. Or, if you made them suspicious, you might – and this is more important – frighten them into killing Colin . . . if, that is, Colin is still alive.'

'Oh, God, I suppose you're right. I – I've not been thinking very straight.' I put a hand to my head. 'If you'd seen Sofia. That's what really frightened me . . . when Josef didn't come home. You should have seen her face.'

Incoherent as I was, she understood me. 'You mean that she's not worrying in case he's broken his neck out there on the mountain-side, but because she's afraid of what he may be doing?'

'Yes. And there are only two things I can think of that he might be doing.'

She was blunt. 'Meaning that if Josef is your Cretan murderer – and I'd risk a bet on it myself – he's either still out hunting for Mark, to kill him, or he's mounting guard over Colin somewhere?'

'And she's terrified.' I swallowed. 'If he's with Colin, and she knows it, and she's afraid of what he may be doing . . . Well, there it is.'

My voice trailed off, miserably. She didn't answer, and we trudged along for some minutes in silence. The sun had gone now, dipping swiftly into the sea, and the shadow of the cliffs had reached after us. The breeze had dropped. At the other side of the bay there was a light in the hotel. It seemed a long way away.

I said at length: 'You're right, of course. Mark told me to keep out, and he meant it. Unless I actually found Colin—'

'That's it, you see. That's why he wouldn't go to the authorities, he told you that. If any question were asked, or if Mark and Lambis came here openly, or if anyone shoved the affair to the point where accusations were made – I wouldn't give you twopence for the boy's chances of surviving to tell his part of the story. He's the hostage.'

'I see that. Mark told me himself, after all. All right, I – I'll stay put, Frances, don't worry. But all the same—'

'Well?'

'There's nothing to stop me *looking* for him, is there? If I'm terribly careful? I – I can't just put him out of my head, can I?'

'No, love. You go ahead. I don't see how you could stop looking, even if you wanted to. It isn't just a thing one forgets overnight, like losing a pencil. All you can do, for the sake of your own peace of mind, is to assume he's still alive, and keep your eyes open. One thing, for a start; if he's alive, he's got to be fed.'

'Of course! And not too far away, at that. If one kept a tight eye on Sofia – I'll bet it's she who feeds him ... though it could be Tony, I suppose.'

She smiled. 'My bet's on Sofia. Whoever does it probably has to get up at crack of dawn to avoid being seen, and I don't just see Little Lord Fauntleroy frisking around in the dew.'

'Well, I shall, and tomorrow as ever was. I'll go for an early-morning swim near the hotel, and keep my eyes skinned.'

'You do that,' said Frances. 'Look, there's someone out there now. That's the little boat putting out, isn't it? The man in it – is that Stratos Alexiakis?'

A man, a dim figure in the fast-falling dusk, had been stooping over the small boat, which was now moored beside the rocks by the hotel. He climbed in, and cast her off. He busied himself over something in the stern, and presently we heard the splutter of an engine. The boat started towards us, keeping well inshore.

'I think so,' I said. 'He must have taken an out-board motor down ... I wonder where he's going?'

We had both stopped to watch him. He was standing well forward, and, as we drew nearer, we could see that the rudder had a long lever attached, to enable him to steer while peering over the shoulders of the boat into the lighted water. The huge lamps were in their places in the bows, but were as yet unlit.

She was drawing level with us, and he had seen us. It was Stratos. He grinned and waved, then he moved aft for a minute, and the engine slowed to a soft *put-put*, so that the boat seemed to be just drifting by. I could make out the white letters on her bows: ΨΥΧΗ.

His voice came cheerfully over the water. 'Hullo there! Would you like to come?'

'Another time!' We both grinned and waved in what we hoped was a cordial refusal. 'Thanks all the same! Good fishing!'

He raised a hand, stooped again to the engine, and *Psyche* veered away in a long, lovely curve for the tip of the headland. Her wash lapped the shore beside us, and the small shingle hissed and grated.

'Hm,' said Frances, 'very matey.'

'I asked him about light-fishing before.'

'Well, there's something for us, anyway. Detection without tears.

Colin's not along that way, or Stratos would hardly welcome visitors.'
She turned to go, then said quickly: 'What's the matter?'

I was standing still, like a dummy, with the back of my hand to my
mouth.

'Frances! The *Eros!*'

'The what?'

'He's got a boat, a big one, lying in the harbour! *That's* where he'll
be!'

She said nothing for a moment, regarding me with a frowning look I
couldn't quite read. Then she nodded. 'Yes, that's something we could
try. If we're allowed near the *Eros*, we may be sure she's innocent; if not,
then I think you can certainly go straight up to look for Mark tomorrow.
It would be the easiest thing in the world for those two to bring their
caique in after dark, and board the *Eros*, and search her. They could be
clear away in no time. We could do something about keeping Stratos and
Co. away from the harbour – burn down the hotel, or something like
that.'

I laughed, then looked curiously at her. 'Do you know, I believe you
meant that?'

'If it was the only thing that would do the trick,' said Frances crisply,
'why not? There's a boy being frightened and hurt by a bunch of thugs,
and what's more, he probably believes, all this time, that his brother's
dead. Oh, yes, if a little arson would help, I don't mind in the least
burning Mr. Alexiakis' hotel, with him inside it. Meanwhile, we can
certainly take a look at the *Eros*. We'll go straight down tonight, if only
to put your mind at rest.'

'We?'

'Why not? It'd look more natural. Look, is that Tony on the terrace,
waiting for us?'

'Yes.'

'Then for heaven's sake let's start looking natural straight away. I'm
supposed to be a botanist, and you seem to have given me a build-up that
would have flattered Linnaeus. Now, would you like to pause one
moment, and peer passionately at this plant here – no, *here*, you owl, the
one in the rock!'

'Is it rare?'

'Darling, it grows in every wall in the South of England. It's pellitory-
of-the-wall, but you can bet your boots Tony won't know that! Go on,
pick a bit, or one of those mesembryanthemums or somethings. Show
willing.'

'The ice-daisies?' I stooped obediently. Tony was waiting under the
tamarisks, not fifty yards away. 'Look,' I said, holding it out to her,
'they've shut. Don't they look like tiny plastic parasols?'

'Dear heaven,' said Frances devoutly, 'and to think I once hoped to
make a naturalist of you! And another thing, that egret you mentioned;
according to the books, there are no egrets in Greece.'

'I know that.' Without looking his way, I knew that Tony had come out from under the tamarisks, and was standing at the edge of the gravel. My voice must be carrying clearly to him. 'Just as there aren't any golden orioles, either – officially. But I've seen them at Epidaurus, and honestly, Frances, I saw a pair today between Chania and Kastelli, and I couldn't be wrong about a golden oriole; what else could they have been? I admit I might be wrong about the egret, but I can't think what else that was, either!'

'A squacco heron? They look white in flight. Oh, no, you said black legs and yellow feet . . . Why, hullo, Tony, something smells good.'

I said cheerfully: 'I hope it's not the octopus I saw down at the harbour today?'

'No, my dears, it's a *fricassée*, my very own *fricassée* of veal . . . done with wine, and mushrooms, and tiny, tiny peas. I call it *veau à jouer*.'

'Why on earth?'

'Well, veal by Gamble,' explained Tony. 'Now, ladies, dinner's almost ready, I'll have your drinks waiting for you when you come down. What's it to be?'

CHAPTER ELEVEN

What bird so sings, yet so does wail?
O 'tis the ravish'd nightingale.
Jug, jug, jug, jug, tereu, she cries,
And still her woes at midnight rise.

LYLY: *Campaspe*

The caique was still where she had been, lying without movement in the still waters of the harbour. There was a riding-light on the mast; its reflection glimmered, stilly, feet below the level of her keel. Another light, bigger, glowed in its iron tripod at the end of the pier. Apart from these, all was darkness, and the dank, salt smell of the harbour water.

The youth, Alkis, must have left the caique for the night, for the dinghy no longer nuzzled her sides. It lay alongside the pier, at our feet. We regarded it in silence.

Then a voice spoke suddenly from somewhere beside my elbow, nearly startling me straight into the harbour.

'You want to row out?' asked Georgi. 'I'll take you!'

I glanced at the caique again, lying so quietly in the darkness. Stratos was away fishing, Tony was in the bar, Alkis had presumably gone home. On the face of it, it looked like the sort of chance that shouldn't be missed . . . But – with Georgi? If Alkis had made the offer, well and good. That would have been proof enough, and we could have refused him, with another possibility safely eliminated. But to row across now, and, perhaps, actually find Colin there . . . in the village . . . at this time of night . . .

'What's he saying?' said Frances.

I told her of Georgi's offer, and my own conclusions.

'I'm afraid you're right. We'll have to wait till morning to find out. If we did find him on board—' a little laugh – 'the only solution would be to up anchor, and sail full speed away, *Eros* and all, to meet the other caique. No doubt that's exactly what your capable friend would do, but let's face it, this is one of the occasions where being a woman has its limitations. I suppose you *can't* drive one of those things, can you?'

'Well, no.'

'That's that, then.'

'There is the rowing-boat.' I offered the suggestion with a marked lack of conviction, and she made a derisive sound.

'I can just see us rowing along the coast of Southern Crete in the pitch darkness, looking for a caique that's been hidden in a creek somewhere. I'm sorry, but we'll have to accept our female limitations and wait till morning.'

'As usual, you're so right.' I sighed. 'Well, I'll tell Georgi that we'll ask Stratos properly, in the morning.' I looked down at the boy, who had been following this incomprehensible exchange wide-eyed. 'Thanks a lot, Georgi, but not tonight. We'll ask Mr. Alexiakis tomorrow.'

'We can ask him now,' said Frances dryly. 'Here he comes . . . and how nice it would have been, wouldn't it, if we'd both been on the *Eros*, struggling madly with the gears and the starting-handle? I think, Nicola, my pet, that you and I must definitely keep to the less strenuous paths of crime.'

The soft *put-put* of the light-boat's engine sounded clearly, now as she rounded the pier.

'Here he is!' announced Georgi buoyantly, skipping to the extreme edge of the concrete, where he stood on tiptoe. 'He's been spear-fishing! *Now* you will see the big fish, the sea-bass! He must have got one, or he wouldn't have come back so soon!'

I found myself watching the boat's approach with, ironically, relief: at least now there was no question of heroics. Moreover, they were unnecessary. We could find what we wanted to find, the easy way. We didn't have to wait till morning.

We didn't even have to ask: Georgi did it for us. The boat, with its engine cut, glided alongside, and Stratos threw Georgi a rope, sending us a cheerful greeting.

'What did you get?' demanded Georgi.

'I wasn't spear-fishing. I've been to the pots. Well, ladies, out for another walk? It's Miss Scorby, is it not? How do you do? I see you lose no time in exploring our big city. It's a pity you didn't take the trip with me, it's a lovely night.'

'The ladies were wanting to go to the *Eros*,' said Georgi. 'Shall I carry those up for you?'

'No, I'm taking the boat round again to the hotel. I came to put some gear on the *Eros*.' He stood easily in the rocking boat, looking up at us. 'Do you really want to have a look at her? She's not much of a boat, but if you're interested—' A gesture of invitation completed the sentence.

I laughed. 'As a matter of fact, it was Georgi's idea, he wanted to row us out. I would like to see her, of course, but let's wait till daylight, when we take that trip. What have you caught?'

'*Schâros*. You'll have it tomorrow; it's very good.'

'I've heard of it, but I've never had it. Is that it? How do you catch them?'

'You set pots rather like lobster-pots, and bait them with green-stuff. I assure you, they're better than lobster, and handsome too, aren't they? Here, Georgi, you can take this to your mother . . . How that boy guessed I'd be coming in this way . . .!' This with a grin and a grimace, as Georgi ran happily off, clutching the fish.

'Was that what he was waiting for?'

'Sure. He knows everything, that child; he'd be a godsend at Scotland Yard. You ladies don't want a lift back to the hotel, then?'

'Oh, no, thank you, we're doing a tour of the town.'

Stratos laughed. ' "Agios Georgios by Night?" Well, you'll hardly need a guide, or a bodyguard, or I'd offer to come with you. Good night.'

He thrust with an oar against the pier, and the boat drifted away towards the silent bulk of the *Eros*.

We walked back towards the houses.

'Well, I suppose that's something,' I said at length. 'The caique's innocent, and our tour of the village doesn't worry him, either. *Or* the fact that our nosy little Georgi's sculling around the place night and day, and nattering Greek to me nineteen to the dozen. In fact, I'd have said Stratos hadn't a care in the world. Wherever Colin is, Stratos isn't worrying about his being found.'

'No,' was all Frances said, but not quite guardedly enough. We were passing a lighted doorway, and I saw her expression. My heart seemed to go small, painfully, as flesh shrinks from the touch of ice.

I said it at last. 'You've been sure all along that Colin's dead, haven't you?'

'Well, my dear,' said Frances, 'what possible reason can they have for keeping him alive?'

The night was very dark. Though it would soon be midnight, the moon was not yet up, and the stars were veiled by cloud. I had borrowed Frances' dark-blue poplin coat, and, hugging this round me, waited at the head of the stone steps outside my room.

There was still a light in Sofia's cottage. Though I had forced myself to admit that Frances might be right about Colin, I wasn't prepared to accept it without an effort, and I was ready to ride herd on Sofia all night if need be, and, if she left the cottage, to follow her. But midnight came, and the next slow half-hour, and still the lamplight burned, though every other house in the village was darkened.

It was twelve-thirty before a move was made, and then it was a harmless one; the crack of light round the cottage door vanished, and a small light flowered behind the thick curtains of the bedroom window. She had sat up late, perhaps to wait for Josef, and now she was going to bed. But I stayed where I was: if Sofia had not stirred from her cottage and the yard behind it, it might be for a good reason. I would give her a few minutes longer, and then, Frances or no Frances, I was going to take a look at that yard myself.

I went like a ghost down the steps, and skirted the open ground like a stealthy cat, hugging the shelter of the pistachio-trees. The dust underfoot made silent walking, and I slipped soundlessly past Sofia's garden wall, and round the end of her house into the narrow lane that twisted up from the end of the village towards the meagre vineyards under the cliff.

Here was the yard gate, in the wall behind the cottage. Beyond it, visible only as dimly-looming shapes, were the huge cone of the baking-oven, the great spiky pile of wood in a corner, and the shed backed against the rough wall that edged the lane.

I wondered if the gate would creak, and put a cautious hand down to it, but the hand met nothing. The gate stood wide already.

I paused for a moment, listening. The night was very still. I could hear no sound from the cottage, and no window faced this way. My heart was beating light and fast, and my mouth felt dry.

Something moved beside my feet, almost startling me into a cry, until I realized it was only a cat, on some errand as secret as my own, but apparently quite ready to welcome a partner in crime. It purred softly, and began to strop itself on my ankles, but when I stooped it slid away from my touch, and vanished.

It seemed I was on my own. I took a long breath to steady those heart-beats, then went in through the gate.

The door of the shed must lie to the right. I felt my way towards it, treading cautiously among the debris underfoot.

Somewhere beyond the cottage, across the square, a door opened suddenly, spilling light, and throwing the squat shape of the cottage into relief. As I shrank back towards the shadow of the wood-pile, the light was lopped off again as the door shut, and I heard rapid steps cross a strip of board flooring, then tread quickly across the square through the dust, coming this way.

Stratos, coming over from the hotel to see his sister. If Colin were here – if Stratos came into the yard . . .

He didn't. He pushed open the garden gate and went quietly to the cottage door. It wasn't locked. I heard the latch click, then the soft sound of voices, question and answer. Sofia must have brought the lamp out of the bedroom again, to meet him at the door, for again I could see the faint glow of light from beyond the dark bulk of the cottage.

His visit was certainly not secret, and his purpose, therefore, not likely to be sinister, but while through my confusion I realized this, I wasn't taking any chance of being found by him in Sofia's yard at nearly one in the morning. If I had to be found much better be found in the lane . . .

From what I had seen of this in daylight, it was a dirty and unrewarding little cul-de-sac that led up between clumps of cypress, to peter out in a small vineyard under the cliff. What excuse I could give for being there I didn't know, but since Stratos had no earthly reason for suspecting me, no doubt I could get away with the age-old excuse of sleeplessness, and a walk in the night air. And anything was better than being caught lurking here. I melted quickly out of the gate and into the lane.

There I hesitated. One glance towards the hotel was enough to tell me I couldn't get that way without being seen; the light from the cottage door fell clear to the garden wall, and I could even see the moving edge of Stratos' shadow. It would have to be the lane.

I trod softly, hurrying away from the gateway, and almost immediately stepped on a loose stone that nearly brought me down. Before I had recovered, I heard the cottage door shut, and Stratos' quick steps to the gate.

I stood still, face turned away. I could only hope that, coming fresh from the lamplight, his eyes would not yet be adjusted to the dark. Otherwise, if he looked this way as he passed the corner of the wall, he would be bound to see me.

My fists were pressed down hard into the pockets of Frances' blue coat, while my mind spiralled like a feather in a current of air. What could I say to him? What plausible reason could I give for a midnight stroll up this unappetizing dead-end of a lane?

The answer came, piercingly sweet and loud, from a clump of cypresses beyond the wall, a nightingale's song, pouring into the silence from the crowded spires of the grove, and straight away it seemed as if the whole of that still night had been waiting, just for this. I know I held my breath. The trills and whistles and long, haunting clarinet-notes poured and bubbled from the black cypress. The bird must have sung for two full minutes while I stood there, blessing it, and waiting, with one ear still tuned for Stratos' retreating steps.

The nightingale stopped singing. Clearly, ten yards away, I heard the rattle of loose change in a pocket, then the scrape of a match. Stratos had stopped at the corner, and was leisurely lighting a cigarette.

The flaring match seemed unnaturally bright. If he looked up now . . .

He was lifting his head to inhale the first breath of smoke. My hand, thrust down in the pocket of Frances' coat, met the shape of a packet of cigarettes.

I turned. 'Mr. Alexiakis?'

His head jerked round, and the match dropped into the dust, and fizzled out. I moved towards him, with one of Frances' cigarettes in my hand. 'Do you mind? Have you a light, please? I came out without one.' 'Why, Miss Ferris! Of course.' He came to meet me, and struck and held a match for me. 'You're out very late, aren't you? Still exploring?' I laughed. ' "Agios Georgios by Night?" Not really. I did go up to bed, but then I heard a nightingale, and I had to come out to track it down.'

'Ah, yes, Tony told me you were keen on birds.' He sounded unworried to the point of indifference. He leaned a shoulder back against the wall behind him, gesturing with his cigarette in the direction of the cypresses. 'Up there, was it? They always sing there, ever since I was a boy I remember them. I don't notice them now. Was there one tonight? It's a little early for them.'

'Just one, and he seems to have stopped.' I smothered a yawn. 'I think I'll go to bed now. It's been such a long day, but such a lovely one. Perhaps tomorrow—'

I stopped short, because he moved with a sharp, shushing gesture, as if some sound had startled him. I had heard it, too, but it had not registered with me as quickly as it had with Stratos; for all that relaxed, indifferent air, the man must be as alert as a fox.

We had been standing close against the wall of the shed that I had come to search. This was built of big, rough stones, crudely plastered, and with many gaps between. The sound had come apparently through some gap just beside us – a small, scraping sound, then a soft rustle as of spilled dust. Something moving, inside Sofia's shed.

Stratos had stiffened, head cocked. I could see the sideways gleam of his eyes in the tiny glow of his cigarette.

I said quickly: 'What is it?'

'I thought I heard something. Wait.'

Colin, I thought wildly, *it's Colin* ... but then I saw that fear was making me stupid. If it were indeed Colin, then Stratos would know it, and would certainly not have informed me of the boy's presence in the shed. But if there was someone in the shed, I knew who it would be ... I didn't even think of Lambis, who might very well have hung around till dusk to start a close search of the village; my mind jumped straight to Mark. There was no reason why I should have been so sure, but, as clearly as if I had heard him speak, I knew he was there, just on the other side of the wall, waiting and listening, and trying, after that one betraying movement, not even to breathe ...

I moved away quickly, scraping my feet carelessly among the stones. 'I didn't hear a thing. Are you going back now? It may just have been—'

But he was already moving, and, close to him as I was, I could see that his hand had dropped, quite casually, to his hip. As he went through the yard gate I was on his heels.

I had to stop him somehow, somehow give warning. I cried out, 'Good heavens, is that a gun?' and put a detaining hand on his arm, holding him back, trying to sound merely nervous and feminine, and, with the genuine tremor in my voice, probably succeeding. 'For goodness' sake!' I quavered. 'You don't need that! It'll be a dog or something, and you really can't just shoot it! Please, Mr. Alexiakis—'

'If it is a dog, Miss Ferris, I shall not shoot it. Now, please, you must let me – ah!'

From the shed had come a whole series of sounds, now quite unmistakable. A scrape and a clatter, a curious clucking noise, and the thud of a small, soft body landing from a height. Then from the half-open door shot a vague, slim shape which slid mewing between our feet, and was gone into the shadowed lane.

Stratos stopped, and his hand dropped from his hip. He laughed. 'A cat! This is the criminal on my sister's property! You may calm yourself, Miss Ferris, I shall certainly not shoot *that!*'

'I'm sorry,' I said shamefacedly. 'That was silly of me, but guns and things do panic me. Besides, you might have got hurt or something. Well, thank goodness that's all it was! I was talking to that cat in the lane a while ago; he must have been ratting.'

'Nothing so useful,' said Stratos cheerfully. 'My brother-in-law keeps a decoy quail in there. The cats can't get at it, but they keep trying. Well, we'll shut the door, shall we?'

He pulled it shut, and turned out of the yard. We walked back to the hotel together.

Sofia's yard seemed darker than ever. The shed door was still shut. The cat had gone, and the nightingale was silent in the cypresses. A cracked bell from somewhere near the harbour tolled three.

The door opened with only the slightest creak. I slipped through it into the shed, and pulled it shut behind me.

'Mark?' It was only a breath.

No reply. I stood still, listening for his breathing, and hearing only my own. There was brushwood stacked somewhere; I could smell rosemary, and dried verbena, and all the sweet sharp scents of the bed he and I had shared last night.

'Mark?' I began to feel my way cautiously over to the wall that skirted the lane. A small sound behind me brought me round sharply, with eyes straining wide against the dark, but it was only the scrabbling of claws, and a small rustling movement from a corner where the quail's cage must be. No other sound.

I groped my way over to the wall. As my hands met the stone the nightingale, outside in the grove, began to sing again. The sound filled the darkness, full and near. I felt along the wall. Stone, rough stone, cold stone. Nothing else; and no sound but the rich music from the cypress-grove. I had been wrong; Mark hadn't been here after all; the strong sense I had had of his presence had only been something evoked by the

verbena-scents of the piled brushwood. It had been the cat, and only the
cat, that we had heard.

My hand met something that wasn't stone, something smooth and
sticky, and still faintly warm, that made the hair rise up the back of my
neck, and my stomach muscles tighten sharply. I pulled the hand away
and stood there, holding it stiffly before me, fingers splayed.

So instinct had been right, after all. Mark had been there, leaning
against the wall within inches of Stratos and me, perhaps betrayed by
exhaustion into some revealing movement, while his shoulder bled against
the stone. In sudden fear I stooped to feel if he had fallen there, at the
foot of the wall. Nothing. The shed was empty. There was only his blood.

Outside, the nightingale still sang in the cypresses.

I don't remember getting back to the hotel. I know I took no care. But
I met no one, and no one saw me running back across the square, with
one hand closed tightly over its smeared palm.

CHAPTER TWELVE

... One clear day when brighter sea-wind blew
And louder sea-shine lightened, for the waves
Were full of god-head and the light that saves ...

SWINBURNE: *Thalassius*

The water was smooth and gentle, but with an early-morning sting to
it, and a small breeze blew the salt foam splashing against my lips. The
headland glowed in the early sunlight, golden above the dark-blue sea
that creamed against the storm-beach at its feet.

Here, where I swam, the water was emerald over a shallow bar, the
sunlight striking right down through it to illumine the rock below. It
threw the shadow of the boat fully two fathoms down through the clear,
green water.

Psyche rocked softly at her old moorings, orange and blue. I swam up
to her, and threw an arm over the side. She tilted and swung, but held
solid, squatly-built and fat-bellied, heavier than she looked. I waited a
moment to get my breath, then gripped and swung myself in.

The boat rocked madly, bucked round on her rope, then accepted me.
I thudded down on the bottom-boards, and sat there, dripping and
panting, and rubbing the salt drops from my eyes.

I had had no reason for coming out to Stratos' boat, except that a boat
anchored in a bay is a natural challenge to an idle swimmer. I sat on the
broad stern-seat, resting in the sun, and reflecting that this was as good
a place as any from which to watch the hotel.

If I had had any doubts about the innocence of Stratos' fishing-trip
last night, one look at the boat would have dispelled them. There was
no hiding-place for anything larger than a puppy, and nothing to be seen

except the small-boat clutter that one might expect; oars, carefully laid along the sides, a baling-tin, a rope basket for fish, a kind of lobster-pot – the *scháros*-pot, I supposed – made of cane, a coil of rope, some hollow gourds for use as floats, and a folded tarpaulin. The only things strange to me were the fish-spear – a wicked double trident, with five or six barbed prongs set in a circle – and the glass. This was a sort of sea-telescope, a long metal tube with a glass the size of a dinner-plate set in the end. The fisherman lies in the bows, pushes this thing under water as far as it will go, and watches the depths.

I fingered it curiously, then lifted it, and lay down on the flat boarding behind the big brackets that hold the lights. I carefully lowered the glass into the sea, and peered down through it.

You might, in a simpler world, have said it was magic. There was the illuminated rock of the sea-bed, every pebble clear, a living surface shifting with shadows as the ripples of the upper sea passed over it. Sea-weeds, scarlet and green and cinnamon, moved and swayed in drowsy patterns so beautiful that they drugged the eye. A school of small fish, torpedo-shaped, and barred like zebras, hung motionless, then turned as one, and flashed out of sight. Another, rose-coloured, and whiskered like a cat, came nosing out of a bed of grey coralline weed. There were shells everywhere.

I lay and gazed, with the sun on my back, and the hot boards rocking gently under me. I had forgotten what I had come out for; this was all there was in the world; the sea, the sun hot on my skin, the taste of salt, and the south wind . . .

Two shadows fled across the glimmering underworld. I looked up, startled.

Only two birds, shearwaters, flying low, their wings skimming the tops of the ripples; but they had brought me back to the surface. Reluctantly, I put the glass back where it had been, and turned to look at the hotel.

People were beginning to move now. A shutter was thrown back, and presently a wisp of smoke curled from the chimney. In the village a black-clad woman carried a jar to the well, and a couple of men were making for the harbour.

I sat there for a little longer, prolonging the moment, basking in the sheer physical joy brought by the salt water and the sun. Then I slid over the boat's side, and swam back to the hotel.

I picked up my towel from under the tamarisks, and padded up the steps to my room. Sofia's cottage door was open, and I caught a glimpse of her moving inside. She was sweeping. Below me, in the restaurant, Tony was singing *'Love me tender'* in a passionate counter-tenor. Stratos, in his shirt-sleeves, was outside in the square, talking to a couple of half-naked workmen with buckets and trowels. In the other cottages, people were moving about.

I went in to dress.

'Not a move out of place,' I reported to Frances. 'Everything as innocent as the day. I'm beginning to think the whole thing was a mirage.' I stretched, still feeling the luxurious physical pleasure of the salt water, and the mood it had inspired. 'And, oh my goodness, how I wish it was! I wish we had nothing in the world to think about except tramping off into the hills and looking at the flowers!'

'Well,' said Frances, reasonably, setting down her coffee-cup – she was finishing her breakfast in bed, while I sat on the edge of the table, swinging my legs – 'what else *is* there? We can hardly plan anything. We've done all that lies ready to hand, and it does look now as if Lambis and your Mark have given the village a good going-over between them.'

'That's at least the fourth time you've called him my Mark.'

'Well, isn't he?'

'No.'

Frances grinned. 'I'll try to remember. As I was saying, all we can do now is behave as we normally would, and keep our eyes open. In other words, we go out for the day, and take the camera.'

I remember that I felt a kind of shame-faced relief. 'Okay. Where d'you want to go?'

'Well, since we've seen the shore and the village, the mountain seems the obvious choice, so we can extend our search there quite nicely. Anyway, nothing will keep me away from those irises you told me about last night.'

'So thick on the ground that you had to tread on them,' I said cheerfully, 'and cyclamens, all over the rock. And wild gladioli and tulips. And three colours of anemone. A yellow oxalis as big as a penny. Rock-roses the size of breakfast-cups and the colour of Devonshire cream. And, of course, if you go really high, those purple orchids that I told you about—'

Frances gave a moan, and pushed her tray aside. 'Get out of this, you little beast, and let me get up. Yes, yes, yes, we'll go as high as you like, and I only hope my aged limbs will stand it. You're not pulling my leg about the orchids?'

'No, honestly. Lady's-slippers, or something, as big as field-mice, and trailing things, like the ones in shops that you can never afford.'

'I'll be with you in half an hour. Get Ceddie to have some lunch put together. We may as well take the whole day.'

'Ceddie?'

'Little Lord Fauntleroy. I forgot, your generation never reads,' said Frances, getting out of bed. 'A thumping good lunch, tell him, *and* some wine.'

The on-shore breeze had found its way well inland, and it was deliciously cool by the river-bridge. We went along the river, up the path that I had taken yesterday.

Our progress was slow. Frances, as I had known she would be, was enraptured by everything she saw. The sugar-canes, standing deep along the ditches, rustling. A pair of turtle-doves, flying up out of a patch of melon-flowers. A jay, vivid and chattering. A nest of rock-nuthatches that I found on a broken wall. And the flowers ... Soon she stopped exclaiming, and in a short while managed to overcome the feeling that one ought not to touch – let alone pick – the pale lilac anemones with indigo hearts, the miniature marigolds, the daisies purple, yellow, and white. Between her delight, and my own delight at her pleasure (for Greece was, I liked to think, my country, and I was showing her round it), we reached the upper plateau with its fields and windmills before I even had time to remember my preoccupations of yesterday.

There were a few people at work among the fields. We saw a man and his wife working with primitive long-handled hoes, one on either side of a furrow of beans. In another field a donkey stood patiently beside the ditch, waiting for its owner. Further on, a child sat on a bank beside a patch of crude pasture where vetches and camomile grew, watching over this little flock of four goats, two pigs, and a ewe with her lamb.

We left the main track and picked our way along the narrow beaten paths between the fields, pausing frequently for Frances to use her camera. Everything made a picture – the child, the beasts, the men bent over their work; even the long views of the plateau and the upper mountain were brought alive by the whirling sails of the windmills. There were everywhere on the plateau, dozens of them, skeleton structures of iron like small pylons, ugly in themselves, but now, with their white canvas sails spread and spinning in the morning's breeze, they looked enchantingly pretty, like enormous daisies spinning in the wind, filling the hot morning with the sigh of cool air and the sound of spilling water.

Then Frances found the irises.

These were the same as I had seen further up the hill-side, tiny irises three inches high, lilac and bronze and gold, springing out of ground baked as hard and – you would have sworn – as barren as fireclay. They grew on the stony banks, on the trodden pathway, in the dry verges of the bean-field, and swarmed as thick as butterflies right up to the walls of the windmill.

This, as luck would have it, was no ugly iron pylon, but a real mill, one of the two corn-mills that served the plateau. It was a solidly-built, conical structure, much like the windmills we know, with a thatched roof, and ten canvas sails. The sails unlike those of the water-mills, were furled along their spokes, but this idle mill, with its arched doorway and dazzling whitewash, was beautiful. The irises – in places crushed and trodden – were thick around it, and just beside the doorstep stood a clump of scarlet gladioli. Behind the white mill crowded the lemon-groves that edged the plateau, and beyond these rose the silver slopes of Dicte.

Muttering strange oaths, Frances reached for her camera yet again. 'My God, I wish I'd brought five miles of film, instead of five hundred miserable feet! Why didn't you tell me that the very *dust* of this country was so damned photogenic? If only there was some movement! Why aren't the sails going?'

'It's a corn-mill. The owners only run it when somebody hires them to grind the corn. Each settlement has two or three, to serve everyone.'

'Oh, I see. Well, look, would *you* go into the picture, and – ah, that's lucky, there's a peasant woman . . . just what it needs, the very job . . .'

The door of the mill had been standing half open. Now it gaped wider, and a Greek woman, clothed in the inevitable black, and carrying a cheap rexine shopping-bag, came out. She turned, as if to pull the door shut, then she saw us, and stopped short in the act, with her hand still out to the big old-fashioned key that jutted from the lock.

Frances' camera whirred on, unconcernedly; but my heart had started to beat in erratic, painful thuds, and the palms of my hands were wet.

I thought: If I tell Frances that's Sofia, that'll be two of us acting our heads off, instead of only one. Frances, at least, must be left to behave naturally . . .

The camera stopped. Frances lowered it, and waved and smiled at Sofia, who stood like stone, staring at us, with her hand still out to the door.

'Nicola, go and tell her it's a movie, will you? There's no need to pose, I want her moving. Ask her if she minds. And get in the picture yourself, please; I want that turquoise frock beside the gladioli. Just walk up to her and say something. Anything.'

Just walk up to her and say something. Dead easy, that was. *'Have you got Colin Langley hidden in the mill, Sofia?'* The sixty-four-thousand-dollar question.

I swallowed. I was scrubbing my hands surreptitiously on my handkerchief. 'I'll ask her,' I said, steadily enough, 'to show me into the mill. You'll get a good picture as we go into that dark archway.'

I walked across the irises to greet Sofia.

Frances still has the film. It is the only one, of many which she has of me, in which I walk and behave as if quite oblivious of the camera. As a rule, in front of a camera, I am stiff and shy. But on this occasion I wasn't thinking about Frances and her film; only about the woman who stood unmoving in the bright sunlight, with that half-shut door beside her, and her hand on the big key. It is a very effective piece of film, but I have never liked watching it. This was not a day that I care, now, to remember.

I trod through the irises, and smiled.

'Good morning, *kyria*. I hope you don't mind being photographed? This is my cousin, who's very keen, and she'd like a picture of you and the mill. This is your mill?'

'Yes,' said Sofia. I saw her tongue wet her lips. She bobbed her half-curtsey at Frances, who made some gesture of greeting, and called out 'How do you do?' I hoped that both would assume that an introduction had been made.

'It's a moving picture.' My voice sounded strained, and I cleared my throat. 'She just wants us to stand and talk here for a moment . . . there, you can hear the camera going again . . . and then, perhaps, walk into the mill.'

'Walk – into the mill?'

'Why, yes, if you don't mind? It makes a bit of action, you see, for the film. May we?'

For one long, heart-stopping minute I thought she was going to refuse, then she put a hand flat against the door, and pushed it wide. With an inclination of the head, and a gesture, she invited me in. It was a movement of great dignity, and I heard Frances give a little grunt of satisfaction as the camera got it.

I mounted the single step, and went into the mill.

Just inside the door a stone stairway, built against the wall, spiralled upwards. Within its curve, on the ground, stood sacks of grain, and a pile of brushwood for repairing the thatch. Against the wall was a stack of tools; a rough hoe, a spade, something that was probably a harrow, and a coil of light rope. A sieve hung from a nail.

I couldn't hear if the camera was still going. Sofia was just behind me. I looked up the curling stairway.

'May I go up?' Already, while I was speaking, I had mounted two steps, and my foot was on a third before I paused to glance back at her. 'I've always wanted to see inside a mill, but the only other one I've been to was derelict. That was on Paros . . .'

Sofia had her back to the light, and I couldn't see her face. Again I sensed that hesitation, and again my pulses thudded, while I gripped the narrow handrail. But she could hardly, without a boorishness comparable to my own, have refused.

'Please do.' Her voice was colourless. She put her bag down on the floor, and followed me closely up the stairs.

The chamber on the first floor was where the flour was weighed. Here were the old-fashioned scales, a contraption of chains and bar and burnished bowls, which would be slung from a hook on the massive wooden beam. All about the floor stood the big square tins which caught the milled flour as it came down the chute from the grindstones. Some of the tins were full of a coarse, meal-coloured flour. Here, too, were sacks of grain.

But no Colin Langley. And no place to hide him.

So much I took in while I was still climbing out of the stair-well. The place was as innocent as Stratos' boat had been. There was no hiding-place for anything much bigger than a mouse. As I stepped out on to the boarded floor, a mouse did indeed whisk out of the way between two tins, carrying some titbit in its mouth.

But there was another stairway, and another floor . . .

Beside me Sofia said, still in that colourless voice that was so unlike her: 'Since you are interested, *thespoinís* . . . That is the chute down which the flour comes. You see? These are the scales for weighing it. You hang them up, so . . . '

I watched her in the light from the single window. Was it imagination, or was she more waxen-pale than ever in the bright glare of morning? Certainly she was acting with a reserve which might have been construed as uneasiness, or even anxiety, but her stolid peasant dignity had come to her aid, and I could see nothing in her face that I could put a name to; except that, today, my intrusion and interest in her doings were less than welcome.

She had finished whatever she was explaining to me, and began to dismantle the scales with an air of finality.

'And now, if the *thespoinís* will excuse me—'

'Oh, don't put them away yet!' I cried, 'I know my cousin'll want to see this – it's terribly interesting! Frances!'

I ran to the stairs and called down, adding warmly, as poor Sofia hesitated, scales in hand: 'It's awfully good of you; I'm afraid we're being a lot of trouble, but it really is marvellous to see all this, and I know my cousin will love it all! Here she comes. Now I must just go up *quickly*, and see the rest—'

'*Thespoinís*—' Something had touched that colourless voice at last. It was sharp. '*Thespoinís*, there is nothing up there except the millstones, nothing at all! Do not go up; the floor is rotten!'

This was true. From below I had seen the holes in the boards.

I said cheerfully, not even pausing: 'It's all right, I'm not afraid. After all, I suppose it holds you when you have to come up here to work, doesn't it? I'll be careful. Heavens, are these the grindstones? It's a marvel there's ever wind enough to move them at all!'

I hadn't yet paused to think what I would do if Colin were there, but the small, circular room was empty – if one could apply that word to a space almost filled by the giant millstones, and crowded with primitive machinery.

The ceiling was conical, and was the actual roof of the mill. From the apex of this wigwam-like thatch down the centre of the chamber, like a tent-pole, ran the huge axle on which the millstones turned. These, some eight to ten feet across, looked as if no power short of a steam-turbine could ever move them. Jutting out from the wall was a metal lever by which the whole roof could be swung round on its central pivot, to catch any wind that blew; and a vast, pegged wheel, set at right angles to the millstones, no doubt transferred the drive to them from the sails. This driving-wheel was of wood, hand-hewn and worm-eaten, like the floor. But everything was clean, and the room was fresh and very light, for there were two windows cut in the thick walls, one on either side, at floor-level. One of these was shuttered, and fastened with a wooden peg; and, beside it, pushed back into a rough pile against the wall, was a jumble of brushwood left over – as was apparent – from a recent job of thatching.

I stepped over the hole in the aged flooring, and looked thoughtfully down at the brushwood. A clay jar hung from a nail near by, and a short-handled broom stood underneath it. The brushwood looked as if it had just been bundled back against the wall, and the floor had been newly swept . . .

I wondered how recently the jar had been used, and whether, if I tilted it, I would find a few drops of water still in the bottom . . .

I had no chance to try, for now Sofia was at the head of the stairs, and I could hear Frances coming up.

I turned quickly. 'Frances! This is wonderful, it's like the Bible or Homer or something. Bring the camera up, there's plenty of light!' Then, brightly, to Sofia: 'I'm so glad we've seen this! We have nothing like this, you know, in England – at least, I believe there still are some windmills, but I've never seen inside one. May my cousin take a picture? Would it be all right to open the other window?'

I chattered on at her, as disarmingly as I could. After all, she could only be annoyed: I had shown myself yesterday to be a busybody without manners, and if an extension of this character today would get me what I wanted, then my reputation was gone in a good cause.

Frances came quickly up, exclaiming with pleasure. Sofia, unbending perhaps at her palpably innocent interest, moved willingly enough to unlatch the window, and began to explain the action of the millstones. I translated what she said, asking a few more harmless questions, and then, when Frances had started work with the camera, and was persuading Sofia to mime some of the movements with lever and grain-chute, I left them casually – oh, so casually! – and started down the stairs again.

I had seen what I was looking for. Of that I was sure. Sofia had cleaned up efficiently, but not quite efficiently enough. After all, I myself had just done the self-same job in the shepherds' hut, and my eye was fresh to the signs. Nobody who was not looking for it would have guessed that, until recently, a prisoner had been kept in the mill. But I had known what to look for.

I was sure I was right. The brushwood on the top floor had been ruffled up again, and pushed back, but someone had lain there. And Sofia had swept the floor, but had overlooked the fact of the rotten boards beside the bedding. Some of her sweepings must have fallen through on to the floor below . . .

I ran lightly down the steps, and paused on the landing.

Yes: again I had been right. On the boards beneath the hole were a few fragments of broken brushwood and dusty fronds. This, in itself, would have meant nothing, but among them there were crumbs. It had been a crumb of bread that I had seen the mouse carrying. And here were more, as yet unsalvaged, tiny traces of food which, without the mouse, and the sharpened eyes of suspicion, I would never have seen.

I never thought I should live to be grateful for the time that one has to wait about while Frances takes her films. I could hear her now, conversing with Sofia with – presumably – some success, and much laughter. Sofia, no doubt feeling herself safe, appeared to be relaxing. The whirr of the camera sounded loud in the confined space. I ran on down the stairs.

I had remembered the coil of rope that lay beside the grain-sacks. If you had a prisoner, presumably you tied him. I wanted to see that rope.

I reached the ground floor, and paused for a moment, throwing a swift glance round me. I could hear them still busy with the camera, and, even if they came down, I should have plenty of warning: they could not see me until they were half-way down the stairs. I bent over the rope.

The first thing I saw was the blood.

It sounds simple when I write it like that, and I suppose I had even been expecting it. But what one expects with the reasoning mind, and one's reactions to it as a fact, are two very different things. I think it was the driving need for haste, and secrecy, that saved me. Somehow, I managed to stay cool enough, and, after the first moment or so, to look more closely.

There was very little blood; only (I told myself) the sort of stain one might get from bound wrists scraped raw with struggling. The slight staining came at intervals along one of the ropes, as it might if this were coiled round someone's wrists.

Somehow, I fumbled among the coils to find the ends of the rope. They were unfrayed, still bound.

As I let them fall back where they had lain, Sofia's shopping-bag caught my eye, standing near. Without a second's compunction I pulled the mouth wide, and looked inside.

There wasn't much; a bundle of the faded, red-and-green patterned cloth that I had seen in her house, a crumpled newspaper stained with grease, and another strip of the cloth, much creased, and stained as if with damp.

I opened the bundle of cloth; there was nothing in it but a few crumbs. The newspaper too; the marks on it could have been made by fat, or butter. She must have brought the boy's food wrapped in paper, then bundled up in a cloth. Then there was the other cloth, the creased strip, that looked as if it had been chewed . . .

Just that, of course. The boy could hardly have been left here, lying bound. They would have had to gag him.

I dropped it back into the bag, with hands that shook, then pushed the other things back after it, and straightened up.

It was true, then. Colin had been here: and Colin had gone. The unfrayed rope told its own tale; there had been no escape, no bonds sawn through. The rope had been untied, then neatly coiled away, presumably by Sofia when she had cleared away the gag, the bedding, and the traces of food.

But if Colin was still alive – my brain was missing like a faulty engine, but it hammered on, painfully – if they still had Colin, alive, then surely he would still be bound? If the rope was here, discarded, then might it not mean that Colin had been set free deliberately, and that he might now, in his turn, be looking for Mark?

. I had been standing, staring blindly down at the clutter of stuff beside the wall. Now, my eyes registered, with a jerk that was almost physically painful, the thing at which they had been staring, unseeingly; the thing that stood there beside the rope gleaming in its obviousness.

The spade. Once I had seen it, I could see nothing else.

It was an old spade, with a well-worn handle, but the blade shone, with recent use, as if it were new. There was still earth clinging to it. Some of this had dried and crumbled, and lay in little piles on the floor. The spade had been used very recently, and for deep digging: not just the dry, dusty topsoil, but the deep, damp earth that would cling . . .

I shut my eyes on it then, trying to push aside the image that was forming. Someone had been digging; all right, that was what a spade was for, wasn't it? The fields had to be tilled, hadn't they? It needn't mean a thing. Anybody could have been using it, for a variety of reasons. Sofia could have been digging vegetables, or Josef, or Stratos . . .

And now the picture, unimportant, unremembered until this moment, showed complete – yesterday's picture of these tranquil fields: the sleeping boy; the man, alone, digging behind that patch of sugar-cane, beyond the mill. He had been a broad-shouldered man, with a red kerchief round his neck. He had not noticed me, nor I him. But now, in my mind's eye, I could see him again, clearly.

As I had seen him later, when he had finished his work and had come down to Sofia's cottage to tell her what he had done, and that she could come up to the mill to clear away.

Somehow, I got outside. The sun was brilliant on the irises, and a sulphur butterfly quested among the purple petals.

The back of my hand was pressed so hard to my mouth that my teeth hurt it.

'I'll have to tell Mark,' I said, against the bitten flesh. 'Dear God, I'll have to tell Mark.'

CHAPTER THIRTEEN

'Nicola – Nicky, honey – what is it?'

'It's all right. Give me a minute, that's all.'

'I knew there was something. Look, we can sit down here. Take your time.'

We had reached the wayside shrine above the lemon-grove. The fields were out of sight; the windmill no more than a gleam of white through the trees. I could not remember getting here: somehow, I must have taken a civil leave of Sofia; somehow waited, while she and Frances exchanged farewell compliments; somehow steered a blind way up through the trees, to stop by the shrine, staring wordlessly at Frances.

'Here,' she said, 'have a cigarette.'

The sharp smell of the match mingled, too evocatively, with the scents of verbena and lavender that grew beside the stones where we sat. I ran my fingers up a purple spike of flowers, shredding them brutally from the stem, then let the bruised heads fall; but the scent of lavender was still stronger on the flesh of my hand. I rubbed it down my skirt, and spoke to the ground.

'They've killed Colin. You were right. And they've buried him down there . . . just near the mill.'

There was a silence. I was watching some ants scurrying to examine the fallen flower-heads.

'But—' her voice was blank – 'how do you know? Do you mean you saw something?'

I nodded.

'I see. The mill. Yes, why not? Well, tell me.'

When I had finished, she sat a little longer in silence, smoking rather hard. Then I saw her shake her head sharply, like someone ridding themselves of a stinging insect. 'That nice woman? I can't believe it. The thing's fantastic.'

'You didn't see Mark, lying up there in the dirt, with a bullet-hole in him. It's true enough, he's dead. And now I'll have to tell Mark. We can get the police on it, now that it's too late.' I swung round on her, anxiously. 'You said you guessed something was wrong. You mean I showed it? Would Sofia guess I knew something?'

'I'm sure she wouldn't. I wasn't sure myself, and I know you pretty well. What could she have guessed, anyway? She's not to know you knew anything about it; and there was nothing to see, not unless someone was deliberately looking for traces.'

'It was the mouse. If I hadn't seen the mouse with that bit of bread, I'd never have found anything. I'd have wondered about the brushwood, but it would never have entered my head to hunt for crumbs, or to look at that rope.'

'Well, she didn't see the mouse, so it wouldn't occur to her, either. I should stop worrying about that side of it. She'll have gone off quite satisfied with the result of her tidying-up, and you and I are still well in the clear.'

The ants were scurrying about aimlessly among the lavender-flowers.

'Frances, I'll have to tell Mark.'

'Yes, I know.'

'You agree I should, now?'

'I'm afraid you'll have to, darling.'

'Then – you think I'm right? You think that's what's happened?'

'That Colin's dead? I'm afraid it looks like it. In any case, Mark ought to hear the evidence. It's got well beyond the stage at which he can deal with things himself. Are you going now?'

'The sooner I get it over, the better. What about you?'

'You'll be better on your own, and in any case, I ought to be here to cover up for you if you're late back. I'll stay around taking film and so on, and then go back for tea, as arranged. I'll tell them that you've gone farther than I cared to, but that you'll keep to the paths, and be back by dark.' She gave me an anxious smile. 'So take care of yourself, and see that you are. I'm not at all sure that I could be convincing if you chose to spend another night up there!'

'You needn't worry about that, I'll be even less welcome than I was last time.' I hadn't meant to speak quite so bitterly. I got quickly to my feet, adding prosaically: 'Well, the sooner the better. How about dividing the lunch-packet?'

My plan, if it could be called a plan, was relatively simple.

It was possible that Mark and Lambis, after last night's foray, had gone back for the rest of the night to the shepherds' hut, sooner than undertake the long trek over to their caique. But, if the blood in Sofia's shed was evidence, Mark might not have been able to face the stiff climb to the hut. He and Lambis could have holed up till morning somewhere nearer the village, and it might even be that Mark (if his wound had broken open badly) would have to stay hidden there today.

Whatever the case, it seemed to me that my best plan was to find the track which led across to the ruined church – the track on which the first murder had been committed – and follow that along the lower reaches of the mountain-side. It was a reasonable way for a tourist to go, it would lead me in the same general direction that Mark and Lambis would have to take, and it was, as I knew, visible for long stretches, not only from the alp and the ledge, but from a wide range of rocks above.

I remembered how clearly the Cretan had stood out, yesterday, against the stand of cypresses beside the track. If I stopped there, and if Mark and Lambis were anywhere above me, they would surely see me, and I could in some way make it apparent that I had news for them. No doubt – since I had promised that I would only interfere again if I had vital news – they would show some sign, to let me know where they were, and after that I could make my way up to them as cautiously as I could. If no signal showed from above, then I would have to decide whether to go up and look at the ledge and the hut, or whether to push on along the track, and try to find the caique. It was all very vague and unsatisfactory, but for want of more exact knowledge, it was the best I could do.

As for the murderer, whom I was determined, now, to identify with Josef, I had coldly considered him, and was confident that there I ran very little risk. If I should meet him on the track, I had every excuse (including Stratos' own advice to visit the Byzantine church) for being there. It was only after I had exchanged signals with Mark that I should need caution, and then no doubt Mark and Lambis would make it their business to protect me. It was odd that this idea didn't irk me, as it would have done yesterday. Today, I could think of nothing beyond the moment when I should have discharged my dreadful burden of news, and with it the responsibility for future action.

From the shrine, where I had left Frances, a narrow path led up through the last of the lemon-trees, on to the open ground above the plateau. Like the track from the bridge, it looked as if it was much used by the village flocks, so it occurred to me that it might eventually join the old mountain road which led towards the church and the 'ancient harbour'.

This proved to be the case. Very soon my narrow path took me upwards over bare, fissured rock where someone had tried to build a dry wall, to join a broader, but by no means smoother, track along the mountain-side.

It was already hot. On this stretch of the hill there were no trees, other than an occasional thin poplar with bone-white boughs. Thistles grew in the cracks of the rock, and everywhere over the dry dust danced tiny yellow flowers, on thread-like stalks that let them flicker in the breeze two inches above the ground. They were lovely little things, a million motes of gold dancing in a dusty beam, but I trudged over them almost without seeing them. The joy had gone: there was nothing in my world now but the stony track, and the job it was taking me to do. I plodded on in the heat, weary already. There is no one so leaden-footed as the reluctant bringer of bad news.

The track did not bear steadily uphill. Sometimes it would twist suddenly upwards, so that I had to clamber up what was little more than a dry water-course. Then, out of this, I would emerge on to a stretch of bare, hot rock that led with flat and comparative ease along some reach of the mountain's flank. At other times I was led – with an infuriating lack of logic – steeply downhill, through drifts of dust and small stones where thistles grew, and wild fig-trees flattened by the south wind. Now and again, as the way crossed an open ridge, or skirted the top of a thorn-thicket, it lay in full view of the high rocks that hid the shepherds' hut: but whether I could have seen Mark's ledge, or whether he, if he was still there, could have seen me, I did not know. I kept my eyes on the nearer landscape, and plodded steadily on. It would be time enough to expose myself to the gaze of the mountain-side when I had reached the grove of cypresses.

It was with curiously conflicting feelings of relief and dread that, following the track round a jutting shoulder, I saw at length, dark against the long open wing of the mountain, the block of cypresses.

They were still a fair distance off. About half-way to them I could see the jagged scar, fringed with the green of tree-tops, which was the narrow gully running roughly parallel to the big ravine up which I had first adventured. It was at the head of this gully, in the hollow olive-tree, that Lambis had hidden the provisions yesterday.

It was downhill all the way to the gully. I paused at the edge at last, where the track took a sudden sharp run down to the water. At this point the stream widened into a shallow pool, where someone had placed stepping-stones. Downstream from this, the stream-bed broadened soon into a shallow trough where the water tumbled from pool to pool among the bushy scrub, but upstream, the way I might have to go, was a deep, twisting gorge crowded with the trees whose tops I had glimpsed from the distance. It was the thickest cover I had seen since I had left Frances in the lemon-grove, and now, though reason told me that I had no need of cover, instinct sent me scrambling thankfully down towards the shady pool with the thought that, if I must rest anywhere, I would do so here.

Where the track met the pool it widened, on both banks, into a flattened area of dried mud, beaten down by the feet of the flocks which, year in and year out, probably since the time of Minos, had crowded down here to drink, on their journey to the high pastures. There had been a flock this way recently. On the far side the bank, sloping gently up from the water, was still muddy where the sheep had crowded across, splashing the water up over the flattened clay. Superimposed on the swarming slots in the mud I could see the blurred print of the shepherd's sandal. He had slipped in the clay, so that the print was blurred at the toe and heel, but the convoluted pattern of the rope sole was as clear as a photograph.

A rope sole. I was balanced on the last stepping-stone, looking for a dry place to step on, when the significance of this struck me, and – after a horrible moment of teetering there on one leg like a bad imitation of Eros in Piccadilly – I stepped straight into the water. But I was too startled even to care. I merely squelched out of the stream, carefully avoiding that beautiful police-court print, and stood there shaking my soaking foot, and thinking hard.

It was very possible that, as I had first thought, this was the print of the shepherd's foot. But if that was so, he had the same kind of shoes as Mark.

This, again, was possible, but seemed unlikely. Most of the Greek country-folk appeared to wear either canvas slippers with rubber soles, or else a kind of cheap laced plimsoll; and many of the men (and some of the women) wore boots, as in summer the dry fields were full of snakes. But rope soles were rare; I knew this, because I like them, and had been trying both in Athens and Heraklion to buy some for this very holiday, but with no success.

So, though it was possible that a Cretan shepherd was wearing these rope soles, it was far more likely that Mark had been this way.

The thought brought me up all standing, trying to revise my plans.

The print was this morning's, that much was obvious. Whatever had happened last night, this meant that Mark was fit enough to be on his feet, and heading away from the village – not for the hut, but back towards the caique.

I bit my lip, considering. Could he – *could* he have already found out what I was on my way to tell him? Had he somehow found his way into the mill, before Sofia had been able to remove traces of its occupant?

But there I checked myself. I couldn't get out of it that way. I still had to try to find him ... But it did look as if the job might be simplified, for there were other prints ... A second much more lightly-defined than the first, showed clearly enough; then another, dusty and blurred; and another ... then I had lost him on the dry, stony earth of the bank.

I paused there, at fault, staring round me at the baked earth and baking stone, where even the myriad prints of the tiny, cloven hoofs were lost in the churned dust. The heat, unalloyed in the gorge by any breeze, drove down from the fierce sky as from a burning-glass.

I realized, suddenly, how hot and thirsty I was. I turned back into the shade, set down my bag, and stooped to drink ...

The fourth print was a beauty, set slap down in a damp patch under a bush, right under my eyes.

But not on the track. He had left it here, and headed away from it, up the gully-bottom, through the tangle of trees beside the water. He wasn't making for the caique. He was heading – under cover – up in the direction of the shepherds' hut.

I gave a heave to the bag over my shoulder, and stooped to push after him under a swag of old-man's-beard.

If it had been shelter I wanted, there was certainly plenty of it here. The cat-walk of trodden ground that twisted up under the trees could hardly have been called a path; nothing larger than rats seemed to have used it, except for the occasional blurred prints of those rope-soled feet. The trees were spindly, thin-stemmed and light-leaved; aspens, and white poplars, and something unknown to me, with round, thin leaves like wafers, that let the sun through in a dapple of flickering green. Between the stems was a riot of bushes, but luckily these were mostly of light varieties like honeysuckle and wild clematis. Where I had to push my way through, I was gratified to notice various signs that Mark had pushed his way through, too. Old Argus-Eyes, I thought, momentarily triumphant. Girl Crusoe in person. Not such a slouch at this sort of thing after all. Mark would have to admit . . . And there the mood faded, abruptly, back to its dreary grey. I plodded doggedly on.

The stream grew steeper, the way more tangled. There were no more signs now, and if there were footmarks I never saw them. The air in the bottom of the gully was still, and the shade was light, letting a good deal of sunshine through. I stopped, at length, to have another drink, then, instead of drinking, turned from the water with sudden resolution, sat down on a dry piece of fallen tree-trunk in the shade, and opened my bag.

I was hot, tired, and exhausted by depression. It was going to help no one if I foundered here. If the news I was bearing (I thought crudely to myself) had knocked the guts out of me, better have a shot at putting them back in working order.

I uncorked the bottle of *King Minos, sec,* and, with a silent blessing on Frances, who had insisted on my taking it, took a swig that would have done credit to Mrs. Gamp and her tea-pot. After that I felt so much better that – in homage to the gods of the place – I poured a few drops on the ground for a libation, then tackled lunch with something like an appetite.

Frances had also given me at least two-thirds of Tony's generous lunch-packet. With a little more help from King Minos, I ate a couple of the fresh rolls crammed with roast mutton, some olives from a poke of grease-proof paper, and then a rather tasteless apple. The orange I would not face, but dropped it back into the bag.

A little stir of the breeze lifted the tree-tops above me, so that the sun-motes spilled dazzlingly through on to the water, and shadows slid over the stones. A couple of butterflies, which had been drinking at the water's edge, floated off like blown leaves, and a goldfinch, with a flash of brilliant wings, flirted its way up past me into some high bushes in an overhanging piece of cliff.

I watched it, idly. Another slight movement caught my eye, a stir of light colour among some piled boulders below the overhang, as if a stone had moved. Then I saw that there was a lamb, or a ewe, lying up there, under a tangle of honeysuckle. The breeze must have lifted the fleece, so that the ruffling wool had shown momentarily above the boulders.

I watched, attentive now. There it was again, the stroking finger of the breeze running along the wool, and lifting it, so that the light caught its edge and it shone softly for a moment, like bloom along the stone.

I had been wrong, then. The foot-print had not been Mark's. The sheep were somewhere near by, and with them, no doubt, would be the shepherd.

I began quickly to pack the remnants of lunch away, thinking, more confusedly than ever, that now I had better revert to my first haphazard plan, and make for the cypress grove.

I got to my feet warily, then stood, listening.

No sound except the chatter of the water, and the faint hushing of the wind in the leaves, and the high liquid twittering of the goldfinches somewhere out of sight . . .

I had turned back downstream, to find a place where I could clamber more easily out of the gully, when it occurred to me that the sheep had been oddly still and quiet, all through the time that I had been eating. I glanced back. It lay on the other side of the stream, some way above me, half under the overhang. It could have slipped from above, I thought, unnoticed by the shepherd, and it might well be dead; but if it was merely trapped on its back, or held down by thorns, it would only take me a few moments to free it. I must, at least, take time to look.

I stepped across the stream, and clambered up towards the boulders.

The sheep was certainly dead; had been dead some time. Its fleece was being worn as a cloak by the boy who lay curled under a bush, in the shelter of the boulders, fast asleep. He wore torn blue jeans and a dirty blue shirt, and the sheepskin was pulled over one shoulder, as the Greek shepherds wear it, and tied into place with a length of frayed string. This, not Mark, was the quarry I had been stalking. The mud on his rope-soled shoes was hardly dry.

The noise of my approach had not disturbed him. He slept with a sort of concentration, deep in sleep, lost in it. A fly landed on his cheek, and crawled across his eye; he never stirred. His breathing was deep and even. It would have been quite easy to creep quietly away, and never rouse him.

But I made no such attempt. I stood there, with my heart beating in my throat till I thought it would nearly choke me. I had seen that kind of sleep before, and recently – that almost fierce concentration of rest. I thought I had seen those eyelashes before, too; I remembered the way they lay on the brown cheeks in sleep. And the way the dark hair grew.

The thick lashes lifted, and he looked straight at me. His eyes were blue. There was the quick flash of alarm shown by any sleeper who is startled awake to find himself being stood over by a stranger; then a second look, half-relieved, half-wary, as he registered my harmlessnes.

I cleared my throat, and managed a hoarse *'Châirete.'* It is the country greeting, and means, literally, 'Rejoice.'

He stared for a moment, blinking, then gave me the conventional 'Good day.'

'Kalí méra.' His voice sounded stupid and slurred. Then he thrust his knuckles into his eyes, and pushed himself into a sitting posture. He moved, I thought, a little stiffly.

I wetted my lips, and hesitated. 'You're from Agios Georgios?' I still spoke in Greek.

He was eyeing me warily, like a shy animal. *'Óchi.'* The denial was hardly audible, a thick mutter as he got quickly to one knee, and turned to grope under the bush, where he had put down his shepherd's stick. This was the genuine article, gnarled fig-wood, polished by years of use. Shaken by a momentary doubt, I said sharply: 'Please – don't go. I'd like to talk to you ... please ...'

I saw his body go tense, just for a second; then he had dragged the stick out from where it lay, and was getting to his feet. He turned on me that look of complete and baffling stupidity that one sometimes sees in peasants – usually when one is arguing the price of some commodity for which they are over-charging by about a hundred per cent. *'Thén katalavéno* (I don't understand),' he said, *'adío,'* and jumped past me, down the bank towards the stream. Round the wrist of the hand that held the stick was tied a rough bandage of cloth in a pattern of red and green.

'Colin—' I said, shakily.

He stopped as if I had struck him. Then, slowly, as if to face a blow, he turned back to me. His face frightened me. It still looked stupid, and I saw now that this was real; it was the blank look of someone who is beyond feeling punishment, and who has long since stopped even asking the reason for it.

I went straight to the root of the matter, in English. 'Mark's alive, you know. It was only a flesh wound, and he was quite all right, last time I saw him. That was yesterday. I'm on my way to find him now, I – I'm a friend of his, and I think I know where he'll be, if you'd care to come along?'

He didn't even need to speak. His face told me all I wanted to know. I sat down abruptly on a boulder, looked away, and groped for a handkerchief to blow my nose.

CHAPTER FOURTEEN

'Wonder of time,' quoth she, 'this is my spite,
That, thou being dead, the day should yet be light.'

SHAKESPEARE: *Venus and Adonis*

'Do you feel better now?' I asked.

It was a little time later. I had made him sit down then and there, by the stream, and drink some of the wine, and eat the rest of the food I had brought. I hadn't asked him any questions yet, but while he ate and drank I told him all I could about Mark's end of the story, and my own.

He said very little, but ate like a young wolf. They had fed him, I gathered, but he 'hadn't been able to eat much.' This was all he had said so far about his experiences, but the change in him – since the news about Mark – was remarkable. Already he looked quite different; the bruised look was gone from his eyes, and, by the time the *Minos Sec* was half down in the bottle, there was even a sparkle in them, and a flush in his cheeks.

'Now,' I said, as he gave the neck of the bottle a final wipe, corked it, and set it down among the wreck of papers that was all he had left of my lunch, 'you can tell me all your side of it. Just let me get all this rubbish stowed away, and you can tell me as we go. *Were* you in the windmill?'

'I'll say I was, tied up like a chicken and dumped on a bundle of rubbish,' said Colin warmly. 'Mind you, I hadn't a clue where I was, when they first took me there; it was dark. In fact, I didn't know till today, when I left, except that I'd got the impression I was in a sort of round tower. They kept the shutters up all the time – in case I saw them, I suppose. What are you doing?'

'Leaving the crumbs for the mice.'

'Crumbs for the *mice*?'

I laughed. 'You'd be surprised how much the mice have done for us today. Never mind, skip it. How did you get away? No, wait, let's get on our way. You can tell me while we go; and start at the very beginning, when Mark was shot at, and the gang jumped on you.'

'Okay.' He got to his feet eagerly. He was very like his brother to look at; slighter, of course, and with a frame at once softer and more angular, but promising the same kind of compact strength. The hair and eyes, and the slant of the brows were Mark's, and so – I was to discover – were one or two other things.

'Which way are we going?' he asked briskly.

'For the moment, back down the gully for a bit. There's a place quite near, a clump of cypresses, which you can see from anywhere higher up. I'm going over to that. If he and Lambis are somewhere about, they'll be keeping a lookout, and they'll surely show some sort of signal, then we can go straight up to them, via the gully. If not, then we'll aim for the caique.'

'If it's still there.'

This thought had been worrying me, too, but I wasn't going to admit it. 'It will be. They knew, if you were free, that you'd make straight for it; where else could you go? Even if they've moved it again, you can bet your life they're keeping a good lookout for you.'

'I suppose so. If you're going up into the open to signal them, had I better stay down here?'

'Oh, yes. And whichever way we go, we'll stay in cover. Thank goodness, anyway, one of my problems is gone – you'll know the way from the old church to the caique. Come on.'

'How did you find me, anyway?' asked Colin, scrambling after me across the stream, and down the narrow gully-path.

'Followed your tracks.'

'*What?*'

'You heard. That's one of the things we'll have to put right before we go. You left some smashing prints down by the stepping-stones. You can sweep them out while I go up to the cypress-grove.'

'Well, but how did you know they were mine?'

'Oh, I didn't; I thought they were Mark's. You've the same sort of shoes.'

'Have a heart, Nicola, he takes nines!'

'Well, I wasn't really thinking. Anyway, you'd slipped in the mud, and the toe and heel were blurred, so the prints looked longer. If it hadn't been for recognizing Mark's shoes, I'd never have noticed them. He was – a bit on my mind, at the time. All the same, you'd better wipe them out.'

'Gosh—' Colin sounded thoroughly put out at this evidence of his inefficiency – 'I never thought of prints. I suppose, with its being dark, and then I was pretty well bushed—'

'You had other things to think about. Here we are. There, see them? Now, I'll go up, and if there's no one to be seen, then I'll give the all-clear, and you can come out and deal with the evidence, while I show myself up yonder and wait for the green light.' I paused, and looked at him uncertainly. In the shadow of the trees he looked disconcertingly like his brother. 'You – you will still be here, won't you, when I come back?'

'You bet your sweet life I will,' said Colin. 'But look here—'

'What?'

He was looking uneasy. 'Look, I don't like you going out there, it mightn't be safe. Can't we think of some other way?'

'*I'm* quite safe, even if I bump head-on into Josef, as long as *you* keep out of sight,' I said firmly. 'You're very like your brother, aren't you?'

'For my sins,' said Colin, and grinned.

He waited there in the dappled shade while I climbed to the rim of the gully. I looked about me. The landscape was as bare of life as on the first four days of Creation. I gave Colin a thumbs-up sign, then set off briskly for the cypress-grove.

The track was smooth, the sun brilliant, the sky a glorious, shining blue. The tiny yellow flowers danced underfoot, like jewels in the dust. The goldfinches flashed and twittered over the lavender-bushes, and the freckled snake slipping across the path was as beautiful as they ...

Everything, in fact, was exactly the same as it had been an hour before, except that now I was happy. My feet were as light as my heart, as I almost ran across the rocks towards the dark, standing shadow of the grove.

I had been wondering how to attract the men's attention quickly. It now occurred to me, for the first time, that there was no reason why I should not simply make a noise. I felt like singing. Well, why not sing?

I sang. The sound echoed cheerfully round the rocks, and then was caught and deadened by the cypresses. Remembering how sound had carried on this same hillside yesterday, I was certain that I would be heard clearly by anyone in the reaches immediately above.

I took my stance, deliberately, in front of the thickest backdrop of cypress, then paused, as if to look at the view. At last I was able to tilt my head, shade my eyes, and stare towards the head of the main ravine. Even knowing the place as well as I did, it took some time to get my bearings. I had to start from the ravine, and let my eye travel to the rock where the naiad's spring was . . . yes, there was a recess – looking absurdly small – where the flower-covered alp must lie. The shepherds' hut would be back in that corner, out of sight. And the ledge . . .

The ledge defeated me. It might have been in any one of half a dozen places; but I had the general direction right, and I watched patiently and carefully, for something like six minutes.

Nothing stirred. No movement, no flicker of white, no sudden flash of glass or metal. Nothing.

The test was far from satisfactory, but it would have to do. I gave it another minute or two, then turned to hurry back. Overriding even my desire to find Mark quickly was the fear – irrational, perhaps, but nevertheless strong – that Colin, in some mysterious manner, would vanish again while I was away from him. But no, he was there, sitting under a bush. He rose to greet me, his face eager.

I shook my head. 'Not a sign. I honestly didn't expect it. They'll have gone to the caique. So we'll go after them, and we'd better hurry, because I've got to get back.'

'Look, you don't have to fag yourself going all that way. I can manage on my own,' said Mark's brother.

'I dare say, but I'm coming with you. For one thing, I've got a lot that Mark ought to know; for another, even Josef might think twice before shooting you in front of me.'

'Well,' said Colin, 'let me go in front. I can clear the way a bit with this stick. And give me that bag; I oughtn't to be letting you carry it.'

'Thank you.' I surrendered the bag meekly, and followed him up the path through the trees.

He went at a fair speed. Every moment he seemed more himself again, and obviously all he wanted now was to find his brother with the least possible delay, and shake the Cretan dust off his rope soles. I didn't blame him.

'What did you sing that for?' he asked, over his shoulder.

'Sing what? I can't even remember what I *was* singing.'

'*Love me tender.*'

'Was it? Oh, yes, I believe it was.'

'No wonder Mark didn't come out!' he said, laughing.

It was a crudity I wouldn't have expected of him, young as he was. I felt the blood sting my cheeks. 'What *do* you mean?'

'He's so square he's practically a cube. Nothing more tuneful than

Wozzeck will do for Mark, or somebody-or-other's concerto for three beer-glasses and a bassoon. Charlie's the same, but with her it's show-off; too RADA for words, Charlie is. Charlie's my sister Charlotte. Julia and I like pop – she's the next youngest to me. Ann's tone-deaf.'

'Oh, I see.'

'You're a bit out of date, though, aren't you?'

'I suppose so. But look, I'm dying to hear what happened to you. Suppose you tell me, and we might be able to get some sort of a story pieced together before we find Mark.'

So he told me, in snatches, breathlessly, as we toiled up the gully.

When Mark had fallen, wounded, from the track, Colin had run to him, only to be dragged back by Stratos and Josef. In the resulting struggle Colin had been knocked on the temple, and had fainted, but only for a few minutes. When he came to, they had secured him with some sort of rough bonds, stuffed a rag in his mouth, and were carrying him downhill, he could not tell in which direction. He kept as limp and still as he could, in the hazy hope that they might leave him for dead, or even relax sufficiently to give him a chance to get away.

It was a long way, and rough, and by now it was fairly dark, so his captors used most of their energy for the trek, and a good deal of their talk was in Greek, but he gathered that they were disagreeing violently about something.

'I can't be absolutely sure I remember properly,' he said, 'because of course I was muzzy in the head, and scared because I thought they'd murder me any minute – and besides, I was half crackers about Mark . . . I thought he was either dead, or lying bleeding to death somewhere. But some of the argument was in English – when the ones that called themselves Stratos and Tony got going – and I do remember quite a bit of what was said.'

'Try, anyway. It could be important.'

'Oh, I've tried. I had nothing else to do for three days except think what it was all in aid of; but it's more *impressions* than actual *memory*, if you see what I mean. I do know that Tony was blazing mad at them for shooting Mark and taking me along. We'd never have traced them, he said, we hadn't seen them properly; and in any case they could give each other alibis, "but taking the boy like this – it's stupid!" '

'Well,' I said, 'so it was. I still don't know why they did it.'

'Sofia,' said Colin, simply. 'I'd had this cut on the head, and I was bleeding like a pig. She thought if they left me, I'd bleed to death, and she made such a fuss and she was so cut up about the whole thing, I gathered, that they gave in, and just hustled me away. It was partly Tony, too. In the end he said that they might get away with Mark's shooting, as an accident, but if we were both found dead, or badly hurt, there'd be a fuss that might take in the whole district, and uncover "Alexandros' murder", and that would get back to them, and "the London affair".'

' "The London affair"?' I asked sharply.

'I think that's what he said. I can't be sure.'

'It could be. And the man who was murdered was "Alexandros", was he? It certainly sounds as if he might be someone catching up on Stratos and Tony from their London life, doesn't it? I wonder if he was Greek or English? He talked English to Tony, but then Tony's Greek isn't good.'

'He'd be Greek, surely, if his name was – oh, I see, you mean they may just have been, what's the word? giving his name the Greek form?'

'Hellenizing, yes. But it doesn't matter; if you heard right, then he was killed for something that happened in London. I remember now, Tony did say something about London "not being healthy" – not to me, he was only joking, to some children, but it struck me at the time. Well, to get back to Saturday night, what on earth did they intend to do with you?'

'Quite honestly, I think they were in such a general flap about what had happened, that they were just getting away from it as quickly as they could. I gathered that Stratos and Tony were livid with Josef for losing his head and shooting Mark, and that Josef was all for cutting their losses and killing me as well, then and there, but Stratos was swithering a bit, and Tony and Sofia were dead against it. In the end they sort of gave up, and bundled me off – clear out first and think later; you know. In fact, Tony was all for bolting – really bolting, I mean, getting right away. He wanted to get straight out. I remember all that bit clearly, because I was praying he wouldn't go; with him being English, I thought I might stand a better chance talking to him than the others. And he *hadn't* a part in it, really.'

'You mean Tony wanted to clear out on his own?'

'Yes. I remember exactly what he said. "Well, once you shot that tourist, you landed yourselves, whatever you do with the boy. I had nothing to do with it, or with Alex, and you know that's true. I'm getting out. I'll take my cut here and now, and don't pretend you'll not be glad to see the last of me, Stratos, dear." That was the way he talked, in a kind of silly voice; I can't quite describe it.'

'Don't bother, I've heard it. What did Stratos say?'

'He said, "They're no use to you, they're still hot. You can't get rid of them yet." Tony said. "I know that. You can trust me to be careful," and Stratos gave a beastly sort of laugh and said, "I'd as soon trust you as I'd" —' Colin stopped abruptly.

'Yes?'

'Oh, just an expression,' said Colin. 'A – a slang expression, I can't quite remember what. Meaning that he wouldn't trust him, you know.'

'Oh, yes. Well, go on.'

The gorge had widened out as we climbed higher. There was room now to walk two abreast.

'Then Stratos said where could he go, he had no money, and Tony

said, "For a start, you can give me some," and Stratos said, "Blackmail?"
and Tony said, "Well, I could talk quite a lot, couldn't I? And *I've* done
nothing that matters. There's such a thing as Queen's Evidence." '
'He's got a nerve,' I said, half-admiringly. 'Fancy coming out with
that one, to old Stratos, with two dead men behind you, and a bleeding
boy on your hands. I – er, I meant that literally.'
Colin grinned. 'I was, too, buckets of it, and it wasn't much of a cut,
when all came to all. Well, I thought Stratos would blow his lid at that,
but he must have known Tony didn't mean it, because he didn't answer,
and then Tony laughed in that silly way and said, "Dear boy, we were
going to split anyway, so come through with the stuff now, and we'll call
it a day. Where is it?" Stratos said, "When I think it's time to come
through, I'll tell you. And not so much of the holier-than-thou stuff,
either. What about Alex?" Tony said, "You mean the other time? I only
helped afterwards; it was nothing to do with me," and Stratos gave that
laugh again and said, "Nothing ever is. You'd like to stand by looking
like the Queen of Hearts and keeping your lily hands clean, wouldn't
you? Well, you'll get them dirty soon enough. We've got to get the pair
of them buried yet. So save your breath." '
'And that was all?'
'Tony just laughed and said, "You poor sweets, I'll have some coffee
and sandwiches ready for you when you get back from the graveyard."
Then,' said Colin, 'we got to the mill. I just knew it was a building of
some sort, because I heard a door creak open, and then they humped me
up the stairs. It was foully bumpy.'
'It can't be exactly easy to carry a body up a narrow spiral staircase.'
'It's beastly for the body,' said Colin cheerfully. 'They got a rope from
somewhere, and one of them tied me up properly. By that time, Tony
had gone. I heard him say, "I said you could count me out. I had nothing
to do with it, and I'll have nothing to do with this, either. If you touch
him, you're bigger fools than I thought you were." And he went.'
'The Levite,' I said.
'What? Oh, passing by on the other side, you mean? I suppose so, but
he may have been some use, because after he'd gone there was another
really terrific argument, and the woman started sort of screaming at the
men, till it sounded to me as if someone had put a hand over her mouth.
It was dark, of course; they used their torch in flashes, and kept well
back where I couldn't see them. When Sofia insisted on doing my head,
she had her veil pulled right up so's I could only see her eyes. She cleaned
my face and put something over the cut. It had stopped bleeding. Then
she took that horrible gag out of my mouth and gave me a drink, and
made them put a more comfortable one on. She was crying all the time,
and I think she was trying to be kind. The men were arguing in whispers,
in Greek. In the end Stratos said to me, in English, "You will be left
here, and we will not hurt you. You cannot escape, even if you get the
ropes off. The door will be watched, and you will be shot." I had a

feeling that it might be bluff, but I wasn't wild keen to call it, not just then, anyway. And later, when I did try to get free, I couldn't.' He paused. 'That was all. In the end, they went.'

'If I'd only known. I passed your mill twice when you were in it.'

'Did you? I suppose,' said Colin wisely, 'that if there'd been only the one, you'd have thought of it straight away, but with those dozens, all with their sails going, and so conspicuous, you wouldn't even notice them. If you see what I mean.'

'Oh, yes. *The Purloined Letter.*'

'The what?'

'A story by Poe. A classic about how to hide something. Go on. What happened next day?'

'Sofia came very early and gave me food. She had to loose my hands and take the gag off for that, so I tried to ask her about Mark, and begged her to let me go. Of course she would know I'd be asking about Mark, but all she would do was shake her head and dab her eyes on her veil, and point up the mountain. In the end, I latched on to it somehow that the men had gone up to look for him by daylight.'

'Josef had, anyway.'

'Yes, and found him gone. But I wasn't to know that, more's the pity. Mind you, I'd a pretty good idea that once they'd made sure Mark was dead, I'd be for the high jump myself, but I couldn't get any more out of Sofia, when she came again. That night, when she brought my food, she wouldn't talk at all. Her eyes just looked scared, and sort of dumb. Then yesterday morning I knew they'd decided to kill me. I'm sure they had. That's what made me sure Mark was dead.'

He might have been discussing the weather. Already the past had slipped away from him in the moment of happiness and present hope. In spite of that tough independence he was, I thought, still very much a child.

He went on: 'I didn't think it all out at the time, but, looking back, I think I can see what had happened. They'd been worrying themselves sick about where Mark had got to; Josef must have spent the whole two days out raking the countryside, and found no trace. You said he'd been up to the hill-villages too, and he'd have drawn blank there; and of course nothing had happened in Agios Georgios. So they'd reckoned they could count Mark dead. I don't think Josef would ever have thought twice about murdering me, but I expect Sofia made trouble with Stratos, and Tony may have been against it, too – if he ever bothered to mention it again that is. He may just have shut his eyes and let them get on with it.'

'Perhaps. I think you're right, though; I don't see how they could ever have let you go – I know Frances just assumed they'd have murdered you. What happened?'

'It was Josef, not Sofia, who brought the food yesterday. I'd heard a man's boots coming up the stairs and I managed to roll over and peek down through those holes in the floor. He was in that Cretan rig, with a knife in his belt, and the rifle in one hand and my food in the other. He stopped on the floor below, stood the rifle against the wall, and – you remember those square tins?'

'Yes.'

'He pulled an automatic out of his pocket, and hid it down behind one of them.'

'An automatic? You mean a pistol?'

'Well, I think they're the same. This, anyway.'

His hand reached under the sheepskin cloak, to produce a deadly-looking gun. He paused, weighing it on his hand, and grinning at me with the expression of a small boy caught with some forbidden firework.

'Colin!'

'I suppose it's Alex's. Pity he didn't get time to use it first. Heavy, isn't it?' He held it out obligingly.

'I wouldn't touch it if you paid me! Is it loaded?'

'No, I took them out, but I brought them along. See?'

'You seem to know how to handle the thing,' I said, reassured.

'Not really, but we mess around with rifles in the Cadets, and one can guess. Not much use against a rifle, of course, but it makes you feel sort of better to have it, doesn't it?'

'For heaven's sake!' I stared at this capable child with – it must be confessed – a touch of exasperation. The rescue was going all wrong. Colin, it now seemed, was escorting me to Mark. No doubt Lambis would be detailed to see me home . . .

'As a matter of fact,' said Colin frankly, 'I'm terrified of it.' He put it away. 'I say, haven't we climbed far enough? It's getting pretty open here.'

We were approaching the head of the gorge. Some way farther up I could see where the stream sprang out of the welter of rocks and trees under the upper ridge. I thought I recognized the old, arthritic olive-tree where Lambis had hidden the food.

'Yes, this is where we leave cover. For a start, you can let me show myself first again, in case anyone's about.'

'Okay. But d'you mind if we have a rest first – just for a minute? Here's a decent place to sit.'

He clambered a little way up the south side of the gully, where there was some flattish ground, and lay down in the sun, while I sat beside him.

'Finish your story,' I said.

'Where was I? Oh, Josef hiding the gun. Well, he picked up his rifle and came on upstairs. While I was trying to eat, he just sat there, with the rifle across his knees, watching me. It put me off my food.'

'I can imagine.'

'I'd been trying to think up some Greek, but I don't really know any.'

He grinned. 'You just about heard my full repertoire when you woke me up.'

'You did wonders. If I hadn't known, I'd just have thought you were dim, and a bit sulky. Where'd you get the fancy dress? Sofia?'

'Yes. Anyway, in the end I managed to think up a bit of classical Greek, and tried that. I remembered the word for "brother" – "*adelphós*" – and tried that on him. Apparently it's still the same word. I'd never have thought,' said Colin ingenuously, 'that Thucydides and all that jazz would ever have come in useful.'

'It worked, then?'

His mouth thinned, no longer young-looking. 'I'll say it did. He said, "*Nekrós*", and even if it hadn't been obvious what that means, he drew his hand across his throat, like this, as if he was cutting it. Then he grinned, the stinking little sod. I'm sorry.'

'What? Oh – it's all right.'

'Mark always goes down my throat with his boots on if I swear.'

'*Mark* does? Why?'

'Oh, well—' He rolled over, staring down the gully – 'I mean, naturally one swears at school, but at home, in front of the girls, it's different.'

'If Charlotte's at RADA,' I said dryly, 'I'd have thought she'd have caught up with you by now.'

He laughed. 'Oh, well, I told you he was a bit of a square. But he's all right, old Mark, as brothers go.' He returned briskly to his narrative. 'After that, Josef just shut me up when I tried to speak. It was after he'd gone that I realized he'd let me see him. He'd sat there in full view, with daylight coming through the shutters. The only reason for that I could think of was that they were going to kill me anyway. I tried pretty hard to get away, that day, but I only hurt my wrists. But it wasn't Josef, that evening, after all, it was Sofia. She came very late – nearly morning, it must have been – and she untied me. I didn't realize at first that she'd done it – I couldn't move. She rubbed my legs, and put oil on my wrists, and bandaged them, then she gave me some soup. She'd brought it all the way in a jug, and it was only just warm, but it was awfully good. And some wine. I ate a bit, wondering how soon my legs would work, and if I could get away from her, then I realized she was signing me to go with her. Mind you, I was scared to, at first. I thought this might be – well, the pay-off. But there wasn't any future in staying where I was, so I followed her downstairs. She went first, and I managed to sneak the pistol from behind the tin, then went down after her. It was pretty dark, just breaking dawn. It was then I saw I'd been in a windmill. The other mills were all standing quiet, like ghosts. It was beastly cold. Oh, I forgot, she'd brought this sheepskin thing, and the stick, and I was jolly glad of them both, I may tell you; I was as shaky as a jelly for the first few minutes. She took me quite a long way, I had no idea where, through some trees and past a little cairn affair—'

'The shrine. There's a Madonna in it.'

'Oh, is there? It was too dark to see that. We went quite a way, and then it was light enough to see, more or less, and we'd got to that wide track, so she stopped. She pointed the way to me, and said something I couldn't make out. Perhaps she was telling me it was the track to the church, where they'd first found us; she'd think I'd know the way from there. Anyway, she sort of pushed me on my way and then hurried back. The sun came up with a bang, and it was light, and you know the rest.'

'So I missed her, after all. If only I'd pulled myself together, and stayed on watch! Well, then, I suppose you just decided it was safer to lie up in the gully and hide during daylight?'

'Yes. As a matter of fact, I was too tired and stiff to get far, so I thought I'd hole up out of sight and rest for a bit. I had the gun, after all; it made me feel a lot safer.' He laughed. 'I certainly never meant to go "out" like that! It must have been hours!'

'You were dead to the wide. Are you all right now? Shall we go on?'

'Sure. Man, oh man, *get* those birds! What are they?'

The shadows had moved across the uneven ground below us, swinging smoothly in wide, easy circles. I looked up.

'Oh, Colin, they *are* lammergeiers! Bearded vultures! I thought I saw one yesterday! Aren't they rather gorgeous?'

I could find time, today, to be moved and excited by this rare, huge bird, as I had been moved by the beauty of the speckled snake. I had seen the lammergeier before, at Delphi, and again yesterday, but never so close, never so low, never the two of them together.

As I stood up, they swung higher.

'It's the biggest bird of prey in the "old world",' I said. 'I believe the wing span's nearly ten feet. And they're rather handsome, too, not like the other vultures, because they haven't got that beastly bare neck, and – Colin? Is anything the matter? Aren't you well?'

He had made no move to rise when I did, and he wasn't watching the birds. He was staring, fixed, at something near the foot of the gully.

I looked. At first, I saw nothing. Then I wondered why I hadn't seen it straight away.

Near a little clump of bushes, not very far from where we sat, someone had recently been digging. The earth lay now in a shallow, barrow-shaped heap, and someone had thrown stones and dry thorns over it to obliterate the marks of recent work. But it had been a hasty job, done perhaps without the right tools, and, at the end nearest to us, the crumbling stuff had already fallen in a bit, exposing an earthy shape that could have been a foot.

The shadows of the vultures crawled across it; and again, across it.

Before I could speak, Colin was on his feet, and slithering down the slope.

'Colin!' I was stumbling after him. 'Colin, don't go over there! Come back, *please*!'

He took no notice. I doubt if he heard me. He was standing over the grave. It was a foot, no doubt of that. I grabbed him by the arm.

'Colin, please come away, it's beastly, and there's no point in poking around here. It'll be that man they killed, that poor Greek, Alexandros ... I suppose they had to bring him across here, where there was enough soil—'

'He was buried in the field by the mill.'

'What?' I said it blankly, my hand falling from his arm.

'He was buried in the field by the mill.' Colin had turned to stare at me, with that stranger's face. You'd have thought he'd never seen me before. 'I heard them digging. All the first night, I heard them digging. And then again yesterday, someone was there, tidying up. I heard him.'

'Yes. Stratos. I saw him.' I looked at him stupidly. 'Well, who can it be? It's so - so recent ... you'd think—'

'You were lying to me, weren't you?'

'I? Lying to you? What do you mean?' Then the look in his face shocked me into understanding. I said sharply: 'It's not *Mark*, don't be so silly! I wasn't lying, it was only a flesh-wound, and he was better - *better*, do you hear? And last night, even if the wound *was* bleeding again, it - couldn't have been as bad as *that*!' I found I had hold of his arm again, and was shaking it. He stood like stone. I dropped the arm, and said, more quietly: 'He'd be all right. Lambis wouldn't be far off, and he'd look after him. It *was* healing cleanly, Colin, I'll swear it was.'

'Well, then, who's this?'

'How do I know? It *must* be the man they killed.'

'I tell you, he was buried in the field. I heard them.'

'All right, you heard them. That still doesn't make it Mark. Why should it?'

'Josef shot him. That was why Josef didn't get back for me last night, when I'll swear he meant to. He was up here, burying Mark. Or else Stratos ... What time was Stratos at that shed with you last night?'

'One o'clock, twenty past, I hardly know.'

'Stratos went back to kill him later. He knew it hadn't just been the cat. He only wanted to put you off and get you back to the hotel, so's he could—'

'Mark might have had something to say about that!' I was still trying to sound no more than reasonable. 'Give him a little credit!'

'He was hurt. And if he'd been raking round the village for hours, he'd be flaked out, you know he would. If it comes to that, the blood mayn't have been from his shoulder at all. Perhaps that was where Stratos—'

'Colin! Shut up and don't be silly!' I could hear the nerves shrilling through my voice like wires. I swallowed, and managed to add, more or less evenly: 'Stratos didn't leave the hotel again before I went back to the shed and found Mark gone. Do you think I wasn't watching? Give me some credit, too! And they'd hardly have killed him in the village and carried him up here to bury him ... Anyway, what about Lambis? Where's he in all this?'

'Perhaps they killed him, too. Or he got away.'

'He wouldn't run away.'

'Why not? If Mark was dead, and he thought I was, too, why should he stay? If he'd any sense at all, he'd go ... with the caique.'

His stony insistence was carrying through to me. I found I was shaking. I said, more angrily than I had meant to: 'This is all bilge! You haven't a thing to go on! It isn't Mark, I tell you it isn't! It ... this could be anyone. Why, it mightn't even *be* anyone. Just because a bit of soil looks like a – Colin, what are you doing?'

'I have to know. Surely you see that? I've got to know.' And with a stiff, abrupt little movement, that somehow had whole chapters of horror in it, he reached out a foot, and dislodged a little of that dry dirt.

A small cascade of it trickled down with a whispering sound. It was the foot that was exposed, and the ankle, in a sock that had been grey. There was no shoe. A bit of the trouser-leg was showing. Dark grey flannel. There was a triangular tear in it that I remembered well.

There was a moment's complete stillness, then Colin made a sound, a small, animal noise, and flung himself to his knees at the other end of the mound, where the head should be. Before I had quite realized what he was about, he was tearing at the bushes and stones with his hands, flinging them aside, careless of cuts and scratches, digging like a dog into the pile of dirt. I don't know what I was doing: I believe I tried to pull him back, but neither words nor frantic hands made any impression at all. I might as well not have been there. The dust rose in a smoking cloud, and Colin coughed and scrabbled, and then, as he dug lower, the dust was caked ...

He was lying on his face. Under the dirt now was the outline of his shoulders. Colin scooped a drift of stony earth away, and there was the head ... Hiding it, half-buried, was a branch of withered scrub. I stooped to pull this aside, but gently, as if it could have scratched the dead flesh. Its leaves crumpled in my hands, with the smell of dried verbena. And then, sticking up in obscene tufts from the red dust, I saw the dark hair, with the dirt horribly matted over a sticky blackness ...

I'm not clear about what happened next. I must have flinched violently back, because the branch I was grasping came dragging out from the piled earth, dislodging as it did so a fresh heap of stuff which came avalanching down from above over the half exposed head and shoulders. My own cry, and Colin's exclamation as his wrists and hands were buried deep in the falling debris, were followed, sharply, by another sound that split the still air with its own kind of terror. A shot.

I think I simply stood there, stupid and sick, with the branch in my hand, and Colin, startled into a moment's immobility, kneeling at my feet. Then he moved. Vaguely I remember him dragging his hands out of the earth, and more stuff tumbling with its choking cloud of dust, and the branch being torn from my hands and flung down where it had been ... then I was crouching in the shelter of a thicket a little way off, with my head in my hands, sweating and sick and cold, till Colin came pelting after me, to seize me by the shoulder and shake me, not gently.

'Did you hear the shot?'

'I – yes.'

He jerked his head seawards. 'It came from over there. It'll be them. They may be after Lambis.'

I merely stared. Nothing that he said seemed to mean very much. 'Lambis?'

'I'll have to go and see. I – can come back for him later.' Another jerk of the head, this time towards the grave. 'You'd better stay out of sight. I'll be okay, I've got this.' His face still had that stunned, sleepwalker's look, but the gun in his hand was real enough.

It brought me stumbling to my feet. 'Wait. You're not going alone.'

'Look, I've got to go that way anyway, I've got to find the caique, it's all I can do. But for you – well, it's different now. You don't have to come.'

'I do. I'm not leaving you. Go on. Keep right up under the cliffs where the bushes are.'

He didn't argue further. He was already scrambling up the side of the gully, where the cover was thickest. I followed. I only asked one more question, and then I didn't quite dare make it a direct one. 'Was he – was he covered right up again?'

'Do you think I'd leave him for those stinking birds?' said Colin curtly, and swung himself up among the trees at the gully's edge.

CHAPTER FIFTEEN

No spectre greets me—no vain Shadow this:
Come, blooming Hero ... !

WORDSWORTH: *Laodamia*

The ruined church was tiny. It stood in a green hollow full of flowering weeds. It was just an empty shell, cruciform, the central cupola supporting four half-cups that clung against it like a family of limpets clinging to the parent, and waiting for the rising tide of green to swamp them. This, it threatened soon to do: a sea of weeds – mallow and vetch, spurge and thistle – had washed already half up the crumbling walls. Even the roof was splashed with green, where the broken tiles had let fern-seeds in to mantle their faded red. A wooden cross, bleached by the sea-winds, pricked bravely up from the central dome.

We paused at the lip of the hollow, peering down through the bushes. Nothing moved: the air hung still. Below us now we could see the track running past the door of the church, and then lifting its dusty length through the maquis towards the sea.

'Is that the way to the caique?' I whispered.

Colin nodded. He opened his lips as if to say something, then stopped abruptly, staring past me. As I turned to look, his hand shot out to grip my arm. 'Over there, see? I saw someone, a man. I'm sure I did. Do you see where that streak of white runs down, above the knot of pines? To the right of that . . . no, he's gone. Keep down, and watch.'

I flattened myself beside him, narrowing my eyes against the bright afternoon glare.

His hand came past me, pointing. 'There!'

'Yes, I can see him now. He's coming this way. Do you think?'

Colin said sharply: 'It's Lambis!'

He had half-risen to one knee, but I shot out a hand and pulled him down. 'You can't be sure at this distance. If it was Lambis, he'd be keeping under cover. Hang on.'

Colin subsided. The small figure came rapidly on; there must have been a path there; he made good speed along the hillside towards where the main track must lie, and he was certainly making no attempt at concealment. But now I saw him more clearly; brown trousers, dark-blue seaman's jersey and khaki jacket, the way he moved . . . Colin was right. It was Lambis.

I was going to say as much when I saw, a little way beyond Lambis and above the path he was following, another man emerging from a tangle of rocks and scrub where he must have been concealed. He began to make his way more slowly along, above Lambis' path, converging downhill upon it. He was still hidden from the advancing Lambis, but he was plain enough to me . . . the loose breeches and bloused jacket, the red Cretan cap, and the rifle.

I said hoarsely: 'Colin . . . above Lambis . . . that's Josef.'

For seven or eight paralysed seconds we watched them: Lambis, unaware of his danger, coming steadily and rapidly on; Josef, moving slowly and carefully, and, as far as I could make out, already within easy range . . . The gun nosed forward beside me, light trembling on the barrel, which was not quite steady.

'Shall I fire a shot to warn him?' breathed Colin. 'Or would Josef—?'

'Wait!' My hand closed on his wrist again. I said, unbelievingly: 'Look!'

Lambis had paused, turned, and was looking around him as if expecting someone. His attitude was easy and unafraid. Then he saw Josef. He lifted a hand, and waited. The Cretan responded with a gesture, then made his way unhurriedly down to where Lambis awaited him.

The two men stood talking for a few minutes, then I saw Lambis' arm go out, as if he were indicating some path, and Josef lifted the field-glasses to his eyes, and turned them eastwards. They swept past the church, the hollow, the bushes where we lay, and passed on. He dropped them, and presently, after a little more talk, he moved off again, alone, at a slant which would by-pass the hollow, and take him straight down towards the coastal cliffs.

Lambis stood watching him for a moment, then turned towards us, and came rapidly on his way. His course would lead him straight to the church. And – I saw it, as he came nearer – he now had Josef's rifle.

Colin and I looked at one another.

'*Lambis?*'

Neither of us said it, but the question was there, hanging between us, in the blank, frightened bewilderment of our faces. Vaguely, I remembered Lambis' evasive replies when I asked him about his birthplace. It had been Crete; was it here, perhaps? Agios Georgios? And had he used Mark and Colin as the cover for bringing his caique here, for some purpose connected with Stratos and his affairs?

But there was no time to think now. Lambis was approaching fast. I could hear his footsteps already on the rock beyond the hollow.

Beside me, Colin drew in his breath like a diver who has just surfaced, and I saw his hand close round the butt of the gun. He levelled it carefully across his wrist, aiming at the point where Lambis would appear on the track beside the church.

It never occurred to me to try to stop him. I simply found myself wondering what the range of an automatic was, and if Colin was a good enough shot to get Lambis at the fore-shortened angle he would present.

Then I came to myself. I put my lips to Colin's ear. 'For heaven's sake, hang on! We've got to talk to him! We've got to know what's happened! And if you fire that thing, you'll bring Josef back.'

He hesitated, then, to my relief, he nodded. Lambis came out into the clearing below us. He was walking easily, without even a hand on his knife – as well he might, I thought bitterly. I remembered the way he had followed Josef out of sight yesterday – to have a conference, no doubt. Another thought struck me: if Josef had been to the village, then he would have told Stratos and Sofia that I was involved. But they had not known . . . or they surely could not have behaved the way they did. So he hadn't yet been back to the village . . . and now we would do our best to see that he never got back there again.

The rights and wrongs of it never entered my head. Mark was dead, and that thought overrode all else. If Colin and I could manage it, Josef and the treacherous Lambis would die, too. But first, we had to know just what had happened.

Lambis paused at the door of the church to light a cigarette. I saw Colin fingering the gun. There was sweat on his face, and his body was rigid. But he waited.

Lambis turned, and went into the church.

There was the sound, magnified by the shell of the building, of stone against stone, as if Lambis were shifting pieces of loose masonry. He must have used this place as a cache, and he had come this way to collect something he had hidden there.

Colin was getting up. As I made to follow, he whispered fiercely: 'Stay where you are!'

'But, look—'

'I'll manage this on my own. You keep hidden. You might get hurt.'

'Colin, listen, put the gun out of sight. He doesn't know we saw him with Josef – we can go down there openly, and tell him you're found. If he thinks we don't suspect him, we can get the rifle from him. *Then* we can make him talk.'

As clearly as if the boy's face were a screen, and a different picture had flashed on to it, I saw the blind rage of grief give way to a kind of reason. It was like watching a stone mask come alive.

He pushed the gun back out of sight under his cloak, and made no objection when I stood up with him. 'Pretend you're a bit shaky on your pins,' I said, and slipped a hand under his elbow. We went down into the hollow.

As we reached level ground, Lambis must have heard us, for the slight sounds inside the church stopped abruptly. I could smell his cigarette.

I squeezed Colin's elbow. He called out, in a voice whose breathlessness (I thought) wasn't entirely faked:

'Mark? Lambis? Is that you?'

Lambis appeared in the doorway, his eyes screwed up against the sun. He started forward. '*Colin!* How on earth—? My dear boy – you're safe! Nicola – *you* found him?'

I said: 'Have you anything to drink, Lambis? He's just about done.'

'Is Mark there?' asked Colin, faintly.

'No. Come inside out of the sun.' Lambis had Colin's other arm, and between us we steered him into the church's airy shade. 'I was just on my way down to the caique. There's water in the flask. Sit the boy down, Nicola . . . I'll get him a drink.'

Mark's haversack lay in one corner, where Lambis had dragged it from its hiding-place in a tumble of masonry. Apart from this, the place was empty as a blown egg, the stone-flagged floor swept clean by the weather, and the clustered domes full of cross-lights and shadows, where the ghost of a Christos Pantokrator stared down from a single eye. The rifle stood where Lambis had set it, against the wall by the door.

He was stooping over the haversack, rummaging for the flask. His back was towards us. As Colin straightened, I let his arm go, and moved to stand over the rifle. I didn't touch it; I'd as soon have touched a snake; but I was going to see that Lambis had no chance to grab it before Colin got control. The automatic was levelled at Lambis' back.

He had found the thermos. He straightened and turned, with this in his hand.

Then he saw the gun. His face changed, almost ludicrously. 'What's this? Colin, are you mad?'

'Keep your voice down,' said Colin curtly. 'We want to hear about Mark.' He waved his gun. 'Go on. Start talking.'

Lambis stood like a stone, then his eyes turned to me. He was looking scared, and I didn't blame him. Colin's hand wasn't all that steady, and the gun looked as if it might go off at any moment. And Lambis' question hadn't been quite idle: Colin did indeed look more than a little unhinged.

'Nicola,' said the Greek sharply, 'what is this? Have they turned his brain? Is that thing loaded?'

'Nicola,' said Colin, just as sharply, 'search him. Don't get between him and the gun – Lambis, stand still, or I promise I'll shoot you here and now!' This as Lambis' eyes flicked towards his rifle. 'Hurry up,' added Colin, to me. 'He hasn't a gun, but he carries a knife.'

'I know,' I said feebly, and edged round behind Lambis.

Needless to say, I had never searched anyone before, and had only the vaguest recollection, from films and so on, of how it was done. If it hadn't been for the grim relics buried in the gully, and for the look in Colin's face, the scene would have been pure farce. Lambis' English had deserted him, and he was pouring forth a flood of questions and invective which Colin neither heeded nor understood, and to which I didn't even listen. I found the knife straight away, in his pocket, and dropped it into my own, feeling stupid, like a child playing pirates. I stood back.

Lambis said furiously, in Greek: 'Tell him to put that thing down, Nicola! What the hell are you playing at, the pair of you? He'll shoot someone! Has he gone crazy with what they did to him? Are you mad, too? Get hold of that bloody gun, and we'll get him down to—'

'We found the grave,' I said, in English.

He stopped in mid-tirade. 'Did you?' The anger seemed to drop from him, and his face looked strained all at once, the dark sunburn looking almost sickly in the queer cross-lights of the church. He seemed momentarily to have forgotten Colin and the gun. He said hoarsely: 'It was an accident. I would have you to understand that. You know I would not mean to kill him.'

I was standing back against the door-jamb – the unheeded Doric column – fingering in my pocket the knife I had taken from him. Under my hand I could feel the casing of the handle, and remembered suddenly, vividly, the pattern of the blue enamelling on the copper shaft. I remembered his using this very knife to slice the corned beef for Mark . . .

'*You* did it?' I said.

'I did not want him dead.' He was repeating himself in a kind of entreaty. 'When you get back to your people in Athens, perhaps you will help me . . . if you tell them that this was an accident . . .'

Something broke inside me. Where I found the Greek words I do not know: looking back, what I spoke was probably mainly English, with bits of Greek and French thrown in. But Lambis understood, and so – he told me later – did Colin.

'*Accident?*' I forgot the need for quiet, and my voice rose sharply.

'Accident? Then I suppose it's an accident that you're running round now on the hillside with that swine who shot at Mark and wanted them to murder Colin? And don't think I don't know all about you and your precious friends, because I do! You can take it from me, I know every move your filthy gang have been making – Stratos, and Tony, and Sofia, and Josef . . . and now you! And don't try to pretend you're not in it up to your neck, because we *saw* you – no, hold your damned mouth, and let me finish! Help you? You want shooting out of hand, and I shan't raise a finger to stop Colin doing it, but first of all we want to know just what you're doing in all this. Who pays you, and why? Why did you have to bring him here? And why did you kill him? Why did you have to pretend to save his life, you filthy Judas? Was it because I happened along? If I'd stayed – he was such a marvellous person – if only I'd known – I'd have murdered you myself before I'd have let you hurt him! If only I'd stayed . . .'

The tears came, then, uncontrollably, but the blurring of my vision didn't prevent me from seeing, over the speechless, half-comprehending stupefaction of Lambis' face, the flash of a different expression, as his eyes flickered from my face to something just beyond me. Behind me, and beyond, outside the door . . .

A shadow moved in the doorway. Baggy breeches and a Cretan cap. A man coming in fast, with a knife in his hand.

I shrieked: 'Colin! Look out!'

Colin whirled, and fired. Lambis shouted something at the same moment, and jumped for him. The shot thudded into the door-jamb, midway between the newcomer and me, and the noise slammed, deafeningly, round and round the walls. Then Lambis had Colin's gun-hand; his other arm was tight round the boy's body; the gun went flying to the floor. I never moved. In the same moment that I cried out, I had seen the newcomer's face.

Now, I said: 'Mark!' in a high, silly voice that made no sound at all.

The shot had stopped him just inside the doorway. Lambis let Colin go, and stooped to pick up the gun. Colin stood blinking against the light, looking dazed and stupid, as if a touch would have knocked him over.

'Colin,' Mark said.

Then Colin was in his arms, not saying a word, not making a sound, you'd have sworn not even breathing. 'What have they done to you? Hurt you?' I hadn't heard that voice from Mark before. The boy shook his head. 'You're really all right?' The boy nodded. 'That's the truth?' 'Yes.' 'Then we'll go. This is the end, thank God. We'll go straight to the caique.'

I didn't hear if there were any more. I turned and walked past them, and out of the church. Lambis said something, but I took no notice. Regardless now of who could see me, I started up the slope of the hollow, back towards Agios Georgios.

The tears still blurred my eyes, and twice made me stumble; stupid tears, that need never have been shed. I dashed them away. I had cried more over this affair than I remembered having done for years. It was time I got out of it. It was over.

Besides, it was getting late, and Frances would be wondering what had happened to me.

CHAPTER SIXTEEN

This done, he march'd away with warlike sound,
And to his Athens turn'd.

DRYDEN: *Palamon and Arcite*

Before I had gone thirty yards, I heard him behind me.

'Nicola!'

I took no notice.

'Nicola . . . please wait! I can't go at this speed.'

I faltered, then looked back. He was coming down the track with no noticeable difficulty. The only sign of his recent injury was the sling, made from the hanging fold of the Cretan head-dress, that cradled his left arm. He looked very different from the unkempt, half-bearded invalid of yesterday; he had shaved, and washed his hair, but – as with Colin – it was the relief and happiness of the moment that altered his appearance so completely. My first thought was a vague surprise that I should have recognized him so quickly; my second, that the 'heroic' costume suited him disturbingly well.

'Nicola—' he sounded breathless – 'don't hurry off, please; I've got to thank you—'

'You shouldn't have bothered. It's all right.' I thrust my damp handkerchief out of sight into a pocket, gave him a smile of a sort, and turned away again. 'You and Colin had better get down to the caique, and away. You're all right now? You look a whole lot better.'

'Lord, yes, I'm fine.'

'I'm glad. Well, all the best, Mark. Good-bye.'

'Wait, please. I—'

'Look, I've got to get back. Frances will be sending out search parties, and it'll take me all of three hours to get home.'

'Nonsense!' He was standing in front of me now, squarely in the middle of the path. 'Two hours downhill, if that. Why did you run away like that? You must know—'

'Because it's all over and done with, and you don't want me mixed up in it any more. You and Lambis and Colin can go to your b-boat and sail away, and that is that.'

'But, my dear, for goodness' sake give us time to thank you! It's you who've done everything, while I was laid up there, about as useful as a pint of milk! And now everything's wonderful – mainly thanks to you. Look, don't be so upset—'

'I'm not upset at all. Don't be absurd.' I sniffed, and looked away from him at the level brilliance of the sun. To my fury, I was beginning to cry again. I rounded on him. 'We thought he'd murdered you. We found that grave, and ... *it* ... had your clothes on. It was quite horrible, and I was sick. If that isn't enough to upset me—'

'I know. I'm desperately sorry that you should have come across that. It's the man Colin calls Josef; you'll have guessed that. Lambis killed him, yesterday morning, when he followed him down the hill, remember? He didn't mean to; naturally what we wanted out of Josef was information about Colin, but it happened accidentally. Lambis had been stalking him, not daring to get too close, because of the rifle, when he came suddenly round a bend of that gully, and there was Josef having a drink, with the gun laid to one side. I suppose the noise of the stream had prevented his hearing Lambis coming. Well, catching him like that, Lambis jumped him. Josef hadn't time to reach the rifle, and pulled his knife, but Lambis was on top of him, so he didn't get a chance to use it. He went down, hard, with his head against the rock, and that was that.'

'I ... see. Yesterday? When Lambis came back, and sent me away, for the food ... he told you then?'

'Yes. He'd hidden the body behind some bushes, and come back to report.'

'You never said a word to me.'

'Of course not. But you see why we didn't dare to go down and stir up the local police? We didn't even know who the man was, or where he was from. And Lambis was worried sick, naturally. I thought it best to let it alone, until we knew where we were.'

'If I'd known ...' I was thinking about the spectre of Josef, which had stalked so frighteningly behind my shoulder this last twenty-four hours. 'You could have trusted me.'

'Good God, you know it wasn't that! I just thought the less you knew about that, the better. I didn't want you involved.'

That did it. I said furiously: 'Involved? Heaven give me strength, *involved*? I suppose I hadn't been involved enough already? I'd been scared to death by Lambis, I'd spent a perfectly beastly night with you, and I'd ruined a very expensive petticoat. I'd also dressed your horrible shoulder, and cooked and slaved and – and *worried* myself silly! About Colin, I mean. And all you could think of was to get rid of me because I'm a g-girl, and girls are no use, and you were too damned bossy and stiff-necked to admit I *could* help! Well, Mr. Godalmighty Mark Langley, I *did* find Colin, and if he'd still been locked up in that filthy windmill, I'd *still* have found him! I *told* you I could go about on the mountain and in the village safely, and I can, and I have, and I've found out more than you and that horrible Lambis have in *days*. And you needn't think I'm going to tell you *any* of it, because you can just go and find it out for yourselves! *You* didn't tell me anything, so of course I thought he'd murdered you, and Colin and I were going to shoot you both, and you're jolly lucky we didn't!'

'I'll say we are. That bullet was pretty near on target as it was.'

'Stop laughing at me!' I cried furiously. 'And don't think I'm crying about *you*, or that I meant a *single word* I said about you to Lambis just now! I couldn't have cared less if it *had* been you in the g-grave!'

'I know, I know—'

'And I'm not crying, I never cry, it was only that awful body . . . and . . . and—'

'Oh, Nicola, darling, I'm sorry, truly I am. I'm not laughing. I'd give anything if the pair of you hadn't had that shock, and I'm desperately sorry you had that fright just now, over Lambis and me. But we'd been planning to go down into the village, you remember, and I thought Josef's clothes might just help me to get by, in the dark.' He grinned. 'In any case, my own were pretty well past it. Those pants were hardly decent as it was.'

'I saw the tear in them when Colin pulled the earth off, and the s-socks had a h-hole in.'

And I sat down on a stone, and wept bitterly.

He dropped down beside me, and his arm went round my shoulders, 'Oh, Nicola . . . Dear heaven, can't you see, this is just the sort of thing I was trying *not* to let you in for?' He shook me, gently. 'And they weren't my socks, darling, I did draw the line at his footgear and underthings! We took everything else he had, and buried the boots . . . All right, go on, cry, you'll feel better just now.'

'I'm not crying. I never cry.'

'Of course you don't. You're a wonderful girl, and if you hadn't come along when you did, we'd have been sunk.'

'W-would you?'

'Certainly. I might have died of Lambis' poultices, or Josef would have found me in the hut, or Colin might never have got to us safely . . . What's more, you saved me from getting shot last night, though you didn't know it. I was in that shed, along with the cat, when you stopped to have a smoke with your fierce friend in the lane.'

'I know. I went back later. There was blood on the wall.'

'You went back?' His arm moved as a muscle tightened, and I heard his voice change. 'You *knew*? So – when you tried to stop that chap coming in—?'

'He's Josef's friend.' I was crumpling my wet handkerchief into a small, tidy ball. I still hadn't looked at Mark. 'He's one of them. I told you I'd found them.'

There was a sharp silence. I heard him draw in his breath to speak, and said quickly: 'I'll tell you all about them. I – I didn't really mean it when I said I wouldn't; of course I will. But tell me about you first.

When I found the blood last night I thought . . . I'm not sure what I thought. Are you really all right?'

'Yes, perfectly. I knocked my shoulder, swanning around there in the dark, and started it bleeding, but it stopped soon enough, and there seems to be no damage.'

'What happened yesterday after I'd left you?'

'Nothing, really. After Lambis had seen you down to the cultivation, he doubled back to meet me, and we buried Josef after a fashion. It took a fair time, and when we'd finished I was so knocked up that I wasn't much use for anything, but I wasn't going to waste any more time before we took a look at the village. I told you Lambis hadn't been sure which way Josef was heading when he killed him, but the odds were it was Agios Georgios . . . Anyway, we went down as far as we dared, and lay up above the village and watched till dark. I felt better after the rest, so we got down into the place and did the best kind of search we could. I thought the Cretan clothes a good idea – if anyone caught a glimpse of me skulking up a back alley, I wouldn't look so blatantly foreign, and I might just have got by with grunting "good night" in Greek. Well, we neither of us found a trace of Colin, as you know. You said he was in a windmill?'

'Yes. But go on; what happened when you got out of the shed?'

'Nothing whatever. I met Lambis as arranged, and we got up into the rocks again and holed up till morning. I was very little use to anyone by that time, and getting pretty sure we'd never find Colin . . .' A pause. 'This morning Lambis went down again, but all I could do was get up to the church to cache our stuff, then take the rifle and hide where I could watch the track where the first murder took place. I thought someone might possibly come to look for Josef, or for traces of me. If they had come, in Josef's clothes I could probably have got well within range before they saw it wasn't him. But never mind that now. Nobody came – not even you. You must have by-passed the track. Which way did you come?'

'We stayed under cover, in the little gully where the body was. Didn't you hear me singing? After I'd found Colin I tried to locate you.'

He shook his head. 'Not a thing. I wish I had. And Lambis drew blank, too. He'd gone to look at the cultivation.'

'This morning? We were there, Frances and I.'

'I know. He saw you both at one of the windmills. Was that the one?' He smiled. 'There's irony for you. He saw you go in, so he didn't bother about that one; he just hung around till you'd gone, and the Greek woman, then broke into the other mill. And found nothing, of course. Then he made his way back to me. That was all. A fine, useless effort.'

'I begin to see why this is such good guerilla country. If it hadn't been so awful it would be comic – the whole boiling of us climbing about on the mountain, with never a glimpse of each other. Was it you who fired a shot?'

'Yes, to guide Lambis to me. A shot's safer than shouting; it's a sound one takes for granted in the country. Did that frighten you, too?'

I shook my head, but said nothing. I wasn't going to explain to Mark that the shot had been the least of my worries at the time. I stuffed the handkerchief away into my pocket, rubbed the back of my hand hard over my eyes, and smiled at him.

'All right now!' he said gently.

'Of course.'

'That's my girl.' His arm came round me again in a quick, hard hug, then let me go. 'Now come back with me, and we'll have our council of war.'

Colin and Lambis were sitting by the bushes that edged the hollow. They had chosen a flat little clearing, where the small flowers grew, and baby cypresses like thin dark fingers pointed up through the green. These smelt delicious in the hot sunshine. Below us, the bank was thick with the creamy rock-roses. The track wound down through them, to disappear among the folded ridges that marked the coast. Here and there, a gap showed a blinding wedge of sea.

As we came up, Colin was laughing at something Lambis had said. The haversack was open between them, and Colin was already rootling purposefully through what food was there. He waved my wine-bottle at Mark as we approached.

'Hurry up, Marco Polo, if you want any of this. It's nearly all gone.'

'Then I suggest you leave some for Nicola. Where'd you get it, anyway?'

'She brought it.'

'Then most certainly she ought to drink it. Hand it over. Here, Nicola, have some now.'

'It was for you,' I said.

' "My wine is dew of the wild white rose",' misquoted Mark, 'and what could be nastier, come to think of it? No, really, I'm getting almost used to water; drink it yourself.'

As I obeyed, I saw Colin grin at Lambis' puzzled look. 'Don't listen to Mark. That was just Keats. Go on, Lambis, this one's a classic, say "What are Keats?" '

Lambis grinned. It was obvious that he was used to being Colin's butt, and for the moment the two of them seemed much of an age. Lambis, like the others, looked quite different; much younger, and with the heavy, sullen set gone from his mouth. I realized that it had been put there by worry, and felt more than ever ashamed.

'Well,' he was saying placidly, 'what are they?'

Colin opened his mouth to whoop with mirth, then quickly shut it again. 'So I should think,' said his brother. 'If you did but know it, Lambis' English is a darn' sight better than yours. The Lord alone knows where you get it, things must have changed a lot since I was at that Borstal of yours myself. A Borstal—' to Lambis – 'is an English school.

Now, attention all, this is serious, and we haven't a lot of time. Nicola, here's a place to sit.'

As the Greek moved aside to make room for me, I smiled at him a little shyly. 'Lambis, I ought to have known. I'm sorry, I truly am. It was only because we'd had such a shock, Colin and I . . . and I honestly couldn't imagine who else *could* be buried there. And then there were the clothes. I said some awful things. Can you forgive me?'

'It does not matter. You were a little disturbed with seeing the dead body. Such things are not nice for ladies.' And on this masterly piece of understatement Lambis grinned amiably, and dismissed the matter.

'Well,' said Mark crisply, taking charge, 'we can't keep you very long, so if you could bear to start . . .'

I said: 'I've been thinking. I really think you'd better hear Colin's side of it first. One or two things he overheard, when he was actually in the lions' den, seem to provide a clue to the rest.'

So Colin told them the story he had told to me, and afterwards Mark – a rather grimmer-faced Mark – detailed him to keep a look-out with the field-glasses, while he and Lambis turned back to me.

'I don't know quite where to start' – I felt suddenly shy – 'because a lot of it may mean nothing. Shall I just try to tell you more or less all that's happened, and let you draw conclusions?'

'Please. Even if it's irrelevant.'

'*Oriste?*' from Lambis.

'Even if it's rot,' translated Colin, over his shoulder.

'Even if it doesn't seem to matter,' amended his brother. 'Don't take any notice of the brat, Lambis, he's above himself.'

'And that,' said Colin, 'is an idiom, meaning—'

'Belt up or I'll do you,' said Mark, coming down to Colin's level with a rush. 'Nicola?'

I told them then, as briefly as I could, all that had happened since I had left the mountain-side on the previous day. When I had finished, there was silence for perhaps a minute.

Then Mark said, slowly: 'It makes a picture, of a sort. I'll try to sum up, shall I, from the fragments we've got? I think you were right – the bits that Colin overheard provide the clue to the rest. The main thing is, that something Stratos had, and had promised to divide later, was "hot".' He glanced at Lambis. 'That's a slang expression – thieves' language, if you like. It means that they had stolen property in their possession, which the police were on the look-out for, and which could be identified if found.'

'In the plural,' I said. ' "They" were hot.'

'Yes, in the plural. Things small enough, in the plural, to be portable; small enough to come through the Customs (we'll look at that later, but we can assume they brought them from London); things small enough to hide, even in Agios Georgios.'

'Jewels?' suggested Colin, bright-eyed. I could see that, for him, this

was becoming simply an adventure – something with a happy ending
already settled by his brother's presence, to be stored up, and talked about
next term at school. At least, I thought thankfully, he didn't seem the
type to store up nightmares.

Mark saw it too. He gave Colin a fleeting grin. 'All the treasures of
the East, why not? But I'm afraid it doesn't really matter terribly what
it is . . . for the moment, anyway. All *we* need is a coherent story that
we can present to the Consul and the police in Athens . . . something
that'll tie Stratos and Co. up good and hard with Alexandros' murder.
Once that's done, our end of the story'll be accepted, however many alibis
are cooked up in Agios Georgios. If we can establish the fact that Josef
was a criminal and a murderer, then Lambis will get away with justifiable
homicide, or self-defence, or whatever they do get away with here. And
that's all I'm bothered with just now. He wouldn't be in this mess, but
for us, and all I care about is to see he gets clear out of it.'

Lambis glanced up, caught my eye, and grinned. He had his knife out,
and was whittling away at a curly piece of wood, carving it to a shape
that looked like a lizard. I watched, fascinated, as it began to take shape.

Mark went on: 'Now, it's the London end of it that'll give us the
connection . . . Colin heard them say that any investigation would 'get
back to the London affair'. This is what's valuable – we can be sure the
connection between Stratos and the murdered man is originally a London
one, and it sounds to me as if the London police are on the job already
– or have been. The stuff was "hot", after all.' He paused. 'Let's see how
much we can assume. Stratos and Tony came from London six months
ago, and brought with them this "hot" stolen property. They have
arranged to settle here, probably until the hue and cry has died down;
then Tony will take his share, and go. They must have intended to leave
England anyway, since Stratos apparently wound up his affairs, and
what better cover could they have than Stratos' own home, where he'd
come naturally, and where Tony might very well come to help him start
up his business? You know—' looking up '—it does sound as if the loot,
whatever it is, must be pretty considerable.'

'You mean because it's worth a long wait.'

'Exactly. You can't tell me your friend Tony wants to spend years of
his life in Agios Georgios. Do you think for one minute that that tin-pot
hotel is worth his while?'

'Oh, it's a change from the dear old Vicarage,' I said.

' "The loot," ' said Lambis. 'What is that?'

'The swag,' said Colin. 'The lolly, the pickings, the—'

Lambis put a hand to the side of his head, and pushed him over into
a rosemary bush.

'The stolen property,' I said, laughing.

'Order, children,' said Mark. 'Stratos and Tony, then, are concerned
in some crime in London, presumably a top-flight robbery. They blind
off with the – they leave the country with the stolen property (how good

you are for us, Lambis) and settle down here to wait. Stratos must be the leader, or senior partner, since he has the stuff hidden away, and Tony doesn't know where it is. Then we come to Alexandros.'

'He came looking for Stratos,' I said. 'He knew Tony, and talked English to him, and Tony took him along to meet Stratos. I'll bet Alexandros came from London, too.'

Colin rolled over eagerly. 'He was their partner in the robbery, and they did him down, and he came to claim his share, so they murdered him!'

'Could be,' said Mark, 'but Stratos did appear quite happy to cut his sister in on the deal – I mean, divide the, er—'

'Loot,' said Lambis.

'—the loot with his sister. So it doesn't seem likely that he'd murder a partner just because he claimed his share. Tony doesn't seem to think there's much risk, anyway.'

I said, hesitantly; 'Couldn't it be quite simple – that it did happen much as Colin says, but that they did quarrel, and Stratos just lost his temper? I'll swear he's that kind of man; one of those big, full-blooded toughies – *pallikaráthes*, Lambis – who can suddenly lose all their self-control, and who're strong enough to do a lot of damage when they do. And in a country where everybody carries guns as a matter of course . . . Mark, you saw the actual murder. You said they were shouting. Wasn't it done like that?'

'Well, yes, it was. They were arguing violently, then the whole thing seemed to explode . . . but don't ask me who exploded first, or how. The murder does seem likely to have its roots back in something that happened in London; this 'affair', whatever it is, that they're so afraid is going to catch them up. Apparently that, let alone the Alexandros murder, is serious enough to frighten them into a dashed silly action like taking Colin along. I imagine that Stratos probably – and Tony certainly – hold British passports. It would be interesting to know if we have an extradition treaty with Greece.'

'I can tell you that,' I said. 'We have.'

'Ah,' said Mark. He glanced at his watch. 'Let's cut this short. I think we've got all we need. We can give the police a lead to Stratos and Co. long before they suspect we're even operative. It shouldn't be hard for the London end to identify a couple of Soho Greeks and a – well, Tony; they're probably marked down as "wanted" anyway, only they've just not traced them. Then, if the police here slap a watch on to them immediately, they may find the stuff . . . and there's your connection, your motive . . . *and* Lambis in the clear for attacking a potential murderer.'

'The police'll have to be quick,' I said uneasily. 'Stratos must know Colin'd go straight for help.'

'If he knows he's escaped. But if Colin was right – and I think he was – then they did mean to kill him, and Sofia knew this. She may let Stratos think Colin has been disposed of. We can't count on it, but she might keep her mouth shut for a while, for her own sake. Stratos'll worry about where Josef has got to, but I doubt if – yet – he'll take the desperate step of bolting from Agios Georgios.'

'If I were Stratos,' I said, 'I'd shift the body – Alexandros', I mean – just in case of an inquiry. It was silly to bury it on their own land.'

'If you'd tried burying someone up here in four inches of dust,' said Mark, 'you'd see their point. But I agree. He very well may. The fact that they put him there at all might mean that they didn't intend Colin to get away, after what he'd seen and heard.'

'They *were* going to kill me?'

'I don't see how else they'd be safe,' said Mark frankly. 'They could be fairly sure I was lying dead somewhere. Without Lambis, I would have been. You can be sure they were only waiting for definite news of me. Even if Sofia had persuaded Stratos to let you alone, she must have known she couldn't protect you for ever . . . not from the kind of man Josef appears to have been, anyway . . . so she decided to let you go.'

Colin looked anxious. 'Will she be all right when they do find out I've gone?'

Mark glanced at me.

I said slowly: 'I'm sure Stratos wouldn't harm her, even if he dared. I've been thinking about it, and I don't think you need worry seriously. He might hit her in a temper, but he'd never kill her. And she's used to rough treatment, poor soul. What's more, the fact that she did save you, may save *her* from quite a lot, once the police inquiries get going.' I glanced at Lambis. 'And you . . . you can be pretty sure she'll be happier and better off as a widow than she ever has been since she married that beastly waster.'

'That is good to hear,' was all Lambis said, but I thought his expression was lighter as he bent again over the little lizard.

'It's true. Look, I must go.'

'Lord, yes, you must,' said Mark. 'Sister Ann, do you see anyone coming?'

Colin put the glasses to his eyes again.

'Not a sausage.'

'Not a what?' Lambis looked up, blade suspended again over the lizard's spine.

'Not a sausage,' repeated Colin. 'You know quite well what—'

'I know quite well what not a sausage is,' retorted Lambis. '*Óchi loukánika*. But I do not know that you have an idiom where it walks about in the mountains. I like to learn.'

'Get you!' said Colin, admiringly. I reflected that by the time Lambis had spent a month in the company of the brothers Langley, his knowledge of the odder byways of the English language would be remarkable.

Mark was getting to his feet. I noticed all at once that he was looking tired. There were lines from nostrils to mouth, and a shadow round his eyes. He put a hand down to me, and pulled me to my feet. 'I wish you hadn't to go down there.'

'The way I feel now,' I said frankly, 'if it weren't for Frances, I'd go down to your caique with you now, luggage or no luggage, and hightail it straight for Athens! But that's only the way I *feel*. Cold reason tells me that none of them will even think of suspecting that I know anything about it!'

'I'm sure they won't.' But the look he gave me was doubtful. 'The only thing is . . . I don't feel we can just set off now for Athens, without making quite certain that you and your cousin really are safe.'

'Well, but why shouldn't we be?'

'No reason at all. But we've no possible way of knowing what's been going on down there since Colin got away, and I – well, I just don't like cutting communications altogether, without knowing what sort of situation we're leaving behind us. You'll be pretty isolated, if anything should happen, and you're right in Stratos' territory.'

I realized then why he was watching me so doubtfully; he was waiting for me to assert my independence. For once, I had not the least desire to do so. The thought of leaving these capable males, and walking down alone to Stratos' hotel, was about as attractive as going out unclothed into a hail-storm.

'When are your friends calling for you?' asked Mark.

'On Monday.'

He hesitated again. 'I'm sorry, but I really think . . . I'd be inclined not to wait until Monday.'

I smiled at him. 'I'm with you there. All else apart, I quite definitely do *not* want to be around when the police start nosing about. So I think we'll find a good excuse for leaving, tomorrow as ever was. The sooner I see the bright lights of Heraklion, the happier I shall be!'

'That's very wise.' He looked immeasurably relieved. 'Can you invent a good reason?'

'Easily enough. Don't worry, we'll think up something that won't alarm your birds. They'll be so glad to get rid of us, all things considered, that they won't ask any questions.'

'True enough. Can you get in touch with the boat that was going to pick you up?'

'No, but it's calling at Heraklion first for supplies, and to let the party visit Cnossos and Phestos. Frances and I can have a car sent for us tomorrow, and we'll go to the Astir Hotel and wait for them . . .' I laughed. 'And I defy any harm to come to us there!'

'Fine,' said Mark. 'The Astir? As long as I know where you are . . . I'll get in touch with you just as soon as I can.'

We had begun, as we talked, to walk slowly back down the slope towards the church. 'What will you do when you leave?' I said. 'Go to Heraklion, or make for Athens straight away?'

'I'd like to get straight to Athens, to the British Authority there, and

get the London inquiries started, but I don't know. Lambis, how long
will it take us to Athens?'

'In this weather, anything from twelve to fifteen hours.'

'Fair enough. That's what we'll do. I imagine the Embassy will rally
round with flags flying, when they hear one of their ewe lambs is a
witness in the middle of a capital crime.'

'They'll be furious, more like,' I said ruefully.

'Which brings me to the last thing.' We had reached the church, and
stopped there, by the door.

'Yes?'

'I said before that I don't want to leave the place tonight, without
knowing you're all right.'

'I know you did, but how can you? Once I'm clear away from here,
you can take it for granted.'

'I'm not taking anything about your safety for granted.'

It was odd, but this time his cool assumption of responsibility never
raised a single bristle: not a stir. All I felt was a treacherous glow,
somewhere in the region of the stomach. I ran a hand down the genuine
Doric column, rubbing an abstracted thumb along the raw edge of the
bullet-hole. 'I don't see how.'

'Well, I've been thinking how. Listen, everyone. Lambis is going with
Nicola now, to see her safe down to the fields. Colin and I'll wait here
for you, Lambis, in the church. I – I'll rest till you get back. Then we
three are going down to the caique, and we'll put straight out from shore.
It'll be dusk before long, so we'll wait for that, then move along, well
out, till we get west of Agios Georgios. After dark, we'll put in nearer,
and lie off for a while. The sea's like glass, and looks like staying that
way, thank heaven. Lambis, d'you know anything about the coast west
of the village?'

'A little only. It is much like this, small bays at the foot of rocks like
these. Near the village there is shallow bays, sandy.'

'Is there anywhere where a caique could put in, if necessary?'

Lambis frowned, considering. 'I do not know. I have noticed a bay, a
little way to the west—'

I said: 'I think there is. There's a bay the children called the Dolphins'
Bay, past the second headland along from the village. There are rocks
running right out into deep water: I saw them from a distance, a sort of
low ridge running out like a pier. It must be deep alongside, because the
children told me you could dive from them.'

Lambis nodded. 'I think that is the bay I saw. Past the second headland
to the west of the village? Yes, I notice the place as we come by.'

'Could you put in there, if necessary?' asked Mark.

'I can use my lights, once we have the headland between us and the
hotel?'

'Surely.'

Lambis nodded. 'Then in this weather it should be quite easy. Okay.'

'Fine.' Mark turned to me. 'Now, how about this? If, when you get down there this evening, you think there's the least thing wrong – any sort of suspicion, any danger . . . oh, you know what I mean . . . In other words, if you get the feeling that you and Frances ought to get out of there, and fast, without waiting for morning, then we'll be waiting at the mouth of your Dolphins' Bay till, what shall we say? – two in the morning. No, half-past: that should give you time. Have you an electric torch? Good. Well, any time between midnight and two-thirty a.m., we'll be watching for it. We'll have to fix a signal . . . say, two long flashes, then two short, then pause half a minute, and repeat. We'll answer. That do?'

I grinned at him. 'Corny.'

'Oh, sure. Can you think of anything better?'

'No.'

'What happens if the bay's full of light-fishers?' asked Colin.

'It won't be,' I said. 'There are *scháros*-pots there, and they're collected before that time. No, it's fine, Mark. I can hardly wait.'

'Man, oh man, it's terrific!' Colin still had that boys'-adventure-story glow about him.

Mark laughed. 'It's pretty silly, really, but it's the best we can do, short of putting into Agios Georgios and scaring every bird within miles.'

'It won't be necessary, anyway,' I said. 'It's just a flourish, to go with that pirate's rig of Mark's. Now I'll go. Anybody coming, Sister Ann?' This to Colin, who had mounted some sort of decaying buttress outside the church wall, and was once again raking the hillside beyond the hollow with Josef's glasses.

'*Óchi loukánika.*'

'Then I'll be off. Heavens, if I make the hotel by dinner-time it's all I'll do! *What* excuse can I give for staying out till now? No, don't worry, I'll simply say I came over to see the church – Stratos suggested it to me himself, so he'll probably be pleased. Nothing succeeds like the truth.'

'You told me,' said Colin, from above us, 'that you were supposed to be collecting flowers.'

'Oh, lord, yes! Well, I'll grab a handful or two on the way down.'

'Have this for a start . . . and this . . . and this . . . ' Colin had already yanked half a dozen random weeds from the overgrown stones above his head. 'And I'm sure *this* one's as rare as rare . . . ' He stretched to pull down a straggling handful from a high vertical crack.

'Frances is going to be very impressed by that lot,' said Mark drily. 'And so's Stratos, come to that.'

'Why not? All these are probably howlingly rare in England.'

'Including the dandelion? Don't forget he's lived twenty years there, and Tony's English.'

'Well, Londoners.' Colin scrambled down, unabashed. 'They won't know any better. You can tell them it's a Cretan variety, only found here at two thousand feet. And look at that purple thing, dash it, I'll bet they haven't even got *that* at Kew! There, Nicola—' and he pushed the bunch of exotic weeds at me— 'and don't forget this is "*dandeliona Langleyensis hirsuta*", and fearfully rare.'

'Well, I wouldn't know any better.' I accepted them gratefully, refraining from pointing out that *dandeliona Langleyensis* was, in fact, a hawkweed. 'Thanks a lot, I'm sure Frances will love them.'

'I'll ring you up at the Astir,' said Mark, 'and let you know what's going on. Then I suppose we meet in Athens?'

'If we don't all foregather in Dolphins' Bay tonight,' I said cheerfully. ' 'Bye for now. See you both in Athens. Be good, Colin, take care of Mark. And stop worrying about me. I'll be all right.'

'Famous last words,' said Colin gaily.

'Shut up, you clot,' said Mark, quite angrily.

CHAPTER SEVENTEEN

But having done whate'er she could devise,
And emptied all her Magazine of lies
The time approach'd . . .

DRYDEN: *The Fable of Iphis and Ianthe*

Lambis left me at the stepping-stones, which was just as well. Tony was waiting for me at the shrine, sitting on the rocks among the verbena, smoking.

'Hullo, dear. Had a nice day?'

'Lovely, thanks. I suppose my cousin gave up, and went back for tea?'

'She did. She seemed quite happy about you, but I was trying to make up my mind to come and look for you. These aren't the hills to be messing about on by oneself.'

'I suppose not.' I sat down beside him. 'But I stayed pretty well on the track, and anyway, if one goes high enough, one can see the sea. I couldn't really have got lost.'

'You could have turned an ankle. Cigarette? No? Then we'd have had to spend all night looking for you, Calamity!'

I laughed. 'I suppose so. But one can't spend one's whole life expecting the worst, and I did so want to get over to see the church.'

'Oh, so that's where you've been?'

'Yes. My Danish friend told me about it, and Mr. Alexiakis said it was easy to find if one kept to the track, so I went over. It's a long way, but it's well worth the trek, isn't it?'

Tony blew a smoke ring, and tilted his head gracefully to watch it widen, blur, and wisp off into the sunlight. 'Me, I wouldn't know, dear, I've never been further than this. Mountains are not, but not, my thing.'

'No? They're not Frances' thing either. At least, they used to be, but she broke her ankle once, and it's a bit gammy, so she doesn't do much scrambling now.' This was true.

'So she said. Are those for her?'

'Yes.' I allowed myself a dubious look at the flowers in my hand. Lambis and I had added what we could on the way down, but even the eye of faith could hardly have called it a selection to excite a botanist. I had intended to root out the more obvious undesirables before I got to the hotel; as it was, I could only hope that Tony hadn't noticed that most of the gems of my collection grew right down as far as the village street. 'I don't know if she'll want any of these.' I looked hopefully at him. 'Do you know anything about flowers?'

'I can tell a rose from a lily, and an orchid from either.'

'Oh, well, I don't know much about them myself. I just brought what I saw. Birds are more my line, but Frances says I don't know much about them, either.' I turned the bunch of flowers over. 'These are probably common as mud, most of them.'

'Well, that's a dandelion, for a start. Really, dear—'

'Hawkweed, quite a different thing. Variety *Langleyensis hirsuta*, and only found above two thousand feet. I do know *that* one. Frances told me where to look for it.'

'Oh? Well, you seem to have had quite a day. Did you see anyone else up there?'

'Not a soul.' I smiled. 'You said we'd come to the right place if we wanted peace and quiet. There wasn't a sign of life, unless you count the birds – and all I saw of *them* was a hoodie, and a pair of lesser kestrels, and a mob of goldfinches near the stepping-stones.'

Tony, it appeared, did not count the birds. He got up. 'Well, are you rested? Shall we go down?'

'Good heavens, did you come right up here just to meet me?'

'I wanted a walk. The lemons smell good, don't they?' We left the lemon-grove, and skirted the field where the cornmill stood. A swift glance showed me that the door was tightly shut, and that no key jutted from the lock. I looked away quickly, my mind racing. Had Tony really come up here to meet me, perhaps to find out where I had been and what I had seen; or had he come up to the mill? Did he know that Colin was no longer there? If so, did he suspect Sofia, or would he assume that Josef had taken the boy up into the hills to silence him? It was even possible that Sofia herself had confided in him; he, like her, had been opposed to the idea of further murder. I stole a glance at him. Nothing in his face or bearing betrayed that he was thinking of anything more serious than how to avoid the mule-droppings in the track. Certainly there was no hint that he was engaged in a kind of verbal chess with me.

Well, so far we had each made the move we wanted. And if I could, I would avoid letting him make another. Quickly, I tried a diversion. I pointed up into an ilex-tree. 'Look, there's a jay! Aren't they pretty things? They're so shy at home that you hardly ever see them properly.'

'Is that what it was?' He had hardly glanced at it. He made his next move; pawn advancing to queen's square: 'Don't you think these windmills are just ducky?'

'They're lovely.' I hoped the queen's hesitation wasn't showing. But whatever he knew, or didn't know, I must say and do the natural thing. I said it, with a rough-and-ready compromise. 'We took some ciné-film up here this morning – there were people working in the fields, and Frances got some lovely shots of that mill.'

'Was Sofia up here?'

'Mr. Alexiakis' sister? Yes, she was. She's very nice, isn't she? I'd never have taken her for his sister; she looks so much older.'

'That's the difference between the fleshpots of Soho and the empty fish-nets of Agios Georgios, dear. Especially if your husband's a fisherman who won't fish. Josef's idea of bringing home the bacon is to slope off into the hills armed to the teeth like a Cretan brigand. Not that there's anything to shoot in these parts. If he brings home a rock-partridge once a month he thinks he's done his bit towards the happy home.'

I laughed. 'Have I seen him yet? Does he spend his time playing backgammon at the hotel?'

'Not he. No, he's off somewhere just now on a ploy of his own. I thought you might have seen him up yonder. That's why I asked. Did Sofia let you into the mill?'

Check to the queen. This diversion hadn't worked, either. Then I saw that my trapped feeling came only from myself, from the guilty knowledge of my own involvement. Tony could have no possible reason for suspecting I knew anything at all. The only reason he would be asking me these questions was if he really wanted to know.

Sofia, then, had told him nothing. For one frantic moment I wondered what to say. Then I saw, sharply, that Sofia would have to protect herself. It was my job to look after my own side, and that included me. It would be no help to Tony and Stratos, now, to know that Colin had gone. They couldn't get him. And Sofia would have to face them some day. Meanwhile I must look after myself, and Frances. The truth was the only armour for innocence.

I had stooped to pick an iris, and this had given me the moment I wanted. I straightened up, tucking the flower into the bunch I carried. 'Into the mill? Yes, she did. She was awfully kind, because I think she was in a hurry, but she showed us round, and Frances got some lovely shots of the interior. We were awfully lucky to run across her; I'd never have known whose mill it was, and it's usually kept locked, I suppose?'

'Yes,' said Tony. The light eyes showed nothing but mild interest. 'You saw the whole works, then? How nice. The millstones and all that?'

'Oh, yes. She showed Frances how they worked.'

'Ah,' said Tony. He dropped his cigarette on the dusty path, and ground it out with his heel. He smiled at me: Tony, to whom it didn't matter whether or not Colin had been murdered in the small hours of the morning; Tony, the passer-by on the other side; the chess-expert who was enjoying a game that made my palms sweat with the effort of being natural. 'Well, dear', he said lightly, 'I'm glad you had a good day. Ah, there's the bridge, not far to go now. You'll just about have time to change before dinner, *and* it's octopus, which you'll adore, if you've a taste for flavoured india-rubber.'

So the game was over. Relief made me as gay as he was. 'I don't mind it, but it's not the main dish, surely? Oh, Tony, and I'm ravenous!'

'I gave you each enough lunch for two.'

'You certainly did. I ate nearly all of it, what's more, and left the rest for the birds. If you'd given me less, I'd have been down a couple of hours ago. I hope you didn't want the bottle back?'

'No. I hope you buried it out of sight? It offends the gods of the place,' said Tony, blandly, 'if undesirable objects are left unburied hereabouts.'

'Don't worry, I buried it under some stones – after pouring the correct libations with the last of the wine.'

'Correct libations?'

'One for Zeus – he was born up there, after all. And then my own private one for the moon-spinners.'

'The what?'

'The moon-spinners. Three ladies who spin the moon away every month, to bring a good dark night at the end of it. The opposite of the hunter's moon – a night that's on the side of the hunted things . . . like Josef's rock-partridges.'

'A night of no moon,' said Tony. 'Well, isn't that interesting? What my dear old father used to call a night for the Earl of Hell.'

I raised my eyebrows. 'That seems an odd expression for a Vicar.'

'A what?' For one glorious moment I saw Tony disconcerted. Then the pale eyes danced. 'Oh, yes. But then my father was such an *odd* Vicar, dear. Ah, well, I dare say your libation will work. There'll be no moon tonight. Black enough,' he added cheerfully, 'to hide anything. Or anybody.'

Frances was sitting in the garden, but the door to the hall was open, and as soon as Tony and I entered the hotel, she saw us, and came hurrying in.

'My dear! Practically a search-party! Tony was sure you'd be lying with a broken leg, surrounded by vultures, but I assured him you'd be all right! Had a good day?'

'Wonderful! I'm sorry if I worried you, but I decided while I was up there that I'd make for that old Byzantine ruin I told you about, and it's positively miles! But I had a marvellous day!'

Tony had lingered to watch our meeting, but now disappeared through the door behind the reception table. He left it ajar. I heard Stratos' voice say something in soft Greek which I couldn't catch.

Frances' eyes were on my face, worried and questioning. I must have looked very different from the depressed messenger she had seen off that morning.

'Are those for me?' She was conscious, as I was, of the open door.

'Yes . . . If only you'd come a little bit farther up, I found the very thing we were looking for! Brought it back, too, alive and undamaged. Here, hawkweed *Langleyensis hirsuta*, as good as new.'

I detached the common little hawkweed from the bunch, and handed it to her. I saw a spasm pass across her face, to be followed swiftly by something like understanding. Her eyes came up to mine. I nodded, every muscle of my face wanting to grin with triumph; but I fought them into stillness. I saw her eyes light up. 'It should be all right, shouldn't it?' I said, touching the yellow petals. 'It's quite fresh and undamaged.'

'Darling,' said Frances, 'it's a treasure. I'll put it straight away. I'll come up with you.'

I shook my head at her quickly. It might be better not to look as if we wanted to hurry off together into privacy. 'Don't bother, I'll bring the things down for you when I've changed. Here are the rest. I don't suppose there's much that matters, but there wasn't much time. Order a *tsikóuthia* for me, will you, like a lamb? I'll join you out there till dinner, and let's pray it's soon, I'm starving.'

I ran upstairs to my room, where the last of the sunlight still lingered as a rosy warmth on the walls. The shadows of the vine were blurred now, ready to fade and spread into the general darkness.

I took off my linen jacket, and dropped it on the bed, then kicked off my dusty shoes. Only now did I begin to realize how tired I was. My feet were aching, and grimed with dust that had seeped through my canvas shoes. The thin straw matting felt gratefully smooth and cool to my bare feet. I pulled off my frock and threw it after the jacket, then went over to the window, pushed it wide, and leaned on the cool stone sill, looking out.

In the distance, above their gold-rimmed bases, the cliffs towered, charcoal-black. Below them, the sea lay in indigo shadow, warmed, where the sun still touched it, to a deep shimmering violet. The flat rocks near the hotel, lying full in the lingering light, were the colour of anemones. The ice-daisies had shut, and the mats of leaves that covered the rocks looked dark, like seaweed. The wind had changed with evening, and a light breeze blew off-shore, ruffling the water. Two gulls sailed across the bay, shadows identifiable only by their long, grieving cry.

I looked out towards the open sea. A caique was setting out for the night's fishing, with its *gri-gri*, the unpronounceable little Indian file of small boats following behind it, like ducklings behind the mother duck, light-fishers being towed out to the good fishing-grounds. Presently, away out, the lights would scatter and bob on the water like points of phosphorus. I watched them, wondering if the mother-boat were the *Eros*, and looked beyond her, straining my eyes over the dimming sea for a glimpse of another caique, a stranger, slipping lightless along, far out

Then I pulled myself up. This wouldn't do. If I was to play the innocent, I must clear my mind of any thoughts of the others. In any case, they were out of my picture. Lambis' caique would slip past in the darkness towards the Bay of Dolphins, with three people on board who had probably forgotten all about me, and had their faces and thoughts thankfully set for Athens, and the end of their adventure. And meanwhile I was tired, hungry, and dusty, and I was wasting time. If Stratos' hotel would run to a hot bath . . .

It would. I bathed fast, then, back in my room, hurried into a fresh frock, and quickly did my face and hair. The bell sounded just as I was slipping on my sandals. I seized my handbag, and ran out, almost colliding with Sofia on the landing.

I had apologized, smiled, and asked how she did, before it struck me, like a fresh shock, that this very day I had seen her husband's grave. The thought caught at my speech, and made me trail off into some stammered ineptitude, but she seemed to notice nothing wrong. She spoke with her former grave courtesy, though, now that I was looking for them, I could see the strain lines, and the smudges of sleepless terror under her eyes.

She looked past me through the open door of my room.

'I'm sorry, I should have tidied it,' I said hurriedly, 'but I've only just got in, and the bell went . . . I did clean the bathroom.'

'But you should not trouble. That is for me.' She walked into my room and stooped to pick up my shoes. 'I will take these down and brush them. They are very dirty. You went far today, after I saw you at the mill?'

'Yes, quite a long way, right across to the old church your brother told me of. Look, don't bother about those old things—'

'Yes. They must be cleaned. It is no trouble. Did you meet anybody . . . up there?'

I wondered if it was Josef she was worrying about, or Colin. I shook my head. 'Nobody at all.'

She was turning the shoes this way and that in her hands, as if studying them. They were navy canvas, much the same colour as the ones Colin had been wearing. Suddenly, I remembered the way his foot had prodded at that dreadful grave. I said, almost sharply: 'Don't bother about those, really.'

'I will do them. It is no trouble.'

She smiled at me as she said it, a gesture of the facial muscles that accentuated, rather than hid, the strain below. Her face looked like yellowed wax smeared thinly over a skull, all teeth and eye-sockets. I remembered Colin's brilliant blaze of happiness, the vivid change in Mark, and the light-hearted way the two of them had fooled with Lambis. This, we owed to Sofia. If only, if only it were true that Josef had been a brute, and could die unmourned. If only it were true that she had hated him . . . But could one ever really, honestly, hate a man with whom one had shared a bed, and to whom one had borne a child? I thought not, but then, one thinks like that at twenty-two . . .

I lingered for a moment longer, fretted by that feeling of guilt which
was surely not mine, then, on an awkward 'Thank you,' I turned and
hurried down the outer stair and round the side of the hotel to where
Frances awaited me with a vermouth for herself and a *tsikóuthia* for me.
'How you can drink that stuff. It's quite revolting.'
'All true Philhellenes cultivate the taste. Oh, that's *good*.' I stretched
back in my chair, and let the drink trickle back over my palate and into
my throat. I lifted the glass to Frances, and at last allowed the triumph
of the day to reach my mouth and eyes. 'It's been a lovely day,' I said,
'a wonderful day. Here's to . . . us, and our absent friends.'
We drank. Frances regarded me smilingly. 'I'll tell you something else,
you ignorant little blighter. Among that first-class bunch of weeds you
brought me, you have put, by – I am sure – the merest chance, a thing
that is really quite interesting.'
'Great Zeus almighty! Good for me! D'you mean Hairy Hawkweed?'
'I do not. It's this.' A few plants stood in a glass of water at her elbow.
She detached one of them gently, and handed it to me. 'It was clever of
you to bring the root as well. Careful, now.'
The plant had round leaves, furry with white down, and purple,
trailing stems, vaguely familiar. 'What is it?'
'*Origanum dictamnus*,' said Frances.
'Oh?'
'You may well look blank. Dittany, to you, a kind of marjoram. You
may even have seen it in England – not that you'd have noticed, but it's
found sometimes in rock-gardens.'
'Is it rare, or something?'
'No, but it's interesting that you found it here. It's a Cretan plant –
hence the name. *Dictamnus* means that it was first found in this very
spot, on Dicte.'
'Dicte? The birthplace of Zeus! Frances, this is exciting!'
'And *Origanum* means "joy of the mountain". Not because it's anything
much to look at, but because of its properties. The Greeks and Romans
used it as a healing herb, and as a dye, and for scent. They also called
it "the herb of happiness" and used it to crown their young lovers. Nice,
isn't it?'
'Lovely. Have you just been looking all this up to impress me with?'
'I have, actually.' She laughed, and picked up the book that lay on the
table beside her. 'It's a book on Greek wild-flowers, and it quotes some
rather nice things. There's a long bit about *Origanum*, quoted from a
medical book by a first-century Greek, Dioscorides. It's in a rather
heavenly seventeenth-century translation. Listen'. She turned a page and
found the place—
' "*Dictamnus, which some call Pulegium Sylvestre (but some Embac-
tron, some Beluocas, some Artemidion, some Creticus, some Ephemeron,
some Eldian, some Belotocos, some Dorcidium, some Elbunium, ye
Romans Ustilago rustica) is a Cretian herb, sharp, smooth, like to*

Pulegium. But it hath leaves greater, and downy and a kind of woolly adherence, but it bears neither flower nor fruit, but it doeth all things that the Sative Pulegium, but more forcibly by a great deal, for not only being drank but also being applied and suffumigated it expells the dead Embrya. And they say also that ye goats in Crete being shot, and having fed on the herb do cast out ye arrows . . . Ye root of it doth warm such as taste it; it is also a birth hastener, and likewise ye juice of it being drank with wine helpeth ye bitten of serpents . . . But ye juice of it, being dropt into a wound, it forthwith cures." What are you looking like that for?'

'Nothing. I was just wondering if the Cretans still used it for healing. I mean, a thing that'll do anything, "from abortion to snake-bite—" '

'Nothing more likely. They'll have lores passed down, time out of mind. Ah, well, so that's "the joy of the mountain".' She took it from me and replaced it in water. 'Well, it's nothing very great, I suppose, but it would be very interesting to see it actually growing. Do you remember where you got it?'

'Oh, my goodness, I'm not sure.' Lambis and I had, so to speak, grazed in motion, like harried deer. 'But I could probably pin it down to within a couple of square miles. Very steep,' I added kindly, 'about one in three . . . and occasionally perpendicular. Would you have liked – I mean, do you really want to go and see it?' Mark's plan for our leaving was humming in my head like a knell. Poor Frances; it seemed hard. And what danger, what possible danger could there be?

'I would, rather.' Frances was watching me with a slightly puzzled look.

'I – I'll try to remember where it was,' I said.

She watched me a moment longer, then got briskly to her feet. 'Well, let's go and eat. You look dog-tired. Tony has promised octopus, which he says is a delicacy unknown even to the better London restaurants.'

'Understandably.'

'Oh? Oh dear. Well, all experience is an arch wherethrough,' said Frances. 'Oh give me the polythene bags, will you? It doesn't matter about the rest, but I'd like to get *Origanum* safely under hatches. I'll look at it later.'

'Oh, lord, I forgot them. I did get them from your room, but I dropped them in my jacket pocket, and then came down without it. I'll get them now.'

'Don't bother; you've done enough for one day; it can wait.'

'No, really, it'll only take a second.' As we traversed the hallway I caught a glimpse of Sofia, with my shoes in her hand, vanishing through Stratos' office door. She must have finished upstairs, so, I thought thankfully, I shouldn't run into her again. Disregarding Frances' protest, I left her at the restaurant door, and ran up to my room.

Sofia had left it very tidy: my jacket hung behind the door, the discarded dress lay neatly over the chair-back, the towels had been folded, and the coverlet taken off the bed. Frances' polythene bags weren't in the first pocket I tried – when was anything ever? – but I found them in the other, and ran downstairs again.

Dinner was a cheerful meal, and even the octopus passed muster, as we ate it under Tony's apparently anxious surveillance. The lamb which followed it was wonderful, though I had not even now grown reconciled to eating the tender, baby joints from the suckling lambs. 'They can't afford to let them graze,' I said, when I saw that Frances was distressed. 'There just isn't enough pasture to let them grow any bigger. And if you're going to be in Greece over Easter, I'm afraid you'll have to get used to seeing the Paschal lamb going home with the family to be eaten. The children treat it as a pet, and play with it, and love it; then its throat is cut, and the family weeps for it, and finally feasts on it with rejoicing.'

'Why, that's horrible! It's like a betrayal!'

'Well, that's what it's symbolizing, after all.'

'I suppose so. But couldn't they use our sort of symbols, bread and wine?'

'Oh, they do. But the Easter sacrifice in their own homes – well, think it over. I used to think the same as you, and I still hate to see the lambs and calves going home to their deaths on Good Friday. But isn't it a million times better than the way we do it at home, however "humane" we try to be? Here, the lamb's petted, unsuspicious, happy – you see it trotting along with the children like a little dog. Till the knife's in its throat, it has no idea it's going to die. Isn't that better than those dreadful lorries at home, packed full of animals, lumbering on Mondays and Thursdays to the slaughterhouses, where, be as humane as you like, they can smell the blood and the fear, and have to wait their turn in a place just reeking of death?'

'Yes. Yes, of course.' She sighed. 'Well, I don't feel so dreadful for having enjoyed that. The wine's rather good; what did you say it was?'

'*King Minos.*'

'Then here's to the "herb of happiness".'

'Here's to it, and to *hawkweed Langleyensis* – oh!'

'Now what?'

'I've just remembered where I found it, your dittany.'

'Oh? Good. I hope it's somewhere I can get at.'

I said slowly: 'I think it is. It was actually growing at the old church; in fact, it was growing *on* it. And I'm sure there was more where that piece came from.'

'That's fine; I'd very much like to see it growing. Did you say there was a reasonable track the whole way?'

'There's a track, yes, but I wouldn't call it "reasonable". It's beastly rough in places. You'd be all right though, if you watched your step. All the same—' I smiled at her, my illogical feeling of guilt fading – 'it would be much easier, and far more fun, going by boat. Apparently there's an old harbour not too far from the church. We might take a caique along the coast one day, and just walk straight into the hills from there.' I was thinking, thankfully, that now I needn't feel so guilty about having to drag Frances away from here in the morning. We could take a car over from Heraklion to Agia Gallini, and hire a caique from there, and I would show her the exact spot where Colin had pulled the dittany off the wall of the little church.

'We'll have to fix it up,' said Frances, 'but it can wait a day or two; you won't want to go straight to the same place tomorrow. Oh, Tony, may we have coffee on the terrace, please? If you're ready, Nicola . . . ?'

'I think I'll get my jacket after all,' I said, as I rose. 'Give *Origanum* to me; I'll put him out of harm's way upstairs.'

I laid the polythene bag with its precious plant carefully on my table, and lifted my jacket down from behind the door. As I put it on, something – something hard – in one of the pockets, swung against a corner of the table with a dull little thud. I put my hand in, and touched cold metal; the thin, sharp blade of a knife.

The cold shape met my palm with the tingle of a small electric shock. Then I remembered. I brought the thing out of my pocket, and looked at it. Lambis' knife, of course; the one I had taken from him during that ghastly, serio-comic skirmish up there in the ruined church. I should have remembered to return it. Well, I could still do so, when my gay 'see you in Athens' came true.

I was turning to put the thing out of sight in my case, when something occurred to me that brought me up all standing, with a little formless fear slipping over my skin like ice-water. When I had come up to get the polythene bags for Frances, surely I had felt in both pockets of the jacket? Surely I had? I frowned, thinking back. Then certainty came; I had my hand in both pockets; I could not have missed the knife. It hadn't been there.

Sofia. It was the only explanation. Sofia must have found the knife when she hung my jacket up. She had taken it . . . why? To show to Stratos and Tony? Had she taken it with her, that time I saw her vanishing into Stratos' office, only to return it quietly while I was at dinner? *Why?*

I sat down abruptly on the edge of the bed, furious at the wave of panic which swept over me, trying to think coherently.

Lambis' knife. It didn't matter; I must remember that. It didn't matter. Nobody here would recognize it: nobody here had seen Lambis, or even knew of his existence. The knife could not possibly link me with the affair; not possibly.

Why, then, had Sofia done what she had done? Simply because, I told myself, she and her companions were, like all criminals, touchy at the least thing. It wasn't usual for the ordinary, innocent woman tourist to carry an unsheathed and very business-like knife. She had thought it worth showing to her brother; but that was, surely, as far as it would go? There was no reason why I should not have bought such a thing as a souvenir; business-like though it was, it was also rather pretty, with the

copper hilt worked with blue enamel, and a sort of filigree chasing on
the root of the blade. I turned it over in my hand, examining it. Yes, that
was the story: if anyone asked me, I would say that I had bought the
thing in Chania, partly as a toy, and partly because I knew I should
want some sort of tool to dig up plants for Frances. That was why I had
taken it with me today . . . Yes, that would do . . . I had used it today . . .
that would account for the used look of the thing, and the couple of chips
and notches that showed in the enamel of the handle.

I stood up, relieved, and ready to dismiss my fears. That story would
do, and meanwhile I would put it away, and I must certainly remember
to return it to Lambis. He would have been missing it.

The thing slipped from my fingers, and fell, to quiver, point down, in
the floor-boards. I was sitting on the bed again, my hands to my cheeks,
my eyes shut in a vain effort to blot out the picture that my memory had
conjured up . . .

Lambis, relaxed in the sunshine beside Colin, whittling away at the
little wooden lizard. After we had left the church; after I had taken this
knife from his pocket. He hadn't missed it at all; his own knife, his
accustomed knife, had had a wooden handle . . . I remembered it now,
and remembered the sheath of embossed leather that he had worn thrust
into his waistband, and which lay beside him as he did his carving . . .

And this knife? This enamalled copper affair that I had taken from
his pocket, and forgotten to return? This pretty, deadly bit of Turkish
enamel-work?

'*He pulled his knife*,' Mark had said, '*and then went down hard, with
his head on the rock, and that was that . . . We took everything else he
had, and buried the boots.*'

Josef. Josef's weapon, marked and notched into unmistakability. Found
in my pocket by Josef's wife. Shown to Tony; shown to Stratos. Then
quietly slipped back where they had found it.

I didn't stop then to consider what they might make of it, or if I could
invent some story of finding it on the hillside. I just sat there, fighting
off the waves of senseless panic that bade me get away, myself and
Frances, get away, straight away, that very night, to friends and lights
and normal places and people and sanity.

To Mark.

After a bit, I put the knife in my suitcase, steadied myself, and went
down the stairway.

CHAPTER EIGHTEEN

Thus far her Courage held, but her forsakes:
Her faint Knees knock at ev'ry Step she makes.

DRYDEN: *Cinyras and Myrrha*

'Ah, Miss Ferris,' said Stratos.

He was in the hallway, behind the table, not doing anything, just standing there, waiting for me. From behind the closed door of the office came voices, Tony's and Sofia's, the latter lifted on a high, urgent note, which stopped abruptly as Stratos spoke.

'I hope you had a pleasant day,' he said.

'Very, thank you,' I smiled, hoping he couldn't tell that my lips were stiff, and the nerves tingling in my finger-tips. 'A pretty long one, but I've enjoyed it thoroughly.'

'So you've been across to the old church, Tony tells me?' His tone was quite normal, friendly even, but something in it drove me to respond as if to an accusation.

'Oh, yes, I did.' My voice was hoarse, and I cleared my throat. 'The track was quite easy to follow and the church was well worth visiting – you were quite right about that. I was only sorry I hadn't a camera with me.'

'Ah, yes, it is Miss Scorby who is the photographer, is it not?' Still nothing in the even voice that I could put a name to. The black Greek eyes watched me. I find it hard at the best of times to read in them any but the more normal expressions: Stratos' eyes, now, might as well have been behind smoked glass.

I smiled into those blank eyes, and put another brick of truth on the wall of innocence I was trying to build. 'We got some marvellous pictures this morning, up in the fields. I think the one of your sister at the mill should be a winner. Did she tell you she'd been playing film star?'

It was difficult to keep myself from glancing towards the office door. Behind it, Sofia was talking again, on a dreadful wailing note. Stratos' eyelids flickered, and he raised his voice. 'Sofia told me about it, yes. She showed you over the mill, I believe.' Behind him the sounds sank abruptly to a murmur; then I heard Tony speaking softly and urgently. 'I hope you found it interesting,' said Stratos politely.

'Oh, very. I only wish I could have seen it working, but I suppose that only happens when someone wants some corn grinding?'

'Perhaps that will happen while you are here.' His voice was non-committal, his eyes suddenly alive, intent and wary.

I saw it then. He had not yet had time to think, to assess what had happened. Tony must just have told him that Colin was no longer in the mill, and Sofia – bewildered and no doubt frightened by the discovery of Josef's knife in my pocket – had walked into the conference, to be met with angry accusations, and a startled reassessment of the situation. What I was hearing now from behind the office door must be the tail-end of quite a pretty scene. And it was apparent that Stratos himself was considerably shaken; he was confused, alarmed, and very ready to be dangerous, but for the present, wariness held him back. He wasn't prepared, yet, to be bolted into the open. He wanted time to think. And all he needed from me, for the moment, was reassurance on two points: namely, that nothing had happened to make me suspicious and therefore dangerous: and – a corollary to this – that I was prepared to stay placidly in Agios Georgios, under his eye, until my holiday came to its natural end. The one would presuppose the other. I only hoped that the knowledge would content him.

I said, smoothly enough: 'If it does, I hope you'll let me know.'

I smiled at him again, and turned away, but he made a slight movement as if he would have stopped me. 'Tell me this, Miss Ferris—'

He was interrupted. The office door opened, and Tony came out. He didn't come far; just shut the door, very softly, behind him, and stayed there leaning back against the jamb, loose-limbed and graceful as ever. He was smoking, the cigarette hanging from the corner of his mouth. He neither smiled nor greeted me, just stood there, and when he spoke he didn't trouble to remove the cigarette.

'Were you asking Miss Ferris about the fishing?' he said.

'Fishing?' The Greek's head jerked round, and the men's eyes met. Then Stratos nodded. 'I was just going to.' He turned back to me. 'You were asking me before about the fishing.'

'Fishing?' It was my turn to sound blank.

'You said you would like to go fishing, did you not?'

'Oh. Yes, I did. Of course.'

'Would you care to come out tonight?'

'Tonight?' For a moment, both thought and speech were beyond me. My brain felt light and empty as a bubble. Then I saw what to say. Whatever he suspected, whatever he was trying to find out about me, it could do nothing but good to establish those two facts for him here and now.

I said: 'Why, I'd love it! Thank you so much! You mean light-fishing?'

'Yes.'

'But you've missed the *gri-gri*.'

'Oh, you saw them? I do not go with them. I told you I fish for pleasure, not for food. I stay near the shore. Then you will come?'

'I'd love it,' I said enthusiastically. 'What about Frances?'

'I have spoken to her. She does not wish to go.'

'Oh, I see. Then—'

'I'll come with you.' Tony had removed the cigarette at last, and was smiling at me, his eyes light and cold.

I smiled back at him. I was sure, now, that they weren't going to mention the knife, and relief made me genuinely gay. 'Will you really? That'll be fun! I didn't think boats would have been your thing, somehow.'

'Oh, they're not. But this is a trip I wouldn't miss for worlds, dear. I can crew for Stratos.'

'There's no need.' The Greek spoke roughly. His big hands moved sharply among some papers on the table in front of him, and I saw a vein beating in his temple, up near the hair-line. I wondered just what was going on; if Tony was insisting on coming along in order to keep a tight eye on his companion, or merely to help him in whatever plans he might have for me . . .

'Will you be going tomorrow night?' I asked.

'Tomorrow night?'

I moistened my lips, looking from one to the other in what I hoped was pretty apology. 'The thing is . . . if it's all the same to you . . . I think I honestly am a bit tired tonight. I've had a long day, and now that heavenly dinner's made me sleepy. *Would* you be going out tomorrow night?'

A tiny pause. 'I might.'

'Then would you – yes, I think I *would* rather leave it till then, if it's all the same to you?'

'Of course.' Of all the emotions, relief is the hardest to conceal, and I thought there was relief in the gesture with which he dismissed the plan. He was sure of me now. He smiled. 'Any time. The boat is at your service.'

I lingered, hesitating. There was no harm in making him even surer. 'There was one thing I was going to suggest, Mr. Alexiakis. You remember how you said we might make a sea-trip one day in the Eros? Well, I did wonder if we might hire it some day soon? I wondered if it would be possible to take a trip along the coast, that way' – I waved vaguely eastwards – 'to where the ancient harbour was? The thing is, I found a plant growing on the ruins, today, that's got my cousin all excited. She says it's Cretan dittany, do you know it?'

He shook his head.

'Well, she wants to see it growing, and to photograph it, but I think it would be too far and too rough for her to go the whole way over by the track. I did wonder if it wouldn't be rather fun to take the sea-trip. I thought if we could land at the old harbour, then we could simply walk inland to the church; it can't be far, I could see the sea from just above it. Then she could see the dittany growing, and get her pictures. Come to that, I'd like some pictures of the church myself, and of the harbour. Do you think we could do that? There's no hurry,' I finished, 'any day will do, when you're not wanting the caique.'

'Of course,' he said heartily, 'of course. It is a good idea. I will take you myself. You must just tell me the day before you wish to go. And, for the light-fishing . . . that is settled? Tomorrow night?'

'Yes. Thank you, I'll look forward to it.'

'So shall I,' said Stratos, smiling, 'so shall I.'

This time, he made no attempt to detain me when I went out to where Frances sat with the coffee under the tamarisks. Their boughs were ethereal in the diffused electric light, like clouds. Behind them was the black, murmuring sea, and the black, blank sky. The night of no moon. I thought of Stratos, the *pallikarás*, with that vein beating in his temples, and a murder weighing on his mind. And of Tony. And of myself, out in a small boat with them, alone out there somewhere in the blackness . . .

I didn't really pause to ask myself what he could be planning to do, or whether I really had won for myself a respite until tomorrow. I only knew that somewhere out in that same blackness was a lightless caique, with Mark on board, and that, come hell or high water, Frances and I were getting out of this place tonight.

The stone treads of the stairway were comfortingly silent under our feet. Somewhere, once, a dog barked, and then fell quiet. The sea whispered faintly under the off-shore wind; a wilderness of darkness; a huge, quiet creature breathing in the night.

'Keep to the rocks if you can,' I breathed to Frances. 'The shingle will make a noise.'

We padded, soft-shoed, along the smoothed ridges of the rock, where the mats of ice-daisies muffled our steps. The night was so dark that, even from here, the solid oblong of the hotel was hardly visible – would have been quite hidden if it had not been blocked in with whitewash. No light showed. Further down the village the darkness was thick also; only two pinpricks of light showed where someone was still awake well after midnight. The faintest ghost of a glimmer from the church hinted at lamps left burning in front of the ikons all night.

We felt our way along, each yard an agony of suspense; having to move so slowly, but longing to switch on the torch and hurry, hurry . . .

Now, perforce, we were on shingle. It sounded as loud as an avalanche under our cautious steps. After a dozen slithering paces, I put a hand on Frances' arm, and drew her to a halt.

'Wait. Listen.'

We waited, trying to hear beyond the sound of our own breathing. If we had made any noise loud enough to be heard, so, if we were being followed, would our pursuers.

Nothing; only the breathing of the sea.

'You're sure there'll be no moon?' whispered Frances.

'Sure.' The sky was black velvet, obscured by the veil of cloud drawing slowly across from the White Mountains. Later, perhaps, it would be thick with stars, but now it was black, black and comforting for the hunted. The moon-spinners had done their work. Somewhere out beyond the black horizon, the drowned moon was waiting to unspin in stranded light towards the shore. But not tonight.

I touched Frances' arm again, and we went on.

It is only when one has been out in the night for some time that one begins to see the different densities, even the colours, of darkness. The sea, a living darkness; the shingle, a whispering, shifting, clogging darkness; the cliffs that rose now on our right, a looming lamp-black mass that altered the sound of our footsteps, and of our very breathing. Our progress here was painfully slow, with the cliffs pressing close on our right, thrusting out jagged roots of rock to trip us, and, on the other side, barely a yard away, the edge of the sea, giving a foot, taking a foot, always moving, only visible as a faintly luminous line of pale foam; the only guide we had.

I have no idea how long this part of the journey took. It seemed like hours. But at last we had traversed the full curve of the bay, and towering in front of us was the high, cathedral-like cliff that stuck out into the sea, right out into deep water that lapped hollowly round its base, creaming up among the fallen boulders of the narrow storm-beach which provided the only way round. We had clambered round the point by daylight; could it be done in the dark?

It had to, of course. But, as a form of exercise, I cannot recommend carrying a suitcase for a mile or so along sand and shingle at dead of night, and then edging one's way along a narrow path where a false step will mean plunging into a couple of fathoms of sea that, however quiet, is toothed like a shark with jagged fangs of rock.

I glanced back as I reached the point. The last pinprick of light from the village had disappeared; the bay we had traversed showed only as a gap of darkness.

Frances, behind me, said breathlessly: 'Out to sea . . . lights. All over the place.'

I turned to look, disconcerted to see the blackness alive with tiny lights. Then I realized what it was.

'It's the light-fishers,' I told her. 'They're a long way out. I saw them going. I suppose we were too low to see them from the bay. Can you manage this? We oughtn't to show the torch yet.'

'Faint yet pursuing,' she said cheerfully. 'Actually, I can see fairly well; I've got my night-sight now.'

The second bay was small, only an inlet, paved with beautifully firm, pale sand that showed up well in the gloom, and provided safe walking. We made good time, and in ten more minutes we had reached the second headland, where, too, the going was comparatively easy. A fairly obvious path had been beaten along the narrow storm-beach which lay piled against the point like the foam under a moving prow. I made my way cautiously round the cliff, then down to the hard sand of the Bay of Dolphins. I could see Frances, still on the path, as a vaguely moving shadow, feeling her way carefully down to where I waited.

'All right?'

'Yes.' She was breathing rather heavily. 'Is this the bay?'

'Yes. The spit of rock runs out from the far side of it. We'll have to get out along that, over the deep water. Now we can use the torch, thank heaven. Here—' I pressed it into her hand – 'you'd better have it. Give me your case.'

'No. I can easily—'

'Don't be daft, it isn't far, and my own weighs nothing. The going's tricky here . . . it looks as if there are rock-pools and things. . . so one of us had better be mobile, and light the way. You can take my shoulder-bag; here. I'll follow you.'

Reluctantly, she handed me her case, and took the bag and the torch. The beam of light looked brilliant after the unalleviated blackness; it threw the sand and rocks into such vivid relief that for the first few moments the sense of distance and proportion was almost annulled.

At least, that was how it seemed to me, and I must suppose that is what happened to Frances, for she had taken only three or four steps when, suddenly, with a bitten-off exclamation of pain, she seemed to lurch forward, then pitched down on to the sand as if shot. The darkness came down like a blanket as the torch flew from her hand, to be doused on the nearest rock with the ominous, the final sound of breaking glass.

I dropped the cases and was down beside her. 'Frances! What is it? What happened?'

Such had been the havoc wrought on my nervous system during the last three days that I honestly believe that, for a mad moment, I expected to find her dead.

But she was very much alive, and swearing. 'It's my blasted ankle. Did you ever *know* such a fool, and I had the torch, too. Is the bloody thing broken?'

'I'm afraid so. But your foot—'

'Oh, it's the same old ankle. It's all right, don't worry, it's only wrenched; the usual. If I sit here a moment and swear hard enough, it'll pass off. Hell, and I'm wet! You were right about the rock-pools; the sand just seemed to shelve straight down into one, or something. I couldn't see. And now, if the torch has gone—' She broke off, aghast. 'Nicky, *the torch!*'

'Yes, I know. It can't be helped. He – he'll surely come close in to look for us, anyway, and we can hail him.'

'If we see him.'

'We'll hear, surely?'

'My dear girl, he won't use his engine, will he?'

'I don't know. He might; there are those other boats out fishing, it wouldn't be the sort of sound that people would notice. It'll be all right, Frances, don't worry.'

'It'll have to be,' she said grimly, 'because *our* boats are nicely burned. I can't see us trekking all the way back, somehow, not now.'

'If the worst comes to the worst,' I said, falsely cheerful, 'I'll stagger back with the cases and unpack, sharpish, then go and tell them we've been having a midnight swim, and will they please come out and collect you.'

'Yes,' said Frances, 'and then they'll come streaming along in force, and run into Mark and Co.'

'Then it'd be over to Mark. He'd like that.'

'Maybe. Well, it serves me right for not bringing you up better. If I'd taught you to mind your own business—'

'And pass by on the other side?'

'Yes, well, there it is. If we will be anti-social, and come to the god-forsaken corners of the earth in order to avoid our fellow-trippers, I suppose we have to take what comes. You couldn't have done anything else, even to this horror-comic episode tonight. One can't touch murder, and not be terrified. We can't get out fast enough, in my opinion. *Damn* this ankle. No, don't worry, it's beginning to cool down a bit. What's the time?'

'Nearly half-past one. Have you any matches?'

'No, but there's my lighter. That might do it. I *am* sorry about the torch.'

'You couldn't help it.'

'Give me a hand now, and help me up, will you?'

'There. Manage? Good for you. I'll tell you what, I'll dump the cases here, back against the cliff, and we'll get you along the "pier," if we can – as far as we can, anyway. Then I can come back for them . . . or maybe we'd better leave them till we see Mark coming in. Sure you can make it?'

'Yes. Don't worry about me. Look, is that the torch?'

A tiny edge of starlight on metal showed where it lay. Eagerly I picked it up and tried it. Useless. When I shook it gently, there was the rattle of broken glass.

'*Kaput?*' asked Frances.

'Very *kaput*. Never mind. The luck couldn't run all the way all the time. Press on regardless.'

It was a slow, dreadful progress across the bay, our steps less certain than ever after the brief illumination and the fall. Frances hobbled along nobly, and I tried to seem unhurried, and perfectly confident and at ease; but the night was breathing on the back of my neck, and I was flaying myself mentally for having tried this final escapade at all. Perhaps I had been stupid to panic so, over the discovery of Josef's knife. Perhaps they hadn't even seen it; it had been in my pocket all the time. Perhaps Stratos' manoeuvre to get me to himself out in the light-boat had been no more than the host's anxiety to please, and there had never been any danger except in my own imagination. I need never have subjected Frances to this ghastly trek, this schoolboys' escapade that probably wouldn't even work. If I'd kept my head and waited till tomorrow . . . Tomorrow, we could have telephoned for a car, and then walked to it, in sunlight, through the public street.

But here we were in the dark, committed. It must have been all of thirty minutes more before I had got Frances out along the ridge of rock. With my help, she shuffled, half-crawling, along it, until she had found a place to sit, a few feet above deep water. She fetched a long sigh of relief, and I saw her bend, as if to massage her ankle.

'You were marvellous,' I told her. 'Will you give me the lighter now?'

She felt in her pocket, and passed it to me. I went a little further along the rock-ridge. Its top sharpened presently into a hog's-back, then dropped steeply to deep water, where the ridge had been broken and split by the sea. Ahead of me I could see the fangs of rock which marked the broken ridge, running straight out to sea, their bases outlined with ghostly foam, as the breeze freshened beyond the immediate shelter of the cliffs.

I found a flat place to stand, then, with the lighter ready in my hand, faced out to sea.

They should see the flame quite well. I remembered hearing how, in the blackout during the war, flyers at some considerable height could see the match that lit a cigarette. Even if I couldn't manage the pattern of flashes that we had agreed upon, surely a light, any light, from this bay at this time, would bring Mark in . . . ? And once he was near enough, a soft hail would do the rest.

I cupped a hand round the lighter, and flicked it. Flicked it again. And again . . .

When my thumb was sore with trying, I allowed myself to realize what had happened. I remembered the splash with which Frances had fallen, and the way she had wrung out the skirts of her coat. The lighter had been in the pocket. The wick was wet. We had no light at all.

I stood there, biting my lips, trying to think, straining eyes and ears against the darkness.

The night was full of sound. The sea whispered and hummed like a great shell held to the ear, and the dark air around me was alive with its noise. There were more stars now, and I thought I should even be able to see if any craft bore shorewards. The great space of the sea ahead looked almost light, compared with the thick blackness of the cliffs towering round me.

Then I heard it; or thought I did. The slap of water against a hull; the rattle of metal somewhere on board.

Stupidly, I was on tiptoe, straining forward. Then, some way out, well beyond the encircling arms of the bay, a light came past the point from my right, bearing eastward. A small boat, not using an engine, moving slowly and erratically across the black void, the light making a dancing pool on the water. One of the *gri-gri*, standing in nearer the shore; that was all. I thought I could see a figure outlined against the light, crouching down in the bows. At least, I thought, he wasn't likely to spot Lambis' caique, riding lightless somewhere out in the roads; but, with the light-boat so near, I dared not risk a hail for Mark to hear.

I went back to Frances, and told her.

'Then we'll have to go back?'

'I don't know. He'll have seen the light-boat, too. He may think we daren't flash our signal because of that. He – he may stand in to the bay, just to see.' I paused, in a misery of indecision. 'I – I don't see how we *can* go back now, Frances. They may have found out – that man—'

'Look!' she said sharply. 'There!'

For a moment I thought she was just pointing at the light-boat, which, pursuing its slow course across the mouth of the bay, would soon be cut off from view by the eastern headland.

Then I saw the other boat, low down in the water; a shape, silent and black, thrown momentarily into relief as the light passed beyond it. The unlighted boat lay, apparently motionless, a little way outside the arms of the bay.

'That's it!' My voice was tight in my throat. 'That's him. He's not coming in. He's doing just what he said he would; waiting. There, the light-boat's out of sight; Mark would expect us to signal now, if we were here . . . And we can't afford to wait any longer to see if he will come in . . . It's ten past two already. Can't you do it, either?'

'Afraid not.' She was working away at the lighter. 'It's had a pretty fair soaking. I'm afraid it's no use – what *are* you doing, Nicola?'

I had dropped my coat on the rock beside her, and my shoes went to join it. 'I'm going out after him.'

'My dear girl! You can't do that! Look, can't we risk shouting? He'd hear us, surely?'

'So would anyone else within miles, the way sound carries over water. I daren't. Anyway, we've no time to try: he'll be away in twenty minutes. Don't worry about me, he's well within range, and the water's like glass in the bay.'

'I know, the original mermaid. But don't for pity's sake go beyond the headland. I can see the white-caps from here.'

My frock, and the jersey I had been wearing over it, went down on the pile. 'All right. Now don't *worry*, I'll be okay. Heaven knows I'll be thankful to be doing something.' My petticoat dropped to the rock, then my socks, and I stood up in briefs and bra. 'Not just the correct dress for calling on gentlemen, but highly practical. I've always longed to swim naked, and I dare say this is as near as I'll get. Here's my watch. Thanks. See you later, love.'

'Nicky, I wish you wouldn't.'

'Damn it, we've got to! We can't go back, and we can't stay here. Needs must – which is the only excuse for heroics. Not that these are heroics; if you want the truth, nothing could keep me out. I'm as sticky as all-get-out after that horrible walk. Keep working at that beastly lighter, it may yet function. *Adío, thespoinís.*'

I let myself down into the water without a splash.

The first shock of it was cold to my over-heated body, but then the silky water slid over my flesh with the inevitable shiver of pure pleasure.

The filmy nylon I was wearing seemed hardly to be there. I thrust away from the rock into the smooth, deep water, shook the hair back from my eyes, and turned out to sea.

I swam steadily and strongly, making as little splash as I could. From this angle, the cliffs stood up even more massively against the night sky.

I headed straight out to sea, with the ridge of rock to my right as a guide, and soon drew level with the place where I had stood with the lighter. Beyond this spot, the ridge of rock was split and broken by the weather into a line of stacks and pinnacles. As I left the shelter of the inner bay, I could feel that the breeze had stiffened slightly: I could see foam creaming at the bases of the rock-stacks, and now and again a white-cap slapped salt across my mouth. Where I swam, fairly near the rocks, the lift and fall of the water against them was perceptible.

Another fifty yards or so, and I paused, resting on the water, stilling my breathing as best I could, and trying to see and hear.

Now more than ever I was conscious of the fresh breeze blowing out from the land. It blew steadily across the water, bringing with it, over the salt surface, the tang of verbena, and the thousand sharp, sweet scents of the maquis. I wondered if it would set up any currents that might make it hard for me to get back, if I should have to . . .

From my position, low down in the water, I could no longer see the outline of the caique – if, indeed, I had ever seen it. It might, I told myself, have drifted in-shore a little, until its black silhouette was merged in the dense blackness of the eastern headland; but this, with the off-shore breeze, was unlikely. Even to keep her from drifting seawards, they would have to use anchor or oars.

I strained across the moving, whispering darkness. As before, it was full of sounds, far fuller than when, on the ridge, I had stood insulated by the air from the subdued and roaring life of the sea. Now, the humming was loud in my ears, drowning all other sounds, except the suck and slap of water against the rock-stacks hard to my right . . .

Meanwhile, time was running out. And I had been right. Lambis was making no attempt to stand into the bay. Why should he, indeed? If I was to find the caique, I would have to leave the line of the ridge, and swim across the open bay, with the tip of the headland as a guide.

I hesitated there, treading water, strangely reluctant, all at once, to leave even the cold shelter of the stacks for the undiscovered darkness of the open bay. I suppose there is nothing quite so lonely as the sea at night. I know I hung there in the black water, suddenly frightened, doubtful, half-incredulous of the fact that I was there at all; conscious only that behind me was an alien country where I had behaved foolishly, and where folly was not tolerated; and that before me was the limitless, empty, indifferent sea.

But I was committed. I had to go. And, if they weren't there, I had to come back . . .

I took a breath, and turned away from the rock-ridge, bearing steadily seawards, towards the dim outline of the headland, the point where I thought the caique might be lying. I swam fast. It might take me ten minutes to come within distance of a soft hail. And in about ten minutes he would up anchor, and go . . .

I had travelled, I suppose, not more than thirty yards, when I was brought up sharply in my course by a new sound, not of the sea; the sound – unmistakable, and near – of metal on wood. A boat's sound. But this came, not from ahead of me, but from the right, further out to sea.

I stopped, treading water again, conscious now of the fast beating of my heart. A line of foam ran past me. The sea hummed. I was inside its great, roaring shell, rocked to and fro in an echoing confusion of din like the noises in a hollow cave. Under my body, fathoms down, throbbed the organ-pipes of the sea.

Another moment of deep fear, loneliness, and confusion swept over me with a cold splash like spray. But I dared not hesitate. If this were not he, I might be too late. I must try a hail now. . . But, if it were not he . . .

Then I saw it, unmistakably, and near. A boat, a dim shape, dark against darkness, the froth running white from her slowly-dipping oars. No light; no sound, save for the rattle of rowlocks that had caught my ear. She was seaward of me, standing across the bay towards the outer fangs of the rock-ridge. Lambis was coming in after all, without the signal; no doubt to reconnoitre the ridge before finally turning for the open sea, and Athens.

I put my head down, made a diving turn, and went at my fastest crawl back towards the ridge. My hand touched rock, I surfaced, clung, and turned, with my body held against the stack by the lifting water.

I had crossed the boat's course with plenty to spare; she was still slightly to seaward of me, but closing in, bearing for shore. And now she was level with me, looming between me and the stars. I shook the water out of my eyes, tightened my grip on the rock, and hailed her.

It came very breathlessly: 'Ahoy there! Sailor!'

Silence. She bore on her way. The wind must have caught my voice and eddied it away in the rush and lap of the water. She was passing, soon to be lost again in the darkness. I could feel her wash lifting me against the rock.

I let myself go with it, hauling on my hand-grip as I did so. The wash carried me back, and up, against my rock-stack; a crevice gave me another handhold, then a slippery foothold. I reared myself up out of the water, and let it hold me there, spread by it against the rock, where my body would show paler. I dared not leave the rock, for fear of being run down. I called again, not caring how loudly, and heard how this time the rock caught the cry, and echoed it uncannily across the black water.

'Ahoy! Ahoy! *Náfti!*'

The jerking clack of wood on wood, and she came up as sharply as a checked horse. Then the high prow slanted, swung, and she had veered head on to me.

I gave a little sobbing breath of relief. It was over. And of course it was Mark. I had had time, now, to realize that no other boat would have put into this bay, along this perilous ridge, in this unlighted and stealthy silence. Only a few minutes more, and Frances and I would both be safely aboard, and that would be that . . .

He was looming right over me. The faint line of frost under the bows seemed to brush my thighs. Then he swung broadside again, within feet of me, and the oars bit water. The boat halted, slid a little, backed water. I heard an exclamation, half of surprise, half of what sounded like fear.

I called softly: 'It's all right. It's me, Nicola. I was swimming out.'

There was silence. Feet away, the boat loomed.

'Mark—' I said.

Then, suddenly, a light flashed on; an enormous, blinding light; a pharos of a light. Straight above my head twin massive lamps were suspended in nothing. The beams, converging in a glaring ring, stabbed down on to the water, on to me. I was blinded, pinned down, held, dazzled and helpless to move or think, in that appalling light.

I believe I cried out, cowering back against the rock, and, at the same moment, I heard him shout. It was a rough voice, and it spoke in Greek, but there was no time for this to register with me. Fear stabbed through at a purely instinctive level, and already, before he had moved, I had dived away into the dark beyond the floodlit pool.

I heard an oar strike rock, as he thrust against it, and the nose of the boat turned with me. The light followed. I had seen, in that sharp, immediate flash of terror, what this was: it was a light-boat, too small (but the dark had hidden this) for an inter-island caique; too furtive – surely – for one of the *gri-gri*. And I thought I knew whose light-boat.

A moment later, I was proved right. Noise ripped the night open, as the motor started. No, this wasn't one of the harmless *gri-gri* that the caique had towed out to sea; this was a boat with an outboard. Like Stratos'.

Stratos' own. I heard him shout: '*You? I knew it! And Josef?*' He was standing there now, brilliantly lit beside the lanterns, and the six-pronged trident flashed as he drove it down, straight at me.

CHAPTER NINETEEN

It was that fatal and perfidious bark . . .

MILTON: *Lycidas*

No time to think, certainly no time to cry out through the choking swirl of water; impossible to shout to him, ask what he was doing, what danger I could be to him, now that the others were safely away . . .

The harpoon went by me with a hiss; bubbles ripped back from the blades in a sparkling comet's-tail. I twisted aside, kicking my way frantically out of the merciless light.

The spear reached the bottom of its run, jerked the rope tight; then he hauled it back, as the boat swerved after me. The rope touched me as he dragged it up; the small graze, even through the rip of the water, touched the skin with terror, like a burn. I had a glimpse of him, towering beside the lanterns, hauling in the glittering coils of rope with rapid, practised hands. Momentarily, he had had to let the tiller swing, and the light swerved away. Dark water swirled in the shadow of the boat, hiding me. I jack-knifed away again, towards the deep, black water. But *Psyche* came up to the tiller with a jerk, and turned with me, as if locked to my wake by radar . . .

For a split, crazy second, I thought of diving under her; then I knew it would be a dive to certain death: if the screw didn't get me, I would be a sitter for Stratos and the light as I came up. As it was, this could only have one end, and that a quick one . . . He needn't even risk another miss with the spear; another half-minute of this dreadful, uneven hunt, and I should be done, gasping on the surface, ready to be spitted . . .

Full in the glare, I turned to face the spear, and threw an arm up towards him. I was trying, I think, to get my breath to shout; to gain a little time in which his crazy anger might be checked, reasoned with. But even as I turned, he swung his spear-arm up again. The long shaft gleamed golden, the barbed blades glittered; the light beat me down, hammered me into the water, held me there, like a moth frying on a flame. His other hand was on the tiller. If the spear missed this time, the boat, swinging on that radar-beam, would run me down, and plough me back into the sea.

I gulped air, watching for the first flash of metal as his muscles tensed for the throw. The flash came: I turned and dived for the darkness. Nothing followed, no blades, no rope; he must have missed. I held myself under as long as I could, thrusting down and away, steeply, into deep water . . .

The moment came when I had to turn upwards. I was rising towards the light . . . it was everywhere . . . the sea paled to a luminous green, to a wavering of blue and gold, barred with the ripples of the boat's passage, blocked with the formidable shadow of her keel.

The turquoise and gold thinned, lightened, fizzed with sparks as the foam ran from her screw . . .

Just before I broke surface I saw him, a shadow towering above a shadow, tall on the thwarts, huge, distorted, wavering like a pillar of cloud. He was up there, waiting, the spear still poised. I don't pretend I saw anything except the moving shadows above the light, but I knew, as surely as if the sea were clear glass, that he still had the spear. He hadn't thrown it before, it had been a feint. He would get me now, as, gasping and exhausted, I surfaced for the last time.

Then something touched me, drove at my outstretched hand, breaking my dive, and sending me sprawling untidily to the surface. The boat rocked past, her bow-wave piling. The spear drove down at the same moment, a flash among the million flashing and glittering points of light; stars, water-drops, splashing foam, the dazzle of my water-filled eyes. There was a crack, a dreadful jarring, a curse. The world swam, and flashed, and was extinguished, as the massive shape of blackness surged up between me and the light. I hadn't even known what had knocked me to the surface, but the animal in me was already clinging, gasping and sobbing for air, to solid rock. That last, long dive had taken me into the wake of one of the stacks of the rock-ridge. The spear, striking prematurely, had hit it, and the prow of Stratos' boat, following me too closely, had taken it with a jarring graze, and was even now, roughly headed off by the rock, swerving fast away.

The moment's respite, the solid rock of my own element, were enough. My mind cleared of its helpless terror as the air poured into my body, and I saw that I was safe, as long as I kept among the rocks.

Psyche turned again, wheeling for my side of the stack. I dropped back into the sea, and plunged round into the darkness at the other side.

I reached out for a handhold, to rest again until she could come around.

Something caught at me then, holding me back from the rock; something under the water . . . It was thin and whippy as a snake, and it wrapped round my legs, dragging me down like the weight roped to the feet of a man condemned to die by drowning.

I fought it, with the new strength born of instinctive terror. I had forgotten the other danger; the light and the spear were of the upper air, this horror came from the world below. This was the swimmer's nightmare, the very stuff of horror; the weed, the tentacle, the rope of a net . . . It held me fast, pulled me down, choking. And now the light was coming back.

My flailing hand met rock again; clung, with the thing dragging at my knees. I was done; I knew it. The light was coming.

Then it vanished, switched off. The sudden darkness, printed with its image still, roared and dazzled. But the roaring was real, the night suddenly shaking with a confused uproar of engines, a medley of shouting, the sharp crack of a backfiring motor – and then I saw other lights, small and dim and moving wildly across the water. The darkened light-boat hung between me and the stars, as if hesitating, then, suddenly, her motor was gunned, and the jet of white foam that shot from her stern almost dragged me off my rock. Her wake arrowed away, to be lost under the dark. In its place, came, gently, a biggish shadow, with riding-lights steady at mast and prow.

Someone said: 'Hang on, sweetheart,' and someone else said, in Greek: 'God protect us, the sea lady,' and Colin's voice said breathlessly: 'She's hurt.'

Then a boat-hook ground into the rock beside me, and the boat swung in gently. Hands reached, grabbed. The side of the caique dipped, and I managed to grab it and was dragged half inboard, to hang gasping and slack over the side until the hands gripped again and lifted me in, and whatever it was that had twined round my legs and tried to drown me, came too.

I was down in the well of the caique, hunched on the thick rope matting, gasping and shivering and sick. Vaguely I was aware of Mark's voice and hands; something dry and rough rubbed me smartly into warmth, something sharp and aromatic was forced down my throat, while the caique swung and ground against the rock, and Mark cursed steadily under his breath in a way I hadn't thought he was capable of. Then came the dry roughness of a tweed coat round my bare shoulders, and another mouthful of the heady Greek brandy, and I was sitting up, with Mark's sound arm around me, feeling the warmth of his body comforting my own, and clutching his coat to my nakedness with numbed and flaccid fingers.

'Stay quiet; it's all right, just stay quiet.' It was the voice he had used to comfort Colin.

I shook, clinging to him. 'The spear,' I said, 'the weeds.'

'I know. It's all right now. He's gone.' Reassurance seemed to flow from him in tangible waves. 'It's all finished; you're quite safe. Now relax.'

'It was because of Josef's knife. I took it out of Lambis' pocket in the church, when we held him up. I forgot it. It was in my pocket. They saw it. H – he must have come after us.'

A moment or so, while he assessed this. 'I see. But it still doesn't explain why he—'

'*Mark!*' A shadow that I recognized as Colin dropped down to squat beside us.

'What?'

'This stuff that came up with her. It isn't weeds, it's rope.'

'Rope?' I shivered again, uncontrollably, and the protecting arm tightened. 'You mean a – a *net?*'

'No. It's a length of rope, with a float, and a sort of lobster-pot at the other end.'

The *scháros*-pots; of course. It seemed like a memory from another life.

I said: 'He has pots laid along there. I forgot. That was all it was, then. It felt horrible, like weed.'

'Chuck it back in,' said Mark.

'But there's something inside.' Colin sounded suddenly excited. 'Not fish. A sort of package.'

Mark let me go. 'Send a light down, Lambis.' He got down on his knees beside Colin. The wicker pot lay between them, a dark stain of water spreading from it. Gingerly Mark thrust his fingers in, and brought out a package, which he laid on the boards. Colin leaned close. Lambis, from his place beside the engine, peered in over their shoulders. The three faces were grave, absorbed, tense with a curiosity that was just about to break into excitement. The caique throbbed softly, swinging away from the rocks in a long, gentle drift seawards. We had all completely forgotten Frances.

Mark unwrapped the package. A layer of oilskin or polythene; another; a third. Then a bag of some soft species of skin, chamois-leather, I supposed, drawn together at the neck. Its coverings had kept it quite dry.

Mark pulled the draw-string loose, then up-ended the bag. There was a glitter and a coloured flash, a gasp from Colin and a grunt from Lambis. Mark picked up a kind of chain, very heavily ornate, and worked in gold; as he ran it through his fingers, red glowed and burned among the gold. Colin reached out, gingerly, and picked up something – it looked like an eardrop – with a hoar-frost glitter round a flash of green.

'I said it was jewels,' he said breathlessly.

'This is the loot?' Lambis' voice, over our shoulders, was deep with satisfaction.

'This is the loot, the highly identifiable loot.' Mark let the gold and ruby necklace trickle back into the mouth of the bag. 'It begins to make sense now, doesn't it? We wanted evidence, and oh boy! what evidence we've got! If this isn't why Alexandros was murdered, then I'm the Queen of the May!'

' "The London job",' I quoted.

'Big deal, eh?' Colin still sounded almost awe-stricken. He was turning the emerald drop from side to side, letting it catch the light. 'I wonder how many pots he's got?'

'That's a question that can wait for the police. Let's put these things back. Drop that in here, will you?' Mark held out the bag for the earring, then pulled the drawstring tight, and began to tie it.

I said slowly: 'He must have thought that's what I was after. The knife made him suspicious, but he thought we were safe under his eye for a bit. Then he came out here to check over his pots, and found me beside them, in the water. I'm not surprised, after all that's happened recently, that he saw red, and went for me regardless. I wonder if he even thought Josef might be double-crossing him? With me, I mean. He did shout something about him, and of course he must be wondering like mad where he is.'

'What *were* you doing in the water?'

'We broke the torch, so we couldn't signal. I was coming for you. I – *Mark!*' I put a hand to my head, which was only just beginning to clear of the sea-noises and the confused terror of the chase. 'I must have gone crazy myself! Get Lambis to put back to the rocks! There's—'

'You're hurt?' Lambis interrupted me sharply. 'That is blood, no?'

'No . . .' I must have looked at him with vague surprise. I had felt nothing, was feeling nothing even now; my flesh was still cold and damp to the touch, and too numb to feel pain. But as Mark snatched up the antern, and swung its light round to me, I saw that there was, indeed, blood on my thigh, and a dark line of it creeping down on to the deck. He must have got me with the edge of the spear,' I said, faintly, because was beginning to shake again. 'It's all right, it doesn't hurt. We'd better go back—'

But I was interrupted again, this time by Mark, who leaped – no, surged – to his feet. 'The bloody-minded *bastard!*' Colin and I – crouched at his feet like famine, sword and fire at the heels of the war-god – gaped up at him, dumbly.

'By God, I'll not stand for this!' Mark towered over us, possessed, apparently, by one sudden, glorious burst of sheer, uninhibited rage. 'I'm damned if we cut and run for Athens after this! We're getting after him, if it's the last thing we do! Lambis, can you catch him?'

I saw a grin of unholy joy split the Greek's face. 'I can try.'

'Then get weaving! Colin, throw me the first-aid box!'

I began feebly: 'Mark, no—'

I might have known they would take no notice of me, and this time it was three to one. My feeble protest was drowned by the roar of the caique's engine, as she jumped forward with a jerk that set every board quivering. I heard Colin shout: 'Man, oh *man*, Lambis, cool it wild!' as he dived into the cabin. Mark dropped back to his knees beside me, saying, simply and rudely: 'Shut up. We're going back, and that's that. Hell's teeth, do you think I'd have sat there and let them do all they've done, if they hadn't had Colin to hold me to ransom with? What d'you take me for, a bloody daffodil? Now I've got you and Colin safe under hatches, I'm going to do what I'd have done in the first place, if I'd been fit, and the pair of you hadn't been a sitting target for them. And now shut up, and for a change you can sit quiet and let *me* bandage *you*! Colin! Where the – oh, thanks!' This as the first-aid box hurtled from the cabin door. Mark caught it, and pulled it open. 'And find the girl something to wear, will you? Now, keep still, and let me get that tied up.'

'But Mark, what are you going to do?' I sounded infuriatingly humble, even to myself.

'Do? Well, my heaven, what d'you think? I'm going to hand him over to the police myself, personally, and if I've got to paste the living daylights out of him to do it, well, that'll suit *me*!'

I said meekly: 'Do you have to be quite such a sadist with the Elastoplast?'

'What?' He stared at me quite blankly. He really was looking very angry indeed, and quite dangerous. I smiled at him happily, well away now (as I was aware) on what Frances would have called Stage Three. Then the black look faded, to be succeeded by a reluctant grin. 'Was I hurting? I'm very sorry.' He finished the job quite gently.

'Not so much as I hurt you, I expect. Look, do you really think this is a good idea? I know how you feel, but—'

A quick look up, where, even in the lantern-light, I could read irony
'Darling, I admit I lost my temper, but there's more to it than a simple
desire to clobber this thug. For one thing, this is the chance to connect
him here and now with the jewels and Alexandros' murder – if we can
catch him and identify him before he gets the chance to run home and
cook up alibis with Tony. What's more, if we don't get straight back and
alert the village elders, what's to stop Stratos and Tony lifting whatever
other lobster-pots they've got, and being a hundred miles away, with
bulk of said loot, before we even sight Piraeus?'

'I see.'

He shoved the things back in the box, and clipped the lid shut. 'Mad
at me?'

'What on earth for?'

'Because when my girl gets hurt, I've got to have another reason for
hitting the chap that did it?'

I laughed, without answering, and slipped painlessly into Stage Four
– a stage Frances wouldn't have recognized, as it was new to me, too.

'Will these do?' Colin emerged from the cabin, clutching a thick
fisherman's-knit jersey, a cotton-mesh vest, and a pair of jeans. 'You can
put them on in the cabin, it's warm there.'

'They look marvellous, thanks awfully.' I got up stiffly, Mark helping
me, then Colin put the clothes into my hands, and retired modestly af
into the shadows.

The cabin was warm after the smartly-moving breeze on deck. I took
off Mark's jacket. The wisps of nylon which – I suspected – had been
almost non-existent as garments when wet, had now more or less dried
on me, and were ready to reassume their functions as clothing. I rubbed
my cold flesh again vigorously with the rough towel, then wriggled into
the jeans. They must be Colin's; they would be tight on him, and were
even tighter on me, but they were warm, and fitted comfortably enough
over the Elastoplast. The jersey – Mark's, at a guess – was wonderfully
warm and bulky, and came fairly well down over the jeans. I pushed
open the cabin door, and peered out.

A rush of starry wind met me, the roar of the motor, the slap and rac
of water ... We had swerved, close in, round the second headland, and
were tearing across the mouth of the bay towards Agios Georgios. I could
see, low down, a few dim lights, and a yellow gleam that must mark the
harbour mouth. Our own riding-lights were out. Lambis, at the tiller
was hardly visible, and Mark and Colin, standing together in the well
were two shadows peering intently forward. The caique jumped and
bucked like a bolting horse as the cross-wind met her round the headland

I opened my mouth to say 'Can I do anything?' then shut it again
Common sense suggested that the question was a purely rhetorical
gesture, and therefore better unasked. Besides, I knew nothing about
boats, and these three were a team which, freed now of everything bu

a single purpose, looked a formidable proposition enough. I stayed quietly in the shelter of the cabin door.

To seaward of us, the light-boats bobbed and twinkled. Some had worked their way in-shore, and one – probably the one that had passed so close to the Bay of Dolphins – was barely fifty feet from us as we roared past.

I could see the faces of its two occupants, open-mouthed and curious, turned towards us. Lambis yelled something, and their arms shot out, pointing, not towards Agios Georgios, but at the inner curve of the bay, where the hotel lay.

Lambis called something to Mark, who nodded, and the caique heeled till she lay hard over, then drove towards the looming crescent of cliff that held the bay.

Colin turned and saw me, and flashed a torch. 'Oh, hullo! Were the things all right?'

'Fine, I'm as warm as anything now. The pants are a bit tight, that's all, I hope I don't split them.'

'They don't look it, do they, Mark?'

Mark turned, looked obediently, and said, simply: 'Boy, oh *boy*!'

Colin, laughing, vanished past me into the cabin.

'Well, well,' I said, 'something tells me you must really be feeling better.'

'Sure. Try me. Just one hundred per cent – *there he is!*'

I dived after him to the side, peering to starboard. Then I saw it, too, barely a hundred yards ahead of us, a small shape, a dark tip on an arrow of white, hurtling into the curve of the bay.

'They're right, he's making for home!'

'Nicola!' Lambis hailed me from the stern. 'What is it like? Is there a landing-place?'

'No, but there's flat rocks right to the edge of the water. It's quite deep, right up to them.'

'How deep?' This was Mark.

'I can't say, but deep enough for a caique. He takes the *Eros* in himself, and it's bigger than this. I've swum there; I'd say eight feet.'

'Good girl.' I must be far gone, I thought, when this casual accolade from an obviously preoccupied man could make me glow all through. Stage Five? Heaven alone knew – and heaven alone could care, because I didn't . . .

Next moment a more substantial warmth met my hands, from the mug which Colin thrust into them. 'Here, it'll warm you up, it's cocoa. I'd say you've just time, before we waltz in to clobber the bastards.'

This got through. Mark half-turned, but at that moment the note of the caique's engine changed, and Lambis spoke, urgently and quietly:

'Here, we go in now. See him? He will make fast in a moment. Colin, light the lamp again; he must have seen us now. When we get in, you make her fast; I will go to help Mark. Take the boat-hook; you know what to do.'

'Yes.' But the boy hesitated a moment. 'If he has a gun?'

'He won't use it,' said Mark. 'He can't know who we are, for a start.'

This was undoubtedly true, but it had already occurred to me that Stratos might be making a fairly shrewd guess. In any case, whether or not he guessed whose caique was pursuing him, he must know that its owners had rescued me from his murderous attack, and were bound on an errand, if not of violent retribution, then, at the least, of angry inquiry – which would lead to the very uproar he wanted to avoid. We were, in other words, hard on the heels of a man both angry and involved to the point of desperation.

'Anyway,' Mark was saying, 'we've got one too, remember. Now, don't worry, here we go.'

I pushed the empty mug back into the cabin, and shut the door. I half expected to be told to go in after it, but nobody even noticed me. Lambis and Mark were both leaning out, watching the dim rocks of the shore rush to meet us. Colin, on the prow, held the boat-hook at the ready. The caique heeled more sharply still, then drove in.

Stratos had seen us, of course. But even at the cost of helping us, he had to have a light. As the light-boat ran in to the landing, he switched on the huge lamps, and I heard Lambis give a grunt of satisfaction.

Stratos cut his engine, and the boat lost way abruptly, slipping alongside the rocks. I saw him, the figure of my nightmare, rope in one hand, boat-hook in the other, poised beside the lights. Then his boat touched, kissed stone, and jarred to a rocking halt as the boat-hook flashed out and held her. I saw him glance back, and seem to hesitate. Then the lights went out.

'Ready?' Lambis' voice was almost inaudible, but it affected me like a shout.

'Okay,' said Mark.

The three of them must, of course, have worked together at berthing the caique many times before. This time, done fast and in semi-darkness, it was a rough berthing, but still surprisingly slick.

The engine accelerated briefly, and was killed. The caique jumped forward, then skidded sideways against the moored boat, using her as a buffer. I heard poor *Psyche* grind against the rock as the caique scraped along her sides. She was empty. Stratos was already on shore: I saw him, caught momentarily in our lurching lights, bending to fling a couple of rapid loops of rope round a stanchion.

Then Mark, in a standing leap from the caique's bows, landed beside him.

As the Cretan swung to face the challenge, Mark hit him. I heard the blow connect, sickeningly, and Stratos went staggering back. Mark jumped after him, and then they were beyond the reach of our lights, a couple of plunging, swearing shadows, somewhere in the scented darkness under the tamarisks.

Lambis pushed past me, scrambling ungracefully on the thwarts to leap ashore. Colin said urgently: 'Here, *you* tie her up,' shoved a rope into my hand, and jumped after Lambis, belting across the gravel into the darkness, where the roughhouse of the century was now playing havoc with the peaceful island night. Tables hurtled over, chairs went flying, someone shouted from a near-by house, dogs barked, cocks crew, Stratos was shouting, Colin yelled something, and then a woman cried out from somewhere, shrill and frightened. Stratos' homecoming could not have been more public if he had had television cameras and a brass band.

A light flashed on in the hotel.

I could hear a babel of other shouts, now, in the village street, and running footsteps, and men's voices, curious and excited. They were bringing lights ...

I suddenly realized that the caique – with me in it – was beginning to drift away from shore. Shaking like a leaf with cold, nerves and reaction, I managed somehow to find the boat-hook, pull her in, and crawl out on to the rock. I went stiffly to my knees, and began to wind the rope round the stanchion. I remember that I wound it very carefully, as if the safety of us all depended on how neatly I curled the rope round the metal. Four, five, six careful turns ... and I believe I was even trying solemnly to knot the thing – all the while straining to see what was happening out there under the tamarisks – when the shadowy mêlée grew dimmer still, and I realized that the light in the hotel had gone out again.

Feet came running, lightly. I heard a quick tread on gravel, then he was coming, fast, along the rock towards me, dodging through the shadows. A glimmer of light from one of the advancing lanterns touched him. It was Tony.

I was full in his way, sitting there numbly, holding my rope. I don't even remember being afraid, but even if I had been, I doubt if I could have moved. He must have been armed, but he neither touched me nor turned aside for me – he simply jumped straight over me, so lightly that one almost expected Weber's long harp *glissandos* to pour spectrally from the wings.

'Excuse me, dear—' His voice was quick and high, and only a little breathless. Another leap landed him in the frantically-rocking *Psyche*. There was a jerk at her rope as he cut it, the engine burst raucously into life, and *Psyche* lurched away from the rock so sharply that she must have shipped water.

' ... High time to leave.' I thought I heard the light, affected voice quite plainly. 'Such a *rough* party ...'

Then lights everywhere, and men shouting, and the dogfight was coming my way.

Here was Mark, with a stain spreading across his shirt, reeling backwards from a blow, to trip over a chair, which, collapsing, crashed with him to the ground. Stratos aimed a kick at his head, which went wide as Lambis, charging through a tangle of metal tables, knocked him aside; and then the pair of them hurtled, furniture flying, through a crackling fog of tamarisk-boughs, to fetch up hard against a tree-trunk. A *pithos* of carnations went rolling wildly: Stratos, who must know, even in semi-darkness, the hazards of his own territory, side-stepped it, but it struck Lambis full in the legs, just as the Cretan managed, at last, to pull his knife.

Lambis, lunging for the knife-hand, trod on the rolling pot, missed, and went down, tangled with carnations, and swearing lamentably. And now Mark, on his feet again, was lurching forward through the cheval-de-frise of tables, with behind him a crowd of milling, shadowy figures responding enthusiastically – if blindly – to Lambis' shouts.

Stratos didn't wait. He must have seen Tony, heard *Psyche's* engine, and thought the boat was ready there, and waiting. He swept aside the tamarisk-branches with one powerful arm, and, knife at the ready, came racing for the edge of the sea.

He had suffered a good deal of damage; I saw that straight away, but it didn't seem to affect the speed of this final, express-train rush for freedom. Then he saw me, crouching there over the stanchion, full in his path . . . and, in the same moment, he must have seen that *Psyche* had gone . . . but the caique was there, and he hesitated only fractionally before he came on.

The knife flashed as he lifted it, whether for me or the rope I was never to know, for Colin flew yelling out of the dark like a mad terrier, and fastened on the knife-arm with – apparently – arms, legs, and teeth combined.

It hardly checked the Cretan. He stumbled, half-turned, brought his free hand round in a smashing blow which brushed the boy off like a fly from a bull's flank, then, a mad bull charging, he hurtled towards me down the last stretch of rock.

I lifted the rope I was holding, and it caught him full across the shins.

I have never seen a man go such a purler. He seemed to dive forward, full length, towards the rocks. The breath was driven out of him in a gasping cry, then, out of nowhere, Mark plummeted down on top of him in a sort of flying tackle, rolled over with him, then let his arms drop, and got rather unsteadily to his feet.

'One more to you,' he said, and grinned. Then he pitched down on top of the Cretan's unconscious body, and went out like a light.

CHAPTER TWENTY

Tho' much is taken, much abides ...

The cabin of the caique was very full. There was Mark, rather white, and newly bandaged; myself looking, in Colin's pants and Mark's enormous sweater, like a beatnik after a thick night; Lambis, looking rough and collected, but still smelling exotically of carnations; Colin, with a new bruise on his cheek, silent, and rather close to Mark's side. That was the crew. With us, at the tiny cabin table, sat the headman of Agios Georgios, and three of the village elders, old men dressed in the savage splendour of Cretan heroic costume, which I suspected (from the speed with which they had arrived on the scene with every button in place) that they slept in. These were our judges – the Lord Mayor and all the Commissioners of Assize – while outside, in the well of the deck, and sitting on the engine coamings, and along the rocks, sat the whole array of jurors, the entire male population of Agios Georgios.

Four men had taken Stratos up to the hotel, there to watch over – and watch – him. Tony had, in the general confusion, got clear away. Although by this time most of the light-boats – attracted by the bedlam of noise and lights at the hotel – were converging on us across the bay, none of those near enough had had an engine, so Tony had dodged his way to freedom with the utmost ease and – it was reported – all the loose cash from the hotel, together with a sizeable number of his own portable possessions. But it should be simple, they said, to pick him up ...

Myself, I rather doubted this. The cool-headed Tony, with his genius for dissociating himself from trouble, at large in the Aegean with a good boat, and the coasts of Europe, Africa, and Asia Minor to choose from? But I said nothing. We ourselves had need of all the sympathetic attention we could command.

It had not taken long for the four of us to tell our story. We had omitted nothing, down to the smallest detail of Josef's death. Over this, there were grave looks, and some head-shaking, but I could see that the main climate of opinion was on our side. It seemed obvious that the actual acts of violence which Stratos had committed meant little, in themselves, to these men, and it might have gone differently with us if we had killed Stratos himself, whatever he had done in the course of his own private feud. But the death of Josef the Turk – and a Turk from Chania, at that – was (one gathered) quite a different thing. And in the matter of poor Sofia Alexiaki, who would have enough to bear when her brother's story came to light, it could be seen as the mercy of heaven that now, at last, as a widow, she could once more be a free woman, and a

Christian. She could even – Christ be praised – make her Communion this very Easter Sunday ...

The rest was to be as easy. When Stratos later recovered consciousness to be confronted with the discovery of the jewels in his fishing-grounds, the body of Alexandros (which was in fact found buried in the field by the mill), the guilty defection of Tony, and, finally, the death of Josef, he took the easiest way out for himself, and told a story which, in essentials, seemed to be an approximation of the truth.

He and Alexandros were not (as Colin's theory had had it) thieves, but had for some years been partners as 'fences', or receivers of stolen goods, with Tony as a kind of assistant and liaison officer. Stratos, running an honestly profitable little restaurant in Frith Street, had provided unimpeachable 'cover', and he and Alexandros had apparently had no connection other than a friendship between compatriots. Even this friendship had a perfectly natural explanation, for Alexandros was a Cretan, too, a native of Anoghia, the village which lay in the heights beyond the ruined Byzantine church. So things had gone on prosperously for a time, until the affair of the big Camford House robbery.

But Stratos had the good business man's instinct for getting out of the deal at the right moment, and, well before the robbery at Camford House, he had set about realizing his assets at leisure, and in good order, ostensibly to retire with his 'pile' to his native village. Alexandros – who could see only that a highly lucrative partnership was packing up in the moment of its greatest prosperity – bitterly opposed Stratos' move. Argument after argument supervened, culminating in a violent quarrel on the very eve of Stratos' departure, when Alexandros was driven to utter threats which he almost certainly had no intention of carrying out. The inevitable happened; tempers snapped, and knives were drawn – and Alexandros was left for dead in a back alley at least two miles from Frith Street, while Stratos and Tony innocently embarked that same night on the flight for Athens, for which their bookings had been made at least six weeks previously.

Recovering slowly in a London hospital, Alexandros held his tongue. Possibly he realized now – in the hue and cry over the disappearance of the Camford jewels – that Stratos' withdrawal had been opportune. The only thing was, Stratos had taken the lot ...

As soon as he was fit, and was sure that the police had not yet connected the obscure stabbing affair in Lambeth with the Camford robbery, Alexandros in his turn retired – armed – to his native land.

If it could ever be said that stupidity rated a punishment as final as murder, it would seem that Alexandros asked for what he got. Stratos and Tony received him – understandably – with a certain wariness, but soon, somehow, the affair was patched up, and there followed a scene of reconciliation and apology, made more plausible by the presence of Sofia and Josef. Stratos would, in good time, divide the spoils, and the three men would go their separate ways, but meanwhile it was only reasonable

for all three to lie low for a period, until the jewels could, in some form
or other, find their way gradually on to the market. This agreed, the
family party (well wined and dined, Soho-fashion, by Tony) set out to
escort Alexandros over to his own village, but on the way an argument
had arisen, over the disposal of the jewels, which had sprung almost
immediately into a quarrel. And then, Alexandros had laid a hand to his
gun . . .

It is probable, even, that Alexandros was not quite so stupid or
credulous as the story made him. Stratos swore, and continued to swear,
that he himself had never intended murder. It was Josef who had killed
Alexandros, Josef who had shot at Mark, and who had gone, on his own
initiative and without orders from Stratos, to make sure of Mark's death.
As for Colin, who had been dragged off in a moment of panic-stricken
and drunken confusion, Stratos swore that it was he himself who had
given the order for Colin's release, and here (he said, and nobody doubted
him) his sister would bear him out.

And, finally, the attack on me . . . Well, what did anyone expect? He
had gone to make a routine check of his spoils, and had found a girl
whom he suspected of some connection with Josef's mysterious absence,
diving after his pots. He had only done what any man would have done
in his place – and here, it was obvious, the meeting rather agreed with
him – and in any case he had only been trying to frighten, not to kill me.

But all this was for morning. Now, the first explanations over, our
story pieced together, weighed, and at last accepted, someone came across
from the hotel with coffee for everyone, and glasses of spring water. By
the time dawn broke, Agios Georgios had settled happily down to the
greatest sensation since the Souda Bay landing.

I sat, weary, drowsy, and warm, with the cut in my thigh throbbing
painfully, and my body relaxed into the curve of Mark's arm. The air
of the cabin was slate-grey with smoke, and the walls vibrated with the
noise of talking, and the clash of glasses as emphatic fists struck the little
table. I had long since stopped trying to follow the thick, rapid Greek.
Leave it to Mark, I thought sleepily; leave it all to Mark. My part in
it was over; let him cope with the rest, then, soon, we could all sail away,
free at last to salvage what remained of our respective holidays . . .

A memory cut through the smoky cabin like a knife-blade of cold air.
I sat up abruptly, out of the circle of Mark's arm.

'*Mark! Mark*, wake up! There's Frances!'

He blinked. 'Do you mean to tell me – dear heaven, of course, I'd
clean forgotten! She must be back there in the bay!'

'Well, of course she is! She's sitting there on a rock with a twisted
ankle. Frances, I mean, not the rock. Oh dear, how could we? That's
twice I've remembered – at least forgotten, but—'

'Pull yourself together,' said Mark kindly. 'Look, sweetie, don't start
another panic; she'll be all right. Believe it or not, it's barely an hour and
a half since we picked you up. If we go straight back there now—'

'It's not that! She'll be wondering what happened! She must be half out of her mind!'

'Not she,' he said cheerfully. 'She'd see us haul you in. She was yelling for help while you were in the water, with Stratos after you. It was the noise she made that brought us in – that, and the odd way his light was behaving, so near our rendezvous. Then, once we got near enough, there was too much to do, and I clean forgot her. Oh, and she threw a rock at Stratos.'

'*Did* she? Good for her! Did she hit him?'

'Did you ever know a female hit anything? That she aimed at, I mean? She hit me,' said Mark. He got to his feet, and addressed the concourse in Greek. This was to the effect that there was another English lady to be rescued, some way westwards along the coast, and that they would have to trust him and his party not to run away, but we must immediately go and fetch her.

Instantly every man present was on his feet. I am not quite sure what happened, amid the passionate babel of Cretan Greek, but in a very few minutes, as the caique swung away from shore, she was as well attended as a Cunarder edging her way out into Southampton Water. Not a man in Agios Georgios but would have died on the spot sooner than stay behind. Those light-boats that possessed engines had now caught up with us, lights blazing. Those that had not bobbed valiantly in our wake. Astern of us loomed the bigger mother-shapes of the *Agia Barbara*, and the innocent *Eros*. It was a noble procession.

To Frances, sitting nursing her sore ankle on her lonely rock, we must have been a brave sight, a pack of lighted boats swinging round the headland, our lamps yellow against the growing dawn.

One caique drew ahead of the rest, and slid alongside the rock-ridge. Colin shot out the boat-hook, and held us fast. Mark hailed her, cheerfully.

'Ahoy, there, Andromeda! Perseus here, with apologies, but there was a little matter of a dragon.'

I ran to the side. 'Frances! Are you all right? I'm most dreadfully sorry—'

'Well,' said Frances, 'I can see you're all right, which is all that matters, though I did have information to that effect. How nice to be rescued in style! I'm glad to see you, Perseus. You're a little late for the other dragon but, as you see, he did me no harm.'

Mark's brows knitted. 'The other dragon?'

I put my hand to my mouth. 'Tony? You mean Tony? *Here?*'

'As ever was.'

'What happened?'

'He came to collect the remainder of the jewels. The Camford House robbery, I understand.' Frances was bland. 'How well I remember the fuss when it happened.'

'But he didn't know where they were,' I said blankly. 'I *know* he didn't. Colin said—'

'Yes, he did.' Mark's voice was grim. 'Fool that I am, I heard Stratos tell him tonight. He shouted out something about the *schâros*-pots, when we were crashing around in the hotel garden like demented buffaloes. I don't know whether he was just cursing me, or whether he was letting Tony know, so that he could pick them up. But Tony heard, and it seems he didn't waste any time.' He looked at Frances. 'Do you mean to tell me that while we've been sitting jabbering like monkeys in Agios Georgios, he's just calmly walked away with the rest of the jewels?'

'Not all of them; only one pot-full. I don't know how many there are, and neither did he. He didn't even know where the pots were laid, and of course, even with the lights, it wasn't easy to find them. He hauled up four in turn, and only one of them had what he was looking for. The rest were fish-pots, quite genuine. He was quite – er – picturesque about them. Then we heard the flotilla coming, and he cut his losses, and went. He said he'd got quite enough to make the whole thing worth while.'

' "He said"? You mean he saw you?'

'He could hardly avoid it, could he? At least one of the pots was almost at my feet. Don't look so horrified, my dear, he was very polite, and quite amusing. He simply kept nicely out of range – not that I could even have begun to try to stop him – and told me all about it. He really did seem pleased that Colin had got safe away.'

'Small thanks to him,' I said tartly.

'So I told him. But I gather you've quite a lot to thank Sofia for. Apparently she refused from first to last to take anything from Stratos, because she thought it was all the proceeds of crime. She wouldn't have given him away, but it seems she did threaten to turn the lot of them in, Josef and herself included, if they hurt Colin. Master Tony passed that on to me, so that I could put in a word for her. And he sent you his love, Nicola; he was sorry to have to pass out of your life, but you'll get a picture postcard from the Kara Bugaz.'

'From the what? Where on earth's that?'

'I doubt if it need worry you. I've a strong feeling that we'll never hear of Little Lord Fauntleroy again, from the Kara Bugaz or anywhere else. Oh yes, and I was to tell you how much he approves of your trousers.'

'Well,' said Mark, 'that's one thing over which he and I see eye to eye. Aren't you coming off your rock? I know we're pretty crowded, but I can guarantee Lambis to get you back without foundering, and Colin makes a smashing cup of cocoa.'

Frances smiled at the three of them. 'So that's Lambis . . . and this is Colin. I can hardly believe we've never met till now, I seem to know you so well.' She put out a hand, and Mark jumped to the ridge, and helped her to her feet. 'Thank you, Perseus. Well, Nicola, so this is your Mark?'

'Why, yes,' I said.

Nine
Coaches
Waiting

For
Elizabeth Manners

First and Second Coaches

CHAPTER ONE

O, think upon the pleasures of the palace!
Securèd ease and state! The stirring meats
Ready to move out of the dishes, that e'en now
Quicken when they are eaten. . . .
Banquets abroad by torchlight! music! sports!
Nine coaches waiting – hurry – hurry – hurry –
Ay, to the devil. . . .

TOURNEUR: *The Revenger's Tragedy*

I was thankful that nobody was there to meet me at the airport.

We reached Paris just as the light was fading. It had been a soft, grey March day, with the smell of spring in the air. The wet tarmac glistened underfoot; over the airfield the sky looked very high, rinsed by the afternoon's rain to a pale clear blue. Little trails of soft cloud drifted in the wet wind, and a late sunbeam touched them with a fleeting underglow. Away beyond the airport buildings the telegraph-wires swooped gleaming above the road where passing vehicles showed lights already.

Some of the baggage was out on the tarmac. I could see my own shabby case wedged between a brand new Revrobe and something huge and extravagant in cream-coloured hide. Mine had been a good case once, good solid leather stamped deeply with Daddy's initials, now half hidden under the new label smeared by London's rain. Miss L. Martin, Paris. Symbolic, I thought, with an amusement that twisted a bit awry some-where inside me. Miss L. Martin, Paris, trudging along the tarmac between a stout man in impeccable city clothes and a beautiful American girl with a blond mink coat slung carelessly over a suit that announced discreetly that she had been to Paris before, and recently. I myself must have just that drab, seen-better-days shabbiness that Daddy's old case had, dumped there among the sleek cabin-class luggage.

But I was here, home after nine years. Nine years. More than a third of my lifetime. So long a time that now, pausing in the crush beside the Customs barrier, I felt as strange as I suppose anybody must feel on their first visit abroad. I found I even had to make a conscious effort to adjust my ears to the flood of French chatter going on around me. I even found myself, as all about me uttered little cries of recognition, excitement and pleasure, and were claimed by waiting friends and relations, scanning the crowd of alien faces for one that I knew. Which was absurd. Who would there be to meet me? Madame de Valmy herself? I smiled at the thought. It was very good of Madame de Valmy to have provided me with the money for a taxi into Paris. She was hardly likely to do much more for the hired help. And that was what I was. I had better start remembering it, as from now.

The *douanier*, chalk in hand, was pausing over my shabby case. As I stepped forward to claim it an airport official, hurrying past, bumped against me, sending my handbag flying to the floor.

'*Mille pardons, mademoiselle. Excusez-moi.*'

'*Ce n'est rien, monsieur.*'

'*Je vous ai fait mal?*'

'*Pas du tout. Ce n'est rien.*'

'*Permettez-moi, mademoiselle. Votre sac.*'

'*Merci, monsieur. Non, je vous assure, il n'y a pas de mal . . .*' And to my repeated assurances that nothing was lost and that I was not irretrievably damaged, he at length took himself off.

I stared after him for a moment, thoughtfully. The trivial little incident had shown me that, after all, that nine-years' gap had not been so very long. Ear and brain had readjusted themselves now with a click that could be felt.

And I must not let it happen. It was another thing I must remember. I was English. English. Madame de Valmy had made it very clear that she wanted an English girl, and I hadn't seen any harm in letting her assume that my knowledge of France and things French was on a par with that of the average English girl who'd done French at school. She had made rather a lot of it, really . . . though probably, I thought, I'd been so anxious to get the job that I'd exaggerated the importance of the thing out of all measure. After all, it could hardly matter to Madame de Valmy whether I was English, French or even Hottentot, as long as I did the job properly and didn't lapse into French when I was supposed to be talking English to young Philippe. And I could hardly be said to have deceived her, because in fact I *was* English; Daddy had been English and Maman at least a quarter so . . . and even to me those early years were faded and remote, the years when Maman and I lived out at Passy with Grand'mère, and the Boche was in Paris, and Daddy was away somewhere unspecified but highly dangerous and we never allowed ourselves to speak or even think in English . . . even for me those years had sunk well back into the past, so far back that now they seemed hardly to belong to me at all. Infinitely more real were the last nine years in England – seven of them spent at the orphanage in Camden Town, and the last two in a qualified independence – a travesty of freedom – as general help and dogsbody at a small prep. school for boys in Kent. Those endless green-linoleumed corridors, the sausage on Mondays and Thursdays, the piles of dirty sheets to count, and the smell of chalk and carbolic

soap in the classroom where I had taught elementary French ... these
were a very much more present memory than the lovely old house at
Passy or even the top flat in the Rue du Printemps, where we had gone
after the war was over and Daddy came home. ...

The *douanier* said wearily: '*Vous n'avez rien à déclarer?*'

I started and turned. I said firmly, in English: 'Nothing to declare.
No, none of those things. Nothing at all. ...'

There were taxis waiting outside. To the driver I said: 'Hôtel Crillon,
please,' and derived my third twinge of amusement from the slight air
of surprise with which he received the august address. Then he heaved
the old brown case in beside me; the car door slammed, the gears raced,
and we were off.

If there had been any strangeness left in me, it would have vanished
now. The taxi swung round into the main road with a screech of brakes,
skidded as a matter of course on the wet tarmac, and roared towards
Paris. I sat back in the familiar reek of Gauloises, disintegrating leather,
and stale exhaust, and the old world closed round me in a cloud of
forgotten impressions which seemed in a moment to blot out the last nine
years as if they had never been. The taxi was Pandora's box, and I had
not only lifted the lid, I was inside it. Those sweet, those stinging
memories ... things I had never before noticed, never missed, until now
I saw them unchanged, part and parcel of that life that stopped nine
years ago. ...

The driver had been reading a newspaper; it was thrust into a
compartment beside the dash. I could see the familiar black blurred print,
and the corner of an out-of-focus picture. A bus approached, its direction-
board already lit: SENLIS. I saw the crowd of girls and workmen standing
on the rear platform, crushed together and lurching with the movement
against rails and rope. And now the ugly suburbs were closing in; tall
houses with wrought-iron balconies and slatted shutters; hoardings with
their peeling posters, Bonbel, Sunil, Ancre Pils; shabby little tabacs with
their lights reflected orange and gold in the damp pavements; in a café-
bar, bright light on rows of glittering bottles and a huddle of metal tables
behind steamy glass; Dubo, Dubon, Dubonnet ... and there ahead of
us, down the long straight stretch of the Route de Flandre, Paris was
lighting up.

My eyelids stung suddenly, and I shut my eyes and leaned back against
the shabby upholstery. But still through the open window Paris met me,
assailed, bombarded me. The smell of coffee, cats, drains, wine and wet
air ... the hoarse voices shouting *France-Soir, Paris-Presse* ... someone
selling lottery tickets ... the police-whistles ... the scream of brakes.
Something was missing, I thought vaguely, something had changed ...
but it was only when the taxi swerved violently and I opened my eyes
to see it miss a pack of cyclists by inches that I realised what it was. He
wasn't using his horn; the incessant blare of Paris was gone. I found

myself looking about me all at once as if I were a stranger and this were a new town and a new experience.

Something inside me welcomed the change. Quite deliberately I turned my thoughts away from the easy path they were treading, and made myself think about the future. I was back in France; that much of the dream of the past nine years had come true. However prosaic or even dreary my new job might be, at least I had come back to the country I had persisted in regarding as my home. If I had deceived Madame de Valmy, I had done so under a pressure that was to me a necessity. Well, here I was. This was France. The lighted suburbs that were swimming past me were those of my home. Not very long now and we would be in the heart of Paris, thrusting our way down the confusion of the Rue Royale to shoot out into the great glittering spaces of Concorde, where the windows of the Crillon look out through the still-bare chestnut branches towards the Seine. Then tomorrow we would set off again, deeper into France, across her pastures and vineyards and hills and high alps till we reached the Château Valmy, perched above its forests by the little village of Soubirous in High Savoy. .... I could see it in my mind's eye now, as I had pictured it a hundred times since the journey started – the fairy-tale castle of a dream, something remote and romantic and impossible – a sort of Walt Disney advertisement for Gibbs Dentrifice. Of course it wouldn't be like that, but all the same. .... The taxi checked, then ground to a reluctant halt behind a stationary bus. I clutched my handbag tightly on my knee and leaned forward, staring out of the window. Now that I was here, even this tiny delay became suddenly intolerable. The bus moved a yard or so and pulled to the right. The taxi shot past with three centimetres to spare, did a quick in-and-out between two terrified pedestrians, and tore on its way. *Hurry.* ...

Suddenly, unbidden, verses were spinning in my brain.

Nine coaches waiting – hurry – hurry – hurry—But here, surely, the quotation was desperately inappropriate? What was it, anyhow? I racked my brain, remembering. ... Something about *the pleasures of the palace, secured ease and state ... banquets abroad by torchlight! music! sports! nine coaches waiting – hurry – hurry – hurry* ... some tempter's list of pleasures, it had been, designed to lure a lonely young female to a luxurious doom; yes, that was it, Vendice enticing the pure and idiotic Castiza to the Duke's bed. ... (*Ay, to the devil*). ... I grinned to myself as I placed it. Inappropriate, certainly. This particular young female was heading, I hoped, neither to luxury nor the devil, but merely to a new setting for the same old job she'd abandoned in England. Miss Linda Martin, nursery-governess to Philippe, Comte de Valmy, aged nine.

In a few minutes now I would be there. Madame de Valmy, silver and elegant and so upright in her chair that you thought a draught would sway her – Madame de Valmy would receive me. I abandoned fairy-tales, dragged a mirror from my bag, and began to tidy my hair, making myself recall, as if it were a lesson, what I could remember of my new employers.

Madame de Valmy, when I had talked to her in London, had not told me a great deal about the family I was to serve, but I had gathered the essentials of what seemed to have been a fairly complicated story. The old Comte de Valmy, Philippe's grandfather, had been enormously wealthy, and on his death the property had been divided between his three sons, the new Comte Étienne, Léon, and Hippolyte. To Étienne went the bulk of the fortune, the Château Valmy, and the Paris house; to Léon, among other things, a lovely little estate in Provence called Bellevigne, and to Hippolyte a large property on the edge of Lac Léman, a few kilometres below the Valmy estate. At the time of the old Comte's death the eldest son, Étienne, had not been married, and had been thankful when his brother Léon offered to stay on at Valmy and run the estate for him. Étienne preferred Paris, so to Paris he went, while Léon stayed on at Valmy and managed it, running his own Midi property from a distance. The younger brother, Hippolyte, who was (I gathered) an archaeologist of some standing, lived quietly at his house in Thonon-les-Bains, in between bouts of travelling and 'digging' abroad.

So things had gone on for some years. Then, long after anyone had ceased to expect him to do so, Étienne had married and within a couple of years Philippe had been born. The family had stayed on in Paris until, last year, when Philippe was almost nine years old, tragedy had struck at him even as it had struck at me. His parents had been killed together in an air crash on their way back from a holiday in Italy, and Philippe had left Paris to live with his uncle Hippolyte in Thonon. Hippolyte was still unmarried, 'but,' said Madame de Valmy to me, poised in that silver elegance of hers beside a Regency mirror in her sitting-room at Claridge's, 'but the child had seen a lot of him, and is very fond of him. Hippolyte – my brother-in-law – wouldn't hear of his coming to us at Valmy, even though, officially, Valmy is Philippe's home. ....' She smiled then, that remote sweet smile of hers that was about as cosy as an April moon, so that I thought I saw Hippolyte's point. I couldn't exactly picture the exquisite Héloïse in a romp with a nine-year-old boy. Philippe was certainly better off at the Villa Mireille with Uncle Hippolyte. Even an archaeologist, I thought, must be more approachable than Madame de Valmy. At least he would share the normal small boy's passion for grubbing in the mud.

But an archaeologist must occasionally grub to order. Philippe had been only a few months at the Villa Mireille when Monsieur Hippolyte had to fulfil an engagement which took him to Greece and Asia Minor for some months. The Villa Mireille was perforce shut up, and Philippe went up to Valmy to stay with his other aunt and uncle for the duration of Hippolyte's tour. And his Paris-bred Nanny, restless enough in the little town of Thonon, had struck at the prospect of perhaps half a year's sojourn in the remote Savoyard valley, and had removed herself, with tears and reproaches, back to Paris. . . .

So here was I. And it was curious that, in spite of the familiarity with which Paris invaded me, I didn't yet feel at home. I was a stranger, a foreigner, going to a strange house and a strange job. Perhaps loneliness was nothing to do with place or circumstance; perhaps it was in you, yourself. Perhaps, wherever you were, you took your little circle of loneliness with you. . . .

The taxi swerved across the Rue Riquet and swung right-handed into streets I knew. Away on the right I could see the dome of Sacré-Coeur sharp against the daffodil sky of evening. Somewhere below it, in the spangling blue dusk of Montmartre, was the Rue du Printemps.

On an impulse I leant forward, my hands tight on the clasp of my shabby handbag.

'Do you know the Rue du Printemps? It's off the Avenue Verchoix, Eighteenth Arrondissement. Take me there, please. I – I've changed my mind.'

I stood on the damp pavement outside the open door and looked up at Number 14, Rue du Printemps. The paint was peeling off the walls; the wrought-iron of the balconies, that I remembered as a bright turquoise, showed in this light as a patched and dirty grey. A shutter hung on one hinge beside the first-floor window. Monsieur Bécard's canaries had long since gone; there wasn't even a patch of darker colour on the wall where the cage had hung. The top balcony, our balcony, looked very small and high. There were pots of straggling geraniums arranged round its edge, and a striped towel hung over the railing to air.

How stupid to have come! How unutterably stupid to have come! It was like finding the glass empty when you lifted it to drink. I turned away.

Someone was coming down the stairs. I could hear the click of high-heeled shoes. I waited, perhaps still in some faint hope that it might be somebody I knew. It wasn't. It was a young woman, cheap and smart, with that tight-black-sweater-and-skirt smartness made to look very Place Vendôme with ropes of improbable pearls. She was blonde, and chewed gum. She eyed me with slight hostility as she crossed the lobby to the concierge's desk by the door and reached to the rack for a bundle of papers.

'You looking for someone?'

'No,' I said.

Her eyes went beyond me to my suitcase on the pavement. 'If you're wanting a room—'

'I wasn't,' I said, feeling suddenly foolish. 'I was just – I used to live hereabouts, and I thought I'd just like to look at the place. Is – is Madame Leclerc still here? She used to be the concierge.'

'She was my aunt. She's dead.'

'Oh. I'm sorry.'

She was leafing through the papers, still eyeing me. 'You look English.'

'I am English.'

'Oh? You don't sound it. But then I suppose if you lived here. . . . In this house, you mean? What name?'

'My father was Charles Martin. The poet Charles Martin.'

The blonde said: 'Before my time,' licked a pencil, and made a careful mark on one of the papers she held.

I said: 'Well, thanks very much. Good evening,' and went back to where my case stood on the pavement. I looked up the now darkening street for a taxi. There was one coming, and I lifted a hand, but as it came nearer I saw that it was engaged. A street-lamp shone into the back as it passed me. A middle-aged couple sat there, a whispy woman and a stoutish man in city clothes; two girls in their early teens sat on the drop-seats. All four were laden with parcels, and they were laughing.

The taxi had gone. The street was empty. Behind me I heard the blonde's footsteps receding up the stairs of Number 14. I glanced back over my shoulder once at the house, then turned back to the street to watch for another taxi. Neither house nor street looked even remotely familiar any more.

Quite suddenly I ceased to be sorry I had come. It was as if the past, till then so longed-after, so lived-over, had slipped off my shoulders like a burden. The future was still hidden, somewhere in the lights that made a yellow blur in the sky beyond the end of the dark street. Here between the two I waited, and for the first time saw both clearly. Because of Daddy and Maman and the Rue du Printemps I had made myself a stranger in England, not only bereaved, but miserably *dépaysée*, drifting with no clear aim, resenting the life I had been thrust into with such tragic brutality; I had refused to adapt myself to it and make myself a place there, behaving like the spoilt child who, because he cannot have the best cake, refuses to eat at all. I had waited for life to offer itself back to me on the old terms. Well, it wasn't going to. Because of my childhood I had rejected what England had for me, and now the Paris of my childhood had rejected me. Here, too, I had been dispossessed. And if I was ever to have a place, in whatever country – well, nobody ever wanted you anyway unless you damned well made them. And that was what I would have to do. I had my chance in front of me now, at the Château Valmy. As yet I knew nothing of the family but their names; soon those names would be people I knew, the people I lived with; the people to whom I would matter. . . . I said their names over slowly to myself, thinking about them: Héloïse de Valmy, elegant and remote with that chilly grace that would – surely – melt in time; Philippe de Valmy, my pupil, of whom I knew nothing except that he was nine years old and not very strong; his uncle, the acting master of the château, Léon de Valmy. . . .

And then a queer thing happened. Whether it was because now for the first time I said the name over to myself, coupled with the fact that I was standing in the street where a million unconscious memories must be stirring, I don't know; but now, as I said the name, some trick of the subconscious drew some of those memories together as a magnet draws pins into a pattern so that, clear, and till now unrecollected, I heard them speak. 'Léon de Valmy,' Maman was saying, and I think she was reading from a newspaper, 'Léon de Valmy. It says he's crippled. He's cracked his back at polo and they say if he recovers he'll be in a wheel-chair for the rest of his life.' Then Daddy's voice, indifferently: 'Oh? Well, I'm sorry to hear it, I suppose, though I can't help feeling it's a pity he didn't break his neck. He'd be no loss.' And when Maman said: '*Charles!*' he added impatiently: 'Why should I be a hypocrite about the man? You know I detest him.' And Maman said: 'I can't think why,' and Daddy laughed and said: 'No. You wouldn't. . . .'

The memory spun away into silence, leaving me tingling with something that might have been apprehension, wondering if I had really remembered it at all, or if it were some new trick of that romantic imagination of mine. A taxi had appeared and I must have signalled it because here it was swerving in towards the kerb with a screech of brakes. Once again I said: 'Hôtel Crillon, please,' and climbed in. The taxi moved off with a jerk, swung left out of the Rue du Printemps and accelerated down a dark shuttered street. The sound of the engine swelled and echoed back from the blind houses. *Nine coaches waiting, hurry, hurry, hurry. . . . Ay, to the devil . . . to the devil. . . .*

It wasn't apprehension, it was excitement. I laughed to myself, my spirits suddenly rocketing. To the devil or not, I was on my way. . . .

I rapped on the glass.

'*Hurry,*' I said.

Third Coach

CHAPTER TWO

This castle hath a pleasant seat; the air
Nimbly and sweetly recommends itself
Unto our gentle sense . . .

SHAKESPEARE: *Macbeth*

The raven himself is hoarse
That croaks the fatal entrance of Duncan
Under our battlements . . .

IBID

The little town of Thonon-les-Bains lies some twelve miles east of Geneva, on the southern shore of Lac Léman. Our plane had been met at Geneva by the big black Chevrolet from Valmy, which wafted us smoothly through the expensively-polished streets of Geneva, across the bridge at the end of the Lake, through gardens where magnolias already bloomed, and then turned east for the French border and Thonon.

Madame de Valmy had talked very little to me on the journey from Paris, for which I was grateful, not only because my eyes and mind were busy with new impressions, but because – although she had been kind and pleasant in the extreme – I could not yet feel quite at ease with her. There was that curious remoteness about her which made her difficult to approach, or even to assess. Conversation with her had an almost long-distance touch about it; far from feeling that she had come half-way to meet you, you found her suddenly abstracted, all contact withdrawn. I wondered at first whether she was deliberately keeping me at a distance, but when she had twice asked me a question, only to lose interest before I had answered, I decided that she had graver matters on her mind than Philippe's governess, and myself retired contentedly enough into silence.

The car was purring along through flat, densely-cultivated country. Everywhere were prosperous-looking farms, and tree-bordered fields where red-and-white cattle fed sleekly. To our left, through thickets of poplar and willow, the gleam of water showed and hid and showed again; on the right the country rolled green and gradual to wooded foothills, then swooped dramatically up to the great ranges of the Alps and the dazzle of the colossal snows. One of them, I supposed, was Mont Blanc itself, but this, I thought, stealing a glance at Héloïse de Valmy beside me, was not the time to ask.

She was sitting with shut eyes. I thought as I looked at her that I had been right. She looked both tired and preoccupied, though nothing, it seemed, could impair her rather chilly elegance. She was, I supposed, about fifty-five, and was still a beautiful woman, with the sort of beauty that age seems hardly to touch. Bone-deep, that was the phrase; it was in the shape of her head and temples and the thin-bridged, faintly aquiline nose with its fine nostrils; it was only at another glance that you saw the tiny wrinkles etching eyes and mouth. Her skin was pale and clear, and expertly tinted; her brows delicately drawn and arched with a faint arrogance above the closed lids. Her hair was sculptured silver. Only her mouth under the curve of its expensive rouge, and the hands which lay grey-gloved and still in her lap, were too thin for beauty. She looked expensive, a little fragile, and about as approachable as the moon.

I sat back in my corner. In front of me were the square shoulders of Madame's chauffeur. Beside him, equally square and correct, sat Madame's maid Albertine. If I – as the classic tales of governessing led me to expect – was to be insecurely poised between the salon and the servant's hall, at least I was now at what might be called the right end of the car. For which I was grateful, as I didn't much like what I had seen of Albertine.

She was a dark sallow-faced woman of perhaps forty-five, with a sullen, secretive expression and ugly hands. Although she had been most of the time about Madame de Valmy's rooms last night when I had been there, she had not once spoken to me and I had seen her watching me with a sort of stony resentment which had surprised me, but which I now realized was probably habitual and without meaning. She sat rigidly beside the chauffeur, gripping Madame's jewel-case tightly on her lap. Neither she nor the man spoke. Neither, as far as I could tell, was remotely aware of the other's presence. They seemed so admirably suited that I found myself wondering, quite without irony, if they were a married couple; (I found later that they were, in fact, brother and sister). Bernard, the chauffeur, had impeccable manners, but he, too, looked as if he never smiled, and he had the same dark-avised, almost resentful air as the woman. I hoped it wasn't a common Savoyard characteristic . . . I stole another look at Madame's still face. It didn't look as though, for gaiety, there was going to be much to choose between the drawing-room and the servants' hall. . . .

Well, after all, the schoolroom was to be my domain. I looked out of the window again, to wonder a little about Philippe, and more than a little about Léon de Valmy, the cripple, whom his wife had hardly mentioned, and of whom Daddy had said, indifferently: 'It's a pity he didn't break his neck.'

I hadn't noticed the road-barrier until the car slowed to a sliding halt, and two men in uniform emerged from a green-painted hut and came towards us.

Héloïse de Valmy opened her eyes and said in her cool high voice: 'This is the frontier, Miss Martin. Have your passport ready.'

The frontier-guards quite obviously knew the car. They greeted Madame de Valmy, flicked a casual glance across my passport, and I heard them joking with the chauffeur as he opened the boot for what was the briefest and most formal of glances at the luggage there.

Then we were moving again, across the strip of no-man's-land that divides the two countries, to pause once more for the same formalities at the French barrier.

Soon after this we reached Thonon, where our road turned south towards the mountains. The main part of the town lies fairly high above the Lake. As we climbed, the ground fell sharply away to the left, spilling a huddle of bright roofs and budding fruit-boughs down towards the belt of trees that bordered the water. Through the mist of still bare branches showed, here and there, the chimneys of some biggish houses. One of these – Madame de Valmy surprised me by rousing herself to point it out – was the Villa Mireille, where the third Valmy brother, Hippolyte, lived. I could just see its chimneys, smokeless among the enveloping trees. Beyond, mile upon glimmering mile, stretched Lac Léman, lazily rippling its silk under the afternoon sun. Here and there a slim sickle of white or scarlet sail cut the bright field of water, and clear on the distant shore I could see Montreux, etched in faint colours like a picture-book town against that eternally dramatic background of towering snows.

It was a warm afternoon, and the little town through which we drove was gay in the sun. Pollarded trees lined the streets, linking pleached branches where buds were already bursting into green. Shops had spilled their goods onto the pavements; racks of brightly printed dresses swung in the warm breeze; red and green peppers shone glossy among last season's withered apples; there was a pile of gaily-painted plant-pots and a small forest of garden tools in brilliant green. And at the edge of the pavement there were the flowers; tubs of tulips and freesias and the scarlet globes of ranunculus; box after box of polyanthus, vivid-eyed; daffodils, sharply yellow; the deep drowned-purple of pansies; irises with crown and fall of white and ivory and blue and deeper blue ... oh, beautiful! And all packed and jammed together, French-fashion, billowing and blazing with scent as thick as smoke in the sunlight.

I must have made some exclamation of pleasure as we slid past them and into the square, because I remember Madame de Valmy smiling a little and saying: 'Wait till you see Valmy in April.' Then we had swung to the right and the road was climbing again through a sparse tree-crowded suburb towards the hills.

Very soon, it seemed, we were in a narrow gorge where road, river, and railway, crossing and re-crossing one another in a fine confusion, plaited their way up between high cliffs hung with trees. After a few miles of this the railway vanished, tunnelling away on the right, not to reappear, but the river stayed with us to the left of the road, a rush of green-white water that wrestled down its boulder-strewn gully, now close beside us, now dropping far below as our road wound its way along the cliff under the hanging trees. The gorge was deep; the road was most of the time in shadow, only the higher trees netted the westering sun in branches where the faintest green-and-gold hinted at the spring. The cliffs closed in. Ugly grey bulges of some pudding-like stone showed here and there between the clouds of shadowed, March-bare trees. The road began to climb. Away below us the water arrowed loud and white between its boulders.

A grim little valley, I thought, and a dangerous road . . . and then we rounded the bend called Belle Surprise, and away in front of us, like a sunlit rent in a dark curtain, lay the meadows of Valmy.

'That's Soubirous,' said Madame de Valmy, 'there in the distance. You'll lose sight of it again in a moment when the road runs down into the trees.'

I craned forward to look. The village of Soubirous was set in a wide, green saucer of meadow and orchard serene among the cradling hills. I could see the needle-thin gleam of water, and the lines of willows where two streams threaded the grassland. Where they met stood the village, bright as a toy and sharply-focused in the clear air, with its three bridges and its little watch-making factory and its church of Sainte-Marie-des-Ponts with the sunlight glinting on the weathercock that tips the famous spire.

'And Valmy?' I said, as the car sailed downhill again and trees crowded thickly in on either side of the road. 'We must be near it now?'

'Those are the Valmy woods on your left. They stretch most of the way back to Thonon. The Merlon – that's the name of the river – marks the boundary between Valmy and Dieudonné, the estate to the right of the road. We cross the river soon and then' – she smiled faintly – 'you'll see Valmy.'

She spoke as usual in that cool flute-clear voice, with nothing ruffling the silvery surface. But I thought, suddenly, she's excited – no, perhaps nothing so strong as that, but there's anticipation there and something more . . . I had been wrong in my judgment of her a while back; in spite of the rather fragile urban charm, she loved this lonely valley, and came back with pleasure to it . . . I felt a little rush of warmth towards her, and said, impulsively: 'It's lovely, Madame de Valmy! It's a beautiful place!'

She smiled. 'Yes, isn't it? And you're lucky, Miss Martin, that spring has come early this year. It can be bleak and grim enough in winter, but it's always beautiful. At least, I think so. It has been my – our home for many years.'

I said impetuously: 'I shall love it here! I know I shall!'

The gloved hands moved in her lap. 'I hope you will, Miss Martin.'

The words were kind, but formally spoken, and the smile had gone. She was withdrawn again, cool and remote. She looked away from me. I might be at the right end of the car, but it seemed I must keep to my own side.

I threw her a doubtful little look that she didn't see, and turned again to my own window. And at that moment I saw the château.

We had been running for a little time along the bottom of the valley, with the Dieudonné plantations – tall firs with the sun and wind in their crests – on our right, and beyond the river the steep woods of Valmy, a wild forest where holly gleamed among oak and birch, and great beeches rose elephant-grey from a tangle of hawthorn and wild clematis. Above these banked and ravelled boughs hung a high plateau; and there, backed by more forest and the steep rise of another hill, stood the Château Valmy, its windows catching the sunlight. I had only a glimpse of it, just enough to show me that here was no romantic castle of turrets and pinnacles; here was the four-square classic grace of the eighteenth century, looking, however, wonderfully remote, and floating insubstantially enough up there in the light above the dark sea of trees. It also looked inaccessible, but I had barely time to wonder how it was approached when the car slowed, turned gently off the main road onto a beautiful little stone bridge that spanned the Merlon, swung again into a steep tunnel of trees, and took the hill with a rush.

The Valmy road was a zigzag, a steep, rather terrifying approach which the big car took in a series of smooth upward rushes, rather like the movement of a lift, swooping up through woodland, then open hillside, and running at last under the high boundary wall that marked the end of the château's formal garden. At the top was a gravel sweep as big as a small field. We swung effortlessly off the zigzag onto this, and came round in a magnificent curve to stop in front of the great north door.

The chauffeur had Madame de Valmy's door open and was helping her to alight. Albertine, without a glance or a word for me, busied herself with wraps and hand-luggage. I got out of the car and stood waiting, while my employer paused for a moment talking to Bernard in a low rapid French that I couldn't catch.

I did wonder for a moment if her instructions could have anything to do with me, because the man's little dark eyes kept flickering towards me almost as if he weren't attending to what his employer said. But it must only have been a natural interest in a newcomer, because presently he bent his head impassively enough and turned without a further glance at me to attend to the luggage.

Madame de Valmy turned to me then. 'Here we are,' she said unnecessarily, but with such grace that the cliché took on almost the quality of a welcome. She gave me her sweet, fleeting smile, and turned towards the house.

As I followed her I got only the most confused impression of the size and graciousness of the place – the great square façade with the sweep of steps up to the door, the archway on our left leading to courtyard and outbuildings, the sunny slope beyond these where orderly kitchen gardens climbed towards another tree-bounded horizon ... I saw these things only vaguely, without noticing. What met me with the rush almost of a wind was the sunlight and space and the music of the trees. Everywhere was the golden light of late afternoon. The air was cool and sweet and very pure, heady with the smell of pines and with the faint tang of the snows.

A far cry, certainly, from Camden Town.

I followed my employer up the wide flight of steps and past a bowing manservant into the hall of the château.

CHAPTER THREE

His form had not yet lost
All her original brightness, nor appeared
Less than Archangel ruin'd.

MILTON: *Paradise Lost*

My first thought was, he lied in every word,
That hoary cripple, with malicious eye
Askance to watch the working of his lie
On mine ...

BROWNING: *Childe Roland*

At first I did not see the woman who waited for us a few paces inside the great door.

The hall seemed immense, but this was mainly because it was very high and full of shadows. The floor was a chilly chessboard of black and white marble, from which, opposite the door, a staircase rose to a wide landing lit by a window whose five tall lancets poured the sun downwards in dazzling shafts. At the landing the staircase divided, lifting in twin graceful curves towards a gallery. So much I saw, but the light, falling steeply through the speartips of the high windows, threw all but the centre of the hall into deep shadow.

I was still blinking against the glare when I heard a voice greeting Madame de Valmy, and then a woman came towards us in welcome. I supposed she was the housekeeper. She was a stout body of sixty-odd, with a fat comfortable face and grey hair worn neatly in an old-fashioned bun. She was dressed in severe black, her only ornament – if it could be called that – being a pair of gold-rimmed pince-nez which stuck out of a pocket high on her bosom, and were secured by a chain to a plain gold pin. Her pleasant face, her plodding walk, her whole appearance were solid respectability personified. This was no secret dark Savoyard, at any rate.

She looked at me curiously as she greeted Madame de Valmy. She had a cheerful voice that sounded perpetually a little out of breath, and surprisingly, her French, though fluent, was atrociously bad.

Madame answered her greeting absently. In that merciless cascade of light the lines in her face showed up clearly. She said abruptly, her eyes sliding past the woman in black towards the dimmer background of the hall: 'The Master: he's well?'

'Oh yes, madame. He's been – oh, quite his old self the last few days, madame, if you'll forgive my saying so . . . interested in what's going on, the way he hasn't been for long enough, and full of plans. Oh, quite like old times, madame.'

She spoke with the ease of an old servant, and her face showed her very real pleasure in the good news she could give her employer. More pleasure, indeed, than Madame de Valmy's own face reflected. I thought I saw a shadow pass over it as she said: 'Plans?'

'Yes, madame. I don't rightly know what they are, myself, but he and Armand Lestocq were talking it over for long enough, and I do know there's extra hands busy in the garden, and a man came today to look round the place and give his estimate for the jobs the Master was talking about last winter. He's here now, as it happens, madame. He went up to take a look at the stonework on the west balcony, and I think the Master went with him. The Master's lift wasn't at the ground floor when Seddon made up the library fire.'

Madame de Valmy was pulling off her gloves with quick nervous movements. She said abruptly: 'Do you know if he has heard from Monsieur Hippolyte?'

'I think so, madame. There was a letter a week ago, on Tuesday . . . no, it was Wednesday; it was your letter came from London on Tuesday about the young lady.' She paused, puffing a little, and then nodded. 'That's right. The one from Athens came on the Wednesday, because I remember Armand Lestocq was up here that very day, and—'

'Very well, Mrs. Seddon, thank you.' Madame de Valmy might hardly have been listening. 'You said the Master was upstairs? Please send someone to tell him I'm here with Miss Martin.'

'I've already done that, madame. He most particularly asked to be told the minute you arrived.'

'Ah, thank you.' Madame de Valmy turned then towards me, still with those abrupt, slightly nervous movements, and spoke in English. 'Now, Mrs. Seddon, this is Miss Martin. I wrote to you about her when I informed the Master. Miss Martin, Mrs. Seddon is the housekeeper here. She is English, so you need not feel too much alone. Her husband is our butler, and he and Mrs. Seddon will do what they can to help you.'

'That we will,' said Mrs. Seddon warmly. She beamed at me and nodded, so that the gold chain on her bosom bobbed and glittered. 'You're very welcome, I'm sure.'

'Miss Martin's rooms are ready?'

'Oh, yes, madame, of course. I'll take her up now, shall I, and then show her round myself, seeing that perhaps she's a little strange?'

'Thank you, yes, if you will, but not straight away. She will come upstairs presently. Perhaps you will wait for her?'

'Of course, madame.' Mrs. Seddon nodded and beamed again, then retreated, puffing her way steadily up the stairs like a squat determined tug.

Madame de Valmy turned as if to speak to me, but I saw her eyes go past my shoulder, and her hands, which had been jerking her gloves between them, stilled themselves.

'Léon.'

I heard nothing. I turned quickly. Even then it was a second or so before I saw the shadow detach itself from the other shadows and slide forward.

Though I had known what to expect, instinctively my eye went too high, and then fell – again by instinct, shrinkingly – to the squat shape that shot forward, uncannily without sound, to a smooth halt six feet away.

Pity, repulsion, curiosity, the determination to show none of these ... whatever feeling struggled in me as I turned were swept aside like leaves before a blast of wind. The slightly dramatic quality of his entrance may have contributed to the effect; one moment a shadow, and the next moment silently there ... But, once there, Léon de Valmy was an object for no-one's pity; one saw simply a big, handsome, powerful man who from his wheel-chair managed without speaking a word to obliterate everybody else in the hall – this literally, for almost before the wheelchair stopped, the servants had melted unobtrusively away. Only Mrs. Seddon was still audible, steaming steadily up the right-hand branch of the staircase towards the gallery.

It was a tribute to Léon de Valmy's rather overwhelming personality that my own first impression had nothing to do with his crippled state; it was merely that this was the handsomest man I had ever seen. My experience, admittedly, had not been large, but in any company he would have been conspicuous. The years had only added to his extraordinary good looks, giving him the slightly haggard distinction of lined cheeks and grey hair that contrasted strikingly with dark eyes and black, strongly-marked brows. The beautifully-shaped mouth had that thin, almost cruel set to it that is sometimes placed there by pain. His hands looked soft, as if they were not used enough, and he was too pale. But for all that, this was no invalid; this was the master of the house, and the half of his body that was still alive was just twice as much so as anybody else's. . . .

He was smiling now as he greeted his wife and turned to me, and the smile lit his face attractively. There was no earthly reason why I should feel suddenly nervous, or why I should imagine that Héloïse de Valmy's voice as she introduced us was too taut and high, like an over-tight string.

I thought, watching her, she's afraid of him ... Then I told myself sharply not to be a fool. This was the result of Daddy's intriguing build-up and my own damned romantic imagination. Just because the man looked like Milton's ruined archangel and chose to appear in the hall like the Demon King through a trap-door, it didn't necessarily mean that I had to smell sulphur.

It was disconcerting to reach downwards to shake hands, but I hoped I hadn't shown it. My self-command, as it happened, was a mistake. He said gently: 'You were warned about me?' The dark eyes, with a question in them, slid to his wife standing beside me.

I felt rather than saw her small movement of dissent. A glance passed between them and his brows lifted. He was too quick by half. With a guilty memory of my own secret I said uncertainly: 'Warned?'

'About Lucifer's fall from heaven, Miss Martin.'

I felt my eyes widen in a stare. Was the man a thought-reader? And was he determined I should smell sulphur? Or ... did he really see himself as the thunder-scarred angel he quoted? Oddly, the last thought made him more human, more vulnerable.

Before I could speak he smiled again, charmingly. 'I'm sorry. I shouldn't have tried to be so cryptic. I was referring to the accident that, as you see. ...'

I said hastily and a bit too ingenuously: 'I know. I was only surprised because that's what I was thinking myself.'

'Was it indeed?' His laugh held a tiny note of self-mockery, but I thought he looked pleased. Then the laugh died and his eyes were on me, intent, appraising. I remembered perhaps rather late that I was a servant and this was my employer. I felt myself colour, and said quickly, almost at random: 'Someone told me about your accident – someone I met on the plane from London.'

'Oh? An acquaintance of ours, perhaps?'

'I think so. We talked. When I told her I was coming here she remembered having met you.'

'She?' said Héloïse de Valmy.

I said: 'I never knew her name. She was elderly, and I think she came from Lyons or somewhere like that. I don't remember.'

Léon de Valmy abandoned the catechism abruptly. 'Whoever it was, it's just as well she told you.' He hesitated a moment, looking down at his hands, then went on slowly: 'You must think this very odd of us, Miss Martin, but I believe my wife does not care to speak of my – deformity. Consequently it is apt to meet people with a shock. And I myself – even after twelve years – am absurdly sensitive of meeting new people and seeing it in their eyes. Perhaps both my wife and I are foolish about this ... Perhaps already you are condemning me as a neurotic ...

But it is a very human folly, Miss Martin. We all of us spend some of
our time pretending that something that *is*, is not – and we are not
grateful to those who break the dream.'

He looked up and his eyes met mine. 'One day, perhaps, it will cease
to matter.' He shrugged, and smiled a little wryly. 'But until then. . . .'

He had spoken quite without bitterness: only that small wryness
touched his voice. But the speech was so little what I would have expected
from him that I found myself, embarrassed and disarmed, shaken into
some stupid and impulsive reply.

I said quickly: 'No, please – you mustn't mind. Deformity's the wrong
word, and it's the last thing anybody'd notice about you anyway . . .
honestly it is.'

I stopped, appalled. From Linda Martin to Monsieur de Valmy the
words would have been bad enough. From the new governess to her
employer they were impossible. I didn't pause then to reflect that it was
the employer who had – deliberately, it seemed – called them up. I stood
biting my lip and wishing myself a thousand miles away. Through my
sharp discomfort I heard myself stammering: 'I – I'm sorry. I shouldn't
have said that . . . I only meant—'

'Thank you, my dear.' His voice was still grave, but I saw the
unmistakable flash of amusement in his eyes. Then he was saying easily:
'It seems, Héloïse, that your excessively silly friend Lady Benchley has
justified her existence at last in recommending Miss Martin to us. We
were indeed lucky to find you, Miss Martin, and we're delighted to
welcome you to Valmy. I hope we'll manage to make you feel at home.'
He paused. That gleam again. 'Not perhaps quite a felicitous expression.
Shall I say rather that I hope Valmy will become a home for you?'

I said rather stiffly: 'Thank you. You're very kind. I was happy to
have the chance to come, and I'll try my best to—'

'Endeavour to give satisfaction? That's the usual bromide, isn't it?
What are you staring at?'

'I'm sorry. It was impertinent of me. It was just – your English is so
frightfully good,' I said lamely. Damn the man; was I never to regain my
lost poise? I finished the sentence coldly – 'Sir.'

He laughed outright then, a quite delightful laugh that at once conceded
a point and abandoned the game, whatever it was. He began then to
inquire quite naturally, and very kindly about the journey and my
impressions of the valley; Madame de Valmy joined in, smiling, and
soon, under their renewed phrases of welcome, I found my embarrassment
relaxing into naturalness once again. More, into liking. The man's charm
was palpable, and he had taken the trouble to turn it on full blast . . .
and I was all the more vulnerable for being tired, lonely, and a bit
bewildered. By the time the three of us had talked for a few minutes
longer I was back on top of the world again with my shattered poise
restored and all the tensions and uneasinesses of the past half-hour
dismissed as figments. Monsieur and Madame de Valmy were a handsome

nd delightful couple and I was going to like them and love living at
almy and belonging even in this humble sort to a family again.

Sulphur? Poppycock.

But all the same, I reflected, it hadn't taken me long to see what had
een implied in that remembered snatch of conversation. '*You wouldn't,*'
)addy had said, and I saw what he meant. The man was damnably
ttractive, no doubt of that . . . and I used the adverb deliberately; it was
1e *mot juste*. And, charm or no, the faintest of resentments still pricked
1e. Léon de Valmy had played a game with me, and I hadn't liked it.
had been shaken into offering pity and comfort where none was
eeded . . . and he had been amused.

Nor did I attempt to explain, even to myself, why I had launched so
nerringly on that sea of lies about the elderly lady from Lyons, or how
knew I would never, never have the courage to tell Léon de Valmy that
spoke French even better than he spoke English, and had understood
erfectly well what he said to Héloïse when, at length dismissed, I had
one upstairs to meet Mrs. Seddon on the gallery landing.

He had said softly, and I knew he was staring after me: 'All the same,
Iéloïse, it is possible that you've made a very great mistake. . . .'

My rooms were lovelier than anything I had imagined, certainly than
ny I had ever been in. They had tall windows facing west, which gave
nto a balcony and the view across the valley.

This drew me straight away. I stood leaning on the stone balustrading
nd looking out over that incredible view. So high-perched we were that
seemed to be looking level at the crest of the Dieudonné forest beyond
1e Merlon; below, along the zigzag, the bare tree-tops moved like clouds.
`he balcony was afloat in a golden airy space. Soubirous, to the south,
linted like a jewel.

I turned. Mrs. Seddon had followed me to the window, and waited,
miling, plump hands clasped under plump bosom.

'It's – wonderful,' I said.

'It's a pretty place,' she said comfortably. 'Though some don't like the
ountry, of course. Myself, I've always lived in the country. Now I'll
how you the bedroom, if you'll come this way.'

I followed her across the pretty sitting-room to a door in the corner
pposite the fireplace.

'These rooms are built in a suite,' she said. 'All the main rooms open
nto this corridor, or the south one. You saw how the balcony runs the
vhole length of the house. These rooms at the end have been made into
he nursery suite, and they open out of one another as well. This is your
iedroom.'

It was, if possible, prettier than the sitting-room. I told her so, and she
poked pleased. She moved to a door I had not noticed, half-concealed as
t was in the ivory-and-gold panelling. 'That door's to the bathroom and

Master Philip's bedroom opens off it the other side. You share the bathroom with him. I hope you don't mind?'

At the Constance Butcher Home we had queued for baths. 'No,' said, 'I don't mind. It's beautifully up-to-date, isn't it? Baths behind the panelling. Did all the ghosts leave when the plumbing was put in, Mr Seddon?'

'I never heard tell of any,' said Mrs. Seddon, sedately. 'This was powder-closet in the old days; it runs the whole way between the two rooms. They made half of it into a bathroom and the other half's a little pantry with an electric stove for making nursery tea and Master Philip's chocolate at night.' I must have looked surprised, because she added 'This was always the schoolroom wing; the Master and his brothers were brought up here, you see, and then these alterations, with the electricity and all that, were done when Mr. Rowl was born.'

'Mr. . . . Raoul?' I queried.

'The Master's son. He lives at Bellyveen. That's the Master's place in the Midi.'

'Yes, I knew about that. I didn't know there was a son, though Madame de Valmy didn't – well, she didn't talk to me much. I know very little about the family.'

She gave me a shrewd look, and I thought she was going to make some comment, but all she said was: 'No? Ah well, you'll find everything out soon enough, I dare say. Mr. Rowl isn't Madame's son, you understand. The Master was married before. Mr. Rowl's mother died twenty-two years ago this spring, when he was eight. It's sixteen years ago now that the Master married again and you can't blame him at that. It's a big place to be alone in, as you may well imagine. Not that,' said Mrs. Seddon cheerfully, chugging across the room to twitch a curtain into place, 'the Master was ever one in those days for sitting alone in the house, if you take my meaning. Fair set Europe alight between them, him and his oldest brother, if all tales be true, but there, wild oats is wild oats, and the poor Master'll sow no more of them even if he wanted to, which I doubt he doesn't, and poor Mr. Étienne's dead, God rest him, and long past thinking of the world, the flesh and the devil, or so we'll hope. . . .' She turned to me again, a little out of breath with these remarkable confidences; it appeared that Mrs. Seddon, at any rate, didn't share Madame de Valmy's habit of reticence. 'And now would you like to see over the rest of the place, or will you wait till later? You'll be tired, I dare say.'

'I'll leave it till later, if I may.'

'It's as you wish.' Again the shrewd twinkling glance. 'Shall I send Berthe to unpack for you?'

'No, thank you.' That look meant that she knew quite well that wouldn't want a maid exploring my meagre suitcase. Far from resenting the thought, I was grateful for it. 'Where's the nursery?' I asked. 'Beyond Master Philip's bedroom?'

'No. His bedroom's the end one, then yours, then your sitting-room, then the nursery. Beyond that come Madam's rooms, and the Master's are round the corner above the library.'

'Oh, yes. He has a lift there, hasn't he?'

'That's so, miss. It was put in soon after the accident. That'd be, let's see, twelve years ago come June.'

'I was told about that. Were you here then, Mrs. Seddon?'

'Oh, yes, indeed I was.' She nodded at me with a certain complacency. 'I came here thirty-two years ago, miss, when the Master was first married.'

I sat down on the edge of the bed and looked at her with interest. 'Thirty-two years? That's a long time, Mrs. Seddon. Did you come with the first Madame de Valmy, then?'

'That I did. She was from Northumberland, the same as me.'

'Then she was English?' I said, surprised.

'Indeed, yes. She was a lovely girl, Miss Deborah. I'd been in service at her home ever since she was a little girl. She met the Master in Paris one spring, and they was engaged in a fortnight, just like that. Oh, very romantic it all was, very romantic. She said to me, she said: "Mary" – that's my name, miss – "Mary," she said, "you'll come with me, won't you? I won't feel so far from home then," she said.' Mrs. Seddon nodded at me, with an easy sentimental moistening of the eye. 'So, seeing as I was courting Arthur – that's Mr. Seddon – meself at the time, I married him and made him go along too. I couldn't let Miss Debbie adventure all by herself to foreign parts, like.'

'Of course not,' I said sympathetically, and Mrs. Seddon beamed, settling her arms together under the plump bosom, obviously ready to gossip for as long as I would listen. She gave the appearance of one indulging in a favourite pastime whose rules were almost forgotten. If I had been delighted to see her pleasant English face after the secret countenances of Albertine and Bernard, it was obvious that Mrs. Seddon had been equally pleased to see me. And the governess, of course, was not on the proscribed list: this could not be called Gossiping with the Servants. I supposed that, for me, Mrs. Seddon was hardly on the proscribed list either. At any rate I was going to gossip all I could.

I prompted her: 'And then when your Miss Debbie ... died, you didn't go back to England? What made you stay on, Mrs. Seddon?'

As to that, it seemed that she was not quite sure herself. Miss Debbie's father had died meanwhile and the house in England had been sold, while here at Valmy Mrs. Seddon and her husband had excellent jobs which 'the Master' seemed quite disposed to let them keep. .... I also gathered that Miss Debbie's interest had lifted them into positions which in another house they might never have filled; Seddon himself had been on my one sight of him impeccably polished, neutral and correct; Mrs. Seddon, too, had all the trappings of the competent and superior house-keeper; but her voice and some of her mannerisms had, gloriously defying gentility, remained the homely and genuine voice and ways of Mary Seddon, erstwhile second-gardener's daughter.

I listened to a long description of Miss Debbie, and others of Miss Debbie's home, father, pony, clothes, jewellery, wedding, wedding-presents and wedding-guests. When we appeared to be about to launch (via how much Miss Debbie's mother would have liked to be at the wedding if only she had been alive) on a description of Miss Debbie's mother's clothes, jewellery, wedding, and so on, as observed by Mrs. Seddon's mother – then I thought it was time to prod her gently back to foreign parts.

'And there was Miss Debbie's son, wasn't there? Of course you wanted to stay and look after him?'

'Mr. Rowl?' She primmed her lips a little. 'French nurses they had for him. Such a quiet little boy as he was, too – a bit like Master Philip here, very quiet and never a mite of bother. You'd never had thought—' But here she stopped, sighing a little wheezily, and shook her head. 'Eh, well, miss, he's half foreign, say what you will.'

There was all rural England in the condemnation. I waited, gravely expectant, but she merely added, maddeningly: 'But there, I never was one to gossip. And now, if you'll excuse me, I'll have to be getting about my work and leaving you to unpack. Now, miss, if there's anything you want you've only to ask me or Seddon and we'll do our best to help you.'

'Thank you very much. I'm awfully glad you're here, Mrs. Seddon.' I added naïvely.

She looked pleased. 'Well, now, that's very nice of you, miss, I'm sure. But you'll soon feel at home and pick things up. I couldn't speak a word of French when I came here first, and now I can talk it as fast as they can.'

'I heard you. It sounded wonderful.' I stood up and clicked back the locks of my suitcase. 'As you say, thirty years is a long time, especially when one's away from home. You didn't feel tempted to go back to England, say, when Monsieur de Valmy married again?'

'Oh, we talked of it, Seddon and I,' she said comfortably, 'but Seddon's that easy-going, and we liked the new Madam, and she was satisfied, so we stayed. Besides, I've had the asthma terrible bad since a girl, and, say what you like, none of these new-fangled things they give you, anti-hysterics and such-like, seem to do me any good. I used to get it terrible bad at home, but up here it cleared up something wonderful. It still comes now and again, but it soon goes off. It's the air. Wonderful healthy it is up here, and very dry.'

'It's certainly lovely.'

'And then,' said Mrs. Seddon, 'after the Master had his accident, she wouldn't hear of us going. He couldn't stand changes, you see.'

'I did gather that from what he said to me in the hall. Does he – does he have much pain, Mrs. Seddon?'

'Pain? No. But he has his days,' said Mrs. Seddon cryptically. 'And you can't blame him, the way things are.'

'No, of course not. He's bound to get depressed at times.'

'Depressed?' She looked at me blankly. 'The Master?'

I was still trying to equate the self-confessed 'neurotic' with the impression of easy and competent power that Léon de Valmy gave. 'Yes. Does he get sort of sorry for himself at times?'

She gave a sound suspiciously like a snort. 'Sorry for himself? Not him! Mind you, this last few years he's not been just as sweet-tempered as he might be, but he's all there, miss, you may be sure. He'd never be the one to give up because of a little thing like being crippled for life!'

'I think I can see that. In fact you never think of that when you talk to him.' (I didn't add 'unless he reminds you', but the thought persisted.)

'That's so.' She nodded at me again. 'And he forgets it himself, most times. What with that electric chair of his, and the lift, and the telephone to every corner of the place, and that there Bernard to be the legs of him, there's nothing he can't do. But now and then, just like *that*, something'll bring it home to him, and then. . . .'

I said, still thinking of the scene in the hall: 'What sort of thing?'

'Dear only knows. It might be a bad night, or a report coming in that something's gone wrong or been neglected in some place he can't get to himself to see to it, or something that needs doing and no money to do it with, or Mr. Rowl—' As before, she stopped abruptly.

I waited. She pulled unnecessarily at the chair-cover to straighten it. She said vaguely: 'Mr. Rowl runs the other estate for him, Bellyveen, in the Midi, and there's always trouble over money, and it upsets the Master, and besides . . . ah, well, he's not often here, which is as it should be, seeing he's the one that reminds the Master most often that he's a helpless cripple for all the powerful ways he has with him.'

I stirred. 'Reminds him? That's rather beastly.'

She looked shocked. 'Oh, not on purpose, you understand. I didn't mean that! It's only that he – well, Mr. Rowl might be the Master like he was twenty years ago, you see.'

'Oh, I see what you mean. He does all the things his father used to like doing. Polo, for instance?'

She shot me a surprised look. 'Did they tell you about that?'

'No. I heard it from someone who knew them – someone I met on the plane.'

'Oh, I see. Yes, that sort of thing. He could put his hand to anything, the Master.' She smiled reminiscently and a little sadly. 'Miss Debbie always did say he'd break his neck one day. He was such a one for sport – all sorts, motor-cars, horses, speed-boats . . . fighting with swords, even. He's got a shelf of silver cups for that alone.'

'Fencing?'

'That's it. But cars and horses were the chief thing. I've often thought he'd break his own neck and everyone else's, the way he'd come up that zigzag from the Valmy bridge. Sometimes,' added Mrs. Seddon surprisingly, 'you'd think a devil was driving him ... like as if he had to be able to do everything – *and* do it better than anybody else.'

Yes, I thought, I can believe that. And even crippled he has to be a crippled archangel. ...

I said: 'And now he has to sit and watch his son riding and driving and fencing—?'

'As to that,' said Mrs. Seddon, 'Mr. Rowl hasn't got the money ... which is just as well, or maybe he'd go the same way as his father. And like I said, he's not here very often anyway. He lives at Bellyveen. I've never been to Bellyveen myself, but I've heard tell it's very pretty.'

I said 'Oh?' with an expression of polite interest as she began to tell me about Bellevigne, but I wasn't really listening. I was reflecting that if Raoul de Valmy was really a younger copy of his father it was probably just as well he visited Valmy only rarely. I couldn't imagine two of Léon de Valmy settling at all comfortably under the same roof ... I stirred again. There was that same damned romantic imagination at work still. ... And what had I to go on, after all? A vague snatch of memory twelve years old, and the impression of an overwhelming personality in some odd way playing with me for its own amusement, for some reason concerned to give me a picture of itself that was not the truth. ...

It struck me then, for the first time, that there had been a notable omission from my welcome to the Château Valmy.

And that was the owner of all this magnificence, the most important of the Valmys, Monsieur le Comte, Philippe.

And now Mrs. Seddon was preparing to go about her own affairs.

She plodded firmly away to the door, only to hesitate there and turn. I bent over my case and began to lift things out onto the coverlet. I could feel her eyeing me.

She said: 'You ... the Master ... he seemed all right with you, did he? I thought I heard him laugh when I was waiting upstairs for you.'

I straightened up, my hands full of folded handkerchiefs. 'Perfectly all right, Mrs. Seddon. He was very pleasant.'

'Oh. That's good. I'd like to have been able to have a word with you first and warn you what like he sometimes was with strangers.'

I could well understand her slightly anxious probing. It was obvious that the emotional temperature, so to speak, of the Château Valmy, must depend very largely on Léon de Valmy and 'his days'.

I said cheerfully: 'Thanks very much, but don't worry, Mrs. Seddon. He was awfully nice to me and made me feel very welcome.'

'Did he now?' Her eyes were anxious and a little puzzled. 'Oh, well, that's all right, then. I know he was very pleased when Madam's letter came about you, but as a rule he hates changes in the house. That's why we were so surprised when Master Philip's Nanny was dismissed after

eing with the family all those years, and they said a new girl was coming
rom England.'

'Oh, yes, Madame de Valmy told me about her.' I put the handkerchiefs
own and lifted some underwear out of the suitcase. 'But she wasn't
lismissed, surely? I understood from Madame that she didn't want to
ive in the wilds at Valmy and, as Madame was in London at the time,
Monsieur de Valmy wrote urgently and asked her to find an English
:overness while she was there.'

'Oh, no.' Mrs. Seddon was downright. 'You must have misunderstood
vhat Madam said. Nanny was devoted to Master Philip, and I'm sure
he broke her heart when she had to go.'

'Oh? I was sure that Madame said she'd left because the place was
o lonely. I must have been mistaken.' I found myself shrugging my
houlders, and hastily abandoned that very Gallic gesture. 'Maybe she
vas just warning me what it would be like. But she did seem very
unxious to engage someone to teach him English.'

'Master Philip's English is excellent,' said Mrs. Seddon, rather primly.

I laughed and said: 'I'm glad to hear it. Well, whatever the case, I
uppose if Philippe's nine he's old enough to graduate from a Nanny to
a governess of sorts. I gathered from Monsieur de Valmy that that was
he idea. And for a start I'm going to try and remember to call the nursery
he "schoolroom". I'm sure one's too old for a nursery when one's nine.'

'Master Philip's very young for his age,' she said, 'though there's times
vhen he's too solemn for my liking. But there, you can't expect much
ifter what's happened, poor mite. He'll get over it in the end, but it takes
ime.'

'I know,' I said.

She eyed me for a moment and then said, tentatively: 'If I might ask
- do you remember your own folks, now?'

'Oh, yes.' I looked across the room and met the kindly inquisitive gaze.
air was fair, after all. She must be every bit as curious about me as I
vas about the Valmys. I said: 'I was fourteen when they were killed. In
un air accident, like Philippe's. I suppose Madame de Valmy told you
.'d been at an orphanage in England?'

'Indeed, yes. She wrote that she'd heard of you through a friend of
iers, a Lady Benchley, who comes up every year to Évian, and Lady
3enchley thought very highly of you, very highly.'

'That was very nice of her. Lady Benchley was one of the Governors
it the orphanage for the last three years I was there. Then when I left
.o be assistant at a boys' school it turned out she had a son there. She
:ame up to me on Visitors' Day and talked to me, and when I told her
I hated the place she asked me if I'd ever considered a private job abroad,
)ecause this friend of hers – Madame de Valmy – was looking for a
;overness for her nephew and had asked her if she knew of anyone from
he Home. When I heard the job was in France I jumped at it. I – I'd
ilways fancied living in France, somehow. I went straight up to London

next day and saw her. Lady Benchley had promised to telephone abou
me, and – well, I got the job.' I didn't add that Madame must have take
Lady Benchley's recommendation to be worth a good deal more than
actually was. Lady Benchley was a kindly scatterbrain who spent a goo
deal of her time acting as a sort of private labour-exchange between he
friends and the Constance Butcher Home, and I doubt if she had eve
known very much about me. And I had certainly got the impression tha
Madame de Valmy had been so anxious to find a suitable young woma
for the post during her short stay in London that she hadn't perhap
probed as far back into my history as she might have done. Not, of course
that it mattered.

I smiled at Mrs. Seddon, who was still eyeing me with that faintl
puzzled look. Then all at once she smiled back, and nodded, so that th
gold chain on her bosom glittered and swung. 'Well,' she said, 'well,' an
though she didn't actually add 'You'll do,' the implication was there. Sh
opened the door. 'And now I really will have to be going. Berthe'll b
up soon with some tea for you; she's the girl that looks after these room
and you'll find she's a good girl, though a bit what you might call flighty
I expect you'll make yourself understood to her all right, and Maste
Philip'll help.'

'I expect I shall,' I said. 'Where is Master Philip, Mrs. Seddon?'

'He's probably in the nursery,' said Mrs. Seddon, her hand on th
door. 'But Madam particularly said you weren't to bother with hir
tonight. You were to have a cup of tea – which I may say *is* tea, thoug
it took near thirty years to teach them how to make it – and settle yourse
in before dinner and you'll be seeing Master Philip tomorrow. But no
to bother yourself tonight.'

'Very well,' I said. 'Thank you, Mrs. Seddon. I shall look forward t
that tea.'

The door shut behind her. I could hear the soft plod of her steps alon
the corridor.

I stood where I was, looking at the door, and absently smoothing th
folds of a petticoat between my hands.

I was thinking two things. First that I was not supposed to have hear
Mrs. Seddon mentioning the lift in her conversation with Madame d
Valmy, and that if I was going to make mistakes as easily as that I ha
better confess quickly before any real damage was done.

The second thing was Mrs. Seddon's parting admonition: 'not to bothe
with him tonight.' Had that really been Héloïse de Valmy's phrase? 'No
to bother with him.' And he was 'probably' in the nursery. ... I laid th
petticoat gently in a drawer, then turned and walked out of my prett
bedroom, across the roses-and-ivory sitting-room, towards the schoolroo
door. There I hesitated a moment, listening. I could hear nothing.

I tapped gently on the door and then turned the gilded handle. I
opened smoothly.

I pushed it wide and walked in.

CHAPTER FOUR

O my prophetic soul!
My uncle!

SHAKESPEARE: *Hamlet*

My first thought was that he was not an attractive little boy.

He was small for his age, with a thin little neck supporting a round dark head. His hair was black, and cut very short, and his skin was sallow, almost waxen. His eyes were black, and very large, his wrists and knees bony and somehow pathetic. He was dressed in navy shorts and a striped jersey, and was lying on his stomach, reading a large book. He looked small and a little drab on the big luxurious rug.

He looked round in inquiry and then got slowly to his feet.

I said, in English: 'I'm Mademoiselle Martin. You must be Philippe.'

He nodded, looking shy. Then his breeding asserted itself, and he took a short step forward, holding out his hand. 'You are very welcome, Mademoiselle Martin.' His voice was small and thin like himself, and without much expression. 'I hope you will be happy at Valmy.'

It came to me again, sharply, as I shook the hand, that this was the owner of Valmy. The thought made him, oddly enough, seem even smaller, less significant.

'I was told that you might be busy,' I said, 'but I thought I'd better come straight along and see you.'

He considered this for a moment, taking me in with the frankly interested stare of a child. 'Are you really going to teach me English?'

'Yes.'

He said: 'You do not look like a governess.'

'Then I must try and look more like one, I suppose.'

'No, I like it as you are. Do not change.'

The de Valmys, it seemed, started young. I laughed. '*Merci du compliment, Monsieur le Comte.*'

He gave me a swift look upwards. There was glimmer in the black eyes. But all he said was: 'Do we have a lesson tomorrow?'

'I expect so. I don't know. I shall probably see your aunt tonight, and no doubt she'll tell me just what the programme is.'

'Have you seen – my uncle?' Was there, or was there not, the faintest of changes in that monotonous little voice?

'Yes.'

He was standing quite still, small hands dangling from their bony wrists in front of him. It came to me that he was in his own way as un-get-at-able as Héloïse de Valmy. My task here might not be a very easy one. His manners were beautiful; he was not, it was patent, going to be a 'difficult' child in the sense of the word as usually used by governesses;

but would I ever get to know him, ever get past that touch-me-not electric fence of reserve? That, and his unchildlike habit of stillness, I had already met in Madame de Valmy, but there the resemblance ended. Her stillness and remoteness was beautiful and poised; this child's was ungraceful and somehow disturbing.

I said: 'I must go and unpack now, or I'll be late for dinner. Would you like to help?'

He looked up quickly. 'Me?'

'Well, not help, exactly, but come and keep me company, and see what I've brought you from London.'

'You mean a present?'

'Of course.'

He flushed a slow and unbecoming scarlet. Without speaking, he walked sedately past me through my sitting-room towards my bedroom door, opened it for me, then followed me into the room. He stood at the foot of the bed, still in silence, staring at my case.

I stooped over it, lifted a few more things out onto the bed, then rummaged to find what I had brought.

'They're nothing very much,' I said, 'because I haven't much spare cash. But – well, here they are.'

I had brought him, from Woolworth's, a cardboard model of Windsor Castle – the kind that you cut out and assemble, together with a box, as big as I could afford, containing a collection of men in the uniform of the Grenadier Guards.

I looked a little uncertainly at the silent owner of the Château Valmy, and handed him the boxes.

He regarded the optimistic pictures on the lids.

'An English castle?' he said. 'And English soldiers?'

'Yes. The kind they have at Buckingham Palace.'

'With the fur hats, to guard the Queen. I know.' He was still looking raptly at a picture of a full regiment of Guards, drilling in an improbable fashion.

'They're – they're not much,' I said. 'You see—'

But I saw he was not listening. He had opened the lids and was fingering the cheap toys inside. 'A present from London,' he said, touching one crudely-painted toy soldier. It came to me, suddenly, that it would not have mattered if they had been home-made paper dolls.

I said: 'I brought you a game too, called Peggitty. You play it with these pegs. Later, I'll show you how. It's a good game.'

From the schoolroom a girl's voice called: '*Philippe? Où es-tu, Philippe?*'

He started. 'It's Berthe. I have to go.' He shut the boxes and stood up, holding them tightly to him. He said, very formally: 'Thank you. Thank you, mademoiselle.' Then he turned and ran to the door. '*Me voici, Berthe. Je viens.*' On the threshold he stopped and swung round. His face was still flushed, and he clutched the presents hard.

'Mademoiselle.'

'Yes, Philippe?'

'What is the name of the game with the pegs?'

'Peggitty.'

'Peg-it-ee. You will show me how to play it?'

'Yes.'

'You will play this Peg-it-ee when I have had my supper before I go to bed?'

'Yes.'

'Tonight?'

'Yes.'

He hesitated as if he were going to say something else. Then instead he went quickly out, and shut the door gently behind him.

However strange and luxurious my new surroundings, life at Valmy soon settled itself into a simple and orderly routine. Every morning Monsieur Bétemps, Philippe's tutor, arrived, and the two were closeted together till lunch-time. Once my various morning jobs about the school-room suite were finished I could count myself free, and for the first few days I occupied myself happily in exploring the gardens and the nearer woods, or in reading – hours and hours of reading, a luxury so long denied me at the Home that I still felt guilty whenever I indulged in it.

The library at the château almost certainly contained English books, but since it was Léon de Valmy's private study-cum-office, I could not – or would not – ask permission to use it. But I had brought as many of my own books as I could carry, and in the schoolroom there were shelves to the ceiling full of an excellent miscellany – children's books thrust cheek by jowl with English and French classics and a good deal of lighter reading. I wondered a little at the odd collection until I saw in some of the volumes the name *Deborah Bohun*, or the message '*To Debbie*', and once I took down a battered old copy of *Treasure Island* to find it inscribed in a flamboyant young hand *Raoul Philippe St. Aubin de Valmy* . . . of course, Léon's son was half English and had used these very rooms. I found Buchan, too, and Conan Doyle, and a host of forgotten or never-known books that, gratefully, I devoured – forcing myself to ignore the irrational feeling drilled into me in the seven years at the Home that Reading was a Waste of Time.

On one occasion my guilty feeling was justified. When I read French, I read it in secrecy, and once I was nearly caught out over *Tristan et Iseut*. I was devouring it, rapt and oblivious in my bedroom, when Berthe knocked and, receiving no reply, came in to dust the room. She noticed nothing, but I cursed myself and vowed yet again to be careful and wished for the hundredth time that I had never embarked on the silly deception that had seemed at the time to matter so much, and became daily more difficult to confess.

I no longer imagined seriously that anyone would mind; Philippe and

I got on well together, and Madame de Valmy, in her aloof way, seemed to like me; I was certainly very completely trusted with Philippe's well-being. But I didn't particularly want her to know that I had deceived her – systematically, as it were, schemed to deceive her. And, as with all deceptions, the thing grew bigger daily. I had to make myself understood to Berthe, the schoolroom maid, and did this in elementary schoolgirl French which amused her and even made Philippe smile. Luckily, I never had to do this with my employers; invariably in my presence they spoke in their flawless and seemingly effortless English. And so the days went by and I said nothing. I dared not risk their displeasure; I loved the place, I could easily cope with the job, and I liked Philippe.

He was a very quiet, self-controlled child, who never chattered. Every afternoon, unless it rained too hard, we went for a walk, and our 'English conversation' mainly consisted of my comments on the country or the gardens where we took our walks. That electric fence of his was still up: it was not a consciously-erected barrier – the gift of the toys had won his alliance if not his heart – but it was there, the obstruction of a deep natural reserve. I imagined that his naturally undemonstrative nature had been made even more so by the sudden loss of his parents, to whom he had never referred. This was not a child one could readily 'get to know'. I soon stopped trying, and kept both his and my own attention on things outside ourselves. If I was ever to win his confidence, it would only be done by very gradual and natural degrees: by custom, as it were. And there was, indeed, no reason why I should push my way into his fenced and private world; I had suffered so much from lack of privacy in the Home that I deeply respected anybody's right to it, and would have looked on any attempt at intimacy with Phillipe as a kind of mental violation.

His reserve showed itself not only towards me. Each evening, at half-past-five, I took him down for half an hour to the small salon where his aunt sat. She would politely put aside her book or writing-paper, pick up instead her exquisite and interminable *petit-point*, and hold conversation with Philippe for the half-hour. I say 'hold conversation' advisedly, because that phrase does perfectly imply the difficult and stilted communication that took place. Philippe was his usual quiet and withdrawn self, answering questions readily and with impeccable politeness, but asking none and volunteering nothing. Madame de Valmy was the one, it seemed to me, who had to violate her personality here: she, also naturally withdrawn, had to unbend, almost to chatter.

I suppose, though, that it was I who loathed those half-hours most, and who suffered the most. Madame de Valmy and Philippe talked, naturally, in French, and this exchange I was supposed not to understand. But occasionally she would revert to English, either for my benefit or to test my pupil's knowledge of that tongue, and then I was drawn into the conversation, and had the awkward task of betraying no knowledge of the exchange in French to which I had just been listening. I don't remember if I made any mistakes; she certainly appeared to notice none, but then, she never gave the appearance of more than the most superficial attention to the whole routine; it was, for her, the discharge of a duty to a charge she hardly knew. Madame de Valmy, certainly, could not be accused of trying to violate anybody's confidence.

Her husband was never there. His only meetings with Philippe seemed to be the purely chance ones of encounters in corridors, on the terrace, or in the gardens. At first I found myself blaming Philippe's uncle for his lack of interest in a lonely and recently-bereaved little boy, but soon I realized that it wasn't entirely Léon de Valmy's fault. Philippe systematically avoided him. He would only go down the library corridor with me when we had seen the wheel-chair safely out beyond the ornamental ponds or at the far side of the rosery; he seemed to have the faculty for hearing the whisper of its wheels two corridors away, when he would invariably drag at my hand, persuading me with him to vanish out of his uncle's sight.

There seemed to be no good reason for this steady aversion; on the two or three occasions during my first week when we did, unavoidably, meet Monsieur de Valmy, he was very nice to Philippe. But Philippe was, if possible, more withdrawn than ever; in front of his uncle the child's reserve appeared to be little more than the sulks. This was natural enough in a way; in Léon de Valmy's overwhelming presence anyone as awkward and unattractive as Philippe was bound to be made to feel doubly so, and, consciously or not, to resent it. Moreover his uncle's tone towards him was kind with the semi-indifferent indulgence he might have accorded to a not-very-favourite puppy. I could never make out whether Philippe noticed or resented this; I know that on one or two occasions I found myself resenting it on his behalf. But I still liked Léon de Valmy; Philippe, on the other hand – and this I came only gradually to realize – disliked his uncle very much indeed.

That this was irrational I tried on one occasion to tell him.

'Philippe, why do you avoid your Uncle Léon?'

The stone-wall expression shut down on his face. *"Ne comprends pas."*

'English, please. And you do understand quite well. He's very good to you. You have everything you want, don't you?'

'Yes. Everything I want I have.'

'Well, then—'

He gave me one of his quick, unreadable looks. 'But he does not give it to me.'

'Who then? Your Aunt Héloïse?'

He shook his head. 'It is not theirs to give to me. It was my father's and it is mine.'

I looked at him. This, then, was it. Valmy. I remembered the little gleam in the black eyes when I had laughingly addressed him as Comte de Valmy. This was another thing at which it seemed the de Valmys started young. 'Your land?' I said. 'Of course it's yours. He's keeping it for you. He's your trustee, isn't he?'

He looked puzzled. 'Trustee? I do not know trustee.'

'He takes care of Valmy till you are older. Then you have it.'

'Yes, until I am fifteen. Is that trustee? Then my Uncle Hippolyte is also trustee.'

'Is he? I didn't know that.'

He nodded, with that solemn look that sat almost sullenly on his pale little face. 'Yes. *Tous les deux* – both. My Uncle Léon for the property and my Uncle Hippolyte for me.'

'What do you mean?' I asked involuntarily.

The gleam in the look he shot me might have been malice or only mischief. 'I heard papa say that. He said—'

'Philippe,' I began, but he wasn't listening. He was wrestling with a translation of what Papa had said, only to abandon it and quote in French in a rush that spoke of a literal and all-too-vivid memory:

'He said "Léon'll keep the place going, trust him for that. God help Valmy if it was left to Hippolyte." And Maman said "But Hippolyte must have the child if anything happens to us. Hippolyte must look after the child. He is not to be left to Léon." That's what Maman—' He stopped, shutting his lips tightly over the word.

I said nothing.

He slanted that look at me again and said in English: 'That is what they said. It means—'

'No, Philippe, don't try and translate,' I said gently, 'I don't suppose you were meant to hear it.'

'N – no. But I wish I had not had to leave my Uncle Hippolyte.'

'You're fond of him?'

'Of course. He has gone to *la Grèce*. I wanted to go with him but he could not take me.'

'He'll come back soon.'

'Yes, but it is a long time.'

'It'll pass,' I said, 'and meanwhile I'll look after you for him, and your Uncle Léon'll look after Valmy.'

I paused and looked at the uncommunicative little face. I didn't want to sound pompous or to alienate Philippe, but I was after all in charge of his manners. I said, tentatively: 'He does it very well, Philippe. Valmy is beautiful, and he cares for it, *ça se voit*. You mustn't be ungrateful.'

It was true that Philippe had no cause to complain of his uncle's stewardship. Léon seemed to me to spend his whole time, indeed, his whole self, on the place. It was as if the immense virility that was physically denied its outlet was redirected onto Valmy. Day after day the wheel-chair patrolled the terraces and the gravel of the formal gardens, the conservatories, the kitchen gardens, the garages . . . everywhere the chair could possibly go it went. And in the château itself the hand of a careful master was everywhere apparent. No plan was too large, no detail too small, for Léon de Valmy's absorbed attention.

It was also true that, as Comte de Valmy, Philippe might legitimately claim that he was a cypher in his own house, but he was only nine, and moreover a Paris-bred stranger. His uncle and aunt did ignore him to a large extent, but his daily routine with its small disciplines and lack of what one might call cosy family life was very much the usual one for a boy in his position.

I added, rather lamely? 'You couldn't have a better trustee.'

Phillipe shot me one of his looks. The shutters were up in his face again. He said politely and distantly: 'No, mademoiselle,' and looked away.

I said no more, feeling myself unable to deal with what still seemed an unreasonable dislike.

But one day towards the end of my second week at Valmy the situation was, so to speak, thrust on me.

Philippe and I had, as usual, been down for our five-thirty visit to Madame de Valmy in the small salon. Punctually at six she dismissed us, but as we went she called me back for some reason that I now forget. Philippe didn't wait, but escaped without ceremony into the corridor.

A minute or so later I left the salon, to walk straight into as nasty a little scene as I had yet come across.

Philippe was standing, the picture of guilt and misery, beside a table which stood against the wall outside the salon door. It was a lovely little table, flanked on either side by a Louis Quinze chair seated with straw-coloured brocade. On one of the chair-seats I now saw, horribly, a thick streak of ink, as if a pen had rolled from the table and then across the silk of the chair, smearing ink as it went.

I remembered, then, that Philippe had been writing to his uncle Hippolyte when I called him to come downstairs. He must have come hurriedly away, the pen still open in his hand, and have put it down there before going into the drawing-room. He was clutching it now in an ink-stained fist, and staring white-faced at his uncle.

For this time of all times he hadn't managed to avoid Monsieur de Valmy. The wheel-chair was slap in the middle of the corridor, barring escape. Philippe, in front of it, looked very small and guilty and defenceless.

Neither of them appeared to notice me. Léon de Valmy was speaking. That he was angry was obvious, and it looked as if he had every right to be, but the cold lash of his voice as he flayed the child for his small-boy carelessness was frightening; he was using – not a wheel, but an atomic blast, to break a butterfly.

Philippe, as white as ashes now, stammered something that might have been an apology, but merely sounded like a terrified mutter, and his uncle cut across it in that voice that bit like a loaded whip.

'It is, perhaps, just as well that your visits to this part of the house are restricted to this single one a day, as apparently you don't yet know how to behave like a civilized human being. Perhaps in your Paris home you were allowed to run wild in this hooligan manner, but here we are accustomed to—'

'This is my home,' said Philippe.

He said it still in that small shaken voice that held the suggestion of a sullen mutter. It stopped Léon de Valmy in full tirade. For a moment I thought the sentence in that still little voice unbearably pathetic, and in the same moment wondered at Philippe, who was not prone to either drama or pathos. But then he added, still low, but very clearly: 'And this is my chair.'

There was a moment of appalling silence. Something came and went in Léon de Valmy's face – the merest flick of an expression like a flash of a camera's shutter – but Philippe took a step backwards, and I found myself catapulting out of the doorway like a wildcat defending a kitten.

Léon de Valmy looked up and saw me, but he spoke to Philippe quietly, as though his anger had never been.

'When you have recovered your temper and your manners, Philippe, you will apologise for that remark.' The dark eyes lifted to me, and he said coolly but very courteously, in English: 'Ah, Miss Martin. I'm afraid there has been a slight contretemps. Perhaps you will take Philippe back to his own rooms and persuade him that courtesy towards his elders is one of the qualities that is expected of a gentleman.'

As his uncle spoke to me, Philippe had turned quickly, as if in relief. His face was paler than ever, and looked pinched and sullen. But the eyes were vulnerable: child's eyes.

I looked at him, then past him at his uncle.

'There's no need,' I said. 'He'll apologise now.' I took the boy gently by the shoulders and turned him back to face his uncle. I held him for a moment. The shoulders felt very thin and tense. He was shaking.

I let him go. 'Philippe?' I said.

He said, his voice thin with a gulp in it? 'I beg your pardon if I was rude.'

Léon de Valmy looked from him to me and back again.

'Very well. That is forgotten. And now Miss Martin had better take you upstairs.'

The child turned quickly to go, but I hesitated. I said: 'I gather there's been an accident to that chair, and that Philippe's been careless; but then, so have I. It was my job to see that nothing of the sort happened. It was my fault, and I must apologise too, Monsieur de Valmy.'

He said in a voice quite different from the one with which he had dismissed Philippe: 'Very well, Miss Martin. Thank you. And now we will forget the episode, shall we?'

As we went I was very conscious of that still, misshapen figure sitting there watching us.

I shut the schoolroom door behind me, and leaned against it. Philippe and I looked at one another. His face was shuttered still with that white resentment. His mouth looked sulky, but I saw the lower lip tremble a little.

He waited, saying nothing.

This was where I had to uphold authority. Curtain lecture by Miss Martin. Léon de Valmy had been perfectly right: Philippe had been stupid, careless, and rude. . . .

I said: 'My lamb, I'm with you all the way, but you are a little owl, aren't you?'

'You can't,' said Philippe, very stiffly, 'be a lamb and an owl both at the same time.'

Then he ran straight at me and burst into tears.

After that I did help to keep him out of his uncle's way.

CHAPTER FIVE

Ay, now the plot thickens very much upon us.
BUCKINGHAM: *The Rehearsal*

The spring weather continued marvellous. There was still snow on the nearer hills, and the far high peaks that unrolled below the clouds were great dazzling beds of white as yet untouched by the spring. But the valley was green, and yet greener; the violets were out along the ditches, and all the urns and stone tubs that lined the château terraces held their constellations of narcissus and jonquil that danced with the wind.

Philippe and I went out every afternoon, coated and scarved against the breeze that blew off the snow. The mountain air seemed to be doing him good; colour came into the sallow cheeks: he even, occasionally, laughed and ran a little, though for the most part he walked stolidly at my side, and answered in his slow but excellent English my dutiful attempts at conversation.

One of our walks was a steep but easy track down through the meadows towards the village. At the foot of the slope a narrow wooden bridge crossed the Merlon, deep here and placid in its wandering from one wide and gleaming pool to the next. From the bridge the track led straight through water-meadows and budding orchards to the village.

On the occasions when it was known that our walk would take us to Soubirous, we were given small commissions to execute there, usually for Mrs. Seddon or Berthe, and sometimes for Albertine, but occasionally for Madame de Valmy herself.

One morning – it was the first of April – Philippe and I set out for the village soon after breakfast. It was Monday, and as a rule on Monday morning Monsieur St. Aubray, the curé of Soubirous, came up to the château to instruct the young Comte in Latin, Greek and the Roman Catholic religion. But M. le Curé had twisted an ankle, and, since it did not seem desirable for Philippe to miss his instruction, I took him down to the presbytery beside the church and left him there.

It was the first time I had been on my own in the village, with time to spare. I stood in the little square outside the church and looked about me.

The day was warm, the sunlight as it beat up from flags and cobbles was bright and almost hot. There was a white cat sunning itself on top of a low wall below which someone had planted primulas. The single *bistro* had put out its red-and-black striped awning, and in spite of faded paint and peeling walls the houses looked gay with their open doors and the coloured shutters fastened back from the windows. A canary, in a small cage hanging outside a shop, sang lustily. Some small children, black-haired and brown-limbed, were intent on something in a gutter. Outside a food-shop cabbage and cheeses and tired-looking oranges made a splash of colour. A boy on a bicycle shot past me, with a yard or so of bread under one arm.

It was a pleasant, peaceful, light-hearted little scene, and my own heart was light as I surveyed it. It was a lovely morning; I was free to do as I wished with it for two hours; I had some money in my pocket; the shadow of the Constance Butcher Home for Girls dwindled and shrank to nothing in the warm Savoyard light. It was also – as a stray warm breeze stirred fragrance from the primulas and brought a shower of early cherry-blossom floating out over the presbytery wall – it was also spring.

I walked slowly across the square, made sure that it was only marbles, and not a frog or a kitten, that was occupying the children in the gutter, then turned into the pharmacy beside the *bistro* to carry out what commissions I had for the day.

'Madamoiselle Martin?' The apothecary came out of his dark cave at the back. He knew me well by this time. Mrs. Seddon, in the intervals of anti-histamine, seemed to live exclusively on aspirin and something she called Oh Dick Alone, while I (after half a lifetime of White Windsor) had developed a passion, which had to be satisfied frequently, for the more exotic soaps.

I said gaily, in my most English French: 'Oh, good morning, Monsieur Garcin. It is a fine day, is it not? It was a fine day yesterday. It will be a fine day tomorrow. Not? I am looking at the soaps, as usual.'

I said *par usuel*, and the chemist's thin lips pursed. It was his weekly pleasure to correct my French, always with that pained, crab-apple face, and I didn't see why I should deny him anything.

'*Comme d'habitude,*' he said sourly.

'*Plaît-il?*' I said, very fluently. He had taught me that one last week.

'*Comme d'habitude,*' said Monsieur Garcin, raising his voice as to the slightly deaf.

'*Comme quoi?* I do not understand,' I said carefully. I was behaving badly and I knew it, but it was a heavenly day and it was spring, and

Monsieur Garcin was prim and dry and a bit musty, like herbs that have been kept too long, and besides, he always tried to put me in what he thought was my place. I raised my voice, too, and repeated loudly: 'I said I was looking at the soaps, *par usuel.*'

The chemist's thin nose twitched, but he restrained himself with an effort. He looked at me dourly across a pile of laxatives. 'So I see. And which do you want?' He heaved up a box of Roger and Gallet from behind the counter. 'There is a new box this week. Rose, violet, cologne, sandalwood, clove pink—'

'Oh, yes, please. The clove pink. I love that.'

A slight gleam of surprise showed in the oyster-like eyes. 'You know what flower that is? *Oeillet mignardise?*'

I said composedly: 'The name is on the soap. With a picture. *Voilà.*' I reached across to pick the tablet out, sniffed it, smiled at him, and said kindly: '*C'est le plus bon, ça.*'

He rose to that one. '*Le meilleur.*'

'*Le meilleur,*' I said meekly. 'Thank you, monsieur.'

'You are doing quite well,' said Monsieur Garcin, magnanimously. 'And have you any little commissions for your employers today?'

'Yes, if you please. Madame de Valmy asked me to get her medicine and the tablets – her pills for sleeping.'

'Very well. Have you the paper?'

'Paper?'

'You must give me the paper, you understand.'

I puckered my brows, trying to remember if Albertine had given me a prescription along with the shopping-list. The chemist made a movement of ill-concealed impatience, and his mouth drew up and thinned till it disappeared. He repeated very slowly, as to an imbecile: 'You - must - have - a paper - from - the - doctor.'

'Oh,' I said evilly, 'A prescription? Why didn't you say so? Well, she didn't give me one, monsieur. May I bring it along next year?'

'Next *year?*'

'I mean next week.'

No,' he said curtly. 'I cannot give you the drugs without the prescription.'

I was already regretting having teased him. I said distressfully: 'Oh, but Madame asked specially for the medicine. I'll bring the paper as soon as I can, or send it or something, honestly I will! Please, Monsieur Garcin, can't you trust me for a day or two?'

'Impossible. No.' His bony fingers were rearranging the tablets of soap. 'And what else do you want?'

I glanced down at the list in my hand. There were various things on it, listed – luckily for Monsieur Garcin's patience and my own ingenuity – in French. I read them out to him carefully: someone wanted tooth-powder and Dop shampoo: someone else (I hoped it was the sour-faced Albertine) demanded corn-plasters and iodine, and so on to the end, where came the inevitable aspirin, eau-de-cologne, and what Mrs. Seddon simply listed as 'my bottle'.

'And Mrs. Seddon's pills,' I said finally.

The chemist picked up the packet of aspirin.

'No,' I said, 'the others.' (I wouldn't know the word for asthma, would I? And I genuinely didn't know the word for anti-histamine.) 'The pills for her chest.'

'You got them last week,' said Monsieur Garcin.

'I don't think so.'

'I know you did.'

His voice was curt to rudeness, but I ignored it. 'Perhaps,' I said politely, 'she has need of more?'

'She cannot have, if she got them last week.'

'Are you so sure she did, monsieur? She put them herself on the list today.'

'Did she give you the paper – the prescription?'

'No,' I said.

He said impatiently: 'I told you she got them last week. You took them yourself. You were in a hurry and you handed me a list with a prescription for Madame Sed-don. I sent the tablets. Perhaps you forgot to give them to her. I have an excellent memory, me; and I remember handing them to you. Moreover, I have a record.'

'I am sorry, monsieur. I just don't remember. No doubt you're right. I thought – oh, just a minute, here's a paper in my bag! Here it is, monsieur, the prescription! *Voyez-vous.* Is this it?'

I handed him the paper, carefully keeping anything of I-told-you-so out of my voice. Which was just as well, because he said tartly: 'This is not for Madame Sed-don. It is the paper for Madame de Valmy's heart-medicine.'

'Oh? I hadn't realized I had it. It must have been with the list. I came out in a hurry and didn't notice. I'm so sorry.' I smiled winningly at him. 'Then you can give me the medicine after all, monsieur. I'll get the tablets in Thonon on Friday.'

He shot me a queer look out of those oyster eyes, and then, by way of teaching me (I suppose) that servants shouldn't argue with their betters, he proceeded to put on his spectacles and read the prescription through with exaggerated care. I watched the sunlight beyond the doorway and waited, suppressing my irritation. He read it again. You'd have thought I was Madeleine Smith asking casually for half a pound of arsenic. Suddenly I saw the joke and laughed at him.

'It's all right, monsieur. It's quite safe to let me have it. I'll see I deliver it promptly where it belongs! I don't often eat digitalis, or whatever it is, myself!'

He said sourly: 'I don't suppose you do.' He folded the paper carefully and pushed my purchases towards me. 'There you are then. I'll give you the drops, and perhaps you will also see that Madame Seddon gets the tablets I sent up on Wednesday?' As I gathered the things up without replying I saw him throw me that queer, quick look yet again. 'And I must congratulate you on the way your French has improved, made moiselle,' he added, very dryly.

'Why, thank you, monsieur,' I said coolly. 'I try very hard and study every day. In another three weeks you won't even guess that I'm English.'

'*Anglaise?*' The word was echoed, in a man's voice, just behind me. I looked round, startled. I had heard nobody come in, but now realised that a newcomer's large body was blocking the door of the pharmacy, while his enormous shadow, thrown before him by the morning sun, seemed to fill the shop. He came forward. 'Excuse me, but I heard you say "*Je suis anglaise*". Are you really English?'

'Yes.'

'Oh, I – that *is* a relief!' He looked down at me half-shyly. Seen properly now, and not just as a colossal silhouette framed in the shop door, he still appeared a very large young man. He was dressed in khaki shorts and a wind-cheater. His head was bare, and covered with an untidy thatch of fair hair, very fine and thick. His eyes were blue in a tanned face. His hands and legs were tanned, too, and on them in the sunlight the fair hair glinted, pale as barley in September.

He groped in an inner pocket and produced a tattered old envelope. 'I wonder – could you possibly help me, d'you think? I've got a whole list of stuff to get, and I was wondering how on earth to ask for it. My French is non-existent, and yours seems terribly good—'

I said firmly: 'My French may sound wonderful to you, but it sounds like nothing on earth to Monsieur Garcin.'

I sent a bright smile to the chemist, who still watched me, sourly, from behind the stack of laxatives. No response. I gave it up and turned back to the Englishman, who was saying, unconvinced: 'It seems to get results anyway.' He gestured towards my purchases.

I grinned. 'You'd be surprised what a fight it is sometimes. But of course I'll help – if I can. May I see your list?'

He surrendered it relievedly. 'This is awfully good of you to let me bother you.' He gave his disarmingly shy grin. 'Usually I just have to beat my breast like Tarzan and point.'

'You must be very brave to come holidaying here without a word of French.'

'Holidaying? I'm here on a job.'

'Paid assassin?' I asked, 'or only M.I.5?'

'I – I beg your pardon?'

I indicated the list. 'This. It sounds a bit pointed.' I read it aloud. 'Bandages; three, one-and-a-half, and one-inch. Sticking plaster. Elastoplast. Burn-dressing. Boracic powder. ....' I looked at him in some awe. 'You've forgotten the probe.'

'Probe?'

'To get the bullets out.'

He laughed. 'I'm only a forester. I'm camping off and on in a hut at four thousand feet, so I thought I'd set up a first-aid kit.'

'Do you intend to live quite so dangerously?'

'You never know. Anyway I'm a confirmed hypochondriac. I'm never happy till I'm surrounded by pills and boluses and thermometers marked in degrees Centigrade.'

I looked at his six-feet-odd of solid bone and muscle. 'Yes. One can see that you should take every care. Do you really want me to struggle with sticking-plaster and burn-dressings for you?'

'Yes, please, if you'd be so good, though the only item I'm really sure I shall need is the last one, and I could ask for that myself at a pinch.'

'Cognac? Yes, I see what you mean.' Then I turned to Monsieur Garcin and embarked on the slightly exhausting procedure of describing by simple word and gesture articles whose names I knew as well as he did himself. Monsieur Garcin served me reservedly, and as with Philippe, his reserve sometimes bore a strong resemblance to the sulks. I had twice tried the *amende honorable* of a smile, and I was dashed if I would try again, so we persevered in chilly politeness to the last-but-one item on the Englishman's list.

At last we had finished. The Englishman, weighed down with enough pills and boluses to satisfy the most highly-strung *malade imaginaire*, stood back from the doorway and waited for me to precede him into the sunlight.

As I picked up my own parcels and turned to go the chemist's voice said, as dry as the rustle of dead leaves: 'You are forgetting the drops for Madame de Valmy.' He was holding out the package across the counter.

When I reached the sunny street the young man said curiously: 'What's biting him? Was he being rude? You're – forgive my saying so – but you're as pink as anything.'

'Am I? Well, it's my own fault. No, he wasn't rude. It was just me being silly and getting what I deserved.'

'I'm sure you weren't. And thank you most awfully for being such a help. I'd never have managed on my own.' He gave me his shy grin. 'I still have to get the cognac. I wonder if you'd help me to buy that too?'

'I thought you said you could ask for that yourself.'

'I – well, I rather hoped you'd come with me and let me buy you a drink to thank you for taking all that trouble.'

'That's very nice of you. But really, there's no need—'

He looked down at me rather imploringly over his armful of packages. 'Please,' he said. 'Apart from everything else, it really is wonderful to talk English to someone.'

I had a sudden vision of him up in his lonely hut at four thousand feet, surrounded by pills and boluses and thermometers in degrees Centigrade.

'I'd like to very much,' I said.

He beamed. 'That's fine. In here? It's Hobson's choice anyway – I think this is the only place apart from the Coq Hardi half-a-mile away.'

The *bistro* with its gay awning was next door to the pharmacy. Inside it looked dim and not very inviting, but on the cobbles outside there were two or three little metal tables, and some old cane chairs painted bright red. Two small clipped trees stood sentinel in blue tubs.

We sat down in the sun. 'What will you have?' He was carefully disposing his life-saving parcels on an empty chair.

'Do you suppose they serve coffee?'

'Surely.' And it seemed, indeed, that they did. It arrived in large yellow cups, with three wrapped oblongs of sugar in each saucer.

Now that we were facing one another more or less formally across a café table, my companion seemed to have retreated once more behind a rather English shyness. He said, stirring his coffee hard: 'My name's Blake. William Blake.' On this last he looked up with a trace of defiance.

I said: 'That's a good name to have, isn't it? Mine's only Belinda Martin. Linda for short – or for pretty, my mother used to say.'

He smiled. 'Thank you.'

'For what? Making you free of my name?'

'Oh – yes, of course. But I meant for not making a crack about the *Songs of Innocence*.'

' "Little lamb, who made thee?" '

'That one exactly. You'd be surprised how many people can't resist it.'

I laughed. 'How awfully trying! But me, I prefer tigers. No thank you, Mr. Blake' – this to a proffered cigarette – 'I don't smoke.'

'Mind if I do?'

'Of course not.'

Across the spluttering flare of a French match he was looking a question. 'If one may ask – what are you doing in Soubirous? Not a holiday, I take it?'

'No. I'm here on a job, too. I'm a governess.'

'Of course. You must be the English girl from the Château Valmy.'

'Yes. You know about me?'

'Everybody knows everybody else hereabouts. Anyway I'm a near neighbour, as things go round here. I'm working on the next estate, in the plantations west of the Merlon.'

'Oh,' I said, interested. 'Dieudonné?'

'That's it. The château – it's only a country-house really, a quarter of the size of Valmy – lies in the valley a bit beyond the village. The owner's hardly ever there. His name's St. Vire. He seems to spend most of his time in Paris or down near Bordeaux. Like your boss, he gets a lot of his money from his timber and his vineyards.'

'Vineyards? Valmy?'

'Oh, yes. They own chunks of Provence, I believe.'

'Of course,' I said. 'Bellevigne. But that's Monsieur de Valmy's own property, and Valmy isn't. Even he wouldn't spend its income on Valmy.'

'*Even* he?'

To my surprise my voice sounded defensive. 'I believe he's an awfully good landlord.'

'Oh, that. Yes, second to none, I imagine. He's pretty highly thought of hereabouts, I can tell you. And the gossip goes that most of the Bellevigne income did get diverted up here until a few years back; there used to be plenty of money, anyway.'

'There, still is,' I said, 'or so it seems.'

'Yes. Things are waking up again, I gather. Two good vintages, and you get the roof repaired. . . .' He laughed. 'Funny how everyone in these places minds everyone else's business, isn't it?' He looked at me. 'Governessing. Now that's a heck of a life, isn't it?'

'In story-books, yes; and I suppose it could be in real life. But I like it. I like Philippe – my pupil – and I love the place.'

'You're not lonely – so far from home, I mean, and England?'

I laughed. 'If you only knew! My "home in England" was seven years in an orphanage. Governessing or not, Valmy's a wild adventure to me!'

'I suppose so. Is that what you want, adventure?'

'Of course! Who doesn't?'

'Me, for one,' said Mr. Blake firmly.

'Oh? But I thought all men saw themselves hacking their way with machetes through the mangrove swamps and shooting rapids and things. You know, all hairy knees and camp-fires and the wide wide world.'

He grinned. 'I got over that pretty young. And just exactly what is a machete?'

'Goodness knows. They always have them. But seriously—'

'Seriously,' he said, 'I don't know. I'd like to get around, yes, and I like travel and change and seeing new things, but – well, roots are a good thing to have.' He stopped himself there and flushed a little. 'I'm sorry. That was tactless.'

'It's all right. And I do see what you mean. Everybody needs a – a centre. Somewhere to go out from and come back to. And I suppose as you get older you enjoy the coming back more than the going out.'

He gave me his shy, rather charming smile. 'Yes, I think so. But don't listen to me, Miss Martin. I have a stick-in-the-mud disposition. You go ahead and chase your tigers. After all, you've done pretty well up to now. You've found one already, haven't you?'

'Monsieur de Valmy?'

His eyebrows lifted. 'You were quick onto that. He *is* a tiger, then?'

'You did mean him? Why?'

'Only that he seems a little fierce and incalculable by reputation. How do you get on with him? What's he like?'

'I – he's very polite and kind – I'd even say charming. Yes, certainly he's charming. He and Madame seem terribly anxious that I should really feel at home here. I don't see an awful lot of them, of course, but when I do they're awfully nice. . . .'

I looked away from him across the square. Two women came out of the boulangerie, and paused to glance at us curiously before they moved off, their sabots noisy on the stones. Someone called, shrilly, and the group of children broke up, chattering and screaming like jays. Two of them raced past us, bare feet slapping the warm cobbles. The clock in the church tower clanged the half-hour.

I said: 'And what made you come here? Tell me about your job.'

'There's nothing much to tell.' He was drawing little patterns on the table-top with the handle of his spoon. And indeed, the way he told it, his life had taken a very ordered course. A pleasant, reasonably well-to-do suburban home; a small public school; two years in the Army, doing nothing more eventful than manoeuvres on Salisbury Plain; then the University – four years' hard work, with holidays (more or less of the busman variety) in Scandinavia and Germany; finally a good degree and the decision to go on to a further two years' research on some Conifer diseases, which he proceeded to explain to me very carefully and with much enthusiasm. . . . Far from lacking adventure, it appeared that (what with butt rot, drought crack, larch canker, spruce bark beetle, and things with names like *Phomopsis* and *Megastismus* and even *Ips*) life in a conifer forest could positively teem with excitement. I gathered that Mr. Blake himself was seriously involved with the Pine Weevil . . . there was a magnificent infestation of these creatures (*Hylobius*, mark you, not *Pissodes*), in a plantation west of the Merlon. . . .

But here he recollected himself and flushed slightly, grinning at me. 'Well, anyway,' he finished, 'that's why I'm here. I'm busy getting the best of both worlds – thanks to Monsieur de St. Vire, who's a remarkably decent chap for a Frenchman.' He added, seeming to think this phenomenon worth explaining: 'My father knew him in the War. He's given me a job here of a sort – at any rate I'm paid a bit for doing what's really my own research programme anyway. I'm getting some valuable material as well as experience, and I like working in this country. It's small-scale stuff hereabouts, but these people – at any rate the Valmys and St. Vires, really do care about their land. But there's a lot to learn.' He looked wistful. 'Including the language. It seems to escape me, somehow. Perhaps I've no ear. But it would be a help.'

'If you're living alone, with thermometers,' I said, 'I can't see why.'

'Oh, I'm not up at the hut all the time. I work up there mostly, because it's near the plantation I'm "on" at present, and it's quiet; I keep all my stuff up there, and I sleep there when I'm short of cash.' He grinned. 'That's quite often, of course. But I do come down to the Coq Hardi pretty frequently. It's noisy, but the boss speaks English and the food's good . . . ah, is that your little boy?'

From where we were sitting we could see the high wall of the presbytery garden, and now the gate in it opened, and Philippe appeared in the archway, with the broad figure of the curé's housekeeper behind him.

'Yes, that's Philippe,' I said. 'I'll have to go.'

I got to my feet, and the child saw me, said something over his shoulder to the woman, and then ran across the square in our direction.

'I'm glad you waited. I told Madame Rocher you would go – would have gone for a walk. But here you are.'

'Here I am. You're early, aren't you, Philippe? Did Monsieur le Curé get tired of you?'

'I do not know tired of.'

'*Ennuyé*.'

He was solemn. 'No. But he is not very well. He is tired, but not at – of – me. Madame Rocher says I must come away.'

'I'm sorry to hear that,' I said. 'Philippe, this is Monsieur Blake, who works for Monsieur de St. Vire. Mr. Blake, the Comte de Valmy.'

They shook hands, Philippe with the large gravity that sat on him rather attractively.

'What do you work at, monsieur?'

'I'm a forester.'

'Forest – oh, yes, I understand. There are foresters at Valmy also.'

'I know. I've met one or two of them. Pierre Detruche, Jean-Louis Michaud, and Armand Lestocq – he lives next door to the Coq Hardi.'

'As to that,' said Philippe, 'I do not know them myself yet. I have not been here very long, *vous comprenez*.'

'Of course not. I – er, I suppose your uncle manages these things.'

'Yes,' said Philippe politely. 'He is my trustee.'

The look he shot me was merely one of minor triumph that he should have remembered the word, but it tinged the reply with a sort of smug stateliness that brought the beginnings of amusement to Mr. Blake's face. I said hastily: 'We'd better go, I think. Mr. Blake, thank you so much for the coffee. I'm awfully glad we met.' I held out my hand.

As he took it, he said quickly: 'I say, please – don't just vanish. When can we meet again?'

'I'm not a very free agent. Sometimes I've a morning, but I don't often get as far as this.'

'Are you free in the evenings?'

'No, not really. Only Fridays, and a Sunday here and there.'

'Then that's no good,' he said, sounding disappointed. 'I've arranged to meet some pals of mine this week-end. Perhaps later on?'

Philippe had given a little tug to my hand. 'I really must go,' I said. 'Let's leave it, shall we? We're sure to meet – the valley isn't all that big. And thank you again. . . .'

As we crossed the square I glanced back, to see him laboriously gathering up the bandages and the sticking-plaster and all the homely remedies which were to reassure life at four thousand feet.

I hoped he would remember to get the cognac.

CHAPTER SIX

Something will come of this. I hope it
mayn't be human gore.

DICKENS: *Barnaby Rudge*

That evening the quiet run of our existence was broken. Nursery tea
was over; the early April dusk had drawn in against the uncurtained
windows where lamp and firelight were cheerfully reflected. Philippe
was on the hearthrug playing in a desultory fashion with some soldiers
and I was sitting, as I often did at that time, reading aloud to him, when
I heard a car climbing the zigzag. It was a mild evening, and one of the
long balcony windows was open. The mounting engine roared, changed,
roared again nearer. As I paused in my reading and glanced towards the
window, Philippe looked up.

'*Une auto! Quelqu'un vient!*'

'English,' I said automatically. 'Philippe, what are you doing?'

But he took no notice. He jumped up from the rug, while his toys
scattered unheeded. Then he flew out of the window like a rocket and
vanished to the right along the balcony.

I dropped the book and hurried after him. He had run to the end of
the balcony where it overlooked the gravel forecourt, and was leaning
over eagerly and somewhat precariously. I stifled an impulse to grab him
by the seat of his pants and said instead, as mildly as I could: 'You'll fall
if you hang over like that. . . . Look, the dashed thing's loose anyway
– this coping moved, I'm sure it did. This must be one of the bits they
were talking about repairing. Philippe—'

But he didn't seem to be listening. He still craned forward over the
stone coping. I said firmly: 'Now come back, Philippe, and be sensible.
What's the excitement for, anyway? Who is it?'

The car roared up the last incline, and swung with a scrunch of tyres
across the gravel. She had her lights on. They scythed round, through
the thin dark thorns of the rose-garden, the flickering spear-points of the
iron railings below us, the carefully-planted pots on the loggia, came to
rest on the stableyard archway, and were switched off.

A door slammed. I heard a man's voice, low-pitched and pleasant.
Another voice – I supposed the driver's – answered him. Then the car
moved off softly towards the stableyard, and the newcomer crossed the
gravel and mounted the steps to the great door.

I waited with mild curiosity for the door to open and the light from
the hall to give body, as it were, to the voice. But before this happened
Philippe ducked back behind me and retreated along the balcony towards
the schoolroom windows. I turned, to see in the set of the thin back and
shoulders the suggestion of some disappointment so sharp that I followed

him in without a word, sat down again in my chair by the fire, and picked up my book. But Philippe didn't settle again to his toys. He stood still on the hearthrug, staring at the fire. I think he had forgotten I was there.

I leafed through a few pages of the book and then said very casually: 'Who was it, did you know?'

The thin shoulders lifted. 'Monsieur Florimond, I think.'

'Monsieur Florimond? Do you mean the dress-designer?'

'Yes. He used to visit us a lot in Paris and he is a friend of my aunt Héloïse. Do you know of him in England?'

'Of course.' Even in the Constance Butcher Home we had heard of the great Florimond, whose 'Aladdin' silhouette had been the rage of Paris and New York years before and had, it was rumoured, caused Dior to mutter something under his breath and tear up a set of designs. I said, impressed: 'Is he coming to stay?'

'I do not know.' His voice sufficiently also expressed that he did not care. But the general impression of poignant disappointment prevailed so strongly that I said: 'Did you expect someone else, Philippe?'

He glanced up momentarily, then the long lashes dropped. He said nothing.

I hesitated. But Philippe was my job: moreover, he was a very lonely little boy. Who was it who could expect that headlong welcome from him?

I said: 'Your cousin Raoul, perhaps?'

No answer.

'Is anyone else supposed to be coming?'

He shook his head.

I tried again. 'Don't you like Monsieur Florimond?'

'But yes. I like him very much.'

'Then why—?' I began, but something in his face warned me to stop. I said gently: 'It's time we went down to the salon, *petit*. I haven't been told not to, so I suppose, guests or not, that we'll have to go. Run and wash your hands while I tidy my hair.'

He obeyed me without a word or look.

I went slowly across to shut the balcony window.

In a small salon a log fire had been lit, and in front of it sat Madame de Valmy and Monsieur Florimond on a rose-brocaded sofa, talking.

I looked with interest at the newcomer. I don't know what I expected one of fashion's Big Five to look like; I only know that the great Florimond didn't look like it. He was vast, baldish, and untidy. His face in repose had a suggestion of tranquil melancholy about it that was vaguely reminiscent of the White Knight, but no-one could ever doubt Monsieur Florimond's large sanity. Those blue eyes were shrewd and very kind: they also looked as if they missed very little. He wore his conventional, superbly cut clothes with all the delicate care one might accord to an old beach-towel. His pockets bulged comfortably in every direction, and there was cigar-ash on his lapel. He was clutching what looked like a folio-society reprint in one large hand, and gestured with it lavishly to underscore some story he was telling Madame de Valmy.

She was laughing, looking happier and more animated than I had seen her since I came to Valmy. I realised sharply how lovely she had been before time and tragedy had drained the life from her face.

On the thought, she turned and saw myself and Philippe by the door, and the gaiety vanished. The boredom and annoyance that shut down over it were humiliatingly plain to see. I could have slapped her for it, but then realised that Philippe had probably not noticed. He was advancing solemnly and politely on Florimond, who surged to his feet with noises indicating quite sufficient delighted pleasure to counter Héloïse's obvious irritation.

'Philippe! This is delightful! How are you?'

'I am very well, thank you, m'sieur.'

'H'm, yes.' He tapped the boy's cheek. 'A little more colour there, perhaps, and then you'll do. Country air, that's the thing, and the Valmy air suits you, by the look of it!' He didn't actually say 'better than Paris', but the words were there, implicit, and Philippe didn't reply. It wasn't easy to avoid mistakes just then with him. Florimond registered this one, I could see, but he merely added amiably: 'Mind you, I don't wonder that Valmy's good for you! When one is lucky enough to have a beautiful young lady as one's constant companion, one must expect to flourish!'

The perfect politeness of Philippe's smile indicated how completely this gallant sally went over his head. It had perforce, since they were speaking French, to go over mine too. I looked as non-committal as I could and avoided Florimond's eye.

Héloïse de Valmy said from the sofa: 'Don't waste your gallantries, Carlo. Miss Martin's French improves hourly, so I'm told, but I don't think she's reached the compliment stage yet.' Then, in English: 'Miss Martin, let me introduce Monsieur Florimond. You will have heard of him, I don't doubt.'

I said composedly as I shook hands: 'Even in my English orphanage we had heard of Monsieur Florimond. You reached us perhaps some six years late, monsieur, but you did reach us.' I smiled, remembering my own cheap ready-made. 'Believe it or not.'

He didn't pretend to misunderstand me. He made a largely gallant gesture with the book which was, I saw, *The Tale of Genji*, and said: 'You, mademoiselle, would adorn anything you wore.'

I laughed. 'Even this?'

'Even that,' he said, unperturbed, a twinkle in the blue eyes.

'The size of that compliment,' I said, 'strikes me dumb, monsieur.'

Madame de Valmy said, sounding amused now, and more naturally friendly than I had yet heard her: 'It's Monsieur Florimond's constant sorrow that only the old and faded can afford to be dressed by him, while

the young and lovely buy dresses *prêtes à porter* – there's a phrase . . .
(my English is slipping in the excitement of talking to you, Carlo) –
what's the phrase you have for "ready-made"?'

' "Off the peg?" ' I suggested.

'Yes, that's it. You buy your dresses off the peg, and still show us up.'

'Your English *is* slipping, Madame,' I said. 'You're getting your
pronouns all wrong.'

As she lifted her eyebrows Florimond said delightedly: 'There, *chère
madame*, a real compliment! A compliment of the right kind! So neat you
did not see it coming, and so *subtil* that you still do not see it when it has
come.'

She laughed. 'My dear Carlo, compliments even now aren't quite so
rare that I don't recognise them, believe me. Thank you, Miss Martin,
that was sweet of you.' Her eyes as she smiled at me were friendly,
almost warm, and for the first time since I had met her I saw charm in
her – not the easy charm of the vivid personality, but the real and
irresistible charm that reaches out halfway to meet you, assuring you
that you are wanted and liked. And heaven knew I needed that assurance. . . . I was very ready to meet any gesture, however slight, with the
response of affection. Perhaps at last. . . .

But even as I smiled back at her it happened again. The warmth
drained away as if wine had seeped from a crack and left the glass empty,
a cool and misted shell, reflecting nothing.

She turned away to pick up her embroidery.

I stood with the smile stiffening on my lips, feeling, even more sharply
than before, the sense of having been rebuffed for some reason that I
couldn't understand. A moment ago I could have sworn the woman liked
me, but now . . . in the last fleeting glance before the cool eyes dropped
to her embroidery I thought I saw the same queerly apprehensive quality
that I had noticed on my first day at Valmy.

I dismissed the idea straight away. I no longer imagined that Madame
de Valmy feared her husband; on the contrary. Without any overt
demonstration it was obvious that the two were very close: their personalities shared a boundary as light and shadow do: they marched. It was
probable (I thought pityingly and only half-comprehendingly) that
Héloïse de Valmy's keep-your-distance chilliness was only a by-product
of the sort of Samurai self-control that she must have learned to practise
elsewhere. With the inability of youth to imagine any temperament other
than my own, I felt that life must be a good deal easier for Léon de
Valmy himself than for his wife. . . .

And her attitude to me – to Philippe as well – must only be part of
the general shut-down. . . . It would take time for the reserve to melt,
the door to open. That look of hers wasn't apprehension: it was a kind
of waiting, an appraisal, no more. It would take time. Perhaps she was
still only wondering, as I was, why Léon de Valmy thought she'd made
'a very great mistake. . . .'

She was setting a stitch with delicate care. There was a lamp at her elbow. The light shone softly on the thin white hand. The needle threaded the canvas with moving sparks. She didn't look up. 'Come and sit by me, Philippe, on this footstool. You may stay ten minutes ... no, Miss Martin, don't slip away. Sit down and entertain Monsieur Florimond for me.'

The mask was on again. She sat, composed and elegant as ever over her needlework. She even managed to appear faintly interested as she put Philippe through the usual catechism about his day's activities, and listened to his polite, painstaking replies.

Beside me Florimond said: 'Won't you sit here?'

I turned gratefully towards him, to find him watching me with those mild eyes that nevertheless seemed to miss nothing. He may have noticed the ebb-and-flow of invitation and rebuff that had left me silent and stranded; at any rate he now appeared to lay himself out to amuse me. His repertoire of gently scandalous stories was extremely entertaining and probably at least half true, and – as I knew his Paris better than he realised – I was soon enjoying myself immensely. He flirted a very little, too – oh, so expertly! – and looked slightly disconcerted and then delighted when he found that his gallantries amused instead of confusing me. He would have been even more disconcerted if he'd known that, in a queer sort of way, he was reminding me of Daddy: I hadn't heard this sort of clever, over-sophisticated chatter since I'd last been allowed in to one of Daddy's drink-and-verses jamborees nine years before. I may be forgiven if I enjoyed every moment of the oddly nostalgic rubbish that we talked.

Or would have done, if every now and again I hadn't seen Héloïse de Valmy's cool eyes watching me with that indefinable expression which might have been appraisal, or wariness, or – if it weren't fantastic – fear.

And if I hadn't been wondering who had reported on the 'hourly' improvement of my French.

The entry of Seddon with the cocktail tray interrupted us. I looked inquiringly at Madame de Valmy, and Philippe made as if to get to his feet.

But before she could dismiss us Florimond said comfortably: 'Don't drive the child away, Héloïse. Now he's said his catechism perhaps you'll deliver him over to me.'

She smiled, raising her delicate brows. 'What do you want with him, Carlo?'

He had finally put down *The Tale of Genji* on the extreme edge of a fragile-looking coffee-table, and was fishing in one untidy pocket with a large hand. He grinned at Philippe, who was watching him with that guarded look I hated to see, and I saw the child's face relax a little in reply. 'Last time I saw you, my lad,' said Florimond, 'I was trying to initiate you into the only civilised pastime for men of sense. Ah, here we

are. . . . ' As he spoke he fished a small folded board out of one pocket.
It was a traveller's chess-set, complete with tiny men in red and white.

Madame de Valmy laughed. 'The ruling passion,' she said, her cool
voice almost indulgent. 'Very well, Carlo, but he must go upstairs at a
quarter past, no later. Berthe will be waiting for him.'

That this was not true she knew quite well, and so did I. Though the
conversation was now in French, I saw her give me a quick glance, and
kept my face non-committal. It was interesting that I wasn't the only one
who schemed to keep Philippe out of his uncle's way.

Philippe had dragged his stool eagerly enough across to Florimond's
chair and the two of them were already poring over the board.

'Now,' said Florimond cheerfully, 'let's see if you can remember any
of the rules, *mon gars*. I seem to recollect some erratic movements last
time you and I were engaged, but there's a sort of wild freshness about
your conception of the game which has its own surprising results. Your
move.'

'I moved,' said Philippe demurely, 'while you were talking.'

'Did you, *pardieu*? Ah, the king's pawn. A classic gambit, monsieur . . .
and I, this pawn. So.'

Philippe bent over the board, his brows fiercely knitted, his whole
small being concentrated on the game, while above him Florimond,
leaning back vast in his chair, with cigar-ash spilling down his beautifully-
cut jacket, watched him indulgently, never ceasing for a moment the
gentle, aimless flow of words, of which it was very obvious that Philippe,
if indeed he was listening at all, would understand only one in three.

I sat quietly and watched them, feeling a warm, almost affectionate
glow towards this large and distinguished Parisian who, among all his
other preoccupations, could bother to make a lonely small boy feel he
was wanted. From the couturier's talk you would suppose that he had
had nothing to do for the past year but look forward to another game
with Philippe.

I noticed then that Madame de Valmy wasn't sewing. Her hands lay
idle in the tumble of embroidery in her lap. I thought that she was
interested in the game until I saw that she wasn't watching the board.
Her eyes were fixed on the back of Philippe's down-bent head. She must
have been deep in some faraway thoughts, because when Philippe made
a sudden exclamation she jumped visibly.

He gave a little whoop of glee and pounced on the board. 'Your queen!
Your queen! Monsieur, I've got your queen!'

'So I see,' said Florimond, unperturbed. 'But will you kindly tell me,
Capablanca, by what new law you were able to move your piece straight
down the board to do so?'

'There was nothing in the way,' explained Philippe kindly.

'No. But the piece you moved, *mon vieux*, was a bishop. I'm sorry to
be petty about it, but there is a rule which restricts the bishop to a

diagonal line. Nugatory, you will say; trifling ... but there it is. Medes and Persians, Philippe.'

'A bishop?' said Philippe, seizing on the one word that made sense.

'The ones with the pointed hats,' said Florimond tranquilly, 'are the bishops.'

'Oh,' said Philippe. He looked up at his opponent and grinned, not in the least abashed. 'I forgot. You can have your queen back then.'

'I am grateful. Thank you. Now, it's still your move and I should suggest that you observe again the relative positions of your bishop and my queen.'

Philippe concentrated. 'There is nothing between them,' he said, uncertainly.

'Exactly.'

'Well – *oh!*' The small hand hastily scooped the lawless bishop out of the queen's path. 'There. I move him there.'

Florimond chuckled. 'Very wise,' he said. 'Very wise.' From the way he leaned forward to scan the board through a thoughtful cloud of tobacco-smoke you would have thought he was matched with a master instead of a small boy who didn't even know the rules.

I glanced at the clock. Sixteen minutes past six. I looked in surprise at Madame de Valmy, whom I had suspected of a clock-watching nervousness almost equal to my own. She had dropped her hands in her lap again and was staring at the fire. She was a hundred miles away. I wondered where ... no pleasant place, I thought.

I said: 'Madame.'

She started, and picked up her embroidery so quickly that she pricked her finger. I said: 'I'm sorry, madame, I startled you. I think it's time I took Philippe upstairs, isn't it?'

I had my back to the door so I neither saw nor heard it open. It was the quick turn of Philippe's head and the widening of the black eyes that told me. Léon de Valmy's beautiful voice said:

'Ah, Philippe. No, don't move. Carlo, how delightful! Why don't we see you more often?'

The wheel-chair glided silently foward as he spoke. For such a quiet entrance the effect was remarkable enough. Philippe jumped off his footstool and stood staring at his uncle like a mesmerised bird, Monsieur Florimond hoisted himself again to his feet, Héloïse de Valmy dropped her embroidery and turned quickly towards her husband, while I slid out of my place as his chair passed me and retired towards my usual distant window-seat.

I didn't think Léon de Valmy had noticed me, but Philippe had. He, too, made a movement as if to escape, but was netted, so to speak, with a word.

'No, indeed, Philippe. It's all too rarely that I get a chance to see you. We must thank Monsieur Florimond for bringing me in early. Sit down.'

The child obeyed. The wheel-chair slid up beside the sofa and stopped.

Léon de Valmy touched his wife's hand. 'Your devotion to duty touches me, Héloïse. It does really.'

Only an ear that was tuned to it could have detected the taunt in the smooth voice. I saw their eyes meet, and Héloïse de Valmy smiled, and for the second time that evening I felt the scald of a little spurt of anger. Did they find even half-an-hour out of the day intolerably much to give to Philippe? And did they have to make it plain? This time Philippe didn't miss it. I saw the swift upward slant of his lashes at his uncle, and the too-familiar sullenness settle on the pale little face, and thought: why don't you pick someone your own weight, damn you . . . ?

The next second the incident might have been illusion. Léon de Valmy, obviously in the best of spirits, was welcoming Monsieur Florimond almost gaily. 'It's very nice of you to look us up, Carlo. What brought you to Geneva?'

Florimond lowered himself once more into his chair. 'I came on the track of a material.' He made another of his large gestures, this time towards *The Tale of Genji*, which promptly fell onto the floor. 'Take a look at those pictures some time, Héloïse, and tell me if you ever saw anything to touch that elegance, that courteous silverpoint grace just on the hither side of decadence . . . Ah, thank you, *mon lapin*.' This to Philippe, who had quietly picked up the book and was handing it to him. 'Give it to your aunt, *p'tit. C'est formidable, hein?*'

She glanced at it. 'What's this, Carlo?'

'A threat to your peace of mind and my pocket,' said Léon de Valmy, smiling. 'The "mandarin" line, or some such thing, I don't doubt, and just on the hither side of decadence at that. I confess I can't see you in it, my dear. I doubt if I shall permit it.'

Florimond laughed. 'Only the material, I do assure you, only the material! And that's as much as I shall tell you. Rose Gautier and I have concocted something between us that ought to flutter the dovecotes next November, and I came up to keep a father's eye on it in the making.' He grinned amiably at his host. 'At least, that's the excuse. I always try to desert Paris at this juncture if I possibly can.'

'How's the collection going?' asked Madame.

Florimond dropped a gout of ash down his shirt-front, and wiped it placidly aside across his lapel. 'At the moment it's hardly even conceived. Not a twitch, not a pang. I shall not be in labour for many months to come, and then we shall have the usual lightning and half-aborted litter to be licked into shape in a frenzy of blood and tears.' Here his eye fell on Philippe, silent on his stool, and he added, with no perceptible change of tone: 'There was thick mist lying on the road between here and Thonon.'

Léon de Valmy was busy at the cocktail tray. He handed his wife a glass. 'Really? Bad?'

'In places. But I fancy it's only local. It was clear at Geneva, though of course it may cloud up later along the Lake. Ah, thank you.'

Léon de Valmy poured his own drink, then as his chair turned again
into the circle round the hearth he caught sight of the chessboard on the
low table.

The black brows rose. 'Chess? Do you never move without that thing,
Carlo?'

'Never. May I hope you'll give me a game tonight?'

'With pleasure. But not with that collection of dressmakers' pins, I
beg of you. I don't play my best when I've to use a telescope.'

'It's always pure joy to play with that set of yours,' said Florimond,
'quite apart from the fact that you're a foeman worthy of my steel –
which is one way of saying that you beat me four times out of five.'

'H'm.' Léon de Valmy was surveying the board. 'It would certainly
appear that Red was playing a pretty short-sighted game in every sense
of the word. I knew you were not chess-minded, Héloïse, my dear, but
I didn't know you were quite as bad as that.'

She merely smiled, not even bothering to deny it. There was no need
anyway. He knew who'd been playing, and Philippe knew he knew.

'Ah, yes,' said Florimond calmly. He peered at the miniature men.
'Dear me, I have got myself into an odd tangle, haven't I? Perhaps I
need spectacles. You're quite right, my dear Léon, it's a mistake to
underrate one's opponent. Never do that.' The big hand shifted a couple
of men with quick movements. The mild clever face expressed nothing
whatever except interest in the Lilliputian manoeuvres on the board.

I saw Léon de Valmy glance up at him swiftly, and the look of
amusement that came and went like the gleam on the underside of a
blown cloud. 'I don't.' Then he smiled at Philippe, silent on his stool.
'Come and finish the game, Philippe. I'm sure your aunt won't drive you
upstairs just yet.'

Philippe went, if possible, smaller and more rigid than before. 'I – I'd
rather not, thank you.'

Léon de Valmy said pleasantly: 'You mustn't allow the fact that you
were losing to weigh with you, you know.'

The child went scarlet. Florimond said, quite without inflection: 'In
any case we can't continue. I disarranged the pieces just now. The
situation wasn't quite as peculiar as your uncle supposed, Philippe, but
I can't remember just what it was. I'm sorry. I hope very much that
you'll give me the pleasure of a game another time. You do very well.'

He pushed the board aside and smiled down at the child, who responded
with one quick upward look. Then he leaned back in his chair, and,
smiling amiably at his host, launched without pausing straight into one
of his improbable stories, thus effectively forcing the general attention
back to himself. Philippe remained without moving, small on his stool,
the picture of sulky isolation. I watched him, still feeling in my damn-
them mood. He must have felt my glance, because eventually he looked
up. I winked at him and grinned. There was no answering gleam. The
black lashes merely dropped again.

Then the door opened, and Seddon, the butler, came in. He crossed the floor to Madame de Valmy's side.

'Madame, a telephone message has just come through from Monsieur Raoul.'

I saw her flash a glance at her husband. 'From Monsieur Raoul? Yes, Seddon?'

'He asked me to tell you he was on his way up, madame.'

The base of Léon de Valmy's glass clinked down on the arm of his chair. 'On his way? Here? When? Where was he speaking from?'

'That I couldn't say, sir. But he wasn't at Bellevigne. He said he would be here some time tonight.'

A pause. I noticed the soft uneven ticking of the lovely little clock on the mantel.

Then Florimond said comfortably: 'How very pleasant! I don't know when I last set eyes on Raoul. I hope he'll be here for dinner?'

Seddon said: 'No, monsieur. He said he might be late, and not to wait for him, but that he would get here tonight.'

Léon de Valmy said: 'And that was all the message?'

'Yes, sir.'

Madame de Valmy stirred. 'He didn't sound as if there was anything wrong . . . at Bellevigne?'

'No madame. Not at all.'

Florimond chuckled. 'Don't look so worried, my dear. They've probably had a week of the mistral and he's decided to cut and run for it. The original ill wind.'

'He doesn't usually run in this direction,' said his father, very dryly. 'Very well, Seddon, thank you.'

Madame de Valmy said: 'Perhaps you'll be good enough to see Mrs. Seddon straight away about a room?'

'Of course, madame.' Seddon, expressionless as ever, bent his head. I saw Héloïse de Valmy glance again at her husband. I couldn't see his face from where I sat, but she was biting her bottom lip, and to my surprise she looked strained and pale.

A nice gay welcome for the son of the house was, it appeared, laid on. Him and Philippe both . . . As a cosy family home the Château Valmy certainly took some beating. The Constance Butcher also ran.

Then the central chandelier leaped into a lovely cascade of light. Seddon moved forward to draw curtains and replenish drinks. Glasses clinked, and someone laughed. Philippe moved cheerfully to help Florimond pack away the tiny chessmen . . . and in a moment, it seemed under the bright light, the imagined tensions dissolved and vanished. Firelight, laughter, the smell of pine-logs and Schiaparelli, the rattle of curtain-rings and the swish as the heavy brocades swung together . . . it was absurd to people the lovely Château Valmy with the secret ghosts of Thornfield.

The Demon King turned his handsome grey head and said in English: 'Come out, Jane Eyre.'

I must have jumped about a foot. He looked surprised, then laughed and said: 'Did I startle you? I'm sorry. Were you very far away?' 'Pretty far. At a place in Yorkshire called Thornfield Hall.' The black brows lifted. 'So we're *en rapport*? No wonder you jumped.' He smiled. 'I shall have to be careful ... And now will you take your charge away before Monsieur Florimond corrupts him with vermouth? No, Philippe, I do assure you, you won't like it. Now make you adieux – in English, please, and go.'

Philippe was on his feet in a flash, making those adieux correctly, if rather too eagerly. I think I was almost as thankful as he was when at length, his hand clutching mine, I said my own quiet goodnights and withdrew.

Léon de Valmy's 'Goodnight, Miss Eyre,' with its wholly charming overtone of mockery, followed me to the door.

Philippe was a little subdued for the rest of the evening, but on the whole survived the ordeal by uncle pretty well. After he was in bed I dined alone in my room. It was Albertine, Madame de Valmy's sour-faced maid, who brought my supper in. She did it in tight-lipped silence, making it very clear that she was demeaning herself unwillingly.

'Thanks, Albertine,' I said cheerfully, as she set the last plate down just a shade too smartly. 'Oh, and by the way —'

The woman turned in the doorway, her sallow face not even inquiring. She radiated all the charm and grace of a bad-tempered skunk. 'Well?'

I said: 'I wonder if you can remember whether I got Mrs. Seddon's tablets for her last week, or not?'

'*Non*,' said Albertine, and turned to go.

'Do you mean I didn't or do you mean you don't remember?'

She spoke sourly over her shoulder without turning. 'I mean I do not know. Why?'

'Only because Mrs. Seddon asked me to get the tablets today and Monsieur Garcin said he gave them to me last week. If that's the case you'd think I must have handed them to her with her other packages. I've no recollection of them at all. D'you know if there was a prescription with the list you gave me?'

The square shoulders lifted. 'Perhaps. I do not know.' The shallow black eyes surveyed me with dislike. 'Why do you not ask her yourself?'

'Very well, I will,' I said coldly. 'That will do, Albertine.'

But the door was already shut. I looked at it for a moment with compressed lips and then began my meal. When, some little time later, there came a tap on the door and Mrs. Seddon surged affably in, I said, almost without preamble:

'That Albertine woman. What's biting her? She's about as amiable as a snake.'

Mrs. Seddon snorted. 'Oh, her. She's going about like a wet month of Sundays because I told her to bring your supper up. Berthe's helping Mariette get a room ready for Mr. Rowl seeing as how Mariette won't work along with Albertine anyhow and she's as sour as a lemon if you ask her to do anything outside Madam's own rooms. Her and that Bernard, they're a pair. It's my belief he'd rob a bank for the Master if asked, but he'd see your nose cheese and the rats eating it before he'd raise a little finger for anybody else.'

'I believe you. What I can't understand is why Madame puts up with her.'

'You don't think she has that sour-milk face for Madam, do you? Oh no, it's all niminy-piminy butter-won't-melt *there*, you mark my words.' Conversation with Mrs. Seddon was nothing if not picturesque. 'But she's like that with everyone else in the place bar Bernard, and it's my belief she's as jealous as sin if Madam so much as smiles at anybody besides herself. She knows Madame likes you, and that's the top and bottom of it, dear, believe you me.'

I said, surprised: 'Madame likes me? How d'you know?'

'Many's the nice thing she's said about you,' said Mrs. Seddon comfortably, 'so you don't have to fret yourself over a bit of lip from that Albertine.'

I laughed. 'I don't. How's the asthma? You sound better.'

'I am that. It comes and goes. This time of year it's a nuisance, but never near so bad as it used to be. I remember as a girl Miss Debbie's mother saying to me—'

I stopped that one with the smoothness of much practice. 'I'm afraid Monsieur Garcin wouldn't give me the anti-histamine today. He said I got it last week. Did I give it to you, Mrs. Seddon? I'm terribly ashamed of myself, but I can't remember. D'you know if it was with the other things I got for you? There was some Nestlé's chocolate, wasn't there, and some buttons, and some cotton-wool – and was it last week you got your watch back from the repairers?'

'Was it now? Maybe it was. I can't mind just now about the pills, but I know there were a lot of things and the pills may have been with them.' She laughed a little wheezily. 'I can't say I took much notice, not wanting them till now, but Mr. Garsang's probably right. He's as finicky as the five-times-table, and about as lively. I'll have a look in my cupboard tonight. I'm sorry to give you the bother, dear.'

'Oh, that doesn't matter. I did get you the aspirins and the eau-de-cologne. They're here, with your change.'

'Oh, thanks, dear – miss, I mean.'

I said: 'Is Monsieur Florimond staying, or is he only here for dinner?'

'He only came for dinner, but I dare say he'll stay on late to see Mr. Rowl. It might yet be they'll ask him to stay the night if the fog gets any thicker.'

I got up and went over to the balcony windows.

'I don't see any fog. It seems a fine enough night.'

'Eh? Oh yes. I think it's only down by the water. We're high up here. But the road runs mostly along the river, and there's been accidents in the valley before now in the mist. It's a nasty road, that, in the dark.'

'I can imagine it might be.' I came back to my chair, adding, with a memory of the recent uncomfortable session in the drawing-room: 'Perhaps Monsieur Raoul won't get up here after all tonight.'

She shook her head. 'He'll come. If he said he was coming he'll come.' She eyed me for a moment and said: 'Did they – was there anything said downstairs, like?'

'Nothing. They wondered what brought him, that was all.'

'They've not much call to wonder,' she said darkly. 'There's only one thing'll make him set foot in the place and that's money.'

'Oh?' I said, rather uncomfortably. There were limits to gossip, after all. 'I thought – I got the impression it might be some business to do with Bellevigne.'

'Well,' said Mrs. Seddon, 'that's what I mean. It's always Bellyveen and money.' She sighed. 'I told you, Mr. Rowl manages it for him and now and again he comes up and talks to him about it and then' – she sighed again – 'there's words. It's trouble every time, what with Mr. Rowl wanting money for Bellyveen and the Master wanting it for Valmy and before you know where you are it's cat and dog, or maybe I should say dog and dog because nobody could say Mr. Rowl's like a cat, the horrible sneaking beasts, but a dogfight it's always been, ever since Mr. Rowl was big enough to speak up for himself and—'

'He – he must be a careful landlord,' I said hastily.

'Oh, I don't deny he makes a good job of Bellyveen – he's too like his father not to, if you see what I mean – but they do say he rackets about the place plenty between times. There's stories—'

'You can't believe everything you hear,' I said.

'No, indeed, that's true,' said Mrs. Seddon, a shade regretfully, 'and especially when it's about Mr. Rowl, if you follow me, miss, because he's the sort that'd get himself talked about if he lived in a convent, as the saying is.'

'I'm sure you're right,' I said.

'And where does he get the money, I ask you that?' Mrs. Seddon was now fully and enjoyably launched. 'Where did he get the car he was driving last time he was here? As long as the Queen Mary and a horn like the Last Trump, and you can't tell me he got anything out of the Master so I ask you, where?'

'Well,' I said mildly, 'where?'

'Ah,' said Mrs. Seddon darkly, 'you may well ask. I heard the Master ask him that very question, sharp-like, the last time he was here. And Mr. Rowl wouldn't tell him; just passed it off in that way he has with something about a lucky night and a lucky number.'

I laughed. 'It sounds to me as if he won it at roulette. Good luck to him.'

She looked a little shocked. 'Well, miss! I don't say as how I think a little flutter does any harm and I'm as partial to a nice game of whist as anyone, but – well, many's the time I wonder what Miss Debbie would have said. Many's the time she said to me "Mary," she said—'

'Forgive me,' I said quickly, 'but it's time for Philippe's chocolate. I left him reading in bed and I must put his light out.'

'Eh? Oh, yes, to be sure, how time goes on, doesn't it? And it's long past time I ought to be seeing if Berthe and Mariette have put that room properly to rights. . . .' She heaved herself onto her feet and plodded to the door, which I opened for her. 'Have they remembered the milk?'

'It was on the tray.'

'Ah, yes. That Berthe, now, do you find she does her work all right, miss? If there's anything to complain of, you must be sure to let me know.'

'I've no complaints,' I said. 'I like Berthe very much, and she keeps the rooms beautifully. You've only to look in the pantry here.'

She followed me into the tiny pantry, where the light gleamed on the spotless enamel of the little stove, and saucepan, beaker and spoon stood ready. I poured milk into the pan, set it on the stove and switched on. Mrs. Seddon ran a practised eye over the tiny room, and an equally practised finger over the shelf where the tins of chocolate, coffee and tea stood, and nodded her head in a satisfied manner.

'Yes, Berthe's a good girl, I must say, if she'll keep her mind on her work instead of running after that there Bernard . . . The sugar's here, miss.'

'No, not that. I use the glucose for Philippe, you remember – that's his special tin, the blue one. Oh, thank you. D'you mean to tell me there's something between Berthe and Bernard? I hope it's not serious? It would be an awful pity. He's too old for her, and besides—'

I stopped, but she took me up.

'Well, miss, you never said a truer word. A pity it is. If that Albertine wasn't his sister born, I'd have said why not them, they wouldn't spoil two houses, and them as alike as two hogs in the same litter. A sour-faced, black-avised sort of chap he is and all, for a bonny young girl like Berthe to be losing her head over. But there, human nature's human nature, believe it or not, and there's nothing we can do about it. What are you looking for now?'

'The biscuits. They've been moved. Ah, here they are.' I put three into Philippe's saucer, looking sidelong at Mrs. Seddon. 'Extra rations tonight. It was a slightly sticky session in the drawing-room.'

'That's right. He could do with a bit of spoiling, if you ask me. And now I'll have to go, really. I've enjoyed our little chat, miss. And I may say that Seddon and me, we think that Philip's a whole lot better for

aving you here. He likes you, that's plain to see, and it's my belief that
rhat he needs is somebody to be fond of.'

I said softly, half to myself: 'Don't we all?'

'Well, there you are,' said Mrs. Seddon comfortably. 'Not but what
is other Nanny wasn't a very nice woman, very nice indeed, but she did
aby him a bit, say what you will, which was only natural, seeing as
ow she'd brought him up from a bairn in arms. Maybe the Master was
ight enough like you said in thinking he ought to have a change,
specially after losing his Mam and Dad like that, poor bairn. And
ou're making a grand job of him, miss, if you'll excuse the liberty of me
aying so.'

I said with real gratitude: 'It's very nice of you. Thank you.' I lifted
'hilippe's tray and grinned at her over it. 'And I do hope all goes well
ownstairs. At least there's one person who'll be pleased when Monsieur
Laoul arrives.'

She stopped in the doorway and turned, a little ponderously. 'Who?
1r. Florimond? Well, I couldn't say—'

'I didn't mean him. I meant Philippe.'

She stared at me, then shook her head. 'Mr. Rowl hardly knows him,
iiss. Don't forget Philip only came from Paris just before you did, and
1r. Rowl's not been over since he was here.'

'Then Monsieur Raoul must have seen something of him in Paris, or
lse when he was with Monsieur Hippolyte.'

'He didn't. That I do know. And I'd go bail him and Mr. Rowl hardly
aw each other in Paree. Paree!' said Mrs. Seddon, reverting to form,
Paree! He'd not be the one to bother with Philip *there*. He had other
ettles of fish to fry in Paree, you mark my words!'

'But when we heard the car coming up the zigzag tonight with
Monsieur Florimond, Philippe flew out onto the balcony like a rocket
and he certainly wasn't hoping to see *him*. He looked desperately
isappointed . . . more than that, really; "blighted" would almost describe
: . . . Who else could he be looking for if it wasn't his cousin Raoul?'

Then I looked at her, startled, for her eyes, in the harsh light, were
rimming with sudden, easy tears. She shook her head at me and wiped
er cheeks with the back of a plump hand. 'Poor bairn, poor bairn,' was
ll she would say, but presently after a sniff or two and some action with
handkerchief, she explained. The explanation was simple, obvious, and
readful.

'He never saw them dead, of course. Nor he wasn't allowed to go to
he funeral. And it's my belief and Seddon's that he won't have it they're
eally gone. They were to have driven back from the airport, you see,
nd he was waiting for them, and they never came. He never saw no
1ore of them. It's my belief he's still waiting.'

'That's dreadful.' I swallowed. 'That's - dreadful, Mrs. Seddon.'

'Yes. Every car that comes up, he'll fly out yonder. I've seen him do
:. It's lucky there's not more coming and going than there is, or he'd do

it once too often, and end up on the gravel on his head, or else stuck on those spikes like a beetle on a pin.'

I shivered. 'I'll watch him,' I said.

'You do,' said Mrs. Seddon.

Fourth Coach

CHAPTER SEVEN

A Being, erect upon two legs, and bearing all the outward semblance of a man, and not of a monster.

DICKENS: *Pickwick Papers*

Philippe was already asleep, curled in an extraordinarily small bundle under the bedclothes. The light was still on, and his book had slid to the floor. Something was clutched in his hand, and I drew the sheet aside to see what it was – one of the Queen's soldiers with the fur hats.

I picked up the book, straightened the bedclothes, turned off the light and went softly out, taking the unwanted chocolate back to the pantry.

Back in my room, I walked straight through it onto the balcony, letting the curtains fall behind me to cut off the light. The night was calm, and unexpectedly warm. There was still no sign of fog, but I thought that could see a paler darkness away in the valley's depths. The damp of spring hung in the air. An owl called below me, down in the woods, called again. Its muted melancholy found too ready an echo in me. I felt tired and depressed. Too much had happened today; and the pleasant things – the morning's encounter with William Blake, my gay little flirtation with Florimond in the salon – had somehow faded back out of mind and left me with this queerly flattened feeling.

I know what it was, of course. I'd lived with loneliness a long time. That was something which was always there . . . one learns to keep it at bay, there are times when one even enjoys it – but there are also times when a desperate self-sufficiency doesn't quite suffice, and then the search for the anodyne begins . . . the radio, the dog, the shampoo, the stockings-to-wash, the tin soldier. . . .

I bit my lip and took myself sharply to task. Just because I had had two pleasantly off-duty encounters – not to mention a cosy and entertaining gossip with the housekeeper – I didn't have to feel let-down and left out when they were over and I had to put in the evening by myself. I didn't have to stand here glooming at the spring dusk and picturing myself for the rest of my life relegated to the edge of the room, the frame of the conversation-piece.

And what did I want, for heaven's sake? To retreat on the illusion that Florimond's courtesy had created, that he and I and Madame de Valmy could share a fireside on equal terms? To be where Madame de Valmy was? Where I might still have been if the thing that happened nine years ago hadn't happened? Well, *that* was out, and the sooner I accepted once and for all the fact that the jamboree was over, the sooner I would stop riding this uneasy see-saw of moods and memories.

I turned deliberately and walked along to the southern end of the balcony until I stood above the salon.

The light from the long windows, muted by gold curtains, streamed softly across the loggia and onto the terrace. The bare rose-bushes stood out, thorn and twig in a naked mesh netting the light. Their shadows raked away like besoms over the freshly-dug beds. One window had been opened to the mild night, and here the light streamed out boldly, and with it the sound of talk and laughter. I could imagine the spurting glow of the log fire, the gleam of rummers, the smell of coffee and brandy, and cigars. . . .

Goodnight, Miss Eyre . . . amusement supervened and with it sanity. I grinned to myself as I walked softly back to my own window. If I did have to spend the rest of my life sitting in the corner of someone else's drawing-room, knitting and wearing black bombazine – whatever that was – then by God it would be the best bombazine. The very best bombazine.

Ignoring the anodynes of book, radio and stockings-to-wash, I got my coat and went out.

I went down the zigzag very slowly, for in the faint moonlight the slope was deceptive, and the slight dampness made the surface slippery. There was a way down through the wood itself – a steep track of alternate step-and-slope that short-circuited the zigzag – but it would have been too dark under the trees, so I avoided it and kept to the road.

The air was very still. Below me, in the valley-depths where the river ran, I could see, quite distinctly now, the pale drift of mist. The owl cried again once, very sadly, from the wood. There was a strong wet smell of earth and growing things; the smell of spring . . . not softness, not balm-and-blossoms, but something harsh and sharp that pierced the senses as the thrust of new life broke the ground. *The cruellest month, breeding Lilacs out of the dead land* . . . yes, that was it. That was *it*. Not for the first time I was sharply grateful to Daddy for making poetry a habit with me. *The best words in the best order* . . . one always got the same shock of recognition and delight when someone's words swam up to meet a thought or name a picture. Daddy had been right. Poetry was awfully good material to think with.

Something rustled in last year's beech-leaves and poetry fled as, absurdly, I remembered that there were still bears in France. And boars. And probably wolves. And werewolves and vampires too, no doubt ... by mocking myself I got at length safely down to river-level and the bridge to the main road.

The bridge was an elegant affair of the eighteenth century, with carved balustrading that opened in graceful curves towards the river-banks. The mist was thick here, but only in patches. Where I stood it was waist-high, but beyond the parapet to my right it slanted down like a snowbank to lie low over the water, pinned through here and there by spikes of bulrush and the black spars of dead boughs.

The water itself was invisible. The sound of it was dark and deep, a lovely liquid undertone to the night. The owl's breathy call fell less sadly now, less hollowly through the dim boughs.

I stood still in the centre of the bridge, my hands deep in my pockets, and gazed up at the steeply wooded slope on the other side of the main road. Rank upon rank of pines, I knew, crowded up those rocky heights, with here and there a bare crag jutting through, where in daylight the hawks mewed and circled. Now, in the faint moonlight, the forest was no more than a looming darkness, a towering cloud faintly luminous where the crescent moon feather-edged the rims of the pines. The scent drifted down, spicy and sharp and somehow dark like the pines themselves.

A car was coming up the valley. I heard the sound of the engine grow and fade and grow again as the curving road and the mist cut off and distorted the sound. It came round Belle Surprise, high above the mist, before I saw its lights. I saw them turn then, tilt, and drive down into the darkness, to bend this way and that among the trees, brightening and then blurring as the fog-clouds blunted them. I watched the stems of the trees outline themselves sharply against the light, to reel away like logs tumbling over a waterfall, then swoop back and up into the towering shadow behind the glare where still the tree-stems blanched, drifted, and darkened. ...

Only a late lorry driving up to Soubirous. ... The headlights went steadily past the end of the bridge, and the mist tossed and whirled in the red of the tail-lamp.

I was turning to go back up the zigzag, when my eye was caught by a tiny light high up among the Dieudonné trees. A minute before it had not been there, but now it pricked through the cloud of pines like a small yellow star.

I stopped and looked up at it. The trees along the roadside were busy in their ghostly dance as another lorry roared up the valley, but that tiny light hung there high above them, warm and steady. No, not a star: a planet, and lived-on at that. It might very well not be William Blake's little hut at four thousand feet, but somehow I thought it was. I smiled to myself picturing him sitting up there with his bandages and boluses (what *was* a bolus?) and thermometers in degrees Centigrade.

The second lorry thundered past the end of the bridge.

And the cognac – had he remembered the cognac?

I hadn't noticed the car travelling quietly behind the enormous lorry. I didn't see it until it turned sharp onto the narrow bridge and came at me like a torpedo.

It was an easy corner, and he took it fast. The main beam leaped out and pinned me full in the glare. I heard his brakes shriek as they bit metal. I jumped for the edge of the road. The lights lurched and tyres screeched and ripped the tarmac. One yard: that was all the leeway he had. Something grabbed at me; tore. I slipped on the greasy road and fell flat in the gutter under the parapet as the car went by with a foot and a half to spare and screamed to a skidding halt beyond the bridge.

The engine cut. The door slammed. Léon de Valmy's voice said: 'Where are you? Are you hurt? I didn't touch you, did I?' Quick footsteps sounded on the tarmac. 'Where are you?'

I had risen to my knees in the wet gutter, and was holding rather hard to the parapet. At the sound of the footsteps and that familiar voice I thought I must have been hit and gone mad. I was blind, too. I couldn't see anything, anyone. I was blinking in a dazed sort of panic as I pulled myself shakily to my feet. . . .

I wasn't blinded after all; the mist sank and dwindled and swirled waist-high again as I turned, leaning back for support against the parapet.

Nor was I mad. The man who was striding towards me in the moonlight was not Léon de Valmy, though thirty years ago Léon de Valmy had probably looked exactly like him. As with his father, my first impression of Raoul de Valmy was that he was remarkably good-looking; but where age and illness had given the older man's looks the fine-drawn, fallen-angel quality he had mocked to me on our first meeting, there was nothing in the least fine-drawn about Raoul. He merely looked tough, arrogant, and (at the moment) furious. It wasn't exactly the time to judge whether he possessed the charm which his father could apparently radiate at will, though his personality certainly made (this without irony) as strong an impact. But the difference was there again: where Léon de Valmy kept himself banked down, so to speak, and burning secretly, Raoul was at full blaze. And just now he was blazing with something more than personality. He was as shaken as I was, and it had made him angry.

I sat down suddenly on the parapet, and waited. He loomed over me, tall and formidable-looking in the misty moonlight.

Tall, dark and handsome . . . the romantic cliché repeated itself in my head – so automatically and irresistibly that I braced myself to dislike him on sight.

He said sharply: 'Are you hurt?'

'No.'

'Did I hit you?'

'No.'

'Not even touch you?'

I was smoothing my coat down with unsteady fingers. 'N – no.'

'You're sure you're all right?'

'Yes. I – yes. Thank you.'

I heard his breath expelled in quick relief. He relaxed and his voice warmed then into anger. 'Then will you kindly tell me what the bloody hell you were doing standing in the middle of the road in a fog? You came damned near being killed and if you had you'd have deserved it!'

Shock was reacting on me too, and I wasn't used to being sworn at. I stopped fussing with my clothes and lifted my head to glare straight back at him. 'It's not a public road and I've a perfect right to stand in the middle of it or sit in the middle of it or lie in the middle of it if I want to! I wasn't expecting you – at least I'd quite forgotten you were coming and in any case you've no business to come at that speed, whether it's a private road or not!'

There was a fractional pause, during which I had the impression that he was distinctly taken aback. Then he said mildly: 'I was only doing fifty, and I know the road like the back of my hand.'

'*Fifty!*' I heard my voice rise to a squeak, and was furious. 'Why, that's – oh, kilometres, of course.'

'What else?'

'It's still far too fast and there was mist.'

'I could see the way quite well and that car sits down on the corners like a broody hen.' He was beginning to sound amused, and that made me angrier.

I snapped: 'Broody hen or no, it very nearly ran me down!'

'I'm quite aware of that. But I would hardly expect to find anyone standing on the bridge at this time of night—'

He stopped and then went on, the amusement now clear in his voice: 'I'm damned if I see why I should have to stand here defending myself for not having run you over! Perhaps now you'll be good enough to tell me why you consider you've a perfect right to stand – or was it lie down? – in the middle of this particular private road? This is my – this is the Valmy estate, you know.'

I was busy wiping my muddy hands on a handkerchief. 'Yes,' I said, 'I live here.'

He made a little movement of surprise, and I saw his eyes narrow on me in the moonlight. 'Surely,' he said, 'you're not one of the, er—?'

'Servants? In a way,' I said. 'I'm Philippe's governess.'

'But,' said Raoul de Valmy, slowly, 'they told me she was to be an English girl.'

I felt as if he had dealt me a sharp blow in the stomach. For the first time I realised that the whole of the exchange had been in French. Literally thrown off my balance as I had been, I had answered him without thinking in the tongue that he had first used.

I said feebly: 'I – I forgot.'

'You are English?' he said, in a tone of great surprise.

I nodded. 'Linda Martin, from London. I've been here three weeks.'

His voice was a little dry. 'Then allow me to congratulate you on your progress, Miss Martin.'

But this second shock had shaken me quite out of all composure. The dry note in his voice was so like Léon de Valmy's that I found myself saying, in a taut little voice that was pitched a shade too high: 'You must know perfectly well that I haven't learned all my French in the last three weeks, Monsieur de Valmy, so don't add insult to injury by baiting me as well as knocking me down!'

This was palpable injustice and I half-expected the annihilation I deserved. But he merely said: 'I'm sorry. And now do you feel recovered enough to move? I shouldn't keep you here talking any more. You must have had a nasty shaking. We'll get you into the car and I'll drive you up to the house.'

Like his father, he knew how to disarm. . . . I found myself obediently sliding off the parapet to my feet, while he put a steadying hand under my elbow.

'I'm all right,' I said.

But when I tried to move towards the car I found that my knees were very shaky still, and I was thankful for his support.

He said quickly: 'You're limping. You *are* hurt.'

I found myself reassuring him. 'Not by you. I slipped and fell when I tried to jump out of the way. It's only a bumped knee or something. Honestly, that's all.'

He said, sounding worried. 'Well, I think the sooner I get you up to the château and find you a drink, the better. You'll have to get in by the driver's door, I'm afraid. The other one's rather difficult of access just at present.'

This was, I saw, only too true. The big car, in swerving to avoid me, had skidded slightly on the damp tarmac, and run up onto the right-hand verge of the road beyond the bridge. The verge at this point was a muddy grass bank, mercifully not very steep, but quite steep enough to cant the car at a crazy-looking angle.

I looked at it guiltily, and then up at Raoul de Valmy's impassive face.

'I – it isn't damaged, is it?'

'I don't think so. Would you rather wait on the road while I straighten her out, or had you better get in and sit down?'

'I think if it's all the same to you I'll sit down.'

'Of course.' He opened the nearside door. I got in – with just a little difficulty, as my knee was undoubtedly stiff, and got myself somehow past the wheel and into the passenger's seat. He leaned into the car and groped in the darkness under the dash. There was a click, and the headlamps flashed on, so that just in front of the car the first bend and slope of the zigzag strode forward at us, a ragged white wall of tree and rock, not six feet from the front bumper.

He didn't even glance at it. 'Just a minute,' he said. He slammed the door and went round to the back of the car.

I closed my eyes to shut out the sight of that looming rock-wall, and lay back in the deep seat, relaxing as well as I could. The car was very big and very comfortable, even tilted as it was at that odd angle. It smelled faintly of cigarettes and expensive leather. I opened my eyes again. In the light reflected back off the rock ahead the bonnet gleamed long and black – plenty of horses under that, I thought, and remembered Mrs. Seddon's description: '*As long as the Queen Mary and a horn like the Last Trump.*' I wondered what Raoul de Valmy's lucky number was. . . .

I settled my shoulders back in the luxurious seat. The shaky feeling had almost gone. Suddenly out of nowhere I remembered something I had once heard at the Constance Butcher – a piece of servant-girls' lore which had amused me at the time and now came back with an added point. *If you ever get run over, be sure and pick a Rolls-Royce.* . . . Well, there was something in that, I reflected . . . and a Cadillac was perhaps not a bad second choice, especially when it had as good a driver as Raoul de Valmy at the wheel. Now that the first shock had subsided I realised perfectly well how near I had been to being badly hurt, through my own silliness. Moreover it was no thanks to me that Monsieur Raoul's expensive Cadillac hadn't smashed itself against the parapet.

I became aware that Raoul de Valmy was still behind the car. I peered back through the swirls of mist to see him bending over a rear wing, while torchlight moved slowly over the metal. I bit my lip, but before I could speak he had straightened up, switched off the torch, and come swiftly round to the driver's door.

He slanted a quick look at me as he slid in beside me. 'All right?' I nodded. 'We'll soon get you home. Hold tight.'

He touched the starter button and the engine snarled to life. He thrust the big car very gently forward and to the left; she moved, jerked, hesitated, and then the front wheels swooped down with a plunge to the level of the road. The back wheels seemed to mount for a moment, then slid down after them, and the car rolled onto the level road and stopped there, rocking gently on her superb springs.

'*Et voilà,*' said Raoul de Valmy, and smiled at me.

As his hand moved on the hand-brake I said, in a small voice: 'Monsieur de Valmy.'

The hand paused. 'Yes?'

'Before you take me back I – I'd like to apologise. I'm most awfully sorry, really I am.'

'Apologise? And for what? My dear ma'am—'

I said: 'Don't be so *nice* about it, *please*! I know it was really my fault and you're making me feel a *worm*!' I heard him laugh, but I went on doggedly and not very clearly: 'I had no business to be in the road and you saved my life by doing what you did and then I went and was rude to you and you were nothing but nice to me when ninety-nine drivers out of a hundred would have blasted me from here to Madagascar, and it's true, I do feel a worm. An utter *crawling* worm! And' – I took breath and finished idiotically – 'if you've damaged your car you can stop it out of my wages!'

He was still laughing at me. 'Thank you. But it's not damaged, as it happens.'

'Is that the truth?' I asked suspiciously.

'Yes. Not a scratch. I thought I heard something as she skidded, but it was only a bit of a fallen branch hitting the wheel. Not a mark. So no apologies please, Miss Martin. If anybody should apologise, it's I. I believe I swore at you. I'm sorry.'

'That's all right,' I said, a little awkwardly. 'We were both a bit shaken up, I suppose. I didn't quite know where I was or what I was saying.'

He said nothing. He seemed to be waiting. He made no move to start the car. I stole a sidelong look at him and saw that he was watching me steadily, with the amusement gone from his face. It was an oddly daunting look, and, though he had been much nicer to me than I deserved, I found that I was gripping my hands between my knees to give myself courage to go on.

I said: 'I knew so little about what I was saying that I'm afraid I gave myself away to you.'

'When you spoke to me in French.' It was not a question.

'Yes.'

His hand moved to the ignition, and the engine died. He cut off the headlights, so that the car stood islanded in the little glow of side and tail-lamps. He half-turned towards me, his shoulder propped back against the door. I couldn't see his face now, and his voice told me nothing. He said: 'This is interesting. So I was right?'

'That they didn't know I was partly French when I got the job? Yes.'

He said: 'I'm not your employer, you know. You don't have to explain. But as a matter of curiosity, do I understand that you did deliberately deceive my father and Madame de Valmy over this?'

'I – I'm afraid so.'

'Why?'

'Because I wanted the job.'

'But I don't see why—'

I pressed my hands tightly together, and said carefully: 'I *needed* the job. I – I'll try and tell you why, though I don't suppose you'll understand. . . .' He started to say something but I went on quickly and not very coherently: 'I'm partly French and I was brought up in Paris. When I was fourteen Maman and Daddy were killed in a plane crash. Daddy was writing a script for a film to be made in Venice, and Maman went with him for the holiday. The – oh, the details don't matter, but

I finished up in an orphanage in London. . . . I don't know if you've ever been inside an orphanage?'

'No.'

'Well, the details don't matter there, either. They were very kind to me. But I wanted – oh, to *live*, to find some place in the world that was mine, and somehow I seemed to be getting nowhere. My schooling was all to blazes, what with the war and – and everything, so I can't do much, but I got a job at a small private school. I – I wasn't very happy there, either. Then when one of our governors heard that Madame de Valmy wanted an English governess it seemed like a gift from heaven. I told you I'm not qualified to do much, but I can look after children and I knew I could make a good job of Philippe's English and I thought it would be so wonderful to be in France and living in a real home again.'

He said, very dryly: 'So you came to Valmy.'

'Yes. That's all.'

There was a pause. He said: 'I do understand, I think. But there was no need to explain all this to me, you know. I've no right to question you.'

I said shyly: 'I felt I sort of owed you something. And you did ask me why I wanted the job.'

'No. You misunderstand me. I asked you why you had deceived my father and Héloïse about it.'

I began, rather stupidly: 'I told you—'

'I should have said, rather, why you *had* to deceive them. I'm not concerned in the least with the fact that you did do so.' I caught the glimmer of a smile. 'I merely find myself wondering why it was necessary. Are you trying to tell me that you concealed the fact you were partly French because you wouldn't in that case have got the job?'

'I – yes, more or less.'

A little silence. 'Indeed.'

'It wasn't put like that,' I said hastily, 'not said in so many words. But – but I honestly did get the impression that it might have mattered. I mean, once we had got past the point where I should have told Madame de Valmy I couldn't very well go back and confess or she'd have thought there was something queer about me and she'd never have looked at me. And she'd made rather a lot of the fact that I wouldn't be tempted to lapse into French when I was talking to Philippe – I'm supposed always to talk to him in English, you see. I didn't really see that it mattered, myself, because I could have taken care to speak English with him anyway, but – well, she was so emphatic about it that I – oh, I just let it slide. I know I was silly,' I finished miserably, 'and it's such a stupid little thing, but there it is.'

'And I suppose I'm to understand,' he said, still rather dryly, 'that they still don't know.'

'Yes.'

'I see.' To my relief he was beginning to sound amused again. 'Haven't you found that such a deception – I'm sorry I started by using such a harsh term for it – has its socially embarrassing moments?'

'You mean overhearing things I'm not meant to? No, because Monsieur's and Madame's manners are too good.' Here he laughed outright, and I said rather confusedly: 'I mean – when I meet them without Philippe they always talk English, and when I take Philippe to see them they talk about his lessons, which I know about anyway; and in any case I don't listen.'

He said: 'Well, I should stop worrying about it. As far as I can see it can hardly matter one way or the other.' He turned in his seat and started the engine. The lights sprang up. I could see him smiling. 'And I certainly didn't mean to add insult to injury by turning this into an inquisition! Forgive me; it's not my affair.'

'Monsieur,' I said quickly, in a rather small voice.

'Yes?'

'I – I wonder if you'd not – I mean—' I floundered and stopped.

He gave me a quick glance. 'You wondered if I'd not give you away?'

'Yes. Please,' I added, feeling even smaller.

There was a fractional pause. 'For what it's worth,' said Raoul de Valmy, slowly, 'I shan't. . . . And now I think we'd better make tracks. . . .'

The car moved forward and took the first slope at a decorous speed.

He drove in silence, and I had time to reflect with wry surprise that shock produces some very odd after-effects. What on earth had impelled me to blurt out that naïve and stumbling betrayal of my pathetic needs to Raoul de Valmy's no doubt hard-bitten sophistication? *Daddy and Maman . . . they were very kind to me at the orphanage. . . .* What did it matter to him? A dreary little fool, that was what he'd think of me. And that's what I was, anyway, I thought, remembering my depression of earlier that evening. I bit my lip. What did it matter anyway? He probably hadn't even been listening. He had more important things than Philippe's governess on his mind. Bellevigne, for instance, or whatever had driven him up to see his father in the face of what appeared to be his normal welcome at the Château Valmy.

I found myself remembering Florimond's presence with a species of relief, and then felt amused. Raoul de Valmy would hardly need the same kind of protection as Philippe.

I said: 'Monsieur Florimond's here this evening.'

'Oh? Is he staying long?'

'I think he only came to dine, but if the mist gets thicker he'll probably stay.'

'Ah,' said Raoul, 'that's something else to put down to the fog's account. It's an ill wind, they say.'

I was still working that one out when the Cadillac swung off the last rise and came to a whispering halt at the foot of the steps.

Seddon was crossing the hall as we came in. He turned when he saw Raoul and came hurrying to meet him, then his eye fell on me, and a slight twitch of dismay crossed his impassive features.

'Mr. Raoul! Miss Martin! Has there been an accident?'

'I nearly ran Miss Martin over on the Valmy bridge. I suggest that you get her some brandy now, and send someone upstairs—'

'No, please,' I said quickly, 'I don't want any brandy. I'm all right now, Seddon. Mr Raoul never touched me; I slipped and fell as I was getting out of the way. It was all my fault. I'll just go upstairs and have a bath and then make some tea in the pantry.'

Seddon hesitated, glancing at Raoul, but I said firmly: 'It's all right, really it is. I don't want a thing.'

'Well, miss, if you're sure. . . .' He looked at Raoul. 'I'll have your things taken straight up, sir. You're in your usual room.'

'Thank you. How are you, Seddon? And Mrs. Seddon? The asthma keeping away?'

'Yes, thank you, sir, we're both well.'

'That's fine. I'll come upstairs in a moment. Where's everyone? The small salon?'

'Yes, sir. Monsieur Florimond is here, sir, and he's staying the night. Shall I tell Madame you've arrived?'

'If you will. Say I'll join them in a few minutes.'

'Very good, sir.' And, with a final glance at me, he went.

As I turned to follow him, Raoul said: 'You've torn your frock.'

I looked down, unable to suppress a movement of dismay. My coat was open. At the hem of my frock a tear showed.

'Oh, yes. I remember now. I felt it catch on something. But it's nothing much. It'll mend.'

He was frowning. 'The bumper must have caught you. I really am most—'

'Raoul?'

The voice came from behind me. I jumped and spun round. Raoul must have been inured to his father's methods of approach, for he merely turned, said 'How d'you do, sir?' and held out a hand. As Léon de Valmy took it his brilliant dark gaze turned to me.

'What's this? Did I hear something about a bumper catching you?'

I said: 'It's nothing.'

'Miss Martin and I,' said Raoul, smiling, 'met – rather abruptly – down on the Valmy bridge.'

His father's eyes went to the torn hem of my frock; went lower to a laddered stocking and the stain of a muddy graze on my leg. 'You mean you knocked her over?'

I said quickly: 'Oh, no, nothing like that! I fell down and bumped my knee, that's all. Monsieur Raoul didn't touch me. It—'

'That tear wasn't done by falling down. That stuff's been ripped. Was that done by that damned great car of yours, Raoul?'

Temper flicked suddenly, patently, through the words, like a whip. For a moment I was reminded of the way I had heard him speak to Philippe, pilloried beside the yellow-brocaded chair, and, damn it, Raoul was – what? thirty? I felt myself going hot with embarrassment, and glanced at him.

But this was not Philippe. He merely said, unruffled: 'I imagine so. I had only just noticed it. I was abasing myself when you came in.' He turned back to me, 'Miss Martin, I really am most terribly sorry—'

'Oh, please!' I cried. 'It was nothing. It was my own fault!'

Monsieur de Valmy said: 'What were you doing down on the bridge at this time of night?'

'I went out for a walk,' I said. 'It was damp in the woods so I went down the road.'

'What happened?'

Raoul began to speak but I said hastily: 'I stopped in the middle of the bridge. I was going to turn back and I stood for a minute or two listening to the water. It was a silly thing to do, because there was a drift of mist there over the river, and Monsieur Raoul ran slap into it. But I'd forgotten he was coming.'

'Forgotten?'

I looked at him in faint surprise. Then I remembered that the conversation in the salon had been in French. I said steadily, hoping my colour hadn't risen: 'Mrs. Seddon told me this evening that he was coming.'

'Ah. Yes.' The dark eyes were unreadable under the heavy black brows. He looked at Raoul. 'And then?'

I said quickly: 'So of course Monsieur Raoul didn't see me – he couldn't have seen me till he was just about running me down. It was entirely my own fault and I'm lucky to get away with a bruise and a torn frock. If it was the car that tore it that's all it touched, honestly. The bruise I got myself by slipping and falling in the gutter.'

Léon de Valmy was still frowning. 'That's a bad corner . . . as we all know.' The cutting-edge was back on his voice. 'Raoul, if you must come up that road on a night like this—'

Raoul said gently: 'I have already told Miss Martin how sorry I am.'

Something sparked inside me. My employer had a perfect right to catechise me, but not to make his son look a fool in front of me. And I'd seen a little too much of his tactics tonight already. I said hotly: 'And I have explained to Monsieur Raoul that the fault was mine and mine only. So please may we drop the subject? It isn't fair that he should be blamed. If he'd been any less brilliant a driver I'd have been killed!'

I stopped. I had seen the faintest, least definable shade of amusement in Raoul's face, and in his father's something that was, less mistakably, anger. He said smoothly, but with the edge still on the carefully pedantic words: 'A brilliant driver should not have to call upon his skill to that extent at such a dangerous corner.'

Raoul smiled at him and said, very pleasantly: 'The corner was relaid last autumn . . . by the Bellevigne estate, remember? And are you sure you're qualified to criticise my driving? You forget that both roads and cars have altered considerably since you were last able to drive.'

In the sharp little silence that followed I saw the lines round Léon de Valmy's mouth deepen, and the white hands moved on the arms of the chair. He said nothing. Raoul smiled lazily down at him. No, this was not Philippe. No wonder he'd been amused when I wild-catted to his defence. I thought, with an absurd rush of pleasure: *that for Philippe, Monsieur the Demon King!*

Raoul turned to me and said easily: 'Are you sure you won't have something sent up to you, Miss Martin?'

'Quite sure.' I looked from one to the other a bit uncertainly. 'Goodnight, Monsieur de Valmy. Goodnight, Monsieur Raoul.'

I went quickly upstairs, leaving the two of them together.

Fifth Coach

CHAPTER EIGHT

Thou art more deep damn'd than Prince Lucifer:
There is not yet so ugly a fiend of hell
As thou shalt be, if thou didst kill this child.

SHAKESPEARE: *King John*

Next day all traces of mist had gone, and the trees moved lightly in their Lenten green. Since the winds of March had whipped some of the buds into tiny leaf, our favourite walk had been the way through the woods that stretched northwards down the valley, and this afternoon we went that way again.

We started down the path that short-circuited the zigzag. For all its steepness it was not bad walking, as the path itself was ribbed across with sunken logs to give a foothold, and the occasional flights of steps were in good repair, with wide flat treads scored and clear of moss. Here and there the path crossed a trickle of water; sometimes the bridge was only a step, a slab of stone over a mossy trough where water chuckled; but in places some streamlet had cut deeply through the rock into miniature cascades, spanned by sturdy little bridges no more than two planks' width, with a single handrail of untrimmed pine.

It was on these bridges that Philippe loved to linger, gazing down at the ferns and grasses swaying in the wind of the cascade, and counting what he fondly imagined to be the fish attempting to leap up the spray. This afternoon we hung happily together over the biggest of the pools where fingers of bright sunlight probed the ferns and made an iridescent bloom of fine spray.

'Three,' said Philippe, triumphantly. '*Voilà*, did you see her? Beside the stone there, where the waves are!'

I peered down at the whirling pool some fifteen feet below us. 'I can't see anything. And it's not *her*, Philippe.'

'It was. Truly it was. I am seeing her—'

'I'm sure you are. But a fish isn't *her*, it's *it*.'

'A trout is her in French,' said Philippe firmly. It was a great source of pride to him that my French was worse than his English.

'No doubt,' I said, 'but not in English. Oh, look, there's one, Philippe, definitely! I saw her – it jump!'

'Four.' Philippe knew when to pursue his triumphs and when to hold his tongue. 'Four and a half, because I do not know if that shadow is a *truite* – trout, or a shadow.' He gripped the rail and leaned over, peering eagerly down.

'Let's go on,' I said. 'If it's still there when we come back, it's a shadow. Let's go down into the big wood again.'

He turned obediently off the bridge onto the wide level path that led along the hillside deeper into the trees. 'All right. To look for wolves?'

'*Wolves?*'

He was trotting ahead of me. He turned, laughing. 'Mademoiselle, you sounded quite frightened! Did you think there were really wolves?'

'Well, I—'

He gave a crow of laughter and a comic little skip that shuffled up last year's dead leaves. 'You did! You did!'

'Well,' I said, 'I've never lived in a place like this before. For all I know Valmy might be crawling with wolves.'

'We have got bears,' confided Philippe, in the tone of one inviting congratulations. He looked earnestly up at me. 'We truly have. This is not a *blague*. Many bears of a bigness incredible.' His scarlet-gloved hands sketched in the air something of the dimensions of an overgrown grizzly. 'I have never seen one, *vous comprenez*, but Bernard has shot one. He told me so.'

'Then I hope to goodness we don't meet one today.'

'They are asleep,' said Philippe comfortingly. 'There is no danger unless one treads on them where they sleep.' He jumped experimentally into a deep drift of dead leaves, sending them swirling up in bright flakes of gold. The drift was, fortunately, bearless. 'They sleep very sound,' said Philippe, who appeared to find it necessary to excuse this failure, 'with nuts in the pocket, like an *écureuil*.'

'Squirrel.'

'Skervirrel. Perhaps you prefer that we do not look for bears?'

'I would really rather not, if you don't mind,' I said apologetically.

'Then we will not,' he said generously. 'But there are many other things to see in the woods, I think. Papa used to tell me of them. There is chamois and *marmottes* and the foxes, oh, many! Do you think that when I have ten years—'

' "When I am ten".'

'When I am ten years I can have a gun and shoot, mademoiselle?'

'Possibly not when you're ten, Philippe, but certainly when you're a bit older.'

'Ten is old.'

'It may be old, but it's not very big. You wouldn't be of a bigness – I mean you wouldn't be big enough to use the right gun for a bear.'

'Skervirrels, then.'

'Squirrel.'

'Skervirrel. I could have a small gun for skervirrel when I am ten?'

'Possibly, though I should doubt it. In any case, it's what they call an unworthy ambition.'

'*Plaît-il?*' He was still jigging along slightly in front of me, laughing back over his shoulder, his face for once flushed and bright under his scarlet woollen ski-cap. He said cheekily: 'English, please.'

I laughed. 'I meant that it's a shame to shoot squirrels. They're charming.'

'Char-ming? No, they are not. They eat the young trees. They cause much work, lose much money. The foresters say it. One must shoot them.'

'Very French,' I said dryly.

'I *am* French,' said Philippe, skipping gaily on ahead, 'and they are *my* trees, and I shall have a gun when I am older and go out every day to shoot the skervirrels. Look! There's one! *Bang!*' He proceeded, with gestures, to shoot down several squirrels very loudly, singing meanwhile an extremely noisy and shapeless song whose burden was something like:

> *Bang, bang, bang,*
> *Bang, bang, bang,*
> *Got you, got you,*
> *Bang, bang, bang.*

'If you don't look where you're going,' I said, 'it'll be you who'll – look *out*, you silly chump!'

Then three things happened, almost simultaneously.

Philippe, laughing back at me as he jigged along, tripped over a tree-root and fell headlong. Something struck the tree beside him with the sound of a hand smacking the bark, and, a fraction later, the sharp crack of a rifle split the silence of the woods.

I don't know how long it took me to grasp just what had happened. The unmistakable crack of the gun, and the child's body flat in the path ... for one heart-stopping moment terror zigzagged like pain through my blood. Then even as Philippe moved the significance of that sharp smack on the tree's bole struck me, and I knew he was not hit.

I found myself shouting into the silent woods that sloped above us: 'Don't shoot, you fool! There are people here!' Then I was beside Philippe, bending over him, making sure. . . .

The bullet had not touched him, of course; but when I looked up and saw the hole in the tree just above where he lay, I realised how nearly he had been missed. The silly little jigging song that had tripped him up had saved his life.

He lifted a face from which all the bright gaiety and colour had gone. There was mud on one thin little cheek and his eyes were scared.

'It was a gun. Something hit the tree. A bullet.'

He spoke, of course, in French. This was no moment to insist either on his English or my own false position. In any case he had just heard me shouting in French at the owner of the gun. I put my arms round him and spoke in the same tongue. 'Some silly fool out with a rifle after foxes.' (Did one shoot foxes with a rifle?) 'It's all right, Philippe, it's all right. A silly mistake, that's all. He'd hear me shout and he'll be far more scared than we were.' I smiled at him and got up, pulling him to his feet. 'I expect he thought you were a wolf.'

Philippe was shaking, too, and I saw now that it was with anger as much as fright. 'He has no business to shoot like that. Wolves don't sing, and in any case you don't shoot at *sounds*. You wait till you can *see*. He is a fool, an imbecile. He should not have a gun. I shall get him dismissed.'

I let him rage on in a shaken shrill little voice, a queer and rather touching mixture of scared child and angry Comte de Valmy. I was scanning the slopes of open wood above us for the approach of an alarmed and apologetic keeper. It was quite a few seconds before I realised that the wood was, apparently, empty. The path where we walked ran between widely-spaced trees. Above us sloped some hundred yards of rough grass – an open space of sunlight and sparse young beeches, where brambles and honeysuckle tangled over the roots of felled trees. At the crest of the rise was a tumble of rock and the dark ridge of a planted forest. Nothing moved. Whoever was at large there with a rifle had no intention of admitting the recent piece of lunatic carelessness.

I said, my jerking heart shaking my voice a little: 'You're right. He shouldn't be allowed out, whoever he is. You wait here. Since he won't come out I'm going to see—'

'*No!*' It was no more than a breath, but he caught hold of my hand and held it fast.

'But Philippe – now look, son, you'll be all right. He's miles away by now and getting further every second. Let me go, there's a good chap.'

'*No!*'

I looked up through the empty wood, then down at the small pinched face under the scarlet cap.

'All right,' I said, 'we'll go home.'

We were hurrying back the way we had come. I still held Philippe's hand. He clutched at me tightly. I said, still shaken and angry: 'We'll soon find out, Philippe, don't worry, and your uncle'll dismiss him. Either he's a careless fool who's too scared to come out, or he's a lunatic who thinks that sort of thing's a joke, but your uncle can find out. He'll be dismissed, you'll see.'

He said nothing. He half-trotted, half-shuffled along beside me, silent and sober. No skipping now, or singing. I said, trying to sound calm and reasonable above the blaze inside me: 'Whatever the case, we're going straight to Monsieur de Valmy.'

The hand tucked in mine twitched slightly. 'No.'

'But, my dear Philippe—!' I broke off, and glanced down at the averted scarlet cap. 'All right, you needn't, but I must. I'll get Berthe to come and give you some five-o'clock and stay with you till I get back to the schoolroom. I'll ask Tante Héloïse if she'll visit you upstairs instead of making you go down to the salon, and then we'll play Peggitty till bedtime. How's that?'

The red cap merely nodded. We trudged on in silence for a bit. We came to the bridge where we had counted the trout, and Philippe walked straight over it without a glance at the pool below.

The blaze of anger licked up inside me again. I said: 'We'll get the stupid criminal fool dismissed, Philippe. Now stop worrying about it.'

He nodded again, and then stole a queer little look up at me.

'What is it?'

'You've been talking French,' said Philippe. 'I just noticed.'

'So I have.' I smiled at him. 'Well, I could hardly expect you to remember your English when you were being shot at like a *skervirrel*, could I?'

He gave the ghost of a little smile.

'You say it wrong,' he said. 'It's *squirrel*.'

Then, quite suddenly, he began to cry.

Madame de Valmy was alone in the rose-garden. Early violas were already budding beside the path where she walked. There were daffodils out along the edge of the terrace. She had some in her hands.

She was facing in our direction, and she saw us as soon as we emerged from the woods. She had been stooping for a flower, and she stopped in mid-movement, then slowly straightened up, the forgotten daffodil trailing from her fingers. Even at that distance – we were still some hundred yards away – she must have been able to see the mud on Philippe's coat and the general air of dejection that dragged at him.

She started towards us.

'Philippe! What in the world has happened? Your coat! Have you fallen down? Miss Martin' – her voice was sharp with real concern – 'Miss Martin, not another accident, surely?'

I was breathless from the hasty ascent, and still angry. I said baldly: 'Someone shot at Philippe in the wood down there.'

She had been half-bending towards the little boy. At my uncompromising words she stopped as if she had been struck.

'Shot ... at Philippe?'

'Yes. They only missed him because he tripped and fell. The bullet hit a tree.'

She straightened up slowly, her eyes on my face. She was very pale. 'But – this is absurd! Who could. ... Did you see who it was?'

'No. He must have known what had happened, because I shouted. But he didn't appear.'

'And Philippe?' She turned shocked eyes to him. '*Comment ça va, p'tit? On ne t'a fait mal?*'

A shake of the red cap and a quiver of the hand in mine were the only answers. My own hand closed on his.

'He fell down,' I said, 'but he didn't really hurt himself. He's been very brave about the whole thing.' I didn't feel it necessary to insist in front of the child that, but for the tumble, he would probably now be dead. But Madame de Valmy understood that. She was so white that I thought she would faint. The pale eyes, watching Philippe, held a look, unmistakably, of horror. So she did care after all, I thought, surprised and a little touched. She said faintly: 'This is ... terrible. Such carelessness ... criminal carelessness. You – saw nothing?'

I said crisply: 'Nothing. But it shouldn't be too hard to find out who it was. I'd have gone after him then and there if I'd been able to leave Philippe. But I imagine Monsieur de Valmy can find out who was in the woods this afternoon. Where is Monsieur, Madame?'

'In the library, I expect.' She had one hand to her heart. From the other the daffodils fell in an unheeded scatter. She really did look dreadfully shocked. 'This is – this is a dreadful thing. Philippe might have – might have—'

'I think,' I said, 'that I'd better not keep him out here. Will you excuse us from coming down tonight, madame? Philippe had better have a quiet evening and early bed.'

'Of course. Of course. And you, too, Miss Martin. You have had a shock—'

'Yes, but I'm angry too, and I find it helps. I'll go and see Monsieur de Valmy as soon as I've taken Philippe in.'

She was nodding in a shocked, half-comprehending way. 'Yes. Yes, of course. Monsieur de Valmy will be terribly – annoyed. Terribly annoyed.'

'I hope,' I said grimly, 'that that's an understatement. Come on, Philippe, let's go and find Berthe. Madame. ...'

As we left her I glanced back to see her hurrying away, towards the corner of the terrace. To tell Léon de Valmy herself, no doubt. Well, the sooner the better, I thought, and swept Philippe into the house and upstairs to the haven of the schoolroom.

Berthe was in the pantry, busy with some cleaning. After a swift explanation that shocked her as much as it had Héloïse, I would have left Philippe with her, but he clung to me, and looked so suspiciously like crying again that I stayed with him. Madame de Valmy had certainly taken the tale straight to her husband, who would, no doubt, put the necessary machinery in motion to discover the culprit. For me, Philippe was the first concern.

So I stayed with him and talked determinedly light-hearted nonsense to distract him till at length, fresh from a hot bath, he was safely ensconced with a book on the rug by the schoolroom fire. He made no objection when Berthe brought in her mending and prepared to keep him company while I went down to see his uncle.

Léon de Valmy was alone in the library. I had not been in the room before. It was a high room, lit with two long windows, but warmed and made darker by the oak bookshelves lining it from floor to ceiling. Above the fireplace a huge portrait glowed against the panelling; my first glance told me that it was a young portrait of Raoul de Valmy, looking very handsome in riding-clothes, one hand holding a whip, the other the bridle of a grey Arab pony with large soft eyes and a dark muzzle. I wondered why his father kept it there. Below the portrait a log fire burned in the open hearth, which was flanked by a single armchair. The room contained, apart from its thousands of books and a big desk beside one window, very little furniture. I realised the reason for this as Léon de Valmy's wheel-chair turned from a side-table where he had been leafing through a pile of papers, and glided towards the fire, there to stop in the vacant place opposite the single armchair.

'Come and sit down, Miss Martin.'

I obeyed him. The first rush of my anger had long since ebbed, but nervousness tightened my throat and made me wonder a little desperately how to start.

Not that there was anything even slightly intimidating about him today. His voice and face were grave and friendly as he turned towards me. It came to me then, with a sense of almost physical shock, that the portrait above the mantel was not of his son, but of Léon himself.

He must have caught my involuntary glance upwards, for his own followed it. He sat in silence for a moment, regarding the picture sombrely, then he turned to me and smiled. 'It seems we are an ill-starred race, we Valmys.'

There was the same wryness in voice and smile that I remembered from our first encounter. The slightly dramatic phrasing, no less than the repeated and deliberate reference to a state he ostensibly wanted ignored, jarred on me sharply. Did he see everything then, purely in relation to his own misfortune? I said nothing, but looked away from him to the fire.

He said: 'I am told we have barely escaped another tragedy this afternoon.'

I looked up. (*Another tragedy.*) I said stolidly: 'Has Madame de Valmy seen you?'

'She came straight to me. She was very much shocked and upset. It has made her ill. Her heart, I am afraid, is not robust.' He paused and the dark eyes scanned my face. There was nothing now in his own but gentleness and concern. 'You, too, Miss Martin. I think you had better have a drink. Sherry? Now supposing you tell me what happened.' He reached a hand to the tantalus at his elbow.

'Thank you.' I took the glass gratefully. My nervousness had gone. I was left with an empty feeling of reaction and fatigue. In a voice drained of any emotion I told him briefly of the afternoon's events. 'Do you know who was out with a gun today?' I asked in conclusion.

He lifted his sherry-glass. 'Off-hand, no. Armand Lestocq told me – no, that won't do. He went to Soubirous this afternoon to the sawmill. In any case Armand is never careless with a gun.'

'But you'll be able to find out, won't you? He shouldn't be allowed—'

'I am doing my best.' A glance. 'My active work is mainly done by telephone. And when I do find out he'll be dismissed.'

He was turning the glass round and round in his long fingers, watching the gleam and shift of the firelight in the amber liquid. Behind him the mellow brown-and-gold of the books glinted in the firelight. Outside the dusk fell rapidly; the windows were oblongs of murky grey. Soon Seddon would come to draw the curtains and turn on the lights. Now in the flickering glow of the logs the room looked rich and pleasant, even – in this book-lined bay where the fire burned – cosy.

I said: 'Someone's been out already to look around?'

He glanced up. 'Of course. But the chances are that the culprit would make straight back when he saw what he had done – or nearly done. He wouldn't want to be caught out with the gun.' He gave a little smile. 'You do realise that whoever it is is going to take quite a bit of trouble to cover his tracks, don't you? Good jobs aren't as easy to get as all that round here.'

'If he'd been going to come forward he'd no doubt have come running when he heard me shout,' I said. 'But I quite see why he's scared to. It might even be a question of police proceedings.'

The dark brows rose. 'Police? If there had actually been an accident – yes. But as it is—'

'I don't think it was an accident.'

He looked considerably startled. 'What in the world are you suggesting, then?' Then, as I made no immediate reply, he said in a voice where anger flickered through derision and disbelief? 'What else, Miss Martin, what else? Deliberate murder?'

Mockery – but through it I felt anger meeting me, palpable as the beat of a hot wind. The words bit through the air between us. I merely gaped at him, surprised.

Then it drew off. He said, his voice smooth and cold: 'You're being a little hysterical, aren't you? Who would want to kill a child? Philippe has no enemies.'

No, I thought, and no friends either. Except me. I sat up and met Léon de Valmy's hard stare. I said coolly: 'You take me up too quickly, Monsieur de Valmy. I wasn't suggesting anything quite as silly as that. And I am not hysterical.'

His mouth relaxed a little. 'I apologise. But you gave me a shock. Go on. Explain yourself.'

I drank sherry, regarding him straightly. 'It's only that I can't quite see how it could have been pure accident. The place was so open and he *must* have been able to hear us fairly easily. I think it was some silly prank – some youth, perhaps, showing off or trying to startle us. And he got nearer than he meant to, and then was so scared of what he'd done that he made off.'

'I see.' He was silent for a moment. 'You had better fill in the details for me. Exactly where were you?'

'We went down the path that short-cuts the zigzag towards the Valmy bridge. We left it about half-way down, where you cross a deep ravine and turn right down the valley.'

'I know it. There's a cascade and a trout-pool.'

Some fleeting surprise must have shown in my face, for he said quietly: 'I have lived at Valmy all my life, Miss Martin.'

It was an almost physical effort to keep from looking at the picture above our heads. I said quickly: 'Of course. Well, you know how the path runs along the hillside down the valley? After about half a mile it's quite wide, and flat, and there are thick trees on the left going down towards the river, but on the right, above you, they thin out.'

'I know. An open ride, with grass and beech rising to a ridge of rock. Above the rock is the planted forest.'

I nodded. 'The pines are about twenty feet high now, and very thick. We were going along the path; Philippe was singing and hopping about ahead of me, not looking where he was going.'

'Fortunately, it seems,' said Léon de Valmy dryly.

'Yes. Well, just as he tripped and fell flat, a bullet went slap into the tree that had tripped him, and I heard the report from above us, to the right.'

'From the ridge?'

'I suppose so. It was the best cover, and where it happened there was nothing between us and the ridge except brambles and a few stumps covered with honeysuckle.'

'You saw nothing?'

'Nothing. I shouted, and then, of course, I had to attend to Philippe.

suppose I assumed that whoever it was would have had a bad fright, nd would come pelting down to see if we were hurt. But he didn't. I'd ave gone up to investigate, only I thought I ought to get Philippe traight home.'

He was watching me curiously. 'You would have done that?'

'Of course. Why not?'

He said slowly: 'You are a courageous young woman, are you not?'

'Where's the courage? We both know it couldn't have been deliberate. Vhy should I be afraid of a fool?'

A pause, then all at once his face lighted with that extraordinarily harming smile. 'A young woman might well be afraid to approach a ool armed with a rifle. Don't be angry with me, mademoiselle. It was neant as a compliment.'

'I'm sorry.' I swallowed, and said as an afterthought: 'Thank you.'

He smiled again. 'Tell me, just how much do you know about guns?'

'Nothing whatever.'

'I thought as much. You seem, when you talk of an "accident", to be icturing a singularly unlikely one. You think, in fact, that this fool with he gun fired more or less at random through the trees at a barely-seen arget, or even at a sound?'

'Yes. And I can't quite see how he didn't know—'

'Exactly. The place was open and you said Philippe was shouting or inging.'

'Yes. That's why I thought it must have been meant as a joke.'

'Some unauthorized youth with a talent for excitement? Hardly. No, he explanation's far simpler than that. An "accident" with a gun usually nly means one thing—a carelessly-held gun, a stumble (as Philippe tumbled) over a stone or a root ... and the gun goes off. I think, myself, hat he must have seen Philippe fall, and have thought he had hit him. io ... he panicked, and ran away.'

'Yes, of course. That does seem to be the answer.'

'Well, you can be sure it'll be looked into. The culprit may even come orward when he hears that no damage was done – but personally I lon't think he will.' The long fingers toyed with the glass. He said, kindly it could surely not be amusement that so faintly warmed his voice?): My poor child, you've had a strenuous couple of days, haven't you? Ve're very grateful to you, my wife and I, for your care of Philippe. I'm orry it's been such a frightening burden today.'

'It's not a burden. And I'm very happy here.'

'Are you? I'm glad. And don't worry any more about this business. After all, whether we find the man or not, it's not likely to happen again. Ias Philippe got over his fright?'

'I think so.'

'There's no need to call a doctor, or take any measures of that kind?'

'Oh no. He's perfectly all right now. I doubt if he really knows how

– how near it was. He seemed quite happy when I left him, but I did
have to promise to go back and play a game before bed-time.'

'Then I won't keep you. But finish your sherry first, won't you?'

I obeyed him, then set the glass down and said carefully: 'Monsieur
de Valmy, before I go, I have a confession to make.'

An eyebrow lifted. I was right. It was amusement.

I said: 'No, I'm serious. I – I've been deceiving you and Madame de
Valmy, and I can't do it any longer. I've got to tell you.'

The glint was still there. He said gravely: 'I'm listening. How have
you deceived us?'

I said, in French: 'This is how I've deceived you, monsieur – ever
since I came into the house, and I think it's high time I came clean.'

There was a short silence.

'I see,' he said. 'Not just good French, either; the French of France,
Miss Martin. Well, let's have it. Come clean.'

The murder was out. It was over. My useless deception was confessed,
and nothing had happened except that Léon de Valmy had laughed
rather a lot – not only at the shifts I had been put to, but at the idea that
my job should be contingent on an ignorance of French. Shamefacedly,
I laughed with him, only too ready, in my relief, to admit my own folly.
But. . . .

Somewhere, deep inside me, something was protesting faintly. But. . . .

But now the Demon King laughed good-temperedly, and, thankfully,
I laughed with him.

It was into this scene of hilarity that Raoul de Valmy came a few
moments later. I didn't hear him come in until he said from the door.
'I'm sorry. I didn't know you were engaged.'

'It's all right,' said his father. 'Come in.'

With a click, the lights sprang to life. Raoul came round the bookcase
into the bay where we sat. 'I've just got in—' he began, then saw me
sitting there, and paused.

'Good evening, mademoiselle.' He glanced from me to his father. 'I
believe you wanted to see me, sir?'

I got quickly to my feet.

'I was just going,' I said. I spoke in French, and I saw Raoul's brows
lift, but he made no comment. Then I paused, glancing back diffidently
at my employer. 'Perhaps Monsieur Raoul has found something about
the shooting? Has he been out to look for this man?'

'No,' said Monsieur de Valmy. He nodded a pleasant dismissal. 'Well
Miss Martin, thank you for coming. Goodnight.'

'Shooting?' said Raoul sharply.

He was speaking to me. I hesitated and looked uncertainly at Monsieur
de Valmy. Raoul said again: 'What's this about shooting? Who should
I have been looking for?'

'Oh,' I said awkwardly – I had, after all, been already dismissed the library – 'I thought perhaps ... then you don't know what happened this afternoon?'

Raoul had moved between his father's chair and the fireplace and was reaching for the sherry decanter.

'No. What did happen?'

Léon said coldly: 'Some fool out with a rifle in the woods has narrowly missed killing your cousin.'

Raoul's head jerked up at that. Some sherry splashed. '*What?* Philippe? Someone shot at Philippe?'

'That's what I said.'

'Was he hurt?'

'He wasn't touched.'

Raoul straightened, glass in hand, his shoulders back against the mantel. He looked from one to the other of us. 'What did the chap think he was doing?'

'That,' said his father, 'is what we would like to know.' He tilted his head back to look at his son. 'You've been out, you say. Did you see anyone?'

'No.'

'Which way did you go?'

'East. I told you I was going up through the new plantations. I went up from the kitchen gardens. I never saw a soul. Where did it happen?'

'On the track through the beechwood, half a mile north of the bridge.'

'I know the place.' He looked at me. 'This is – shocking. He really wasn't hurt at all?'

'Not at all,' I said. 'He fell down, and the bullet missed him.'

'And you? I take it you were there?'

'I was with him. It didn't go near me.'

He stood looking down at the glass between his fingers, then set it carefully on the mantelpiece beside him. 'Don't go yet, please. Sit down again. D'you mind telling me just what happened?'

Once more I told the story. He listened without moving, and his father leaned back in his chair, one hand playing with the stem of his empty glass, watching us both. When I had finished Raoul said, without turning his head: 'I assume you have the matter in hand?'

For a moment I thought he was speaking to me, and looked up, surprised, but Léon de Valmy answered: 'I have,' and proceeded to outline the various instructions he had given by telephone. Raoul listened, his head bent now, staring into the fire, and I sat back in my chair and watched the two of them, wondering afresh at the queer twisted relationship that was theirs. Today all seemed quite normal between them; last night's perverted cut-and-thrust might never have been. The two voices, so alike; the two faces, so alike and yet so tragically different ... my eyes lifted to the devil-may-care young face above the mantelpiece, with the pictured smile and the careless hand on the pony's bridle. No, it wasn't Raoul; it could never have been Raoul. There was something in his face, something dark and difficult that could never have belonged to the laughing careless boy in the picture. I had the feeling, watching Raoul as he talked to his father, that the young man of the picture would have been easier to know. . . .

I came back to reality with a jerk. Léon de Valmy was saying: 'We seem to treat our employees a little roughly. I would have liked to persuade Miss Martin to take the evening off, but she feels it her duty to entertain Philippe.'

'I must,' I said. 'I promised.'

'Then go out afterwards. Not' – that flash of charm again – 'for a walk, as we seem so determined at Valmy to dog you with malice, but why not shake our dangerous dust from your feet, Miss Martin, and go down to Thonon? It's not late. A café, a cinema—'

'By the time she has put Philippe to sleep there'll be no buses to Thonon,' said Raoul.

'It doesn't matter,' I said quickly, surprised at the desire to escape that had swept over me. An evening outside Valmy – supper in a crowd, lights, voices, music, the common comings-and-goings of café and street – suddenly I longed desperately for these. I had had enough of drama this last two days. I got to my feet, this time decisively.

'It's very kind of you, but I did promise Philippe, and he's been upset. . . . I mustn't disappoint him. I'll rest after dinner.'

'Tea alone in your room again and an early bed?' Raoul straightened his shoulders. 'Are you sure you wouldn't rather go out?'

'Well, I—' I hesitated, laughing. 'I can't can I?'

'There are two cars at Valmy, and the requisite number of people to drive them.' He glanced down at Léon. 'I think we owe Miss Martin her escape, don't you?'

'Assuredly. But I'm afraid Jeannot has the big car in Geneva on my business, and the shooting-brake isn't back yet from the sawmill.'

'Well,' said Raoul, 'there's mine.' He looked at me. 'Do you drive?'

'No. But look, you mustn't think – I wouldn't dream—'

'You know,' said Raoul to the ceiling, 'she's pining to go. Aren't you?'

I gave up. 'It would be heaven.'

'Then take my car.' He looked at his father. 'You can spare Bernard to drive it?'

'Of course.'

'Where is he?'

'Out. I sent him straight away to look for traces of this fool with the gun, but it's dusk now so he should be back. No doubt he'll be in soon to report. . . . That's settled, then. Excellent. It only remains for me to wish you – what, Miss Martin? A pleasant evening, an evening to remember?'

I said, thinking of Philippe's face streaked with mud and tears: 'I thought it was to be an evening to forget.'

Léon de Valmy laughed.

Raoul crossed the room and opened the door for me.

'At eight, then?'

'Thank you. Yes.'

'I'll see he's there. I – er, I gather we now speak French?'

I said, low-voiced: 'I told him just now.'

I didn't add that I was pretty sure my confession had been quite unnecessary. The Demon King had known already.

Punctually at eight the lights of the car raked the darkness beyond the balcony rail. Philippe was already sound asleep, and Berthe sat sewing beside the fire in my sitting-room. It was with a light step and a light heart that I ran downstairs towards my unexpected evening of freedom.

The Cadillac was standing there, its engine running. The driver, a tall silhouette against the lights, waited by the off front door. I got in and he slammed it after me, walked round the front of the car, and slid into his seat beside me.

'You?' I said. 'That wasn't in the bond, was it?'

The car glided forward, circled, and dived smoothly into the zigzag. Raoul de Valmy laughed.

'Shall we talk French?' he said in that language. 'It's the language I always take girls out in. Construe.'

'I only meant that I don't see why you should chauffeur me. Couldn't you find Bernard?'

'Yes, but I didn't ask him. Do you mind?'

'Of course not. It's very nice of you.'

'To follow my own inclinations? I warn you,' he said lightly, 'I always do. It's my *modus vivendi*.'

'Why "warn"? Are they ever dangerous?'

'Sometimes.' I expected him to smile on the word, but he didn't. The light mood seemed to have dropped from him, and he drove for a while in an abstracted, almost frowning silence. I sat there rather shyly, my hands in my lap, watching the road twist and swoop up to meet us.

The car dropped down the last arm of the zigzag, turned carefully off the bridge and gathered speed on the valley road.

He spoke at length in a formal, almost cool tone. 'I'm sorry you should have had such a bad two days.'

'Two days?'

'I was thinking about last night's episode on the bridge back there.'

'Oh, that.' I gave a little laugh. 'D'you know, I'd almost forgotten it.'

'I'm glad to hear it. But perhaps that's only because what happened this afternoon has overridden it. You seem to have got over your scare now.' He threw me a quick glance and said abruptly: 'Were you scared?'

'Today? Ye-es. Yes, I was. Not of being shot or anything, because that part was over before I knew anything about it, but somehow – just scared.' I twisted my fingers together in my lap, thinking back to that heart-stopping point of time, trying to explain. 'I think it was the moment when I heard the shot and there was Philippe flat on the path . . . the moment before I realized he wasn't hurt. It seemed to last for ever. Just the silence after the shot, and the world spinning round out of gear with no noise but the tops of the trees sweeping the air the way you hear a car's tyres when the engine's off.'

We were sailing up the curve towards Belle Surprise. The trees streamed by, a moment drenched in our flowing gold, then livid, fleeing, gone. I said: 'Have you ever thought, when something dreadful happens, "a moment ago things were not like this; let it be *then*, not *now*, anything but *now*"? And you try and try to remake *then*, but you know you can't. So you try to hold the moment quite still and not let it move on and show itself. It was like that.'

'I know. But it hadn't happened after all.'

'No.' I let out a long unsteady breath. 'It was still *then*. I – I don't think I'll forget the moment when Philippe moved as long as I live.'

Another of those quick glances. 'And afterwards?'

'Afterwards I was angry. So blazing angry I could have killed someone.'

'It takes people that way,' he said.

'Because they've been scared? I know. But it wasn't only that. If you'd seen Philippe's face –' I was seeing it myself a little too clearly. I said, as if somehow I had to explain: 'He's so quiet, Philippe. It's – it's all wrong that he should be so quiet. Little boys shouldn't be like that. And today was better; he was playing the fool in that silly maddening way children have, shouting rubbish and hopping about, only I was so pleased to see him like that that I didn't mind. And then . . . out of the blue . . . that beastliness. And there was mud on his face and he didn't want to stop to look at the trout and then he – he cried.' I stopped then. I bit my lip and looked away from him out of the window.

'Don't talk about it any more if you'd rather not.'

'It . . . gets me a bit. But I feel better now I've told someone.' I managed a smile. 'Let's forget it, shall we?'

'That's what we came out for.' He smiled suddenly, and said with an abrupt, almost gay change of tone: 'You'll feel quite different when you've had dinner. Have you got your passport?'

'What?'

'Your passport. I suppose you carry it?'

'Yes, it's – here it is. This sounds serious. What is it, a deportation?'

'Something like that.' We were approaching the outskirts of Thonon now. Trees lined the road, and among them globed lamps as bland as melons made fantastic patterns of the boughs. 'What d'you say,' said Raoul, slowing a little and glancing at me, 'shall we make a night of it? Go into Geneva and eat somewhere and then dance or go to a cinema or something like that?'

'Anything,' I said, my mood lifting to meet his. 'Everything. I leave it to you.'

'You mean that?'

'Yes.'

'Excellent,' said Raoul, and the big car swept out into the light and bustle of Thonon's main square.

I am not going to describe that evening in detail though, as it happens, it was desperately important. It was then, simply, one of those wonderful evenings. . . . We stopped in Thonon beside a stall where jonquils and wallflowers blazed under the gas-jets, and he bought me freesias which smelt like the Fortunate Isles and those red anemones that were once called the lilies of the field. Then we drove along in a clear night with stars aswarm and a waxing moon staring pale behind the poplars. By the time we reached Geneva – a city of fabulous glitter and strung lights whose reflections swayed and bobbed in the dark waters of the Lake – my spirits were rocketing sky-high; shock, loneliness, the breath of danger all forgotten.

Why had I thought him difficult to know? We talked as if we had known each other all our lives. He asked me about Paris and I found myself, for the first time, talking easily – as if memory were happiness and not regret – of Maman and Daddy and the Rue du Printemps. Even the years at the orphanage came gaily enough to hand, to be remembered with amusement, more, with affection.

And in his turn Raoul talked of his own Paris – so different from mine; of a London with which it seemed impossible that the Constance Butcher Home for Girls could have any connection; of the hot brilliance of Provence, where Bellevigne stood, a little jewel of a château quietly ruining down among its dusty vines. . . .

Anything but Valmy. I don't think it was mentioned once.

And we did do everything. We had a wonderful dinner somewhere; the place wasn't fashionable, but the food was marvellous and my clothes didn't matter. We didn't dance there, because Raoul said firmly that food was important and one must not distract oneself with gymnastics, but later, somewhere else, we danced, and later still we drove back towards Thonon, roaring along the straight unenclosed road at a speed which made my blood tingle with excitement, yet which felt, in that wonderful car, on that wonderful night, like no speed at all. The frontier checked us once, twice, momentarily, then the big car tore on, free, up the long hill to Thonon. Along the wide boulevard that rims the slope to the Lake, through the now-empty market-place, past the turning that led up to Soubirous. . . .

'Hi,' I said, 'you've missed the turning.'

He glanced at me sideways.

'I'm following one of my dangerous inclinations.'

I looked at him a little warily. 'Such as?'

He said? 'There's a casino at Évian.'

I remembered Mrs. Seddon, and smiled to myself, 'What's your lucky number?'

He laughed. 'I don't know yet. But I do know that this is the night it's coming up.'

So we went to the casino, and he played and I watched him, and then he made me play and I won and then won again and then we cashed our winnings together and went out and drank *café-fine* and more *café-fine*, and laughed a lot and then, at last, drove home.

It was three in the morning when the great car nosed its way up the zigzag, and – whether from excitement or sleepiness or the *fines* – I might have been floating up it in a dream. He stopped the car by the side-door that opened off the stable-yard, and, still dreamily and no doubt incoherently, I thanked him and said goodnight.

I must have negotiated the dark corridors and stairways to my room still in the same trance-like daze. I have no recollections of doing so, nor of the process by which eventually I got myself to bed.

It wasn't the brandy; the coffee had drowned that effectively enough. It was a much more deadly draught. There was one thing that stood like stone among the music and moonfroth of the evening's gaieties. It was stupid, it was terrifying, it was wonderful, but it had happened and I could do nothing about it.

For better or worse, I was head over ears in love with Raoul de Valmy.

Sixth Coach

CHAPTER NINE

Never seek to tell thy love,
Love that never told can be.

WILLIAM BLAKE: *Poem from MSS.*

It was to have been expected. It would be a very odd Cinderella indeed who could be thrown out of such dreary seclusion as the orphanage had offered me, into contact with Raoul de Valmy, without something of the sort happening. A man whose looks and charm were practically guaranteed to get him home without his even trying, had exerted himself to give a very lonely young woman a pleasant evening. *An evening to remember.*

That it was no more than that I was fully aware. In spite of a quantity of romantic reading and a great many wistfully romantic (and very natural) dreams, I had retained a good deal of my French commonsense. That, along with the nastily-named English quality called phlegm, would have to help me to control the present silly state of my emotions. I had had my evening. Tomorrow would be another day.

It was. Soon after breakfast the big Cadillac disappeared down the zigzag; Raoul, I supposed, gone back to Bellevigne. I tore my thoughts resolutely away from a Provençal idyll where he and I drove perpetually through moonlit vineyards with an occasional glimpse of the Taj Mahal and the Blue Grotto of Capri thrown in, and concentrated rather fiercely on Philippe.

Nobody owned to the rifle incident, and there was little hope of tracing the culprit. But Philippe seemed to have got over his fright so the matter was allowed to drop. Life fell back into its accustomed pattern, except for the exciting prospect of the Easter Ball, which now provided a thrilling undercurrent to conversation below stairs. This function had for many years been held at Valmy on Easter Monday. Mrs. Seddon and Berthe, when they were about the schoolroom domain, delighted to tell me of previous occasions when the Château Valmy had been *en fête*.

'Flowers,' said Berthe (who seemed to have taken serenely for granted my sudden acquisition of fluent French), 'and lights everywhere. They even used to string lights right down the zigzag to the Valmy bridge. And there's floodlights in the pool, and they turn the big fountain on, and there are little floating lights in the water, like lilies. Of course,' pausing in her dusting to look at me a little wistfully, 'it isn't as grand as it used to be in the old days. My mother used to tell me about it when the old Comte was alive; they say he was rolling in money, but of course it's not the same anywhere now, is it? But mind you, it'll be pretty grand, for all that. There's some as says it's not quite the thing to have a dance this Easter seeing as Monsieur le Comte and Madame la Comtesse were killed last year, but what I says is them that's dead is dead (God rest their souls)' – crossing herself hastily – 'and them that's alive might as well get on with the job. Not wanting to sound hard-hearted, miss, but you see what I mean?'

'Of course.'

'Anyway, Madame says it'll be just a small private party – not but what *they* call a small private party'd make your eyes stand out on stalks, as the saying is . . . if you'll excuse the expression, miss. But' – here she brightened, and picked up a brass tray which she began to polish with vigour – 'we'll have *our* dance just as usual.'

'You have one, too?'

'Oh yes. All the tenants and the château staff. It's the night after the château dance, on the Tuesday, down at Soubirous. Everybody goes.'

This, not unnaturally, left me wondering which dance I would be invited to attend, but it was very soon made clear to me by Madame de Valmy that for this occasion at any rate I was above the salt . . . So I, too, succumbed to the universal feeling of pleased anticipation, a pleasure shot through with the worry of not having a dance frock to wear.

I didn't worry about this for long. I am French enough where my needle is concerned, and I had been – there was nothing else to do with it – saving the greater part of my salary for the last weeks. I didn't doubt that I could achieve something creditably pretty, even though it might not stand comparison with the Balmains and Florimonds with which the ballroom would probably be crowded. It would be pretty enough to sit out in, I told myself firmly, thrusting back a vision of myself *en grande tenue*, dancing alone with Raoul in a ballroom about the size of Buckingham Palace. But it would *not* (this with a memory of Jane Eyre's depressing wardrobe and Léon de Valmy's mocking eye) it would *not* be 'suitable'. I wasn't down to bombazine yet.

My next half-day off fell some three days after the incident with the rifle, and I went down to Thonon on the afternoon bus, with the object of buying stuff and pattern for a dance-frock. I didn't think it would be much use looking for a ready-made in so small a place as Thonon, and Évian or Geneva prices were beyond me. So I hunted happily about for the best material I could afford, and at last was rewarded with a length of some pretty Italian stuff in white, webbed with gossamer silver threads, at what the saleswoman called a bargain price, but to me represented a horrifying proportion of my savings. I fought a swift losing battle with the remnants of my commonsense, and firmly planted the money down on the counter with no trace of regret. Then, clutching the parcel to me, I pushed my way out through the shop door into the windy street.

It was almost five o'clock, one of those dark, rain-laden April days with a warm gusty wind blowing. There had been showers earlier, but now a belated gleam from the west glissaded over the wet housetops and etched the budding chestnuts of the square in pale gold against a slaty sky. Many of the shop-windows were bright already, harshly-lit grocery-stores and *boucheries* mirrored to soft orange and copper in the damp pavements. Over the flower-stall where Raoul had bought me the freesias a naked gas-jet hissed and flared in the gusty wind, now a snake-long lash of brilliant flame, now a flattened mothswing of cobalt and sulphur-yellow. The tyres of passing cars hissed softly on the wet tarmac. Here and there among the bare chestnuts an early street-lamp glowed.

I was longing for a cup of tea. But here my sense of economy, subconsciously outraged, no doubt, by the recent purchase, stepped in to argue the few francs' difference between tea and coffee. A *salon de thé* would be expensive, while coffee or an apéritif were at once far better quality and half the price.

I abandoned the tea and walked across the square towards a restaurant where a glass screen protected the tables from the fitful wind.

As I gained the pavement and paused to choose a table, a diffident voice spoke beside me.

'Miss Martin?'

I turned in some surprise, as the voice was unmistakably English. It was the fair young man of my encounter in Soubirous. He was dressed in a duffel coat supplemented by a shaggy scarf. His thick fair hair

opped in the wind. I had forgotten what an enormous young man he
was. The general effect was that of a huge, shy blond bear, of a bigness
ncredible, as Philippe would have said.

He said: 'D'you remember me? We met in Soubirous on Monday.'

'Of course I remember you, Mr. Blake.' I could have added that I was
hardly likely to have forgotten him – the one English lamb in my pride
of French tigers – but thought it was, perhaps, not tactful ... 'I hope
you haven't had to use any of those bandages and things?'

He grinned. 'Not yet. But I expect to daily. Were you – were you
thinking of going in here for a drink? I wonder if you would – may I
– I mean I'd be awfully glad if—'

I rescued him. 'Thank you very much. I'd love to. Shall we sit out
here where we can watch what's going on?'

We settled ourselves at a table next to the glass screen, and he ordered
offee in his laborious English-French. His look of triumph when in
ctual fact coffee did arrive, made me laugh. 'You're coming on fast,' I
aid.

'Aren't I? But really, you know, it's hard to go wrong over *café*.'

'Are you managing your shopping all right today?'

'Oh, yes. You can usually find someone who understands English in
Thonon. Besides,' he said simply, 'it's cheaper. I usually shop in the
market. I don't need a lot.'

'Are you living up at the hut now?'

'For the time being. I sleep at the Coq Hardi in Soubirous a couple
of nights in the week, and I have the odd meal there, but I like the hut.
I get a lot of work done, and I can come and go and eat and sleep when
I like.'

I had a momentary and irresistible vision of him curling up in straw,
nuts in the pocket, like a bear, for the winter. This made me think of
Philippe. I said: 'Does anyone from your side of the valley ever bring a
gun over to Valmy?'

'Only if invited. There are shooting-parties in the autumn, I believe.'

'I didn't mean that. Would the foresters or keepers or anyone ever go
stalking foxes or chamois or something with a rifle?'

'Good Lord, no. Why?'

I told him in some detail just what had occurred on Tuesday afternoon
with Philippe. He listened with great attention, shocked out of his shyness
by the end into sharp expostulation.

'But that's frightful! Poor kid. It must have been a beastly shock – and
for you, too. The best you can say of it is that it's bl—er, criminal
carelessness! And you say they've found no trace of the chap?'

'No-one admits it, even now it's known that nobody was hurt. But
that's easy to understand; he'd lose his job just like *that*, and jobs aren't
all that easy to come by up here.'

'True enough.'

'What's more,' I said, 'when Monsieur de Valmy sent a couple of men

down to look at the place where it happened, they found that the bullet
had been dug out of the tree.'

He whistled. 'Thorough, eh?'

'Very. D'you see what it means? Those men were sent down there as
soon as Philippe and I got back to the house. It means, first, that the
chap with the gun knew what had happened when he loosed it off; and
second, that he didn't run away. He must have sat tight waiting for
Philippe and me to go, then skated down to remove the evidence.' I looked
at him. 'The thought of him hiding up there in the wood watching us
is rather – nasty, somehow.'

'I'll say. What's more, the man's a fool. Accidents do happen, and if
he'd done the decent thing and come tearing down to apologise and see
you both home the odds are he'd have got off with just a rocket from the
boss. He must have lost his head and then not dared own up. As it is,
I hope they do get him. What's de Valmy doing about it?'

'Oh, he's still having inquiries made, but I don't think they'll produce
anything now. All we've got so far is lashings of alibis, but the only two
I'm prepared to believe are Monsieur de Valmy's and the butler's.'

William Blake said: 'The son was here, wasn't he?'

His tone was no more than idle, but I felt the blood rushing hotly to
my cheeks. Furious with myself, I turned away to look out through the
glass at the now twilit square. If I was going to blush each time his name
was mentioned, I wouldn't last long under the Demon King's sardonic
eye. And this sort of nonsense I couldn't expect him to condone. I fixed
my gaze on the brilliant yellows and scarlets of the flower-stall, and said
indifferently: 'He was; he went away the morning after it happened. But
you surely can't imagine—' In spite of myself my voice heated. 'It
certainly couldn't have been *him!*'

'No? Cast-iron alibi?'

'No. It – it just couldn't!' Logic came rather late in the wake of
emotion: 'Dash it, *he'd* have no reason to sneak about digging bullets out
of trees!'

'No, of course not.'

I said, rather too quickly: 'How are the weevil-traps?'

That did it. He was the last person to see a reference to his work,
however abruptly introduced, as a mere red herring. Soon we were once
more happily in fully cry ... I listened, and asked what I hope were the
right questions, and thought about the Valmy dance. Would he be there?
Would he? *Would* he?

I came out of my besotted dreaming to hear William Blake asking me
prosaically which bus I intended to take back to Valmy. 'Because,' he
said, 'one goes in about twelve minutes, and after that you wait two
hours.'

'Oh Lord, yes,' I said, 'I mustn't miss it. Are you getting the same
one?'

'No. Mine goes just before yours. I'm sloping off this weekend to meet some friends at Annecy.' He grinned at me as he beckoned the waiter. 'So forget you saw me, will you, please? This is A.W.O.L. but I couldn't resist it. Some pals of mine are up in Annecy for the week and they want me to go climbing with them.'

'I won't give you away,' I promised.

Here the waiter came up, and Mr. Blake plunged into the dreadful struggle of The Bill. I could see all the stages; understanding the waiter's total, translating it mentally into English money, dividing by ten for the tip, reckoning to the nearest round number for simplicity, slowly and painfully thumbing over the revolting paper money, and finally handing over a sheaf of it with the irresistible feeling that so much money cannot possibly be the fair amount to pay for so little.

At last it was over. He met my eyes and laughed, flushing a little. 'I'm all right,' he said defensively, 'until they get to the nineties, and then I'm sunk. I have to make them write it down.'

'I think you're wonderful. By the time you've been here another month you'll talk it like a native.' I stood up. 'Thank you very much for the coffee. Now you'd better not bother about me if you want to dash for that bus.'

'You're right. I'm afraid I'll have to run.' But he still hesitated. 'It was – awfully nice meeting again . . . Could we – I mean, when do you have your next afternoon off?'

'I don't quite know,' I said, not very truthfully. Then I relented. 'But I'm often in Thonon on a Friday afternoon and – look, for goodness' sake . . . isn't that your bus? The driver's getting in! Go on, run! Is this yours? And this? . . . Goodbye! Have a good weekend!'

Somehow he dragged his paraphernalia up from the floor, lurched, with rope and rucksack perilously swaying, between the crowded tables, thrust his way through the swing door I grabbed and held wide for him, then waved a hand to me and ran. He reached the bus just as the driver's door slammed and the engine coughed noisily into life. Then wedged – it seemed inextricably – on the narrow steps of the bus, he managed to turn and wave again cheerily as the vehicle jerked and roared away.

Feeling breathless myself, I waved back, then turned hurriedly to cross the road to where my own bus waited. But before I could step forward a big car slid to a halt beside me with a soft hush of wet tyres. A Cadillac. My heart, absurdly, began to race.

The door was pushed open from inside. His voice said: 'Going my way?'

He was alone in the car. I got in beside him without a word, and the car moved off. It swung round the corner of the square where the Soubirous bus still stood beside its lamp, and turned into the tree-lined street that led south.

It was odd that I hadn't really noticed till now what a beautiful evening it was. The streetlamps glowed like ripe oranges among the bare boughs. Below in the wet street their globes glimmered down and down, to drown in their own reflections. *He hangs in shades the orange bright, like golden lamps* . . . and on the pavements there were piles of oranges, too, real ones, spilled there in prodigal piles with aubergines and green and scarlet peppers. The open door of a wine-shop glittered like Aladdin's cave with bottles from floor to roof, shelf on shelf of ruby and amber and purple, the rich heart of a hundred sun-drenched harvests. From a brightly-lit workmen's café nearby came music, the sound of voices loud in argument, and the smell of new bread.

The last lamp drowned its golden moon in the road ahead. The last house vanished and we were running between hedgeless fields. To the right a pale sky still showed clear under the western rim of the rain-clouds, and against it the bare trees that staked the road stood out black and sheer. The leaves of an ilex cut the half-light like knives. A willow streamed in the wind like a woman's hair. The road lifted itself ahead, mackerel-silver under its bending poplars. The blue hour, the lovely hour. . . .

Then the hills were round us, and it was dark.

Raoul was driving fast and did not speak.

I said at last, a little shyly: 'You're back soon. You haven't been to Bellevigne, then?'

'No. I had business in Paris.'

I wondered what kettles of fish he'd (in Mrs. Seddon's unlikely idiom) been frying. 'Did you have a good time?'

He said 'Yes', but in so absent a tone that I hesitated to speak again. I leaned back in silence and gave myself up to the pleasure of being driven home.

It was not for some time that I – absorbed in my dreaming – noticed how he was driving. He always travelled fast and there was a slickness about the way the big car sliced through the dark and up the twisting valley that demonstrated how well he knew the road; but there was something in his way of handling her tonight that was different.

I stole a glance at his silent profile as we whipped round and over a narrow bridge that warped the road at right-angles. He had done nothing that was actively dangerous; in the dark we would have had ample warning of an approaching car, but we were skirting danger so closely that it now occurred to me a little sickeningly to wonder if he were drunk. But then our headlamps swung across a curve of rock overhanging a corner and in the meagre light that was reflected back into the car I saw his face. He was sober enough; but that something was the matter was quite evident. He was frowning at the road ahead, his eyes narrowed in the flying dark. He had forgotten I was there. It seemed quite simply as if something had put him into a bad temper and he was taking it out on the car.

'What were you doing down in Thonon?' The question was no more than a *quid pro quo*, but he spoke so abruptly out of the silence that it sounded like an accusation, and I jumped and answered almost at random.

'What? Oh, it's my afternoon off.'

'What do you usually do on your afternoon off?'

'Nothing very much. Shopping – a cinema, anything.'

'You go out to friends sometimes?'

'No,' I said, surprised. 'I don't know anyone. I told you when we . . . I told you on Tuesday.'

'Oh. Yes. So you did.'

We had run into another shower, and big drops splashed and starred the windscreen. The car slewed overfast round a sharp bend in the road, and rubber whined on the wet tarmac. The headlights brushed a brilliant arc across a wall of rock. Reflected light swirled through the car, showing his face abstracted, still frowning. He hadn't once so much as glanced at me. He was probably hardly aware of who it was he had in the car. So much for Cinderella.

I sat quietly beside him and nibbled the bitter crusts of commonsense.

We had gone two-thirds of the way to Valmy before he spoke again. The question was sufficiently irrelevant and surprising.

'Who was that chap?'

I was startled and momentarily at a loss. I said stupidly: 'What chap?'

'The man you were with in Thonon. You left the café with him.'

'Oh, him.'

'Who else?' The phrase, brief to the point of curtness, made me glance at him in surprise.

I said shortly: 'A friend of mine.'

'You told me you didn't know anyone hereabouts.'

'Well,' I said childishly, 'I know him.'

This provoked a glance, quick and unsmiling. But he only said: 'How is Philippe?'

'All right, thank you.'

'And you? No more mishaps?'

'No.'

My voice must have sounded subdued and even sulky, but I was having a fight to keep it level and unbetraying. Pride had joined forces with commonsense, and the two were flaying me. The phantoms of those idiotic dreams wavered, mockingly, in the dark. . . . I don't know quite what I had expected, but . . . that man, and this: the change was too great; it was unnerving.

I was also making a grim little discovery that frightened me. The dreams might be moonshine, but the fact remained. I was in love with him. It hadn't been the wine and the starlight and all the trappings of romance. It hadn't even been the charm that he'd been so lavish with that night. Now I was undoubtedly sober and it was raining and the charm wasn't turned on . . . and I was still in love with this cold-voiced stranger who was making futile and slightly irritated conversation at me. At least I'd had the sense all along to try and laugh at my own folly, but it was no longer even remotely amusing.

I bit my lip hard, swallowed another choking morsel of that bitter
bread, and wished he would stop asking questions that needed answering.
But he was persisting, still in that abrupt tone that made his queries –
harmless enough in themselves – sound like an inquisition.

It seemed he was still curious about William Blake, which, in view of
my promise to say nothing, was awkward.

'Who is he? English?'

'Yes.'

'He took the Annecy bus, didn't he? A climber?'

'He's climbing from Annecy this weekend.'

'Staying there?'

'Yes.'

'Did you know him in England?'

'No.'

'Oh. Then he's been to Valmy?'

'Not that I'm aware of.'

'Is he staying hereabouts for long?'

'Look,' I said, cornered, 'does it matter? What's the inquisition for?'

A pause. He said, sounding both stiff and disconcerted: 'I'm sorry. I
wasn't aware I was trespassing on your private affairs.'

'They're not private. It's just – I – I didn't mean . . . I didn't want to
tell you . . .' I floundered hopelessly.

He threw me an odd look. 'Didn't want to tell me what?'

'Oh – nothing. Look,' I said desperately, 'I don't want to talk. D'you
mind?'

And now there was no doubt whatever about his mood. I heard him
say 'God damn it,' very angrily under his breath. He wrenched the
Cadillac round at the Valmy bridge and hurled her up the zigzag about
twice as fast as he should have done. The car snarled up the ramp like
a bad-tempered cat and was hauled round the first bend. 'You mistake
me.' Still that note of barely-controlled exasperation. 'I wasn't intending
to pry into what doesn't concern me. But—'

'I know. I'm sorry.' I must have sounded nearly as edgy as he did,
shaken as I was, not only by his anger and my failure to understand it
but by a humiliation that he couldn't guess at. 'I expect I'm tired. I
trailed about Thonon for a couple of hours looking for some dress-
material—oh!' My hands flew to my cheeks. 'I must have left it – yes
I left it in the café. I put it on the ledge under the table and then William
had to run for the bus and – oh dear, how stupid of me! I suppose if I
telephone – *oh!*'

His hand had moved sharply. The horn blared. I said, startled: 'What
was that?'

'Some creature. A weasel, perhaps.'

The trees lurched and peeled off into darkness. The next corner
steeply embanked, swooped at us.

I said: 'Do you have to go so fast? It scares me.'

The car slowed, steadied, and took the bend with no more than a splutter of gravel.

'Did you tell him about the shooting down in the beechwood?'

'What? Who?'

'This – William.'

I drew a sharp little breath. I said clearly: 'Yes, I did. He thinks that probably you did it yourself.'

The car whispered up the slope and nosed quietly out above the trees. He was driving like a careful insult. He didn't speak. The devil that rode me spurred me to add, out of my abyss of stupid self-torment: 'And I didn't know that I was supposed to account to my employer for everything I said and did on my afternoon off!'

That got him, as it was meant to. He said, between his teeth: '*I am not your employer.*'

'No?' I said it very nastily because I was afraid I was going to cry. 'Then what's it to do with you what I do or who I see?'

We were on the last slope of the zigzag. The Cadillac jerked to a stop as the brakes were jammed on. Raoul de Valmy swung round on me.

'This,' he said, in a breathless, goaded undertone. He pulled me roughly towards him, and his mouth came down on mine.

For a first kiss it was, I suppose, a fairly shattering experience. And certainly not such stuff as dreams are made on. . . . If Cinderella was out, so decidedly was Prince Charming. . . . Raoul de Valmy was simply an experienced man shaken momentarily out of self-control by anger and other emotions that were fairly easily recognisable even to me. I say 'even to me' because I discovered dismayingly soon that my own poise was a fairly eggshell affair. For all my semi-sophistication I emerged from Raoul's embrace in a thoroughly shaken state which I assured myself was icy rage. And certainly his next move was hardly calculated to appease. Instead of whatever passionate or apologetic words should have followed, he merely let me go, re-started the car, opened the throttle with a roar, and shot her up the slope and onto the gravel sweep without a word. He cut the engine and opened his door as if to come round. I didn't wait. I whipped out of the car, slammed the door behind me and in a silence to match his own I stalked (there is no other word) across the gravel and up the steps.

He caught up with me and opened the big door for me. He said something – I think it was my name – in an undervoice sounding as if it were shaken by a laugh. I didn't look at him. I walked past him as if he didn't exist, straight into a blaze of light, and Léon de Valmy, who was crossing the hall.

He checked his chair in its smooth progress as I came in, and turned his head as if to greet me. Then his eyes flicked from my face to Raoul's and back again, and the Satanic eyebrows lifted, ever so slightly. I turned abruptly and ran upstairs.

If it had needed anything else to shake me out of my daydreams, that glance of Léon de Valmy's would have done it. I leaned back against the door in my darkened bedroom and put the back of my hand to a hot cheek. There was blood bittersweet on my tongue from a cut lip ... Léon de Valmy would have seen that too. The whip flicked me again. Not only my face, my whole body burned.

I jerked myself away from the door's support, snapped on the light, and began to tug savagely at my gloves. Damn Raoul; how dared he? How *dared* he? And Léon de Valmy – here the second glove catapulted down beside the first – damn Léon de Valmy, too. Damn all the Valmys. I hated the lot of them. I never wanted to see any of them again.

On the thought I stopped, half-way out of my coat.

It was more than possible that I wouldn't have the chance. The Demon King didn't have to be *en rapport* with me to guess what had happened tonight, and it was quite probable that he would take steps to dismiss me.

It didn't occur to me at once that, if there were any hint of trouble, Raoul would certainly tell his father the truth, that I had been kissed against my will, and that since for the greater part of the year Raoul was not at Valmy to trouble the waters I would probably be kept on.

I only know that as I hung my coat with care in the pretty panelled wardrobe I felt depressed – more, desolate – at the prospect of never seeing any of the hated Valmys again.

My lip had stopped bleeding. I put on fresh lipstick carefully, and did my hair. Then I walked sedately out and across my sitting-room to the schoolroom door.

I opened it and went in. The light was on, but no-one was there. The fire had burned low and the room had an oddly forlorn look. One of the french windows was ajar and the undrawn curtains stirred in a little breeze. On the rug lay an open book, its pages faintly vibrant to the same draught.

Puzzled, I glanced at the clock. It was long past time for Philippe's return from the salon. Madame de Valmy would be upstairs, dressing. Well, I reflected, it wasn't my affair. On this night of all nights I wasn't going to see why he was being kept late below stairs. No doubt he would come up when his supper did.

I was stooping for a log to throw on the fire when I heard the sound. It whispered across the quiet room, no more loudly than the tick of the little French clock or the settling of the woodash in the grate.

A very slight sound, but it lifted the hair on my skin as if that, too, felt the cold breath from the open window. It was no more than a voiced sigh, but, horribly, it sounded like a word ...

'*Mademoiselle.* ...'

I was across the schoolroom in one leap. I ran out onto the dark balcony and turned to peer along the leads. To right and left the windows were shut and dark. From behind me the lighted schoolroom thrust a bright wedge across the balcony, making my shadow, gigantic and grotesque, leap and posture before me over the narrow leads.

'Philippe?'

The ends of the balcony were in deep darkness, invisible. I plunged out of my patch of light and ran along past the windows. The balcony floor was slippery with rain.

'Philippe? Philippe.'

That terrible little whisper answered me from the darkest corner. I was beside it, kneeling on the damp leads. He was crouched in a tiny huddle up against the balustrade.

Or rather, where the balustrade had been. It was no longer there. In its place was merely the workman's ladder I had wedged that very day across below the unsteady coping. Beyond this frail barrier was a gap of darkness and a thirty-foot drop to the gravel and that terrible line of iron spikes. . . .

My hands were on him, my voice hoarse and shaking.

'Philippe? What happened? You didn't fall. Oh, God, you didn't fall . . . oh my little Philippe, are you all right?'

Small cold hands came up and clung. 'Mademoiselle. . . .'

I had him in my arms, my face against his wet cheek. 'Are you all right, Philippe? Are you hurt? I felt his head shake. 'Sure? Quite sure?' A nod. I stood up with him in my arms. I am not big myself, but he seemed a feather-weight, a bundle of birds'-bones. I carried him into the schoolroom, over to the fireplace, and sat down in a wing-chair, cuddling him close to me. His arms came up round my neck and clung tightly. I don't know what I was saying to him: I just hugged and crooned rubbish over the round dark head that was buried in my neck.

Presently he relaxed his stranglehold and stopped shivering. But when I tried to stoop for a log to put on the fire he clutched me again.

'It's all right,' I said quickly, 'I'm only going to build the fire up. We must get you warm, you know.'

He suffered me to lean forward, throw some faggots onto the sullen fire, and stir it until some little tongues of flame crept up around the new wood and began to lick brightly at it. Then I sat back in the chair again. It seemed to me that the reassurance of my arms was of more importance at the moment than bed or hot drinks or any of the remedies that would follow shortly. I said gently: 'Was it the car, Philippe?'

That little nod again.

'But I warned you the stone was loose. I told you not to go galloping along there, didn't I?'

He said in a voice that sounded thinner and more childish than ever: 'I heard the horn. I thought . . . Daddy always used to . . . on the drive . . . to tell me he was coming. . . .'

I bit my lip, then winced. Of course, the horn. I remembered that arrogant blare on the zigzag. I had seen nothing on the road. It had merely been part, no doubt, of the flare of temper and excitement that had driven Raoul to kiss me ... and driven Philippe out into the darkness, running in a stubborn, passionate hope to fling himself against the rotten stone.

I said, as much to myself as him: 'I'd no idea the coping was as dangerous. It only seemed to move such a little. I thought it would hold. Thank God I put the ladder across. Why I did ... oh, thank God I did!' Then a thought struck me. 'Philippe, where was Berthe? I thought she was with you.'

'Bernard came for her. Something she'd forgotten to do.'

'I see.' I waited for a moment, holding him. 'Look, Philippe, we've got a lovely fire now. What about warming those frozen paws?'

This time he unclasped himself without demur, and slipped down onto the rug beside me, holding out his hands obediently to the now bright blaze of the fire. I ruffled his hair. 'This is wet, too. What a beastly night to go running out in! You are a little ass, aren't you?'

He said, his voice still too tight and sharp: 'I hit the stone and then it wasn't there. It went over with a bang. I bumped into something. I couldn't see it. I fell down. I couldn't see anything.'

'It was the ladder you bumped into, Philippe. You couldn't have fallen over, you know. There wasn't really a gap. You couldn't see the ladder, but it's a very solid one. It was really quite safe. Quite safe.'

'It was awful. I was frightened.'

'I don't blame you,' I said, 'I'd have been scared stiff. It was awfully sensible of you not to move.'

'I didn't dare. I knew you'd come.' The plain, pale little face turned to me. 'So I waited.'

Something twisted inside me. I said lightly: 'And I came. What a good thing I came up in your cousin Raoul's car instead of waiting for the bus!' I got up and bent over him, slipping my hands under his arms. 'Now, come and get these things off. Up with you.' I swung him to his feet. 'Goodness, child, you've been lying in a puddle! What about a hot bath and then supper in bed with a fire in your bedroom as a treat?'

'Will you be there?'

'Yes.'

'Have your supper in my room?'

'I'll sit on your bed,' I promised.

The black eyes glinted up at me. 'And play Peggitty?'

'Oho!' I said. 'So you're beginning to make capital out of this, are you? What's more, you're getting too dashed good at Peggitty. All right, if you'll promise not to beat me.' I swung him round and gave him a little shove towards the door. 'Now go and get those things off while I run the bath.'

He went off obediently. I rang the bell for Berthe, and then went to turn on the bath. As I watched the steam billowing up to cloud the tiles

I reflected a little grimly that now I should have to face Léon de Valmy again tonight.

Above the noise of the taps I heard a knock on the door that led from my sitting-room. I called: 'Come in.' Berthe had been very quick.

I turned then in surprise, as I saw that it wasn't Berthe, but Madame de Valmy. She never came to these rooms at this hour, and as I caught sight of her expression my heart sank. This, then, was it. And I hadn't had time to think out what to say.

I twisted the taps a little to lessen the gush of water, and straightened up to meet whatever was coming.

'Miss Martin, forgive me for interrupting you while you're changing—' Hardly a frightening opening, that; her voice was apologetic, hurrying, almost nervous: 'I wondered – did you remember to get me my tablets in Thonon this afternoon?'

I felt myself flushing with relief. 'Why, yes, madame. I was going to give them to Berthe to put in your room. I'm sorry, I didn't realise you'd want them straight away.'

'I'm out of them, or I wouldn't trouble you.'

'I'll get them now,' I said. 'No, really, it's no trouble, madame. You're not interrupting me; this bath isn't for me. Philippe!'

I bent to test the water, then turned off the taps. 'Oh, there you are, Philippe. Hop in, and don't by-pass your ears this time. . . . I'll get your tablets straight away, madame. My bag's through in my sitting-room.'

As I came out of the bathroom and shut the door behind me I was wondering how to tell her about the recent near-tragedy. But as I looked at her all idea of this melted into a different consternation. She looked ill. The expression that I had thought forbidding was revealed now as the pallor, set lips, and strained eyes of someone on the verge of collapse.

I said anxiously: 'Are you all right? You don't look well at all. Won't you sit down for a few minutes? Shall I get you some water?'

'No.' She had paused by the fireplace, near a high-backed chair. She managed to smile at me; I could see the effort it took. 'Don't worry, my dear. I – I didn't sleep well last night, that's all. I don't manage very well nowadays without my medicine.'

'I'll get it straight away.' Throwing her another doubtful look I ran towards my sitting-room, only to remember that the tablets were after all still in the pocket of my coat. I turned swiftly.

'*Madame!*' The horrified anxiety of the cry was wrenched out of me by what I saw.

She had put a hand on the chair-back, and was leaning heavily on it. Her face was turned away from me, as if she were listening to Philippe splashing in the bathroom, but her eyes were shut, and her cheeks were a crumpled grey. No beauty there. She looked old.

At my exclamation she started, and her eyes flew open. She seemed to make an effort, and moved away from the chair.

I ran back to her. 'Madame, you *are* ill. Shall I call someone? Albertine?'

'No, no. I shall be all right. My tablets?'

'In my coat-pocket in the wardrobe. Yes, here they are. . . .'

She almost grabbed the box I held out to her. She managed another smile. 'Thank you. I'm sorry if I alarmed you . . . these things pass. Don't look so worried, Miss Martin.' In the bathroom Philippe had set up a shrill tuneless whistling that came spasmodically between splashes. Héloïse glanced towards the noise and then turned to go. She said, with an obvious attempt at normality: 'Philippe sounds . . . very gay.'

'Oh, yes,' I said cheerfully, 'he's fine.'

I opened the door for her, straight onto Berthe who had paused outside, one hand lifted to knock. . . .

'Oh, miss, you startled me! I was just coming.' Her eyes went past me and I saw them widen. I said quickly: 'Madame isn't too well. Madame de Valmy, let Berthe see you to your room. I only rang for her to light Philippe's bedroom fire, but I'll do that myself. Berthe,' I turned to the girl, who was still looking curiously at Héloïse de Valmy's drawn face, 'take Madame to her room, ring for Albertine and wait till she comes. Then come back here, please.'

'Yes, miss.'

As I knelt to light Philippe's bedroom fire my mind was fretting at a new problem – a minor one, which I suppose I had seized on almost as a relief from the other worries that beat dark wings in my brain. What were those tablets that were apparently the breath of life to Madame de Valmy? Did she drug? The ugly thought swirled up through a welter of ignorant conjectures, but I refused to take it up. The things were only sleeping-tablets, I was sure; and presumably some people couldn't live without sleeping-tablets. But – the flames spread merrily from paper to sticks and took hold with a fine bright crackling – but why did she want the tablets now? She had looked as if she were suffering from some sort of attack, heart or nerves, that needed a restorative or stimulant. The sleeping-tablets could hardly be the sort of life-savers that her anxiety had implied.

I shrugged the thoughts away, leaning forward to place a careful piece of coal on the burning sticks. I was ignorant of such matters, after all. She had certainly seemed ill, and just as certainly old Doctor Fauré must know what he was about. . . .

Another burst of whistling and a messy-sounding splash came from the bathroom, and presently Philippe emerged, his hair in damp spikes, and his usually pale cheeks flushed and scrubbed-looking. He had on his nightshirt, and trailed a dressing-gown on the floor behind him.

Something absurd and tender took me by the throat. I looked austerely at him. 'Ears?'

He naturally took no notice of this poor-spirited remark, but came over to the hearthrug beside which the fire now burned brightly. He said, with palpable pride: 'I escaped death by inches, didn't I?'

'You did indeed.'

'Most people would have fallen over, wouldn't they?'

'Decidedly.'

'*Most* people wouldn't have had the presence of mind to stay quite still, would they?'

I sat back on my heels, put an arm round his waist, and hugged him to me, laughing. 'You odious child, don't be so conceited! And look, Philippe, we won't tell Berthe when she comes back, please.'

'Why?'

'Because your aunt isn't well, and I don't want any alarming rumours getting to her to upset her.'

'All right. But you'll – *you'll* tell my uncle Léon, won't you?'

'Of course. It's a marvel to me that he didn't hear the coping fall himself. He was in the hall when I got in, and that was only a few moments after – ah, Berthe. How is Madame?'

'Better, miss. She's lying down. Albertine's with her and she knows what to do. She says Madame will be well enough to go down to dinner.'

'I'm glad to hear it. She ... she took her tablets, Berthe?'

'Tablets, miss? No, it was her drops. She keeps them in the cabinet by her bed. Albertine gave her them.'

'I – see. By the way, Berthe, weren't you supposed to be around the schoolroom wing while I was out?'

'Yes, miss, but Bernard came for me.' She shot me a sidelong glance. 'There was some linen I'd been sewing. Bernard wanted it for the Master, and couldn't find it, though I'd told him where it was.'

'I see. Well, that shouldn't have kept you very long.'

'No, miss. But it wasn't where I'd put it. Somebody'd moved it. Took me quite a while to find.' She was eyeing me as she answered, obviously wondering why I questioned her so sharply.

I said: 'Well, Master Philippe went outside to play on the balcony and got wet, so he's had a bath and is to have supper in bed. Do you mind bringing it in here, Berthe, and mine as well, please?'

'Not a bit, miss. I'm sorry, miss, but you see Bernard was in a hurry and—' She broke off. She was very pink now and looked flustered.

I thought: 'But in no hurry to let you go, that's obvious. And I don't suppose you insisted.' I said aloud: 'It's all right, Berthe, it doesn't matter. Master Philippe's not a baby, after all. It was his own fault he got a wetting, and now he gets the reward, and you and I have the extra work. That's life, isn't it?'

I got up, briskly propelling Philippe towards the bed. 'Now in you get, brat, and don't stand about any longer in that nightshirt.'

I had supper with Philippe as I had promised, and played a game with him and read him a story. He was still in good spirits, and I was glad to see that his own part in the accident was assuming more and

more heroic proportions in his imagination. At least nightmares didn't
lie that way.

But when I got up to go out to the pantry to make his late-night drink
he insisted a little breathlessly on coming with me. I thought it better to
let him, so he padded along in dressing-gown and slippers and was set
to watch the milk on the electric ring while I measured the chocolate and
glucose into the blue beaker he always used. We bore it back to the
bedroom together and I stayed with him while he drank it. And then,
when I would have said goodnight, he clung to me for a moment too
long, so that I abandoned my intention of seeing Léon de Valmy that
night, and spent the rest of the evening in my own room with the
communicating doors open so that the child could see my light.

When finally I was free to sit down beside my own fire I felt so tired
that the flesh seemed to drag at my bones. I slumped down in the
armchair and shut my eyes. But my mind was a cage gnawed by formless
creatures that jostled and fretted, worries – some real, some half-recog-
nised, some unidentified and purely instinctive – that wouldn't let me
rest. And when, very late, I heard a car coming up the zigzag I jumped
to my feet, nerves instantly a-stretch, and slid quietly through the shadows
to the door of Philippe's room.

He was asleep. I went wearily back into my bedroom and began to
undress. I was almost ready for bed when someone knocked softly on the
door.

I said in some surprise: 'Who is it?'

'Berthe, miss.'

'Oh, Berthe. Come in.'

She was carrying a parcel, across which she looked at me a little oddly.
'This is for you, miss. I thought you might be in bed, but I was told to
bring it straight up.'

'No, I wasn't in bed. Thank you, Berthe. Good night.'

'Good night, miss.'

She went. I sat down on the bed and opened the parcel in some
mystification.

I sat there for some time, looking down at the silver-webbed folds of
Italian stuff that glimmered against the coverlet. Then I saw the note.
It read:

*'For the kiss I can't honestly say I'm sorry, but for the rest I do. I was
worried about something, but that's no excuse for taking it out on you.
Will you count the fetching of your parcel as penance, and forgive me,
please?*

R.

P.S. Darling, don't be so Sabine about it. It was only a kiss, after all.'

Before I got to sleep that night, I'd have given a lot, drugs or no, for
some of Madame de Valmy's tablets.

CHAPTER TEN

I told my love, I told my love,
I told him all my heart. ...

WILLIAM BLAKE: *Poem from MSS.*

Next morning it might all have been illusion. Raoul left Valmy early, this time for the south and Bellevigne. I didn't see him go. Whether or not he and Léon had spoken of last night's incident I never discovered; certainly nothing was said or even hinted to me. When I braved my employer in the library to tell him about Philippe's second escape, he received me pleasantly, to darken as he listened into a frowning abstraction that could have nothing to do with my personal affairs.

He was sitting behind the big table in the library. When I had finished speaking he sat for a minute or two in silence, the fingers of one hand tapping the papers in front of him, his eyes hooded and brooding. I had the feeling that he had forgotten I was there.

When he spoke it was to say, rather oddly: 'Again.'

I said, surprised: 'Monsieur?'

He glanced up quickly under his black brows. I thought he spoke a little wearily. 'This is the second time in a very few days, Miss Martin, that we have had cause to be indebted to you for the same rather terrible reason.'

'Oh. I see,' I said, and added awkwardly: 'It was nothing. Anyone—'

'Anyone would have done the same?' His smile was a brief flash that failed to light his eyes. 'So you said earlier, Miss Martin, but I must insist as I did before that we are lucky to have so ...' a little pause ... 'so foresighted a young woman to look after Philippe. When did you put the ladder there?'

'Only yesterday.'

'Really? What made you do it?'

I hesitated, choosing my words. 'The other day I went out myself along the balcony – to wait for a car coming. I remembered the coping had felt a bit loose before, and tried it. It was loose, but I'd have sworn not dangerously. I intended to mention it to you, but honestly I'd no idea it was as bad. Then the car came, and ... I forgot about it.'

I didn't add that the day had been Tuesday and the car Raoul's. I went on: 'Then yesterday, just before I was due to leave for Thonon I went out again, to see if it was going to rain. The ladder was lying on the balcony and I wondered if workmen had been there. I remembered then about the coping, but I was in a tearing hurry for the bus, so I just shoved the ladder along in front of the balustrade and went. I – I vowed I'd remember to tell you as soon as I got back. I – I'm terribly sorry.' I finished lamely.

'You needn't be. You were not to know that the stone was as rotten as that. I did have a report on the stonework of that balcony some time ago, but there was no suggestion that the repair was urgent. There'll be trouble about this, you may be sure. But meanwhile let us just be thankful for whatever inspired you to put the ladder across.'

I laughed, still slightly embarrassed. 'Perhaps it was Philippe's guardian angel.'

He said dryly: 'Perhaps. He seems to need one.'

I said: 'There's a phrase for it, isn't there? "Accident-prone".'

'It seems appropriate.' The smooth voice held a note that, incongruously, sounded like amusement. I looked sharply at him. He met my look. 'Well? Well, Miss Martin?'

'Nothing,' I said confusedly. 'I – it's just that – you take it so calmly. I'd have expected you to be angry.'

'But I am,' he said, 'very angry.' And meeting his eyes squarely for the first time during the interview I realised with a shock that he spoke a little less than the truth. He smiled again, and quite without amusement. 'But being a rational man, I keep my anger for those who are to blame. It would ill become me, mademoiselle, to vent it on you. And I cannot spend it in protests, because that is . . . not my way.'

He swung the wheel-chair round so that he was turned a little away from me, looking out of the window across the rose-garden. I waited, watching the drawn, handsome face with its fine eyes and mobile mouth, and wondering why talking with Léon de Valmy always made me feel as if I were acting in a play where all the cues were marked. I knew what was coming next, and it came.

He said, with that wry calmness that was somehow all wrong: 'When one is a cripple one learns a certain . . . economy of effort, Miss Martin. What would be the point of raging at you here and now? You're not to blame. How's Philippe?'

The question cut across my thoughts – which were simply that I'd have liked him better indulging in some of that profitless rage – so abruptly that I jumped.

'Philippe? Oh, he's all right, thank you. He was frightened and upset, but I doubt if there'll be any ill effects. I imagine it'll soon be forgotten – though at the moment he's inclined to be rather proud of the adventure.'

He was still looking away from me across the garden. 'Yes? Ah well, children are unpredictable creatures, aren't they? *Le pauvre petit*, let's hope he's at the end of his "adventures", as you call them.'

'Don't worry, Monsieur de Valmy. He's having a bad spell, but it'll get over.' I added, inconsequentially: 'When does Monsieur Hippolyte get home?'

He turned his head quickly. The chair moved at the same moment so suddenly that the arm struck the edge of the desk. His exclamation was lost in my cry.

'You've knocked your hand!'

'Its nothing.'

'The knuckle's bleeding. Can I get you—?'

'It's nothing, I tell you. What were you saying?'

'I forget. Oh yes, I wondered if you knew just when Philippe's Uncle Hippolyte gets home?'

'I have no idea. Why?'

My eyes had been on his grazed hand. I looked up now to see him watching me, his face as usual calmly shuttered, but with something in that quiet gaze that held me staring without reply.

Then the brilliant eyes dropped. He moved a paper-knife an inch or two and repeated casually: 'Why do you ask?'

'Just that Philippe keeps asking me, and I wondered if you'd heard from Monsieur Hippolyte.'

'Ah. Yes. Well, I don't know exactly, I'm afraid. My brother has always been slightly unpredictable. But he'll be away for another three months at least. I thought Philippe knew that. I believe his scheduled lecture-tour finished just before Easter, but he plans to stay for some time after that to assist the excavations at – as far as I remember – Delphi.' He smiled. 'My brother is a remarkably poor correspondent. ... I imagine that Philippe knows just about as much as I do.' He lifted the paper-knife, placed it exactly where it had been before, looked up at me and smiled again, charmingly. 'Well, Miss Martin, I won't keep you. I still have to divert some of that anger into its proper channels.'

He was reaching for the house-telephone as I escaped.

It occurred to me with wry surprise that 'escape' was exactly the right word for my relieved exit from the library. The discovery annoyed me considerably. Damn it, the tiger played velvet-paws with me, didn't he?

But, unreasonable as it was, I couldn't rid myself of the impression that some of that much-discussed anger had been – whatever he said, whatever the probabilities – directed straight at me.

It was only a fortnight now to the Easter Ball, and I had to work fast. The weather was bad, so walks with Philippe were not obligatory, and though I took him several times to the stables to play on wet afternoons, we had a good deal of spare time indoors when I cut and sewed. Philippe and Berthe both appeared fascinated by the idea of making a dance-dress, and hung over me, fingering the stuff and exclaiming over every stage in its manufacture. Berthe was of rather more practical help than Philippe, as she gave me the use of her machine, and – since she was of my height and build – let me fit the pattern on her, never tiring of standing swathed in the glinting folds while I pinned and pulled and experimented.

As the days went by the château hummed with activity and pleased expectation. If there was indeed any shortage of money here, it could not have been guessed at. I did gather, from odd snippets of gossip to which I was careful to pay no attention, that much of the cost of the ball must be borne by Monsieur de Valmy himself. Monsieur Hippolyte, it was whispered, didn't care for such things, and whereas in past years Philippe's father had willingly financed the affair and had invariably, with his wife, come from Paris to attend it, now that Monsieur Hippolyte was Philippe's co-trustee he was (I gathered) inclined to sit down rather tightly on the money-bags. Whatever the case, it seemed that Monsieur de Valmy was determined to recall at least some of the splendours of 'the old Comte's' time. To my unaccustomed eye the preparations seemed lavish in the extreme. Rarely-used bedrooms were opened and aired – for there were to be guests over Easter weekend – the great ballroom and the big drawing-room were thrown open, chandeliers were washed, lustre by lustre, mirrors were polished, furniture and rugs spirited from one place to another, all, it seemed, under the eagle eye of Monsieur de Valmy. His chair was everywhere; if a servant dropped a piece of silver he was cleaning, the Master heard it; if a table was pushed along a parquet floor instead of being lifted, the Master spoke angrily from a corner of the room; he was even to be seen constantly on the upper corridors, swiftly propelling himself in and out of bedrooms and along corridors not commonly used by the family.

And so, bit by bit, corner by corner, the great house was prepared for the event of the year, and excitement seemed to thicken in the air as Easter drew nearer. Then came the final touches; flowers were carried in from the hot-houses, camellias and lilies and gorgeous blooms I didn't recognise, with tub after tub of bluebells and narcissi and tulips looking cool and virginal among the heavy-scented exotics. In one of the galleries there was even a miniature grove of willows over a shallow basin where goldfish glided, with cyclamens clustering like butterflies at the water's edge. Outside, floodlights had been fitted up, and a fountain like a firework shot its sparkling trails thirty feet towards Saturday's big yellow moon. For on Easter Eve the weather cleared, and Easter itself came in bright and beautiful, with a soft wind blowing that set the wild daffodils dancing in the woods, and put the seal on the success of the affair.

The Château Valmy was *en fête*.

On Sunday night after Philippe had gone to bed I put the finishing-touches to my frock. Berthe had stayed to help me, and now paraded it delightedly before me, while I sat on the floor among a scatter of pins and watched her with critical eyes.

'Ye—es,' I said. 'Turn round again, will you? Thanks. It'll do, I think, Berthe.'

Berthe twirled a curtsy in it, gay and graceful. It was amazing how she had shed her prim servant-maid attitude along with her uniform. In the shimmering dress she looked what she was, a pretty country-girl, slim and young and – just now – flushed with excitement.

'It's *lovely*, miss, it's really lovely.' She spun round so that the full skirt swirled and sank. She lifted a fold and fingered it almost wistfully. 'You'll look beautiful in it.'

'I've an awful feeling it'll look pretty home-made alongside the collection downstairs.'

'Don't you believe it,' said Berthe stoutly. 'I've seen some of them; Mariette and me did most of the unpacking. The prettiest frock I think belongs to the Marquise in the yellow guestroom, and she's no oil-painting herself by a long chalk.'

'Hush, Berthe,' I protested, laughing, 'you mustn't say things like that to me!'

She began to waltz round the room, humming a tune. 'Of course Madame's always nice. She looks lovely in *grande toilette* – like a Queen. And that Madame Verlaine gets herself up very smart, doesn't she? Hers is black.'

'Is Monsieur Florimond here?'

'Oh, he always comes. He says he wouldn't miss it for worlds. He dresses half the ladies, anyway.'

I began to pick up the scattered pins, asking casually: 'And Monsieur Raoul? Does he come to this affair as a rule?'

There was a tiny pause. At the edge of my vision I saw Berthe's circling form check and turn. I looked up to catch a sidelong glance before her eyes slid from mine. She plucked at a fold of the skirt. 'He hasn't been for years. But they're expecting him – this time.'

I said nothing, and picked up pins.

She came over to where I sat, her voice warming into naturalness again. 'Why don't you try it on now, miss? Don't bother with those, I'll pick them up after.'

'It's done,' I said. 'There, that's the lot, I think.'

'Don't you believe it,' she said darkly. 'We'll be finding them for weeks. Go on, miss, put it on, do. I want to see you in it, with the silver shoes and all.'

I laughed and got up. 'All right.'

'It's a shame you haven't got a decent mirror. That one in the wardrobe door's no good at all, not for a long frock.'

'It's all right. I told Madame I was making a frock and she said I might use the glass in her room. I'll just go along now and give it the final check-up. Tomorrow night I'll have to make do in here.'

She followed me into my bedroom, speaking a little shyly. 'May I help you to dress tomorrow?'

'Why, Berthe, how nice of you! But you'll have so much to do! And I could manage quite well, really. I'm not used to luxuries, you know.'

'I'd like to. I would really.'

'Then thank you very much. I'd be awfully glad to have you.'

Back in her uniform, she helped me pleasedly with the dress. At last I stood surveying myself in the narrow wardrobe mirror.

'Oh, miss, it's lovely!'

'We put a lot of work into it, Berthe. I'm terribly grateful to you for helping. I couldn't have managed without you.'

I turned this way and that, eyeing the line and fall of the material, and wondering just how amateurish it was going to look against the other gowns downstairs. Then I saw Berthe's eyes in the glass. They were brilliant with uncomplicated excitement and pleasure. Her delight, it was obvious, wasn't fretted by the shades of Balenciaga and Florimond. 'Oh, miss, it's lovely! There won't be one prettier! You'll look a picture! Wait, I'll get the shoes!'

She was scurrying towards a cupboard but I stopped her impulsively. 'Berthe. . . .'

She turned.

'Berthe, would *you* like to wear it too, for your own dance on Tuesday? You've probably got another just as pretty, but if you'd like it—'

'Oh, *miss!* Her eyes grew enormous and she gripped her hands together. 'Me? Oh, but I *couldn't*. . . . *Could* I?'

'Why not? You look lovely in it, and it was practically made on you, after all. If you'd really like it, Berthe, I'd be terribly pleased for you to take it. I don't suppose anyone'll recognise it.'

'No, they won't,' she said ingenuously. 'It'll be hired waiters here tomorrow, and Ber – the servants won't be about. If – if you really mean it—' She began to thank me again, but I said quickly:

'Then that's settled. Fine. Now I'll better fly if I'm to get to that looking-glass before Madame comes upstairs.'

Berthe dived once more for the cupboard.

'Your shoes! Put on your new shoes with it!'

'No, no, don't bother,' I said hastily, making for the door, 'I must run. Thanks again, Berthe! Goodnight!'

Madame de Valmy's bedroom adjoined a small sitting-room which she used in the mornings. I went through, leaving the connecting-door ajar.

Her bedroom was a beautiful room, all soft lights and brocade and elegant Louis Seize, with a positively fabulous glitter of silver and crystal on the toilet-table. An enormous Venetian mirror flanked the bathroom door, apparently held to the silk panelling by the efforts of the whole cherub choir.

I stood in front of this. The long window-curtains mirrored behind me were of rose-coloured brocade. The lighting was lovely. As I moved I saw the gleam of the cobwebbed silver thread shift and glimmer through the white cloud of the skirt the way sunlight flies along blown gossamer.

I remember that the thought that surfaced first in my mind was that now Cinderella had no excuse to stay away from the ball. And – at midnight?

Impatiently I shook my thoughts free, angry that I could still fool around even for a moment with the myth that I knew was nonsense. I'd burned myself badly enough on that star already.

Someone was at the sitting-room door. Berthe must have come along with the silver sandals. I called: 'Come in. I'm through here,' and made a face at myself in the glass. Here were the glass slippers. Damn it, I didn't stand a chance. . . .

A quick tread across the sitting-room. Raoul's voice said: 'Héloïse, did you want me?'

Then he saw me. He stopped dead in the doorway.

'Why – hullo,' he said. He sounded a little breathless, as though he'd been hurrying.

I opened my mouth to answer him, then swallowed and shut it again. I couldn't have spoken if I'd tried. I must just have gaped at him like a schoolgirl caught out in some escapade. I know I went scarlet.

Then I gathered up my skirts in clumsy hands and moved towards the doorway which he still blocked.

He didn't give way. He merely leaned his shoulders back against the jamb of the door and waited, as if prepared to settle there for the evening.

I took two more hesitating steps towards him, and then stopped.

'Don't run away. Let me look at you.'

'I must. I mean, I'd better—'

He said: 'Sabine,' very softly, and the laugh in the word brought hotter colour to my face and my eyes up to his.

I'm not sure what happened next. I think he moved a little and said: 'All right. So you really want to run away?' And I think I said, somehow: 'no,' and then 'Raoul,' as his shoulders came away from the doorpost in a kind of lunge, and then he was across the room and had me in his arms and was kissing me with a violence that was terrifying and yet, somehow, the summit of all my tenderest dreams.

I pushed away from him at last, both hands against his chest. 'But Raoul, *why*?'

'What d'you mean why?'

'Why me? Your father called me "Jane Eyre", and he wasn't far wrong. And *you* – you could have anyone. So . . . why?'

'Do you want to know why?' His hands turned me round to face the mirror again, holding me back against him. I could feel his heart hammering against my shoulder-blade. His eyes met mine in the glass. 'You don't have to be humble, *ma belle*. That's why.'

An odd sensation took me, part triumphant and part forlorn. I said nothing. The cherubs peered at us blind-eyed. Behind us the rose and gold and crystal of the lovely room glowed like the Bower of Bliss. Raoul was watching my face.

He opened his mouth as if to say something, but before he could speak there came a slight sound from the other room. He turned his head sharply, and for a moment his hands tightened on my shoulders. Then he let me go and turned, saying coolly: 'Ah, Héloïse. I was looking for you. I believe you wanted me.'

I jumped and spun round. I felt the quick heat wash and ebb in my cheeks, leaving me cold and pale. We had been standing in full view of anyone entering the sitting-room. Héloïse de Valmy was there now, just inside the door, with Albertine beside her. She was speaking over her shoulder to someone – presumably one of the guests – behind her in the corridor, beyond my range of vision.

A woman's voice returned a soft reply and I heard skirts rustle away. It was impossible to tell if Madame de Valmy had seen Raoul holding me, but I knew Albertine had. Avoiding her dark malicious eyes I came quickly out of the bedroom with Raoul behind me.

I said, stammering: 'Madame ... I was using your glass to – to try my frock. You said I might ...'

It was impossible to tell whether she had seen. Her light-grey eyes looked me up and down without expression. As usual, they were unsmiling, but I could detect no hint of displeasure in her face.

She said, in her cold composed voice: 'Of course. Is that the dress you have made, Miss Martin? It's very pretty. You must be an accomplished needlewoman. Perhaps one day you might do some work for me?'

So she had seen. I felt Raoul, beside me, make a little movement. The burning colour washed back into my face. I said quickly: 'It would be a pleasure, madame. Good night, madame. Good night, monsieur.'

I didn't look at him. I slipped past Héloïse de Valmy into the welcome dimness of the corridor, and ran back to my room.

The next day passed in a whirl. I spent all my time with Philippe, who, alone of all the people in the house, seemed untouched by the general excitement, and was, indeed, indulging in a bout of the sulks at being left out of the Easter revels.

Luckily I didn't have to face Madame de Valmy. Just after lunch Albertine – was there a spark of malice in the smooth voice and face as she said it? – brought me a message which asked if we could please direct our afternoon's walk to the village to make some small purchases, as none of the servants (had she or had she not hesitated on the phrase "other servants"?) could be spared?

I agreed politely, and chided myself, as I took a reluctant, foot-trailing Philippe down to Soubirous, for being over-sensitive. Madame de Valmy would surely not put me so brutally in my place a second time, and as for Albertine, a servant's malice couldn't affect me.

But I began to wonder, a few minutes later, if this last was true. As I paused in the sunshine outside Monsieur Garcin's shop to fish in my bag for Albertine's note, the bead curtains over the chemist's doorway rattled aside, and Albertine herself came out. Albertine who 'could not be spared' today; for whom I was playing errand-boy. She must have set out for Soubirous almost immediately after briefing me.

I stared at her in amazement. She showed no sign of confusion, but
lipped by me with one of her dark sidelong looks and small-lipped Mona
Lisa smiles. She went into the *confiserie* just beyond the café.

When I pushed through the swinging beads myself into the spicy
dimness of the shop, I was tense and nervous and very ready to discover
in Monsieur Garcin's voice and attitude that same sidelong malice that
had now certainly seen in Albertine.

I told myself firmly that this was only fancy. But as I emerged from
the pharmacy I came face to face with Madame Rocher, the curé's
housekeeper, and this time there was no doubt about the chilliness of the
greeting. If the good Madame could have passed by on the other side she
would undoubtedly have done so. As it was she simply stared, nodded
once, and gave me *bonjour* in a tone nicely calculated (as from virtuous
matron to viper-in-the-bosom) to keep me in my place, while at the same
time allowing just the faintest loophole for a possibly legitimate future.
Philippe she greeted, quite simply, with pity.

And later, when I bought some chocolate in the *confiserie*, I thought
Madame Decorzent's fat smile was a little stiff today, and her prune-
black eyes were curious, almost avid, as she said, glancing from Philippe
to me: 'And when are you leaving us, mademoiselle?'

I said coolly, through the sudden hammering of my heart: 'We don't
go to Thonon for a good while yet, madame. Monsieur Hippolyte doesn't
get back for three more months, you know.'

And I almost swept Philippe out through the tinkling curtain of beads
into the hot sunlight. Albertine had done her work all right. The news,
with its attendant rumours, was all over Soubirous.

I ran the gauntlet of sundry other stares and whispers before I reached
the bridge and faced – with poor Philippe maddeningly a-whine beside
me – the long trudge up through the water-meadows.

I hadn't realised before what hard going it must have been for
Cinderella.

After tea I went to look for Mrs. Seddon, to talk to her about whatever
rumours were being put about below stairs, only to be told that the fuss
and overwork occasioned by the ball had brought on 'one of her attacks',
and that she had gone to bed, unfit to speak to anyone. So I stayed with
Philippe, my mind hovering miserably between remembered (and surely
disastrous?) ecstasy, and my apparently imminent dismissal from Valmy.
I am glad to remember that some of my worry was on behalf of
Philippe. . . .

By the time Berthe came up that evening to serve Philippe's supper,
I was in a fairly lamentable state of nerves, and more than half inclined
to shirk facing my host and hostess downstairs. Then Philippe chose to
throw a tantrum, and refused with tears to go to bed at all unless I
would come up later 'in the middle of the night' and take him to peep

at the dancing from the gallery. I promised, and satisfied, he disappeare
quietly enough with Berthe.

I shut the door on them, and went to run my bath.

Dressing for my first dance ... and Raoul somewhere among th
throng of dancers ... I should have been happy, eager, excited. But m
fingers shook as I opened a fresh tablet of scented soap, and later o
when I was sitting in my petticoat brushing my hair, and a knock sounde
on the door, I turned to face it as if it were a firing-squad.

'I'll go,' said Berthe, who had disposed of Philippe and was helpin
me. She opened the door a little way, had a short muffled colloquy wit
whoever was outside, then shut the door and came back into the roor
holding a box.

I was still sitting at the dressing-table, hair-brush suspended. Berth
came over to me. She looked a little flushed as she handed me the bo
and she avoided my eye.

'This is for you.' Her tone – like her whole bearing that evening – wa
subdued and a little formal.

For a moment I thought of asking her what was being whispered, the
I held my tongue. I didn't want to meet him – and Monsieur an
Madame – fresh from Albertine's brand of backstairs gossip. Th
woman's glance had been smirch enough.

Et tu, Berthe, I thought, and took the box from her.

It was light and flat, with a cellophane lid glassing the dark heartshape
leaves and fragile blossoms of white violets; milk-white blooms, moth
white, delicate in dark-green leaves. There was the faintest veining o
cream on throat and wing.

A card was tucked among the leaves. Without opening the lid I coul
see the single letter in an arrogant black scrawl: – *R*.

I finished dressing in silence.

Then I pinned the violets on, said quietly: 'Thank you, Berthe,' an
went towards the music and the laughter.

CHAPTER ELEVEN

I am two fools, I know,
For loving, and for saying so.

JOHN DONNE: *The Triple Fool*

The ball was well under way, and I was thankful to see that Monsieu
and Madame de Valmy had finished receiving. Their place near th
banked flowers at the foot of the great staircase was empty. Now the hal
was brilliant with a shifting mass of people. I hesitated on the gallery
having no mind to make an entrance alone down that impressive fligh
of steps; then three young women came chattering past me from som

room along the corridor, and I followed as inconspicuously as I could in their wake.

It was easy enough to slip unremarked through the throng and into the ballroom itself, where I found a corner sheltered by a pillar and a bank of azaleas, and settled down quietly to watch the dancers.

I couldn't see Léon de Valmy's chair anywhere, but Héloïse, looking wonderful in a gown the colour of sea-lavender, was dancing with an elderly bearded man on whose breast the blue ribbon of an Order showed. I saw Florimond over by one of the windows talking, or rather listening, to a terrifying-looking old woman with a beak of a nose and improbable blue hair. He was leaning forward slightly, that flattering air of his assuring her that she was the most amusing and intelligent woman in the room. For all I know she may have been. But had she been the dreariest hag on earth I am sure that Florimond would have looked exactly the same.

I turned to look for Raoul. On a swirl of music the dancers near me swung and parted and I saw him. He was dancing with a blonde girl with slanting eyes and a beautiful mouth. She was in black, with a high neck and a straight-cut skirt that spoke of Madame Fath and made her look incredibly slender and fragile. She was dancing very close to him and talking rapidly, with flickering upward glances through her long lashes. I didn't see him speak, but he was smiling. They were a striking couple, and danced so beautifully that more than one glance was thrown in their direction and – I had nothing to do but see it – more than one significant eyebrow lifted in their wake. It would seem that Mrs. Seddon had been right: where Raoul went, rumour walked. I wondered who the girl was. When – if – he danced with me, what would the eyebrows do then? *Who's the new girl? My dear, nobody, obviously. And my dear, the dress ... The governess? ... Oh ... Oh, I see ...*

The music stopped, and people drifted to the sides of the ballroom. I was hidden by the crowd. Nobody had noticed me. I sat still, glad of the sheltering pillar and the massed azaleas. Beside me a trickle of water ran down a little scale, soulless as the music of a spinet. There was a tank of fish here, too, and the water dripped into it from a bank of moss. The azaleas threw patterns on the water, and gold and silver fish moved warily underneath.

The music started again, obliterating talk, laughter, and the tiny tinkle of water. The glittering dresses took the floor. This time he led out an elderly woman with a dreadful gown of royal blue and magnificent diamonds. And then a dark hawk of a woman with a clever hungry face and hands like yellow claws. And then the lovely blonde girl again. And then a well-corseted woman with dyed hair who wore dramatic black with emeralds. And then a white-haired woman with a gentle face. And then the blonde again.

The fish hung suspended in water green as serpentine, fins moving rhythmically. A petal, loosed from a pink azalea, floated down to lie

upon the surface. I remembered my promise to Philippe. I got up, shaking
out the folds of my skirt. The fish, startled, shuttled about the tank under
the hanging mosses.

When a voice said: 'Mademoiselle,' just behind me, I started like a
guilty thing upon a fearful summons, and dropped my handbag, missing
the tank by millimetres.

The owner of the voice stooped a little ponderously to pick it up for
me. I might have known he would come sooner or later to comfort the
wallflower.

'Monsieur Florimond!' I said. 'You startled me.'

'I'm sorry.' He handed me the bag with a smile. 'But you must not
fly away now, mademoiselle. I'm depending on you for an alibi.'

'An alibi?'

He made one of his wide gestures. 'My dear, I don't dance, and I've
talked myself to a standstill. I thought perhaps if I cornered you quickly
we could resume our flirtation, which is something I can do at any time
without effort.'

'And,' I said, watching how his hand hovered already over his pocket,
'have a quiet smoke at the same time? All right, Monsieur Florimond,
I'll be your chimney-corner.'

'A sympathetic woman,' said Florimond, unabashed, taking out his
case, 'is above rubies.'

'Don't you believe it. No woman is above rubies,' I said, sitting down
again. 'No thank you, I don't smoke.'

'Above diamonds, pearls, and rubies,' said Florimond, lowering himself
into the chair beside me with a sigh, and proceeding, as to an elaborate
ritual, to light a cigarette. He beamed at me through the resultant cloud
of smoke. 'That's a very pretty gown, my dear.'

I laughed at him. 'Shakespeare,' I said, 'congratulating Minou Drouet
on a neat phrase? Thank you, monsieur.'

His eyes puckered at the corners. 'I meant it. But you're rather hiding
your light under a bushel, aren't you? I've been watching for you, but
I haven't seen you dancing.'

'I don't know anyone.'

'Oh, *là-là*! And didn't Héloïse introduce any young men?'

'I haven't seen her to speak to. I came down late.'

'And now she is – ah, yes, there she is, dancing with Monsieur de St.
Hubert.' He scanned the floor. 'Then where's Raoul? He knows everybody. Perhaps he—'

'Oh, no, please!' The exclamation burst out quite involuntarily. I met
Florimond's eye of mild inquiry and finished lamely: 'I – I was just
going upstairs. I promised Philippe to go and see him. I – don't bother
Monsieur Raoul, please.'

'Upstairs? And not to come down again, is that it?' The kind eyes
surveyed me. 'And is that also why you came down so late and then hid
among the flowers?'

'I don't – what d'you mean?'

His gaze fixed itself on the violets. He didn't answer. My hand moved in spite of me to cup the flowers, a curiously defensive gesture and quite futile. I said: 'How did you know?' and touched the violets with a finger-tip. 'These?'

He shook his head. 'My dear,' he said gently, 'haven't you learnt yet that every breath the Valmys take is news in the valley?'

I said bitterly: 'I'm learning.' I looked away from him. A fish was nosing at the azalea-petal, butting it gently from underneath. I watched it absorbedly. The dance-music seemed to come from a great way off. Here among the flowers was a little walled garden of silence broken only by the liquid arpeggios of the dripping mosses.

At length he spoke. 'You're very young.'

'Twenty-three.' My voice tried hard not to sound defensive.

'Mademoiselle' – he seemed to be choosing his words – 'if you ever thought of leaving Valmy, where would you go?'

I stared at him through a moment of whirling silence. Here, too. It was true. It hadn't been imagination to see those dragon's-teeth of scandal springing up in Albertine's malicious wake. Madame de Valmy or (something caught at my breathing) Monsieur himself had said something, hinted something about dismissing me. And Florimond the kind had sought me out to talk to me about it. Everybody, it seemed, was making my connection with Raoul their business.

I don't quite know what I was thinking about it myself. I couldn't see beyond the fact that I loved him; that he had kissed me; that he was here tonight. I wanted to see him; dreaded seeing him. About Raoul's feelings and purpose – his 'intentions' – I didn't think at all. He was here, and I loved him. That was all.

I pulled myself together to hear Florimond saying, kindly: 'Have you friends in France, or are you on your own over here, mademoiselle?'

I said in a tight little voice: 'I don't know anyone in France, no. But I am not on my own, monsieur.'

'What do you mean?'

'Monsieur Florimond, you are being very kind, and don't think I don't appreciate it. But let's be frank, now that we've gone so far. You are concerned about me because I was seen kissing Raoul de Valmy, and I'm to be dismissed. Is that it?'

'Not quite.'

I said, surprised: 'Then what?'

He said gently: 'Because you are also in love with Raoul de Valmy, child.'

I said, rather breathlessly: 'So – what?'

'What I said. You are too young. You have nobody here to run to. You are too much alone.'

'No. I told you. I'm not alone.'

He looked a query.

I said very evenly: 'Is it so very impossible that I should be able to run – as you put it – to Raoul?'

There was a pause. The words seemed to repeat themselves into the silence. The clasp of my bag was hurting my fingers when I gripped it. I looked at him. 'Yes, monsieur. We are being frank, you and I. Is it so very impossible that Raoul should – care for me?'

'My dear—' said Florimond, and stopped.

'Yes, monsieur?'

He took a deep breath. 'You and Raoul? . . . No, mademoiselle. No and no and no.'

I said, after a little pause: 'Just how well do you know him, monsieur?'

'Raoul? Well enough. Not intimately, perhaps, but—' he stopped again and one large hand tugged at his collar. He didn't meet my eyes. He said: '*Hell!*' unexpectedly and explosively, and began to grind out his cigarette in the earth of the azalea-tub.

I was too angry to let him off. 'Then since you don't know him so very well, perhaps you'll explain what you meant.'

He looked at me then. 'My dear, I can't. I should never have said it. I've already done the unforgivable. I mustn't go further.'

'Monsieur de Valmy being your host?'

He almost jumped. 'You're a little too quick for me, my dear. Yes, that and other reasons.'

Our eyes met, in a curious half-ashamed comprehension. But I was still angry. I said: 'Since we're talking in riddles, monsieur, what makes you think that all tigers breed true?'

'Mademoiselle—'

'All right,' I said, 'we'll leave it. You've warned me. You've eased your conscience and it was very kind of you to bother. Shall we just wait and see?'

He breathed a great, gusty sigh. 'I was wrong,' he said. 'You're not as young as I thought.' He was groping for another cigarette, grinning amiably at me. 'Well, I've said my piece – unwarranted cheek, and you've been very nice about it. And don't forget, when you do do that running you've got at least one other person in France to run to.'

My anger died. 'Monsieur Florimond—'

'There,' he said, 'and now we'll drop the subject. What about that flirtation we were in the middle of? Do you remember just where we'd got to? Or would you rather have a quick game of chess?'

I gave a shaken little laugh. 'It would certainly be quick. Compared with me, Philippe's a master. You'd mop me up in three minutes.'

'A pity. There's nothing like chess and tobacco, judiciously mixed, for taking the mind off the advice of a doddering old fool who ought to know better.' A large hand patted mine paternally, and was withdrawn. 'Forgive me, child. I couldn't help it, could I, if the advice came too late?'

I smiled at him. 'Monsieur Florimond, even if this isn't the right moment in our flirtation to say so, you are a darling. But yes ... much too late.'

Raoul's voice said, above me: 'So here you are! Carlo, what the devil d'you mean by hiding her away in this corner? Damn it, I've been watching the doors for a couple of hours! I'd no idea she was finding you and the goldfish such fascinating company. What was the sombre discussion, *mon vieux*? What's much too late?'

'You, for one thing,' said Florimond, calmly. 'Now take Miss Martin away and dance with her and try and atone for leaving her to the goldfish.'

Raoul grinned. 'I'll do that. Linda, come here.'

I went.

Florimond's eyes followed me, still with that pucker of trouble about them. Then I forgot them as the music took us.

His voice said at my ear: 'It's been an age. Had you been there long?'

'Not really.'

'Why were you so late?'

'I was scared to come down.'

'Scared? My God, why? Oh, of course, Héloïse.'

'She saw us; you know that.'

'Yes.' He laughed. 'D'you mind?'

'Of course.'

'You'll have to learn not to.'

My heart was beating anyhow up in my throat. 'What d'you mean?'

But he only laughed again without replying and swept me round with the music in a quick turn. A pillar swirled past, a group of men, a wheelchair. . . .

Léon de Valmy.

He was watching us, of course. A shadow at the centre of the kaleidoscope; a spider at the knot of the bright web ... the stupid fancies rose from nowhere in a stinging cloud. I shook my head a little, angrily, as if that would dispel them. Damn the man, I wasn't afraid of him ... was I?

As, momentarily, the dance took me round to face him again, I looked straight at him and gave him a brilliant smile.

He was taken aback: there was no doubt about that. I saw the black brows lift sharply, then his mouth twitched and he smiled back.

The other dancers came between us and cut him off from view. I was left with the sharp impression that my employer's smile had been one of quite genuine amusement, but that it was amusement at some joke I couldn't see. It was an impression that was quite particularly unpleasant.

'Raoul,' I said suddenly, urgently.

'Yes?'

'Oh – nothing.'

'Just *Raoul*?'

'Yes.'

He slanted a look down at me and smiled. '*Soit,*' was all he said, but I had the odd feeling that he understood.

When the dance finished we were at the opposite end of the room from Léon de Valmy, and beside one of the long windows. Raoul showed no sign of leaving me. He waited beside me in silence. He seemed to be oblivious of the crowd surrounding us, though the eyebrows were certainly at work. I caught a few curious looks cast at us, but I wasn't worrying about them. I was busy trying to locate Madame de Valmy in the crowd and to see her without actually catching her eye. But she wasn't there.

The music started again. Raoul turned back to me.

I said feebly: 'Now look, you don't really have to bother about me. I'm—'

'Don't be idiotic,' said he crisply, taking hold of me.

This lover-like speech naturally reassured me completely. I laughed. I forgot Héloïse de Valmy, the raised eyebrows, even Léon and his amusement. I said meekly: 'No, monsieur,' and was swept out onto the floor again.

'I've done more than my share tonight, by God,' said Raoul with feeling. 'I've danced with every dowager in the place. Don't try and thwart me now, my girl. . . . It's just as well I couldn't find you before or I might have neglected my duty.'

We were dancing at the edge of the room, near the french windows which stood open to the mild night.

'As,' he finished, 'I am about to neglect it now. . . .'

And before I knew quite what he was about we were out of the ballroom and on the loggia, slipping as easily and unnoticeably out of the throng as a floating twig slides into a backwater. The music followed us through the long windows; and there was the Easter moon, and the ghosts of jonquils dancing in the dark garden. My skirt brushed the narcissi on the terrace's edge. Raoul's shoulder touched jasmine and loosed a shower of tiny stars. We didn't speak. The spell held. We danced along the moonlit arcade of the loggia, then in through the dark windows of the salon, where firelight warmed the deserted shadows, and the music came muted as if from a great way off.

We were in the shadows. He stopped and his arms tightened round me. 'And now . . .' he said.

Later, when I could speak, I said shakily: 'I love you. I love you. I love you.' And, of course, after that singularly ill-advised remark it was impossible to speak or even breathe for a very long time indeed.

When at length he let me go and spoke, I hardly recognised his voice. But, slurred and unsteady as it was, it still held that little undertone of laughter that was unmistakably his. 'Well, aren't you going to ask it?'

'Ask what?'

'What every woman in the world asks straight away. The vow returned. "*Do you love me?*" '

I said: 'I'll settle for whatever you want to give.'

'I told you before not to be humble, Linda.'

'I can't help it. It's the way you make me feel.'

He said: '*Oh God!*' in that queer wrenched voice and pulled me to him again. He didn't kiss me but held me tightly and spoke over my head into the darkness. 'Linda ... Linda, listen.'

'I'm listening.'

'This love thing. I don't know. This is honest. I don't know.'

Something twisted at my heart that might – if it were not absurd – have been pity. 'It doesn't matter, Raoul. Don't'

'It does. You have to know. There've been other women – you know that. Quite a few.'

'Yes.'

'This is different.' A silence. The ghost of a laugh. 'I'd say that anyway, wouldn't I? But it is. It is.' His cheek moved against my hair. 'Linda. That's the hell of a name for a Frenchwoman, isn't it? So now you know. I want you. I need you, by God I do. If you'd call that love—'

'It'll do,' I said. 'Believe me, it'll do.'

Another silence. The fire burned steadily, filling the room with shadows. In one of the logs I could hear the whine and bubble of resin.

He gave a queer little sigh and then loosened me, holding me at arm's length. His voice was his own again, cool, casual, a little hard. 'What were you and Carlo talking about?'

The question was so unexpected that I started. 'I – why, I hardly remember. Things. And – oh, yes, my frock. Yes, we talked about my frock.'

I saw him smile. 'Come now, confess. You talked about me.'

'How did you know?'

'Second sight.'

'Oh, murder,' I said. 'Don't tell me you've got it as well.'

'As well?'

'Your father's a warlock; didn't you know?'

'Oh? Then shall we just say that I've got excellent hearing. Did Carlo warn you that my intentions were sure to be dishonourable?'

'Of course.'

'Did he, by God?'

'More or less. It was done by implication and with the nicest possible motives.'

'I'm sure of it. What did he say?'

I laughed at him and quoted: ' "You and Raoul, no and no and no." And you are not to be angry. I adore Monsieur Florimond and he was only talking to me for my own good.'

He was looking down at me soberly. 'I'm not likely to be angry. He was too damned near right. I don't mean about my motives, but that probably you and I—' He stopped. 'I've told you how I feel. But you; you say you love me.'

I said: 'Yes and yes and yes.'

I saw him smile. 'Again thrice? You're very generous.'

'I was cancelling Carlo out. Besides, we have a poem in English which says: "What I tell you three times is true".'

Another pause. Then he said, still holding me: 'Then you will take a chance on marrying me?'

I began to tremble. I said huskily: 'But your father—'

His hands moved so sharply that they hurt me. 'My father? What's it to him?'

'He'll be so angry. Perhaps he'll do something about it – make you leave Bellevigne, or—'

'So what? I'm not tied to him or to Bellevigne.' He gave a short, half-angry laugh. 'Are you afraid of harming my position? My prospects? By God, that's rich!'

I said falteringly: 'But you love Bellevigne, don't you? You told me you did, and Mrs. Seddon said—'

'So she's been talking about me, too, has she?'

'Everybody does,' I said simply.

'Then did she tell you I hadn't any future except Bellevigne, and that only until Philippe gets Valmy?'

Yes.'

'Well, she's right.' He added more gently: 'Does that three-times-true love allow you to take a chance on a barren future?'

'I said I'd settle for what you had to give, didn't I?'

Another of those little silences. 'So you did. Then you'll marry me?'

'Yes.'

'In the teeth of the warnings?'

'Yes.'

'And without prospects?'

'Yes.'

He laughed then, still on that curious note of triumph. 'You needn't worry about that,' he said cryptically. 'Fair means or foul, I'll always have prospects.'

'An adventurer, that's what you are,' I said.

He was looking down, and the black eyes were veiled again. 'Aren't you?'

I said slowly: 'Yes, I believe I am.'

'I know you are,' said Raoul, 'Diamond cuts diamond, my darling. Kiss me and seal the bargain.'

Afterwards he let me go. I said uncertainly: 'Do we have to – tell them?'

'Of course. Why not? I'd like to shout it from the house-tops now, but if you like we'll wait till tomorrow.

'Oh yes, *please*.'

I saw his teeth gleam. 'Does it need so much hardihood, *ma mie*? Are ou afraid of my father?'

'Yes.'

He gave me a quick, surprised look. 'Are you? You've no need. But 'll tell them myself if you'd rather. You can just keep out of the way ntil it's done.'

I said: 'They'll be – so very angry.'

'Angry? You undervalue yourself, my dear.'

'You don't understand. I'm – I was due to be sacked anyway. That loesn't make it any easier to tell them.'

'Due to be *sacked*? What on earth do you mean?'

'What I say. I was rather expecting to be told tomorrow. That's why didn't want to come down to the dance.'

'But – why? What's the crime?'

I looked up at him and gave a little smile. 'You.'

It took him a moment to assimilate this. 'Do you mean because Héloïse aw me kissing you? You were to be sacked for that? Rubbish,' he said urtly.

'It's true. At least I think so. You – well, you heard how Madame poke to me just afterwards, and when I went into Soubirous today it vas quite obvious that the story had got round.' I told him about the eception I had had in the village. 'Albertine – the maid – may just have een scandalmongering because she doesn't like me, but I think she probably knows what Madame intends to do.'

He lifted a shoulder indifferently. 'Well, it doesn't matter, does it? You needn't let it worry you now. In any case I'm sure you're wrong. Héloïse would never want to let you go.'

I said rather shyly: 'I thought that myself. I did think it – odd, because of Philippe.'

He said quickly: 'Philippe?'

'Yes. I – don't get me wrong; I don't think I did anything very great for Philippe. The shooting business in the wood was nothing. I just didn't ose my head and fuss him too much, but I – well, I did save him the ime he nearly fell off the balcony, and your father said—'

Raoul said: 'What time? What are you talking about?'

'Didn't you know?' I said, surprised. I told him about the grim little incident that had crowned my shopping trip to Thonon. He listened, his face turned away from me towards the fire. In the flickering light I couldn't read his expression. He reached abstractedly for a cigarette and lit it. Over the flare of the match I could see he was frowning. I finished: 'And your father knew that night that you'd kissed me. I'm sure he did. You remember?'

A glint through the frown. 'I remember.'

'There wasn't any talk then about sending me away. But there is now, really.'

He laughed: 'Well, my love, we've given them more cause, haven't

we? Let that be a comfort to you. It's very probable that everybody i
the ballroom knows by this time that you've gone out with me, and
speculating wildly on the whys and wherefores.'

I said tartly: 'I don't suppose they have any doubt at all about th
whys and wherefores. It's all very well you carrying off your love affai
en grand seigneur, Monsieur de Valmy, but I'm only the governess. N
don't laugh at me. I've got to face them tomorrow.'

'With me, *chérie*, remember. And now let's forget tomorrow. This i
tonight, and we are betrothed.' He took my hands. 'If we can't shout
from the housetops at least we can celebrate it to ourselves. Let's go an
get some champagne.'

'And some food,' I said.

'You poor child! Haven't you fed?'

'Not a bite. I sat in my corner while you danced and drank and enjoye
yourself—'

'More fool you,' said Raoul unsympathetically. 'You had only to sho
yourself to be trampled to death by partners avid to let you dance an
drink and enjoy yourself with them. Come on, then. Food.'

The great dining-room was brilliant with people and gay with chatte
and the popping of corks. Raoul made his way through the crowd wit
me in his wake. Several people hailed him, and I saw a few curiou
glances cast at me, but he didn't stop. As we reached the big table all a
gleam with silver I remembered something and touched his sleeve.

'Raoul, I'd forgotten. I promised to go up and see Philippe half-wa
through the dance. I must go.'

He turned quickly, almost as if I had startled him. 'Philippe? Wha
on earth for?'

'I think he felt left out of things. At any rate I did promise to go u
at "dead of night". I can't disappoint him.'

'You ... do look after him a little beyond the line of duty, don't you?

'I don't think so. Anyway I think I ought to go straight away, in cas
he goes to sleep and thinks I've forgotten.'

'But I thought you were starving?'

'I am.' I looked wistfully at the laden table. There was a silver dis
of crab patties just beside me, creaming over pinkly under their crimpe
fronds of parsley. 'But a vow's a vow.'

'And you always keep your vows?'

'Always.'

'I'll remember that.'

I laughed. 'They're only valid if you'll let me keep the one I made t
Philippe. His came first.'

'Then I suppose I must. But I insist on coming too, and I'm not lettin
you faint with hunger by the wayside.' He glanced at his wrist. 'It's clos
on midnight – that's "dead of night", isn't it? Why don't we break a fe
more rules and take some food upstairs? Then Philippe will get hi
excitement and we our celebration.'

'Oh, Raoul, that's a wonderful idea! Let's do that!'

'All right. I'll fix some food and drink. What d'you like?'

I looked again at the table. 'Everything,' I said simply.

He looked startled. 'You must be hungry!'

'I am. Even if I weren't' – I sighed – 'I couldn't by-pass that. I never saw anything so wonderful in my life.'

He was looking at me with a curious expression. 'Do you mean to say you've never been to a dance before?'

'This sort of thing? Never.'

'One forgets,' he said.

'I try to,' I said lightly, 'at any rate the dreary past never produced anything like this. May I have one of those meringues?'

'If you must. And I suppose you've never had champagne either? That's a thought. . . . Well, you shall have it tonight. Meringues and champagne, may God forgive me. Well, you go along up to Philippe and I'll follow as soon as I've organised the food. I'll bring a bit of everything.'

'That's a vow,' I told him, and made my way out through the crowd.

My main fear was of coming across Léon de Valmy. I turned away from the hall and main staircase and ran down a corridor towards the secondary stair that Philippe and I commonly used.

But I needn't have worried. I reached the stairs unnoticed and mounted them hurriedly, holding up my filmy skirts. The staircase gave onto the upper corridor almost opposite Madame de Valmy's bedroom door. I was nearly at the top when I half-tripped as the catch of my sandal came loose. The sandal came off. I had to stop to pick it up.

As I straightened up, sandal in hand, two women came out of Madame de Valmy's sitting-room. My heart seemed to catch in mid-beat, then I saw that neither was Héloïse. They were elderly women who had not been dancing. I recognised one of them as an inveterate eyebrow-raiser – first at the blonde, then at me. I wondered how high her overworked brows would go if she knew I had an assignation with Raoul upstairs, however closely chaperoned by Philippe.

The sandal was my alibi. I waited politely for them to pass me before I proceeded to my own room for the ostensibly-needed repairs. I smiled at them, receiving in return two courteous and beautifully-calculated inclinations as they sailed by me, making for the main staircase.

The corridor emptied itself of the last rustle. With a wary eye on Héloïse's door I picked up my skirts again and turned towards Philippe's room.

Somewhere a clock whirred to strike. Midnight. I smiled. Dead of night exactly. I hoped Philippe was still awake.

The clock was beating twelve as I moved quietly along the corridor. Then a thought touched me out of nowhere and I stopped short, staring down at the sandal in my hand. Midnight. The dropped slipper. The escape from the ball.

I realised that I was frowning. The thing was so absurd as to be obscurely disquieting. Then I laughed and shrugged.

'Bring on your pumpkins,' I whispered cheerfully, and laid a hand on Philippe's door.

CHAPTER TWELVE

These delicates he heaped with glowing hand
On golden dishes and in baskets bright
Of wreathed silver; sumptuous they stand
In the retired quiet of the night.

KEATS: *Eve of St. Agnes*

Drink to heavy Ignorance!
Hob-and-nob with brother Death!

TENNYSON: *The Vision of Sin*

Philippe was awake. When I let myself quietly into his bedroom I found him sitting bolt upright in bed in his dressing-gown, with his eyes on the door. The fire, which should have been out hours ago, was burning merrily. The curtains over the long balcony windows were drawn back, so that the moonlight flowed in bright dramatic slant across the head of the bed.

Full in its path sat the little boy, his skin blanched to a waxy pallor by the white light, the black eyes huge and brilliant. He looked very frail.

But he seemed animated enough. He said immediately: 'You've been ages.'

'You said "dead of night", remember. It's just midnight now.'

'Midnight? Is it really?' He looked pleased. 'I kept the fire on. I knew you'd come.'

'Of course I came. How d'you manage to be so wide awake at this hour?' I saw the untouched tumbler of chocolate on the bedside table, and laughed. 'Oh, I see. Cunning, aren't you? Didn't you feel sleepy at all?'

'I did a bit,' he confessed, 'but it kept me awake looking after the fire.'

'Is that why you kept it on?'

The big eyes slid sideways from mine and he plucked at the coverlet. 'I sort of hoped – I wondered if you'd stay for a bit.'

I sat down on the bed. 'Why, Philippe? Is anything the matter?'

A vigorous shake of the head was followed by one of those little sidelong looks that contradicted it. I reached out and laid a hand over his. 'What is it, brat?'

He said in a sort of furious mutter: 'Nightmares.'

'Oh dear, I didn't know. How beastly! What sort of nightmares?'

'People coming in,' said Philippe, 'and touching me.'

This, oddly enough, was more shocking than any more usual horror
of pursuit and desperately hindered flight could be. I shifted my shoulders
a little, as if with cold, and said rather too heartily: 'Oh well, it's only
dreams, after all. It's not real – unless you mean me. I come in sometimes
after you're asleep.'

'No,' said Philippe rather wanly, 'not you. I wouldn't mind you.'

'Do you have the same dream often?'

He nodded.

'It doesn't wake you up? If it does, you should call. I'd come.'

'I do call, but there's no noise.'

I patted the hand. It seemed very small and cold. 'That means you're
still asleep. It's a horrid feeling, but it *is* only a dream. And it might
easily be me, Philippe; I usually do look in last thing at night. You're
always sound asleep.'

'Am I?'

'Like a top. Snoring.'

'I bet I'm not.'

'I bet you are. Now listen, I've a treat for you, Monsieur le Comte de
Valmy. Since your honour wouldn't deign to come down for supper on
the night of the ball, would you like supper to come up to you?'

'Supper? But I've had supper!'

'That was hours ago,' I said, 'and I haven't had mine. Wouldn't you
like to entertain your cousin Raoul and me to a midnight feast?'

'A midnight feast? Oh, Miss *Martin*.' The big eyes sparkled in the
moonlight, then looked uncertain. 'Did you say my cousin Raoul?'

I nodded. 'He said he'd bring the food, and – oh, here he is.'

The door had opened quietly and now Raoul came in, delectably laden
with bottles, and followed by one of the hired waiters with a tray. Raoul
lifted a gold-necked aristocrat of a bottle in mock salute. *'Bon-soir,
Monsieur le Comte.* Put the tray down there, will you? Thanks. Do you
suppose you could collect the debris later on? Secretly, of course.'

Not a muscle of the man's face moved. 'Of course, monsieur.'

Something passed from Raoul's hand to his. 'Excellent. That's all,
then. Thank you.'

'Thank you, sir. M'sieur, 'dame.' The man sketched a bow, aimed
between the bed and me, and went out, shutting the door.

'Then it really is a midnight feast?' said Philippe, eyeing his cousin
a little shyly.

'Undoubtedly.' Raoul was dealing competently with the gold-topped
bottle. 'As clandestine and – ah, that's it! A grand sound, eh, Philippe?
– cosy as one could wish it. That's an excellent fire. Are you warm
enough, Linda?'

'Yes, thank you.'

He was pouring champagne. Philippe, his doubts forgotten, came out
of bed with a bounce. 'Is that lemonade?'

'The very king of lemonades.'

'It's jolly fizzy, isn't it? It went off like a gun.'

'Gun or no, I doubt if it's your tipple, *mon cousin*. I brought some rea[lemonade for you. Here.'

'That's more like it,' said Philippe, accepting a tall yellow drink tha[hissed gently. 'Mademoiselle, wouldn't you like some of mine?'

'It looks wonderful,' I said, 'but I daren't hurt your cousin's feelings.

Raoul grinned and handed me a glass of champagne. 'I doubt if thi[is your tipple either, my little one, but I refuse to pledge you in anythin[less.'

'Pledge?' said Philippe. 'What's that?'

'A promise,' I said. 'A vow.'

'And there's our toast,' said Raoul, lifting his glass so that the fireligh[spun and spangled up through its million bubbles. 'Stand up, Philippe click your glass with mine ... now Miss Martin's ... so. Now drin[to our vows, and long may we keep them!'

Philippe, puzzled but game, drank some lemonade, then, hesitating looked from Raoul to me and finally down at the tray which the servan[had set on a low table before the fire. 'When do we start?'

'This minute,' I said firmly, and sat down.

Even without the influence of the king of lemonades it would hav[been a wonderful feast. My betrothal supper, held between firelight an[moonlight in a little boy's bedroom – to me a feast every bit as magica[as the banquet Porphyro spread for his Madeleine on that "ages lon[ago" St. Agnes' Eve. And the food was a lot better. I don't remembe[that St. Agnes' lovers – perhaps wisely – ate anything at all, but Philipp[and I demolished an alarming number of the delicates that Raoul' glowing hand had heaped upon the tray.

He had made a very creditable attempt to bring 'everything'. remember thin curls of brown bread with cool, butter-dripping asparagus scallop-shells filled with some delicious concoction of creamed crab; cris[pastries bulging with mushroom and chicken and lobster; *petits four* bland with almonds; small glasses misty with frost and full of som[creamy stuff tangy with strawberries and wine; peaches furry and glowin[in a nest of glossy leaves; grapes frosted with sugar that sparkled in th[firelight like a crust of diamonds....

Phillipe and I ate and exclaimed, and chatted in conspiratorial whis pers, while Raoul lounged beside the fire and smoked and drank cham pagne and watched us indulgently for all the world as if I and Philipp[were of an age, and he a benevolent uncle watching us enjoy ourselves

'Or an overfed genie,' I said accusingly, having told him this, 'bringin[a feast to Aladdin starving in his garret, or was it cellar?'

'As far as I recollect he was still,' said Raoul lazily, 'in his mother' wash-house. Romance is running away with you tonight, Miss Martin is it not?'

'Remind me to resent that another time when I feel more earthly.'

He laughed. 'More champagne?'

'No, thank you. That was wonderful. Wonderful champagne, wonderful supper. Philippe, if you get a nightmare after this, let it comfort you to know that you've asked for it!'

'I rather think,' said Raoul, 'that Monsieur le Comte is all but asleep already.'

Philippe, curled up on the rug with his head against my knee, had indeed been rather silent for some time. I bent over him. The long lashes were fanned over the childish cheeks, and he was breathing softly and evenly. I looked up again at Raoul and nodded. He rose, stretched, and pitched his cigarette into the dying fire.

'We'd better put him to bed.' He stood for a moment looking down at the child. He looked very tall in the firelight with Philippe curled at his feet. 'Does he have nightmares?'

'He says so. People come in in the night and touch him. Rather horrid.'

His eyes rested on me for a moment, but I had the odd impression that he didn't see me.

'As you say.' He stopped then and picked the child up, holding him easily in his arms. He carried him towards the bed.

The side of the room where we had been sitting was in deep shadow, lit warmly by the now-fading fire. Behind us the white shaft from the moonlit windows had slowly wheeled nearer. The bed lay now full in the sharp diagonal of light.

Raoul carried the sleeping child across the room. He was just about to step into the patch of light – a step as definite as a chessman's from black to white – when a new shadow stabbed across the carpet, cutting the light in two. Someone had come to the window and stopped dead in the path of the moon.

The shadow, jumping across his feet, had startled Raoul. He swung round. Philippe's face, blanched by the moon, lolled against his shoulder. Héloïse de Valmy's voice said, on a sharp note of hysteria: '*Raoul! What are you doing here? What's wrong?*'

She was backed against the light, so I couldn't see her face, but the hand gripping the curtain was tight as a hawk's claw. The other hand went to her heart in a gesture I had seen before.

He said slowly, his eyes on her: 'Nothing. What should be wrong?'

She said hoarsely: 'What's the matter with Philippe?'

'My dear Héloïse. Nothing at all. He's asleep.'

I thought it better not to wait for discovery. I got to my feet.

The movement of my white dress in the shadows caught her eye and she jerked round. '*Oh!*' It was a little choked scream.

'Easy,' said Raoul. 'You'll wake him up.'

I came forward into the moonlight. 'I'm sorry I startled you, madame.'

'You here? What's going on? *Is* there something wrong?'

Raoul grinned at her. 'A carouse, that's all. An illicit night out *à trois*. Philippe was feeling a bit left out of the festivities, so Miss Martin and

I tried to include him in, that's all. He's just gone to sleep. Turn the bed down, Linda, and help me get his dressing-gown off.'

Héloïse de Valmy gave a rather dazed look about her. 'Then I did hear voices. I thought I heard someone talking. I wondered. . . .' Her eye fell on the tray at the fireside, with its bottles and empty glasses and denuded silver dishes. She said blankly: 'A carouse? You really *did* mean a carouse?'

Raoul pulled the bedclothes up under Philippe's chin and gave them a final pat before he turned round. 'Certainly. He may suffer for those lobster patties in the morning, but I expect he'll vote it worth while.' He looked across the bed at me. 'Let me take you down again now.'

His eyes were confident and amused, but I looked nervously at Madame de Valmy. 'Were you looking for me, madame?'

'I? No.' She still sounded rather at a loss. 'I came to see if Philippe was asleep.'

'You – don't mind our coming up here . . . bringing him some of the supper?'

'Not at all.' She wasn't even looking at me. She was watching Raoul.

He said again, rather abruptly: 'Let me take you downstairs,' and came round the bed towards me.

Downstairs? Léon de Valmy, Monsieur Florimond, the eyebrows? I shook my head. 'No, thank you. I – it's late. I'll not go down again. I'll go to bed.'

'As you wish.' He glanced at Madame. 'Héloïse?'

She bent her head and moved towards the door. I opened it and held it for her. As she passed me I said hesitantly: 'Good night, madame. And thank you for . . . the dance. It was – I enjoyed it very much.'

She paused. In the dim light her face looked pale, the eyes shadowy. She had never looked so remote, so unreachable. 'Good night, Miss Martin.' There was no inflection whatever in the formal words.

I said quickly, almost imploringly: 'Madame . . .'

She turned and went. The rich rustle of her dress was as loud in the silence as running water. She didn't look back.

Raoul was beside me. I touched his sleeve. 'It was true after all. You see?'

He was looking away from me, after Héloïse. He didn't answer.

I said urgently, under my breath: 'Raoul . . . don't tell them. I can't face it. Not yet. I – just can't.'

I thought he hesitated. 'We'll talk about it tomorrow.'

I said quickly: 'Let them send me away. I'll go to Paris. I can stay there a little while. Perhaps then we can—'

His hands on my shoulders turned me swiftly towards him, interrupting me. 'My dear, if I'm not to tell Héloïse tonight, I'd better leave now. Don't worry, it'll be all right. I'll say nothing until we've talked it over.' He bent and kissed me, a brief, hard kiss. 'Good night, *ma mie*. Sleep well. . . .'

The door shut behind him. I heard him walk quickly down the corridor after Héloïse, as if he were in a hurry.

CHAPTER THIRTEEN

'Yes,' I answered you last night;
'No,' this morning, sir, I say.
Colours seen by candlelight
Will not look the same by day.

ELIZABETH BARRETT BROWNING: *The Lady's Yes*

Next morning a note was brought up to the schoolroom at breakfast-time by Bernard, Léon de Valmy's man. It looked as if it had been written in a tearing hurry, and it read:

My dear,

I can't stay today as I'd hoped. I find I must go back to Paris – a damnable 'must'. Forgive me, and try not to worry about anything. I'll be back on Thursday morning without fail, and we can get things worked out then.

Héloïse said nothing to me, and (as I'd promised you I wouldn't) I didn't talk to her. I don't think you need worry too much about that side of it, *m'amie*; if they have anything to say they'll undoubtedly say it to me, not you. Till Thursday, then, pretend, if you can – if you dare! – that nothing has happened. I doubt if you'll see much of Héloïse anyway. She overdid things, and I imagine she'll keep her bed.

Yours,
R.

As a first love-letter, there was nothing in it to make my hands as unsteady as they were when I folded it and looked up at the waiting Bernard. He was watching me; the black eyes in that impassively surly face were shrewd and somehow wary. I thought I saw a gleam of speculation there, and reflected wryly that it was very like Raoul to send his messages by the hand of the man who hadn't been out of Léon de Valmy's call for twenty years. I said coolly: 'Did Monsieur Raoul give you this himself.'

'Yes, mademoiselle.'

'Has he left already?'

'Oh yes, mademoiselle. He drove down to catch the early flight to Paris.'

'I see. Thank you. And how is Mrs. Seddon today, Bernard?'

'Better, mademoiselle, but the doctor says she must stay quiet in her bed for a day or two.'

'Well, I hope she'll soon be fit again,' I said. 'Have someone let her know I was asking after her, will you please?'

'Yes, mademoiselle.'

'Bernard,' said Philippe, putting down his cup, 'you have a dance tonight, don't you?'

'Yes, monsieur.'

'Down in the village?'

'Yes, monsieur.'

'Do you have supper there as well?'

'Yes, monsieur.'

'What sort of things do you have for supper?'

The man's dark face remained wooden, his eyes guarded – unfriendly, even. 'That I really couldn't say, monsieur.'

'All right, Bernard,' I said. 'Thank you.'

As he went I wondered, yet again, what pretty little Berthe could see in him.

It was a very unpleasant and also a very long day.

I felt curiously bereft. Raoul had gone. Florimond left soon after breakfast. Mrs. Seddon did as Bernard had prophesied and kept her room, and Berthe went about her tasks all day with that withdrawn and rather shamefaced expression which seemed – if it were possible – faintly to image Bernard's sullen mask.

Small wonder, then, that when Philippe and I were out for our afternoon walk, and a jeep roared past us carrying several men and driven by William Blake, I responded to his cheerful wave with such fervour that Philippe looked curiously up at me and remarked:

'He is a great friend of yours, that one, *hein?*'

'He's English,' I said simply, then smiled at myself. 'Do you know what irony is, Philippe? *L'ironie?*'

'No, what?'

I looked at him doubtfully, but I had let myself in for a definition now and plunged a little wildly at it. '*L'ironie*. . . . I suppose it's Chance, or Fate (*le destin*), or something, that follows you around and spies on what you do and say, and then uses it against you at the worst possible time. No, that's not a very good way of putting it. Skip it, *mon lapin*; I'm not at my best this afternoon.'

'But I am reading about that this morning,' said Philippe. 'It has a special name. It followed you *comme vous dîtes* and when you do something silly it – how do you say it? – came against you. It was called Nemesis.'

I stopped short and looked at him. I said: 'Philippe, my love, I somehow feel it only wanted that. . . . And it's practically the Ides of March and there are ravens flying upside down on our left and I walked the wrong way round Sainte-Marie-des-Ponts last Thursday afternoon, and—'

'You didn't,' said Philippe. 'It was raining.'

'Was it?'

'You know it was.' He chuckled and gave a ghost of a skip. 'You do say silly things sometimes, don't you?'

'All too often.'

'But I like it. Go on. About the ravens flying upside down. Do they really? Why? Go *on*, mademoiselle.'

'I don't think I can,' I said. 'Words fail me.'

On our way in from the walk we met Monsieur de Valmy.

Instead of coming up the zigzag itself we took the short cut which ran steeply upwards, here and there touching the northerly loops of the road. We crossed the gravel sweep at the top. As we went through the stableyard archway, making for the side door, the wheel-chair came quietly out of some outbuilding and Léon de Valmy's voice said, in French: 'Ah, Philippe. Good afternoon, Miss Martin. Are you just back from your walk?'

The quick colour burned my face as I turned to answer. 'Good afternoon, monsieur. Yes. We've just been along the valley road, and we came back up the short cut.'

He smiled. I could see no trace of disapproval or coolness in his face. Surely if I were privately under sentence of dismissal, he wouldn't act quite so normally – more, go out of his way to greet us in this unruffled friendly fashion? He said, including Philippe in the warmth of his smile: 'You've taken to by-passing the woods now, have you?'

'Well, we have rather.' I added: 'I'm nervous, so we keep near the road.'

He laughed. 'I don't blame you.' He turned to Philippe with a pleasant twinkle. 'And how are you this morning, after your excesses of last night?'

'Excesses?' said Philippe nervously.

'I'm told you had a midnight feast last night ... an "illicit night out *à trois*" was the phrase, I believe. No nightmares afterwards?'

Philippe said: 'No, *mon oncle*.' The amused dark gaze turned to me.

I said, almost as nervously as Philippe: 'You don't mind? Perhaps it was a little unorthodox, but—'

'My dear Miss Martin, why should I? We leave Philippe very completely to your care and judgment, and so far we've been amply proved right. Please don't imagine that my wife and myself are waiting to criticise every move that's out of pattern. We know very little about the care of children. That's up to you. And a "special treat,' now and again is an essential, I believe? It was kind of you to spare time and thought to the child in the middle of your own pleasure. ... I hope you enjoyed the dance?'

'Yes, oh yes, I did! I didn't see you last night to thank you for inviting me, but may I thank you now, monsieur? It was wonderful. I enjoyed it very much.'

'I'm glad to hear it. I was afraid you might feel rather too much a stranger among us, but I gather that Raoul looked after you.'

Nothing but polite inquiry. No glint of amusement. No overtone to the pleasant voice.

'Yes, monsieur, thank you, he did. . . . And how is Madame de Valmy this afternoon? She's not ill, is she?'

'Oh, no, only tired. She'll be making an appearance at the dance in the village tonight, so she's resting today.'

'Then she won't expect us – Philippe and me – in the salon tonight?'

'No. I think you must miss that.' The smile at Philippe was slightly mischievous now. 'Unless you'd like to visit me instead?'

Philippe stiffened, but I said: 'As you wish, monsieur. In the library?'

He laughed. 'No, no. We'll spare Philippe that. Well, don't let me keep you.' The wheel-chair swivelled away, then slewed back to us. 'Oh, by the way. . . .'

'Monsieur?'

'Don't let Philippe use the swing in the big coach-house, Miss Martin. I see that one of the rivets is working loose. Keep off it until it's mended. We mustn't have another accident, must we?'

'No indeed. Thank you, monsieur, we'll keep out of there.'

He nodded and swung the chair away again. It moved off with that disconcertingly smooth speed towards the gate to the kitchen garden. Philippe ran ahead of me towards the side door with the air of one reprieved from a terrible fate.

He wasn't the only one. I was reflecting that once again my imagination had betrayed me. That smile of Monsieur de Valmy's last night . . . Madame's coldness . . . my interpretation of them had been wildly wide of the mark. A guilty conscience, and a too-ready ear for gossip had given me a few bad hours. It served me right. There was obviously no idea of dismissing me; if there had been Monsieur de Valmy would never have spoken to me as he had. All was well . . . and even if there were snags in the future, Raoul would be here beside me.

'Mademoiselle,' said Philippe, 'you look quite different. *Qu'est-ce que c'est?*'

'I think I've seen a raven,' I said, 'flying the right way up.'

The rest of the day limped through without incident. I put Philippe to bed a little earlier than usual, and later on, as soon as I had taken him his late-night chocolate, I went thankfully to bed myself and slept almost straight away.

I don't remember waking. Straight out of deep sleep, it seemed, I turned my head on the pillow and looked with wide open eyes towards the door. The room was dark and I could see nothing, but then there came the stealthy click of the door closing, and soft footsteps moved across the carpet towards the bed. I think that for a moment or two I didn't realise I was awake, but lay still listening to the ghostly approach in a sort of bemused half-slumber.

Something touched the bed. I heard breathing. I was awake and this was real. My heart jerked once, in a painful spasm of fear, and I shot up in the bed, saying on a sharply rising note: 'Who's that?'

As I grabbed for the bedside switch a voice that was no more than a terrified breath said: 'Don't put the light on. Don't!'

My hand fell from the switch. The intruder's terror seemed to quiver in the air between us, and in the face of it I felt myself growing calm. I said quietly: 'Who is it?'

The whisper said: 'It's Berthe, miss.'

'*Berthe?*'

There was a terrified sound that might have been a sob. 'Oh, *hush*, miss, they'll hear!'

I said softly: 'What's the matter, Berthe? What's up?' Then a thought touched me icily and I put a hand to the bedclothes.

'Philippe? Is there something the matter with Philippe?'

'No, no, nothing like that! But it's – it's – I thought I ought to come and tell you—'

But here the distressful whispering was broken unmistakably by gulping sobs, and Berthe sat down heavily on the end of the bed.

I slipped from under the covers and padded across the room to lock the doors. Then I went back to the bed and switched on the bedside lamp.

Berthe was still crouched on the bottom of my bed, her face in her hands. She was wearing the silver-netted frock, with a coat of some cheap dark material thrown round shoulders which still shook with sobs.

I said gently: 'Take your time, Berthe. Shall I make you some coffee?'

She shook her head, and lifted it from her hands. Her face, usually so pretty, was pinched and white. Her cheeks were streaked with tears and her eyes looked dreadful.

I sat down beside her on the bed and put an arm round her. 'Don't, my dear. What is it? Can I help? Did something happen at the dance?' I felt the shoulders move. I said on a thought: 'Is it Bernard?'

She nodded, still gulping. Then I felt her square her shoulders. I withdrew my arm but stayed beside her. Presently she managed to say, with rather ragged-edged composure: 'You'd better get back into bed, miss. You'll get cold like that.'

'Very well.' I slipped back into bed, pulled the covers round me, and looked at her. 'Now tell me. What is it? Can I help?'

She didn't answer for a moment. Nor did she look at me. Her eyes went round the room as if to probe the shadows, and I saw terror flick its whiplash across her face again. She licked her lips.

I waited. She sat for a moment, twisting her hands together. Then she said fairly calmly, but in a low, hurried voice: 'It is Bernard . . . in a way. You know I'm – I'm going to marry Bernard? Well, he took me to the dance tonight, and I wore your frock and he said I looked a princess and he started – oh, he was drinking, miss, and he got . . . you know—'

'I know.'

'He was drunk,' said Berthe, 'I've never seen him that way before. I knew he'd taken a good bit, of course: he often does, but he never shows it. I – we went outside together.' Her eyes were on her fingers, plaited whitely in her lap. Her voice thinned to a thread. 'We went to my sister's house. She and her man were at the dance. It – I know it was wrong of me, but—' She stopped.

I said, feeling rather helpless and inadequate: 'All right, Berthe. Skip that part. What's frightened you?'

'He was drunk,' she said again, in that thin little voice. 'I didn't realise at first . . . he seemed all right, until . . . he seemed all right. Then . . . afterwards . . . he started talking.' She licked her lips again. 'He was boasting kind of wild-like about when we were married. I'd be a princess, he said, and we'd have money, a lot of money. I'd – I'd have to marry him soon, now, he said, and we'd buy a farm and be rich, and we'd have . . . oh, he talked so wild and silly that I got frightened and told him not to be a fool and where would the likes of him get money to buy a farm. And he said—'

Her voice faltered and stopped.

I said, wondering where all this was leading: 'Yes? He said?'

Her hands wrung whitely together in the little glow of the lamp. 'He said there'd be plenty of money later on . . . when Philippe – when Philippe—'

'Yes?'

'—was dead,' said Berthe on a shivering rush of breath.

My heart had begun to beat in sharp slamming little strokes that I could feel even in my finger-tips. Berthe's eyes were on me now, filled with a sort of shrinking dread that was horrible. There was sweat along her upper lip.

I said harshly: 'Go on.'

'I – I'm only saying what he said. He was drunk . . . half-asleep. He was—'

'Yes. Go on.'

'He said Monsieur de Valmy had promised him the money—'

'Yes?'

'—when Philippe died.'

'*Berthe!*'

'Yes, miss,' said Berthe simply.

Silence. I could see sweat on her forehead now. My hands were dry and ice-cold. I felt the nails scrape on the sheets as I clutched at them. The pulse knocked in my fingertips.

This was nonsense. It was nightmare. It wasn't happening. But something inside me, some part of brain or instinct listened unsurprised. This nightmare was true: I knew it already. On some hidden level I had known it for long enough. I only wondered at my own stupidity that had not recognised it before. I heard myself saying quietly: 'You must finish now, Berthe. Philippe ... so Philippe is going to die later on, is he? How much later on?'

'B – Bernard said soon. He said it would have to be soon because Monsieur Hippolyte cabled early today that he was coming home. They don't know why – he must be ill or something; anyway he's cancelling his trip and he'll be here by tomorrow night, so they'll have to do it soon, Bernard says. They've tried already, he says, but—'

I said: 'They?'

'The Valmys. Monsieur and Madame and Monsieur—'

'No,' I said. 'No.'

'Yes, miss. Monsieur Raoul,' said Berthe.

Of course I said: 'I don't believe it.'

She watched me dumbly.

'*I don't believe it!*' My voice blazed with the words into fury. But she didn't speak. If she had broken into protestation perhaps I could have gone on fighting, but she said nothing, giving only that devastating shrug of the shoulders with which the French disclaim all knowledge and responsibility.

'Berthe. Are you sure?'

Another lift of the shoulders.

'He said so? Bernard said so?'

'Yes.' Then something in my face pricked her to add: 'He was drunk. He was talking—'

'I know. Kind of wild. That means nothing. But this can't be true! It can't! I know that! Berthe, do you hear me? *It – simply – isn't – true.*'

She said nothing, but looked away.

I opened my lips, then shut them again, and in my turn was silent.

I don't intend – even if I could – to describe the next few minutes. To feel something inside oneself break and die is not an experience to be re-lived at whatever merciful distance. After a while I managed, more or less coherently, to think, spurred to it by the savage reminder that Philippe was what mattered. All the rest could be sorted out, pondered, mourned over, later; now the urgent need was to think about Philippe.

I pushed back the bedclothes. Berthe said sharply: 'Where are you going?'

I didn't answer. I slipped out of bed and flew to the bathroom door. Through the bathroom ... across the child's darkened bedroom. ... Bending over the bed, I heard his breathing, light and even. It was only then, as I straightened up on a shaking wave of relief, that I knew how completely I had accepted Berthe's statement. What was it, after all? A frightened girl's version of the drunken and amorous babbling of a servant? And yet it rang so true and chimed in with so many facts that without even half a hearing it seemed I was ready to jettison the employers who had shown me kindness and the man with whom an hour ago I had been in love.

Stiffly, blindly, like a sleep-walker, I went back to my own room, leaving the connecting-doors ajar. I climbed back into bed.

'Is he all right?' Berthe's whisper met me, sharp and thin.

I nodded.

'Oh, miss, oh, miss. . . .' She was wringing her hands again. I remember thinking with a queer detached portion of my mind that here was someone wringing her hands. One reads about it and one never sees it, and now here it was. When at length I spoke it was in a dead flat voice I didn't recognise as my own. 'We'd better get this clear, I think. I don't say that I accept what Bernard says, but – well, I want to hear it . . . all. He says there's a plot on hand to murder Philippe. If that's so, there's no need to ask why; the gains to Monsieur and Madame and – the gains are obvious.'

The words came easily. It was like a play. I was acting in a play. I didn't feel a thing – no anger or fear or unhappiness. I just spoke my lines in that dead and uninflected voice and Berthe listened and stared at me and twisted her hands together.

I said: 'You say "they've tried already". I suppose you mean the shot in the woods and the balcony-rail?'

'Y – yes.'

'So.' I remembered then the white expectancy on Madame de Valmy's face as Philippe and I came up from the woods that day. And the night of the balcony-rail: she hadn't come upstairs that night to get any tablets; she had come because she couldn't stand the suspense any longer. Léon de Valmy, stationed in the hall, must have heard the crash from the forecourt. My mind leaped on from this to recollect those two interviews with my employer in the library. I said harshly: 'This could be true. Oh, my dear God, Berthe, it could be true. Well, let's have it. Who fired the shot? Bernard himself?'

'No. That was Monsieur Raoul. Bernard dug the bullet out.'

I forgot about its being a play. '*I don't believe it!*'

'Miss—'

'Did Bernard say so?'

'Yes.'

'In so many words?'

'Yes.'

'Then he's lying. He probably did the shooting himself and—' But here I saw her face and stopped. After a while I said fairly calmly: 'I'm sorry. I did ask you to tell me just what he said, after all. And I – I'm pretty sure that what he said is true in the main. It's just that I can't quite bring myself to – to believe—'

'Yes, miss. I know.'

I looked at her. 'Oh, Berthe, you make me ashamed. I was so wrapped up in my own feelings that I forgot the way you'd be feeling, too. I'm sorry. We're both in the same boat, aren't we?'

She nodded wordlessly.

Somehow the knowledge steadied me. I said: 'Well, look, Berthe. We've got to be tough about this for Philippe's sake, and because there isn't much time. Later on we can work it out and – and decide who's guilty and who isn't. At present I suppose we must assume they're all in it, whether or not we can believe it in our heart of hearts. And I'm pretty sure that Monsieur and Madame are guilty – in fact I know they are. I'm very much to blame for not seeing it before, but who on earth goes about suspecting an impossible outlandish thing like *murder*? That's something that happens in books, not among people you *know*. I suppose I ought to have seen it straight away, when Philippe was shot at in the woods. And Raoul . . . Raoul was out there; he admitted it himself, and Bernard was sent straight out, and I suppose he removed the bullet then and went back later with someone else to "discover" it. Yes, and I was right in thinking that Monsieur de Valmy knew I spoke French; I'd shouted it at – at the murderer in the beech-wood, and talked it to Philippe all the way home. Then the affair of the balcony-rail, Berthe – I suppose that and the swing in the barn were extras? Off-chances? Booby-traps that might work sooner or later?'

'Yes.'

'And then the Cadillac's horn blasting at – perhaps at nothing – brought Philippe out to his death?' I added shakily: 'Do I have to believe that, too?'

'I don't know what you're talking about, miss. What horn? Bernard never said anything about any horn.'

'Oh? Well, skip it. It's over, thank God, without harm. Now we have to think what to do.'

I looked down at my hands while I tried to marshal my thoughts. And the pattern was forming in a way I didn't want to examine too closely. It was all there. I tried to make myself look at it all quite coldly and in order, from the time when Philippe had been sent up to Valmy and so delivered by the unsuspecting Hippolyte straight into the hands of murder. . . .

The first step – and it was taken immediately – had been to get rid of the only person close to Philippe and trusted by Hippolyte – the child's nurse. Someone must replace her, and it was judged better to find a young woman without family or guardian who, in the event of an 'accident' to her pupil, wouldn't be able to call upon friends and relatives to exonerate her from possible charges of carelessness (or worse) should there be a mistake and doubts arise. So Madame de Valmy had made inquiries of a friend in London who was known to supply her friends with domestic help from an orphanage. Who better than an orphan, and a foreigner at that – someone who, in the accumulated bewilderments of a new job, a new country, and a foreign language, would hardly be in a position to observe too much or defend herself too readily. . . . There had in sober fact been that slight over-emphasis on my Englishness . . . my instinct to hide my Continental origin had, absurd though it had seemed, been right.

So the scapegoat had been found and brought to France. They waited. There was plenty of time. I had been allowed to settle in; my life with Philippe formed its own quiet pattern, an ordinary day-to-day pattern which appeared pleasantly normal except that Monsieur de Valmy couldn't quite keep his bitter tongue off the child who stood between him and so much. So it had gone on. I had stayed there three weeks, settled and happy, though still not quite at ease with my employers. Then the attempt was made and, by the purest chance, it failed. The second was a longer chance, but quite safe for them – the rotten coping had already been reported, so Bernard had made sure of the stone's collapse and then waited for an accident to happen when none of the interested parties was anywhere near. And the second 'accident' failed too, because of me. If the first, or even the second, had come off, 'accident' would almost certainly have been the verdict ... and no doubt an entirely baffling series of alibis was in any case available. Certainly the one person who couldn't be found guilty was the interested party, Léon de Valmy. It would have been a tragedy, and it would have blown over, whispers and all, and Léon would have had Valmy. It was even possible that there'd have been no whispers at all. ... Léon was highly thought of, and a first-rate landlord: the country folk would for many years past have regarded him as the *seigneur*, and they might have been only too pleased when the custody of Valmy passed unequivocally into his hands.

Berthe was still crouching at the foot of my bed, watching me dumbly. I said: 'And now, Berthe, what's next?'

'I don't know. I don't know.'

'You must. This is what matters. Think. Bernard let so much out; he must have told you that.'

'No. I don't think he knew himself. I think it wasn't to be him. That's all.' She floundered, gulped, and began to sob again.

Out of nowhere, unbidden, unwanted, a picture flashed onto the dark screen of my mind. Philippe's sleeping head lolling back against Raoul's shoulder, and Héloïse's voice saying hoarsely: '*What's the matter with Philippe?*' And Raoul giving her that hard quelling look. '*Nothing at all. He's asleep.*'

I said shakily: 'And Bernard said nothing to indicate when? Or how?'

'No, honestly he didn't. But it was to be soon because of Monsieur Hippolyte's coming back. The cable came early this morning and it really put the Master out, Bernard said.'

'And Hippolyte's coming back tomorrow?' I caught my breath. '*Today*, Berthe. It's today, d'you realise that? *Today*?'

'Why – yes, I reckon it is. It's nearly one o'clock, isn't it? But I don't rightly know when Monsieur Hippolyte'll get here. I think it won't be till night, and then he mayn't get up to Valmy till Thursday.'

I said quietly: 'Monsieur Raoul has gone to Paris till Thursday,

Berthe. If the cable came "early" this morning he would probably know about it, but he still went to Paris. So he can't be in it, can he? Bernard was wrong.'

She said in that dull voice that was stupid with shock and succeeded in sounding stubborn: 'Bernard said he was in it. Bernard said he fired the shot.'

It was useless – and cruel – to spend myself in protests. I said: 'All right. The point is that if we're to decide how to protect Philippe we must have some idea where the danger's coming from. I mean, nobody's going to listen to us unless we have some sort of a case which, God knows, we haven't got yet. Let's begin with the things we know. You say it's not to be Bernard.'

She gulped and nodded. She was steadier now, I saw, and her breathing was less ragged. Her hands had stopped wrenching at each other. She was listening with some sort of attention.

I said: 'I think we can count out the idea that there are any more booby-traps waiting about. They've got to make quite certain this time; they can't wait for chance to act for them. And in any case, too many "accidents" of the same kind might make people begin to think. That was why Monsieur de Valmy warned me about the swing in the barn . . . yes, he did that this afternoon, *after* he'd heard that Hippolyte was coming back. He was as nice as ninepence, though I'd been quite sure that he and Madame – oh, well, that doesn't matter. Well, Bernard's out, and booby-traps are out. There are limits to what Monsieur de Valmy can do himself, and from the way things have gone up to now I have a feeling he'll keep well out of it, since he's the person who stands most obviously to gain. And Raoul isn't here, so it can't be Raoul.' In spite of myself my voice lightened on the words. I said almost joyously: 'That leaves Madame, doesn't it?'

'Are you sure?' said Berthe.

'That it's Madame? Of course I'm not. But—'

'That he's gone,' said Berthe.

I stared at her. 'What *do* you mean?'

She gave a little boneless shrug. 'It's a big place.'

Something crept over my skin like a cold draught. 'You mean . . . he may still be here somewhere . . . hiding?'

She didn't speak. She nodded. Her eyes, watching me painfully, were once more alive and intelligent.

I said almost angrily: 'But he went. People must have seen him go. Bernard said – oh, that's not evidence, is it? But his car's gone. I noticed that when we came through the stableyard this afternoon.'

'Yes, he left. I saw him. But he could have come back. There's such things,' added Berthe surprisingly, 'as alibis.'

I said slowly: 'Yes, I suppose there are. But that he should be here – hiding – no, it's too far-fetched and absurd.'

'Well,' said Berthe, 'but it's absurd to think Madame would do it, isn't it?'

'Oh God,' I said explosively, 'it's absurd to think anyone would do it! But I can't believe the thing hinges on Raoul. No' – as she was about to speak – 'not only for the reason you think, but because if he is in it, I can't see where I come in at all. *That's* fantastic if you like.'

'How d'you mean?'

'If he was involved in this murder thing, why get involved with me? You know he was, of course?'

'Everybody knew.'

I said bitterly: 'They did, didn't they? Well, why did he? Surely it was a dangerous and unnecessary thing to do?'

'Perhaps,' she said disconcertingly, 'he just can't help it. You're awfully pretty, aren't you, and Albertine says that when they were in Paris she heard—'

'Ah, yes,' I said. 'Albertine hears an awful lot, doesn't she? You mean that he automatically turns the power on for every young female he meets? His father's like that, have you noticed? He's got a technique all his own of disarming you with his affliction and then switching on charm like an arc-light. Well, it could be, but I don't think so. Raoul's not like his father; he's got no need to waste himself where it doesn't matter. And in this case it might have been actually dangerous to get involved with me if he *was* . . . Third Murderer.'

'If he is in it with them, and he started to – well, to—'

'To make love to me?'

'Yes, miss. If he did that, and, like you said, it wasn't safe, mightn't that be why Monsieur and Madame were so annoyed about it?'

'I thought they were at first, but they weren't. I told you. Monsieur was awfully nice to me this afternoon.'

'Oh, but they were, miss. Albertine said you were to be sent away. Everyone knew. They were all talking about it. And why should they bother to send you away, unless Monsieur Raoul was in with them, and it wasn't safe, like you said? Otherwise you'd hardly think they'd trouble their heads about his goings-on, because – oh, I'm sorry, miss, I do beg your pardon, I'm sure.'

'It's all right. "Goings-on" will do. Well, they might be annoyed even so, because Philippe was in their charge and I – no that won't do. If they're all set to murder the child they won't give a damn about the moral code of his governess. But no, Berthe, it won't fit. It doesn't make sense. I still can't throw Monsieur Raoul in, you know. And not just because of the way I feel, either. It went too far, our affair – beyond all the bounds of reason if he *was* involved in his father's game. He asked me to marry him at the ball.'

'Yes, I know.'

'*You know?*'

'Yes, miss. Everybody does.'

I don't think I spoke for a full five seconds. 'Do they? Second sight or just more gossip?'

'I don't know what you mean. Bernard told Albertine and she told the rest of us.'

'When was this?'

She looked uncomfortable. 'Well, she'd been saying things about you for quite a time. She'd been saying you were, well—'

'Yes?'

'She said you were out to get him, miss, and that Monsieur and Madame were furious and you were going to be sent away. And then yesterday she was saying it had happened, like.'

'Yesterday? You mean after the ball?'

'That's right.'

'Did she say she knew for certain?'

'I don't know. She was sounding sure enough about it. She said – oh, well, never mind. She's a nasty one sometimes, that one.'

'Yes. Let it pass. I've had my fill of Albertine. But let's think,' I said a little desperately, 'if she and everyone else were talking about our engagement, then, even if they hadn't been actually told, you'd think Monsieur and Madame would know too?'

'That's right, you would.'

'But you said they were genuinely furious before that – when it was known that he and I were, well, interested in each other.'

'Oh yes. I'm sure of that.'

'But I tell you it doesn't make sense. I told you, I saw Monsieur de Valmy yesterday – when presumably he knew as much about it as everyone else – and he was extremely nice to me. And neither of them sent for me to ask me about it or – or anything. I – I can't work it out, Berthe. My head's spinning and it feels as if it's going to burst. If they *knew*, and didn't mind, then Raoul can't be in it, can he? When I saw him, Monsieur Léon must have already laid his plans because he'd already had Hippolyte's cable. . . .'

My voice trailed away into nothing. I swallowed hard. I repeated, unrecognisably: '*He'd already had Hippolyte's cable.*'

In the silence that followed she stirred and the bed creaked.

I said slowly: 'He and Madame *were* angry with me before; I know they were. I believe they *were* planning to send me away. But Hippolyte's cable changed all that. They had to make a plan in a hurry and that plan included me. How does *that* fit?'

'Well—'

'It does, you know. But how? *How?* Are you sure Bernard said nothing?'

'I'm sure,' she said desperately. 'Don't you fret, miss. I'd go bail you'll be in no danger.'

'What makes you think I'm worrying about that?' I said, almost sharply. 'But we must get this straight, don't you see? It's the only way we'll be able to do anything to help Philippe. What can they be planning to do that includes me? What the sweet hell can they be planning?'

She said: 'Maybe you've nothing to do with it at all. Maybe they just think it'd look funny if something happened to Philippe the day you were sent off, so they've decided they'll have to keep you.'

'Yes, but marriage is a bit—'

'Maybe they want to make sure you'll hold your tongue if you suspect anything,' said Berthe.

'Oh, dear God,' I said wearily, 'they surely can't imagine that I'd suspect a child was murdered and do nothing about it?'

'But if you were going to marry him, and everyone knew—'

'What difference would that make? They'd never be idiot enough to think I'd *help* them? No, it's nonsense. They'd never use marriage as a bait to make me hold my tongue. Why, good heavens—'

'I wasn't going to say that.' There was some new quality in Berthe's voice that stopped me short. She was still speaking softly, but there was some curious vibrancy in the tones that held me. She said: 'Everybody knows you're engaged to Monsieur Raoul. If Philippe died, you'd be Madame la Comtesse de Valmy one day. If the cable really came *before* the ball—'

'What do you mean?' Then I saw. I finished in a voice that wasn't a voice at all: 'You mean that when the cable came and they made their plan, it *did* include me? That they've given me a motive for murder? That they can't risk another "accident" without a scapegoat ready to hand in case things go wrong and people ask questions? Is that what you mean?'

Berthe said simply: 'Why else should he ask you to marry him?'

'Why else indeed?' I said.

I had checked up again on Philippe. He still slept peacefully. The house was quiet. I tiptoed back into my bedroom and reached for my dressing-gown.

Berthe said: 'Is he all right?'

I was putting the dressing-gown on with hands that shook and were clumsy. 'Yes. You realise, I suppose, that the likeliest time for anything to happen is tonight, now, and everybody's out at the dance except Mrs. Seddon?'

'Mr. Seddon didn't go. He stayed with her.'

'Oh? Well, I'd trust them all right, but she's ill and I doubt if he'd be much use – even if they'd believe us, which isn't likely.' I found my slippers and thrust my feet hastily into them. 'Will you stay with Philippe and mount guard over him? Lock his door and window now.'

'What are you going to do?'

'The only possible thing. What's the time?'

'Going on quarter past one. I – we came away early.'

'Did Bernard come up with you?'

'Yes.' She didn't look at me. 'I persuaded him to bring me up in the brake. It wasn't difficult. He – he's asleep now in my room.' She finished in a thin little voice: 'It was awful, driving up that zigzag with him so drunk still. . . .'

I was hardly listening. I was reflecting that, apart from the Seddons, we were alone in the house with Léon de Valmy and Bernard. Thank God the latter still had to sleep it off. I said: 'Was Madame de Valmy at the dance?'

'Yes, but she'll have left by now. She never stays long.'

'I see. Now can I get to the telephone in Seddon's pantry without being heard or seen? Does he lock it?'

'No, miss. But he goes to bed at midnight and he always switches it through to the Master's room then.'

Something fluttered deep in my stomach. I ignored it. 'Then I'll switch it back again. How d'you do it?'

'There's a red tab on the left. Press it down. But – he might hear it. Miss – what are you going to do?'

'There's only one thing I can do. We must have help. D'you mean that if I use the telephone it'll ting in the Master's room or something? Because if so I can't use it. And I can't go out and leave Philippe. You may have to go for the police yourself if you can—'

'*The police?*'

I was across at the door that gave on the corridor, listening. I turned and looked back at her in surprise.

'Who else? I must tell the police all this. They may not believe me, but at least I can get them up here and if there's a fuss it'll make it impossible for another attempt on Philippe to be made. And tonight or tomorrow Monsieur Hippolyte gets back and he can take care of Philippe when the row's over and I've been sent – home.'

'*No!*' said Berthe so violently that the syllable rang, and she clapped a hand to her mouth.

'What d'you mean?'

'You're not to go to the police! You're not to tell anyone!'

'But my dear girl—'

'I came to tell you because you'd been kind to me, because I liked you and Philippe. You've been so good to me – always so nice, and there was the dress and – and all. I thought you might have got mixed up in it somehow, with Monsieur Raoul and all that. . . . But you mustn't let on I told you! You mustn't!'

The new fear had sharpened her voice, so that I said urgently: 'Be quiet, will you! And don't be a fool! How can you expect me to say nothing—?'

'*You are not to tell them about Bernard!* You can go away if you're afraid!'

I must have looked at her blankly. 'Go away?'

'If it's true what we said, and you're likely to be blamed for a murder!

You can make an excuse in the morning and leave straight away! It's easy! You can say you don't want to marry him after all, and that you know you can't stay as governess after what's happened. It's likely enough. They can't make you stay anyway, and they won't suspect.'

'But, Berthe, stop! That's only guesswork! And even if it's true you can't seriously suggest that I should *run away* and leave Philippe to them?'

'I'll look after him! I'll watch him till Monsieur Hippolyte gets back! It's only one day! You can trust me, you know that. If you upset their plans and they've nobody to blame, maybe they won't do anything!'

'Maybe they will,' I rejoined grimly, 'and blame you instead, Berthe.'

'They wouldn't dare. Bernard wouldn't stand for it.'

'You're probably right. But I'm not risking Philippe's life on any "maybes". And you don't understand, Berthe. The thing to be stopped isn't *my* being involved, but Philippe's murder! I know you came to warn me, and I'm grateful, but there's simply no question of my leaving. I'm going to ring the police now.'

Her face, paper-white, had flattened, featureless; starched linen with two dark holes torn for eyes. 'No! No! No!' Hysteria shook her voice. 'Bernard will know I've told you! And Monsieur de Valmy! I daren't! You can't!'

'I must. Can't you see that none of these things *matter*? Only the child.'

'I'll deny it. I'll deny everything. I'll swear he never said a word or that I spoke to you. I'll say it's lies. I will! I will!'

There was a little silence. I came away from the door.

'You'd do – that?'

'Yes. I swear I would.'

I said nothing for a bit. After a few seconds her eyes fell away from mine, but there was a look in her face that told me she meant what she said. I fought my anger down, reminding myself that she had lived all her life in Valmy's shadow, and that now there was the best of reasons why Bernard should still be willing – and free – to marry her. Poor Berthe; she had done a good deal: more I could hardly expect. . . .

'Very well,' I said, 'I'll leave you out of it and I won't mention Bernard. We'll let the past die and just deal with the future. I'll put it to the police as simply my own suspicions. I'll think of something. And then I'll go straight along to Léon de Valmy and tell him that I've spoken to them. That should put paid to him as effectively.'

She was staring at me as if I were mad. 'You'd – *dare*?'

I had a sudden inner vision of Philippe in Raoul's arms. 'Oh yes,' I said, 'I'd dare.'

She was shivering now, and her teeth were clenched as if she was cold. 'But you mustn't. He'd guess about Bernard – and me. Someone'd tell him Bernard was drunk tonight. He'd know. You can't do it.'

'I must and will. Don't be a fool, Berthe. You know as well as I do that I've got to. . . .'

'No, no, no! We can look after him! With two of us he'll be all right.
It's only for one day. We can watch Bernard—'

'And Madame? And Léon de Valmy? And God knows who else?'

She said blindly, hysterically: 'You are not to tell! If you don't swear
not to go to the police I shall go to Bernard now! He'll be sober enough
to stop you!'

I took three strides to the bedside and gripped her by the shoulders.
'You won't do that, Berthe! You know you won't! You can't!'

Under my hands her shoulders were rigid. Her face, still pinched and
white, was near my own. My touch seemed to have shaken the hysteria
out of her, for she spoke quietly, and with a conviction that no scream
could have carried: 'If you tell the police, and they come to see the
Master, he'll guess how you found out. And there'll be a fuss, and he'll
just deny everything, and laugh at it. They'll say that you – yes! they'll
say you tried to marry Monsieur Raoul and were slighted and you're
doing it out of spite, and then the police will laugh too and shrug and
have a drink with the Master and go away. . . .'

'Very likely. But it'll save Philippe and a bit more slander won't hurt
me.'

'But what do you suppose will happen to me when it's all over?' asked
Berthe. 'And Bernard? And my mother and my family? My father and
my brothers have worked at Valmy all their lives. They're poor. They've
got nothing. Where can they go when they're dismissed? What can we
do?' She shook her head. 'You must please – *please* – do as I say. Between
us we can keep him safe all right. It's best, miss, honestly it's best.'

I let my hands drop from her shoulders.

'Very well. Have it your own way. I'll keep my mouth shut.' I looked
at her. 'But I swear to you that if anything happens to Philippe – or if
any attempt is made – I'll smear this story, and the Valmys, across every
newspaper in France until they – and Bernard – get what they deserve.'

'Nothing will happen to Philippe.'

'I pray God you're right. Now go, Berthe. Thank you for coming as
you did.'

She slid off the bed, hesitating. 'The frock?'

I said wearily: 'Keep it. I'll have no use for it where I'll be going.
Good night.'

'Miss—'

'Good night, Berthe.'

The door clicked shut behind her, and left me alone with the shadows.

CHAPTER FOURTEEN

Fill the cup, Philip,
And let us drink a dram.
Anonymous Early English Lyric.

There was only one possible plan that would make certain of Philippe's safety. He had to be removed from Léon de Valmy's reach and hidden till help came.

There wasn't a minute to lose. Léon de Valmy might well assume that one-thirty would be a dead hour in the schoolroom wing. And the servants would be coming back from the dance between three and four. If anything was to be done tonight it would be done soon.

I was back at my bedside, tearing off my dressing-gown with those wretchedly shaky hands, while my mind raced on out of control. I couldn't think; I didn't want to think; there were things I didn't want to face. Not yet. But Philippe had to be got away. That was all that mattered. I had decided that I didn't dare use the telephone; it might somehow betray me to Léon de Valmy, and besides, it was possible that Berthe would wait to see if I approached the pantry – and in her present shaken and terrified mood I couldn't answer for her reactions. And there was no help in Valmy. Mrs. Seddon was ill; Seddon himself was elderly, conventional and (I suspected) none too bright. Berthe and I between us might have guarded Philippe if we had only known from what danger, but as it was . . . no, he had to be got away to the nearest certain help, and then, as soon as possible, to the police. I didn't let the promise Berthe had blackmailed from me weigh with me for a second; being a woman, I put commonsense in front of an illusory 'honour', and I'd have broken a thousand promises without a qualm if by doing so I could save Philippe.

I had flung my dressing-gown down and was reaching for my clothes when I heard the sound from the corridor.

Even though I had been listening for it I didn't at first know what it was. It came as the thinnest of humming whispers through the turmoil of my brain. But at some level it must have blared a warning, for my hand flashed to the bedside light and switched it off just as Philippe's door opened very quietly, and I knew what the whisper had been. The wheel-chair.

I stayed where I was frozen, one hand still on the light-switch. I don't think I was even breathing. If there had been the slightest sound from the other room I think I'd have been through there like a bullet from a gun, but the wheel-chair never moved, so I stayed still, waiting.

Nothing. No movement. After a while Philippe's door shut once more very softly. The whisper was in the corridor again.

I don't know what instinct thrust me back into my bed and pulled the clothes up round me, but when my bedroom door opened I was lying quite quietly with my back to it.

He didn't come in. He simply waited there in silence. The seconds stretched out like years. I thought: I wonder what he'd do if I turned over, saw him, and screamed? The employer caught creeping into the governess's bedroom, the lights, the questions, the scurrying feet in the corridor ... could you laugh that one off, Monsieur de Valmy? Tiny bubbles of hysteria prickled in my throat at the thought of Léon de Valmy pilloried in the role of vile seducer – then I remembered how pitifully he was insured against the risk, and lay still, all my perilous amusement gone. In its stead came a kind of shame and a pity that, rather horribly, did nothing to mitigate my fear. There was something curiously vile about the mixture of emotions. My muscles tensed themselves against it and I started to tremble.

He had gone. The door had closed noiselessly behind him. I heard the whisper of the wheels fade along the corridor towards his room.

I slipped out of bed and padded across to the door, where I stood listening until, far down the corridor, I thought I heard another door shut softly. Seconds later, I heard the faint whine of the lift. He had been checking up, that was all. But he had also told me all I wanted to know. The story was true. And I had to get Philippe out of it, and fast. Somehow I was calm again. I shut and locked my door, then with steady hands drew the curtains close and turned on the bedside light. I dressed quickly, picked up my coat and strong shoes, and went through the bathroom into Philippe's room.

This was going to be the hardest part of the job. I put the coat and shoes down on the chair where I had sat for last night's midnight feast, then, with a glance at the sleeping child, I crossed to the door and locked it. Deliberately, I refused to hurry. If this was to succeed at all it must be taken calmly.

The room was light enough. The long curtains hung slightly apart, and between them a shaft of light fell, as it had done last night, to paint a bright line across the carpet. Something struck my foot as I crossed the floor, and rolled a little way, glittering. A frosted grape. Berthe had scamped the cleaning today, it seemed.

I pushed aside the heavy curtain, and latched the window. Behind me Philippe moved and sighed, and I paused and looked over my shoulder towards the bed, with one hand still on the window-catch, and the other holding back the curtain.

The shadow falling across me brought me round again like a jerked puppet to face the window. Someone had come along the balcony, and was staring at me through the gap in the curtains. I stood there, held rigid in the noose of light that showed me up so pitilessly. I couldn't move. My hand tightened on the window-catch as if an electric current held it there. I looked straight into Héloïse de Valmy's eyes, a foot from my own.

She showed no surprise at my presence, nor even at the fact that I was fully dressed. She merely put a hand to the window-fastening, as if expecting to find it open. She shook it, and then her hands slid over the glass is if trying to push a way in. Then she took hold of the latch once more, rattling it almost impatiently.

I could hardly refuse to let her in. I noticed that there were no pockets to her long ivory-coloured robe, and that her hands were empty. Besides, if she was here to harm Philippe she would hardly demand entry from me in this unruffled fashion. Wondering confusedly how I was going to explain the fact that I was up and dressed at one-thirty in the morning, I opened the window. I said, as coolly as I could: 'Good evening, madame.'

She took no notice, but walked calmly past me into the room. Her robe whispered across the carpet. She stopped near the head of the bed. In the dim room her shadow threw a yet deeper darkness over the sleeping child. She put out a hand slowly, almost tentatively, to touch his face. It was a gentle touch, a meaningless gesture, but I recognised it. This was Philippe's nightmare. This had happened before.

If she had had some weapon, if her approach had been at all stealthy – anything but this apparently calm and routine visit – no doubt I would have moved more quickly. As it was, her hand was still hovering over the boy's face when I flew after her. I reached Philippe just as her fingers touched him. He didn't move. She drew her hand back, and straightened up. I went round the bed and reached a protective hand to draw the sheet up to the child's face. I faced her across the bed. Whatever my feelings towards the Demon King, I was not afraid of his wife. I said: 'What is it, madame? What do you want?'

She didn't answer. She hadn't even acknowledged my presence. This was carrying ostracism a bit too far. I began to say something angry, then stopped, bewildered, to watch her.

She had turned to the little table that stood beside the bed. Her hands moved now over the clutter of objects on the table – a lamp, a book, a little clock, the tumbler that had held Philippe's chocolate, a couple of soldiers, a biscuit. ... I thought she was going to switch the light on, and made a half-movement of protest. But her hands, groping in a curious blind fashion, passed the lamp, moved softly over the clock and the tin soldiers, and hovered over the tumbler. She picked this up.

I said: 'Madame de Valmy—'

She turned at that. She had lifted the tumbler as if to drink from it, and across the rim her eyes met mine again. With her back to the moonlight, her face was a pale blur, her eyes dark and expressionless, but as I looked at her, bewildered and beginning once more to be frightened, I understood. The goose-pimple cold slid, ghost-handed, over my skin.

The open eyes, no less than the smooth stealthy hands, were indeed blind. . . . I stared into the woman's expressionless face for one eerie moment longer, while the child breathed gently between us, then, very quietly, I moved to one side, down to the foot of the bed.

She stood still, with the tumbler held to her face, staring at the place where I had been. . . . *You see, her eyes are open: Ay, but their sense is shut.* . . . I stood and watched her as if she were a ghost on a moonlit stage. The verses marched on through my brain as if someone had switched on a tape-recorder and forgotten it. I remember feeling a sort of numb surprise at their aptness. *Lo you, here she comes! This is her very guise, and upon my life, fast asleep.* . . .

So Héloïse de Valmy, like Lady Macbeth, had that weighing on her heart which sent her sleep-walking through the night to Philippe's room. And would she, like that other murderess, give away what she had seen and known? I knew nothing about sleep-walkers except what I remembered of that scene in *Macbeth*. And Lady Macbeth had talked. Was it possible that I could get Héloïse de Valmy to do the same? *Observe her, stand close.*

I was gripping the rail at the foot of Philippe's bed. Without it, I think I would have fallen.

I said hoarsely: 'Madame.'

She took no notice. She put the tumbler down surely and quietly, and turned to go. The moonlight rippled along the lovely folds of her robe; it caught her face, gleaming back from eyes wide and glossy as a doll's.

I said: 'Héloïse de Valmy, answer me. How will you kill Philippe?'

She was on her way to the window. I walked with her. She went smoothly, and at the right moment her hand went up to the curtain. For one fearful moment I thought I had been mistaken and she was awake, but then I saw her fumble the curtains and hesitate as a fold tangled in her robe. The fixed eyes never moved, but she fetched a sigh and faltered. *Heaven knows what she has known.* The obsessive question burst from me. 'Is Raoul helping you to kill Philippe?'

She paused. Her head inclined towards me. I repeated it urgently in her ear: '*Is Raoul helping you?*'

She turned away. It wouldn't work. She was going, and her secrets with her, still locked in sleep. I reached an unsteady hand and drew the curtain aside for her.

She walked composedly past me and out of sight along the balcony.

But she had told me one thing. I saw it as soon as I turned.

God, God forgive us all. I stood over Philippe in the moon-dappled darkness, with the tumbler in my hand.

I woke him quietly. I used a trick I had read about somewhere in John Buchan – a gentle pressure below the left ear. It seemed to work; he opened his eyes quite naturally and lay for a moment before they focused on me in the moonlight. Then he said, as if we were resuming a conversation: 'I had another nightmare.'

'I know. That's why I came in.'

He lifted his head, and then pushed himself into a sitting position. 'What's the time?'

'Half-past one.'

'Haven't you been to bed yet? Have you been to the dance in the village? You didn't tell me.'

'No, I haven't been out. I got dressed again because—'

'You're not going out now?' The whisper sharpened so abruptly that my finger flew to my lips.

'Quiet, Philippe. No – that is, yes, but I'm not leaving you alone, if that's what you're afraid of. You're coming too.'

'I am?'

I nodded, and sat down on the edge of the bed. The big eyes watched me. He was sitting very still. I couldn't tell what he was thinking. God knows what my voice sounded like. I know my lips were stiff. I said: 'Philippe.'

'Yes, mademoiselle?'

'Do you – feel all right? Not – not sleepy or anything?'

'Not really.'

'Quite fit and wide-awake?'

'Yes.'

I said hoarsely: 'Did you drink your chocolate?'

His eyes slid round in that narrow sidelong look towards the tumbler, then back to me. He hesitated. 'I poured it away.'

'You *what*? Why?'

'Well ...' he said uncertainly, eyeing me, then stopped.

'Look, Philippe, I don't mind. I just want to know. Was it nasty or something?'

'Oh no. At least I don't know.' Again that look. Then a sudden burst of candour: 'They left the bottle last night and I found it and kept it. I didn't tell you.'

I said blankly: 'Bottle?'

'Yes,' said Philippe, 'that smashing lemonade. I had that instead. It wasn't fizzy any more but it was fine.'

'You ... never said anything when I went to make your chocolate.'

'Well,' said Philippe, 'I didn't want to hurt your feelings. You always made the chocolate and – what's the matter?'

'Nothing. Nothing. Oh, Philippe.'

'What *is* it, Miss Martin?'

'I guess I'm tired,' I said. 'I had a late night last night and I haven't slept much tonight.'

'You don't mind?'

'No, I don't mind.'

'Why haven't you slept tonight?'

I said: 'Now listen, *mon p'tit*. Did you know your Uncle Hippolyte is coming home tomorrow – today?'

I saw the joy blow across his face the way a gleam runs over water
nd felt, suddenly, a deep and calm thankfulness. There was port in this
torm, it seemed.

Philippe was saying in a quick, excited whisper: 'When is he coming?
Vhy is he coming back? Who told you? When can we go to see him?'

'That's what I came to wake you for,' I said, as if it was the most
easonable thing in the world. 'I thought that we might go straight away.
The – the sooner the better,' I finished lamely, all my half-thought-out
xcuses dying on my lips under that steady wide stare.

'Do you mean we are going to the Villa Mireille *now*? To meet my
Jncle Hippolyte?'

'Yes. He won't be there yet, but I thought—'

Philippe said, devastatingly: 'Does my Uncle Léon know?'

I swallowed. 'Philippe, my dear, I don't expect you to understand all
his, but I want you to trust me, and come with me now as quickly and
juietly as you can. Your Uncle Léon—'

'You are taking me away from him.' It was a statement, not a question.
His face was expressionless, but his eyes were intent, and he was
preathing a little faster.

'Yes,' I said, and nerved myself for the inevitable 'Why?' But it didn't
ome. The child supplied the terrible answer for himself.

He said in that sombre, unsurprised little voice: 'My Uncle Léon hates
ne. I know that. He wishes I was dead. Doesn't he?'

I said gently: 'Philippe, *mon lapin*, I'm afraid he might wish you
1arm. I don't like your Uncle Léon very much either. I think we'll both
)e better away from here, if you'll only trust me and come with me.'

He pushed back the bedclothes without a second's hesitation, and
;rabbed at the back of his nightshirt, ready to haul it over his head. In
he act he stopped. 'The time I was shot at in the wood, that was not an
iccident?'

The question, coming grotesquely out of the folds of the nightshirt,
nade me gasp. There was no need, it appeared, to pretend, even about
his. I said: 'No, it wasn't an accident. Here's your vest.'

'He tried to kill me?'

'Yes.' The word sounded so flat that I added quickly: 'Don't be afraid,
Philippe.'

'I'm not afraid.' He was fighting his way into his shirt now. As he
emerged from the neck of it I saw that he spoke the truth. He was taut
is a wire, and the long-lashed black eyes – Valmy eyes – were beginning
:o blaze. 'I've been afraid for a long time, ever since I came to Valmy,
Jut I didn't know why. I've been unhappy and I've hated my Uncle
Léon, but I didn't know why I was afraid all the time. Now I know, and
I'm not frightened any more.' He sat down at my feet and began to pull
his socks on. 'We'll go to my Uncle Hippolyte and tell him all this, and
then my Uncle Léon will be guillotined.'

'*Philippe!*'

He glanced up at me. 'What would you? Murderers go to the guillotine
He's a murderer.'

Tigers breed true, I thought wildly, *tigers breed true*. He had even, fo
a flash, had a look of Léon de Valmy himself. But he was only a child
he couldn't know the implications of what he was saying. I said: 'He'
not, you know. You're still alive, and going to stay that way. Only w
must hurry, and be terribly quiet. Look, your shoes are here. No, don'
put them on. Carry them till we get out.'

He picked them up and got up, turning towards me, then, with ;
sudden duck back into childhood, he reached for my hand. 'Where ar
we going?'

'I told you. To your Uncle Hippolyte.'

'But we can't go to the Villa Mireille till he's there,' he said uncertainly
'That's where they'll look for us straight away in the morning.'

'I know.' His hand quivered in mine, and I pulled him against my
knees and put an arm round him. 'But we'll be quite safe. We'll follow
our star, Philippe. It'll not let us down. D'you remember Monsieu
Blake, the Englishman?'

He nodded.

'Well, he has a cabin up in Dieudonné woods where he spends th
night sometimes. I know he's there tonight, because I saw his ligh
shining like a star before I went to bed. We'll go up there straight away
and he'll look after us and take us to your uncle's house tomorrow. It'l
be all right, you'll see. I promise you it will.'

'All right. Shall I take this scarf?'

'Yes. Was that your warm jersey you put on? Good. We'll lock th
balcony window, I think. . . . Okay now? Be terribly quiet.'

I paused by the door, my hand on the key, and listened. Philipp
drifted to my elbow like a ghost. His eyes looked enormous in a pal
face. I could hear nothing. Beyond the door the great house stretche
dark and almost untenanted. And Madame de Valmy was certainly
asleep, and Bernard was drunk, and the tiger himself – waiting dow
there for death to be discovered – the tiger himself was crippled. . . .

With a hand that slipped a little on the doorknob I eased the doo
open, then took Philippe's hand and tiptoed with him out into the dar
corridor. Past the clock that had sounded midnight for us, down the stair
where I had lost my slipper, along the dim stretches of corridor walle
with blind doors and the side-long painted eyes of portraits . . . the grea
house slid past us in the darkness as insubstantial as scenery in a Cocteau
fantasy, until our breathless and ghostly flight was blocked by the heavy
door that gave onto the stableyard and freedom.

It was locked. There must be some other way left for the servants to
come in, but I didn't dare turn aside to explore. The heavy key turned
easily and quietly, but still the door wouldn't move. My hands slid over
the studded wood in the darkness, searching for a bolt. Beside me I hear
Philippe take a little breath and begin to shiver. Standing on tiptoe

groping above my head, I found the bolt, and pulled. It moved with a
scream like a mandrake torn up in a midnight wood. The sound seemed
to go on and on, winding back along the corridor in a creeping echo. I
pulled at the door with shaking hands, listening all the time for the whine
of the wheel-chair. The door wouldn't budge. Still it wouldn't budge. I
tried to feel if it had a spring lock beside the key, but couldn't find one.
He would be coming any minute now, to find us cornered in this dark
passage-way. It didn't need the shrieking bolts to tell him where we were
and what we were doing. I could almost hear my panic-stricken thoughts
pouring down the corridor to shout it at him. He would know. Oh yes,
he would know. We were *en rapport*, the Demon King and I. . . .

'It's all right,' whispered Philippe, 'I brought my torch. Look.'

He stooped down to the other bolt, drew it quietly, and the door
opened.

We went out into the night air.

CHAPTER FIFTEEN

Enter these enchanted woods,
You who dare.

GEORGE MEREDITH: *The Woods of Westermain*

I had no idea how to find William Blake's forest hut, but from my
window at Valmy I had noticed that the light seemed to be very near a
broad, straight ride that slashed up through the pines from somewhere
near the Valmy bridge. Philippe and I had only to cross the bridge and
climb up from the road, bearing slightly right, and we were bound to
strike the open ride. Once in this we must follow it up towards the first
ridge, and no doubt sooner or later the light itself would guide us to the
hut.

It sounded easy, but in practice it was a long and exhausting climb.
I dared not use Philippe's torch so near the road, nor later in the ride,
open as this was to every window on Valmy's west front.

In the forest it was very dark. My eyes had by now adjusted themselves,
and we were able to pick our way between the trees without actual
mishap, but very slowly, and with many stumbles and grazes, as the
thick carpet of pine-needles was criss-crossed, and in places piled, with
dead and spiky branches left when the woods were thinned. Once Philippe
tripped and was only saved from falling by my hand, and once I had to
bite back a cry of pain as I stumbled against some fallen snag of wood
that stabbed at my leg for all the world like a sword. But Philippe made
no complaint and, crazy though it may sound, I myself, with every yard
of midnight wood put between me and Valmy, felt safer and happier.
This wild mountain-side, tingling with the smell of the pines, was for
all its secret and murmurous life no place of fear: that was Valmy with

its lights and luxury. I realised that once again the word in my mind was 'escape': it was as if the brilliance and comfort of life at Valmy had been closing in, subtle, stifling, over-sophisticated. Now I was free. . . . The darkness took us. The air was cool and the silence was thick with peace.

My guess had been right. After perhaps twenty minutes of our steep, stumbling progress we came at a climbing angle upon the open ride. This was some fifteen yards wide, and ran in a dead-straight slash from top to bottom of the hillside. I supposed it was a fire-break, or a road left open for tractors – whatever its purpose, it would be easier going for Philippe and myself.

It was, we found, very little better underfoot, as here, too, the dead boughs were thickly strewn. But at least we could see to pick our way. Clutching at my hand, and panting, Philippe climbed gamely beside me. We turned once to look at Valmy. On the far side of the valley the château, catching the moon, swam pale above its own woods, its side stabbed with a single light. Léon de Valmy still waited.

With a little shiver I turned my face back towards the sweet-smelling wild mountain of Dieudonné, and we plodded on up the moonlit canyon between the pines.

'All right, Philippe?'

'Yes, mademoiselle.'

If any other creature moved in the forest that night, we never saw it. The only eyes that glittered at us were the stars, and the million drops of stardew that shivered on the fallen boughs. The breeze was failing, and in its pauses the breaking of the dead stuff under our feet sounded like thunder. I found myself, absurdly, with a quick over-the-shoulder glance at Léon de Valmy's remote little light, trying to tread more softly, and eyeing in some dread the gaunt black shadows that the moon flung streaming behind us down the open ride.

But no new terror waited under the swimming moon, and, when we stopped to rest, no sound came to us except the laboured sound of our own breathing, and the age-old singing of the pines, and the rustle of wind-made showers as the dew shook down from the boughs.

It was Philippe who saw the hut. I had been straining my eyes upwards through the trees on our left for a glimpse of William's light, and as we neared the summit of the hill, had begun to worry to myself in case we had already passed it hidden from us by the thick pines.

Then, as we stopped for one of our now frequent breathers, Philippe tugged at my hand.

'There,' he said breathlessly, and nodded towards a break in the southern wall of trees.

I turned thankfully, only to pause and stare, while a little chill slid over me.

It was certainly a hut – *the* hut, as it was placed pretty well where I had expected to find it. It was small and square, beautifully made, chalet-fashion, of hewn pine-logs, with a railed verandah round it, a steep-

pitched overhanging roof, and slatted wooden shutters. At back and sides
the pines crowded so closely up to the eaves that you would have thought
a lamp would be burning even by day.

But now the windows showed no light at all. At one there was a tiny
glow, as of firelight, but the welcoming lamp – the star – was out. I stood
clutching the boy's hand, and staring at those blank windows.

I noticed all at once how black the trees were and how they crouched
and crowded over the hut. I saw how our shadows streamed back from
us grotesque and ink-black down the open ride. I moved, and a giant
gesture mocked me. The night was full of whispering.

'He'll be fast asleep,' said Philippe cheerfully, and not whispering at
all.

I almost jumped, then looked down at him. I had to control an impulse
to hug him. 'Why, of course,' I said, not too steadily. 'Of course. I – I
was forgetting it'll soon be daylight. I hope he doesn't mind being knocked
up again! Come along, Monsieur le Comte!'

He set off sturdily, ahead of me this time, for the hut. I followed him
thankfully. We were here, safe, at our star. It was Valmy now whose
alien glimmer showed a crow's mile away. I spared a last quick glance
for that cold point of light. Already it seemed remote, distance-drowned.
I would never go there again.

I found my eyes were full of tears. Not one, but a swarm of stars
swam in the liquid distance. Angrily, I put up a hand to brush the tears
away, and looked again.

Not one, but a swarm of stars.

Three lights now glared from the white bulk that was Valmy. And
even as I stared, with the quick hot thrill twisting belly-deep inside me,
another window sprang to life, and another. My bedroom, my sitting-
room, the schoolroom . . . and then I saw two tiny lights break from the
shadows below and slide away as a car came out of the courtyard. The
alarm had been given. Dear God, the alarm had been given. He hadn't
waited till morning. He'd checked on us again, and now Valmy was up.
I could almost hear the quick footsteps, the whispering, the whine of the
wheel-chair, the humming telephone-wires. The bright windows stared
with their five eyes across the valley. Then, even as I wondered through
my sick panic why he should have roused the place, the lights went out
quickly, one by one, and Valmy sank back into quiet. Only the single
point of brilliance still showed, and below, the car's lamps dropped down
two quick flicking curves of the zigzag and then vanished as they were
switched off.

I'd been wrong. There had been no alarm. He'd found us gone, made
sure, and then gone back to wait by his telephone. He had the rest of the
night, and his hound was out after us. Bernard, drastically sobered?
Raoul?

I turned and ran in under the darkness of the pines, as Philippe's soft
rapping sounded on the door of the hut.

Half a minute went by; three-quarters. I stood beside Philippe, trying to still that little twist of terror deep inside me. In a moment now it would be over; the Englishman's feet would tread comfortably towards the door; the hinges would creak open; the firelit warmth would push a wedge into the cool night across the verandah floor.

The forest was still. The air breathed cold at my back. A minute; a minute and a half. No sound. He would be still asleep.

'Shall I knock again?'

'Yes, Philippe. Harder.'

My nerves jumped and tingled to the sharp rap of knuckles on wood. The sound went through the stillness like the bang of a drum. It seemed to me that it must startle the whole forest awake.

In the backwash of the silence that followed I heard, away below us on the road, the snarl of a car going fast.

There was no sound from the hut.

'There's no one in.' The quiver in the child's voice – he must be very tired after all – made me pull myself together.

'He's sound asleep,' I said calmly. 'Let's see if we can get in. He won't mind if we wake him.'

Philippe lifted the latch and pushed. A little to my surprise the door opened immediately. He took a step forward, hesitating, but I propelled him gently in front of me straight into the room. The sound of that engine reiterated from the valley was making my skin crawl.

'Mr. Blake!' I called softly as I shut the door. 'Mr. Blake! Are you there?'

Silence met us, the unmistakably hollow silence of an empty house.

I knew from what William had told me that the hut only had one room, with a pent-house scullery at the back. The door which presumably led to this was shut. The room in which we now stood was the living, eating, and sleeping-room of the place.

He could not have been gone long. It didn't need the memory of the lighted window to prove that he had been there and until quite late. The wood-stove still glowed faintly, and the smell of food hung in the air. He must have been working up here, made himself a meal, and then decided, late as it was, to go down to the Coq Hardi. The blankets on the bed in the corner were neatly folded in a pile.

It was a bare little room, its walls, floor, and ceiling all of pine, still, in the heat from the stove, smelling faintly of the forest. There were a sturdy, hand-made table, a couple of wooden chairs, and a hard-looking bed with a box underneath. A small cupboard hung in one corner, and a shelf over the bed held a few books. On pegs near the stove was a miscellany of things – ropes, a rucksack, an old khaki coat. Some spare tools lay beneath on a pile of clean sacking. In the far corner an upright ladder led to a small square trap-door.

'Can't we stay here?' There was the faintest suspicion of a whine in Philippe's voice; he must be very nearly exhausted, and indeed, the thought of going further appalled me. And where could we go? This must be what the mired fox felt like when it found its way to earth with the last calculated ounce of strength. I glanced at the shut door, at the glowing stove, at Philippe.

'Yes, of course.' The car would be raking the road to the Villa Mireille. They would never look for us here. I said: 'D'you think you could climb that ladder?'

'That? Yes. What's up there? Why do we have to go up there?'

'Well,' I said, 'there's only one bed down here, and that's Mr. Blake's. He may come back and need it. Besides, we'd be better hidden away there, don't you think? Can you keep as still as a mouse if anybody comes in?'

He looked up at me, big eyes in a pinched little face. He was biting his lip. He nodded. I think if Léon de Valmy had come in at that moment I could have killed him with my bare hands. As it was I said briskly: 'Well, we mustn't leave any sign we've been here, just in case somebody else comes looking for us before Mr. Blake gets home. Are your shoes wet? Ah, yes, they are a bit, aren't they? So are mine. We'll take them off – no, stay on the mat, *petit* – that's fine. Now, you carry them and perch here by the stove while I reconnoitre the loft.'

Luckily the trap-door was light, and, it seemed, in frequent use. At any rate it opened easily and quietly, and, standing on the ladder with my head and shoulders through the opening, I raked the loft with the beam of Philippe's torch. I had been praying fervently as I climbed that the place would be not too bad. Now I gave a sigh of relief. The loft was almost as clean as the living-room, and quite dry. It was used as a store-room, and I could see some boxes and canisters, some more rope, a drum of wire, and – what was more to the purpose – a pile of tarpaulins and sacking on the chimney side of the steep-roofed little chamber.

I went quickly down again and reported this to Philippe. 'It's beautifully warm,' I said cheerfully, 'right over the stove. Can you shove your shoes in your pockets and swarm away up while I collect some blankets? I'll pass them up to you. I can't spare the torch for a moment, so don't explore too far.'

As I had hoped, there were extra blankets in the box under the bed. I dragged these out with wary flashes of the torch, and with some little trouble got them one by one up the ladder and into Philippe's waiting grasp. At last I pulled myself up beside him, and sent a final beam raking the little room. ... Nothing betrayed us; the floor was dry, the bed undisturbed, the door shut but not locked. ...

We shut the trap-door quietly and crawled – only in the centre of the loft could one stand – to make our bed. The warmth from the chimney was pleasant, the blankets thick and comforting; the little dark loft with its steep-pitched roof gave an illusion of safety.

So presently, having shared a stick of chocolate and said our prayers,

from both of which exercises we derived immense comfort, we settled
down for what remained of the night.

Philippe went to sleep almost immediately, curled in his usual small
huddle up against me. I tucked the blankets thankfully round him, and
then lay listening to his light breathing, and to the million tiny noises of
the large silence that wrapped us in.

The breeze seemed finally to have dropped, for the forest – so close to
us lying up under the shingles – was still. Only a faint intermittent
murmur, like a long sigh, came from the pines. Inside the cottage came,
from time to time, the tiny noises of a building stirring in its sleep; the
creak of a settling board, the fall of charred wood in the stove, the tiny
scratting of a mouse in the wall. I lay there, trying to empty my mind
of worry and speculation about the coming day. It was Wednesday; only
the one day to go and then I could deliver my charge, either at the Villa
Mireille itself, or, if that proved difficult, by any telephone. The thing
was easy. Easy.

And if, as seemed likely, William Blake called at the mountain-hut in
the morning, then it became easier still. Once we had him as escort the
last shred of danger vanished. All I had to do now was relax and try to
sleep. Neither Léon de Valmy nor Bernard would think of looking for
us here. I had once spoken of 'William' to Raoul (the thought brought
me momentarily awake again) and he might connect the name – but of
course Raoul wasn't in it. Raoul was in Paris. He had nothing to do
with it. We were safe here, quite safe. . . . I could sleep. . . .

The lifting of the door-latch sounded, in that sleepy silence, like a
pistol-shot.

Even as one part of my mind stampeded in panic like the mice now
scurrying from the sound, the other rose light and dizzy with relief. It
was William Blake, of course. It couldn't be anyone else. I must have
slept longer than I'd thought, and now it was early morning, and he had
come back.

I lifted my head to listen, but made no other movement. Something
else which had nothing whatever to do with my mind and its conclusions
kept me clamped down like a hare in her form.

I waited. Philippe slept.

Below us the door shut very softly. The newcomer took two or three
steps, then stopped. I could hear him breathing hard, as if he'd been
hurrying. He stood perfectly still for a long time. I waited for the homely
sounds of a log in the stove, the rasp of a match, the opening of the
scullery door, but there was nothing except the stillness, and the rapid
breathing. And then there was a pause of complete silence, as even the
breathing stopped.

I think mine did too. I knew now it wasn't William Blake. I knew
why he had paused with held breath, standing with ears at the stretch

and probably a torch-beam raking the darkness. He had been listening for sounds of the quarry. It couldn't be true, but it was. The hound was here already.

Then his breath came out again with a gasp, and he moved across the floor.

Now came the quiet *chunk* of closing shutters, the chink of the lamp-globe, the scrape of a match; but the sounds were about as homely as the click of a cocked gun.

I heard the slight clatter of the globe sliding into its socket, then a muttered curse as, I suppose, the wick went out again. Seconds later came the scrape of another match.

It couldn't be morning yet, and it certainly wasn't William Blake. The curse had been in French, and in a voice I thought I recognised. Bernard's. The hunt was up with a vengeance.

The lamp was burning now. I could see, here and there, tiny threads of light between the ceiling-boards. He was moving about, with a slow deliberation that was far more terrifying than haste. Only his breathing still hurried, and that, surely, should have been under control by now. . . .

I found that I was shaking, crouched together in my form of blankets. It wasn't the climb up the mountain-side that had hurried Bernard's breathing and made his big hands clumsy on the lamp. It was excitement, the tongue-lolling excitement of the hound as it closes in. He knew we were here.

He crossed the floor to the base of the ladder.

But he was only making for the scullery. I heard the door open, then more sounds of that deliberate exploration. A bolt scraped: he was barring the back exit. He was coming back.

My bitten lips tasted salt; my hands were clenched so tightly on a fold of blankets that my nails scored the stuff. I hadn't told Philippe about Bernard, had I? If he should wake, he might not be frightened . . . but let him sleep, dear Lord, let him sleep. . . . Perhaps Bernard doesn't know about the loft; perhaps he won't notice the ladder . . . if only Philippe doesn't wake up and give us away. . . .

He came out of the scullery and shut the door. This time he didn't pause to look round. He took two unhurried strides across to the ladder. I heard the wood creak as he laid hold of it.

Someone trod rapidly across the verandah outside. I heard Bernard jerk out an oath under his breath. The door opened again. A strange voice said: "*Que diable?* Oh, Bernard, it's you. What the devil are you doing up here?'

The ladder creaked again as Bernard released it '*Holà*, Jules.' He sounded sober enough, but his voice was thick and not too steady. He seemed disconcerted, almost shaken. 'I might ask you the same, mightn't I? What brings you up here at this hour?'

The other shut the door and came across the room. 'Night-patrols, a curse on it. Ever since we had that fire up in Bois-Roussel we've had them. The boss is convinced it's wilful damage and he won't listen to anything else. So I have to tramp up and down between Bois-Roussel and Soubirous the whole bloody night, and me only a fortnight wed. Dawn's a lousy time to be out in anyway, and when I think where I might be—'

Bernard laughed and moved away from the ladder. 'Hard luck, friend. I expect you make out, *tout de même.*'

'As to that,' said Jules frankly, 'I can go to bed the whole bloody day, can't I? Here, let's make this stove up ... aha, that's better! Now, tell me what brings you up here at this hour? It's gone five, surely? If you're wanting the Englishman he's down at the Coq Hardi for the night. What's he done?'

Bernard said, so slowly that I could almost hear the calculation clicking behind the words: 'No, it's not the Englishman.'

'No? What then? Don't tell me you're my fire-raiser, Bernard?' Jules laughed. 'Come now, what's up? Come clean or I'll have to take you in for trespass. It's bound to be either duty or a woman, and I'm damned if I can see why either should bring you up here.'

'As it happens, it's both,' said Bernard. 'There's queer doings at the Château Valmy tonight. You've heard of young Philippe's governess; Martin's her name?'

'The pretty little thing that's been dangling after Monsieur Raoul? Who hasn't? What's she done?'

'She's disappeared, that's what she's done, and—'

'Well, what if she has? And what the devil would she be doing up here anyway? There's an obvious place to look for her, my friend, and that's in Monsieur Raoul's bed, not the Englishman's.'

'For God's sake can't you keep your mind out of bed for two minutes?'

'No,' said Jules simply.

'Well, try. And let me finish what I was telling you. Here. Have a cigarette.'

A match snapped and flared. The sharp smell of the Gauloise came up through the boards to where I lay. I could see the two men as plainly as if the ceiling were of glass, their dark faces lit by the crackling stove, the blue smoke of the cigarettes drifting up through the warm air to hang between them. Bernard said, still in that queer note of over-measured thoughtfulness: 'The boy's gone, too.'

'The boy?'

'Young Philippe.'

A pause, and a long soft whistle. 'Great God! Are you sure?'

'Damn it, of course we're sure! They've both vanished. Madame went along a bit ago to have a look at the boy – he's not strong, you know, and it seems she's been worried about him. She's not sleeping very well ... anyway, she went along, and he wasn't in his room. She went to rouse the governess and found her gone, too. No word, no note, no nothing.

We've searched the château from cellar to roof, the Master and I. No sign. They've gone.'

'But what in the world for? It doesn't make sense. Unless the girl and Monsieur Raoul—'

'You can leave him out of it,' said Bernard sourly. 'I've told you she's not snug in *his* bed. For one thing, what would she want with the boy if that's where she's bound? He'd not be a help, would he?'

'No, indeed,' said Jules, much struck. 'But – well, the thing's crazy! Where would they go, and why?'

'God knows.' Bernard sounded almost indifferent. 'And they'll probably turn up very soon anyway. The Master didn't seem very worried, though Madame was properly upset. It's made her ill – she has a bad heart, you know – so the Master told me to get out and scout around the place for them. I've been down to Thonon, but there's no sign. . . .' He paused, and then I heard him yawn.

Beside me Philippe moved a little and stretched in his sleep. His shoes must have been lying near him, and through the blankets his knee touched one of them and pushed it with a small scraping sound over the boards. It was the slightest of noises, but it seemed to fill the pause like thunder.

But Bernard had heard nothing. He was saying, indifferently: 'Ten to one it's all nonsense anyway. I probably shouldn't have told you about it, but since you've caught me on your land—' He laughed.

'But why should they be up here?'

'The Master's idea. It seems the girl was seen in Thonon with the Englishman. I tell you, the whole thing's crazy. It stands to reason it's only one of two things; either they're both off together on some silly frolic, or the boy's gone out adventuring on his own and the girl's found him gone and set off to fetch him back.'

Jules sounded dubious. 'It doesn't seem very likely.'

Bernard yawned again. 'No, it doesn't, but boys are queer cattle – almost as queer as women, friend Jules. And he and the Martin girl are very thick. The two of them had a midnight feast the other night, so I'm told. They'll not have gone far . . . the boy hasn't got his papers. Depend on it, it'll be some silly lark or other. What else could it be?'

'Well, as long as Monsieur isn't worried,' said Jules doubtfully. There was a little silence, through which I heard the hiss of the stove and the shifting of a man's feet. Then Bernard said briskly: 'Well, I think I'd better be off. Coming?'

Jules didn't answer directly. He said, in a voice which had a tentative, sidelong sound: 'That girl Martin. . . . There was talk. A lot of talk.'

'Oh?' Bernard didn't sound interested. As if you didn't know, I thought, lying in my form not four feet from his head.

'People were saying,' said Jules hesitantly, 'that she and Monsieur Raoul were fiancés.'

'Oh, that,' said Bernard. A pause. 'Well, it's true.'

'*Diable!* Is it really? So she got him?'

'If you put it that way.'

'Don't you?'

'Well,' said Bernard, sounding amused, 'I imagine Monsieur Raoul may have had something to say in the matter. You can't tell me that any girl, however pretty, could lead that one up the garden path unless he very much wanted to go.'

'There's ways and ways,' said Jules sagely. 'He knows what he's about, of course, but damn it, there comes a time. . . .' He laughed. 'And she's nothing like his usual. That gets us every time, doesn't it? Fools.'

'He was never a fool,' said Bernard. 'And if he wants to marry her – well, that's what he wants.'

'You don't persuade me he's really fallen, do you? For the little English girl? Be your age, man. He wants to sleep with her and she won't let him.'

'Maybe. But it's quite a step from that to marriage . . . for such as him.'

'You're telling me. Well, perhaps the reason's more pressing still. Perhaps she has slept with him and now there's a little something to force his hand. It has been done,' said Jules largely. 'I should know.'

'Oh? Congratulations.' Bernard's voice sounded almost absent. 'But I doubt if that's it.'

That's big of you, I thought, biting my knuckles above him while Jules' words crawled like lice along my skin. The stove-top clanked as someone lifted it to drop a cigarette-butt on the logs. Bernard said again: 'Look, I must go. Are you coming?'

'Bernard. . . .' Jules had dropped his voice for all the world as if he knew I was listening. He sounded urgent and slightly ashamed. The effect was so queer, so horrible almost, that my skin prickled again.

'Well?' said Bernard, impatiently.

'The girl—'

'Well?' said Bernard again.

'Are you so sure . . . that she' – Jules paused and I heard him swallow – 'that she means well by the boy?'

'What the devil d'you mean?'

'Well . . . I told you there'd been talk. People have been saying that she . . well, has ambitions.'

'Ambitions? Who hasn't? Very likely she has, but why should that make her "not mean well" by the brat? What d'you—' Bernard's voice tailed off and I heard him draw in his breath. He said on a very odd note: 'You can't mean what I think you mean, friend Jules.'

Jules sounded defiant. 'Why not? Why should her ambitions stop at marrying Monsieur Raoul? What does anyone know about her after all? Who is she?'

'An English orphan – I think of good family. That's all I know.' A pause. 'She's fond of the boy.'

Jules said: 'The boy will not make her Madame la Comtesse de Valmy.'

A longer pause. Bernard's laugh, breaking it, sounded a little strained. 'The sooner you get back to that bed of yours the better, *mon ami*. The night air's giving you fancies. And I must get back. Ten to one the thing's over and they're both safely back in bed. I hope Monsieur gives them hell in the morning for all the trouble they've caused. Come now—'

Jules said stubbornly: 'You may laugh. But I tell you that Monsieur Garcin said—'

'That old woman of a chemist? You should have better things to do than listen to village clack.'

'All the same—'

Bernard said irritably: 'For God's sake, Jules! You can't make every pretty girl a criminal because she makes a play for her betters. Now look, I've got to go. Which way are you bound?'

Jules sounded sulky. 'Down towards Soubirous. It's wearing on for morning.'

'And your trick's over? Right. I'll go down that way with you. I brought the brake up to the end of the track, so I'll run you down. You go on now while I turn the lamp down and close up.'

'Okay.' The stove-top clanked again as the second cigarette-butt followed the first. I heard Jules tread heavily towards the door. Beside me Philippe stirred again and muttered something in his sleep. The footsteps stopped. Jules said sharply: 'What was that?'

'What?'

'I heard something. Through there, perhaps, or—'

Bernard said softly: 'Open the door. Quickly.' Jules obeyed. The fresh grey-morning smell pierced the blue scent of cigarettes and woodsmoke. 'Nothing there.' Jules' voice came as if from a distance. I imagined him out on the verandah peering round the wall.

Bernard, just below us still, laughed his short hard laugh. 'A mouse, friend Jules. You're seeing a tiger in every tree tonight, aren't you?' He stretched noisily and yawned. 'Well I'm for bed as well, though mine'll not be as warm as yours, I'm afraid. What time does the Englishman get up here as a rule?'

'Pretty early – that is, if he's coming up here this morning. I wouldn't know.'

'Ah. Well, let's be going. I hope to God the excitement's over down at Valmy. Why the hell the Master should send me up here anyway I can't imagine. Go on, *mon ami*. I'll turn the lamp down and close up. I'll follow you.'

'I'll wait for you.'

'Eh? Oh, very well ... there, that's it. I suppose the stove's safe? Yes, well ... I'd have thought that bed of yours would have put a bit of hurry into you, friend Jules.' He was going. His voice dwindled towards the door. Beside me Philippe moved his head and his breath touched my cheek softly.

Jules' voice said, with the good temper back in it: 'Ah, that bed of mine. Let me tell you, *copain* ... '

The door shut quietly, lopping off Jules' embroidery of his favourite motif. I heard his voice faintly, fading off into the dawn-hush that held the forest. I hadn't realised how quiet it was outside. Not a bough moved; not a twig brushed the shingles. Philippe breathed softly beside me. From somewhere a woodpigeon began its hoarse roucouling.

Soon the sun would be up. It would be a lovely day. I lay back beside Philippe, shaking as if I had the fever.

The reprieve from terror had been so sudden that it had thrown me out of gear. All through that conversation I had crouched, straining every sense to interpret the two men's intentions, but with my mind spinning in a useless, formless confusion. At one moment it seemed to me that I ought to call out and disclose our presence to Jules, who was not a Valmy employee, and who would at any rate save us from any harm that Bernard might intend. At the next moment I found myself dazedly listening to Jules accusing, Bernard defending me. And what he'd had to say was odd enough: Léon de Valmy was not perturbed; it was known that I was fond of the boy; and Monsieur Raoul 'could be left out of it'. .... Bernard, in fact, had taken some pains to suppress the very gossip that I had imagined he and Albertine had engineered. No wonder I was shaken and confused. Had I been wrong? Could I possibly have been wrong? Surely Léon de Valmy, if he were guilty, must know from my flight with Philippe that I suspected him. If he were guilty, he couldn't be unperturbed; and if he were guilty, why should Bernard defend me to Jules? *And Raoul was out of it.* Dear Lord, had I been wrong?

But something fretted at me still. The whole conversation had had about it a curious air of inversion, something off-key that had sounded in Bernard's defence of me and in that slow, deliberative tone he had used.

I lay there quietly, savouring our safety and the stillness of Dieudonné, while the pigeon cooed peacefully in the pine-tops outside, and the racing blood in my body slowed down to normal. Philippe stirred again and said: 'Mademoiselle?' and relaxed once more in sleep. I smiled a little, thinking with another quick uprush of relief that, had he spoken so clearly before, Bernard must surely have heard him. After all, he had been standing just below us, while Jules was almost at the door. ...

On the thought I came upright in the darkness, dry-lipped, my heart going wild again in my breast.

Bernard must surely have heard him. Of course Bernard had heard him.

Bernard had known we were there.

So that was it. No other explanation would fit the facts and explain the curious overtones to that conversation. No wonder it had seemed off-key. No wonder I had been bogged down between friend and enemy.

Bernard had known. And it hadn't suited him to find us while Jules was there. That was why, though he'd been interrupted on his way up to the loft, he hadn't finished the search. That was why he had refused to 'hear' what Jules had heard; why he had tried to get Jules to go on ahead while he stayed behind to 'close up'.

It also explained very effectively his playing-down of the effect of our flight at Valmy. Whatever was discovered in the morning, it was obvious that Bernard's presence in the forest would have to be explained. The simplest and safest thing to do was obviously to tell some version of the truth. With me crouched not four feet above his head he'd had to play a very careful game. I was listening, and he didn't want to flush the quarry . . . not before he had a chance to come back alone.

Because of course he would come back. I was out of my blankets almost before the thought touched me, and creeping soundlessly across the floor to the trap-door. For all I had heard Jules talking away down the forest path I was taking no risks of a door that closed to leave the enemy inside and waiting. I lay flat beside the trap and slowly, slowly, eased it up till the tiniest crack showed between it and the floor. I peered through as best I could. Some light through the badly-fitting shutters showed an empty room.

I flew back to Philippe's side, but as I put out a hand to shake him awake I checked myself. I knelt beside him, my hands clutched tightly together, and shut my eyes. I could not wake the child on this wave of shaking terror. I must take control again. I must. I gave myself twenty seconds, counting them steadily.

He would come back. He would take Jules home in the shooting-brake, let himself be seen starting for Valmy, and then he would come back. He would be as quick as he could, because the night was wearing on for morning, and the night and the day were all they had.

I didn't take the thought further; I didn't want it put into words. I left it formless, a beat of fear through my body. How they would get away with it I couldn't – wouldn't – imagine, but in my present state of mind and in that dark hole at the top of the lonely forest anything seemed possible. I knelt there and made myself count steadily on through perhaps the worst twenty seconds of my life, while the terror, pressing closer, blew itself up into fantasy . . . the Demon King watching us from behind that bright window a mile away, hunting us down from his wheel-chair by some ghastly kind of radar that tracked us through the forest. . . . I whipped the mad thought aside but the image persisted; Léon de Valmy, like a deformed and giant shadow, reaching out for us wherever we happened to be. Why had I thought I could get the better of him? Nobody ever had, except one.

The silly tears were running down my face. I bent to rouse Philippe.

Seventh Coach

CHAPTER SIXTEEN

Oh Sammy, Sammy, vy worn't there a alleybi!

DICKENS: *Pickwick Papers*

He came awake instantly. 'Mademoiselle? Is it morning?'

'Yes. Get up, chicken. We've got to go.'

'All right. Are you crying, mademoiselle?'

'Good heavens, no! What makes you think that?'

'Something fell on me. Wet.'

'Dew, *mon p'tit*. The roof leaks. Now come along.'

He jumped up straight away, and in a very short space of time we were down that ladder, and Philippe was lacing his shoes while I made a lightning raid on William Blake's cupboards.

'Biscuits,' I said cheerfully, 'and butter and – yes, a tin of sardines. And I brought cake and chocolate. Here's riches! Trust a man to look after himself. He's all stocked up like a squirrel.'

Philippe smiled. His face looked a little less pinched this morning, though the grey light filtering through the shutters still showed him pale. God knows how it showed me. I felt like a walking ghost.

'Can we make up the stove, mademoiselle?'

'Afraid not. We'd better not wait here for Monsieur Blake. There are too many people about in the wood. We'll go on.'

'Where to? Soubirous? Is that where he is?'

'Yes, but we're not going towards Soubirous. I think we'll make straight for Thonon.'

'Now?'

'Yes.'

'Without breakfast?' His mouth dropped and I'm sure mine did too. There had been a tin of coffee in the cupboard and the stove was hot; I'd have given almost anything to have taken time to make some. Almost anything.

I said: 'We'll find a place when the sun's up and have breakfast outside. Here, put these in your pockets.' I threw a quick glance round the hut. 'All right, let's go. We'll make sure no-one's about first, shall we? You take that window ... carefully now.'

We reconnoitred as cautiously as we could from the windows, but anyone could have been hidden in the trees, watching and waiting. If Bernard had taken Jules down to Soubirous he wouldn't be back yet, but even so I found myself scanning the dim ranks of the trees with anxious fear. Nothing stirred there. We would have to chance it.

The moment of leaving the hut was as bad as any we had yet had. My hand on the latch, I looked down at Philippe.

'You remember the open space, the ride, that we came up? It's just through the first belt of trees. We mustn't go across it while we're in sight of Valmy. We must go up this side of it, in the trees, till we've got over the top of the ridge. It's not far. Understand?'

He nodded.

'When I open this door, you are to go out. Don't wait for me. Don't look back. Turn left – that way – uphill, and run as fast as you can. Don't stop for anything or anyone.'

'What about you?'

'I'll be running with you. But if – anything – should happen, *you are not to wait for me.* You are to go on, across the hill, down to the nearest house, and ask them to take you to the police station in Thonon. Tell them who you are and what has happened. Okay?'

His eyes were too big and bright, but he nodded silently.

On an impulse, I bent and kissed him.

'Now, little squirrel,' I said, as I opened the door, '*run!*'

Nothing happened after all. We slipped out of the hut unchallenged, and still unchallenged reached the summit of the ridge. There we paused. We had broken out of our hiding-place with more regard for speed than silence, but now we recollected ourselves and moved quietly but still quickly for a hundred yards more of gentle downhill before we halted on the edge of the ride.

Peering through a convenient hazel-bush we looked uphill and down. The ride was straight and empty. On the far side the trees promised thick cover.

We ran across. Pigeons came batting out of the pine-tops like rockets, but that was all. We scurried deep into the young forest of larch and spruce, still so thickly set that we had to brush a way between the boughs with hands constantly up to protect our eyes.

The wood held the wet chill of early morning, and the boughs dripped moisture. We were soon soaked. But we held on doggedly on a long northward slant that I hoped would eventually bring us to a track or country road heading towards Thonon.

It was Philippe who found the cave. I was ahead of him, forging a way through the thick branches and holding them back for his passage, when I pushed through a wet wall of spruce, to find myself on the edge of an outcrop of rock. It was a miniature cliff that stuck out of the half-grown trees like the prow of a ship. The forest parted like a river and flowed down to either side, leaving the little crag with its mossy green apron open to the sky. I could hear the drip of a spring.

I said: 'Watch your step, Philippe. There's a drop here. Make your way down the side. That way.'

He slithered obediently down. I followed him.

'Miss Martin, there's a cave!'

I said thankfully: 'And a spring. I think we might have a drink and a rest, don't you?'

Philippe said wistfully: 'And breakfast?'

'Good heavens. Yes, of course.' I had forgotten all about food in the haste that was driving me away from Bernard, but now I realised how hungry I was. 'We'll have it straight away.'

It wasn't really a cave, just a dry corner under an overhang, but it provided some shelter from the grey forest-chill, and – more – gave us an illusion of safety. We ate without speaking, Philippe seemingly intent on his food, I with my ears straining for sounds that were not of the forest. But I heard nothing. The screech of a jay, the spattering of waterdrops off the trees, the clap of a pigeon's wing and the trickle of the spring beside us . . . these made up the silence that held us in its safety.

And presently the sun came up and took the tops of the springtime larches like fire.

It may sound a silly thing to say, but I almost enjoyed that morning. The spell of the sun was potent. It poured down, hot and bright, while in front of it the wet greyness streamed off the woods in veils of mist, leaving the spruces gleaming darkly brilliant and lighting the tiny larch-flowers to a red flush along the boughs. The smell was intoxicating. We didn't hurry; we were both tired, and, since we had followed no paths, it would only be the purest chance that would put Bernard onto our trail. And on this lovely morning it was impossible to imagine that such an evil chance existed. The nightmare was as good as over. We were free, we were on our way to Thonon, and Monsieur Hippolyte arrived tonight. . . . And meantime the sun and the woods between them lent to our desperate adventure, not the glamour of romance, but the everyday charm of a picnic.

We held hands and walked sedately. In the older belt of the forest the going was easy. Here the trees were big and widely spaced, and between them shafts of brilliant sunlight slanted down onto drifts of last-year's cones and vivid pools of moss. Ever and again the wood echoed to the clap and flurry of wings as the ringdoves rocketed off their roosting-places up into the high blue.

Presently ahead of us we saw brighter sunlight at the edge of the mature forest. This ended sharply, like a cliff, for its whole steep length washed by a river of very young firs – babies, in all the beauty of rosy stems and a green as soft as woodsorrel. They split the older forest with a belt of open sunshine seventy yards wide. Between them the grass was thick and springing emerald already through the yellow of winter. On their baby stems the buds showed fat and pink.

We halted again at the edge of the tall trees before braving the open space. The young green flowed down the mountainside between its dark borders, plunging into the shadow that still lay blue at the bottom of the Dieudonné valley. Looking that way I could see the flat fields where cattle grazed; the line of willows that marked a stream; a scatter of houses; a farm where someone – tiny in the distance – stood among swarming white dots that must be hens.

No-one was on the hillside. The inevitable woodpigeon played high above the treetops, riding the blue space like surf in ecstatic curved swoops and swallow-dives, wings raked back and breast rounded to the thrust of the air.

Nothing else moved. We plunged – Philippe was chest-high – across the river of lovely young trees. The fresh green tufts brushed hands and knees softly, like feathers; they smelt of warm resin. Half-way across Philippe stopped short and cried: 'Look!' and there was a fox slipping like a leaf-brown shadow into the far woods. He paused as he reached them and looked back, one paw up and ears mildly inquiring. The sun was red on his fur. Along his back the fine hairs shone like gold. Then he slid quietly out of sight and the forest was ours again.

All morning the enchantment held, our luck spinning out fine and strong, like the filigree plot of a fairytale. Almost, at times, we forgot the dark and urgent reason for our journey. Almost.

Some time before noon we came, after a slowish journey of frequent stops, and one or two forced diversions, on the road I had hoped to find. This was a narrow road between steep banks, that wound stonily the way we wanted to go, high above the valley which carried the main traffic route to the south. Our last stage had taken us through a rough tract of thorns and dead bracken, so it was with some thankfulness that we clambered through the wire fence and negotiated the dead brambles that masked the ditch.

Our luck had made us a little careless. As I landed on the gravel surface of the road, and turned to reach a hand to Philippe, the clang of metal and the swish of a car's tyres close behind me brought me round like a bayed deer.

A battered Renault coasted round the bend in a quiet whiffle of dust that sounded a good deal more expensive than it looked. She slithered – with a few bangs and rattles that belied that expensively silent engine – to a stop beside us. The driver, a stout grey-stubbled character in filthy blue denims, regarded us benevolently and without the least curiosity from under the brim of a horrible hat.

He was a man of few words. He jerked a thumb towards the north. I said: *'S'il vous plaît, monsieur.'* He jerked the thumb south. I said:

'*Merci, monsieur*,' and Philippe and I clambered into the back seat to join the other passengers already there. These were a collie-dog, a pig in what looked like a green string bag, and a rather nasty collection of white hens in a slatted box. A large sack of potatoes rode *de luxe* beside the farmer in the front seat. As I began, through the embraces of the collie-dog, to say rather awkwardly: 'This is very kind of you, monsieur,' the Renault lurched forward and took a sharp bend at a fairly high speed and still without benefit of engine, but now with such a succession of clanks and groans and other body-noises that conversation – I realised thankfully – was an impossibility.

He took us nearly two miles, then stopped to put us down where a farm track joined the road.

To my thanks he returned a nod, jerked his thumb in explanation down towards the farm, and the Renault after it. The track down which he vanished was a dirt road of about one in four. We watched, fascinated, until the Renault skated to a precarious standstill some two inches from the wall of a Dutch barn, and then turned to go on our way, much heartened by an encounter with someone who quite obviously had never heard of the errant Comte de Valmy, and who was apparently content to take life very much as it came. He might also, I thought cheerfully, be deaf and dumb. Our luck seemed to be running strongly enough even for that.

Our road ran fairly openly now along the hillside, so we kept to its easier walking. The lift had done something to cheer Philippe's flagging spirits; he walked gamely and without complaint, but I could see that he was tiring, and we still had some way to go . . . and I had no idea what we might yet have to face.

He set off now cheerfully enough, chatting away about the collie and the pig. I listened absently, my eyes on the dusty length of road curling ahead of us, and my ears intent on sounds coming from behind. Here the road wound below a high bank topped with whins. I found myself watching them for cover as we passed.

Half-a-mile; three-quarters; Philippe got a stone in his shoe and we stopped to take it out. We went on more slowly after that. A mile; mile-and-a-quarter; he wasn't talking now, and had begun to drag a bit; I thought apprehensively of blisters, and slackened the pace still further.

I was just going to suggest leaving the road to find a place for lunch when I heard another car. An engine, this time, coming from the north. She was climbing, and climbing fast, but for all that, making very little more noise than the old Renault coasting. A big car: a powerful car . . . I don't pretend I recognised the silken snarl of that engine, but I knew who it was. The sound raked up my backbone like a cruel little claw.

I breathed: 'Here's a car. Hide, Philippe!'

I had told him what to do. He swarmed up the bank as quick and neat as a shrew-mouse, with me after him. At the top of the bank was a thicket of whins, dense walls of green three or four feet high with little gaps and clearings of sunlit grass where one could lie invisibly. We flung ourselves down in one of these small citadels as the Cadillac took a bend three hundred yards away. The road levelled and ran straight below us. He went by with a spatter of dust and the *hush* of a gust of wind. The top was down amd I saw his face. The little claw closed on the base of my spine.

There was no sound in the golden noon except the ripple of a skylark's song. Philippe whispered beside me: 'That was my cousin Raoul, mademoiselle.'

'Yes.'

'I thought he was in Paris?'

'So did I.'

'Is he - couldn't we have - wouldn't he have helped us?'

'I don't know Philippe.'

He said on a note of childish wonder: 'But . . . he was so nice at the midnight feast.'

A pause.

'Wasn't he, mademoiselle?'

'I - yes. Yes, Philippe, he was.'

Another pause. Then, still on that terrible little note of wonder: 'My cousin Raoul? My cousin Raoul, too? Don't you trust him, mademoiselle?'

'Yes,' I said, and then, desperately: '*No.*'

'But why—?'

'Don't, Philippe, please. I can't—' I looked away from him and said tightly: 'Don't you see, we can't take risks of any kind. However sure we are we've got to be - we've got to be sure.' I finished a bit raggedly. 'Don't you see?'

If he saw anything odd in this remarkably silly speech he didn't show it. With a shy but a curiously unchildlike gesture he put out a hand and touched mine. 'Mademoiselle—'

'I'm not crying, Philippe. Not really. Don't worry. It's only that I'm tired and I didn't get much sleep last night and it's long past time for food.' Somehow I smiled at him and dabbed at my face while he watched me with troubled eyes. 'Sorry, *mon p'tit*. You're standing this trek of ours like a Trojan and I'm behaving like a fool of a woman. I'm all right now.'

'We'll have lunch,' said Philippe, taking a firm hold of the situation.

'Okay, Napoleon,' I said, putting away my handkerchief, 'but we'd better stay where we are for a little while longer, just to make sure.'

'That he's really gone?'

'Yes,' I said, 'that he's really gone.'

Philippe relaxed obediently into the shelter of the whins, and lay chin on hand, watching the road below him through a gap in the thick green. I turned on my back so that the sun was on my face, and closed my eyes. Even then I didn't want to face it. I wanted to go on, blind, cowardly, instinct-driven ... but as I lay there listening for the engine of his car the thing that I had been trying to keep back, dammed out of mind, broke over me. And before I had thought further than simply his name I knew how very far I was – still was – from jettisoning him along with the others. Instinct might make me shrink from Léon de Valmy, and keep me a chilly mile away from Héloïse, but – it seemed – whatever evidence, whatever 'proof' I was offered, I still sprang without thought straight to his defence.

Because you want it that way. Haven't you been enough of a fool, Cinderella? I stirred on the warm grass with sharp discomfort, but still somewhere inside me hammered the insistent advocate for the defence. . . .

Everything that had happened since Raoul had entered the affair, everything he had said and done, could bear an innocent interpretation as well as a guilty one ... or so I told myself, groping wearily, confusedly, back through the fogs of memory. A word here, a look there – never did frailer witnesses plead more desperately. He had not known of the attempts to get a non-French-speaking governess; he hadn't been worried, only amused, at the thought that I might have eavesdropped on his father's conversation; he had seemed as shocked as I was over the shooting in the wood; his sharp questions about William Blake, and that curiously touchy temper he had shown, might have been due to jealousy or some other preoccupation, and not to the realisation that the 'friendless' orphan was in touch with a tough-looking Englishman in the neighbourhood; and that blast of the horn that brought Philippe out onto the balcony – that might have been fortuitous. Bernard hadn't spoken of it. As for Bernard's flat statement to Berthe that it had been Raoul who had shot at Philippe in the wood, I didn't regard that as evidence at all. Even in his drunken mood, and however sure he had made himself of Berthe, Bernard might well hesitate to admit that kind of guilt to her. Then at the dance. . . .

But here the pleading memories whirled up into a ragged and flying confusion, a blizzard so blinding that, like Alice among the cards, I came to myself trying to beat them off. And I was asked to believe that these, too, were dead and painted like a pack of cards? Something to put away now in a drawer, and take out again, years hence, dusty, to thumb over in a dreary game of solitaire? Yes, there it was. For Philippe's sake I had to assume Raoul's guilt. I couldn't afford to do anything else. The child had only one life to lose, and I couldn't stake it. Raoul was guilty till he could be proved innocent. In that, if in no other part of my crazy fear-driven plans, I had been right. He was here but we couldn't run to him.

Close to my ear Philippe whispered: 'Mademoiselle.'

I opened my eyes. His face was close to mine. It was scared. He breathed: 'There's someone on the hilltop behind. He's just come through the wood. I think it's Bernard. D'you suppose he's in it too?'

I nodded and put a swift finger to my lips, then lifted my head cautiously and peered through the screening whins towards the hill behind us. At first I saw nothing but the trees and the tangling banks of scrub, but presently I picked him out. It was Bernard. He was above us, about two hundred yards away, standing beside a big spruce. There was no need to tell Philippe to keep close; we both lay as still as rabbits in our thicket of green. Bernard was standing motionless, scanning the slope below him. The moments dragged. He was looking our way. His gaze seemed to catch on us, to linger, to pass on, to return. . . .

He was coming quickly down the hill in our direction.

I suppose a rabbit stays still while death stalks it just because it is hoping against hope that this is not death. We stayed still.

He had covered half the distance, not hurrying, when I heard the Cadillac coming back.

My hand pressed hard over Philippe's on the short turf. I turned my head and craned to stare up the road. My muscles tensed themselves as if they would carry me without my willing it straight down into his path.

I don't know to this day whether I really would have run to him then or not, but before I could move I heard the brakes go on. The tyres bit at the soft gravel of the road and the car pulled up short some fifty yards away from us. I could see him through my screen of whins. He was looking uphill towards Bernard. The horn blared twice. Bernard had stopped. I saw Raoul lift his hand. Bernard changed course and walked quickly down the hill towards the car. He jumped the ditch and hurried up to the door. Raoul said something to him, and I saw Bernard shake his head, then turn with a wide gesture that included all the hill from where we lay back to Dieudonné. Then Raoul gave a sideways jerk of the head and Bernard went round the bonnet and got in beside him.

The Cadillac went slowly by below us. Raoul was lighting a cigarette and his head was bent. Bernard was talking earnestly to him.

I turned to meet Philippe's eyes.

After a while I got up slowly and reached a hand down to him.

'Come along,' I said, 'let's get back from the road and find somewhere to have lunch.'

After we had eaten we took to the woods again without seeing another soul, and some time in the middle of the afternoon our path led us out of a wild tangle of hornbeam and honeysuckle onto a little green plateau; and there, not so very far to the north of us we saw at last, through the tops of the still-bare trees, the blue levels of Lac Léman.

CHAPTER SEVENTEEN

Upon thy side, against myself I'll fight,
And prove thee virtuous . . .

SHAKESPEARE: *Sonnet 88*

'This,' I said, 'is where we stop for a while.'

Philippe was surveying the little dell. It was sheltered and sun-drenched, a green shelf in the middle of the wood. Behind us the trees and bushes of the wild forest crowded up the hill, dark holly and the bone-pale boughs of ash gleaming sharp through a mist of birch as purple as bloom on a grape. Below the open shelf the tangle of boughs fell steeply towards Thonon. Those bright roofs and coloured walls were, I judged, little more than a mile away. I saw the gleam of a spire, and the smooth sweep of some open square with brilliant flowerbeds and a white coping above the lake. Even in the town there were trees; willows in precise Chinese shapes, cypresses spearing up Italian-fashion against the blue water, and here and there against some painted wall a burst of pale blossom like a cloud.

At my feet a small stream ran, and a little way off, under the flank of a fallen birch, there were primroses.

Philippe slipped a hand into mine. 'I know this place.'

'Do you? How?'

'I've been here for a picnic. There were foxgloves and we had *pâtisseries belges.*'

'Do you remember the way down into Thonon? Where does it land us?'

He pointed to the left. 'The path goes down there, like steps. There's a fence at the bottom and a sort of lane. It takes you to a road and you come out by a garage and a shop where they keep a ginger cat with no tail.'

'Is it a main street?'

He wrinkled his forehead at me. 'We – ell—'

'Is it full of shops and people and traffic?'

'Oh, no. It has trees and high walls. People *live* there.'

A residential area. So much the better. I said: 'Could you find your way from there to the Villa Mireille?'

'Of *course*. There's a path between two garden walls that takes you to the road above the lake and then you go down and down and *down* till you get to the bottom road where the gate is. We always went by the funicular.'

'I'm afraid we can't. Well, that's wonderful, Philippe. We're practically there! And with you as guide' – I smiled at him – 'we can't go far wrong, can we? Later we'll see how much I can remember of what you told me about the Villa Mireille, but just for the moment I think we'll stop and rest.'

'Here?'

'Right here.'

He sat thankfully down on the fallen birch. 'My legs are *aching*.'

'I'm not surprised.'

'Are yours?'

'Well, no. But I did miss my sleep last night and if I don't have a rest this minute I shall go to sleep on my feet.'

'Like a horse,' said Philippe, and giggled, albeit a little thinly.

I flicked his cheek. 'Exactly like a horse. Now, you get tea ready while I make the bed.'

'English tea?'

'Of course.'

The grass was quite dry, and the sun stood hot overhead in the calm air. I knelt down beside the birch-log and carefully removed two dead boughs, a thistle, and some sharp stones from our 'bed', then spread out my coat. Philippe, solemn-eyed, was dividing the last of William's biscuits into equal parts. He handed me mine, together with half a stick of chocolate. We ate slowly and in silence.

Presently I said: 'Philippe.'

'Yes, mademoiselle?'

'We'll be down in Thonon pretty soon now. We really ought to go straight to the police.'

The big eyes stared. He said nothing.

I said: 'I don't know where the nearest British Consul is, or we'd go to him. I don't suppose there's one in Évian, and we can't get to Geneva because you've no passport. So it should be the police.'

Still he said nothing. I waited. I think he knew as well as I did that the first thing the police would do would be to face us both with Léon de Valmy. After a while he asked: 'What time will my Uncle Hippolyte get home?'

'I've no idea. He may be here already, but I think we may have to wait till late . . . after dark.'

A pause. 'Where is this Monsieur Blake?'

'I don't know. He may be out somewhere in Dieudonné, or he may have gone back up to the hut. But we – we couldn't very well wait for him there.' He gave me a quick look and I added hastily: 'We might telephone the Coq Hardi from Thonon. They might be able to give him a message. Yes, that's a good idea. We can try that.'

Still he said nothing. I looked at him a little desperately. 'You want to go and look for your uncle first? Is that it?'

A nod.

'Philippe, you'd be quite safe if we went to the police, you know. We – we should do that. They'd be frightfully nice to you, and they'd look

after you till your Uncle Hippolyte came – better than I can. We really
should.'

'No. Please. Please, Miss Martin.'

I knew I ought to insist. It wasn't only the eloquence of Philippe's
silences, and the clutch of the small cold hand that decided me. Nor was
it only that I was afraid of facing Léon de Valmy . . . though, with the
anger spilt out of me and dissolved in weariness, my very bones turned
coward at the thought of confronting him in the presence of the police.

There was another reason. I admitted it out of a cold grey self-
contempt. I might have braved Léon de Valmy and the police, but I
didn't want to face Raoul. I was a fool; moreover, if I allowed any more
risk to the child I was a criminal fool . . . but I would not go to the police
while there was any chance that Raoul might be involved. I wasn't ready,
yet, to test the theories of that advocate for the defence who pleaded still
so desperately through today's tears. I couldn't bring the police in . . .
not yet. If they had to be told, I didn't even want to be there. I was going
to wait for Monsieur Hippolyte and, like a craven, hand the whole thing
to him. Let the *deus ex machina* fly in out of the clouds and do the dirty
work. I was only a woman, and a coward, and not ready, even, to face
my own thoughts.

I gave a little sigh. 'All right. We'll go to the Villa Mireille first. In
any case they've already searched it.'

'How d'you know?'

'Eh? Oh, well, I imagine they have, don't you? But your uncle won't
be there yet, *petit*, of that I'm sure. We'll stay here a little while and rest.
I don't feel fit for very much more just yet. Here, you may as well finish
the last of the chocolate.'

'Thank you.' He gave me a watery smile. 'I'm sleepy.'

'Well, curl up there and sleep. I'm going to.'

'I'm thirsty too.'

'I imagine the stream's all right. It comes straight down the hillside.
Let's risk it anyway.'

We drank, and then lay down in the sun, curled close together on my
coat, and soon we slept.

I needn't have been afraid that any restless ecstacy of the mind would
keep me awake. Sleep fell from nowhere like a black cloud and blotted
me out. I never stirred or blinked until the sun had his chin on the hilltop
beyond Dieudonné valley, and the shadows of the naked trees stretched
long-fingered across the glade to touch us with the first tiny chill of
evening.

Philippe was awake already, sitting with knees drawn up and chin on
them, gazing a little sombrely at the distant housetops, purpling in the
fading light. The lake was pale now as an opal, swimming under the
faint beginnings of mist. In the distance on the further shore we could
see, touched in with rose and apricot, the snows of Switzerland.

Brightness falls from the air. . . . I gave a little shiver, then got to my feet and pulled the silent Philippe to his. 'Now,' I said briskly, 'you show me that path of yours, *petit*, and we'll be on our way.'

His memory proved accurate enough. The path was there, and the narrow country road, and the corner with the garage and the shop, past which we hurried in case anyone should recognise him from his previous visits. He never spoke, and his hand in mine had become perceptibly more of a drag. I watched him worriedly. His frail energy was running out visibly now, sand from the brittle glass. I thought of the long wait that probably still lay ahead of us, and bit my lip in a prolonged pain of indecision.

The dusk had fairly dropped now over the town. We walked along a high-walled street where the pavements were bordered with lopped willows. The lamps had come on, and festoons of gleaming telegraph wires pinned back the blue dusk. Few people were about. A lorry started up from the garage and drove off with a clatter, its yellow lights like lion's eyes in the half-light. A big car purred by on its own hasty business. Two workmen on bicycles pedalled purposefully home. From a side street came the raucous voice of a radio and the smell of frying.

Philippe stopped. His face, lifted to mine, looked small and pale. He said: 'That's the way, mademoiselle.'

I looked to my right where a vennel led off the street between two high ivy-covered walls. It was narrow and unlighted, vanishing into shadow within twenty yards. A loose spray of ivy tapped the wall; its leaves were sharp and black and clicked like metal.

From the opposite side of the road came a burst of laughter, and a woman's voice called something shrill and good-natured. The café door clashed, and with the gush of light came once again the heavenly hot smell of food.

The child's hand clutched mine. He said nothing.

Well, what was luck for if it was never to be tempted?

I turned my back on the black little alley. Two minutes later we were sitting at a red-topped table near the stove while a long thin man with a soiled apron and a face like a sad heron waited to be told what we would have to eat.

To this day I vividly remember the smell and taste of everything we had. Soup first, the first delicious hot mouthful for almost twenty-four hours ... It was *crème d'asperge*, and it came smoking-hot in brown earthenware bowls with handles like gnomes' ears, and asparagus-tips bobbed and steamed on the creamy surface. With the soup came butter with the dew on it, and crusty rolls so new that where they lay on the plastic table-top there was a tiny dull patch of steam.

Philippe revived to that soup as a fern revives to water. When his omelette arrived, a fluffy roll, crisped at the edges, from which mushrooms burst and spilled in their own rich gravy, he tackled it with an almost normal small-boy's appetite. My own brand of weariness demanded something more solid and I had a steak. It came in a lordly dish with the butter still sizzling on its surface and the juices oozing pinky-brown through the mushrooms and tomatoes and tiny kidneys and the small mountain of crisply-fried onions ... if *filet mignon* can be translated as *darling steak* this was the very sweetheart of its kind. By the time that adorable steak and I had become one flesh I could have taken on the whole Valmy clan single-handed. I complimented the waiter when he came to clear, and his lugubrious face lightened a little.

'And what to follow, mademoiselle? Cheese? A little fruit?'

I glanced at Philippe, who shook his head sleepily. I laughed, 'My little brother's nearly asleep. No, no cheese for me, thank you, monsieur. A *café-filtre*, if you please, and a *café-au-lait*. I fingered the purse in my pocket. 'And a benedictine, please.'

'*Un filtre, un café-au-lait, une bénédictine.*'

He swept the last crumb from the table, gave the shiny red top a final polish with his cloth, and turned away. I said: 'Could monsieur perhaps get me some *jetons?*'

'Assuredly.' He took the money I held out and in a short time the cups were on the table and I had a little pile of *jetons* in front of me.

Philippe roused himself to blink at them. 'What are those?'

I gaped at him. Then it came to me that Monsieur le Comte de Valmy had, of course, never had to use a public telephone. I explained softly that one had to buy these little metal plaques to put in the slot of the telephone.

'I should like to do it,' said Monsieur le Comte decidedly, showing a spark of animation.

'So you shall, *mon gars*, but not tonight. Better leave it to me.' And I rose.

'Where are you going?' He didn't move, but his voice clutched at me.

'Only to the corner behind the bar. See? There's the telephone. I'll be back before my coffee's filtered. You stay here and drink your own – and Philippe, don't look quite so interested in those men over there. Pretend you've been in this sort of place dozens of times, will you?'

'They're not taking any notice.'

Neither they were. The only other occupants of the little café besides ourselves were a gang of burly workmen absorbed in some card-game, and a slim youth with hair cut *en brosse* whispering sweet somethings into the ear of a pretty little gipsy in a tight black sweater and skirt. Nobody after the first casual glance had paid the slighest attention to us. The stout patronne who sat over some parrot-coloured knitting behind the bar merely smiled at me and nodded as I picked my way between the tables towards her and asked if I might telephone. Nobody here, at any rate, was on the lookout for a young woman with brown hair and grey eyes, on the run with the kidnapped Comte de Valmy.

It wasn't only luck that protected us, I thought, as I fumbled with the half-forgotten intricacies of the telephone; it was common-sense to suppose that the chances of our being seen and recognised now, here, were very small. One had read dozens of 'pursuit' books, from the classic *Thirty-nine Steps* onwards, and in all of them the chief and terrible miracle had been the unceasing and intelligent vigilance of every member of the population. In sober fact, nobody was much interested. . . .

Here one of the card-players raised his eyes from the game to look at me; then he nudged his neighbour and said something. The latter looked up too, and his stare raked me. My heart, in spite of the soothing logic of my thoughts, gave a painful jerk, as with an effort I forced my gaze to slide indifferently past them. I turned a shoulder and leaned against the wall, waiting, bored, for my connection. From the corner of an eye I saw the second man say something and grin. I realised with a rush of amused relief that any pursuit that those two might offer would have other and quite natural motives that had nothing whatever to do with the errant Comte de Valmy.

'*Ici le Coq Hardi*,' quacked a voice in my ear.

I jerked my attention back to it, and my imagination back to the teeming little inn at Soubirous.

'I want to speak to Monsieur Blake, please.'

'Who?'

'Monsieur Blake. The Englishman from Dieudonné.' I was speaking softly, and mercifully the radio was loud enough to drown my voice. 'I understand he stays with you. Is he there now?'

There was some altercation, aside, that I couldn't make out. Then it stopped abruptly, as if cut off by a hand over the mouthpiece. To my fury I found that my own hand was damp on the receiver.

Then the voice said into my ear: 'No, he's not here. Who's that wanting him?'

'Is he likely to be in tonight?'

'Perhaps.' Was I being jumpy, or was it suspicion that put the edge on that unfriendly voice? 'He didn't say. If you ring back in half an hour. . . . Who is that speaking, please?'

I said: 'Thanks very much. I'll do that. I'm sorry to have—'

The voice said, harsh and sharp: 'Where are you speaking from?'

Suspicion. It bit like an adder. If I didn't answer they could trace the call. I didn't stop to ask myself why they should. It was enough for me that the Coq Hardi was on Valmy land and that presumably the news would reach the château just as quickly as wires could carry it. If I could let them think I was safe for another half-hour. . . .

I said pleasantly, with no perceptible hesitation: 'From Évian. The Cent Fleurs. Don't trouble Monsieur Blake. I'll ring him up later on. Thank you so much.'

And right in the teeth of another question I rang off.

I stood for a moment looking unseeingly at the telephone, biting my lip. Needless to say I had no intention of waiting to ring up again, but in putting off pursuit I had also put off William Blake. If he got my message at all, and if he was aware of the story that must by now be rife in Soubirous, he might realise I needed help and set straight off for Évian and the huge crowded floor of the Cent Fleurs, which certainly wouldn't remember if a young woman accompanied by a small boy had used the telephone at some time during the evening.

Somehow I was very sure of William Blake's desire – and solid capacity to help. Now I had had to cut myself off from that, and only now did I realise how much I had depended on the comfort of his company when the inevitable showdown came. I was well aware that even the interview with Hippolyte wouldn't be altogether plain sailing. Never before had I felt so miserably in need of a friend – someone who, even if they could do nothing, would simply be there. I gave myself a mental shake. I mustn't start this. Just because, for a few short hours, I had laid flesh and spirit in other hands, I didn't have to feel so forsaken now. I'd hoed my own row for long enough – well, it seemed I must go on doing just that. What one has never really had, one never misses. Or so they say.

I went back to my table, unwrapped three lumps of sugar, and drank my coffee black and far too sweet. The benedictine I drank with appreciation but, I'm afraid, a lack of respect. It was the effect, and not the drink I craved. I took it much too quickly, with half a wary eye on the card-players in the other corner.

Then, just as they were nicely involved in a new round of betting, I quietly paid the waiter, nodded a good night to Madame and went (unfollowed except by Philippe) out of the café.

CHAPTER EIGHTEEN

If thou wilt leave me, do not leave me last,
When other petty griefs have done their spite,
But in the onset come ...

SHAKESPEARE: *Sonnet 90*

The Villa Mireille stood right on the shore of Lac Léman. It was one of a row of large wealthy houses – châteaux, almost – which bordered the lakeside, being served to landward by a narrow pretty road some two hundred feet below the town's main boulevards. Most of the houses stood in large gardens plentifully treed and guarded from the road by high walls and heavy gates.

It was dark when we reached the Villa Mireille. The gate was shut and as our steps paused outside there was the rattle of a heavy chain within, and a dog set up a deep barking.

'That's Beppo,' whispered Philippe.

'Does he know you?

'No – I don't know. I'm frightened of him.'

Here the door of the concierge's lodge opened, and the light from it rushed up the trees that made a crowded darkness beyond the gate. A woman's voice called something, shrilly. The barking subsided into a whining growl. The door shut and the trees retreated into murky shadow.

I said: 'Is there another way in?'

'You can get in from the lake-shore. The garden runs right down, and there's a boat-house. But I don't know the way down along the lake.'

'We'll find it.'

'Are we going further?' His voice was alarmed and querulous; tears of pure fatigue were not far away.

'Only to find a way down to the lake. We can't go in past Beppo and Madame – what did you say her name was?'

'Vuathoux.'

'Well, unless you'd like to go straight to her—'

'*No.*'

I said: 'You'd be safe, Philippe.'

'She would telephone my Uncle Léon, wouldn't she?'

'Almost certainly.'

'And my cousin Raoul would come?'

'It's possible.'

He looked at me. 'I would rather wait for my Uncle Hippolyte. You said we could.'

'All right. We'll wait.'

'Would you rather wait for my Uncle Hippolyte?'

'Yes.'

'Then,' said Philippe, swallowing, 'perhaps we will find the way quickly?'

We did – three houses along from the Villa Mireille. A small wicket, swinging loose, gave onto a dim shrubbery, and as we slipped cautiously inside we could see the dim bulk of a house looming unlighted among its misty trees. No dog barked. We crept unchallenged down a long winding path, along beside a high paling bordering an open stretch of grass, and eventually once again between big trees towards the murmur of the lake.

Neither moon nor stars showed tonight. Over the water mist lay patchily, here thick and pale against the dark distances, here no more than a haze veiling the lake's surface as breath mists a dark glass, here as faint as the sheen that follows a finger stroking dark velvet. Long transparent drifts of vapour wreathed up from the water and reached slow fingers across the narrow shore towards the trees. The water lapped hollowly on the shingle beside us as we crunched our way back towards the Villa's garden. The night was not cold, but the water breathed a chill into the air, and the slowly-curling veils of mist brushed us with a damp that made me shiver.

'That's the boat-house,' whispered Philippe. 'I know where the key's kept. Are we going to go in?'

The boat-house was a small square two-storeyed building set, of course, over the water, at the head of an artificial bay made by two curving stone jetties. The shore was very narrow here, and from the yard-wide strip of shingle rose the steep bank crowded with trees that edged the grounds of the Villa Mireille. The rear wall of the boat-house was almost built up against this bank, and the beeches hung their branches right over the roof. Mist and darkness blurred the details, but the general effect of desertion, looming trees, and lapping water was not just exactly what the moment demanded for Philippe and me.

I said briskly: 'I want to go up through the garden and take a look at the house. For all we know he's already here. Would you like to stay in the boat-house? You could lock yourself in, and we'd have a secret signal—'

'*No*,' said Philippe again.

'All right. You can scout up the garden with me. Very carefully, mind.'

'Madame Vuathoux is deaf,' said Philippe.

'Maybe. But Beppo isn't. Come on, *petit*.'

The bank was steep and slippery with clay and wet leaves that lay in drifts between the roots of the beeches. Above it was the rough grass of a small parkland studded with more of the great trees. We crept softly from one huge trunk to the next; the spring grass was soft and damp underfoot, and there was, incongruously, the smell of violets. Elms now, and horse-chestnuts. I could feel the rough bark of the one, and the sticky buds of the other licked at my hand. The hanging fronds of willow brushed us wetly, clung, hindered us. We pushed through into a grove of willows as thick as a tent, and paused. We were almost at the house now. The willows curtained the edges of a formal lawn; the terrace of the house lay beyond this, thirty yards away. Near us was the metallic gleam of a small pool and I could see something that looked like a statue leaning over it.

I took Philippe's hand and we crept softly up behind the plinth of the statue, where the willows hung like an arras down to the water's surface. I pulled the trailing stems aside and scanned the façade of the house. None of the windows showed light, but there appeared to be a lamp over the front door, illuminating the drive. The door itself was out of our range of vision, but the glow of the lamp showed part of a circular gravel sweep, and banks of rhododendrons. Up here the mist was still only a blurring of the air, a thickening of the lamplight that lay like hoar-frost on the wet leaves.

I said softly: 'The windows on the terrace. What room's that?'

'The salon. It's never used. My Uncle Hippolyte has his study upstairs. The end window. There's no light in it.'

I looked up at it. 'Then I'm afraid he's not home yet.'

'Are we going in?'

I thought for a moment. 'Where's the back door?'

'Round the other side, near the lodge.'

'And near Beppo? Then that's out. And I doubt if there are any windows open. And there's that light over the front door. ... No, Philippe, I think we'll wait. What do you think?'

'Yes. I – *there's a car!*'

His hand gripped mine almost painfully. The road was not more than twenty yards away on our right. A car was coming along it, slowing down rapidly through its gears. Brakes squealed. A door slammed. Footsteps. A bell clanged. Seconds later through the clamour of the dog we heard the chink of iron and the squeak of a hinge, as Madame Vuathoux hastened to open the gates.

Philippe's grip tightened. '*My Uncle Hippolyte!*'

A man's voice said something indistinguishable beyond the banked shrubs.

'No,' I said on a caught breath. 'Raoul.'

The cold hand jerked in mine. I heard the concierge say, in the loud toneless voice of the very deaf: 'No, monsieur. Nothing, monsieur. And has there been no trace of them found?'

He said curtly: 'None. Are you sure they couldn't have got in here? This is where they'll make for, that's certain. Is the back door locked?'

'No, monsieur, but I can see it from my window. Nobody has been there. Or to the front. Of that I am sure.'

'The windows?'

'Locked, monsieur.'

'No telephone call? Nothing?'

'Nothing, monsieur.'

There was a pause. In it I could hear my own heart hammering.

'All the same,' he said, 'I'll have a look round. Leave the gates open, please. I'm expecting Bernard here any minute.'

Another heart-hammering pause. Then the car started up and the lights turned in slowly off the road, slithering metallically across the sharp leaves of the rhododendrons. He parked it in front of the door, and got out. I heard him run up the steps, and then the door shut behind him. The dog still whimpered and growled a little. Back at the lodge, the concierge called something to it, and after a few moments it fell silent.

I felt the cold hand twitch in mine. I looked down. The child's face was a blur with great dark pools for eyes. I whispered: 'Keep close behind the statue. He may put some lights on.'

I had hardly spoken before the salon windows blazed to brilliant oblongs, and the light leaped out across the terrace to touch the lawn. We were still in shadow. We waited, tense behind the statue. It was the figure of a boy, naked, leaning over to look at himself in the pool; a poised, exquisite Narcissus, self-absorbed, self-complete. ...

Room after room leaped into light, was quenched. We followed his progress through the house; light and then black darkness. The windows on the terrace facing us remained lit. Finally they were the only ones. He came to one of the long windows, opened it, and stepped out onto the terrace. His shadow leaped across the lawn to the edge of the water. He

stood there for a minute or two, very still, staring at the night. I put a
gentle hand on Philippe's head, pushing it down so that no faint probe
of light would touch his face. We were crouching now. My cheek was
against the stone of the plinth. It was cold and smooth and smelt of
lichen. I didn't dare lift my head to look at Raoul. I watched the tip of
his shadow.

Suddenly it was gone. In the same moment I heard another car come
fast along the road. Lights swept in at the gate. The salon windows went
black, blank. I lifted my head and waited, straining my ears.

Steps on the gravel. Raoul's voice, still on the terrace, saying: 'Bernard?'

'Monsieur?' The newcomer came quickly round the corner of the
house. I heard Raoul descending the terrace steps. He said in that quick
hard voice he had used to Madame Vuathoux: 'Any sign?'

'None, monsieur, but—'

I heard Raoul curse under his breath. 'Did you go back to the hut?'

'Yes. They weren't there. But they'd been, I swear they—'

'Of course they had. The Englishman was up there last night till
midnight. I know that. They'd go to find him. Have you found out where
he is?'

'He's not back yet. He went out with a party up to the plantation
beyond Bois-Roussel early this morning and they're not back yet. But,
monsieur, I was trying to tell you. I rang up just now, and they told me
she'd telephoned him at the Coq Hardi. She—'

'She telephoned him?' The words flashed. 'When?'

'Thirty to forty minutes ago.'

'*Sacré dieu.*' I heard his breath go out. 'Where was she speaking from?
Did the fools think to ask?'

'Yes, indeed, m'sieur. They had heard the scandal from Jules, you
understand, and—'

'*Where was she speaking from?*'

'The Cent Fleurs, in Évian. They said—'

'Half-an-hour ago?'

'Or three-quarters. No more.'

'Then the Englishman can't have heard anything. He must be still
away with the party. She's not with him yet.'

He turned away abruptly and Bernard with him. Their voices faded
but I heard him say roughly: 'Get over to Évian immediately with that
car. I'm going myself. We have to find them, and quickly. Do you hear
me? Find them.'

Bernard said something that sounded surly and defensive, and I heard
Raoul curse him again. Then the voices faded round the corner of the
house. Seconds later the Cadillac's engine started, and her lights swept
their circle out of the driveway. The dog was barking once more. Madame
Vuathoux must have come out of her cottage at the sound of the second
car, for I heard Bernard speak to her, and she answered him in that

high, overpitched voice: 'He said he'd be here at twelve. Twelve at the
latest.'

Then Bernard, too, was gone. I lifted my head from the cold plinth
and slid an arm round Philippe. I waited for a moment.

Philippe said, with excitement colouring the thin whisper: 'He's coming
at twelve. Did you hear?'

'Yes. I don't suppose it's far off nine now. Only three more hours to
wait, *mon gars*. And they've gone chasing off to Évian.'

'He came down the terrace steps. He must have left a window open.
Shall we go in?'

I hesitated, then said dully: 'No. Only three more hours. Let's play it
quite safe and go back and lock ourselves in the boat-house.'

The boat-house looked, if possible, rather more dismal than before.
Philippe vanished round the back of it and after a minute reappeared
with a key which he displayed with a rather wan air of triumph.

'Good for you,' I said. 'Lead the way, *mon lapin*.'

He went cautiously up the steep outside stair to the loft over the boats.
The treads were slippery with moss and none too safe. He bent over the
door, and I heard the key grate round in the lock. The door yawned,
creaking a little, on a black interior from which came the chill breath of
dust and desertion.

'Refuge,' I said, with a spurious cheerfulness that probably didn't
deceive Philippe at all, and switched on the torch with caution.

The loft, thank heaven, was dry. But that was its only attraction. It
was a cheerless little black box of a place, a dusty junk-hole crowded
with the abandoned playthings of forgotten summers. I found later that
one of the concrete piers of the harbour had a flat platform in its shelter
which in happier days made a small private lido. Here in the loft had
been carelessly thrust some of the trappings that in July's sunshine were
so amusingly gay; striped canvas chairs, a huge folded umbrella of scarlet
and dusty orange, various grubby objects which looked as if, well beaten
and then inflated, they might be air-cushions, a comical duck, a sausage-
like horse with indigo spots. . . . Seen by torchlight in the chilly April
dark, with a vigil ahead of us and fear at our elbow, they looked
indescribably dreary and grotesque.

There was a small square window low down in the shoreward wall.
I propped a canvas chair across it to conceal the torchlight from a possible
prowler, then turned to lock the door.

Philippe said dolefully behind me. 'What are we going to do till twelve
o'clock?'

'Failing Peggitty and chess,' I said cheerfully, 'sleep. I really don't see
why you shouldn't. You must be worn out, and there's nothing now to
worry you and keep you awake.'

'No,' he said a little doubtfully, then his voice lightened. 'I shall sleep
in the boat.'

'Little cabbage, the boat isn't there. Besides, how wet. Now up here,' I said falsely, gesturing with the torch towards the dreary pile, 'it's much nicer. Perhaps we can find—'

'Here it is.' And Philippe had darted past me and was pulling out from under three croquet mallets, a half-deflated beach ball and a broken oar, a flat yellowish affair that looked like a cyclist's mackintosh.

'What in the wide world—?' I said.

'The boat.'

'Oh. Oh, I see. Is it a rubber dinghy? I've never seen one.'

He nodded and spread his unappetising treasure out on the unoccupied half of the floor. 'You blow it up. Here's the tube. You blow into that and the sides come up and it's a boat. I want to sleep in it.'

I was too thankful that he had found something to occupy him to object to this harmless whim.

'Why not?' I said. 'It's a good solid damp-proof groundsheet anyway. And after all, who minds a little dust?'

'It's not a ground-sheet. It's a *boat*.' He was already rootling purposefully behind some dirty canvas in a corner.

'*Ça se voit*,' I said untruthfully, eyeing it.

'You blow it *up*,' explained Philippe patiently, emerging with an unwonted spot of colour in his face, from between an oil-drum and the unspeakable spotted horse.

'Darling, if you think either of us has got enough blow left in them—'

'With *this*.' He was struggling with some heavy-seeming object. I took it from him.

'What is it?'

'A pump. It's *easy*. I'll *show* you.' He was already down on the floor beside the dismal yellow mass, fitting the nozzle of the pump to the mouth of the tube. I hadn't the heart to dissuade him. Besides. . . . I had been uneasily aware for some minutes now of the bitter little draught that crept under the door and meandered along the boards, cutting at my ankles. Philippe was busy with the footpump, which seemed remarkably easy to work. If the blessed boat really would inflate. . . .

It would. Presently Philippe lifted a face flushed with pride and effort and liberally festooned with cobwebs, from a business-like rubber dinghy whose fat sausage-like sides would certainly stem any wandering draughts. I praised him lavishly, managed to parry offers to blow up the horse, the duck, and the beach-ball as well ('just to *show* you'), and finally got us both disposed in our draught-proof but decidedly cramped bed, curled up for warmth together in our coats and preparing to sit out the last three hours or so of our ordeal.

The ghastly minutes crawled by. The night was still, held in its pall of mist. I could hear the occasional soft drip of moisture from the boughs that hung over us, and once some stray current of air must have stirred the trees, for the budded twigs pawed at the roof. Below in the boat-house the hollow slap and suck of water told of darkness and emptiness and a world of nothing. .... Compared with this burial in the outer dark last night's lodging had had a snug homely quality that I found myself remembering – Bernard or no Bernard – with longing.

And it was cold. Philippe seemed warm enough, curled in a ball with his back tucked into the curve of my body and my arms over him; at any rate, he slept almost straight away. But as the minutes halted by I could feel the deadly insidious cold creeping through me, bone by bone. It struck first at my exposed back, then, slowly, slithered through my whole body, as if the blood were literally running cold through the veins and arteries that held me in a chilled and stiffening network. Cramped as I was, I dared not move for fear of waking the child. He had had, I judged, just about as much as he could take. Let him sleep out the chilly minutes before the final rescue.

So I lay and watched the darkness beyond my canvas barrier for a glimpse of light from the villa, and tried not to think, not to think about anything at all.

It was the beach-ball that put an end to the beastly vigil. Disturbed from its winter's rest and moved, I suppose, by some erratic draught, it finally left its place on a pile of boxes and rolled, squashily elliptical in its half-deflated state, off its perch and down onto the floor. It fell on me out of nowhere with a silent, soggy bounce, and jerked me with a yelp out of my stiff, half-dozing vigil. I sat up furiously. Philippe's voice said, sounding scared: 'What was that?'

I reached clumsily for the torch. 'The beach-ball, confound it. I'm sorry, Philippe. Don't be frightened. Let's have a look at the time. .... Quarter to twelve.' I looked at him. 'Are you cold?'

He nodded.

I said: 'Let's get out of here, shall we? There's no light up at the villa yet, so I vote we try that terrace window. Only a few minutes more now. ...'

The mist was thicker now. Our little torch-beam beat white against it. It lay heavy as a cloudbank among the trees, but over the lawn near the house it showed only a pale haze that thinned and shifted in the moving torchlight.

The lamp still glowed over the front door. Its circle of light seemed to have shrunk as the trees crowded and loomed closer in the mist. No other light showed.

We slipped quietly across the lawn and up the terrace steps. The long window stood ajar, and we went in.

The salon was a big room, and in the light of a cautious torch it looked even bigger. The little glow caught the ghostly shapes of shrouded furniture, the gleam of a mirror, the sudden glitter of the chandelier that moved with a spectral tinkle in the draught from the window. The

meagre light seemed only to thicken the shadows and make the room
retreat further into dusk. It smelt of disuse, melancholy, dry-as-dust.

We hesitated just inside the window.

I whispered: 'We'll go to your Uncle Hippolyte's room. That'll have
been prepared, surely? There'll be a fire or a stove. And is there a
telephone in it?'

He nodded and led the way quickly across the salon. If he was scared
he didn't show it. He moved almost numbly, as if in a bad dream. He
pushed open a massive door that gave onto the hall and slipped through
it without a look to right or left into the shadowed corners. I followed.

The hall was a high dim square where I could just make out a graceful
branching staircase. Tiles echoed our quick footsteps hollowly. No other
sound. We fled upstairs. Philippe turned left along a wide gallery and
finally stopped before a door.

'It's Uncle Hippolyte's study,' he whispered, and put a hand to the
knob.

The room, sure enough, was warm. Like pins to a magnet we flew
across the carpet to the big stove and hugged it as closely as we could
with our chilled bodies. I said, sending the torchlight raking round the
room: 'Where does that door lead?'

'There's another salon. Bigger. It's never used now.'

I went across and pushed the door open. The torchlight once more
probed its way over the ghosts of furniture. Like the room downstairs,
this was still shrouded in its winter covers. It smelt musty, and the silk-
panelled walls, as I put up a gentle finger, felt dusty and brittle, like a
dead moth's wing. From the empty darkness above came the now familiar
phantom tinkling of a chandelier.

I crossed the carpet softly and paused by a shrouded shape that seemed
to be a sofa. I lifted the dust-cover and felt underneath it . . . damask
cushions fraying a little, silk that caught on the skin and set the teeth on
edge. 'Philippe,' I called softly.

He appeared beside me like a smaller, frailer ghost. He was shivering
a little. I said very matter-of-factly: 'I don't suppose it'll be needed, but
every fighter has to have a possible line of retreat worked out. If for any
reason we still want to hide, I'd say this is as good a place as any. Under
the dust-cover. It makes a tent, see? And you'd be pretty snug underneath
and quite invisible.'

He saw. He nodded without speaking. I cast him a look as I covered
the sofa again and followed him back into the study. I pulled the salon
door almost, but not quite, shut behind me.

I glanced at my wrist. Five minutes to twelve. One of the windows
looked out over the drive. No sign of a car. I turned to Hippolyte's
desk and picked up the telephone.

CHAPTER NINETEEN

So, uncle, there you are.

A man's voice said: 'Coq Hardi.'

At least it was not the same unpleasant and suspicious voice, but there was no harm in trying to disarm it further. It was five minutes to twelve, but just in case. . . .

I said quickly, eagerly; 'Guillaume? Is that you, *chéri?* It's Clothilde.'

He said blankly: 'Clothilde?'

'Yes, yes. From Annecy. You haven't forgotten? You told me to—'

The voice was amused. 'Mademoiselle, a moment. Who is it you want?'

'I – isn't that Guillaume? Oh *mon dieu*, how silly of me!' I gave a nervous giggle. 'I am sorry, monsieur. Perhaps – if he isn't in bed? – if you will have the goodness to fetch him—'

He was patience itself. 'But of course. With the greatest of pleasure. But Guillaume who, Mademoiselle Clothilde? Guillaume Rouvier?'

'No, no. I told you. Monsieur Blake, the Englishman. Is he there? He did tell me—'

'Yes, he's here. Content yourself, Mademoiselle Clothilde. He's not gone to bed. I'll fetch him.' I heard him laugh as he moved away from the telephone. No doubt William's stock would soar at the Coq Hardi. . . .

Philippe had moved up close to me. In the faint glow that the front door light cast up through the uncurtained window his face looked small and pale, the eyes enormous. I winked and made a face at him and he smiled.

William said in my ear, sounding bewildered and suspicious: 'Blake here. Who is that, please?'

'I'm sorry if I've embarrassed you,' I said, 'but I had to get you somehow, and that seemed the best way. Linda Martin.'

'Oh, it's *you*. The barman said it was a *petite amie.* I couldn't think – what's been going on? Where are you? Are you all right? And the boy—'

'For heaven's sake! Can anyone hear you, William?'

'What? Oh yes, I suppose they can. But I don't think they know English.'

'Never mind, don't risk it. I daren't call you for long because it mayn't be safe, but I . . . I need help, and I thought—'

He said quietly: 'Of course. I heard the local version of what's happened, and I've been hop – expecting you'd get into touch with me. I – I've been terribly worried – I mean, you being on your own, and all that. What is it? What can I do?'

I said gratefully: 'Oh, William ... Listen, I can't explain now, it would take too long. Don't worry any more; we're safe, both of us, and I think the whole thing will be over in a few minutes, but ... I'd be awfully grateful if you'd come along. There's no danger now, but there'll be ... scenes, and I don't somehow feel like facing them alone. I know it's a lot to ask of someone you hardly know, and it's a shocking time of night, but I wondered—'

'Tell me where you are,' said William simply, 'and I'll come. I've got the jeep. *Is* it the Cent Fleurs?'

'No, no. So they told you I'd rung up before?'

'Yes. I've just got back from Évian.'

'Oh, William, no!'

'Well,' he said reasonably, 'I thought you were there. I didn't know anything about this business till we got in tonight, you know. I was up at the hut till late last night, working, but I was due today to go with a couple of men over to the south plantations and we had to make an early start, so I slept at the pub. We were out all day and got back lateish, and then I was told you'd rung up from the Cent Fleurs, and of course I heard all the stories that were going round. I rang up the Cent Fleurs and they didn't remember you, so I skated down to Évian in the jeep—'

'Did you see Raoul de Valmy there?'

'Don't know him from Adam,' said William simply. 'Is he looking for you, too?'

'Yes.'

'Oh. I thought you might have – I mean, someone said—' he stopped, floundering a little.

I said: 'Whichever of the stories you heard, it isn't true. We're on our own.'

'Oh. Ah. Yes. Well,' said William cheerfully, 'tell me where you are now and I'll be straight over.'

'We're in Thonon, at the Villa Mireille. That's Hippolyte de Valmy's place; he's the brother—'

'I know. Have you seen him?'

'He's not back yet. Expected any minute. We're waiting for him. I – I'll explain when I see you why we didn't go straight to the police. Just for the time being, will you not say anything? Just – come?'

'Sure. I'm half-way there already. Repeat the name of the place, please.'

'The Villa Mireille. Anyone'll tell you. It's on the lakeside. Take the lower road. M.I.R.E.I.L.L.E. Got it?'

'Yes, thank you ... sherry.'

'What? Oh, I see. Is the barman listening?'

'Yes.'

'Then you'll have to say goodbye nicely, I'm afraid.'

'I don't know how.'

'Say "*à bientôt, chérie*".'

'Ah biang toe sherry,' said William grimly, and then laughed. 'I'm glad you're in such good spirits, anyway,' he added.

'Yes,' I said drearily. 'See you soon. And thank you, William. Thank you a lot. It's nice not to be . . . quite on one's own.'

'Think nothing of it,' said William, and rang off.

The handset was hardly back in its cradle when the car came down the road. We stood together, just back from the dark window, and watched the lights. It slowed and changed gear for the gate. Its lights swung round in the mist and slid across the study ceiling.

Philippe's hand slid into mine, and gripped. My own was shaking.

He said inadequately: 'Here he is.'

'Yes. Oh, Philippe.'

He said wonderingly: 'You have been afraid too, all the time?'

'Yes. Terribly.'

'I didn't know.'

'I'm glad of that.'

The car had stopped. Lights were cut, then the engine. Feet crunched on the gravel and the car door slammed. Steps, quick and assured, mounted to the front door. We heard the rattle of the handle. Then the sounds weren't outside the house any longer, but inside; the slight sound of the big door opening, a step on the tiled floor. . . .

He had come. It was over.

I said shakily: '*Dieu soit béni*,' and made for the study door.

I hadn't even considered what I was going to say to Hippolyte. It was possible that in some fashion he had already been greeted with the news. It was also possible that he had never even heard of me. I didn't care. He was here. I could hand over.

I flew along the carpeted gallery and down the lovely curve of the stairs.

The hall lights were not on. The front door was ajar, and the lamp that hung outside it over the steps cast a long panel of gold across the tiles. Outside I saw the car gleaming in the mist. The newcomer stood just inside the door, one hand raised as if in the act of switching on the lights. He was silhouetted against the lamplit haze beyond, a tall, powerfully-built man, standing stock-still, as a man does when he is listening.

On the thick carpet my feet made little more noise than a ghost's. I reached the centre stair and hesitated, one hand on the balustrade. I started slowly down the last flight towards him.

Then he saw me, and raised his head.

'So you are here,' he said.

That was all, but it stopped me as if he had shot me. I stood clutching the banister till I thought the wood would crack. For one crazy moment I wanted to turn and run, but I couldn't move.

I said, in an unrecognisable voice that broke on the word: 'Raoul?'

'*Lui-même.*' There was a click as the lights came on – a great chandelier that poured and flashed light from a thousand glittering crystals. They struck at my eyes and I flinched and put up a hand, then dropped it and looked at him across the empty hall. I had forgotten all about Philippe, about Hippolyte, about William Blake even now tearing down from Soubirous; I could see nothing but the man who stood there with his hand on the light-switch, looking up at me. There was nothing except the thing that lay between us.

He dropped his hand, and shut the door behind him. He was quite white, and his eyes were hard as stones. There were lines in his face I hadn't seen before. He looked very like Léon de Valmy.

He said: 'He's here? Philippe?' His voice was very even and quiet, but I thought I could hear the blaze of anger licking through it that he didn't trouble to suppress.

The question was answered by Philippe himself. He had followed me as far as the gallery, and there had stopped, prompted by a better instinct than my own. At his cousin's question he must have moved, for the stir in the shadows above him made Raoul lift his head sharply. I followed his look just in time to see Philippe, a small silent wraith, melt back into the darkness of the gallery.

Then Raoul moved, and fast. He took the hall in four strides and was coming upstairs two at a time. His leap out of immobility had been so sudden that I reacted without reason, a blind thing in a panic. I don't remember moving, but as I let go the banister I fled – was swept – up the stairway in front of him, only to check desperately on the landing and whirl to face him.

I shrieked: '*Run, Philippe!*' and put up frantic, futile hands to break the tempest.

They never touched him. He stopped dead. His arms dropped to his sides. I moved slowly back till I came up against the curve of the banister-rail and leaned there. I don't think I could have stood unsupported. He wasn't looking after Philippe. He was looking at me. I turned my head away.

Behind me, along the gallery, I heard the study door shut, very softly. Raoul heard it too. He lifted his head. Then he looked back at me.

'I see,' he said.

So did I. I had seen even while shock reacting on weariness had driven me stupidly and headlong from him up the stairs. And now I saw the look that came down over his face, bleak bitter pride shutting down over anger, and I knew that I had turned my world back to cinders, sunk my lovely ship with my own stupid, wicked hands. I couldn't speak, but I began to cry – not desperately or tragically, but silently and without hope, the tears spilling anyhow down my cheeks, and my face ugly with crying.

He didn't move. He said, very evenly: 'When I reached the Château Valmy this morning and my father told me that you had gone, he seemed to think you would have come to me for help. I told him no, you thought I was in Paris till Thursday, but I'd left my apartment there on Tuesday evening, and you couldn't know where I was. It was only later that I found you hadn't tried to get in touch with me there at all.' His voice was quite expressionless. 'There was only one reason I could think of why you hadn't telephoned me. When I . . . put this to my father he denied that any harm had come to you. I didn't believe him.'

He paused. I couldn't look at him. I put up a hand to wipe away the tears that streaked my face. But they kept falling.

'I told him then that I intended to make you my wife, and that if anything happened to you, or to the boy and through him to you, I would kill him – my father – with my own hands.'

I looked at him then. 'Raoul. . . .' But my voice died away. I couldn't speak.

He said slowly, answering my look: 'Yes. I believe I did mean it,' and added one word, one knell of a word, 'then.'

We had neither of us heard the other car. When the hall door swung open to admit two people – a man and a woman – we both jumped and turned. The man was a stranger to me; the woman was Héloïse de Valmy. They neither of them saw us above them on the landing, because at that moment Madame Vuathoux, who must this time have seen the lights of the car, came bustling into the hall from the back regions, vociferous with welcome.

'Monsieur – but you are welcome! I was so afraid that, with this mist – oh!' She stopped and her hands went up as if in horror. '*Tiens*, Madame – she is ill? What is the matter? Of course, of course! What horror! Has there still been no word?'

I hadn't noticed till she mentioned it, but Héloïse de Valmy was indeed clinging to Hippolyte's arm as if she needed its support. In the merciless light from the chandelier her face looked ghastly, grey and haggard like the face of an old woman. The concierge surged forward with cries of commiseration.

The little boy – nothing was heard yet, no? And of course Madame was distracted. *La pauvre* . . . Madame must come upstairs . . . there was a stove lit . . . a drink . . . some bouillon, perhaps?

Hippolyte de Valmy interrupted her. 'Monsieur Raoul is here?'

'Not yet, monsieur. He came this evening, and then left for Évian. He said he would be back at midnight to see you. It is after—'

'His car's outside.'

Raoul moved at that, almost idly. He said: 'Good evening, *mon oncle*.'

Madame Vuathoux gaped up at him, at last stricken dumb. Hippolyte turned, eyebrows raised. Héloïse said: 'Raoul!' just as I had done, and with no less horror in her voice. New lines etched themselves in her face and she swayed on her feet, so that Hippolyte tightened his grip on her arm. Then she saw me shrinking behind Raoul against the banister and she cried my name, almost on a shriek: 'Miss Martin!'

Madame Vuathoux found her voice again at that. She echoed the cry. '*La voilà!* There she is! In this very house! Monsieur Raoul—'

Hippolyte said curtly: 'That will do. Leave us, please.'

There was silence until the door had shut behind her. Then he turned again to look up at us. He surveyed me without expression, then he gave a formal little nod and looked at Raoul. 'You found them?'

'Yes, I found them.'

'Philippe?'

'He's here.'

Héloïse said hoarsely: 'Safe?'

Raoul's voice was very dry. 'Yes, Héloïse. Safe. He was with Miss Martin.'

Her eyes fell before his and she gave a little moaning sigh. Hippolyte said: 'I think we had better talk this thing out quietly. Come up to the study. Héloïse, can you manage the stairs, my dear?'

No-one looked at me, or spoke. I was a shade, a ghost, a dead leaf dropped by the storm into some corner. My story was over. Nothing would happen to me now. I would not even be called upon to explain to Hippolyte. I was safe, and I wished I was dead.

Héloïse and Hippolyte were coming slowly up the stairs. Raoul turned past me as if I didn't exist and began to mount the flight to the gallery. I went after him quietly. I had stopped crying, but my face still stung with tears, and I felt tired, so tired. I found I was pulling myself up by the banisters as if I were an old woman.

Raoul had opened the study door and switched on the light. He was waiting. I didn't look at him. I passed him with my head bent, and went straight across the study to the door that gave onto the salon.

I pushed it open.

I said wearily: 'Philippe? It's all right, Philippe, you can come out.' I hesitated, conscious that Raoul, too, had crossed the room and was standing just behind me. Then I said: 'You're quite safe now. Your Uncle Hippolyte's here.'

For some reason – no reason at all – the others had followed us into the salon, ignoring the comfort of the study stove.

Hippolyte had taken the cover from the sofa, and now sat there, with Philippe in the crook of his arm. On the other side of the empty grate Héloïse sat huddled in a small chair of golden brocade. Someone had twitched the dust-sheet off that and it lay in a bundle at her feet.

With its light on, the salon seemed more ghostly than ever. The light of the big chandelier dripped icily from its hundred glittering prisms. It fell coldly on the white shrouds that covered the furniture, and struck back from the pale marble of the fireplace where Raoul stood, one elbow on the mantelpiece, as I had seen him stand in the library at Valmy.

I sat as far away from them as possible. At the end of the long room was a piano, a concert-sized grand encased in green baize; to this I retreated in silence, and sat down on the long piano-bench with my back to the instrument. My hands clutched at the edge of the bench. I felt numb and unutterably weary. There was talking to be done – well, let them do it, the Valmys, and get it over and let me go. It was no longer anything to do with me. I raised my head and looked at them down the length of that beautiful dead room. They might have been a million miles away.

Hippolyte was talking to Philippe in an undertone. In him, too, the Valmy likeness was strong; he was a younger, gentler edition of Léon de Valmy – Lucifer before the fall. He looked kind, and his voice as he talked softly to Philippe sounded pleasant. But for all the gentleness, and the marks of anxiety and fatigue, I thought I could see in him the same hard force as in the other men – cooler, perhaps, and slower, but in the circumstances none the worse for that. My *deus ex machina* would be capable enough, thank God.

He looked up at Raoul and said in his quiet voice: 'As you may have guessed, Héloïse drove into Geneva to meet my plane. She has told me a rather . . . odd story.'

Raoul was selecting a cigarette. He said without raising his eyes. 'You'd better tell me what it was. I've heard several versions of this odd story lately, and I confess I'm a little confused. I'd like to know which one Héloïse is trying to sell now.'

She made a little sound, and Hippolyte's lips tightened. 'My dear Raoul—'

'Look,' said Raoul, 'this thing has gone a long way beyond politeness or the conventions of – filial duty. We'll get on a lot better if we simply tell the truth.' His eyes rested indifferently on Héloïse. 'You know, you may as well cut your losses, Héloïse. You must know my father was pretty frank with me this morning. I suppose he may intend to deny it all now, but I confess I can't see where that'll get him – or you. I don't know what he sent you down to Geneva to say, but the thing's over, Héloïse. You can abandon your – attitudes. There are no witnesses here that matter, and you'll certainly need my Uncle Hippolyte to help you if the hell of a scandal is to be avoided. Why not give it up and come clean?'

She made no reply, but sat there in a boneless huddle, not looking at him.

He watched her for a moment without expression. Then his shoulders lifted a fraction and he turned back to Hippolyte. 'Well,' he said, 'since it appears that Héloïse isn't playing, you'd better let me start.'

Hippolyte's face, as he glanced from one to the other looked suddenly very tired. 'Very well,' he said. 'Go ahead. You rang me up in Athens on Monday night to ask me to come home as you were anxious about Philippe. You spoke of accidents, and insisted that Philippe might be in

some danger. You also said something not very clear about Philippe's
governess. Héloïse, too, spoke of her tonight – also not very clearly. I
take it that this is the young woman in question, and that there have
been recent and alarming developments which Héloïse has been attempting to explain to me. I must confess to some confusion. I am also tired.
I hope you will be very brief and very lucid.'

Raoul said: 'You can forget Philippe's governess.' (That was me –
'Philippe's governess.' He hadn't even glanced at me. He was a million
miles away.) He went on: 'She never was in it, except incidentally. The
story begins and ends with my father. That was why I said this thing
had gone beyond convention. Because your starting-point, *mon oncle*, is
this: your brother – my father – with the help or at any rate the
connivance of his wife – has been trying for some time past to murder
Philippe.'

I heard Héloïse give a faint sound like a moan, and I saw the child
turn his head to look at her from the shelter of Hippolyte's arm. I said
in a hard little voice I didn't recognise as my own: 'Philippe is only nine
years old. Also he has just been through a considerable ordeal and is very
tired and probably hungry. I suggest that you allow me to take him
downstairs to some reliable person in the kitchen.'

They all jumped as if one of the shrouded chairs had spoken. Then
Hippolyte said: 'Certainly he should go downstairs. But I should like
you to remain here, if you will. Ring the bell, please, Raoul.'

Raoul glanced at me, a look I couldn't read, and obeyed.

We waited in silence, and presently the door opened. It wasn't Madame
Vuathoux who stood there, but an elderly manservant with a pleasant
face.

'Gaston,' said Hippolyte, 'will you please take Master Philippe downstairs and see he gets something to eat? Have Madame Vuathoux or
Jeanne get a room ready for him ... the little dressing-room off my
own, I think. Philippe, go with Gaston now. He'll look after you.'

Philippe had jumped up. He was smiling. The grey-haired servant
returned the smile. 'Come along,' he said, and put out a hand. Philippe
ran to him without a backward look. The door shut behind them.

Hippolyte turned back to Raoul. I could see, I'm not sure how, the
rigid control he was exerting over face and hands. His voice was not
quite steady, but it was as pleasant and gentle as ever. He said: 'Well,
Raoul, you'd better go on with your story. And I advise you to be sure
of your facts. You ... he's my brother, remember.'

'And my father,' said Raoul harshly. He knocked the ash off his
cigarette into the empty fireplace with an abrupt movement. 'As for my
facts, I haven't a great many, but you can have them. I only really came
into the story myself' – here his eyes lifted and met mine; they were like
slate – 'this morning.'

He paused for a moment. Then he began to talk.

He said: 'I don't have to tell you the background to the story; that my father, if Philippe had never been born, would have succeeded to Valmy, where he has lived all his life and which he loves with what (particularly since his accident) is an obsessive love. When his elder brother didn't marry he assumed that Valmy would be some day his, and he never hesitated to divert the income from his own estate, Bellevigne, into Valmy. I have run Bellevigne for him since I was nineteen, and I know just how steadily, during those early years, the place was milked of everything that might have made it prosperous. My father and I have fought over it time and again ... after all, it is my heritage as well, and I wasn't as sure as he that Étienne wouldn't get himself a son one day.'

Hippolyte said: 'I know. Léon would never listen.'

'Well,' said Raoul, 'Étienne did marry, and got Philippe. I don't intend to distress you with my father's reactions to that fact; mercifully he had the sense to keep them from Étienne ... possibly so that Étienne would let him go on living at Valmy. But the immediate result was that Bellevigne's income was put back where it belonged, and I had the job of trying to build up what had been steadily ruined for years.' Something like a smile touched the hard mouth. 'I may say I enjoyed the fight ... But last year, Étienne was killed.'

He looked down at Hippolyte. 'And immediately Valmy started to take the money out of Bellevigne again.'

The older man made a little movement. 'As soon as that?'

Raoul smiled again. It wasn't a nice smile. 'I'm glad you're so quick in the uptake. Yes. He must have decided then and there that something had to be done about Philippe. There were six years before the child inherited. The chance would come.'

Hippolyte said, hard and sharp: 'Be sure of your facts.'

'I am. It'll save time and heart-searching if you know here and now that my father has admitted his intention of murdering Philippe.'

A pause. Hippolyte said: 'Very well. I'll accept that. To whom did he admit this?'

Raoul's mouth twisted. 'To me. Content yourself, *mon oncle*, it's still only a family affair.'

'I – see.' Hippolyte stirred in his chair. 'And so I went off to Greece and handed Philippe over.'

'Yes. Somewhat naturally I hadn't tumbled to the significance of what had happened over Bellevigne. One doesn't,' said Raoul evenly, 'readily assume one's father is a murderer. I was merely puzzled and furious – so furious at being thrown back to the foot of the cliff I'd been climbing that I didn't stop to think out the whys and wherefores. I just spent all my energy on one blazing row after another. When I went up to Valmy at the beginning of April I thought I'd find out how Philippe was getting on there. I don't pretend for a moment that I thought there was anything wrong; I told you, one doesn't think in that sort of way of one's own family and the people one knows. But – anyway, I went up to Valmy to "sound" things, as it were. And things seemed all right. I'd heard

Philippe had a new governess, and I wondered—' Here his glance crossed mine momentarily and he paused. He added: 'Valmy was never a house for children, but this time it seemed all right. Then, next day, there was an accident that might have been fatal.'

He went on, in that cold even voice, to tell Hippolyte about the shooting in the woods, while Hippolyte exclaimed, and Héloïse stirred in her chair and watched the floor. She made no sound, but I saw that the fragile gold silk of the chair-arm had ripped under her nails. Raoul was watching her now. There was no expression whatever on his face.

'Even then,' he said, 'I didn't suspect what was really going on. Why should I? I blamed myself bitterly for that later, but I tell you, one doesn't think that way.' He dropped his cigarette-stub onto the hearth, and turned away to crush it out with his heel. He said a little wearily, as if to himself: 'Perhaps I did suspect; I don't know. I think I may have fought against suspecting.' He looked at his uncle. 'Can you understand that?'

'Yes,' said Hippolyte heavily. 'Yes.'

'I thought you would,' said Raoul. 'A damnable exercise, isn't it?' He was already lighting another cigarette.

Hippolyte said: 'But you suspected enough to make you go back pretty soon? And again at Easter?'

Raoul's attention was riveted on lighting the cigarette. 'It wasn't altogether suspicion that drove me back. Nor did I see anything to rouse me into active worry until the Easter Ball – the night I rang you up. But that night two things happened, Miss Martin told me that there'd been another accident – a coping of the west balcony was suddenly dangerously loose overnight, and only the fact that she noticed it and shoved something across the broken bit saved Philippe from a particularly nasty end on some spiked railings underneath.'

This had the effect of making Hippolyte turn and look at me. The expression in his face made me wonder, for the first time, what Héloïse had been telling him about me on the way from Geneva. From the look on his face it had been nothing to my credit. As Raoul went on to speak of the midnight feast with Philippe I saw the expression deepen – as if Hippolyte were being given a very different picture of me from the one he had got from Héloïse. 'And there was something so odd about Héloïse that night,' said Raoul. 'She seemed frightened, if that were possible, and then there was Miss Martin's talk of nightmares. ... But it was really the second accident that shook me. I went straight to the telephone in the small hours, and eventually got hold of you. It seemed the best thing to do, for us to tackle him together and find out what was going on and force him to ... see reason. I thought you might also hand the child over to my care if you had to leave again. I've no authority at all where Philippe's concerned, and for obvious reasons I preferred not to enlist official help at that point. Hence the S.O.S. to you.' He gave his uncle that fleeting, joyless smile. 'In any case, as far as the police were concerned, my father still held the winning card, which was that nothing had happened. He had, and has, committed no provable crime. But I thought that if you cabled you were coming home it would put paid to whatever he might be planning. If even then,' he finished very wearily, 'he really was planning anything.'

There was another of those silences. Hippolyte looked across at Héloïse. Raoul went on: 'It seems odd, now, that I should ever have been so slow to believe him capable of murder. I should have known. . . but there it is. I tell you it's not the sort of thing one readily accepts. It certainly wasn't the sort of thing I felt I could tax him with – and I doubt if that would have done much good anyway. If the interview I had with him this morning is anything to go by—' He broke off, and then gave a little shrug. 'Well, I had sent for you. I'd done what I could to silence my own uneasiness, and I knew Miss Martin was dependable. I told myself I was being a fool. I didn't want to leave Valmy next morning, but I got an early call from Paris, and had to go. It was to do with some money I'd been trying to raise on Bellevigne, and the chap I wanted was passing through Paris that afternoon. I had to catch him. So I went. I'd intended to stay in Paris till Wednesday afternoon, then to come over here and meet you when you got in from Athens, and go up to Valmy with you on Thursday. But once I got away from Valmy I found I was worrying more and more; it was as if, once I got out of his range, I could see him more clearly. Anyway, I think I saw for the first time that this impossible thing might be true, and there might really be danger – immediate danger. I did ring up Valmy in the afternoon and got my – got him. I made some excuse – I forget now what it was – and asked a few questions. He told me about your cable, and I'll swear he even sounded pleased at the prospect of seeing you. Everything seemed to be normal, and when I rang off I was convinced yet again that the whole thing was a bag of moonshine.' He drew on his cigarette and the smoke came out like a sigh. 'But – well, by the evening I couldn't stand it any longer. I rang up the airport and was lucky. There was a seat on a night flight. I'd left my car at Geneva, and I drove straight up to Valmy. I got there early this morning, to find that Miss Martin and Philippe had disappeared.'

He flicked ash from his cigarette. 'Just as a matter of interest, Héloïse, how did you account for that to my uncle when you met his plane?'

Still she didn't speak. She had turned away her head so that her cheek was pressed against the wing of the chair. She looked as if she were hardly listening. Her face was grey and dead. Only her fingers moved, shredding, shredding the gold silk under them.

Hippolyte began, looking so uncomfortable that I had a rough idea what the story had involved: 'It wasn't very coherent. I did gather—'

I said: 'It doesn't matter. I'll tell you what did happen. I found out on Tuesday night what Monsieur de Valmy was planning. Bernard got drunk at the dance and told Berthe, one of the maids. She told me. I had to get Philippe away. I – I didn't know where to go. We hid, and then came here to wait for you. That's all.'

I could feel Raoul's eyes on me. Between us stretched the empty ghost-filled spaces of that alien room. I said no more. If I never told him the rest, I couldn't do it here.

Hippolyte turned back to Raoul. 'Go on. You got back and found them gone. I assume that at this point you did tackle Léon?'

'I did.' Something new had come into the even voice, something that made me stir on my bench and look away. I didn't want to watch his face, though heaven knew, there was nothing there to read. He said: 'There were various – theories as to why the two had run away, but to me it only meant one thing; that Miss Martin had had some proof that Philippe was in danger, and had removed him from harm's way. I blamed myself bitterly for not having let my own suspicions take root. So I attacked my father.'

'Yes?'

Raoul said: 'It wasn't a pleasant interview. I'll cut it very short. He started by denying everything, and – you know him – he denied it so well that he made me look a fool. But the fact remained that Lin – Miss Martin had bolted. I kept at him and eventually he changed his ground. He suggested then that as far as Philippe's fate was concerned Miss Martin mightn't be entirely disinterested.' He flicked ash off his cigarette, not looking at me.

Hippolyte said: 'What do you mean?'

Raoul didn't answer. I said briefly: 'Monsieur de Valmy had reason to believe that I was in love with Monsieur Raoul.'

I saw Hippolyte raise his brows. In his own way he was as quick as Léon. He said: 'So you might have had an interest in disposing of Philippe? A very long-sighted young lady. And what was your reaction to this – suggestion, Raoul?'

'It was so absurd that I wasn't even angry. I laughed. I then told him that he had got the facts right only so far. The interest was on both sides and it was serious – in other words I intended to make Miss Martin my wife, and if any harm came to her or to Philippe he'd have me to answer to as well as the police.'

Hippolyte flashed a look from Raoul to me, and back again, then his eyes dropped to his hands. There was a long pause. Something in the way the interview was going must have prompted him to ignore the information in Raoul's last speech, for all he said was: 'And then?'

Raoul said, in a very hard, dry voice: 'I'll cut this short. It's pretty unspeakable. He changed his ground again, and suggested cutting me in. Yes. Quite. He pointed out the advantages that I and my wife would get from Philippe's death. He – didn't seem to understand that I might be able to resist them. And he was convinced I would be able to persuade her too, as my wife, to acquiesce in his plans. Between us we could pacify you when you arrived, see you back to Greece, and then take our time over Philippe. We could cook up some story of Linda's having run away to me – everyone was saying that anyway – and get through the bigger scandal by making it a purely sex affair. He then suggested that I find Linda and allow people to believe she had run off to meet me.'

'Yes?'

It was, perhaps, the most horrible thing about the interview that neither Léon's son nor his brother showed surprise. Distress, yes; horror, perhaps; but not surprise. Not even at a wickedness that couldn't conceive of disinterested good.

Raoul said: 'I didn't say much. I – couldn't, or I'd have laid hands on him. I merely said that neither of us would ever connive at harming Philippe, and we had better stop talking nonsense and find the pair of them, or there might be a scandal he'd find it hard to get out of. I thought that Linda might have tried to get in touch with me in Paris, and rang up there and then in front of him, but there hadn't been a call. I left a message with the concierge in case Linda rang up later, but I'd been so sure she'd ring me up that I thought my father had lied about their escape from Valmy, and that something had happened to them, so – oh well, never mind that now. I knew I was wrong almost straight away, because Bernard – you know his man? – came in. Apparently he'd been out looking for them. He got a bit of a surprise to see me, and I lost no time in making it very plain that it was in his best interest to find Linda and Philippe quickly. I thought they might have gone for help to the Englishman who works over on Dieudonné – I'd discovered that Linda knew him, and was glad she had at least one friend in the district. I rang up the Coq Hardi at Soubirous, where he sleeps sometimes, but he'd already gone out, and he wasn't expected back till dinner-time. I told Bernard to go up to the hut where the Englishman keeps his things, but he said he'd been already and they weren't there. He told me where else he'd been. I sent him out again with instructions to report to me, and some sort of plan of search, the best I could devise with the little I knew... well, none of this matters now. He knew very well he'd better play in with me, and play safe. When he'd gone I told my father again, quite plainly, that if any harm came to those two even if it looked like the most obvious accident in the world, I would kill him. Then I went out with the car.' His voice was suddenly flat and very tired. 'That's all.'

I sat still, looking down at my feet. That was all. Only sixteen more hours spent combing the valleys, ringing up Paris, making carefully casual inquiries (I found later) of the Consulate, the hospitals, the police. ...

One or two things became plain: first, that Léon de Valmy had had no idea that the convenient rumour of my engagement was, in fact, true: second, that Raoul knew nothing of the final hurried poison-plot, and was unaware that Léon de Valmy had ever had any positive intention of harming me; Bernard, coming in on the interview, must have realised immediately that his master's guns were spiked; somehow, Léon de

Valmy had tipped him the wink that the hunt must be called off, and from then on the man had, perforce, co-operated with Raoul in his search. Whether or not I had been right about our danger last night in the woods, we had been safe since early this morning . . . since Raoul had come home. Because of Raoul, the dogs had been called off. We had been quite safe all day, because of Raoul. I sat very still, watching my feet.

The silence was drawing out. I heard the lustres quiver like the music of a ghostly spinet. I looked down the length of the lovely dead room towards the group by the fireplace.

Both men were watching the woman in the chair.

She was sitting very still, but her stillness wasn't even a travesty of the poise I knew. The delicate flower had wilted to pulp. She lay back in her chair as if she had no bones, and her hands were motionless at last on the shredded silk of the chair-arms. Her pale eyes were fully open now; they moved from Raoul's face to Hippolyte's, painfully. There was no need for her to speak. It was all written in her face, even, I thought, a dreadful kind of relief that now it had all been said.

The door opened and Philippe came in. He was carrying a steaming cup of bouillon very carefully between his hands. He brought it to me and held it out. 'This is for you. You had an ordeal too.'

I said: 'Oh, Philippe. . . .' and then my voice broke shamefully. But he didn't appear to notice this. He was looking at Héloïse, silent and slack in her chair. He said doubtfully: 'Aunt Héloïse, would you like some too?'

That did it. She began to cry, on a thin dry note that was quite horrible to listen to.

I leaned forward, kissed Philippe's cheek, and said quickly: 'Thank you, *p'tit*, but Aunt Héloïse isn't well. Better just run along. Good night now. Sleep well.'

He gave one wondering look, and went obediently.

Héloïse didn't put her hands to her face. She lay back in her chair and sobbed tearlessly on that dreadful, jerky note. Hippolyte de Valmy, now as grey-faced as she, watched her helplessly, touching a handkerchief to his lips with an unsteady hand. Then, after a few moments' hesitation, he moved to a chair beside her, took one of her unresisting hands and began, rather feebly, to pat it. He was murmuring something through her sobs, but the uncertain comfort had no effect.

Raoul stood apart from the two of them, silent, and with the shutters still down over his face. He didn't look at me.

I believe I opened my lips to say something to him, but at that moment Héloïse began at last to speak. Her voice was terrible, thin and shaken and breathless.

She said: 'It's true, yes, it's true what he says, Hippolyte. He made Léon tell him . . . there was a scene . . . dreadful things . . . he had no right. . . .' She turned suddenly towards him and her free hand closed over his, clutching at him. 'But I'm glad you know, Hippolyte. You'll get us out of it, won't you? You'll see there's nothing said? You won't take it further? It's not a police matter! You heard what Raoul told you – it's only in the family! That's it, it's only in the family! Bernard won't dare speak, and Raoul can't say anthing; how can he? Léon's his father, isn't he? Surely that means something?' She shook his arm, leaning nearer, her voice hurrying and breathless: 'You can't let it all come out, you know that! You can't do that to Léon, you and Raoul! There's no harm done . . . the boy's safe and the girl's all right. Don't look like that, Raoul. You know you can put it right between you if you want to! The Martin girl's in love with you; she'll keep her mouth shut, and—'

'Héloïse, please!' This, sharply, from Hippolyte. He had freed himself and moved slightly away from her. He was looking at her almost as if he'd never seen her before. 'You say it's all true? You did know of it? You?'

She had sunk back in her chair. She swallowed another of those sharp convulsive sobs and moved her head to and fro against the chair-back. 'Yes, yes, yes. Everything he told you. I'll admit everything, if only you'll help.' Something in his tone and look must have got through to her here, for her voice changed: 'I – I'm not wicked, Hippolyte, you know that. I didn't want to hurt Philippe, but – well, it was for Léon's sake. I did it for Léon.' She met his stony look and added sharply: 'You know as well as I do that Valmy should be his. Surely he has the best right to it? It's his home. You know that. Why, you've said so yourself! And he's not like other men. You know that, too; you should realise he's not like other people. He should have had Valmy. He should! He'd had enough to bear without being turned out of his home!'

Her brother-in-law moved uncomfortably. 'I cannot see that Léon would be grateful for this special pleading, Héloïse. And at the moment it's beside the point. What we're discussing is a good deal more serious. Attempted murder. Of a child.'

'Yes, yes, I know. It was wrong. It was wrong. I admit that. But it didn't happen, did it? There's no harm done, Raoul said that himself! *That* doesn't have to be taken any further! Oh, you'll have to talk to Léon about it, I can see that, but you'll see he stays on at Valmy, won't you? There's no reason why he shouldn't! People are talking, but it'll soon be forgotten if you stand by us and don't bring things into the open. And I know you won't! You know how Léon feels! You'll see he keeps Valmy, won't you? He should have talked to you before – I wanted him to, instead of trying to arrange things this way. I was sure you'd see his point of view, and you do, don't you? I'm sure there's some way things can be fixed! You can come to some arrangement, can't you? Can't you?'

He started to say something, then bit it back, saying instead, calmly enough: 'It's no use discussing it any more here. This is getting us nowhere. Héloïse—'

'Only promise me you won't take it to the police!'

'I can't promise anything. All I can say is that we'll try and compromise between what's right and what's best.'

She seemed not to be listening. Something had broken in her, and now she couldn't stop. She was out of control; her hands and lips were shaking. The pleading voice poured on, admitting with every desperate syllable what must never – even in her mind – have been in words before.

'It'll kill him to go to Bellevigne! And all our money's in Valmy! We looked after Valmy, you can't say that we didn't! Every penny went into the estate! You can't say he was a bad trustee!'

'No,' said Hippolyte.

She didn't even notice the irony. The dreadful single-mindedness she showed was ample explanation of how Léon had persuaded her to help him against what better instincts she must have possessed. She swept on: 'It was for Léon's sake! Why shouldn't he get something – just this thing – out of life? Valmy was his! You know it was! Étienne had no right to do this to him, no right at all! That child should never have been born!'

Raoul said suddenly, as if the words were shaken out of him: 'God pity you, Héloïse, you've begun to think like him.'

This stopped her. She turned her head quickly towards him. I couldn't see her eyes, but her hands clenched themselves on the arms of the chair. Her voice went low and breathless: 'You,' she said, 'you. You always hated him, didn't you?'

He didn't answer. He had taken out another cigarette and was making rather a business of lighting it.

'He's your father,' she said. 'Doesn't that make any difference? Can you stand by and see him ruined? Doesn't it mean anything to you that he's your father?'

Raoul didn't speak. For all the expression on his face he mightn't even have been listening. But I saw his brows twitch together as the match burned him.

Suddenly her hands hammered the chair-arms. She shouted at him: 'Damn you, are you condemning your own father?' Even the vestiges of common self-control had gone; her voice rose to the edge of hysteria. '*You* to stand there and call him a murderer! *You* who have everything, everything, and he a cripple with nothing to call his own but that ruined relic of a place in the south! You condemn him, you talk fine and large of right and wrong and murder and police, and who's to say what you'd have done if you'd been in his place? How do you know what *you'd* have been if you'd smashed your car up one fine day on the zigzag and cracked your spine and two lives along with it? Yes, two! Would she have looked at you then? Ah yes, it only takes one look from you now, doesn't it, but would she? Would she have stayed with you and loved you the way I've loved him all these years and done for you what I've done for him – and glad to, mind that, *glad to*? Oh, no, not you!' She stopped and drew a long, shivering breath. 'Oh, God, he's a better man with half a body than you'll ever be, Raoul de Valmy! You don't know ... oh dear God, how can you know ...?'

Then she put her hands to her face and began to weep.

Quite suddenly, the scene was unbearable. And I didn't belong in this anywhere any more. I stood up abruptly.

It was at this moment that the door went back with a slam against the silk-panelled wall, and William Blake came in with a rush like an angry bear.

Eighth Coach

CHAPTER TWENTY

Death has done all death can.

BROWNING: *After*

'Who the devil are you?' said Raoul.

Since he said it in French, William Blake took not the slightest notice. He stopped just inside the door, breathing hard. He looked, as ever, enormous; very English, with the untidy blond hair, and very safe. He looked down the room at me, ignoring everyone else.

'Linda? What's going on here? Are you all right?'

I said, between a laugh and a sob: 'Oh, William!' and ran to him down the length of the room, bouillon and all.

He didn't exactly fold me in his arms, but he did catch me, and, with some presence of mind, hold me away from him, so that the bouillon didn't spill all over his ancient jacket, but only on the priceless Savonnerie carpet.

'Here, steady on,' he said. 'Are you sure you're all right?'

'Yes, quite all right.'

Hippolyte had turned and risen in surprise at the interruption, but Héloïse was past caring for the presence of a stranger. She was weeping freely now, the sobs tearing at the atmosphere of the beautiful over-civilised room. Hippolyte paused, looking helplessly from the newcomer back to her. Raoul said, without moving: 'It's the Englishman. I told you about him.'

I saw William wince from the sound of sobbing, but he stood his ground, his jaw jutting dangerously. 'Did they hurt you?'

'No, oh no. It's not them, William, it's all finished, honestly.'

'Anything I can do?'

'Not a thing, except ... take me out of here.'

Behind me I heard Hippolyte say with a kind of controlled desperation: 'Héloïse, please. My-dear, you must try and pull yourself together. This is doing no good, no good at all. You'll make yourself ill. Héloïse!'

William said: 'Okay. We'll get you out of this. And fast.' He put an arm round my shoulders, and turned me towards the door. 'Let's go.'

I saw Hippolyte take half a step towards us. 'Miss Martin—'

But here Héloïse sobbed something incoherently and caught at his sleeve, a desperate little gesture that broke something inside me.

I said: 'I can't stand this, William. Wait.'

I thrust the half-empty pot of bouillon into his hands, and went back to Madame de Valmy. Hippolyte stood aside and I went down on my knees in front of the little gold chair. I was kneeling at Raoul's feet. I didn't look up at him, and he never moved. Her hands were still over her face. The sobs were less violent now. I took her wrists gently and pulled them down and held her hands.

I said: 'Madame, don't. Don't cry any more. We can talk this thing over quietly when you're feeling better. It won't do any good to make yourself ill.' Then to Hippolyte: 'Can't you see she's beside herself? There's no point in letting this go on. She doesn't know what she's saying. She must be got to bed ... Madame, there'll be some way to arrange everything, you'll see. Don't cry any more. Please.'

The sobbing caught in her throat. She looked at me with those pale, drowned eyes. The beauty had all gone. The delicately rouged cheeks sagged slack and grey, and her mouth was loose and blurred with crying. I said: 'There've been enough tears over this, madame. Don't distress yourself any more. Nothing's going to happen to you. It's all over now. Here, take my handkerchief ... Why, you're cold! I don't know why you're sitting here when there's a stove in the study; and you haven't been well lately, have you? Shall we go in there, and perhaps we can get Gaston to bring some coffee? Can you get up? Let me help you ...'

She got to her feet slowly, stiffly, and I led her across to the study door. She came obediently, as if she were sleep-walking. The others followed. Nobody spoke. She was weeping still, but quietly, into my handkerchief. I put her into a chair near the stove, and knelt again beside her on the rug.

I don't know quite what else I said to her, but the sobbing stopped, and presently she lay back in the chair quietly, and looked at me. She looked exhausted, dazed almost. She said abruptly, in a flat, sleep-walker's tone: 'I liked you, Miss Martin. I liked you from the first.'

I said soothingly: 'I know you did. It's all right. Don't worry now. We'll get you home, and—'

'You wouldn't really have been blamed for the accidents, you know. We didn't mean to blame you. We never meant at the beginning to make you responsible.'

'No.'

'Léon liked you too. He said you were gallant. That was the word. He said: "She's a gallant little devil and it'd be a pity if we had to bring her down." '

Raoul said very quietly, from behind me: 'And just what did he mean by that?'

Madame de Valmy took no notice. She seemed oblivious of anyone but herself and me. She held my hands and looked at me with those pale dazed eyes, and talked in that tired monotone that she didn't seem to be able to stop. 'He said that just a day or so ago. Of course, after the second accident on the balcony we were going to have to dismiss you, you know. He said you were too wide-awake and now you'd begin to suspect us if anything else happened. We were pleased when you gave us the excuse to send you away. You thought I was angry, didn't you?'

'Yes, madame.'

'Then we got the cable. We had to do something in a hurry. There were the rumours in the village about you and Raoul, and about your being dismissed, but Léon said it might come in useful later anyway, if the village had been linking your names.'

Behind me I heard Raoul take in his breath as if to speak. I said quickly, to divert her: 'Yes, madame, I know. Albertine started to talk, didn't she? Well, don't think about that now.'

'She never knew what we were trying to do,' said Madame de Valmy. 'But she didn't like you. She never liked you. It was she who told me about the muddle you'd made with the prescriptions that time. She only told me to show you up. She thought I'd think you careless and silly. It was only spite. But that's what made us think of the poison, you see. That was the only reason we thought of using those pills. We weren't trying to fix it on you, Miss Martin. It was to have looked like an accident. It was in the glucose, you understand. The poison was in the glucose that you used every night to make his chocolate with.'

'Madame—'

'Luckily there wasn't much left in the tin, so we soaked the blue colour off the tablets and powdered them up and made a strong mixture. Too strong perhaps. It may have been bitter. He didn't take it, did he?'

'No. But that wasn't why.' I turned desperately to Hippolyte, who was standing silently over by the desk. 'May I ring and ask for some coffee, Monsieur de Valmy? I really think—'

'We hadn't time to think of anything better,' said Héloïse. 'It was to look like an accident. If he had taken it and died they might not have thought of murder. Those anti-histamine pills are blue. The doctor might have thought he'd taken them as sweets. Children do. We meant to empty out the rest of the glucose and leave one or two pills by his bed. There were some in a jar on your mantelpiece, where he might have found them and eaten them. You mightn't have been blamed. They would have thought you'd forgotten to give them to Mrs. Seddon. Léon said you might not be blamed even then.'

Behind me Raoul said: 'Just what are you talking about, Héloïse?'

She looked up at him with that dead, sleep-walker's look. She seemed to have forgotten her outburst. She answered him mechanically: 'The poison. It wasn't a very good plan, but we had to be sure and it was all we could think of that might look like an accident. But he didn't take it. It's all right. She said so. I was just explaining to her that we didn't mean her any harm. I like her. I always did.'

I said quickly: 'Madame, you're upset. You don't know what you're saying. Now we're going to have some coffee, and we'll see you home.'

Across me Raoul said: 'And if Miss Martin *had* been blamed? If murder *had* been suspected? You had made it common knowledge, hadn't you, that she and I – that there might be an interested reason to get rid of Philippe?'

She said nothing. She stared up at him.

'Was that what my father meant when he said that the gossip "might have been useful later"?'

I heard Hippolyte begin to say something, but Raoul cut across it. 'On Tuesday night, Héloïse . . . who was it found Philippe had gone?'

'Léon did. He stayed awake. We were going to empty out the rest of the glucose and—'

'So you said. He found Philippe gone. And then?'

'He thought he must have felt ill and gone for Miss Martin. But there was no light there. She'd gone too.'

'And when he couldn't find them, what then?'

'He sent Bernard out to look for them.'

Raoul said: 'With what instructions?'

She said nothing. Under the hammering of his questions she seemed to have come partly to life again. Her eyes were conscious now, blinking nervously up at him.

'With what instructions, Héloïse?'

Still she didn't answer. She didn't need to. Her features seemed to flatten out and melt like candlegrease. Hippolyte said, harshly: 'That's enough, Raoul.'

'Yes,' said Raoul. 'I think it is.'

He walked out of the room and shut the door behind him.

For a moment nobody moved. Then Héloïse came to her feet, thrusting me aside so that I fell over on the rug.

She stood there with her hands slack at her sides. She said, almost conversationally: 'Léon. He's gone to kill Léon.' Then she crumpled beside me on the rug in a dead faint.

I left her there. I remember leaping to my feet, to stand like a fool on the rug beside her, gaping at the shut door. I remember Hippolyte starting forward and shouting: '*Raoul! Come back, you fool!*' He was answered by the slam of the front door. He turned with a sound like a groan and jumped for the telephone. I remember that, as he touched it, it began to ring.

Before it had threshed once I was out on the gallery and racing for the head of the stairs. There were steps behind me and William's hand caught at my arm. 'Linda, Linda. Where are you going? Keep out of this. You can't do a thing.'

Outside, an engine roared to violent life. A door slammed. The Cadillac gained the road, paused, whined up through her gears, and snarled away into silence.

I shook off William's hand and fled down the curving stairs. Across the hall, and struggling with the heavy door . . . William reached over my shoulder and yanked it open. The lamp over the door showed the dark circular drive walled in with misty trees . . . a big black car . . . a battered jeep . . . the scored grooves in the gravel where the Cadillac's tyres had torn their circle. The smell of her exhaust hung in the air.

I ran out.

William caught at my arm. 'For God's sake, Linda—'

'We've got to stop him! We've got to stop him!'

'But—'

'Didn't you understand? He's gone to kill Léon. He said he would, and they'll have to kill him for it. Don't you understand?'

He still held me. 'But what can you do? You've been mixed up in enough of their dirty game as it is. Let me take you away. There's nothing you can do. You said yourself it was finished. What's it to you if they murder each other?'

'Oh, dear God, what's it to me? William' – I was clinging to him now – 'William, you have to help. I – I can't drive a car. Please, William, please, *please—*'

The night, the misty trees, the solitary lamp in its yellow nimbus, were all part of the roaring horror that enveloped me, that was only my own blood pounding in my ears . . .

He said quietly: 'Very well, let's go,' and his hand closed over mine for a moment. As the world steadied around me I saw that he was opening the door of the jeep.

I said shakily: 'No. The other.' I ran to the big Chevrolet and pulled the door open. It was the Valmy car. Héloïse must have had it down to the airport to meet Hippolyte.

William followed me. His voice was doubtful. 'Ought we to?'

'It's faster. The key's in. Oh, William, hurry!'

'Okay.'

And then we were away. Our wheels whined round in the same circle, skidding on the gravel. Our lights raked the trees, the lodge, the willows fronded with weeping mist . . . We took the gate cautiously, gained the road, and swung right.

Along the narrow, fog-dimmed road with its soaring dark trees; a sharp turn left, a steep little climb between echoing walls; right again, then a series of dizzy, whipping turns through the steep streets that climbed up to the town. Now we had reached the upper level, and were clear of the mist. We swept along a wide curved boulevard where lamps flickered by among the pollard-willows . . . A sharp swing right, and we scudded across the empty market-place where cobbles gleamed damply and a few flattened cabbage-leaves lay in a gutter like a drift of giant leaves. William had got the feel of the car now. We swirled right-handed into a badly-lit avenue and gathered speed. The lopped chestnuts flicked past us one by one, faster, faster, faster. . . .

We were out of the little town. Our headlights leaped out ahead of us, and the engine's note rose powerfully, and held steady.

Ahead of us the road forked. A signboard flashed up in the white light and tore towards us.

We took the left for Valmy.

William was, I thought, as good a driver as Raoul, but Raoul had not only a start, but a faster car which was, moreover, the one he was accustomed to drive. But after a while I began to hope that even these advantages might not help him too much, for very soon after leaving Thonon we met the mist again. Not the tree-haunting grey mist that had risen from the lake to moat the Villa Mireille, but little clouds and clots of white brume, breathed up from the river to lie in all the hollows of a road that was never far from the water. Each time the car's nose dipped a dazzling cumulus of white struck back the light at us, swept over us, blinded, engulfed us, then even as the engine slowed and hesitated we roared up out of cloud again into the calm black air. At first the experience was unnerving; the moment of blindness was like a great white hand thrust against your face, so that you flinched backwards against the upholstery, and were conscious of your eyes' catlike dilation. But with each succeeding dive into the cloud the car's hesitation became less apparent and after a while I realised that William was losing very little speed. He seemed to know unerringly just how the road lifted and curved, where the mist would lie for fifty yards and where for five, and he sliced through the fog-patches with the confidence of the man who – literally – knows his road blindfold. He must have driven up and down it scores of times in the course of his job; it was even probable that he knew it better than Raoul, who for some time had lived most of his year between Bellevigne and Paris. We might catch him yet. . . .

So at any rate I told myself, huddled down in the seat beside William and staring with eyes that winced through the marching clouds of mist to catch a glimpse of a vanishing tail-light round some curve ahead.

William said: 'What was all that about, Linda?'

'What d'you mean? Oh – I keep forgetting you don't speak French.' I gave a shaky little laugh. 'I'm sorry, William. I – I'm not thinking very clearly tonight. I haven't even said thank you for coming. I've just rushed you into my affairs and used you like this. I – I'm terribly grateful. I really am.'

'Think nothing of it. But you'd better put me in the picture, hadn't you?'

So I told him the story from the beginning – not very clearly, I'm afraid, and with halts and pauses due to weariness and the fear that clawed at me, while the car roared on up that wicked valley-road and the night went by us smoothly as a dream. The dark road fell away, streamed, poured away behind us; the thin grey trees reeled past us into nothingness; the mist-clouds marched, fled, broke and streamed away from us in mackerel flakes like rack in the wind.

The red tail-light struck at my eyes like a dagger.

I said hoarsely: 'There. William. Look, there.'

He didn't answer, but I knew he'd seen it. Then it vanished and a moment later the blinding white swamped us again. Out into a patch of clear darkness, and then another cloud was on us, but this time thin, so that our yellow-dimmed lights made rainbows in it that wisped away along our wings, and we were through.

The car gathered speed up a steady straight rise. And the fleeing red light was there, not three hundred yards ahead.

He didn't seem to be travelling so very fast. We were gaining, gaining rapidly. Two hundred yards, a hundred and fifty . . . the gap dwindled. We were coming up fast. Too fast.

'It's only a lorry,' said William, and lifted his foot.

We ran up close behind it and asked to be by.

It was one of those appalling monsters so common in France, far too high and wide for any road, and far too fast for their size. And it became obvious very soon that this one had no intention of allowing us the road. Ignoring the flickering of our lights it roared along, rocking a little on the bends, but never yielding an inch of the crown of the road.

I don't know how long we were behind it. It seemed a year. I sat with my nails driving holes into the palms of my hands, and my teeth savaging my lip while I stared with hatred at the dirty back-board of the lorry held in our lights. It was carrying gravel, which dripped through the cracks onto the road. Someone had chalked a face like a gremlin on the left-hand panel. To this day I can see the number-plate with the chip off the corner and read the number. 920-DE75 . . . I stared at it without consciously seeing it at all, and thought of the Cadillac roaring on ahead, of Raoul and Léon and the terrible little scene that, unbelievably, was so soon to be acted out in the Valmy library.

I said again: 'William . . .'

'If the Caddy passed him,' said William calmly, 'we can. Hold on.'

There wasn't even a trace of impatience in his voice. He drew out to the left, flickered his lights again, and waited. The lorry lumbered on. We were on an up-grade now, and the lorry was slowing. It held the road, and once again we drew patiently in behind it.

So we went in procession up the hill. A sob rose and burst in my throat and I put the back of my hand hard against my teeth in an effort for self-control.

The lorry slowed, slowed again, and checked as it was rammed into bottom gear. We crawled towards the head of the rise.

The trees that crowned the hill-top swelled into light that soared towards us. Lights were coming up the other side of the hill, and coming fast. Their grey aurora spread, splayed brighter, lifted into gold. The lorry topped the crest of the road, black against the approaching glare, and swung sharply over to its right to make way for the oncoming car.

Our own lights flashed once, and dimmed. Something hit me in the small of the back as the Chevrolet shot forward like a torpedo into the gap.

Lights met lights with a clash that could be felt. Then we whipped to the right almost under the lorry's front bumper. I heard the yell of a horn and something that might have been a shout, but we were through with a little to spare and dropping downhill with the rush of a lift.

'Oh, you honey,' said William affectionately to the car, and then sent me a grin. I had bitten the back of my hand but his breathing wasn't even ruffled. 'It's nice,' he said mildly, 'to have the horses. . . .'

The road lifted once more, to shake itself clear of mist. William's foot went down and those horses took hold. My eyes strained through the darkness ahead for that tell-tale light among the trees.

But no light showed till we rounded the curve where the road begins the long drop to the Valmy bridge, and saw the lurch and sway of lights that cut their way up the zigzag nearly half-a-mile ahead.

I must have made some small sound, for William gave me a glance and said: 'Don't fret, my dear. They'll talk it over, surely?' But he didn't sound convinced, and neither was I. We'd both seen Raoul's face. And the way those distant headlights now slashed their way up the zigzag was some indication that the mood still held.

I saw them vanish at the top under the château's bright windows. William accelerated, and we shot down the last hill, met a wall of mist bonnet-high, slowed, sank down to second for the turn onto the bridge – and then stopped short, with brakes squealing.

I said breathlessly: 'What is it?'

'Can two cars pass on that road?'

'The zigzag? No. But—'

He nodded towards it. I followed his gaze and said: 'Oh, dear Lord,' on a dreary little sob. A car had nosed its way down off the driveway and was taking the first hairpin with some caution. It got round, and came on its decorous way down . . .

'Where are you going?' asked William sharply.

I was fumbling with the door. 'There's a path straight up from the bridge through the wood . . . steps . . . I think I could—'

He reached across and his hand closed over mine. 'Don't be silly. You'd break your heart and I'd still be there before you. Sit still.'

'But William—'

'My dear girl, I know. But there's nothing else to do.' His voice was calm. 'Look, he's nearly down. Sit still.'

I was shaking uncontrollably. 'Of course. It – it doesn't matter to you, does it?'

His eyes were grave and gentle. 'And it does to you? It really does?'

I said nothing. The descending car swung round the last bend, and her lights sank towards the bridge. There was mist lying as it had lain that night.

William said gently: 'I'm sorry, Linda.'

The car was crossing the bridge, nosing through the mist. It paused, and moved out into the road with a lamentable crash of gears. William's hand shifted and the Chevrolet leaped for the gap and went over the bridge with the mist flying out from the headlamps like spray in the teeth of a destroyer.

For a fleeting second before the cliff cut it off from view I lifted my eyes and saw the Château Valmy, brightly lit against the night sky. That was what William meant; I knew it. The castle in the air, the Cinderella-dream – nonsense for a night. *Banquets abroad by torchlight, music, sports, nine coaches waiting!*

Not for you, Linda my girl. You get yourself back to Camden Town.

The Chevrolet lurched up and round the final curve, and skidded wildly as her wheels met the gravel of the drive. She came to a rocking halt just behind the parked Cadillac.

There was another car in the drive and a van of sorts, but I hardly noticed them. I had my door open before our wheels had shrieked to a stop, and was out and stumbling up the steps to the great door.

Seddon was in the hall. He started forward when he saw me and I heard him say: 'Oh, Miss Martin—' but I fled past him as if he didn't exist, and down the long corridor that led to the library.

The door was slightly ajar and a light showed. As I reached it my panic courage spilt out of me like wine from a smashed glass and I stopped dead with my hands actually on the panels ready to push.

Inside the room there was no sound.

I pushed the door open softly, took three steps into the room, and stopped short.

There were several men in the room, but I only saw two of them.

Raoul de Valmy was standing with his back to the door, staring down at his father.

For once Léon de Valmy was not in his wheel-chair. He had fallen forward and out of it onto the floor. His body lay clumsily, pulled a little crooked by whatever harness he wore under his clothes. His head was turned to one side, his cheek against the carpet. His face was smooth, wiped clean of every line and shadow; beauty and evil had emptied themselves from it together. Now there was nothing there at all.

From where I was you could hardly see the blackened hole in the temple.

I would have fallen where I stood but that William's arm came round me from behind and swept me up and out of the silent room.

Ninth Coach

CHAPTER TWENTY ONE

Look you, the stars shine still.

JOHN WEBSTER: *The Duchess of Malfi*

... Warmth, and the sound of liquid, and the smell of azaleas ... And someone was patting my hand. But there was no music, and the voice that said my name was not Florimond's. Nor was Raoul there waiting to sweep me out onto the terrace and under the moon ...

William said: 'Here, Linda, drink this.'

The liquid burned sourly on my tongue and made me gasp. I opened my eyes.

I was in the small salon, lying on the sofa before the fire. Someone had made this up recently. Tongues of pale flame licked round the new logs. I stared at them dazedly. I had never fainted before, and the memory of the roaring dizziness frightened me and I put an unsteady hand up to my eyes. The salon still swam round me, too bright and a little out of focus.

'Finish it,' urged William.

I obeyed him meekly. It was detestable stuff, whatever it was, but it ran into my body warm and potent, so that in a few moments more my eyes and fingers and even my brain were mine again. And my memory.

'How d'you feel now?' asked William.

I said drearily: 'Oh, fine. Just fine. I'm sorry, William. That wasn't a very useful thing to do.'

He took the glass from my hand and put it on the mantelpiece. Then he sat down on the sofa beside me. 'Nothing we've done tonight has been so terribly useful, has it?'

I found myself staring at him in a kind of daze. Of course. It was nothing to him. I said, dragging the words up from the depths: 'Have they ... taken him away yet?'

'Not yet.'

'William. I've got to ... see him. Just for a moment. I've got to.'

I heard stupefaction in his voice. 'But my dear Linda—'

'When will he go?'

'I've no idea, the police are still busy. The ambulance is waiting.'

I gave a little gasp and turned my head sharply. 'Ambulance? Is he hurt? What's happened?' I sat up and gripped his arm. The bright roaring mist was there again. Dimly through it I saw William's eyes, puzzled and a little shocked. Dimly I heard him say: 'But Linda. Didn't you realise? I thought you knew. He's dead.'

My grip must have been savaging his sleeve. His hand came up to cover mine, quietly. 'He shot himself,' said William, 'some time before Raoul and you and I got here.'

'Oh,' I said, in a silly high voice, 'Léon. Léon shot himself. The ambulance is for Léon.'

'Why – who else?'

I heard myself give a cracked breathless little laugh. 'Who indeed?' I said, and burst into tears.

It was hard luck on William. And for a shy British amateur, he was certainly doing very well. He produced some more of that filthy drink, and patted my hand some more too, and put a large comforting arm round me.

'I thought you'd grasped the situation,' he was saying. 'I thought it was just the shock of seeing, er, Monsewer Léon that made you faint . . . The butler chap was telling me all about it just now when he brought the drink for you. I thought you heard. I'd no idea you were right out.'

'I – I wasn't really. I heard you talking. But I didn't take it in. It was like voices in a dream . . . coming and going.'

The arm tightened momentarily. 'You poor kid. Better now?'

I nodded. 'Go on, tell me. What did Seddon say?'

'Is that his name? Thank God he's English! Well, he told me he'd gone in to look at the library fire soon after eleven, and found him dead on the floor, the way you saw him. Nobody heard the shot. He called the police and the doctor straight away, and then the Villa Mireille, but got no answer there.'

'That would be before Philippe and I got into the house.'

'Oh? They tried again later, twice. I suppose the first time was while you were telephoning me, and then they finally got Monsewer Hippolyte. That would be the call that came through as we left the house. Hippolyte's on his way up. He'll be here before long.'

'If he knows how to drive the jeep.'

'Oh, murder,' said William. 'I never thought of that.'

I said: 'Are you sure it was suicide?'

'Oh, quite. The gun was in his hand, and there's a letter.'

'A letter? Léon de Valmy left a letter?'

'Yes. The police have it. Seddon didn't read it, but from what the police asked him he pretty well gathered what it said. It admitted the first two attempts to murder Philippe, involving Bernard, but nobody else. He states categorically that neither Raoul or Madame de Valmy knew anything about them. He never mentions this last affair of the poison – I suppose that would almost certainly involve his wife. He simply says that Bernard must have let something out to you about the two earlier attempts, and you got in a panic and bolted with Philippe. I think that's about the lot. You've certainly nothing to worry about.'

'No.' I was silent for a moment. 'Well, I shan't volunteer anything else unless they ask me. I don't somehow want to pile anything more onto Madame de Valmy, whatever she did. *He's* dead, you see. She's got that to go on living with. Funny, one somehow imagines her snuffing quietly out now, the way the moon would if the sun vanished. Somehow it's like Léon to let her out, and me, and yet to turn the wretched Bernard in … though I suppose it was impossible to hide his part in it. And Bernard failed, after all.'

'That's not why,' said William. 'When Bernard found you both gone and Raoul on the trail he must have realised that Léon de Valmy's bolt was shot and that there'd never be a future and a fortune for him the way he'd been promised. He moved onto the winning side, probably with an eye to the future, and played in with Raoul all day, looking for you and Philippe. Then last night – three or four hours ago – he came and tried to retrieve that lost fortune by putting the black on Monsewer Léon.'

'Blackmail?'

'Yes. It's in the letter. He threatened to turn informer. If you ask me, that's what tipped Léon de Valmy's scales towards suicide in the end. I mean, there's no end to blackmail, is there?'

I said slowly: 'You're probably right. I was wondering what had made him kill himself instead of waiting to see what Raoul and Hippolyte would do. After all, it was still all in the family. But when one thinks about it … Even if Raoul and Hippolyte and I had agreed to hush the whole thing up for Philippe's sake and the sake of the family – what was there left for Léon de Valmy? Hippolyte would be able to put any sort of pressure on that he liked, and he might have insisted on Léon's leaving Valmy. Even if Léon was allowed to stay, Hippolyte would start sitting down tight on the money-bags, and presumably Raoul would be in a position to stop Léon milking Bellevigne any more. . . . And in any case Léon would have had to get out in five years' time. And we all – even Philippe – knew what he'd done and what he was. . . . And then, finally, the wretched tool Bernard started to blackmail him. Yes, one can see a desperate moment for Léon, and no future. Certainly he wasn't the kind of man to submit to blackmail; he'd literally die sooner, I'm sure of it. It only surprises me that he didn't kill Bernard first, but I suppose Bernard would be on guard against that, and he did have certain physical advantages. What did happen to Bernard anyway? *Did* Léon kill him?'

'No, he's disappeared. There'll be a hue and cry, but I suppose it's to be hoped that he gets away, and the rest of the story with him.'

I said: 'Yes. Poor little Berthe.'

'Who's that?'

'Oh, nobody. Just one of the nobodies who get hurt the most when wicked men start to carve life up to suit themselves. You know, William, I doubt if I was altogether right about why Léon de Valmy killed himself. . . . I imagine all those things would be there, part of it, in his mind, but it would be something else that tipped him over. I think I knew him rather well. He'd been beaten. He'd been shown up. And I don't think he could have taken that, whatever happened later. He was – I think the word's a megalomaniac. He had to see himself as larger than life . . . everything that happened was seen only in relation to him. . . . He sort of focused your attention on himself all the time, and he could do it, William. I believe he liked to think he could play with people just as he wanted to. He *couldn't* ever have taken second place to anyone. To shoot himself, making that magnanimous gesture with the letter . . . yes, that was Léon de Valmy all right.' I leaned back wearily. 'Well, whatever his reasons, it made the best end, didn't it? Oh, God, William, I'm so tired.'

He said anxiously: 'Are you all right? What about some more brandy?'

'No, thanks. It's all right. This is just the anticlimax hitting me.'

'D'you want to go now? Perhaps we could—'

'Go. Where to?'

He pushed his fingers through his hair. 'I – yes, I hadn't thought of that. They didn't exactly get the red carpets out at the Villa Mireille, did they? Though if you ask me they owe you a ruddy great vote of thanks, and I'll tell them so myself if nobody else does!'

'They know, for what it's worth,' I said.

'But you don't want to stay here, do you?'

'What else can I do? When Monsieur Hippolyte gets around to it, he'll see that I get my passage paid back to England.'

'You'll go home?'

'Yes.' I looked at him and gave a smile of a sort. 'You see, when you're in my position you can't afford to make the grand gesture, William. I can't just swep' out. I'm afraid I must wait here till the police have asked all their questions. I think I'll go along and see Berthe now, and then come back here and wait for them.'

'Hang on, here's someone coming,' said William. 'Yes, here they are.'

I must still have been in a semi-dazed condition, because, although I remember quite well exactly what the police inspector looked like, I can't recall our interview with any accuracy. I did gather that after Léon de Valmy's death the frightened servants had poured out the story of Philippe's and my disappearance and all the accompanying rumours, but that the suicide's letter, together with what Hippolyte de Valmy had said over the telephone and (finally) an interview with Raoul, had strangled stillborn any doubts about myself. This much I understood soon enough: the inspector's manner with me was gentle and even respectful, and I found myself answering his questions readily and without any anxiety other than the dreadful obsessional one – the fox under my cloak that kept my eyes on the open door all through the half-hour or so of question and answer, and made my heart jump and jerk every time anyone passed along the corridor.

The inspector left us eventually when Hippolyte arrived. I saw them pass the door together on the way to the library. Hippolyte was still pale and tired-looking, but very composed. It was easy to suppose that, once the shock was over, the news would prove a relief.

I wondered fleetingly about Héloïse, and then again, sharply, about Berthe. But as I got to my feet to go in search of her Seddon came in with coffee, and in response to my inquiries told me that the police had dealt with her very kindly, and had (when the interview was over) sent her in one of their cars down to her mother's house in the village. I supposed this was the car that had held us up at the zigzag. There was nothing more to be done for Berthe except to hope that Bernard could be forgotten, so I sat wearily down again while Seddon poured me some coffee. He lingered for a while, asking me about Philippe, to vanish at length in the direction of the hall when Hippolyte came into the room.

William got to his feet a little awkwardly. I put my coffee-cup down on the floor and made to follow suit, but Hippolyte said quickly: 'No, please,' and then, in English, to William: 'Don't go.'

I began to say: 'Monsieur de Valmy, I – we're awfully sorry—'

But he stopped me with a gesture, and coming over to the sofa he bent over me and took both my hands in his. Then, before I knew what he was about, he kissed them.

'That is for Philippe,' he said. 'We owe you a very great deal, it seems, Miss Martin, and I have come belatedly to thank you and to ask you to forgive me for my rather cavalier treatment of you at the Villa Mireille.'

I said rather feebly: 'You had other things on your mind, monsieur.' I wanted to tell him not to bother about me but to go back to his own worries and his own personal tragedy, but I couldn't, so I sat and let him thank me again with his grave courteous charm, and tried not to watch the door while he talked, or to think how like Raoul's his voice was.

I realised suddenly that he had left the past and was talking about the future.

'. . . He will stay with me at the Villa Mireille for the time being. Miss Martin – dare I hope that after your very terrible experience you will stay with him?'

I stared at him for some time, stupidly, before I realised what he was asking me. He must, in his own tragic preoccupation, have forgotten Raoul's confession concerning me. I said: 'I – I don't know. Just at the moment—'

'I quite see. I had no right to put it to you now. You look exhausted, child, and no wonder. Later, perhaps, you can think it over.'

There was a queer sound from the corridor, a kind of slow, heavy shuffling. Then I knew what it was, Léon, leaving the Château Valmy. I looked down at my hands.

Hippolyte was saying steadily: 'If under the circumstances you prefer not to spend the night here, there's a place for you as long as you choose to stay at the Villa Mireille.'

'Why, thank you. Yes, I – I would like that. Thank you very much.'

'Then if we can find someone to take you down—?'

He had glanced at William, who said immediately: 'Of course.' Then he stammered and added awkwardly: 'I say, sir, I'm terribly sorry about taking the car. We thought – that is, we were in a hurry. I really am awfully sorry.'

'It's nothing.' Hippolyte dismissed the theft with a gesture. 'I believe you thought you might prevent a tragedy – a worse one than what actually happened.' His eyes moved sombrely to the door. 'I'm sure you will understand me when I say that – this – was not altogether a tragedy.' Another glance at William, this time with the faintest glimmer of a smile underlying the sombre look. 'You'll find your own – extraordinary vehicle – outside. And now good night.'

He went. I picked up my coffee-cup absently, but the stuff was cold and skinning over. I set it down again. A log fell in with a soft crash of sparks. No movement now outside in the corridor. I looked at the clock. It had stopped. *The world-without-end hour. . . . Nor dare I chide the world-without-end hour, whilst I (my sovereign) watch the clock for you. . . .*

'Linda,' said William. He came and sat beside me on the sofa. He reached out and took both my cold hands in his. Safe, gentle hands; steady, sensible hands. 'Linda,' he said again, and cleared his throat.

I woke to the present as to a cold touch on the shoulder. I sat up straighter. I said: 'William, I want to thank you most awfully for what you've done. I don't know what I'd have done without you tonight, honestly I don't. I'd no business to call you in the way I did, but I was so terribly on my own, and you were my only friend.'

'It's a friend's privilege to be used,' said William. He loosed my hands. There was a pause. He said: 'If you are going to stay with Philippe, I might see you now and again, mightn't I?'

'I don't suppose I'll be staying.'

'No?'

'No.'

'I see.' He got to his feet and smiled down at me. 'Shall I run you down to the Villa Mireille now in the jeep?'

'No, thanks, William. I – think I'll wait.'

'Okay. I'll say good night, then. You'll look me up before you leave, won't you?'

'Of course. Good night. And – thanks a lot, William. Thank you for everything.'

I forgot him almost as soon as the front door shut behind him. Someone had come out of the library. I could hear Hippolyte's voice, and Raoul's, talking quietly. They were coming along the corridor together.

My heart was hurting me. I got up quickly and moved towards the door. Hippolyte was talking, saying something about Héloïse. I shrank against the wall to the side of the door so that they wouldn't see me as they passed.

'. . . A nursing-home,' said Hippolyte. 'I left her with Doctor Fauré. He'll look after her.' There was something more – something about an allowance, a pension, and 'somewhere away from Valmy, Paris or Cannes,' and finally the words, dimly heard as they moved away along the corridor: 'her heart,' and 'not very long, perhaps. . . .'

They had reached the hall. Hippolyte was saying good night. I went softly out into the corridor and hesitated there, waiting for Hippolyte to leave him. I was shaking with panic. Léon and Héloïse might have faded already into the past, poor ghosts with no more power to terrify, but I had a ghost of my own to lay.

Raoul's voice, now, asking a question. Seddon's answer, almost indistinguishable. It sounded like '*Gone.*' A sharp query from Raoul, and, clearly, from Seddon: 'Yes, sir. A few minutes ago.'

I heard Raoul say, grimly: 'I see. Thank you. Good night, Seddon.'

Then I realised what he had been asking. I forgot Hippolyte's presence, and Seddon's. I began to run down the corridor. I called: 'Raoul!'

My voice was drowned in the slam of the front door.

I had reached the hall when I heard the engine start. Seddon's voice said, surprised: 'Why, Miss Martin, I thought you'd gone with Mr. Blake!' I didn't answer. I flew across the hall, tore open the great door, and ran out into the darkness.

The Cadillac was already moving. As I reached the bottom of the steps she was wheeling away from the house. I called again, but he didn't hear – or at least the car moved, gathering speed. Futilely, I began to run.

I was still twenty yards behind it when it slid gently into the first curve of the zigzag, and out of sight.

If I had stopped to think I should never have done what I did. But I was past thinking. I only knew that I had something to say that must be said if I was ever to sleep again. And I wasn't the only one that had to be healed. I turned without hesitation and plunged into the path that short-circuited the zigzag.

This was a foot-way, no more, that dived steeply down the hillside towards the Valmy bridge. I had taken it with Philippe many a time. It was well-kept, and the steps, where they occurred, were wide and safe, but it could be slippery, and in the dark it could probably be suicide.

I didn't care. Some kind freak of chance had made me keep Philippe's

orch in my pocket, and now by its half-hearted light I went down that
tizzy little track as if all my ghosts hunted me at heel.

Off to the left the Cadillac's lights still bore away from me on the first
ong arm of the zigzag. He was driving slowly. The engine made very
ittle sound. I hurtled, careless of sprains and bruises, down through the
wood.

It couldn't be done, of course. He was still below me when he took the
irst bend and the headlights bore back to the north, making the shadows
of the trees where I ran reel and flicker so that they seemed to catch at
ny feet like a net.

The path twisted down like a snake. The whole wood marched and
shifted in his lights like trees in a nightmare. Just before he wheeled
away again I saw the next segment of my path doubling back ten feet
below me. I didn't wait to negotiate the corner with its steps and its
handrail. I slithered over, half on my back, to the lower level, and gained
seven precious seconds before the dark pounced again in the wake of the
retreating car.

The third arm of the zigzag was the longest. It took him away smoothly
o the left without much of a drop. . . . I would do it. At the next northern
bend I could be in the road before he got there.

I flung myself down a steep smooth drop, caught at a handrail to
steady myself, and then went three at a time down a straight flight of
steps. The rail had driven a splinter into my hand, but I hardly felt it.
A twig whipped my face, half-blinding me, but I just blinked and ran
on. Down the steps, round, along over a little gorge bridged with a
flagstone . . . and the great headlights had swung north again and the
shadows were once more madly wheeling back and away from me.

But I was below him now. I could do it. Only fifty yards away the
track ran right to the bend of the road, where a high bank held the
cambered corner.

The shadows blurred and wavered, caught at me like the ropes of a
great web. My breath was sobbing; my heart-beats hammered above the
sound of the oncoming car.

Here was the bank, head-high. Beyond it the road lay like a channel
of light in front of his headlamps. I had done it.

But even as I put my hands on the bank-top to pull myself over into
the road, I heard the engine's note change. He was gathering speed. Some
devil of impatience had jabbed at him and he let the Cadillac go for just
those few seconds – just those few seconds.

She went by below me with a sigh and a swirl of dust and I fell back
into the darkness of the wood.

If reason had spoken to me then I would have stayed where I was. But
reason could not be heard for the storm of my heartbeats and the silly
little prayer on my lips. '*Please, please, please,*' it was, and it spun in my
brain like a prayer-wheel to the exclusion of any kind of sense or thought.

I didn't stop. Two more sweeps of the zigzag, and the Valmy bridge and – he was away. I left the path and simply went down the shortest way between my bank and the next northerly hairpin. That it was a reasonably smooth slope carpeted with nothing worse than dog's-mercury and last year's beech leaves was my luck – and better than I deserved. I fetched up against the trunk of a beech near the banked-up road while the car was still only half-way down to it, but I made no attempt this time to climb the bank into the road.

My beech-tree was at the edge of a rocky little drop, and below me lay the bridge itself. The white mist that marked the river swirled up into silver as the Cadillac took the bend beside me and bore away again for the last steep bend to the Valmy bridge.

I went over the drop. The stone glowed queerly in the light that came off the mist. The rock was rough and steeply-piled, but it was solid enough, and easy to scramble on. I suppose I got scratches and knocks. I don't know. I do know that I slipped once and gripped at a holly-bush to save myself and even as I bit the cry off I heard the shriek of the Cadillac's brakes.

I found out later that something had run across the road. I like to think it was the same anonymous little creature that had been there the first time Raoul kissed me. At any rate it stopped the car for those few precious seconds. . . . They were enough.

I dropped into the road just as his lights swept round the last curve.

I ran onto the bridge. The mist swirled up waist-high. It was grey, it was white, it was blinding gold as the glare took it.

I shut my eyes and put both hands out and stayed exactly where I was.

Brakes and tyres shrieked to a stop. I opened my eyes. The mist was curling and frothing from the car's bonnet not three yards from me. Then the headlights went out and the grateful dark swept down. In the small glow of the car's sidelights the mist tossed like smoke. I took three faltering, trembling steps forward and put a hand on her wing. I leaned against it, fighting for breath. The little prayer-wheel still spun, and the prayer sounded the same: *'Please, please, please'*. . . . But it was different.

He got out of the car and walked forward. He was on the other side of the bonnet. In the uncertain, fog-distorted light he looked taller than ever.

I managed to say: 'I was . . . waiting. I've got to . . . see you.'

He said: 'They told me you'd gone.' He added unemotionally: 'You little fool, I might have killed you.'

My breathing was coming under control, but my legs still felt as if they weren't my own. I leaned heavily on the wing of the car. I said: 'I had to tell you I was sorry, Raoul. It's not exactly – adequate – to tell a man you're sorry you suspected him of murder . . . but I am. I'm sorry I even let it cross my mind. And that was all it did. I swear it.'

He had his driving-gloves in his hand and he was jerking them through and through his fingers. He didn't speak.

I went on miserably: 'I'm not trying to excuse myself. I know you'll not forgive me. It would have been bad enough without what – was between us, but as it is ... Raoul, I just want you to understand a little. Only I don't somehow know how to start explaining.'

'You don't have to. I understand.'

'I don't think you do. I was *told*, you see, told flatly that you were in it, along with your – with the others. Bernard had said so to Berthe. He told her that you had done the shooting in the wood. I imagine he realised, even when he'd gone so far, that he'd better not own to *that*. And he may have thought you *would* condone the murder once you saw the advantages of it. I didn't believe it, even when she told me flatly. I couldn't. But the rest was so obvious, once I knew, about ... them, I mean, and there was nothing to prove you weren't in it with them. Nothing except the – the way I felt about you.'

I paused, straining my eyes to see his expression. He seemed a very long way away.

I said: 'I don't expect you to believe it, Raoul, but I was fighting on your side. All the time. I've been through a very private special little hell since Tuesday night. You called it a "damnable exercise", remember? Everything conspired to accuse you, and I was half silly with unhappiness and – yes, and doubt, till I couldn't even trust my own senses any more. ... Oh, I won't drag you through it all now; you've had enough, and you want to be done with this and with me, but I – I had to tell you before you go. It was simply that I couldn't take the chance, Raoul! You do see that, don't you? Say you see that!'

He jerked the gloves in his fingers. His voice was quite flat, dull, almost. 'You were prepared to take chances – once.'

'Myself, yes. But this was Philippe. I had no right to take a chance on Philippe. I didn't dare. He was my charge – my duty.' The miserable words sounded priggish and unutterably absurd. 'I – was all he had. Beside *that*, it couldn't be allowed to matter.'

'What couldn't?'

'That you were all I had,' I said.

Another silence. He was standing very still now. Was it a trick of the mist or was he really a very long way away from me, a lonely figure in the queerly-lit darkness? It came to me suddenly that this was how I would always remember him, someone standing alone, apart from the others even of his own family. And, I think for the first time, I began to see him as he really was – not any more as a projection of my young romantic longings, not any more as Prince Charming, the handsome sophisticate, the tiger I thought I preferred. ... This was Raoul, who had been a quiet lonely little boy in a house that was 'not a house for children', an unhappy adolescent brought up in the shadow of a megalomaniac father, a young man fighting bitterly to save his small inheritance from ruin ... wild, perhaps, hard, perhaps, plunging off the beaten track more than once ... but always alone. Wrapped up in my loneliness and danger I hadn't even seen that his need was the same as my own. He and I had hoed the same row, and he for a more bitter harvest.

I said gently: 'Raoul, I'm sorry. I shouldn't have bothered you with this just now. I think you've had about all you can take. What can I say to you about your father, except that I'm sorry?'

He said: 'Do you really think I would have shot him?'

'No, Raoul.'

A pause. He said in a very queer voice: 'I believe you do understand.'

'I believe I do.' I swallowed. 'Even the last twenty-four hours – with the world gone mad and values shot to smithereens – I must have known, deep down, that you were you, and that was enough. Raoul, I want you to know it, then I'll go. I loved you all the time, without stopping, and I love you now.'

Still he hadn't moved. I turned back towards the château. I said: 'I'll leave you now. Good night.'

'Where are you going?'

'Someone'll take me to the Villa Mireille. Your Uncle Hippolyte asked me to go there. I – I don't want to stay at Valmy.'

'Get into the car. I'll take you down.' Then, as I hesitated: 'Go on, get in. Where did you think I was going?'

'I didn't think. Away.'

'I was going down to the Villa Mireille to look for you.'

I didn't speak; didn't move. My heart began to slam again in slow painful strokes.

'Linda.' Under the quiet voice was a note I knew.

'Yes?'

'Get in.'

I got in. The mist swirled and broke as the door slammed. Swirled again as he got in and slid into the seat beside me. It was dark in the car. He seemed enormous, and very near.

I was trembling. He didn't move to touch me. I cleared my throat and said the first thing that came into my head. 'Where *did* you get this car? Roulette?'

'Écarté. Linda, do you intend to stay at the Villa Mireille for a while with Philippe?'

'I don't know. I haven't thought things out yet. I'm awfully fond of him, but—'

Raoul said: 'He'll be lonely, even with Hippolyte. Shall we have him with us at Bellevigne?'

I said breathlessly: 'Raoul. Raoul. I didn't think—' I stopped. I put shaking hands up to my face.

'What is it, sweetheart?'

I said, very humbly, into my hands: 'You mean you'll still ... have me?'

I heard him take a quick breath. He didn't answer. He turned suddenly towards me and pulled me to him, not gently. What we said then is only for ourselves to remember. We talked for a long time.

Later, when we could admit between us the commonplace of laughter, he said, with the smile back in his voice: 'And you've still not made me own it, my lovely. Don't you think it's time I did?'

'What are you talking about? Own what?'

'That I love you, I love you, I love you.'

'Oh, *that*.'

'Yes, damn it, *that*.'

'I'll take a chance on it,' I said. And those were the last words I spoke for a very long time.

And presently the car edged forward through the mist and turned north off the Valmy bridge.

The
Ivy Tree

A north country maid up to London had stray'd
  Although with her nature it did not agree;
She wept, and she sighed, and she bitterly cried:
  'I wish once again in the North I could be!
Oh! the oak and the ash, and the bonny ivy tree,
  They flourish at home in the North Country.

'No doubt, did I please, I could marry with ease;
  Where maidens are fair many lovers will come:
But he whom I wed must be North Country bred,
  And carry me back to my North Country home.
Oh! the oak and the ash, and the bonny ivy tree,
  They flourish at home in my own country.'

Seventeenth Century Traditional.

CHAPTER ONE

Come you not from Newcastle?
Come you not there away?
Oh, met you not my true love?

Traditional.

I might have been alone in a painted landscape. The sky was still and blue, and the high cauliflower clouds over towards the south seemed to hang without movement. Against their curded bases the fells curved and folded, blue foothills of the Pennines giving way to the misty green of pasture, where, small in the distance as hedge-parsley, trees showed in the folded valleys, symbols, perhaps, of houses and farms. But in all that windless, wide landscape, I could see no sign of man's hand, except the lines – as old as the rig-and-furrow of the pasture below me – of the dry stone walls, and the arrogant stride of the great Wall which Hadrian had driven across Northumberland, nearly two thousand years ago.

The blocks of the Roman-cut stone were warm against my back. Where I sat, the Wall ran high along a ridge. To the right, the cliff fell sheer away to water, the long reach of Crag Lough, now quiet as glass in the sun. To the left, the sweeping, magnificent view to the Pennines. Ahead of me, ridge after ridge running west, with the Wall cresting each curve like a stallion's mane.

There was a sycamore in the gully just below me. Some stray current of air rustled its leaves, momentarily, with a sound like rain. Two lambs, their mother astray somewhere not far away, were sleeping, closely cuddled together, in the warm May sunshine. They had watched me for a time, but I sat there without moving, except for the hand that lifted the cigarette to my mouth, and after a while, the two heads went down again to the warm grass, and they slept.

I sat in the sun, and thought. Nothing definite, but if I had been asked to define my thoughts they would all have come to one word. England. This turf, this sky, the heartsease in the grass; the old lines of ridge and furrow, and the still older ghosts of Roman road and Wall; the ordered, spare beauty of the northern fells; this, at my feet now, was England. *This little world. This other Eden, demi-paradise* ...

It was lonely enough, certainly. We had it to ourselves, I and the lambs, and the curlew away up above, and the fritillaries that flickered like amber sparks over the spring grasses. I might have been the first and only woman in it; Eve, sitting there in the sunlight and dreaming of Adam ...

'Annabel!'

He spoke from behind me. I hadn't heard him approach. He must have come quietly along the turf to the south of the Wall, with his dog trotting gently at heel. He was less than four yards from me when I whirled round, my cigarette flying from startled fingers down among the wild thyme and yellow cinquefoil that furred the lower courses of the Roman stones.

Dimly I was aware that the lambs had bolted, crying.

The man who had shattered the dream had stopped two yards from me. Not Adam; just a young man in shabby, serviceable country tweeds. He was tall, and slenderly built, with that whippy look to him that told you he would be an ugly customer in a fight – and with something else about him that made it sufficiently obvious that he would not need much excuse to join any fight that was going. Possibly it is a look that is inbred with the Irish, for there could be no doubt about this young man's ancestry. He had the almost excessive good looks of a certain type of Irishman, black hair, eyes of startling blue, and charm in the long, mobile mouth. His skin was fair, but had acquired that hard tan which is the result of weathering rather than of sunburn, and which would, in another twenty years, carve his face into a handsome mask of oak. He had a stick in one hand, and a collie hung watchfully at his heels, a beautiful creature with the same kind of springy, rapier grace as the master, and the same air of self-confident good-breeding.

Not Adam, no, this intruder into my demi-Eden. But quite possibly the serpent. He was looking just about as friendly and as safe as a black mamba.

He took in his breath in a long sound that might even have been described as a hiss.

'So it is you! I thought I couldn't be mistaken! *It is you* . . . The old man always insisted you couldn't be dead, and that you'd come back one day . . . and by God, who'd have thought he was right?'

He was speaking quite softly, but just what was underlying that very pleasant voice I can't quite describe. The dog heard it, too. It would be too much to say that its hackles lifted, but I saw its ears flatten momentarily, as it rolled him an upward, white-eyed look, and the thick collie-ruff stirred on its neck.

I hadn't moved. I must have sat there, dumb and stiff as the stones themselves, gaping up at the man. I did open my mouth to say something, but the quiet, angry voice swept on, edged now with what sounded (fantastic though it should have seemed on that lovely afternoon) like danger.

'And what have you come back for? Tell me that! Just what do you propose to do? Walk straight home and hang up your hat? Because if that's the idea, my girl, you can think again, and fast! It's not your grandfather you'll be dealing with now, you know, it's me . . . I'm in charge, sweetheart, and I'm staying that way. So be warned.'

I did manage to speak then. In face of whatever strong emotion was burning the air between us, anything that I could think of to say could hardly fail to sound absurd. What I achieved at last, in a feeble sort of croak that sounded half paralysed with fright, was merely: 'I – I beg your pardon?'

'I saw you get off the bus at Chollerford.' He was breathing hard, and the fine nostrils were white and pinched-looking. 'I don't know where you'd been – I suppose you'd been down at Whitescar, blast you. You got on the Housesteads bus, and I followed you. I didn't want you to recognise me coming up the field, so I waited to let you get right up here, because I wanted to talk to you. Alone.'

At the final word, with its deliberately lingering emphasis, something must have shown in my face. I saw a flash of satisfaction pass over his. I was scared, and the fact pleased him.

Something, some prick of humiliation perhaps, passing for courage, helped me to pull myself together.

I said, abruptly, and a good deal too loudly: 'Look, you're making a mistake! I don't—'

'*Mistake?* Don't try and give me that!' He made a slight movement that managed to convey – his body was as eloquent as his face – a menace as genuine and as startling as his next words. 'You've got a nerve, you bitch, haven't you? After all these years . . . walking back as calm as you please, and in broad daylight! Well, here am I, too . . .' His teeth showed. 'It doesn't necessarily have to be midnight, does it, when you and I go walking at the edge of a cliff with water at the bottom? Remember? You'd never have come mooning up here alone, would you, darling, if you'd known I was coming too?'

This brought me to my feet, really frightened now. It was no longer imagination to think that he looked thoroughly dangerous. His astounding good looks, oddly enough, helped the impression. They gave him a touch of the theatrical which made violence and even tragedy part of the acceptable pattern of action.

I remember how steep, suddenly, the cliff looked, dropping sharply away within feet of me. At its foot Crag Lough stirred and gleamed under some stray breeze, like a sheet of blown nylon. It looked a long way down.

He took a step towards me. I saw his knuckles whiten round the heavy stick. For a mad moment I thought I would turn and run; but there was the steep broken slope behind me, and the Wall at my right, and, on the left, the sheer cliff to the water. And there was the dog.

He was saying sharply, and I knew the question mattered: 'Had you been down to the farm already? To Whitescar? *Had* you?'

This was absurd. It had to be stopped. Somehow I managed to grab at the fraying edges of panic. I found my senses, and my voice. I said flatly, and much too loudly: 'I don't know what you're talking about! *I don't know you!* I told you you'd made a mistake, and as far as I'm concerned you're also behaving like a dangerous lunatic! I've no idea who you think you're talking to, but I never saw you before in my life!'

He hadn't been moving, but the effect was as if I'd stopped him with a charge of shot. Where I had been sitting I had been half turned away from him. As I rose I had turned to face him, and was standing now only two paces from him. I saw his eyes widen in startled disbelief, then, at the sound of my voice, a sort of flicker of uncertainty went across his face, taking the anger out of it, and with the anger, the menace.

I followed up my advantage. I said, rudely, because I had been frightened, and so felt foolish: 'And now will you please go away and leave me alone?'

He didn't move. He stood there staring, then said, still in that edged, angry tone that was somehow smudged by doubt: 'Are you trying to pretend that you don't recognise me? I'm your cousin Con.'

'I told you I didn't. I never saw you in my life. And I never had a cousin Con.' I took a deep, steadying breath. 'It seems I'm lucky in that. You must be a very happy and united family. But you'll excuse me if I don't stay to get to know you better. Good-bye.'

'Look, just a minute – no, please don't go! I'm most terribly sorry if I've made a mistake! But, really—' He was still standing squarely in the path which would take me back to the farm track, and the main road. The cliff was still sheer to one side, and the water, far below us, smooth once more, glassed the unruffled sky. But what had seemed to be a dramatic symbol of menace towering between me and freedom, had dwindled now simply into a nice-looking young man standing in the sunshine, with doubt melting on his face into horrified apology.

'I really am most desperately sorry! I must have frightened you. Good God, what on earth can you think of me? You must have thought I was crazy or something. I can't tell you how sorry I am. I, well, I thought you were someone I used to know.'

I said, very drily: 'I rather gathered that.'

'Look, please don't be angry. I admit you've every right, but really – I mean, it's pretty remarkable. You could be her, you really could. Even now that I see you closely . . . oh, perhaps there are differences, when one comes to look for them, but – well, I could still swear—'

He stopped abruptly. He was still breathing rather fast. It was plain that he had indeed suffered a considerable shock. And, for all his apology, he was still staring at me as though he found it difficult to believe me against the evidence of his eyes.

I said: 'And I'll swear too, if you like. I don't know you. I never did. My name isn't Arabella, it's Mary. Mary Grey. And I've never even been to this part of the world before.'

'You're American, aren't you? Your voice. It's very slight, but—'
'Canadian.'

He said slowly: '*She* went to the States . . .'

I said violently and angrily: 'Now, look here—'

'No, please, I'm sorry. I didn't mean it!' He smiled then, for the first time. The charm was beginning to surface, now, through what I realised had been still a faint filming of disbelief. 'I believe you, truly I do, though it gets more fantastic every minute I look at you, even with the foreign accent! You might be her twin . . .' With an effort, it seemed, he dragged his uncomfortably intent stare from my face, and bent to caress the dog's ears. 'Please forgive me!' The swift upward glance held nothing now but a charming apology. 'I must have scared you, charging up like that and looming over you like a threat from the past.'

'My past,' I retorted, 'never produced anything quite like this! That was some welcome your poor Prodigal was going to get, wasn't it? I – er, I did gather you weren't exactly going to kill the fatted calf for Arabella? You did say Arabella?'

'Annabel. Well, no, perhaps I wasn't.' He looked away from me, down at the stretch of gleaming water. He seemed to be intent on a pair of swans sailing along near the reeds of the further shore. 'You'd gather I was trying to frighten her, with all that talk.'

It was a statement, not a question, but it had a curiously tentative effect. I said: 'I did, rather.'

'You didn't imagine I meant any of that nonsense, I hope?'

I said calmly: 'Not knowing the circumstances, I have no idea. But I definitely formed the impression that this cliff was a great deal too high, and the road was a great deal too far away.'

'Did you now?' There, at last, was the faintest undercurrent of an Irish lilt. He turned his head, and our eyes met.

I was angry to find that I was slightly breathless again, though it was obvious that, if this excessively dramatic young man really had intended murder five minutes ago, he had abandoned the intention. He was smiling at me now, Irish charm turned full on, looking, I thought irritably, so like the traditional answer to the maiden's prayer that it couldn't possibly be true. He was offering me his cigarette-case, and saying, with a beautifully-calculated lift of one eyebrow: 'You've forgiven me? You're not going to bolt straight away?'

I ought, of course, to have turned and gone then and there. But the situation was no longer – if, indeed, it had ever been – dangerous. I had already looked, and felt, fool enough for one day; it would look infinitely more foolish now to turn and hurry off, quite apart from its being difficult to do with dignity. Besides, as my fright had subsided, my curiosity had taken over. There were things I wanted to know. It isn't every day that one is recognised – and attacked – for a 'double' some years dead.

So I stayed where I was, returned his smile of amused apology, and accepted the cigarette.

I sat down again where I had been before, and he sat on the wall a yard away, with the collie at his feet. He was half-turned to face me, one knee up, and his hands clasping it. His cigarette hung in the corner of his mouth, the smoke wisping up past his narrowed eyes.

'Are you staying near by? No, I suppose you can't be, or everyone would be talking ... You've a face well known in these parts. You're just up here for the day, then? Over here on holiday?'

'In a way. Actually I work in Newcastle, in a café. This is my day off.'

'In *Newcastle*?' He repeated it in a tone of the blankest surprise. 'You?'

'Yes. Why on earth not? It's a nice town.'

'Of course. It's only that ... well, all things considered, it seems odd that you should have come to this part of the world. What brought you up here?'

A little pause. I said sharply: 'You know, you still don't quite believe me. Do you?'

For a moment he didn't reply, that narrow gaze still intent through the smoke of the cigarette. I met it squarely. Then he unclasped his hands slowly, and took the cigarette out of his mouth. He tapped ash off it, watching the small gout of grey feathering away in the air to nothing.

'Yes. I believe you. But you mustn't blame me too much for being rude, and staring. It's a queer experience, running into the double of someone you knew.'

'Believe me, it's even queerer learning that one *has* a double,' I said. 'Funnily enough, it's a thing one's inclined to resent.'

'Do you know, I hadn't thought of that, but I believe you're right! I should hate like hell to think there were two of me.'

I thought: and I believe *you*; though I didn't say it aloud. I smiled. 'It's a violation of one's individuality, I suppose. A survival of a primitive feeling of – what can one call it – identity? Self-hood? You want to be *you*, and nobody else. And it's uncomfortably like magic. You feel like a savage with a looking-glass, or Shelley seeing his *doppel-gänger* one morning before breakfast.'

'Did he?'

'He said so. It was supposed to be a presage of evil, probably death.'

He grinned. 'I'll risk it.'

'Oh lord, not your death. The one that meets the image is the one who dies.'

'Well, that is me. You're the image, aren't you?'

'There you are,' I said, 'that's just the core of the matter. That's just what one resents. We none of us want to be "the image". We're the thing itself.'

'Fair enough. You're the thing itself, and Annabel's the ghost. After all, she's dead.'

It wasn't so much the casual phrasing that was shocking, as the lack of something in his voice that ought to have been there. The effect was as startling and as definite as if he had used an obscene word.

I said, uncomfortably: 'You know, I didn't mean to ... I should have realised that talking like this can't be pleasant for you, even if you, well, didn't get on with Annabel. After all, she was a relative; your cousin, didn't you say?'

'I was going to marry her.'

I was just drawing on my cigarette as he spoke. I almost choked over the smoke. I must have stared with my mouth open for quite five seconds. Then I said feebly: 'Really?'

His mouth curved. It was odd that the lineaments of beauty could lend themselves to something quite different. 'You're thinking, maybe, that there'd have been very little love lost? Well, you might be right. Or you might not. She ran away, sooner than marry me. Disappeared into the blue eight years ago with nothing but a note from the States to her grandfather to say she was safe, and we none of us need expect to hear from her again. Oh, I admit there'd been a quarrel, and I might have been' – a pause, and a little shrug – 'well, anyway, she went, and never a word to me since that day. How easily do you expect a man to forgive that?'

You? never, I thought. There it was once more, the touch of something dark and clouded that altered his whole face; something lost and uncertain moving like a stranger behind the smooth façade of assurance that physical beauty gives. No, a rebuff was the one thing he would never forgive.

I said: 'Eight years is a long time, though, to nurse a grudge. After all, you've probably been happily married to someone else for most of that time.'

'I'm not married.'

'No?' I must have sounded surprised. He would be all of thirty, and with that exterior, he must, to say the least of it, have had opportunities.

He grinned at my tone, the assurance back in his face, as smoothly armoured as if there had never been a flaw. 'My sister keeps house at Whitescar; my half-sister, I should say. She's a wonderful cook, and she thinks a lot of me. With Lisa around, I don't need a wife.'

'Whitescar, that's your farm, you said?' There was a tuft of sea-pink growing in a crevice beside me. I ran a finger over its springy cushion of green, watching how the tiny rosettes sprang back into place as the finger was withdrawn. 'You're the owner? You and your sister?'

'I am.' The words sounded curt, almost snapped off. He must have felt this himself, for he went on to explain in some detail.

'It's more than a farm; it's "the Winslow place". We've been there for donkey's ages ... longer than the local gentry who've built their park round us, and tried to shift us, time out of mind. Whitescar's a kind of enclave, older than the oldest tree in the park – about a quarter the age of that wall you're sitting on. It gets its name, they say, from an old quarry up near the road, and nobody knows how old those workings are. Anyway, you can't shift Whitescar. The Hall tried hard enough in the old days, and now the Hall's gone, but we're still there ... You're not listening.'

'I am. Go on. What happened to the Hall?'

But he was off at a tangent, still obviously dwelling on my likeness to his cousin. 'Have *you* ever lived on a farm?'

'Yes. In Canada. But it's not my thing, I'm afraid.'

'What is?'

'Lord, I don't know; that's my trouble. Country life, certainly, but not farming. A house, gardening, cooking – I've spent the last few years living with a friend who had a house near Montreal, and looking after her. She'd had polio, and was crippled. I was very happy there, but she died six months ago. That was when I decided to come over here. But I've no training for anything, if that's what you mean.' I smiled. 'I stayed at home too long. I know that's not fashionable any more, but that's the way it happened.'

'You ought to have married.'

'Perhaps.'

'Horses, now. Do you ride?'

The question was so sudden and seemingly irrelevant that I must have looked and sounded almost startled. 'Horses? Good heavens, no! Why?'

'Oh, just a hangover from your looking so like Annabel. That was her thing. She was a wizard, a witch I should say, with horses. She could whisper them.'

'She could *what?*'

'You know, whisper to them like a gipsy, and then they'd do any blessed thing for her. If she'd been dark like me, instead of blonde, she'd have been taken for a horse-thieving gipsy's changeling.'

'Well,' I said, 'I do know one end of a horse from the other, and on principle I keep clear of both ... You know, I wish you'd stop staring.'

'I'm sorry. But I – well, I can't leave it alone, this likeness of yours to Annabel. It's uncanny. I *know* you're not her; it was absurd anyway ever to think she might have come back ... if she'd been alive she'd have been here long since, she had too much to lose by staying away. But what was I to think, seeing you sitting here, in the same place, with not a stone of it changed, and you only changed a little? It was like seeing the pages of a book turned back, or a film flashing back to where it was eight years ago.'

'Eight years is a long time.'

'Yes. She was nineteen when she ran away.'

A pause. He looked at me, so obviously expectant that I laughed. 'All right. You didn't ask ... quite. I'm twenty-seven. Nearly twenty-eight.'

I heard him take in his breath. 'I told you it was uncanny. Even sitting as close to you as this, and talking to you; even with that accent of yours ... it's not really an accent, just a sort of slur ... rather nice. And she'd have changed, too, in eight years.'

'She might even have acquired the accent,' I said cheerfully.

'Yes. She might.' Some quality in his voice made me look quickly at him. He said: 'Am I still staring? I'm sorry. I was thinking. I – it's something one feels one ought not to let pass. As if it was . . . meant.'

'What do you mean?'

'Nothing. Skip it. Tell me about yourself. You were just going to. Forget Annabel; I want to hear about you. You've told me you're Mary Grey, from Canada, with a job in Newcastle. I still want to know what brought you there, and then up here to the Wall, and why you were on that bus from Bellingham to Chollerford today, going within a stone's throw of the Winslow land.' He threw the butt of his cigarette over the cliff, and clasped both hands round the uplifted knee. All his movements had a grace that seemed a perfectly normal part of his physical beauty. 'I'm not pretending I've any right to ask you. But you must see that it's an odd thing to accept, to say the least. I refuse to believe that such a likeness is pure chance. Or the fact that you came here. I think, under the circumstances, I'm entitled to be curious' – that swift and charming smile again – 'if nothing else.'

'Yes, of course I see that.' I paused for a moment. 'You know, you may be right; about this likeness not being chance, I mean. I don't know. My people did come from hereabouts, so my grandmother told me.'

'Did they now? From Whitescar?'

I shook my head. 'I never heard the name, that I remember. I was very little when Granny died, and she only knew what my great-grandmother told her, anyway. My own mother was never much interested in the past. But I know my family did originally come from somewhere in Northumberland, though I've never heard Granny mention the name Winslow. Hers was Armstrong.'

'It's a common name along the borders.'

'So she said, and not with a very savoury history, some of them! Wasn't there an Armstrong once who actually lived just here, in the Roman Fort at Housesteads? Wasn't he a horse thief? If I could only "whisper" horses like your cousin Annabel, you might suppose—'

'Do you know when your people left England?' he asked, not so much ignoring my red herring as oblivious of it. He seemed to be pursuing some very definite line of his own.

'I suppose in my great-grandfather's time. Would that be somewhere about the middle of the last century? About then, anyway. The family settled first at a place called Antigonish, in Nova Scotia, but after my father married, he—'

'What brought you back to England?' The singleness of purpose that seemed to be prompting his questions robbed the interruption of rudeness. Like an examiner, I thought, bringing the candidate back to the point . . . Certainly his questions seemed to be directed towards some definite end. They had never been quite idle, and now they were sharp with purpose.

I said, perhaps a little warily: 'What brings anyone over? My people are dead, and there was nothing to keep me at home, and I'd always wanted to see England. When I was little, Granny used to talk and talk about England. She'd never seen it, but she'd been brought up on her own mother's stories of "home". Oh yes, I heard all about "bonny Northumberland", and what an exciting city Newcastle was – I almost expected to see the sailing-ships lying along the wharves, and the horse-trams in the streets, she'd made it all so vivid for me. And Hexham, and Sundays in the Abbey, and the market there on Tuesdays, and the road along the Tyne to Corbridge, and the Roman Wall with all those lovely names . . . Castle Nick and Borcovicium and Aesica and the Nine Nicks of Thirlwall . . . I read about it all, too. I've always liked history. I'd always promised myself that some day I'd come over, maybe to visit, maybe – if I liked it – to stay.'

'To stay?'

I laughed. 'That's what I'd told myself. But I hadn't seen myself coming back quite like this, I'm afraid. I – well, I was left pretty badly off. I got my fare together, and enough to tide me over till I got a job, and that's my situation now. It sounds like the opposite of the usual story, doesn't it? Usually the lone wolf sets out to the New World to make his way, but I – well, I wanted to come over here. The New World can be a bit wearing when you're on your own, and – don't laugh – but I thought I might fit in better here.'

'Because your roots are here?' He smiled at my look. 'They are, you know. I'm sure I'm right. There must have been someone, some Winslow, 'way back in the last century, who went to Canada from here. Probably more than one, you know how it was then; in the days when everybody had thirteen children, and *they* all had thirteen children, I'm pretty sure that one or two Winslows went abroad to stay. Whitescar wouldn't have been big enough, anyway, and nobody would have got a look-in except the eldest son . . . Yes, that's it, that explains it. Some Winslow went to Canada, and one of his daughters – your great-grandmother, would it be? – married an Armstrong there. Or something like that. There'll be records at Whitescar, surely? I don't know, I wasn't brought up there. But that must be it.'

'Perhaps.'

'Well,' he said, with that charmingly quizzical lift of the eyebrow that was perhaps just a little too well practised, 'that does make us cousins, doesn't it?'

'Does it?'

'Of course it does. It's as plain as a pikestaff that you must be a Winslow. Nothing else would account for the likeness; I refuse to believe in pure chance. You're a type, the Winslow type, it's unmistakable – that fair hair, and your eyes that queer colour between green and grey, and those lovely dark eyelashes . . .'

'Carefully darkened,' I said calmly. 'After all, why go through life with light lashes if you don't have to?'

'Then Annabel's must have been darkened, too. By heaven, yes, they were! I remember now, when I first came to Whitescar she'd be only fifteen, and I suppose she hadn't started using that sort of thing. Yes, they were light. I don't even remember when the change took place! I was only nineteen when I came, you know, and straight from the back of beyond. I just took her for granted as the most beautiful girl I'd ever seen.'

He spoke, for once, quite simply. I felt myself going scarlet, as if the tribute had been aimed at me. As, in a way, it was.

I said, to cover my embarrassment: 'You talk of me as being a "Winslow type". Where do you come in? You don't seem to conform.'

'Oh, I'm a sport.' The white teeth showed. 'Pure Irish, like my mother.'

'Then you are Irish? I thought you looked it. Is Con short for Connor?'

'Sure. She was from Galway. I've her colouring. But the good looks come from the Winslows. We're all beauties.'

'Well, well,' I said drily, 'it's a pity I haven't a better claim, isn't it?' I stubbed out my cigarette on the stone beside me, then flicked the butt out over the cliff's edge. I watched the place where it had vanished for a moment. 'There is . . . one thing. Something I do remember, I think. It came back as we were talking. I don't know if it means anything . . .'

'Yes?'

'It was just – I'm sure I remember Granny talking about a forest, some forest near Bellingham. Is there something near your "Winslow place", perhaps, that—?'

'*Forrest!*' He looked excited. 'Indeed there is! You remember I told you that Whitescar was a kind of enclave in the park belonging to the local bigwigs? That's Forrest Park; the Park's really a big tract of land enclosed in a loop of the river, almost an island. The whole place is usually just spoken of as "Forrest" – and the Forrests, the family, were there for generations. It was all theirs, except the one piece by the river, in the centre of the loop; that's Whitescar. I told you how they tried to winkle us out of it. The big house was Forrest Hall.'

'Was? Oh, yes, you said the Hall had "gone". What happened? Who were they? This does sound as if my great-grandmother, at any rate, may have come from hereabouts, doesn't it?'

'It certainly does. I knew it couldn't be sheer chance, that likeness. Why, this means—'

'Who were the Forrests? Could she have known the family? What happened to them?'

'She'd certainly have known them if she lived at Whitescar. The family wasn't an especially old one, merchant adventurers who made a fortune trading with the East India Company in the seventeenth century, then built the Hall and settled down as landed gentry. By the middle of the nineteenth, they'd made another fortune out of railway shares. They extended their gardens, and did a spot of landscaping in the park, and built some rather extravagant stables (the last owner ran it as a stud at one time), and did their damnedest to buy the Winslows out of Whitescar. They couldn't, of course. Another cigarette?'

'No, thank you.'

He talked on for a few minutes more about Whitescar and Forrest; there had been in no sense, he said, a "feud" between the families, it was only that the Winslows had held their small parcel of excellent land for generations, and were fiercely proud of it, and of their position as yeoman farmers independent of the family at the Hall, which, in its palmy days, had managed to acquire all the countryside from Darkwater Bank to Greenside, with the single exception of Whitescar, entrenched on its very doorstep.

'Then, of course, with the mid-twentieth century, came the end, the tragic Fall of the House of Forrest.' He grinned. It was very evident that, whatever tragedy had touched the Hall, it didn't matter a damn if it hadn't also touched Whitescar. 'Even if the Hall hadn't been burned down, they'd have had to give it up. Old Mr. Forrest had lost a packet during the slump, and then after his death, what with taxes and death duties—'

'It was burned down? What happened? When you said "tragic", you didn't mean that anyone was *killed*?'

'Oh, lord, no. Everyone got out all right. There were only the Forrests themselves in the house, and the couple who ran the garden and house between them, Johnny Rudd and his wife, and old Miss Wragg who looked after Mrs. Forrest. But it was quite a night, believe me. You could see the flames from Bellingham.'

'I suppose you were there? It must have been awful.'

'There wasn't much anyone could do. By the time the fire brigade could get there the place was well away.' He talked about the scene for a little longer, describing it quite graphically, then went on: 'It had started in Mrs. Forrest's bedroom, apparently, in the small hours. Her poodle raised the place, and Forrest went along. The bed was alight by that time. He managed to drag the bedclothes off her – she was unconscious – and carry her downstairs.' A sideways look. 'They were damned lucky to get the insurance paid up, if you ask me. There was talk of an empty brandy-bottle in her room, and sleeping-pills, and of how there'd been a small fire once before in her bedroom, and Forrest had forbidden Miss Wragg to let her have cigarettes in her room at night. But there's always talk when these things happen – and heaven knows there'd been enough gossip about the Forrests ... of every sort. There always is, when a couple doesn't get on. I always liked him, so did everybody else for that matter, but the old woman, Miss Wragg, used to blackguard him right and left to anyone who'd listen. She'd been Crystal Forrest's nurse, and had come to look after her when she decided to be a chronic invalid, and she had a tongue like poison.'

'Decided to be – that's an odd way of putting it.'

'Believe me, Crystal Forrest was a damned odd sort of woman. How any man ever – oh well, they say he married her for her money anyway. Must have, if you ask me. If it was true, he certainly paid for every penny of it that he'd put into that stud of his, poor devil. There can't have been much money, actually, because I know for a fact that when they left England after the fire they lived pretty much on the insurance, and on what he'd got for the horses. They went to live in Florence – bought a small villa there, but then she got worse, went right round the bend, one gathers, and he took her off to some man in Vienna. Till she died, two years ago, she'd been in one psychiatric clinic after another – or whatever is the fashionable name for the more expensive loony-bins – in Vienna, and that had taken everything. When Forrest got back from Austria eventually, to finish selling up here, there was nothing left.'

'He's back, then?'

'No, he's not here now. He only came over to sell the place. The Forestry Commission have the park-land, and they've planted the lot, blast them. That's the whole point. If I'd been able to lay my hands on a bit—' He broke off.

'The whole point?'

'Skip it. Where was I? Oh, yes. The Hall's gone completely, of course, and the gardens are running wild. But the Rudds – they were the couple who used to work at the Hall – the Rudds have moved across to the other side of the Park, where the West Lodge and the stables are. Johnny Rudd runs the place now as a sort of small-holding, and when Forrest was over here last year, he and Johnny got the old gardens going again, as a market-garden, and I believe it's doing quite well. Johnny's running it now, with a couple of local boys.'

He was gazing away from me as he talked, almost dreamily, as if his attention was not fully on what he was saying. His profile was as handsome as the rest of him, and something about the way he lifted his chin and blew out a long jet of smoke, told me that he knew it, and knew I was watching him, too.

'And Mr. Forrest?' I asked idly. 'Does he live permanently in Italy now?'

'Mm? Italy? Yes, I told you, he has this place near Florence. He's there now ... and the place is abandoned to Johnny Rudd, and the Forestry Commission ... and Whitescar.' He turned his head. The long mouth curved with satisfaction. 'Well? How's that for a dramatic story of your homeland, Mary Grey? The Fall of the House of Forrest!' Then, accusingly, as I was silent: 'You weren't even listening!'

'Oh, I was. I was, really. You made a good story of it.'

I didn't add what I had been thinking while I watched him; that he had told the dreary, sad little tale – about a man he liked – with rather less feeling and sympathy than there would have been in a newspaper report; had told it, in fact, as if he were rounding off a thoroughly satisfactory episode. Except, that is, for that one curious remark about the Forestry Commission's planting programme.

He had also told it as if he had had no doubt of my own absorbed interest in every detail. I wondered why ...

If I had some suspicion of the answer, I wasn't prepared to wait and see if I was right. I looked round me for my handbag.

He said quickly: 'What is it?'

The bag was on the ground at the foot of the Wall. I picked it up. 'I'll have to go now. I'd forgotten the time. My bus—'

'But you can't go yet! This was just getting exciting! If your great-grandmother knew about Forrest, it might mean—'

'Yes, I suppose it might. But I'll still have to go. We work Sunday evenings at my café.' I got to my feet. 'I'm sorry, but there it is. Well, Mr. Winslow, it's been interesting meeting you, and I—'

'Look, you can't just go like this!' He had risen too. He made a sudden little movement almost as if he would have detained me, but he didn't touch me. The rather conscious charm had gone from his face. He spoke quickly, with a kind of urgency. 'I'm serious. Don't go yet. My car's here. I can run you back.'

'I wouldn't think of letting you. No, really, it's been—'

'Don't tell me again that it's been "interesting". It's been a hell of a lot more than that. It's been important.'

I stared at him. 'What *do* you mean?'

'I told you. This sort of thing isn't pure chance. I tell you, it was meant.'

'Meant?'

'Ordained. Destined. Kismet.'

'Don't be absurd.'

'It's not absurd. This thing that's happened, it's more than just queer. We can't simply walk away in opposite directions now and forget it.'

'Why not?'

'*Why not?*' He said it almost explosively. 'Because – oh, hell, I can't explain, because I haven't had time to think, but at any rate tell me the address of this place where you work.' He was searching his pockets while he spoke, and eventually produced a used envelope and a pencil. When I didn't answer, he looked up sharply. 'Well?'

I said slowly: 'Forgive me, I can't explain either. But ... I'd rather not.'

'What d'you mean?'

'Just that I would rather – what did you say? – that we walked away in opposite directions now, and forgot all about it. I'm sorry. Please try to understand.'

'I don't even begin to understand! It's perfectly obvious to me that this likeness of yours to Annabel Winslow *isn't* pure chance. Your people came from hereabouts. I wasn't only joking when I said we were long-lost cousins ...'

'Possibly we are. But can't you grasp this? Let me be blunt. Whitescar and Winslows and all the rest may mean a lot to you, but why should they mean anything to me? I've been on my own a good long time now, and I like it that way.'

'A job in a café? Doing what? Waiting? Cash desk? Washing up? *You?* Don't be a fool!'

'You take this imaginary cousinship a bit too much for granted, don't you?'

'All right. I'm sorry I was rude. But I meant it. You can't just walk away and – after all, you told me you were nearly broke.'

I said, after a pause: 'You – you take your family responsibilities very seriously, don't you, Mr. Winslow? Am I to take it you were thinking of offering me a job?'

He said slowly: 'Do you know, I might, at that. I ... might.' He laughed suddenly, and added, very lightly: 'Blood being thicker than water, Mary Grey.'

I must have sounded as much at a loss as I felt. 'Well it's very nice of you, but really ... you can hardly expect me to take you up on it, can you, even if our families *might* just possibly have been connected a hundred years or so ago? No, thanks very much, Mr. Winslow, but I meant what I said.' I smiled. 'You know, you can't have thought. Just what sort of a sensation would there be if I did turn up at Whitescar with you? Had you thought of *that*?'

He said, in a very strange voice: 'Oddly enough, I had.'

For a moment our eyes met, and held. I had the oddest feeling that for just those few seconds each knew what the other was thinking.

I said abruptly: 'I must go. Really. Please, let's leave it at that. I won't annoy you by telling you again that it's been interesting. It's been – quite an experience. But forgive me if I say it's one I don't want to take any further. I mean that. Thank you for your offer of help. It was kind of you. And now this really is good-bye ...'

I held out my hand. The formal gesture seemed, in these surroundings, and after what had passed, faintly absurd, but it would, I hoped, give the touch of finality to the interview, and provide the cue on which I could turn my back and leave him standing there.

To my relief, after a moment's hesitation, he made no further protest. He took the hand quite simply, in a sort of courteous recognition of defeat.

'Good-bye, then, Mary Grey. I'm sorry. All the best.'

As I left him I was very conscious of him standing there and staring after me.

CHAPTER TWO

Whisht! lads, haad your gobs
An' Aa'll tell ye aal an aaful story.

C. F. LEUMANE: *The Lambton Worm*

The woman was there again.

For the last three days, punctually at the same time, she had pushed her way through the crowded aisles of the Kasbah Coffee House, and had found herself a seat in a corner. This last fact alone argued a good deal of stubborn determination, since at half past five in the afternoon the Kasbah was always crowded. But, either owing to her own fixity of purpose, or to the good manners of the students who, at that time of day, made up most of the Kasbah's clientèle, she got her corner seat every day, and there she sat, sipping her Espresso very slowly, and working her way through a Sausageburger Special, while the brightly-lit café-crowd swirled round her table, the deafening babel of young voices earnestly and dogmatically discussing love, death, and the afternoon's lectures against an emphatic background of Messrs. Presley, Inc., and what I had learned to recognise as the Kool Kats' Klub.

I myself had not noticed the woman until she was pointed out to me. I was on table-duty that week, and was too occupied in weaving my laden way through the crowds to clear the dirty cups away and wipe the scarlet plastic table-tops, to pay much attention to a dull-looking woman in country clothes, sitting alone in a corner. But Norma, from her position behind the Espresso machine, had observed her, and thought her 'queer'. It was Norma's most deadly adjective.

'She stares, I'm telling you. Not at the students, though take it from me what I see from up here's nobody's business sometimes; the things you see when you haven't got your gun. I mean, take a look at that one, that blonde in the tartan jeans, and when I say *in* she's only just to say in, isn't she? And I happen to know her da's a professor up at the University. Well, I don't know about a professor, exactly, but he works up in the Science Colleges and that shows you, doesn't it? I mean to say. Two coffees? Biscuits? Well, we've got Popoffs and Yumyums and – oh yes, two Scrumpshies ... ta, honey. Pay at the cash desk. The things some people eat, and look at her figure, it stands to reason. Oh yes, the woman in the corner, she's off her rocker, if you ask me, fair gives you the creeps the way she stares. Don't say you hadn't noticed her, it's you she's watching, love, take it from me. All the time. Not so's *you'd* see it, but every time you're looking away there she is, staring. Nutty as a fruit cake, love, take it from me.'

'Stares at *me*, d'you mean?'

'That's what I'm telling you. Three coffees, one tea. Pay at the desk.

Stares at you all the time. Can't seem to take her eyes off you. No, not that girl, *she's* with that black haired chap in the Antarctic get-up who's over at the juke-box, would you credit it, he's got that tune *again* ... Yes, that woman over there under the contemp'ry Crusaders. The middle-aged one with the face like blotting-paper.'

I turned to look. It was true. As my eyes met hers, the woman looked quickly down at her cup. I lowered my tray of dirty crockery slowly till the edge rested against the bar-counter, and considered her for a moment.

She could have been anything between thirty-five and forty – 'middle-aged', to Norma, meant anything over twenty-six – and the first adjective I myself would have applied to her would have been 'ordinary', or, at any rate, 'inconspicuous', rather than 'queer'. She wore goodish, but badly-chosen country clothes, and a minimum of make-up – powder, I guessed, and a touch of lipstick which did little to liven the dull, rather heavy features. Her hair under the slightly out-of-date felt hat was dark, and worn plainly in a bun. Her eyebrows were thick and well-marked, but untidy-looking over badly-set eyes. The outer corners of brows, eyes and mouth were pulled down slightly, giving the face its heavy, almost discontented expression. The general effect of dullness was not helped by the browns and fawns of the colour-scheme she affected.

I saw at once what Norma had meant by that last, graphic phrase. One got the curious impression that the woman only just missed being good-looking; that the features were somehow blurred and ill-defined, as if they had been drawn conventionally enough, and then the artist had smoothed a light, dry hand carelessly down over the drawing, dragging it just that fraction out of focus. She could have been a bad copy of a portrait I already knew; a print blotted off some dramatically sharp sketch that was vaguely familiar.

But even as I tried to place the impression, it slid away from me. I had never, to my recollection, seen her before. If I had, I would scarcely have noticed her, I thought. She was the kind of woman whom, normally, one wouldn't have looked at twice, being at first sight devoid of any of the positive qualities that go to make up that curious thing called charm. Charm presupposes some sort of vivacity and spark, at least what one might call some gesture of advance towards life. This woman merely sat there, heavily, apparently content to wait while life went on around her.

Except for the tireless stare of those toffee-brown eyes. As I let my own gaze slide past her in apparent indifference, I saw her eyes lift once more to my face.

Norma said, in my ear: 'D'you know her?'

'Never seen her before in my life. Yes, I know who you mean, the woman in the brown hat; I just didn't want her to see *me* staring, that's all. Are you sure, Norma? She's not just sitting there kibitzing in general?'

''Course I'm sure. What else have I got to do –' here she laid hold of the Espresso handle with one hand, reached for a couple of cups with the other, filled them, slapped them on to their saucers and the saucers on to a tray, supplied the tray with sugar and teaspoons, and pushed the lot across to Mavis, the waitress on duty in the inner room – 'What else have I got to do, but watch what's going on?'

Mavis, I noticed, had passed quite close to the corner table, bound for the inner room with the coffee-cups. The woman didn't glance at her.

'Still watching you . . .' murmured Norma. 'You see?'

'You must be mistaken. It's a nervous mannerism, or she thinks I'm someone she knows, or – ' I broke off short.

'Or what?'

'Nothing. It doesn't matter anyway. Let her stare if it gives her pleasure.'

'Sure. I should worry. Poor old thing's going round the bend, I shouldn't wonder,' said Norma kindly. 'All the same, you watch it, Mary. I mean to say, kind of uncomf'able, isn't it? Someone staring at you all the time, stands to reason.' She brightened. 'Unless she's a talent scout for films, or the T.V. Now, there's a thing! D'you think it might be that?'

I laughed, 'I do not.'

'Why not? You're still pretty,' she said generously, 'and you must have been lovely when you were young. Honest. Lovely.'

'That's very sweet of you. But anyway, talent scouts hang round the infant-school gates these days, don't they? I mean, you're practically crumbling to pieces at anything over nineteen.'

'You've said it. On the shelf with your knitting at twenty-one,' said Norma, who was eighteen and a half. 'Well, all the same, you watch it. Maybe she's one of *those*, you know, slip a syringe into your arm and away with you to worse than death before you know where you are.'

I began to laugh. 'Who's out of date now? I believe you have to queue for a place these days. No, I hardly see her putting that one across, Norma!'

'Well, I do,' said Norma stubbornly. 'And you may well laugh, not but what it makes you wonder who said it was worse than death. A man, likely. Well, there's no accounting for tastes, is there, not but what I wouldn't just as soon have a good square meal, myself. Three coffees? Here you are. Sorry, I'll give you a clean saucer. Ta. Pay at the desk. For crying out loud, he's got that tune *again*.'

Compelling, piercing, and very skilful indeed, the saxes and (surely) the cornets of the Kool Kats bullied their way up triumphantly through the noises of the café and street outside.

I said hurriedly: 'I'll have to take these through to the kitchen. See you later. Keep your eye on the White Slaver.'

'Sure. All the same, it's all very well to laugh, but she's got that kind of face. Stodgy, but clever, and more to her than meets the eye. Must be something, anyway, stands to reason. I mean, I'm telling you, the way she stares. Oh well, maybe you *are* just like someone she knows, or something.'

'Maybe I am,' I said.

I picked up the tray and, without another glance at the corner under the contemporary Crusaders, I pushed my way through the swing door into the steamy cubby-hole that the Kasbah called its kitchen.

Next day she was there again. And the next. And Norma was right. Now that I knew, I could feel it, the steady gaze that followed me about the place, pulling my own eyes so strongly that I had to will myself not to keep glancing back at her, to see if she was still watching me.

Once or twice I forgot, and my look did cross hers, to see her eyes drop just as they had before, and the heavy face, expressionless, stare down at the slow swirl of brown in her coffee-cup as she stirred it. Another time when I caught the edge of her steady, obstinate stare, I stopped, cloth in hand – I was wiping a table-top – and let myself look surprised, and a little embarrassed. She held my gaze for a moment, then she looked away.

It was on the third afternoon that I decided that there must be more in it than a chance interest. My recent encounter on the Roman Wall was still very much in the front of my mind, and I felt strongly that that afternoon's mistakes would hardly bear repeating.

When the bar-counter was quiet, I paused by it, and said to Norma: 'She's still at it, your White Slaver in the corner. And I'm tired of it. I'm going over to speak to her and ask her if she thinks she's ever met me.'

'Well, you needn't bother,' said Norma. 'I been trying to get a minute to tell you ever since a quarter to six. She's bin asking about you. Asked Mavis who you were.'

'*Did* she?'

'Uh-huh. Right out. Got hold of Mavis while you were in the kitchen. What's up?'

'Nothing. No, really. What did Mavis tell her?'

'Well, she didn't see nothing wrong in it, the old girl said she thought she knew you anyway, and asked if you came from these parts and if you were living in Newcastle. So Mavis said who you were and that you'd come from Canada and had a fancy to stay up north for a bit, seeing as your family'd come from round here hundreds of years ago, and that you were just working here temp'ry, like, till you got yourself sorted out and found a proper job. Mavis didn't see anything wrong in telling her, a woman like that, sort of respectable. It's not as if it was a *man*, after all, is it?'

Another time I would have appreciated the way Norma said the word, as if describing a dangerous and fascinating kind of wild beast; but just now I had room for only one thing. 'No,' I said, 'it's all right. But – well,

it's odd, Norma, the whole thing, and I don't like mysteries. Did Mavis
find out anything about *her*? Who she is, where she come from?'

'No.'

I looked unseeingly down at the tray of crockery in my hand. Fleetingly,
I was there again: the Roman Wall in the sunshine, the babble of the
curlews, the smell of thyme, the swans preening and dipping in the lough
below, and, facing me, that hard blue stare, as genuinely dangerous, I
felt sure, as anything that Norma could have dreamed up . . .

I said abruptly: 'I want to know who she is. But I don't want to speak
to her. Look, Norma, she's got a dress-box or something with her, and
it's labelled. I'm going into the kitchen again, now, because I don't want
to look as if I've any interest in it. Will you ask Mavis to go over, say
something – any excuse will do – and get a look at that label?'

'Sure. You leave it to me. Anything for a spot of excitement. Oh, and
tell them to get a move on in there: I'll be out of cups in a minute.'

When I got back from the kitchen with the cups, the corner table was
empty. Mavis was at the counter with Norma. I said, a little anxiously:
'Did she see you looking?'

'Not her,' said Mavis. 'Funny sort of woman, eh? Norma says you
don't know her.'

'No.' I set the tray down on the counter. 'The box was labelled, then?
What was the name?'

'Dermott. A Miss Dermott.'

I turned slowly to look at her. 'Dermott?'

'Does it mean anything?' asked Norma.

Mavis said: 'Dermott? That's an Irish name, isn't it?'

'What's the matter?' said Norma quickly. 'Mary, *do* you know her?'

I said sharply: 'Did you see the address? Was there one? Did you see
where she was from?'

Mavis was looking at me curiously. 'Yes, I did. Some address near
Bellingham, a farm. White-something Farm, it was. Mary, what—?'

'*Whitescar?*'

'Yes, that was it. Then you *do* know her?'

'No. I've never seen her in my life. Honestly. But—' I took in my
breath – 'she must know someone I know, that's all. I – I've met someone
from Whitescar . . . she must have heard I worked here, and came to
see. But what an odd way of doing it, not to speak, I mean . . . Oh, well,'
I managed a smile, speaking lightly. 'That's *that* little mystery solved,
and nothing to it after all. Thanks a lot, Mavis.'

'Think nothing of it.' And Mavis, dismissing the incident, hurried
away. But Norma, lifting the piles of clean cups and saucers from the
tray I had brought, and stacking them slowly in place, eyed me
thoughtfully.

'Nothing to it, eh?'

'Nothing at all. If she's here tomorrow I'll speak to her myself.'

'I would,' said Norma. 'I would, too. Find out what she's playing at . . . Friend of a friend of yours, eh?'

'Something like that.'

Something like that. I could see the likeness now: the poorish copy of that dramatically handsome face, the sepia print of Connor Winslow's Glorious Technicolor. *'My half-sister keeps house at Whitescar . . .'* She would be some half-dozen years older than he, with the different colouring she had probably got from her Dermott father, and none of the good looks that his Winslow blood had given Connor. But the likeness, ill-defined, shadowy, a characterless travesty of his vivid charm, was there, to be glimpsed now and then, fleetingly, by anyone who knew. I thought, suddenly: I wonder if she minds.

'I wouldn't let it upset you,' said Norma. 'Really I wouldn't.'

'I won't. Thanks, Norma. Don't worry.'

She wasn't looking at me. She began to rearrange a carefully stacked pile of chocolate biscuits.

'There's a man in it, isn't there?'

'Well, you could hardly – ' I paused. It was easier that way, after all. 'Yes, I suppose there is.'

'Oh *well*.' This, for Norma, would apparently have explained behaviour a good deal odder than Lisa Dermott's. 'Well, you take it from me, dear, have done with it if it bothers you. If she's here tomorrow I'd walk right up to her, if I was you, and just ask her straight out what she's playing at and what she wants.'

'All right,' I said, 'I will.'

But I wasn't there next afternoon to watch for her coming. I gave my notice in that night.

CHAPTER THREE

Go fetch me some of your father's gold,
And some of your mother's fee,
And I'll carry you into the north land,
And there I'll marry thee.

Ballad: *Mary Colvin*

When the knock came at my bedroom door I knew who it was even before I looked up from my packing.

My landlady, Mrs. Smithson, was out: I had been to look for her as soon as I came in, only to remember that Wednesday was her regular evening for the cinema and late supper with a friend. Even without this knowledge I could never have mistaken the tentative, even nervous quality of this knock for Mrs. Smithson's forthright rapping. As clearly as if the thick, shiningly varnished door were made of glass, I could see who stood there; the toffee-brown eyes under the brown, undistinguished hat, and the drawn-down corners of the soft, obstinate-looking mouth.

I hadn't heard anyone come upstairs, though the bare and echoing linoleum of the two flights to my room was a more than sufficient herald of approach. She must have come up very softly.

I hesitated. She must know I was here. I had seen no reason for silence, and the light would be showing under my door.

As the soft, insistent rapping came again, I threw a swift look round the room.

The ash-tray by the bed, almost full . . . the bed itself, disordered . . . evidence of the hours spent smoking, thinking, counting the stains on the fly-spotted ceiling, before I had finally risen to drag out and pack the cases that stood – proof of a more tangible kind of disturbance – in the middle of the floor.

Well, it was too late to do anything about them now. But there, on the table near the window, was a more cogent witness still – the telephone directory, borrowed from downstairs, and open at the page headed: 'Wilson – Winthorpe . . . '

I went silently across the room, and shut it. Then I turned back to the dressing-chest and pulled open a drawer.

I said, on a note of inquiry: 'Yes? Come in.'

When the door opened, I had my back to it, lifting clothes out of the drawer. 'Oh, Mrs. Smithson,' I began, as I turned, then stopped short, my brows lifted, my face registering, I hoped, nothing but surprise.

She said, standing squarely in the doorway: 'Miss Grey?'

'Yes? I'm afraid – ' I paused, and let recognition dawn, and with it puzzlement. 'Wait a moment. I think – don't I know your face? You were in the Kasbah this afternoon, the café where I work, weren't you? I remember noticing you in the corner.'

'That's right. My name's Dermott, Lisa Dermott.' She pronounced the name Continental-fashion, '*Leeza*'. She paused to let it register, then added: 'From Whitescar.'

I said, still on that puzzled note: 'How do you do, Miss – Mrs.? – Dermott. Is there something I can do for you?'

She came into the room unasked, her eyes watchful on my face. She shut the door behind her, and began to pull off her plain, good hogskin gloves. I stood there without moving, my hands full of clothes, plainly intending, I hoped, not to invite her to sit down.

She sat down. She said flatly: 'My brother met you up on the Roman Wall beyond Housesteads on Sunday.'

'On the Ro – oh, yes, of course I remember. A man spoke to me. Winslow, he was called, from somewhere near Bellingham.' (*Careful now, Mary Grey; don't overplay it; she'll know you'd not be likely to forget a thing like that.*) I added slowly: 'Whitescar. Yes. That's where he said he came from. We had a rather – odd conversation.'

I put the things I was holding back into the drawer, and then turned to face her. There was a packet of Players in my handbag lying beside me on the dressing-chest. I shook one loose. 'Do you smoke?'

'No, thank you.'

'Do you mind if I do?'

'It's your own room.'

'Yes.' If she noticed the irony she gave no sign of it. She sat there solidly, uninvited, in the only chair my wretched little room boasted, and set her handbag down on the table beside her. She hadn't taken her eyes off me. 'I'm Miss Dermott,' she said, 'I'm not married. Con Winslow's my half-brother.'

'Yes, I believe he mentioned you. I remember now.'

'He told me all about *you*,' she said. 'I didn't believe him, but he was right. It's amazing. Even given the eight years, it's amazing. I'd have known you anywhere.'

I said, carefully: 'He told me I was exactly like a young cousin of his who'd left home some eight years ago. She had an odd name, Annabel. Is that right?'

'Quite right.'

'And you see the same resemblance?'

'Certainly. I didn't actually know Annabel herself. I came to Whitescar after she'd gone. But the old man used to keep her photographs in his room, a regular gallery of them, and I dusted them every day, till I suppose I knew every expression she had. I'm sure that anyone who knew her would make the same mistake as Con. It's uncanny, believe me.'

'It seems I must believe you.' I drew deeply on my cigarette. 'The "old man" you spoke of . . . would that be Mr. Winslow's father?'

'His great-uncle. He was Annabel's grandfather.'

I had been standing by the table. I sat down on the edge of it. I didn't look at her; I was watching the end of my cigarette. Then I said, so abruptly that it sounded rude: 'So what, Miss Dermott?'

'I beg your pardon?'

'It's an expression we have on our side of the Atlantic. It means, roughly, all right, you've made your point, now where is it supposed to get us? You say I'm the image of this Annabel of yours. Granted: I'll accept that. You and Mr. Winslow have gone to a lot of trouble to tell me so. I repeat: so what?'

'You must admit – ' she seemed to be choosing her words – 'that we were bound to be interested, terribly interested?'

I said bluntly: 'You've gone a little beyond "interest", haven't you? Unless, of course, you give the word its other meaning.'

'I don't follow you.'

'No? I think you do. Tell me something frankly, please. Does your brother still persist in thinking that I might *actually be* Annabel Winslow?'

'No. Oh, no.'

'Very well. Then you have to admit that this "interest" of yours does go far beyond mere curiosity, Miss Dermott. He might have sent you to take a look at me, Annabel's double, once, but not more than' – I caught myself in time – 'not more than that. I mean, you'd have hardly followed me home. No, you're "interested" in quite another sense, aren't you?' I paused, tapped ash into the waste-basket, and added: ' "Interested parties," shall we say? In other words, you've something at stake.'

She sounded as calm as ever. 'I suppose it's natural for you to be so hostile.' There was the faintest glimmer of a smile on her face: perhaps not so much a smile, as a lightening of the stolidity of her expression. 'I don't imagine that Con was exactly, well, tactful, to start with . . . He upset you, didn't he?'

'He frightened me out of my wits,' I said frankly. I got up from the table, and moved restlessly to the window. The curtains were undrawn. Outside, the lights and clamour of the street made a pattern two storeys below, as remote as that of a coastal town seen from a passing ship. I turned my back on it.

'Look, Miss Dermott, let me be plain, please. Certain things are obvious to me, and I don't see any advantage in playing stupid about them. For one thing, I don't want to prolong this interview. As you see, I'm busy. Now, your brother was interested in me because I look like this Annabel Winslow. He told you about me. All right. That's natural enough. But it isn't just pure coincidence that brought you to the Kasbah, and I know darned well I never told him where I worked. It sticks out a mile that he followed me home on Sunday, and either he came here and asked someone where I worked, or he saw me go on for the late Sunday shift at the café, and then went back and told you. And you came next day to have a look at me . . . Yes, I admit I did see you before today. How could I help noticing you, the way you stared? Well, no doubt he and you had a talk about it, and today you've followed me home. Am I right?'

'More or less.'

'I told you I was being frank, Miss Dermott. I don't like it. I didn't like the way your brother talked to me on Sunday, and I don't like being watched, and I'm damned if I like being followed.'

She nodded calmly, as if I had said something a little pettish, but fairly reasonable. 'Of course you don't. But if you'll just be a little patient with me, I'll explain. And I'm sure you'll be interested then . . .'

All this time she had been watching me, and there was some quality about her steady gaze that I associated with something I couldn't place. It made me feel uncomfortable, and I wanted to look away from her. Con Winslow had had the same look, only his had held a frankly male appraisal that made it more understandable, and easier to face.

She looked away at last. Her gaze shifted from me to the appointments of the shabby little room; the iron bedstead, the garish linoleum, the varnished fireplace with its elaborately ugly overmantel, the gas-ring on the cracked tiles of the hearth. She looked further, as if wondering, now, whether something of me, personally, was anywhere superimposed on the room's characterless ugliness. But there were no photographs, and what books I had had with me were packed. The questing look came to rest, defeated, on the clothes untidily hanging from the drawer I had been emptying, on the handbag I had pulled open to get my cigarettes, from which had spilled a lipstick, a pocket-comb, and a small gold cigarette-lighter whose convoluted initials caught the light quite clearly: *M.G.*

Her eyes came back to my face. I suppressed a desire to say tartly: 'Satisfied?' and said instead: 'Are you sure you won't smoke?' I was already lighting another for myself.

'I think I might, after all.' She took cigarette and light with the slight awkwardness that betrayed it as an unaccustomed action.

I sat down on the table again and said, uncompromisingly: 'Well?'

She hesitated, looking for the first time not quite at ease, but it wasn't discomfort that touched the heavy face; it looked, incongruously, like excitement. It was gone immediately. She took a rapid puff at the cigarette, looked down at it as if she wondered what it was there for, then said in that flat voice of hers:

'I'll come to the main point first, and explain afterwards. You were right in saying that our interest in you was more than the normal curiosity you'd expect the likeness to arouse. You were even right – terribly right – when you said we had "something at stake".'

She paused. She seemed to be waiting for comment.

I moved again, restlessly. 'Fair enough. You want something from me. Your brother hinted as much. Well, what? I'm listening.'

She laid her cigarette carefully down in the ash-tray I had placed near her on the table. She put her hands flat down on her thighs and leaned forward slightly. 'What we want,' she said, 'is Annabel, back at Whitescar. It's important. I can't tell you how important. She must come back.'

The voice was undramatic: the words, in their impact, absurdly sensational. I felt my heart give a little painful twist of nervous excitement. Though I had suspected some nonsense of this kind – and of course it *was* nonsense – all along, the knowledge did nothing to prevent my blood jerking unevenly through my veins as if driven by a faulty pump. I said nothing.

The brown eyes held mine. She seemed to think everything had been said. I wondered, with a spasm of genuine anger, why people with some obsessive trouble of their own always thought that others should be nerve-end conscious of it, too. A cruel impulse made me say, obtusely: 'But Annabel's dead.'

Something flickered behind the woman's eyes. 'Yes, she's dead. She can't come back, Miss Grey, she can't come back ... to spoil anything for you ... or for us.'

I watched the ash from my cigarette float and fall towards the waste-basket. I didn't look at her. I said at length, with no expression at all: 'You want me to go to Whitescar. As Annabel Winslow.'

She leaned back. The basket chair gave a long, gasping creak like a gigantic breath of relief. It was obvious that she had taken my apparent calmness for compliance.

'Yes,' she said, 'that's it. We want you to come to Whitescar ... Annabel.'

I laughed then. I couldn't help it. Possibly the laughter was as much the result of taut nerves as of the obvious absurdity of her proposal, but if there was a suggestion of hysteria in it, she took no notice. She sat quite still, watching me with that expression which, suddenly, I recognised. It was the look of someone who, themselves uninvolved, coolly assesses a theatrical performance. She had all this time been weighing my looks, my voice, my movements, my reactions, against those of the Annabel Winslow of whom she knew so much, and whom she and her brother must have spent the greater part of the last three days in discussing.

I felt some nerve tighten somewhere inside me again, and deliberately relaxed it. My laughter died. I said: 'Forgive me, but it sounded so absurd when it finally got put into words. It – it's so theatrical and romantic and impossible. Impersonation – that old stuff? Look, Miss Dermott, I'm sorry, but it's crazy! You can't be serious!'

She said calmly: 'It's been done.'

'Oh, yes, in stories. It's an old favourite, we know that, from the *Comedy of Errors* on. And that's a point, too: it may be all right in books but on the stage, where one can *see*, and still one's supposed to be deceived, it's absurd. Unless you do really have identical twins ... or one person plays both parts.'

'That,' said Miss Dermott, 'is the whole point, isn't it? We *have* got identical twins. It could be done.'

'Look at it this way,' I said. 'It's something, you say, that has been done. But, surely, in much simpler times than these? I mean, think of the lawyers, handwriting, written records, photographs, and, if it came to the point, police ... oh, no, they're all too efficient nowadays. The risks are too great. No, it belongs in stories, and I doubt if it's even readily acceptable there any more. Too many coincidences required, too much luck ... That vein was worked out with *The Prisoner of Zenda* and *The Great Impersonation*. Pure romance, Miss Dermott.'

'Not quite worked out,' she said, on that note of soft, unshaken obstinacy. 'Haven't you read *Brat Farrar*, by Josephine Tey? You couldn't say *that* was "pure romance". It could have happened.'

'I have read it, yes, and it probably is the best of them all. I forget the details, but doesn't Brat Farrar, who's the double of a boy that's dead go to the family home to claim a fortune and an estate? I agree, it was wonderfully convincing, but damn it, Miss Dermott, it was a *story*. You can't *really* do that sort of thing and get away with it! Real life is – well it's not Brat Farrar, it's the Tichborne Case, and Perkin Warbeck. I forget just what the Tichborne Claimant got, but poor Perkin – who in fact may have been just what he claimed to be – got chopped.'

'The Tichborne Case? What was that?'

'It was a *cause célèbre* of the eighties. A certain Roger Tichborne had been presumed drowned; he was heir to a baronetcy and a fortune. Well, years later a man turned up from Australia claiming to be Roger Tichborne – so convincingly that to this day there are people who still think he was. Even Roger Tichborne's mother, who was still alive, accepted him.'

'But he didn't get the estate?'

'No. The case went on literally for years, and cost thousands, and pretty well split the country into two camps, but in the end he lost it. He got a prison sentence. *That's* the real thing, Miss Dermott. You see what I mean?'

She nodded. Arguing with her was like battering a feather pillow. You got tired, and the pillow stayed just the same. 'Yes, of course. There has to be luck, certainly, and there has to be careful planning. But it's like murder, isn't it?'

I stared at her. 'Murder?'

'Yes. You only know about the ones that are found out. Nobody ever hears about the ones that get away with it. All the counting's on the negative side.'

'I suppose so. But—'

'You say that *Brat Farrar's* only a story, and that in real life anyone who walks into a family claiming to be a – well, a long-lost heir, would merely land in trouble, like this Tichborne man.'

'Yes. Certainly. The lawyers—'

'That's the whole point. That's not what you'd be doing. The lawyers wouldn't come into it, I'm sure of that. The point is that you'd not be *claiming* anything from anybody; there'd be nobody to fight you. The only person who'd lose by your reappearance is Julie, and she has enough of her own. Besides, she adored Annabel; she'll be so pleased to see you, that she'll hardly stop to think what it'll mean in terms of money ...'

'Julie?'

'Annabel's young cousin. She's not at Whitescar now, but she'll be coming some time this summer. You needn't worry about her, she was only ten or eleven when Annabel went away, and she'll hardly remember enough about her to suspect you. Besides, why should she? I tell you, it's not a risk, it's a certainty. Take it from me, Con and I wouldn't dare take risks, either! We've everything to lose. You wouldn't even find it nerve-racking. Apart from the daily help, and the farm-hands you need hardly see, you'll be mostly with Con and myself, and we'll help you all we can.'

'I don't understand. If Julie isn't there, who are you trying to — ?'

'And the point about the old man is that he's never believed Annabel was dead. He simply won't have it. He'll never even question you, believe me. You can just walk in.'

I was staring at her, my cigarette arrested half-way to my mouth. 'The old man? Who? Who are you talking about?'

'Old Mr. Winslow, her grandfather. I spoke of him before. He thought the world of her. He kept half a dozen pictures of her in his room — '

'But surely . . . I understood he was dead.'

She looked up in surprise. 'Where did you get that idea? No, he's very much alive.' Her mouth twisted suddenly, incongruously, into a likeness of that not-so-pleasant smile of Con's. 'You might say that's the whole cause of this – situation. What made you think he was dead?'

'I didn't think. But I somehow got the impression . . . When you spoke of "the old man" before, you used the past tense. You said "*he was* Annabel's grandfather".'

'Did I? Possibly. But, of course, the past tense,' she said softly, 'would be for Annabel.'

'I see that now. Yes. But it was added somehow to an impression I got on Sunday . . . your brother said something, I forget what . . . Yes, of course, he said – implied, I suppose, would be more accurate – that he owned the farm. No, he stated it flatly. I'm sure he did.'

She smiled then, genuinely, and for the first time I saw the warmth of real feeling in her face. She looked amused, indulgent, affectionate, as a mother might look when watching the pranks of a naughty but attractive child. 'Yes, he would. Poor Con.' She didn't take it further, merely adding: 'No, he doesn't own Whitescar. He's old Mr. Winslow's manager. He's . . . not even Mr. Winslow's heir.'

'*I see.* Oh, lord, yes, I see it now.'

I got up abruptly, and went over again to the window. Opposite, in one of the tall, drab houses, someone came into a bedroom and switched on the light. I caught a too-familiar glimpse of yellow wall-paper with a writhing pattern of green and brown, a pink plastic lampshade, the gleam of a highly polished radio, before the curtains were twitched across the window. The radio was switched on, and some comedian clacked into the night. Somewhere a child wailed, drearily. In the street below, a woman was shouting a child's name in a wailing northern cadence.

'What do you see?'

I said, slowly, still staring out at the dark: 'Not much, really. Just that Mr. Winslow – Con – wants Whitescar, and that somehow he thinks he can fix it, if I go back there as Annabel. I take it that Julie must be the heir now, if he isn't. But how on earth it's going to help Con to bring back Annabel, and put two people in the way instead of one . . .' I finished heavily: 'Oh, lord, the whole thing's fantastic anyway. I can't think why I've bothered to listen.'

'Extraordinary, perhaps, but not fantastic.' The colourless voice behind me might have been discussing a knitting-pattern. I didn't turn. I leaned my forehead against the glass and watched, without seeing them, the moving lights of the traffic in the street below. 'But then, families are extraordinary, don't you think? And with all their faults, the Winslows have never been exactly dull ... Listen for a little while longer, and you'll understand what Con and I are getting at.'

I let her talk. I just leaned my head against the glass and watched the traffic, and let the soft, unemphatic voice flow on and on. I felt, suddenly, too tired even to try and stop her.

She told me the recent family history very briefly. Old Matthew Winslow (she said) had had two sons: the elder had one daughter, Annabel, who had lived with her parents at Whitescar. When the girl was fourteen, her father was killed in an accident with a tractor, and her mother died soon afterwards, within the year, of pneumonia, leaving her as an orphan in her grandfather's care. The latter was then only in his early sixties, but had been for some time handicapped by arthritis, and found it heavy work to manage the place on his own. His younger son had been killed some years previously in the Battle of Britain, leaving a widow, and a month-old daughter, Julie. Matthew Winslow had immediately invited his daughter-in-law to Whitescar, but she had chosen to remain in London. She had eventually re-married, and gone out, with her small daughter, to live in Kenya. Later, when Julie was some seven years old, she had been sent back to England to school; she spent the winter vacations with her parents in Africa, but her spring and summer holidays had been passed with her grandfather at Whitescar, which she regarded as her English home.

It had not been for some time after his elder son's death that Mr. Winslow thought of offering a home and a job to Connor Winslow, his only surviving male relative. Matthew Winslow had had a nephew, the son of his younger brother, who had worked at the Forrest stud as trainer in old Mr. Forrest's time, but who had eventually left Whitescar and gone to Ireland to a big training-stable in Galway. There he had married a young widow, a Mrs. Dermott, who had a five-year-old daughter, Lisa. A year later, Connor was born, to become the spoiled darling of his parents, and also, surprisingly, of his half-sister, who had adored him, and had never dreamed of resenting her mother's preference for the good-looking only son. But this apparently safe and happy circle had been rudely shattered when Connor was thirteen. His father broke his neck one day over a big Irish in-and-out, and exactly ten months later the inconsolable widow cheerfully married for the third time.

The young Connor found himself all at once relegated to the background of his mother's life, and kept there by an unsympathetic step-father and (very soon) by the even stronger claims of a new young family, consisting of twin boys and, later, another daughter. Con's father had left no money, and it became increasingly obvious that his step-father, and now his mother, were not prepared to spare either time, or material help, on the son of the earlier marriage. There was only Lisa, and she was as badly off as he. But at least she could feel herself needed. There is plenty for a plain unmarried daughter to do in a house with three small children.

So when Matthew Winslow, the great-uncle whose existence he had half-forgotten, wrote out of the blue to ask Connor, then aged nineteen, to make his home at Whitescar and be trained for farm-management, the boy had gone like an arrow from a bow, and with very little in the nature of a by-your-leave. If Lisa wept after he had gone, nobody knew; there was plenty for Lisa to do at home, anyway . . .

Small wonder that Con arrived at Whitescar with the determination to make a place for himself, and stay; a determination that, very soon, hardened into a definite ambition. Security. The Winslow property. Whitescar itself. There was only Annabel in the way, and Con came very quickly to think that she had no business to be in the way at all. It didn't take him long to find out that the place, backed by Matthew Winslow's not inconsiderable private income, could be willed any way that the old man wished.

So Connor Winslow had set to work. He had learned his job, he made himself very quickly indispensable, he had worked like a navvy at anything and everything that came along, earning the respect and even the admiration of the slow, conservative local farmers, who at first had been rather inclined to regard the good-looking lad from Ireland as an extravagant whim of Matthew's, showy, perhaps, but bound to be a poor stayer. He had proved them wrong.

Matthew himself, though he had never publicly admitted it, had had the same doubts, but Con defeated his prejudices first, then proceeded to charm his great-uncle 'like a bird off a tree', (so Lisa, surprisingly). But charm he never so wisely, he couldn't quite charm Whitescar from him, away from Annabel. 'Because Con tried, he admits it,' said Lisa. 'The old man thought the world of him, and still does, but he's like the rest of the English Winslows, as stubborn as the devil and as sticky as a limpet. What he has, he hangs on to. He wanted her to have it after him, and what he wants, goes. The fact that she's dead,' added Lisa bitterly, 'doesn't make a bit of difference. If the old man said black was white, he'd believe it was true. He can't be wrong, you see; he once said she'd come back, and he won't change. He'll die sooner. Literally. *And* he'll leave everything to Annabel in his Will, and the mess'll take years to clear up, and the odds are that Julie's the residuary beneficiary. The point is, we just don't know. He won't say a word. But it does seem unfair.'

She paused for a moment. I had half-turned back from the window, and was standing leaning against the shutter. But I still didn't look at her, or make any comment on the story. I felt her eyes on me for a few moments, then she went on.

There wasn't much more. Con's next move had been the obvious one. If Annabel and Whitescar were to go together, then he would try to take both. Indeed, he was genuinely (so Lisa told me) in love with her, and an understanding between them was such an obvious and satisfactory thing to happen that the old man, who was fond of them both, was delighted.

'But,' said Lisa, hesitating now and appearing to choose her words, 'it went wrong, somehow, I won't go into details now – in any case, I don't know a great deal, because I wasn't there, and Con hasn't said much – but they quarrelled terribly, and she used to try and make him jealous, he says, and, well, that's only too easy with Con, and he has a terrible temper. They had a dreadful quarrel one night. I don't know what happened, but I think Con may have said something to frighten her, and she threw him over once and for all, said she couldn't stay at Whitescar while he was there, and all that sort of thing. Then she ran off to see her grandfather. Con doesn't know what happened between them, or if he does, he won't tell me. But of course the old man was bound to be furious, and disappointed, and *he* never was one to mince his words, either. The result was another dreadful row, and she left that night, without a word to anyone. There was a note for her grandfather, that was all. Nothing for Con. She just said she wasn't coming back. Of course the old man was too stubborn and furious even to try and find her, and persuade her, and he forbade Con to try either. Con did what he could, quietly, but there was no trace. Then, a month later, her grandfather got a note, post-marked New York. It just said she was quite safe, had got a job with friends, and she wasn't ever coming back to England again. After that there was nothing, until three years later someone sent Mr. Winslow a cutting from a Los Angeles paper describing an accident in which an express had run into a bus at some country crossing, and a lot of people had been killed. One of them was a "Miss Anna Winslow" of no given address, who'd been staying at some boarding-house in the city, and who was thought to be English. We made inquiries, and they were all negative. It could have been Annabel. It would certainly be enough, with the long absence, to allow us to presume her dead. After all this time, she must be; or else she really isn't ever coming back, which amounts to the same thing, in the end.' She paused. 'That's all.'

I turned my head. 'And you? Where do you come in?'

'After she'd gone,' said Lisa Dermott, 'Con remembered me.'

She said it quite simply. There was no hint of self-pity or complaint in the soft, flattened voice. I looked down at her, sitting stolid and unattractive in the old basket chair, and said gently: 'He got Mr. Winslow to send for you?'

She nodded. 'Someone had to run the house, and it seemed too good a chance to miss. But even with the two of us there, doing all that we do, it's not the slightest use.'

The impulse of pity that had stirred in me, died without a pang. I had a sudden vivid picture of the two of them, camped there at Whitescar, hammering home their claims, Con with his charm and industry, Lisa

with her polish and her apple pies . . . She had called it 'unfair', and
perhaps it was; certainly one must admit they had a right to a point of
view. But then so had Matthew Winslow.

'You see,' she said, 'how unjust it all is? You do see that, don't you?'

'Yes, I see. But I still don't see what you think I can do about it! You
want me to go to Whitescar, and somehow or other *that* is going to help
Con to become the heir, and owner. How?'

I had left the window as I spoke, and come forward to the table again.
I saw that fugitive look of excitement touch her face once more as she
leaned towards me, looking up under the brim of the brown hat.

'You're interested now, aren't you? I thought you would be, when you
heard a bit more.'

'I'm not. You've got me wrong. I was interested in your story, I admit,
but that was because I think your brother may be right when he says I
must come originally from some branch of the same family. But I never
said I was interested in your proposition! I'm not! I told you what I
thought about it! It's a crazy idea straight out of nineteenth-century
romance, long-lost heirs and missing wills and – and all that drivel!' I
found that I was speaking roughly, almost angrily, and made myself
smile at her, adding, mildly enough: 'You'll be telling me next that
Annabel had a strawberry-mark—'

I stopped. Her hand had moved, quickly, to the telephone directory
on the table beside her. I saw, then, that I had shut it over a pencil which
still lay between the leaves.

The book fell open under her hand, at the page headed '*Wilson –
Winthorpe*'. She looked at it without expression. Then her blunt, well-
kept finger moved down towards the foot of the second column, and
stopped there.

'*Winslow, Matthew. Frmr. Whitescar . . . Bellingham 248.*'

The entry was marked, faintly, in pencil.

I said, trying to keep my voice flat, and only succeeding in making it
sound sulky: 'Yes, I looked it up. It puzzled me, because your brother
had said he owned the farm. It isn't an old directory, so when you
first spoke of "the old man", I assumed he must have died quite
recently.'

She didn't answer. She shut the book, then leaned back in her chair
and looked up at me, with that calm, appraising look. I met it almost
defiantly.

'All right, I was interested before. Who wouldn't be? After that
business on Sunday . . . oh, well, skip it. Call it curiosity if you like, I'm
only human. But my heaven, there's no reason why it should go further
than curiosity! This – proposition – you appear to be suggesting, takes
my breath away. No, no, I don't want to hear any more about it. I can't
even believe you're serious. *Are* you?'

'Quite.'

'Very well. But can you give me any conceivable reason why *I* should be?'

She looked at me almost blankly. There it was again; that merciless all-excluding obsession with their personal problems. 'I don't understand.'

I found that I was reaching, automatically, for another cigarette. I let it slip back into the packet. I had smoked too much that evening already; my eyes and throat felt hot and aching, and my brain stupid. I said: 'Look, you approach me out of the blue with your family history, which may be intriguing, but which can really mean very little to me. You propose, let's face it, that somehow or other I should help you to perpetrate a fraud. It may mean everything to you; I don't see how, but we'll grant it for argument's sake. But why should it mean a thing to me? You tell me it'll be "easy". Why should I care? Why should I involve myself? In plain words, why on earth should I go out of my way to help you and your brother Con to anything?'

I didn't add: 'When I don't much like you, and I don't trust him,' but to my horror the words seemed to repeat themselves into the air of the room as clearly as if I, and not the tone of my voice, had said them.

If she heard them, she may have been too unwilling to antagonise me, to resent them. Nor did she appear to mind my actual rudeness. She said, simply: 'Why, for money, of course? What other reason is there?'

'For *money*?'

She gave a slight, summing, eloquent glance round the room. 'If you'll forgive me, you appear to need it. You said so, in fact to my brother; that was one of the reasons why we felt we could approach you. You have so much to gain. You will forgive my speaking so plainly on such a short acquaintance?'

'Do,' I said ironically.

'You are a gentlewoman,' said Miss Dermott, the outmoded word sounding perfectly normal on her lips. 'And this room ... and your job at that dreadful café ... You've been over here from Canada for how long?'

'Just a few days.'

'And this has been all you could find?'

'As far as I looked. It took all I had to get me here. I'm marking time while I get my bearings. I took the first thing that came. You don't have to worry about me, Miss Dermott. I'll make out. I don't have to work in the Kasbah for life, you know.'

'All the same,' she said, 'it's worth your while to listen to me. In plain terms, I'm offering you a job, a good one, the job of coming back to Whitescar as Annabel Winslow, and persuading the old man that that is who you are. You will have a home and every comfort, a position, everything; and eventually a small assured income for life. You call it a fraud: of course it is, but it's not a cruel one. The old man wants you there, and your coming will make him very happy.'

'Why did he remove the photographs?'

'I beg your pardon?'

'You said earlier that he used to keep a "whole gallery" of this girl's photographs in his room. Doesn't he still?'

'You're very quick.' She sounded appreciative, as of a favourite horse who was showing a pretty turn of speed. 'He didn't get rid of them, don't worry; he keeps them in a drawer in his office, and he still has one in his bedroom. He moved the others last year, when he had one done of Julie.' She eyed me for a moment. 'She'll be coming up for her summer holiday before very long. You see?'

'I see why you and your brother might want to work quickly, yes.'

'Of course. You must come home before Julie persuades him to be reasonable about Annabel's death ... and to put Julie herself in Annabel's place. Whatever happens, it'll happen soon. It's doubtful if the old man'll see the year out, and I think he's beginning to realise it.'

I looked up quickly. 'Is he ill?'

'He had a slight stroke three months ago, and he refuses to take very much care. He's always been strong, and very active, and he seems to resent any suggestion that he should do less. He takes it as an encroachment ...' Her lips tightened over whatever she had been going to say, then she added: 'The doctor has warned him. He may live for some time, but he may, if he does anything silly, have another stroke at almost any moment, and this time it might be fatal. So you see why this is so urgent? Why meeting you like that seemed, to Con, like a gift from heaven?'

I said, after a pause: 'And when he's gone?'

She said patiently: 'It's all thought out. We can go into details later. Briefly, all you have to do is to establish yourself at Whitescar, *be* Annabel Winslow, and inherit the property (and her share of the capital) when the old man dies. I tell you, there'll be no question. Don't you see, you'll not actually be coming back to *claim* anything, simply coming home to live? With luck you'll be able to settle quietly in and establish yourself, long before there's any sort of crisis, and by the time the old man does die, you'll have been accepted without question. Then, after a decent interval, when things seem settled, you'll turn over your legacy to Con. You'll get your cut, don't worry. Annabel's mother left her some money, which she could have claimed when she was twenty-one; it brings in a nice little independent income. You'll have that – in any case, it would look absurd if you attempted to hand *that* over. As for the main transaction, the handing over of Whitescar, that can be arranged to look normal enough. You can say you want to live elsewhere ... abroad, perhaps ... whatever you'd planned for yourself. In fact, you'll be able to lead your own life again, but with a nice little assured income behind you. And if "Annabel" decided to live away from Whitescar again, leaving the place to her cousin, who's run it for years anyway, there's no reason why anyone should question it.'

'The young cousin? Julie?'

'I tell you, you needn't be afraid of her. Her step-father has money, there's no other child, and she'll certainly also get a share of Mr. Winslow's capital. You'll rob her of Whitescar, yes, but she's never given the slightest hint that she cares anything about it, except as a place to spend a holiday in. Since she left school last year, she's taken a job in London, in the Drama Department at the B.B.C., and she's only been up here once, for the inside of a fortnight. All she could do, if the place was hers, would be to sell it, or pay Con to manage it. You needn't have Julie on your conscience.'

'But surely—' it was absurd, I thought, to feel as if one was being backed against a wall by this steady pressure of will— 'But surely, if the old man realised that he was ill, and still Annabel *hadn't* come back, he would *leave* things to Con? Or if he left them to Julie, and she was content to let Con go on as manager, wouldn't that be all right?'

Her lips folded in that soft obstinate line. 'That wouldn't answer. Can't you see how impossible – ah, well, take it from me that it wouldn't work out like that. No, my dear, this is the best way, and you're the gift straight from the gods. Con believes he'll never get control of Whitescar and the capital except this way. When you've said you'll help, I'll explain more fully, and you'll see what a chance it is for all of us, and no harm done, least of all to that stubborn old man sitting at Whitescar waiting for her to come home . . .'

Somehow, without wanting it, I had taken the cigarette, my hands fidgeting with carton and lighter in spite of myself. I stood silently while she talked, looking about me through the first, blue, sharp-scented cloud of smoke . . . the sagging bed, the purplish wallpaper, the wardrobe and dressing-chest of yellow deal, the table-cloth with the geometric flowers of Prussian blue and carmine, and the stain on the ceiling that was the shape of the map of Ireland. I thought of the high moors and the curlews calling and the beeches coming into leaf in the windbreaks. And of the collie-dog waving his tail, and the straight blue stare of Connor Winslow . . .

It was disconcerting to feel the faint prickle of nervous excitement along the skin, the ever-so-slightly quickened heartbeat, the catch in the breath. Because of course the thing *was* crazy. Dangerous and crazy and impossible. This silly, stolid pudding of a woman couldn't possibly have realised how crazy it was . . .

No, I thought. No. Go while the going's good. Don't touch it.

'Well?' said Lisa Dermott.

I went to the window and dragged the curtains shut across it. I turned abruptly back to her. The action was somehow symbolic; it shut us in together, story-book conspirators in the solitary, sleazy upstairs room that smelt of too much cigarette-smoke.

'Well?' I echoed her, sharply. 'All right. I am interested. And I'll come, if you can persuade me that it can possibly work . . . Go on. I'll really listen now.'

CHAPTER FOUR

Or take me by the body so meek,
Follow, my love, come over the strand—
And throw me in the water so deep,
For I darena go back to Northumberland.

Ballad: *The Fair Flower of Northumberland*

It took three weeks. At the end of that time Lisa Dermott vowed that I would do. There was nothing, she said, that she or Con knew about Whitescar and Annabel that I, too, didn't now know.

My handwriting, even, passed muster. The problem of the signature had been one of Lisa's worst worries, but she had brought me some old letters, written before Annabel's disappearance, and when I showed her the sheets that I had covered with carefully-practised writing, she eventually admitted that they would pass.

'After all, Lisa—' I used Christian names for her and Con, and made a habit of referring to Matthew Winslow as "Grandfather"— 'I shan't be doing much writing. The person who matters is Grandfather, and I shan't have to write to him. As far as the bank's concerned, the signature is all that's needed, and I've got that off pretty well, you must admit. In any case, even a signature might change a bit in eight years; it'll be easy enough to account for any slight differences, one would think.'

We were in another boarding-house room, this time in a big house in the tangle of busy streets east of the Haymarket. I had left my previous lodgings the day after my first meeting with Lisa, and, on her recommendation, had taken this room under the name of Winslow.

'Because,' said Lisa, 'though I don't imagine for a moment that anyone will see us together who knows me, or knew Annabel, if they *should* happen to see us before you turn up at Whitescar, or if they do make inquiries, at least they won't find that Lisa Dermott and Con Winslow were seeing an awful lot of one Mary Grey just before "Annabel" turned up at home to eat the fatted calf.'

'You seem awfully sure of that fatted calf,' I said drily. 'Let's hope you're right. You'll have to be completely honest with me, both of you, about Grandfather's reactions when he gets the news I'm coming. If he seems to have the slightest suspicion of a doubt – and if he so much as *mentions* having me investigated – you're to tell me, and—'

'We'll think again, that's understood. You don't imagine *we'd* be too keen on an investigation, either? We'll look after you, you know. We have to. It cuts both ways.'

I laughed: 'Don't think I haven't realised that! The possibilities for mutual blackmail are unlimited, and quite fascinating.'

She gave her faint, unreadable smile. 'The point is, surely, that it *is* mutual?' She patted the book which lay on the arm of her chair. *Brat Farrar* had become, for her, the text-book of our enterprise. 'It was the same in this book ... only you've less to worry about than the impostor there; you're not coming back just to claim a fortune, and it's easier to make your story – the reasons for your flight and your return – hang together.'

'Is it? You know, Lisa, there is one point at which the story doesn't hang together at all well.'

I thought she looked wary. 'Where?'

'Well, unless Con intends to come through with some pretty convincing reasons for a most almighty row the night she went, I can't believe that a normal "lovers' quarrel", however bitter, would drive a girl away for good, from the only home she had, even if her grandfather didn't side with her over it. I'd even have thought that Con might have been the one to be shown the door.'

It was a moment or two before she replied. Then she said slowly: 'I expect that Con intends to tell you exactly what passed, when he – when he gets to know you better. I don't know it all myself, but I believe it does (what was the phrase?) hang together, quite well, really.'

'All right. We'll leave it to Con. Well, at least,' I said cheerfully, 'I'll be able to relax and tell the truth about my travels abroad. The truth, wherever possible ... There never was a better alibi. Let's go through our stuff again, shall we?'

And, for the fiftieth time, we did.

She was the best possible teacher for the purpose, with an orderly mind, and very little imagination. Her patience, her almost Teutonic efficiency, never failed to amaze me, and her matter-of-fact calmness began to have its effect on me. In her company, any doubts I had seemed to become merely frivolous; moral quibbles were hardly worth the trouble of thought; apprehensions were baseless, mists to be blown aside by the steady gusts of common sense.

With the methods outlined in *Brat Farrar* as our *modus operandi*, Lisa had taught me all the facts about Whitescar, its environs, and the house itself, in those afternoon sessions during my three-weeks' appren-ticeship. And, like the impostor-hero of the book, I soon found myself to be not only involved, but even excited by the sheer difficulties of the deception. The thing was an adventure, a challenge, and, I told myself (with how much self-deceit I didn't pause to consider), I would, in the long run, do no harm. As for Julie ... But I didn't let myself think much about Julie. I shut my mind to the future, and kept to the task in hand, pitting my wits against Lisa's day after day, hour after hour, in those interminable cross-examinations.

'Describe the drawing-room ... the kitchen ... your bedroom ...'

'What does your grandfather eat for his breakfast?'

'What was your mother's Christian name? The colour of her hair? Where was her home?'

'The day your father was killed, and the news was brought, where were you?'

'Go from the kitchen door to the hay-loft . . .'

'Describe the front garden; what plants did you put in? Your favourite flowers? Colours? Food? The names of the horses you rode at the Forrest stables? The dogs? Your old cat? The name of the farmer at Nether Shields . . . the head cattleman at Whitescar . . . 'the horse-keeper at Forrest . . .?'

'Describe Mrs. Forrest . . . her husband . . .'

But as a rule, the personalities of the game were left to Connor to bring to life for me.

He managed, on several occasions (once when Lisa was there, but usually alone), to come out for an hour or so while his great-uncle was resting in the afternoons.

The first time he came was when Lisa had already been with me for a couple of hours. We had expected him that day, and had been listening for the sound of his car stopping in the quiet street. When he came at length, I was absorbed, over the teacups, in describing for Lisa the old Forrest Hall grounds as she had taught me them, and as Annabel would remember them, before the house had been burned down and the Forrests gone abroad.

I was concentrating hard on what I was saying, and had failed to hear anyone mount the stairs. It was the sudden change in Lisa's impassive, listening face that told me who was at the door.

It was she who called 'Come in!' before I had even turned my head, and she was on her feet as he entered the room.

I saw then why we had missed hearing the car. He must have walked some distance from the place where he had parked it. His hair, and the tweed of his jacket, were misted with raindrops.

This was my first meeting with him since our strange encounter on the Roman Wall, and I had been half-dreading it; but I need not have worried. He greeted me with imperturbable friendliness, and the same unquestioning acceptance of my partnership in his affairs that I had seen in his sister.

If my own greeting was a little uncertain, this went unnoticed in Lisa's exclamation. 'Con! Is it raining?'

'I think so, I hardly noticed. Yes, I believe it is.'

'You believe it is! Why, you're soaking! And no coat on. I suppose you left the car three streets away. Really, Con! Come to the fire, dear.'

I had to stop myself from staring at her in amazement. This was a totally different Lisa from the one I had known up to now. Gone was the silent, stodgy-looking watcher of the Café Kasbah, the single-minded juggernaut of my Westgate Road lodgings, the crisply efficient tutor of the last few days. This was the hen fussing over its chick, or the anxious shepherd with the weakling lamb . . . She had bustled across the room to meet him, had brushed the raindrops from his shoulder with her hands, and drawn him nearer to the fire, almost before the door was shut behind him. She pressed him into the room's best chair, which she had just vacated, then hurried (without so much as a by-your-leave to me) to make fresh tea for him. Con accepted the fuss without even appearing to notice it; he stood patiently while she fluttered round him, as a good child stands still while its mother fusses its clothes into order, took the chair she pointed him to, and the tea she had made for him. It was a totally new facet of Lisa, and an unexpected one. It also went, I thought, quite a long way towards completing the picture of Con that I had had in my own mind.

He was, in his own way, as good a teacher as Lisa. It fell to him to give me some sort of picture of life at Whitescar when Annabel had been there, and to round out, in his own racy, vivid way, the two most important portraits, that of Matthew Winslow, and of the girl herself.

I waited for him to mention the final quarrel, and the night of Annabel's flight. But when he did come to it he added very little to what I had already heard from Lisa. I asked no questions. Time enough when he knew me better. He would have to come to it sooner or later, since the point at which the young Annabel had walked out of her grandfather's life was, obviously, the point at which I came in. But I wondered, increasingly, what reasons he could give me for a 'lovers' quarrel' severe enough to drive a girl to three thousand miles of flight, and years of silence.

The explanation was, in fact, left to my last 'lesson' with Lisa.

This fell on the Thursday of the third week, and I had not been expecting her. When I opened the door and showed her into my room, I thought that something was ruffling her usually stolid calm, but she took off her gloves and coat with her customary deliberation, and sat down by the fire.

'I didn't expect you, I said. 'Has something happened?'

She sent me a half-glance upwards, in which I thought I could read uneasiness, and even anger. 'Julie's coming, that's what's happened. Some time next week.'

I sat on the table's edge, and reached for a cigarette. 'Oh?'

She said sourly: 'You take it very calmly.'

'Well, you said you expected her some time during the summer.'

'Yes, but she's taking her holiday much earlier than we'd expected, and I've a feeling that the old man's asked her to come, and she's getting special leave. He doesn't say so; but I know she *had* originally planned to come in August ... You see what it means?'

I lit the cigarette deliberately, then pitched the dead match into the fire. (The gold lighter, with its betraying monogram, lay concealed at the bottom of a suitcase.) 'I see what it might mean.'

'It means that if we don't get moving straight away, Julie'll have wormed her way into Whitescar, and he'll leave her every penny.'

I didn't answer for a moment. I was thinking that Con, even at his most direct, was never coarse.

'So you see, this is it,' said Lisa.

'Yes.'

'Con says it must mean the old man's a bit more nervous about his health than he's admitted. Apparently Julie wrote to him once or twice while he was ill, and he has written back, I know. I'm sure he must have asked her to come up early, for some reason, and he certainly seems as pleased as Punch that she can get away so soon. She said she'd be here next week, some time, but would ring up and let us know. Normally we'd have had till July or August, and anything,' said Lisa, bitterly, 'could have happened before then. As it is—'

'Look,' I said mildly, 'you don't have to hunt round for motives to frighten yourselves with. Perhaps he does just want to see Julie, and perhaps she does just want to see him. It could be as simple as that. Don't look so disbelieving. People are straightforward enough, on the whole, till one starts to look for crooked motives, and then, oh boy, how crooked can they be!'

Lisa gave that small, tight-lipped smile that was more a concession to my tone than any evidence of amusement. 'Well, we can't take risks. Con says you'll have to come straight away, before Julie even gets here, or heaven knows what Mr. Winslow'll do.'

'But, look, Lisa—'

'You'll be all right, won't you? I'd have liked another week, just to make certain.'

'I'm all right. It isn't that. I was going to say that surely Con's barking up the wrong tree with Julie. I don't see how she can possibly be a danger to him, whether she's at Whitescar or not.'

'All I know is,' said Lisa, a little grimly, 'that she's as like Annabel as two peas in a pod, and the old man's getting more difficult every day ... Heaven knows what he might take it into his head to do. Can't you see what Con's afraid of? He's pretty sure Julie's the residuary beneficiary now, but if Mr. Winslow alters his Will before Annabel gets home, and makes Julie the principal ...'

'Oh yes, I see. In that case, I might as well not trouble to go any further. But is it likely, Lisa? If Grandfather abandons Annabel at last, and re-makes his Will at all, surely, now, it will be in Con's favour? You said Julie's only been to Whitescar for holidays, and she's London bred. What possible prospect—?'

'That's just the point. Last year, when she was here, she was seeing a lot of one of the Fenwick boys from Nether Shields. It all seemed to blow up out of nothing, and before anyone even noticed it, he was coming over every day, getting on like a house on fire with Mr. Winslow, and Julie ... well, *she* did nothing to discourage him.'

I laughed. 'Well, but Lisa, what was she? Eighteen?'

'I know. It's all speculation, and I hope it's nonsense, but you know what a razor's-edge Con's living on, and anything could happen to the old man. Once you're there, things should be safe enough: he'll certainly never leave anything to Julie over *your* head, but as it is – well, she's his son's child, and Con's only a distant relative ... and he likes Bill Fenwick.'

I regarded the end of my cigarette. 'And did Con never think to set up as a rival to this Bill Fenwick? An obvious move, one imagines. He tried it with Annabel.'

Lisa stirred. 'I told you, it never occurred to anyone that she was even adult! She'd just left school! I think Con thought of her as a schoolgirl. Mr. Winslow certainly did; the Fenwick affair amused him enormously.'

'And now she's had a year in London. She'll have probably got further than the boy-next-door stage,' I said cheerfully. 'You'll find you're worrying about nothing.'

'I hope so. But once you're there at Whitescar, things will be safe enough for Con. Julie won't be seriously in the way.'

I looked at her for a moment. 'No. Well, all right. When?'

There, again, was that surreptitious flash of excitement.

'This weekend. You can ring up on Sunday, as we'd arranged. If you ring up at three, the old man'll be resting, and I'll take the call.'

'You know, I'll have to see Con again before I come.'

She hesitated. 'Yes. He – he wanted to come in and see you himself, today, but he couldn't get away. You'll realise there are one or two things ...' she paused, and seemed to be choosing her words ... 'that you still have to be told. We've – well, we've been keeping them back. We wanted to be quite sure, first, that you saw how easy it was all going to be. So I – we – ' She stopped.

I didn't help her. I waited, smoking quietly. Here it came at last. She needn't have worried, I thought drily, whatever I'd been telling myself, whatever she had to say, I knew I wouldn't back out now. The moment when I had consented to move my rooms, and see Con again, had been the point of no return.

She spoke as if with difficulty. 'It's the real reason for Annabel's doing as she did, and leaving home. You asked about it before.'

'Yes. I was beginning to wonder if you knew yourself.'

'I didn't. Not till recently, not fully.'

'I see. Well, I'll have to know it all, you must realise that.'

'Of course. I may as well be honest with you. We *did* deliberately avoid telling you, until you were more or less committed. We didn't want to risk your throwing the whole thing up, just because there was something that was going to make it, not exactly more difficult, but a little awkward.'

'A little awkward? Lord, Lisa, I thought it must be murder at least, being kept from me so carefully all this time! I confess I've been burning to know. Let's have it, for pity's sake! No, all right, you needn't worry. I'm not throwing anything up at this stage in the proceedings. I couldn't for the life of me pack up and go quietly away, without at least having one look at Whitescar. Besides, I'd feel a fool and a quitter if I did. Silly, considering what it is we're planning to do, but there it is. Take it that I am completely committed.'

She gave a little sigh, and the hands stirred in her lap and relaxed. 'That's what I told Con! The girl's straight, I said, she won't let us down, not now.'

I raised an eyebrow. 'Sure. Straight as a corkscrew. Try me. Well, let's have your "awkward" news. It's been sticking out a mile that there must have been something extra-special about that last row with Con, hasn't it? What had finally gone wrong?'

That little smile again, tight and secret and – I thought, startled – malignant.

'Annabel,' she said.

I stopped with the cigarette half-way to my lips and stared at her. The pudgy hands lay without moving in her lap, but somehow, now, they looked complacent. 'Annabel?' I said sharply. 'I don't follow.'

'It was a vulgarism, I'm afraid. I shouldn't have allowed myself to use it. I only meant that the girl had played the fool and got herself pregnant.'

'*What?*'

'Yes.'

They say that words make no difference; it isn't true, they make it all. I found I was on my feet, looking, I suppose, as shocked as I felt. 'Oh, my God,' I said, 'this is . . . this is . . .' I turned abruptly and went over to the window and stood with my back to her. After a bit I managed to say: 'I quite see why you didn't tell me sooner.'

'I thought you would.'

Her voice sounded as calm as ever, but when after a moment or so I turned, it was to see her watching me with a wariness that was almost sharp enough for apprehension. 'Are you so very shocked?'

'Of course I'm shocked! Not at the fact, particularly – I should have expected something like that, after the build-up – but at realising, flat out, what I've let myself in for. It didn't seem to be really true, till I heard it in so many words.'

'Then it had occurred to you? I thought it might. In fact I hoped it might.'

'Why?'

'I should say, I hoped it *had*. Then I knew that you'd thought about it, and still decided to go on with this.'

'Oh lord, yes,' I repeated it almost wearily, 'I said I would, you needn't worry. I'd look fine, wouldn't I, proposing to lie and cheat my way into the share of a fortune, and then holding up hands of horror at a lapse from grace eight years old.' The setting sun was behind me; she couldn't see me except as a silhouette against the window. I stayed where I was. After a moment or two more, I managed to say, quite evenly: 'Well? Go on. Did they find out who it was?'

She looked surprised, 'Why, good heavens, Con, of course!'

'*Con?*'

'Well, of course!' She was looking at me in the blankest astonishment. Then her eyes dropped, but I had, for one moment, seen the flash of an emotion more shocking than anything which had passed up to now. 'Who else?' she asked in a flat colourless voice.

'Well, but Lisa—!' I stopped, and drew a long steadying breath. 'Con.' I repeated it softly. 'My God . . . *Con.*'

There was a very long silence, which Lisa didn't attempt to break. She was watching me again, and the firelight, striking a gleam from her eyes, made them brilliant and expressionless. I stayed where I was, with my back to the now fading sun. I had been leaning back against the window-sill. I found that my hands were behind me, pressed hard against the edge of the wood. They were hurting. I drew them away, and began slowly to rub them together.

Lisa said, eventually: 'Are you very upset? Why don't you say something?'

'That,' I said, 'was what is known as a silence too deep for words.'

'Annabel—'

'And you thought I might find it a little awkward, did you? I really can't think why.'

She sat forward almost eagerly. 'You mean you *don't* mind?'

'Mind? A little thing like that? My dear Lisa, what a – a *fusspot* you must think me!'

'You don't have to worry about Con's being embarrassed, because he won't be. He . . .'

I said shakily: 'I – I'm glad to hear it. D-don't let's embarrass Con, shall we?'

She said suddenly: 'You're laughing!'

'No, oh no, Lisa. I – I'm only struggling to control myself. I mean, there are possibilities that I feel you can't have thought of. You know, I quite see why Con was being the least bit coy about telling me himself.'

She said, sounding almost resentful: 'I can't imagine why you think it's funny.'

'I don't, really.' I left the window at last, and came across to the table. I pulled a chair out and sat down. 'Don't imagine I was amused at what happened eight years ago; not for a moment. It's my own part in this that has its funny side. I'd have thought you'd be thankful I was amused, Lisa, instead of filled with pious horror at the thought of playing the part of someone who once, in your own charming phrase, "went wrong".'

She gave a little gasp. 'Then it won't make any difference? You do really mean you'll still do it?'

'I said I would. Though this isn't going to make it any easier to face Con again, is it?'

'Con won't mind.'

'So you said. Big of him. But Grandfather's the one who matters. Did he ever know?'

'Oh yes. Con told him.'

'*Con told him?*'

'Yes. You see, after she'd run away, he had to give some sort of explanation to Mr. Winslow. The old man knew she'd been with Con that night, before she came running to him. She'd told her grandfather that she and Con had been quarrelling again, and that this time it was serious, but when he asked why, all she would say was that she wasn't going to stay in the same house with Con any longer, and she begged her grandfather to send him away. Well, of course, Mr. Winslow wanted a reason. He knew Con had been wanting to marry her, and when she wouldn't say anything further, he seems to have assumed that Con had just been – well, too importunate, to put it mildly. He wasn't sympathetic. Then, when it was found in the morning that Annabel had run away, of course Con had to supply an explanation. A mere "lovers' quarrel", as you've said, wasn't enough. In the end, Con thought it was better to admit the truth.'

' "In the end"?'

'Well, yes. Con didn't tell his great-uncle straight away, naturally. The old man was in a dreadful state, and he might easily have fired Con.'

'Unless he'd kept him there, to make him marry her when she came home.'

'There was no need to "make" him. Mr. Winslow knew that. Con would have married her all along. You're not to think it was *that*.'

'I believe you. There was Whitescar, after all.'

A quick look up under her lids, surprisingly unresentful. 'Yes, there was.'

'So Con didn't tell Mr. Winslow straight away? When did he actually confess about the baby?'

'Much later, after it became obvious that she really was gone for good. When she finally wrote from New York, and it was obvious she really meant what she said about not coming home, Con was furious. It made him look such a fool.'

'Yes,' I said, rather drily, 'I see what you mean. So after that, he told Mr. Winslow that Annabel was probably going to have a child, and that he was the father?'

'Yes.' She stirred in her chair. 'He had to, don't you see? It had obviously been so much more than just a violent quarrel. He simply made a clean breast of it, said he'd been her lover, and was still willing to marry her when she came home. Of course there was a terrible row, with the old man raging at Con, as you might expect; but Con stuck to his guns, and swore he'd been ready to marry her any time, and still would. So, in the end, Mr. Winslow accepted it. I don't think it occurred

to him, then, to send Con away. He was the only one still at home, you
see.'

'I see.'

'They waited to hear from her again, but nothing happened. I told
you about that. Just the one note, to say she'd taken a job with a friend
who'd gone to the States, and that she was never coming back. That was
all.'

'No mention, then, of any baby on the way?'

'No.'

'And she hadn't told her grandfather, the night she left home?'

'No.'

'In fact, it never came from Annabel at all?'

'She told Con.'

'Ah, yes,' I said, 'she told Con.'

A quick glint from under her lids. 'I don't quite see—'

'Never mind. Only a line of thought. But there's still something *I*
don't quite see, and we'd better get it straight. Go back to when she
told Con. The night of the quarrel. You'd better tell me exactly what
happened.'

'I don't know just what passed,' said Lisa. 'Con won't say. Maybe
he'll tell you, now that you know the worst.' Her lips tightened again
into that thin travesty of a smile. 'I'd better tell you all I know, as far
as he told me. He says that she had just found out that day about the
baby. She'd been into Newcastle that afternoon to see a doctor, and had
been told she was pregnant. She got back late, and it was dark. She came
back to Whitescar across the fields; there's a path that leads to the
footbridge below the garden. She met Con by chance, somewhere along
the river, where the path skirts it high up, under the trees. I suppose she
hadn't had time to regain her balance or self-control; the news must have
been a dreadful shock to her, and when she ran into Con she just told
him, flat out, and then, of course, there was a scene, with Con trying to
persuade her to listen to him, and Annabel half-crazy with worry about
telling her grandfather, and raving at Con, and just refusing to listen
when he insisted that now they would have to marry, and that it would
work out right in the end.'

'You know, it's not the end of this affair that's the bother,' I said, 'it's
the beginning. From all I've heard, I can't imagine how it ever started.'

She gave me a glance I couldn't interpret. 'Can't you? With Con so
handsome, and Annabel, from what I hear—' an infinitesimal pause.
'She was very young, after all. I suppose it was one of those short, wild
affairs that can blow themselves out as violently as they start. She'd never
let on in public that she cared for him. No one knew – though people
must have guessed, I suppose. But it seems she was never prepared to
settle down, not with Con. And when this happened, and she blamed
Con, and said that she still wouldn't marry him, she could never live
with him, and now one of them would have to leave the place . . . well,

Con had had a shock, too, and he's terribly hot-tempered, like all th
Winslows, so I gather that the scene just went from bad to worse
Eventually she broke away from him, and ran home, shouting that she'
tell Mr. Winslow everything, that it was all Con's fault, and that she'
see he was thrown out.'

'But, in fact, she didn't tell Mr. Winslow "everything".'

'No. Her nerve must have failed her when it came to the point. I
seems that all she did was cry, and rage about Con, and say he must b
sent away; and because Mr. Winslow wanted her to marry Con anyway
all he would do was tell her not to be a fool, and that the sooner sh
made it up with Con the better. I think he suspected, even then, that Co
was her lover. That's all I know.' Her hands moved on her lap in a littl
smoothing movement, as if wiping something away. 'And all I want t
know, I must admit. But I think it's enough, isn't it?'

'Quite enough.' I sat looking down at the table in front of me. I wa
thinking: 'And I know, too. Something you don't. Something Con neve
told you. I know just what did happen that night, in the dark, above th
edge of the deep river ...' I remembered Con's face, and the smoot
voice saying: '*It doesn't necessarily have to be midnight, does it, whe
you and I go walking at the edge of a cliff with water at the bottom.
Remember?*' I remembered the look in his eyes as he spoke, an
the poison-bubbles of fear pricking in my blood; and I wondered how
Con would equate that with the story he had told Lisa and Mr
Winslow.

I looked across at Lisa, who was watching her hands. Yes, for her i
was enough. Whatever Con had done, Lisa would accept it, shutting he
eyes. Even if there had been no subsequent letter from New York, t
show that the girl was still alive after she vanished from Whitescar, Lis
would still not want to know more.

The silence drew out, while I watched the flickering of the flames i
the grate. A coal fell in with a dry, crumbling sound. A rocket of yellow
flame shot up past it with a hiss, and died.

'That was all?' I said at length.

'Yes. People talked, but it's forgotten now, and nobody ever actually
knew anything. Only Con and Mr. Winslow. Con never even told me
till now.'

'I see.' I straightened up, saying briskly: 'Well, that's that, as far as
it goes. All right, Lisa, I'll play; but on my own terms.'

'Which are?'

'The obvious ones. I'll accept everything, except this last thing; and
that, I'll deny.'

'But – you can't do that!'

'Meaning because it might make Con look a fool? All right, you tell
me, where's the baby?'

'Dead. Stillborn. Adopted. We can easily invent—'

'No.' At my tone, I saw her eyes flicker, and that wary look come into her face. I said slowly: 'Lisa, I've said I'll go the whole way with you and Con. But I can't, and won't, take this. I'm not going to invent for myself the sort of tragedy that – that's totally outside my experience. Apart from everything else, it would be too difficult. It's a – a raw sort of situation, and I'm not prepared to react to it. Don't you see? I'm not prepared to play, in front of Grandfather, the part of someone who's borne a child, living or dead, to Con. It – that sort of thing – matters too much. Besides, if it were true, I should never have come home. Con as ex-lover; yes. Con as – this; no. That's all.'

'But what explanation—?'

'It's perfectly simple to say that it was a mistake. That by the time I found out I was wrong, I'd gone abroad, and was too proud to come home – and too unwilling to face Con and Grandfather again.'

'And the other thing? You'll accept that?'

'Having had a lover? I said I would.'

Lisa said, watching me: 'You are – what did you say? – "prepared to react" to that?'

I looked at her straightly. 'I've no objection, if that's what you mean, to having Con as my ex-lover. As long as the emphasis remains on the "ex".'

She dropped her eyes again, but not before I had seen, quite clearly, what had now and then stirred those unexpressive features with that sudden gleam of malignancy; it was jealousy, still alive and potent, of an unhappy girl whom she had believed dead for years. And by the same token, I saw why Lisa and her brother had all along accepted the fact that I was prepared to come in with them on what was at best a crazy and hazardous adventure. Their need was obvious; but I was under no compulsion. The very fact that I was what Lisa had called 'straight' might make me safe to employ, but should have made them pause to wonder why I had thrown my lot in with theirs. I had been sure all along that they didn't really think of me as the type who would do anything for money. And even this last disclosure had not been expected to put me off. Lisa had been wary, even uneasy, but never downright apprehensive.

But now I saw it, simply and infuriatingly through Lisa's eyes. She couldn't understand that any woman could resist for a moment the prospect of an association – any sort of association – with the wonderful, the handsome, the fascinating Connor Winslow.

And Con? Well, as far as I could judge, Con thought exactly the same.

Fatted calf or no fatted calf, Annabel's homecoming would certainly be a riot.

CHAPTER FIVE

Oh, the oak, and the ash, and the bonny ivy tree,
They are all growing green in the North Country.

Traditional

The approach to Whitescar was down a narrow gravelled track edged with hawthorns. There was no gate. On the right of the gap where the track left the main road, stood a dilapidated signpost which had once said, *Private Road to Forrest Hall*. On the left was a new and solid-looking stand for milk-churns, which bore a beautifully-painted legend, WHITESCAR. Between these symbols the lane curled off between its high hawthorns, and out of sight.

I had come an hour too early, and no one was there to meet the bus. I had only two cases with me, and carrying these I set off down the lane.

Round the first bend there was a quarry, disused now and overgrown, and here, behind a thicket of brambles, I left my cases. They would be safe enough, and could be collected later. Meanwhile I was anxious to make my first reconnaissance alone.

The lane skirted the quarry, leading downhill for perhaps another two hundred yards before the hedges gave way on the one side to a high wall, and on the other – the left – to a fence which allowed a view across the territory that Lisa had been at such pains to picture for me.

I stood, leaning on the top bar of the fence, and looked at the scene below me.

Whitescar was about eight miles, as the crow flies, from Bellingham. There the river, meandering down its valley, doubles round leisurely on itself in a great loop, all but enclosing the rolling, well-timbered lands of Forrest Park. At the narrow part of the loop the bends of the river are barely two hundred yards apart, forming a sort of narrow isthmus through which ran the track on which I stood. This was the only road to the Hall, and it divided at the lodge gates for Whitescar and the West Lodge which lay the other side of the park.

The main road, along which my bus had come, lay some way above the level of the river, and the drop past the quarry to the Hall gates was fairly steep. From where I stood you could see the whole near-island laid out below you in the circling arm of the river, with its woods and its water meadows and the chimneys glimpsed among the green.

To the east lay Forrest Hall itself, set in what remained of its once formal gardens and timbered walks, the grounds girdled on two sides by the curving river; and on two by a mile-long wall and a belt of thick trees. Except for a wooded path along the river, the only entrance was through the big pillared gates where the main lodge had stood. This, I knew, had long since been allowed to crumble gently into ruin. I couldn't see it from where I was, but the tracks to Whitescar and West Lodge branched off there, and I could see the latter clearly, cutting across the park from east to west, between the orderly rows of planted conifers. At the distant edge of the river, I caught a glimpse of roofs and chimneys, and the quick glitter of glass that marked the hot-houses in the old walled garden that had belonged to the Hall. There, too, lay the stables, and the house called West Lodge, and a footbridge spanning the river to serve a track which climbed through the far trees and across the moors to Nether Shields farm, and, eventually, to Bellingham.

The Whitescar property, lying along the river-bank at the very centre of its loop, and stretching back to the junction of the roads at the Hall gates, was like a healthy bite taken out of the circle of Forrest territory. Lying neatly between the Hall and West Lodge, it was screened now from my sight by a rise in the land that only allowed me to see its chimneys, and the tops of its trees.

I left my view-point, and went on down the track, not hurrying. Behind the wall to my right now loomed the Forrest woods, the huge trees full out, except for the late, lacy boughs of ash. The ditch at the wall's foot was frilled with cow-parsley. The wall was in poor repair; I saw a blackbird's nest stuffed into a hole in the coping, and there were tangles of campion and toad-flax bunching from gaps between the stones.

At the Hall entrance, the lane ended in a kind of cul-de-sac, bounded by three gateways. On the left, a brand-new oak gate guarded the Forestry Commission's fir plantations and the road to West Lodge. To the right lay the pillars of the Hall entrance. Ahead was a solid, five-barred gate, painted white, with the familiar WHITESCAR blazoning the top bar. Beyond this, the track lifted itself up a gentle rise of pasture, and vanished over a ridge. From here, not even the chimney-tops of Whitescar were visible; only the smooth sunny prospect of green pasture and dry-stone walling sharp with blue shadows, and, in a hollow beyond the rise somewhere, the tops of some tall trees.

But the gateway to the right might have been the entrance to another sort of world.

Where the big gates of the Hall should have hung between their massive pillars, there was simply a gap giving on to a driveway, green and mossy, its twin tracks no longer worn by wheels, but matted over by the discs of plantain and hawkweed, rings of weed spreading and overlapping like the rings that grow and ripple over each other when a handful of gravel is thrown into water. At the edges of the drive the taller weeds began, hedge-parsley and campion, and forget-me-not gone wild, all frothing under the ranks of the rhododendrons, whose flowers showed like pale, symmetrical lamps above their splayed leaves. Overhead hung the shadowy, enormous trees.

There had been a lodge once, tucked deep in the trees beside the gate. A damp, dismal place it must have been to live in; the walls were almost roofless now, and half drifted over with nettles. The chimney-stacks stuck

up like bones from a broken limb. All that had survived of the little
garden was a rank plantation of rhubarb, and the old blush rambler that
ran riot through the gaping windows.

There was no legend here of FORREST to guide the visitor. For those
wise in the right lores there were some heraldic beasts on top of the
pillars, rampant, and holding shields where some carving made cushions
under the moss. From the pillars, to either side, stretched the high wall
that had once marked the boundaries. This was cracked and crumbling
in many places, and the copings were off, but it was still a barrier, save
in one place not far from the pillar on the lodge side of the gate. Here
a giant oak stood. It had been originally on the inside of the wall, but
with the years it had grown and spread, pressing closer and ever closer
to the masonry, until its vast flank had bent and finally broken the wall,
which here lay in a mere pile of tumbled and weedy stone. But the power
of the oak would be its undoing, for the wall had been clothed in ivy, and
the ivy had reached for the tree, crept up it, engulfed it, till now the
trunk was one towering mass of the dark gleaming leaves, and only the
tree's upper branches managed to thrust the young gold leaves of early
summer through the strangling curtain. Eventually the ivy would kill it.
Already, through the tracery of the ivy-stems, some of the oak-boughs
showed dead, and one great lower limb, long since broken off, had left
a gap where rotten wood yawned, in holes deep enough for owls to nest
in.

I looked up at it for a long time, and then along the neat sunny track
that led out of the shadow of the trees towards Whitescar.

Somewhere a ring-dove purred and intoned, and a wood-warbler
stuttered into its long trill, and fell silent. I found that I had moved,
without realising it, through the gateway, and a yard or two up the drive
into the wood. I stood there in the shade, looking out at the wide fields
and the cupped valley, and the white-painted gate gleaming in the sun.
I realised that I was braced as if for the start of a race, my mouth dry,
and the muscles of my throat taut and aching.

I swallowed a couple of times, breathed deeply and slowly to calm
myself, repeating the now often-used formula of *what was there to go
wrong, after all?* I was Annabel. I was coming home. I had never been
anyone else. All that must be forgotten. Mary Grey need never appear
again, except, perhaps, to Con and Lisa. Meanwhile, I would forget her,
even in my thoughts. I was Annabel Winslow, coming home.

I walked quickly out between the crumbling pillars, and pushed open
the white gate.

It didn't even creak. It swung quietly open on sleek, well-oiled hinges,
and came to behind me with a smooth click that said *money*.

Well, that was what had brought me, wasn't it?

I walked quickly out of the shade of the Forrest trees, and up the
sunny track towards Whitescar.

In the bright afternoon stillness the farm looked clean in its orderly
whitewash, like a toy. From the top of the rise I could see it all laid out,
in plan exactly like the maps that Lisa Dermott had drawn for me so
carefully, and led me through in imagination so many times.

The house was long and low, two-storied, with big modern windows
cut into the old thick walls. Unlike the rest of the group of buildings, it
was not whitewashed, but built of sandstone, green-gold with age. The
lichens on the roof showed, even at that distance, like patens of copper
laid along the soft blue slates.

It faced on to a strip of garden – grass and flower-borders and a lilac
tree – whose lower wall edged the river. From the garden, a white
wicket-gate gave on a wooden footbridge. The river was fairly wide here,
lying under the low, tree-hung cliffs of its further bank with that still
gleam that means depth. It reflected the bridge, the trees, and the banked
tangles of elder and honeysuckle, in layers of deepening colour as rich
as a Flemish painter's palette.

On the nearer side of house and garden lay the farm; a courtyard –
even at this distance I could see its clean baked concrete, and the freshness
of the paint on doors and gates – surrounded by byres and stables and
sheds, with the red roof of the big Dutch barn conspicuous beside the
remains of last year's straw stacks, and a dark knot of Scotch pines.

I had been so absorbed in the picture laid out before me, that I hadn't
noticed the man approaching, some thirty yards away, until the clang of
his nailed boots on the iron of the cattle-grid startled me.

He was a burly, middle-aged man in rough farm clothes, and he was
staring at me in undisguised interest as he approached. He came at a
pace that, without seeming to, carried him over the distance between us
at a speed that left me no time to think at all.

I did have time to wonder briefly if my venture alone into the Winslow
den was going to prove my undoing, but at least there was no possibility
now of turning tail. It was with a sense of having the issue taken out of
my hands that I saw the red face split into a beaming smile, and heard
him say, in a broad country voice: 'Why, Miss Annabel!'

There was the ruddy face, the blue eyes, the huge forearm bared to
the elbow, and marked with the scar where the bull had caught him.
Bates, head cattleman at Whitescar. *You'll know him straight away*, Con
had said. But I didn't venture the name. The lessons of the past three
weeks still hummed in my head like a hive of bees: *Take it slowly. Don't
rush your fences. Never be too sure....*

And here was the first fence. *Tell the truth wherever possible.* I told
it. I said with genuine pleasure: 'You knew me! How wonderful! It
makes me feel as if I were really coming home!'

I put out both hands and he took them as if the gesture, from me, was
a natural one. His grip nearly lifted me from the ground. The merle
collie running at his heels circled round us, lifting a lip and sniffing the
back of my legs in a disconcerting manner.

'Knew you?' His voice was gruff with pleasure. 'That I did, the minute you come over the top there. Even if Miss Dermott hadn't tell't us you were coming, I'd 'a known you a mile off across the field, lass! We're all uncommon glad to have you back, and that's a fact.'

'It's marvellous to be here. How are you? You look fine, I don't think you can be a day older! Not eight years, anyway!'

'I'm grand, and Mrs. Bates, too. You'd know I married Betsy, now? They'd tell you, maybe? Aye ... Well, she's in a rare taking with your coming home, spent all morning baking and turning the place upside down, and Miss Dermott along with her. You'll likely find there's tea-cakes and singin' hinnies for your tea.'

'Singin' hinnies?'

'Nay, don't tell me you've forgotten! That I'll not believe. You used to tease for them every day when you was a bairn.'

'No, I hadn't forgotten. It was just – hearing the name again. So – so like home.' I swallowed. 'How sweet of her to remember. I'm longing to see her again. How's Grandfather, Mr. Bates?'

'Why, he's champion, for his age. He's always well enough, mind you, in the dry weather; it's the damp that gets at his back. It's arthritis – you knew that? and there's times when he can hardly get about at all. And now they say there's this other trouble forby. But you'll have heard about that, too, likely? Miss Dermott said you'd telephoned yesterday and asked them to break it gentle-like to your Granda. They'd tell you all the news?'

'Yes. I – I didn't quite know what to do. I thought of writing, but then I thought, if I telephoned Con, it might be easier. Miss Dermott answered; the others were out, and, well – we had a long talk. She told me how things were, and she said she'd get Con to break it to Grandfather. I hadn't known about Grandfather's stroke, so its just as well I didn't just write to him out of the blue. And anyway, I wouldn't have dared just walk right in here and give everyone a shock.'

His voice was rough. 'There's not many dies of that sort of shock, Miss Annabel.'

'That's ... sweet of you. Well, Miss Dermott told me quite a lot of the news.... I'm glad Grandfather keeps so well on the whole.'

'Aye, he's well enough.' A quick glance under puckered eyelids. 'Reckon you'll see a change, though.'

'I'm afraid I probably shall. It's been a long time.'

'It has that. It was a poor day's work you did, Miss Annabel, when you left us.'

'I know,' I said. 'Don't blame me too much.'

'I've no call to blame you, lass. I know naught about it, but that you and your Granda fell out.' He grinned, sourly. 'I know what he's like, none better, I've known him these thirty years. I never take no notice of him, rain or shine, and him and me gets on, but you're too like your dad to sit still and hold your tongue. Winslows is all the same, I reckon.

Maybe if you'd been a mite older, you'd 'a known his bark was always worse than his bite, but you were nobbut a bit lass at the time, and I reckon you'd troubles of your own, at that.'

A short, breathless pause. 'Troubles – of my own?'

He looked a little embarrassed, and stabbed at the ground with his stick. 'Maybe I didn't ought to 'a said that. I only meant as everyone knew it wasn't all plain sailing with you and Mr. Con. Happen one takes these things too hard at nineteen.'

I smiled. 'Happen one does. Well, it's all over now. Let's forget it, shall we? And you mustn't blame Con and Grandfather either, you know. I was young and silly, and I suppose I thought I'd like to get away on my own for a bit. I didn't want to be tied down to Whitescar or – or anything, not just then, not yet; so when the time came, I just went without thinking. One doesn't think very straight, at nineteen. But now I'm back, and I'm going to try and forget I've ever been away.'

I looked away from him, down towards the farm. I could see white hens ruffling in the straw of the stackyard, and there were pigeons on the roof. The smoke from the chimneys went straight up into the clean air. I said: 'It looks just the same. Better, if anything. Or is that absence, making the heart grow fonder?'

'Nay, I'll not deny it's well looked after. As well every way, nearly, as in your Granda's time.'

I stared at him. 'As in – you talk as if that was past.'

He was prodding at the earth again with his stick. 'Happen it is.'

'What d'you mean?'

That quick, almost surly glance upwards again. 'You'll see, Miss Annabel. I don't doubt but what you'll see. Times change.'

I didn't pursue it, and he turned the subject abruptly. He nodded past me, the way I had come, towards the towering woods that surrounded the site of Forrest Hall. 'Now, there's the biggest change you'll find, and none of it for the better. Did she tell you about Forrests?'

'Yes.' I looked back to where the crest of the ivied oak reared above the skyline, the glinting darkness of the ivy making it stand up like a ruined tower against the young summer green of the woods. 'Yes, Miss Dermott told me. Four years ago, wasn't it? I thought the old lodge looked even more dilapidated than it should. I never remember anyone living there, but at least the drive looked reasonable, and the gates were on.'

'They went for scrap, after the fire. Aye, we miss the Hall, though it's not all gone, you mind. They're using some of the stable buildings over at West Lodge for poultry, and the old garden's going strong. Mr. Forrest got that going himself, with Johnny Rudd – you'll mind Johnny? He's working there still, though there's nobbut one horse in the stables. Mr. Forrest kept that one when the stud went; he's one of the old "Mountain" lot, and I reckon Mr. Forrest couldn't bear to part, but I doubt he'll have to be sold now. He's just running wild there, and eating his head off, and

there's no one can hardly get near him.' He grinned at me. 'You'll have
to get to work on him yourself, now you're back.'

'Me? Not on your – I mean, not any more. Those days are past, Mr.
Bates.'

'How's that?'

The story that Lisa and I had concocted came glibly enough. 'I had
a bad fall in the States, and hurt my back – nothing drastic, you know,
but not a thing I'd dare risk doing again.'

'That's a shame, now! I reckoned Johnny'd be rare pleased when he
heard you were back. He hasn't the time to bother on wi' horses now,
not at this time of year; and the colt's spoiling. Mr. Con's been along to
take a hand to him, now and then, but the youngster's taken a rare
scunner at him, seemingly. Won't let him near. There's naught else fit
for a ride at Whitescar.'

'I expect I've lost my touch, anyway.'

'Eh, well,' he said, 'it's like we said. Things change, more's the pity.
Every time I walk up this road I think on the way it was. It's sad to see
the old places falling down, and the families gone, but there it is.'

'Yes.' Beyond the ivy-clad oak, behind a sunny tracery of tree-tops, I
could see a chimney. The sun glinted warm on the mellow stone. There
was the glimpse of a tiled roof through the boughs. A wisp of cloud,
moving slowly, gave the illusion of smoke, rising from a homely fire.
Then it moved on, and I saw that the roof was broken.

Bates said, beside me, so suddenly that I jumped. 'You've changed. I
was wrong, maybe, I didn't think you had, not that much, but now I can
see.'

'What can you see?'

'I dunno. It's not only that you're older. You're different, Miss
Annabel, no offence.' The kindly blue eyes surveyed me. 'Happen you'll
have had a hard time of it, out there?'

He made it sound as if the Atlantic were the water of Styx, and the
lands beyond it the Outer Darkness. I smiled. 'Happen I have.'

'You didn't marry?'

'No. Too busy earning my keep.'

'Aye. That's where it is. You'd 'a done better to stay here at home,
lass, where your place was.'

I thought of Con, of the scandal, of the lonely crumbling ruin in the
Forrest woods. 'You think so?' I laughed a little, without amusement.
'Well, I'm back, anyway. I've come back to my place now, and I expect
I'll have the sense to stick to it.'

'You do that.' The words had an emphasis that was far from idle. He
was staring at me fixedly, his eyes almost fierce in the rubicund face.
'Well, I'll not keep you here talking. They'll be looking for you down
yonder. But you stay here, Miss Annabel, close by your Granda – and
don't leave us again.'

He nodded abruptly, whistled up the collie, and strode past me up the track without looking back.

I turned down towards Whitescar.

The end of the barn threw a slanting shadow half across the yard gate. Not until I was within twenty paces of it did I see that a man leaned there, unmoving, watching my approach. Con.

If Bates had been the first fence, this was the water-jump. But Lisa had been so sure he 'wouldn't mind'....

Apparently he didn't. He straightened up with the lazy grace that was so typical of him, and gave me a brilliant smile that held no trace of embarrassment whatsoever. His hand went out to the latch of the gate.

'Why, Annabel,' he said, and swung the gate open with a sort of ceremony of invitation. 'Welcome home!'

I said feebly: 'Hullo.' I was trying to see, without looking too obviously round me, if there was anyone else within earshot. The yard was apparently deserted, but I didn't dare risk it. I said, feeling perilously foolish: 'It – it's nice to be back.'

'You're earlier than we expected. I intended to meet you with the car. Where's your luggage?'

'I left it in the quarry. Could someone fetch it later?'

'I'll go myself. You know, you really should have let me come into Newcastle for you.'

'No. I – I wanted to come alone. Thanks all the same.' I found to my fury that I was stammering like a schoolgirl. I did manage to reflect that if anyone happened to be watching us, they would see merely that there was something stilted and constrained about our greeting. As well there might be, I thought, bitterly. Damn Lisa. She should have told me earlier, let me get this over, find some sort of working arrangement with Con, before I was pitchforked into greeting him in public.

I still hadn't met his eyes. He had shut the gate behind me, but I stayed standing by it, talking, still feebly and rather madly, about luggage. 'Of course, you know, my main baggage is in Liverpool. I can get it sent –'.

'Of course.' I heard the laugh in his voice, then, and looked up. Outrageously, he was looking amused. Before I could speak again he had put out both hands and taken mine in them, smiling delightfully down at me. His voice was warm and, one might have sworn, genuinely moved. 'This is wonderful ... to see you here again after all this time. We never thought ...' he appeared to struggle for a moment with his emotions, and added, deeply: 'This is a pretty shattering moment, my dear.' '*You're telling me, blast you.*' I didn't dare say it aloud, but he read it in my eyes quite easily. His own were dancing. He gave me that deliberately dazzling smile of his, then pulled me towards him, and kissed me. He must have felt my startled and instinctive resistance, because he slackened his hold straight away, saying quickly under his breath: 'There are windows looking this way, Mary, my dear. I think, under the circumstances, that I'd have kissed her, don't you? Strictly cousinly and affectionate, of course?'

He was still holding my hands. I said equally softly, and through shut teeth: 'And don't you think, dear cousin Connor, that she might even have hauled off and slapped your face, hard? Strictly cousinly and affectionate, of course.'

I felt him shake with laughter, and pulled my hands away. '*Is* there someone watching, then? Can they hear us?'

'Not that I'm aware of.'

'Well, *really* – !'

'Ssh, not so loudly. You never know.' He had his back to the house, and was looking down at me. 'Are you really as mad as blazes at me?'

'Oh course I am!'

'I wouldn't blame you, either. Lisa told me you took it terribly well. I wouldn't have dared tell you, myself. You wouldn't think I was shy, to look at me, would you?'

'Oddly enough, no. I wonder why all the most aggressive personalities insist on telling one how shy they really are underneath it all?' I considered him thoughtfully. 'Yes. Lisa was quite right. She kept telling me that *you* wouldn't mind.'

The laughter went out of his face as if a light had been switched off. 'Why would I, now? What man ever minded being known to be a girl's lover?'

A pigeon rustled down beside us, and strutted, arching its neck. The iridescent colours shifted and gleamed along its feathers, like a witch's oils spilling on moving water.

'You silence me,' I said at length.

The light was back, a glimmer of it. 'Not really. You're quite right. I was behaving badly, but the occasion kind of went to my head. Forgive me.'

'It's all right.'

Suddenly, it seemed, we were over the water-jump and moving easily into the straight. I relaxed, leaning back against the gate. We smiled at one another with a certain amount of understanding. To an observer the scene would still be perfectly in character. Even from the house, I thought, the scarlet in my cheeks could be seen quite easily; and Con stood in front of me in an attitude that might have suggested hesitation, and even humility, if one hadn't been able to see his eyes.

He asked abruptly: 'Do you mind so very much?'

'This rôle of ex-lover that you've wished on me at the last minute? No, not really, since nobody knows except Grandfather. Though whether I mind or not is obviously going to depend entirely on you.'

'Meaning?'

'I mean that I don't intend to play this as though I'd come back ready to fall at your feet and make it up, Con Winslow.'

He grinned. 'No. That would be asking a bit too much, I can see that.'

'You might have thought of it before you kissed me.' I leaned back against the gate and added, coolly: 'Do you really want to find yourself waiting for me at the altar steps, at the wrong end of Grandfather's shotgun?'

There was a startled silence. It was something, I thought, not without satisfaction, to have shaken that amused assurance. I tilted my head and smiled up at him. 'Yes, it's a wonder you and Lisa didn't think of that one. It's just possible that Grandfather might think it's never too late to mend. And I might accept you this time.'

Silence again, two long beats of it.

'Why, you little *devil!*' It was the first genuine feeling he had shown during the interview. 'Who'd have thought – ?' He broke off, and the long mouth curved. 'And what if I call your bluff, girl dear? It might be the perfect ending to our little game, after all, and it's just a marvel that I never thought of it before. Sweet saints alive, I can think of a lot worse fates than ending up on the altar steps with you!' He laughed at my expression. 'You see? Don't pull too many bluffs with me, acushla, or you might find them called.'

'And don't get too clever with me, Con, or you'll cut yourself. Shotgun or no, I could always quarrel with you again, couldn't I? And this time, who knows, Grandfather might even throw *you* out instead of me.'

'All right,' said Con easily, 'we've called each other's bluff, and that's that.' His eyes were brilliant under the long lashes: it was obvious that, however the game went, Con was going to enjoy it to the full. The eight-years'-old tragedy was now nothing more than a counter in that same game. If it had ever touched him, it did so no longer. 'We'll play it your way,' he said. 'I'll watch my step, really I will. I didn't mean to upset you.'

'It's the only way to play it.'

'Yes, I see that. And I really am sorry about this. I know Lisa and I ought to have told you this last thing much sooner, but, to tell you the sober truth, I didn't dare. I'd not have blamed you if you'd backed down straight away, though somehow I didn't think you were the girl to do that. And I was right. You still came.'

'Oh yes, I came.'

He still had his back to the house windows, which was just as well. His face, expressive as ever, was alight with uncomplicated excitement. 'Whatever the terms – and you can set them – this is going to be the hell of a partnership, Mary Grey! You're a wonderful girl! You know, you and I have a lot in common.'

I said, just a little dryly: 'Why, thank you. Praise indeed.'

He ignored that, or perhaps he didn't see it. 'A hell of a partnership! I told you, you'll call the tune. You'll have to, if it comes to that: you'll know better than I would what a girl's reactions would be, after – well, coming back like this. I'll play it any way you say. But we'll have to play it together: it's a duet, not a duel. A duet for you and me, with Lisa turning the pages.'

I wondered, fleetingly, what Lisa would have thought of the rôle so lightly assigned to her. 'Very well. And to start with, kisses, cousinly or not, are out. Did you ever read *Count Hannibal*?'

'Certainly I did. And I know what you're thinking of, the bit where the hero says: "Is it to be a kiss or a blow between us, madame?"'

'That's it. And she says: "A thousand times a blow!" Well, that's the way it is, monsieur.'

'Yes, all right. But then, if you remember what happened next –'

'He slapped her face. Yes, so he did. But that's going a bit too far, don't you think? If we just keep it calm and cousinly –'

'You're enjoying this, aren't you?'

'What?' The abruptness of the question had startled me out of laughter. I must have gaped at him quite blankly. 'Enjoying it?'

'Yes. Don't pretend you're not. You're as excited as I am.'

'I – I don't know. I'm certainly a bit tensed up, who wouldn't be? Hang it, I'm only human.' His hand moved up to cover my wrist where it lay along the top bar of the gate. 'All right, my pulse is racing. Wouldn't yours be?' I pulled the hand away from under his. 'Now, we've talked long enough. When will Grandfather be around?'

'He won't be expecting you quite yet. Don't worry. Lisa says he'll wait upstairs and see you in his room after he's had his rest. Shall I show you round now, before you see him?'

'Good heavens, no. I wouldn't want to look round first, you know. People first, places later. You'd better take me in and introduce me to Lisa, and I'll see Mrs. Bates.'

'You keep your head, don't you?'

'Why not? I've taken the first hurdle, anyway.'

'Was I a hurdle?'

I laughed. 'You? You were the water-jump. No, I meant that I'd met Bates when I was on my way down from the road.'

'Oh, God, yes, I'd forgotten. I saw him go up, but of course I'd no idea you were coming so early. I take it you got away with it? Good for you. You see how easy it's going to be.... Did you greet him by name?'

'Not till he mentioned his wife. Better safe than sorry, though I felt pretty sure, and of course the scarred arm made it a certainty.'

'Where did you meet him?'

'Crossing High Riggs.'

I saw his eyes widen, and laughed a little. 'My dear Con, you'll have to learn not to look startled. Give Lisa some credit. Why shouldn't I recognise High Riggs? It's been called that, time out of mind.'

He drew a long breath. 'Fair enough. I'm learning. But it's – even more disconcerting, now that I see you actually here ... in this setting.'

'We'd better go in.'

'Yes, Lisa'll be in the kitchen, and Mrs. Bates with her.'

'I can smell baking, even from here. Do you suppose she'll have made singin' hinnies for my tea?'

I had spoken quite naturally, as I turned to go, but the naked shock in his face stopped me short. He was staring at me as if he'd never seen me before.

His lips opened, and his tongue came out to wet them. 'You can't – I never – how did you – ?'

He stopped. Behind the taut mask of shock I thought I glimpsed again what I had seen in his face at our first meeting.

I lifted my brows at him. 'My dear Con, if you're beginning to have doubts about me yourself, after all this time, I *must* be good!'

The strain slackened perceptibly, as if invisible guys had been loosened. 'It's only, it sounded so natural, the sort of little thing she might have said.... And you standing there, by the yard gate. It's as if it were yesterday.' He took a breath; it seemed to be the first for minutes. Then he shook his head sharply, like a dog coming out of water. 'I'm sorry, stupid of me. As you say, I'll have to learn. But how in the world did you know a silly little thing like that? I hadn't remembered it myself, and Lisa wouldn't know, and it's ten to one Mrs. Bates never mentioned it to her till today, if she has even now.'

'Yes, she has. Bates told me she'd be making them for my tea. He nearly caught me right out. What the dickens are they, anyway?'

'Oh, a special kind of girdle-cake.' He laughed, and the sound was at once elated, and half-relieved. 'So you just learned it ten minutes ago, and you come out with it as to the manner born! You're wonderful! A hell of a partnership, did I call it? My God, Mary Grey – and it's the last time I'll ever call you that – you're the girl for my money! You're a winner, and didn't I know it the minute I clapped eyes on you, up there on the Wall? If it wouldn't look kind of excessive, besides going back on our pact and making you mad as fire, I'm damned if I wouldn't kiss you again! No, no, it's all right, don't look at me like that; I said I'd behave, and I will.'

'I'm glad to hear it. And now we've been out here quite long enough. Shall we go in?'

'Sure ... Annabel. Come along. Headed straight for the next fence; Becher's Brook this time, wouldn't you say?' His hand slid under my arm. Physical contact seemed to come as naturally to Con Winslow as breathing. 'No, not that way. You ought to know they never use the front door on a farm.'

'I'm sorry.' I gave a quick glance round the deserted yard, and up at the empty windows. 'No harm done.'

'Not scared at all?'

'No. Edgy, but not scared.'

The hand squeezed my arm. 'That's my girl.'

I withdrew it. 'No. Remember?'

He was looking down at me speculatively, charmingly, still with that glint of teasing amusement, but I got the feeling that it was no longer something pleasant that amused him. He said: 'Girl dear, if you only knew....'

'Look,' I said, 'if I only knew, as you put it, I imagine I wouldn't be here at all. And we agreed to drop it all, didn't we? It's going to be quite embarrassing enough having to face you in front of Grandfather, without your amusing yourself by teasing me when we're alone.'

'I only said – '

'I know what you said. And I'm saying that we'll drop the subject as from now. If I were Annabel, would you want to be reminding me? Would you ... *dare*? Or, for that matter, would you want *me* to be reminding Grandfather?'

There was a tiny pause.

'Well, well,' said Con, and laughed. All right, Annabel, my dear. A thousand times a blow. Come along into the lion's den.'

CHAPTER SIX

She can make an Irish stew,
Aye, and singin' hinnies, too ...

North Country Song: *Billy Boy*

When Con showed me along the flagged passage, and into the kitchen, Lisa was just lifting a fresh batch of baking out of the oven. The air was full of the delectable smell of new bread.

The kitchen was a big, pleasant room, with a high ceiling, a new cream-coloured Aga stove, and long windows made gay with potted geraniums and chintz curtains that stirred in the June breeze. The floor was of red tiles, covered with those bright rugs of hooked rag that make Northern kitchens so attractive. In front of the Aga was an old-fashioned fender of polished steel, and inside it, from a basket covered with flannel, came the soft cheepings of newly-hatched chickens. The black and white cat asleep in the rocking-chair took no notice of the sounds, or of the tempting heavings and buttings of small heads and bodies against the covering flannel.

I stopped short, just inside the door.

At that moment, more, I think, than at any other in the whole affair, I bitterly regretted the imposture I was undertaking. For two pins I'd have bolted then and there. What had seemed exciting and even reasonable in Newcastle, simple in High Riggs, and intriguing just now in the yard outside, seemed, in this cheerful, lovely room smelling of home, to be no less than an outrage. This wasn't, any more, just a house I had come to claim for Con, or a counter in a game I was playing; it was home, a place breathing with a life of its own, fostered by generations of people who had belonged here. In the shabby Newcastle boarding-house, with my lonely and prospectless Canadian life behind me, and a dreary part-time job doing nothing but stave off the future, things had looked very different: but here, in Whitescar itself, the world of second-class intrigue seemed preposterously out of place. Things should be simple in a place like this, simple and good; sunshine through flowered curtains, the smell of new bread, and chickens cheeping on the hearth; not a complicated imposture, a fantastic Oppenheim plot hatched out in a shabby bedroom with this Irish adventurer, and this stolid woman with the soft, grasping hands, who, having put down the baking-tray, was moving now to greet me.

They must have noticed my hesitation, but there was no one else to see it. Through a half-shut door that led to the scullery came the sounds of water running, and the chink of crockery. Mrs. Bates, I supposed. Perhaps, with instinctive tact, she had retired to let me meet the current mistress of Whitescar.

It seemed it was just as well she had, for to my surprise the stolid, ever-reliable Lisa seemed, now it had come to the point, to be the least composed of the three of us. Her normally sallow cheeks were flushed, though this may only have been from the heat of the oven. She came forward, and then hesitated, as if at a loss for words.

Con was saying, easily, at my elbow: 'Here she is, Lisa. She came early, and I met her at the gate. I've been trying to tell her how welcome she is, but perhaps you'll do it better than me. She's finding it all a bit of a trial so far, I'm afraid.' This with his charming smile down at me, and a little brotherly pat on the arm. 'Annabel, this is my half-sister, Lisa Dermott. She's been looking after us all, you knew that.'

'We've already had a long talk over the telephone,' I said. 'How do you do, Miss Dermott? I'm very glad to meet you. It – it's lovely to be back. I suppose I needn't tell you that.'

She took my hand. She was smiling, but her eyes were anxious, and the soft hand was trembling.

She spoke quite naturally, however. 'You're welcome indeed, Miss Winslow. I dare say it seems odd to you to have me greet you like this in your own home, but after all this time it's come to feel like home to me as well. So perhaps you'll let me tell you how glad everybody is to see you back. We'd – you must know – I told you yesterday – we'd all thought you must be dead. You can imagine that this is a great occasion.'

'Why, Miss Dermott, how nice of you.'

'I hope,' she said, rather more easily, 'that you'll call me Lisa.'

'Of course. Thank you. And you must please drop the "Miss Winslow", too. We're cousins, surely, or is it half-cousins, I wouldn't know?' I smiled at her. The chink of crockery from the scullery had stopped as soon as I spoke. Through the half-shut door there came a sort of listening silence. I wondered if our conversation were sounding too impossibly stilted. If this had genuinely been my first introduction to Lisa, no doubt the situation would have been every bit as awkward. There would have been, literally, nothing to say.

I went on saying just that, in a voice that sounded, to myself, too high, too quick, too light altogether. 'After all, I'm the stranger here, or so it feels, after all this time, and I'm sure you've given me a better welcome than I deserve! Of course it's your home. . . .' I looked about me . . . 'more than mine, now, surely! I never remember it looking half as pretty! How lovely you've got it . . . new curtains . . . new paint . . . the same old chickens, I'll swear, they were always part of the furniture . . . oh, there's the old tea-caddy, I'm so glad you didn't throw it out!'

Lisa had certainly never thought fit to mention the battered old tin on the mantelpiece, but, since it was decorated with a picture of George V's Coronation, they would recognise it as a safe bet. 'And the Aga! That's terrific! When was that put in?'

'Five years ago.' Lisa spoke shortly, almost repressively. Con was watching me with what seemed to be amused respect, but Lisa, I could see, thought I was jumping a bit too fast into that attentive silence from the scullery.

I grinned at her, with a spice of mischief, and moved over to the hearth. 'Oh, lord, the old rocking-chair . . . and it still creaks. . . .' I creaked it again, and the sleeping cat opened slitted green eyes, looked balefully at me, and shut them again. I laughed, almost naturally, and stooped to stroke him. 'My welcome home. He looks a tough egg, this chap. What happened to Tibby?'

'He died of old age,' said Con. 'I buried him under your lilac tree.'

'He'd have died of middle age long before that, if I'd had my way.' Lisa was back at the table, scooping hot rolls off the tin on to the baking-sieve. She seemed relieved to be back in action. She didn't look at Con or me. 'The place for cats is in the buildings, and they know it.'

'You didn't try to keep *Tibby* outside?'

'Tibby,' said Con cheerfully, 'was so hedged about with the sanctity of having been your cat, that he was practically allowed to live in your bedroom. Don't worry about Tibby. He got even Lisa down in the end, and lived his life out in the greatest possible honour and luxury.'

I smiled and stroked the cat's ears. 'Not like Flush?'

'Flush?' This was Lisa. I caught the sudden quick overtone of apprehension, as if she had caught me speaking without the book.

Con grinned at her. 'Elizabeth Barrett's dog. When Elizabeth bolted, early one morning, just like Annabel, her father is said to have wanted to destroy her little dog, as a sort of revenge.'

'O – oh . . . I see.'

He looked at me. 'No, Annabel, not like Flush. Revenge wasn't . . . our first reaction.'

I let it pass. 'And this one?' I said. 'What's his claim to the best chair in the kitchen?'

'Tommy? That fat, lazy brute?' Lisa was patently feeling the strain.

A conversation about cats at this juncture was, obviously, the last straw in irrelevance. Lisa's Teutonic thoroughness wanted to get on with the task in hand, lay the next brick or so, and slap a few more solid lies in to mortar the brand-new structure together. She said, almost snappily: 'Heaven knows I throw him out often enough, but he will come in, and I haven't had the time today to shift him.'

Con said lazily: 'His personality's stronger than yours, Lisa my dear.' He, apparently, shared my belief that the bricks of deception could be perfectly well made with the smallest straws of irrelevance. He took a roll off the rack and bit into it. 'Mmm. Not bad. They're eatable today, Lisa. I suppose that means Mrs. Bates baked them?'

His sister's forbidding expression broke up into that sudden affectionate smile that was kept only for him.

'Oh, have some butter with it, Con, do. Or wait until tea-time. Won't you ever grow up?'

'Isn't Mrs. Bates here?' I asked.

Lisa shot me a look, three parts relief to one of apprehension. 'Yes. She's through in the scullery. Would you like—?'

But before she could finish the sentence the door was pushed open and, as if on a cue, a woman appeared in the doorway, a round squat figure of the same general shape as the Mrs. Noah from a toy ark, who stood on the threshold with arms in the traditional 'akimbo' position, surveying me with ferocious little boot-button eyes.

Lisa led in hastily. 'Oh, Mrs. Bates, here's Miss Annabel.'

'I can see that. I ain't blind, nor yet I ain't deaf.' Mrs. Bates' thin lips shut like a trap. The fierce little eyes regarded me. 'And where do *you* think you've been all this time, may I ask? And what have you been a-doing of to yourself? You look terrible. You're as thin as a rail, and if you're not careful you'll have lost all your looks, what's left of 'em, by the time you're thirty. America, indeed! Ain't your own home good enough for you?'

She was nodding while she spoke, little sharp jerking movements like one of those mandarin toys one used to see; and each nod was a condemnation. I saw Con flick an apprehensive look at me, and then at his sister. But he needn't have worried; Lisa's briefing had been thorough. '*She adored Annabel, cursed her up hill and down dale, wouldn't hear anyone say a word against her; had a frightful set-to with Mr. Winslow after she ran away, and called him every tyrant under the sun. ... She's frightfully rude – plain-spoken she calls it – and she resents me, but I had to keep her; Bates is the best cattleman in the county, and she's a marvellous worker. ...*'

'A fine thing it's been for us, let me tell you,' said Mrs. Bates sharply, 'thinking all this time as you was lost and gone beyond recall, but now as you *is* back, there's a few things I'd like to be telling you, and that's a fact. There's none can say I'm one to flatter and mince me words, plain-spoken I may be, but I speak as I find, and for anyone to do what

you gone and did, and run off without a word in the middle of the
night –'.

I laughed at her. 'It wasn't the middle of the night, and you know it.'
I went up to her, took her by the shoulders and gave her a quick hug,
then bent and kissed the hard round cheek. I said gently: 'Make me
welcome, Betsy. Don't make it harder to come home. Goodness knows
I feel bad enough about it, I don't need you to tell me. I'm sorry if it
distressed you all, but I – well, I was terribly unhappy, and when one's
very young and very unhappy, one doesn't always stop to think, does
one?'

I kissed the other cheek quickly, and straightened up. The little black
eyes glared up at me, but her mouth was working. I smiled, and said
lightly: 'And you must admit I did the thing properly, dreadful quarrel,
note left on the pincushion and everything.'

'Pincushion? What did you ever want with a pincushion? Never did
a decent day's work in your life, always traipsing around after horses
and dogs and tractors, or that there garden of yours, let alone the house
and the jobs a girl ought to take an interest in. Pincushion!' She snorted.
'Where would you be finding one of them?'

'Well,' I said mildly, 'where did I leave it?'

'On that mantelpiece as ever was, *which* well you remember!' She
nodded across the kitchen. 'And when I come down that morning I was
the one found it there, and I stood there fair pussy-struck for five mortal
minutes, I did, afore I dared pick it up. I knew what it was, you see. I'd
heard you and your Granda having words the night before, *and* I heard
you go to your room just after, which well you know I did. I didn't never
think to have the chance to tell you this, but I folleyed you along, Miss
Annabel, an' I listened outside your door.' Another nod, more ferocious
than the last. 'I did that. *Which* I won't take shame to meself for doing
it, neither. If you'd a' bin upset-like, which you being only a girl, and
your Granda playing Hamlet with you, there's times when a girl needs
a woman to talk to, even if it's nobbut Betsy Bates, as was Betsy Jackson
then. But if I'd had any idea as you was in real trouble, which I never
thought –'

I was very conscious of Con just at my shoulder. I said quickly: 'Betsy,
dear –'

I saw Con make a slight, involuntary movement, and thought: he
doesn't want me to stop her; he thinks I'll learn something from all this.

He needn't have worried, she had no intention of being stopped until
I had heard it all.

'But there wasn't a sound, not of crying. Just as if you was moving
about the room quiet-like, getting ready for your bed. So I thought to
meself, it's only a fight, I thought, the old man'll be sorry in the morning,
and Miss Annabel'll tell him she won't do it again, whatever she done,
riding that Everest horse of Mr. Forrest's maybe, or maybe even staying
out too late, the way she has been lately, and the old man not liking it,

him being old-fashioned that way. But I thinks to meself, it'll be all right in the morning, the way it always has been, so I just coughs to let you know I'm there, and I taps on the door and says: "I'm away to bed now, Miss Annabel," and you stopped moving about, as if I'd frightened you, and then you come over to the door and stopped inside it for a minute, but when you opened it you still had all your things on, and you said: "Good night, Betsy dear, and thank you," and you kissed me, you remember, and you looked so terrible, white and ill, and I says, "Don't take on so, Miss Annabel," I says, "there's nought that doesn't come right in the end, not if it was ever so," and you smiled at that and said "No." And then I went off to bed, and I never heard no sound, and if anyone had tell't me that next morning early you'd up and go, and stay away all these years, and your Granda fretting his heart out after you, for all he's had Mr. Con here, and Julie as is coming this week, which she's the spitting image of you, I might say –'

'I know. Lisa told me. I'm longing to meet her.' I touched her hand again. 'Don't upset yourself any more. Let's leave it, shall we? I – I've come back, and I'm not going again, and don't be too angry with me for doing what I did.'

Lisa rescued me, still, I gathered, trying to bring the straying runner back on course. 'Your grandfather'll be awake by now. You'd better go up, he'll want to see you straight away.' She was reaching for her apron strings. 'I'll take you up. Just give me time to wash my hands.'

I saw Mrs. Bates bridle, and said smoothly enough: 'Don't trouble, Lisa. I – I'd sooner go up by myself. I'm sure you'll understand.'

Lisa had stopped half-way to the sink, looking irresolute, and rather too surprised.

Mrs. Bates was nodding again, with a kind of triumph in the tight compression of her mouth. Con took another new roll, and saluted me with a tiny lift of the eyebrow as he turned to go. 'Of course you would,' he said. 'Don't treat Annabel as a stranger, Lisa my dear. And don't worry, Annabel. He'll be so pleased to see you that he's not likely to rake up anything painful out of the past.'

Another lift of the eyebrow on this masterly *double-ententre* of reassurance, and he was gone.

Lisa relaxed, and seemed to recollect something of her lost poise. 'I'm sorry.' Her voice was once more even and colourless. 'Of course you'll want to go alone. I was forgetting. It isn't every day one gets a – an occasion like this. Go on up now, my dear. Tea'll be ready in half an hour. . . . Mrs. Bates, I wonder if you would help me with the tea-cakes? You're a much better hand at them than I am.'

'Which is not to be wondered at, seeing as how I'm north country bred and born, *which* no foreigner ever had a good hand with a tea-cake yet,' said that lady tartly, but moving smartly towards the table.

Lisa had stooped again to the oven. Her back was towards us. I had

to say it, and this was as good a moment as any. 'Betsy, bless you, singin'
hinnies! They look as good as ever!'

Lisa dropped the oven shelf with a clatter against its runners. I heard
her say: 'Sorry. Clumsy,' in a muffled voice. 'It's all right, I didn't spill
anything.'

'You don't think,' said Mrs. Bates crisply, 'that them singin' hinnies
is for you? Get along with you now, to your Granda.'

But the nod which went along with the briskly snapping voice said,
quite plainly: 'Don't be frightened. Go on. It'll be all right.'

I left the kitchen door open behind me.

It was obvious that no questions of identity were going to rouse
themselves in the minds of Mrs. Bates and her husband; but the
real ordeal was still ahead of me, and if there were ever going to be
questions asked, my every movement on this first day was going to be
important.

So I left the door open, and was conscious of Lisa and Mrs. Bates
watching me as I crossed the flagged back lobby, pushed open the green
baize door which gave on the front hall, and turned unhesitatingly to the
right before the door swung shut behind me.

'It's a very simple house,' Lisa had said. 'It's shaped like an L, with
the wing shorter than the stem of the L. The wing's where the kitchens
are, and the scullery, and what used to be the dairy, but all the dairy
work's done in the buildings now, so it's a laundry-house with a Bendix
and an electric ironing machine. There's a baize door that cuts the kitchen
wing off from the main body of the house.

'It's not the original farm-house, you know, it's what you might call
a small manor. It was built about a hundred and fifty years ago, on the
site of the old house that was pulled down. You'll find a print of the
original farm-house in Bewick's *Northumberland*: that was a square,
grim-looking sort of building, but the new one's quite different, like a
small country house, plain and sturdy, certainly, but graceful too . . .
The main hall's square, almost an extra room . . . a wide staircase
opposite the front door . . . drawing-room to one side, dining-room to
the other with the library behind; that's used as an office . . . your
grandfather's bedroom is the big room at the front, over the drawing-
room . . .'

As the baize door shut, I leaned back against it for a moment, and let
myself pause. It could not have been more than three-quarters of an
hour since I had met Bates in High Riggs, but already I felt exhausted
with sustained effort. I must have a minute or two alone, to collect myself
before I went upstairs . . .

I looked about me. The hall had certainly never been built for an
ordinary farm-house. The floor was oak parquet, and the old blanket-
chest against the wall was carved oak, too, and beautiful. A couple of
Bokhara rugs looked very rich against the honey-coloured wood of the

floor. The walls were plain ivory, and there was a painting of a jar of marigolds, a copy of the Sartorius aquatint of the Darley Arabian, and an old coloured map of the North Tyne, with *Forreſt Hall* clearly marked, and, in smaller letters on a neat segment of the circle labelled *Forreſt Park*, I identified *Whiteſcar.*

Below the map, on the oak chest, stood a blue ironstone jug, and an old copper dairy-pan, polished till its hammered surface gleamed like silk. It was full of blue and purple pansies and wild yellow heartsease.

Whitescar had certainly not suffered from Lisa's stewardship. I reflected, in passing, that Lisa had been wrong about Mrs. Bates. Mrs. Bates by no means disliked her; her attitude of armed neutrality was a faint reflection of the ferocious affection she had hurled at me. Anyone who could keep a house as Lisa had, had almost certainly won Mrs. Bates' loyalty, along with as lively a respect as a Northumbrian would care to accord a 'foreigner'.

I went slowly up the wide oak staircase. The carpet was moss-green and thick; my feet made no sound. I turned along the landing which made a gallery to one side of the hall. At the end of it a window looked over the garden.

Here was the door. Oak, too, with shallow panels sunk in their bevelled frames. I put out a finger and ran it silently down the bevel.

The landing was full of sunlight. A bee was trapped, and blundering, with a deep hum, against the window. The sound was soporific, dreamy, drowning time. It belonged to a thousand summer afternoons, all the same, long, sun-drenched, lazily full of sleep . . .

Time ran down to nothing; stood still; ran back . . .

What did they call those queer moments of memory? *Déjà vu?* Something seen before, in a dream perhaps? In another life I had stood here, facing this door, with my finger on the carving that, surely, I knew as well as the skin on my own hands . . . ?

The moment snapped. I turned, with a sharp little movement, and thrust open the casement beside me. The bee bumbled foolishly about for a moment or two, then shot off into the sunlight like a pebble from a sling. I latched the window quietly behind it, then turned and knocked at the door.

Matthew Winslow was wide awake, and watching the door.

He lay, not on the bed, but on a broad, old-fashioned sofa near the window. The big bed, covered with a white honeycomb quilt, stood against the further wall. The room was large, with the massive shiny mahogany furniture dear to the generation before last, and a thick Indian carpet. The windows were charming, long and latticed, and wide open to the sun and the sound of the river at the foot of the garden. A spray of early Albertine roses hung just outside the casement, and bees were busy there. For all its thick carpet, cluttered ornaments, and heavy old furniture, the room smelt fresh, of sunshine and the roses on the wall.

On a small table beside the bed were three photographs. One was of Con, looking dramatically handsome in an open-necked shirt, with some clever lighting throwing the planes of his face into relief. Another, I guessed, was Julie; a young, eager face with vivid eyes and a tumble of fair, fine hair. I couldn't see the third from where I stood.

But all this was for the moment no more than a fleeting impression. What caught and held the eye was the figure of the old man reclining against the cushions on the sofa with a plaid rug across his knees.

Matthew Winslow was a tall, gaunt old man with a thick mane of white hair, which had once been fair. His eyes, puckered now and sunken under prominent brows, were grey-green; they had once been exactly the same colour as my own; now the edges of the iris had faded, but the eyes still looked bright and hard as a young man's. His mouth, too, was hard, a thin line between the deep parallels that drove from nostril to jawline. It would have been, for all its craggy good looks, a forbidding face, had it not been for a gleam of humour that lurked somewhere near the corners of mouth and eyes. One would certainly not, at first glance, take Matthew Winslow for a man who needed to be guarded from anything. He looked as tough as pemmican, and nobody's fool.

In response to his gruff summons I had entered the room, and shut the door quietly behind me. There was a pause of complete stillness, in which the buzzing of the bees among the pink roses sounded as loud as a flight of aircraft.

I said: 'Grandfather?' on a note of painful hesitation.

His voice was harsh when he spoke, and the words uncompromising, but I had seen him wet his lips and make the attempt twice. 'Well, Annabel?'

There was surely, I thought confusedly, some sort of precedent for this, the prodigal's return? *He ran, and fell on his neck, and kissed him* . . .

Well, Matthew Winslow couldn't run. That left me.

I went quickly across the room and knelt down beside the sofa, and put my hands on his lap, on top of the plaid rug. His thin hand, with its prominent, blue-knotted veins, came down hard over mine, surprisingly strong and warm.

In the end it was easy to know what to say. I said quite simply: 'I'm sorry, Grandfather. Will you have me back?'

The hand moved, holding mine together even more tightly. 'If I said no,' said Grandfather crisply, 'it would be no more than you deserve.' He cleared his throat violently. 'We thought you were dead.'

'I'm sorry.'

His other hand reached forward and lifted my chin. He studied my face, turning it towards the light of the window. I bit my lip and waited, not meeting his gaze. He said nothing for a long time, then, as harshly as before: 'You've been unhappy. Haven't you?'

I nodded. He let me go, and at last I was able to put my forehead down on the rug, so that he couldn't see my face. He said: 'So have we,' and fell silent again, patting my hand.

Out of the corner of my eye I could see Con's portrait, the fine mouth just moving into that smile of his, full of challenge, and something that was more than mischief; an exciting, and, yes, a dangerous face. Well, Con, it was done now, all behind me, the burned boats, the Rubicons. We were over Becher's Brook, the Canal Turn, the lot, and into the straight. Home.

Con's eyes watched. What good would it do now to lift my head and say: 'Your beloved Con's betraying you. He's paying me to come and pretend I'm your grand-daughter, because he thinks you'll die soon, and he wants your money, and your place.' And something in me, some little voice I'd never listened to before, added: 'And once he's made certain of that, I wouldn't give twopence for your life, Grandfather, I wouldn't really ...'

I stayed where I was, not speaking.

The old man said nothing. The bees had gone. A small bird flew into the roses by the open window; I heard the flirt of its wings, and the tap and swish of the twigs as it alighted.

At length I lifted my head, and smiled at him. He removed his hands, and looked at me under the thrust of his brows. If there had been any sign of emotion in his face, it had been banished now.

'Get a chair.' He spoke abruptly. 'And sit where I can see you.'

I obeyed him. I chose an upright chair, and sat correctly and rather primly on it, knees and feet together, back straight, hands in lap, like a small girl about to recite her catechism.

I thought I saw a glimmer of appreciation in his eyes. 'Well?' he said. Without moving, he seemed all at once to sit up straighter, even to tower over me. 'You've got a lot of talking to do, girl. Supposing you start.'

CHAPTER SEVEN

Some men has plenty money and no brains, and some
men has plenty brains and no money. Surely men with
plenty money and no brains were made for men with
plenty brains and no money.

From the Notebook of the Tichborne Claimant

'Well?' said Lisa softly, like an echo.

She was waiting at the foot of the stairs. A shaft of sunlight through the hall window dazzled along the edge of the copper bowl of pansies. She had her back to the light, and I couldn't see her expression, but even in the one softly-uttered word I could hear some of the trembling uncertainty she had showed in the kitchen. 'How did it go off?'

I had paused when I saw her waiting, and now came reluctantly down the stairs.

'All right. Far better than I'd have expected.'

She gave her withdrawn, close-lipped smile. It was as if, with this quiet lying-in-wait, these careful whispers, she was deliberately putting me back where I belonged; inside a dusty little cell of conspiracy, able to share my thoughts and hopes only with herself and Con, bound to them in a reluctant but unbreakable intimacy.

She said: 'I told you there was nothing to be afraid of.'

'I know. But I suppose conscience makes cowards of us all.'

'What?'

'Nothing. A quotation. Shakespeare.'

She looked faintly resentful, as she had in the kitchen when Con and I had seemed to be moving too fast for her. Perhaps the quotation irked her, or the realisation that I hadn't come from Grandfather's room bursting with confidences; or perhaps she didn't like to be reminded that I had once had a conscience. At any rate she slammed the door of the conspirators' cell hard on me once again. 'You're very literary today. You want to be careful. It isn't in character.'

I smiled. 'I've had plenty of time to settle down and improve my mind abroad.'

'Hm. He didn't – he wasn't suspicious at all?'

'No.' I spoke a little wearily. 'It's exactly as you and Con foretold. There's no reason why he should be. It never even entered his head.'

She pursed her lips with satisfaction. 'Well, what did happen?'

My mind went back to the scene upstairs. Well, they couldn't buy everything.

I said slowly: 'You can have the main outlines, if you like. I told him where I'd been since I left here, and how I'd been living. You know we'd arranged to tell the simple truth about that, as much as possible.'

'Did he say much about . . . the trouble? The reason why you went?'

'If you mean the baby, he never mentioned it until I did. I simply told him I'd been mistaken, and that I'd found out my mistake after I'd gone abroad. And of course I never wrote to tell him so, since I'd no idea that Con had told him about it, and that he'd been worrying. That was all. He was so relieved, and . . . oh, well, skip that. I was quite right, you know, Lisa. It would have been unforgivable to tell him anything else. As it is, we can forget all that part of the story. I don't suppose he'll refer to it again.'

'And Con?' Her voice had lifted perceptibly.

'I tried to make it clear that, whatever had happened in the past, nothing in the world would persuade me to – well, to take up with Con again.' I saw the look in her face, and added smoothly: 'That, of course, was to protect Con and myself. It was quite possible, you know, that

Grandfather was nursing some hopes of a reconciliation. I had to insist that there could never be anything between Con and myself except –' I hesitated '– you might call it armed neutrality.'

'I see. Yes, that would have been –' she stopped. That conspirators' look again. 'I'm sure you're right. There was nothing more? Nothing about the – the future?'

'Nothing at all.'

She looked about her. 'Well, you can't say much more just now, that's obvious. He'll be coming down soon. Later tonight, when we're alone, you can tell me all that was said.'

'Make my report? No,' I said gently.

Her mouth opened, with as much surprise as if I had struck her. 'What d'you mean? You surely don't think that you can –'

'You probably wouldn't understand what I mean. But let's put it like this. I've a difficult rôle to play, and the only way to play it is to *be* it, to live in it, breathe it, think it, try to dream it. In other words, not to have to keep stepping out of Annabel's skin to remember that I'm just someone pretending to be Annabel. I can't act this thing in a series of little scenes, Lisa, with commentaries to you and Con in the intervals. If there's anything vital, or if I should want your help, believe me, I won't hesitate to come to you. But the biggest help you can both give me is simply to forget all that's happened in the last three weeks, and think of me, if you can, just as Annabel, come back to take my accustomed place in my own home. If you keep asking me questions, jerking me back out of my part into the part of Mary Grey, impostor. ... Well, then, Lisa, some day I may get my parts mixed up, and go wrong. And I could go very wrong indeed, very easily.'

I paused, and added, lightly enough: 'Well, there it is. Forget Mary Grey. Forget she ever existed. Believe me, I'm right. This is the only way to take it.'

She said doubtfully: 'Well, yes, but ...'

I laughed. 'Oh, Lisa, stop looking at me as if you were Frankenstein, and the monster had just got away from you! I'm only talking common sense! And you've only to remember that Con and I are mutually committed, even to the extent of signing those deadly little "confessions" for each other to keep, just in case. I've no doubt Con keeps mine next to his skin, day and night. Call it remote control if you like, but it's there! Even if Annabel Winslow *is* home again, at least you know that she's got to bat on Con's side this time!'

'I – well, yes, of course. Forgive me, I didn't really doubt you, but this afternoon has been disconcerting, to say the least. You ... you're so very *good* at this. I've been the one to be nervous.'

'I assure you, I'm quaking inside! It's all right. I won't double-cross you, you know, Lisa, even if I dared.'

'Dared?'

I didn't answer, and after a moment her eyes dropped. 'Well, that's that, then. And you're quite right. I'll try and do as you say, and forget it all, unless there's anything urgent. But it certainly doesn't look as if you're going to need much help, my dear. If you got away with that –' A movement of her head towards the upper landing completed the sentence for her.

'Well, I did. Now let's forget it. Did you say something about tea?'

'I was just going to make it.'

'Do you want any help?'

'Not on your first day home.'

'Then I think I'll go upstairs for a little. Am I in my old room?'

She smiled. 'Yes. D'you mind using the nursery bathroom? You'll be sharing it with Julie.'

'Of course not. Does she know about me?'

'Yes. She rang up last night, to say she'd be here on Wednesday, and Mr. Winslow told her about you. That's all I know.'

'Wednesday . . .' I paused with a foot on the lowest stair. 'Ah well, that give us two more days. Oh, Lisa, I forgot, my cases –'

'Con brought them in just now, and took them up.'

'Oh? It was good of him to get them so quickly. I'll see you at tea, then. Where d'you have it?'

'When I'm alone, in the kitchen as often as not. But for today, the drawing-room. Your grandfather'll be down, I expect. Did he say?'

'Yes. He – he wants to show me round the place himself after tea.'

The brown eyes held mine just a moment longer than was necessary.

'Of course,' said Lisa, abandoning comment with what looked like an effort, 'he would want to do that. Naturally. Well – I'll see you later.'

I turned and went back upstairs. I could see her watching me as, unhesitatingly, I took the left-hand passage past the head of the gallery.

'*Yours is the second door*' . . . It was a pleasant room, with a long latticed window like Grandfather's, and the same Albertine rose nodding outside it. There was a wide window-seat, covered with chintz in a pretty, Persian-looking pattern of birds and flowers and trellis-work, done in deliberately-faded colours. The same chintz appeared for curtains and bedspread. The furniture was plain deal, white-painted; originally it would speak of 'nursery', but now a new coat of paint made it merely cottagey and very charming. The floor was of polished boards with a couple of rugs, and the walls and ceiling were plain ivory-white.

Con had dumped my baggage on the floor near the foot of the bed. He had also thoughtfully brought up my handbag, which I must have left in the kitchen, and this lay on the bed.

I wasn't prepared to cope with unpacking yet. I picked up the handbag and carried it across to the window-seat. I sat down, opened the bag, and took out my cigarettes.

As I shook one loose from the pack, I glanced at the door. There was a key in the lock. So far, so good. I had a feeling that I was going to need frequent doses of privacy to recover from the rounds of a game which, though so far it had proved a walk over, might well get stickier as time went on.

I put the cigarette in my mouth, and felt in the little mirror-pocket in my bag where I had carried a flat book of matches. It wasn't there. My fingers met merely a slip of paper. Surely, I thought, irritably, I had had one? I had been smoking in the bus coming from Newcastle ... I pulled the bag wider to look for it. I saw it immediately, then, a little scarlet book labelled *Café Kasbah*, tucked deep in the pocket on the other side of my bag, where I kept bills and shopping-lists and oddments of that sort.

I lit the cigarette slowly, and sat contemplating the bag, open on my lap. Now that I had noticed it, there were other signs. The top had come loose on one of my lipsticks; the few papers that I carried were shuffled hastily back into their places as I didn't think I had put them; the slip of paper where I had scribbled down the Whitescar telephone number, which had been among the other papers, was pushed into the mirror-compartment where normally the matches were kept. Whoever had scrabbled hastily through my handbag, had taken few pains to cover his tracks.

Con? Lisa? I grinned to myself. What was it they called this kind of thing? Counter-espionage? That, I was sure, was how it would rank in Lisa's mind. Whatever you call it, it was surely a little late, now, for them to be checking on my *bona-fides*.

I went quickly through what was there. The telephone number; it was natural enough that I should have scribbled that down; numbers change in eight years. A bus time-table, acquired that day on my way here. The receipt for my lodgings near the Haymarket, also received that morning. That was all right; it was addressed to 'Miss A. Winslow'.

Then I hesitated, with it in my hand. Was it all right, after all? It was admittedly unlikely that Grandfather would ever see it, or check on it if he did, but both Con and Lisa had visited me there. It was better out of the way. I crumpled the paper up, and threw it into the empty fireplace. I would burn it before I went downstairs.

I turned over the other papers. A few shopping chits; a couple of used bus tickets; a folded paper of pale green ...

I picked it out from among the others, and unfolded it. '*Passenger Motor Vehicle Permit ... Mary Grey ...*' and the address near Montreal. There it lay, clear as a curse, the Canadian car permit; the owner's licence that you carry daily, yearly, and never even see, except when the time comes round to renew it ...

Well, I thought, as I crumpled it in my hand, Con and Lisa must realise what an easy mistake this had been to make. I wondered, not without amusement, how on earth they would manage to warn me about it, without having to confess that they had searched my belongings. At least they could not also have searched my cases; the key hung on a chain round my neck, and there it was going to stay . . .

From somewhere outside I heard Lisa calling, and Con's voice in reply. I heard him cross the yard towards the house. There was a low-voiced colloquy, then he went back towards the buildings.

I got up, and set a match to the crumpled bill in the fireplace, then carefully fed the car permit into the flames. I picked up the poker, and stirred the burned fragments of paper till they flaked and fell away to nothing, through the bars of the grate. Then I went back to the sunny window, picked up my half-smoked cigarette, and sat for some minutes longer, trying to relax.

The window looked out over the small front garden. This was a simple square bounded by low sandstone walls, and sloping slightly towards the river. From the front door a gravel path, weedy and unraked, led straight to the white wicket-gate that gave on the river-bank and the bridge that spanned the water. The path was bordered by ragged hedges of lavender, under which sprawled a few hardy pansies and marigolds. Behind these borders, to either side, the unkempt grass reached back to what had once been the flower-beds.

Here was confusion indeed. Lupins had run wild, all the gay colours faded back to their pristine blue; peonies crouched sullenly under the strangling bushes of fuchsia and flowering-currant, and everywhere ivy, bindweed, and rose-bay willow-herb were joyously completing their deadly work. At first glance, the riot of colour might deceive the eye into thinking that here was a pretty garden still, but then one saw the dandelions, the rampant rose-bushes, the docks in the rank grass under the double-white lilac trees . . .

Beyond the far wall, and the white wicket, was a verge of sheep-bitten grass and the wooden bridge that was Whitescar's short cut to town. From the other end of the bridge the track wound up through the trees that crowded the far bank, and vanished eventually into their shadow.

My eye came back, momentarily, to the tangled garden. Two blackbirds had flown into the lilac tree, quarrelling furiously. The great heads of milky blossom shook and swayed. I could smell lilac from where I sat.

(*'Annabel's garden. She planted it all. Remember to ask Con what's in it . . . if he knows.'*)

He had not known.

I leaned to stub out my cigarette on the stone sill outside the window-frame.

It was time to go down. Act Two. Back into the conspirators' cell with Con and Lisa.

I found myself hoping passionately that Con wouldn't be in to tea.

He wasn't, and it was still, it seemed, going to be easy. Grandfather came down a little late, opened the drawing-room door on me discussing amiably with Lisa what had happened to various neighbours during my long absence, and thereafter acted more or less as though the eight years' gap had never been.

After tea he took me outside, and led the way towards the farm buildings. He walked fairly rapidly, and held his gaunt body upright apparently without effort. With the westering sun behind him, shadowing the thinned, bony face, and making the grey hair look blond as it must once have been, it wasn't difficult to see once more the active, opinionated, quick-tempered man who had done so much through his long life to make Whitescar the prosperous concern it now was. I could see, too, why Con – in spite of the old man's favour – walked warily.

Grandfather paused at the yard gate. 'Changed much?'

'The farm? I – it's hard to tell.'

A quick look under the jutting white brows. 'What d'you mean?'

I said slowly: 'Oh, some things, yes. The new paint, and – that wall's new, isn't it? And the concrete, and all that drainage. But I meant – well, I've been gone a long time, and I suppose I've lived so long on a memory of Whitescar, that now it's bound to look strange to me. My picture of it – my imagined picture, I mean – has become almost more real than the thing itself. For one thing,' I laughed a little, 'I remember it as being always in sunshine. One does, you know.'

'So they say. I'd have thought you'd be more likely to remember it the way you left it. It was a vile day.'

'Yes. I went before it was fully light, and you can imagine what it looked like. Rain and wind, and the fields all grey and flattened. I remember how awful that one looked – at least, was it in corn that year? I – I forget.'

'Turnips. But you're quite right. The corn was badly laid everywhere that year.'

'The odd thing is, I said, 'that I hardly really remember that at all. Perhaps the psychologists would say that the rain and wind, and that grey early morning, were all mixed up in my mind with the misery of leaving home, and that I've allowed myself to forget it.' I laughed. 'I wouldn't know. But all the years I was away, I remembered nothing but sunshine . . . fine, lovely days, and all the things we used to do . . . childhood memories, mostly.' I paused for a little. 'I suppose you could say that my actual memories of home got overlaid, in time, with dream-pictures. I know that, after a few years, I'd have been hard put to it to give a really accurate description of . . . this, for instance.'

I gestured to the tidy yard, the shadowy cave of the barn, the double stable doors with the tops latched back to the wall.

'If you'd even asked me what sort of stone it was built of, I couldn't have told you. And yet, now that I'm back, I notice everything. Tiny things that I must have taken for granted all my life, and never really seen before.'

'Mm.' He was staring at me fixedly. There was neither gentleness nor affection, that I could see, in the clear grey-green gaze. He said abruptly. 'Con's a good lad.'

I must have sounded slightly startled. 'Yes, of course.'

He misunderstood the wariness of my manner, for his voice had a harsher note as he said, with equal abruptness: 'Don't worry. I'm not harking back to that business eight years back. I'd hardly hold Connor in affection for that, would I? Only thing I have against him, but at least he came out into the open, and tried to make amends like a decent man.'

I said nothing. I saw him glance sideways at me, then he added testily as if I had been arguing: 'All right, all right. We've already spoken about that. We'll drop it now. I said we'd forget it, and we will. But apart from things that are over and forgotten, Con's a good lad, and he's been a son to me this last eight years.'

'Yes.'

Another of those bright, almost inimical glances. 'I mean that. After you'd played the fool and left me, he stayed, and made a clean breast of things. Told me what he thought was the truth. I don't deny that there were words, but once everything had been said and done, what else was there for me to do? I'd have done badly without him for a long time now, and this last year or two, it'd have been impossible. He's more than made up for what's past. He's put everything he knows into the place.'

'Yes. I know.'

The white brows jutted at me. 'Well? Well?'

I smiled at him. 'What do you expect me to say, Grandfather? It's quite true. I played the fool and left you, and Con played the fool and stayed. One up to Con. Not forgetting, though, that it took me rather longer to get over my folly than it took him ... or you.'

There was a little silence. Then he gave a short bark of laughter. 'You don't change,' he said. 'So you've come back to quarrel with me, have you?'

'Grandfather darling,' I said, 'no. But I don't quite see what you're getting at. You're trying to tell me how wonderful Con is. All right; I'll give you that. He's been telling me himself. But you can't blame me for being a bit wary. Eight years ago, all this would have been leading up to a spot of match-making. I hoped I'd made it clear that that was impossible.'

'Hm. So you said, but one never knows how much one can believe a woman, especially when she starts talking all that clap-trap about love turning to hate, and so forth.'

'I said nothing of the sort. I don't hate Con. If I felt strongly about him at all, I couldn't have come back while he was still here, could I? I told you how I felt; indifferent, and more than a bit embarrassed. I'd give quite a lot not to have had to meet him again, but since he's here, and not likely to go ...' I smiled a little. 'All right, Grandfather, let it pass. I had to see you, and it'd take more than Con to keep me away.

Now, you don't usually hand out compliments for the fun of the thing. You're leading up to something. What is it?'

He chuckled. 'All right. It's this. You always knew Whitescar would be yours when I died, didn't you? Should have been your father's, and then it would have been yours.'

'Yes. I knew that.'

'And had it occurred to you that I might have made other arrangements during the time you were away?'

'Well, of course.'

'And now that you've come back?'

I turned half to face him, leaning against the gate, just as I had leaned to talk to Con earlier that day. 'Come to the point, Grandfather dear.'

The old eyes peered down at me, bright, amused, almost malicious. For some reason I was suddenly reminded of Con, though there was no outward resemblance whatever. 'I will. It's this. They'll have told you I'm not expected to live a great while – no,' as I made some movement of protest, 'don't bother. We all know what this confounded condition of mine means. Now, you cleared out eight years ago, and, for all we knew, you were dead. Well, you've come back.' He paused. He seemed to be waiting for a reply.

I said steadily: 'Are you accusing me of coming back for what I think I can get?'

He gave his sharp crack of laughter. 'Don't be a fool, girl. I know you better than that. But you *would* be a fool if you hadn't thought about it, and wondered where you'd stand. Have you?'

'Of course.'

He gave a nod, as if pleased. 'That's a straight answer, anyway. And I'll be straight with you. Look at it this way. You walked out eight years ago; Con stayed. Do *you* think it right that you should just walk back like this, after the work that Con's put into this place meantime – and that fool Lisa Dermott for that matter – and just scoop it all up from under his very nose? Would you call that fair? I'm hanged if I would.' His head thrust forward suddenly. 'What in thunder are you laughing at?'

'Nothing. Nothing at all. Are you trying to tell me that you've left everything to Con and Lisa?'

Again that glint of mischief, that could have been malice. 'I didn't say that. And don't you go letting them think it, either. I'm not dead yet. But is there any reason that you can think of why I shouldn't?'

'None at all.'

He looked almost disconcerted, staring at me under his white brows. I realised then what the fleeting likeness had been between him and Con; it was a matter of expression, nothing else; an impression of arrogance, of deliberately enjoying a moment of power. Matthew Winslow was enjoying the situation just as much as Con, and for allied reasons. He liked the power that it gave him.

He said testily: 'I wish I knew what the devil there was in all this to laugh at.'

'I'm sorry,' I said. 'I was thinking of Con. "The engineer hoist with his own petard." '

'What? What are you talking about, girl?'

'It was a quotation,' I said, helplessly, 'I'm sorry, Grandfather. I'm serious, really I am.'

'You'd better be. Quotation, indeed. You've been wasting your time abroad, I can see that. Some modern rubbish, by the sound of it. Well, what were you thinking about Con?'

'Nothing, really. Aren't you going to tell him that you've made a Will in his favour?'

'I didn't say I had. And I forbid you to speak to him about it. What I want is to get things straight with you. Perhaps I should have left it till you'd been home a bit longer, but as it happens, I've been thinking a good deal about it lately. You knew Julie was coming up here?'

'Yes. Lisa told me.'

'I wrote and asked her to come as soon as she could, and the child tells me she can get leave straight away. When she comes, I want to get things fixed up. Isaacs – do you remember Isaacs?'

'I – I'm not sure.'

'The lawyer. Nice chap. I'm sure you met him.'

'Oh, yes, of course. I remember now.'

'He's coming on Friday, and then again next week. I suggested the twenty-second.'

'The twenty-second? That's your birthday, isn't it?'

'Good God, fancy your remembering.' He looked pleased.

'Lisa's planning a party, she told me, since we'll all be here, Julie too.'

'Yes. A family gathering. Appropriate.' He gave that dry, mischievous chuckle again.

I tilted my head and looked up at him, all amusement gone. 'Grandfather—'

'Well?'

'At this – appropriate – family gathering . . .' I paused . . . 'do you intend to tell us all where we stand?'

'A nice, old-fashioned gathering of the vultures round the old man's bones? How do you think I like all this talk of what's to happen after I'm dead?'

I grinned at him. 'You started it, and you told me to be a realist. But, look, Grandfather—' I fought not to let my voice sound too urgent – 'if you do intend to – to make Con your heir . . . would you tell him so? Please?'

'Why the devil should I?'

'It – it would make things easier for me.'

'Easier for *you*? What d'you mean?'

'Only that he – well, he'd resent me less. You can't blame Con for being a realist, too, can you? You must know he'll have had expectations.'

'If he has,' said Grandfather drily, 'then he's an optimist.' He caught my expression, and laughed. 'What I do with my property's my own affair, Annabel, and if I choose to allow people to confuse themselves, that's their funeral. Do I make myself clear?'

'Very clear.'

'Good. You'll gather that I intend to keep my affairs to myself.'

'Yes. Well, you've a perfect right to.'

There was a pause. He seemed to be choosing his words, but when he spoke, it was bluntly enough: 'You know I always wanted you to marry Connor.'

'Yes, I know. I'm sorry, Grandfather.'

'It always seemed to me the best answer.'

'For Whitescar; yes, I see that; but not for me. And not really for Con, Grandfather. Honestly, it wouldn't work. Ever.'

'Not even after – no; I said I'd drop that subject, and I will.'

'Not even after that,' I smiled. 'And it does take two to make a match, you know. I don't think you'll find Con in the same mind as he was eight years ago.'

The old eyes were suddenly very sharp and shrewd. 'Not even if Whitescar went with you?'

'Of course not!' But I was disconcerted, and showed it. 'Don't be so mediaeval, Grandfather!'

He still peered down at me, bright-eyed. 'And if it went with Connor?'

'Is that a threat or a bribe?'

'Neither. You've shown me how little effect it would have. I'm thinking about your future, if the place were Con's. Would you stay?'

'How could I?'

'Is that meant to be a pistol at my heart?'

'Good heavens, no. You don't have to worry about me. I'd have Mother's money.'

'And Whitescar?'

I was silent.

'Wouldn't you care?'

'I – I don't know. You've just pointed out that I can hardly expect to walk straight home after eight years.'

'Well, that's true enough. I'm glad you seem to have faced it. I shan't be here for ever, you know.'

'I know. But at least I can be here as long as you are.'

He snorted. 'Soft soap, child. That'll get you nowhere. And don't glare at me like that, it cuts no ice! So you expect me to cut you right out, do you, leave Julie to her own devices, and hand the place lock, stock and barrel, to young Connor? That it?'

I pushed myself upright, away from the gate.

I said: 'Grandfather, you always were insufferable, and you were never fair in all your born days. How the devil do you expect me to know what you plan to do? You'll do as the mood takes you, fair or no, and Con and I can take what comes, charm we never so wisely.' I added: 'That was another quotation. And don't say I've been wasting my time again, because that's from the Psalms.'

Grandfather's face never changed, but something came behind the eyes that might have been a grin. He said mildly, 'Don't swear at me, Annabel my girl, or old as you are, I'll soap your mouth out.'

'Sorry.' We smiled at one another. There was a pause.

'It's good to have you back, child. You don't know how good.'

'I don't have to tell you how good it is to be here.'

He put a hand to the latch of the gate. 'Come down to the river meadows. There's a yearling there you'll like to see.'

We went down a lane between hedgerows whispering with budding meadowsweet. The hawthorn was rusted thickly over with bunches of dried flowers hardening to fruit.

At the end of the lane a gate opened on a field deep with buttercups and cuckoo-flowers. A grey mare moved towards us, swishing her tail, her sides sleek and heavy. From the shade of a big beech a yearling watched us with eyes as soft and wary as a deer.

'He's a beauty.'

'Isn't he?' There was satisfaction and love in the old man's voice. 'Best foal she ever dropped. Forrest kept a three-year-old out of her by the same sire, but they'll make nothing of him. Yes, she's a grand mare: I bought her from Forrest three years ago, when the stud was sold up. Give over, Blondie, give over, now.' This to the mare, who was pushing at his chest with her muzzle as he opened the gate and held it for me. 'Come through. The grass is dry enough. You'll have to find some better shoes for this tomorrow.'

I followed him into the field. 'What's wrong with the three-year-old?'

'What? Oh, Forrest's horse? Nothing, except that nobody's had time to do anything about him. Only kept him out of sentiment, I suppose, as he's one of the old "Mountain" lot. Everest got him; you'll remember Everest? He's gone to the Chollerford stud now; getting long in the tooth, the old devil, but his get's as good as it ever was; look at that yearling. And Forrest's colt could be a winner, too, if they'd time to school him. Rowan, they called him.' He chuckled, and clapped the mare's neck. 'By Everest, out of Ash Blonde.'

'Mountain Ash?'

'That's it. Sort of nonsense Forrest always went in for with his names. You knew the stud was gone?'

'Oh, yes. What have you called this one? You said he was the same breeding.'

'We haven't named him yet. That'll be for his owners.'

The mare threw her head up to avoid his caressing hand, and swerved a little, flicking her tail pettishly. She pricked her ears at me, and reached out an inquiring muzzle.

I said, ignoring it: 'He's sold, then?'

'Yes. I'm afraid you'll find nothing here to ride now. Blondie's heavy at foot, as you can see, and the youngster'll be away next month.' He laughed. 'Unless you try your hand with Forrest's three-year-old. I've no doubt he'd let you if you asked him.'

The mare was pushing close to me. The yearling, looking interested, was coming to join her. From behind me, some way along the lane, I heard footsteps approaching. I backed away from the mare's advance until I was right up against the gate. She pushed her head at me again, and breathed gustily down the front of my dress.

I said breathlessly: 'Ask who?'

'Forrest, of course. What the devil's the matter with you, Annabel?'

'Nothing. What should be the matter?' The footsteps were nearer.

Grandfather was regarding me curiously. 'You're as white as a sheet! Anyone'd think you were afraid of the mare!'

I managed a little laugh. 'Afraid of her? How absurd! Here, Blondie ...' I put out a hand to her head. I hoped he wouldn't see how unsteady it was. The mare was nibbling the buckle of my belt. The yearling had come right up to her shoulder, and stood staring. Any minute now he would close in too ...

I looked away from Grandfather's curious, puzzled stare, and said quickly: 'I thought Mr. Forrest was in Italy.'

'He's coming back some time this week, so Johnny Rudd tells me. They didn't expect him quite yet, but I imagine the sale of the place in Italy went through quicker than he'd expected.'

I gave the mare's head a shove away from me. I might as well have shoved an elephant. I said, unsteadily: 'I – I understood he'd left for good. I mean, with the Hall gone, and – and everything—'

'No, no. He's planning to settle at West Lodge now, Johnny tells me, with the Rudds to look after him. He came back last year to clear up the rest of the estate, and he and Johnny set to work and got the old gardens going; I believe that's what he plans to do now.'

'Yes, Con did say—'

Con's voice, from beyond the bend in the lane, called: 'Uncle Matthew? Annabel?'

'Here!' called Grandfather.

The mare was nibbling at my frock, and, retreating from her advance, I was pressed so hard against the gate, that the bars bit into my back. Grandfather gave a quick little frown. 'Annabel—'

'I thought as much!' Con said it, mercifully, from just behind me. 'I might have known you'd bring her straight down here!'

He must have summed up the situation at a glance as he rounded the bend in the lane: Grandfather, his attention divided between the yearling and my own odd behaviour; myself backed against the gate, chattering

breathlessly, and trying, with patently unsteady hands, to stop the mare
from blowing lovingly down the breast of my frock.

I saw the flash of amusement in Con's eyes, and then he had leaned
over the gate beside me, handed off the importunate mare with one strong
thrust and a 'Give over, now,' that sent her swerving straight away, ears
flattened and tail switching. The yearling threw up his lovely head and
veered after her. As I relaxed, Con pushed open the gate and came
through.

Grandfather, fortunately, was watching the yearling as it cantered
away into the shade of the tree. 'Moves well, doesn't he?' he said fondly.

'He's a little beauty,' agreed Con.

'Little?' I said shakily. 'He looks enormous!'

A flicker in Con's eyes showed me the ineptitude of this remark for
someone who was supposed to have lived and breathed horses for most
of her life. Then he covered up as smoothly as a practised actor, the
amusement warming his voice so faintly that only I would hear it. 'Yes,
he's pretty well-grown, isn't he, seeing he's barely a year old . . .' And
he plunged easily off into technicalities with Mr. Winslow, no doubt to
give me time to recover my poise.

Presently Grandfather said: 'I was telling Annabel that she'll have to
see Forrest about some riding if she wants it.'

'Forrest? Oh, is he back?'

'Not yet. Some time this week. Johnny Rudd told me they didn't look
for him before autumn at the soonest, but apparently he's sold the villa,
and he's coming back to live at West Lodge.'

Con was leaning on the gate beside me. He sent a slanting look down
at me, with a lurking smile behind it. 'That's a bit of luck, Annabel.
He'll let you ride the Mountain colt.'

I was still shaken, but I had no intention of letting Con amuse himself
further at my expense. I said immediately, with every evidence of
enthusiasm: 'Do you really think he would? That's wonderful!'

Con's eyes widened. Grandfather said shortly: 'Of course he would,
unless you've lost your touch completely! Want to come across and look
at him now?'

'I'd love to.'

'Can't it wait?' said Con. 'You look tired.'

I looked at him, slightly surprised. 'I'm all right.'

Con straightened up with that lazy grace of his that looked deliberate,
but was in reality as natural as breathing. At the movement, slow though
it was, the mare, who was grazing near, rolled a white-rimmed eye and
moved away.

'Doesn't like you, does she?' said Matthew Winslow. 'Come along
then, my dear. Coming, Con?'

Con shook his head. 'No, I've a lot to do. I really only came down to
see if you'd come up into the seventeen-acre and take a look at the cutter

for me. She's been running rough, and I don't seem to be able to get to the bottom of the trouble. I could take you up in the car.'

'The cutter? Good God, can't you put that right without running to me?' But the old man had stopped and turned, looking far from displeased. 'Well, in that case—' He looked at me. 'Some other time, perhaps? Unless you go along there yourself? He's at grass, two fields along from the bridge, you know the place, beyond the wood.'

'Yes,' I said, 'I know it. I'll go now.'

My one desire was to get away, to be alone, not even to have to walk back to the house in their company. But even as I spoke, half-turning to go, I saw a shade of what looked like genuine anxiety on Con's face.

I realised then, suddenly, that his timely appearance on the scene had not been a matter of chance. He had not come down to see about the repair of the cutter, and then stayed to tease me; his coming had been a deliberate rescue bid. He had guessed that I had been brought down to the paddock; guessed, too, what might be happening there, and that the prolonged interview with Grandfather might be too much of a strain. He had come down solely to get me out of it, to draw Mr. Winslow off. In all probability there was nothing wrong with the cutter at all . . .

And if, once here, he had been unable to resist teasing me a little, it was no more than he was entitled to, under the circumstances. He was standing now with grave patience, listening to a crisp lecture on the incompetence of a young man who could not, in twenty seconds, diagnose and correct every fault in every piece of machinery in use on the estate.

Well, fair was fair. I wouldn't worry him further. I interrupted the lecture: 'I don't think I will go, after all. I'll go back to the house. I – I've done enough for today.'

Matthew Winslow looked at me, still with that crinkle of puzzlement round his eyes. 'Something *has* upset you, child. What is it?'

Suddenly, absurdly, I wanted to cry. 'Nothing, truly. Nothing. Con's right. I'm tired.' I made a little gesture. 'It's been wonderful playing the prodigal returning, and everyone's been so kind. . . too kind. But, you know, it's terribly exhausting. I feel as if I'd been back a year already, things have crowded in so fast.'

We were back in the lane. As Con pulled the gate shut behind me, he took my arm as if in reassurance.

'Of course it's a strain. We all understand that. You should go in now, and rest till supper.'

He spoke, as before, gently. I saw Grandfather glance quickly from his face to mine, and back again. It must be obvious to anyone that Con's solicitude was quite genuine, and I knew the reason for it, but I wasn't going to have Matthew Winslow leaping to the wrong conclusion. I withdrew my arm and said quickly:

'I think I will.' Then I turned to the old man. 'Have you still got the cribbage-board?'

His face lightened to a grin. 'Of course. You remember how to play?'

'How could I forget?' (*She used to play with him often: it's an old-fashioned game; you know it? Good ...*') I added: 'I also remember that you owe me a vast sum of money, Grandfather.'

'Nonsense. I always beat you.'

'Ah well,' I said cheerfully, 'I've improved, in eight years. I'll win your house and lands off you yet, so watch your step!'

At his dry little chuckle I felt Con stiffen beside me. He said abruptly: 'Well, you'll not be playing tonight, at all events, I hope?'

'No, no. The child will want an early night. Besides, I'll probably stay up in the seventeen-acre with you. How are you getting on there?'

Con answered him, and the two of them talked across me as we walked slowly back towards the yard where the car stood. Con's manner with his great-uncle was charming; relaxed and easy and familiar, but with just the hint of a deference which obviously flattered the old man, coming from someone as vital and as capable as Con, to a man who, for all his deceptive appearance of power, was a frail husk that the first chill wind might blow away.

Grandfather was saying: 'Nonsense! I can give you a hand when we've got the cutter running properly.'

Con gave him that flashing, affectionate smile. 'You'll do no such thing. Come along, by all means, and bully us, but I'm afraid that's all we'll let you do!'

'You coddle me. I'm not senile yet, and I won't be treated like a girl.'

Con grinned. 'Hardly that. In any case, the girl's going to work, once she's got herself run in again! Can you drive a tractor – still, Annabel?'

'I dare say I might manage, even if I have rather lost my touch with horses,' I said evenly.

We had reached the gate of the main courtyard. Grandfather climbed, a little stiffly, into the big Ford that stood waiting there. Con shut the car door on him.

In the distance, from the fields beyond High Riggs, came the steady, smooth whirr of the grass-cutter. Unless I was very much mistaken, there was nothing wrong with it at all. As Con shut the car door and turned, his eyes met mine. There was a smile in them.

He said: 'Over to me,' very softly, and then: '*Do* you drive a tractor, by the way?'

'I have done.'

'And,' said Con, 'a car?'

I studied him for a moment, then I smiled. He had earned it, after all. I said: 'I had a car in Canada; I've just burned the permit, and I don't know where my licence is, but that doesn't mean a thing. I dare say I'd qualify for a British one, if I needed to.'

'Ah,' said Con. 'And now, if you wouldn't mind shutting the gate behind us ...?'

CHAPTER EIGHT

'Tis down in yonder garden green,
Love, where we used to walk,
The finest flower that ere was seen
Is wither'd to a stalk.

Ballad: *The Unquiet Grave*

Supper with Lisa and Grandfather was not the ordeal I had feared it might be. The old man was in excellent spirits, and, though he was in something of a 'do you remember' vein, and Lisa's eyes, under their lowered lids, watched us both over-anxiously, it went off smoothly enough, with no hitch that I could see. Con wasn't there. It was light late, and he was at work long hours in the hayfield while the weather lasted.

Shortly after supper Grandfather went into the office to write letters, and I helped Lisa wash up. Mrs. Bates went off at five, and the girl who helped in the kitchen and dairy had gone home when the milking was over. Lisa and I worked in silence. I was tired and preoccupied, and she must have realised that I didn't want to talk. She had made no further attempt to force a tête-à-tête on me, and she didn't try to detain me when, soon after nine o'clock, I went up to my room.

I sat there by the open window, with the scent from the climbing roses unbearably sweet in the dusk, and my mind went round and round over the events of the day like some small creature padding its cage.

The light was fading rapidly. The long flushed clouds of sunset had darkened and grown cool. Below them the sky lay still and clear, for a few moments rinsed to a pale eggshell green, fragile as blown glass. The dusk leaned down slowly, as soft as a bird coming in to brood. Later, there would be a moon.

It was very still. Close overhead I heard the scratch and rustle of small feet on the sloping roof-tiles, then the throaty murmur as the pigeons settled back again to sleep. From the garden below came the smell of lilac. A moth fluttered past my cheek, and a bat cut the clear sky like a knife. Down in the neglected garden-grass the black and white cat crouched, tail whipping, then sprang. Something screamed in the grass.

I brushed the back of a hand impatiently across my cheeks, and reached for a cigarette. Round the side of the house, in the still evening, came the sharp sounds of a door opening and shutting. A man's footsteps receded across the yard, and were silenced on turf somewhere. Con had been in for a late meal, and was going out again.

I got up quickly, and reached a light coat down from the hook behind the door. I dropped the packet of cigarettes into the pocket, and went downstairs.

Lisa was clearing up after Con's meal in the kitchen. I said quickly: 'I'm going out for a walk. I – I thought I'd take a look round on my own.'

She nodded, incuriously. I went out into the gathering dusk.

I caught him up in the lane that led down to the river-meadow. He was carrying a coil of wire, and hammer and pliers. He turned at the sound of my hurrying steps, and waited. The smile with which he greeted me faded when he saw my expression.

I said breathlessly: 'Con. I had to see you.'

'Yes.' His voice was guarded. 'What is it? Trouble?'

'No – at least, not the kind you mean. But there's something I have to say. I – I had to see you straight away, tonight.'

I was close to him now. His face, still readable in the thickening dusk, had stiffened almost into hostility, arming itself against whatever was coming. So much, I thought, for Con's co-operation; it was fine as long as you stayed in line with him, but the moment he suspected you of deviating . . .

'Well?' he said.

I had meant to start reasonably, quietly, at the right end of the argument I had prepared, but somehow the abrupt, even threatening sound of the monosyllable shook my resolution into flinders. Woman-like, I forgot reason and argument together, and began at the end.

'This can't go on. You must see that. It can't go on!'

He stood very still. 'What do you mean?'

'What I say! It'll have to stop! We were mad, anyway, even to have thought of starting it!' Once begun, it seemed I couldn't check myself. I had had more of a shaking that day than I cared to admit, even to myself. I stumbled on anyhow, growing even less coherent in the face of his unresponding silence.

'Well – we'll have to think of some other way – something to tell Grandfather – I'm sure we can think something up! You must see there's no point in my staying, now, you must see! Even if I could have got away with it—'

I heard him breathe in sharply. '*Could have* got away with it? Do you mean he's found you out?'

'No, no *no!*' I heard my voice rising, and checked it on a sort of gulp. We were near the gate where we had been that afternoon. I took a step away from him, and put out a hand to the gate, gripping it hard, as if that might steady me. I said, shakily: 'Con . . . look, I'm sorry—'

His voice said coldly, behind me: 'You're hysterical.'

Since this was undoubtedly true, I said nothing. He put the tools and wire down beside the hedge, then came up to the gate beside me. He said, as unpleasantly as I had ever heard him speak: 'Getting scruples my dear, is that it? A little late, one feels.'

His tone, even more than what his words implied, was all the cure my nerves needed. I turned my head sharply. 'Does one? I think not!'

'No? Think again, my pretty.'

I stared at him. 'Are you trying to threaten me, Connor Winslow? And if so, with what?'

It was almost dark now, and he was standing with his back to what light there was. He had turned so that he was leaning his shoulders against the gate, seemingly quite relaxed. I felt, rather than saw, his look still on me, watchful, intent, hostile. But he spoke lightly.

'Threaten you? Not the least in the world, my love. But we're in this together, you know, and we work together. I can't have you forgetting our ... bargain ... quite so soon. You're doing splendidly, so far; things have gone even better than I dared to hope ... *and* they're going to go on that way, darling, till I – and you, of course – get what we want. Fair enough?'

'Oh, quite.'

The moon must be rising now beyond the thick trees. I could see the first faint glimmer on the river. The sky behind the black damask of leaf and bough was the colour of polished steel. The mare, grazing thirty yards away, had lifted her head and was staring towards us, ears pricked. Under the eclipsing shadow of hedgerow and tree she gleamed faintly, like some palladic metal, cool and smooth. The yearling was beside her, staring too.

I regarded Con curiously, straining my eyes against the dark. 'I wonder ...'

'Yes?'

I said slowly: 'I wonder just how far you would go, to get what you wanted?'

'I've sometimes wondered that myself.' He sounded amused. 'You'd maybe be surprised what you can bring yourself to do, little cousin, when you've never had a damned thing in your life but what you could make – or take – with your own two hands. And what's wrong with that, anyway? A man who knows he can—' He broke off, and I thought I saw the gleam of a smile. 'Well, there it is, girl dear. I'm not going to be sent on my travels again ... fair means if I can, but by God, I'll see foul ones if I have to!'

'I see. Well, we know where we are, don't we?' I brought the packet of cigarettes out of my coat pocket. 'Smoke?'

'Thanks. You smoke too much, don't you?'

'I suppose I do.'

'I knew you'd more sense than to panic at the first hint of something you didn't like. What is the trouble, anyway? I've a light. Here.'

In the momentary flare of the match I saw his face clearly. In spite of the light words, and the endearments with which he was so lavish, I could see no trace of liking, or even of any human feeling, in his expression. It was the face of a man concentrating on a job; something tricky, even dangerous, that called for every ounce of concentration. Me. I had to be got back into line.

The match went out. I thought I must have been mistaken, for his voice when he spoke was not ungentle. 'Supposing you tell me exactly what's upset you? Something has, hasn't it? What was it? The horses this afternoon? You looked like seven sorts of death when I came down.'

'Did I?'

'You know, you don't have to go near Forrest's horse if you don't want to.'

'I know I don't. It's all right, it wasn't that.' I leaned back against the gate beside him, and drew deeply on my cigarette. 'I'm sorry I started this at the wrong end, and scared you. I don't have to tell you, I hope, that I'm not planning to let you down. I – I've had a hell of a day, that's all, and I was letting it ride me. I'll try and explain now, like a reasonable human being, which means not like a woman.'

'You said it, honey, not me. Go ahead; I'm listening.'

'It's true, though, that I did want to talk to you about altering our plans. No, wait, Con; the point is, things have changed.'

'Changed? How? Since when?'

'Since I had my talk with Grandfather down here this evening.'

'I . . . thought there had been something.' I heard his breath go out. 'I told you, you looked like death. I thought it was that fool of a mare.'

'No.'

'Well?'

'The point is, Con, that all this may have been for nothing. It shook me, rather. I – I think he's going to leave Whitescar to you anyway.'

'*What?*'

'That's what he said.'

'*He said so?*'

'Almost. I'll swear that's what he meant. Did you know that his lawyer, his name's Isaacs, isn't it? – is coming down here on Friday?'

'No, I didn't know.' He sounded dazed. His voice was blurred at the edges.

'Well, he is. Julie gets here on Wednesday, and Mr. Isaacs comes on Friday. Grandfather didn't say anything definite, but he hinted like mad. I've a feeling he wants to have some sort of family gathering on his birthday, and he's asked the lawyer here before that, so it's a fairly resonable guess that it's to be about his Will. He said "I want to get things fixed up".'

He moved sharply, and the gate creaked. 'Yes, but this *is* only a guess! What about Whitescar? What did he actually say?'

'Not very much, but – Con, it's all right. I wouldn't have mentioned it to you, if I wasn't sure. I'll swear that's what he means to do. Oh, no, he didn't quite commit himself, not in so many words, even to me. But he was as definite as he'd ever be.'

'How?'

'Well, he reminded me first of all that Whitescar had always been promised to Annabel. "It should have been your father's, and then it would have been yours." '

' "Would have been?" ' he asked, sharply.

'Yes. Then he began to praise you. You'd been a son to him, he couldn't have done without you – oh, all sorts of things. He really does recognise your place here, Con. Then he said, would it be right if I were allowed simply to walk back home, and claim Whitescar over your head. Yes, over your head. "Would you call that fair? I'm hanged if I would!" Those were his very words.'

'My God, if you're right!' he breathed. 'And Julie? Did he say anything about her?'

'Nothing you could be clear about. He wouldn't even say definitely that he intended to tell us all on the twenty-second, and when I tried to pin him down – asked flat out if he was re-making his Will in your favour – he just wouldn't give a straight answer. I couldn't press it, you know what he's like. He seems to like to keep people guessing, doesn't he?'

'He does, damn him!'

He spoke with such sudden, concentrated viciousness, that I stopped with my cigarette half-way to my lips. I was reminded sharply, shockingly, of the charming way he had talked to the old man that afternoon. Oddly enough, I thought that both attitudes were equally genuine.

I said gently: 'The thing is, Con, don't you see, he's old? I think he *minds* not being able to do things the way he used to. He's always been – well, I've gathered he's a pretty domineering type, and now his property and his money's the only kind of power he's got left. That's why he won't commit himself; I don't think he realises just how unfair he's being to younger people ... to you, anyway. He just thinks – quite rightly – that it's his property, and he'll play Old Harry with it if he wants to. But he's made up his mind now. He must have, since he's sent for Mr. Isaacs.'

I could see Con's cigarette smouldering unheeded between his fingers. He hadn't stirred. I got the impression that only the essentials of what I'd been saying had got through.

He said painfully, as if the readjustment of ideas was somehow a physical effort: 'If he's made a decision, it's happened since you got here ... or rather, since he knew you were coming back. He went to the telephone soon after Lisa broke the news to him. I remember her telling me so. It must have been to get hold of Isaacs.' He lifted his head. 'My God, but you must have got this the wrong way round! Why should he send for him now, *except to cut me out and include you in?*'

'He isn't doing that. Be sure of that. I tell you, he kept asking me, harping on it almost, if I thought it was fair for me to walk straight home after eight years and expect to take up as I left off. That was almost the very phrase he used. Yes, he asked flat out if I thought I

ought to be allowed to walk straight home and scoop Whitescar from
under your nose, after all the work you'd put into it.'

'Did he, by God?' A long breath, then he laughed, a sharp exultant
crack of sound. 'And what did you say?'

'Well, I thought it would be less trouble if I just said no. I may say
he seemed surprised.'

'And well he might! Annabel would never have parted with a penny-
piece to me, and what's more, she'd have seen that he didn't, either!'

'Well,' I said, 'she could have learned sense in eight years, couldn't
she? Found out what really mattered most?'

'You call that sense? Letting her rights go, for want of a fight?'

' "Rights?" Annabel's? What about Mr. Winslow's? Hasn't he as
much "right" to leave his own property any way he pleases?'

'No.'

'Oh? Well, I'm not breaking any lances with you over Annabel. You've
staked a claim of your own, and I won't argue with that, either. In any
case, it looks very much as if you're going to get what you want.'

'Do you know something?' said Con slowly. 'You're a very much nicer
person than Annabel ever was.'

'Good heavens, why on earth? Because I encouraged Grandfather to
give you the poor girl's property?'

'No. Because I honestly believe you want me to have it. And not just
for the "cut" you'll stand to get, either.'

'Don't you believe it. I'm as mercenary as hell,' I said cheerfully.

He ignored that. 'You said she "might have learned sense in eight
years", and found out what really mattered. What really does – to you?'

I knew he couldn't see my face, but all the same, I looked away. I said
shortly: 'I'm a woman. That should answer it.'

Through the ensuing silence I heard a horse's steady cropping,
now quite close at hand. At the bottom of the pasture the river glimmered. Something drifted across like a shadow, shimmering at the edges,
shapeless and quiet as a ghost. The yearling, moving up nearer, beside
his mother.

I had just had time to realise how Con could have interpreted my last
remark, when he spoke again, mercifully ignoring it, and coming sharply
back to the matter in hand.

'And there really was nothing more about Julie?'

'Nothing.' I dropped my cigarette, and trod it out. 'Well, there it is.
I think it's true. For one thing, he told me not to tell you anything about
it.'

I caught the gleam of a grin. 'Did he now?'

I said tartly: 'And don't just accept it as if you expected me to let him
down automatically. I wouldn't have told you if – if I hadn't wanted to
ask you to change our ... plans.'

He didn't follow this up. He seemed to have a truly remarkable power
of only attending to what he wanted to. He was saying thoughtfully: '

can't quite understand it, if it's true. Ironic, isn't it, how our little conspiracy has turned out? I find you, import you into Whitescar at great trouble and some risk, expose myself and my ambitions to your uneasy female conscience . . . and all for nothing. He'd have left it to me all along.' His cigarette went fizzing down into the damp grass. 'Funny, you'd have expected it to act the other way. I mean, it seems absurd to have kept you in his Will all these years, in spite of me, only to cut you out when you actually do turn up. I – well, I don't get it. I wish I understood.'

'I think I do. I think – how shall I put it? – he's been keeping a sort of dream alive all these years, almost in spite of what he suspected to be the truth. You've all insisted that Annabel was dead, and, being who he is, and also because he must know you wanted Whitescar, he's simply got stubborn about it. He's hung on to his dream and his belief out of sheer obstinacy, even though probably in his heart he's known it wasn't true . . . And perhaps, partly, to keep some sort of hold over you, too. Yes, I think that might have come into it . . .' I paused. 'Well, now I've come back; he finds he was right all along. But also, mark you, he finds himself facing the *reality* of the dream that he's been using as a threat to stop you getting too sure of yourself. He's kept telling you that he'll leave the place to Annabel, come what may. Well, now she's here, having pretty well demonstrated that she doesn't give much of a damn for Whitescar, disappearing for eight years without a trace. You, on the other hand, have proved yourself the obvious legatee. So he's had to make his mind up in a hurry; and he's going to do, at last, what he knows he ought to have done all along.'

'You may be right. It's illogical enough to be likely.'

'What's more,' I said, 'there's one thing I'm pretty sure of.'

'What's that?'

'I think you've been a residuary beneficiary all along. Maybe with Julie, maybe not. I think that, underneath it all, he's believed Annabel was dead. He's obstinate enough to have left her named as his heir, but it's my belief he's expected you to inherit any time these last few years. But my coming home has given him a jolt. He's realised he's got to do something quickly, and make it stick.'

'You might be right. My God, you might be right.'

'I don't see why not.'

'If only we knew where Julie comes in.'

'Yes, Julie's the unknown quantity. Did you hear when I told you he sent for her? He did invite her, as Lisa thought. He wrote to to her. Did you know?'

'No.' I heard the twist to his voice. 'You see? You've been back here – twelve hours, is it? and, claim or no claim, he tells you more than he'd tell me in twelve months.'

'Con, please. Don't tear yourself up so.'

I spoke quite without thinking. Unexpectedly, he laughed, and his voice lightened. 'All right, darling, what the hell. We'll wait and see, and pray you're right. And irony or no, I still say you're my lucky star!'

'I don't know about that. If I'd never come, your luck would have still been in. You'd have got what you wanted the way you've got everything else; just as you said, with your two hands.' I half-turned towards him. In spite of myself, my voice tightened. 'Con . . . you still haven't heard what I came to say.'

'What else? Oh, lord, you're still upset, and now you feel it's all been for nothing. Is that it? Or are you beginning to worry in case I get what I want without you, and don't keep my side of the bargain? Relax, honey. I'll keep it, never fear. You'll get your cut, just the same.' I heard the smile in his voice. 'I'd not trust you else, sweetie, you could do me too much damage.'

'No, I'm not worried about that. I'd do you no harm. I only want to go. I told you, didn't I?'

'*Go?*'

'Yes. Cut right out. Leave. Straight away.'

He said blankly: 'You're – crazy!'

'No. It's obvious that I'm not needed any more, so – '

'Now look – '

'No, Con, listen to me, please! It's true that you *might* have got all this without my coming at all, or, on the other hand, my coming may have forced the decision on Grandfather. We weren't to know which way he'd decide. The game was worth playing, as far as it went. But now it isn't necessary. We've seen that. And since I'm not needed here any more, I really would rather go. No, please don't be angry; you know I'd never have let you down if I'd been needed, but I'm not. I – I want to go. Don't ask me to explain any more, I can't, you'd only laugh at me for – for scruples or something, and I couldn't take it, not tonight. Won't you just accept the fact – ?'

'I'll accept nothing!' We were back where we had been, with enmity sharp and open between us. 'If it's your conscience that's bothering you, for heaven's sake forget it! You've just found out that you're not robbing anyone after all – you're not even going to have to hand Annabel's share of Whitescar over to me! You came into this with your eyes wide open, and if this is the way you intend to react after one day, then I can only say it's turned out better for you than you deserve!' He paused, and added, more pleasantly: 'Now relax, for pity's sake. You're hurting nobody, and the old man's as pleased as a dog with two tails to have you here.'

'I know, but – '

'And how could you walk out now? Tell me that. What d'you think people – let alone Mr. Winslow – would say? What possible excuse could there be, short of the truth?'

'It's simple enough. I've only to go to Grandfather tonight and tell him that I came back to see him, but that on second thoughts I can see how silly it was of me to come . . . because of you, I mean. After all, Con, he can't expect me to find it easy to face you, can he? He'll accept that; he might even think I'm sulking because of his decision to leave Whitescar to you.'

I waited a moment, but he didn't speak. I turned to face the gate, gripping the top bar hard with both hands. 'Con, it's best, really it is. It'll work. The luck's running our way; today's proved it. We'll think up what to say to Grandfather, then I'll go, tomorrow. I can stay in Newcastle till Wednesday – it'd look queer if I didn't stay to meet Julie – and I can come for Grandfather's birthday. Then I'll go to London. I can always come back if – if he's ill or anything.' My voice was going out of control again. I stopped and took a steadying little breath that caught somehow in my throat, and must have sounded like a sob. 'You – you can't want me here, Con. Can't you see, if I go, it'll do you nothing but *good*? If I go straight away again, now, that'll clinch it as far as Grandfather's concerned, surely? He'd never leave me anything at all, not even money. You'd get the lot, you and Julie.'

He had made a quick movement in the dark. His hand came down over mine in a kind of pounce, and gripped it hard against the bar. 'Stop this!' He spoke sharply. 'You're hysterical. Think, can't you? What the hell's the matter with you tonight? You know quite well this is nonsense. If you go now, what sort of questions d'you think will be asked? Then heaven help us both, and Lisa too.'

'I don't see how they could find out – '

'Another thing. There's no possible excuse you could give for going now. You'd see that, if you'd behave like a reasonable human being instead of a hysterical girl.'

'I told you – '

'Oh, don't be a fool.' He sounded exasperated, and thoroughly angry. 'When you came back here – you, Annabel, I mean – you must have known you'd have to face me. If, after twenty-four hours, you decide you can't "take" me any more, what's Mr. Winslow going to think? He's no fool. He's going to assume that I've made myself objectionable – made another pass at you . . . raked up the past and upset you . . . something, anyway – and this time he mightn't be prepared to forgive me. No.'

'Oh. Yes. Yes, I do see that. Well, we could think of something else –'.

'I tell you, *no*! For one thing, we still don't know for certain about the terms of this Will, or even if there *is* to be a new Will. Even if you're right, do you think I want him cutting you right out, as he certainly would if you left tomorrow?'

I stared painfully at the shadow beside me. 'What do you mean?'

'My dear little conscience-stricken nitwit, do you think I want to see him splitting his capital two ways instead of three? If you stay, I get your share as well as my own. If you go, I go halves, if I'm lucky, with Julie . . . I'm talking about money now. I need the money to run the place. It's as simple as that.' His hand moved over mine, holding it hard down on the bar. 'So, darling, you'll stay. You'll go on playing the sweet repentant prodigal. And you'll play it till you collect at least Annabel's rightful share of what money's going. Is that clear?'

'No.'

'Girl dear, do I have to give it to you in a children's comic strip? I can't put it any clearer. And in any case, it doesn't matter. You'll do as I say.'

'No.'

Silence.

I said shakily: 'I didn't mean I didn't understand. I just meant no.'

For a moment I thought his stillness would explode into violent anger. I could feel it running through his wrist and hand into mine. Then the tension changed in quality. He was peering at me, as if he would pierce the dusk to read my face.

He said slowly: 'You still haven't told me the reason for all this. Now, supposing you do . . . Well? Something's scared you, and badly, hasn't it? No . . . not the horses; something important . . . And I'd give a lot to know just what . . .'

His voice had altered completely. The anger had vanished, and in its place was only a kind of curiosity; no, more than that; a kind of speculation.

Where his anger had failed to frighten me, it was absurd, now, suddenly, to be afraid. I said hurriedly: 'Nothing's scared me. It's just . . . I told you, I've had a rather ghastly day . . . I'm sorry, I – oh, don't ask me any more questions, *please*! I – I've done quite a lot for you today. Do this for me. We *can* think of some way, I know, if you'll only help . . .'

For the first time, I touched him of my own volition. I reached my free hand and laid it over his, where it held mine over the bar of the gate.

Then, suddenly, the moon was there, swimming up behind the tree-tops into a milky sky, and the shadows of the trees bored towards us, blue and hard as steel, across grass awash with silver.

I could see his face clearly, bent to mine. The expression of his eyes was hidden; the moonlight threw back a glint from their curved, brilliant surfaces, hiding everything but an impression of blackness behind. I was again sharply aware of that terrifying single-track concentration of his. The bright, blank eyes watched me.

Then he said, quite gently: 'You mean this? You really want to give it up, and go?'

'Yes.'

'Very well, my dear. Have it your own way.'

I must have jumped. He smiled. I said, incredulously: 'You mean, you'll help me? You'll let me go – give it up, and you'll just wait and see . . . fair means?'

'If that's the way you want it.' He paused, and added, very kindly: 'We'll go straight in now, and tell your grandfather that you're not

Annabel at all. We'll tell him that you're Mary Grey of Montreal, an enterprising tramp on the make, who wanted a peaceful niche in life in the Old Country, and a spot of assured income. We'll tell him that the three of us, Lisa, myself and you – all of whom he trusts – have plotted this thing up against him, and that we've been laughing at him all day. I don't know what passed between you in his bedroom this afternoon, but I imagine that he might be quite sensitive about it, don't you? ... Yes, I thought so. And when we've assured him, at the end of this long, happy day, that Annabel's as dead as mutton for all we know, and has been this last five years ... Do you see?'

The horses moved nearer, cropping the long grass. Through the hanging trees the river glittered in the growing moonlight. Across it a heron lumbered up on to its wings, and flapped ponderously down-river.

Eventually I said: 'Yes. I see.'

'I thought you would.'

'I should never have started it.'

'But you did. With your eyes open, sweetie.'

'It would kill him, wouldn't it? Whatever sort of scene ... I mean, if we told him, now?'

'Almost certainly. Any shock, any sudden strong emotional reaction, such as anger, or fear ... Oh yes, I think you can be sure it would kill him. And we don't want him dead – yet – do we?'

'*Con!*'

He laughed. 'Don't worry, sweetheart, that's not the plan at all. I only said it to wake you up to the – er – realities of the situation.'

'To frighten me, you mean?'

'If you like. If I want something badly enough, you know, I get it. I don't count small change.'

I said, before I thought: 'I know that. Don't think I haven't grasped the fact that you once tried to murder Annabel.'

A long, breathless pause. Then he straightened up from the gate. 'Well, well. You *have* put two and two together and made five, haven't you? Well, go on believing that; it'll keep you in line ... That's settled then. We carry on as planned, and you, my lovely, will do as you're told. Won't you?'

'I suppose so.'

His hand was still over mine. The other hand came up under my chin, and lifted my face to the moonlight. He was still smiling. He looked like every schoolgirl's dream of romance come true.

I moved my head away. 'Don't hold this against me, honey, will you? I've said some pretty hard things to you, but – well, you know as well as I do what's at stake, and it seemed the only way. I'm not worrying really that you'll let me down when it comes to the push ... This was bound to happen; I was expecting it. It's reaction, that's all. It's a highly emotional set-up, and you've taken more than enough for one day. So we'll forget it, shall we? You'll feel fine in the morning.' His hand touched my cheek, and he gave a little laugh. 'You see how right I was to choose a nice girl? That conscience of yours does give me the slightest advantage in this mutual-blackmail pact of ours, doesn't it?'

'All right. You've made your point. You're unscrupulous and I'm not. 'Vantage to you. Now let me go. I'm tired.'

'Just a minute. Do you think the blackmail would run to just one kiss?'

'No. I told you this afternoon – '

'Please.'

'Con, I've had enough drama for one day. I'm not going to gratify you by struggling in your arms, or whatever. Now let me go, and let's call the scene off.'

He didn't. He pulled me nearer to him, saying, in a voice nicely calculated to turn any normal woman's bones to pulp: 'Why do we waste our time quarrelling? Don't you know yet that I'm crazy about you? Just crazy?'

'I've gathered,' I said drily, 'that you've your very own way of showing it, as a rule.'

His grip slackened. I thought, with satisfaction: that's spoiled your routine, anyway. But it hadn't quite thrown him out of gear. He gave a little laugh that managed to make what I had said an intimate joke between us, and drew me closer once more. His voice sank to a murmur, somewhere near my left ear. 'Your hair looks like melted silver in this light. Sure, and I'm –'

'Oh, Con, don't!' How, short of cruelty, could one get through? I added, a little desperately: 'Con, I'm tired – '

Then, even as Con himself had rescued me that afternoon, rescue came. The grey mare, who had been browsing her way, unnoticed, steadily nearer and nearer the gate, suddenly lifted her beautiful head, and thrust it between us, blowing gustily, and still chewing. A froth of grass-stains went blubbering down the front of Con's white shirt.

He swore lamentably, and let me go.

The mare rubbed her head hard against me. Trying not to laugh, I ran a hand up to her forelock, and with the other hand held her gently by the muzzle, keeping her head away from Con. I said, shakily: 'Don't be angry! She – she must have been jealous.'

He didn't answer. He had taken a pace away from me, to pick up the tools and the coil of wire.

I said quickly: 'Please don't be angry, Con. I'm sorry I've been a fool tonight, but I was upset.'

He straightened, and turned. He wasn't looking angry. His face held no expression whatever, as he regarded me and the mare.

'So it appears. But not, apparently, by the horses.'

'The – oh, well,' I said, pushing the mare's head to one side, and coming away from the gate, 'I told you it wasn't that, didn't I? And she's awfully gentle really, isn't she?'

He stood there, looking at me. After a moment or two he said in a curiously dry, abrupt tone: 'Well, so long as you know just where you are.'

'Oh yes,' I said wearily, 'I know just where I am.'

I turned away and left him standing there in the lane, with the fencing-wire in his hand.

The path to Forrest Hall looked as if nobody had been that way for a hundred years.

I don't remember consciously deciding to take it: I only wanted to get away from Con, and not to have to encounter Lisa for a little while longer. I found myself, with no clear idea why I had come this way, walking rapidly away from the house, along the river-path that led towards the Hall.

The moss was silent underfoot. To my left, the sliding sparkle of the water lit the way. Big trees edged the path, lining the river-bank. The track was ribbed with the shadows of their trunks, thrown slanting by the moon. Now last year's beech-mast crackled under my feet, and I thought I could smell lime-blossom, until the path led me up to the high wall that girdled Forrest, and there the neglected overgrowth crowded in, with its stronger scents of ivy and rotting wood and wild garlic and elder-flowers.

Set deep in the tangle was the gate leading through into the Hall grounds. The elder-bushes, and the ivy cascading over the wall, had almost hidden it from sight. It creaked as I pushed it, and opened crookedly on one hinge.

It was darker in the wood, but here and there, in some chance patch of moonlit sky framed by the branches, burned a star, sparkling blue-white, like frost. The air was still, and the vast trees kept quiet their tangled boughs. The river made all the sound there was.

You could easily have missed the summer-house if you didn't know where it was. It stood a little back from the path, under the trees, and rhododendrons had run wild up the bank in front of it, until its entrance showed only as a gaping square of blackness behind the other shadows. I had gone straight by it when an owl, sweeping past me low down, like the shadow of a flying cloud, startled me into turning. Then I saw the hard edge of the moonlight on the tiles of the roof. A flight of shallow steps, blurred by moss, let up through the bushes.

I paused for a moment, looking at it. Then I left the path, and made my way up the steps, pushing aside the sharp leaves of the rhododendrons. They were as stiff as leather, and smelt bitter and narcotic, of autumn and black water.

The summer-house was one of those once-charming 'follies' built by some eighteenth-century Forrest with a taste for romance. It was a small, square pavilion, open in front, and pillared with slender Ionic columns of peeling plaster. The floor was marble, and round the three sides ran a broad seat. A heavy, rustic-seeming table still stood in the centre of the floor. I touched it with an exploratory finger. It felt dry, but thick with dust, and, I suspected, birds' droppings. In the sunlight of high summer, with the bushes trimmed back, and the view of the river, and cushions on the benches, the place would be charming. Now it was a home not even for ghosts. Pigeons would nest there, and perhaps a blackbird or two, and the owl in the roof. I left it and went down the steps to regain the path.

There I hesitated, half inclined, now, to go back. But the events of the day still pressed on me, and the woods were quiet and fresh. If they were not full of comfort, at least they offered solitude, and a vast indifference.

I would go on, I thought, a little further; as far as the house. The moonlight was strong, and even when the path turned (as it soon did) away from the river, I could see my way fairly easily.

Presently the timber thinned again, and the path shook itself free of the engulfing rhododendrons, to skirt a knoll where an enormous cedar climbed, layer upon layer, into the night sky. I came abruptly out of the cedar's shadow into a great open space of moonlight, and there at the other side of it, backed against the far wall of trees, was the house.

The clearing where I stood had been a formal garden, enclosed by artificial banks where azaleas and berberis grew in a wild tangle. Here and there, remains of formal planting could be seen, groups of bushes and small ornamental trees, their roots deep in the rough grass that covered lawns and flower-beds alike. Sheep had grazed the turf down to a close, tufted mat, but underneath this, the formal patterning of path and lawn (traced by their moon-slanted shadows) showed clear. At the centre of the pattern stood a sundial, knee-deep in a riot of low-growing bushes. At the far side of the garden, a flight of steps mounted between urns and stone balustrading to the terrace of the house.

I paused beside the sundial. The scent of the small, frilled roses came up thick and sweet, and mixed with honeysuckle. The petals were wet, and the dew was heavy on the grass where I stood.

The shell of the house gaped. Behind it, the big trees made a horizon, against which the moon sketched in the shapes of the broken walls and windows. One end of the house, still roofed and chimneyed, thrust up looking almost intact, till you saw the forest through the window frames.

I crossed the damp, springy grass towards the terrace steps. Somewhere an owl hooted, and a moment later I saw it drift past the blind windows, to be lost in the woods beyond. I hestitated, then slowly climbed the steps. Perhaps it was here that I would find the ghosts. . . .

But they were not there. Nothing, not even a wisp of the past, stirred in the empty rooms. Peering in through the long windows, I made out the shapes of yesterday . . . The drawing-room – a section of charred panelling, and the wreck of a door, and what remained of a once lovely fireplace. The library, with shelves still ranked against the two standing walls, and a damaged chimney-piece mounted with what looked like a coat of arms. The long dining-room, where a young ash-sapling had thrust its way up between broken floor-boards, and where ferns hung in the cracks of the wall ... On an upper landing, one tall window had its lancet frames intact, standing sharply against the moonlight. For a moment it seemed as if the leaded tracery was there still, then you could see how the ferns grew in the empty sockets, with a plant of what might in daylight show to be wild campanula, its leaves and tight buds as formal as a design in metal.

No, there was nothing here. I turned away. The weedy gravel made very little sound under my feet. I paused for a moment at the head of the terrace steps, looking back at the dead house. The Fall of the House of Forrest. Con's mocking words came back to me, cruelly, and, hard after them, other words, something once read and long forgotten ...

Time hath his revolutions, there must be a period and an end of all temporal things, finis rerum, an end of names and dignities, and what-soever is terrene, and why not of De Vere? For where is Bohun? Where's Mowbray? Where's Mortimer? Nay, which is more and most of all, where is Plantagenet? they are intombed in the urnes and sepulchres of mortality ...

Magnificent words: far too magnificent for this. This was no noble house ruined, no Bohun or Chandos or Mortimer; only the home of a line of successful merchant-venturers, with a purchased coat-of-arms that had never led a battle-charge; but they had built something here of beauty and dignity, and cared for it, and now it had gone: and beauty and dignity had gone with it, from a world that was content to let such things run through its fingers like water.

There was a movement from the bushes at the edge of the clearing; the rustle of dead leaves underfoot, the sound of a heavy body pushing through the thicket of shrubs. There was no reason why I should have been frightened, but I jerked round to face it, my heart thudding, and my hand on the stone balustrade grown suddenly rigid ...

...Only a ewe with a fat lamb nearly as big as herself, shoving her way between the azaleas. She saw me, and stopped dead, head up, with the moon reflecting back from her eyes and from the dew on her clipped fleece. The lamb gave a startled cry that seemed to echo back into the woods and hang there for ever, striking the sounding-board of their emptiness. Then the two of them vanished like clumsy ghosts.

I found that I was shivering. I walked quickly down the steps and across the clearing. As I hurried under the layered blackness of the cedar, my foot struck a cone as solid as a clock-weight, and sent it rolling among the azaleas. A roosting blackbird flew out of the bushes with a clatter of alarm-notes that set every nerve jumping, and jangled on and on through the trees like a bell that has been pulled and left swinging.

It brought me up short for the second time. I was just at the entrance to the river-path, where it plunged out of the moonlight into the wood.

I took half a step forward towards those shadows, then paused. I had had my hour of solitude; enough was enough. I had a home of a sort, and it was time I went back to it.

I turned aside to where the main drive entered the clearing, then hurried down its wide avenue, past the banked rhododendrons, past the ruined lodge and the ivy tree, till I reached the painted gate marked WHITESCAR, and the well-kept road beyond it.

CHAPTER NINE

Alang the Roman Waal,
Alang the Roman Waal,
The Roman ways in bygone days are terrible to recaal.

NORMAN TURNBULL: *Northumbrian Song*

Julie arrived just before tea on a drowsy afternoon. Everywhere was the smell of hay, and the meadowsweet was frothing out along the ditches. The sound of the distant tractor was as much a part of the hot afternoon as the hum of the bees in the roses. It made the sound of the approaching car unnoticeable, till Lisa looked up from the table where she and I had been slicing and buttering scones for the men's tea, and said: 'There's a car just stopped at the gate. It must be Julie.' She bit at her lower lip. 'I wonder who can be bringing her? She must have got Bill Fenwick to meet her train.'

I set down my knife rather too carefully. She gave me one of her thoughtful, measuring looks. 'I shouldn't worry. This'll be nothing, after the rest.'

'I'm not worrying.'

She regarded me a moment longer, then nodded, with that little close-lipped smile of hers. In my two-days' sojourn at Whitescar, Lisa seemed to have got over her odd fit of nerves. Indeed, she had taken my advice to her so much to heart that sometimes I had found myself wondering, but only momentarily, if she really had managed to persuade herself that I was Annabel. At any rate she seemed to have adopted me as genuine; it was a sort of protective colouration for herself.

'I'll go out and meet her,' she said. 'Are you coming?'

'I'll let you meet her first. Go ahead.'

I followed her down the flagged passage to the back door, and waited there, just in the door's shadow, while she went out into the sunlight.

Julie was at the wheel of an open car, a battered relic almost as old as she was, carefully hand-enamelled a slightly smeared black, and incongruously decorated in dazzling chrome – at least, that was the impression one got – with gadgets of blatant newness and dubious function. Julie dragged ineffectually at the hand-brake, allowing the car to slide to a stop at least four yards further on, then hurled herself out of the door without even troubling to switch off the engine.

'Lisa! What heaven! We've had the most *sweltering* run! Thank God to be here, and I can smell new scones. How's Grandfather? Has she come? My dear, you don't mind Donald, I hope? It's his car and he wouldn't let me drive because he says I'm the world's *ghastliest driver*, but he had to at the end because I wouldn't get out and open the gates. I asked him to stay – I hope you don't mind? He can have the old nursery and I'll do every *stroke* of the work myself. *Has* she come?'

She had on a white blouse, and a blue skirt belted tightly to a slim waist with a big leather belt the colour of new horse-chestnuts. Their simplicity did nothing to disguise the fact that they were expensive. Her hair, which was fair and fine, shone in the sun almost as pale as cotton-floss, and her eyes were grey-green, and very clear, like water. Her face was tanned golden, and her arms and legs, which were bare, showed the same smooth, amber tan. A heavy gold bracelet gave emphasis to one slim wrist.

She was holding Lisa's hands, and laughing. She hadn't kissed her, I noticed. The ecstasy of welcome was not personally for Lisa, but was so much a part of Julie's own personality that it sprang, as it were, unbidden. Fountains overflow. If people are near enough, the drops fall on them, sparkling.

She dropped Lisa's hands then, and turned, with a swirl of her blue skirt, towards the man whom I now noticed for the first time. He had been shutting the yard gate behind the car. Now, before responding to Julie's hail of 'Donald! Come and meet Lisa!' he walked quietly across to where the car stood, with her chrome glittering in the sun as she shook to the vibrations of the engine. He switched the engine off, took out the key, put it carefully into his pocket, and then approached, with a slightly diffident air that was in startling contrast to Julie's ebullience.

I found later that Donald Seton was twenty-seven, but he looked older, having that rather solemn, withdrawn look that scholarship sometimes imposes on the natural reserve of the Scot. He had a long face, with high cheekbones, and eyes set well under indecisively-marked brows. The eyes were of indeterminate hazel, which could look shallow or brilliant according to mood. They were, indeed, almost the only indication that Donald Seton ever varied his moods. His face seldom changed from its rather watchful solemnity, except to let in, like a door opening on to bright light, his rare and extremely attractive smile. He had fine, straight hair that refused discipline, but tumbled forward in a thick mouse-brown thatch that showed reddish lights in the sun. His clothes were ancient and deplorable, and had never, even in their fairly remote past, been 'good'. They reminded me somehow of his car, except that his person was not ornamented to a similar extent. He was the kind of man who would, one felt, have stigmatised even the most modest band of Fair Isle as 'a bit gaudy'. He looked clever, gentle, and about as mercurial as the Rock of Gibraltar. He made a most remarkable foil for Julie.

She was saying, with that same air of delighted improvisation: 'Lisa, this is Donald. Donald Seton. Darling, this is Lisa Dermott; I told you, she's a kind of cousin, and she's the most *dreamy* cook, you've no idea! Lisa, he can stay, can't he? Where have you put *her*?'

'Well, of course he may,' said Lisa, but looking faintly taken aback. 'How do you do? Have you really driven Julie all the way up from London? You must both be tired, but you're just in time for tea. Now, Mr. – Seton, was it? –'

'Didn't Grandfather *tell* you?' cried Julie. 'Well, really, and he's always jumping on me for being scatter-brained! I *told* him on the phone that Donald was bringing me! Why, it was the whole *point* of my coming now, instead of August, or almost, anyway. Donald's the most terrific big bug in Roman Remains, or whatever you call it, and he's come to work up at West Woodburn where there's a Roman camp –'

'Fort,' said Mr. Seton.

'Fort, then, isn't it the same thing? Anyway,' said Julie eagerly, 'I thought if I came *now*, I'd be up here when he was, *and* be here for the birthday party Grandfather's talking about, and anyway, June's a heavenly month and it always rains in August. *Has* she come?'

For once, Lisa's not very expressive face showed as a battle-ground of emotions. I could see relief at Julie's gay insouciance about her reasons for coming to Whitescar and the birthday party; avid curiosity and speculation about Donald; apprehension over the coming meeting between Julie and myself; pure social embarrassment at having another visitor foisted on her without notice, and a swift, house-proud calculation that she would manage this, as she managed everything. Besides – I could see her assessing the smile Julie flung at Donald – it might be worth it.

'Of course we can put you up, easily,' she said, warmly, for her. 'No, no, it doesn't matter a bit, there's always room, and any friend of Julie's –'

'It's very good of you, but I really wouldn't dream of putting you to the trouble.' Mr. Seton spoke with a quiet lack of emphasis that was as definite as a full stop. 'I've explained to Julie that I'll have to stay near my work. I'll be camping up there on the site, when the students come, but for a night or two, at any rate, the hotel expects me.'

'Ah well,' said Lisa, 'if that's what you've arranged. But of course you'll stay and have tea?'

'Thank you very much. I should like to.'

'That's *absurd*!' cried Julie. 'Donald, I *told* you, it would be *much* nicer staying here. You don't have to do the polite and refuse just because Grandfather forgot to tell Lisa you were coming, for goodness' sake! As a matter of fact I may have forgotten to tell Grandfather, but then I was so excited about Annabel and then it was three minutes and it's a call-box in my digs and you know Grandfather's always been as mean as stink about reversing the charges. Anyway, Donald, darling, you can't *possibly* camp at West Woodburn, it's the *last* place, and I've seen that site of yours; there are *cows*. And you've got to escape your dreary old Romans sometimes, so obviously you'll stay here. That's settled, then. Lisa I can't bear it another moment. Where *is* she?'

I hadn't moved from the shadows of the passage. But the fraction before Julie turned, Donald, looking past her shoulder, saw me standing there. I had been prepared for surprise, shock, even, in the recognition of everyone who had known Annabel before, but the startled amazement in Donald Seton's eyes jolted me, until I realised that, to him, I was a ghost of Julie. The look went, banished from his eyes immediately, but I wondered just what he had seen; a Julie grown older, thinner; not greyer, that would have been absurd, but somehow greyed? The eight years were dry in my throat, like dust.

Julie had seen me. I saw her eyes widen, then the same look spring in them.

I came out into the sunlight.

'*Annabel*!'

For a moment she stayed poised, as it seemed, between welcome and something else. The moment hung suspended for ever, like the wave before it breaks. I thought, Lisa was wrong, this is the worst yet: I can't bear it if she hates me, and God knows, she may be the one to have the right.

'Annabel *darling*!' said Julie, and dived straight into my arms and kissed me. The broken wave washed over me; the salt drops tingled and smarted in my eyes. She was laughing and hugging me and holding me away from her and talking, and the moments slid past with all the other moments, and was gone.

'Annabel, you *devil*, how *could* you, it's been such *hell*, and we were so unhappy. Oh, I could kill you for it, I really could. And I'm so thankful you're not dead because now I can *tell* you. That's the worst of people dying, they get away ... Oh, lord, I'm not crying – these must be those tears of joy they always shed like *mad* in books, only I've never believed them ... Oh, it's terrific, it really is! You've come back!' She gave me a little shake. 'Only *say* something, darling, for pity's sake, or I *will* think you're a ghost!'

I noticed that Donald had turned away, tactfully to examine the side of the Dutch barn. Since this was made of corrugated iron, it could hardly be said to provide an absorbing study for an archaeologist; but he seemed to be finding it quite fascinating. Lisa had withdrawn a little behind Julie, but she was watching unashamedly.

I looked at Julie, feeling suddenly helpless. What was there to say, after all?

I cleared my throat, smiled uncertainly, and said the only thing that came into my head. 'You – you've grown.'

'I suppose I have,' said Julie blankly.

Then we both laughed, the laughter perhaps a little high and overpitched. I could see Lisa looking at me with her mouth slightly open. I came to me suddenly that she was staggered and dismayed at the ineptitude with which I was playing this scene; all the more feeble since she had seen the way I dealt with Grandfather. As far as it was possible for me to do so at that moment, I felt amused. Of course there wa nothing to say. Here at least, Lisa was a bad psychologist. What did she expect me to do? Make a charmingly social occasion out of this? My part in the scene had been far more convincing than she knew.

The next second, uncannily, Julie was echoing my thought. 'You know, isn't it silly? I've noticed it before, about meeting anyone one hasn't seen for a long time. You long and long for the moment, like mad and then, when it comes, and you've got the first hullos said, there' nothing whatever to say. All that comes later, all the *where have you been and how did you get on?* stuff. For the moment, it's quite enough to have you here. You do understand, don't you?'

'Of course. I'm just thanking heaven you do. I – I can't think of much in the way of conversation, myself.' I smiled at her, and then at Donald now gravely waiting on the outskirts of the conversation. 'I'm still English enough to regard tea as a sort of remedy for any crisis. Shall we go in and have it? How do you do, Mr. Seton?'

'Oh, lord, I'm sorry,' said Julie, and hastily made the introduction 'Only for pity's sake call him Donald, everybody does, at least, everybody he *likes*, and if he doesn't like them, he never speaks to them at all which comes to the same thing.'

I laughed as I shook hands with him. 'It sounds a marvellous way of getting along.'

'It works,' said Donald.

'Oh,' said Julie, at my elbow, 'Donald has his very own way of getting through life with the minimum of trouble to himself.'

I glanced at her quickly. Nothing in Donald's expression showed me whether this was intended to have a sharp edge to it, or anything in Julie's, for that matter. She looked very lovely and gay, and she was laughing at him.

She thrust an arm into mine. 'Where's Grandfather? Surely he's no up in the field in this weather? It's far too hot.'

'He's lying down. He does every afternoon now.'

'*Does* he? I mean, does he *have* to?'

Lisa had gathered Donald up, so to speak, and, with the usual polite murmur about washing his hands before tea, was shepherding him ahead of us towards the house.

I said: 'It's only a precaution. He has to be careful. He might be risking another stroke if he did anything too energetic, or had any sort of an upset. Go gently with him, Julie. I think my coming back has been a bit of a strain, but he's taken it remarkably well.'

'And Con?' The sideways glance was disconcertingly shrewd.

I said lightly: 'He's taken it very well, too.' I wondered, by no means for the first time, how much the eleven-year-old Julie had known about her cousin's disappearance. 'You'll see him later. I imagine he'll take his tea up in the field with the men.'

'Are you going to take it up? I'll help if you like, or we can make Donald come and carry everything – you don't exactly look as if you ought to be hiking loads around in this heat, if I may say so. What on earth have you been doing to yourself, you look so thin, and your figure used to be heaven, at least *I* thought so, which might mean anything, because when I was eleven my ideal was the Angel Gabriel and they're not supposed to have figures anyway, are they?'

'Julie! At least you didn't piffle on at that rate when you were eleven, or if you did, I don't remember it! Where on earth did you learn?'

Julie laughed. 'Donald.'

'That I don't believe.'

'Well, he never speaks at all unless it's necessary, so I have to do enough for two on one person's sense. Result, half my talk is piffle, whereas Donald's silence is a hundred per cent solid worth. Or would it be two hundred per cent? I never know.'

'I see.'

'And there was you.'

'I?'

'Yes. Nobody could piffle quite so well. The stories you used to make up. I can still remember them, and the funny thing is, a lot of them seemed somehow more real than you, or at any rate they seemed the reallest part of you.'

'Perhaps they were.'

She gave me a swift look as we went into the house, and squeezed my arm. 'When you look like that you break my heart.'

'I don't see why.'

'You look unhappy, that's why. Whenever you're not actually smiling. It's just a look you have. It's not like you ... I mean, you weren't like that before.'

'I meant, I don't see why you should worry over the way I feel.'

'Don't you?'

'No. Why should you care what happened to me? I lighted out regardless, didn't I? And now I come back, like a ghost to trouble sleep. Why should you care?'

The grey-green eyes were open and candid as a child's. 'Because I love you, of course,' said Julie, quite simply.

The passage was dim after the glare of the sun. I was glad of this. In a moment I said, lightly: 'Better than the Angel Gabriel?'

She laughed. 'Oh, he stopped being top pop years ago. Much better.'

In a way, Julie's homecoming was as exacting as my own.

Mrs. Bates was, inevitably, lying in wait in the kitchen: 'And very nice it is to see you, Julie, and very smart you're looking, quite London,

I'm sure. A real shame I call it, the way they make you work at the
B.B.C. – not a chance to come up and see your poor Granda, *not* to
mention others as I could name what would have liked a sight of you any
time this past year. But there it is, birds leave the nest, which you might
say is only natural, and them that is left has only to lump it, as the
saying goes . . . And that was your young man that went through with
Miss Dermott? "Not official?" And what does that mean, may I ask? In
my day, if we were courting, we knew we was courting, and believe me,
we knew just where we *was*. Now don't you bother, Miss Annabel, love.
Cora's taking the men's tea up, which you may be sure ain't no bother
for *her*, seeing as Willie Latch is along helping this afternoon. Go on in,
then. I'll bring the trolley as soon as the tea's mashed, if you'll take the
cake-stand . . .'

Then there was Con, who came down unexpectedly from the hayfield,
ostensibly impatient to welcome Julie, but curious, I knew, to see who
had driven her down.

It was amusing to watch the meeting between him and Donald. We
were quietly settled, waiting for Mrs. Bates and the tea-trolley, when
Con walked in. He had presumably conformed by washing his hands,
but he was still in his working clothes – old breeches, and a white shirt,
short-sleeved and open at the neck. He brought with him, into the rather
charmingly old-fashioned room, the smell of sunshine and hay, and – it
must be confessed – a faint tang of horses and outdoor, sunbaked sweat.
He looked magnificent.

He greeted Donald with none of the curiosity that I knew he was
feeling. If he had been wondering about Julie's new escort as a potential
threat to his own position, the worry, I could see, was dispelled as soon
as he entered the room, and saw the unobtrusive figure sitting quietly in
the old-fashioned chintz-covered chair by the fireplace. I could also see,
quite well, that he was pleased – as Donald rose to greet him – to find
himself the taller of the two by at least three inches. The contrast between
the two men was certainly remarkable, and I saw an odd expression in
Julie's eyes as she watched them. Lisa's face, for once, was much more
transparent: one almost expected to hear the proud, contented clucking
with which the mother-hen regards the swan that she has just personally
hatched. The only person in the room who seemed unconscious of Con's
overwhelming physical splendour was Donald. He greeted the other man
serenely, and then turned back to resume his conversation with me.

Grandfather came in then, followed immediately by Mrs. Bates with
the tea. The old man was using a stick, which I hadn't seen him do
before, and I thought he looked more finely-drawn than usual, with a
waxy tinge to the skin.

'Grandfather, it's lovely to see you!' Julie, as she rose to greet him,
gave him a fond, anxious look. 'How are you?'

'Hm. You've controlled your anxiety remarkably well, haven't you?
How long is it since you were here? Twelve months?'

'Only ten,' said Julie. 'Grandfather, this is Donald Seton. He's a London friend of mine who drove me up, such luck, and he's going to be up here all summer, working at West Woodburn.'

'How d'ye do? Good of you to bring the child. Glad you could stay to tea. Working at West Woodburn, eh? What sort of work?'

As Donald answered, I noticed that Con, ostensibly talking to Julie, was listening carefully. Mrs. Bates, lingering beside Lisa, hadn't taken her eyes off Donald.

'Thank you, Mrs. Bates,' said Lisa, pouring tea. 'That's everything, I think ... Annabel, I wonder if you'd help hand the cups?'

'Let me, please,' said Donald quickly, getting to his feet. Con slanted a lazy look up at him, and stayed where he was.

Lisa – with great restraint – poured tea for Julie and Grandfather before she attended to Con, but when she did come to Con's cup, I noticed that she not only put sugar in, but even stirred it, before giving it to Donald to hand to him. Donald carried it across with no change of expression, and Con took it without even looking away from Julie, who was telling some story or other which involved a lot of laughter.

Mrs. Bates had made no move to go, but busied herself rather ostentatiously, handing scones. The little black eyes had never left Donald.

'London, eh?' This came as soon as he left his chair, and was detached, so to speak, from Grandfather's orbit. 'So you've come up north for the summer, from what I hear?'

'Yes.'

'And what d'you think of the North?' This in the tone of a champion throwing down a rather well-worn glove. 'I suppose you Londoners think we've not even got electric light in these parts yet?'

'Haven't you?' said Donald, startled into a vague glance at the ceiling.

I said quickly: 'Mrs. Bates regards all Londoners as ignorant southerners who think the Arctic Circle begins at Leeds, or something.'

'One wonders,' put in Julie from the sofa, 'if they mayn't be right, sometimes. Not this year, it's been heaven *everywhere*.'

'Even here?' said Grandfather, rather drily.

I saw a glance pass, like a spark across points, between Con and Lisa.

I said quickly: 'Betsy, dear, Mr. Seton isn't a southerner, really; he's from Scotland.'

'Oh?' She appeared only slightly mollified. 'I've never been up in them parts. But you *live* in London, like?'

'Yes, I've got rooms there. But I usually spend the summer somewhere out on a – well, in the country. This year I'm at West Woodburn.'

'For the whole summer?' I hoped the calculating glance that Mrs. Bates shot at Julie wasn't as obvious to him as it was to me. But she underlined it. 'How long are *you* staying, Julie?'

'Mm?' Julie had been laughing at some remark of Con's. 'Who, me? As long as I can. I've got three weeks.'

'Mrs. Bates,' said Lisa, 'there's the telephone, I think. Do you mind? ... I'm sorry, Mr. Seton, but she's been a member of the family for so long, and of course she's known Julie since she was very small ... I think she puts all Julie's friends into the same age-group.'

'And that,' said Julie cheerfully, 'stays at about thirteen plus. Donald doesn't mind, do you, darling?'

'Not in the least.' Mr. Seton, who had, during the cross-examination, been handing sandwiches and scones round with unruffled good humour, now sat down, and took one himself. Somehow, I noticed, the stand of sandwiches and cakes had finished up in a position mid-way between his chair and mine, and within easy reach of both. No mean strategist, I thought, watching him finish his sandwich, and quietly take another. They were very good; I had made them myself.

'Now,' said Grandfather, who, being a Winslow male, obviously thought it was time he was back in the centre of the stage, 'about this Roman camp at West Woodburn ...'

'Fort, actually,' said Donald.

'Fort, then. Habitancium, isn't that the Roman name for it?'

'Habitancum.' Donald took another sandwich in an absent sort of way while managing to keep a keenly interested gaze fixed on his questioner. 'That's the name on the various inscriptions that have been uncovered. There are no other references, and the place is named solely from the inscriptions, so, in fact,' that sudden, charming smile, 'your guess is as good as mine, sir.'

'Oh. Ah. Well, what I want to know is this –'

But Mrs. Bates, laden with more scones, and big with news, re-entered the room briskly.

'The way things gets around in these parts is like magic, it is that. Here's Julie only been at home five minutes before her young man's ringing her up on the phone. He's waiting.' She slapped the plate of scones down on the trolley, and stared pointedly at Julie.

The latter looked blank for a moment, then I saw the faintest tinge of pink slide up under her skin. 'My – young man?'

'Aye,' said Mrs. Bates a little sourly. 'Young Bill Fenwick from Nether Shields. Saw you pass, he says, when they was working up near the road.'

'Young Fenwick?' said Grandfather. 'Nether Shields? What's this? What's this?'

'I've no idea.' Julie spoke airily, setting down her cup. 'Did he say it was for me?'

'He did, and well you know it. Never talked about anyone else since last time you were here, and if you ask me –'

'Oh, Mrs. Bates, *please*!' Julie, scarlet now, almost ran out of the drawing-room. Mrs. Bates gave a ferocious nod that was aimed somewhere between Grandfather and Donald. 'He's a nice lad, Bill Fenwick is, but he's not for the likes of her, and *that's* the truth and no lie!'

'Mrs. Bates, you really mustn't –' began Lisa.

'I speak as I find,' said that lady tartly.

'Hm,' said Grandfather. 'Pity you find such a lot. That'll do, now, Betsy. Go away.'

'I'm going. Enjoy your teas, now, I made those scones meself. You'll not get the likes of *them* in London,' with a nod at Donald, '*nor* in Scotland, neither, let me tell you. Now, did I see that cat come in or did I not?'

'Cat?' said Lisa. 'Tommy? Oh, no, surely not, he's never allowed in here.'

'I thought I seed him run past when I opened the door.'

'Nonsense, Betsy, you're imagining things.' Grandfather was poking about testily under the sofa with his stick. 'There's no cat in here. Don't make excuses, now, just go away, do. The scones are excellent. Perhaps you'll get Julie to bring the hot water in, when she's finished her telephone call?'

'All right,' said Mrs. Bates, unoffended. 'There's nobody can say I can't take a hint as well as anyone.' But, pausing at the door, she fired her last shot. 'Mr. Forrest, too, did I tell you? He's back already. Didn't expect *him* till Friday, but he's flown. Maybe *he'll* be on the phone soon.' And, with a chuckle, she disappeared.

There was a pause.

'Ah, well,' said Con, reaching out a lazy hand, 'the scones are worth it.'

'Hm,' said Grandfather, 'she's all right. Trust Betsy with my last halfpenny, and that's a thing you can't say of many, nowadays. Now, Seton, where were we?'

'Habitancum,' said Con, 'just about to start digging.'

'Ah, yes. Well, what are you going to find? Tell me that? If there's anything worth finding round here, I wish you digging Johnnies would find it at Whitescar. No likelihood of *that*, I suppose?'

I saw a sudden look of surprise flicker over Donald's face, to be followed by what looked like rather furtive embarrassment. Grandfather, drinking tea, hadn't noticed, but Con had. I saw his eyes narrow momentarily in a speculative look. Then I saw what was hidden from anyone else in the room. Donald's hand, with a portion of ham sandwich, had been hanging down over the arm of his chair while he talked. The skirts of his armchair almost touched the ground. From under the edge of this crept a stealthy, black and white paw, which once again patted the edge of the ham sandwich.

'There's nothing marked hereabouts on any existing map,' said Donald, now serenely ignoring this phenomenon, 'but that's not to say there *was* nothing here, of course. If you start turning up Roman coins with the plough, sir, I hope you'll send straight for me.' As he spoke, he had returned the sandwich to the plate, and then his hand went, oh, so idly, over the arm of the chair, holding a substantial portion broken off. The paw flashed out and took it, not too gently. Tommy, it appeared, had had to learn to snatch what bits he got.

'And how long are you to be here?'

'Possibly until August, on this particular job.'

'I doubt,' said Con with a grin, 'if we'll be doing much ploughing before you go, then.'

'No?' said Donald, adding, apologetically, 'I'm afraid I'm very ignorant. Your – er, Mrs. Bates was perhaps not so far out in her judgment of Londoners.'

'Well,' said Grandfather, 'if you can tell wheat and barley apart, which I've no doubt you can, then you'll be one up on me and Connor. I wouldn't know a Roman inscription from a whisky advertisement, and neither would he.'

Con's protest, and my 'Are you sure?' came simultaneously, and everyone laughed. Into the laughter came Julie, so blandly unconcerned, and so fussily careful of the hot-water-jug she was carrying, that the attention of everyone in the room switched straight to her with an almost audible click. It was all Con could do, I knew, not to ask her outright what Bill Fenwick had had to say.

'Julie?' Old Mr. Winslow had no such inhibitions. 'What did the boy want?'

'Oh, nothing much,' said Julie airily, 'just how was I and how long was I here for, and – and all that.'

'Hm. Well, now, let's have a look at you, child. Come and sit by me. Now, about this job of yours ...'

Conversation began to flow again, Con and Lisa both listening with some interest to Julie's account of her first year's work at Broadcasting House. Beside me, the skirts of Donald's chair began to shake in a frustrated fashion. I said gently: 'Won't you have another sandwich, Mr. Seton? These are crab. They – er, go down rather well.'

I saw the glimmer in his eyes as he took one. Half a minute later I saw the paw field a piece, very smartly, and, in a matter of three-quarters of a second, come out for more. Tommy, flown with good living, was getting reckless.

'You're not eating anything,' said Lisa to me. 'Have another sandwich. There's one left –'

Even as she turned to look, the paw shot out, and the last of the crab sandwiches vanished, whole, from the plate on the bottom tier of the trolley.

'I'm so sorry,' said Donald, blandly, to me. 'I took it myself. Have a macaroon.'

CHAPTER TEN

O wherefore should I tell my grief,
Since lax I canna find?
I'm stown frae a' my kin and friends,
And my love I left behind.

Ballad: *Baby Livingston*

Julie and I went out together that evening. Lisa's eyes followed us to the door, but she said nothing. Donald, not to be moved from his decision, had driven off to West Woodburn soon after tea. Grandfather, whom the heat was tiring, I thought, more than he would admit, had gone early to bed. Con had not come in again. No doubt he would come back at dusk for a late supper. The sound of the tractor wound on and on through the soft evening into the dusk.

Though it would have seemed the natural pilgrimage to take her to see the mare, I had had enough of the lane. We went the other way, through the garden towards the wicket-gate and the river-path that led towards West Lodge. In the half-light the rank borders looked and smelt heavy with flowers. The swifts were out, and flying high. Their screaming was thin and ecstatic, and exciting, like all the sounds that one feels one is not meant to hear; the singing of the grey seal and the squeak of a bat and the moaning of shearwaters under the ground at night on the wild sea's edge.

Now that we were alone together there still seemed curiously little to say. She had told the truth when she said that the major things of life had no need to be talked over. I supposed that for her the return of the idolized cousin from the dead was one of these. Never by word or look had she betrayed any consciousness that my advent might make the least difference to her future. It might not even have occurred to her ... but it soon would; it must. If it didn't occur to her, it might occur to Donald.

We had been filling up the eight years' gap – I with completely truthful reminiscences of my life in Canada, and Julie with a lively and (it is to be hoped) libellous account of the year she had spent in the Drama Department at Broadcasting House.

' ... No, *honestly*, Annabel, it's gospel truth!'

'I don't believe it. It sounds as if you wouldn't even know what "gospel" means.'

' "Good tidings".'

'Heavens!'

'I thought that'd shake you,' said Julie complacently.

'I suppose you got that from Donald too?'

' "All good things–?", I expect so.' Her voice had abruptly lost its sparkle.

I looked at her. 'He's very nice,' I said, tentatively.

'Yes, I know.' She spoke without enthusiasm. She had picked a dead dry stalk of last year's hedge-parsley, and switched it idly through the buttercups that lined the river-path where we walked.

'You mustn't mind Mrs. Bates, Julie. Marrying and burying is meat and drink to her.'

'I know. I don't mind. I suppose I did let her jump to conclusions, rather.'

'Here's the boundary. Shall we go on?'

'No. Let's find somewhere to sit.'

'The stile will do. It's quite dry.'

We climbed the two steps of the stile and sat side by side on the broad cross-bar, facing away from the house. It was another quiet evening, and the trees that edged the meadows were still in the dusky air. The path had left the river some way to our right; along it, here, the willows streamed un-trimmed, their long hair trailing in the water.

I said: 'You know, I'm afraid I jumped to conclusions myself. I was hoping they were correct.'

'Were you?'

I laughed. 'I fell for your Donald, from a great height.'

Her face came alight for a moment. 'One does. That's how it happened, with me. He's such a – a poppet. Even when I'm a bit foul to him, like today, he's just the same. He's – oh, he's so *safe* . . .!' She finished on a note that sounded more despondent than anything else: 'And I do adore him, I·do, really.'

'Then what's wrong?'

'I don't know.'

I waited.

She extended a sandalled foot, and regarded it. 'It's true; I do want to marry him. And most times I want nothing better than to marry him *soon*. And then, sometimes, suddenly . . .' A little pause. 'He hasn't asked me, actually.'

I smiled. 'Well, you've got three weeks.'

'Yes.' She dimpled, then sighed. 'Oh, Annabel, it's all such *hell*, isn't it? If only one could *tell*, like *that*, the way they do in books, but when it comes to the real thing it's actually quite *different*. I mean—'

'I wouldn't have thought you need worry quite so hard. You've loads of time, after all. You're only nineteen.'

'I know.' Another sigh, and a despondent silence.

I said, after a minute: 'Would you rather talk about something else? You don't need to tell me anything you don't want to.'

'Oh, but I do. In a way it was one of the things I was so longing to see you again for. I thought you'd know, you see.'

'My dear,' I said helplessly.

'Oh, I know you don't know him yet. But when you do—'

'That wasn't what I meant. I meant why the blazes should you imagine

I could be of any help to you? I – I made a pretty fair mess of my own life, you know.'

I half expected the routine and automatic response of kindness and reassurance, but it didn't come. She said immediately: 'That's why. It isn't the people who've had things their own way who – well, who get wisdom. And they haven't the time to think about what life does to other people, either. But if you've been hurt yourself, you can imagine it. You come alive to it. It's the only use I can ever see that pain has. All that stuff about welcoming suffering because it lifts up the soul is rot. People ought to avoid pain if they can, like disease . . . but if they have to stand it, its best use might be that it makes them kinder. Being kind's the main thing, isn't it?'

'Julie, I wouldn't know. I've never got these things straight with myself yet. And on a rainy day I find I believe quite different things from on a fine one. But you might be right. Being cruel's the worst thing, after all, so kindness might be the best. When you come to think about it, it covers nearly everything, doesn't it? One's whole duty to one's neighbour.'

'And the other whole duty?'

'My dear, I don't even pretend to know what that duty is. My duty to my neighbour will have to do. Maybe it'll count.'

She had reached out an idle hand to the bush beside her, and broken off a small spray of hawthorn-blossom, not yet dead. The milky heads hung bunched; I could smell their thick, sleepy scent. She twisted the stem between her fingers, so that the flower-heads swung out and whirled like a tiny roundabout. She seemed all at once very young and uncertain as she hesitated, apparently on the brink of some confidence.

I spoke almost nervously. 'Julie.'

'Mm?' She seemed absorbed in the twirling flowers.

'Julie – don't ask me about it at the moment, but . . . well, just keep quiet for the moment about the state of affairs between you and Donald, will you? I mean, if people want to jump to conclusions, like Betsy, let them.'

The flowers stopped twirling. She turned her head, her eyes wide and surprised. 'Heavens, why?'

'I'm sorry. I can't explain. But if you've really made up your mind to have Donald when he asks you – and if you can't make him in the next three weeks, I wash my hands of you – well, quarrel with him all you like in private, but don't let other people see you having too many doubts.'

'Honey!' To my relief she sounded amused. 'Is this Aunt Agatha's advice to young girls, or do you really mean anyone special when you say "other people"?'

I hesitated. I believe that at that moment I very nearly told Julie the whole story. But I said, merely: 'You might say I meant Grandfather. I think this stroke he's had has frightened him, rather, and he's fretting a bit about the future – our future.'

She sent me a glance that was all at once adult and wise. '*My* future, do you mean, now that you've come home?'

'Yes. You know what men of his generation are like, they think there's really nothing but marriage ... I know you're still very young, but I – I know he'd like to think of your being settled with someone like Donald. I'm sure he liked him, too. So – don't rock the boat too much, Julie, at any rate not while you're here.'

'The boat? Mr. Isaacs and all?' She laughed suddenly. 'I *thought* there was something in the wind! Don't you start worrying about that, Annabel, good heavens, all *I* want is to get on with my own life in my own way, and I think – I *think* – that includes Donald!' She dropped a hand over mine where it lay on the bar. 'But don't you ever go away again. Promise?'

I said nothing, but she took this for assent, for her hand squeezed mine softly, and then withdrew. She added, cheerfully now: 'All right, I won't rock any boats. All the storms of my love-life shall be – passed? blown? raged? waged? – up at the Roman camp.'

'Fort.'

'Oh, lord, yes. I *must* learn to be accurate about the more important things of life. Fort. Look, there's Mr. Forrest's horse, over there, like a shadow. He looks awfully quiet. Don't you love the way everyone shakes their heads over him and says "He won't be easy to school"?'

'I do rather. But I expect it's true. Blondie's foals do have that reputation.'

'Do they?'

'Didn't you know? And Grandfather tells me this one is by Everest.'

'By Everest? Oh, I see, you mean that's the name of the father?'

'The sire, yes. Don't you remember him? He was a bit of a handful, too, like all the old "Mountain" lot.' I glanced at her, amused. It seemed that Con had been right; this was not Julie's *métier*. She had shown the same cheerful ignorance in the drawing-room over tea, when the talk had turned on the affairs of Whitescar. Grandfather had noticed; I had seen him eyeing her; and Con had noticed too. And now she had made it obvious that she realised my return would deprive her of her place here; she had also made it apparent that she didn't care. She wasn't only making things easy for me: I was sure it was true. For Julie, this place was a holiday, no more. I felt a real rush of relief, not only for my conscience' sake, but because Con could now bear no grudge against her. What sort of grudge, or what shape that grudge would take, I hadn't yet allowed myself to guess at.

She was holding the flowers close to her face, watching Rowan with the uncritical admiration of complete ignorance.

'He's lovely, isn't he?' she said dreamily. 'Like something in a book. And the field smells like heaven. Pegasus, in the Elysian fields. He ought to have a manger of chalcedony and a bridle of pearl.'

'Have you the faintest idea what chalcedony is?'

'Not the faintest. It sounds wonderful. Have you? It ought to be like marble shot with fire and gold. What is it?'

'Something looking a bit like soap, the healthy kind. As big a let-down as jasper, anyway. The gates of Paradise are made of that, according to Revelations, but really it's the most—'

'Don't tell me! Let me keep my gates of jasper just as I've always seen them! Is this what the New World does to you? Have a heart, won't you? And admit that he *ought* to have a manger made of fire and gold and cedar-wood and turquoises at *least*!'

'Oh, yes,' I said. 'I'll give him that.'

The horse was grazing steadily along the hedge where a tall guelder-rose broke the yard-high barrier of hawthorn. His shoulders brushed the pale saucers of bloom, and, through the leaves, the growing moonlight touched him here and there, a dapple of light shifting over moving muscle; then a sudden liquid flash from the eye as he raised his head to stare.

I heard him blow a soft greeting through whickering nostrils. He seemed to eye us uncertainly for a moment, as if he might come forward, then he lowered his head again to the grass. 'I thought he was coming,' said Julie breathlessly. 'They all used to, to you, didn't they? Will you help school him? Johnny Rudd says he'll be the very devil, he won't let anyone near him in the stable, and he's next to impossible to catch in the field.'

'He sounds a useful sort of beast,' I said drily.

She laughed. 'What a way to speak of Pegasus! You can't deny he's a beauty.'

'No, he's that all right. What colour is he in daylight?'

'Red chestnut, with a pale mane and tail. His name's Rowan. Aren't you going in to speak to him?'

'I am not. This isn't my night for charming wild stallions.'

'It seems a dreadful pity that all the horses had to go. It must have been a dreadful wrench for Mr. Forrest – though I suppose it would only come as a sort of last straw, considering everything else that had happened.'

'Yes.'

There was a little pause. Then she said, with a curious soft abruptness, her eyes still on the horse: 'You know, you don't have to pretend with me. I know all about it.'

The dusky trees, the shapes of hawthorn, the ghost of the grazing horse, all seemed to blur together for a moment. I didn't speak.

'I – I just thought I'd let you know I knew,' said Julie. 'I've known all along. Have you ... have you spoken to him yet?'

The confusion in my mind blurred again, swung into another shape. I said: 'Have I – what do you mean? Spoken to whom?'

'Mr. Forrest, of course.'

Silence again. I couldn't have spoken if I'd tried. Before I could grope for words, she looked at me again, fleetingly, sideways, and said, like a nice child who confesses to something that she may be punished for: 'I'm sorry. But I did want to tell you that I knew all the time. I knew that you and Mr. Forrest were lovers.'

I said: 'Oh dear sweet *heaven*.'

'I'm sorry.' She repeated the words with a kind of desperation. 'Perhaps I shouldn't have told you I knew. But I wanted you to know. In case it was difficult or – or anything. You see, I'm on your side. I always was.'

'Julie—'

'I didn't spy on you, don't think that. But I saw you together sometimes, and people don't always notice a kid of eleven hanging about. I was always around, all that spring and summer, in the hols, and I knew you used to leave letters in the ivy tree at the old Hall gate. I thought it wonderfully romantic. But I can see now that it must have been pretty awful. For you, I mean. You were younger than I am now.'

My hands were pressing down hard to either side of me on the bar of the stile. 'Julie ... you ... we ... I didn't ...'

'Oh, I know there wouldn't ever be anything *wrong*. I mean, really wrong ...'

Let her talk, I thought, let her tell me just what she saw, what she knew. At worst she might only remember having drifted like a shadow round the edges of romance. Romance? Adam Forrest? *Con*? The two names burned in front of me, as if they had been branded in the bars of the stile ...

'You couldn't help it. One can't help who one falls in love with.' Julie was offering this shabby cliché as if it were the panacea still sealed all glittering in its virgin polythene. 'It's what one does about it that matters. That's what I meant when I said I knew you'd had a bad time; I mean, if one falls in love with a married man there *is* nothing to do, is there?' It seemed that, to Julie, falling in love was an act as definable and as little controlled by the will, as catching a disease in an epidemic. That there came a moment when the will deliberately sat back and franked the desire, was as foreign to her as the knowledge that, had the will not retreated, desire would have turned aside and life, in the end, have gone as quietly on.

'One can only go away,' said Julie. 'It's all there is to do. I knew why you'd gone, and I thought it marvellous of you. Do you know, I used to cry about it?'

I said, in a very hard, dry voice: 'You needn't have done that.'

She gave a little laugh: 'Oh, it wasn't all tragedy to me at that age. It was sad, yes, but beautiful too, like a fairy-tale. I used to try and make up happy endings to myself in bed, but they could never really work, because they meant that she – his wife, I mean – would have to die. And even if she *was* awful, it's always cheating, in a story, to kill off the person who prevents the happy ending. And I suppose I did see it more as a story, in those days, than as something that was really happening to people I knew. Was it so very dreadful, that time?'

'Yes.'

'I've sometimes wondered, since,' said Julia, 'if life isn't just a little too much for all of us. Sometimes one thinks . . . oh well, never mind. You don't mind my having told you? I rather wanted you to know I knew. That was all. We won't speak of it again if you like.'

'It doesn't matter. It's over.'

She looked almost shocked. 'Over?'

'My God, Julie, what d'you take me for? One can't tear a great hole in one's life pattern and expect the picture to be unspoiled till one chooses to come back and finish it. One can't fit straight back into the space one left. Nor does one want to. Of course it's over!'

'But I thought—'

I said, and I could hear myself how nerves had sharpened my voice: 'Do you seriously think I'd have *dreamed* of coming back if I'd know he was still here?'

'*Didn't* you know?'

'Of course I didn't! I thought I'd made very sure he wasn't, or I'd never have come, except perhaps just a flying visit to see Grandfather again, and make things up with him. But as for coming here to stay . . . *No*.'

'But . . .' her voice sounded all at once as frankly disappointed as a child's . . . 'but it's not the same now, is it? I mean, now that you *have* come, and he *is* here, and . . .' The sentence trailed off.

'You mean because Crystal Forrest's dead?' I said flatly.

I heard her give a little gasp. 'Well . . . yes.'

I laughed. 'Poor Julie. Your happy ending at last. I'm sorry.'

'Annabel—'

'Forget it, darling. Oblige me by forgetting it. And remind me one day to thank you for forgetting it as far as Con and the rest are concerned. I'd have rather hated them to know. Con has his own – theories – as to why I left.'

Her voice was suddenly mature, and curious. 'You dislike Con. Why?'

'Heaven knows. And "dislike" 's the wrong word. Say I distrust him. Julie . . .'

'Mm?'

'Just what, exactly, did you know about me and – about me and Adam?'

'Only what I told you. I knew you met, and I knew you wrote quite regularly, and put the notes in the hole in the ivy tree. And I think I knew that it – it was a hopeless passion – what are you laughing at?'

'I'm sorry. Your vocabulary. Go on, it was a hopeless passion.'

'All right,' she said without rancour. 'I suppose I do read all the wrong books. But *you're* taking this the wrong way. I believe you really don't care any more.'

'No.'

'Ah, well.' It was a sigh almost of disappointment. 'I'd hoped it would come right in the end. You see, everybody knew they were unhappy, him and his wife, I mean. You couldn't ever tell what *he* was thinking, but she didn't try very hard to pretend, did she? I mean, it got sort of painful when they were anywhere together in public. Even I noticed, though I was only a kid. It's true, isn't it?'

'Yes.'

'But there wasn't even any talk of their separating. Everybody used to say they ought to divorce, but that he wouldn't divorce her money.'

'They would.'

'Yes. And of course I thought it was so obvious that he would fall in love with you. Anybody would.'

'Julie, my love, you and I ought to be fairly careful how we compliment one another on our looks in public.'

She grinned. 'True enough. All the same, between ourselves, you were pretty smashing at nineteen. Confess!'

She was laughing at me in the light of the rising moon. I looked at her appraisingly. 'I'm beginning to think I must have been.'

'You're nice, aren't you?' she said naïvely. 'Well ... I still can't help having the feeling that I oughtn't to talk to you about it, for fear of making you unhappy, but still ... I've wondered since, money or no money, why he didn't divorce her. She wasn't an R.C., so it can't have been that. *Could* it have been the money, Annabel? I'm not being foul, but after all, he couldn't ever have kept Forrest going—'

'I doubt if he cares that much about Forrest.' I realized as soon as I had spoken how oddly my reply was framed, but she didn't notice.

'Then why? Why did they stay together? Why was she so filthy to him, almost as if he'd done something dreadful? It wasn't you, because it was going on for years before that. Why?'

'How could I know? He – he never discussed it.' Then, out of nowhere, came a guess like a certainty: 'She had no child.'

'I – see,' said Julie, slowly. 'And he ...?'

'Some men take life itself as a responsibility. Maybe that was it. Maybe he took her unhappiness as his. How could he leave her? You can't leave people who have nothing else.'

'You know,' she said, 'you talk about it all as if it was sort of remote, just a story about someone else.'

'That's what it feels like,' I said. 'Look, why don't we go in? Come along, you're yawning like a baby. You've had a long journey today, and you must be tired. There'll be plenty of time to talk. Is Donald coming down tomorrow?'

'I expect so.'

'I'm looking forward to meeting him again. Tell me all about him tomorrow. I seem to have kept you on my affairs tonight, but we'll forget them, as from now, shall we?'

'If that's the way you want it.'

'Okay.' She yawned again, suddenly and unashamedly, like an animal or a child. 'Oh lord, I *am* sleepy. No need to drink mandragora to sleep out the great gap of time my Donald is away.' She giggled. 'Funny how he simply will not fit into any romantic context.'

'Maybe you're safer that way, considering the kind of thing you appear to read.'

'Maybe. Oh Annabel, it *is* good to have you here. Did I say?'

'Yes. Thank you, Julie. Sleep well.'

'Oh, I shall. But this ghastly hush is *devastating* after London, and if that blasted owl starts up I shall shoot it, I swear I will, even if it *is* a mother with seven starving babies in the ivy tree.'

'That sort of owl has three.'

She unlatched the garden gate and pushed it open. 'You always did know everything about everything.'

'Oh no, Julie! You make me sound like some ghastly Nature Girl hobnobbing with the owls, and charming wild horses, and flitting about the woods at night—' I stopped.

If Julie had noticed she made no sign. 'Aren't you coming in?'

'Not yet. It's a lovely night, and I'm not tired. Nature Girl on the prowl. Good night.'

'Good night,' said Julie.

CHAPTER ELEVEN

The wind doth blow to-day, my love,
And a few small drops of rain;
I never had but one true-love;
In cold grave she was lain.

Ballad: *The Unquiet Grave*

If you stood on the low piece of crumbling wall that enclosed the trunk, you could just reach your hand into the hole. I held on to the writhen stems of the ivy with one hand and felt above my head into the hollow left by some long-decayed and fallen bough.

I put my hand in slowly, nervously almost, as I might have done had I known that Julie's owl and seven mythical young were inside, and ready to defend it, or as I might have invaded a private drawer in someone's desk. The secret tryst; Ninus' tomb; the lover's tree; what right had a ghost there, prying?'

In any case there was nothing to pry into. Whatever secrets the ivy tree had held in the past, it was now only a tree, and the post-box was an empty hole, the bottom cracked and split, its fissures filled with crumbling touchwood as dry as tinder. Some twigs and rotting straw seemed to indicate that a starling had once nested there. The ivy, brushing my face, smelt dark and bitter, like forgotten dusty things.

I climbed down from the wall and wiped my hands on my handkerchief.

Beside me, skirting the ruins of the lodge, the neglected avenue curled away into the shadows. I turned my head to look where, in the strong moonlight beyond the blackness cast by the trees, the white gate glimmered. I could almost make out the neat black letters on the top bar. WHITESCAR. I made a half-movement in that direction, then checked myself. *If it be now, 'tis not to come.* Well, let it be now.

I put away my handkerchief, and walked quickly past the ruined lodge, up the silent mosses of the drive, towards the house.

The moon was fuller tonight, and it was later. The skeleton of the house stood up sharply, with the dramatic backcloth of trees cutting its lines and angles, and throwing into relief the tracery of the bare windows. One or two sheep grazed among the azaleas. The little tearing sounds they made, as they cropped the grass, sounded loud in the windless air.

I could smell the roses and honeysuckle that smothered the sundial. I went slowly down the moss-furred steps, and over the grass towards it. The dial was covered with a thick mat of leaves and tendrils. I picked one of the tiny chandeliers of the honeysuckle and held it to my face. The long stamens tickled, and the scent was thick and maddeningly sweet, like a dream of summer nights. I dropped it into the grass.

I sat down on the lowest step where the pediment jutted into the encroaching grass, and pushed aside the trailing honeysuckle with gentle hands, till the shaft of the sundial lay bare. The moonlight struck it slantingly, showing the faint shadows of carving under the soft rosettes of lichen.

I scratched a little of the moss away, and traced the letters with a slow, exploratory finger.

TIME IS.   TIME WAS ...

Another line below. No need to trace that out.

TIME IS PAST ...

It didn't need the startled swerve of a ewe ten yards away, or the rustle and patter of small hoofs retreating, to tell me that I had been right. He had come, as I had guessed he would.

My hands were pressed flat on the dry mosses. I could feel the blood in them jump and beat against the chill of the stone. I waited for a moment, without moving, crouched there on the step of the sundial, my hands hard against the stone.

Well, let it come. Get it over with. Learn just where you stand. *If it be now now, yet it will come.*

I turned slowly round, and, as stiffly as a puppet on strings, got to my feet.

He was standing not twenty yards away, at the edge of the the wood.

He was just a shadow under the trees, but it could be no one else. He had come, not by the drive, but up the path from the summer-house.

I stood without moving, with the moon behind my shoulder, and my back to the sundial. I think that I had a hand on it still, as if for support, but oddly enough, the emotion that struck at me most vividly at the sight of him was that of relief. This was the worst thing that had happened, and I had had no time to be ready for it; but now it had come, and it would get over. Somehow, I would find the right things to say . . .

It seemed a very long time before he moved. The moonlight fell strongly on him as he came forward, and even at that distance I could see that he was staring as if he had seen a ghost. His features were blanched and dramatised by the white slanting light, but even so it was apparent that some violent emotion had drained his face to a mask where the flesh seemed to have been planed from the strong-looking bones, leaving it a convention, as it were, of planes and angles, lights and shadows. The eyes looked very dark, and the brows made a bar of black across them. I could see the deeply incised lines down his cheeks, and the thin line of a mouth schooled to reserve or patience. But when his lips parted to speak, one saw all at once how thin the defences were. His voice sounded vulnerable, too, half hesitating. This was a man who was by no means sure of his reception. And why should he be? Why indeed?

He spoke at last, in a half-whisper that carried no expression. 'Annabel?'

'Adam?' Even as I said it, I thought the name sounded exploratory, tentative, as if I'd never used it before.

He had stopped a yard or so away. There was a pause, painfully long. Then he said: 'I came as soon as I knew.'

'Did you expect to find me here?'

'I didn't know. I thought . . . I don't know what I thought. Does it matter? You came.'

'Yes,' I said, 'I – I had to see you.'

I found that I had braced myself for his response to this, but he made none. His voice was so flattened and expressionless that it sounded barely interested. 'Why did you come home?'

'Grandfather's ill. He – he may not have long to live. I had to see him again.'

'I see.' Another pause. That flat, empty voice again. 'You never told me you were coming.'

He might have been talking to a stranger. Between lovers there are such situations, so highly charged that words are absurd; but then lovers have their own language. We had none. Adam Forrest's love was dead, and there was nothing to say.

I answered him in the same way. 'I didn't know you were still here. I only heard it by chance, the other night, from something Grandfather said. I'd understood you lived permanently in Italy now. In fact, when I came back to England, I'd no idea that your—' I stopped, swallowed,

and finished stupidly on a complete *non sequitur*: 'I didn't even know
that Forrest Hall had gone.'

'You never did have much regard for logic, did you? What you started
to say was, that you didn't know that Crystal had died.'

'I—'

'Wasn't it?'

'Yes. I – I hadn't heard. I'm sorry.'

He acknowledged this with a slight movement of the head, and let it
go. He was standing perhaps six feet away. The moonlight fell between
us, slantingly, from behind my left shoulder. The angled shadows it cast
made his expression difficult to read. They also, which was more
important, made it impossible for him to see me clearly. But he was
watching me steadily, without moving, and the close unwavering regard
was discomforting.

He said slowly: 'Are you trying to tell me that if you had known – that
I was here at Forrest, I mean, and free – you would not have come
back?'

Behind me the edge of the sundial, rough with dried lichen, bit into
my hands. Was this, after all, easier than I had imagined, or was it
worse? His voice and face gave nothing away. There was nothing to
indicate that he cared, any more than I did. Why should he? Eight years
was a long time. I said, almost with relief: 'Yes. Just that.'

'I see.' For the first time the steady gaze dropped, momentarily, then
came back to me with a jerk. 'But you came tonight to meet me?'

'I told you. I came, hoping you'd come along. I had to see you. After
I found out last night that you were coming back from Italy, that you
still lived here, I knew I – well, I couldn't just wait around and meet you
in public.'

'That was nice of you.' The flat voice held no irony.

I looked away, Beyond the massed shadows of the forsaken garden,
the house stood up, raw-edged and broken. 'Your home,' I said, not very
evenly, '. . . I'm sorry about that, too, Adam. That sounds a bit inadequate, but what can one say? It's been a bad time all round, hasn't it?
You must have been very unhappy.'

For the first time his face changed. I saw the ghost of a smile. 'You
say that?'

I stirred. Easy? This was intolerable. Heaven knew I had dreaded the
interview, and heaven knew I could hardly have expected to get through
it more smoothly than this. I had expected questions, recriminations,
anger even . . . anything but this calm, dead voice and steady stare that
(since the moment when I had turned momentarily into the moonlight
to glance up at the house) had narrowed sharply as if he were only just
bringing me into focus.

I stood away from the sundial and began to rub my scored palms
together.

'I must go.' I spoke hurriedly, nervously, looking down at my hands. 'It's late. I – I can't think that we have anything more to say. I—'

'Why did you go?'

The question came so suddenly that, although it was softly spoken, I looked up at him, startled. He was still watching me with that steady, unreadable stare. 'You know,' he said, 'you can't simply walk out like this. I would have thought we had a very great deal to say. And I'd like to go right back to the beginning. Why did you go like that?'

'You know why I went!' I could hear how my voice shook, edged with nerves, but I couldn't control it. I tried to thrust him back again, off the dangerous ground. 'Don't let's go back over it, please! I – I couldn't stand it! That's all over, you know that as well as I do. It was over eight years ago, and it – it's best forgotten. *Everything's* best forgotten . . .' I swallowed. 'I've forgotten it, I truly have. It's as if it had happened to someone else. It – it doesn't seem to mean anything to me any more. People change, you know. In all that time, people change. You've changed yourself. Can't we . . . just *leave* it, Adam? I didn't come to see you tonight because I hoped . . . because I wanted . . .' I floundered desperately for words . . . 'I knew you'd feel just the same as I do, now. I only came tonight so that we could – we could – '

'Agree that it was forgotten? I know, my dear.' His voice was very gentle. There was no reason why I should have to bite my lips to keep the tears back, or why I should have to turn sharply aside and jerk a spray from the yellow rose, and be twisting it round and round in my fingers. This was nothing to me, after all. 'You don't have to worry,' he said. 'I shan't torment you. There's someone else, isn't there?'

'No!' I hadn't meant to say it quite like that. I saw his brows lift a fraction.

'Or has been?'

I shook my head.

'In eight years?'

I looked down at the bruised rose in my fingers. 'No. It's not that. It's only—'

'That people change. Yes. I understand. You've changed a good deal, Annabel.'

I lifted my head. 'Have I?'

His mouth twisted. 'So it would seem. Tell me; do you – or perhaps I should say *did* you – intend to stay at Whitescar, now that you're back?'

At least here was a safe and easy path. I scuttled down it breathlessly, talking too fast. 'I hadn't really made any firm plans. I told you I only came to see Grandfather. Until I got here, up North, I mean, I had no idea he was so frail. You knew he'd had a stroke? Actually, I'd decided to come back and see him before I knew of that. I hadn't been sure if he – if they'd want me back at Whitescar, but I wanted to see him if he'd let me. I didn't know what the situation would be, but he's been very kind.' I hesitated. 'They all have. I'm glad I came back. I'd like to stay till . . . as long as Grandfather's here. But afterwards . . .' I stopped.

'Afterwards?'

'I don't think I'll stay afterwards.'

A pause. 'And the place? Whitescar?'

'There'll be Con.'

I was unwinding the split and twisted rose-stem with great care. A thorn had drawn blood on my thumb. I stared unseeingly at the tiny black gout of blood that blobbed and spilt glossily over the flesh. I didn't know he had moved until his shadow slithered forward a pace, slantingly, and fell across the grass beside me.

'You'd leave Whitescar to Connor Winslow?'

I smiled. 'I may have to.'

'Don't beg the question. You know what I mean. If the place were yours, would you stay?'

'No.'

'Has that decision anything to do with me?'

I swallowed. 'You know it has.'

Quite suddenly, his voice came alive, the way flesh does after frostbite. He said: 'You came back because you thought I had gone. When you found I was still here, you decided to go again. You make things very clear, Annabel.'

I said, as steadily as I could: 'I try to. I'm sorry.'

There was a pause. He spoke almost as if he were reasoning quietly with me about something that didn't matter very greatly. 'You know, I've regretted everything I said and did that night, far more bitterly than you could have done. I doubt if I'll ever quite forgive myself. Not only for losing my head and saying all that I said to you that last time we met, but for ever having allowed things to . . . get to the stage they did. You were very young, after all; it was I who should have known better. The sort of life I led with Crystal was no excuse for – for losing my head over you, when I could do nothing but hurt you.'

'Don't, please, there's no need—'

'Don't think I'm trying to excuse myself for the way I spoke and acted that last night. I'd just about come to the end – or so I thought; except that, of course, one never does.' He took in his breath. 'So I finally lost my head, and begged you – bullied you – to go away with me, away from Whitescar and Forrest, and to hell with everybody, including my wife. And you refused.'

'What else could I do? Look, there's no need to go back over this. I've told you it's best forgotten. It should never even have started. We should have realised where it would take us.'

'That's what you said then, that night, isn't it? True enough, of course, but as far as I was concerned, much too late. I remember that you even promised to keep out of my way.' He gave a brief smile that was more like a grimace. 'So then,' he said, 'I told you that, if you weren't prepared to do as I asked, I never wanted to see you again. Oh no,' at my involuntary movement, 'I suppose I didn't put it quite so crudely, but I dimly remember a good many wild and whirling words, to the effect that either you would have to leave the neighbourhood, or I would, and since I was tied to Forrest and to my wife ...' He drew in his breath. 'But heaven help me, Annabel, I never dreamed you'd go.'

'It was better. You must see it was better.'

'Perhaps. Though I wonder, looking back. No doubt, in the end, I'd have behaved like a reasonable mortal, and we could have found some ... comfort. Fundamentally, I suppose, we're both decent human beings, and you, at least, kept your moral sense intact. Then, six years later ...' He paused, and seemed to straighten his shoulders. 'Well, there it is. You were young, and I behaved badly, and frightened and hurt you, and you went. But you're older now, Annabel. Surely you must understand a little more than you did then, about the kind of life I led with Crystal, and the reasons why I was driven to act the way I did?'

'I do, oh, I do. It isn't that. Please don't think I – I'm bearing a grudge or – or anything. This, the way I feel now, has nothing to do with what happened then, try and believe that.' I added, quietly: 'Whatever was said or done, it's over, eight years over. There was nothing to forgive... and now, let's pretend there was nothing to remember, either. Let it go, Adam. From now. It's better not to talk about it any more. Good night.'

I turned quickly away from him, but his shadow moved again across the turf, this time with something like a pounce. His hand caught at my arm, and, almost before I realised what was happening, he had pulled me round to face him.

'Wait. Listen. No, I can't let you go like this. You've got to listen to me. It's only fair.'

'I don't see that—'

'If you'd rather wait till you're less upset, I'll let you go now. But I've got to see you again.'

I said breathlessly, trying to pull away from him: 'No!'

'What do I have to do? Grovel?'

'Adam, I've been trying to explain—'

'My God,' he said, 'what did I do that made you hate me so?'

'I don't, I don't! I told you.'

'Then stay one minute, and listen. Look, Annabel, don't cry. It's all right. Just let me – wait just one minute, and let me tell you ... You've told me it's all over for you; you don't love me. Very well, I'll accept that. Don't worry, I'll accept it. Good grief, how can I expect anything else? But you can't imagine that I'll just retire quietly to West Lodge and do nothing about it, can you?'

Somewhere, far off behind the cedar tree, the owl hooted. I said waveringly: 'Do nothing about what?'

'About trying to see you again.' His other hand came up now, and he had me by both arms, lightly, holding me a little away from him. 'You see,' he said, 'there's still one thing that we haven't made plain. It isn't over for me.'

I felt myself stiffen, and so must he have done, for he went on quickly: 'No, all right, I've told you I'll accept the fact that you want to forget the past. But there's still the future, my dear, and you've told me there's no one else; you can't expect me to stand by and do nothing, now that you've come home.' He smiled suddenly, and for the first time there was warmth and even lightness in his voice. 'And I owe you a courtship, don't I? We'll have no more clandestine romance, my love! No more notes sneaked into the old ivy tree, no more damned chilly moonlit meetings in the summer-house, with the rhododendron leaves sopping wet, and you fussing about bats getting into your hair!' He shook me gently, and his smile widened. 'No, this time I'll woo you properly, by daylight, according to the book. I'll even start by calling on your grandfather—'

'*No!*' This time he must have felt the genuine shock of panic that kicked through me, jerking me rigid against the light clasp of his hands. Here was something I hadn't thought of. I had come to meet him tonight, with no very clear idea of what would be said, but only with the knowledge that the eight-years'-past love-affair must, somehow, be kept from Con. Eight years was a long time, and it hadn't for a moment occurred to me that passion might be still there, smouldering, ready to flare up – into danger. It had seemed so easy: all I had had to do, after all, was to tell Adam Forrest the simple truth – that I did not care for him; that the past was dead and buried, and that I wanted it to remain so.

Then, the interview once over, the friendly, civil goodbyes of long-estranged lovers given . . . I had hoped, more, known, that betrayal would not come from this direction. Yet here it was: after the days of smooth, too-easy masquerading, here, where it had been least expected, was danger.

Desperately I tried to marshal my thoughts. But the only coherent thing that came to me was that Con must not know. I had a sudden vision of his face as he had looked at me, down in the lane beside the meadowsweet . . . and behind him Lisa's watchful, toffee-brown eyes.

'Please,' I said shakily, 'you mustn't do that. You mustn't come to Whitescar. Promise me that you won't come to Whitescar!'

'My dear, all right.' He had dropped his hands when I spoke, and was staring at me now, the smile gone, and a deep crease gathering between his brows. 'Just as you wish. Heaven knows I don't want to tease you. I'll promise anything you like, except not to try to see you again. You can't ask me to go quietly away and do nothing, knowing you're there at Whitescar. For one thing, we're bound to meet, and I—' the flicker of a smile again – 'am bound to see that that happens as often as possible. But don't worry. I think I understand the way you feel, and I'll respect it . . . only you mustn't deny me the chance of trying to change it, now that we're free.'

'Free?' The visions crowded in again, Con, Lisa, Grandfather, Julie . . . I said, bitterly: 'Which of us is ever free?'

'My dear—'

The very quietness of his insistence was terrifying. Something, that could have been panic, mushroomed up inside me, and burst into words I had never meant to say. 'You mean, now that *you're* free! You mean you think you can dismiss me when it's convenient – forget me for eight years – and then, when I come back, just calmly expect to take up where you left off? You like to keep your mistresses in your own time, is that it? "It isn't over for you!" ' I mimicked him, cruelly – 'No, I dare say not! Now that you're home for good, and your wife's dead, no doubt it'll suit you to have me around! Well, it doesn't suit me! How much plainer do I have to be? I've tried to put it kindly, but you won't take it. It's over. *Over.* So will you please, please, *please*, let me go and leave me alone?'

Even in that uncertain light, I saw the change in his face, and stopped, half-afraid. Then my thoughts steadied. There was danger here; I must not forget that. Whatever happened, whatever I told him, whether or not I tried to go on with the masquerade, there was danger. Why not take the risk, and get it over now? Everything ought only to have to die once. Adam Forrest had gone through all this years ago; he mustn't be allowed to start it again, and for nothing. There was only one way to prevent that. Con had shown me how to play my cards, after all.

But for the moment I could find no way to do it. I stood silent, staring at him.

Then the decision was taken from me. He spoke so pat on my thoughts that he might have been taking a cue. 'If it weren't absurd,' he said, very slowly, 'if it weren't something so crazy as to sound like black magic . . . I'd have said you couldn't be Annabel. Even in eight years, I wouldn't have thought you'd change so much.'

I drew a sharp little breath, and choked over it, then I said quickly, and perhaps too loudly: 'That's silly! Who else could I be?'

'That,' he said, even more slowly, 'is what I'm wondering.'

I suppose the interview had got through what poor defences I had had. I simply stood there, and stared at Adam Forrest, with a curious sense of drifting, of destiny. Those dark gods who watch over the moonlit trysts of lovers had helped, cajoled, and then betrayed me to this final irony. I made no attempt to speak, just stared at Adam Forrest, and watched the thing dawning, incredulously, in his face.

Even when he took a rapid step that brought him within a foot of me, I didn't move. He said slowly: 'I must be going mad. It can't be possible. It can't.' He put out his hands and turned me round, quite gently, to face the moon. I didn't meet his eyes. I looked down, shutting my lips tightly to stop them trembling. There was a long pause.

Then he dropped his hands again, and turned away abruptly. He took several rapid strides away from me, and I thought he was going to leave me there and then, and wondered in a brief moment of panic where he was going, but he stopped suddenly, and stood for a few seconds with his back to me, looking at the ground.

Then he turned, churning his heel in the grass, and came back. His face looked quite impassive.

'Is this true?'

I hesitated painfully. The moment stretched like a year. Then I saw that the hesitation had answered for me. I nodded without speaking.

'You're not Annabel Winslow?'

I cleared my throat and managed to say, steadily enough, even with a kind of relief: 'No, I'm not Annabel Winslow.'

'You're ... not ... Annabel.' He said it again, the sharpness of his questions blurred now into bewilderment.

This time I said nothing. The irrational feeling of escape, of relief, persisted. The flooding moonlight; the backcloth, as motionless and silent as paint, of the ruined house and towering trees; the little sundial with its sharply-etched shadow thrown beside our own, these lent the scene an air of complete unreality. We were not people who ate and worked and talked through the sunlit days: we were beings from a fantasy world, creatures of a moonlit stage, living only by our passions, able to talk about love and death and pain, only in the subtle and rarefied voices of poetry. This was the world of the doomed black sail, the enchanted cup, the swallow flying through the casement with the single gold hair in his beak. We were Pervaneh and Rafi, floating like ghosts through the night-time garden, and to us the death of love would come as poetry; not fear, and quarrelling, the grimy commonplaces of the station platform, the unanswered telephone, the letter gone astray, the years of dragging loneliness ...

The moonlight struck the sundial as sharply as the sun. Time was.

I was still facing the light. He had come close to me again, and was scrutinising my face. 'You look like her, you move like her. But your voice is different ... and there's something else ... Don't ask me what. But it's ... extraordinary. It's beyond reason.'

I said gently: 'But it's true.'

He gave a little laugh that had no relationship with mirth. 'You've spent a lot of time tonight assuring me of various truths. At least this one is the easiest to accept.' He half turned away, and thrust the tangle of tendrils aside from the dial's face. 'Who are you?'

'Does that matter?'

'Probably not. But it matters a great deal why you are here, and why you're doing this – whatever it is you are doing. At least you don't seem to be trying to hedge. You might as well tell me the lot; after all, I have every right to know.'

'Have you?'

He turned his head as if in exasperation. 'Of course. You must know a good deal about my affairs, or you wouldn't have been here to meet me tonight. Who told you? Annabel?'

'Annabel?' I said blankly.

'Who else could it have been?' He had turned back to the sundial, and appeared to be tracing out the figures with a forefinger. His voice was abrupt. 'Tell me, please. Where you met her, what happened, what she told you. What you know of her.'

'It wasn't that!' I cried. 'It didn't happen like that! I never met Annabel! It was Julie who told me!'

'*Julie?*'

'Yes. Oh, don't worry, she didn't know anything, really, about you and Annabel; but she'd seen you meet and talk in the wood, and she knew about the post-box in the ivy tree. She saw Annabel put a letter in there one day, and take another out. She – she just thought it was a perfectly natural and very romantic way of conducting a love-affair. She never told anyone.'

'I see. And just what has she told you?'

'Only this – about the meetings and the ivy tree. She wanted me to know she knew. She – she rather imagined I'd be wanting to see you again, straight away.'

'Hm.' He had turned back to the sundial, and seemed absorbed in chipping a flake of moss away with a finger-nail. 'A bit of luck for you, wasn't it? That she knew, and told you? Otherwise you'd have been a little startled at our first meeting.' A piece of moss came away, and he examined the inch or so of bronze beneath it with great care. 'Are you sure that was all Julie told you? I'm not suggesting that she deliberately played the spy; she was only a child at the time, and would hardly realise what was going on. But one doesn't like to think that anyone, least of all a child—'

'Honestly, there was nothing else.'

'Yet you played your part so very well.' His voice, now, had an edge to it that would have engraved the bronze dial he was fingering. 'I find it hard to believe that you knew so little. Perhaps Connor Winslow found out somehow—'

'No!' I said it so sharply that he glanced at me, surprised. 'At least, he's said nothing to me. He hardly mentions you.' I added, lightly: 'I'm a very good actress, of course; you'll have guessed that. I merely played to the cues I got. It wasn't difficult. After all, it's what one expects to have to do when one's involved in this kind of game. If you think back over what was actually said, you'll find that I merely played your service back. All the *statements* were made by you.'

He dropped the flake of moss on to the dial. It fell with a tiny rustling click. I saw him straighten as if with relief, but he still sounded grim. 'Oh yes, you'd have to be clever. But not, it appears, quite clever enough.

The sudden appearance of a lover must have been something of a shock I grant you courage, too; you did very well ... And now, please, back to my question. Who are you, and what is this "game" you say you're playing?'

'Look,' I said, 'I've told you the truth and played fair with you. I do assure you I needn't have let you guess. I'm not going to harm anybody. I'm only out to do myself a bit of good. Can't you let it go ... at any rate till you *see* me harming someone? Why should it concern you, what goes on at Whitescar?'

'You ask, why should it concern me? You come back here posing as Annabel, and ask why it should concern me?'

'Nobody knows about you and her except Julie, and I've already told Julie that we're not—'

'That's not the point.' The words snapped. 'Don't hedge. What's your name?'

'Mary Grey.'

'You're very like her, but of course you know that.' A long look. 'The thing doesn't seem possible. Mary Grey. My God, this sort of thing doesn't happen outside the pages of fiction! Am I seriously to believe that you have somehow got yourself into Whitescar, and are masquerading as Annabel Winslow?'

'Yes.'

'Why.'

I laughed. 'Why do you think?'

There was a silence. He said, not pleasantly: 'Funny, you don't look venal.'

'Try earning your living the hard way,' I said. 'You never know how you'll turn out till you've been down to half a dollar and no prospects.'

His lips thinned. 'That's true enough.'

'Oh, yes, I forgot. You do know. You work for your living now, and hard, too, they tell me. Well, didn't you mind having to spoil your hands?'

'I – beg your pardon?' He sounded considerably startled, I couldn't imagine why.

'Wouldn't *you* perhaps have taken a chance to step into some easy money, if the chance came, and it did no harm?'

'I did once. But they'll have told you about that, too. And how can we expect to calculate what harm we do? Who's briefing you?'

The question came so sharply that I jumped. 'What?'

'You couldn't do this on your own. Someone's briefed you and brought you in. Julie, I suppose, wanting to spoil Connor's chances?'

I laughed. 'Hardly. Con himself, and his sister.'

He stared at me unbelievingly. 'Con? And Lisa Dermott? Do you really expect me to believe that?'

'It's true.'

'Connor Winslow bring back "Annabel" to cut him out of what he expects? Don't take me for a fool; he'd as soon slit his own throat.'

'I'm not cutting Con Winslow out.'

'No. Julie, then?' His voice hardened.

'No. Annabel herself.'

'Annabel's dead.' Only after he had spoken them, did he seem to hear the words, as if they had been said by someone else. He turned his head almost as if he were listening, as if he expected to hear the last heavy syllable go echoing through the woods, dropping, ripple by ripple, like a stone through silence.

'Mr. Forrest, I'm sorry . . . If I'd known—'

'Go on.' His voice was as hard and sharp as before. 'Explain yourself. You say Connor has brought you in to impersonate Annabel, in order to cut Annabel out of her rights in Whitescar land. What sort of a story is that, for heaven's sake?'

'It's simple enough. Grandfather has refused to believe she's dead, and he's refused to alter his Will, which leaves everything to her. As things stand now, Whitescar goes to Annabel, with reversion to Julie. I think it seems pretty obvious that, in the end, Grandfather would have done the sensible thing, admitted that Annabel must be dead, and willed the place to Con; in fact, I think he intends to do just that. But he's ill now, really ill; and you know him, he may play about with the idea, just to torment people, until it's too late. Con *might* have got Whitescar anyway, after some sort of legal upheaval, because I'm pretty sure Julie doesn't want it, but he'd only get a proportion of Grandfather's money along with it, not enough for what he'd want to do.'

'I . . . see.'

'I thought you might.'

'And just what do you get out of it?'

'A home, at the moment. That's a new thing for me, and I like it. A competence.'

'A competence!' he said, explosively, 'Why, you lying little thief, it's a small fortune?'

I smiled. If the interview had seemed unreal at first, when the ghosts and dreams of passion had hung between us, how infinitely less real it was now, with me standing there, hands deep in pockets, looking composedly up at Adam Forrest, and talking about money. 'Be realistic, won't you, Mr. Forrest? Do you really see Con Winslow bringing me out of sweet charity, and watching me pocket all the money that goes to Annabel?'

'Of course. Stupid of me.' He spoke as if he were discussing the weather. 'You hand the major part to him, and are allowed to keep your "competence". How very neat, always assuming that there's sufficient honour among thieves . . . Where did you meet Connor Winslow?'

I said evasively: 'Oh, he saw me one day. I had a job in Newcastle, and I came out to this part of the country one Sunday, for a day out, you

know, a walk. He saw me, and thought, as you did, that I was his cousin
come back. He followed me, and found out who I was, and we talked.'
I didn't feel it necessary to go into details of the three weeks' planning;
nor did I bother to tell him that I had, to begin with, opposed Con's plan
myself.

'And hatched this up between you?' The contempt in his voice was
hardly veiled. 'Well, so far, I gather, you've been completely successful . . .
as why shouldn't you be? The thing's so fantastic that you'd be almost
bound to get away with it, given the nerve, the information . . . and the
luck.'

'Well,' I said, calmly enough, 'it seems the luck's failed, doesn't it?'

'Indeed it does.' His voice was gentle, calculating. He was watching
me almost with hatred, but I could forgive him that, remembering how
he had betrayed himself to me. He said slowly: 'Yes, you've been clever.
I don't know how easily you managed to deceive the people at Whitescar,
but, after Julie had talked to you, you must have realised you couldn't
hope to get away with such a deception with me. You must have gone
through quite a bad moment when you heard that your erstwhile lover
was coming home.'

'Quite a bad moment,' I said steadily.

'I'm glad to hear it. But you kept your head, clever Miss Grey. You
had to risk seeking me out here and talking to me; you didn't dare wait
to meet me for the first time in public. So you took the chance, and came.
Why didn't you go to the summer-house?'

'The summer-house? Do you mean that little pavilion along the other
end, in the rhododendrons? I didn't realise that had been your meeting-
place, till you told me so yourself.'

'It would hardly have been here,' he said drily, with a glance at the
blank and staring windows.

'I did realise that. But this seemed the obvious spot to wait. I – I
thought if you came at all, you'd come this way to look.'

'Yes, well, I came. So far, you've been right every way, Miss Grey:
but now, what happens? You're taking this remarkably calmly, aren't
you? Do you really imagine that I won't blow the whole thing sky-high
on you?'

I thrust my hands down into my pockets again. I said coolly: 'I have
no idea what you'll do. It's quite possible that tomorrow you'll turn up
at Whitescar, and tell Grandfather what you've learned tonight. You'll
tell him that she's dead after all, and that all these years Con has been
nursing his resentment, and planning to take Whitescar . . . and looking
forward to Grandfather's death. And you might add for good measure
that Julie's thinking of marrying, and that her husband's job will take
her away from Whitescar.'

There was a silence. Adam Forrest said unemotionally: 'You bitch.'

'I thought you'd see it my way.' (Con, smiling at me in the lane, his
voice soft in the whisper that conspirators, and lovers, use. Yes, Con had

taught me how to play it.) 'It's really better for everyone the way it is, isn't it?' I finished, gently.

'Whether a thing is right or wrong doesn't depend on how many people it hurts. This is wrong.'

I said suddenly, violently: 'How the hell dare you sit in judgment on me, Adam Forrest?'

He jumped. I saw his eyes narrow on me suddenly, then he relaxed with a queer little sigh. 'Then what about Julie? I can't see that it's "better" for her. This criminal arrangement of yours may suit everyone else, including old Mr. Winslow, since it means keeping him in a false paradise until he dies. But what about Julie?'

'Julie has money of her own. So has this man of hers, and he's " 'way up in his profession".'

'That,' said Adam Forrest gently, 'is hardly the point.'

'It's the point unless you do propose to – what's the phrase we crooks use? – blow the gaff.'

He was giving me that appraising, narrow stare again. 'I could, you know. In fact, I must.'

'You'd find it very difficult to convince Grandfather. Con and Lisa did a very good job of briefing, and I'm well dug in. And Julie would just laugh at you.'

There was another of those silences. He didn't stir, but I felt the hair prickle along my skin as if I had expected a blow.

When he spoke, his voice sounded quite normal, friendly, almost. 'You speak like an American.'

'Canadian, actually.' I was surprised and wary. 'It's one of my assets, of course, as an impersonator. *She* went to the States, and, according to *my* story, from there to Canada.'

'To come from Canada, Miss Grey, one needs a passport.' He laughed suddenly, not a nice sound. 'Yes, I thought that would get through to you. Nobody else thought of it?'

I said hoarsely: 'Why should they? They accepted me without question. You don't usually ask to see people's papers, unless there's some doubt.'

'That,' he said pleasantly, 'is just what I mean. And I shouldn't destroy it, my dear. They're terribly easy to trace.'

I drove my fists down, and held them steady.

'Mr. Forrest—'

'Well?'

'What are you going to do?'

'What do you think?'

'I don't think you quite understand, you know. Grandfather—'

'I understand perfectly. You and Connor are trading on his age and sickness. That's quite clear. But it's Julie I'm thinking about – Julie, and my own constitutional dislike of seeing anyone get away with this kind of damned lie. If I did agree to hold my tongue now, it would be purely for old Mr. Winslow's sake. But if he dies—'

I said violently: 'How much of a fool can you be? If he dies before he re-makes his Will, and you throw Annabel back into her grave, what do you suppose would happen to Julie?'

This time the silence was electric. The night was so still that I heard my own heart-beats, and I thought he must hear them, too. Ten miles off, a train whistled for a crossing.

As if it had been a signal to wake us both, he said: 'Don't be absurd.' But his voice had slackened with uncertainty.

'I meant it, oddly enough. I think I know Con Winslow a little better than you do.'

'That's very probable,' he spoke with (I thought) a quite undue dryness. 'If this – fantasy – is true, do I take it that you expect to stay on in safety at Whitescar?'

'I'll face that when the time comes.'

'You think he'll marry you? Are you playing for that, too?'

'Look here—!' I began hotly, then stopped and bit my lip. It was an obvious conclusion, after all. 'I am not,' I said clearly, 'anything to Con Winslow, or he to me . . . except accomplices.'

'I beg your pardon.' His apology was surprisingly prompt, and sounded genuine. 'Then am I to take it that you are protecting Julie . . . for a "competence"?'

'You can take it how you like. I've assured you that no one will be harmed by what I'm doing, but I don't expect you to believe me. Why should you? I can only beg you to keep out of what doesn't concern you . . . at least until you see wrong being done.'

He said, all at once sounding very tired. 'I don't understand you.'

'Why should you? But I mean what I say, remember that. And I'm telling you the truth about this. I'm playing this game for my own advantage, that's obvious; I saw a chance to get out of poverty and hard work, to grab what they call a place in the sun, and I took it. It's wrong, I admit that; I'm unscrupulous, I admit that. But I'm not *bad*, and I wouldn't do it if anyone was going to suffer for it. Believe me, they'll have plenty, and the little I'll get will mean a lot to me, and nothing to any of them.'

He said, angrily: 'That's immoral nonsense. It's also quite beside the point.'

'I know that.' I laughed. 'But all the same, you think about it, Mr. Forrest. This is one of those cases where to do the right thing, will be to do nothing but harm. So let well alone, will you? Stifle your conscience, and keep away from Grandfather. It's none of your business, after all.'

'If I could believe you. If I knew what you were playing at.'

'Don't worry about that, or about my future. It has nothing to do with you.'

He let out a breath like a sigh. 'No. All right. I'll keep out of it, for a while at least. But watch your step . . . Annabel.' As I caught my breath, he added, roughly: 'If I'm to play your game, or even watch from the touchlines, I can hardly call you "Miss Winslow".'

'Then you will ... play my game?' I said breathlessly.

'I think so. Though heaven knows why. Let's say I'll go away and think about it, and hold a watching brief. But I promise you that if I plan to – what was it? – "blow the gaff", I'll warn you first.'

I said huskily: 'I don't know why you should do this for me.'

'Nor do I,' he said wearily. 'But ... be careful.'

'I intend to. And I – I'm sorry I said those things to you.'

'What things?'

'About your dismissing Annabel and then wanting to take up your – your love-affair again. It was unkind, but – well, I was scared. You must see that I'd have said anything to ... make you let me go.'

'Yes, I see.'

I hesitated. 'Good night ... Adam.'

He didn't answer. I turned away and left him.

Just before the dark leaves of the rhododendrons hid him from me, I thought I heard him say 'Good night.'

CHAPTER TWELVE

Why should not I love my love?
Why should not my love love me?
Why should not I speed after him,
Since love to all is free?

Traditional

The days went by, warm and cloudless,. Haymaking was in full swing, and the mown fields smelt Elysian, lying ribbed gold under a blue sky. Wild roses tumbled anyhow through all the hedges, and Tommy, the fat black and white cat, startled everyone by confounding the experts and having seven kittens.

And Adam Forrest did nothing.

I had got the passport away to the bank, which made me feel a little better, but it was a day or two after that moonlit meeting before I stopped watching the road between West Lodge and Whitescar. When two days, three days, passed, with no sign from him, I began to think that perhaps, having 'thought it over', he had decided to take me at my word, and, for Grandfather's sake, to hold his tongue and await developments. I had not seen him again, though Julie had once or twice persuaded me to walk through the river-meadows to look at the horse, Rowan: and I had gone, realising that, whatever Adam Forrest's intentions, I might as well behave as normally as possible, and naturally Julie expected my interest in the colt to be intense.

I had made no further attempt at confidence with Julie, and she had offered none, but I could not help suspecting that all was far from well between her and Donald Seton. How far her own feelings were settled, it was impossible to guess. She was young, volatile, perhaps a trifle spoiled, but from what little she had said to me – perhaps because she *had* said so little – I believed her affections to be seriously engaged. I had, on my first sight of Donald, decided that here was a man one could both like and respect; since then he had been down to Whitescar two or three times, and I had liked him better each time, though I thought I could see the cause of tension that appeared to exist, if not between the two of them, then in Julie's mind. I could see that his quietness, his steady reserve, might appear daunting and even formidable to a nineteen-year-old extrovert accustomed to the easy and outspoken admiration of the young men of her own London 'set'. Still waters run deep, but at nineteen one can hardly be expected to appreciate the fact.

The complaint she had made in jest, on that first evening, had its foundations firmly in the truth. Donald Seton would not 'fit into any romantic context'. And Julie, for all her gay sophistication, was young enough still to want her love-affair sprinkled with stardust, and vulnerable enough to be hurt by a reserve which she must mistake for indifference, or at best a reluctance to pursue. Donald was, in other words, a disappointment. Liking affection, comradeship, all growing steadily from the first seed of love – these were not what Julie, at nineteen, was looking for. Not happiness, but intensity, was what she craved. As a lover, the quiet Scot by no means measured up to the standards of Julie's favourite reading, or (more immediately) to those of the unhappy man who, eight years ago, had left notes for his mistress in the old ivy tree. Poor Julie, if she only knew . . . I found myself hoping, with quite startling fervour, that Donald would emerge soon from his Roman preoccupation, and Speak.

Meanwhile, he called at Whitescar in the evenings, after work had packed up, and, on one occasion, Julie went up to West Woodburn to see what was going on there, and even, possibly, in a genuine attempt to learn something about the job.

Although in this, it seemed, she was not successful, it did appear as if Donald had moved at least a little of the way towards her. He had brought her back in the evening, and stayed to dinner, listening silently and in apparent amusement to her lively – and malicious – account of the way he occupied his time.

'Sitting in a hole,' said Julie, 'my *dears*, I mean it, sitting all day at the bottom of a little pit, scraping away at *mud*, and with a thing the size of a teaspoon! Nothing but mud, *honestly*! And every spoonful preserved as if it was the Grand Cham's jewels. I never was so disillusioned in my life!'

'No gold coins? No statues?' I asked, smiling.

'My dear, I think there was a Roman bootlace.'

Donald's eyes twinkled. 'That was our big day. You mustn't expect excitement all the time.'

She opened her lips, and then shut them again. I thought her smile was brittle. I said quickly: 'Just what are you doing, anyway?'

'Only a preliminary bit of dating.'

'Dating?' Grandfather looked up from his cheese.

I saw Donald glance at him, in that diffident way he had, and affirm that this was genuine interest and not mere civility, before he replied. 'Yes, sir. It does consist, as Julie says, of just scratching at the earth. We've dug a trial trench through the wall and rampart of the fort, and we're going down layer by layer, examining the successive ramparts, and whatever debris – in the way of pottery shards and so on – comes to light as we work down. In that way, we can determine what building was done in the fort at different times. Eventually it sorts itself out into a picture of the general history of the place, but at present – ' the glimmer of a smile at her – 'Julie's quite right. It's nothing but scraping at earth, and must seem deplorably dull.'

'*You* seem to find it terribly absorbing, anyway,' said Julie. I don't think she had meant the words to have an edge, but they sounded almost pettish, like the retort of a piqued child.

Donald didn't appear to notice. 'Well,' he said, 'it's like most jobs, I suppose, masses of dull routine most of the time; but the good moments, when they come, can be pretty exciting.'

'Oh?' said Julie, then suddenly laughed, with an attempt at her normal sparkle of good-humour. 'Well, for goodness' sake tell us when that's likely to happen, and we'll all come and watch! At *least* – this to me – 'he's coming up out of the mud on Wednesday. Did I tell you? *And* so am I. We're going into Newcastle, to the Royal.'

'The theatre? How lovely. But, darling, Wednesday . . . it's Grandfather's birthday, had you forgotten? We're making rather an occasion of it, since we're all here – '

'Oh yes, I know, that's why we're going to the matinée. Donald says he can usually only manage Saturdays, but there weren't any seats left, and it's John Gielgud's new play, and I simply *cannot* miss it. So Donald's sneaking Wednesday off, after lunch, and we're going. Grandfather knows, and we'll be back in good time for the party. Donald's staying for that, too.'

'Very sensible of him. I know Lisa's got something wonderful laid on, but she won't tell me what it is.'

Lisa smiled but rather absently. I knew she was fidgeting until she could get out of the dining-room and back to the kitchen, where she could start to prepare Con's supper. When he worked late, she gave him this in the kitchen at whatever hour he came in, and I knew that, for her, this half-hour, when she had him to herself, was the peak of her day.

'Look,' Donald was saying, in that pleasant, unemphatic voice of his, 'it's very nice of you to have asked me, but I hadn't realised it was a family party. I think perhaps I'd better say – '

'Now, don't go crying off,' said Grandfather. 'We'll be thankful to have you. Never known a family gathering yet where the presence of a stranger didn't do a lot of good. Families are usually pretty damned grim when they get together, especially Winslows. We'll have to behave ourselves if you're here.'

Donald laughed. 'Well, if you put it like that ... '

'I do indeed. Anything I have to say to the family as such, can be said in three minutes precisely, on the way to bed.' The fierce, faded old eyes went round the table, lingering momentarily on Con's empty chair. 'And better so. There's been too much talk already, and I can't stomach post-mortems before I'm dead.'

The sheer unfairness of this took my breath away, and I saw Julie open her eyes wide. Donald, to whom these last remarks had been addressed, said rather faintly: 'Oh, quite.'

I rescued him. 'Then we'll see you on Wednesday? That'll be nice. What's the play, Julie?'

Julie, her face lighting, her pique forgotten, plunged happily into an account of it, unaware of the fact (or perhaps uncaring) that she was betraying with every word how far her heart lay from Whitescar and the quiet island of Forrest Park. I saw Grandfather watching her, an odd expression on his face. Ah well, I thought, this was best. I stole a glance at Lisa, to see if this was being stored up for Con, but she was looking at her watch, and murmuring something about coffee in the drawing-room.

'Well,' said Grandfather, a little drily, as he pushed back his chair, 'enjoy yourselves.'

'We will, be sure of that! But till then,' said Julie, dimpling at Donald, 'I'll let you get on with your mudlarking in peace, and put in a bit of work for Con instead. In any case, I think haymaking's more fun, and far more profitable to the human race.'

'Very probably,' said Donald equably.

Sure enough, Julie spent the next two or three days in the hayfield driving the tractor for Con.

Here I watched her rather more anxiously. It was just possible that Julie (provoked, restless, and already slightly bored with the country holiday that wasn't answering its purpose) was hoping to try out the age-old romantic device of making Donald jealous. She had two strings to her bow: Bill Fenwick from Nether Shields, who came over now and again, ostensibly to 'give a hand' in the hayfield when he could be spared from home, but in reality it was obvious, for a chance to be near Julie; and Con. Bill I dismissed without a thought, except to hope that he would not be hurt; but Con was a different proposition. He was not a man who could be used in this sort of way, or in any sort of way that he didn't nitiate. Besides, he was extremely attractive, and older and more sensible girls than Julie had rebounded before now into far less exciting arms. And if Con suddenly decided that three-thirds of the Winslow money was even better than two, and seriously turned his attention to Julie . . .

I need not have worried. At any other time, I suppose, Con would have flirted with her as a matter of course, a purely automatic reaction, as instinctive as that of a cock bird displaying to the female; but, just at present, Con had more important things on his mind. Mr. Isaacs, the lawyer, had been duly summoned to see Grandfather, and had spent Friday morning closeted with him in his office. The old man had said nothing whatever about this interview, but had allowed it to be known that Mr. Isaacs would call again in a few days' time, that is, on the morning of his, Grandfather's birthday. The inference was obvious, and, to my eyes, the effect on Con was obvious, too. The tension in him had increased perceptibly in the last few days; he was quieter than usual, and seemed edgy and strained. We saw very little of him; he rarely even ate with us, but spent all his time in the hayfield, working with an energy and fierce physical concentration that were remarkable, even for him. This was partly, I thought, due to a genuine passion for hard work, partly to work off the tensions he was feeling, and partly, also, to keep out of old Mr. Winslow's way. The die was cast, one way or the other; it seemed likely that it was cast in Con's favour, and Con was taking no risks.

In this he may have been wise. Since the lawyer's visit, there had been a perceptible change too, in Grandfather. Where Con had grown tense and wary, turning that diamond-hard concentration of his on his job, old Mr. Winslow became daily more difficult and less predictable, prone to sudden irritabilities, and even (what was new in him) fits of vagueness and absence of mind. The continued hot weather seemed to trouble him. He was very easily tired, but as he did less, so his fretfulness increased, and it seemed, wherever possible, to be directed at Con. His decision now finally made, it was as if the abdication of that will-to-power, which had been his driving force, had slackened something in him. He even seemed, physically, to have grown smaller. Where before he had been formidable, he now seemed merely fretful, and his resentful nagging at Con (over matters which previously he had been quite content to leave to the younger man) were the grumblings of a pettish old man, no longer the storms of a tyrant.

Lisa was the only person who seemed unaffected by the tensions that snapped the nerves at Whitescar. It was as if she too, had abdicated. It was increasingly obvious to me that Lisa, a determined enough personality in her way, lived only for Con – or, indeed, through Con. His energy and ambition charged her batteries; he steered her into a path, and along that path she ploughed steadily, undeviating, un-judging; but the decisions – and the rewards – were all his. She was more than content to help him to success, as long as she could watch him enjoying it. Her unremitting worship had certainly helped to make him what he was, but sometimes I found myself wondering if, in fact, Lisa wasn't also his prison. It was all he had had, that mothering, smothering love of hers that had driven him so much in upon himself. Con was for Con, and Lisa saw nothing wrong, or even out of the way, in such an attitude.

If she shared her half-brother's wariness and worry, she didn't show it, unless perhaps in a reflection of his relentless industry. Regardless of the heat, she threw herself into a positive frenzy of housewifery and cooking, and we were treated to a magnificent course of *haute cuisine* which drew only the most casual of accolades from the others, which Con, shut in his cold and wary preoccupations, noticed not at all, and which proved a great nuisance to me, who had in common civility to offer my help in whatever job she undertook.

For me, it was something of a relief to find myself abruptly removed from the centre of attention. Con was, for the moment, no longer concerned with me, and Lisa had accepted me completely. What jealous thoughts she may have originally had of me, she had transferred to Julie, who (to do her justice) had done nothing to deserve them. Me, she seemed even to like; I had the odd feeling that, in her stolid, brother-centred way, she was even grateful for my presence at Whitescar, where Mr. Winslow persisted in regarding her as something of a stranger, a sort of paid-housekeeper-cum-poor-relation; Mrs. Bates with a slightly jealous Northern caution; and Con himself with a casual affection that took everything, including the most detailed personal service, completely for granted.

Meanwhile, the heat increased, charging the air with thunder, adding this threat to the other perceptible weights in the air. Day by day the great soapsud clouds built up their slow thunder-towers in the south-west. The trees hung heavily, as if themselves exhausted by the heat, and the sky was a deep, waiting blue.

And Con kept quiet, and watched the clouds, and drove himself and the men like galley-slaves to clear the fields before the weather broke . . . And with that same cold preoccupation, and for a closely analogous reason, he watched Grandfather . . .

Wednesday came, still without the threatened thunderstorm. The air felt a little lighter, as a small breeze had sprung up, though without shifting the towering, beautiful clouds. But the sense of oppression (or was it foreboding?) seemed to have lifted.

Mr. Isaacs came just before midday, and Grandfather took him straight into the office. I gave them ten minutes, then went to the dining-room to get the sherry.

As I crossed the hall, Julie came downstairs, pulling on her gloves.

I paused. 'Why hullo! Are you going now? My, my, don't you look wonderful!'

This was true. She was wearing crisp cotton, the colour of lemon-ice, and her gloves were white. The pale, shining hair was brushed into an elaborate and very attractive style that had been thought up at least two hundred miles from Whitescar. Over one arm she carried a little coat of the same material as the frock.

I said: 'Ve - ery nice! But why so early? I thought Donald couldn't get away till after lunch?'

She tugged the second glove into place, pushing the heavy gold bracelet higher up her wrist with a sharp little movement that looked almost savage. 'Donald,' she said crisply, 'can't get away at all.'

'What?'

'He rang up an hour ago to say that he couldn't go, after all.'

'Oh, Julie, no! Why?'

Her careful composure shivered a bit, like cat-ice wrinkling under the wind. Her eyes were stormy. 'Because he doesn't think what *I* want to do matters a damn, that's why!'

I threw a glance towards the office door. 'Come into the dining-room. I was just going to take Mr. Isaacs and Grandfather some sherry ... '

In the dining-room I said: 'Now come off it, honey. Why can't he come? What's happened?'

'Somebody's turned up from London, that's why. Some beastly man from the Commission, who's working with Donald, and Donald says he'll have to stay and see him. He says - oh, what's it matter, anyway? I didn't listen. It's always the same, I might have known. The one time he *did* say he'd leave his precious blasted Romans - '

'Julie, he'd come if he could. He can't help it.'

'I know! Oh, it isn't *that*! It's just - oh, it's just *everything*!' cried Julie. 'And he sounded so *calm* and reasonable -'

'He always does. He would in a fire. It's a habit men have; they think it calms us, or something.'

'Well, but he seemed to think *I* ought to be reasonable too!' said Julie, furiously. 'How dumb can you get? ... Annabel, if you laugh, I'll kill you!' She gave a reluctant grin. 'Anyway you know *exactly* what I mean.'

'Yes, I know. I'm sorry. But you're not being fair to Donald, are you? The man's got a job to do, and if something crops up that has to be attended to - '

'Oh, I know, I know! I'm not as silly as all that. But he knew how *foully* disappointed I'd be. He needn't have sounded just as if he didn't even *mind* not going out with me.'

'He wouldn't mean to, you know. He's just not the type to spread himself all over the carpet for you to trample on. He'd be as sorry as the next man, but he - well, he just hasn't got the gift of the gab.'

'No, he hasn't, has he?' Her voice was genuinely bitter. She had turned aside to pick up the jacket from the chair where she had thrown it.

'My dear - '

'It's all right. I dare say I'm being stupid about it, but I can't help that. It would be different if he'd ever – if I knew – ' she sounded all at once very young – 'if I was sure he cared.'

'He does care. I'm sure he does.'

'Then why the hell doesn't he *say* so?' cried Julie explosively. She snatched up her coat. 'Oh, what's the *use*?'

'Is he still coming to dinner tonight?'

'He said he'd try. I said he could please himself.'

'Oh, Julie!'

'Oh, I didn't just say it like *that*. I was really quite nice about it.' She gave me a wavering smile. 'Almost reasonable . . . But if he *knew* what hellish thoughts were churning away inside me . . . '

'It's often a good thing they don't.'

'They? Who?'

I grinned. 'Men.'

'Oh, *men*,' she said, in accents of loathing. '*Why* are men?'

'I give you three guesses.'

'The most harmless answer is that there'd be nothing whatever to do if there weren't any, I suppose.'

'There'd be nothing whatever, period,' I said.

'Well, you've got something there,' said Julie, 'but don't ask me to admit it for quite some time. Oh, Annabel, you've done me good. I must go now; there's the car.'

'Car?'

She gave me a little sideways look under her lashes. 'I told you I wasn't going to miss this play. I'm going with Bill Fenwick.'

'I see.'

'And just what do you see?'

I ignored that. 'But surely the play's going to open in London soon? You'll see it there?'

'That,' said Julie, 'is not the point.'

'No, quite. Donald couldn't get away, so you rang up Bill Fenwick, and asked him to take you? That it?'

'Yes,' she said, with a shade of defiance.

'And *he* dropped everything, and promptly came?'

'Yes.' She eyed me. 'What's wrong with that?'

'Nothing at all,' I said cheerfully. 'I hope they've finished leading for the day at Nether Shields, that's all.'

'Annabel,' said Julie, warmly, 'are you trying to be a pig?'

I laughed. 'I was rather. Never mind me, honey, go and enjoy your play. We'll be seeing you at dinner. And, Julie – '

'What is it?'

'If Donald does come, don't make it too obvious that you're a bit fed-up with him, will you? No – ' as she made a little movement of impatience – 'this isn't Advice from Aunt Annabel. What's between you Donald is your affair. I was thinking of something quite different . . . I'll explain later. There's no time now ... But come and see me when you get in, will you? I've something to tell you.'

'Sure,' said Julie.

The front door shut behind her. I found the sherry-glasses, and a tray, but as I set the decanter on this, the office door opened, and Grandfather came out.

He was making for the baize door that led to the kitchen lobby, but, hearing the chink of glass, he stopped, turned, and saw me through the open door of the dining-room. He seemed to hesitate for a moment, then abruptly to make up his mind. He came into the room, and shut the door quietly behind him.

'I was just going to bring you some sherry,' I said. 'Were you looking for me?'

'I was going to get Betsy Bates and that girl Cora to witness my signature,' he said, in a dry, rather harsh voice.

'Oh.' I waited. He stood just inside the door, his head bent and thrust forward, staring at me under his brows.

'Child – ' He seemed not quite to know what he had come to say.

'Yes?'

'I've taken you at your word.'

I tried not to let him see the relief that swept through me. 'I'm glad of that.'

'I believe you are.'

I said earnestly: 'It's right, Grandfather, you said yourself it was only right and fair. It's best for everyone – Con, me, the place, your peace of mind.'

'Julie?'

'And Julie,' I said steadily. 'Julie loves this place, don't think she doesn't, but can you see her running it?'

He gave his little bark of laughter. 'Frankly, no. Must confess I've wondered, though, with young Fenwick in the offing – '

I said quickly: 'There's nothing in that. It's Donald Seton, and you know he lives in London when he's not on field work.'

'Hm. Gathered there was something in the wind. Not quite senile yet. Decent sort of fellow, I thought. Gentleman, and so on. Only thing is, he doesn't look as if he's got a penny to his name.'

I laughed. 'His clothes and car? That's affectation, when he's out on a dig. I'll bet he's formal enough in London. He makes eighteen hundred a year, rising to two thousand five hundred, and his family's got money.'

'How the devil d'you know?'

'Julie told me. She looked him up.'

'Good God,' said Grandfather, impressed. 'Girl's got sense, after all.' He gave a curious little sigh, and then smiled the tight, lipless smile of the old. 'Well, that's that, isn't it? All settled. But I don't mind telling you, I haven't liked it. Boy's all right, don't think I don't know it, but not m'own flesh and blood. Not the same. Young people don't understand that nowadays, but it's true. A bit too much of the damned foreigner about Connor sometimes.'

'Foreigner?' I said blankly.

'Irish,' said Grandfather. I thought of Donald, and smiled to myself, but he didn't see. He was looking past me, out of the window. 'If your father, or Julie's had lived, it would have been a different matter.'

'Yes,' I said gently.

The old eyes came back to me. 'You and Connor should have made a match of it. Should still. I'm not raking up the past, but after what's been between you – '

'I told you, it would never have worked.'

'Not then, no. Too much of the Winslow in both of you, perhaps. But now ... say what you like, the onlooker sees most of the game. I still think it would be the best thing. For the place, for Connor; yes, and for you. Never a woman born yet, that wasn't better for a husband. Don't just stand and smile at me, child. Come here.'

I went and stood in front of him. He put up a hand, and held it against my cheek. It was cool and very dry, and felt as light as a leaf. 'It's made me very happy, your coming back. Don't think for a moment that you're not my favourite, because you are.'

'I always did say you were never fair in your life.'

'I've left you some money,' he said gruffly. 'A good sum, and Julie, too. I want you to know.'

'Grandfather, I – '

'It's settled. We'll have neither thanks nor argument. I've done what I think fair, in spite of what you say about me. Tell you just how it stands. It's tangled up in a lot of lawyers' nonsense, but it amounts to this: Whitescar goes to Connor, with the house, stock, implements, the lot. I take it you won't contest that? Or Julie?'

'No.'

A grin. 'Doubt if you could, anyway. Isaacs' wrapped it all up in legal jargon, with reasons stated. Seems you have to stop anyone being able to say, later on, that you were cranky when you made the Will. So there it is, all laid out: Whitescar goes as an acknowledgement of Connor's "devoted work", for which I've so far made "inadequate recompense". True enough. Well, there it is. Then we come to the recompense for you.'

'For me? What have I ever done, except run away?'

'Recompense for losing Whitescar. Should have been yours. Handed over your head to Connor.'

'Oh.' I waited, helplessly.

'The money,' said Grandfather. He had a hand on the table, and was leaning on it. He sent me a look up under the white brows, a pale counterfeit of his old, bright glance, but recognisably the same. 'I've divided it into three. A third goes to Julie, outright. It's all she ever expected, and I doubt if she'll quarrel with Con over Whitescar. If she marries this man of hers, she'll be well enough found. The other two-thirds I've left in trust, to pay your income for life.'

'In – trust?'

'That's what I said. Worked it all out with Isaacs as the best way. I want you repaid for losing Whitescar, and I want to see you well-provided-for. But I don't want the money to leave the land outright. You said you'd not stay here when I'd gone; remember? So it's left in trust for your lifetime. After your death it comes back to Connor absolutely, or to his heirs. On the other hand, if Connor should die before you, without issue, then Whitescar becomes yours, and the money along with it, absolutely. I take it, if he were gone, you'd look after the place . . . ? Good girl.' His hand lifted. 'No wait, I haven't finished. There's one thing more. If you should marry Connor – '

'Grandfather – '

'If you should marry Connor, and live at Whitescar, the money becomes yours then, absolutely. Clear?'

'Y – yes.'

The only really clear thing was the old man's determination to tie the money to Whitescar; and me, along with it, if he could, to Con. The wrong end of the shotgun, with a vengeance. Dazedly I tried to assess the probable results of what he had just told me. 'But . . . *two-thirds* for me, and a third for Julie? What about Con? If I don't – I mean – ' I floundered, and stopped. It was no use insisting; let him keep his dream.

'I've left him a little, and Lisa, too.'

'But, Grandfather – '

'My good girl– ' he was suddenly irritable – 'anyone would think you were trying to get rid of every penny piece to Connor! Are you mad? If the place comes to him over the heads of you and Julie, he can hardly expect much more! It'll not be easy for him, with only a small capital to back him, but he'll have all the liquid assets of the place, and he'll make out.'

He stopped, breathing rather hard. I noticed all at once how heavily he was leaning on his hand. He pulled a handkerchief, rather fumblingly, from his breast-pocket, and touched it to his mouth. 'Con's a good lad, and a clever lad; he's not afraid of work, and the land's in good heart. I think it's fair enough, all round.'

'Darling, of course it is! More than fair! And now let's stop thinking about it; it's done, let's all forget it, and you forget it, too.' I grinned at him. 'You know I can't stomach these post-mortems.'

He patted my cheek. 'Dear child,' he said, and went abruptly out of the room.

What it cost Con in self-command I shall never know, but he did not come in to luncheon. The lawyer left immediately afterwards, and Grandfather retired to rest. I had promised Lisa to go into Bellingham that afternoon to do some shopping. She was already busy with preparations for dinner, but had refused to allow me to help her 'because,' she said simply, 'I enjoy special occasions, and I'm selfish; but you shall do the table if you like.'

I laughed. 'All right, I've no quarrel with that. If I'm to be allowed to eat your cooking without having to work for it, that's okay by me.'

'Oh, you can wash up,' said Lisa placidly, adding, with that spice of malice that was never far away: 'Julie can help you.'

The shopping did not take long, and I caught the four o'clock bus back from Bellingham, which put me down at the head of the lane. I assembled my rather awkward collection of packages and set off downhill.

When I reached the mouth of the disused quarry where, on the first day, I had left my luggage, I saw a car standing there, an old car with too much chrome winking too brightly in the sun. Donald's car.

I picked my way in at the rutted entrance of the quarry. Donald was there, pipe in mouth, hands deep in trouser-pockets, his head tilted back, apparently surveying the high wall at the back of the quarry. This was of sand-coloured stone, darkened with weathering, and here and there fissured red with iron. It was a big quarry, deep and narrow, consisting of several sections opening out of one another, partitioned off by jutting walls of rock. The cliff tops were crested with woods, whose crowding trees had sown seedlings broadcast, so that every ledge and tumble of rock was hung with green, and young oaks thrust golden frilled leaves above the brambles and foxgloves that hid the edges of the quarry floor. It must have been decades since any stone had been taken out of here.

Donald turned when he heard my footsteps, took the pipe out of his mouth, and smiled.

'Why, hullo.'

'Hullo.' I added, a little awkwardly, with a gesture of the basket and parcels in my hands: 'I saw your car, and yielded to temptation. You were coming down to Whitescar, weren't you?'

'If I hadn't been,' said Donald diplomatically, 'I should be now.'

I laughed. 'You could hardly do anything else. I've an awful nerve, haven't I?' I hoped that my glance at his suit, which was, for once, impeccably formal, had not been too obvious. 'But surely, you're coming to dinner?'

I thought he looked uncertain. I added, quickly: 'Julie said you weren't quite sure if you could manage it after all, but we're hoping you will. It'll be worth it, I promise you. There were rumours about duckling.'

'I'm sure it will. Miss Dermott's a wonderful cook. Well, if you're sure I haven't put things out—'

'Of course you haven't. We were all hoping you'd manage to get away. Julie'll be delighted. She's out just now; she went into Newcastle after all; but she'll be back in time for dinner.'

'Did she? Then she won't miss the play. I'm glad. Did her cousin take her?'

'Con?' No. Bill Fenwick. D'you know him?'

'She's mentioned him. Would you like to put your parcels in the car?' He moved to open the door and take them from me.

'Thanks very much.' I handed them over with a sigh of relief. 'There. At least that's one way of ensuring that you do come to dinner. I only hope I'm not taking you down too early.'

'No; I wasn't going straight there, as it happens; I want to go over and see Mr. Forrest, so I'll take you down via Whitescar, and – ' he grinned ' – it'll be very nice to have someone to open the gates.'

'Fair enough. And there's an extra one now; one of the cattle-grids is damaged, and you have to use the gate.' I added, curiously, for his eyes had returned to the quarry face: 'What interests you here? This is a geologist's sort of thing, not an archaeologist's, surely?'

'Oh, sure. But there is something interesting. This is the local sandstone, the building stone you'll see they've used for all the old houses hereabouts, and most of the walls, too. It's an old quarry. I've been asking about it, and I'm told it stopped working in 1910. I'd like to find out when it started, how far back there are any records of it.'

'I can tell you one thing, though it may be only legend. This is supposed to be the quarry that Whitescar came out of, and I suppose Forrest too, though Whitescar's older. It's supposed to have taken its name from the quarry. When this sort of stone is newly blasted, could it be said to look white?'

'Fairly pale, anyway. Yes, I'd heard of that story. It's in Bewick's *Northumberland*. The first Whitescar was built in the fifteen hundreds, wasn't it?'

'Yes. And the main part of Forrest in 1760, or something like that. At any rate the first working here must be at least four hundred years old.'

'Older than that, by far.' He smiled. 'The quarry was here long before Whitescar was built. When you come to think about it, it is more likely that the place got its name from a quarry – a white scar – that was already a well-known landmark, *before* they took the stone out to build the house.'

'It could be, I suppose. Is this a guess, or can you tell, somehow?' I looked vaguely at the overgrown rock around us.

'I can tell.' I saw, suddenly, a spark of excitement in the deep hazel eyes. 'Come and tell me if you see what I see. Over here, and watch your feet. There are bits of old iron and stuff lying around still. The oldest end of the quarry's along here, and it's flooded. I'll go first, shall I?'

We picked our way through the foxgloves, and the buds of ragwort, where loose stones and shards of rusting iron made going dangerous. A rabbit bolted out of a clump of nettles, and dived out of sight down an unlikely-looking crevice.

'A nice fat one,' said Donald, watching it.

'Were you thinking of the cooking-pot, and Lisa's arts?'

'I was not. I was thinking about myxomatosis.'

'Oh. Seeing the rabbits coming back, you mean?'

'Yes, the destructive little devils. But will you ever forget seeing them hobbling about, dying and in pain, and having to kill them, and not quite knowing how, and being afraid one wouldn't manage it cleanly the first time? One got sickeningly good at it, in the end. It may be the wrong thing to say to a farmer's daughter, but I'm pleased to see them back nice and fat and immune, and I hope they eat every blade of grass belonging to the brutes who deliberately gave them the disease ... But of course, you won't remember it. You weren't here, I keep forgetting. You seem so much a part of the scene at Whitescar. It's a lovely place, isn't it?'

'Do you know,' I said, 'I'm quite aware that that was a *non sequitur*, but it was also a compliment.'

He looked surprised. 'Was it?' He seemed to consider. 'Yes, I've got it. So it was. Well, I didn't see it, but if I had I would have meant it.'

'Fair enough.' I laughed. 'Except that *then* you'd never have said it.'

He smiled slightly. 'Probably not. The curse of Scotland, the padlocked tongue.' But his eyes weren't amused.

I said, before I thought: 'Maybe. But is it any worse than the curse of Ireland; the tongue without a latch, even, let alone a lock?'

He grinned then, spontaneously, and I knew he was thinking as I was too late, about Con. But all he said was: 'Or the curse of England; the double tongue?'

I laughed. 'We had to have that crack, didn't we? The old, old war. What a mercy that neither side means it ... Do you like living in the South?'

'Very much. I've good rooms in London, and my work takes me out as much as anyone could want.'

'Do you think you'd want to settle permanently in London?'

We had clambered over a ridge of fallen stones, jammed by time into a bank of solid clay. Below us, round in another angle of the quarry, I could see water.

He stopped. He still had his pipe in his hand. It had gone out. He examined it carefully, but absently, as if he was not quite sure what it was. Then he stuffed it into his pocket. 'You mean if I married Julie?'

I hadn't been ready for quite such direct dealing. 'Yes. Yes, I did mean that. Perhaps I shouldn't have – '

'If I married Julie, I should still have to go where my work was,' said Donald bluntly, 'and it won't always be at West Woodburn.' He looked at me. 'Are you trying to tell me that she'll want to come and live here?'

'No.'

'Ah. Well, I didn't altogether get the impression that she was wedded to the place.'

'She's not.' I hesitated, then added, equally bluntly: 'Nor likely to be.'

He looked at me sharply. Beside me a tuft of silvery hair-grass had fluffed into a lace of pale seeds. I ran my fingers through them, and then regarded the handful of tiny particles. I took a breath and plunged on. 'You know, I wouldn't dream of saying this sort of thing to you, if it weren't important. You may think I'm speaking out of turn, and if so, I hope you'll forgive me.'

He made the slight, indescribable sound that, in the North, manages to express assent, deprecation, interest, dissent, apology – anything at all that the listener cares to read into it. It sound like 'Mphm,' and you can conduct whole (and perfectly intelligible) conversations with that one sound, anywhere north of the Tyne. As a contribution from Donald, it was unhelpful.

I opened my hand and let the seeds drift down on to the clay. 'Have you said anything to Julie yet?'

He said quite simply: 'No. It's been – so quick, you see ... eight weeks since we met, that's all. I don't mean that *I'm* any the less sure, but I don't know if she ... well, she's so young.'

'She's nineteen. Nowadays girls know their own minds at nineteen.'

'Do they?' I caught a slight hesitation in his manner then, and wondered if he had been suddenly reminded of another nineteen-year-old, eight years ago at Whitescar. He said: 'I rather thought Julie had given every indication of not knowing.'

'Bill Fenwick? He's a nice boy, I think, but I assure you, you needn't worry about him.'

'I wasn't thinking about Bill Fenwick.'

'What do you mean, then?'

'Connor.'

'*Con?*' I stared for a moment, then said flatly: 'If you'd asked me, I'd have said she didn't even like him.'

He had taken out his pipe, and was filling it again, more, I thought, for something to fidget with than because he wanted to smoke. He glanced up across it, and I thought his look sharpened. 'I should have thought he was the very sort of chap a girl would be bound to fall for.'

'Oh, lord, lord, he's attractive,' I said impatiently. 'You might say devastating. But Julie's never shown any signs of falling for him, and she's had plenty of chance to ... Goodness knows, if she wasn't susceptible to sheer blazing good looks like Con's at fifteen or sixteen, then she probably never will be. You forget, she was brought up here; she probably thinks of him like a brother ... and not a particularly favourite one.'

'You think so? I'm not very knowledgeable about these things. It just seemed to be so likely, and so ... suitable.'

'Suitable? I doubt it! Anyway, Julie's not a nitwit, and she's had plenty of time to fall for Con if she was ever going to, instead of which ...' I paused, and brushed a finger idly over a tight purple thistle-top. 'Things are a little – difficult – just now at Whitescar. I can't quite describe why ... it's a sort of emotional climate ...'

'I know,' he said, surprisingly. 'Everyone seems a little too much aware of what other people are doing.'

'You've felt it? Then you know what I mean. It's partly to do with my
coming back, and Grandfather's stroke, and his making a new Will . .
oh, and everything. But it's rather horrid, and definitely unsettling.
know Julie's feeling it, and I'm so afraid she'll do something just plain
silly. If it weren't for that, I'd be quite happy to settle back, and depend
on her good sense and good taste, but just at present . . . ' My voice
trailed off, awkwardly.

'Do you know,' said Donald, 'whether you meant it or not, that was
a compliment?'

I glanced at him. He looked amused, relaxed, confident, calmly pressing
the tobacco down into the bowl of his pipe. I suddenly realised that I had
been tempering the wind to a fully-grown and completely self-possessed
lamb. I had underrated Donald, and so (I thought with amused relief
had Julie.

I took a little breath of relief. Then I grinned maliciously.

'Think nothing of it. That was my double tongue. How do you know
I meant you?'

His eyes twinkled. 'It never occurred to me that you could mean
anyone else. That's one of the blessings of being a Scot, a profound and
unshakable conviction of your own worth.'

'Then hang on to that, and forget about Con,' I said. 'Heavens above
what's got into me? Donald, don't ask me why, and blame me for an
interfering so-and-so if you like, but I wish to goodness that you'd simply
ask the girl!'

He sent me that sudden, transforming grin. 'It'll be a pleasure. Now
come along, and be careful down this slope, there may be loose bits
Here, take my hand. That's it.'

'Goodness, that water's deep, isn't it?'

'It is that. Round here now. It's all right, you can walk on the edge
the rock's safe.'

The water lay still and billiard-green in the shadow of the ledge where
we stood. The edges of the pool were as sharply-quarried as those of a
swimming-bath. On two sides the water was held in by a right-angle of
the high cliff; at the side where we stood, the quarry was floored with
flat, bare rock, as smooth as concrete, which dropped squarely away in
front of us to the water-level some four feet below.

Here the water was in shadow, oil-green, slightly opaque, and somehow
dangerous-looking, but where the sunlight struck it, it was lucid with
grass-green colour streaked with weed, and beneath the surface the planes
of quarried rock showed clearly, coloured according to their depth, green
gold and gold-jade, like peaches drowned in chartreuse.

I said: 'Why is it that even the most awe-inspiring things in nature
like volcanoes and ice-cliffs and deserts and things, look kind and innocent
compared with places where men have worked and built things, and then
abandoned them? This is *sinister.*'

He laughed. 'Professionally speaking, I'd say it all depends if the were abandoned long enough ago. If a thing's old enough, it's purged, I suppose, of all the nastier wreckage – like the rusty iron, and that old boot there; and can you tell me where in the world that pram can have come from? – like finding a nice clean skeleton, instead of a decaying body.'

'For goodness' sake! You give me the creeps. Did you bring me here to show me a body?'

'No.' He pointed down through the water towards one of the slanting slabs of stone that showed like a buttress shoring up the side of the pool. 'Do you see that bit of rock?'

'The one that's lying on a slant? Yes. It looks as if it had been shaped, doesn't it? Such a nice, regular oblong.'

'It has been shaped.' Something in his voice made me look at him. He said: 'Look at it again. Don't you see the marks?'

I peered down: 'I . . . think so. I can't be sure. Do you mean what looks like a sort of rough scoring, diagonally across the block? That's not artificial, surely?'

'I think it was. Those marks would be sharply scored originally; chisel-marks. That block's been under water a long time, and even still water will smooth out a stone surface, given time.'

I stood up and looked at him. 'Given time?'

'I don't know how long, because I don't know when this part of the quarry was flooded. But those stones down there were quarried about two thousand years ago.'

'Two thou – ' I stopped short and said, rather blankly: 'You mean the *Romans*?'

'That's my guess. About two thousand years ago they opened a quarry here. Later, possibly much later, the "white scar" among the woods was re-opened and worked again. Perhaps the Roman workings were already flooded; at any rate, new ones were started, and the original ones left to the weather. And now, this year, with this dry spring, and the drought, the water-level sinks a couple of feet just when I chance to be poking about in this part of the world, and I see the stones. That's how things happen.'

'Is it – is it important? Forgive me, I'm terribly ignorant, but what does it tell you, apart from the fact that they got building stone from here, for the Wall?'

'Not for the Wall. Hardly, when they were driving that along the whin sill anyway. They quarried the stone for the Wall on the spot.'

'For the fort at West Woodburn, then? Habitancum, where you're working?'

'The same applies. There's stone there. They dug the local stuff whenever they could, of course, to save time and transport.'

He seemed to be waiting, eyeing me in amiable expectation. It was a moment or two before the very simple conclusion presented itself.

'Oh! Yes, I get it. But, Donald, there's nothing Roman hereabouts, is there? At least, I've never heard of anything, and surely, if there were, the one-inch map would have it marked?'

'Exactly,' said Donald.

I stared at him stupidly for a moment or two. 'I ... see! You think there *may* be something? Some Roman work that hasn't been found yet?'

He pushed his pipe down into a pocket, and turned away from the water's edge. 'I've no idea,' he said, 'but there's nothing to stop me looking, is there? And now, if you're ready, I'll be taking you down to Whitescar, and then I'll get along and see Mr. Forrest, and ask his leave to go poking around in his policies.'

CHAPTER THIRTEEN

I cannot get to my love if I wad dee,
The water of Tyne runs between him and me.

North Country Song

When we got to the farm, it was to find a slightly distracted Lisa watching for me with some tale of disaster that involved a cream trifle, and Tommy, the black and white cat.

'And I'll wring his neck if he comes near the dairy again,' she said, violently for her.

I said mildly: 'We've got to remember he's eating for eight.'

'Nonsense,' said Lisa, 'he had them days ago. Oh, I see what you mean. Well, even if he *is* feeding seven kittens, and let me tell you if only I can find them I'll drown the lot, that's no excuse for taking the whole top off the trifle I'd made for your grandfather's birthday dinner.'

'Just a minute,' said Donald, 'no doubt I'm not just at my best today, but who has taken the trifle?'

'That beastly Tommy.'

'The black and white cat? The fat one I – the one who was in to tea the other day?' Donald liked cats, and had made friends with them all, even the little half-wild tortoiseshell that lived like a wraith under the hen-house.

'That's the one. And not so fat either, now he's had his kittens, but after half the trifle and a pint of cream – '

I said helplessly, seeing Donald's expression: 'It's all right. Nature has not suspended her laws, not yet. Everyone was wrong about Tommy – except that marmalade brute from West Lodge, at least I suppose it was him, because now that Tommy's unmasked he's the only tom for miles. Oh lord, I'm getting muddled too. And poor Tommy's figure wasn't due to incontinence – at least, not of the kind we thought; it was just kittens. Seven of them.'

'And Annabel saw them in the loft, and didn't tell me till next morning, and by that time the brute had shifted them, and he's too fly to let us see him going to feed them.' Lisa slapped a basket down on the kitchen table.

'You wouldn't really drown them? All?' Donald spoke in the carefully non-committal voice of the man who would sooner die stuck full of arrows than seem to be soft-hearted over an animal.

'I certainly would, and Tommy too, if he gets in the dairy again.'

'You can't change a personal pronoun overnight,' I said apologetically, to Donald. 'I'm afraid Tommy won't even decline to Thomasina. He'll be Tommy till the end of his days.'

'Which are not,' said Lisa, 'so far distant, though even I have not the heart to have the brute put down, and leave those wretched kittens to starve to death somewhere. But if I find them before they're too big, they'll certainly have to drown. Did Mr. Seton say he was going over to West Lodge now? Annabel, would you be an angel and go across with him as far as the gardens, and get some strawberries? I rang up, and Johnny Rudd said he'd keep them for us. They should be ready, so hurry back, if you don't mind; we'll have them all to pick over.'

Something must have shown in my face, for I saw her recollect herself for the first time for days. She must have forgotten that I had not yet been across to the gardens.

I saw her eyes flicker with a moment of calculation, and then she turned to Donald, but he spoke first. He must have seen something too; he saw more than one thought, I reflected; but of course he put my hesitation down to simple physical causes.

'Annabel's tired. Look, I can easily drop in at the market garden for you. You go past it to get to the Lodge, don't you?'

I said: 'It's all right, Donald, thanks all the same. I'm not tired, and if you've to see Mr. Forrest at the Lodge, time will be getting along by the time you manage to get away, and besides, you don't want to have to hurry. I'll come along with you now, if I may, and walk straight back with the strawberries by the short cut, and then we can get on with hulling them. I'd like to see Johnny Rudd, anyway. He'll be in the garden?' This to Lisa.

'Yes.' Her eyes were on me. 'You haven't seen him since you came back, have you? His hair's going grey now, but he hasn't changed much. He's the only one who'll still be working there by this time; he said he'd wait if he could. The two boys go off at five. But if Mr. Forrest should be in the garden – '

'Oh, did I tell you?' I said. 'I saw him the other day.'

'Did you?' The question only just missed being too sharp. 'To speak to?'

'For a moment. I forget what we talked about, but I thought he'd changed, rather a lot.' I picked up the basket. 'I'll be as quick as I can,' I said.

What had been the old walled kitchen-garden of Forrest Hall lay

beside the stables, about a quarter of a mile from the West Lodge, where
Adam Forrest now lived. It was reached by the road that led from beside
the Hall gates, through the plantations above Whitescar, and over a mile
or so of moorland in the centre of the peninsula. A rough track from
Whitescar led steeply up to join this road, which finished at the
Lodge.

Even here, at West Lodge, some pomp remained from the once palmy
days of the Forrests. The entrance to the stableyard – now worked as a
small farm – was a massive archway, with shields bearing the same
heraldic beasts that flaunted their improbable attitudes on the gateposts
at Forrest Hall. Over the arch stood the old clock-tower, with a gilded
weather-vane over it. Trees crowded close on the other side of the lane,
and the river glittered just beyond them. The road was rutted, and green
with weeds, its verges deep in wild flowers, but the cobbles of the yard,
glimpsed through the archway, were sparkling clean, like the shingle on
a seaswept beach. A little way off, beyond a clump of laburnum and
copper beech, the chimneys of West Lodge glinted in the sunlight. Smoke
was rising from one of them. Life at Forrest Park had shifted its focus.

Beyond the stableyard stretched the twelve-foot-high wall of the kitchen
garden. There was a wrought-iron gate set into it.

'This one?'

'Yes.'

Donald stopped the car, and I got out.

'Now, don't bother about me. It's just as quick taking the cut back
across the fields. I'll go that way.'

'If you're sure – '

'Quite sure. Thanks for the lift. I'll see you at dinner.'

The car moved off. I pushed the gate open.

The last stretch of the lane had been deep under trees. Now, I walked
through the gate, between two massive yews, and into a brilliance of
sunshine that made me blink and narrow my eyes.

It wasn't only the brightness, however, that gave me pause. Here, the
contrast with the moonlit derelict at Forrest was both striking and
disturbing. In this garden, filled with sun and warmth and scent inside
its four high walls, everything, at first sight, was as it might have been
in the eighteenth-century heyday of the place.

All along one wall was the glass, and under it I could see the peaches
and apricots and grapes of a more luxurious age, still carefully pruned
and trained, and beneath them the homely forests of tomatoes and
chrysanthemum seedlings, and the occasional splashes of colour that
meant hydrangeas or begonias coming into flower for the market. Along
the other three walls were the espaliered fruit-trees. The fruit, small,
green and shining, crowded thickly on the boughs against the warm
sandstone.

Down the centre of the garden went a broad walk of turf, beautifully
cut and rolled, and to either side of this was a flower border, spired and

splashed and shimmering with all the colours of an English June; lupins, delphiniums, peonies, poppies, irises, Canterbury Bells, all held back by lavender swags of catmint, and backed by a high rustic trellis where climbing roses held up their fountains of bright flowers. At the far end of the walk, at the focal point, as it were, of the vista, I could see the basin of some disused stone fountain, with a couple of bronze herons still on guard over what had been the pool. This was set round with flagstones, between which were clumps of lavender, rosemary, thyme, and sage, in a carefully-planned confusion as old as the garden itself. They must have left the old herb-garden, I thought, and this one avenue of flowers. The rest was all order and usefulness – peas and beans and turnips and potatoes, and regimented fruit-bushes. The only other thing that spoke of the glory that had departed, was a tall circular structure in one corner of the garden, a dove-house, *columbarium,* with honeysuckle and clematis running riot over its dilapidated walls. The pegged tiles of its roof sagged gently over the beams beneath, as canvas moulds itself to the supporting ropes. The tiles showed bronze-coloured in the sunlight, their own smoky blue overlaid and softened by the rings of that lovely lichen that spreads its amber circles, like water-lily leaves, over old and beautiful things. The dove-house door had decayed, and looked like empty eye-sockets; I saw starlings fly out.

But elsewhere all was order. Not a weed. I reflected that if Adam Forrest and Johnny Rudd kept all this themselves, with the help of a couple of boys, I could hardly taunt him with not understanding the meaning of labour. The place must be killing work.

At first I couldn't see anyone about at all, and walked quickly up the grass walk, towards the green-houses, peering through the rose trellis to right and left. Then I saw a man working among raspberry-canes over near one of the walls. He had his back to me, and was stooping. He was wearing faded brown corduroys, and a blue shirt, and I could see an old brown jacket hung near him over a stake. He had dark hair with grey in it.

He didn't seem to hear my approach, being intent on fastening a bird-net back securely over the canes.

I stopped on the path near him. 'Johnny?'

He straightened and turned. 'I'm afraid – ' he began, then stopped.

'You?' For the life of me I couldn't help sounding unbelieving. This was certainly the Adam Forrest I had met and spoken with a few nights ago, but now, facing him in the broad glare of the afternoon, I could see how different he was from my remembered picture of him. What I had seen on that last, almost dreamlike meeting, had been something like seeing a sequence from a film taken years ago, when he had been ten, no, fifteen years younger. Some unreality of the night had lent itself to him: I remembered the fine planes of his face, the smoothness of skin young in the moonlight, the darkness of hair and eyes dramatised in the drained light. In the moonlight he had seemed merely tallish, well enough

built, and had moved easily, with that air of self-confidence that goes
with strength – or with inherited wealth. Now, as he straightened in the
sunlight to face me, it was as if the film had spun along swiftly, and the
actor had, with skilful makeup, confirmed the passage of years. His hair,
which had been very dark, was showing grey; not gracefully, at the
temples, but in an untidy flecking all over, like the dimming of dust. The
fine structure of strong bone couldn't be altered, but there were lines I
hadn't seen by moonlight, and he was thinner than the size of his frame
should have allowed. Before, he had been conventionally dressed, and I
had noticed neither the cut nor the quality of his clothes; but now the
light showed up a working shabbiness that – so unconsciously he wore
it – must have been part of every day. Some part of my mind said that
of course it was only common sense to wear rough clothes for a rough
job, but another part, that I had not known existed, linked the shabbiness
with the lines on his face, and the greying hair, and winced away from
them with a pity I knew he didn't want, and that I had no right to feel.
I noticed that he was wearing gloves, and remembered my taunt about
his hands, and was sorry.

He smiled at me, narrowing his eyes against the sun. They were grey-
blue, and puckered at the corners. He spoke easily, as if there could be
no constraint between us.

'Hullo. Were you looking for Johnny Rudd? I'm afraid he's gone.'

'I came for some strawberries. The cat's been at the trifle, and it's
Grandfather's birthday, so Lisa rang up with an S.O.S., and Johnny
said he'd try to save some.'

'Then he'll have left them up in the packing-shed. Come and see.'

We walked up the path together. I saw him eyeing me, as curious as
I had been, no doubt, to see what the daylight showed.

I said: 'Have you met Julie's young man? Donald Seton?'

'No. Why?'

'He came across with me just now, to see you about something, but
he thought you'd have finished for the day, so he went along to the
Lodge.'

'Oh? What's it about, d'you know?'

'Yes, but I'll leave him to tell you himself.' I caught his quick look,
and smiled a little. 'Oh, don't worry, it's nothing personal. You're still
quite safe.'

We had reached a door in the wall behind the green-houses, which led
to the workrooms of the place – boiler-room, potting-houses, cold frames.
He stopped with his hand on the knob, and turned. I noticed all at once
that his eyes looked tired, as if he didn't sleep well. 'Safe? *I?*'

'Indeed, yes. If you're not an accessory after the fact, I don't know
what you are. You never came after that passport. You never came across
to Whitescar, and tried to trip me up and catch me out in front of
Grandfather, as no doubt you think you could easily have done. You've
done nothing. Why?'

'I don't know. I honestly don't know.' He hesitated, as if to say something more. Then, instead, he merely turned, and pushed the door open for me. 'This way, now; leave the door, it's all right; Seton may come looking for me. Is Julie with him?'

'No. She's gone into Newcastle with Bill Fenwick.'

He shot me a look. 'That troubles you. Why?'

'Because Con won't like it one bit,' I said crisply, 'and Con is a . . . creature of impulse.'

'That's absurd.' He said it as he had done before, but with just a shade less conviction.

'Any situation bordering on violence is absurd – until it suddenly breaks, and then, *wham*, there you are, in the middle of something you'd thought only happened in the Sunday Press.'

'What about this man who's here, Seton, was it?'

'That's different. He'll take her away from Whitescar, and they'll live in London, and spend half the year in a tent somewhere, digging. Con's all for that, as you may imagine – and the further away, the better. Uzbekistan, for instance, or the Desert of Lop, if the Romans went there. I wouldn't know.'

'Does she want to go?'

'Pining to,' I said cheerfully. 'Don't worry, I've practically fixed it. I told you I'd look after Julie.' I caught his eye, and laughed. 'What is it?'

'This – crazy business; and I'm as crazy as any part of it. That's what comes of working by instinct instead of sense; I suppose women do it every day, but I'm not accustomed to it, and I dislike it. There's nothing to assure you that you're still rational. Look at the situation: I'm not sure who you are; I'm not sure what you're doing; I'm certain it's wrong; but for some reason I'm prepared to let you do it.'

'I told you who I was, and what I was doing.'

'Yes, you did. You were honest, as far as that went. And you've got me into a position where I seem to be condoning what you do, even though I'm damned if I do more. I suppose it's because I think rather a lot of old Mr. Winslow, and oddly enough, I'd trust you over Julie, who seems to me to be the only other person who matters. I confess I'd wondered, before you came, just what the set-up would be at Whitescar, when Mr. Winslow died. You say you're "looking after" her interests. Well, as long as Julie comes to no harm, I don't much care how you and Connor fight it out the rest of the way. If you can get it, I shan't grudge you your "competence".'

'You needn't worry; you can trust me over Julie.'

He sighed. 'The odd thing is, that I believe you, and for that alone I deserve to be behind bars as an accessory, just as soon as you are. Here's the packing-shed. Come and see if Johnny's left your strawberries.'

The shed was big and cool, its basic smell, of geraniums and damp peat, dizzily overlaid by that of a tank crammed full with sweet peas. It was as orderly as the garden: there were shelves of plant-pots and boxes, in graded sizes; printed labels in rows (probably in alphabetical order); raffia hanging in loops that looked as if they would never dare tangle or snap; and two or three pairs of clean cotton gloves on a hook beside the window.

I watched Adam Forrest with some awe as he crossed the shed and reached down a pair of these. There were two punnets of strawberries on a bench to the left of the window. 'Enough, do you think?' he asked.

'I think so.'

'There may be a few more ripe, in the bed by the dove-houses. I can pick them, if you've time to wait.'

'No, don't trouble. I'm sure there'll be enough, and I promised to get back quickly. Dinner's at half-past seven, and we'll have them to pick over. Look, I brought a basket. We can tip them all in together, and you can keep the punnets.'

'It comes cheaper that way,' agreed Adam gravely.

I gaped at him for a second, for some absurd reason more embarrassed than at any time in our too-rapidly intimate relationship. Lisa hadn't mentioned money; I had none with me, and hadn't thought about it till now. I said, stammering: 'I – I'm afraid I can't pay for them now.'

'I'll charge them,' said Adam imperturbably. He reached for a note-book, and made a jotting on a meticulously-columned page headed 'Winslow'. He caught my eye on him, and grinned, and suddenly, in the shadowed shed, the years fell away, and there was the lover of the moonlit tryst, the actor of that early film. I caught my breath. He said: 'Whitescar runs an account. They don't seem to have time to grow any vegetables there themselves . . . I doubt if anybody has even touched the garden' – he shut the book and returned it neatly to its place – 'since you left. Careful! You're spilling those! What did I say to make you jump.'

'You know quite well. You did it deliberately. You . . . got under my skin.'

'That makes two of us,' said Adam; at least, that's what I thought he said, but he muttered it under his breath, and the words were swallowed as he turned his head quickly to the door, adding aloud: 'I suppose this is Mr. Seton?'

'Oh . . . hullo, Donald. Yes, Mr. Forrest's still here. Mr. Seton, Adam . . . '

The men exchanged greetings. Donald said: 'You got your strawberries?'

'I did. Your dinner's safe. I told Mr. Forrest you wanted to see him, Donald, but I managed to keep quiet about the reason.'

'You needn't have done that.' He turned to Adam. 'I don't know if Annabel told you, sir, but I'm an archaeologist; I'm attached to the Commission – the Royal Commission on Historical Monuments – and just at present I'm in charge of the work being done up at West Woodburn.'

'I had heard that excavating has started there,' said Adam. 'Just what are you hoping to do?'

'Well, the Commission's job is to list and describe all existing Roman monuments, with maps and photographs and so on – to make a complete survey, eventually covering the whole country. It's worked on a county basis, and I'm one of the team assigned to Northumberland. We haven't got very far, yet, with this particular site; I've got some students from Durham and London working for me on the job, and we're now busy on a trial trench . . .'

I had got the strawberries all tipped into my basket, but lingered a little, interested to hear the outcome of what Donald had to say. He gave Adam a very brief account of the work he was engaged on, and then passed, with an admirably Scottish economy of time and words, to the business of the moment.

When he described how he had seen the 'Roman stones' in the quarry, it was obvious that he had caught Adam's interest. 'And you think it likely, if that quarry *was* originally Roman, that there may be some Roman buildings near by?'

'Fairly near, at any rate,' said Donald. 'There's nothing remarkable about the rock itself – the quarried rock – if you follow me. If it were marble, for example, you might expect it to be worked, even if it had to be carried long distances; but this kind of sandstone is the common local stone. If the Romans did start a quarry there, then they would do so for pure reasons of convenience. In other words, they were building locally.'

'I see,' said Adam, 'and am I right in thinking that there's nothing recorded hereabouts? I've never read of anything, though I've always been interested in local history.'

'Quite right. There's nothing nearer than the camp at Four Laws, and, since that's on Dere Street, the materials for building it would certainly be taken from somewhere on the road, not right across country from here. So it did occur to me that, if the quarry was started here, in the peninsula, when the same stone occurs all along the ridge above the river . . . and is rather more get-at-able there . . . it did occur to me to wonder if whatever was built, was built on the peninsula itself.'

'Somewhere in Forrest Park?'

'Yes. I wanted to ask your permission to have a look round, if I may.'

'With the greatest of pleasure. I'm afraid the Forestry Commission acres are out of my jurisdiction, but the meadowland, and the Hall grounds, by all means. Go where you like. But what exactly will you be looking for? Surely anything there was, will be deep under several feet of earth and trees by now?'

'Oh yes. But I did wonder if you could help me. Can you remember if there's anything else in the way of a quarry, anything that might be an overgrown pit, or artificial bank – you know the kind of thing?'

'Not at the moment, but I'll think it over. The only pit I can think of is the old ice-house near the Forrest Lodge. That's dug deep into the earth under the trees, but that can hardly – wait a minute!'

He broke off, his brows knitted in an effort of memory. I watched him half-excitedly, Donald with the utmost placidity. Doubtless he was very much better aware than I was, that 'discoveries' rarely, if ever, come out of the blue.

'The ice-house,' said Adam. 'Mentioning the ice-house struck a chord. Wait a minute, I can't be sure, but somewhere, some time, when I was a child, I think ... I've seen something at Forrest. A stone ... Roman I'll swear.' He thought a moment longer, then shook his head. 'No, it's gone. Could it have been the same ones, I wonder, that I saw? The ones in the quarry?'

'Not unless there was a very dry season, and you probably wouldn't have noticed them unless they were even nearer the surface than they are now. Wouldn't you say so, Annabel?'

'Certainly. And anyway, nobody but an expert could possibly have guessed those *were* Roman. They looked quite ordinary to me, and to a child they'd mean nothing at all.'

'That's true. You can't remember anything more, sir? What made you think it was Roman stone? Why the ice-house? What is the ice-house anyway?'

'A primitive sort of refrigerator. They usually built them somewhere in the grounds of big houses, in the eighteenth century,' said Adam. 'They were big square pits, as a rule, dug somewhere deep in the woods where it was cool. They had curved roofs, with the eaves flush with the ground, and a door in one end, over the pit. People used to cut the ice off the lake – there's a small pool beyond the house – in winter, and store it underground in layers of straw, to bring out in summer. The one at Forrest's in the woods near the old lodge.'

'Then you may have seen this thing there, surely? It was quite usual for later builders to lay hands on any Roman stones they could, to use again. They were good blocks, well shaped and dressed. If there were a few left stacked in the old quarry, above water-level, a local eighteenth-century builder may well have taken them and – '

'The cellars!' said Adam. 'That was it! Not the ice-house, we weren't allowed in; it wasn't safe, and it was kept locked. We weren't allowed in the cellars, either, but that was different; they were at least accessible.' He grinned. 'I thought there was something surreptitious and candle-lit about the memory, and it also accounts for the fact that we never mentioned it to anyone. I'd forgotten all about it until this moment. Yes, I'm fairly sure it was in the cellars at Forrest. I can't remember any more than that, except that we were rather intrigued for the moment, as children are, by the carving on the stone. It was upside down, which made it harder to make out what it said, even if we could have – '

'What it *said*?' Donald's voice was sharp, for him.

Adam looked surprised. 'Yes. Didn't you say the stones were carved?'

There was some sort of lettering, as far as I remember, and a carving of some kind . . . an animal.'

'I said "chiselled", not "carved",' said Donald. 'If you're right, it sounds as if you may have seen an inscription. All I saw were the ordinary tooling-marks on the stone, the marks made by dressing with chisels. Like this . . .' He fished in his inside pocket, and came out with a thick wad of papers. There seemed to be (besides a wallet, several dozen letters and a driving-licence) an Ordnance Survey map of the North Tyne, and a thin booklet of what looked like – but surely could not be – logarithms. Donald looked at them vaguely, selected an old envelope, on which I distinctly saw a postmark two years old, and restored the rest to his pocket.

Adam handed him a pencil. 'Thanks. This,' said Donald, drawing with beautiful economy and accuracy on the dog-eared envelope, 'is something like the stones I saw.'

He handed the paper to Adam, who studied it. 'I see. No, that conveys nothing to me; I'd never have known that was Roman . . . not even now, let alone at ten years old. Well, the obvious thing to do is to go and look, isn't it? This is really rather exciting. If it turns out to be an inscription of the Ninth Legion or something, will Forrest's fortune be re-made?'

'Well,' said Donald cautiously, 'you might get it on to T.V. . . . The house is a ruin, isn't it? Is it still possible to get into the cellars?'

'I think you'll find you can get down. I don't have to tell you to watch yourself: I'm not sure what sort of condition the place is in. But you may certainly go just where you like. Look, I'll make you a plan.'

He reached to the nearby shelf for a paper – it looked like an invoice-form – and spread it on the bench. Donald handed back the pencil. I came to Adam's elbow to look. He drew a couple of lines, then, with a subdued exclamation of irritation, pulled off the cotton gloves, dropped them on the bench beside him, and picked the pencil up again. 'I can't write in them. Do you mind?'

'Mind?'

Then I saw. His hands were disfigured, most horribly, it must have been by burns. The skin was white and dead-looking, glassed like polythene, and here and there were puckered scars that showed purple; the shape of his hands, like the other bone-structure, had been beautiful, but the injuries had distorted even that, and made them hideous, things to shock. Things to hide, as, until now, he had hidden them. This was something else that the romantic moonlighting had not revealed.

I must have made some small sound, some little gasp of indrawn breath. Adam's pencil checked, and he looked at me.

I suppose most people stared like that, sick and shocked, for a moment or two, then looked quickly away, saying nothing, talking of something else, pretending not to have seen.

I said: 'Adam, your hands, your poor hands . . . What did that to your hands?'

'I burned them.'

The fire at Forrest. His wife. '*The bed was alight by that time. H*
managed to drag the bedclothes off her, and carry her downstairs . . .'

He had reached one of those terrible hands for the discarded gloves
He hadn't taken his eyes off my face. He said gently: 'I'll put them o
again. I'm sorry, I forgot you wouldn't know. It's rather a shock, the firs
time.'

'It – it doesn't matter. Don't, for me . . . I – I've got to go.' I reache
blindly for the basket. I could feel the tears spilling hot on to my cheeks
and couldn't stop them. I had forgotten all about Donald, till I hear
him say 'Here,' and the basket was put into my hands. I said shakily
'I've got to hurry back. Good-bye,' and, without looking at either of them
my head bent low over the basket, I turned and almost ran out of th
packing-shed.

I was conscious of the silence I had left behind me, and of Adam
straightening abruptly, the pencil still in his hand, staring after me.

CHAPTER FOURTEEN

Go with your right to Newcastle,
And come with your left side home;
There will you see these two lovers. . . .

Ballad: *Fair Margaret and Sweet William*

As it turned out, there were more than enough strawberries for supper
Julie didn't come back.

The dinner, though delicious, could hardly be said to be festive. It wa
as if all the accumulated tensions of the last days had gathered tha
evening at the dining-table, building slowly up like the thunderhead
that stood steadily on the horizon outside.

Con had come in early, rather quiet, with watchful eyes, and line
from nostril to chin that I hadn't noticed before. Grandfather seemed t
have recruited his energies with his afternoon rest: his eyes were brigh
and a little malicious as he glanced round the table, and marked the tau
air of waiting that hung over the meal. It was his moment of power, an
he knew it.

If it had needed anything to bring the tensions to snapping-point
Julie's absence provided it. At first it was only assumed that she wa
late, but, as the meal wore through, and it became apparent that sh
wasn't coming, Grandfather started making irritatingly frequent remark
about the forgetfulness and ingratitude of young people, that wer
intended to sound pathetic, but only managed to sound thoroughly bad
tempered.

Con ate more or less in silence, but a silence so unrelaxed as to b
almost aggressive. It was apparent that Grandfather thought so, for h

kept casting bright, hard looks under his brows, and once or twice seemed on the verge of the sort of edged and provocative remark with which he had been prodding his great-nephew for days.

I drew what fire I could, chattering shamelessly, and had the dubious satisfaction of attracting most of the old man's attention to myself, some of it so obviously affectionate – pointedly so – that I saw, once or twice, Con's glance cross mine like the flicker of blue steel. Afterwards, I thought, when he knows, when that restless, torturing ambition is stilled at last, it will be all right; everything will be all right . . .

As Grandfather had predicted, Donald's presence saved the day. He seconded my efforts with great gallantry, making several remarks at least three sentences long; but he, too, was unable to keep his eyes from the clock, while Lisa, presiding over a magnificent pair of ducklings *à la Rouennaise*, and the strawberries hastily assembled into whipped cream *Chantilly*, merely sat unhelpfully silent and worried, and, in consequence, looking sour.

The end of the meal came, and the coffee, and still no Julie. We all left the dining-room together. As Con pushed back his chair, he said abruptly: 'I'm going to telephone Nether Shields.'

'What the devil for?' asked Grandfather testily. 'If the girl chooses to forget, let her be.'

'She's not likely to have forgotten. I'm afraid there may have been an accident.'

'Then what's the use of telephoning Nether Shields? If they knew anything, they'd have rung us up. The girl's forgotten. Don't waste your time.'

'I'll ring, all the same,' said Con, and left the room abruptly. Grandfather's gaze as he watched him was bright and sardonic

To forestall what comment he might make, I said quickly: 'If she did forget, she may have gone back to supper with Bill Fenwick.'

'Nonsense,' said Grandfather roundly, and stumped out of the dining-room.

In the drawing-room Lisa poured coffee, her attention stolidly on the cups. Grandfather mercifully relapsed into silence, fidgeting with his fingers, and forgetting to drink his coffee. Donald was still watching the clock, though I suspected that his motives had altered somewhat. I'd have given a lot, myself, to go for a long, long walk, preferably several miles away from Whitescar.

'If anything has happened to that child – ' began Grandfather, at length.

'Nothing will have happened,' I said. 'You'd have heard if there'd been an accident. She'd have rung up . . . or someone else would. Don't worry, it'll be all right. She'll turn up soon.'

'If a tyre burst when they were miles from anywhere – ' Donald put in a comforting oar – 'that could delay them.'

'As long as this? It's nine o'clock.'

'Mphm,' said Donald.

I glanced anxiously at Grandfather. The bright malice had faded. He looked his age, and more, and the hand with which he pushed aside his untasted coffee was shaking a little.

Con came back into the room.

'Nothing,' he said tersely. 'Mrs. Fenwick knew Julie was due back here for dinner. Bill said he'd be home by seven. No sign.'

'I told you it was no use telephoning!' Grandfather almost snapped it. 'But you know best, as usual.'

Con took the coffee which Lisa had stirred and handed to him. 'It was a chance,' he said, mildly enough. 'And I thought it might save you worrying.'

'You're very solicitous of others, all of a sudden, aren't you, Connor? Why so anxious? Because you want to see the family all assembled together? Lisa tell you what I said at luncheon, eh?'

It was unforgivable enough, especially in front of Donald, but normally it would hardly have worried anyone. Con's reaction was indicative, uncomfortably so, of the pressure that had been building up behind the quiet, sealed front.

He went rather pale, and put down his coffee half-drunk. He didn't even look where he was setting the cup, but put it blindly down on what would have been a vacancy, if Lisa had not quietly taken it out of his hand. For a moment he and Grandfather stared at one another, and I waited, with a sort of horror, for the valves to blow.

Then Con said: 'If I'm wanted, I'll be in the field,' and turned his back on his great-uncle. 'Good night, Seton.' Quietly still, but like one escaping to a freer, purer air, he went out of the room.

Unexpectedly, Grandfather chuckled. 'Good lad,' he said, with a sort of fierce approval, then turned a ghost of his old charming smile on Donald. 'I warned you, didn't I? You'll have to forgive us for thrusting our family squabbles on you.'

Donald returned some sort of polite reply, and, thereafter, the conversation trickled back into fairly normal channels. But half an hour went by, and still there was no sign of Julie, nor did the telephone ring. I must have shown how worried I was, and Grandfather took to saying, at shorter and shorter intervals: 'Where on earth can the child have got to?' or alternatively: 'Why the devil couldn't she have telephoned?' until I could see it was getting across even Donald's admirable nervous system. I wasn't surprised when, almost too soon for civility, he rose to his feet, and said he thought he had better be going.

No one made any attempt to stop him. Lisa got up with rather too patent relief, and let him carry the coffee-cups out to the kitchen for her.

I followed. 'I'll come back in a minute, Lisa, when I've done the gate for Donald. Leave them for me: you said you would.'

It was dusk in the lee of the big barn, where Donald had parked his car. When I reached it, I couldn't see him. Puzzled, I paused beside the car, peering around me into the shadows

Then I heard a soft step, and turned swiftly. Donald came very quietly round the end of the barn, from the direction of the stable-yard. Seeing me waiting beside the car, he stopped abruptly, and even in that light I could see he was out of countenance. I stared at him, completely at a loss for words. He looked like a man who has been caught out in a dubious act.

There was one of those ghastly pauses, then he smiled. 'It's all right, I haven't been hiding the silver behind the barn. I've been visiting friends.'

'Friends?' I said, blankly.

He laughed. 'Come and see.'

I followed him into the yard, where he pushed open the half-door of the empty stable. The interior smelt sweet and dry, of hay and horses. Opposite the door was a big loose-box, the bars down now, since Blondie had gone out to grass. Donald switched on the light, and led the way into the loose-box. There was an iron manger running the breadth of it, deep, and half full of clean straw. I supposed the hens laid there sometimes.

'Here,' said Donald softly, 'meet the family.'

I leaned over the manger. Deep in the straw was a nest, but not of eggs. Seven kittens, some days old, still blind and boneless, all sleeping soundly, lay curled together in a tight, furry mass, black and white and ginger. Donald put down a gentle hand to touch the warm fur. As he did so, a wraith, black and white, jumped on to the iron manger at his elbow, purred softly, and slid down beside the kittens. There was a wriggling, and butting, and readjusting of fur, then Tommy settled down, eyes slitted and happy, paws steadily kneading the rustling straw.

'How on earth did you find them?' I whispered.

'Tommy showed me tonight, when I got back from West Lodge.'

'Well, I'll keep your secret. Nobody'll come in here, while the horses are out . . . Did you really have to leave so early?'

'I thought I'd better.'

'Mm, yes, I see what you mean.' We left the darkened stable quietly, and walked back to the car. Beside it, I hesitated for a moment, then turned quickly to him. 'Look, Donald, don't worry.'

'Aren't you worrying?'

'Well, one can't help it, can one? But nothing'll have happened. Depend on it, they've forgotten, and stayed out to a meal, or something.'

'It seems unlikely.'

'Well, perhaps the car *has* broken down.'

'Mphm,' said Donald.

'Why don't you wait? They really ought not to be long.'

'No, thanks, but I won't. Did I remember to thank Miss Dermott for the supper?'

'You thanked her very nicely. No, I'll do the gate.'

'Oh, thank you . . .' But he lingered, a hand on the car door. He seemed about to say something, then I thought he changed his mind. What he did say, rather tentatively, was: 'Nice chap, Forrest.'

'Yes.'

'He seems interested in this quarry. He says he'll come over himself tomorrow, and hunt up that stone in the cellar with me.'

'I hope you'll find it. Does it sound to you as if it could be the real thing?'

'That's impossible to tell, but I think it may well be, if only because he's kept that strong impression, all these years, that it was Roman. He thinks there must have been at least one or two words that he and his sister would have recognised as Latin, even at the age of nine or ten.' He grinned. 'He reckons that an EST or a SUB would have been about their limit at the time. Let's hope he's right.'

'It's terribly exciting, isn't it?'

'At best,' said Donald cheerfully, 'it'll probably simply say "Vote for P. Varro as quarry foreman. Shorter hours and longer pay." '

I laughed. 'Well, good luck to it, anyway.'

'Would you care to come along tomorrow afternoon and help in the hunt?'

'No, thanks, I won't. I – I have things I've got to do.'

'Mphm,' said Donald. This time it seemed to signify a vague agreement. He hesitated again, and suddenly I found myself wondering if Julie had told him anything about Adam.

I glanced up at him. 'I'm sorry I was upset this afternoon. Did he – did he mind, d'you think?'

'He didn't seem to.' Donald spoke so quickly that I realised that this was exactly what he had been wanting to say, and hadn't liked to broach the subject, even to bring me comfort. 'He said nothing. I'm sure he'd understand. I shouldn't worry.'

'I won't,' I said. 'Good night, Donald.'

'Good night.'

The car's engine started with a roar, and the ancient vehicle jerked forward. I saw Donald lift a hand as he passed me, then the car grumbled its way off into the dusk towards High Riggs and the top of the hill.

The washing-up was done, and we were back in the drawing-room, Lisa with some mending for Con, myself playing a rather abstracted game of cribbage with Grandfather, when at length we heard a car enter the yard. Almost before it had drawn to a halt, one of its doors slammed; there was a short pause, and, faintly, the sound of voices, then the car moved off again immediately, and high heels tapped quickly across the yard to the kitchen door. We heard Julie cross the kitchen lobby and push open the green baize door to the hall. Then the hasty steps tapped their way across the hall, and were on the carpeted stairs.

Grandfather put his cards down with a slam, and shouted: 'Julie!'

The flying steps stopped. There was a pause.

'*Julie!*'

She came slowly down the stairs again, and crossed the hall to the drawing-room door. With another part of my mind I heard the car's engine receding over the hill.

The drawing-room door opened. Julie stood there for a moment before she came in. Her eyes went swiftly round the room, and came to rest on Grandfather. Her hair was ruffled from the ride in the open car; her colour was high, and her eyes shone brilliantly, as the pupils dilated to meet the light. She looked very lovely; she also looked like the conventional picture of the young girl fresh from her lover's embrace, confused by the sudden light and the watching eyes. For a moment I wondered, with a sinking heart, if I had been wrong, and her interest in Bill Fenwick was serious, but then – I'm not quite sure how, except that Julie and I were so much alike – I knew, with relieved certainty, that the confused brilliance of her glance was due, not to love and embarrassment, but to sheer temper.

I saw Lisa's plump hands check in their work, and the sock she was mending sink slowly to her lap, as she stared at Julie with what looked like speculation.

'Julie!' Grandfather sounded angry. 'Where have you been? We've spent the whole evening waiting and watching for you, and worrying in case anything had happened. Heaven knows I don't expect you to remember anything so completely unimportant as your grandfather's birthday, but I do think – '

'I'm sorry, Grandfather.' Her voice was tolerably composed, but I saw how white her hand was on the door-knob. 'I – we meant to get back. I didn't forget – there was an accident.'

'An accident?' The old man's hands had been flat on the table among the cards. I saw them twitch, like a puppet's hands pulled by strings threaded through the arms.

I looked up quickly. 'I take it nobody's hurt?'

She shook her head. 'No, it was a silly thing. It wasn't Bill's fault. We weren't going fast – it was in the speed-limit area, and Bill really was driving quite slowly. Somebody backed out of a garage straight into us.'

'Was Bill's car damaged?'

'Yes. The door panel was dented, and he'd hit the front wheel, and Bill was afraid he'd knocked it out of true, and bent the track rod, or whatever you call it, but he hadn't. Then there was all the fuss, and the police – ' she swallowed ' – you know how it is; and then we had to get the car back to a garage and let them see what the damage was, and Bill had to arrange to take it back later to have it done. I – we couldn't help it, really we couldn't.'

'Of course you couldn't, I said. 'Look, honey, have you had supper? Because – '

'You could have telephoned,' said Grandfather sharply. I noticed he was breathing hard, and the thin fingers twitched among the fallen cards.

'I'm sorry,' said Julie again, but with something too sharp and driven-sounding in her voice. Outside, the yard gate clashed, and I saw her jump. 'I know I should have, but I didn't think of it till we were on the way home. You – you know how it is, with everything happening, and Bill's car, and the other man being foul about it, and telling all sorts of lies to the police, only they did believe Bill and me ...' Her voice quavered and she stopped.

Grandfather opened his mouth to speak, but I forestalled him.

'She'd be too upset to think about it, Grandfather. You know what even the smallest of accidents is like; it shakes you right to pieces. Well, it's lucky it's no worse.' Then, to Julie, 'We thought it might be something like this; we knew you wouldn't have skipped the party unless something had happened. Look, my dear – ' I got to my feet – 'it's obvious you've had a shaking. I think you should get yourself straight upstairs to bed. I'll bring you something to eat; there's plenty left ... That was a wonderful meal you missed – Aylesbury ducklings, and strawberries straight off the straw. Tommy ate the trifle.'

'Did he?' said Julie uncertainly. 'Lisa, really, I'm terribly sorry, but – '

Lisa said: 'Donald Seton was here.' It was impossible to tell, from her composed, colourless tone, whether or not she was actuated by deliberate malice.

The result was the same. Julie bit her lip, stammered, and looked ready to cry. 'Here? I – I didn't think he was coming.'

I said gently: 'I met him when I was on my way back from Bellingham. His London colleague had left early, and he was free, so I told him we were expecting him. He'd obviously been hoping to come, anyway.' I smiled. 'He'd changed into a very respectable suit.'

'He left some time ago,' said Lisa. 'We thought he would wait to see you, but he said he had to go.'

Julie turned to look at her, but vaguely, as if she wasn't really seeing her. I said, as lightly as I could: 'I hope this all happened *after* the play? You saw that all right?'

'Oh, yes. It – it was wonderful.'

'Then I expect, when you've had a rest,' I said briskly, 'you'll vote it was worth it, accident or no. Now, darling, I really think – '

The baize door opened and swung shut on a *whoosh* of air. Con came quickly across the hall, to pause in the open doorway behind Julie.

He had changed back into his work-clothes before he had gone up to the field, and in breeches and open-necked shirt he looked tough, and also extremely handsome. And this for the same reason as Julie. He, too, was in a flaming temper, and it didn't need much gazing in the crystal ball to guess that the pair of them had just had a monumental row.

Julie never even turned her head on his approach. She merely hunched one shoulder a little stiffly, as if he were a cold draught behind her, and said to Lisa, on a strained, high note: 'Did Donald say anything?'

'What about?' asked Lisa.

'No, Julie,' I said.

Grandfather's hand scuffed irritably at the cards on the table in front of him. 'What's all this? What's all this? Young Seton? What's he got to do with it?'

'Nothing,' said Julie. 'Nothing at all!' Her voice went thin and high. 'And nor has Con!' She flung him a glance over her shoulder, about as friendly as a volley of swan-shot.

'Con?' Grandfather's eyes went from one to the other. 'Con?' he repeated querulously. 'Where does Con come into this?'

'That's just it!' said Julie, dangerously. 'He doesn't, for all he seems to think he's the master here, and I'm answerable to him! Can you *imagine* –?' She checked herself, and went on in a voice that trembled insecurely on the edge of self-control? 'Just now, as we came back, Bill had to stop the car for the gate at High Riggs – you know the grid's broken, and you've to use the gate – well, Con saw fit to come over, and ask me where the hell I'd been (I'm sorry, Grandfather, but I'm only saying what *he* said), and why was I so late, and, as if that wasn't bad enough he started pitching into Bill! As if it had been Bill's fault! Even if it *had*, it's not *your* business – ' swinging on her cousin – 'to start anything like that! What put *you* in such a howling temper, for heaven's sake? Speaking to Bill like that, swearing and everything, making a fool of me ... and I'll be very surprised if he shows his face here again! He was furious, and I don't blame him! I had to apologise for you! How do you like *that*?'

'You know, Connor,' said Grandfather, mildly enough, 'you ought not to have done this. Julie's explained it to us. It wasn't young Fenwick's fault that – '

'That's not the *point*!' cried Julie. 'Don't you *see*? Even if it *had* been Bill's fault or mine, it's *none of Con's business*! If I choose to stay out all *night*, that's *my* affair!'

'And mine,' said Grandfather, with sudden grim humour.

'All right,' said Julie, 'yours! But not Con's! He takes too dashed much on himself, and always did! It's time someone said something. It's been going on for years, without anyone noticing, and now this – *this* sort of thing – is the last straw as far as I'm concerned! Being ticked off like a naughty child in front of Bill Fenwick, and all because – ' she mimicked Con's voice – 'it was "vital we should all have been here tonight, and now Great-Uncle Matthew's as mad as fire!" ' She swung back on Con. 'So what?' I've explained to him, and that's all there is to it. Why should you make it your business? You're not the master here yet, and as far as *I'm* concerned you never will be!'

'Julie!' I said sharply. 'That's enough!'

They ignored me. Grandfather thrust his head forward, his eyes intent under scowling brows. 'And just what do you mean by that?'

'Just,' said Julie, 'that this is my home, and Con – why Con doesn't even *belong* here! And I'm beginning to think there isn't room for both of us, not any more! If I'm to be able to go on coming here – '

Grandfather slammed the cards down on the table in front of him. 'And now, perhaps you'll let me speak! What you appear to forget, all of you, is that this is *my* house . . . still! Oh, I know you think I'm old, and sick, and that I'll go at any moment; I'm not a fool, that may be true, and by heaven, from the sort of scene you've made tonight, you appear to be eager to see the last of me! No, keep quiet, you've said enough; you've had a shaking, and I'll excuse you for that reason, and we'll say no more, but let me make this clear; this is my house, and while I'm alive I'll expect civil conduct in it, or you, Julie, and you, Connor, can both of you go elsewhere! And now I'm going to bed.' And he put shaky hands to the arms of his chair.

Julie said raggedly, on a sob: 'I'm sorry, Grandfather. I – I am a bit shaken up, I guess. I didn't mean to upset you. I don't want any food, Annabel. I'm going upstairs.'

She turned past Con as if he didn't exist, and ran out of the room.

Con hadn't moved. It wasn't until that moment, when we were all looking at him, that I realised that, since he had come in, he hadn't spoken. His face seemed to have emptied even of anger, and gone blank. His eyes looked unfocused.

'Well?' said Grandfather, harshly. 'What are you waiting for?'

Con turned on his heel without a word, and went back across the hall. The baize door whispered itself shut behind him.

I stooped over Grandfather's chair. 'Darling, don't upset yourself. Julie's a bit strung-up tonight; she's more shaken than she knows . . . and Con . . . Con's been working far too hard, you know he has, and I guess he's tired. It wasn't very sensible of him to tackle Julie, but if they hadn't both been a bit edgy, it wouldn't have come to anything. I expect they'll apologise in the morning.'

He looked up at me, almost vaguely, as if the effort of that last speech had exhausted him. He looked very old, and tired, and almost as if he didn't quite know who I was. He said, muttering it to himself rather than to me: 'Always the same. Always the same. Too highly-strung, that's what it is, your mother always said so; and Julie's the same. History repeats itself.' The faded eyes focused on me then. 'Annabel. Should have married Con in the first place, as I wanted. Settled the pair of you. Settled this. I'm going to bed.'

I bent to help him rise, but as soon as he was on his feet he shook me off almost pettishly. 'I can manage, I can manage. No, don't come with me. I don't want a pack of women. And that goes for you, too, Lisa. Good God, d'you think I can't see myself to bed?'

He went slowly to the door. I thought, he really is old; the tallness, and the sudden flashes of energy are what deceive us . . . Something closed round me that might have been loneliness, or fear . . .

He went out. Lisa and I were left looking at one another.

I remember thinking, with something like a shock, one forgets she's there; she heard all that; she heard what was said to Con . . .

She had put her work composedly away. For all she showed it, the scene might never have taken place. As she moved towards the door, I said quickly: 'He meant it, you know. I wouldn't upset him by saying anything else.'

'I wasn't going to. I'm going to bed. Good night.'

It didn't even seem strange at the time that it was Lisa who should go unconcernedly upstairs, and I who should look for Con.

He was in the kitchen, sitting in the rocking-chair by the range, pulling on his gumboots. His face still wore that blind, shuttered look that was so unlike him. He glanced up briefly, then down again.

I said: 'Con, don't pay any attention. She's upset because she and Donald quarrelled, and she missed seeing him tonight. She didn't mean a thing. She doesn't really think those things, I'm sure.'

'It's my experience,' said Con woodenly, thrusting his foot down into the boot and dragging it on, 'that when people are upset they say exactly what they do think. She was quite startlingly explicit, wasn't she?'

I said, without quite realising what I was saying: 'Don't let it hurt you.'

'Hurt me?' He looked up again at that. The blue eyes held an odd expression; something puzzled, perhaps, along with a glitter I didn't like. Then he smiled, a deliberately charming smile that made goose-pimples run along my spine. 'You can't know how funny that is, Annabel, my sweet.'

'Well, my dear,' I said calmly, 'funny or not, try to see the thing in proportion. I don't know if anyone told you, but Julie and Bill Fenwick were involved in a sort of minor accident tonight. That's what made her late, and distressed her so much. Bill, too – his car was damaged, so he wouldn't be in too sweet a mood. It'll blow over.'

'What makes you explain to me?' He stood up and reached for the jacket that hung on the back of the door. 'It's none of my business. I don't belong here. Lisa and I are only the hired help.'

'Where are you going?'

'To the buildings.'

'Oh, Con, it's late. You've done enough. Aren't you tired?'

'Flaked out. But there's something wrong with the cooler, and I'll have to get it put right.' That quick, glittering look again. 'I suppose even Julie would be content to let that be my business? Or would it be interfering too much with the running of her home?'

'Con, for pity's sake –'

'Sweet of you to come and bind up the wounds, girl dear, but I assure you they don't go deep.'

'Are you sure?' His hand was already on the door-latch. I said: 'Listen. I ought not to tell you, but I'm going to. You've no need to worry any more.'

He stopped, as still as a lizard when a shadow falls across it. Then he turned. 'What d'you mean?'

'You do belong here. You've made your place . . . the way you said . . . with your two hands; and you do belong. That's all I – ought to say. You understand me. Let it go at that.'

There was a silence. The shutters were up again in his face. It was impossible to guess what he was thinking, but I should have known. He said at length: 'And the money? The capital?' Silence. 'Did he tell you?'

I nodded.

'Well?'

'I don't know if I ought to say any more.'

'Don't be a fool. He would have told us all, himself, tonight, only that damned girl made a scene.'

'I still don't think I should.'

He made a movement of such violent impatience that I was startled into remembering the perilous volcano-edge of the last few days. I had gone so far; let us have peace, I thought.

He was saying, savagely, in a low voice: 'Whose side are you on? By God, you've had me wondering, you're so thick with Julie and the old man! If you've started any thoughts of feathering your own nest – ! How do I know I can trust you? What right have you got to keep this to yourself?'

'Very well. Here it is. It comes out much as you'd expected, except that, nominally, very little of the capital comes to you.'

'How's that?' His gaze was brilliant now, fixed, penetrating.

'He's divided it between Julie and me, except for a small sum, which you get outright. He didn't say how much that was. With you inheriting the property over our heads, he thought that was only fair.' I went on to tell him what Grandfather had said to me. 'The major part is divided into three, as we'd expected, with two-thirds of it nominally mine. That can be passed to you, just as we planned.' I smiled. 'Don't forget the blackmail's mutual.'

He didn't smile back. He hardly seemed to be listening. 'Julie. Will she fight the Will? She'll have grounds.'

'I'm sure she won't. She doesn't want the place.'

'No, she just thinks I should be out of it.' He turned away, abruptly. 'Well, since the boy's not afraid of hard work, he'd better go out and get on with it, hadn't he?'

'Con, wait a minute –'

'Good night.'

He went. I stayed where I was for a moment, frowning after him. For heaven's sake, I thought, suddenly irritable, did I have to add to the tangle by feeling sorry for Con as well? Con was perfectly capable of taking care of himself; always had been; had always had to be . . . I shook myself impatiently. Con, let's face it, was a tough customer. Keep that straight, and keep out of it . . .

I went slowly upstairs, and stood on the landing for a few moments, wondering if it would be better to see Julie now, or wait till morning.

I had tried to set Con's mind at rest, with no very conspicuous success; had I the right to give Donald's confidence away, in an attempt to do the same for Julie? More urgent still was that other problem; how much to tell her of the truth about my own situation. Something had to be told her, I knew that; I hadn't yet decided how much, but it was imperative that she should be made to realise, a little more clearly, the kind of person Con was, and of what he was capable.

I hovered there for some time, between her door and my own, before it occurred to me that, by seeing her now, I could probably kill two birds with one stone: if her mind were cleared with regard to Donald, she would happily leave the Whitescar field open for Con. Let us have peace . . .

I went to the door of her room and knocked softly. There was no reply. No light showed under the door, or from the adjacent bathroom.

She could surely not be in bed yet? I tapped again and said softly: 'Julie; it's me, Annabel.'

No answer. As I stood irresolute, I heard a soft step in the passage beside me. Lisa's voice said, calmly:

'She's gone.'

I looked at her blankly. 'What?'

She smiled. ' "History repeats itself," he said, didn't he? She's run out on us.'

'Don't be absurd!' I was so shocked that I said it very angrily. She only shrugged, a slight uncaring gesture of the heavy shoulders.

'I found her room empty. Look.'

Reaching past me, she pushed the door open, and switched on the light. For a second it felt like an intolerable invasion of privacy, then I saw that, indeed, the bedroom was deserted. Julie had made no attempt to get ready for bed. Even the curtains were undrawn, and this emphasised the vacant look of the room.

'Look,' repeated Lisa. I followed her pointing finger, and saw the pretty high-heeled sandals tossed anyhow on the floor. 'You see? She's changed into flat ones.'

'But she may not have gone *out*.'

'Oh yes, she has. Her door was standing wide when I came upstairs, and then I saw her from my window. She went over the bridge.'

'Over the bridge?' I went swiftly to the window. The moon was not yet strong, and the narrow footbridge that led from the garden gate could barely be seen in the diffused lights from the house. 'But why?' I swung round. 'Lisa, you *were* joking, weren't you? She can't possibly really have – oh, no!' This as I pulled open the wardrobe door. 'Her things are here.'

'Don't worry. She won't have gone far. No such luck.'

So the scene in the drawing-room had gone home. I shut the wardrobe door with a sharp little click. 'But where can she have gone? If she only wanted to escape – go for a moonlight walk – surely she'd have gone into the river-meadows where you can see your way, or along towards Forrest Hall?'

'Heaven knows. Why worry about a silly girl's nonsense? She'll have run off to cry on her young man's shoulder, as likely as not.'

'But that's ridiculous!'

She shrugged again. 'Girls are fools at nineteen.'

'So they are.'

'In any case, I saw her go.'

'But it's miles to West Woodburn!'

Something sharpened for the first time in her gaze. 'West Woodburn? I was thinking of Nether Shields.'

'Good heavens,' I said impatiently, 'Bill Fenwick never came into it, poor chap! I thought you understood that, when you prodded her about Donald Seton tonight.'

'I didn't know. I wondered.' Her voice was as composed and uninterested as ever.

Something I didn't yet recognise as fear shook me with a violent irritation. 'Wherever she's gone, I don't much care for the idea of her wandering about the countryside at this time of night! If it *was* either West Woodburn or Nether Shields, you'd think she'd have taken the car!'

'When Con has the key in his pocket?'

'Oh. No, I see. But if she'd waited to see me –'

'And with you,' said Lisa, 'talking to Con in the kitchen?'

I stared at her for a moment, uncomprehendingly. Then I said: 'For goodness' sake, Julie couldn't be so stupid! Do you mean to say she thought I was ganging up on her? With Con? Just how young and silly can you get?'

My sharp exasperation was partly induced by the fact that I hardly understood my own motives in following Con to the kitchen. When Lisa laughed, suddenly and uncharacteristically, I stared at her for a moment, blankly, before I said slowly: 'Yes, I see that that's funny.'

'What did you say to Con?'

'Nothing much. I wanted to apologise for Julie, but he was in a hurry.'

'A hurry?'

'He was on his way out.'

The toffee-brown eyes touched mine for a moment. 'Oh?' said Lisa. 'Well, I shouldn't wait up. Good night.'

Left to myself, I crossed again to the window. There was no sign of movement from the garden, or the river-path. I strained my eyes for the glimpse of a light coat returning through the trees. Down to my right I could see the reflection of the lights from the byres where Con was working, and hear the hum of machinery. The garden below me was in darkness.

I believe I was trying to clear my mind, to think of the problem as it now faced me – Julie and Donald, Con and Lisa – but for some reason, standing there staring into the dark, I found I was thinking about Adam Forrest's hands ... Some seconds later I traced the thought to its cause; some memory of that first sunlit evening when I had seen the cat pounce in the long grass, and some creature had cried out with pain and fear.

There had been bees in the roses, then; now it was the steady hum of machinery that filled the darkness, unaltering, unfaltering in its beat ... '*History repeats itself*,' Lisa had said.

Something tugged at the skirts of my mind, jerked me awake. A formless frightening idea became certainty. Julie, running to change her shoes, seizing a coat, perhaps, creeping softly downstairs, and out ... Con, in the kitchen, hearing the door, seeing her pass the window ... Then, the girl running along the river in the dark, up the steep path where the high bank shelved over the deep pool ... that pool where the rocks could stun you, and the snags hold you down ...

'*He was on his way out*,' I had said, and Lisa had given me that look. '*Well, I shouldn't wait up.*'

The machinery ran smoothly from the byre. The lights were on.

I didn't wait to grab a coat. I slid out of the room and ran like a hare for the stairs.

CHAPTER FIFTEEN

O where hae ye been, my handsome young man?
Ballad: *Lord Randal*

I didn't even look to see if Con were in the buildings after all. The something that had taken over from my reasoning mind told me he wouldn't be. I had no time to make assurance double sure. I ran across the yard, and down the narrow river-path towards the bridge. The wicket at the end of the bridge was standing open, its white paint making it insubstantial in the dusk, like a stage property.

It was really only a few minutes since Julie had left the house. Con would hardly have had time to go up-river as far as the stepping-stones at the end of the lane, where he could cross, and wait to intercept her on the path above the pool. But the impression of haste that he had given in the kitchen, stayed with me as a spur. I ran.

The path sloped up steeply, runged like a ladder with the roots of trees. The ground was dry and hard. Above me the trees hung in still, black clouds, not a leaf stirring. It was very dark. I stumbled badly, stumbled again, and slowed to a walk, my outstretched hands reaching for the dimly-seen supporting stems of the trees. Julie would have had to go slowly, too; she could not have got so very far ...

I thought I heard a movement ahead of me, and suddenly realised what in my fear I hadn't thought of before. There was no need for silence here. If it were Con, and he knew I was coming, it might be enough.

I called shrilly: 'Julie! Julie! Con!'

Then, not far ahead of me, I heard Julie cry out. It wasn't a scream, just a short, breathless cry, almost unvoiced, that broke off short as if she'd been hit in the throat.

I called her name again, my own cry echoing the same sound of fear and shock, and ran forward as fast as I dared, through the whipping boughs of alder and hazel, and out into the little clearing above the pool.

Julie was lying on the ground, at a point where the path skirted the drop to the pool. She lay half on her back, with one arm flung wide, and her head at the brink of the drop. I saw the loose fall of her hair, pale in the moonlight, and the still paler blur of her face. Con was beside her, down on one knee. He was stooping over her to take hold of her.

I cried: 'Julie! No!' and ran out from under the trees, only to stop short as a shadow detached itself from the other side of the clearing, and crossed the open space in four large strides. Before Con could so much as turn his head, the newcomer's hand shot out, and dragged him back from Julie's body. There was a startled curse from Con, which was swallowed up in the sounds of a brief, sharp struggle, and the crashing of hazel-bushes.

After the first moment of paralysing shock, I had run straight to Julie. Her eyes were shut, but she seemed to be breathing normally. I tried quickly, desperately, straining my eyes in the dimness, to see if there were any bruises or marks of injury on her, but could find none. Where she had fallen, though the ground was hard, there was a thickish mat of dog's mercury, and her head lay in a spongy cushion of primrose-leaves. I pushed the soft hair aside with unsteady gentle fingers, and felt over her scalp.

Her rescuer trod behind me. I said: 'She's all right, Adam. I think she's only fainted.'

He sounded breathless, and I realised that he, too, had heard the cries, and come running. The noise that I had made must have masked his approach from Con. 'What's going on?' he demanded. 'Is this your cousin Julie? Who's the man?'

I said shortly: 'My cousin Con.'

'Oh.' The change in his voice was subtle but perceptible. 'What's he done to her?'

'Nothing, as far as I know. I think you've probably jumped the gun a bit. Is there any way of getting water from the river?'

'Are you trying to tell me –?'

'Be quiet,' I said, 'she's coming round.'

Julie stirred, and gasped a little. Her eyes fluttered and opened fully, dark and alive where her face had been a sealed blank. They turned to me. 'Annabel? Oh, Annabel . . .'

'Hush now, it's all right. I'm here.'

Behind me came the crash and rustle of hazel-boughs. Julie said: 'Con – '

'It's all right, Julie, nothing's going to happen. Mr. Forrest's here with us. Lie quiet.'

She whispered, like a child: 'Con was going to kill me.'

I heard Adam draw in his breath. Then Con's voice said, rather thickly, from behind us: 'Forrest? What the hell was that in aid of?'

He was on his feet, not quite steady, perhaps, with his shoulder against a tree. He put the back of his hand up to his mouth. 'What the bloody hell do you think you were doing? Have you gone mad?'

Adam said quietly: 'Did you hear what she said?'

'I heard. And why you should choose to listen to crap of that sort, without –'

'I also heard her cry out. Don't you think that perhaps it's you who've got the explaining to do?'

Con brought his hand away from his face, and I saw him looking down as if he could feel blood on it. He said violently: 'Don't be a damned fool. What sort of story's that? Kill her? Are you crazy, or just drunk?'

Adam regarded him for a moment. 'Come off it. For a start, you can tell us why she fainted.'

'How the devil do I know? She probably thought I was a ghost. I hadn't spoken a damned word to her, before she went flat out on the path.'

I said to Julie: 'Is this true?'

The scarcely perceptible movement of her head might have meant anything. She had shut her eyes again, and turned her face in to my shoulder. Con said angrily: 'Why don't you tell them it's true, Julie?' He swung back to the silent Adam. 'The simple truth of the matter is, Julie and I had words tonight, never mind why, but some pretty hard things were said. Afterwards I found out that she'd been involved in a car accident earlier in the evening, and I was sorry I'd made the scene with her. I'd seen her go flying out of the house, and I knew how upset she'd been when she went upstairs earlier . . . Annabel, blast it all, tell him this is true!'

Adam glanced down at me. 'Apart from Con's feelings,' I said, 'to which I've never had a clue, it's quite true.'

'So,' said Con, 'it occurred to me to come across and intercept her, and tell her I was sorry for what had happened, only no sooner did she see me in the path than she let out a screech like a frightened virgin, and keeled clean over. I went to see what was the matter, and the next thing was, you were manhandling me into that damned bush. Don't worry, I'll take your apologies for granted, I suppose it was quite natural for you to think what you did. But *you* –' he addressed Julie on a scarcely conciliatory note – 'it's to be hoped you'll see fit to stop making these damned silly accusations, Julie! I'm sorry I scared you, if that's what you want me to say, and I'm sorry if you've hurt yourself. Now for pity's sake try to get up, and I'll help Annabel take you home!'

But as he came towards us, Julie shrank a little against my shoulder. 'Keep away from me!'

Con stopped. Adam was standing between him and Julie, and, though I couldn't see his expression, I realised he was at something of a loss. The situation seemed to be hovering uncertainly between melodrama and farce. Then Con said, on a note of pure exasperation: 'Oh, for God's sake!' and turned on his heel and left the clearing. We could hear him, unhurrying, making his way downstream towards the bridge.

The silence in which he left the three of us was the silence of pure anticlimax. I had a strong feeling that, whatever had happened tonight, Con Winslow had walked off with the honours of war.

Adam started to say something then, I think to ask Julie a question, but I cut across it. 'That can wait. I think we'd better get Julie back to the house. Con told you the truth; she's had a shock tonight, and now a bad fright, and the sooner we get her to bed the better. Can you get up, my dear?'

'I think so. Yes, I'm all right.'

Between us, Adam and I helped her to her feet. She still seemed dazed, and was shivering a little. I pulled her coat close round her. 'Come on, darling, can you walk? We must get you back. Where were you going, anyway?'

'To Donald, of course.' This in the tone of one answering a very stupid question.

'Oh. Well, you'll see him tomorrow. Come along now, and don't worry, you're all right with Adam and me.'

She responded to my urging arm, and went forward across the clearing, but so uncertainly and slowly that Adam's arm soon came over mine to support her.

'I'd better carry you,' he said. 'It'd be quicker.'

'I'm too heavy,' protested Julie, still in that small, shaky voice quite unlike her own.

'Nonsense.' He took her up into his arms, and quite unself-consciously she put her own round his neck and held on. I went ahead of them to hold back the swinging branches, and, when we got to the bridge, opened the gate and held it. Con, even in his anger, had taken the trouble to shut and latch it.

The back door was standing open. The kitchen was dark, and the house seemed quiet. At least, I thought, snapping on the light, there was no sign of Con.

Adam paused inside the door, to say a little breathlessly: 'Shall I take her straight upstairs? I can manage.'

Julie lifted her head, blinking in the light. 'I'm all right now. Really I am. Put me down, I'm fine.'

He set her gently on her feet, but kept an arm round her. I was thankful to see that, though still pale, she didn't look anything like as drawn as she had seemed in the dead light of the moon. She managed a little smile for Adam. 'Thanks very much for . . . everything. I'm sorry to be a nuisance. All right, Annabel, I'll go to bed, but may I just sit down a minute first and get warm?'

I said: 'Put her in the rocking-chair near the stove, Adam. I'll get some brandy. Would you like a drink?'

'Thank you. Whisky, if you have it.'

When I brought the drinks through, Julie was in the rocking-chair, leaning back as if exhausted, but looking every moment more like her usual self. Adam stood by the table, watching me. At the sight of his expression, my heart sank.

'Mix your own, will you, Adam?' I said. 'Here you are, honey.'

'I loathe brandy,' said Julie, with a healthy flicker of rebellion.

'You'll take it and like it.' I lifted the cover off the stove, and slid the kettle over the hot-plate. '*And* a hot-water-bottle in your bed, and some soup or something just as soon as I get you there.' I glanced at Adam. 'It's no wonder she fainted; the silly little ass wouldn't have any supper, and all this on top of a mishap to the car she was in, and a mad quarrel with Con. Julie, there's some of tonight's soup left over. Can you take it? It was very nice.'

'As a matter of fact,' said Julie, showing signs of abandoning the rôle of invalid, 'I should adore it.'

'Then finish your brandy while I put the soup to heat, then I'll take you up to bed.'

Adam, if he heard this very palpable hint, gave no sign. As I brought the pan of soup in, he was saying to Julie: 'You're beginning to look a little better. How do you feel?'

'Not a thing wrong with me, except hunger.'

'You didn't hurt yourself – give yourself a knock or anything – when you fell?'

'I – I don't think I can have. I can't feel anything.' She prodded herself experimentally, and then smiled up at him. 'I think I'll live.'

There was no answering smile on his face. 'Then can you tell us now,' he asked, 'why you said that your cousin was going to kill you?'

I set the soup-pan on the stove with a rap. 'I don't think Julie's fit to talk about it now. I saw what happened, and –'

'So did I. I also heard what she said.' His eyes met mine across Julie's head. They were as hard as slate, and his voice was inimical. I saw Julie look quickly from the one to the other of us, and even, in that moment, spared a flicker of pity for a child's dead romance.

'You seem uncommonly concerned,' he said, 'to stop her telling her story.'

'You've heard what happened,' I said steadily, 'and there's nothing to be gained by discussing it now. If we talk much longer there's a chance we'll disturb Grandfather, and he's had more than enough upset for one

night. I know that most of what Con told you was true, and almost
certainly the last bit was, as well. Julie saw him, got a sudden fright, and
fainted. I'm fully prepared to believe that's just what happened.'

'I'm sure you are,' said Adam, and I saw Julie turn her head at his
tone.

'For heaven's sake!' I said crudely. 'You're surely not *still* trying to
make out it was attempted murder!'

I heard Julie take in a little breath. 'Annabel –'

'It's all right, darling, I know you said it, but you didn't know just
what you were saying. He'd half scared you to death, looming up like
that through the trees. Now, if you're ready –'

'Will you please let your cousin speak for herself?' said Adam.

I looked at him for a few moments. 'Very well. Julie?'

Julie looked doubtfully up at him. 'Well, it's true,' she said. Her voice
held a puzzled uncertainty that was uncommonly convincing. 'I know I
said he was trying to kill me, and I – I think I must really have thought
so, for a moment, though why, I can't quite tell you.' She broke off and
knitted her brows. 'But actually, it happened just as Con said, and
Annabel ... I'm not lying, Mr. Forrest, really I'm not. He – he never
touched me. I know it sounds silly, but I'm sure I'd never have fainted
if it hadn't been for the car accident, and then not having anything to
eat ... and then when I saw him, suddenly, like that, in the dark –' she
gave a tremulous smile – 'and, let's face it, I *was* feeling a bit wary of
him, because I'd said some pretty foul things to him, and ... well, that's
all I remember.'

I said: 'Do you want Mr. Forrest to telephone the police, and report
what happened?'

'Police?' Her eyes widened. 'What on earth for?'

'In case it happens to be true that Con meant to kill you.'

'*Con*? Annabel, how crazy can you get? Why, you don't really think – ?'

'No, honey, no. But I think that's the way Mr. Forrest's mind's
working. He threw Con into a bush.'

'*Did* you?' Julie sounded shocked, then, lamentably, began to giggle.
'Oh dear, thank you very much, but – poor Con! Next time he really *will*
try to murder me, and I don't blame him!'

I didn't dare look at Adam. I said hurriedly, to Julie: 'Darling, it's
time you went upstairs, and don't make a *sound*. Adam, I'm most
desperately sorry you've had all this – oh, my dear sweet *heaven*, the
soup!'

It was hissing gently down the sides of the pan on to the top of the
spotless stove. 'Oh, Lisa's stove, and you should *never* let soup boil! It
just shows –' as I seized a cloth and swabbed madly at the enamel – 'that
you shouldn't mix cooking and high drama. All this talk of murder –
Adam, I'm *sorry* –'

'Think nothing of it.' His face was wooden. 'I'd better go.' He turned
to Julie. 'Good night. I hope you'll feel quite all right in the morning.

Then to me: 'I hope my ill-advised attempts to help haven't made the soup quite undrinkable.'

The door shut very softly behind him.

'Annabel!' said Julie. 'Do you think he *meant* to be nasty?'

'I'm quite certain he did,' I said.

The cooler-house was clean, shining and empty. The floors had been swilled some time earlier, and were not yet dry; they gleamed under the harsh, strong light from the unshaded bulbs. Aluminium shone coldly, and enamel glared white and sterile. The machinery hummed, and this, since there was nobody in sight, gave the place an even barer, emptier appearance.

I stepped over a twist of black hosepipe, and looked through an open door into the byre. There, too, the lights glared on emptiness.

'Con?'

No reply. I crossed the wet floor and threw the switch over. The machinery stopped. The silence seemed to surge in, frightening, thick, solid. Somewhere a tap dripped, an urgent rapping on metal. I went back to the door of the byre and reached for the light-switch. My steps sounded incredibly, frighteningly loud, and so did the snap of the switch as I clicked it off. I turned back into the cooler-house.

Adam came quietly in and stood there, just inside the doorway. I stopped dead. My heart began to jerk. I must have looked white with fatigue, and as guilty as sin. I said nothing.

After a while he said: 'Covering up?'

'What?'

'For your accomplice. You knew what I meant, didn't you'?

'I suppose I did.'

'Well?'

'Look,' I said, striving to sound no more than reasonable, 'I know what you think, but, believe it or not, we told you the truth! For goodness' sake, don't try to take this thing any further!'

'Do you really think I can leave it there, after tonight?'

'But nothing *happened* tonight!'

'No, because I was there, and possibly because you were, too.'

'You surely can't think that I –!' I checked myself. 'But you heard what Julie told you.'

'I heard what you persuaded her to say. I also heard her say that Con was going to kill her.'

'She admitted she had nothing to go by! She was scared of him, and got a sudden fright – what's the use of going over and over it! You can see for yourself how seriously Julie's taking it now!'

'She trusts you. That's something I find particularly hard to take. She's another fool, it seems, but she at least has the excuse of being young, and knowing nothing against you.'

I looked at him rather blankly.

He gave a tight little smile. 'I only mean that Julie has no reason not
to trust you, whereas I had, being merely a fool "sick of an old passion".
Well, that's over. You can't expect to take any more advantage of my
folly, now.'

'But I've *told* you –'

'You've told me very loud and clear, you and Con. And Julie has
echoed you. You showed a touching family solidarity. All right, you can
tell me three more things. One, why Connor went across the river at all.'

'He explained that. He was going –'

'Oh yes, I forgot. He was going to apologise to her, wasn't he?' The
irony bit. 'Well, we'll skip that. Now tell me why he left the machinery
running while he did so? I heard it; it was going all the time, and the
lights were on. Odd, wouldn't you say? A careful type like that, who
shuts gates behind him even when he's just been chucked into a bush and
accused of murder?'

'There's – there's nothing in that. Maybe someone else was here.'

'Who else, at this time of night? No one's here now. But we'll skip
that, too. The third thing is, why did you follow Julie yourself?'

'Well, obviously, I didn't like the idea of her going out alone like that
when she was so upset.'

'Did you know Connor had gone to intercept her?'

'No, of course not! The lights were on in the byre, anyway. I thought
he was working here.'

'Then why,' said Adam, 'did you cry out – sounding so frightened, at
that – as you ran up through the wood?'

'I – I heard her scream. Of course I was frightened!'

'You called out before she made a sound.'

'Did I? I must have wanted to stop her, make her wait for me.'

'Why, in that case, did you call "Julie, Julie! *Con!*"?'

Silence.

'So you did expect him to be there?'

'I thought he might be.'

'And you were frightened.'

'Yes,' I said, 'yes, yes, yes! And don't ask me why, because I've told
you before! It was you who said it was absurd when I told you Con
might be violent.'

'I know I did. I thought you were exaggerating. Which is one of the
reasons I so stupidly believed you, when you said you could look after
Julie. Well, now we know better.'

'Listen, Adam—'

'I've done enough listening. Look at this from my point of view. You
told me you're in some racket or other which will turn out right in the
end. You persuaded me to keep out of it, God knows, how, but you did.
Now, tonight, this happens. Because I chanced to be there, no harm was
done. But you admit that Connor may have intended to do harm. That
he may be dangerous.'

'I've always admitted that.'

'Very well. But the time has come for me to stop trusting you, you must see that. In the first place, I had no reason to, except that . . . I had no reason to. Now after this—' a gesture took in the sterile, gleaming shed, and the now silent machinery – 'I have less than none.'

I said, after a pause: 'Well? I can't stop you. What are you going to do? Telephone the police? Tell them Con tried to frighten Julie to death? Even if you had some sort of case – which you haven't; even if Julie would charge Con – which she won't; even if you had me as a witness – which you haven't, what could you prove? Nothing, because there *is* nothing to prove. All you'd achieve would be a howling scandal, and Grandfather laid out, and all for nothing.'

'I might count it an achievement to have made the police take a look at you.'

'At me?' For a moment I regarded him blankly. 'Oh, *that.*'

It must have been obvious that I genuinely hadn't realised for a moment what he was talking about. I thought he was disconcerted, but he said steadily: 'I promised I'd warn you. Here's the warning, now. I'll give you twenty-four hours, as from now, to make your break with Connor, and leave. I don't care what story you tell, or what excuse you offer, but you must break this thing up, and go. And don't imagine that, in the event of Mr. Winslow's death, you can come back. I promise you that if "Annabel" is a legatee in his Will, and turns up to lay claim to a single penny of it, I'll have you investigated so thoroughly that you won't see the outside of Durham Gaol for ten years. And what will happen to Connor and his sister, I neither know nor care.'

Through the ensuing silence the tap dripped, a small maddening sound, like a reiterated note on a harpsichord, a little out of tune.

'Adam.' Rigid self-control made my voice colourless almost to stupidity. In the harsh light his face was as hard as stone, and as strange. There was nothing in it but weariness and contempt. 'Adam, I – I didn't mean to have to tell you now, because I – I felt as if I couldn't face it just yet. But I can't let you go on thinking . . .' I stopped, and took a breath, as though the place were stuffy, and I needed the air. 'I lied to you the other night by the sundial.'

'Really?' The lift of his brows was cruelly ironic.

'Oh, not the way you think! You got the lies and the truth inverted, and I let it stay that way, because I couldn't stand the truth any longer . . . it was easier to let you believe I was a liar and a cheat than to – have to face you as myself. You see,' I finished, 'I really am Annabel Winslow.'

'Well?'

'You . . . you don't believe me?'

'I find it interesting to try to follow this extraordinary game of yours. But I'm afraid I'm in no mood for it tonight.'

'But I *am* Annabel! I am!'

'I assure you that if you stay around, you'll have plenty of chance to prove it.'

My voice was beginning to shake loose from that precarious control. 'If you forced that on me, mightn't *you* find it a bit embarrassing?'

He laughed. 'All this, and blackmail too?'

'No, oh no! I only meant that there might be questions that only I – and you – could answer. If you tried *that* tack . . .' I struck my hand suddenly against the metal side of the cooler and cried, passionately: 'Why did I ever start this god-damned, stupid thing? I might have known – I *did* know! Talk about Julie being immature and romantic-minded! Will I ever grow up? Letters in the ivy tree, meetings in the summer-house, and now, when I ought to know better, *this* – this stupid, stupid business that was meant to make me feel safe, and it's only frightening me to death!' I blazed round at him. 'All right! So you don't believe me! Go on, call my bluff. What do you want to ask?'

He stood there for a moment longer, his eyes vacant almost, like the eyes of someone suffering from shock. Then, without a word, he turned on his heel and went out of the byre.

I found I was leaning against the chilly metal of the cooler. The shaking had stopped, but I felt cold, with a sweating, empty slackness, like someone who has just vomited. My brain felt bruised, and incapable of any thought except a formless desire to get to bed, and sleep.

'Well, by God!' said Con, just behind me.

Even then, I turned slowly, and stared at him with what must have been a blank and stupid look. 'Where were you?' Then, my voice tautening. 'How much did you hear?'

He laughed, and lounged out of the inner shed into the light. He looked quite composed, even over-composed, and his eyes were brilliant and his expression confident. His mouth was cut a little at the corner, and a graze showed swollen, but it only served to lend him a sort of extra rakish attraction.

He came close to me, and stood there, hands deep in pockets, swaying backwards and forwards on his heels, graceful and collected. 'Oh, I kept my distance! I thought that Forrest and I hadn't much to say to one another, girl dear. And I thought that maybe you'd handle him a bit better than I could. And it seems I was right, me jewel. Was it you switched the engines off?'

'Yes. As an alibi for murder it wasn't bad, on the spur of the moment, Con.'

The brilliant eyes narrowed momentarily. 'Who's talking about murder now?'

'I am. You switched the engines on, and the lights, so that they could be seen and heard from the house, and then you ran upstream and across the stepping-stones, and met Julie in the clearing.'

'And if I did?' The bright eyes were narrow and dangerous. He had

stopped swaying. Suddenly I realised what I should have known even
before he came so near. He was drunk. I could smell whisky on his
breath. 'And if I did?' he said gently.

'Adam was right. You did mean to kill her there, Con.'

There was a little silence. His eyes never wavered. He said again,
softly: 'And if I did?'

I said steadily: 'Only this, that if you thought I'd stand for anything
like that, you must be a fool and an imbecile. Or don't you think at all?
What sort of person d'you think I am? You said yourself not long ago
that you knew I was straight, heaven help us, because otherwise you'd
have been too scared of my trying to twist you in what we're doing. Well,
you blundering criminal fool, did you really think I'd see you kill Julie,
and not send the whole works sky-high, myself included?'

He was laughing now, completely unabashed. 'All right, me darlin',
murder's off the cards, is it? But you know, I'm not the fool you make
me out to be. You weren't supposed to know anything about it. Oh, you
might have suspected all you liked in the morning, when her poor
drowned body came up on the shingle, but what could you prove? You'd
have kept quiet, and held your grandpa's hand, wouldn't you?'

'Oh my God,' I said, 'and to think I felt sorry for you tonight, because
you were so much alone.'

'Well,' said Con cheerfully, 'there's no harm done, is there, except a
little keepsake from Forrest.' He touched his cheek. 'Did you manage to
shut the bastard up after all?'

'I don't know.'

He had begun to rock on his heels again. Somewhere behind the
brilliant gaze was amusement, and wariness, and a speculation that for
some reason made my skin crawl.

' "Adam", wasn't it, now? How do you come to be calling him "Adam",
girl dear?'

My heart gave a jerk that sickened me. I said, and was relieved to find
that my voice sounded nothing but normal, and very tired: 'That was one
thing you and Lisa slipped up on. They must have got to Christian
names. When I went today to get the strawberries, he called me
"Annabel" . . . And now I'm going in. I can't talk to you tonight. I'm
tired, and you're in the wrong kind of mood. Sufficient unto the day.
You're luckier than you deserve that nothing's happened; and I can't
even guess what Adam Forrest'll do tomorrow, but, just at the moment,
I don't care.'

'That's my girl.' He spoke a little thickly. Before I realised what he
was doing, his hands came out and he took me by the shoulders. His eyes
between the beautiful lashes were sapphire-blue and laughing, and only
slightly liquid with drink. 'It's beautiful you are, acushla, did you know?'

'I could hardly avoid it, with Julie in front of me all day.'

His teeth showed. 'Good for you. But you take the shine out of Julie,
bejasus and you do. Look, now—'

I stood stiffly under his hands. 'Con, you're drunk, and you're getting maudlin, and I loathe this stage Irishry anyway. If you think you can plan to murder Julie, and then bat off and drink yourself stupid, and then come and blarney me with a lot of phoney Irish, you can damned well think again. And—' this as he moved, still smiling, and his hands tightened— 'if you try to kiss me, that'll be another slap on the jaw you'll get, so I'm giving you fair warning.'

His hands slackened, and dropped. He had flushed a little but he still smiled. I said levelly: 'Now, for heaven's sake, Con, get to bed and sleep it off, and pray to every saint in heaven that Adam Forrest chooses to hold his tongue. And take it from me, this is the last time I cover up any single thing for you. Good night.'

As I reached the doorway I looked back. He was standing looking after me with an expression where I could only read amusement and affection. He looked handsome and normal and quite sober and very nice.

He smiled charmingly: 'Good night, Annabel.'

I said shortly. 'Don't forget to put the light out,' and went quickly across the yard.

CHAPTER SIXTEEN

I wrote a letter to my love,
And on the way I lost it;
One of you has picked it up,
And put it in her pocket

Traditional

I hardly slept that night. I lay, it seemed for hours, watching the wheeling moonlight outside the open curtains, while my mind, too exhausted for sleep, scratched and fretted its way round the complications of this absurd, this crazy masquerade.

I suppose I dozed a little, for I don't remember when the moon went down and the light came. I remember realising that the dark had slackened, and then, later, a blackbird fluted a piercing stave of song alone in the cold dawn. After he fell silent there was a deep hush, for the space of a long breath, and then, suddenly, all the birds in the world were chattering, whistling, jargoning in a mad medley of sound. In spite of my weariness and my fears, I found myself smiling. I had never heard the dawn chorus before. It was an ill wind, indeed, that blew no good.

My moment of delight must have worked like the Ancient Mariner's spontaneous prayer, for soon afterwards I fell deeply asleep. When I looked at the window again it was full daylight, and the birds were singing normally in the lilacs. I felt wide awake, with that floating bodiless calm that sometimes comes after a night of scanty sleeping. I got up, and went over to the window.

It must be still very early. The dew was thick, grey almost as frost, on grass and leaf. The air smelt thin and cool, like polished silver. It was very still, with the promise of close and thundery heat to come. Far away, from the direction of West Lodge, I heard a cock crow thinly. Through a gap in the trees to my left I saw the distant glint of chestnut, where the Forrest colt moved, cropping the wet grass.

Sometimes, I think, our impulses come not from the past, but from the future. Before I had even clearly thought what I was doing, I had slipped into narrow grey trousers and a pale yellow shirt, had dashed cold water on my face, run a comb through my hair, and was out of my room, sliding downstairs as quietly as a shadow. The house slept on, undisturbed. I tiptoed out through the kitchen, and ten minutes later, bridle in hand, I was letting myself in through the gate of the meadow where Rowan grazed.

I kept clear of the gap in the trees, so that, even if someone else were awake at Whitescar, I couldn't be seen. I moved quietly along under the hedge, towards the horse. He had raised his handsome head as soon as I appeared, and now watched intently, ears pricked forward. I stopped under the guelder-rose, where there was a gap in the hedge and a couple of railings. I sat on the top one and waited, dangling the bridle. The panicles of guelder-rose, thick-coloured as Devonshire cream, spilled dew on to my shoulder, chilly through the thin shirt. I rubbed the damp patch, and shifted along the railing, so that the early sunshine struck my shoulders.

Rowan was coming. He paced forward slowly, with a sort of grave beauty, like a creature out of the pages of poetry written when the world was young and fresh, and always just waking to an April morning. His ears were pricked so far forward that the tips almost met, his eyes large and dark, and mildly curious. His nostrils were flared, and their soft edges flickered as he tested the air towards me. The long grass swished under his hoofs, scattering the dew in bright, splashing showers. The buttercup petals were falling, and his hoofs and fetlocks were flecked gold with them, plastered there by the dew.

Then he was a yard away, pausing: just a large, curious, hardly-broken young horse staring at me with dark eyes that showed, at the edge, that unquiet hint of white. I said: 'Hi, Rowan,' but I didn't move.

He stretched his neck, blew gustily, then came on. Still I didn't move. His ears twitched back, forward again, sensitive as snail's horns, as radar antennae. His nostrils were blown wide, puffing sweet breath at my legs, at my waist, at my neck. He mouthed my sleeve, then took it in his teeth and tugged it.

I put a hand on his neck, and felt the muscles run and shiver along under the warm skin. I ran the hand up to his ears, and he bent his head, blowing at my feet. My hand slipped up to the long tangled forelock, and held it. I slid slowly off the fence-bar, and he didn't try to move away, but put his head down and rubbed it violently up my body, jamming me back against the railing. I laughed at him and said softly: 'You beauty, you love, you lovely boy, stand still now, quiet now . . .' and then turned him, with the hand on his forelock, till his quarters were against the railings, and his forehand free. Then with my other hand, still talking, I brought the bit up to his muzzle.

'Come along now, my beauty, my darling boy, come along.' The bit was between his lips and against his teeth. He held them shut against it for a few seconds; I thought he was going to veer away but he didn't. He opened his teeth, and accepted the steel warm from my hand. The bit slipped softly back into the corners of his mouth, and the bridle slid over his ears; then the rein was looped round my arm and I was fastening the cheek-strap, rubbing his ears, between his eyes, sliding my hand down the springy arch of his neck.

I mounted from the top of the fence, and he came up against it and stood as if he had done it every day of his life. Then he moved away from it smoothly and softly, and only when I turned him towards the length of the field did he begin to gather himself and dance, and bunch his muscles as if to defy me to hold him. I'm not, in fact, quite sure how I did. He went at a canter, that lengthened too quickly towards a gallop, to the far corner of the long meadow, where there was a narrow wicket giving on the flat grass of the river's edge. He was biddable enough at the wicket, so that I guessed that Adam Forrest had taken him this way, and taught him his manners at the gates. But, once through the wicket, he danced again, and the sun danced and dazzled too, down through the lime leaves, and the feel of his bare back warm and shifting with muscle between my thighs was exciting, so that I went mad all at once, and laughed, and said, 'All right, have it your own way,' and let him go; and he went, like a bat out of hell along the flat turf of the river's edge, with that smooth lovely motion that was as easy to sit as an armchair; and I wound my right hand in his mane and stuck on like a burr to his withers with too-long-disused muscles that began to ache before long, and I said, 'Hi, Rowan, it's time we got back. I don't want to get you in a lather, or there'll be questions asked . . .'

His ears moved back to my voice, and for a second or two after I began to draw rein, he resisted, leaning on the bit, and I wondered if I could manage to check and turn him. I slackened the bit for a moment to break his stride, and, as it broke, pulled him in. He came sweetly, ears flickering back to me, and then pointing again as he turned. I sang to him, mad now as the morning: 'Oh, you beauty, you beauty, you love, home now, and steady . . .'

We had come the best part of a mile, round the great curve of the river that led to West Lodge. I had turned him just in time. The chimneys of the Lodge were showing above the nearer trees. I spared a glance for them as the horse wheeled and cantered, sober and collected now, back along the river. His neck was damp, and I smoothed it, and crooned to him, and he flowed along smoothly and beautifully, and his ears twitched to my voice, and then, half-way to his own meadow, I drew him to a walk, and we paced soberly home as if he was a hack hired for the day, and bored with it, and there had been no few minutes of mad delight there along the sward. He arched his neck demurely and fiddled with the bit, and I laughed at him and let him have it, and when we came to the wicket he stopped and moved his quarters round for me to reach, as gentle and dainty as a dancer.

I said: 'All right, sweetheart, that's all for today,' and slid down off him and ducked under his neck to open the wicket. He pushed through, eager now for home. I turned to shut the wicket, and Rowan wheeled with me, and then snorted and threw up his head, and dragged hard at the rein I was holding.

I said: 'Steady, beautiful! What's up?' And looked up so see Adam Forrest a yard away, waiting beside the wicket, watching me.

He had been hidden from me by the thick hawthorn hedge, but of course he would have heard Rowan's hoofs, and seen us coming from some way off. He was prepared, where I was not. I actually felt the colour leave my face, and stood stock still, in the act of latching the gate, like a child in some silly game, one hand stiffly held out, the other automatically holding the startled horse.

The moment of shock snapped, and passed. The wicket clicked shut, and Adam came forward a pace and took Rowan's bridle from me. I noticed then that he had brought a bridle himself; it hung from a post in the hedge beside him, and there was a saddle perched astride a rail.

It seemed a very long time before he spoke. I don't know what I expected him to say; I know that I had time to think of his own reactions as well as my own; to imagine his resentment, shame, anger, bewilderment.

What he said was merely: 'Why did you do it?'

The time had gone past for evasions and pretences; in any case Adam and I had always known rather too well what the other was thinking. I said merely: 'I'd have thought that was obvious. If I'd known you were still at Forrest I'd never have come. When I found I had to face you, I felt caught, scared – oh, anything you like, and when you wouldn't just write it off and let me go, I suppose I got desperate. Then you decided I was an impostor, and I was so shaken that on the spur of the moment I let you go on thinking it. It was – easier, as long as I could persuade you to keep quiet about me.'

Between us the horse threw up his head and fidgeted with the bit. Adam was staring at me as if I were some barely decipherable manuscript he was trying to read. I added: 'Most of what I told you was true. I wanted to come back, and try to make it up with Grandfather. I'd thought about it for some time, but I didn't think he'd want me back. What kept me away was the worst kind of pride, I know; but he's always rather played power-politics with money – he's terribly property-conscious, like a lot of his generation – and I didn't want to be taunted with just coming back to claim my share, or to put in my claim for Mother's money.' I gave a little smile. 'As a matter of fact, it *was* almost the first thing he said to me. Well, there it was, partly pride, partly not being able to afford the passage . . . and, apart from all those considerations, there was you.'

I paused. 'But after a bit I began to see things differently. I wanted desperately to come back to England, and I wanted not to be . . . completely cut off from my home any more. I didn't write; don't ask me why. I suppose it was the same impulse that makes you turn up unexpectedly, if you have to visit a house where you're not sure of your welcome; warning them gives people too much time to think of excuses, and be wary; whereas once you're on the doorstep they've got to welcome you. Maybe you don't know about such things, being a man, but I assure you it's quite commonly done, especially if you're a person who's never sure of their welcome, like me. And as for you, I – I thought I might be able to keep out of your way. I knew that . . . things . . . would be long since over for you, but I thought you'd understand why I felt I had to come back. If I had to meet you, I'd manage to let you know I'd only come on a visit, and was going to get a job elsewhere.'

Rowan jerked his head, and the bit jingled. Adam seemed unconscious of the movement. I went on: 'I'd saved a bit, and when Mrs. Grey – my last employer – died, she left me a little money, three hundred dollars, along with a few trinkets for keepsakes.' I smiled briefly, thinking of the gold lighter, and the car permit left so carefully for Con and Lisa to find. 'She was a cripple, and I'd been with her quite a time, as a sort of housekeeper-chauffeuse. I was very fond of her. Well, with the three hundred dollars, and my savings, I managed to pay for my passage, with something left over. I came straight up to Newcastle from Liverpool, and got myself a room, and a temporary job. I waited a day or two, trying to nerve myself to come back and see how things were. Of course, for all I knew, Grandfather was dead . . .'

Half absently I stooped and pulled a swatch of grass, and began to wisp the horse. Adam stood without moving; I had hardly looked at him. It was queer that when a part of your life, your very self, was dead, it could still hurt you, as they say a limb still does, after it has been cut off.

'I hadn't wanted to make too many inquiries, in case Con somehow got to hear of it. I'd even taken my rooms in the name of my last employer, Mrs. Grey. I didn't know what to do, how to make my approach. I wanted to apply to the lawyers for Mother's money, you see, only I wasn't sure if I dared risk Con's finding out I was home. Well, I waited a day or two, wondering what to do—'

'Just a minute.' Adam, it seemed, was listening, after all. 'Why should you not "dare" let Connor know you were home?'

I ran the wisp along Rowan's neck, and said briefly: 'He tried to kill me one night, along the river, just near where you found him with Julie.'

He moved at that. 'He *what?*'

'He'd wanted to marry me. Grandfather wanted it, too. You knew that. Con hadn't a hope then – or so he thought – of getting the property any other way, so he used – to harry me a bit. Well, that night he threw a bit of a scene, and I wasn't just in the mood for it; I wasn't exactly tactful, and I made it a bit too clear that he hadn't a hope, then or ever, and . . . well, he lost his temper and decided to get rid of me. He chances his arm, does Con.' I lifted my eyes, briefly, from my task. 'That's how I guessed, last night, that he'd have gone to find Julie. That's why I followed her.'

'Why did you never tell me?'

His tone was peremptory, proprietorial, exactly as it might have been eight years ago, when he had had the right.

'There was no chance. It happened the last night I was here. I was on my way home, after I'd left you in the summer-house. You remember how late it was. You know how I always used to go over the river by the stepping-stones, and then home by the path and the bridge, so no one would know I'd been to Forrest. It was just as well I bothered, because that night I ran into Con.'

'Oh, my God.'

'That was the – the other reason why I ran away. Grandfather took his part, you see. He'd been angry with me for months because I wouldn't look at Con, and there'd been scenes because he'd found I was staying out late, and I'd lied once or twice about where I'd been. He – I suppose it was natural, really – he used to storm at me, and say that if I ever got into trouble, I could go, and stay away . . .' I smiled a little. 'I think it was only talk and temper; it was a bit hard on Grandfather, being saddled with an adolescent girl to look after, but of course adolescents take these things seriously. When I got home that night, after getting away from Con, I was pretty nearly hysterical. I told Grandfather about Con, and he wouldn't believe me. He knew I'd been out somewhere, and suspected I'd met somebody, and all he would say was "where had I been?" because it was late, and he'd sent Con to find me himself. I think he just thought Con had lost his head and had been trying to kiss me, and all I was saying about murder was pure hysteria. I don't blame him, but there was a . . . pretty foul scene. There's no point in raking it all up: you can imagine the kind of things that were said. But you see why I ran away? Partly because of what had happened between you and me, and because I was scared stiff of Con . . . and now because Grandfather was taking his part, and I was afraid he and Con would start ferreting about, and discover about you. If Crystal had found out . . . the way she was just then . . .'

Rowan put his head down, and began to graze with a jingling of metal. I paused, leaning one hand against his neck. 'Well, you understand why

I was afraid to come back to Whitescar, even now. If Con *had* been in charge here, alone, I'd never have dared, but once I found that Grandfather was still alive, and still playing at power-politics between me and Con and Julie, and that Julie might be exposed to exactly the same sort of danger as I had been . . .'

'And that I had gone.'

'And that you had gone,' I said steadily, 'I knew I'd have to come back here. It would still have been a pretty sticky thing to attempt, in the teeth of Con and Lisa, and not being sure of Grandfather's reception of me, but then Con himself appeared like Lucifer out of the blue, and presented me with what looked like a nice, peaceful, Connor-proof homecoming. I rather grabbed at it. I only planned, you see, to stay here as long as Grandfather lived.'

'I begin to see. How did you fall in with Connor?'

'I took a risk which I shouldn't have taken, and went to take a look at Whitescar. I didn't even get out of the bus, just went along the top road from Bellingham to Chollerford, one Sunday. I got out at Chollerford, to get the bus along the Roman Road. I – I wanted to walk along the Wall, to – to see it again.'

Nothing in his face betrayed the fact that lay sharply between us; that it was on the Wall that he and I, sometimes, by chance – and oh, how carefully calculated a chance! – had met.

I said steadily: 'Con saw me. He waited his chance and followed me. He recognised me, of course, or thought he did. When he came up on me I was startled, and scared stiff, and then I saw he was just doubtful enough for me to pretend he'd made a mistake. So I gave him the name I'd been using, and got away with it.' I went on to tell him, then, of the interview on the Wall, and the subsequent suggestions that were made to me. 'And finally, when I realised that Con was fairly well "in" with Grandfather, and that he and Lisa had it in for Julie, and that Grandfather himself had had a stroke . . . Well, I thought to myself, this is one way of getting home with Con not lifting a finger to stop me. So I agreed. And it went off well enough, until I found that you *were* still here . . .'

He said with sudden impatience: 'That horse isn't sweating. Leave that alone. We'll turn him loose.'

He began to unbuckle the cheek-strap, adding, with as much emotion as if he were discussing the price of tomatoes: 'Go on. When did you find I was still here?'

'Grandfather mentioned it, quite casually, the first evening. I'd managed to chisel a bit out of Con and Lisa, about the fire, and your taking Crystal to Italy, and then Vienna, and the nursing-homes and everything, and her death, but you know Con, he's interested in nothing but himself, and I didn't dare press too much about you and your affairs. When I heard from Grandfather that you hadn't gone permanently, it gave me a shock. I went that night to Con and said I wanted to back down. He – threatened me. No, no, nothing like that, he just said what was true, that it had gone too far, and that a hint of the "truth" would shock Grandfather. Of course I knew I'd told Grandfather nothing but the truth, but for all they get across one another, he thinks the sun rises and sets in Con, and it would have finished him to know what sort of a swine Con is – can be. It still would. I realised that I'd have to stay, but the thought of having to meet you was ... terrifying. I went over to Forrest that night, the night before you came.'

'To lay the ghosts?'

'I suppose so. But the next night ... I knew you'd come, I don't know how.'

You always did ... Nobody had said the words. He wasn't looking at me; he was sliding the bridle off, over Rowan's ears. The horse, his head free, flung it up and sideways, and swerved away from us, thrusting out into the sunlight at a trot. Then he dropped his head, and began to graze again. Adam looked down at the bridle in his hands as if he wasn't quite sure what it was, or how it had got there. Then he turned, and hung it with great care beside his own. 'And when I came, you found it easier to let me think you – that Annabel was dead.'

'Wasn't she?' I said.

He turned then, and for the first time we really looked at one another. 'Why should you have thought so? After you'd gone, when you'd had time to think ... there'd been so much ... you must have known I ...' His voice trailed away, and he looked down at his feet.

I felt something touch me, pierce almost, the armour of indifference that the hurt of eight years back had shelled over me like nacre. It was not enough to have learned to live with the memory of his cruelty and indifference; I had still to care.

I said, hardly enough: 'Adam, eight years ago, we quarrelled, because we were unhappy, and there was no future unless we did the sort of harm we had no right to do. I told you, I don't want to go back over it. But you remember as well as I do, what was said.'

He said roughly: 'Oh God, yes! Do you think I haven't lived through every minute of that quarrel since? Every word, every look, every inflection? I know why you went! Even discounting Con and your grandfather, you'd reason enough! But I still can't see why you never sent me a single word, even an angry one.'

This time the silence was stretched, like a shining thread that wouldn't snap. The sun was strong now, and fell slanting over the eastward hedge to gild the tops of the grasses. Rowan rolled an eye at us, and moved further away. The tearing sound as he cropped the grass was loud in the early-morning stillness.

When I spoke, it was in a voice already heavy with knowledge; the instinct that sees pain falling like a shadow from the future. 'But you had my letter.'

Before he spoke, I knew the answer. The truth was in his face. 'Letter? What letter?'

'I wrote from London,' I said, 'almost straight away.'

'I got no letter.' I saw him pass his tongue across his lips. 'What did it . . . say?'

For eight years I had thought of what I would have liked to say. Now I only said, gently: 'That if it would give you even a little happiness, I'd be your mistress, and go with you wherever you liked.'

The pain went across his face as if I had hit him. I saw him shut his eyes. He put up a hand to them; it was disfigured and ugly in the clear sunlight. He dropped it, and we looked at one another.

He said, quite simply, as if exhausted. 'My dear. I never even saw it.'

'I realise that now. I suppose I should have realised it then, when I got no answer. I should have known you'd not have done anything quite so cruel.'

'Christ,' he said, without violence, 'I think you should.'

'I'm sorry. It never even occurred to me that the letter might have gone astray. Letters don't, as a rule. And I was so unhappy, and alone, and – and *cut off* . . . girls aren't at their most sensible at such times. Adam, don't look like that. It's over now. I waited a few days; I – I suppose I'd really only gone to London to wait for you; I'd never intended, originally, to go abroad. But then, when I telephoned – did she tell you I'd telephoned?' At his expression, I gave a little smile. 'Yes, I telephoned you, too.'

'Oh, my dear. And Crystal answered?'

'Yes. I pretended it was a wrong number. I didn't think she'd recognised my voice. I rang again next day, and Mrs. Rudd answered it. She didn't know who I was; she just told me the house was shut, and that you and Mrs. Forrest had gone abroad, indefinitely. It was then that I – I decided to go right away. I went to a friend of mine who was emigrating. I had some money. I went along to look after her children, and – oh, the rest doesn't matter. I didn't write to you again. I – I couldn't, could I?'

'No.' He was still looking like someone who has been mortally hurt, and hasn't known it till he sees the blood draining away into the grass. 'No wonder you said what you did, the other night. It seems there's even more than I thought, to be laid at my door.'

'You couldn't help it, if a letter went astray! It was hardly – *Adam*!'

His eyes jerked up to mine. 'What is it?'

I liked my lips, and said, hoarsely: 'I wonder what did happen to that letter? We're forgetting that. I said a minute ago, letters just don't go astray, not as a rule, not for eight years. Do you suppose—' I wet my lips again— '*she* took it?'

'*Crystal*? How could – oh my God, no, surely? Don't look like that, Annabel, the damned thing's probably lying in some dusty dead-letter office somewhere on the Continent. No, my dear, she never knew. I'll swear she never knew.'

'Adam, you can't be sure! If she did—'

'I tell you she didn't know! She never gave any sign of knowing! And

I assure you, that if she could have found a whip like *that* to use on me, she'd have used it.'

'But when she got so much worse—'

'She was no worse than neurotic for years after you went away. It was only after the fire – after I'd taken her to Florence – that you could have called her really "mentally ill", and I had to take her to Vienna. She never once, in all that time, mentioned any sort of suspicion of you.'

'But, Adam, you don't know—'

'I know quite well. Stop this, Annabel!'

'Adam, no one's ever told me – how did Crystal die?'

He said harshly: 'It was nothing to do with this. You can take my word for it. For one thing, no letter turned up among her papers after her death, and you can be sure she kept everything there was.'

I said: 'Then she *did* kill herself?'

He seemed to stiffen himself like a man lifting a weight, only able by stark courage to hold it there. 'Yes.'

Another of those silences. We were standing so still that a wren flew on to a hazel close beside me, chattered a stave of shrill and angry-sounding song, then flew away. I was thinking, without drama, well, here was the end of the chapter; all the threads tied up, the explanations made. There was nothing more to say. Better say good-bye, and go home to breakfast, before tragedy dissolved in embarrassment, and the lovers who had once been ready to count the world well lost, should find themselves talking about the weather.

The same thought showed momentarily in Adam's face, and with it, a sort of stubborn resolution. He took a step forward and the maimed hands moved.

I said: 'Well, I'd better be getting back before Con sees I've been on Rowan.'

'Annabel—'

'Adam, don't make me keep saying it's finished.'

'Don't make me keep saying it isn't! Why on earth d'you think I found myself trusting you against all reason and judgment, liking you – oh, God, more than liking you – if I hadn't known in my blood who you really were, in spite of that bag of moonshine you handed me so convincingly?'

'I suppose because I was like her.'

'Nonsense. Julie's the image of what you were, as I knew you, and she never makes my heart miss a single beat. And tell me this, my dear dead love, why did you cry when you saw my hands?'

'Adam, no, you're not being fair!'

'You care, don't you? Still?'

'I . . . don't know. No. I can't. Not now.'

He always had known what I was thinking. He said sharply: 'Because of Crystal?'

'We'll never know, will we? It'd be there, between us, what we did.'

He said, grimly: 'I could bear that. Believe me, I made my reparations.' He turned his hands over, studying them. 'And this was the least painful of them. Well, my dear, what do you want to do?'

'I'll go, of course. It won't be long, you know. Grandfather's looking desperately frail. Afterwards . . . afterwards, I'll see things straight with Con, somehow, and then I'll go. If he knows I'm leaving, there'll be no danger for me. We needn't meet, Adam.'

'Neither we need.'

I turned away abruptly. 'I'll go now.'

'Take your bridle.'

'What? Oh, thanks. I'm sorry I spoiled your ride, Adam.'

'I doesn't matter. Rowan would much prefer it with you. I've a heavy hand.'

He picked his own bridle from the post, and heaved the saddle up over one arm. Then he smiled at me. 'Don't worry, my dear. I won't get under your feet. But don't go away again, without saying good-bye.'

'Adam,' I said desperately; 'I can't help it. I can't *help* the way I feel. Life does just go on, and you change, and you can't go back. You have to live it the way it comes. You know that.'

He said, not tragically, but as if finishing a quite ordinary conversation: 'Yes, of course. But it would be very much easier to be dead. Good-bye.'

He let himself through the wicket, and went away across the field without looking back.

CHAPTER SEVENTEEN

I lean'd my back unto an aik,
I thocht it was a trustie tree;
But first it bow'd and syne it brak –
Sae my true love did lichtlie me.

Ballad: *Jamie Douglas*

Life goes on, I had told Adam. When I got back to the farm the men were arriving for the day, and the cattle were filing into the byres. I managed to slip into the stables and hang the bridle up again without being seen, then went into the kitchen.

Mrs. Bates was there, waiting for the kettle to boil. She cast me a look of surprise.

'Why, Miss Annabel! You're up early. Have you been out riding?'

'No. I just couldn't sleep.'

Her bright black eyes lingered on my face. 'What's to do now? You look proper poorly.'

'I'm all right. I had a bad night, that's all. I'd love a cup of tea.'

'Hm.' The piercing, kind little eyes surveyed me. 'Piece o' nonsense, getting up at all hours when you don't have to. You want to take care o' yersel'."

'Nonsense, Betsy, there's nothing the matter with me.'

'Never seen anything like you the day you came back.' Here the kettle boiled, and she tipped it, dexterously jetting the boiling water into the teapot. 'If you hadn't 'a' told me you was Miss Annabel, I'd hardly 'a' knowd you, and *that's* a fact. Aye, you can smile if you like, but that's the truth and no lie. Depend on it, I says to Bates that night, depend on it, Miss Annabel's had a bad time of it over in America, I says, and I'm not surprised, I says, judging by what you see on the pictures.'

'It was Canada,' I said mildly.

'Well, they're all the same, aren't they?' She slapped the teapot down on the table, which was laid ready for breakfast, whipped off the lid, and stirred the tea vigorously. 'Not but what you look a lot better than what you did, and you've begun to put a bit of weight on, aye, *and* get some of your looks back, and I'm not the only one that's noticed it. Have you noticed, says Bates to me the other day, that Miss Annabel's almost her pretty self again when she smiles. Which isn't often enough by a long chalk, I says. Well, he says, if she'd but get herself a husband and get herself settled, he says. Go on with you, I says, and her hardly home yet, give her time, I says, not but what men always thinks that's all a woman needs in her life to make her happy, so no offence meant, but all the same, he says to me –'

I managed a laugh that was, I hope, convincing. 'Oh, Betsy dear! Let me get home first, before I start looking round!'

'Here's your tea.' She pushed a steaming cup towards me. 'And you did ought to take sugar in it, not a foreign black mess like that. And let me tell you that if you didn't sleep last night you'll only have yersel' to blame, with soup, and coffee, not to mention whisky and such, *as* I know by the glasses left in the kitchen bold as brass for me to find. Not that I'm one as concerns meself in things that are none of my business, but – oh, here's Mr. Con.'

Con, I noticed sourly, looked attractive and wide awake even with last night's stubble on his chin, and in the clothes, carelessly hustled-into, for his before-breakfast jobs. He threw me a look of surprise as he took a cup of tea from Mrs. Bates. 'Good God. What are you doing up at this hour?'

'Taking a walk, she says,' said Mrs. Bates, spooning sugar into his cup. 'I thought she'd been riding, meself, but she says no.'

His eyes flickered over my trousers and yellow shirt. 'Weren't you? I should have thought Forrest's colt would have tempted you long ago.'

I sipped my tea without replying. Already the scene in the meadow was growing dim, dulled, fading . . . The hot tea was a benison, a spell against dreams. The day had started. Life goes on.

'Those things suit you,' said Con. His glance held undisguised admiration, and I saw Mrs. Bates eyeing him with a sort of sour speculation. She pushed a plateful of buttered rolls towards him. 'Try one o' these.'

He took one, still watching me. 'Are you coming out to lend a hand today?'

'That she is not,' said Mrs. Bates promptly.

'I might,' I said, 'I'm not sure. I – I slept badly.'

'You're not worrying about anything, are you?' asked Con. The blue eyes held nothing but mildly solicitous curiosity.

Mrs. Bates took his cup from him and re-filled it. 'She's worrying herself about her Granda, I shouldn't wonder, which is more than *you* seem to be doing, Mr. Con, *which* I may say you can think shame on yourself, for asking her to work in this heat, when you've as much help as you want up in the field, and that's the truth and no lie!'

'Well,' said Con, with the glint of a smile, 'I doubt if we'll get Bill Fenwick over today, so if you could relieve someone on one of the tractors some time, it would help. The weather'll break soon, you see if it doesn't. We'll have thunder before dark.'

'I'll see,' I said. 'Will you be up there all day yourself?'

'As soon as I've had breakfast. Why?'

'I told you last night. I want to talk to you.'

'So you did. Well, tonight, maybe.'

'I'd rather see you before. I may come up to the field, at any rate when you stop to eat.'

'Oh, sure,' said Con unconcernedly, setting down his cup. 'Be seeing you.'

I went up to my room to change. If he hadn't been in his working-clothes, I thought, he'd have smelled the horse on me. There were chestnut hairs on the grey trousers, and one or two on the shirt where Rowan had rubbed his head against me. I went along and bathed, got into a skirt and fresh blouse, and felt better.

I couldn't eat breakfast when the time came, but there was no one there to remark on the fact. Con wasn't yet in, Grandfather wasn't up, Mrs. Bates was busy elsewhere, and Lisa was invariably silent at breakfast-time. Julie was taking hers in bed – this at my insistence, and more to keep her out of Con's way than for any other reason. She seemed to have completely recovered from last night's experience, and only accepted my ruling about breakfast because, she said, she had no desire to see Con again so soon, and certainly not before she had seen Donald.

Donald rang up shortly before half past eight, to ask for news of last night's truants. I told him only enough to reassure him – that Bill Fenwick's car had been involved in a mishap, and that Julie was unhurt, and wanting to see him some time that day. If, I added with a memory of the colleague from London, he was free . . .

'Mphm,' said Donald. 'I'll be along in half an hour.'

'Donald! Wait a minute! She's not up yet!'

'Half an hour,' said Donald, and rang off.

I warned Julie, who hurled herself out of bed with a shriek and a 'What shall I *wear*?' that reassured me completely as to her well-being and her feelings. I didn't see Donald arrive, but when, some half-hour later, I saw his car in the yard, I went to tell him that Julie wouldn't be long. He wasn't in the car, or indeed, anywhere to be seen; on an inspiration I slipped through the half-door of Blondie's stable, and there, sure enough, he was, stooping to prod a gentle finger into the pile of fur deep in the manger, while Tommy, sitting unconcernedly on top of the partition (which was at least half an inch wide), watched composedly, in the intervals of washing a back leg.

Donald straightened when he heard me come in. 'She really is all right?' It was an unceremonious greeting, and I hoped it was symptomatic of his state of mind. He certainly betrayed no other outward signs of deep emotion.

'Perfectly. She'll be along in a minute or two.'

I told him then rather more fully about the accident, but without mentioning Con, or (of course) what had happened later last night. If Julie chose to tell him, that was her affair, but I hoped she wouldn't. I wanted no more trouble until I had managed that overdue interview with Con, and after that, I hoped, all would be clear.

It was six minutes, in sober fact, before Julie came. She certainly looked none the worse for the stresses of last night. She wore her blue skirt and white blouse, and looked composed and immaculate, not in the least as if she had rushed shrieking for the bathroom only thirty-six minutes before.

She greeted Donald with a composure that amounted almost to reserve, and, when I made a move to go, held me there with a quick, imploring look that filled me with forebodings. These weren't diminished by Donald's attitude; he appeared to have retreated into silence, and, I noticed with exasperation, was even groping in his pocket for his pipe.

I said quickly: 'You can't smoke in a stable, Donald. If you two are going off now – '

'Oh,' said Julie, 'are these Tommy's kittens? Aren't they *adorable*!'

She stooped over the bundle in the manger, exclaiming delightedly over the kittens, with every appearance of intending to remain there for some time. 'And *look* at their tiny *paws*! Two black,' she cried rapturously, 'and three black-and-white, and *two ginger* . . . isn't it a *miracle*?'

'As a matter of fact,' I said, rather sharply, 'it's the ginger tom from West Lodge.'

Julie had detached a ginger kitten from the tangle of fur, and was cuddling it under her chin, crooning to it. 'How old are they? Oh, I'd *adore* to keep one! But they're far too tiny to take, aren't they? Six weeks, isn't it, till they can lap? Oh, isn't it a *darling*? Annabel, d'you suppose either of the ginger ones is a he?'

'They both are,' said Donald.

'How do you – I mean, they're too small to *tell*, surely?'

'I should have said,' amended Donald, carefully, 'that the probability of both ginger kittens being male, is about ninety-nine and nine-tenths per cent. Possibly more. The ginger colour is a sex-linked characteristic.'

The nearest we were going to get to romance today, I thought bitterly, was a discussion on genetics. And while there could, admittedly, be said to be some connection, it was getting us no further with the matter in hand. I sent Donald a quelling look, which he didn't see. He was watching Julie, who, with the kitten still cuddled close to her, was regarding him with respectful wonder.

'You mean you just *can't have* a ginger she?'

'No. I mean, yes.' Donald's uncertainty was only momentary, and of the wrong kind. He stood there like a rock, pipe in hand, calm, slow-spoken, and undeniably attractive. I could have shaken him.

'Isn't that marvellous?' said Julie, awed. 'Annabel, did you know that? Then I *shall* keep this one. Oh, lord, it's got claws like *pins*, and it *will* try and climb up my neck! Donald, look at it, isn't it utterly *adorable*?'

'Adorable.' He still sounded infuriatingly detached and academic. 'I'd be inclined to go further. I'd say beautiful, quite beautiful.'

'Would you?' Julie was as surprised as I was at this sudden plunge into hyperbole. She held the kitten away from her, looking at it a shade doubtfully. 'Well, it *is* the sweetest little love, of course, but do you think the pink nose is quite the *thing*? Cute, of course, with that spot on the end, but – '

'Pink?' said Donald. 'I wouldn't have said it was pink.'

He hadn't, I realised suddenly, even glanced at the kitten. Unnoticed at last, I began to edge away.

'But, Donald, it's *glowing* pink, practically *shocking* pink, and quite hideous, actually, only so terribly sweet!'

'I was not,' said Donald, 'talking about the kitten.'

There was a second's open-mouthed pause, then Julie, her poise in flinders, blushed a vivid scarlet and began to stammer. Donald put his pipe back into his pocket.

I said, unheeded: 'We'll see you both this evening some time,' and went out of the stable.

As I went, Donald was gently unhooking the kitten from the shoulder of Julie's blouse, and putting it back into the manger.

'We don't want to squash the poor little thing, do we?'

'No – no,' said Julie.

Later that morning, after I had done the chores which I had taken on as my contribution to the house-keeping, I went to hunt up my gardening-tools from the corner of the barn where they had always been kept. I had, of course, taken the precaution of asking Lisa where they were. The tools looked almost as if they hadn't been used since I'd last had them out more than eight years ago. It was queer to feel my hand slipping in such an assured way round the smoothed wood of the trowel, and to feel the familiar knot-hole in the handle of the spade. I carried the tools along to the tractor-shed and put in a little first-aid on the shears, and the blades of spade and hoe, then threw the lot into a barrow, and went to see what I could do with the neglected garden.

I worked there all morning, and, since I started on the basic jobs of grass and path, it wasn't long before the place looked as if some care had been spent on it. But work, for once, didn't help. As I sheared the grass, and spaded the edges straight, and then tackled the dry, weedy beds with fork and hoe, memory, far from being dulled by the rough work, cut back at me ever more painfully, as if I had sharpened that, too, along with the garden-tools.

That spring and summer, eight years back . . . the March days when the soil smelt strong and damp and full of growing; May when the lilac was thick on the tree by the gate, and rain lay in each cup, scented with honey; June, with the robin scolding shrilly from the waxy blossoms of the syringa bush, as I dug and planted with my back to the house, dreaming of Adam, and our next meeting . . .

Today, it was June again, and the soil was dry and the air heavy. The lilac was done, and the syringa bush wasn't there, dead these many years.

And Adam and I were free, but that was over.

My fork turned up a clump of bulbs, autumn crocus, fat globes covered with onion-coloured crêpe paper. I went on my knees and lifted them out carefully with my hands.

Then suddenly I remembered them, too. This clump had been in flower the last day I'd been at Whitescar. They had burned, pale lilac flames in the dusk, as I slipped out to meet Adam that last, that terrible evening. They had lain, drenched ribbons of silk, under the morning's rain when, with the first light next day, I had tiptoed down the path and away, across the bridge towards the high-road.

I found I was sitting back on my heels with the tears pouring down my face, and dripping on the dry corms held tightly in my hands.

It was still an hour short of lunch-time when Betsy's voice called me from the house. I thought there was some urgency in her voice, and when I stood up and turned, I could see her, in what looked like considerable agitation, waving for me to hurry.

'Oh, Miss Annabel! Oh, Miss Annabel! Come quickly, do!'

The urgency and distress could only mean one thing. I dropped my weeding-fork, and ran.

'Betsy! Is it Grandfather?'

'Aye, it is that . . .' Her hands were twisted now into her apron, and, with her face paler than usual, and the red of the cheeks standing out like paint, and the black eyes at once alarmed and important, she looked more than ever, as she stood bobbing in the doorway, like a little wooden figure from a Noah's Ark. She was talking even more rapidly than usual, almost as if she thought she might be blamed for what had happened, and had to get her excuses in first.

'. . . And he was as right as rain when I took his breakfast up, as right as a trivet he was, and *that's* the truth and no lie. 'And how many times have I tell't you,' he says, 'if you burns the toast, to give it to the birds. I'll not have this scraped stuff,' he says, 'so you can throw it out now and do some more,' *which* I did, Miss Annabel, and there he was, as right as rain . . .'

I took her breathlessly by the shoulders, with my earthy hands. 'Betsy, Betsy! What's *happened*? Is he dead?'

'Mercy, no! But it's the stroke like before, and that's how it'll end this time, Miss Annabel, my dear . . .'

She followed me up the passage, still talking volubly. She and Lisa, I heard, had been together in the kitchen, preparing lunch, when Grandfather's bell had rung. This was an old-fashioned pulley-bell, one of a row which hung on their circular springs in the kitchen. The bell had jangled violently, as if jerked in anger, or some sudden emergency. Mrs. Bates had hurried upstairs, to find the old man collapsed in the wing-chair near the fireplace. He had dressed himself, all but his jacket, and must have suddenly begun to feel ill, and just managed to reach the bell-pull by the hearth as he fell. Mrs. Bates and Lisa, between them, had got him to bed, and then the former had come for me.

Most of this she managed to pour out in the few moments while I ran to the kitchen and plunged my filthy hands under the tap. I had seized a towel, and was roughly drying them, when a soft step sounded in the lobby, and Lisa appeared in the doorway. She showed none of Betsy's agitation, but her impassive face was perhaps a bit sallower, and I thought I saw a kind of surreptitious excitement in her eyes.

She said abruptly: 'There you are. I've got him to bed and got him covered up. He collapsed while he was dressing. I'm afraid it looks serious. Annabel, will you telephone the doctor? The number's on the pad. Mrs. Bates, that kettle's almost hot enough; fill two hot-bottles as soon as you can. I must go back to him. When you've got Dr. Wilson, Annabel, go and fetch Con.'

'Lisa, I must see him. You do the telephoning. I can – '

'You don't know what to do.' she said curtly. 'I do. It's happened before. Now hurry.'

She turned quickly away, as if there was no more to be said. I flung the towel down, and ran to the office.

The doctor's number was written there, largely, on the pad. Luck was in, and he was at home. Yes, he would be there as quickly as possible. What was being done? Ah, Miss Dermott was with him, was she, and Mrs. Bates was there? Good, good. I was to try not to worry. He wouldn't be long. Smooth with professional reassurances, he rang off.

As I went back into the hall, Lisa appeared at the head of the stairs. 'Did you get him?'

'Yes, he's coming.'

'Good. Now, will you go – ?'

'I want to see him first.' I was already starting up the stairs.

'There's nothing you can do.' She did nothing to bar my way, but her very stolidity, as she waited for me in the middle of the way, had that effect.

I said sharply: 'Is he conscious?'

'No.'

It wasn't the monosyllable that halted me, three steps below her, it was the tone of it. I looked up at her. Even through my agitation I caught the surprise in her look. Heaven knows what she could read in my face and eyes. I had forgotten what lay between me and Lisa; now it whipped back at me, stinging me into intelligence, and caution.

She was saying: 'There's no point in your seeing him. Go and get Con. He's in High Riggs.'

'I know.'

'Well, he must know straight away.'

'Yes, of course,' I said, and went on, past her, straight into Grandfather's room.

The curtains had been half drawn, and hung motionless, shading the sunny windows. The old man lay in bed, his only movement that of his laboured, stertorous breathing. I went across and stood beside him. If it hadn't been for the difficult breathing, I might have thought him dead already. It was as if he, the man I knew, had already gone from behind the mask that lay on the pillow. It, and we, were only waiting.

Lisa had followed me in, but I took no notice of her. I stood watching Grandfather, and trying to calm my agitated thoughts into some sort of order.

Lisa had been in the kitchen when it happened, with Betsy. It had been Betsy who had answered the bell. All that Lisa had done had been correct, and obviously genuine. And Con was far enough away, in High Riggs; had been there since early morning ...

I turned to meet Lisa's eyes. If I had had any doubts about the naturalness of this crisis, coming, as it had done, so pat upon the signing of the Will, they were dispelled by the look on Lisa's face. It was still, as before, obscurely excited, and she made no attempt to hide the excitement from me. And it was now, also, thoroughly surprised and puzzled as she stared back at me.

I could hear Betsy chugging upstairs now, with the hot-bottles. Lisa had moved up to my elbow. Her voice muttered in my ear: 'It's a mercy, isn't it?'

'A mercy?' I glanced at her in surprise. 'But he was perfectly all right – '

'Ssh, here's Mrs. B. I meant, a mercy it didn't happen yesterday, before Mr. Isaacs came. God's providence, you might even say.'

'You might,' I said drily. Yes, I thought, it was there, clear enough to see: Lisa, single-minded, uncomplicated, initiating nothing. The stars in their courses fought for Con; Lisa need only wait. Efficient, innocent Lisa. No doubt at all, when Dr. Wilson came, she would help him in every possible way.

I said abruptly: 'I'll go and get Con.'

The sun beat heavy and hot on High Riggs. A third of the field was shorn, close and green-gold and sweet-smelling. Over the rest of the wide acreage the hay stood thick and still in the heat. The clover, and the plumy tops of the grasses made shadows of lilac and madder and bronze across the gilt of the hay. There were purple vetches along the ditch, and the splashing yellow of ladies' slipper.

One tractor was at the far end of the field, with Con driving. It was moving away from me, the blades of the cutter flashing in the sun.

I began to run towards him along the edge of the cut hay. The men with rakes paused to look up at me. The cutter was turning, out from the standing hay, round, and in once more in a close circle, neatly feathering its corner and re-entering the standing hay at an exact right-angle.

Con hadn't seen me. He was watching the track of the blades, but as the machine came into the straight, he glanced up ahead of him, and then lifted a hand. I stopped where I was, gasping in the heavy heat.

The tractor was coming fairly fast. Con, not apparently seeing in my visit anything out of the way, was watching the blades again. The sun glinted on the dark hair, the handsome, half-averted profile, the sinewy brown arms. He looked remote, absorbed, grave. I remember that I thought with a kind of irrelevant surprise, he looks happy.

Then I had stepped out of his path, and, as the tractor came level with me, I shouted above the noise of the motor: 'Con! You'd better come to the house! It's Grandfather!'

The tractor stopped with a jerk that shook and rattled the cutter-blades. The boy on the reaper hauled on the lever and they lifted, the hot light quivering on the steel. Con switched off the motor, and the silence came at us with a rush.

'What is it?'

I said, shouting, then lowering my voice as it hit the silence: 'It's Grandfather. He's taken ill. You have to come.'

I saw something come and go in his face, then it was still again, but no longer remote. It had gone blank, but it was as if something in him was holding its breath, in a sort of wary eagerness; there was a tautness along the upper lip, and the nostrils were slightly flared. A hunter's face.

He drew a little breath, and turned his head to the boy. 'Uncouple her, Jim. I'm going down to the house. Ted!' The farm foreman came across, not hurrying, but with a curious look at me. 'Ted, Mr. Winslow's ll. I'm going down now, and I may not get back today. Carry on, will you?' A few more hurried instructions, and his hand went to the starter. 'Oh, and send one of the boys across to open that gate for the doctor's car. Jim, get up on the tractor here, then you can drive it back. I'll send news up with Jim, Ted, as soon as I see how he is.'

As the boy obeyed, swinging up behind him, Con started the motor. He gestured with a jerk of the head to me, and I ran round and stepped up on to the back of the tractor. It went forward with a lurch, and then turned sharply away from the ridge of cut hay, and bucketed down across the uneven ground towards the gate. The men paused in their raking to watch curiously, but Con took no notice. He sent the tractor over the grid with hardly any diminution of speed. I was close beside him, standing on the bars and holding on to the high mudguard. He began to whistle between his teeth, a hissing little noise that sounded exactly what it was, a valve blowing down a head of steam. I think I hated Con then, more than I ever had before: more than when he had tried to bully me into marrying him: more than when I had wrenched away from him and run, bruised and terrified, to Grandfather: more than when he had tried to claim Adam's place as my lover, and told the stupid lie about the child: more than when he had brought me back, an interloper, to damage Julie.

He said nothing until we were getting down from the tractor in the yard.

'By the way, wasn't there something you wanted to talk to me about? What was it?'

'It'll keep,' I said.

Grandfather was still unconscious. The doctor had come, stayed, and then, towards evening, had gone again to a telephone summons. This was the number . . . we were to call him back, if there was any change . . . but he was afraid, Miss Winslow, Miss Dermott, he was very much afraid . . .

He lay on his back, propped on pillows, breathing heavily, and with apparent difficulty, and sometimes the breath came in a long, heaving sigh. Now and again there seemed a pause in the breathing, and then my heart would jerk and stop as if in sympathy, to resume its erratic beating when the difficult breaths began again . . .

I hadn't left him. I had pulled a chair up to one side of his bed. Con was on the other. He had spent the afternoon alternately in sitting still as a stone, with his eyes on the old man's face, or else in fits of restless prowling, silent, like a cat, which I had stood till I could stand it no longer, then had curtly told him to go out of the room unless he could keep still. He had shot me a quick look of surprise, which had turned to a lingering one of appraisement, then he had gone, but only to return after an hour or so, to sit on the other side of the old man's bed, waiting. And that look came again, and yet again, as the blue eyes kept coming back to my face. I didn't care. I felt so tired that emotion of any kind would have been an exercise as impossible as running to a wounded man. Heaven knows what was showing in my face. I had ceased to try and hide it from Con, and I could not, today, find it in me to care . . .

And so the day wore on. Lisa, quiet and efficient as ever, came in and out, and helped me to do what was needed. Mrs. Bates finished her work, but offered to stay for a time, and the offer was gladly accepted. Julie hadn't come home. After the doctor's visit, Con went out and sent one of the men up in the car to West Woodburn, but on his return he reported that neither Julie nor Donald had been seen at the site since that morning. They had gone up there some time before luncheon, had walked around for a bit, then had gone off in Donald's car. Nobody had any idea where they had gone. If it was into Newcastle —

'Forrest Hall!' I said. 'That's where they'll be! I'm sorry, Con, I'd quite forgotten.' I explained quickly about the alleged Roman carving that Adam had described. 'Ask him to go to Forrest Hall – he'd better go by the river-path, it's quicker than taking a car up past the gates.'

But the man, when he returned, had found nobody. Yes, he had found the cellars; they were accessible enough, and he thought someone had been there recently, probably today, but no one was there now. Yes, he had been right down. And there was no car parked there; he couldn't have failed to see that. Should he try West Lodge? Or Nether Shields?

'The telephone's easier,' said Con.

But the telephone was no help, either. West Lodge was sorry, but Mr. Forrest was out, and had not said when he would be back. Nether Shields – with a shade of reserve – was sorry, too; no, Julie had not been there that day; yes, thank you, Bill was quite all right; they were sorry to hear about Mr. Winslow; sorry, sorry, sorry . . .

'We'll have to leave it,' I said wearily. 'It's no use. They may have found something at Forrest, and all gone into Newcastle to look it up, or something; or Julie and Donald may have gone off on their own after they left Forrest Hall. But it's only an hour to supper-time now, and surely they'll come then? After last night – was it really only last night? – Julie *surely* won't stay away again without letting us know?'

'Do you know, you sound really worried,' said Con.

I said: 'My God, what do you think –?' then looked up and met the blue eyes across the bed where Grandfather lay. They were bright and very intent. I said shortly: 'Oddly enough, I am. I'm thinking of Julie. She would want to be here.'

His teeth showed briefly. 'I always did say you were a nice girl.'

I didn't answer.

The doctor came back just before seven, stayed a while, then went again. The day drew down, the sky dark as slate, heavy with thunder, and threatening rain.

Still Julie didn't come, and still Grandfather lay there, with no change apparent in the mask-like face, except that I thought the nostrils looked pinched, and narrower, and his breathing seemed more shallow.

Con went over to the buildings shortly after the doctor had gone, and only then, leaving Mrs. Bates in Grandfather's room, did I go downstairs for a short time, while Lisa gave me soup, and something to eat.

Then I went back, to sit there, waiting, and watching the old man's face, and trying not to think.

And, well within the hour, Con was back there, too, on the other side of the bed, watching me.

Mrs. Bates went at eight, and soon afterwards, the rain began; big, single, heavy drops at first, splashing down on the stones, then all at once in sheets, real thunder-rain, flung down wholesale from celestial buckets, streaming down the windows as thickly as gelatine. Then suddenly, the room was lit by a flash, another, and the thunderstorm was with us; long flickering flashes of lightning, and drum-rolls of thunder getting nearer; a summer storm, savage and heavy and soon to pass.

I went over to shut the windows, and remained there for a few moments, staring out through the shining plastic curtain of the rain. I could barely see as far as the buildings. In the frequent flashes the rain shimmered in vertical steel rods, and the ground streamed and bubbled with the water that fell too fast for the gutters to take it.

Still no Julie. They wouldn't come now. They would stay and shelter till it was past. And meanwhile Grandfather ...

I drew the thick chintz curtains and came back to the bed. I switched on the bedside lamp and turned it away, so that no light fell on the old man's face. Con, I saw, was watching him abstractedly, with a deep frown between his brows. He said under his breath: 'Listen to that, damn it to hell. It's enough to wake the dead.'

I was just going to say, 'Don't worry, it won't disturb him,' when Con added: 'It'll have the rest of High Riggs as flat as coconut matting. We'll never get the cutter into it after this.'

I said drily: 'No, I suppose not,' and then, sharply, all else forgotten: 'Con! It *has* woken him!'

Grandfather stirred, sighed, gave an odd little snore, and then opened his eyes. After a long time they seemed to focus, and he spoke without moving his head. The sounds he made were blurred, but clear enough.

'Annabel?'

'I'm here, Grandfather.'

A pause. 'Annabel?'

I leaned forward into the pool of light, and slid a hand under the edge of the bedclothes till it found his.

'Yes, Grandfather. I'm here. It's Annabel.'

There was no movement in the fingers under mine, no perceptible expression in Grandfather's face, but I thought, somehow, that he had relaxed. I felt his fingers, thin and frail, as smooth and dry as jointed bamboo, and no more living, lying in my palm, and remembered him as he had been in my girlhood, a tall, powerful man, lean and whippy and tyrannical, and as proud as fire. And suddenly it was too much, this slow, painful ending to the day. A day that had begun with Rowan, and the brilliant morning, and a secret that was still my own; then Adam, and the knowledge of our betrayal of each other; and now this . . .

The storm was coming nearer. Lightning played for seconds at a time, flashing like some dramatically wheeling spotlight against the shut curtains. I saw Grandfather's eyes recognise it for what it was, and said: 'It's just a summer thunderstorm. I don't suppose it'll last.'

'That noise. Rain?'

The thunder had paused. In the interval the rain came down with the noise of a waterfall. 'Yes.'

I saw his brows twitch, very faintly. 'It'll flatten – High Riggs.'

Something touched me that was partly wonder, and partly a sort of shame. Con was a Winslow after all, and perhaps his reaction had been truer than mine – my dumb fury of grief that was a grief for the passing of, not this old man, but my world, the world I hadn't wanted, and deserved to lose. I said: 'That's just what Con was saying.'

'Con?'

I nodded towards him. 'He's there.'

The eyes moved. 'Con.'

'Sir?'

'I'm – ill.'

'Yes,' said Con.

'Dying?'

'Yes,' said Con.

I felt my lips part in a sort of gasp of protest and shock, but what I might have said was stopped by Grandfather's smile. It wasn't even the ghost of his old grin, it was nothing but the slight tightening and slackening of a muscle at the corner of his mouth; but I knew then that Con was right. Whatever had been Matthew Winslow's faults, he had never lacked dignity, and he was not the man to slide out of life on a soothing flood of women's lies. He and Con had ground where they could meet, and which was forbidden to me.

My moment of protest must have communicated itself to him through our linked hands, for his eyes moved back to me, and I thought he said: 'No lies.'

I didn't look at Con. 'All right, Grandfather, no lies.'

'Julie?'

'She'll be here soon. The storm's kept her. She's been out with Donald all day. She doesn't know you're ill.'

I thought he looked a query.

'You remember Donald, darling. The Scot, Donald Seton. He's the archaeologist digging up at West Woodburn. He was here last night at – ' my voice wavered, but I managed it – 'your party.'

I could see him concentrating, but it seemed to elude him. I had to control myself sharply, not to take a tighter hold on the frail hand in mine. I leaned nearer to him, speaking slowly, and as distinctly as I could. 'You met Donald, and you liked him. He's going to marry Julie, and they'll live in London. Julie'll be very happy with him. She loves him. You needn't worry about — '

An appalling crash interrupted me. The flash, the long, growing rumble and crack of chaos, then, after it, the crash. Through all the other precoccupations in that dim room it hacked like the noise of a battleaxe.

Matthew Winslow said: 'What's that?' in a voice that was startled almost back to normal.

Con was at the window, pulling back the curtains. His movements were full of a suppressed nervous excitement, which gave them more than their usual grace, like the sinewy, controlled actions of ballet. He came back to the bedside, and bent over his great-uncle. 'It was a long way off. A tree, I'm pretty sure, but not here. One of the Forrest Hall trees, I'd say.'

He put a hand on the bed, where Grandfather's arm lay under the blankets, and added carefully and distinctly: 'You don't need to worry. I'll go out presently and find out where it was. But it's not near the buildings. And the lights are still on, you can see that. It's done no damage here.'

Grandfather said, clearly: 'You're a good boy, Con. It's a pity Annabel never came home. You'd have suited well together.'

I said: 'Grandfather –' and then stopped.

As I put my face down against the bedclothes, to hide it from him, I saw that Con had lifted his head once more and was watching me, his eyes narrow and appraising.

There was only myself and Con in the room.

CHAPTER EIGHTEEN

Nor man nor horse can go ower Tyne,
Except it were a horse of tree . . .

Ballad: *Jock o' the Side*

It seemed a very long time before Con cleared his throat to speak.

I didn't raise my head. I could feel his scrutiny, and even through the first rush of grief, the instinct that I had been rash enough to disregard, bade me hide my tears from him. I don't think I had any room, then, for conscious thought about the present danger of my position: the way my stupid, difficult safeguard against him had now become, ironically, a peril. I had known since yesterday that I would have to tell him the truth. To have discussed it today, across Grandfather's unconscious body, would have been unthinkable, like counting him already dead. And now, even if I had been ready to frame what I had to say, it was even less possible to do so.

I never knew what he was going to say. Somewhere, downstairs, a door slammed, and there were running footsteps. He checked himself, listening. I remember thinking, vaguely, that perhaps Lisa had somehow guessed what had happened. But would she have run like that? I had never seen Lisa hurry ... somehow it seemed unlike her, even if she had cared enough ...

Julie: of course, it must be Julie. I pressed my fists hard against my temples, and tried to blot the tears off against the counterpane, steadying my thoughts as best I could. Julie was coming running, just too late, and in a moment I would have to lift my face ...

The steps clattered across the hall, seemed to trip at the bottom stair, then came on up, fast. Even through the thick panels of the door I could hear the hurry of sobbing breathing. She grabbed the knob with fumbling hands. It shook even as it turned.

I lifted my head sharply. There were still tears on my face, but I couldn't help that now. Here was something more. And Con had taken his eyes off me at last, and was watching the door.

It was thrust open – no sick-room entry, this – and Julie ran into the room.

She must have come in so quickly from the dark and streaming night that her eyes had barely adjusted themselves to the light. I thought for a moment that she was going to blunder straight into the bed, and came to my feet in a startled movement of protest; but she stopped just short of the bed's foot, gasping for breath.

I had been right in my swift guess: this panic-stricken haste had had nothing to do with Grandfather. She hadn't even glanced at the bed. Her look was wild, dazed almost, and she groped for a chair-back, to which she clung as if that alone prevented her from falling.

Her hair, and the coat she wore, were soaked, so dark with rain that it took me a moment or two to realise, in that dim light, that the coat was streaked and filthy. The gay summer sandals were filthy, too, and there was dirt splashed over her hands and wrists, and smudged across her jawbone. The flush of haste stood out on her cheeks like paint.

She was looking wildly from me to Con while she fought for breath to speak. Her eyes, her whole head, jerked from one to the other and back again, in a kind of distraction that was painful to watch.

'Annabel ... Con ... Con ...'

The appeal was whispered – the sick-room atmosphere, and whatever news Lisa had given her, had overborne her own distress – but if that distress, whatever it was, had driven her to appeal to Con, then something was seriously the matter.

'Julie!' This time my movement towards her was protective. I came between her and the bed. 'Darling! Whatever's the matter?'

But something in the way I moved had got through to her. For the first time, she looked past me, fully, at the bed. I saw the shock hit her, as a stone hits a man who has been knocked half silly already. She wavered, bit her lip, and said, like a child who expects to be punished for behaving badly: 'I didn't know. Annabel, I didn't know.'

I had an arm round her. 'Yes, darling, I'm sorry. It happened just a few minutes ago. It was very sudden, and he seemed quite content. I'll tell you about it later; it's all right . . . If there's something else wrong, you can tell us now. What is it? Something else has happened? Something's wrong.'

She shook in my arms. She was trying to speak, but could only manage a whispered: 'Could you – please – please – you and Con –'

It was apparent that there would be no sense out of her yet. I spoke across her, deliberately raising my voice to a normal pitch, and making it sound as matter-of-fact as I could: 'Con, you'd better go down and tell Lisa, then would you telephone Dr. Wilson? And you might get the brandy; Julie looks as if she needs it. Julie, don't stay in here; come along to your own room –'

'The phone's off,' said Julie.

'Off?'

'Lisa says so. It went off just now, she says. She's been trying. It'll be the ivy tree. When it came down –'

'The ivy tree?' This was Con.

I said: 'The old tree by the Forrest lodge. That was what we heard come down. Never mind that. Julie –'

'It sounded nearer. Are you sure it's that one?'

'It was split. It just split in two.' Julie's voice sounded thin and empty, but unsurprised, as if the questions were relevant enough. 'Half came down right across the lodge, you see. It brought the rest of the roof down, and a wall, and –'

'That's nowhere near the telephone wires,' said Con. 'If that was all it was, there's no real damage done.'

I said: 'Shut up. This is something that matters. Go on, Julie.' I gave her a little shake. '*Julie!* Con, for God's sake go and get that brandy, the girl's going to faint.'

'There's brandy here.' He was at the bedside table. There was the splash and tinkle of liquid being poured, and he put a tumbler into my hand.

'Here, drink this.' I held the rim of Grandfather's tumbler against her chattering teeth. Behind me I caught the movement as Con drew up the sheet to cover the old man's face. The moment passed, almost without significance. I said sharply: 'Julie, pull yourself together. What's happened? Is it something to do with the ivy tree? Were you near the lodge when it – oh, my God, Con, she'd have been just about passing it when we heard it come down . . . Julie, is it *Donald?*'

She nodded, and then went on nodding, like a doll. 'He's down there. Underneath. Donald. The trees came down. It just split in two –'

'Is he dead?' asked Con.

Again, it seemed, his tactics worked better than mine. I felt the shock run through her, and her eyes jerked up to meet his. She said, sensibly enough: 'No. I don't think so, but he's hurt, he can't get out. We have to go . . . We were in the lodge, you see, and the wall came down when he went down the steps, and he's hurt, there underneath. He can't get out.' Abruptly she thrust the back of one grimy hand against her mouth, as if to stifle a cry. 'We – we'll have to go.' She looked in a kind of childish helplessness at the bed.

I said quickly: 'He doesn't need us, Julie. It's all right. We'll come now. Con, where's the car?'

'I – I brought Donald's,' began Julie, 'only –'

Con said crisply: 'You're not fit to drive. Mine's at the door. You're certain the phone's off?'

'Yes. Lisa was trying again.'

'Come on, then,' I said 'quickly.'

It was odd – I spared a fleeting thought for it as we hurried to the door – how deeply conventions are ingrained in us. Scratch the conventional man and you find the savage; look closely at the primitive, and you see the grain of the wood from which our conventions are carved. It was incredibly hard to go out of that room in a hurry, with the mind bent on violent action. It seemed like desecration, yet only a few minutes ago this had merely been the bedroom of an arrogant, difficult, temperamental old man. By some inverted process the departure of his spirit from him had hallowed the room till, shrine-like, it had become a place where normally-pitched voices and decisive actions seemed shocking.

As we reached the door, I glanced back. The sheeted shape, the single dimmed light, made of the bed a catafalque, and of the room something alien and remote. Outside was a wet night, and a fallen tree, and something urgent to do. There was no time, yet, to sit quietly, and think, either of the past, or how to meet the future. Everything has its mercies.

Lisa was in the hall, having apparently just come out of the office where the telephone was.

She stopped when she saw us. 'I've been trying to get through, Julie. It's definitely gone.'

Julie said: 'Oh *God*,' on a little sob, and stumbled, so that for a moment I thought she would pitch straight down the stairs. I gripped and held her.

'Steady up. We'll be there ourselves in a minute.'

Con, behind me, said surprisingly: 'Don't worry, we'll get him out.' He ran down past us, and across the hall, pausing with a hand on the baize door. 'Go and get into the car. Torches and brandy, Annabel, you know where they are. I'll not be a minute. There's some pieces of timber in the barn: we may need them if there's any shoring-up to be done.'

The door swung shut behind him. We ran downstairs. I paused to ask Lisa: 'Are any of the men still around?'

'No. It's Bates's day off, and Jimmy left as soon as the milking was done. The others went when the rain started. There's only Con here. You'd better go too, hadn't you? I'll go upstairs.'

'Lisa –' She guessed, as soon as I spoke; I saw it in her eyes. I nodded. 'Yes, I'm afraid so; just a few moments ago . . . But would you go up? It seems terrible just to – to run out like this.'

She said nothing. Her eyes took in my face with one of her queer, dispassionate glances, then Julie's. Then she merely nodded, and crossed the hall towards the stairs. I think, in that moment, in spite of everything, I was sincerely and deeply glad I had come home. My own isolation was one thing; Grandfather's had been another. That he had made it himself didn't matter; he hadn't cared, and Con had given him enough . . . but without me here, now, no one at Whitescar would have mourned him.

And, ironically enough, I was at the same time glad of Lisa, calm and impassive as ever, mounting the stairs to his room.

I pushed open the green baize door, and hustled Julie through it. 'Hurry. I'll bring the things. And don't worry, Julie, pet, Con'll look after him.'

It didn't even strike me at the time that the tally of irony was complete.

The big Ford was there in the yard. We had hardly scrambled into it, both close together in the front seat, when Con appeared, a shadowy, purposeful figure laden with some short, solid chunks of timber that could have been thick fencing-posts, together with an axe and a ditcher's spade. He heaved these into the back of the car, slid in behind the wheel, started the motor with a roar, and swung the car round in a lurching half-circle and through the yard gate all in a moment. The lights leaped out along the rising track. Rain, small now but still thick enough and wetting, sparkled and lanced in the light. I realised that the storm had withdrawn already; the lightning was only a faint flicker away to the east, and the thunder was silent.

The track was muddy, and Con drove fast. The car took a rising bend at forty, lurched hair-raisingly across a deep rut, swung into a skid that took her sideways a full yard on to turf, hit a stone with a bouncing tyre, and was wrenched straight to pass between the posts of the first cattle-grid, with scarcely an inch to spare on the off side.

Con said abruptly: 'What happened, Julie? Try to put us right in the picture: just where is he, how is he hurt, can we get to him?'

'It's the cellar,' she said. 'You know the place is a ruin; well, it had all fallen in where the old cellar stairs used to be, so they spent most of the day shifting that, and then –'

'They?' I said.

'Yes. Mr. Forrest had told Donald –'

'Mr. Forrest's there?'

I thought my voice sounded quite ordinary, even flat, but I saw Con turn to look at me, and then away again. The car roared round a curve, slid a little on the clay bank-side, and then straightened up for the next grid. High Riggs now. At the edge of our lights the uncut fringe of hay along the track stood up like the crest of a horse, stiff and glittering under the light rain.

'Yes,' said Julie. 'They'd been to the Hall cellars first – oh, well, never mind, but it turned out it was actually the cellars at the lodge –'

'The Roman stones,' I said. 'Oh dear heaven, yes, of course, they were still looking?'

'Yes, oh yes! When the ivy tree came down it brought down the chimney and most of that end wall, and the bit of the floor that those beams were holding. I – I was waiting outside, and –'

'Is he hurt?'

'I told you. He's down in the –'

'*Adam Forrest.* Is he hurt?'

'I don't know. But when the place came down they were both inside, and when I could get through the dust I tried to pull some of the stuff away from the cellar door, but Mr. Forrest – he was inside – shouted for me to hurry and get help, because Donald was hurt, and not answering him, and he didn't know how much because he hadn't found the torch yet, and couldn't get at him, and the stuff was settling. *Con, the gate's shut!*'

The car had been mounting the hill with a rush like a lift. She reached the crest, topped it, and even as Julie cried out, the lights, shooting out level now, caught the gate full on. The bars seemed to leap up out of the dark, solid as a cliff-wall. Beyond, the headlamps lit a field of staring cattle.

Con jammed everything on, and the car seemed to dig in its hind wheels the way a jibbing horse digs in its hoofs, to come up all standing with her bonnet touching the bars.

Before we had stopped I was out of the car and wrenching at the stiff metal fastening. The gate went wide with a swing. As the car moved slowly forward Con, leaning out of his window, shouted: 'Leave it! Get in quickly.'

I obeyed him, and even before my door was shut, we had gathered speed once more.

I said: 'Con. The cattle. They'll get through.'

'The hell with that.' I glanced at him in surprise. In the light from the dash I could see his face; it was preoccupied, and I thought it was only with the car: he was lost in the moment, in the driving, in holding the lurching, bouncing vehicle as fast as possible on an impossible road. Fast, violent action, a summons coming out of the dark like a fire alarm: that suited Con. Just as (I had had time to see it now) it suited him to save Donald; Donald would take Julie away.

'I'm sorry about that,' he was saying. 'I made sure you'd have left the gate open, Julie.'

'I – I came over the grid.'

'But it's broken.'

'I know.' She gave a little gulp that might either have been a laugh or a sob. 'I – I broke something off the car. There was an awful bang. Donald'll be livid with me . . . if he . . . if he –'

'Hold up, I said sharply. 'We're nearly there.'

'Is the top gate open?' This from Con.

'Yes.'

'Okay,' he said, and a moment later the Ford shot between the posts where the white gate swung wide, and skidded to a splashing halt in front of the looming, terrifying mass of debris that had been the ivy tree.

The lightning had split the great tree endways, so that it had literally fallen apart, one vast trunk coming down clear across the lane that led to the road, the other smashing straight down on to what had remained of the ruined lodge. It was the branches, not the trunk itself, that had actually hit the lodge, so that the masonry was not cleanly hacked through by one gigantic blow, but smashed and scattered by a dozen heavy limbs, and then almost buried from sight under the mass of tangled boughs and leaves, and the heavy, sour-smelling black mats of the ivy.

Con had swung the car slightly left-handed as it stopped, and he left the headlights on. They lit the scene with hard clarity; the huge clouded mass of the tree, its leaves glittering and dripping with the rain, among which the scattered masonry showed white: the raw new gash of the split trunk, where the black trail of the lightning could be clearly seen; and, sticking up through the boughs with a sickening kind of irrelevance, those fragments of the building that still stood. The surviving end wall and its chimney were intact, and half the front of the house, as far as the door with the heavy carved lintel, and the date, 1758 . . .

We thrust ourselves out of the car, and ran to the black gap of the doorway. In my haste I had only found one torch to bring, but there had been another in the car, and with this Con led the way through the doorway, where the car's headlamps served only to throw deeper shadows. Inside the wrecked walls was a black chaos of smashed masonry and tangled wet boughs and splintered beams.

Con hesitated, but Julie pushed past him, one hand up to keep the whipping boughs from her eyes as she thrust through the debris that blocked the hallway.

She called: 'Donald! Donald! Are you all right?'

It was Adam who answered her, his voice sounding muffled and strained. It came from somewhere to the left of the hallway and below it. 'He's all right. Have you brought help?'

'Con and Annabel. Here, Con, they're down here.'

Con had shoved after her, stooping under the barrier of one biggish branch, and was kneeling by what seemed in the torchlight to be a gap in the left-hand wall of the passage. I followed him. This was, I suppose, where the door to the cellars had stood. Now there was merely a hole through the shambles of broken masonry, not quite big enough to admit a man. It gave on darkness.

Con flashed the torch into the gap, lighting the flight of cellar steps.

Twelve steps led steeply downwards, looking undisturbed, and solid enough; at the bottom was a short length of stone-flagged passage which must have led to the cellar door. Now the doorway had disappeared. Where it had been, was a pile of stones and rubble where the ceiling and one wall had collapsed, taking with them the splintered wreckage of the doorposts. But the crossbeam still held. It had fallen where the uprights collapsed, and was wedged now at an angle, within a foot or so of the floor, roofing a narrow, triangular gap of darkness which was the only way through to the cellar beyond. Above the beam pressed the weight of the broken wall, and the broken building above, all thrust down in their turn by the pressure of the fallen boughs. Stones were still falling here and there: I heard the patter of loose stuff somewhere; the other passage-wall showed a frightening bulge; and there was fresh dust dancing in the torchlight.

Adam was lying right underneath the beam, face downwards. His feet were towards us, and the top half of his body was out of sight. I recognised the faded brown corduroys, his working-garb, now thick with dust. For one sickening moment I thought that the great beam had fallen clean across his back, then I saw there was a gap of perhaps four inches between it and his body. He must have been somewhere on the cellar steps when the crash occurred, and he had been trying to creep under the fallen stuff to reach the place where Donald lay.

And, for the moment, the crossbeam held.

'Forrest?' Con's voice was subdued. A shout, it seemed, might bring the whole thing down, irrevocably in ruins. Even as he spoke, there was the slithering sound of something settling, and the whisper of dust chuting on to the steps below us. Somewhere, some timber creaked. I think it was only a broken bough of the ivy tree, but it lifted the hair along my arms. 'Forrest?' called Con softly. 'Are you all right?'

'I'm all right.' Adam spoke breathlessly; it was as if he was making some violent effort, like holding up the beam with his own body; but he didn't move. 'Seton's inside here; there's another pile of the – stuff – just in here, past the beam, and I can't – get any purchase – to move it. He'll be safe enough ... it's a groined ceiling, it won't come down in there, and he's lying clear of this ... I can just reach him if I lie flat, but I can't get – any further – and we'll not get him out till this stuff's moved. How long will the doctor be?'

'We couldn't get him. The lines are down.'

'Dear God. Didn't Julie say –?'

'Look, if Seton's not badly hurt, you'll simply have to leave him, and come out, for the time being.' Con had propped his torch where it could light the gap, and was already, gingerly, beginning to widen this. 'You say the roof's safe over him; if you come back, we could probably shift enough stuff between us to get clear through to him. In any case, first things first, if this place isn't shored up pretty damn quick, I wouldn't give twopence for your own chances. That stuff's settling while you wait.'

I heard Julie take in her breath. Adam said painfully: 'My dear man, you'll have to prop it round me as best you can, and take the chance. Otherwise it's a certainty. I can't leave him. He's torn an artery.'

Beside me, Julie gave a little gasp like a moan. I said: 'Julie! Get a way cleared back to the car, and fetch the props. Pass them to me under that bough.'

'Yes,' she said, 'yes,' and began, with savage but barely effectual hands, to push and break a way back through the tangle to the doorway.

'I've got a tourniquet on, of a sort.' Adam's voice was still muffled, so that I hoped Julie, working a yard or two away, couldn't hear it. 'And it's doing the trick. I don't think he's losing much, now. But it's tricky in the dark, and I can't hold it indefinitely. You'll have to get the doctor straight away. Annabel?'

'Yes?'

'The car's there?'

'Yes.'

'Will you go? If you can't find Wilson straight away –'

Julie had heard, after all. She turned among the wet branches. 'The tree's down across the road, too. We can't take the car, and it's four miles.'

I said: 'The telephone at West Lodge, Adam? It's the same line as Whitescar, isn't it?'

'I'm afraid so.'

I was on my feet. 'I'll go on foot. It's all right, Julie, once I get to the road I'll get a lift.'

'There's never anything along the road at this time of night,' said Julie desperately, 'you know there isn't! If you drove the car into the field, couldn't you get it round the tree, and –?'

'No use. We've nothing to cut the wires with, and anyway she'd bog down in a yard. We're wasting time. I'm going. I'll run all the way if I have to.'

Con said: 'It's more than four miles, it's nearer six. And you might get a lift or you might not. Your best chance is Nether Shields.'

'But there's no bridge!' cried Julie.

'No,' I said, 'but I can drive right up to the footbridge at West Lodge, and then it's barely two miles up to the farm. Yes, that's it, Con.' I turned quickly back. 'Adam?'

'Yes?'

'Did you hear? I'm going to Nether Shields. Their telephone may be

working, and I can get Dr. Wilson from there. If it's not, one of the boys
will go for him. I'll send the others straight over here.'

Julie said, on a sob: 'Oh, God, it'll take an hour. Two miles up from
West Lodge, and all uphill. You'll kill yourself, and it'll be too late!'

'Nonsense!' I said. 'Run and open the gate.'

'It's open. Con left it open.'

'Not that one. It's quicker if I go by the top track through the Park.
If I go down by Whitescar, I've to use the little track up behind the
house, and there's three gates on that. Hurry, let's go!'

But she didn't move. 'A horse! That's it!'

I was propping my torch where it would help Con. I turned. 'What?'

'A horse! If you took the mare you could go straight across the ford
and across the fields, and it's hardly any further than from West Lodge,
and you'd be there much quicker!'

Con said: 'That's an idea,' then I saw it hit him. He paused fractionally,
with his fingers curled round a lump of sandstone, and I caught his bright
sidelong look up at me. He said: 'The mare's not shod.'

Julie cried: 'That doesn't matter! What does the mare matter?'

I said impatiently: 'She'd be lame in half a mile, and I'd get nowhere.'

Con said: 'Take Forrest's colt. He'll let you.' Even then, it took me
two heartbeats to realise what he was doing. Then I understood. I had
been right: none of this touched him. The agonising emergency was
nothing more to him than an exciting job. In this moment of terror and
imminent death, he was unscathed. By everything that had happened,
he was untouched. And I had liked him for it; been grateful for it.

Well, he still had to get Adam out.

I said shortly: 'It would save no time. I'd have to catch him.'

Adam's voice came again from beyond the beam. It sounded, now, like
the voice of a man at the limits of his control. 'Annabel, listen, wait, my
dear ... It's an idea. The colt's in the stable at West Lodge. I brought
him in today. Take the car across there ... if he'll face the water ...
only a few minutes to Nether Shields. He'll go, for you, I think ...'

The gap in the wall was open now. Con laid a stone down, and sat
back on his heels. The twin torchbeams held us, Con and myself, in a
round pool of limelight, one on either side of the gap. We stared at one
another. He was no longer smiling.

I said to Adam, without taking my eyes off Con: 'All right. I'll manage.'

'The second door in the stableyard. You know where the bridles are.'

'Yes. I know.'

Adam said: 'Take care, my dear. He doesn't like thunder.'

'I'll be all right.' I said it straight to that stare of Con's. 'I can manage
him. Don't worry about me.'

'You'll take the horse?' cried Julie.

'Yes. Open the top gate for me. Hold on, Adam, darling.'

As I went, I saw Con sitting there, back on his heels, staring after me.

CHAPTER NINETEEN

The water is rough and wonderful steepe,
Follow, my love, come over the strand –
And in my saddle I shall not keepe,
And I the fair flower of Northumberland.

Ballad: *The Fair Flower of Northumberland*

It was important not to think about the scene I was leaving behind me
in the dark lodge; to blot out Donald, his life ebbing slowly behind a wall
of debris; Julie, helpless, holding panic on a thin thread; Adam, prone
in the dust under that settling mass . . .

And Con there to help. I mustn't even remember that. I didn't know
how that quick brain would work; what he would seize for himself out
of this new situation. Con, if it suited Con, would work like a galley-
slave, and do miracles; but if it didn't, God alone knew what he would
do.

But I put it out of my mind, and ran to the waiting car.

It seemed to take an hour to turn her, reversing out between the pillars
of the gateway, over mosses made slimy with rain, and liberally strewn
with fallen twigs, and fragments of rotten timber, and stray stones
scattered from the smashed lodge. I made myself take it slowly, but even
so, the wheels spun and slithered crazily among the fallen rubbish, and
my hands and arms, shaking now as if with fever, seemed powerless to
control the car. I heard the ominous sound of metal scraping stone, then
we were free of the driveway, and swinging to face west again, and Julie
had run across to open the gate to the upper track.

As I passed her, I called out: 'Keep your eye open for the doctor's car!
He may already be on his way to see Grandfather.'

I saw her nod, looking pale as a ghost in the momentary glare of light,
and her mouth shaped the one word: '*Hurry!*'

I drove my foot down as far as I dared, and tried to remember what
I could of the road.

It was eight years since I had driven along the upper track to West
Lodge. Two fields first, I remembered, then trees bordering the track,
young firs, waist-high, that the forestry people had put in; for even then
Adam had been trying all means to make the estate pay its way. It was
a shock to run suddenly between black walls of spruce that shut out the
lighter night, and towered well above the roof of the car. Time was, and
they had grown a foot a year. The headlamps lit a narrow black canyon
through which we ran at a fair speed, as the track was paved with pine-
needles which had acted as drainage, and the walls of trees had kept off
the worst of the storm.

Then a gate, standing open; a long hill curling down between high banks; an avenue, planted in more leisurely days, of great beeches that soared up silver in the lights, then a twisting, up-and-down quarter-mile along the gully cut by some small stream, where all I could do was hang on grimly to the controls and hope that the track was reasonably well-drained.

It wasn't, and I soon throttled down to a safe and cowardly fifteen miles an hour, which felt slower than walking, and brought the sweat out on my body till my hands slipped on the wheel.

Then a gate, shut, hanging a little crookedly across the way.

It was almost a relief to be out of the car, and running to open it. The lever was stiff, jammed by the sagging of the hinges, but I fought it out of its socket at last, and shoved at the heavy gate. This shifted a couple of inches, and stuck. It had sagged into a muddy rut, but that was not what prevented it from opening. As I bent to heave it forcibly wider, I heard the rattle of a chain. A loop of chain, dark with rust, and with a rusty padlock tightly locked, was fastened round gate and gate-post, holding them together.

A locked gate: no place to turn the car: the choice facing me of either reversing down that dreadful piece of track till I could turn for the long trail back, and round by Whitescar; or of abandoning the car and running the half-mile between here and West Lodge. Either alternative, unthinkable . . .

There are times when your body and nerves think for you. Adrenalin, they tell you nowadays. They used to say, 'Needs must, when the devil drives', or even, 'God helps those who help themselves'.

I seized the chain and yanked at it, with the fury of desperate need, and it came off in my hands. It had only been a loop, flung loosely over the posts, to hold the gate from sagging further open. I think I stood for four precious seconds, staring at it in my hands, as if by some miracle I really had snapped its massive links like horsehair. I should have known that Adam wouldn't have let me come this way, if it had been barred.

Adam. I dropped the chain into the soaking grass by the gatepost, shoved the heavy gate wide as if it had weighed an ounce, scrambled back into the car, and was through the gate and away before the grasses had stopped shaking.

A sharp rise, then, away from the trees: and here was the straight, good half-mile across a high heathy pasture where the dry gravel of the track showed white in the lights, and as clear as if it had been marked with cats'-eyes.

The crest of the moor. A single birch tree, its stem flashing white and then lost again in the darkness behind us. Then the sudden, sharp dip of the descent towards the river, the swift, curling drop into the sheltered saucer of land where West Lodge lay.

I had forgotten just how steep the hill was, and how sharp the turn. As my lights met the crest of the hill, we must have been doing forty-five. I stood on the brake, but as we switch-backed over the top and dived for the river, we were still travelling like a bomb. The car went down the drop like an aircraft making for the touch-down. I saw the bend coming, drove my foot hard down on the brake, and put everything I had of strength and timing into getting her round the corner.

I felt the front wheel mounting the edge, swinging, thrown wide by the force of our turn. I had the steering-wheel jammed hard over to the left. I felt the rear swing, too, mount, pause . . .

We could do it. We were round . . .

On a dry night, we might have done it, even despite my bad judgment. But the track was damp, and the grass; and the wheels, at the very verge, had met mud . . .

The front of the car drifted, slid, swam uncontrollably wide. The wheel topped the bank, was over. The car lurched crazily as she hit the rough turf of the slope to the river. The lights struck the water ten yards away, and the mirror-flash startled my eyes.

I must have straightened the wheel instinctively as we left the track, or we would have turned over. As it was, the car plunged down the last four feet of the bank dead straight, in a dive for the river, lurched over a nine-inch drop to the shingle, hit the edge of the drop with her undercarriage, and stopped dead, with the front wheels on the gravel, and the water sliding by not a yard from the bonnet.

In the silence after the engine stalled, the river sounded as loud as thunder.

I sat there, still gripping the wheel, listening to the tick of cooling metal, and stupidly watching the wipers still wagging to and fro, to and fro, squealing across the dry glass. It had stopped raining some time back, and I hadn't noticed . . .

I don't know how long I sat there. Not more than seconds, I think, though it seemed an age. I was unhurt, and, though I must have been shaken, I had no time to feel it. This was a pause in the movement; no more.

I clambered out of the car. The stableyard lay no more than fifty yards away, at the foot of the hill. I retained enough wit to switch the ignition off, and the headlights, and then I abandoned the car, and ran.

I had forgotten the route, and crashed Con's car in consequence, but when I got to the stable door my hand went automatically to the light-switch, and, as the light snapped on, I reached for the bridle without even looking for it. Leather met my hand, and the cool jingle of metal. I lifted it from its peg, and then stood still for a moment or two, controlling my breathing, letting my eyes get used to the light, and the horse used to the sight of me.

It was no use approaching him like this. A few more seconds now, to let my heart slow down to something near its normal rate, and to control my hands . . . I hadn't realised, till I lifted down that ringing bridle, that my hands were shaking still.

I leaned back against the wall of the stable, and regarded the Forrest colt.

He was in a loose-box opposite the door. He stood across the far corner of it, facing away from me, but with his head round towards me, and ears pricked, inquiring, slightly startled.

I began to talk, and the effort to steady my voice steadied me. When I saw the ears move gently, I opened the loose-box and went in.

He didn't move, except to cock his head higher, and a little sideways, so that the great dark eyes watched me askance, showing a rim of white. I slid a gentle hand on to his neck and ran it up the crest towards his ears. He lowered his head then, and snuffled at the breast of my blouse.

I said: 'Help me now, Rowan, beauty,' and cupped the bit towards him. He didn't even pause to mouth it; he took it like a hungry fish taking a fly. In seven seconds after that, as smoothly as a dream, I had him bridled. In ten more, I was leading him outside into the night. I didn't take time for a saddle. I mounted from the edge of the water-trough, and he stood as quietly as a donkey at the seaside.

Then I turned him towards the river. The way led to his pasture, so he went willingly and straight, with that lovely long walk of his that ate up the yards. I made myself sit quietly. Momentarily blinded by the darkness as I was, I could neither guide nor hurry him. I talked to him, of course; it seemed that this was more for my own comfort than the horse's, but it took us both as far as the faint glimmer of the river, where a path turned off towards the pastures, from the foot of the narrow wooden footbridge.

Now, I had no idea if I could get Rowan to cross the water which, swelled a bit by the recent thunder-rain, was coming down at a fair speed, and with some sound and fury over its treacherous boulders. It would be bad enough crossing by daylight, and in the dark it was doubly hazardous. But there is no horse living, except a circus horse, that will cross the unsafe echoing of a wooden footbridge – even if I had dared put him at the triple step at either end. It was the water or nothing.

At least here we had come out from under the trees, and I could see.

The bank shelved fairly steeply near the bridge. The river was a wide, broken glimmer, with shadows where the boulders thrust up, and luminous streams of bubbling foam where the freshets broke. The sound was lovely. Everything smelt fresh and vivid after the rain. As I put Rowan at the bank I could smell thyme and water-mint, and the trodden turf as his hoofs cut it.

He hesitated on the edge, checked, and began to swerve away. I insisted. Good-manneredly he turned, hesitated again, then faced the drop of the bank. Then, as his fore-hoofs went down the first foot of the drop, he stopped, and I saw his ears go back.

Now, when one rides without a saddle, there are certain obvious disadvantages, but there is one great advantage – one is with the horse; his muscles are joined to, melted in with, the rider's; the rider is part of the beast's power, moves with him, and can think into his body a vital split-second faster than when the impulse has to be conveyed through rein and heels alone.

I felt the colt's hesitation, doubt, and momentary fear, even before the impulses had taken root in his mind, and my own impulse forward was supplied instantaneously. He snorted, then lunged forward suddenly and slithered down into the water.

I held him together as he picked his way across between the streaming boulders. I was saying love-words that I thought I had forgotten. His hoofs slipped and rang on the stones, and the water swirled, shining, round his legs. It splashed against his fetlocks, then it was to his knees; he stumbled once, and in recovering sent one hoof splodging down into a pool that drenched me to the thigh. But he went steadily on, and in no time, it seemed, the small shingle was crunching under his feet, and we were across. He went up the far bank with a scramble and a heave that almost unseated me, shook his crest, then plunged forward at a rough canter to meet the track.

This ran steeply up, here, from the footbridge, and, though rutted and uneven, lay clearly enough marked in the moonlight between its verges of dark sedge. I twisted my right hand in Rowan's mane, set him at the slope, and gave him his head.

He took it fast, in that eager, plunging canter that, normally, I would have steadied and controlled. But he couldn't, tonight, go fast enough for me . . . and besides, there was this magnificent dreamlike feeling, the flying night, the surging power that was part of me, the drug of speed that felt like speed, the desperate mission soon to be accomplished . . .

The canter lengthened, became a gallop; we were up the slope and on the level ground. There was a gate, I knew. We would have to stop and open it. Even if I hadn't been riding barebacked, I couldn't have set him to jump it in the dark. I peered ahead uncertainly, trusting the horse to see it before I did, hoping he knew just where it was . . .

He did. I felt his stride shorten, and next moment saw – or thought I saw – the dim posts of a fence, joined with invisible wire, with the shapes of cattle beyond. Across the road, nothing. The way was clear. The gate seemed to be open . . . yes, I could see it now, set to one side of the track, as if it were lying back, wide open, against the wire fence.

Rowan flicked his ears forward, then back, and hurtled down the track at full gallop.

I had hardly time to wonder, briefly, why the cattle hadn't crowded through the gap, when we were on it, and I saw. The gate for the beasts stood to the side, and was shut, as I should have known it would be. And, clear across the way, where I had thought there was a gap, lay the cattle-grid, eight feet of treacherous, clanging iron grid that, even if it didn't break his legs, would throw us both . . .

No time to stop him now, or swerve him to face the gate. Two tremendous strides, and he was on it.

This time, he thought for me. As the grid gaped in front of his feet, looking, in the dark, like a wide pit across his path, he steadied, lifted, and was over, as smoothly as a swallow in an eddy of air.

And then all at once, ahead of us, were the massed trees, and the lights of Nether Shields.

I learned afterwards that there had been some storm-damage at Nether Shields, and that after the rain was off the men – Mr. Fenwick and his two sons – had come out to take a look round. They were in the yard when I got there, and they must have heard the horse's hoofs coming up the moor at the gallop, for all three were at the gate.

The main track went by some fifty yards from Nether Shields. We cut across the corner, and I sent Rowan headlong for the gate.

It is possible that they thought the horse was bolting with me, for nobody opened the gate. Rowan came to a slithering halt with his breast almost up against the bars, and then, seeing the men, shied violently sideways and began to circle.

Someone swung the gate wide, then, and the three men stood aside. It was all I could do to get Rowan in past them, through the gate, but he went in the end, fighting every inch of the way. One of the men shut the gate behind us, and would have reached for the bridle, but I thought the horse would rear, and said breathlessly: 'Leave him. It's all right. Keep back . . .'

Someone said: 'It's Forrest's,' and another: 'It's the Winslow girl,' and then Mr. Fenwick's voice came quickly: 'What is it, lass? Trouble?'

I found I could hardly speak. I was breathless from effort, but it wasn't that. My teeth were chattering as if I was chilled. I suppose it was shock catching up on me; my whole body was shaking, now, and the muscles of my thighs felt loose against the restless movements of the colt. I think that if I hadn't had a hand in his mane, I would, shamefully, have fallen off him.

I managed to say, somehow: 'There's been an accident at the old lodge. Forrest Hall. A tree's down on the lodge, and someone's hurt, and Mr Forrest's there too. They're both trapped inside, and if they don't get help soon the whole place looks like coming down on them. The phone's off at Whitescar. Is yours working?'

Mr. Fenwick was a man of swift action and few words. He said merely: 'Don't know. Sandy, go and see. Is it for the doctor?'

'Yes. Yes. Tell him a cut artery, we think, and to come quickly. And could you come yourself – all of you, straight away? There's a wall collapsing, and the men underneath, and only Con and Julie there—'

'Aye, Bill, get the Land-Rover out. Ropes, torches, crowbars. Sandy, tell your mother.'

Sandy went in at a run. Bill had already vanished into a shed whose doors, dragged wide, showed the gleam of the Land-Rover's bonnet.

I slipped off the horse's back, and held him. 'Props,' I said. 'Have you anything to shore the stones up?'

'What sort of length?'

'Short. Just to hold them off a man. He's lying underneath. A foot, eighteen inches, anything just to hold them clear.'

'Dear God,' said the farmer.

'We had fencing posts, and Con can push them in sideways,' I said, 'but there weren't enough. And some for the passage, too, if you've any longer ones—'

'There's plenty stuff in the shed, all lengths.' He raised his voice above the sudden roar of the Land-Rover's motor. 'Put your lights on, Bill!'

The lights shot out. Rowan went back in a clattering rear, almost lifting me from the ground. I saw the farmer turn, and cried: 'Never mind! Get on! I can manage him!'

The Land-Rover came out of the shed, and stopped just short of the yard gate, with its engine ticking over and its lights full on. Bill jumped out of the front and ran back to where his father was dragging solid lumps of sawn timber from a wood-stack. I saw the gleam of a metal bar, and the shape of a heavy pick, as they were hurled into the back of the vehicle. A couple of what looked like old railway-sleepers went in after them.

'The rope from the tractor-shed?' asked Bill.

'Aye.' The farmer threw a shovel in after the rest.

Sandy must have told his mother something as he ran to the telephone, for she appeared now in the lighted doorway of the farmhouse. 'Miss Winslow? Sandy's told me of the trouble. He's on the telephone now.'

'*It's working?*'

'Oh, yes.'

'Dear God,' I said, meaning it, and put my forehead against Rowan's hot neck.

'My dear,' she said, 'don't worry. It won't be long. Doctor Wilson's not at home, he's up at Haxby, but Sandy's getting through now. He'll be down at Forrest in something under twenty minutes, and the men will be there in ten. Would you like me to go with them, in case I can help?'

There came to me, the first flush of warmth in an Arctic night, a vague memory that before her marriage to Jem Fenwick of Nether Shields, she had been a nurse. He had broken a leg and spent a month in the Royal Victoria, and taken her back with him when he was discharged. A long time ago now, but if the doctor were delayed ...

I cried: 'Oh, Mrs. Fenwick, could you go with them? *Could* you? There's Julie's young man with a cut artery, and Adam Forrest trying to hold it, and the cellar roof going to come down on them, and only Con and Julie there to try and fix it up.'

She was as decisive as her husband. 'Of course. I'll get some stuff and be with you. Don't you fret, child. Can you leave that horse, and come in?'

'No.'

She wasted no time arguing or persuading. She must have known that I was almost grateful for the job of holding Rowan quiet amid the bustle and shouting in the yard. She turned back into the house, and I heard her calling: 'Betty! Pour some of that tea into the big flask, quickly! And get the brandy. Sandy, go up and fetch blankets – what? Oh, half a dozen. Hurry, now!'

The Land-Rover was loaded; Bill had pulled the gate open, and was in the driving seat. Mr. Fenwick heaved a great coil of rope into the back, and then came over to me.

'I take it you came by West Lodge?'

'Yes. The tree that's down has blocked the lane to the main road. I drove over to West Lodge, and then took the horse.'

'Is the river deep?'

'In places, but it's coming down fastish, and near the bridge it's all boulders. There's no decent crossing, even for that thing.'

'I doubt you're right. We can drive her down and pile the stuff across into your car. It's at the Lodge?'

'No. You can't. I – I crashed it. I'm sorry, but —'

'Dear God,' he said again. 'Are you all right?'

'Yes, quite.'

'Well, we'll have to go the other way. It'll not take much longer; it's a good road. Ah, here we are.' This as Sandy ran past us with a load of blankets, which went on top of the tools and props. Then a girl, with what must have been the hot tea and brandy. And finally, Mrs. Fenwick, diminutive but bustlingly efficient, with a box in her hands, and about her, clad though she was in an old tweed coat, the impression of a comforting rustle of starch.

Everyone piled into the Land-Rover. The farmer turned to me. 'Coming? Shove the colt in the barn, he'll come to no harm. We'll make room somehow.'

I hesitated, but only for a moment. 'No. I'll take the horse back. Someone ought to go to Whitescar and tell Lisa. We'll have beds ready there. Don't bother about me. And – thank you.'

His reply was lost in the roar of the motor. The Land-Rover leaped forward, cut across the field corner, her four-wheel drive sending her through the mud churned by the cattle, as easily as if it were an arterial road. I heard Mrs. Fenwick call something shrill and reassuring, then the vehicle was nothing but a receding roar and a red light in the darkness, making for the high-road.

I only remembered then, with a curious little jolt, that I had forgotten to tell them about Grandfather.

The girl said, shyly, beside me: 'Will you come in, Miss Winslow? Just for a minute? There's tea made.'

'No, my dear. Thanks all the same. I must get back. Will you shut the gate behind me?'

'Surely.'

It wasn't so easy to mount Rowan this time, but I managed it with the aid of the gate itself, and presently, having said good night to the girl, I turned him out of the yard, to face the darkness once again.

It was now, with the job done, that nature went back on me. My muscles felt as weak as a child's, and I sat the horse so loosely that, if he had treated me to a single moment's display of temperament, I'd have slid straight down his shoulders under his hoofs.

But, the two of us alone again, he went as softly as a cat across the grass, let me open the second gate from his back, and after that he walked, with that smooth, distance-devouring stride of his, till we came to the river-bank.

Sooner than have to fight or cajole him, I'd have dismounted and led him across, myself thigh-deep. But he took to the water as smoothly as a mallard slipping off her nest, and in a few minutes more, it seemed, we were striding out at a collected, easy canter for Whitescar.

He swerved only once, as we passed the crashed Ford squatting down on the river-gravel, but a word reassured him, and he went smoothly on.

It was now, when I had no more effort to make, when Rowan was, so to speak, nursing me home to Whitescar, with the sound of his hoofs steady and soft on the turf of the avenue, that the spectres of imagination had time to crowd up out of the dark.

Do what's nearest . . . I had done just that, and I was right. Someone had to go to Whitescar, and warn Lisa what to prepare for. There was nothing I could have done at the lodge. And if I could do nothing for Adam, I could at least care for his horse, who was worth, in hard cash, at least as much as the garden and West Lodge put together . . .

But this way, I should be the last to know what had happened. And in the darkness, as Rowan (whom I would never be able to see as 'hard cash' in my life) strode steadily and softly on, I was forced at last, with nerves sufficiently stripped by shock, to admit openly to myself what I had known at some other level for long enough.

It might have already happened. This night, dark and damp and sweet-smelling, might at this moment be empty of all I cared about. All. If Adam were dead (I acknowledged it now), there was nothing else, nowhere else, nothing. They are fools indeed who are twice foolish. I had had my folly, eight years back, and again this morning in the early dewfall, and now, tonight, it might be that the chance to be a fool again was gone.

The colt stopped, lowered his head, and blew. I leaned over his neck, and pushed open the last gate. The lights of Whitescar were just below us.

A few moments later Rowan clattered into the yard, and stood still.

As I slid from his back, Lisa came hurrying out. 'I thought I heard a horse! Annabel! What's happened?'

I told her everything, as succinctly as I could. I must have been incoherent from sheer fatigue, but at least she knew that a bed, or beds, would be needed, and I must have made it clear that the doctor would soon be on his way. 'I'll be with you in a minute,' I finished wearily, 'When I've put the horse in.'

Only then did I notice how she looked from me to Rowan, and back again. 'Yes,' I said, gently, 'I did manage to ride him, after all. I always did have a way with horses.'

I left her standing there. As I led the lathered horse round the end of the Dutch barn, I saw her turn, and hurry back into the house.

The mare's box stood empty. I put the light on, and led Rowan in.

He went without even a nervous glance round at the strange stable. Even when Tommy lifted her head from the nest in the manger, blinking at the light, Rowan only snorted, blew, and then lowered his nose to forage for hay. I fastened the bars behind him, slipped the bridle off and hung it up, then tipped a measure of feed down in front of him. He blew again, sighed, and began to munch, rolling an eye back at me as I brought the brush and set to work on him. Tired as I was, I dared not leave him steaming, and lathered, as he was, with ripples of sweat like the wave-marks on a beach.

I had my left hand flat against his neck, and was currying his back and ribs vigorously, when, suddenly, I felt the muscles under my hands go tense, and the comfortable munching stopped. Rowan put his head up, and his tail switched nervously. From the corner of my eye I saw a shadow leap from the manger to the top of the partition, and vanish without a sound. Tommy, taking cover.

I glanced over my shoulder.

In the doorway, framed by the black night, stood Con. He was alone. He came quietly into the stable, and shut the half-door behind him.

CHAPTER TWENTY

'I lo'e Brown Adam well,' she says,
'I wot sae he lo'es me;
I wadna gie Brown Adam's love
For nae fause knight I see.'

Ballad: *Brown Adam*

He stopped just inside the door, and I saw him reach back to pull the upper half shut, too.

I hardly noticed what he was doing. There was room for only one thought in my mind just then. I straightened up, saying sharply: 'What's happened?'

'They got him out. The doctor got there just before I left.' He was struggling with the bolt, to thrust it home, but it was rusted, and stuck. He added, over his shoulder: 'I see you did get the colt over to Nether Shields. Congratulations.'

'*Con!*' I couldn't believe that even Con could so casually dismiss what must even now be happening up at the old lodge. '*What's happened? Are they all right? For heaven's sake!*'

He abandoned the bolt, and turned. He came no nearer, but stood there, eyeing me. Beside me, Rowan stood stiffly, not eating, motionless except for that nervously switching tail. I laid an automatic hand on his neck; it was beginning to sweat again.

Con's voice was subdued, even colourless. 'I told you. They got Seton out safely enough in the end. The cut in the artery wasn't too bad; he'd lost a fair amount of blood, and he got a bump on the head, but the tourniquet saved him, and the doctor says it won't be long till he's as right as rain. They'll be bringing him down soon.'

So fierce was the preoccupation in my mind, that only now did Con's manner – and his begging of my question – force itself on my attention. I noticed then that he seemed totally unlike himself; quiet, oddly restrained, not tired – that I could have understood – but damped-down in some way, almost as if his mind were not on what he was saying . . . or as if he was holding back what was in the forefront of it.

It came to me, quite clearly, what he was trying not to say. My hand must have moved on Rowan's neck, for the colt shifted his quarters, and his ears flattened.

I said hoarsely: 'Why did you come down like this, ahead of the rest? What are you trying to tell me?'

He looked aside, for the first time since I had known him refusing to meet my eyes – Con, who could lie his way through anything, and smile in your face while he did it. There was a horseshoe on a nail by the door; hung there for luck, perhaps, the way one sees them in stables. He fingered it idly for a moment, then lifted it down, turning it over and over in his hands, his head bent to examine it as if it were some rare treasure. He said, without looking up: 'The beam came down. I'm sorry.'

I must have been leaning back against the horse, because I remember how cold my own body seemed suddenly, and how gratefully the heat from the damp hide met it through my thin blouse. I began to repeat it after him, stupidly, my voice unrecognisable: 'The beam . . .' Then sharply: '*Adam?* Con, you're lying! It isn't possible! You're lying!'

He looked at me quickly, then down again at the metal in his hands. 'He wouldn't come out. The beam was shifting, you saw it, but he wouldn't leave Seton, he said, he'd have to take the chance. We did what we could, but with just me and Julie there . . .' He paused, and added: 'It happened just before the others got there.'

While I had been riding home. It happened then. *Then* . . .

My hand had slid up the colt's neck, and was twisted in his mane. I think it was all that was holding me up. Next day I found the cuts scored in the hand where the coarse hairs had bitten into the flesh. I said, so violently that the horse started: 'So you let it happen, did you?' Con was looking at me again now. ' "Before the others got there . . ." *Of course it was!* Because you let it happen! You did it, Connor Winslow, you wanted him dead!'

He said slowly: 'Are you crazy? Why should I want that?'

'God knows why! Do you have to have a reason? I've stopped wondering how your mind works. I suppose it suited you to let him die, just as it suited you to get Donald out alive! You think nobody exists but yourself, you think you're God . . . every rotten murderer thinks the same! So Donald's alive, and Adam – ' I stopped, as abruptly as if he had struck me across the face; then I added, quite flatly, without the faintest vestige of drama or even emotion: 'You let him die, and me not there.' And this time I wasn't talking to Con.

It must have been fully twenty seconds later that I noticed the silence. The quality of the silence. Then Rowan shifted his feet on the concrete, and I looked at Con again.

He was standing quite still, the horseshoe motionless in his hands. His eyes were wide open now, and very blue. He said softly, and the Irish was there: 'Well, well, well . . . so it's true, is it? I thought as much, up there in your grandfather's bedroom, but I couldn't quite believe it . . . not quite; not till the clever little girl took the horse.' His knuckles whitened round the horseshoe. 'So that's it, is it? That's everything clear at last.' He smiled. 'Annabel, me darlin', what a fool you've made of me, haven't you, now?'

I didn't answer. The other thing was there in front of me still, a black questioning between myself and God. Con's voice seemed to come from a long way away, like a voice on the wireless, heard from next-door through a wall. Irrelevant. A nuisance only, meaning nothing.

The horse threw up his head as Con took a step nearer. 'So it was Adam Forrest, was it? Adam Forrest? Christ, who'd have thought it? What fools we all were, weren't we, and a damned adultery going on under our very noses?' All at once his face wasn't handsome at all, but convulsed, thinned, ugly. 'And when you heard the wife was dead, you came back, you little bitch. You saw your chance to get me out, by God, and carry on your dirty little affair again into the bargain!'

That got through. 'That's not true!' I cried.

'So, you wouldn't look at me . . . I thought there was someone, I thought there was. Your grandfather thought it was me you were meeting, but you wouldn't look at me, would you, Annabel? Oh no, it had to be Forrest of Forrest Hall, no less, not your cousin, who was only good enough to work for you . . .'

Suddenly, stupid and half-fainting (as I suppose I was) with fatigue and shock, I saw what all this time I had never even guessed: a cold rage of jealousy. Not, I am sure, because Con had ever really wanted me, but simply because I had never wanted him. It had been bad enough that I had pushed him aside without a glance, but to prefer another man ... And the discovery of that man's identity had scored his vanity to the bone. And at that same moment, in that disastrous moment of clarity that had come too late, I saw, too, why Con had told that preposterous lie about the child: out of simple vanity. Everybody in the district had known I would have none of him. After I had gone, his moment came. He had been my secret lover. Grandfather's anger was a small price to pay for his own satisfaction.

He took another step forward. 'I suppose you thought he'd marry you?' His voice was cruel. 'Was that why you came back? Was it? He's married money before, and you're well worth it now, aren't you? What was the game, Annabel? What have you been playing at? Come on, let's have it. You've been playing some game with me, and I want the truth.'

He had come right up to the loose-box bar. Rowan was standing quietly now, head low, and tail still. But his ears moved with each inflection of our voices, and where I leaned against his shoulder I could feel the tiny tremors running up under his skin, like little flickers of flame.

'But Con ... Con ...' It was like groping through fog; there had been something I had to tell Con today: something about the money, that I didn't want it, and never had – that he could have it, just as he had planned, and I would take Mother's money, and go ... Something else, too: that I had torn up his 'confession' to me, and that he was free to destroy mine, with its useless signature, 'Mary Grey' ... But above all, that he could have the money; that I was glad to let him have it for Whitescar, because Adam and I ...

I turned my head into the horse's neck. 'No, Con ... not now. Not any more now. Just go away. *Go away.*'

For answer, he came closer. He was right up at the loose-box bar. He had one hand on it; in the other he still held the horse-shoe.

'You've made a fool of me all this time, so you have.' The low voice was venomous. 'Do you think I'd trust you now, with what you know about me? All that crap you talked about leaving the place, making over the money – what the hell were you playing at? Stringing me along, so you could hand me over? Or contest the Will?'

I said wearily: 'It was true. I wanted you to have it. And you did get Whitescar.'

'How do I know even that was true?' he asked savagely. 'You told me, yes, but why should I believe a word you say?'

'Oh God, Con, not now. Later, if you must ... if I ever speak to you again. Go away. Can't you see ...?'

'Can't *you* see?' asked Con, and something in his intonation got through to me at last. I lifted my head and looked hazily at him. 'Yes,' he said. 'I've taken enough risks over this, and I'm taking no more. I take my chances where they come, and I'm not missing this one. Lisa'll give me all the alibi I'll need, and there'll be nothing to prove. Even clever little Annabel isn't infallible with a young, wild brute like this ... The Fenwicks said he was all over the yard with you at Nether Shields, and they won't stop to think he's so flat out he wouldn't hurt a fly.' As he spoke, he was lifting the loose-box bar. 'Now do you understand?'

Instinct had understood for me, where my failing sense did not. I shrank away from Rowan's shoulder, and came back against the cold iron of the manger. Behind me I heard tiny stirring sounds in the straw, as the sleepy kittens searched for their mother. I believe that the only coherent thought in my mind was that Con mustn't be allowed to find them ...

He was in the box with us. I couldn't have moved if I had tried; and if I had tried, I couldn't have got away. The scene seemed to have very little to do with me. The stable was curiously dark, swimming away into an expanding, airy blackness: it was empty, except for something that moved a little, near my shoulder, and Con, coming slowly towards me with some object held in his hand, and a queer look in his eyes. I thought, but not with any sense of its meaning anything to me: he can't kill me in cold blood. Funny! he's finding it difficult. I wouldn't have thought Con would even have hesitated ...

His hand moved out, in slow motion, it seemed, and took me by the wrist. At that same half-conscious level I knew that he wanted to frighten me into moving, screaming, running, fighting – anything that could spark off in him the dangerous current of violence. But all I could hear was my brain, repeating the words which, since that morning, it had repeated over and over again, like a damaged record: 'It would be easier to be dead ...'

I must have said it aloud. I saw the blue eyes widen and flicker, close to mine, then the hand tightened on my wrist. 'You little fool,' said Con, 'he's not dead. I only said that to make you give yourself away.'

The light caught the edge of the horseshoe as he lifted it. The horseshoe: this was why he had picked it up. He had intended this. This was why he came down, alone. He had lied about Adam. He was not yet a murderer. This was the truth.

Then I screamed. I wrenched violently away from him, to get my wrist free. The movement brought me hard up against the colt's side, and jerked an oath from Con as he dropped my arm and tried to throw himself clear.

But he wasn't quite quick enough.

As I went down into the whirling blackness under the colt's belly, I heard the high scream of the horse like a grotesque mimicry of my own, saw the hoofs flash and strike as he reared straight up over me ... and then the red gloss of blood where, a moment before, Con's blue eyes had stared murder.

They told me later that they heard the scream of the colt above the engine when they were still half-way across High Riggs.

Adam wasn't with them. He, like Con, had not waited. When the horse screamed, he was already at the yard gate, and twelve seconds later he burst into the stable to find Con, thrown clean from the box by that first tremendous slash of the forehoofs, lying in his own blood with, oddly, a loose horseshoe three yards away; and in the box Rowan standing, sweating, but quiet, with me sprawled anyhow right under his feet, and his nose down, nuzzling at my hair.

He must have let Adam into the box to pick me up.

I remember, as in a darkened dream, swimming back through the mist to see Adam's face not a foot from my own. And it was only then that I accepted Con's last statement as the truth.

'Adam ...'

He had carried me out of the loose-box into an adjacent stall, and he knelt there, in the straw, with my head against his shoulder. 'Don't talk now. It's all right. Everything's all right ...'

'Adam, you're not dead?'

'No, dear. Now lie quiet. Listen, there's the Land-Rover coming down the hill. It's all over. You're quite safe. Donald's all right, did you know? Just lie still: the doctor's coming with them, there's nothing we can do.'

'Con's dead, isn't he?'

'Yes.'

'He – he was going to kill me.'

'It seems he nearly succeeded,' said Adam grimly. 'If it hadn't been for Rowan, I'd have been too late.'

'You knew?'

'I guessed.'

'How?'

'God knows. The old radar still working, I suppose. When the Fenwicks turned up, they all set to work and got the cellar walls made as safe as possible, and that beam shored up, then I came out from under, and Mrs. Fenwick – she's tiny, isn't she? – managed to creep through into the cellar to fix Donald up temporarily, till the doctor came. Your cousin was still around, then. Someone had said you were making straight back for Whitescar, to warn Lisa Dermott about beds and so forth. Then the doctor arrived. He couldn't get under the beam, of course, so everyone's attention was concentrated on getting Donald out; and in the general confusion of coming-and-going in the dark, it was some time before I noticed that Winslow wasn't there any longer. It was only then that I realised that I'd given you away to him, and I'm afraid I didn't even stop to wonder if this might have put you in danger. I just had a strong feeling that it was high time I came down here. As it was.'

I shivered, and a muscle in his arm tightened. 'I thought, when I heard you scream, that I'd come just too late.'

He bent his head, and kissed me. The things he said to me then, in the straw of the dusty stable, with the smells of meal, and the sweating horse, all round us, and the damp of the lodge cellars still on his coat, and Con's body lying there in its own bright blood under the raw electric light, were the sort of thing that one only says when one's controls have been violently lifted. They are not for re-telling, or even for remembering in daylight. But they belonged to that night of terror and discovery, when both of us had had to be driven to the very edge of loss, before we could accept the mercy that had saved us and allowed us to begin again . . .

Then the Land-Rover roared into the yard, and Adam lifted his head and shouted, and the world – in the persons of the doctor, the Fenwicks, and a couple of strangers who had come down with the doctor when they heard of the accident at the lodge – bustled in on our tragic little Eden.

Adam neither moved, nor let me go. It was as if those early months of lies and subterfuge were suddenly, now, to be purged and forgotten. He knelt without moving, holding me to him, and, as they exclaimed with horror, and the doctor got down beside Con, told them precisely and in a few words what had occurred. Not the attempt at murder, never that: simply that Con (who had come down ahead of the rest to give Lisa and me the good news) had, not realising the danger, walked into the loose-box, tripped, and startled the colt, which had reared back and accidentally caught him with its forehoofs. And I – explained Adam – had fainted with the shock.

'And this shoe?' Mr. Fenwick had picked it up and was examining it. 'He cast this?'

I had been slow to grasp the significance of Con's choice of weapon. Adam, I saw, got there straight away. If he had noticed the thing earlier, he would no doubt have removed it. He said steadily: 'It doesn't look to me like one of Rowan's. It must have fallen from a nail. Was it in the box? Maybe that was what Winslow tripped over.'

The farmer turned the shoe over in his hand. It was clean. He glanced at Rowan's forefeet, which were (mercifully) out of my sight. 'Aye,' he said, 'likely enough,' and put the thing up on a window-sill.

It was late next afternoon when Julie and I walked up through the fields towards the old lodge.

The air was fresh and sparkling after the storm, the light so clear that each blade of grass seemed to stand separately above its shadow, and there were wild flowers out along the roadside where yesterday there had been only dusty and yellowed turf. We let ourselves out of the gate marked WHITESCAR, and stopped there, looking at the wreckage of the lodge and the ivy tree.

Even this, the day transformed. The great cloud of oak-boughs with their golden leaves as yet unfaded, the dark trails of ivy, the pink roses still rioting over what remained of the stone-work – these, in this lovely light, clothed the scene in an air of pastoral, even idyllic melancholy. Last night's near-tragedy might never have been.

But there were the marks of the tyres where I had turned the car:

there, a few of the timber-props still lying; here, most telling of all, the clearing that the Fenwick boys had had cut through the part of the tree that blocked the roadway, to let the ambulance through.

Julie and I stood looking at this in silence.

'Poor Lisa,' I said at length.

'What will she do?' Her voice was subdued.

'I asked her to stay, but she's going home, she says. I suppose it's best. What's done is done, and we can only try to forget it.'

'Yes.' But she hesitated. I had told her, now, the story of my conspiracy with Con and Lisa, and also the truth of what had happened last night. 'I still don't really understand, you know.'

'Who ever does understand what drives a man to murder? You know what he thought last night, of course? He only had my word for it that Grandfather had left Whitescar to him, and when he discovered that I really was Annabel, he couldn't imagine that I'd have stood by and let Grandfather will it away from me. Then he realised that Adam had been – was still – my lover. I believe he had an immediate vision of my marrying Adam and settling here. I doubt if he took time to think anything out clearly; he just knew that I was in a position to contest the Will if it *was* in his favour, and even to arraign him for trying to get money by false pretences.'

'I see.' She gave a little shiver. 'What I can't make out is why he *didn't* just let the beam down, last night? He could have done, so easily. It would have killed them both, but I don't believe he would have cared.'

'No. But he wanted Donald alive . . . and besides, you were there, watching. It wouldn't have been so easy. And Adam's death would only have solved one problem: mine solved them all. Whether I'd told the truth about the Will or not, Con stood to gain by killing me. There was the money, too, remember. He wasn't sure of anything, but he wasn't risking failure at that stage, and the chance was too good to miss. I said Con was never afraid to chance his arm.'

'With me, for instance, that night by the river?'

'I think so.'

We were silent for a while. Then she touched my arm. 'Why do you look like that?'

'I find it very hard not to blame myself.'

'Blame yourself?' cried Julie. 'Annabel, *darling*, what *for*?'

'I can't help feeling that what happened last night was partly my fault. If I hadn't been so tired and stupid – and if Con hadn't shaken me to pieces with that lie about Adam – I'd have managed to make him see I wasn't hatching plots to do him out of Whitescar. Or if I'd seen him earlier – or even if I hadn't tried to be so clever in the first place, and come back here to outplay him at his own game – '

'Stop this!' She gave my arm a little shake. 'Be sensible, for pity's sake! All the trouble and violence there's been, has come solely from Con! He's to blame from first to last for what happened last night, you know he is!

He went down to the stable with the intention of murdering you, just *on the chance* that you might do him some harm! Yes, it's true, *and you* know it. Even if you'd been fit to talk to him, do you suppose he'd have listened? Not he! And as for deceiving him over the Mary Grey business, whose fault was that? If he hadn't frightened you to death eight years ago you'd never have *dreamed* of trying it! And if you hadn't thought he was a danger to Grandfather and me – which he was – you wouldn't have come at all. Oh, no, honey, let's have no nonsense about blaming yourself. Come off it!'

'All right.' I smiled at her.

'Advice from Aunt Julie.' She squeezed my arm lightly, then let it go. 'Tit for tat. I took yours, so you take mine. Forget all about it just as soon as you can; it's the only thing to do. We've an awful lot to be thankful for, if you ask me!'

'Yes, indeed.' I tilted my head back and looked up where the young oak-leaves glowed golden against the deep blue sky. 'Do you know what I'd like to do, Julie?'

'What?'

'Rescue that blessed oak crossbeam from under this mess when they clear it up, and have something made of it, for Whitescar. Something we'll both of us use, a small table, or a bedhead, or even just a shelf for Adam to keep the stud trophies on, and the cups I got for riding.'

'Why not? It seems a pity to let it rot underground. It saved them both. Keep a bit for me, too.' She smiled a little. 'I dare say there'll be room for an ash-tray or two in our London rooms. What about the tree that caused all the trouble?'

'The ivy tree?' I walked across to where it lay in its massive wreckage. 'The poor old tree.' I smiled, perhaps a little sadly. 'Symbolic, do you think? Here lies the past – all the lies and secrecy, and what you would have called "romance" . . . And now it'll be cleared up and carted away, and forgotten. Very neat.' I put out a gentle hand to touch a leaf. 'Poor old tree.'

'I wish – ' Julie stopped and gave a little sigh. 'I was just going to say that I wished Grandfather could have known that you and Adam would be at Whitescar, but then he'd have had to know the rest, too.'

We were silent, thinking of the possessive, charming old man who had delighted in domination, and who had left the strings of trouble trailing behind him, out of his grave.

Then Julie gave a sudden exclamation, and started forward past me. I said: 'What is it?'

She didn't answer. She climbed on to what remained of the parapet of the old wall, and balanced there, groping into the fissure that gaped wide in the split trunk of the ivy tree. Somewhere, lost now among the crumbling, rotten wood, was the hole which the foolish lovers of so long ago had used as a letter-box. It was with a queer feeling of *déjà vue* that I watched Julie, slight and fair, and dressed in a cotton frock that I might have worn at nineteen, reach forward, scrape and pull a little at the rotten wood-fragments, then draw from among them what looked like a piece of paper.

She stood there on the wall-top, staring down at it. It was dirty, and stained, and a little ragged at the edges, but dry.

I said curiously: 'What is it?'

'It's a – a letter.'

'Julie! It can't be! Nobody else – ' My voice trailed away.

She came down from the wall, and held it out to me.

I took it, glanced down unbelievingly at it, then stood staring, while the writing on it swam and danced in front of me. It was young, hurried-looking writing, and even through the blurred, barely legible ink, and the dirt and mould on the paper, I could see the urgency that had driven the pen. And I knew what the illegible letters said.

> 'Adam Forrest, Esq.,
> Forrest Hall,
> Nr. Bellingham,
> Northumberland.'

And the blur across the top said: '*Private*.'

I became conscious that Julie was speaking.

'. . . And I met the post-woman at the top of the road. You remember her, old Annie? She retired that year. She gave me the Whitescar letters, and I brought them down for her. She shouldn't have done it, but you know how she used to, to save herself the long train . . . Well, I'd seen you and Adam putting notes in the ivy tree, and I suppose, being a kid, I thought it was quite the natural thing to do . . . ' Her voice wavered; I realised that I had turned and was staring at her. 'So I put that one in the ivy tree. I remember now. I never thought another thing about it. I – I climbed up on the wall and shoved it in as far as it would go.'

I said: 'And of course, once he knew I'd gone, he'd never have looked in there again.'

'Of course not. Annabel – '

'Yes?'

'Was it – do you suppose it was a particularly important letter?'

I looked down at the letter in my hand, then up at the ivy tree, where it had lain for eight years. If it had reached him, all that time ago, what would have happened? His wife ill, and heading towards complete breakdown, himself wretched, and an unhappy young girl throwing herself on his mercy and his conscience? Who was to say that it had not been better like this? The time we had lost had, most of it, not been our time. The ivy tree, that 'symbol', as I had called it, of deceit, had held us apart until our time was our own, and clear . . .

Julie was watching me anxiously. 'I suppose it *might* have been important?'

'I doubt it.'

'I – I'd better give it to him, and tell him, I suppose.'
I smiled at her then. 'I'm meeting him this evening. I'll give it to him myself.'
'Oh, would you?' said Julie, thankfully. 'Tell him I'm *terribly* sorry, and I hope it wasn't anything that *mattered*!'
'Even if it was,' I said, 'it can hardly matter now.'

I might have been alone in a painted landscape. The sky was still, and had that lovely deepening blue of early evening. The high, piled clouds over to the south seemed to hang without movement. Against their curded bases the fells curved and folded, smooth slopes of pasture, fresh from last night's rain, and golden-green in the late sunlight.

The blocks of the Roman-cut stone were warm against my back. Below me the lough dreamed and ruffled, unchanged since the day I had first sat here. Two black-faced lambs slept in the sun; the same two, it seemed, that had lain there eight years ago, when it had all begun . . .

Time was. Time is . . .

I sat there, eyes shut, and remembered, in the warm green-and-blue silence. Not a lamb called; the curlews were silent; there was no breeze to stir the grasses, and the bees had gone home from the thyme. It might have been the world before life began, and I might have been the first and only woman in it, sitting there dreaming of Adam . . .

'Annabel.'

Though I had been waiting, I hadn't heard him approach. He had come quietly along the turf to the south of the Wall. He was standing close behind me. The lambs, sleepy-eyed, had not even raised their heads.

I didn't turn. I put up a hand, and when his closed over it, I drew the scarred back of it down against my cheek, and held it there.

Time is to come . . .

Madam,
Will You Talk?

For
My Mother and Father

CHAPTER ONE

Enter four or five players

The whole affair began so very quietly. When I wrote, that summer, and asked my friend Louise if she would come with me on a car trip to Provence, I had no idea that I might be issuing an invitation to danger. And when we arrived one afternoon, after a hot but leisurely journey, at the enchanting little walled city of Avignon, we felt in that mood of pleasant weariness mingled with anticipation which marks, I believe, the beginning of every normal holiday.

No cloud in the sky; no sombre shadow on the machiolated walls; no piercing glance from an enigmatic stranger as we drove in at the Porte de la République and up the sun-dappled Cours Jean-Jaurès. And certainly no involuntary shiver of apprehension as we drew up at last in front of the Hôtel Tistet-Védène, where we had booked rooms for the greater part of our stay.

I even sang to myself as I put the car away, and when I found they had given me a room with a balcony overlooking the shaded courtyard, I was pleased.

And when, later on, the cat jumped on to my balcony, there was still nothing to indicate that this was the beginning of the whole strange, uneasy, tangled business. Or rather, not the beginning, but my own cue, the point where I came in. And though the part I was to play in the tragedy was to break and re-form the pattern of my whole life, yet it was a very minor part, little more than a walk-on in the last act. For most of the play had been played already; there had been love and lust and revenge and fear and murder – all the blood-tragedy bric-à-brac except the Ghost – and now the killer, with blood enough on his hands, was waiting in the wings for the lights to go up again, on the last kill that would bring the final curtain down.

How was I to know, that lovely quiet afternoon, that most of the actors in the tragedy were at that moment assembled in this neat, unpretentious little Provençal hotel? All but one, that is, and he, with murder in his mind, was not so very far away, moving, under that blazing southern sun, in the dark circle of his own personal hell. A circle that narrowed, gradually, upon the Hôtel Tistet-Védène, Avignon.

But I did not know, so I unpacked my things slowly and carefully, while, on my bed, Louise lay and smoked and talked about the mosquitoes.

'And now – a fortnight,' she said dreamily. 'A whole fortnight. And nothing to do but drink, and sit in the sun.'

'No eating? Or are you on a cure?'

'Oh, that. One's almost forgotten how. But they tell me that in France the cattle still grow steaks ... I wonder how I shall stand up to a beefsteak?'

'You have to do these things gradually.' I opened one of the slatted shutters, closed against the late afternoon sun. 'Probably the waiter will just introduce you at first, like Alice – Louise, biftek; biftek, Louise. Then you both bow, and the steak is ushered out.'

'And of course, in France, no pudding to follow.' Louise sighed. 'Well, we'll have to make do. Aren't you letting the mosquitoes in, opening that shutter?'

'It's too early. And I can't see to hang these things away. Do you mind either smoking that cigarette or putting it out? It smells.'

'Sorry.' She picked it up again from the ash-tray. 'I'm too lazy even to smoke. I warn you, you know, I'm not going sight-seeing. I couldn't care less if Julius Caesar used to fling his auxiliaries round the town, and throw moles across the harbour mouth. If you want to go and gasp at Roman remains you'll have to go alone. I shall sit under a tree, with a book, as near to the hotel as possible.'

I laughed, and began putting out my creams and sunburn lotions on what the Hôtel Tistet-Védène fondly imagined to be a dressing-table.

'Of course I don't expect you to come. You'll do as you like. But I believe the Pont du Gard—'

'My dear, I've seen the Holborn Viaduct. Life can hold no more. ...'

Louise stubbed out her cigarette carefully, and then folded her hands behind her head. She is tall and fair and plump, with long legs, a pleasant voice, and beautiful hands. She is an artist, has no temperament to speak of, and is unutterably and incurably lazy. When accused of this, she merely says that she is seeing life steadily and seeing it whole, and this takes time. You can neither ruffle nor surprise Louise; you can certainly never quarrel with her. If trouble should ever arise, Louise is simply not there; she fades like the Cheshire Cat, and comes back serenely when it is all over. She is, too, as calmly independent as a cat, without any of its curiosity. And though she looks the kind of large lazy fair girl who is untidy – the sort who stubs out her cigarettes in the face-cream and never brushes the hairs off her coat – she is always beautifully groomed, and her movements are delicate and precise. Again, like a cat. I get on well with cats. As you will find, I have a lot in common with them, and with the Elephant's Child.

'In any case,' said Louise, 'I've had quite enough of ruins and remains, in the Gilbertian sense, to last me for a lifetime. I live among them.'

I knew what she meant. Before my marriage to Johnny Selborne, I, too, had taught at the Alice Drupe Private School for Girls. Beyond the fact that it is in the West Midlands, I shall say nothing more about the Alice Drupe as it is virtually impossible to mention it without risking a heavy libel action. Louise was still Art Mistress there, and owed her continued health and sanity to the habit I have described, of removing herself out of the trouble zone. As far as it was possible to do this at the

Alice Drupe, she did it. Even there, she saw life steadily. At any rate she saw it coming.

'Don't speak too soon,' I warned her. 'You may yet come across Lloyd-Lloyd and Merridew sipping their Pernod in the restaurant downstairs.'

'Not *together*, my dear. They don't speak now. The Great Rupture paralysed the whole school for weeks. . . .' She paused and wrinkled her nose. 'What a revolting metaphor . . . And *not* Pernod, Charity; Vichy water.' She lit another cigarette.

'What happened?'

'Oh, Merridew put up a notice without asking Lloyd, or Lloyd put one up without asking Merridew, or something desperately frightful like that,' she said indifferently. 'I wasn't there.'

Naturally not.

'Poor things,' I said, and meant it.

Louise flicked her ash neatly into the bowl, and turned her gold head on the pillow.

'Yes, you can say that. You're out of it now for good, aren't you? You're lucky.'

I didn't answer. I laid Johnny's photograph gently back in the case, where I had just come across it, and picked up a frock instead. I shook it out and laid it over a chair, ready to put on. I don't think my expression changed at all. But Louise happens to know me rather well.

She ground out her cigarette, and her voice changed.

'Oh God, Charity, I'm sorry. I forgot. I am a fool. Forgive me.'

'Forget it,' I said, lightly enough, 'I do.'

'Do you?'

'Of course. It's a long time now. I'd be silly and unnatural not to. And I *am* lucky, as you said.' I grinned at her. 'After all, I'm a wealthy widow . . . look at these.'

'My dear girl! What *gorgeous* undies. . . .'

And the conversation slipped comfortably back to the things that really matter.

When Louise had gone to her own room, I washed, changed into a white frock with a wide blue belt, and did my face and hair very slowly. It was still hot, and the late sun's rays fell obliquely across the balcony, through the half-opened shutter, in a shaft of copper-gold. Motionless, the shadows of thin leaves traced a pattern across it as delicate and precise as a Chinese painting on silk. The image of the tree, brushed in like that by the sun, had a grace that the tree itself gave no hint of, for it was merely one of the nameless spindly affairs, parched and dust-laden, that struggled up towards the sky from their pots in the hotel court below. But its shadow might have been designed by Ma Yüan.

The courtyard was empty; people were still resting, or changing, or, if they were the mad English, walking out in the afternoon sun. A white-painted trellis wall separated the court on one side from the street, and beyond it people, mules, cars, occasionally even buses, moved about their business up and down the narrow thoroughfare. But inside the vine-covered trellis it was very still and peaceful. The gravel between the gay little chairs was carefully raked and watered; shade lay gently across the tables, some of which, laid for dinner, gleamed invitingly with glass and silver. The only living thing in the court was a thin ginger cat, which was curled round the base of my spindly tree, like – who was it? Nidhug? – at the root of Yggdrasil.

I sat down by the half-shuttered window and began to think about where I should go to-morrow.

Avignon Bridge, where one dances, of course; and after Avignon itself, the Pont du Gard – in spite of the fact that I, too, had seen Holborn Viaduct. I picked up the Michelin Guide to Provence, and looked at the sketch of the great aqueduct which is on the cover. . . .

To-morrow, I said to myself, I would take things easy, and wander round the ramparts and the Popes' Palace. Then, the day after. . .

Then fate, in the shape of Nidhug, took a hand.

My cue had come. I had to enter the stage.

The first hint I had of it was the violent shaking of the shadows on the balcony. The Chinese design wavered, broke, and dissolved into the image of a ragged witch's besom, as the tree Yggdrasil vibrated and lurched sharply under a weight it was never meant to bear. Then the ginger cat shot on to my balcony, turned completely round on a space the size of a sixpence, sent down on her assailant the look to end all looks, and sat calmly down to wash. From below a rush and a volley of barking explained everything.

Then came a crash, and the sound of running feet.

The cat yawned, tidied a whisker into place, swarmed in a bored manner up an impossible drainpipe, and vanished on to the roof. I got up and looked over the balcony railing.

The courtyard, formerly so empty and peaceful, seemed all of a sudden remarkably full of a boy and a large, nondescript dog. The latter, with his earnest gaze still on the balcony, was leaping futilely up and down, pouring out rage, hatred and excitement, while the boy tried with one hand to catch and quell him, and with the other to lift one of the tables which had been knocked on to its side. It was, luckily, not one of those which had been set for dinner.

The table, which was of iron, was very heavy, and the boy seemed to be having some difficulty in raising it. Eventually he let go the dog, and taking both hands to the job, succeeded in lifting the table almost half-way. Then the dog, who appeared to be a little slow in the uptake, but a sticker for all that, realized that his prey was gone from the balcony and leaped madly in several directions at once. He crashed into the boy. The table thudded down again.

'*Oh Rommel!*' said the boy, surprisingly enough.

Before I could decide what language this was, the boy looked up and saw me. He straightened, pushed his hair back from his forehead, and grinned.

'*J'espère*,' he said carefully, '*que ce n'était pas votre chat, mademoiselle?*'

This, of course, settled the question of his nationality immediately, but I am nothing if not tactful. I shook my head.

'My French isn't terribly good,' I said. 'Do you speak English, monsieur?'

He looked immensely pleased.

'Well, as a matter of fact, I *am* English,' he admitted. '*Stop* it, Rommel!' He grabbed the dog with decision. 'He hadn't hurt the cat, had he? I just saw it jump for the balcony.'

'It didn't look very worried.'

'Oh, that's all right, then. I can't persuade him to behave decently, as – as befits a foreigner. It seems funny to *be* foreigners, doesn't it?'

I admitted that it did indeed.

'Have you just arrived?'

'At about four o'clock. Yes.'

'Then you haven't seen much of Avignon yet. Isn't it a funny little town? Will you like it, do you think?'

'I certainly like what I've seen so far. Do *you* like it here?'

It was the most trivial of small-talk, of course, but his face changed oddly as he pondered the question. At that distance I could not read his expression, but it was certainly not what one might expect of a boy – I judged him to be about thirteen – who was lucky enough to be enjoying a holiday in the South of France. Indeed, there was not much about him at that moment, if you except the outward signs of crumpled shirt, stained shorts, and mongrel dog, to suggest the average boy at all. His face, which had, even in the slight courtesies of small-talk, betrayed humour and a quick intelligence at work, seemed suddenly to mask itself, to become older. Some impalpable burden almost visibly dropped on to his shoulders. One was conscious, in spite of the sensitive youth of his mouth, and the childish thin wrists and hands, of something here that could meet and challenge a quite adult destiny on its own ground, strength for strength. The burden, whatever it was, was quite obviously recognized and accepted. There had been some hardening process at work, and recently. Not a pleasant process, I thought, looking at the withdrawn profile bent over the absurd dog, and feeling suddenly angry.

But he came out of his sombre thoughts as quickly as he had gone in – so quickly, in fact, that I began to think I had been an over-imaginative fool.

'Yes, of course I like it. Rommel doesn't, it's too hot. Do you like the heat?' We were back at the small-talk. 'They said two English ladies were coming to-day; that would be you – Mrs. Selborne and Miss Crabbe?'

'Cray. I'm Mrs. Selborne,' I said.

'Yes, that's it.' His grin was suddenly pure small-boy. 'I'm bad at remembering names, and I have to do it by – by association. It sometimes goes awfully wrong. But I remembered yours because of Gilbert White.' Now most people could see the connection between cray and crab, but not many thirteen-years-olds, I thought, would be so carelessly familiar with Gilbert White's letters from his little Hampshire village, which go under the title of *The Natural History of Selborne*. I had been right about the intelligence. I only knew the book myself because one is apt to be familiar with most of the contexts in which one's name appears. And because Johnny—

'My name's David,' said the boy. 'David Shelley.'

I laughed.

'Well, that's easy enough to remember, anyway. How do you do, David? I shall only have to think of the Romantic poets, if I forget. But don't hold it against me if I address you as David Byron, or—'

I stopped abruptly. The boy's face, smiling politely up at me, changed again. This time there could be no mistake about it. He went suddenly rigid, and a wave of scarlet poured over his face from neck to temples, and receded as quickly, leaving him white and sick-looking. He opened his mouth as if to speak, fumbling a little with the dog's collar. Then he seemed to make some kind of effort, sent me a courteous, meaningless little smile, and bent over the dog again, fumbling in his pocket for string to fasten him.

I had made a mistake, it seemed. But I had not been mistaken when I had sensed that there was something very wrong somewhere. I am not a person who interferes readily in other people's affairs, but suddenly, unaccountably, and violently, I wanted to interfere in this one.

I need not have worried; I was going to.

But not for the moment. Before I could speak again we were interrupted by a woman who came in through the vine-trellis, from the street. She was, I guessed, thirty-five. She was also blonde, tall, and quite the most beautiful woman I had ever seen. The simple cream dress she wore must have been one of Dior's favourite dreams, and the bill for it her husband's nightmare. Being a woman myself, I naturally saw the enormous sapphire on her left hand almost before I saw her.

She did not see me at all, which again was perfectly natural. She paused a moment when she saw David and the dog, then came forward with a kind of eye-compelling grace which would have turned heads in Piccadilly, Manchester, on a wet Monday morning. What it did in Provence, where men make a hobby of looking at women, I hesitated to think. I believe I had visions of the cafés along the Rue de la République emptying as she passed, as the houses of Hamelin emptied a different cargo after the Pied Piper.

She paused by the upturned table and spoke. Her voice was pleasant, her English perfect, but her accent was that of a Frenchwoman.

'David.'

No reply.

'*Mon fils.* ...'

Her son? He did not glance up.

She said, evenly: 'Don't you know what the time is? And what on earth happened to the table?'

'Rommel upset it.' The averted head, the sulky-sounding mumble which David accorded her, were at once rude and surprising. She took no notice of his manner, but touched him lightly on the shoulder.

'Well, put it right, there's a good boy. And hurry up and change. It's nearly dinner-time. Where have you been to-day?'

'By the river.'

'How you can—' She laughed and shrugged, all at once very French, then reached in her bag for a cigarette. 'Well, put the table up, child.'

David pulled the reluctant Rommel towards a tree, and began to tie him to its stem. He said flatly:

'I can't lift it.'

A new voice interrupted, smoothly:

'Permit me, madame.'

The man who had come quietly out of the hotel was dark and singularly good-looking. His clothes, his air, no less than his voice, were unmistakably French, and he had that look of intense virility and yet sophistication – the sort of powerful, careless charm which can be quite devastating. It was all the more surprising, therefore, that the woman, after a glance of conventional thanks, ignored him completely, and lit her cigarette without glancing in his direction. I would have gone to the stake for my conviction that she, where men were concerned, was the noticing type.

The newcomer smiled at David, lifted the heavy table without apparent effort, set it straight, then dusted his hands on a handkerchief.

'Thank you, sir,' said David. He began untying Rommel again from the tree.

'*De rien,*' said the Frenchman. 'Madame.' He gave a little bow in her direction, which she acknowledged with a faint polite smile, then he made his way to a table in the far corner of the courtyard, and sat down.

'If you hurry,' said David's mother, 'you can have the bathroom first.'

Without a word the boy went into the hotel, trailing a somewhat subdued dog after him on the end of the string. His mother stared after him for a moment, with an expresson half puzzled, half exasperated. Then she gave a smiling little shrug of the shoulders, and went into the hotel after the boy.

The Frenchman had not noticed me either; his handsome head was bent over a match as he lit a cigarette. I went quietly back through my window, and stood for a moment in the cool shade of the room thinking over the little scene which, somehow, had hidden in it the elements of oddity. The exquisite film-starry creature, and the dilapidated dog . . . Christian Dior and Gilbert White . . . and she was French and the boy's accent was definitely Stratford-atte-Bow . . . and he was rude to her and charmingly polite to strangers.

Well, it was no affair of mine.

I picked my bag up and went downstairs for a drink.

CHAPTER TWO

Ther saugh I first the derke ymaginyng
Of felonye . . .

CHAUCER

When I got down into the little courtyard, it was beginning to fill up. Louise was not down yet, so I found a table in the shade, and ordered a Cinzano.

I looked about me, resigned to the fact that almost everybody in the hotel would probably be English too. But the collection so far seemed varied enough. I began to play the game of guessing at people's professions – and, in this case, nationalities. One is nearly always wrong, of course, and it is a game too often played by those self-satisfied people who are apt to announce that they are students of human nature . . . but I played it, nevertheless.

The two men at the next table to me were Germans. One was thin and clever-looking, and the other was the fat-necked German of the cartoons. And since I heard him say '*Ach, so?* ' to his companion, it didn't need any great insight to hazard the rest. There was a young couple, honeymooning at a guess, and, at another guess, American. Then there was the handsome Frenchman, drinking his Pernod by himself in the corner, and another man sitting alone near the trellis, reading a book and sipping a bright green drink with caution and distrust. I puzzled for a long time over him – he might have been anything – until I saw the title of the book. *Four Quartets*, by T. S. Eliot. Which seemed to settle it. There were two other parties who might have been anything at all.

At this point Louise joined me.

'I have been kept from my drink.' she complained, bitterly for her, 'by the *patronne*, who is convinced that I cannot wait to know the history, business, and antecedents, of everyone in the hotel. And who, incidentally, was panting to find out mine and yours.'

Her vermouth was brought, and she tilted it to the light with a contented sigh.

'*L'heure de l'apéritif.* What a civilized institution. Ah, that must be M. Paul Véry.' She was looking at the Frenchman in the corner. 'Madame said he was handsome enough to suicide oneself for, and that hardly applies to anyone else here. He's from Paris. Something to do with antiques.'

'This is thrilling.'

'The other lonely male is English, and a schoolmaster. His name is John Marsden and he is almost certainly a Boy Scout and a teetotaller as well.'

'Why on earth?' I asked, startled.

'Because,' said Louise drily, 'any lonely male I ever get within reach of these days seems to be both, and to eschew women into the bargain. Is that the right word, eschew?'

'I believe so.'

'At any rate, one would not suicide onself for *that* one. I wonder why he looks so solemn? Do you suppose he's reading *Whither England*, or something?'

'It's T. S. Eliot,' I said. '*Four Quartets.*'

'Oh *well*,' said Louise, who does not consider poetry necessary. Mr. Marsden was dismissed.

'I suppose that couple are American?' I said.

'Oh yes. Their name is Cornell, or they come from Cornell, or something. My French had a breakdown at that point. And Mama and Papa under the palm tree are hot from Newcastle, Scotland.'

'Scotland?' I said blankly.

'So Madame informed me. Scotland, zat is ze Norz of England, *n'est-ce pas*? I like the daughter, don't you? The Young Idea.'

I looked cautiously round. The couple under the palm tree might have sat anywhere for the portrait of Suburban England Abroad. Dressed as only the British can dress for a sub-tropical climate – that is, just as they would for a fortnight on the North-East coast of England – they sat sipping their drinks with wary enjoyment, and eyeing their seventeen-year-old daughter with the sort of expression that barnyard fowls might have if they suddenly hatched a flamingo. For she was startling to say the least of it. She would have been pretty in a fair English fashion, but she had seen fit to disguise herself by combing her hair in a flat thick mat down over one side of her face. From behind the curtain appeared one eye, blue-shadowed to an amazing appearance of dissipation. Scarlet nails, spike-heeled sandals, a flowered dirndl and a cotton jersey filled to frankly unbelievable proportions by a frankly impossible figure ... Hollywood had come to Avignon by way of the Scotswood Road. And it became apparent that this not inconsiderable battery of charm was turned full on for someone's benefit.

'The man in the corner ...' murmured Louise.

I glanced towards M. Paul Véry, who, however, appeared quite indifferent to the effort being made on his behalf. He had a slight frown between his brows, and he was tracing a pattern with the base of his glass on the table-top as if it were the only thing that mattered in the world.

'She's wasting her time, I'm afraid,' I remarked, and, as if he had heard me (which was impossible) the Frenchman looked up and met my eyes. He held them deliberately for a long moment in a cool, appraising stare, then, just as deliberately, he raised his glass and drank, still with his eyes on me. I looked away to gaze hard at the back of the fat German's neck, and hoped my colour had not risen.

'She is indeed wasting her time,' said Louise softly. She raised an amused eyebrow at me. 'Here's metal more attractive.'

'Don't be idiotic,' I said with some asperity. 'And control your imagination, for goodness' sake. Don't forget this is Provence, and if a woman's fool enough to be caught staring at a man, she's asking for it. That's what's called an *oeillade*, which is French for leer.'

'All right,' said Louise tranquilly. 'Well, that's all that Madame told me. I think the other lot are Swiss – nobody else except Americans could afford a gorgeous vulgar car like that – and are just *en passant*. The only other resident is a Mrs. Bristol, who's either a widow or divorced. *Et voilà tous*. Shall we have another drink?'

Then the blonde appeared, threading her way between the tables, to sit down near the trellis, two tables away from Mr. Marsden. She crossed one exquisite nyloned leg over the other, took out a cigarette, and smiled at the waiter. There was a sort of confusion, which resolved itself into three separate movements – the fat German beat the waiter and Mr. Marsden by a short head – to light her cigarette. But Mr. Marsden won on points, because the German's lighter refused to work, and Marsden had a match. She flung a smile to Fat-Neck, an order for a drink to the waiter, and a look across the flame of the match to Marsden that made the flame look awfully dim. At any rate he read *Burnt Norton* upside down for quite some time afterwards. I had been right about the Pied Piper.

'Eschew,' said Louise, 'was definitely *not* the right word. I suppose that is Mrs. Bristol.'

It was on the tip of my tongue to correct her when the waiter, travelling like a Derby winner, brought the drink.

'Madame Bristole's drink.' He bowed it on to the table, and himself away.

She settled back in her chair, and looked about her. Seen at close quarters, she was as lovely as ever, which is saying a lot. It was a carefully tended, exotic loveliness, like that of a strange flower. That is a hackneyed metaphor, I know, but it describes her better than any other . . . her skin was so smooth, and her heavy perfume seemed part of her. Her eyes, I saw, were a curiously bright blue, and large. Her hands were restless, and at the corners of mouth and eyes I could see the faint lines of worry. These deepened suddenly as I watched her, and then I realized that David had come out from the hotel. He followed the waiter, who was bringing another drink for Louise, and, as he passed our table, saw me. He gave me a sudden little half-apologetic grin, which the waiter masked, I think, from the woman. Then the queer sullen look came down over his face again, and he sat down opposite her. She looked approvingly at his clean shorts and white shirt, and said something, to which he did not reply. She looked at his bent head for a moment, then resumed her casual scrutiny of the tables.

The place was filling up rapidly now, and the waiters were handing round the menus.

'Have you met that boy before?' asked Louise, 'or was that just another leer?'

I said that I had spoken to him for a moment in the courtyard. For some reason which I could not analyse, I did not want to talk about it and I was glad when she dropped the subject without further question.

'We'd better order,' she said.

We studied the menu with some enthusiasm. . . .

But when Louise asked me if I wanted *côte d'agneau* or *escalope de veau*, I replied 'Shelley' in an absent sort of way, and between the *petites pommes de terre sautées* and the *tarte maison* I was still trying to fit the lovely (and French) Mrs. Bristol in with Gilbert White and that appalling dog and the expression on a child's face of something being borne that was too heavy for him to bear.

And I didn't mean the iron table, either.

After dinner Louise announced that she was going to get her book, and sit over her coffee and cognac until bedtime. So I left her to it, and went out to explore Avignon alone.

Avignon is a walled city, as I have said, a compact and lovely little town skirted to the north and west by the Rhône and circled completely by medieval ramparts, none the less lovely, to my inexpert eye, for having been heavily restored in the nineteenth century. The city is dominated from the north by the Rocher des Doms, a steep mass of white rock crowned by the cathedral of Notre Dame, and green with singing pines. Beside the cathedral, taking the light above the town, is the golden stone palace of the Popes. The town itself is slashed in two by one main street, the Rue de la République, which leads from the main gate straight up to the city square and thence to the Place du Palais, at the foot of the Rocher des Doms itself.

But these things I had yet to find. It was dusk when I set out, and the street was vividly lit. All the cafés were full, and I picked my way between the tables on the pavement, while there grew in me that slow sense of exhilaration which one inevitably gets in a Southern town after dark. The shop windows glittered and flashed with every conceivable luxury that the mind of the tourist could imagine; the neon lights slid along satin and drowned themselves in velvet and danced over perfume and jewels and, since I have learned in my twenty-eight years to protect the heart a little against too much pity, I kept my eyes on them, and tried not to think about the beggars who slunk whining along the city gutters.

I went on, carefully not thinking about those beggars, until I reached the end of the street, where the Rue de la République widens out and becomes the main square of the city, and where all Avignon collects at night, together with, one would swear, every child and every dog in France.

The square is surrounded with cafés, which overflow the narrow pavements with a froth of gay little tables and wicker chairs, and even cast up a jetsam of more little tables across the roads and into the centre of the square itself. Here, as I said, Avignon collects at night, and for the price of a cup of coffee, which secures you a chair, you may sit for an hour and watch France parade for you.

I paid for my coffee, and sat in the milk-warm air, marvelling, as one has to in Provence, at the charming manners of the children, and the incredible variety of shapes possible among the dogs, at the beauty of the half-naked, coffee-brown young men in from the fields, and the modest grace of the young girls. One in particular I noticed, an exquisite dark creature who went slowly past with downcast eyes. Her dress was cut low over her breasts, and gathered tightly to a tiny waist, but her face might have been that of a nun, and she walked demurely between her parents, stout, respectable-looking folk who made the girl as difficult of access, no doubt, as Danaë. And she was followed, I could see, by dark-eyed glances that said exactly what had been said to Bele Yolanz and fair Amelot, five hundred years before, when the troubadours sang in Provence.

'Excuse me,' said a woman's voice behind me. 'But didn't I see you at the hotel?'

I turned. It was Mamma from Newcastle, Scotland, and she was smiling at me rather hesitantly from a near-by table.

'I'm Mrs. Palmer,' she said. 'I hope you don't mind me speaking, but I saw you at dinner, and—'

'Of course I don't. My name's Charity Selborne.' I got up and picked up my coffee-cup. 'May I join you?'

'Oh, do.' She moved her chair to make way for me. 'Father and Carrie – they go off walking about the place, exploring they call it – only sometimes they seem to take so long, and—'

'And it seems longer when you don't know anyone to talk to,' I finished for her.

She beamed as if I had said something brilliant. 'That's exactly how I feel! Fancy! And of course it's not like home, and what with people talking French it's different, isn't it?'

I admitted that it was.

'Of course if I go in for a cup of tea at home,' said Mrs. Palmer, 'in Carrick's, you know, or it might be Fenwick's, there's always someone I know comes in too, and you can have a nice chat before you get the bus. That's why it seems kind of funny not knowing anybody here, and of course it isn't tea anyway, not *real* tea, as you might say, but

I just can't seem to fancy this stuff they give you with lemon in, can you?'

I said on the whole, no, and how very brave of her to come all this way for a holiday.

'Well,' said Mrs. Palmer, 'it wasn't really me that suggested it, it was Carrie. I'd never have thought of a grand holiday like this, you know. But I just thought to myself, why not? You always read about the South of France and what's the good of just going every year to Scarborough and reading about the South of France? Well, I just thought, we can afford it, and why not? So here we are.'

I smiled at her, and said why not indeed, and good for her, and what a splendid idea of Carrie's.

'Of course she likes to be called Carole,' said Mrs. Palmer hastily. 'I think it's these films, you know. She will try to dress like them, say what I will.'

I said Carole was a pretty girl, which was true.

'Now that Mrs. Bristol, poor thing,' said Mrs. Palmer. 'She *does* look the part, the way Carrie never will. Of course she *was* on the stage or something, before It Happened.'

I sat up straight.

'Before what happened, Mrs. Palmer?'

'Oh, didn't you know? I recognized her straight away. Her photo was in all the Sunday papers, you know. Before she married that dreadful man, I meant.'

'What dreadful man? *What* happened?'

'The murderer,' said Mrs. Palmer, lowering her voice to a whisper. 'He was tried for murder, the Brutal Murder of his Best Friend, it said in the papers.' The quoted headlines echoed queerly. 'He thought his friend was carrying on with *her* – with his wife – so he murdered him. It was all in the papers.'

I stared at her stupid, kindly, half-excited eyes, and felt a bit sick.

'David's father, you mean?' I asked numbly. 'David's father a *murderer?*'

She nodded.

'That's right. Strangled with a blind cord. Horrible. An Act of Jealous Madness, it said.'

I said, inadequately, looking away from her:

'Poor little boy . . . how long ago was all this?'

'The trial was in April. Of course, she's not the boy's mother, you know, she was his second wife. But of *course* she took the boy away: she couldn't leave David to *him*. Not after what happened.'

'What do you mean? D'you mean he's still alive?'

'Oh yes.'

'In prison?'

She shook her head, leaning a little closer.

'No. That's the awful part of it, Mrs. Selborne. He's At Large.'

'But—'

'He was let off. Insufficient evidence, they called it, and they acquitted him.'

'But perhaps he's not guilty. I mean, the courts of law—'

'Guilty,' said Mrs. Palmer, tapping my arm. 'Guilty as hell.' She broke off and went rather pink. 'That's what Mr. Palmer says, you understand, Mrs. Selborne. And it's my belief he was mad, poor soul, or he'd never have gone for the boy like he did, murder or no murder.'

'Gone . . . for the boy?' I repeated, a bit shakily.

'Yes. Terrible, isn't it?' I could see the easy moisture start into her pale kindly eyes, and I warmed towards her. There was nothing of the ghoul about Mrs. Palmer; she was not enjoying the story, any more than I was. 'They found David unconscious in the bathroom near the bedroom where the body was found. He'd been knocked on the head.'

'Did he say his father had done it?'

'He didn't see who hit him. But it must've been the murderer. Caught in the Act, as you might say. Oh, it was an awful business; I'm surprised you don't remember it, really. The papers went on about it for long enough.'

'No, I don't remember it.' My voice sounded flat, almost mechanical. Poor David. Poor little boy. 'I don't remember hearing the name before at all. It's – it's terrible.'

Mrs. Palmer gave an exclamation, grabbed her handbag, and rose.

'Oh, there's Father and Carrie, off down the other side of the square, they can't have seen me . . . I must run. It's been lovely having a little chat, Mrs. Selborne, really lovely.' She beamed at me. 'And don't take on about poor Mrs. Bristol and the little boy. She's divorced from that Man, you know. He can't do a thing. And children do get over things, they say.'

Over some things, yes.

'I'm glad you told me,' I said, 'I might have said something . . . I had no idea.'

'Well, if you didn't see the photos—' said Mrs. Palmer. 'Of course, Bristol isn't their real name, so you wouldn't have heard it. The real name was Byron. Richard Byron, that was it. And now I must run. Good night, Mrs. Selborne.'

She went across the square, away from me, and I sat there for a long time before I even realized she had gone.

CHAPTER THREE

Sur le pont d'Avignon
L'on y danse, l'on y danse
Sur le pont d'Avignon
L'on y danse, tout en rond.

FRENCH NURSERY RHYME

By ten the next morning it was already as hot as on the hottest day in England, but with no sense of oppression, for the air was clear and light. Louise, true to her word, retired with a book and a sketching pad to the little green public gardens near the hotel.

'You go and play tourist,' she said. 'I'm going to sit under a tree and drink grape juice. Iced.'

It sounded a tempting programme, but to-morrow would be no cooler than to-day, and in any case the heat does not worry me unduly, so I set off for a gentle tour of exploration. This time I went out of the city gate, and turned along under the massive outer walls, towards the quarter where the Rhône races under the Rocher des Doms and then round the western fortifications of the city. It was a dusty walk, and not a very pleasant one, after all, I discovered. The verges of the narrow road were deep in dust and grit, the only vegetation, apart from the trees along the river, being thistles as dry as crumbling paper. Even along the flat edge of the Rhône itself, under the trees, there was no grass, only beaten dirt and stones, where beggars slept at night on the bare ground. A pair of enormous birds dipped and circled above the river.

But presently, round a curve in the city wall, the old bridge of the song came into view, its four remaining arches soaring out across the green water to break off, as it were, in midleap, suspended half-way across the Rhône. Down into the deep jade water glimmered the drowned-gold reflection of the chapel of St. Nicholas, which guards the second arch. Here, held by a spit of sand, the water is still, rich with the glowing colours of stone and shadow and dipping boughs, but beyond the sandbank the slender bridge thrusts out across a tearing torrent. Standing there, you remember suddenly that this is one of the great rivers of Europe. Without sound or foam, smooth and incredibly rapid, it sucks its enormous way south to the Mediterranean, here green as serpentine, there eddying to aquamarine, but everywhere hard in colour as a stone.

And then I saw David, playing with Rommel beside the pool under the chapel. Both boy and dog were wet, David, since he was in bathing trunks, more gracefully so than Rommel, who looked definitely better when his somewhat eccentric shape was disguised by his wool. I was on the bridge, actually, before I saw them below me. They seemed absorbed, David in building a dam, Rommel in systematically destroying it, but almost at once the boy looked up and saw me sitting in the embrasure of the chapel window.

He grinned and waved.

'Are you going to dance up there?' he called.

'Probably not,' I called back. 'It's too narrow.'

'What's in the chapel?'

'Nothing much. Haven't you been up?' I must have sounded surprised.

'No money,' said David, succinctly.

'Tell the concierge I'll pay for you on my way down.'

'I didn't mean that, you know.'

'No, I know. But I did. Only for heaven's sake hang on to Rommel. There's no parapet, and he'd be at Marseilles by tea-time if he fell into this.'

Boy and dog vanished into the concierge's lodge, and presently emerged on to the bridge, slightly out of breath, and disputing over Rommel's right to hurl himself sportingly straight into the Rhône.

But presently Rommel, secured by the inevitable piece of string, was reckoned as being under control, and the three of us cautiously went to the very end of the broken arch – cautiously, because the bridge is only a few feet wide and there is always a strong breeze blowing from the North – and sat down with Rommel between us. We sang '*Sur le pont d'Avignon*' in the style of Jean Sablon, and David told me the story of St. Bénézet who confounded the clerics of Avignon, and built the bridge where the angel had told him, and we watched the two big birds, which were kites, David said, and which soared and circled beautifully up in the high blue air.

Then we went down to the road, and I paid the concierge, and David thanked me again, and we set off back to the hotel for lunch.

It seemed impossible, on this lovely gay morning, that David's father might be a murderer, and that David himself had been struck down, for no reason, in the dark, by a hand that must surely have belonged to a madman.

'Where do you spend most of your days?' I asked.

'Oh, by the river, mostly. You can swim under the bridge at the edge, inside the sand-bank where there's no current.'

'You haven't seen – well, the countryside? The Pont du Gard, and the arena at Nîmes, and so on? Perhaps you don't bother with that sort of thing?'

'Oh *yes*. I'd love to see the arena – do you know they have bull-fights every Sunday and one of the matadors is a woman?'

'Well I should hate to see a bull-fight,' I said decidedly. 'But I intend to go and see the arena to-morrow anyway, and if you'd like to come, there's plenty of room in the car. Do you think your mother would let you?'

'My step-mother,' said David distinctly.

He shot me a little sidelong look and flushed slightly. 'That's why we have different names, you see.'

'I see. Would she let you come? That is, if you would like to come?' He hesitated oddly for a moment, and once again I saw the mask fall across his face, and as before, for no reason that I could guess. It was as if he considered some grave objection, rejected it eventually, and finally shrugged it away.

'I should like it very much, thank you,' he said formally. 'And I don't think my step-mother will object at all. It isn't her kind of thing, you know,' naïvely enough, 'but she doesn't much mind what I do.'

When we reached the hotel, people were gathering for *apéritifs* in the cool courtyard. I came down from my room to find Mrs. Bristol already installed at a table beside an orange tree. She smiled at me, and made a gesture of invitation, so I went over and sat down at her table.

'I hear you have been with David,' she said to me, 'so very kind of you to trouble.'

'Not at all. We met by accident – I enjoyed the morning immensely.' I murmured commonplaces, and she thanked me charmingly for what she called my kindness.

She bought me a drink and we talked nothings about the heat, and the town, and the shops for some time. She was very charming and talkative, but I noticed that the worried lines round her mouth seemed rather more pronounced to-day, and that whenever David's name cropped up in the conversation, there seemed to darken in her eyes the same shadow – of wariness, was it? – that had crossed David's face when I spoke of the trip to the arena at Nîmes.

'I had thought of taking the car to the Pont du Gard to-morrow,' I said at length, 'and then on to Nîmes, to look round a bit. If you have no objection, I should like to take David with me? I don't know whether my friend will want to go, and I should very much like to have David's company.'

She was lighting a cigarette when I spoke, and she paused with the flame of the lighter an inch from the cigarette-end, in the queerest, most exact repetition of David's own deliberation. I saw her assimilate the question, look at it carefully, hesitate, and then decide. For the life of me I couldn't understand why a proposal for a day's sight-seeing tour (which was surely what one came to Roman France for anyway?) should raise such problems as mine apparently did.

'It's so very kind of you,' said Mrs. Bristol, and the lighter finally made contact with the cigarette. 'I'm sure David will enjoy it.' She made a charming grimace. 'These antiquities – they are not for me; I am for Paris, the cities, the people – places where one amuses oneself . . . you understand?'

'Oh yes – but I rather like it both ways,' I laughed. 'And I'm afraid I adore sight-seeing. I'm a born tourist, but I don't like to go in a crowd.

But what on earth do you find to do in Avignon if you don't like – er, antiquities?'

She hesitated again, and sent me a quick look from under her darkened lashes.

'We do not stay long – we pass through to Monte Carlo. We rest a few days in Avignon on the way.'

'Well, thank you for the drink, Mrs. Bristol,' I said, getting to my feet. I had caught sight of Louise, who had taken a corner table, and was looking at the lunch menu. We murmured more civilities, and I turned to go, but the strap of my bag caught on the back of the chair, and as I swung round again quickly to disentangle it, I saw Mrs. Bristol staring at me, with her lovely eyes narrowed against the smoke of her cigarette, and in them a look of half-pleased, half-apprehensive speculation that puzzled me considerably.

That evening, as Louise was no more inclined than formerly to go for a walk, I left her sketching in a café in the city square, and went alone up the little dark street that leads to the Popes' palace and the gardens among the pines, high up on the Rocher des Doms.

Unlike the main square, the Place du Palais was almost empty, the buildings on three sides dark and blank, while on the right the great façade of the Palace soared up out of the living rock, shadowy yet luminous in the starlight. I lingered for a while gazing up at it, then went slowly up the sloping zigzag walk through the pines towards the high gardens, which lie at the very edge of the city, and are girdled in by the city wall itself. Very few people appeared to be up there that evening, and only occasionally, it seemed, I heard the murmur of voices and the soft scrunch of the gravel under someone's foot. The air was still, and the cicadas were quiet at last, but the pines kept up a faint continuous murmuring overhead, almost as if, in sleep, they yet gave back the sound of the wind that sweeps down the river all winter, and, in summer, lingers in them still.

Climbing slowly up through the winding alleys of evergreens, I came at length to the topmost edge of the gardens, above the Rhône, and leaned over the low battlemented wall to rest. Below me the wall dropped away vertically, merging into the solid cliff which bounded the river. The Rhône, beneath, slipped silently under the darkness on its wide and glimmering way.

It was very quiet.

Then suddenly, from somewhere behind me, came a man's voice, speaking low, in French.

'So this is where you are!'

Startled, I turned my head, but behind me was a thick bank of evergreen, and I could see nothing. I was alone in my little high corner of the wall. He must be on the lower walk, screened by the bushes. A woman's voice answered him.

She said: 'You're late. I've been here a long time. Have you a cigarette?'
I heard the scrape of a match, then he said in a voice which sounded
sullen: 'You weren't here when I passed ten minutes ago.'
'I got tired of waiting, and went for a walk.' Her voice was indifferent,
and I heard the gravel scrape, as if he made an angry movement.
I had no intention of letting myself be marooned in my corner while
a love scene went on within hearing, and I determined at this point that,
as I would have to pass them to get back to the main path, I had better
emerge before anything passed that might make my appearance embarrassing. But as I turned to move, the woman spoke again, and I realized,
suddenly, two things: one, that the voice was that of Mrs. Bristol, and
secondly, that she was very much afraid. I suppose I had not recognized
the voice immediately because I had previously only heard her speak in
English, but as her voice rose, edged with fear, I recognized it.
She said: 'It's happened. I knew it would happen. I knew. . . .'
His voice cut in sharply, almost roughly: 'What's happened?'
'He's here. He's come. I had to see you, I—'
He interrupted again.
'For God's sake, pull yourself together. How do you know he's here?'
She spoke breathlessly, still with the tremor in her voice.
'I got a phone call to-night. His car's been seen. They traced it as far
as Montélimar. He must be coming this way. He must have found out
where we are—'
'Loraine—'
'What are we going to do?' It was a desperate whisper. I leaned
against the wall in my little corner; not for anything could I have come
out now. I could only trust they would not seek its greater privacy for
themselves.
I heard the man (I think it was he) draw in a long breath. Then he
spoke quietly and with emphasis.
'There is nothing that we can do, yet. We don't know for certain where
he is, he may be anywhere in Provence. When you saw him in
Montélimar?'
'Yesterday.'
He exploded with wrath. 'God in heaven, the clumsy fools! And they
only telephoned to-night?'
'They weren't sure. It was a big grey car with a GB plate, and they
think it was his. It was the first glimpse they'd had since Chartres.'
'They should have been sure. What the hell are they paid for?' he said
angrily.
'Can't we find out where he is? I – I don't think I can stand much
more of this – this suspense.'
'No, we must do nothing. We'll find out soon enough, I've no doubt.'
His voice was grim. 'And for God's sake, Loraine, take hold of yourself.
You shouldn't have got me up here to-night, you don't know who's about,
and this is such a tiny place. Anybody from the hotel—'

Her voice was sharp with new alarm: 'You don't think he's got someone planted in the hotel? Do you mean . . . ?'

'I don't mean anything,' he returned shortly. 'All I'm saying is, that we mustn't be seen together. You know that as well as I do. Anyone might see us, they might mention it to David, and he has little enough confidence in you anyway, as far as I can see.'

'I do try, I really do.'

'I know you do,' he said more gently. 'And I know David's not easy. But it's not David I'm thinking about, so much as *him*. If *he* ever got to know we were connected I'd be a hell of a lot of use to you, wouldn't I? He'd find a way to get me out of the road first, and then—'

'Don't, please!'

His voice softened: 'Look, my dear, stop worrying. It'll be all right, I promise. I got you out of the mess before didn't I? I got you away from England, didn't I? and the boy too?'

She murmured something I couldn't catch, and he went on: 'And it'll be all right again, I swear it. I know it's hell just sitting around wondering what's going to happen, but I'm in charge and you trust me, don't you? Don't you?'

'Yes. Yes, of course.'

'Here, have another cigarette.' I heard him light it for her, and there was a pause.

'Those damned English police,' she said bitterly. 'If they'd known their job this would never have had to happen. He ought to be dead and done with.' The way she repeated it made me shiver, 'Dead and done with,' she said.

'Well, he's not,' said the man briskly, sounding as if he were dragging back the conversation, with an effort, on to a less dramatic and more practical level. 'He's here, in France. And there's nothing to be scared of. He can't do a thing to you, after all. All you've got to do is keep your nerve and hang on to David. We ought to go back, I think. You go first – come down to the corner with me till we see if there's anyone about.' He must have turned to go, for his voice grew suddenly fainter.

She stopped him for a moment. Her tone was calmer, and the note of fear was gone, but I could hear the tautness of her nerves through it, for all that.

'I meant to ask you – that girl, Selborne I think her name is – she offered to take David out in her car to-morrow. I suppose it's all right?'

There was another pause. I think he took her arm, because I heard them begin to move off together, but I heard his reply, faintly, before they went out of earshot.

'Quite all right, I imagine. In fact, it might be a good idea. . . .'

The palms of my hands, I found, had been pressed so hard against the stone of the parapet that they were sore. I stood perfectly still for some time after they had gone, slowly rubbing my hands together, and thinking.

It was not a particularly pleasant thought, that somewhere near at hand, possibly even in Avignon at this moment, was a man who was probably a murderer; a man vindictive enough, if I had understood aright what I had heard, to pursue the wife who had divorced him after the trial, and dangerous enough to frighten her as Loraine Bristol was being frightened. She was not, I thought, a woman who would frighten easily.

Why was he apparently following her? Did he want her back, was he hoping for reconciliation . . . no, that wouldn't do, she wouldn't be so afraid if that were all. Then was he angry at her action in divorcing him at such a time, was it revenge he was after? No, that was absurd; people just didn't behave that way at all, not rational people . . . that must be it, I thought, and went cold . . . he was *not* rational. Mrs. Palmer had said that he was mad, and no sane man, surely, would have struck down his own son. . . .

David.

It wasn't Loraine he was pursuing at all, it was David.

I pressed my now tingling hands to my cheeks, and thought of David and the dog Rommel, building dams under the Pont St. Bénézet, and as I thought, some of the loneliness of the child's situation dawned on me, and made me feel chilled. I knew a lot about loneliness. And I knew that, come murderers, come hell, come high water, I should have to do something about it.

I slowly descended the zigzag walk to the level of the Palace square, on the alert in case I should run into Mrs. Bristol, who might be waiting about somewhere to give her companion a start.

Her companion? I had not recognized the lowered voice, the rapid French. But that it was someone at the hotel I felt sure.

Then, in the narrow dark little street that skirts the foot of the rock where the palace is built, I saw someone standing, a man. He did not see me, but stood gazing in the direction of the main square, and, as I paused in the darkness under the palace steps, I saw him slip out of the shadows, and saunter down the street and into the light.

I recognized him all right.

It was Marsden.

CHAPTER FOUR

Old moniments ...

SPENSER

Towards mid-morning the next day I eased the Riley down the narrow main street of Avignon, and out on to the perimeter road. Louise sat beside me, and in the back were David and Rommel, wrangling as usual over the necessity of chasing every cat we passed. We skirted Avignon, following my route of the previous day, but before we reached the old bridge of St. Bénézet, I turned the car over the narrow suspension bridge which crosses the Rhône. We crept across its swaying, resounding metal surface, then swung through Villeneuve-lès-Avignon and headed south for Nîmes.

The heart of Roman France ... I thought of the legions, tramping behind their eagles through the pitiless heat and dust, across this barren and hostile country. The road was a white and powdery ribbon that twisted between slopes of rock and scrub. Whin I recognized, and juniper, but most of the shrubs were unfamiliar – dark green harsh foliage that sucked a precarious life from the cracks among the screes and faces of white rock. Here and there houses crouched under the heat, clinging to the edge of the road as if to a life-line; occasionally a grove of olives hung on the slopes like a silver-green cloud, or a barrier of cypress reared its bravery in the path of the mistral, but for the most part the hot and desert slopes rose, waterless and unclothed by any softer green than that of gorse and scrub.

'Mustn't they have felt hot in their helmets?' said David, breaking into my thoughts as if he had known exactly what I was thinking. 'Though I suppose Italy's just as hot.'

'And they fought all summer,' I said. 'In winter they retired—'

'To winter quarters – I remember that,' said David, grinning. 'In my Latin Grammar, if they weren't going to the city to buy bread, they were always retiring to winter quarters.'

'I believe they went to the coast. There's a nice little place east of Marseilles where Caesar made a sort of spa for his veterans.'

'Aren't the Michelin guides wonderful?' murmured Louise. 'And incidentally, Charity – I hate to interfere, but you *have* seen that bus, haven't you?'

'I could hardly avoid it,' I said drily. 'It's in the middle of the road.'

'Oh, I just thought – what's the French for "breakdown"?'

'*Dépannage*. Or in this case, just plain *accident*. Haven't you got used to the French way of driving yet? You should have.'

We were rapidly overtaking a bus which was indeed thundering along in the very centre of the narrow road. But I knew my stuff by now, after the hundreds of heartbreaking miles before I had discovered that the 'courtesy of the road' means very different things in France and England. I swung to the left, bore down on the bus with every appearance of intending to ram it, and put the heel of my hand down hard on the horn. The bus, responding with an ear-splitting klaxon, immediately swerved to the left too, straight into our path. I didn't even brake, but put my hand on the horn and kept it there. The bus, with an almost visible shrug, moved over about a foot to the right, and we tore by.

Louise let out a long breath. 'I'll never get used to that!'

'If he'd seen the GB plates we'd never have done it. The British are despicably easy to bully on the roads.'

'Did you see who was on the bus?' said David.

'No, I was busy. Who was it?'

'That man from the hotel. I think his name's Marsden. He sits at the table by the big palm.'

'Oh. Yes, I've noticed him.'

I eased my foot off the accelerator, and glanced at the bus in the driving-mirror. It might conceivably turn off at Pont du Gard for Tarascon, but I had the idea that the Avignon-Tarascon buses went another way. In which case, this must be the bus for Nîmes, and Marsden was on it. And after what I had heard last night up at the Rocher des Doms, I was not quite sure what I thought about the possibility of Marsden's following us to Nîmes.

I slowed down a little more. With a triumphant screech of its klaxon, the bus overtook the Riley, and demanded the road.

I glanced in the mirror as it loomed up behind the car. Yes, unmistakable, even in mirror-image: NIMES.

I put my foot down again, and we drew away. I was trying to think, but I had too little to go on. It was like groping for a window through curtains of spiders' webs, only to find that it was dark outside the window, and that when the webs were all torn down, the window would be still invisible.

I thrust the problem aside, and passed a small Citroën with concentrated care.

At Pont du Gard we drew in under the shade of the trees, opposite the hotel. Louise began to gather her things together.

'David,' I said. 'Will you do something for me?'

'Of course. What?'

'Ask up at the hotel what time the bus gets here. How long it stays. What time it gets to Nîmes. Will your French stand up to that, do you think?'

David gave me a look, and scrambled out of the car with Rommel.

'Of course,' he said again; then, with a sudden burst of honesty – 'It's not so much *asking*, because you can practise on the way up, but it's understanding what they tell you – 'specially when it's numbers. But I'll try.' He gave me his swift engaging grin, and ran off through the gravel terrace of the hotel.

'Are you sure you don't want to come on to Nîmes, Louise?'

'Quite, thanks, I'll go down by the river and paint the bridge – oh, all right, aqueduct – I'll have lunch here first. What time are you coming back?'

'I'm not sure. When d'you want to be picked up?'

Louise looked through the trees towards the river, where could be seen a glowing glimpse of golden stone.

'I don't know, honestly. I'll tell you what, Charity – we won't tie ourselves down. You go on to Nîmes and look at your remains in your own time. If I'm sitting at one of those tables when you come back, pick me up. If not, I'll have gone back on the bus, so don't bother. You won't want to come back much before dinner-time, anyway, and I'll have finished painting long before that.'

David came panting across the road to the door of the car.

'*Midi-vingt!*' he announced with triumph. 'The bus gets here *midi-vingt*. It waits half an hour, and it gets to Nîmes at half-past one. Is that what you wanted to know?'

'That's fine,' I said, glancing at my watch. 'It's barely twelve now, and the bus doesn't get here till twenty past. We'll have time to look at the bridge – sorry, Louise, aqueduct – after all.'

I took the ignition key out and dropped it into my bag.

'What *do* you mean?' asked Louise. She was looking at me curiously. 'I thought that's one of the things you came for? What's the bus got to do with it?'

I felt the colour creep into my face. I had been thinking aloud, without realizing how queer it must have sounded.

'Nothing,' I said, rather lamely. 'I was thinking about lunch. We'll have lunch in Nîmes, so we won't stay here too long.'

I need not have been afraid that Louise would pursue the subject. She was already rummaging for her pencils, and hardly listened to my reply. But as I turned from the car, I saw David looking at me. A long, unreadable look . . . and again I sensed that all those impalpable defences were up. Then Rommel gave an impatient tug to his string, and we all went down towards the bank of the river, under tall trees harsh with the shrilling of the cicadas.

CHAPTER FIVE

O bloody Richard!

SHAKESPEARE

Whenever I look back now on the strange and terrifying events of that holiday in Southern France, I am conscious of two things which seem to dominate the picture. One is the continuous dry and nerve-rasping noise of the cicadas, invisible in the parched trees, the other is the Roman aqueduct over the Gardon as I first saw it that brilliant day. I suppose the ten or twelve minutes that David and Rommel and I spent gazing at those golden arches spanning the deep green Gardon were like the last brief lull before the thunder.

We stood near the edge of the narrow river, on the water-smooth white rock and watched Louise settle herself in the shade of some willows, where the aqueduct soared above us, its steep angle cutting the sky. On the under-sides of the arches moved the slow, water-illumined shadows, till the sun-steeped stone glowed like living gold. Except for the lazy sliding silver of reflected light under the striding spans, nothing stirred. Not a leaf quivered; there was no cloud to betray the wind. You would have sworn that the gleaming river never moved. . . .

The sound of an engine on the road above recalled me abruptly. We said good-bye to Louise, who hardly heard us, and climbed the dusty track again to the car.

Not until we had swung out on to the road to Nîmes did either of us speak.

Then David gave a queer little sigh, and said:

'I'm glad I did come, after all.' Then he flung a quick glance at me, and flushed, 'I mean – I didn't mean—'

'It doesn't matter. I'm glad you're glad you came.'

He glanced at me again, and I could sense, rather than see, a long and curious scrutiny.

'Mrs. Selborne—'

'Yes?'

He hesitated. I could feel his body beside me, tense as a runner's. I kept my eyes on the road and waited. Then he gave another odd, sharp little sigh, and bent his cheek to Rommel's shoulder.

'Oh, nothing. How far is it to Nîmes?'

And for the rest of the way we talked about the Romans. I was not to be allowed to help, after all. And I knew better than to force confidence from a boy of his age – a boy, moreover, who had so much the air of knowing exactly what he was up against, and what he was going to do about it. But stealing a look down at the childish curve of the thin cheek laid against the dog's fur, I wasn't so sure that he could deal with whatever queer situation he was in. And again, I knew that I wanted most desperately to help. It was irrational, and I can't explain it, even to-day. It was just the way David made me feel. I told myself savagely that I was a fool, I said unpleasant things under my breath about a frustrated mother-complex, and I kept my eyes on the road, my voice casual, and I talked about the Romans.

And so we drove into Nîmes, parked the car off the square outside the church, and had lunch in a restaurant in a side street, out of sight of the place where the buses stop.

'The Arena first!' said David. 'I want to see where they keep the bulls!'

'Bloodthirsty little beast, aren't you? But there's no bull-fight to-day, you know. Sunday nights only. The better the day, the better the deed.'

'Look, there's a poster – a Corrida, and this Sunday, too!' He looked at me wistfully. I laughed.

'*No*, David. I won't. And you wouldn't like it either, really. You're English – you'd be on the side of the bull. And think of the horses.'

'I suppose so. Golly, look! Is that it?'

We climbed the sloping street towards the enormous curve of the Arena, and made our way round half its circumference until we found the way in through its massive and terrible arches. I bought tickets, and we went into the barred shadows of the lower corridor. There were a few other tourists there, staring, chattering, fiddling with cameras. We followed a little group of English people up the main steps, out into the sunlight of the Arena until we emerged in what must have been the ring-side seats, looking down into the great oval where the beasts and the Christians used to meet in blood and terror under the pitiless sun. I went forward to the edge and looked down at the sheer sides of the Arena, just too

high for a man to leap, even if he were in terror of his life. David came to my side. He, at any rate, was not haunted by the things that had been done here. His face was excited and a little flushed and his eyes shining.

'Golly, Mrs. Selborne, what a place! I saw a door down there labelled TORIL. D'you suppose that's the bull? Do they use Spanish names here? Where does the bull come out to fight?'

I pointed to the big double doors at the end of the oval, where, in white letters, the word TORIL stood again.

'*Golly!*' said David again. He leaned over the parapet and gazed down with concentration. 'Do you suppose we could see bloodstains?'

I moved back into the shadow of the stairway. The heat reflected from the stones was almost unbearable. I heard, behind and below me, the monotonous voice of the concierge doling out tickets to a new batch of tourists. Two or three people came up the steps beside me, and another group, I noticed, went through a doorway near the foot of the steps, that apparently led out into the arena itself.

I leaned back against the cool stone in the shadows and watched David idly as he sauntered along the ringside tier, periodically stopping to lean over – looking for bloodstains, I supposed. Well, at least that disposed of an idea that the boy was a neurotic – a healthy desire for bloodstains was, I knew, part of the normal boy's equipment.

I closed my eyes. The concierge's voice rose and fell. There was a murmur of talk in French, in German, in American. Somewhere near me a camera clicked. Some more tourists came up the steps beside me, talking vigorously in German. For once we seemed to be the only English people there. But no sooner had the idle thought crossed my mind than I was proved wrong, for down below, on the arena floor itself, I heard some people talking English. And suddenly, a man's voice, sharp, distinct, edged with bad temper:

'This is *not* the wrong blasted ticket. It was issued at the Maison Carrée.'

Then someone passing on the steps jostled me, and my bag slipped from my lax fingers. I opened startled eyes, and made a grab for it. The culprit – it was a pleasant-looking woman of about forty – stooped for the bag and handed it to me with a soft-voiced apology in a charming American drawl.

'My own fault, I was half asleep.'

'It's this turrible heat,' she said, 'You do better in the shade. Come along, Junior.' As they turned to go, I became aware of David at my elbow. He spoke breathlessly:

'Mrs. Selborne!'

'What – why, what on earth's the matter, David?'

He had hold of my sleeve. His face was flour-white, and in the shadow his eyes looked enormous.

'Don't you feel well?'

'No – I – that is—' The hand on my arm was shaking. He began to pull me down the steps. 'May we go now? I don't want to stay here – do you mind?'

'Of course not. We'll go straight away. I was only waiting for you.'

He hardly waited for me to finish; he went down the steps as if his feet were winged, and out through the gate into the hot street, with Rommel close at his heels.

I followed, to find him heading back the way we had come.

'Why, David, don't you want to see the other things? This is the way back to the car.'

He paused a moment as we rounded the street corner, and put out a tentative hand again.

'I – I don't feel too good, Mrs. Selborne. I suppose it's the heat. D'you mind if I don't see the other things with you? I – I can wait for you somewhere.'

I took him by the arm.

'I don't mind at all. Of course not. I'm sorry you're not feeling well, though. Shall we go back to the car?'

We retraced our steps to the square, then he stopped and faced me again. He looked better now; he was still very pale, but he had stopped shaking, and even smiled at me.

'I'll be fine now, Mrs. Selborne. I'll sit in the church till you come back. It's lovely and cool in there. Please don't worry about me.'

'What about a drink? An iced mint? Here's a café.'

But he shook his head.

'I'll just go and sit in the church.'

'What about the dog?'

'Oh—' he glanced uncertainly at the church door. 'Oh. I expect it'll be all right. I'll sit near the back, and it's not the time for service. He could stay in the porch anyway. . . .'

In the end he had his way. I watched him into the cool shadow of the west doorway, then I turned away to look for the temple and the gardens. At least nobody appeared to have forbidden Rommel's entry, and the church was the best place David could choose in this heat. I realized that, if he thought his indisposition had spoiled my day, he would be very embarrassed, so I decided to continue my sight-seeing tour of Nîmes, but to complete it as quickly as I could.

I saw the lovely pillared Maison Carrée, then I made my way along the stinking street beside the canal to the beautiful formal gardens which are the pride of Nîmes. The heat was terrific, and by the time I reached the gardens – so beautifully laid out around their stagnant and pestilential pools – even my enthusiasm for Roman remains had begun to waver.

I stood for a moment gazing up at the ranks of pine trees on the steep slope which leads up to the Roman Tower. It was very steep; the cicadas were fiddling in the branches like mad; the heat came out of the ground in waves.

'No,' I said firmly.

I turned my back on the tower, and made like a homing bee for the little ruined Temple of Diana – which has a café just beside it, where one can drink long iced drinks under the lime trees.

After two very long, very cold drinks, I felt considerably better. I still could not face the Tour Magne, but out of self-respect, as a tourist, I must use up the part of my tourist's ticket dedicated to the Temple of Diana. I left my chair and went through the crumbled arches into the tiny square of the temple.

It was like being miles from anywhere. Behind me, back through the crumbled archway, was the hot white world with its people and its voices; here, within, was a little square of quiet and green coolness. Trees dipped over the high broken walls, shadows lay like arras in the pillared corners, fronds of ferns lent softness to every niche and crevice. And silence. Such silence. Silence with a positive quality, that is more than just an absence of sound. Silence like music.

I sat down on a fallen piece of carved stone, leaned back against a pillar, and closed my eyes. I tried not to think of Johnny ... it didn't do any good to think of Johnny ... I must just think of nothing except how quiet it was, and how much I liked being alone ...

'Aren't you well?'

I opened my eyes with a start.

A man had come into the temple, so quietly that I had not heard him approach. He was standing over me now, frowning at me.

'What's the matter? The heat?' He spoke with a sort of reluctant consideration, as if he felt constrained to offer help, but hoped to God I wasn't going to need it.

I knew there were tears on my eyelashes, and felt like a fool.

'I'm all right, thanks,' I said crisply. 'I was only resting, and enjoying being alone.'

He raised his eyebrows at that, and the corner of his mouth twitched sourly.

'I'm sorry.'

I got up, feeling still more of a fool.

'I'm sorry too. I didn't mean that – I didn't mean to be rude. I – it was actually the literal truth. I wouldn't have said it, but you caught me a little off balance.'

He did not answer, but stood looking at me; I felt myself flushing like a schoolgirl and, for some idiotic reason, the tears began to sting again behind my eyes.

'I'm not usually rude to perfect strangers,' I said. 'Especially when they have been kind enough to – to ask after my health. Please forgive me.'

He didn't smile, but said, kindly enough:

'It was my fault for catching you – off balance. Hadn't you better have a cigarette to put you back on again before you go out?'

He handed me his case, and added, as I hesitated: 'If you don't accept cigarettes from perfect strangers either, we had better remedy that. My name's Coleridge. Richard Coleridge.'

I took a cigarette. 'And mine's Charity Selborne. Though it ought to be Wordsworth, I feel.'

He lit a match for me, and his look over it was sardonic.

'Don't tell me you feel a bond between us already?'

'No ... though as a matter of fact I did wonder for a moment if we'd met before. There's something familiar—'

He interrupted, his voice rough again: 'We haven't. I don't know any Selborne outside of Gilbert White.'

I lifted my head, startled.

'Gilbert White?'

'Yes. You know the book—'

'Of course. It was just that somebody else the other day connected me with it too, and not so very many people read it now. And I was surprised at David, because he's only a boy.'

I suppose I should have been more careful; I suppose I should have heard the way his voice altered then. But I was still embarrassed, wanting to get away, chattering aimlessly about nothing.

He said, very quietly: 'David?'

'Yes. David Shelley. That's who I was thinking of when I said I should have been called Wordsworth. All the Romantic poets seem to be in—'

'Where did you meet this David Shelley?'

I heard it then. I stopped with my cigarette half-way to my lips and looked at him. His hand was quite steady as he flicked the ash from his cigarette, and his face showed no expression. But there was a look behind his eyes that made my heart jolt once, sickeningly.

He said again, softly, almost indifferently: '*Where did you meet this David Shelley?*'

And looked at me with David's eyes.

Shelley – Coleridge – Byron. I knew now. I was alone in that quiet little temple with Richard Byron, who had been acquitted of murder on the grounds of insufficient evidence, and who was looking at me now as if he would like to choke me.

He threw away his cigarette and took a step towards me.

CHAPTER SIX

Escape me?

BROWNING

'Excuse me, monsieur.'

Richard Byron stopped and swung round. The concierge stood just inside the doorway of the temple, looking at him with a sort of mournful reproach.

'Your ticket, monsieur. You nevaire show it.' His limp moustache drooped with rebuke. His eyes were pale watery brown, and slightly bloodshot. I thought I had never seen anybody I liked better. I ground out my cigarette with shaking fingers, and started – oh, so casually! – for the door. But the concierge must have thought that Richard Byron and I were together, for he stood his ground.

As I fished hurriedly in my bag for my ticket, Byron handed over his slip with an abrupt gesture of impatience. The concierge took it, eyed it with the same spaniel-like reproach, and shook his head.

'It is torn, monsieur. It is defaced. It is perhaps not the right ticket. . . .'

Richard Byron spoke harshly: 'I cannot help its being torn. It was torn when I got it.'

'Where did monsieur get it?'

'At the Maison Carrée.'

Something else jolted in my mind. The voice in the Arena, protesting about the same ticket in almost the same words; and David, who had been leaning over the parapet gazing into the Arena, coming flying down the steps to me, and dragging me away. David, white and shaking, going to hide in the church.

David had seen his father all right, and was even now hiding in the church like a rabbit in its burrow. At the thought of David, I was suddenly not afraid of Richard Byron any more. I held out my ticket again to the concierge, who took it, looked mournfully at it, and clipped it. Then I was out in the sunlight again walking past the café tables, back towards the canal. I was trying desperately to think of some way to get back to David and the car without Byron's seeing me. But the lovely gardens stretched ahead of me, open as a chessboard, and then there were the long, straight streets . . . I began to hurry; if only the concierge would keep him . . . but he must have squared the old man somehow, for I had hardly gone fifty yards towards the canal when I heard his step behind me, and he said:

'Just a minute. Please.'

I turned to face him.

'Look,' I said, pleasantly, casually, 'it's been very pleasant meeting you, and thank you for the cigarette. But I must go now. Good-bye.'

I turned to go, but he was at my elbow again.

'I just wanted to ask you—'

I tried to freeze him – to act as if I thought this was just the usual pick-up, and to get away before he could ask any more questions.

'Please allow me to go,' I said icily. 'I prefer to go alone, as I said to you before.'

'I want to talk to you.'

'I'm afraid I—'

'You said you knew a boy called David Shelley.' He was scowling down at me, and his voice had an edge that I by no means liked. Against this direct attack I felt helpless, and in spite of myself, panic started to creep over me again. I wanted time to think – to think what to do, what to say. 'Where did you see him?'

'Why do you want to know?' I must have sounded feeble, but I could only stall weakly for time.

'I know him,' he said shortly. 'If he's hereabouts, I'd like to look him up. He's – he's the son of an old friend. He'd want to see me.'

Like hell he would, I thought, hiding away like a panic-stricken rabbit in the church, poor little kid.

I said: 'I'm sorry, I don't really know him.'

I could see people approaching up the long flight of steps from the gardens below, and I felt better. He could hardly detain me, make a scene, when there were people there. When they reached us I would break away from him, move off with them, lose myself among the other tourists. . . .

I looked candidly into Richard Byron's angry grey eyes: 'I only met him casually on a sight-seeing trip – the way I met you. I couldn't tell you where he's staying.'

'When was this?'

'Two days ago.'

'Where?' The question was quiet, but somehow I could sense behind it some intolerable strain. I was reminded sharply again of David.

'In Tarascon,' I said, at random, some memory of the morning's encounter with the bus no doubt still in my mind. The people were nearly up the steps now, were pausing on a landing to look back at the view. . . .

'Whereabouts in Tarascon? Did he say if he was staying there?'

'No. I told you I didn't know. I only met him for a short time when we were looking at—' Panic flooded me for a moment. What *was* Tarascon? What did one look at in Tarascon? I plunged on a certainty—'At the Cathedral.'

I heard him take in his breath in a long hiss and looking up I saw his eyes narrowing on me in a look that there was no mistaking. It was not imagination this time to see violent intentions there. If ever a man looked murder at anyone, Richard Byron looked it at me on that bright afternoon between the flaming beds of flowers in the gardens of Nîmes.

Then the little group of tourists was round us, and I turned to go with them. Anywhere, so long as I was among people, safe in a crowd, safe from the danger of betraying David to this hard-eyed man who stood in the sunlight looking like murder.

'Why, hallo,' said a soft American voice. 'Didn't I see you before – down at the bull-ring? Kind of a quaint l'il place, isn't it? Where's yuh li'l boy?'

It was the woman who had picked up my bag. She smiled charmingly at me, but my mouth felt stiff. I just looked at her.

'Mom,' came a plaintive voice, 'Hi, Mom! Can yuh fix this film for me?'

She smiled at me again, and hurried towards Junior, who was wrestling with his Kodak at a café table. I started to follow, but a hand closed round my wrist, and gripped it hard.

'Just a minute,' said Richard Byron again.

He pulled me round to face him. I turned as if I were a wax doll – I had no more resistance. His grip was hurting my wrist, and he pulled me close to him. The group of tourists, self-absorbed and chattering, moved by, paying no attention. He drew me behind a group of statuary.

'Let me go!'

'So you were in the Arena to-day with a boy?'

'Let go my wrist or I'll call the police!'

He laughed, an ugly little laugh. 'Call away.'

I bit my lip, and stood dumb. The police – the questions – my papers, my car – and I still had to get quietly out of Nîmes with David. Richard Byron laughed again as he looked down at me.

'Yes, you'd be likely to call the police, wouldn't you?' His grip tightened, and I must have made a sound, because his mouth twisted with satisfaction before he slackened his hold. 'Now, where's this boy you were with?'

I couldn't think. I said, stupidly: 'She's mistaken. He wasn't with me. I was just talking to him. It wasn't David.'

He sneered at me.

'Still lying? So you were just talking to him, were you? The way you talked to David Shelley in the Cathedral at Tarascon?'

I nodded.

'Would it surprise you to be told,' said David's father, 'that Tarascon is a small and dirty village whose main claim to fame is a castle on the Rhône? And that, though I suppose there must be one, I have never seen a church there?'

I said nothing. I might have known. Johnny always said I was a rotten liar.

'And now, damn you,' said Richard Byron, 'take me to David.'

And he pulled my arm through his own, and led me towards the steps.

He did not speak as we went down the long shallow flight of stone steps to the lower gardens, and I was grateful for the chance to think. Why he was acting like this I could not imagine, and I did not intend to waste time thinking about it yet. I must think of nothing but how to shake him off, and get out of Nîmes and back to Avignon without his following me or seeing David.

One thing was certain, I thought, remembering the boy's panic-stricken flight from the Arena on hearing his father's voice, David was mortally afraid of meeting his father. So all that mattered for the moment was that David should get away. If only he had told me then, we could have left Nîmes straight away. And after meeting Richard Byron, I knew that, sooner than let him get his hands on David, I'd murder him myself.

I stole a glance at his profile, with its expressions of brooding bitterness, and the unpleasant set to the mouth. Then I remembered, with a queer cold little twist of the stomach, what Mrs. Palmer had said.

'He must have been mad . . . they ought to have locked him up . . . *he must be mad!*'

Panic swept over me again, and at the same time a queer sense of unreality that I believe does come to people when they are in fantastic or terrifying situations. This could not be happening to me, Charity Selborne; I was not walking along the canal-side in Nîmes, Provence, with my arm gripped in that of a man who might be a murderer. A man who had hurt me and cursed me, and looked as if he would like to kill me. These things didn't happen . . . my mind spiralled stupidly; I wonder if Johnny thought it couldn't be happening to him, when he came down over France with his wings in flames . . . ?

'Well?' said Richard Byron.

He had paused at the corner leading to the Arena, and looked down at me.

I said nothing, and his brows came down sharply into a scowl.

'Well?' he repeated with the sneer in his voice. 'You beautiful little bitch, what about it?'

Then suddenly, gloriously, I was angry. Someone once described it as a 'chemically useful reaction'; I believe it is. At any rate, my mind cleared at that moment and I forgot to be afraid of him, madman or no. And I knew what to do.

I looked up the street that leads to the Arena, and saw, parked at the extreme end of it, a big grey car, and I remembered Loraine's panicky whisper . . . 'A big grey car with a GB plate . . .' I looked the other way towards the square; there was a bus standing there, and I could see its destination: MONTPELLIER.

Then I put a hand to my eyes, and my lip quivered.

'All right,' I said. 'I was lying to you, but you frightened me, and I wanted to get away. I *was* with David Shelley in the Arena.'

His arm moved sharply under mine.

'That's better. Where is he now?'

'I don't know.'

'Now look here, my girl—'

I shook my head impatiently: 'Can't you see I'm telling the truth now? He didn't want to go up to the Tour Magne with me. He went off on his own.'

'Where are you meeting him again?'

I hesitated, and I could feel him tensing.

'In the square,' I said reluctantly. Oh, David, I prayed, if it doesn't work, forgive me!

'When?'

'In time for the bus. You're making me late.'

He whirled round, his eyes on the square. There was no sign of David.

'The Montpellier bus,' I said sulkily.

His eyes showed satisfaction.

'That's the Montpellier bus standing there now,' he said. 'When does it go?'

I peered towards it, screwing up my eyes. 'Is it? Yes, it is.' I saw the drivers standing about in the sun, as if they had all the time in the world, and once again I took a chance. 'It goes in about ten minutes.' Then I looked up at him, and my eyes really did swim with tears. 'And now, please may I go? I – I'm sorry if I annoyed you, but you scared me so.'

He hesitated, and I tried not to hold my breath. Then he dropped my arm abruptly, and said: 'Very well. I'm sorry I scared you, but I thought

– well, you shouldn't have told me those lies. I'm a little anxious about David, you see, and I thought you were stalling me off. I'll see him at the bus.'

He started quickly up the street towards the parked car. I walked as casually as I could to the corner, then, once out of sight, I broke and ran for the church as if hounds were out and I was the hare.

Luckily there was no one about in the porch to see me tear into the building, as if I were bent on sacrilege. If David weren't there – I couldn't think beyond that possibility. But he was, curled up in a big pew in a side aisle with Rommel asleep at his feet. He straightened up with a jerk when he saw me.

'David,' I said breathlessly. 'Don't ask questions. He's looking for you. Come to the car – quick!'

He threw me one scared and wondering look, and came. As we reached the porch I hesitated for a moment and scanned the square, but could not see the big grey car. We turned right and tore across the open space, and as we ran I saw out of the tail of my eye the bus for Montpellier slide out of the rank and turn on to the Montpellier road.

Then we had found our side street and the car, and were threading a maze of narrow streets away from the square.

'Our luck's in . . .' I breathed. 'The Montpellier bus . . . it left early . . . he'll follow it until he finds out, and by that time—'

Two minutes later the Riley slipped out of Nîmes and took the Avignon road.

CHAPTER SEVEN

Never ——

BROWNING

We were some way out of Nîmes before either of us spoke. Then I said carefully: 'You saw your father at the Arena, didn't you, David?'

'Yes.' His voice was low and expressionless, and I didn't look at him; my eyes hardly ever left the driving mirror, where I was watching for a big grey car with a GB plate. 'I heard him speak first, then I looked over and saw him. I didn't think he'd seen me.'

'He hadn't. I gave you away by mistake. I met him up at the Temple of Diana. Up in the gardens.'

'What happened?'

'Oh, he tried to make me tell him where you were. I told a few lies and got caught out in them – I never did have much luck that way. Then I managed to make him think we were getting the Montpellier bus.'

'I suppose he'll follow it?'

'Yes, I'm hoping so,' I said cheerfully. 'And it's in quite the opposite direction from Avignon.

'Yes, I know.'

Something in his tone made me glance quickly at him. He was sitting, hugging Rommel between his knees, and staring in front of him with an expression I found it hard to read. He was still very white, and there was a look of strain over his cheek-bones, as if the skin were stretched too tight. His eyes looked enormous, and as he turned to answer my look I could see in them misery and a kind of exaltation, through the tears that were slipping soundlessly down his cheeks. My heart twisted uncomfortably, and I forgot to be casual any more. I put out my left hand and touched him on the knee.

'Never mind, David. Is it very bad?'

He did not answer for a bit, and when he did his voice was coming under control again.

'How did you find out about my father?'

'I'm afraid there was some gossip at the hotel. Someone who'd followed the – the case recognized your step-mother. Did you know he might be in Nîmes?'

'No. I thought he might be following us down here, but I didn't know ... I thought it couldn't do any harm to have one day out. You – you didn't tell him we were staying in Avignon?' The terror was back in his voice as he half turned to me.

'Of course not. It's very important that he shouldn't find you isn't it?'

He nodded hard over Rommel's head.

'Terribly important. I can't tell you how important. It – it's a matter of life and death.' And somehow the hackneyed over-dramatic words, spoken in that child's voice with a quiver in it, were not in the least ludicrous, and were uncommonly convincing.

'David.'

'Yes.'

'Would it help you to talk about it?'

'I don't know. What did they tell you at the hotel?'

'Not very much. Just what was in the papers at the time. You see, if you'd told me about your father when you saw him first in Nîmes, this needn't have happened. From what I had heard at the hotel, I gathered that it might be – undesirable – for your father to find you again, and then when I met him in Nîmes and realized that it was his voice that had frightened you in the Arena, I knew that whatever happened you didn't want him to catch you. That's all.'

The driving mirror was still blank of anything but a narrow white road snaking away from the wheels.

'That's all there is,' said David at length. 'Except for one thing. Mrs. Selborne, there's one thing that's terribly important too.'

'What's that, David?'

He spoke with a rush: 'Don't tell anyone – *anyone*, what's happened to-day!'

'But, David – how can I help it? Your step-mother ought surely—'

I saw his hands move convulsively in the dog's fur, and Rommel whined a protest. 'No! Oh, please, Mrs. Selborne, *please* do as I say. It would only worry her terribly, and it couldn't do any good. It won't happen again, because I won't go out, and anyway, we leave in a few days for the coast. So please keep it a secret! I wouldn't ask if it didn't matter.'

I was silent for a moment, and the Riley sang up a steep rise in the road. A little way ahead I could see the deep trees and the golden arches of Pont du Gard.

'All right,' I said. 'I don't know why, but I'll do as you say. Though I still think I ought to tell your step-mother. But I won't.'

'Cross your heart?' I don't suppose the childish oath had ever been administered with such an agony of urgency. I smiled at David.

'Cross my heart.'

There was a little sigh beside me. 'You're awfully nice, aren't you?' said David naïvely.

'Thank you.'

'How – how did he look?'

I slowed down and pulled in behind a big brake van with a Vaucluse plate. Still nothing in the mirror. But in front of my eyes rose Richard Byron's face, dark and angry, with scowling brows and hard mouth, and I could feel the bruises on my wrist where he had hurt me.

'He looked well enough,' I said carefully, 'but of course he was pretty angry, and so he wasn't too pleasant. I don't blame you for being scared, you know; I was scared silly. I wondered—' I broke off abruptly.

'You wondered if he was mad?' said the small voice beside me. 'Well, I think he is – I think he must be. Quite mad.'

And we drove into Pont du Gard and drew up in front of the hotel.

A hasty look through the tables on the terrace satisfied us that Louise must have already gone home, so we set off once more for Avignon. On the second half of the journey we hardly spoke; I watched the driving mirror and drove as fast as I dared, while David sat crouched together beside me holding the dog. We swung through Villeneuve-lès-Avignon shortly before six o'clock, and crawled over the suspension bridge. It was queer, after only two days, how much coming back into Avignon felt like coming home; I suppose that after the events of the day the hotel was a refuge, a bolt-hole, where one could hide and lock a door.

I took the car straight in through the Porte del'Oulle this time, feeling that another ten minutes of exposed driving on the perimeter road was more than I could stand. We threaded the narrow streets as fast as a homing cat, and the Riley ran into the garage and stopped with a little sigh, just as the clock in the Place de l'Horloge struck the hour.

L'heure de l'apéritif. And Louise would be sitting in the quiet courtyard drinking her vermouth, just as she had done yesterday and the day before.

I smiled at David, and got out of the car.

'I think a bath before dinner, don't you? And we had a very pleasant, very ordinary day in Nîmes. You were very impressed with the Arena, I remember.'

He managed a smile. 'Thank you for taking me,' he said.

I watched him through the court into the hotel, then I turned sharply, and went back into the street. I almost ran back to the gate which commanded the suspension bridge, and there, in a crowded little café, sitting well inside, against the wall, I had my drink – a cognac, this time. For half an hour I sat there, watching the narrow bridge that joined the city with Villeneuve-lès-Avignon.

But no big grey car with a GB plate crossed the bridge. So after a while I got up and went back to the hotel.

I found Louise, not in the courtyard, but in her room, thumbing through her sketch-book. The inevitable vermouth stood on her dressing-table.

'I just came to make sure you were back. I thought you must be when we didn't see you at Pont du Gard.'

'I came back after the light began to change,' she said. 'Did you have a good day, or were you broiled alive?'

I pushed the hair back off my forehead, and sat down on the edge of the bed.

'It was fearfully hot,' I admitted, 'I didn't finish the course, I'm afraid. I just could *not* climb the last long mile to the Roman tower. But the other things were well worth a visit. How did the sketches go?'

Louise knitted her smooth brow at her sketch book.

'Oh, so-so. The shapes are wonderful, but oh Lord, the light. It can't be got. If you leave out the reflections the arches look like American cheese, and if you put them in they look like fat legs in fish-net nylons. The colours just aren't there in the box.'

She sipped her drink, and her eyes considered me. 'Are you sure you haven't overdone it a bit, Charity? You look done up. Don't forget you're not quite as tough as you think you are.'

'I'm all right.'

'Well, be careful, that's all. This isn't the climate to take risks with—'

'I'm all right,' I said again. 'Or at least I shall be when I've had that dinner I'm beginning to dream up.'

I went to my room to change. I hadn't time for a bath, but I took a quick cool sponge down, and put on my pale green dress. I looked in the mirror as I brushed my hair, and saw with a faint surprise that under their faint tan my cheeks were quite without colour. I leaned closer to the mirror. Something about the eyes and the corners of the mouth reminded me vividly of David's face as he had turned to me in the car, some trace seemed to be there of strain – and fear. I frowned at my reflection, and then fished in a drawer for some rouge, annoyed that my encounter with David's father, which I had been trying to put out of my mind until I could think it over without disturbance, should have apparently had such a profound effect on me. After all, what did it amount to? A bruised wrist and some abuse? The natural fear of a sane person confronted with the unreasonable? For certainly no sane man – even discounting David's terrible little confession to me on the homeward drive – would have behaved in that way to a strange woman, even if she were apparently obstructing him in his desire to see his son.

I smoothed the rouge faintly over my cheek-bones, back towards the hair-line, then dusted over with powder. That was better. My coral lipstick next, and the face that looked back at me was an altogether braver affair. Thank God for cosmetics, I thought, as I put them into my bag; one not only looks better, one *feels* better, with one's flag at the top of the mast again. I would not think about Richard Byron again this evening. He had not come to Avignon, of that I was sure. David had only to lie low for a few days more, then he was to go to the coast, and surely France was big enough for a small boy to get lost in? There was nothing more that I could do, and up to date, even if I was left with food for a nightmare, I hadn't done so very badly.

I picked up my bag, and as I did so, I caught sight of the blue marks on my wrist. I turned the arm over, and examined the dark prints where Richard Byron's fingers had bitten into the flesh. Then I remembered my wide silver bracelet, and, hastily searching for it, clasped it round my wrist, over those tell-tale bruises. To my fury, I found that I was shaking again.

'Oh *damn* everything!' I said aloud, with unwonted viciousness, and went to get Louise.

The dinner that I had dreamed up proved to be every bit as good as the dream. We began with iced melon, which was followed by the famous *brandade truffée*, a delicious concoction of fish cooked with truffles. We could quite contentedly have stopped there, but the next course – some small bird like a quail, simmered in wine and served on a bed of green grapes – would have tempted an anchorite to break his penance. Then *crêpes Suzette*, and, finally, coffee and armagnac.

We sat over this for a very long time, and then we went up to the Place de l'Horloge and had more coffee and sat again. Louise talked a bit about light, and reflections, and a picture by Brangwyn of the Pont du Gard that she had seen in a Bond Street exhibition, but I was not listening very hard. I was not even thinking, at any rate not usefully. I just sat and drank black coffee and felt very, very tired.

We went back to the hotel at about half-past ten, to find the courtyard empty save for the thin cat at the foot of the tree Yggdrasil. I said good night to Louise and went to my room. The tired feeling still persisted, and it was with slow mechanical movements that I took off the green frock, creamed my face, brushed my hair, and went through all the motions of getting ready for bed. I was even too tired to think, and with the edge of my mind I remember feeling glad about this.

Finally I wrapped my housecoat round me, and went along the corridor to the bathroom, which was at the far end from my room.

I was in the bathroom, and was in the act of closing the door softly behind me, when I heard a quick tread in the corridor, a man's tread. A door opened, and I heard an urgent whisper:

'*Loraine!* '

I froze. It was the voice of the man I had overheard with Loraine Bristol on the Rocher des Doms.

'*Loraine!* '

'*You! What is it? What has happened?* '

'*Loraine, he's here! I saw him. To-day. In Nîmes.*'

There was a sound like a deep-drawn breath of terror. Then the door shut behind him, and I heard the click of a lock.

I shut the bathroom door and leaned against it for a moment, my brain revving up like a tired engine.

Marsden. On the bus to Nîmes. I had forgotten all about Marsden.

I must ask David where Marsden came into the picture. I crept out of the bathroom without a sound, and paused outside Loraine Bristol's door. There was the barest murmur inside, of voices. I tip-toed on, round the angle of the corridor, to David's door, and lifted my hand to scratch at the panel, wondering as I did so if Rommel slept in the room with him, and if he would bark.

Then I stopped, with my hand half-way to the panel, and froze again.

From inside the room came the sound of a child's desolate sobbing.

I stood there for a long moment, then my hand dropped to my side and I went back to my own room.

CHAPTER EIGHT

While I am I, and you are you,
So long as the world contains us both ...
While the one eludes, must the other pursue:

BROWNING

All things considered, I did not sleep too badly. I was awakened at about nine o'clock the next morning by Louise, who stopped to knock on my door on her way down to breakfast.

I got up slowly, and dressed. The shadows under my eyes were still there, and so were the marks on my wrist, but I put on my coffee-cream linen dress and my silver bracelet, and felt pretty well able to face what might come. I went down to the courtyard for breakfast.

David was there, looking as if he had not slept too well, but he gave me a gay little smile of greeting, and Rommel, under the table, wagged his silly tail. Loraine Bristol looked up from lighting one cigarette from the half-smoked butt of another. She, too, looked as if she had not slept, and the lines from nostril to mouth were sharply etched on her lovely face, giving her suddenly an older, harder look. I felt sorry for her.

She said: 'Good morning, Mrs. Selborne. It was so good of you to take David yesterday. He has been telling me how much he enjoyed the day.' I said, lightly: 'That's all right, it was a pleasure. Nîmes is a lovely place, except for the smells. I hope David will be able to come with me for another trip some day.'

I saw David's swift upward glance, then Mrs. Bristol said: 'It's so nice of you. Perhaps. But we plan to leave Avignon soon, and we will go then to Nice.'

'I hope you enjoy it,' I said, and we smiled at one another like two mechanical dolls, and then I went to our own table and sat down.

Over the coffee and *croissants* I looked round me. Mamma and Papa from Newcastle were there, and Mamma waved cheerfully when she caught my eye. Carole, apparently, was not up yet, or perhaps it took her a long time to complete her fearsome toilette. The young American couple, each-in-other-absorbed, sat with heads close together in their corner. The Frenchman, Paul Véry, was nowhere to be seen. But Marsden sat at his table beside the vine-covered trellis, imperturbably eating his *croissants* and reading *Little Gidding*.

'At breakfast!' said Louise in an awed voice. 'A man who can read poetry at breakfast would be capable of anything.'

You're probably right at that, I thought, remembering the decisive voice in the dark ... *I got you out of the mess before, didn't I? ... I'm in charge, and you trust me, don't you?*

'More sight-seeing to-day?' came Louise's voice. I shook myself free of my thoughts, and poured another cup of coffee.

'I'll do what you do,' I said.

'Sit in the shade and drink iced grape-juice?'

'Just that.'

'Tired?'

'A bit. You were right. The heat did take it out of me yesterday. I'll stay at home to-day and think up something good for to-morrow.'

Presently people began to move, the tourists discussing the day's programme. The Germans went off, arguing over a guide book, and soon afterwards the American couple strolled out into the Rue de la Répub-lique, arm-in-arm. David got up then, and went into the hotel with Rommel, and in a few moments Marsden went in too. Loraine Bristol lit another cigarette and stared in front of her. I made some excuse and got out of my chair. Perhaps now I could get to David's room and ask him about Marsden – why Loraine Bristol, if she did know Marsden, and if he had helped her and David in the first place, had not told David of the connection. Perhaps David would feel safer if he knew that there was a man on guard between him and Richard Byron.

It was possible, of course, I thought as I climbed the stairs, that David did know, but he had betrayed no such knowledge yesterday when we had seen Marsden on the bus, nor had any sign of recognition passed between Marsden and himself, beyond the casual recognition of fellow-guests in a hotel.

Marsden was in the upper corridor, so, without going near David's door, I went into my own room, and collected the things I should want for the morning, my sun-glasses, a book, my Michelin guide. Then, after a few minutes, I went out again into the corridor, only to find that my plan of having a private word with David would have to wait, for he and Rommel and Marsden were together, making for the stairs.

' . . . So I thought I'd go up there this morning,' David was saying, 'instead of to the river.'

'I'm walking up that way myself,' said Marsden. 'Mind if I come with you?'

'Not at all, sir . . .' The voices faded. I went back into my room, thinking that it certainly did not sound as though David knew of any intimate connection between Marsden and his own affairs. Then I heard them come out into the courtyard, below the balcony, and I moved towards the window.

' . . . The tower at the north corner,' said Marsden. 'Though how he ever got a mule up it I don't know. Have you ever been in?'

'No,' said David. I saw him stop beside his step-mother's table. 'I'm going up to the Rocher des Doms,' he told her. 'Mr. Marsden's coming too. You get a marvellous view of the ferry-boat from there; it has to cross with a rope, in case it gets swept away.'

Yes, I thought, watching them go together up the Rue de la République, and you also get a marvellous view of the suspension bridge that leads in from Nîmes and Montpellier. And I wondered just how much of his day David would spend up on the battlements, watching for a big grey car with a GB plate.

The day dragged by. Louise and I spent the morning in the gardens, according to plan, drinking iced grape-juice and idly watching the circular sprays watering the vivid lawn. Then she got out her sketch book and began to make rapid clever little drawings – of the children, thin and brown, of the old women who sat squarely on the narrow seats, knitting and watching them, of the ragged-trousered half-naked men who raked the gravel, of the frocked priests moving to and from the church across the way. I took out my book and tried to read, but between my eyes and the page swam perpetually two angry grey eyes under their black brows, and a mouth twisting with sudden murderous fury. I blinked it away and began to read with steady concentration, only to find after several minutes that I had read the same page over and over again, and had not taken in a single word of it, and that my brain was mechanically repeating, like a damaged record ... *you little bitch, you little bitch, you little bitch.* I pushed back my hair as if by the action I could brush my mind clean of memories, but I gave up the attempt to read after a while, and sat, fidgeting with my sun-glasses, and wishing I could draw – do anything to take my mind off the wheel that it was treading, over and over again.

'Louise.'

'Mm?'

'Let's go and have lunch.'

'Already?'

'It's time. We may as well go back to the hotel, don't you think?'

But though we sat for a long time in the court, over a leisurely lunch and cigarettes, David did not appear and nor did Marsden. Paul Véry was in his corner, and smiled at me over his *apéritif*, but apart from him and ourselves, all the other residents, including Loraine Bristol, seemed to be lunching elsewhere. At length I got up.

'I think I'll go and rest,' I said, and went up to my room.

To my own surprise I slept deeply and dreamlessly for a long time, and woke in the late afternoon, feeling refreshed and in my right mind. As I washed and slipped into the pale green dress I felt singularly light-hearted, as if some heavy cloud had lifted off the landscape, and had left nothing but a shining prospect of sun upon the wet spring grass. I had had an unpleasant experience, which had upset me considerably; very well, now it was over, and the memory of Richard Byron's crazy furious behaviour could be thrust back with all the other nasty things into the woodshed. I sang as I clipped the silver bracelet on over the bruises, and I smiled at my reflection as I brushed my hair.

And as for David – the lifting cloud cast a momentary shadow there; but the fresh wind of common sense blew it away into rags. David's problem was a tragic one, certainly, but a comparatively simple one, after all. There were two adults to look after him, and, if the conversation on the Rocher des Doms meant anything, Loraine Bristol would eventually marry her helper. The only problem was to keep David out of his father's way, and surely that wouldn't be so very difficult to manage? And, whatever I felt about it, I could do nothing for David. It was Mrs. Bristol's problem, and I was a stranger. And I would see the last of them in a few days' time anyway. There was only one sane thing to do, and that was to forget the whole business.

I went lightly along to Louise's room, and found her doing her hair.

'Louise, I've had an idea. I'm feeling as restless as a gipsy, and I'm sick of doing nothing. I'm going to take the car and drive up to Les Baux for a night – or even a couple of nights. D'you want to come?'

'Les Baux? Where's that and what is it?'

'It's a ruined village, a hill village south of Avignon. I believe it's a queer wild sort of place – just ruins and a deserted village and an inn and a wonderful eerie view. It's just what I feel like, anyway, miles from anywhere.'

Louise put away her brush and comb and began to do her face.

'Do you want me to come – I mean, do you *not* want to go alone?'

'I don't mind whether I go alone or not. That's not why I was asking. If you'd like the drive, come by all means. If not, I'll be perfectly happy.'

She looked at me in the mirror. 'Sure?'

'Perfectly. I take it you *don't* want to come?'

'Not particularly. I'd rather laze about here and draw. But if you—'

'Then forget it. It was a sudden idea, and it suits the way I'm feeling, but you needn't let if affect you. I'll go and ring up and see if they've a room at the inn, and I'll drive up there for dinner.'

Louise sat down to put on her sandals. 'You know,' she said, with an upward look at me, 'I was wondering last night – well, is anything up?'

'Not a thing,' I lied cheerfully. 'I was tired, but after that sleep this afternoon I feel wonderful. But I feel a bit stifled in Avignon, and I want to be off up to Les Baux to-night. You're sure you don't want to come?'

Louise shook her head.

'No. You go off and commune with nature and the ghosts in the ruined houses. It sounds terrible. I'll see you when I see you, I suppose.'

So I went downstairs and telephoned the inn at Les Baux, where I was lucky in being able to secure a room for one night at least, with the probability of the next, if I should wish it. Feeling something like a released prisoner, I hurried back to my room, pushed a nightdress and a few toilet necessities into my big handbag, went down again and saw Madame, then said good-bye to Louise and went out to get the car.

It was all done so quickly, and I was out of Avignon and heading for Orgon, before I really had time to think what I was doing. But when I did think about it, pushing the car along at a comfortable speed in the evening light, it still seemed a good thing to do. I wanted, above all things, to be out of Avignon, out of that *galère*, even for a short time. And I wanted to be alone. I was glad Louise had elected not to come, though, knowing Louise, I had never really for a moment suspected that she might want to. Somehow, the picture I had formed of Les Baux, the empty little mountain village, where night was so quiet and dawn so beautiful, just represented the sort of thing I very much needed.

About David Byron I steadfastly refused to think, and about Richard, his father, I did not think at all, except for a little twist of wry amusement when I looked at the map and saw that soon I would be turning on to the Tarascon road.

The evening was drawing down, and the light deepened. Away behind me I caught a last glimpse of the towers of Avignon, like torches above the trees. Around me the landscape grew wilder and more beautiful, muted from the white and dusty glare of day to the rose and purple of evening. The sun set, not in one concentrated star of fire, but in a deep diffusion of amber light, till the sharp black spires of the cypresses seemed to be quivering against the glow, and flowing upwards like flames formed of shadows.

It did not seem long before the Riley climbed the last hill, and I berthed it ouside the inn not long before seven o'clock.

CHAPTER NINE

Oi deus, oi deus, de l'alba! tan tost ve.
(Ah God, ah God, but the dawn comes soon)

MEDIEVAL FRENCH LYRIC

The deserted town of Les Baux, in medieval times a strong and terrible fortress, stands high over the southern plains. The streets of eyeless houses – little more than broken shells – the crumbling lines of the once mighty bastions, the occasional jewel of a carved Renaissance window, clothed with ferns, have an uncanny beauty of their own, while something of the fierce and terrible history of the 'wolves of Les Baux', the lords of Orange and Kings of Arles, still seems to inhere in these broken fortifications. The prospect is wild enough, and strange enough, to satisfy anyone who, like myself that evening, felt so pressingly the need for quiet and my own company. With faint amusement I perceived slowly creeping over me the mood of melancholy in which the not-quite-romantics of the eighteenth century in England found such gentle pleasure.

I sat near the window of the little inn's dining-room, watching the evening light on the distant slopes, and enjoying my lonely dinner. I ate slowly, and the light was dying from the land when at length I took my coffee and chartreuse outside on to the little terrace, and prepared to let the past have its way with me.

I got out my book, and read the *chansons de toile* again, the songs of lovely Isabel, Yolande the beautiful, Aiglentine the fair, who had sat at their embroidery, singing, so very long ago, in this same land. Then I shut the book, and sat dreaming, with my eyes on the broken lines and ghost-filled terraces of the town, trying to pave the streets and cut back the vegetation and fill the empty ways with horses and men and the glint of armour and the scarlet of banners.

I sat there till darkness had drawn over the scene, and then I went down to the car and drove it away from the inn door, round the open sweep to face the road again. I left it parked there, two wheels on the verge. Then I went up to my room.

Where was it that I had read that to watch the dawn over the ruined town was one of the sights of the world? Looking out of my window into the darkness, tracing the imperceptibly darker shapes of rock and hill, I thought that whatever the book had said it was probably right. I would go out early and wait for the sun to rise, and see if the ghosts of the Kings of Arles really did ride at cock-crow. So I did not undress, but merely took off frock and shoes, and lay down on one of the beds. I was asleep almost at once.

I must have slept for three or four hours, because when I woke and turned my head to look at the window, I could see, not light, but a faint lifting of the darkness. I put a light on and looked at my watch, only to find that I had forgotten to wind it the night before. I put the light off again, got up, and went to the window to lean out. My room faced south-east, and away to my left I could see what looked like the beginnings of a rift in the night, a soft pencilling of light on the underside of a cloud. The air was chill and clear and silent.

I closed the shutters, put on the light again, and got into my frock and shoes. I rinsed my face and hands in cold water to wake myself up properly, then put on my coat, and went quietly out of my room and down the stairs.

I must have made some slight noise, but nobody seemed to hear, or at any rate to bother about it. I supposed the people at the hotel were used to dawn-watchers in Les Baux. The door of the inn was not locked, so apparently there was nothing tangible, at any rate, to fear from the ghostly princes of Orange. Wishing I had a torch, I let myself out with caution and moved carefully towards the deserted buildings. My feet made no sound upon the grass.

How long I sat out there, in a coign of carved stone and rough rock, I do not know. Long enough, I suppose, for my vigil did at length bring in the dawn. I saw the first light, fore-running the sun, gather in a cup of the eastern cloud, gather and grow and brim, till at last it spilled like milk over the golden lip, to smear the dark face of heaven from end to end. From east to north, and back to south again, the clouds slackened, the stars, trembling on the verge of extinction, guttered in the dawn wind, and the gates of day were ready to open at the trumpet . . .

> *oi deus, oi deus, de l'alba! tan tost ve* . . .

Suddenly I was cold. The pleasant melancholy had faded, and in its place began to grow, unbidden, the little germ of loneliness which could, I knew, mature in these dark and wild surroundings all too soon into the flower of desolation. I began to wish violently for a cigarette.

I got up, stretched, stood for a moment looking at the growing light. Waiting, perhaps, unconsciously, for the trumpet to blow its shrill aubade across the stars.

Something moved behind me.

Moved and spoke.

As I whirled, my heart stampeding, my hands to my throat—

'So I've found you again,' said Richard Byron.

He was standing barely three yards away from me. In the darkness

I could see him only as a looming shape on the slope above me, but I would have known that voice anywhere, hard, incisive, with an edge to it, and an unpleasant undertone of mockery. He stood where he was, above me in the dark, and I knew that I was as securely trapped in my corner of rock as if I had been in a locked room. To the left of me, and at my back, the rock wall and the remains of a towering buttress; to my right, the sheer drop to the southern plain; and before me, Richard Byron.

I stood still, and waited.

He lit a cigarette, and in the hissing flare of the match I saw again the face of my nightmare, the dark hair falling over the frowning brow, the hard eyes narrowed against the flame.

The match lit a brief arc over the cliff. The cigarette glowed red as he drew on it.

'How did you get here?' I asked, and was annoyed because my voice was not my own at all.

He said: 'You stopped for petrol at St-Rémy. You went across the road and had a drink in a boulevard café while they put oil in and cleaned up for you.'

'Yes, I did. Were – were you in St-Rémy?'

'I was. I was, like you, having a drink while they did something to my car. I went to your garage and waited for you, but when I heard you ask the man for the road up to Les Baux I knew you were safe, so I thought I'd wait. It isn't so public here as it was in St-Rémy, and you and I have something that we want to discuss, haven't we?'

'Have we?'

His voice was unemotional: 'You god-damned little bitch, you know we have. Where's David?'

So there we were again, except that the issue, for me, was slightly clearer. I knew that I was not going to tell him where David was, but I also knew what before I had only suspected, that he was crazy, and would stop at nothing to get what he wanted.

'Where's David?'

'Asleep in bed, I hope,' I said.

He made an impatient movement, and my throat tightened.

'You know what I mean. Where is he?'

'I'm not going to tell you,' I said levelly. If it maddened him, I couldn't help it, but I judge it better to be downright than to prevaricate.

He was silent for a moment, and I saw the cigarette glow again, twice, in rapid succession.

The next question, when it came, took me completely by surprise.

He said abruptly: 'Is it money you want? If so, how much?'

'I've as much money as I want,' I said, when I could speak. 'What were you going to offer – thirty pieces of silver?'

I could feel him staring at me through the darkness. He dragged on his cigarette again.

'But I wouldn't refuse a cigarette,' I said.

I heard him fumble for it, and again a match rasped and flared. This time his eyes were watchful on me across the flame. He lit the cigarette and, coming a step nearer, handed it to me.

'What's the matter?' I said contemptuously. 'Are you afraid I'll push you over if you come any nearer?'

'Listen, my dear,' said Richard Byron evenly. 'This won't get either of us anywhere. I want to know where David is. You do know, and you refuse to tell me. Very well, then I shall have to make you tell me.'

The cigarette wasn't much help after all; I threw it over the cliff. My brief moment of initiative was over, and he was attacking again.

I said, more bravely than I felt: 'And how do you propose to do that? Torture? Be your age, Mr. Byron.'

He said savagely: 'My God, I'd like to try. If I lay hands on you again I'll not answer for myself. I'd like to wring your lovely neck.'

'I see. Gestapo stuff.' But my voice shook.

'And why not? I've seen it done, and to women. It works, as often as not.'

'Don't be a fool,' I said sharply. The nightmare terror was seeping into me again, cold, cold. I could see him a little better now, towering over me, silhouetted against the faintly glowing east, like some shadow of fear. 'If you so much as moved a finger towards me, I'd scream the place down.'

'Don't worry. I'm not going to hurt you. Not yet. But I think we'll get things plain and clear, you and I.

He flung away his cigarette, and at the sharp movement my inside twisted over with a little thrill of fear, and I began to feel sick. Cold and sick. I put a shaking hand backwards on to the firm stone, and the hand slipped a bit. It was clammy.

Richard Byron spoke without emphasis, but his voice beat at me with the wince of hammer on steel.

'I gather that you know who I am. I told you I was a friend of David's. That was not true, as presumably you know. I am David's father, and I have an idea that that gives me a right to know where David is.'

I said nothing. I was leaning back against the stone, fighting off the same feeling of unreality and nightmare that I had experienced in the streets of Nîmes. And fighting off, too, waves of sickening blackness that kept washing over me out of the cold night.

'I did a murder once,' said Richard Byron pleasantly, 'and got away with it. They say it's easier the second time. And I assure you, you stupid little fool, that I'd do another to-day as easily as I'd stub out a cigarette, to get hold of my son.'

The gates of the eastern sky were opening behind him; the aubade must have blown, and I had never heard it ... Pure and piercing, the first fingers of the dawn stabbed the sky. Then they were blotted out again by another wave of darkness which washed up from the damp ground at my feet. I was falling . . . I clawed at the stones . . . they were slipping sideways from me . . . the whole world was slipping sideways, away from the sun.

From a great way off, a voice spoke in the blackness.

'Nothing could be easier than murder, you know. . . .'

I put out my hands in a futile little gesture, and his shadow towered over me, then stooped like a hawk. . . .

And I fainted.

I was buried, and they had put a heavy stone on top of me. But I was not dead, and I was struggling to lift it, only they had tied my hands as well, and I could not move . . . I could not even open my eyes. Then, of itself, the stone lifted off me, and I could move my head and my hands a little, in the silence and the darkness. I must have been crying, or had I died of drowning? . . . my face was wet and cold.

I struggled back to the edge of consciousness, and opened my eyes to find that the darkness, at any rate, was real, and so were the tears on my face. Tears? I slowly put up a hand, and found that not only my cheeks, but my forehead and hair were damp – someone had put cold water on me. That was it. I had fainted, for some reason, and someone had put cold water on my face to bring me round.

Hazily I turned my head. I was lying on a bed beside a window whose slatted shutters were barring out the faint grey light of early morning. I looked into the room. In the darkness I could see the shape of a chest of drawers . . . another bed . . . Someone was lying on the other bed, smoking. I saw the cigarette glow and fade, glow and fade.

I murmured: 'Johnny?'

The voice that answered me dispelled the dream, and brought reality back with a rush. It said: 'So you're round again. Who's Johnny? Is he in this too?'

I didn't answer for a bit. Then I said: 'You can't get away with this, you know.'

'With what?'

'What are you doing in here? Why won't you leave me alone?'

He said lazily: 'This is as comfortable a way of keeping an eye on you as any. And I've told you why I won't leave you alone. You're my link with David, and I'll keep my hand on you till I get what I want.'

I said: 'But this is my room. Don't you imagine the folk at the inn will want to know who you are? You can't get away with this sort of thing, even in France. What if I start to scream?'

The cigarette glowed placidly, and I could hear the smile in his voice, as he said: 'Scream away.'

I bit my lip. Of course I couldn't scream; I could see in my mind's eye the result if I did – the fuss, the explanations, the recriminations, perhaps the police – then names . . . and addresses. No, I couldn't scream.

He laughed in the darkness. 'I'm your husband, anyway. I got here late last night, and didn't want to disturb them. After all, I don't imagine you specified a single room, did you? And all the rooms here are double, which was lucky.'

'What are you going to do?' I said again.

'Stick to you like a leech, my dear, like a lover.' He settled himself comfortably on his bed. I stared into the dark, somehow too exhausted to be afraid; I felt empty and tired. I remembered to be glad that I had not told Madame where I had come from, and that I had registered merely '*en passant*'. He would get no information either from the inn or from the register.

'Won't they think it a bit odd that we each arrive in our own cars?'

'I didn't bring mine up,' he said. 'I left it a couple of hundred yards down, round the bend out of sight. I wasn't going to let you see it, if by any chance you happened to be about when I arrived. Don't worry about that.'

I did not bother to explain how little I was worrying. I turned away towards the window, and turned the pillow over, so that the dry side was against my cheek. This would have to wait till morning. I could do nothing, and common sense told me that if Richard Byron wanted information out of me, at least he would not murder me in my sleep. Neither, I thought, would he risk trying anything approaching violence, now that people were within call, and now that, if I were frightened enough, I would risk police investigation. I was still in coat and shoes, of course, so I slipped the latter off and wrapped the former warmly round me, and curled up with my back to the other bed.

Richard Byron said: 'Who's Johnny?'

I said shortly: 'I don't want to talk to you. I'm going to sleep.'

I heard a faint scrunching sound as he ground out his cigarette in a tray between the beds. He said nothing. The springs of the other bed creaked heavily, and I tensed myself unconsciously. But he was only settling himself down and relaxing.

After a while, to my own vague surprise, I drifted off to sleep.

CHAPTER TEN

And Charity chased hence by Rancour's hand

SHAKESPEARE

I awoke to an empty room, dredged with sunlight through the shutters, and the comforting sounds of breakfast on the terrace below the windows. For a long drowsy moment I wondered why I should be lying so uncomfortably curled up on the top of the quilt, wrapped in my coat. Then I remembered, and sleep fled incontinently as I turned over to look at the other bed. It had not been a nightmare, that strange interview among the dark ruins, my fainting, the implacability of the man who was going to stick to me like a lover – I could see the impression where he had lain on the other bed, the dent left by his head in the pillow, and a little pile of cigarette-butts in the ash-tray between the beds.

I sat up and swung my legs over the side of the bed. I felt a little stiff from sleeping curled up, and as if I had not slept long enough, but otherwise the night's adventures did not seem to have affected me physically to any great extent. But mentally I was in a turmoil. Where was Richard Byron now? What did he propose to do to-day? And how, how, *how* was I going to get away from him?

I crossed to the door, locked it, then took off my coat and frock and washed, afterwards patting cold water into my cheeks till the skin tingled and I felt fresh and invigorated. I brushed my hair hard, then shook out the green dress, thanking heaven and the research chemists for uncrushable materials, and put it on again. The familiar routine of doing my face and hair did a good deal to restore my confidence. Somehow I would get away from him, get back to Avignon, make some excuse to Louise, and we would drive off somewhere else for our holiday, at any rate until Loraine and the boy had left for the coast. Or at worst, if I could not shake my enemy off, I could lead him astray, away from Avignon . . . though I felt a little cold quiver of the familiar fear to think what he might do if I thwarted him again.

At any rate I would get ready for whatever opportunity might come. I put my book, my dark glasses, my toothbrush, all the small things I had brought for the night, into my bulky handbag, glanced round the room to see that nothing was forgotten, then put my coat round my shoulders and unlocked the door and went out into the corridor.

Richard Byron was waiting for me at the foot of the inn's single flight of stairs. He was leaning against the newel-post, smoking the inevitable cigarette, and as I came hesitantly down the stairs he looked up and gave me a sardonic good morning.

'I hope you slept well?' he said, straightening up.

'If we are husband and wife,' I said, 'you ought to know. And I should like a cigarette, please.'

He gave me one, and we went out on to the terrace. One or two people were still breakfasting, but I had slept late, and most of the guests had already gone into the ruined town, or had left in their cars.

He followed me to a table near the edge of the terrace, and held a chair for me.

I sat down in the shade without looking at him or speaking, and watched the smoke from my cigarette curling up in delicate blue fronds towards the hanging vines that clothed the terrace wall. We sat for some minutes in silence, but it was not the comforting silence of companionship; I could feel his eyes on my face, and was intensely conscious of his presence on the other side of the little table, and between us the air positively sizzled with unasked questions and ungiven answers.

So I watched the tip of my cigarette, and then the waiter came with the coffee and *croissants*.

The coffee was smoking hot and delicious, and smelt wonderful in that sunny still air. I put one of the flat oblongs of sugar into my cup, and stirred it slowly, enjoying the smell and the swirl of the creamy brown liquid in the wide-mouthed yellow cup.

'Have a roll,' suggested Richard Byron, and handed me the flat basket where the new hot *croissants* reposed on their snow-white paper napkin. There was something in the ordinary familiar little gesture over the breakfast table that made me suddenly still more sharply conscious of the queer and uncomfortable situation that I was in now, deeply in. I took a roll, still without looking at him, but memory stirred queerly . . . Johnny passing me the toast-rack, the marmalade . . . I bit my lip. Johnny had never seemed so far away, so utterly gone. I said it to myself, deliberately: so dead.

I was alone. Any help I got now would only come from myself, and I was well aware that I am not the stuff of which heroines are made. I was merely frightened and bewildered, and deeply resentful of the situation in which I found myself.

Which is why I sat eating my rolls without really tasting them, and staring at the golden distance of the southern plain beyond the rocks, without really making any plans at all. With every mouthful of hot and fragrant coffee, I felt better, but my brain was numb, and I dared not look at Richard Byron, in case he should see how afraid of him I was. Though, I told myself, if he doesn't know by now that you panic every time he comes near you, my girl, he must be mad.

Mad. The coffee suddenly tasted vile, and I put down my cup unsteadily on the saucer. That was the root of the matter, of course – even a heroine might legitimately be afraid of a mad-man, and a mad-man who had cheerfully, not very long before, admitted to a murder. I had to get away. I didn't know how, but I had to get away.

Then my eyes fell on my car, which was standing where I had left it, facing down the hill, about fifty yards from the terrace steps. And I remembered something Richard Byron had said last night . . . something about leaving his car a short way down the road, parked off the track. If I could somehow get to my car without him, get a start, I might get away. The Riley was fast and utterly reliable; I had not seen, in Nîmes, what make of car he drove, but I knew the Riley could be depended upon to give the average touring car a run for its money. And I had filled up last night with petrol and oil. Everything I had brought with me was in my handbag . . . I had only to go.

And if Richard Byron had posed as my husband, then Richard Byron could do the explaining, and pay the bill.

My heart was beginning to thump again, and I dared not look at him. I fumbled in my bag, ostensibly for a handkerchief, but in reality to make sure of my car keys. I took out my book of Provençal poetry, and laid it on the table, while I rummaged beneath my nightdress in the bag. My fingers closed over the keys, and I slipped them into a top compartment where I would be able to reach them easily, then I took out my handkerchief and a cigarette, put the book back, and closed the bag.

Richard Byron struck a match and held it for me across the table. I tried not to look at him, but something drew me to raise my eyes across the flame, and I saw that he was watching me with a curious expression on his face.

'What did you come up here for anyway?' he asked.

I tried to speak lightly: 'What does anyone come up here for? To see the lair of the wolves of Orange.'

'I can't help wondering,' he said slowly, 'just where you come into all this. And who is Johnny?'

My fingers tightened on my bag. 'Do you mind?' I said. 'I don't particularly want to talk to you. And I don't feel too good this morning.'

I saw his hand make an abrupt movement of impatience, and he bit back something he had been going to say. We were alone on the terrace now, and the waiter had vanished. A couple of sightseers came out of the inn, paused for a moment in the shade of the terrace roof, then stepped out into the blinding morning sun. The girl was wearing white, and swung a scarlet bag in one hand. The man, in khaki shorts and a loose linen jacket, carried an enormous camera. They were laughing. They strolled past us, below the terrace, and away towards the ruins, and disappeared round a high wall of rock, and as they went, the normal safe and happy world seemed to go with them and suddenly I was, again, alone with Richard Byron, caught in the dark circle of his little personal hell.

For a short while we sat there, in the hot silence, while the sunlight moved a fraction, and laid its slanting glare across the toe of my sandal. Somewhere, a cicada started to rasp, dry and rhythmic.

I dropped my half-smoked cigarette and ground it out gently on the floor. I leaned my forehead on my hand.

'Is there any more coffee?' I said, as if with difficulty.

I felt him glance sharply at me.

'No. It's finished. What's the matter?'

I shook my head a little. 'It's nothing. It's only—' My voice trailed away, and I said nothing.

There was another short silence, while I could feel him staring at me. I sensed the puzzlement and suspicion that must be in his glance, but this time I had an advantage I had not had in Nîmes – there must have been no possible doubt about the genuineness of my faint last night, and I must be looking quite definitely the worse for it this morning. I lifted my head and looked at him, and I know my eyes were strained and shadowed, and my lips, under the brave coral paint, were dry.

'I'm all right, thanks,' I said, 'but would you ask the waiter for some water – or a cognac; yes, a cognac?'

I don't know quite what I was planning to do. I had some general idea of establishing the fact that I was too rocky to make any violent attempt at escape; I think, too, that with hazy memories of thrillers I had read, I toyed with the idea of throwing the cognac into his eyes and making a run for it before he could recover.

But suddenly the opportunity was there, and for once, like every other heroine, I took it, and took it fast.

Richard Byron called the waiter, called again. I drooped in my chair, indifferent. But the waiter, whether because he did not hear, or because he was busy and we were so late – I suspect he helped in other ways in that little inn besides waiting at table – at any rate, the waiter did not come. After calling, and going up to the inn door to peer into the empty lobby, Richard Byron, with a long backward look at me, went into the inn.

It was all the start I needed.

As I ran the fifty yards between the terrace and the car, I snatched out the keys. It took three seconds to open the door and slip into the driving seat, leaving the car door silently swinging. That blessed engine came to life at a touch, and the Riley slid forward on the slope as I lifted the brakes.

As she gathered way I saw, out of the tail of my eye, Richard Byron, with the *patronne*, emerging from the inn door. He started forward, and I slammed the car door and went into gear. As the car rounded the first bend, gathering speed, I saw the *patronne*, gesticulating wildly, catch Byron's sleeve, so that he had to turn and speak to her. . . .

Well, let him do the talking, I thought grimly, then I began to laugh. Let him explain why his wife bolts without a word, let him get out of the silly mess of his own making – *and* pay the hotel bill into the bargain.

The Riley sighed down the curling hill, round another sweeping bend, and there, by the verge, parked in a bay of rock, stood a big grey car. A Bentley.

A Bentley, I thought savagely, braking hard. It would be. Something that could give me a fairly alarming chase, unless I did something drastic to it first. I slipped out of the car, with thoughts of tyre-slashing, taking sparking-plugs, and other acts of thuggery storming through my mind. But there was a garage at the hotel, and who knew what spares might be available? As I stumbled across the stones to the grey car I thought wildly. Not the rotor-arm, for the same reason – and I had nothing to slash tyres with anyway. . . . The bonnet was unlocked, and I lifted it, with half an eye on the road behind me.

It came automatically after all; it was the way Johnny had taught me to immobilize the car during the war, when we had to leave it parked for hours at the R.A.F. Station dances, and when the young officers, after about one in the morning, thought nothing of 'winning' someone else's car for a joy-ride with a girl in the blackout. Not a usual method at all, but one very difficult to detect, and which could give an awful lot of trouble. . . . And so simple. I whipped off the distributor-cap, gave one of the screws a turn and a half with the end of my nail-file, to break the electric contact, put back the cap, closed the bonnet, and raced back to the Riley, all in less time than it takes to tell.

My hands were shaking and slippery on the wheel but when the car leaped forward again down the slope, I began to feel steadier. Down a bank, with a rush like a lift, along an uneven stretch of flat, round another high walled bend . . . and we were out of sight and well away . . . and it might take him some time to find out why the Bentley spluttered and would not start, with everything, apparently, intact.

Presently we dropped gently round the last bend, and swung on to the good surface of the Tarascon road. I turned to the right in St.-Rémy, twisted through back streets till I thought I might have confused my trail a little, then, still keeping generally eastwards, hummed along the narrow country roads with elation in my heart.

CHAPTER ELEVEN

Exit, pursued by a Bear

SHAKESPEARE

Anywhere but Avignon. I might have given him the slip altogether, I hoped at any rate that I had delayed him considerably, but I could not risk leading him straight back to Avignon, and to David. Or, for that matter, back on to my own trail, which from Avignon, wherever I went, would be an open book. I sent the car at what speed I dared over the rough narrow roads, between their blinding high hedges of thorn and cypress, while I thought of where to go and what to do.

I would get clear away, if I could, then I would telephone Louise, tell her as much as I knew, and ask her to pack up and come to meet me. She could hire a car; I would pay for it, and it would save her having to wrestle on the crowded trains with two people's luggage. But where would she meet me? I puzzled over it as the Riley crept cautiously over a narrow and manifestly unsafe river-bridge. Then I made up my mind, taking the simplest solution as being also the best. Marseilles. I had always heard, and indeed it was reasonable enough, that a big city was the easiest place to hide in, and here was I within fairly easy reach of one of the biggest cities in France. Another thing, Louise and I had originally intended to visit Marseilles for a day or so, so the obvious thing to do was to ask her to leave Avignon to meet me in Marseilles.

Even as I made the decision, the Riley ran into a small country town

– a large village, by English standards – and a glance at a road sign
showed me that it was Cavaillon. I turned off the road into a strait little
alleyway and berthed the car. Then after I had lowered the hood and
made it fast, I got back into my seat and took out the map.

For Marseilles, I saw, I should not have crossed the river, but have
turned sharp south at Orgon on to the main Marseilles road. That much
of my way, at any rate, I must retrace. I sat biting my lip, gazing down
the narrow alley, which gave at the far end on to the main street of the
town, and wondering what to do next. If I went back the way I had
come, by the side-roads, and Richard Byron had picked up the trail, I
would run straight into his jaws. If, on the other hand, he had not
followed my actual tracks, he would be on the main road, and if I took
that way I should deliver myself neatly into his hands. He had only the
two alternatives, I knew, and, now, so had I.

I sat gripping the wheel, in an agony of indecision. Two alternatives . . .
and I was wasting time. I looked at the map again, desperately tracing
out with my finger the possible routes to Marseilles. There were three
things, it appeared, after all, that were possible. I could take a chance,
and go back by one of the two ways across the river Durance, on
to the main road for Marseilles, or I could go east through Apt, on
route 100, by an involved and roundabout way; or I could go back to
Avignon.

The last did not count so I dismissed it straight away. And I was
through with taking chances; I was through with trusting my luck. I was
not going back across the Durance, to meet Richard Byron. I would go
east, and take the long road to the coast. With a heavy heart I folded the
map, and started up the Riley. We crept along the alley, which was
barely car-width. It was roughly cobbled, and gleamed with stinking
puddles where thin cats prowled and rummaged in the gutters. The
plaster on the houses was peeling, the shutters hung crookedly on rusty
hinges. We crawled along towards the main road.

Then stopped dead as I jammed on all the brakes and sat shaking.

In the slash of vivid sunlight which was the main road at the alley's
end, a big grey car flashed past, heading east for Route 100.

It was the Bentley.

My first thought was, absurdly enough, a sort of admiration for the
speed he had made, even with my spanners in the works. My second was
a sharp elation for myself. At any rate, the road to Orgon was now clear,
and I could double on my tracks. I pushed the Riley forward to the brink
of the alley, then braked again, and getting out of the car, ran forward
to peer up the main street of Cavaillon.

The sun was blinding. The street was narrow, and crowded with the
usual French country market crowd. There were women with baskets
and string bags clustering round the street-stalls piled high with melons
and beans and oranges and sleek purple aubergines. There were mule

carts and lorries and big gleaming cars. There were dogs and children and half-naked brown men in berets and faded blue trousers.

But the Bentley had disappeared. I fancied I could see its dust still hanging in the hot quivering air at the east end of the street.

I ran to the Riley, and in a flash we were out of the alley and scudding west for the river bridge and Orgon, where one turns south-east for Marseilles.

Now that the Riley had her hood down, I was grateful for the breeze which, with our speed, fanned my cheeks and lifted my hair. But for the wind of our movement, the day was utterly still; under the pitiless sun of late morning the leaves of the planes that lined the road hung heavy, in thick lifeless clusters of yellow-green. The lovely stems of the trees with their dapplework of silver and russet-peeled bark, shone in their long colonnades like cunningly worked pillars. The blinding road was barred by their shadows.

Regular as the pulse of a racing metronome, the shadow-bars flicked along the bonnet and back over my shoulder. We sailed out of Cavaillon on the verge of the speed-limit, tore through a dusty section of untidy ribbon-building, then suddenly the road writhed out from the plane-trees, and there, in the full glare of the sun, was the Durance and the long river-bridge.

And a queue of vehicles waiting to be allowed to pass over it.

With a sinking heart I took my place in the queue. The bridge, it appeared, was only a temporary one, three hundred yards of wooden boarding, narrow and unsteady, between the newly erected iron spans. At each end was a sentry-box, from which a man in uniform controlled the passage of traffic. At the moment, the stream from the opposite end of the bridge was being given the way, and cars, lorries, and carts crawled slowly and painfully across the narrow boards, while the white baton of the *agent de police* stretched implacably in front of us.

The heat poured down. I could feel it striking up in waves from the upholstery of the car, and gently prickling out in sweat on my body. I could not relax; I sat rigid, with my eyes switching like a doll's eyes from that forbidding white baton to my driving mirror, and back again.

And still the baton held us back, and the opposite stream of traffic crept forward, and all round me, before, behind, and edging forward to the left, impatient French drivers hooted and raced their engines and stamped on their klaxons, and got ready for a mad rush for first place on the narrow bridge.…

Behind me, in the tiny mirror, a gigantic lorry quivered and roared, almost on my rear bumper; behind him again I could see a mule cart with a round canvas top. To my left a yellow Cadillac had edged up and was ready to slip in ahead, between the Riley and the brake van in front of me.

My nerves began to stretch. The roaring exhausts, the heat, the klaxons, the undisciplined traffic of the French highways ... would the white baton never drop? The impatient racing of motors round us suddenly became feverish, and again the imperceptible movement forward began; I saw that the other end of the bridge was now barred, and only three or four vehicles were still coming across; presumably as soon as the way was empty we would be allowed to go.

I gripped the wheel tighter, with an eye on the white baton, and another on the yellow Cadillac.

The last lorry lumbered off the reverberating boards. The white baton dropped, and a hand waved us on. The brake van leaped at the gap, and the yellow Cadillac, with a triumphant blare, cut across the Riley's bows and roared in behind it.

I was third in line on to the bridge, when I looked in the mirror again.

And saw the grey Bentley nosing out from behind the covered mule-cart.

At the far side of the bridge stood the other queue now, with wind-screens flashing like morse in the sun. We crawled towards it. Behind me the green lorry edged on to the boards, shaking the whole contraption in a hair-raising manner. And the Bentley—

Richard Byron had reckoned without the Frenchman's utter lack of anything that might be called conscience or courtesy on the road. For as the Bentley drew out to pass the mule-cart, the driver glanced round and saw him, and immediately, with what looked like an imprecation, lashed at his mule, and hauled at its head, so that the cart swung drunkenly across the Bentley's bonnet. The Bentley checked abruptly, and the driver, lashing his mule again, crammed into the vacant place behind the lorry.

I reckoned afterwards that it gave me a good five miles' start. When I slipped off the bridge on to the western bank, the mule-cart was still plodding, only a third of the way over, with the grey car, held fuming, at less than a walking pace behind it.

I put my foot down and kept it there. The Riley tore up the straight good road like a storm. We passed the brake van as if it were standing, and then I put a thumb hard down on my horn and left the yellow Cadillac blinding through my dust at fifty miles an hour.

The needle flicked up ... sixty ... seventy ... seventy-three ... and ahead in the glare I could see trees across the way ... A turn sharp to the left. I lifted my foot off the accelerator....

Mercifully there was nothing coming. We took the turning on the wrong side, and the back of the car skidded round it in the dust. There was a protesting scream from the tyres, and then the car straightened out and roared along the crown of the road. I felt no fear any more, I could not afford to think of anything but my driving ... the world had narrowed down to the blinding straight ribbon of the *route nationale*, and the shadow-flecks across it that blurred now into one long flicker of shadows, like an old film.

I don't even remember Orgon. I suppose I must have slowed down for it, and gone through it with some care, but we were through it before I knew, and out on the road again, with my blessed good engine pulling like the horses of the sun.

We flashed by a little farmstead, set among its bronzed ryefields, swung out for a cruising car, and passed a cart as if it did not exist. A long white hill loomed up, between slopes of baking scrub, and then we were up the hill with the smooth rush of a lift, and dropping down the other side as if the hill had never been.

A little hamlet, pink-painted among dark cypress, hurtled towards us, closed in on us, was gone. Two oncoming cars went by, with a smack like the rattle of a drum.

And the long road writhed and turned and rose and fell beneath the roaring tyres to whip back and away in the driving mirror like a flying snake. And in all the world there was nothing but the racing engine and the rushing air and the road that streamed and streamed towards us.

CHAPTER TWELVE

And southward aye we fled

COLERIDGE

Then, suddenly, we were not alone any more. Out of the tail of my eye, to the right, I saw the plume of white smoke that meant a railway engine. The line was running parallel to the road, about fifty paces away, and an express came steaming out of a wooded defile, placidly heading south, like a pompous and attendant sprite.

My mind leaped ahead; I tried vainly to envisage the map. Would there be a railway bridge, or would it be one of those level crossings so common in southern France? So common, and so slow. Dear God, I thought to myself, *so slow.* I had waited before now a full twenty minutes for the bar of a crossing-gate to lift on an apparently quite empty line. And I might have grabbed a good start, but I had had some taste of the speed Richard Byron could make. I couldn't lose him on this road, and my only chance was to get into Marseilles with sufficient start to lose him there. Five minutes would do in those swarming streets, I thought grimly, and, with a hunted glance at the train, I put my foot down again.

To this day I do not know whether the driver of that train really did try and race my car or not. It seems impossible that he should have done so, and yet it really seemed to me, pelting along beside the rattle of the express, that the train gave a lurch and a sharp wail, and thereafter really entered into the spirit of the thing. The engine and I had it neck and neck for perhaps four hundred yards, while the driver and his mate leaned out of the cab and waved, and I sat over the wheel and looked neither to right nor left. Then we began to gain. The engine, panting, fell behind, and its pursuing rattle was deadened and then lost round a wooded bluff. For another span of minutes that seemed like hours, I held the car to its speed, then suddenly we slashed up a swift hill between two banks of olive-trees, and away ahead, two miles off down a straight stretch of road, I saw, like a brightly painted toy in the distance, the sentry-box and the red and white bars of the level crossing.

It was still open.

But someone, a tiny figure dim in the quivering heat of the distance, was moving out to lower the bars.

I heard myself give a little sound like a groan, as the Riley hurtled down that road like a rocket-bomb.

The sentry-box came towards us with the sickening speed of a hangar towards a homing aircraft. The man lifted his arm to the crank that would release the bars. I put the heel of my hand down hard on the horn, and kept on.

I saw the startled jerk of his head, the white blur as his face turned towards us, his instinctive leap further out of the way.

Then with a roar and a rush and a sickening jerk and sway of springs, we were through.

I heard the bar crash into its socket behind us.

We had come down that two-mile stretch in one-and-a-half minutes dead.

We ran into Salon at a decorous pace, and threaded the main street with innocent care. In my mind's eye I saw the grey Bentley, fuming, stuck behind that maddening red and white bar until long after the train had passed.

I warned myself, through my relief, that I couldn't count on it. Richard Byron was quite capable of bribing the official to lift the bar as soon as the express was through, and the official was no doubt quite capable of obliging him.

So I did not pause in Salon, but held straight on.

But I had begun to feel tired.

So far, I thought, as I held the car at a comfortable fifty between the flickering avenues of plane-trees, so far the breaks had been about even. And the last good break had been mine. I began, I think for the first time, seriously to believe that I might be able to get clean away, lose myself where Richard Byron could not catch up with me, go right away with Louise until the storm-centre moved, and resume our disrupted holiday elsewhere.

Later on, perhaps, when I had time to think about it, I should begin to be angry at the way my time, my liberty – yes, and my person (I smiled wryly at the out-dated phrase) had been tampered with. I had got embroiled in the affair through no fault of my own, but through an impulse I still could not fully understand, the impulse that had led me in the first place to seek David's company, and in the second, to attempt to protect him. But I had certainly not deserved the kind of thing that had recoiled upon me. I ought to be angry, but just at present I was too preoccupied with my immediate problem to indulge in righteous indignation. The fact that Richard Byron was a murderer, and possibly of unsound mind, rendered null and void any prospect of talking reasonably with him. I had to escape, and then, perhaps, I could think.

The road was climbing steadily, towards the band of hills that lies between the Etang de Berre and Marseilles. It was unbearably hot, and I was hungry, but I put the thought aside, and pressed on through that deserted landscape, in a slow steady climb towards the crest of the rocky hills.

Towards the top the air grew fresher, and clumps of pines, looking cool and northern and beautiful, grew here and there beside the road. Then, some way ahead of me, I saw a little *bistro*, just a small yellow-washed house with three Continental pines to the back of it, a red petrol pump, and some small tables outside under a striped awning. Suddenly I felt unbearably thirsty. I tried to persuade myself that my lead from Richard Byron was such that I could afford ten minutes – no, five – with a long cold drink under that gay awning; that I had at any rate time to stop and buy some rolls and a bottle of red wine. But it was no use; I was definitely through with taking chances; it was Marseilles first stop. So I went relentlessly up the last hundred yards of that hill without looking at the *bistro* any more.

Then the decision was taken rudely out of my hands, because I was barely twenty yards short of it when I felt the Riley swerve across the road. I told myself that I must be more tired than I knew, and I straightened her up and crept on towards the crest of the long rise. Then I felt her pull and veer again, and once again I got her into line. It was only as I actually topped the rise that the dismal truth filtered through into my preoccupied and tired mind.

The breaks were even again, and this one was against me. I had picked up a puncture.

But not so badly against me, after all. The Riley, true as ever, had chosen to have her puncture within a hundred yards of an outpost of civilization, so, grateful for this unlooked-for fortune, I backed her slowly in on to the little flat stretch of gravel in front of the *bistro*.

A big stoutish man in shirt-sleeves and a white apron was rubbing glasses behind the bar in the shady interior. I leaned over the door of the car.

'Monsieur....'

He put down the glass he was polishing, and came out into the sun with a grin.

'Please, monsieur, I have a puncture as you see. Is there by any chance a garage? I see you sell petrol. Is there anyone here who could change my wheel while I have something to eat?'

He looked a little doubtful.

But he was French, and I gambled on that. I laid a hand on his arm, looked desperately up at him, and said, with a quiver in my voice that was not entirely assumed: 'Monsieur, it's very urgent. I – I'm running away from someone, and he isn't far behind me. I daren't let him see me, and if I'm stuck here with a puncture he—'

The most complete comprehension flashed across his face.

'Your husband?'

'Yes, my husband. He's following me, and – and, oh, monsieur, *do* help me!'

He was wonderful. In two minutes we had the Riley parked round at the back of the house, in two more he had routed out a lanky and capable youth from (I think) his afternoon siesta, and started him jacking up the car. Within seven at most I was inside the house, in a cool little room at the back, and he was asking me what I would have to eat.

'And madame need have no fear,' he said largely, with gestures, 'for to-night she will sleep with her lover in safety.'

I didn't argue, but I asked for an iced mint drink, a long, long one, and whatever food he could manage in the time it would take to change the tyre.

'An omelette? A herb omelette? It will only take five minutes. We will find something for madame. Madame is tired? She should have something reviving with her omelette, yes?'

In a very little more than five minutes it was there, a fluffy fragrant omelette, flanked with fresh rolls, butter, honey and coffee. I swallowed down my cold drink and started on it. I don't think I have ever tasted anything so wonderful as that perfect little meal that I ate hastily in the little back room of that *bistro*, while Jean-Jacques, outside the window, was yanking off my wheel.

I was actually getting up to go, gulping the last of my coffee, when I heard the whine of another car coming up the hill outside, and the check and deepened note as she changed gear. Then the swish of gravel under her tyres as she turned off the road and stopped in front of the *bistro*.

I stood frozen, with the cup half-way to my mouth.

His voice came quite clearly through the nearly shut door. After the conventional greetings—

'No, nothing to drink, thank you,' he said, but I heard the rustle of notes. 'I haven't time. I stopped to ask you if you had seen an English car pass here within the last half-hour, a dark green car with the hood down. Did you happen to notice?'

There was another rustle.

'A dark green car ...' repeated the *patron* slowly. I heard the clink of a glass, and could imagine him picking it up and deliberately starting to polish it again while he considered.

'A dark green car, English ...' he paused, and I don't know which must have waited in the most tension, I or Richard Byron, one on either side of the door. 'With a young demoiselle driving?' asked the *patron*.

'Yes.' I could almost see the flicker in Richard Byron's eyes as he leaned forward.

The *patron* said, indifferently: 'A young woman driving a dark green open car went by here some time ago. She was going fast. Would that be the one monsieur means?'

'That's the one. How long ago?'

In a voice that sounded like a shrug: 'About twenty minutes, twenty-five, half an hour – who knows, monsieur? I paid no attention, but I remember the car you speak of because of the speed ... and the pretty girl.'

Something passed with a rustle, I heard a mumble of thanks from the *patron* and then, almost immediately, the roar of the Bentley's engine and the sound of rapidly engaged gears. The engine sang across the crest of the hill, and dwindled and died, so that soon the only sound was the rustle of the pines in the little hill-top breeze, and the clink of a glass from the bar.

The *patron* came back grinning.

'He was not far behind you, that one,' he said. 'But if you give him time now he will lose himself ahead of you. Madame cannot go back now the way she came?'

I thought for a moment, then shook my head. I would not lead the chase back into the Avignon area, come what might.

I would wait here, smoke a couple of cigarettes, then drive into Marseilles by the side road, and go to ground and call Louise. And I would tell Louise everything, when I saw her again; I was tired of playing this alone. I didn't feel that David would hold me to my promise of not speaking, after what had happened.

I said: 'Is there another way into Marseilles besides by the main road?'

'Yes, there are many. After one has passed Les Assassins—'

'*Les assassins?*' I asked, startled.

'It is a place at the top of these hills, where one begins to go down into Marseille. The road goes between walls of rock, a little gorge.'

'But why is it called Les Assassins?'

'Because much rock has fallen there, and the old road used to wind in among the cliffs and boulders, and it was the place where brigands waited, in ambush, for the coaches and the carts of merchants.'

'And after that?'

'Then there is the long run down into Marseille, and before one reaches the suburbs there are roads which branch and which, if one has a map, will take one into the city by a different way. There is no need to go down the main road into the town.' He smiled suddenly. 'He is to meet you there, *hein*?'

'He – who? Oh, yes, of course,' I said. I had momentarily forgotten that I had a date with a lover in Marseilles that night. 'You have been more than kind,' I told the *patron*, and he shrugged expansively.

'It is nothing, nothing at all. If one cannot help a *belle demoiselle* in distress – what would you? One might as well be dead.'

He went out, beaming good-will, and I sat for a while, quietly smoking, while time passed softly. I felt, gradually, a sense of peace descending on me, a feeling that this was a safe little harbourage that I should be sorry to leave. I sat, relaxed, and I believe I even dozed a little, for over an hour or longer. And then, when I saw my watch that it was nearly three o'clock, I rose reluctantly, and prepared to go.

I found the *patron*, and paid for what I had had, renewing my thanks, and including a thousand-franc note, over and above what I owed him, and a substantial tip for Jean-Jacques.

I found that the latter had occupied his time not only in changing my wheel, but, when told there was no need to hurry, in finding and mending the puncture in the discarded wheel. This, mended now and serviceable, was strapped in place as spare. I thanked him gratefully, and, pursued by good wishes, and frank promises of joy to come from the *patron*, I drove the Riley back round the house and out again on to the road.

Soon the little *bistro* was lost to sight behind us, round a bend in the track, and we were off on our travels again, with the sun for company, and the tall pines whispering above the humming engine. I did not hurry. For one thing, there was now no need, and I would not unnecessarily abuse the car on the rather stony road, and risk picking up another puncture – which I would have to deal with myself. For another, the strain of the previous night, and of the hectic and nerve-racked morning, were beginning most definitely to tell on me. My head was aching a little, and a sort of lassitude, an almost don't-care-ishness, bred of fatigue and lack of sleep, was making itself felt. I knew that, even if the occasion should arise, I would be quite unequal now to the sort of demands that had been made on me that morning. If suddenly called upon for headlong speed, I would probably drive the car off the road at anything over fifty miles an hour.

So I nursed the engine up the long inclines, and took the car gently over the rough surface, with half of my mind on my driving, and the other half trying to recall the street plan of Marseilles and the way I had planned to take.

The white rocks gave way, as we climbed higher, to red. The country, deserted before, was here desolate, stripped even of its olives and its vines. The red rocks, slashed with hard cobalt shadows, rose sheer from the road on either hand, and the only green was the dark cresting of the pines, swaying richly against the dazzling blue. As we approached what appeared to be the summit of the hill, I could see how the cliffs had split and crumbled, till on either side of the road were bare boulders and pylons of rock. Among the strewn red fragments to the left I saw where the old track had wound tortuously across the hill-crest behind the pines and fallen rocks. But the new road went through the sheer red cliff like a white slash.

Les Assassins.

And, in the blue distance, the Mediterranean.

As the Riley gained the summit, I changed up, and she slipped into the long descent with a sigh. Before me the road sank in an interminable and gentle hill towards the enormous untidy sprawl of Marseilles, set on the edge of the loveliest shore in the world.

We started slowly down the last stretch. To the left of the road, several yards ahead, I saw where the old track emerged again on to the road, behind a knot of pines. We slid past it and down.

I suppose I should have seen it coming, but I confess I had not. There was no reason I could see why Richard Byron should not believe the *patron* of the *bistro*, and race on towards Marseilles in the hope of catching me. But of course, he had not believed him.

The grey Bentley glided out of that knot of pines, and closed in behind my car without a sound.

CHAPTER THIRTEEN

Re-enter Murderer

STAGE DIRECTION

There was nothing to be done, of course.

Even if I had not been so tired, I still could not have hoped to drive away from him with no start, and no advantage. I was beaten, and I knew it. I would go quietly.

Without thinking very much of anything at all, except that my head ached and I would be glad to stop driving and get out of the sun, I went on down the long stretch towards Marseilles as if there were no grey car behind me, and no angry man in it who had, by this time, quite a big account to settle with me.

In a very short time we were in the suburbs of Marseilles. The main road runs for perhaps two miles or more through streets of tattered houses and little grubby shops, where the plaster and the paint hangs in peeling festoons, and where beautiful ragged children and hideous mongrel dogs play together among the refuse of the gutters. Soon the tramlines begin, and the traffic of the city begins to close in. Lorries, mules, carts of all shapes and sizes, cars of assorted vintages and nationalities

– all the world on wheels seems to drive through the narrow streets of Marseilles, hooting, shouting, pushing for places, in a rich and strange confusion.

I steered mechanically through it all, changing gear, stopping, swerving, going through all the rapid actions necessary to getting a vehicle more or less undamaged through that incredible *tohu-bohu*. Behind me, like a shadow, the big grey Bentley swerved and checked and swept forward again on my track, never more than ten yards behind me, never less than four.

I didn't even bother to watch it, except as I would watch anything so close on my tail, in order to give it the necessary signals.

I was finished. I wasn't trying any more. My temples throbbed and I felt as if a heavy weight were pressing down on my shoulders. My mind, even had I tried to make it, would have refused to contemplate what was going to happen after this.

Which is why, when the miracle happened, I did not even notice it.

The first I knew of it was when it gradually filtered through to my stupid senses that there was no grey car reflected in the driving mirror. There was only a mule-cart, and nothing behind that that I could see.

I stared stupidly for three seconds, then I stole a look back over my shoulder. I had come about a hundred yards from where it had happened. A lorry, emerging from a blind side street, had swung across the path of the Bentley, and grazed a passing tram. The Bentley, caught between the two, had had to stop, but whether it was touched or not, I could not, of course tell. But it was stuck fast enough, that much was apparent. Already the beginnings of a crowd had gathered, and excitement was mounting ... And there were the police. ...

It might take him minutes, or even hours, to get himself out of that.

Like a fainting man who makes a last desperate conscious effort before he goes under, I turned the Riley down a side street, and trod on the accelerator ... left, right, right, left again – no, that was a cul-de-sac – right, in and out like a twisting hare ... then before me was a garage, where behind a row of pumps yawned the dark cave of an enormous shed, half filled with lorries, cars, buses, in varying stages of repair. I turned in, ran the car as deep into the shadow as I could, and berthed it finally behind a solid rank of wagons.

Still mechanically, I switched off the engine, collected my bag, maps, glasses and coat, and got out of the car.

I cannot remember what instructions I gave to the proprietor, who had hurried up, but I paid him something in advance, and only just retained enough wit to ask for his card with the address of the garage. I tucked this inside my bag, and went slowly out into the sunshine of the back street.

I turned right, away from the city centre, towards where I imagined the sea to lie, and walked for some way through shabby streets that nevertheless seemed moderately respectable. And soon the name of a little hotel caught my eye, a name I had seen in the Michelin guide. It would, in that case, be clean and comfortable, so I went into its cool tiled lobby, signed my name, and climbed a steep spiral of marble steps to a stone landing on the third floor, where Madame showed me a small and spotless room.

The door clicked shut behind her. I sat down slowly on the bed, and for a full five minutes I don't suppose I even moved an eyelash. The shutters were closed against the sun, and so were the windows, so that the hum and clash of traffic from Europe's noisiest city surged up, muted and drowsy, into the high little room. There was a wash-basin, a foot-bath, a narrow comfortable bed with a snow-white cover a carafe of water on the table beside the bed. . . .

I drank deeply. I stood up, and after I had locked the door, I slowly undressed, shaking out my clothes one by one, and laying them neatly on the bed. I had a leisurely cool wash, bathing and drying my whole body, standing on the warm floor with the slatted sunlight barring me from head to foot. Then I slipped on my fresh nylon nightdress, and brushed my hair thoroughly.

I moved my clothes to the back of a chair, had another long drink, and lay down on the bed.

The day began to recede, grow confused, grow dim, as the sound of the traffic blurred with distance . . . Richard Byron might be miles away, he might be in jail, he might be just outside the door . . . it didn't matter at all.

I slept.

It was just before six when I awoke, and at first, swimming up from the warm depths of sleep, I could not tell where I was, lying on a strange bed with the deepening rays of the sun slanting through the shutters. The light had mellowed from gold to amber, and the sound of the traffic below, too, seemed to have mellowed its note to a subdued rushing like the rushing of an underground sea.

I lay still for a while, enjoying the relaxed warmth of my body and the softness of the bed. Then I got up and began leisurely to dress again in the green frock. It looked fresh enough, considering the wear and tear of the last night and day, I thought, as I buckled the wide belt round it, and slipped into my shoes.

I was hungry, and the first problem I intended to face was that of finding a meal. I toyed with the idea of buying food and wine, and locking myself safely in my room to eat, but decided I might as well eat at a café if I was going out to buy food. And Marseilles was a big and crowded city, not like Nîmes, or Avignon. I would go out, avoiding the main streets, and dine in some small restaurant where I was not likely to be seen. Then I would come back to the hotel and ring up Louise.

I remembered what I had read of Marseilles – that the city was sliced in two by the straight line of the Canebière, the busiest street in Europe, where, sooner or later, all the world passed by. It was said that if you sat in the Canebière long enough, you would see passing by you every soul that you knew. If I were Richard Byron, I thought, that's where I'd go. I'd select a table in a boulevard café on the Canebière, and sit and watch for the girl in the pale green dress.

So the girl in the pale green dress would go elsewhere.

I took my key downstairs, spoke politely to Madame and the marmalade cat in the foyer, and went down the three stone steps into the street. It was still warm, but the sunlight was deep copper-gold, and the shadows lay long on the pavements.

The exhausted feeling had passed, leaving only, as an aftermath of that deep sleep, a profound sensation of unreality, as if I were moving, effortlessly and bodiless, through a dream. People passed me, traffic rattled by, but these movements seemed to have no connection with the world in which I found myself; men were 'likes trees walking', without character or feature or sound, irrelevant creations in the background of my nightmare. The only living person was myself, Charity Selborne, to whom none of these things could possibly be happening. . . .

I walked fairly rapidly to the end of the street and glanced to right and left. To the right a vista of still meaner streets and warehouses met my eyes, so I turned left through a narrow way towards the sea. After a while I realized that I was making for the harbour – I could see masts and the gleam of a gull's wing and a flash of early neon lights at the end of the street.

I hesitated. One had heard such tales of Marseilles, the wicked city . . . and was it not near the harbour that the wickedness congregated? A street led off to my left, and I paused in my walk, and glanced up it.

Then made for the harbour without another second's hesitation. For he was there, my enemy, hesitating like myself at the far corner of that street, which, I found later, gave straight on to the Canebière: – I had been right, as far as it went. I did not think he had seen me, but the hunt was up again, and I made for the Old Port of Marseilles without another thought of the wickedness there abounding. I believe I would almost have welcomed the offer of a free trip to Buenos Aires at that moment.

Where the street led into the harbour I hesitated again. It was so open. The Old Port was a vast open space, criss-crossed by tram-lines and railway tracks, bounded on three sides by houses and restaurants all flashing their gaudy neon signs in the face of the sunset, and open on the fourth side to the sea. The harbour waters were crowded with boats of all shapes and colours, and in the amber light the forest of masts swayed and bobbed amid the glancing web of their ropes.

I only hesitated for a second, then made across the open square towards the nearest crowd of people, hoping to lose myself among them, and get somehow to the other side of the square. There were about twenty or thirty people standing there, talking and laughing, between the railway tracks and the edge of the quay. I reached them and joined the crowd, ignored a pressing invitation from a couple of sailors obviously ashore for the evening, and took refuge behind what appeared to be a family party, papa, mamma, and two little boys in sailor suits with red pompoms on their bonnets. I threw a cautious glance at the mouth of the street I had just left. He was not there.

Then I discovered why the crowd had collected there on the quay.

An old boatman, with scarlet cheeks, a quantity of white whiskers, and a liquid and lascivious eye, suddenly appeared up a short gangplank which led from the quay beside us to the stern of a motor-boat moored below.

'This way!' he yelled. 'This way for the Château d'If!'

Simultaneously, another old man, with whiskers slightly less white, and an eye proportionately more lascivious, shot up in rivalry in the next boat.

'This way,' he screamed. '*This* way for the Château d'If!'

The crowd, showing neither fear nor favour, turned as one and began to file down the twin gangplanks. It looked as if, my cover gone, I was going to be left high and dry on the edge of the Old Port.

I flung a look at the street corner, just in time to see Richard Byron emerge, glance once back over his shoulder, then turn to scan the square, but he was not looking at the quay; he was looking the other way towards the din of the Canebière.

I scuttered down the nearest gangplank and sat down under the awning, as far forward as I could get. The boat lay well below the level of the quayside, and I knew he could not see me from where he stood. But it looked as if, bating Buenos Aires, I were going on a trip to the Château d'If.

The boatman, with a good deal of quite unnecessary noise, cast off, and soon we were churning through the milky waters of the bay towards the harbour mouth.

I cannot pretend that I enjoyed any part of that trip to the Château d'If. I was caught again in the noose of the old fear, and now it was worse, threaded through as it was with the drab strands of hoplessness. It seemed that I literally could not get away from him, almost as if there were something so linking this dark and dangerous man with myself, that wherever I went, he was there. In the whole of Marseilles, to meet him the first moment I ventured out: in the whole of Provence, to meet him in the ruins of Les Baux. To whatever shifts I resorted, he found me: whatever falsehoods my brain devised, he knew the truth behind ... this, at any rate, is how I was thinking, and how much was due to hunger and how much to inescapable fate I was in no fit state to judge. ...

I sat on the lower parapet of the turret of the Château d'If, watching the white stone slowly flush to a tender rose. I watched the softly breaking water of the tideless sea wash and wash across the whispering white pebbles, aquamarine rippled through with liquid gold.

I saw it all in a kind of dream; and the whisper of the sea came like a dream's echo.

The boat went, and I sat where I was. Another came, and discharged its noisy cargo of sightseers, who streamed chattering into the castle, and crowded through the prison-cells and across the wide flat roof where I was sitting. I got up suddenly, and went down to the boat which was waiting. My watch told me I had been on the island already over an hour: he would have gone, I said to myself, without conviction. With rather more conviction, and a good deal more common sense, I told myself that this state of numbed fatalism was the result of hunger and fatigue, and the sooner I got back and got a meal the better I should be.

The journey back seemed much shorter than the outward trip. It was almost dark by now, and along the shore the lights were strung out like a necklace. There were no waves, but bars of darkness slid softly towards the land to lap against the dim rock.

We shut off our engine and drifted towards the quay followed by our arrowing wake. The port was gemmed with neon lights, white, scarlet, green and amethyst, and under the more subdued orange glow of the street lamps the evening crowds were gathering. The city of the night-time was waking up. I sat in the silently moving boat, relaxed now, still in the trance-like drifting state of acute reaction from strain. I scarcely bothered to scan the quay in the twilight, to see if this last absurd bid for escape had worked. I knew it could not. I knew that there was something far stronger than anything I had known before, that would lead Richard Byron straight to the gang-plank to wait for me.

We were tying up at the quay-side. The boatman yelled to a boy on shore, and between them they threw out the gangway. The other people in the boat got up, calling to one another and laughing, and trod awkwardly up the plank. I followed.

I hardly even looked at Richard Byron as he took my arm and helped me on to the quay.

CHAPTER FOURTEEN

Fate, I come, as dark, as sad
As thy malice could desire;
Bringing with me all the fire
That Love in his torches had.

MARVELL

I walked across the quay beside him, his hand under my elbow. People passed us, walked at our shoulders, even jostled us, but we might as well have been alone. I saw the crowd vaguely, darkly through a glass, and the sounds of them were remote, in an anaesthetized distance. The only sound I heard in all the clamour was the tread of our feet on the cobbles, and the breathing of Richard Byron beside me.

He said, not ungently: 'We still have to have our little talk, you know.'

Something deep inside me seemed to snap. The anger I had been too scared, too tired to feel, suddenly jetted up. I stopped abruptly, and swung to face him. People streamed past us, but they were not there at all; there was only myself and my enemy, in a little circle of anger.

I looked him straight in the eyes. I said furiously: 'We can have as many little talks as you want, since you seem prepared to make such a damned nuisance of yourself to get them. But I can tell you one thing now, and it's the most important thing of all, and it's this. *I am not going to tell you anything about David.* I know perfectly well where he is, and you can bully me and threaten me as much as you like, but you'll find out nothing. Nothing.'

'But I—'

I swept on as if he hadn't spoken: 'You told me outright that you were a murderer. Do you think I am going to be party to handing a child over to you, a child who, for all I know to the contrary, you *did* bash over the head in the dark the night you murdered your friend? Think again, Mr. Richard Byron. David is a darling, even if he *is* your son, and I – I'd murder you myself if you laid a finger on him!'

The hot tears were welling up in my eyes, tears of anger, anxiety and strain. I felt them spill over and begin to run down my cheeks. I could not see his face through them, and he did not speak for a long moment.

'My God,' said Richard Byron at length in a curious voice. But I hardly heard him.

'Apart from which,' I finished, 'you – you've ruined my holiday, and I've been looking forward to it for ages.'

After which remarkably silly speech I suddenly broke; I began to cry helplessly, with my hands to my face, and the tears dripping out between my fingers. I turned blindly away from Richard Byron, stumbled over a rail-track, and would have fallen, but that his hand caught me again by the elbow and steadied me.

Then he said, in the same curious voice: 'You'll feel better when you've had something to eat. Come along.'

The neon-lighted cafés were a blur. I felt him piloting me along the sidewalks, and I fought for self-control, groping in my bag for a handkerchief. Then suddenly we were in out of the street, in a little, beautifully appointed restaurant where the tables were set back in alcoves, lit softly by wall-lights. I caught a confused glimpse of napery and glass and silver, and a great spray of yellow flowers, then I was comfortably settled on a deep wall-seat upholstered with wine velvet, and Richard Byron was putting a glass into my hand. My own was shaking, and his hand closed on it, holding it steady until I regained sufficient control to raise it to my lips.

I realized, as from a great distance, that his voice was very gentle. He said: 'Drink it up. It'll make you feel better.'

I gulped some of it down. It was spirit of some kind, and it seemed to burst and evaporate inside my mouth and throat in an immediate aromatic warmth, so that I gasped and choked a little, but my breath came more evenly afterwards, and I found I could control the little shaking sobs that were racking me.

'All of it,' urged Richard Byron. I obeyed him, and lay back against the deep cushions with my eyes closed, letting my body relax utterly to the creeping warmth of the drink and the smell of food and wine and flowers. My bones seemed to have melted, and I was queerly content to lie back against the yielding velvet, with the soft lights against my eyelids, and do nothing, think of nothing. I was quiet and utterly passive, and the awful beginnings of hysteria were checked.

Still from that same dimensionless distance, I heard him speaking in French. I suppose he was ordering food. And presently at my elbow I heard the chink of silver, and opened my eyes to see the big glittering trolley of *hors d'oeuvre* with its hovering attendant.

Richard Byron said something to him, and without waiting for me to speak, the man served me from the tray. I remember still those exquisite fluted silver dishes, each with its load of dainty colours ... there were anchovies and tiny gleaming silver fish in red sauce, and savoury butter in curled strips of fresh lettuce; there were caviare and tomato and olives green and black, and small golden-pink mushrooms and cresses and beans. The waiter heaped my plate, and filled another glass with white wine. I drank half a glassful without a word, and began to eat. I was conscious of Richard Byron's eyes on me, but he did not speak.

The waiters hovered beside us, the courses came, delicious and appetizing, and the empty plates vanished as if by magic. I remember red mullet, done somehow with lemons, and a succulent golden-brown fowl bursting with truffles and flanked by tiny peas, then a froth of ice and whipped cream dashed with kirsch, and the fine smooth caress of the wine through it all. Then, finally, apricots and big black grapes, and coffee. The waiter removed the little silver filtres, and vanished, leaving us alone in our alcove.

The liqueur brandy was swimming in its own fragrance in the enormous iridescent glasses, and for a moment I watched it idly, enjoying its rich smooth gleam, then I leaned back against the cushions and looked about me with the eyes of a patient who has just woken from the first long natural sleep after an anaesthetic. Where before the colours had been blurred and heightened, and the outlines undefined, proportions unstable, and sounds hollow and wavering, now the focus had shifted sharply, and drawn the bright little restaurant into sharp dramatic outline.

I looked across at Richard Byron.

He was sitting, head bent, watching the brandy swirl in the bottom of his glass, the light of the subdued wall-lamp falling upon him from behind and to the left. I found myself for the first time really looking at him without any underlay of fear and suspicion to colour my picture of him. The light lit sharply the angles of cheek-bone and jaw, and the fine line of the temple, throwing a dramatic slant of shadow from his lowered lashes – David's lashes – across the hard line of his cheek. And the first thing that struck me was the deep unhappiness of that face; it was unhappiness rather than harshness that had driven those furrows down his cheeks, and given the eyes such sombre shadowing. As he sat with his head bent, obliviously toying with his brandy-glass, the angry lines of brow and mouth were smoothed away, and instead there was a withdrawn and brooding look, an aspect harsh and forbidding enough, until it was betrayed by the unhappiness of the mouth.

His lashes lifted suddenly and he looked at me. I felt my heart jolt once, uncomfortably, then I met his gaze squarely.

'How do you feel now?'

I said: 'Much better, thank you. It was good of you to salvage the wreck – I must look like—'

He laughed, and it was suddenly like coming face to face with a complete stranger, where you had been talking to someone you thought you knew.

He said: 'You must be feeling better, if you're beginning to worry about how you look. But don't let it distress you. You'll pass, indeed you will.'

He lit a cigarette for me, and suddenly his eyes were grave over the flame and very intent. He said, quietly: 'There are only two things I want to ask you just at this moment—'

My face must have changed, because he added sharply: 'Don't look like that. Please. I've been every kind of damned fool, and I'm sorry, but for God's sake don't look at me like that any more. They're very harmless questions, but if you'll tell me the answers, I'll leave you alone till you feel like telling me the rest.'

He paused, and all of a sudden it was as if the room were as still as the pole.

Here it comes again, I thought. He looked down at his glass, so that I could not see his eyes, but under the noncommittal voice I could feel the urgency that had frightened me before.

He said: 'How is David? Does he seem well – and happy?'

I looked at him in surprise; I had expected a very different question. I said: 'As far as I could see, he is very well indeed. But I don't imagine that he's happy. For one thing, he's lonely, and for another, he's too scared.'

'*Too scared?*' He looked at me this time. He set his glass down so sharply that the brandy splashed and sparkled, and then his hands came down to grip the table's edge, the whites of the knuckles showing. From the ash-tray, where his cigarette burned unheeded, a pencilled blue line of smoke spiralled up between us. Richard Byron stared at me through the smoke, and he repeated, very softly: 'Too scared – of what?'

I raised my eyebrows. 'Of you, of course.'

There could be no doubt about his first reaction to that uncompromising reply; it was stupefaction, sheer, speechless stupefaction. He stared at me across the table, and his eyes widened. Then, suddenly, as if he had understood or remembered something, the old bitter look was back in his face, and he seemed to withdraw once more into himself. He said, in a curiously flat voice:

'Of me? Are you sure it's of me? Did he say so?'

Then suddenly, I knew. I felt my own eyes widening as his had done, and I sat staring at him like an owl.

'Why,' I whispered, 'why, I don't believe you killed your friend. I don't believe you ever hurt David in your life. I believe you love him. Don't you. *Don't you?*'

Richard Byron gave me a queer little twisted smile that hurt. Then he picked up his cigarette again and spoke lightly.

'I love him more than anything else in the world,' he said, quite as if it didn't matter.

Then suddenly, the bubble was broken, and the illusion of privacy dispelled. The head waiter came hovering, his face split with a smile, his hands fluttering before him like large pursy moths.

'Madame has enjoyed her dinner? Monsieur has fed well? The *Chapon marseillais*, he is good, yes? He is the *spécialité de la maison*, you understand, Madame. . . .'

We assured him that everything had been perfect, and, wreathed in smiles and mothlike swoops of the hand, he bowed himself off, and another waiter, with the faint air of apology that is worn by a man committing an act in questionable taste, sidled up with the bill.

Richard Byron glanced at it, put a quite staggering amount of money down on the salver, and waved the bowing waiter aside. Then he hesitated oddly, and looked at me.

'I know it's useless saying I'm sorry for what has happened,' he said, 'but as far as the inadequate phrase can go, I *am* sorry. I've been a damned fool and a blind one. I should have known that someone like you wouldn't have been mixed up in this thing. I promise not to pester you again – but could we go somewhere, take a walk or something, and will you let me explain? It's quite a long story, and somehow I'd rather you knew it.'

His face looked white and strained in the subdued light. I had a sudden sharp memory of David's face, wearing much that same look, and of a hesitating childish voice asking me: '*How did he look?*'

I said: 'If it concerns David, I'd like to hear it. And as for what's in the past, shall we forget it for a while? It looks as if you're not the only one who's made mistakes – and mine, perhaps, were the bigger.'

'You had the more excuse.'

He smiled his sudden warm smile, and to my own amazement, I smiled back, and rose.

'If I promise not to climb out of a back window, may I go and powder my nose?'

'You—' he bit off something he had been going to say. 'Yes, of course.'

As I went I saw him get out another cigarette, and settle back in his chair to wait for me.

We went out into the dark streets that ray from the Old Port and turned, instinctively and as if by mutual consent, towards the sea. Presently we found ourselves in a cobbled street which slanted along the sea front, with tall houses to the left of us, and a low sea-wall to the right. Away ahead, floating in the starlit air like a vision, glimmered the gold statue of Our Lady who stands high on the summit of Notre Dame de la Garde.

The houses were dark and secret, and the occasional lamps cast only a furtive light on the cobbles. Boats bobbed and curtseyed at the water's edge, rubbing each other's shoulders, the sea lipping at them with small sucking sounds. Where the shamefaced lamplight let fall a reflection on the water, the shifting surface cast a pattern of light upwards on to the bellies of the boats, so that they seemed to be swimming, netted in a wavering luminous mesh. Further out in the bay, the green and red and golden riding-lights of the bigger ships drowned themselves in long liquid shadows. The ropes looked as fragile and as magical as gossamer.

We stood looking over the sea-wall. A group of sailors, noisily talking and laughing, went past, then a man and a girl, absorbed. Nobody seemed to pay any attention to us, and once again I felt the beginnings of that strangely dreamlike feeling I had experienced before, only this time it was not brought about by weariness, but by something else I could not quite understand. It was as if Richard Byron and I were alone in a bubble of glass, enclosed in its silence, into which nothing could break, and out of which we might not go. People, like the dim denizens of some under-sea-world in which our bubble was suspended, came and went, floating, soundlessly, amorphous, outside the glass, peering in perhaps, but having no power to intrude upon the silence that enmeshed us. To this day I still remember Marseilles, the noisiest city in the world, as a noiseless background to that meeting with Richard Byron, a silent film flickering on a screen in front of which we two moved and stood and talked, the only living people there.

I turned to face him.

'You said there were two questions you were going to ask me, and you've only asked one. What was other?'

He looked at me without speaking, and in that dim light his expression was unreadable, but I got the impression that he was oddly at a loss.

I said: 'I think I know; in fact, I can hardly help knowing, can I? It should have come first, shouldn't it? – it's the more important.'

I saw the corner of his mouth lift in a smile.

'Possibly.'

I said, deliberately: 'David is at the Hôtel Tistet-Védène, Avignon.'

For a long moment he was motionless, then suddenly his body swung round to face me, and his hands shot out to grip my wrists. Again, as in Nîmes, his grip hurt me, but this time I made no attempt to get away. I could feel his heart beating in his hands.

'Charity,' he said roughly, 'why did you tell me that? Why – suddenly? I haven't told you the story yet – haven't explained. I haven't even told you I was lying when I said I'd murdered Tony. You've no reason on earth to think you can trust me – I've bullied you and hurt you and abused you and all but made you ill. Why the hell should you suddenly make a present of this before I've even started to say my piece?'

It was as if his heart was an engine, and its pounding was driving mine as well. It started to race.

'I – I don't know,' I said lamely, and tried to pull my hands away.

He shifted his grip, and his eyes fell on my bruised wrist. For a second or two he stood with his head bent, staring at the ugly dark mark, then his mouth suddenly twisted, and he pulled me into his arms and kissed me.

After a long while he let me go, and I leaned back against the low parapet, while he turned abruptly and gazed out to sea.

'I suppose that was why,' I said shakily.

'The hell of it is,' he said, 'that I've wanted that ever since I walked into the Temple of Diana and saw you sitting there, with tears on your eyelashes. And all the time I thought you were a crooked little—'

'Bitch.'

He grinned a little. 'Quite,' he said. 'Yes, all that time, when I thought you were in with them, a cheap little crook mixed up in a particularly filthy game of murder – the sort of game that plays with a child's life and sanity as if it were a – a plastic counter you could lose, and never miss it.'

He looked away from me suddenly.

'Your refusing to tell me where to find David – was it because *David* wanted you to?'

'Yes,' I said gently.

'And I thought you were helping them to keep him away from me. You looked so guilty, so guilty and scared, and of course I'd no idea that David himself—' He broke off sharply.

'I'm sorry, but that's how it was. He wanted to – to avoid you, so I helped. I thought I was doing the right thing.'

He gave me a little smile. 'Yes, I see that now. But you must see how all the evidence went against you, even while every instinct I've ever had rose up and screamed that the evidence was wrong ... It was just one more thing, after all those that had happened, one more thing which could shake one's values to smithereens, and make yet another safe road as shifty as sand. Another thing that *couldn't* be, but *was.*'

'I know,' I said. 'How does it go—?

> *Sith there is yet a credence in my heart,*
> *An esperance so obstinately strong,*
> *That does invert the attest of eyes and ears;*
> *As if those organs had deceptious functions,*
> *Created only to calumniate. . . .*

Isn't that what you mean?'

He smiled again, more naturally. 'Yes, exactly, though I can't say it puts it much more clearly. Poor Troilus – he says it better later on, you know—

> *If beauty have a soul, this is not she . . .*
> *If there be rule in unity itself,*
> *This is not she. . . .*

But I was luckier than Troilus, wasn't I? For me, the rules did hold good – that no one who looks and moves and speaks as you do *could* be the bitch you seemed to be. But it was hell while it lasted, reason and instinct at war, and both violated.' He turned his head. 'You do understand, don't you?'

'Of course. Didn't it happen to me too? I thought you were a beast and a murderer, I was scared of you, and yet – this happened.'

'This happened,' he repeated, 'and reason goes out of court – for both of us.'

'Yes.'

He said slowly, looking down at the dark opaque shifting of the water: 'But you got the question wrong, Charity. You didn't really think I was going to throw that one at you again, did you, before I'd explained why I still had the right to an answer?'

'I got it wrong? You weren't going to ask where David was?'

'No.'

'What were you going to ask, then?'

He stood, watching the water, leaning on his elbows on the low wall. He said, heavily, for the fourth time:

'Who's Johnny?'

CHAPTER FIFTEEN

Madam, will you walk——?

OLD SONG

The dark water heaved below the wall, oily looking, webbed with a flotsam of straws and pieces of cork. It was strangely fascinating, as well as soothing, to watch the lift and fall and sway of the drifting fragments in the shallow gleam of the street-lamp.

I said: 'Johnny was my husband.'

'Was?'

'Yes,' I said.

'Oh, I see. I'm sorry.'

I turned, like him, to face the sea, leaned my elbows on the wall and concentrated on the moving water.

'He and I were married in the war – he was in the R.A.F. We had two years, so I suppose we were lucky. Then he was killed over Pas de Calais.'

'Bomber?'

'No. Fighter escort.' Away out over the sea the milky haze had begun to withdraw from the moon. The horizon swam up out of darkness to meet her faint light.

'Some day,' I said, 'I'll tell you about Johnny. But not now.'

He glanced at me quickly.

'Because of this – because of what's happened?'

'Because you kissed me, do you mean?'

'Because I love you, Charity.'

'No,' I said. 'Not because of that. What happens to me now doesn't alter what happened to me before. What was between me and Johnny was a real thing that we built very carefully for ourselves, and, when we built it, it was perfect and satisfying. But because it was blasted to bits by a German shell, that doesn't mean I'm never to try and build anything else among the ruins. Johnny isn't a ghost, you know, tagging along at my elbow, reminding me to mourn.'

'When I first saw you,' he said softly, 'you were crying.'

'I know,' I said. And it's true I was thinking about Johnny. But the memory of my life with him isn't likely to get up and forbid me to live any more, or any differently ... One ought to build even better the second time, and I can still build. And Johnny—' I said, turning to Richard Byron, why, Johnny would have egged me on.'

He straightened up, and his arms went round me, this time very gently. He was smiling, and his eyes had a little steady flame deep in the grey. He held me a little away from him and looked at me, his lips curving.

'I love you, Charity,' he said again. 'You're so sweet and you're so sane. My God, I think you could almost make the world seem a sweet, sane place again, the way it used to be . . . Am I to take it that you're telling me to go ahead and kiss you again?'

'Why, no, I—'

'Because I'm planning to,' said Richard Byron.

And did.

It seemed hours later, and the moon had laid her trail of silver out to sea, when we stood again, side by side, elbows on the wall again, and began to talk.

' . . . Enough of this side-tracking,' said Richard. 'I've got to think, and you've got to help me, so you've got a right to know the story. It's a pretty filthy one to drag you into—'

'It seems to me,' I said mildly, 'that I'm in fairly deep as it is, and entirely through my own efforts.'

He mused a little, and I could see the lines etch themselves again deeply round his mouth, those bitter little lines that made his face suddenly harsh and frightening.

He began to talk. . . .

It was certainly not a pretty story, and as I listened, I could feel some of the anger that burned even now in Richard's voice, licking along my own veins.

Briefly, it was this.

Richard Byron, who was reasonably well-to-do, lived at Deepings, in Surrey, and had acquired some reputation among those who knew, as a dealer in various kinds of antiques. 'It started in a strictly amateurish sort of way,' he said. 'I bought things I liked, and occasionally sold again to people who saw them and wanted them; then bit by bit I came into it as a business, because I got interested. I didn't have to make a living that way, but I gradually learned more about it, and began to travel after stuff, and in time became really keen on certain aspects of the business – old silver and jewellery particularly. I'm supposed to know quite a lot about it now.'

The war had put a stop to it, of course, and he had joined the Air Force – 'Flying a ruddy great Lanc. over the Ruhr,' said Richard. 'That was where I got to know Tony, of course.'

'Tony?'

'Tony Baxter. The lad I'm supposed to have murdered.'

'Oh.'

'He was my navigator, and one of the nicest chaps you could ever know. The idea that he could ever have fallen for Loraine—'

'You did, yourself,' I reminded him. 'After all, you married her.'

He shot me a look from under his brows. 'Yes, I married her. David was twelve and Mary had been dead seven years, and I thought—' he broke off. 'Well, hell, you've seen her, and if you don't know why I married her you ought to.'

I had a sudden vivid memory of Loraine Byron's lovely face and blue eyes, of her long white throat and the full breasts outlined by the silk of her dress.

'I can guess,' I said.

He sent me another look. 'I met her in Paris,' he said. 'I opened my Paris office in the spring of last year, and I was over there several times during the year. In September I went over to attend a big sale of silver, and I took Tony with me, with some idea of showing him the ropes and persuading him to come in and work for me. Loraine was at the sale – I didn't see who with. Then I met her again soon afterwards at a party; she was there with a man I knew, Louis Meyer, the London representative of a big Paris dealer. He introduced me to Loraine. We met again, several times. I was at a horribly loose end, just then, and I—' he paused. 'Anyway, I married her about a month later, and took her back to Deepings at the end of October.'

His mouth twisted, and his voice took on the hard unpleasant undertone I had first heard in it.

'It didn't work,' he said shortly. 'Naturally. As soon as we were married I knew I'd been a fool. In the first place, she hadn't wanted to go to England at all: she wanted me to settle in France, in the South. But there was Deepings – and David – and I insisted. Then of course there was trouble. And – again of course – it just didn't work with David; she couldn't be bothered with him, and he had no time for her. He's a courteous little devil, and he said nothing to me, but I could see he was unhappy about it. . . . We had a highly unpleasant few weeks, and then Tony came to stay for Christmas.' His voice went flat and dead. He might have been reading out of the police report. 'He was found dead in his bed at three o'clock on the morning of January 19th. He had been strangled. There was a thin cord knotted tightly round his neck. It was the cord from my window-blind, and my finger-prints were on the little acorn gadget that you pull the blind down with.'

'Of course they were,' I said. 'I expect you'd pulled the blind down at some time or other, hadn't you?'

'Yes. That's the sort of thing that saved my neck in the end. They could think what they liked, but there was an innocent reason as well as a guilty for most of the things they found. Then ten minutes after Loraine discovered the body—'

'Loraine found him!' I exclaimed.

'Yes,' he said, with the edge back on his voice. 'She went to his room – at three o'clock in the morning. She was quite open about it, all in the cause of justice. The police were impressed. She'd admitted she'd been there before – often: it was a lovely motive for me to kill him, handed to the police on a plate. What do you think about that?'

'I think that three o'clock on a January morning's an awfully funny hour to be waking your lover up,' I said.

He gave a hard little laugh. 'You're right at that, sweet Charity. It's a hell of a funny hour. But she did, and then when she had fainted with shock, and someone went to the bathroom to get some water, they found David there; my little David, unconscious and as cold as ice. When I got there, I thought for a minute that he was dead too.'

The hard voice stopped, and he stared at the sea. But I knew he was not seeing the white path the moon paced across the water, but a small body, huddled on a cold tiled floor.

'He couldn't remember much about it,' he said at length. 'When he was fit to talk he told them that he'd woken with the tooth-ache, and gone along to the bathroom to fill a hot-water bottle. He didn't remember the time. But as he switched on the bathroom light somebody struck him from behind.'

'He had no idea at all? He didn't hear anything – a skirt swishing, or high heels? Nothing to tell him whether it was a man or a woman?'

He gave a wry smile. 'Believe me, if there'd been the faintest scrap of evidence that could have pinned it on Loraine, I'd have pinned it,' he said viciously. 'Because she was in it, all right. You can't live with a woman for half a year, even the way we lived, and not know when she's lying in her teeth. She knew all about it. But she didn't hit David. It was a man. David was facing the bathroom mirror – it hangs opposite the door, and he just saw the arm raised over him, for a fraction of an instant, before it happened. It was a man's arm, in a navy sleeve.'

'Not a dressing-gown?'

'No, not a dressing-gown.' He grinned a little, and his hand moved till it covered mine. 'You're very quick on the evidence in my defence, aren't you? Yes, that was one small thing: I'd been wearing a grey suit that day, as well. And I don't possess a navy one.'

'Well, why—?'

'They didn't attach much importance to David's testimony, you see. He's only a child, he'd had a bad shock, the glimpse he'd had was too slight and might have been imagined, and besides, he might be expected to be a pretty partial witness, of course. He insisted from the very beginning that it couldn't possibly have been me – not for any reason, except that it just couldn't.'

'And so you were arrested?'

'After a bit, yes. Oh, the police were very thorough and really very decent over the whole thing. It was all done by kindness. But one thing and another mounted up, and everything pointed the same way – so I was arrested.'

He regarded the water sombrely.

'I'll spare you the next part. Standing your trial for murder, even when you get off, isn't a thing to go back to, even for a moment, in your mind. It's like having a filthy and contaminating disease – degrading, exhausting, leaving pock-marks on your spirit that never smooth out. Again, everybody was very decent – surprisingly decent. And, though I got to hate the prosecuting Counsel more than anyone else on earth, it was fair trial. The fact that I'm here proves that ... oh, I've nothing against the police, even if she did lead them right up the garden path, and back again. Other mugs had taken that walk before them.'

'But, Richard, did *she* do it? The murder, I mean? And *was* there a man in a navy suit? Who was he?'

'I wish I knew,' he said heavily, 'I wish I knew. They never traced him. But I think there was a man there with her, an accomplice, whom she let in to do the job. He may have come in through the bathroom window – it was open, by the way – and have hidden behind the door when he heard David coming. It was he who knocked David out, to prevent his seeing him. Then either he or Loraine killed Tony. I myself think that he, not she, did it – or why did she have him there at all?'

'Her lover?'

'Possibly. But even if he were spending the night with her – you'll have gathered that she and I had stopped sharing a room – and even if Tony had found out, that's hardly a motive for murder. No, she let him in to do the job.'

'Burglary, perhaps? And Tony—'

'Nothing was touched. And Tony had never moved from his bed. They said he was strangled as he slept.'

'But why—'

'That's it, Charity, that's the big thing. Why?' His voice exploded suddenly. 'My God, *why*? Night after night after night I've spent wondering *why*? If I only knew that ... he was one of the decentest souls God ever sent, Charity. An ordinary, decent boy that nobody on this earth would want to kill, you'd think. They must have meant to do it, planned to do it, quite deliberately, but what the motive was I do not know. That was the strongest thing against me, of course – the fact that there wasn't a shadow of motive for anyone else to do it. And when Loraine confessed to being Tony's mistress that gave me the strongest motive there is.'

He was silent for a moment, his brows drawn. Then he gave his head a little shake, as if to rid it of the thoughts crowding through his brain.

'Try as I will,' he said, 'I can't see why Loraine should either do it herself, or connive at its being done.'

'What if he'd turned her down?' I suggested. 'It can take women that way, can't it?'

'*Hell hath no fury?* I suppose it could ... but then what about the other man? Why should he help in that situation?'

'You seem very sure there *was* a man.'

'Yes,' he said. 'David may be only a kid, but he's intelligent, and he doesn't get rattled easily. If he said there was a man's arm then there was a man's arm.'

'Couldn't he have been trying to divert suspicion from you?'

'He told them the story as soon as he was fit to talk, and he had no idea what had happened, or that I'd even be remotely suspected. No, he told the truth. He thought he'd surprised a burglar.'

There was a pause.

'It's a stinker, isn't it?' said Richard.

'It certainly is.'

'And that's only half the story. I don't know yet why Tony was murdered, or why, apparently, Loraine should be so very anxious to see me dead.'

'But how can you be sure—?' I interrupted, then broke off as, like a whispering echo, I remembered her voice repeating in the frightened dark: *he ought to be dead and done with, dead and done with, dead and done with. . . .* What was it they did to murderers? Buried them in quicklime, so that there was nothing of them left?

I shivered in the still warm air, and his hand closed sharply over mine, warm and strong and very much alive.

His voice was sombre, and he spoke with a conviction that chilled me again.

'Because,' he said, 'I'm next on the list. She couldn't get me hanged, but she staged another murder. And the second time, I was the victim.'

CHAPTER SIXTEEN

Madam, will you talk—?

OLD SONG

'It was after the trial,' he went on. 'I was allowed to go, of course, and someone handed me a note as I was leaving the court, to say that Loraine wanted to see me at Claridge's, where she had a room. I got a taxi and went to see her. She was alone, and she had some news for me. Good news. She told me, quite plainly, that she was going back to France, and that there was no need for me to institute divorce proceedings.'

'No need? What did she mean?'

'She had just discovered, she said, that her previous husband, who had been missing and presumed dead since 1943, was still alive. Our marriage, therefore, was never valid.'

'But – was this true?'

'She showed me her marriage certificate – naturally, I knew she had been married before – and then a letter from a Paris lawyer. The certificate, of course, was genuine; about the letter I don't know yet.'

'What was his name – the husband's, I mean?'

'Jean Something-or-other, I think.' He reached for a cigarette. 'To tell you the truth I hardly bothered. I'd come straight from the dock, I hadn't even had a chance to wash the prison smell off my hands, I felt as if I never wanted to see her or speak to her again – and I wanted most damnably to get home and see David. He was still at Deepings, of course, and I imagined he must be half out of his mind.'

I must have made some inarticulate sound.

He said: 'Yes, I know. Well, I slammed the papers down and snarled that I hoped to God it was true, and that I didn't care what she did as long as she kept out of my way, and she could leave it to the lawyers because I didn't particularly want to stay and talk to her. And a few other things. It wasn't pretty, I can tell you.'

'I don't blame you. I'd have wrung her neck.'

'She wasn't frightened. She knew I wasn't the neck-wringing sort.'

I said drily: 'You don't give a bad imitation of it, at times.'

He grinned a little at that, then seemed suddenly to recollect the cigarette-case in his hand. We lit cigarettes.

'Well, our loving talk finished with Loraine throwing the car keys at me, and telling me she'd left the Rolls at Redmanor station and would I *ficher le camp* – only the phrase she used was more – direct, shall I say? – than that.'

I laughed. 'I get it.'

'You shock me. Well, I did as she suggested; I got the hell out of it, and, what with one thing and another, by the time I got down to Redmanor I was half sick with worry and reaction, and in a flaming temper into the bargain. The Rolls was there, all right, and I went off at the hell of a lick, with only one thought in my head: David.'

'And there was an accident?'

'Right first guess; there was an accident. There's a place where you turn off the main road, about a mile from my house, where the road skirts a quarry. There's a sharp bend about half-way down, with the quarry on your left, and a bluff of rock to the right – the road swings right-handed round it. In general it's safe enough, because above the bluff it's open, and before you reach the bend you can see if anything's on the road below. Well, as I say, I was going the hell of a lick. I could see the chimneys of Deepings through the trees in the valley, and there was nothing on the road, so I took a run at the hill. And just half-way round that bend I met another car, on its wrong side. I was well over to the left, but there wasn't time, and he held on . . . There was just room, only just, if I went into the verge; and he kept coming. I yanked the wheel over, something snapped with a crack like a gun, and we went clean over the edge.'

'Richard!'

'Oh, they had no luck,' he said grimly. 'The off-side door wasn't caught – I'd been in such a hurry that I hadn't noticed – and it fell open as we went over. I fell out. The car dropped to the bottom of the quarry and went on fire, but some bushes broke my fall, and I only got concussed on a ledge.'

'But – are you sure – couldn't it have been a real accident?'

'I've told you I'd seen there wasn't a car on the road. He must have had it parked, waiting for me. I've had plenty of time to think about it, there in hospital, and this is what I think happened. There's a phone box a mile or so along the road, and he could have been waiting there as soon as he heard the trial was over. They must have known I'd make straight for Deepings.'

'But, Richard, why bother to tell you about the marriage business, if they'd planned to kill you?'

'She had to know just when I started for Deepings, and besides, she wanted to give me the keys and make sure I'd take the car. Then, when I left her, I think she must have phoned him. He had his car parked behind the barn near the foot of the hill, and waited for me with field glasses. It was a cream-coloured Rolls coupé, and pretty unmistakable. He had only to time himself, so that he'd meet me on the bend, and he could reckon it would happen just like that, if the steering had been damaged beforehand. I tell you, it went with a crack like a gun, and the wheel just spun in my hands.'

'Wasn't he taking a big risk of being hurt himself?'

'You have to take risks to get away with murder,' returned Richard grimly. 'But, after all, the risk wasn't so very great. He may have meant to swerve at the last minute, if I didn't try to crowd into the edge, but he could be pretty well certain that I'd pull as far to the left as I could, and of course, with the steering column damaged, it was a hundred to one I'd go over.'

'Didn't the police find what had been done to the steering column?'

'No. That was Loraine's one piece of luck. The car burned right out – there was hardly a piece left recognizable, they told me.'

'I suppose her accomplice had damaged the steering while the Rolls was in the station yard?'

'I imagine so. I found the car unlocked, anyway, and my own keys inside it. But that proved nothing. No, my story was more than the police could swallow, I think; after all, motiveless murders, and an invisible, elusive murderer – it was too much. They were quite right, of course, it *was* too much. I'd started by insisting I was being framed for Tony's murder – *why?* Then I'd talked of an attempt on my own life – *why?* It wouldn't wash, Charity. We're back where we were – where is the motive for these attempts?' He gave a sharp little sigh, and threw his cigarette-stub out into the water. 'The police were very patient, all things considered, but I could see their minds were beginning to run in all sorts of curious channels, so eventually I shut up and allowed them to write it off as accident.'

'What sort of curious channels?'

'Oh . . . suicide, for instance.'

'Richard!' I cried again.

'Oh, yes. Disgraced Man's Mind Unhinged by Trial ... you know. The papers got it, of course, and said as much as they dared. But again, there was no proof.'

'And David?'

'The last time I saw David,' he said slowly, and with great bitterness, 'was when they arrested me and took me away. I wouldn't let him visit me in prison, of course. Then, when I was in hospital after the smash, Loraine did as she'd promised. She went back to France. But she did more, as you know. She took David with her. He never even came to see me in the hospital before he went. ...'

He stopped, apparently absorbed in watching the floating butt of his cigarette discolour, split, and disintegrate into a little mess of sodden tobacco, among the débris floating below the wall. I said nothing.

'As soon as the doctors would let me, a fortnight ago, I came over. I traced them as far as Lyons, heading south ... and the rest you know.'

'But, Richard, I don't understand. David didn't believe all that about suicide, did he? And he thought you were innocent of murder; you said so. Why did he go with Loraine?'

Richard's voice tautened. 'I don't know. I suppose, if she never told him she wasn't legally my wife, he'd assume that, as his step-mother, she had the right to look after him when I was ill. And he's only a child. He'd do as he was told.'

'But why didn't he *write*? Why did you have to "trace" them? Why didn't—?'

He turned to look at me, and the slanting lamplight slid over his face, sharpening the finely drawn angles of cheek and jaw-bone, and setting his face into a mask of great unhappiness. His eyes were full of such misery and uncertainty that I looked away.

He said, heavily: 'I don't know, Charity. I don't know. Don't you see, that's what's such a hell for me? I've stopped giving one single damn about Loraine or her precious confederate, or her shots at killing me, or even poor Tony's death. I want to see David again, and get things straight with him. I want to find out what lies they've told him to make him go off like that without a word. Perhaps, in the end, they got him to believe it all ... that I was a murderer, I mean ... and he didn't dare to wait and see me—' He broke off.

His voice, when he spoke again, was very quiet.

He said, his head bent low, watching the water:

'But you know that side of it, don't you, Charity? You said he *was* afraid of me, didn't you?'

I saw the sudden gleam and shift of his knuckles as he clenched them, and a wave of compassion went over me, so real – I mean so physical – that it left me shaking. I could not speak.

He looked at me sharply. 'Well?'

'Oh, Richard,' I said miserably, 'I don't want to hurt you any more.

It's all such a muddle, and I don't know what anything means, or what to believe at all.'

His face softened a little, and he touched my hand again, a feather-light touch.

'We can't work the muddle out until we get all the facts, my dear. Tell me your end of it – tell me everything he said, what both he and Loraine have been doing and saying. Don't worry about my feelings – they should be pretty tough by now. Just tell me what you know, from the first moment you met him.'

I saw, as if a brush had suddenly sketched it in across the moonlight, the slight delicate branches and paper-thin leaves of the tree Yggdrasil ... that shook and swayed as the cat clawed up the stem, then dissolved again into moonlight. I said, suddenly: 'Do you know a man called Marsden?'

He frowned, thinking.

'Marsden? No, I don't think so. What's he like? Why?'

'I remembered something,' I said abruptly. 'I think David was perfectly right about there being a man in the house that night.' I began to tell him about the conversation I had overheard up at Rocher des Doms. 'And I remember his very words,' I finished. 'He said: *I got you out of the mess before, didn't I? I got you out of England, didn't I, and the boy too?*'

Richard had turned sharply as I spoke, and his eyes were very intent. When I had finished he was smiling, with a kind of grim satisfaction.

'So we were right. So far, so good. It's only a very little, Charity, but it's something. I wonder just where this man Marsden could tie in with Loraine's missing husband, Jean-Something-or-other, who appeared so providentially?'

'If he did appear.'

'If, as you say, he did appear.' He straightened up suddenly. 'We'll soon know if *that* part of the story's true: I've got someone investigating it in Paris. It's beginning to matter, rather, too.'

He grinned.

'Well, who knows what else you've seen and heard? We'll have it cleared up before dawn at this rate – long before dawn, my dear, because you look tired, and no wonder. Come and get a drink, and we'll find somewhere to sit while you tell me your story.

CHAPTER SEVENTEEN

Madam, will you walk and talk with me?

'I shall probably get it very muddled,' I said, 'because of course a lot happened before I began to notice things particularly. And I doubt if I have the gift of narrative. But I'll do my best.'

So I began to tell him what I could remember: David and the dog, Mrs. Palmer and her account of the Byron trial, the trip to Nîmes, and David's reactions to his father's presence. The drive home, and David's half-confidence and strange childish insistence that I should tell Loraine Byron nothing at all. The snatch of conversation heard in Loraine's bedroom that night. And everywhere, the presence of the man Marsden – lighting Loraine's cigarette, loitering in the dark at the foot of the Rocher des Doms, driving to Nîmes in the bus, going up to the gardens with David next morning. . . .

Richard Byron listened in silence, tracing little patterns in spilt wine on the table-top, his head bent, his brows frowning.

'So you see,' I said finally, 'why I behaved in the silly way I did. I didn't even tumble to the fact that David hated her when he insisted that his name wasn't the same as hers. I just thought I had to keep you away from him. I – I rather fell for David,' I finished lamely.

He shot me a look that brought the blood to my cheeks, then returned to his drawing on the table-top.

'Yes, David,' he said slowly. 'We always come back to David. And the old questions: why he went away like that without a word; what he believes, now, about that horrible night; why he's afraid to meet me. . . . Why, d'you know, I even thought they might have done away with him, too, until I got the anonymous letter from Paris.'

'Anonymous letter?'

'I got dozens,' said Richard briefly. 'The usual filth that always starts flowing when a murder trial opens the sewer. This one was posted in Paris, and whoever wrote it apparently knew me, and knew David, and had seen him there. It included, of course, a lot of abuse about – oh, well, that doesn't matter, does it?'

'Richard, how beastly!'

'But it gave a clue, you see. My housekeeper had told me that David went off with Loraine, and Loraine had told me she was going to France. This gave me a start. So I raised heaven and earth and the R.A.C. and shipped the car across on the next boat. And at my *appartement* in Paris – I have a room over my office – there was another letter waiting.'

'But who on earth—?'

'Loraine,' he said, grimly. 'Dear Loraine. This time it was signed, and it was written, not typed, but there was something about the style that made it just a continuation of the first one.'

'Was it still about David?'

'It was. She and I, it said, must have a long talk, some time, about his future. But, as David didn't want to see me, and she herself didn't feel like facing me yet, she was taking him away from Paris, and would get in touch with me later. That wasn't all, but that was the gist of it.'

'What did you do?'

'The letter was postmarked Lyons, so of course I went down there. I hunted about for a couple of days, café-haunting, and asking questions, until I picked up what looked like a clue. Loraine's pretty conspicuous, as you know, and the barman at one of the hotels remembered seeing her, and remembered too, that she'd spoken of going south. I won't bore you with the rest of it, but I traced them fairly easily as far as Bollène, and then I went wrong. They had been seen on the road to Pont St. Esprit, and that, as you know, is across the Rhône from Bollène, and on the way to Nîmes. Well, I followed my nose, and landed in Nîmes on a chance. It was a wrong chance, as it happened, but it turned out to be near enough.'

I said: 'No wonder you wanted to kill me when you got so near to David, and I got in the way.'

He said, remorsefully: 'I thought you must be in with them. You see, I didn't believe for a moment that David himself didn't want to see me. I thought she – they – must be keeping him under some sort of duress so that he couldn't write. I thought you were part of it, and I wanted to kill you.' He smiled. 'Poor little Charity, did I scare hell out of you?'

'You did. Is that why you told me you'd done the murder?'

'Of course. I didn't know how much they'd told you of the truth, and I wanted to frighten you. And I did. I made you faint. I want whipping for that.'

'It's done with,' I said. 'I was really scared because I thought you were—' I stopped abruptly.

'You thought I was what?'

'Nothing.'

'Come on. All the facts. You promised.'

'I thought you were mad,' I said, not looking at him.

He did not speak, but I saw his hand arrested in the middle of drawing a circle on the table.

'I only knew what Mrs. Palmer had told me,' I said quickly. 'And then when you – you were so violent, and David was so frightened, I thought you must be mad. I thought you'd have to be mad to have hit David that night. ... After I'd met you in Nîmes,' I finished miserably, 'I thought you'd done it, you see.'

There was a little pause.

'Charity.'

'Oh, Richard—'

'Charity, tell me something.'

'What?' I asked. Here it comes, I thought, here it comes.

'Did David say anything that led you to believe that I was mad?'

'I – I don't know,' I floundered.

'You're lying, Charity. You ought to know by now that you can't lie to me. Did David tell you I was mad?'

'Yes,' I said.

When I looked at him at last, he was smiling.

'You silly little owl,' he said. 'Don't worry so. It makes it reasonably simple.'

'Simple?' I echoed stupidly. 'But I thought you'd—'

'I mean, its something definite,' he said. 'Something we can fight. He did say it himself?'

'Yes.'

'In so many words?'

'Yes.'

'I see. Well, that means simply this: they've persuaded him to believe that it was I who bashed him on the head and/or tried to commit suicide with the Rolls. That's all that could be construed as mad, unless they threw in the actual murder for good measure. And, since I'm morally certain that they couldn't get him to believe either that I killed Tony or attacked David himself, then it's probably the attempted suicide.'

'So?'

'Well, as I see it, we're now in a fairly strong position to fight this belief. He trusts you, doesn't he?'

'I think so. Yes, I'm sure he does, after the way I helped him at Nîmes – to get away from you.'

'Don't look so rueful. You'll have to go back and talk to him, convince him, somehow, that I'm as sane as you are, and get him to meet me somewhere and talk to me. Then we'll get this thing straight, and have done with it once and for all.'

'You mean, take him straight away?'

'Of course. D'you think I'd let him go back to her? She and her lover – husband, what you like – can go their way, and David and I will go ours. . . .' His glance met mine. 'And yours.'

'It sounds easy when you put it like that,' I said. 'But, Richard, if they *are* determined somehow to kill you – well, will Deepings be any safer now than it was before?'

He put a hand to his head, in a gesture at once indescribably weary and very youthful.

'It's the same old answer, Charity,' he said. 'I don't know. My own home . . . and for some strange reason it's no longer safe for me or for my son . . . *for some strange reason*: that's the centre of the matter. This whole crazy story – it's like a tale told by an idiot, held together by some lunatic logic that we can't follow till we've delved back through his mad past and found—'

'Freud in the woodshed?'

He grinned a little at that, and finished his drink at a gulp. 'If you put it that way, yes.'

By now the café was almost empty, and the steady flow of people on the broad pavement had dwindled perceptibly. A few Negro sailors went by, arm in arm with brightly dressed girls. An Arab boy, slim and golden-brown, who might have sat to Polyclites as Hylas, slipped between the tables, begging. People flung him lumps of sugar, which he caught with quick, greedy, graceful fingers, while his monotonous degraded voice mumbled for more.

'Sometimes lately I've thought I really would go mad,' said Richard suddenly. 'The murder and the trial, then the car-smash and the weeks in hospital, and the appalling headaches I still get. And David. A sudden and complete disruption of my whole life, and David's life, out of the blue. And it's the basic unreason of the business that's getting me down; certain facts are there, but they can't *be* facts; there's no sane pattern to which they fit. That's what I meant before, Charity, that's what made me behave like a devil; I find my values slipping till my brain – how does it go? – *suffers then the nature of an insurrection*. Nothing makes sense; things have turned upside down.'

'*And nothing is*,' I quoted softly, '*but what is not*.'

He said quickly, half eagerly: 'Yes, that's it. That's what *Macbeth*'s about, isn't it? Nothing keeping to the rules any more?'

I said: 'But you forget. Macbeth broke the rules first and upset the balance. There was a logic in it, after all; and Richard, there still is. There must be an explanation, a reason, for your idiot's tale, only we just haven't hunted deep enough in the woodshed.'

He did not speak, but his eyes lifted to mine for a moment, and something in them made me speak urgently.

'Richard. I *know* I'm right. Don't you remember, only an hour ago, on the quay, when you said the same thing – about me – and you said that the rules *did* hold good, no matter what the evidence to the contrary seemed to be? It's *true*, my dear. You'll find there *is* a pattern that'll fit the facts. There always is.'

'But if it's an idiot's tale – if you're dealing with the borderland of sanity—'

'You're not,' I said flatly. 'And even if you were . . . why, in Looking-Glass Land itself they kept to the rules of chess. The rules don't break themselves, Richard.'

'In fact—'

'In fact,' I repeated, 'there is no such thing as "basic unreason".'

His eyes were on me, and they were suddenly very bright. He said, softly: '*Charity never faileth*. Yes, you're right. You're right. How very right you are. . . .' He laughed then, and straightened in his chair. 'Forgive me, my darling. I've been living so long on the edge of nothing that it's addled my wits. Let's have some coffee, shall we? What'll you take with it this time?'

'The same, please.'

'*Garçon. Deux cafés-cassis.* No' – the vigour was back in his voice as he spoke to me – 'nothing really matters except David, and that part of it'll soon be straightened out. Once I've seen him. . . . How tired are you, Charity?'

The abrupt turn startled me. 'Tired? I don't feel tired now.'

'Sure?'

'Quite.'

He smiled his sudden, devastatingly attractive smile. 'Then, on your quite unwomanly assumption that there's a logic in everything, we'll begin again at the beginning, rake over the ashes till we discover what makes them tick, probe every avenue to the bone—'

'I get you,' I said. 'Leave no hole and corner unturned. All right. I'm on.'

CHAPTER EIGHTEEN

The mordrynge in the bedde . . .

CHAUCER

Half an hour and two coffees later, our minds were almost as mixed as our metaphors had been. We had taken out every fact we knew, aired it, shaken it, and set it in its place, and, while certain things had become clearer, the centre of the mystery remained dark.

'The motive,' said Richard for the twentieth time. 'Tony murdered, and two attempts to murder me – and no motive.'

'Murder needs a pretty strong motive,' I said stoutly. 'There's one somewhere, if we knew where to look. What do they say are the recognized motives – gain, passion and fear? It's not murder for money, or for love, apparently, but the third motive's the strongest of the lot.'

'Fear? But who's so afraid of me that they've got to kill me?'

'Obviously someone is, because they've tried. Is that logic, Richard?'

He smiled, though the smile was a little strained. 'All right. Go on from there. You're not going to tell me that Loraine's sufficiently afraid of me to want to murder me?'

'No. I thought we'd decided she was working for somebody else.'

'Our old friend X; the man in the car. Yes?'

'X tries to kill you,' I said, 'not for gain, not for jealousy, but because of something you can do to him. You, alive, constitute a threat to him, to his liberty – or livelihood – or life.'

The glint of amusement in his eyes was genuine enough. 'In fact, we're arrived at another hoary old friend; there's something I know that I don't know I know?'

'Well, it happens,' I said stubbornly. 'Don't try to muddle me. There's something else that struck me, too, about your chase after Loraine and David.'

He shot me a quick look. 'Yes?'

'It was too easy, Richard. If they had really wanted to hide—'

He gave a little nod, as if of satisfaction. 'Exactly. That's one of the things that puzzled me. It was too easy by half. She told me she was going to France, she sent me the letters, clearly postmarked as she knew they must be ... she left a trail, in fact, up to a point.'

'You see what it means?' I said. 'She – or X – wanted you over here. You told me she tried to get you to come here after you were married. She still wanted that. That's why she took David in the first place. You'd never have followed Loraine herself, would you? If she'd written to ask you to meet her again you'd have left it to a lawyer—'

'I certainly should,' he remarked grimly.

'So, to make sure of you, she took David to act as bait, and headed you neatly to the South of France.'

'Towards X, I suppose? You're implying, are you, that having failed to kill me in England, X is getting ready to have another shot over here? Laying a trap?'

'Granted they brought you over here deliberately,' I said uneasily, 'and it looks as if they did, then I don't see why else they should have done it.'

'All right, we'll grant that. They lead me to the South of France, but lose me at Pont St. Esprit, either by accident or design.'

'Which do you think it was?'

He said slowly: 'I rather think it was an accident. The wrong trail that I followed to Nîmes was genuine enough; another couple had been seen setting out for Nîmes, a couple that might have been Loraine and David from the description I got. I must have gone tearing off after them before Loraine's clue, whatever it was, had a chance to reach me.' He laughed shortly. 'So there they were, marking time in Avignon, while I lost myself chasing red herrings!'

'No wonder she began to lose her nerve,' I said. 'She sounded really frightened that night at the Rocher des Doms.'

'And no wonder they were quite pleased to let you take David about,' returned Richard. 'With me loose in the vicinity, looking for him, there was quite a chance I'd see him, and pick up the trail again.'

I objected to this. 'What was to stop you talking to David, putting things straight with him, and just taking him away?'

'Mr. X,' said Richard simply.

I looked at him, startled. He nodded. 'Loraine, who had lost her nerve, was better out of the way in Avignon. But where David went, you may be sure Mr. X went too.'

I drew a long breath. 'On the Tarascon bus,' I said.

Richard nodded again, and his eyes gleamed. 'D'you know, I believe we're getting somewhere. If we're right, it must have been a bitter moment for Mr. X when you so neatly scooped David out of my reach again, sweet Charity – and incidentally led me right away from X and all his works! It seems I may owe you quite a lot.'

'But what could he possibly hope to do in Nîmes?' I protested.

He shrugged. He sounded almost indifferent. 'God knows. It's a wild half-deserted country. Anything could happen. A body could lie in that scrub for months, and the kites would—'

'Don't!'

'Well, there it is. It's a good part of the world for a quiet murder; and that, no doubt, is why I'm being decoyed here.' He smiled without mirth. 'I wonder where the trap was to be sprung originally? Avignon? It seems unlikely.'

'Loraine said they were going south in a day or so,' I said quickly. 'Nice and Monte Carlo.'

'Did she indeed? If that was true, it could mean anything . . . there's some lovely lonely country down here, with nice dangerous cliffs—'

'And a nice dangerous city,' I put in.

He lifted an eyebrow. 'Marseilles? Well? Why not? X fails twice in law-abiding Surrey, so he—'

'Gets you on to his own ground,' said I.

'You're jumping at this thing, aren't you?' said Richard, amused. 'So Mr. X lives in Marseilles now?'

'He may call himself Marsden,' I said doggedly, 'and read T. S. Eliot – which, incidentally, I saw him doing upside down – but I'll bet he's French, and I'll bet he's Loraine's first husband Jean Something-or-other, and I'll bet he has some definite reason for wanting you down in this part of the country!'

The amusement in his eyes deepened. 'So it's all solved, is it? If only I could remember what I know that I don't know I know!'

'Well, *try*, Richard!' I said, hopelessly. 'No, don't laugh at me. I thought this was serious! Think!'

'My dear child, certainly? But what about?'

I hesitated. 'Tony's murder. Murder's the only thing serious enough to make X go to such lengths, isn't it? I mean – if you knew something that would hang him?'

But Richard shook his head. 'That horse won't run, Charity dear. There's nothing there, I'm certain of it. The police went into everything, and I – God knows I've had long enough to turn it all over in my mind, every grain, every particle, every atom of fact in my possession. You get a lot of time to think in prison, you know.'

'Yes, I suppose so. I'm sorry I reminded you.'

'Don't worry; it doesn't matter nearly so much as it did half an hour ago.' He gave me a brief smile. 'But we're forgetting one thing, you know. Tony was murdered too, and also without apparent motive. What if X wants, not me for anything connected with Tony's murder, but *both Tony and me* for something we were in together?'

'The antique trade?' I said hopelessly. 'Here we go round the prickly pear.'

He shrugged again, and reached for his cigarette-case. 'Well, there it is. That's all the connection Tony and I ever had, except the War.'

'Had you flown together for long?'

'Not really. It was fairly near the start of my third tour that I pranged. Tony had been with me since half-way through the second.'

'That, and your meeting after the War – that was absolutely all?'

'Absolutely.'

'No shady dealings in Paris?'

'Not more than usual.'

'No witnessing a grisly crime in Montmatre?'

'No.'

'But you must have done,' I insisted. 'Think again. You and Tony must at least have witnessed a murder.'

He grinned. 'No.'

'Not even a very small one?'

'Not even a –' He checked suddenly in the act of striking a match, and his voice changed. 'How very odd!'

'What?' My voice must have sounded excited, because he shook his head quickly and struck the match.

'It's nothing; nothing to do with this affair. But, oddly enough, Tony and I did once see murder done.' He held a match to my cigarette, and smiled at my expression. 'No, really, it's nothing to do with this. It was during the War; part of the general frightfulness.'

'You don't mean the bombing?'

'Lord, no. I wasn't young enough to class that as murder; that was just a job. No, this was cold-blooded murder, rather particularly beastly.'

'Tell me about it. It might, after all, have something to do—'

'I very much doubt it. And it's not a nice story.'

'Never mind that. Tell me, just the same.'

'Very well. It was when Tony and I were being taken up to Frankfurt for interrogation after the crash – we were the only two commissioned in the air-crew – and there'd been some bomb-damage on the main line, so we were hitched on to a little goods train that went by another route, up the Lahn valley. We had to stop in a siding to let an express go past. It was a filthy grey winter's afternoon, with snow everywhere, and a sky like a dirty dish-cover clamped down over it. God, it was cold. . . .'

He was staring at the cigarette between his fingers, talking more to himself than me. I think, indeed, that he had forgotten me completely, and was back in that desolate little siding beside the Lahn.

' . . . There was another train waiting, too – a lot of boarded-up trucks, with some chalk-marks scrawled across them. We didn't tumble to it until we saw a little bunch of S.S. guards standing about, and then we realized what was going on. It was a train-load of Jews going East to the slaughter-houses.'

He drew on his cigarette, and expelled the smoke almost fiercely. 'For a long time, nothing happened, and then, everything seemed to happen at once. We heard the express whistle a short way off. Then there was a yell, a shot, a whole babel of shouts, and the S.S. guards seemed to be running in all directions. All, that is, but the officer; he never even turned his head. I heard two more shots, and a man screaming. Then the screaming stopped, as if he'd bitten his tongue, and the guards were dragging him out from between the trucks of the other train. I suppose he'd made a break for it, poor little bastard. Just a little chap he was, a little thin scarecrow of a man, bleeding a bit, and scared silly. He was crying when they dragged him up to the officer, and they hit him in the face to stop him.' He shifted in his chair. 'It was all so quick – far quicker than I've been able to describe it: There were we, hardly grasping what was going on, stuck with our guard behind the carriage-windows, and outside – that, all over as quickly as a curse. There wasn't a sound but the screech of the express, and the little chap crying. And the officer hadn't even bothered to turn round.'

'What happened?' I was feeling sick, but I had to know.

'Oh, one of them spoke, and he turned and looked at the little man, and smiled. Quite a pleasant smile. Then he just moved a hand, idly enough, and said something. We couldn't hear what it was, because the express was coming up, roaring between the sheds, but the little Jew screamed again, and began to struggle.'

'Oh God,' I said.

'They threw him down across the line,' said Richard. 'He seemed to lie there for ever, like a little black broken golliwog in the snow, then that damned great express engine burst out from behind the sheds and went by like a shrieking guillotine. I – I don't know what we were doing. Our carriage was locked, of course, but I remember battering at the door and cursing like a fool and our guard trying to stop me, because he knew the officer and was afraid of him – and of course we weren't supposed to have been there at all.'

'Did the officer see you?'

'Yes. After the express was gone he heard the racket we were making, and he turned and saw us. We were hauled up in front of him then and there, and I think we'd have been shot out of hand if we hadn't been on our way to being interrogated by General von Lindt, who was a bit more important even than Herr Oberfürer Kramer.'

'That was the officer's name?'

'Yes. Max Kramer. A great big blond handsome brute with eyes like slate. He stood there, staring at Tony and me, and I think it was the worst couple of minutes I ever had in my life. He wanted to shoot us – my God, how he wanted it! His mouth went wet, and his gun-hand was shaking a little.' He shook his head sharply, as if to dodge a memory. 'I can see it at this moment – that gun pointing at us like a wicked little eye, and that hideous hand curled round the butt; there was an ugly scar running right down the forefinger, and the nail was twisted and deformed. I remember how the scar showed white, and the whole thing, hand and gun, shook with a kind of lust. . . .'

I broke across it. 'But he had to let you go.'

'Oh yes. We went. I never saw him again. Our train moved off straight away, and we ended up, conventionally enough, in Oflag XIV. But Charity—'

'What is it?' The shadow was deep in his eyes. I wanted to tell him to forget it all, to stop talking about it, but I knew that the time had not yet come when he would be able to forget. 'What is it?' I said.

'The little Jew. I recognized him.'

I stared back in a kind of horror. 'You mean, you *knew* him?'

'Oh, no, not like that. I'd met him once, that's all, in a Bond Street gallery. He was a painter – a good painter, too. His name was Emmanuel Bernstein.'

'I see. Yes, that does make it worse.'

Richard's mouth twisted as he stabbed out his cigarette viciously in the ash-tray. 'One of the best things he'd done,' he said, 'was called *Landscape under Snow.*'

CHAPTER NINETEEN

*I say, there is no darkness but ignorance; in which thou
art more puzzled than the Egyptians in their fog.*

SHAKESPEARE

It was very late. It seemed absurd that it was only a few hours since I had stepped on to the Marseilles quay straight into Richard Byron's arms. Then he had been my enemy, my nightmare, and now . . .

'I seem to have been sitting talking to you over café tables all my life,' I said inconsequentially.

He looked up at that, and seemed all at once to come out of his dream. He smiled, 'And I've been talking too much,' he said. 'I shouldn't have told you that beastly story. It's over and done with, and, as you see, it has nothing to do with this affair.'

'It certainly doesn't seem to,' I agreed. 'And there's one thing certain, that Mr. X is not Kramer – at least Marsden isn't Kramer. He was never a big blond in his life.'

'So that's that.' Richard looked at his watch. 'Time for bed. More coffee?'

'I couldn't drink another drop.'

'I'm with you there. Now we're going to decide what's the next thing to do, and then I shall see you back to your hotel.'

His plan was very simple. I was to return next day to Avignon, tell Louise what had happened, and get David to go sightseeing with me once more. I was to deliver him into his father's hands, and then Louise and I were to remove ourselves quietly from Avignon, to a hotel Richard knew in Aix. Here we were to lie low for a day or so. Richard would take David to some friends of his, the Dexters, who were spending the summer at Hyères, further along the coast, and then would get into touch with me again.

'Now that I'm forewarned to some extent,' he said, 'I should be able to deal with Mr. X, or whoever is following David about, providing he's on the job alone. And then, when I've put things straight with David, and got him tucked safely away with Bill Dexter, I'll be able to work out what to do. With David still in the open, my hands are tied.'

'It's all nice and clear and simple when you put it like that,' I said, 'if only it works. Where shall I take David sightseeing to meet you?'

He gave me a grin of pure malice. 'What about the Cathedral at Tarascon?'

'Beast!' I said, with feeling. 'I wish I was a good liar. Don't remind me of it!'

'Well, what about Arles – the arena, above the main gate? I'll be there by ten-thirty, and I'll wait all day if necessary. Of course, if you could lose Mr. X on the way . . . but don't take any risks. If anything should go wrong, you can ring up the *Légionnaire* at Nîmes, and leave a message – for Richard Coleridge, remember. Right?'

'Right.'

We stood up, and he paid the waiter. Then we moved out into the bustling throng of the Canebière. There was still, for me, something dreamlike in the teeming, sparkling, roaring streets of Marseilles. The crowd flowed round us, jostling and chattering, the buses clanged past, the cafés were hives of laughter and music, but for me, still, the only real thing in all that glittering pageant was the feel of Richard's hand on my arm.

'This way,' he said, and we were suddenly out of the throng and walking up a dark, half-empty street. 'Where did you leave your car?'

I fished in my bag for the little paste-board slip, and read it aloud: '*Bergère Frères, 69 Rue des Pêcheurs.* But I haven't the foggiest idea where it is, I'm afraid.'

'I know it. I'll call at your hotel in the morning, say eight-thirty; we'll have breakfast somewhere, and I'll take you to get your car. Then we'll go in procession again up the road to Avignon.' He grinned. 'And don't try running away again, my girl.'

'I won't.'

'You nearly foxed me at Cavaillon, you know. Who on earth taught you to drive, by the way? You're pretty good.'

'Johnny.'

'Oh, of course. It would be.'

'It was his hobby,' I said. 'It had been his job, before he joined the R.A.F. He'd raced cars practically ever since he'd had a licence. He was wonderfully good.'

'He certainly taught you a thing or two.'

'Did you pay my bill at Les Baux?' I asked suddenly. 'Because I ought to ring up—'

'I had to,' said he, with grim amusement. 'I'd asked for it, after all, hadn't I, after spending the night in your room? I managed to avert arrest by some story about your being ill recently, and a bit unstable—'

'Dash it—!'

'Don't worry, you're getting better rapidly, but you're still prone to sudden impulses: it was quite a good story, anyway, and she believed it, mainly because it was less trouble to believe it than otherwise, and I was paying anyway. The French are realists; so don't you bother about Les Baux.'

'I'll never dare go back again.'

'One of the things that really began to puzzle me about you,' said Richard, 'was why the devil you should go up there at all; and why you should go armed with a book of medieval French poetry in any case. I somehow couldn't see an accomplice of Loraine's sitting alone up there reading the *chansons de toile*. And there you were, admiring the dawn like any tourist. . . . You're a woman of parts, aren't you, Charity? Did Johnny teach you to read Middle French as well?'

'I taught French before I was married,' I said, 'and there are translations in the book anyway.'

'Well, I thought—' Then his voice broke off, and I heard his breath drawn sharply between his teeth. His hand gripped my arm, and I felt him stiffen. He stopped.

'What on earth—?' I said startled.

There was no one to be seen. We were half-way down a narrow, badly lit street, which curled its seedy way to join two wider thoroughfares. It was a street of tallish, fainty furtive-looking houses, which had seen better days, and now masqueraded as offices, garages, warehouses, and even shops. It was at one of the latter that Richard was staring now. I followed his gaze. The shop-window we had been passing was the only lighted one in the street, but apart from that I could, at first, see nothing remarkable about it. It was long and low, and was crammed with an artful and rather attractive confusion of chairs and tables, faldstools, jugs, and ivory chessmen.

I read the legend above the window: '*Werfel et Cie, Paris et Marseille, Objets d'art* . . . Antique dealers!' I said reproachfully. 'Richard, you shop-hound—'

And then I saw it, too.

It was lying, beautifully placed on the sweep of a velvet drape, glittering in the light of the single lamp. It was a silver bracelet, where the arms of a noble house were wrought about with lilies and griffins and the wings of birds. And I had seen it before.

Richard's arm had relaxed under mine, and he gave a little sigh. 'How odd to see it there!' he remarked. 'I gave that bracelet to Loraine before we were married. She must have sold it in Paris, and it's found its way here. It startled me to see it, I don't know why.' He turned away. 'Let it lie,' he said.

I said: 'If she sold it, then she sold it to-day in Marseilles.'

He swung round at that. 'What d'you mean?'

'I mean I've seen it before, too – or one very like it.'

'It's unique,' he said shortly. 'Fifteenth-century Italian. It was made for Lucrezia di Valozzi, and there isn't another like it.'

'Then Loraine was wearing it yesterday morning,' I said.

There was a pause. I was angry to find myself beginning to shake. Richard's hand, hard and excited, gripped my arm. His voice was apprehensive, but I knew the fear in it was not for himself. 'David,' he said. 'We've got to find out what's happened to David. This means Loraine's in Marseilles already.'

'The trap,' I said shakily. 'The trap . . .'

'Trap be damned,' said Richard curtly. 'They'd take a shorter chance to catch me than this. They've none of them seen me since Nîmes, I'll be bound, and Marsden wasn't on the road to-day. Now listen—' He had drawn me back from the lighted window, and his voice was low and urgent: 'I'm going in to see who hocked that bracelet, and when. Your hotel is in the street at the end of this one, the Rue Mirabell; turn to the right, and it's about fifty yards along. Go straight there, and telephone your friend Louise at the Tistet-Védène. Find out from her when Loraine left, if Marsden's with her, and David – anything she can tell you. You know what to ask. Then come back here. Got any change?'

'Plenty. But, Richard, I don't want—'

He loomed over me in the darkness. His face was all at once grim, remote, frightening, the face of my enemy. His voice, too; it was hard, and the edge was back on it.

'You'll do as I tell you,' he said, and pulled me towards him and kissed me hard upon the mouth.

Then I was half walking, half running up the dark street, and, as I went, I heard the shop-door open and shut behind him.

Louise's voice, across ninety-five kilometres of crackling French telephone-wire, sounded surprisingly clear, and blessedly unruffled.

'Why, Charity! I'd been wondering if you meant to come back to-day. How's the ghastly village with the ghosts?'

'Not too bad,' I said. 'Louise, can anyone hear you?'

'Only the concierge, and he's as deaf as a post,' said Louise very sensibly.

'Well, listen: I'm speaking from Marseilles—'

'From *where*?'

'Don't repeat it aloud, for goodness' sake; Marseilles. Listen, Louise, I haven't time to explain now, but I just want you to answer me a few questions; it's terribly important. I'm in a bit of a jam, and—'

Louise's calm voice spoke in my ear. 'Is David with you?'

So it was true. She had taken David away. The damned woman had taken David away.

' . . . Charity? Are you there?'

'Yes.'

'Are you all right? You sound a bit odd.'

'I'm all right. Are you trying to tell me that the Bristols have left the hotel?'

'Yes indeed. Such a flap,' said Louise placidly, 'as you ever saw. Mrs. Bristol screaming and throwing hysterics and swearing you'd abducted him, and Mr. Palmer and the Germans and that handsome Paul Véry out searching—'

'Louise! Do you mean that David's *run away*?'

'This morning. He left a polite note for his mamma, and moved out, complete with dog. They found out at lunch-time. So he's *not* with you?'

'Of course he's not!'

'Well, I just wondered,' said Louise reasonably. 'You've been so thick with him, and then you suddenly announced that you wanted to go to Les Boos, or whatever it is, which seemed an odd thing to do. However, I'm glad you're not a kidnapper.'

I was thinking furiously. 'Louise, I suppose it's all genuine? I mean, he really *has* run away?'

'My lord, yes! There was nothing phoney about the way Mrs. B. went for me to-day and demanded to know where you'd gone. She was as white as a sheet, and—'

'Did you tell her?'

'No,' returned Louise calmly. 'I didn't imagine you'd kidnap anyone without due cause, and I don't like the woman anyway. What's the matter?'

'Nothing,' I said. 'Nothing at all. Louise, you are the most wonderful woman in the world.'

'Well, it wasn't anything to laugh about. In fact, the hotel was so awful that I just went away for the rest of the day. Naturally.'

Naturally. 'Go on. Tell me what's happened. Is Mrs. Bristol still there?'

'No. Apparently she champed around all day while the various men hunted about in cars and things, and then she left just before dinner.'

'Alone?'

'As far as I know. I didn't get in till after dinner. I must say I was glad to find everyone gone.'

'Everyone?' I asked sharply. 'Has Mr. Marsden gone too.'

'Yes. He left this morning. And the Germans—'

'Before David disappeared or after?' My hand was sticky on the receiver.

'Nobody knows. He checked out at about ten, but of course no one saw David go.'

'I – see.' I leaned against the wall of the telephone booth, with my free hand pressed to my brow, trying to sort it out. David had vanished. And Marsden too. That didn't look so good. But then, I thought confusedly, Marsden couldn't have gone *with* David, or Loraine Bristol wouldn't be so upset that she had gone to the lengths of accusing me of kidnapping.

'Was there any suggestion of going to the police?' I asked.

'Well, there was, of course,' said Louise. 'Madame wanted to, but Mrs. Bristol wouldn't hear of it. She quietened down after a bit, and said she'd been hysterical with shock – which was true – and she apologized for what she'd said about you. Then, apparently, she said she thought she knew where he might have gone, and that no one was to worry further about a boy's prank, and she herself would go to find him. So she packed up, according to Mrs. Palmer, and left on the seven o'clock train for Marseilles. If I were you, I'd come straight back to Avignon, Charity, my dear.'

'I shall, very soon. Has anyone else left the hotel?'

'I wouldn't know. I wasn't in to dinner, and the Palmers were the only people in the court when I got back. I can't say I was sorry; it's been a trying day, on the whole. I say, Charity?'

'Yes?'

'Do you know anything about this business?'

'A little,' I acknowledged, 'but I didn't know David had bolted; and I don't know where he is. I wish I did. Had he any money, d'you know?'

'That's just it,' said Louise's tranquil, faraway little voice. 'He hadn't. That's why he took Mrs. B's bracelet. He pinched that *and* his passport. He explained in the note that he needed the money and he'd send her the pawn-ticket.'

'I – see,' I said again. My heart had begun to jolt, painfully. Two facts: David was in Marseilles, and Loraine was on her way. And Mr. X. . . .

'Louise, I must go. One more thing – did David say anything else in the note?'

'No. I saw it. She was brandishing it all over the place. It just said he was going, he was taking the bracelet because she'd never liked it anyway, and good-bye. Charity, tell me—'

'Dear Louise,' I said rapidly, 'be the utmost angel that you always are and forgive me, but I can't explain now. Don't ask me about it; I've got to go. I'll ring up later on. Angel. Good-bye.'

The voice in the telephone rose the barest fraction of a tone. 'I wasn't going to ask you about it, whatever it is. But please just tell me where you're staying. If,' finished Louise on the faintest note of interrogation, 'that's not a secret too?'

'No. The Belle Auberge, Rue Mirabell. Got it?'

'Yes, thank you. Good-bye.'

And she rang off.

CHAPTER TWENTY

By the pricking of my thumbs,
Something wicked . . .

SHAKESPEARE

When I came out of the telephone booth I found, in spite of the warmth of the night, that I was shivering. I hesitated, wondering if I dared spare the time to fetch my coat. I looked at my watch. The call had taken less than ten minutes. My room was on the second floor, and the lift was standing empty; it was the work of three more minutes to go to my room, pick up my coat, and reach the lobby again. I said a polite and, I hope, normal, good night to the concierge, and ran out into the Rue Mirabell, hugging the comfort of my coat close round me as I turned the corner and plunged once more into the dimness of the narrow street. Round the next bend in the road, past the shuttered Boucherie Chevaline, past the double warehouse doors and the heap of sand and stone where the pavement was being repaired, and there, across the street, was the long low window of the antique shop, with the bracelet on its velvet drape under the lamp. My steps faltered, slowed, and stopped. I stood in the shadows, staring across the road, while the night seemed suddenly colder.

The bracelet was still there. I could see it, pale against the velvet. But the lamp was out, and the shop had the still, deserted look of emptiness. Richard was nowhere to be seen.

I don't know how long I stood there, stupidly staring at the shop, gazing up the street and down the street, alternately, as if somehow I could conjure his presence out of empty air. I even started back the way I had come, as if I could have passed him unseen on my way from the hotel, but I told myself sharply not to be a fool, and went back to my post in the shadows. Firmly I thrust back the stupid, formless fear that was fumbling at me with chilly fingers. I was over-excited, I told myself; I had had an exhausting day, and, before that, a shocking night. There was no reason to suppose that anything untoward had happened at all. I must simply wait. It was only fifteen minutes since I had left him, and after all – with a lovely wave of relief the simple explanation burst over me – after all, Richard had probably gone through to the back of the shop, into the proprietor's office. I bent forward, peering, and then smiled to myself. There was, indeed, a line of light on the floor at the rear of the shop, that seemed to come from under a door.

I hesitated for a moment. Richard had told me to come back here. Should I wait where I was till he came out, or go across into the shop myself? I stood in the shadows, undecided.

Streets away, the traffic's roar sounded like the surging of a distant sea. Twenty yards off, on business or pleasure bent, a scrawny cat slunk purposefully across the pavement. Somewhere near at hand an engine coughed, and a car moved away with a roar and a shocking gear-change. I realized that I was shivering again, whether from apprehension, or nerves, or cold, I did not know. But I was not, I decided, going to stand in the street any longer.

Sometimes, even now, I dream of that moment, of what would have happened if I had walked across the road, and of what it might have meant. And sometimes, in my dream, I do actually walk out of the shadows, over the road, into the shop . . . then, if I am lucky, I wake up screaming. . . .

I was actually beginning to move forward when the blare of a car's horn, as it swung into the little street, startled me, and made me take an instinctive backward step. The oncoming car was a taxi, and it shot down the narrow road, skidding to a stop beside me. Almost before it had stopped the far door opened, and a woman got out. She thrust money into the driver's hand, and hurried across the pavement into the antique shop. The taxi jerked forward and roared away. I heard the shop door slam behind her, and the tap-tap-tap of her heels across the shop. I saw the door at the rear of the shop open, and she stood for a second, as brightly lit as if she had been on the cinema screen. It was Loraine.

I no longer had any desire to move out of the shelter of my doorway. Thankful for my dark coat, I crouched back, my mind racing, wondering how Loraine had traced David so quickly, wondering if Richard was still in the office, and, if so, what sort of a scene was taking place in there at this moment.

I was to know soon enough. The office door opened again, and swung wide. There were three people in the room. I saw Loraine quite clearly; she was standing gesturing furiously with a cigarette, talking to a man who sat in an arm-chair with his back to the door. I could see his arm in a short blue shirt-sleeve, and one navy-blue trouser-leg. It was certainly not Richard. There was another man, whom I took to be the owner of the shop; he it was who had opened the door, and now he paused for a moment to fling a remark at Loraine before he moved out of the lighted office towards me. He was big and broad, and, though his hair was grey, he did not walk like an elderly man. He closed the office door behind him, and came forward to the shop-front.

Really frightened now, I pressed myself back, closer into the shadows. But he did not come out into the street; he was only locking up. I heard the sharp *click* of the doorlock, and then he moved to the window and reached for the blind to pull it down. It came slowly and quietly, hiding his head, his chest, his body, until the whole shop-window was a blank, but for the big white hand that gripped the edge of the blind. In that uncertain light the hand, disembodied, looked like some monstrous white sea-beast, a squid or octopus, floating in the nebulous murk behind the glass. A monstrous, deformed creature of the dark . . . *deformed.*

I pressed the back of one shaking hand to my mouth, as I leaned against the wall, cold and sick. Even at that distance, and in that light, it showed quite clearly. The hand was crooked, and an ugly, puckered scar ran across the back of it, and down to the twisted finger-nail.

The blind clicked down.

It was the trap.

CHAPTER TWENTY-ONE

Will you walk into my parlour?

NURSERY RHYME

I don't believe I thought at all. There was certainly no plan in my head. I just stood there, in the dark doorway, looking at the shop. It did not occur to me that I had exactly no chance at all against them, that I was a woman, alone, unarmed; that even if I had had a weapon I would not have known what to do with it. It did cross my mind, since I am a normal law-abiding person, to go to the police, but imagination quailed before the prospect of explaining, in a foreign tongue, an incredible situation to a sceptical officialdom. And there was not time. Richard and David were in there, and they must be got out.

I walked quietly across the road towards the shop.

The street was luckily still deserted, and no sound came from within the locked and shuttered shop. I had noticed, two doors from it along the street, a broken door which seemed to give on to a narrow tunnel running through the block of buildings to the back. I pushed this open. It creaked slightly, and I slipped through, groping my way down the tunnel into what seemed to be a warehouse yard. The dark shapes of buildings loomed up to right and left; there were piles of old boxes, and an orderly stack of crates; ahead of me I could make out a pair of solid double gates, and, beside them, the darker cavern of an open garage.

I waited for a moment in the mouth of the alley, until I had got my bearings, and in a very few seconds I found that I could see fairly clearly. The moon that Richard and I had watched rise was dispensing a faint light from somewhere beyond the roof-tops, and, in rivalry, the glow of the city streets threw the same chimneys into warmer silhouette. One lighted window on my left cast a line of light like a yellow bar across the blackness, but it was a smallish window, about ten feet up, and the shaft of light went high, to be lost among the deeper shadows of the open garage.

I threw one apprehensive glance at this window, which I guessed to be that of the antique-dealer's office, and then I started on a hurried tiptoe search of the yard buildings. The garage offered the only real hiding-place, and I slid into its black cave like a ghost. Save for some boxes and a few drums of oil, it was empty. But a smell of stale exhaust still hung in the air, and with a flash like the springing open of a door I remembered the car I had heard drive off only a few minutes ago. I bit my lip in an agony of indecision and frustration. Perhaps Richard was no longer on the shop premises. Perhaps he – his body . . . I thrust the thought back into the limbo whence it peered and grimaced, and tried to discipline my thoughts. *He was not dead: he could not be dead . . .* with a little sob of a prayer that was not so much a supplication as a threat to the Almighty, I turned to leave the garage, and found myself staring down at a dark stain that spread hideously on the concrete floor.

It gleamed faintly under the oblique light from the office window. Its surface was thick and slimy. I don't know how long it took me to realize that it was only oil. My flesh seemed to shrink on my bones as I bent down, put a testing finger into the viscous pool, and sniffed at it. Oil. Nothing worse. I was straightening up when, out of the corner of my eye, I saw something on the floor of the garage. It had fallen behind an oil-drum, and, if I had not stooped, I should not have seen it. It showed squarish and pale in the shadows.

Now was the time, I thought, with the tiny remnant of irony that insisted on denying the realities of my situation – now was the time to discover the monogrammed handkerchief with the message scrawled in blood – or oil, amended the other part of my mind, rather hurriedly. I picked up the pale object, which was, at any rate, certainly not a handkerchief, because it was hard, oblong, and about a quarter of an inch thick. It felt as if it could be a book.

It was a book. It was a smudged and ruffled copy of T. S. Eliot's *Four Quartets*.

In something less than twelve seconds I was across that yard, and crouching in the shelter of some crates under the lighted window, with Marsden's book thrust deep into the pocket of my coat. Suspicion, then, was certainty. Marsden had been in that garage; Marsden, in fact, might have been driving the car that I had heard.

But in this last supposition, it soon appeared, I was wrong, for, quite clearly from some four feet above my head, came the voice I had heard that night on the Rocher des Doms.

' . . . Why you had to behave as if all hell was let loose, Loraine. Couldn't you—?'

I had not missed much. They were still discussing Loraine's outburst at the hotel. Her voice cut in, petulant and brittle: 'It *was* all hell. That hotel . . . you don't know what it was like—'

'Don't I? I was staying there myself.'

'Yes, but you had something to *do*. Following that damned kid around. I hadn't. I tell you—'

'You still needn't have lost your nerve to quite that extent, my dear.' He spoke cuttingly, and she flared back:

'It's all very well for you, blast you. What d'you think I've been through, this last few months? You were sitting pretty while I – I've had nothing; no fun, nothing to do except cope with that – that bad-tempered iceberg, damn him. Then *l'affaire Toni*, and the police, and now this last business . . . all that waiting: d'you wonder it's got me down? I tell you, *I couldn't help it.* I've done my best, and for God's sake, Jean, leave me alone.'

Jean. Jean Something-or-other, the husband. John Marsden.

A new voice cut across the interchange, a deep voice, speaking a guttural French that I found hard to follow.

'Stop it, both of you. Loraine, pull youself together; and you, Jean, leave her alone. She's behaved like a fool, but there's no harm done; what's happened to-day has cancelled out any mistakes either of you may have made.'

Jean spoke soberly: 'My God! we've been lucky! When I think of it – the kid walking in here as large as life, and his father after him!'

The antique dealer was curt: 'All right, we've been lucky. Then it seems my luck has got to make up for your carelessness.'

'Damn it, Max—'

Max. Max Kramer; John Marsden. The pieces fitting smoothly into place. The rats in the woodshed.

There was a crash as a fist hit the table. Kramer snarled: '*Lieber Gott*, will you listen to me? This isn't the time to wrangle over what's past. We've got those two to dispose of, and it isn't until I see them offically reported as accidental deaths that this thing's over. *When* that happens, and not before, you'll get your money.'

'And the papers,' put in Loraine sullenly.

'And the papers; and we'll cry quits, and you two can go to perdition in your own way, and leave me to go mine. Is that understood?'

'All right. What do we do?' This from Jean.

Loraine said, still sullen: 'I don't even know what's happened yet. Are they dead?'

'No,' said Kramer, and I felt a muscle jump and tighten in my throat. 'The boy's asleep; he should stay that way for quite a time; I gave him enough to keep him quiet till it's over.' He laughed. 'I've always had a kind heart. His father's had something to keep him quiet, too; perhaps it wasn't administered quite so gently, but then Jean and I were hardly prepared . . . He'll be out for a bit – quite long enough, unless we waste any more time.'

His voice dropped, and I strained closer. 'Now listen. I've been thinking hard since this happened, and I've seen how we can use things the way they've played themselves. It works out pretty well with what we planned before. The boy and his father will be found dead at the foot of the cliffs – at our arranged spot. They'll be together in the wreck of Byron's car.'

'Have you got it?'

'His keys were in his pocket, along with the garage chit. It's in one of Bériot's lock-ups.'

'And the story,' said Jean, with triumph lighting his voice, 'will be that the boy bolted to meet his father; the two of them set off – for Italy, perhaps; and *pff* – an accident in the darkness!'

'Exactly,' said Kramer, with satisfaction. 'The child really played into our hands by running away. He even stole his passport to take with him. There'll be no reason why anyone should think about – murder. No one will look in that boy's body for drugs.'

'And any signs of violence on the man will be accounted for—'

'Exactly,' said Kramer again.

Then the purr of satisfaction faded, and his voice went hard and precise: 'André's taken the two of them, tied up in the van. He's been gone about fifteen minutes. We should be there almost as soon as he is. He's a bit of a fool, as you know, and he's afraid of trouble; I told him we'd have to wait for you, Loraine, but that one of us would go after him as soon as possible, Jean—'

'What?'

'My car's in the garage on the other side of the street. Here are the keys.' I heard the jingle as he threw them. 'You get straight after André. See that he parks well out of sight.'

'Right. And you?'

'I've got to get Byron's car; it won't take me long. If either of them wakes up and makes trouble—'

'I'll know what to do.'

'*So,*' said the German.

Loraine said: 'What about me? Can't I come? I want to watch.'

Jean sounded amused. 'Chief mourner? What on earth did the poor sod do to you, *ma belle?*'

'You'll go with me,' said Kramer flatly. 'I want Jean's mind on his job. Get going, Jean.'

'Okay. Throw me my coat.'

I heard the chair-springs creak as he got up. I heard the small jingle of the car keys as he dropped them into his pocket. He was going. He took three steps, and the door opened. They were on their way to kill Richard and little David, and there was nothing I could do. Nothing. Somewhere out in the night, along that cruel coast, Richard and his son would hurtle to their deaths, and I would not even know where they lay, until I saw the headlines in the morning papers.

I suppose I was praying. I only know that my cheeks and lips were wet, and my hands were gripping the edge of a crate until the bones seemed to crack. *Dear God, don't let them die* . . . not Richard, not little David; there must be something I can do . . . perhaps, even now, the police . . . there must be something I can do. There must be. If only I knew where they'd been taken, I'd find something, somehow . . . if only I knew where they were. *Dear God, won't you tell me where they are?*

'Max,' said Jean's voice above me, half laughing, half casual, 'I'm damned if I can remember whether it's the first fork right after Aiguebelle, or the second.'

'*Lieber Gott!* The second!' said Kramer. 'The first only goes to a cottage on the cliff. The track you want drops steeply away from the road just beyond those big parasol pines on the left. This is a hell of a time to ask a question like that!'

'Isn't it?' said Jean insolently, and went out, whistling, into the shop.

I heard Kramer say: 'Loraine. Quickly now. Get on the telephone to that hotel of yours—' and then I was across the yard and fumbling for the catch of the double gates that opened on to the back alley. With Jean at the street door I dared not go that way. I must chance finding my way through the alley, back to the Rue Mirabell, and thence to locate my car. The road to Italy, the coast road, past Aiguebelle . . . I found myself whispering frantically as my hands clawed at the heavy catch of the gate: '*Bergère Frères, 69 Rue des Pêcheurs* . . . *69 Rue des Pêcheurs* . . . my car, please, quickly . . . the second on the right after Aiguebelle; on the left the parasol pines,' And then, again, like a refrain: '*Bergère Frères.* . . .'

The bolt was rusty, and my fingers slipped and strained. There was sweat on my hand. I thought I heard the outer door of the shop open and shut in the distance. I thought I heard a soft whistle in the street. I couldn't move the bolt. I strained and tugged to move it, and it would not come, and something inside me strained too, and stretched to snapping-point. I couldn't get out. They were going to murder Richard, and I couldn't get out.

In another moment I'd have broken: I'd have been caught by Kramer screaming in his warehouse yard and beating the gates with my hands, but, just as the panic inside me swelled to bursting-point, a little door in the gate swung open like magic in front of me, and I was free. It was one of those little man-doors they cut into bigger ones, to save having to haul the latter open every time somebody wants to get out; and it swung wide in front of me, creaking ever such a little.

I bent down and stepped through it into the narrow back alley-way.

As I straightened up, something hit me. It caught me full on the chest, and I staggered back against the gates, pinned there by my assailant's weight, and with his breath on my cheek.

CHAPTER TWENTY-TWO

Needs must when the Devil drives

PROVERB

Before I had time to do more than draw breath for the scream I dared not utter, my attacker gave a little snuffling whine and began licking my face.

'*Rommel!*' Relief made me weak. My legs shook, and I wanted, insanely, to laugh. I pushed the delighted dog down with a warning whisper and a hand over his muzzle, while my other hand groped for his collar. The inevitable piece of string was there, about two feet of it, the end snapped and frayed. David must have tied the dog up when he went into the shop, and the poor beast had eventually broken the string and come wandering in search of him. As I ran down the back alley in the direction of the Rue Mirabell I was busy with the new and minor problem; what on earth could I do with the dog?

I could abandon the poor beast, of course, if he would let me, but something in me shrank from such an action. I could leave him in my hotel, but the thought of the fuss, the explanations, the waste of time, was more than I dared face. He was running happily beside me, panting with the pleasure of having at last found a friend, and it occurred to me, too, that I was in no position to reject help of any sort. I might yet be glad, even, of Rommel's friendship.

I was proved right about thirty seconds later, as we plunged across the Rue Mirabell into another dark little alley, and a drunken Negro rose straight out of the shadows to lurch across my path. I tried ineffectually to dodge him and slip by, but, even as he gripped my sleeve, Rommel gave a snarl, and leaped for him, hitting him in the groin. The man doubled up and staggered back with a curse, reeling against the wall. I fled by, and Rommel with me, the pleasure on his silly face greatly enhanced by the satisfactory little episode. For me, remembering suddenly the reputation of the city through whose dubious streets I was adventuring alone, the sound of the dog's lolloping feet and excited panting were now enormously comforting. I gripped the frayed string more tightly, and we ran out of the alley into a street that I vaguely remembered.

This was a main street, well lighted, the road, in fact, down which I had come from Avignon into Marseilles. I had turned off it some way further west, in my attempts to dodge Richard, so the garage of Bergère Frères must lie somewhere in the maze of streets between this one and the docks. It couldn't be far, I thought hopefully, as Rommel and I crossed the street and hesitated on the further pavement; I remembered that I had not walked a great distance before re-crossing this street and finding the hotel in the Rue Mirabell.

I looked round me. It was not a street of cafés, and there were surprisingly few people about. The newspaper kiosk at my elbow was shut, so was the *boulangerie* in front of me, but thirty yards away was an open garage, the lights of its petrol-pumps glowing like beacons. Someone there would certainly know the way to the garage in the Rue des Pêcheurs. I tugged Rommel in that direction.

One garage-hand was busy at the pumps, attending to a car, but as I hurried forward another emerged from the garage door, carrying a bucket. He put this down, and, at my breathless query, pushed the beret back on his head and scratched his hair.

'Rue des Pêcheurs, mam'selle? Why yes, but—' he eyed me dubiously. 'It's no sort of place for you to be going, this time of night.'

'But I must!' My insistence was such that his stare became curious. 'It's most urgent. Which is the way?'

He rubbed his ear, still staring. 'I'll point the way out to you, sure enough. But I tell you—'

'I must!' I cried again. He meant kindly, no doubt, but my heart was hammering in my throat, and the engine of every car that passed was like the whining hum of a minute-gong. I took a step towards him. 'Please, m'sieur!'

His stare was all over me now, taking in my smudged hands, my dusty sandals, the plaster-marks on my coat, the desperation in my face. There was a glint in his eyes now that was more than curiosity. 'I'll tell you what I'll do.' He passed his tongue over his upper lip, and smiled quite pleasantly. I wondered if he were thinking of telephoning the police. 'I'm off in ten minutes,' he said. 'If you like to wait I'll take you there myself.'

I grabbed at the edges of my patience and politeness. 'M'sieur, you are kindness itself. But I repeat, this is urgent; I cannot wait. I have to leave Marseilles immediately, and I must have my car. So—'

'Car?'

'Yes. At Bergère's garage. It's in the Rue—'

'I know that. But it's shut.' He spoke curtly; he was losing interest. He half turned away and picked up his bucket.

'*Shut?*' The world stood still, then began to spin. 'Are you sure?'

He shrugged slightly. '*Mais certainment.* It's a repair garage: it shuts at eight.'

'Perhaps someone – it's so very important . . . where do they live?' I found myself beginning to stammer; I was groping for words, my French slipping from me as my brain panicked again: 'I could go to the house—'

He spoke a little more gently: 'I don't know where they live. You could perhaps ask at the house near the garage.'

A tram bucketed down the street behind me, the noise of its speed mocking me. A car turned in beside the petrol pumps, and the swish of its tyres on the gravel made the hairs prickle along the nape of my neck. I dropped Rommel's string on the ground, set my foot on it, and began to grope in my handbag with shaking hands.

'No, that's no use. I've no time. I must go now. I must hire a car. Please get one out immediately and fill it up. How much—'

'There is no car.' Interest, curiosity, perhaps even compassion, these were still in his eyes, but deepening there, too, was suspicion. Heaven knows I didn't blame him: if he could read my face as I read his, he must be able to see something sufficiently out of the ordinary. My whole bearing must speak my fear. I dragged at a handful of notes and held them out, 'A car, m'sieur, for God's sake—'

He eyed the notes, but made no move to take them. 'It is the truth. We have no car for hire. I am sorry.' His shrug of regret was genuine, and final. He turned away.

I just stood there, numbly, clutching the notes, and in me, the hope that had never been a hope at all, drooped and died. It was no use. Richard was dead. I could go to the Rue des Pêcheurs, I could knock from door to door, breathless, hurrying, desperately fumbling for words. I could find M. Bergère; I could explain to him: I could persuade him to open his garage. I could get my car out, and drive along the coast road to Aiguebelle and the parasol pines, I and this silly fluffy dog of David's. And when I got there there would be nothing to see except the moonlight on some car-tracks in the dust, and nothing to hear except the grating roar of the sea on the shingle at the foot of the cliff. I was too late. . . .

Rommel turned his head and wagged his ridiculous tail. Someone spoke behind me.

'Mrs. Selborne!'

I turned, as in a dream. A tall man in a dark suit was standing by the petrol-pumps, looking at me. He spoke again, in English, and took a step towards me.

'It *is* Mrs. Selborne, isn't it?'

I knew him now: it was the handsome Frenchman from the Tistet-Védène. I smiled mechanically. 'Monsieur – Véry?'

He smiled back and gave a charming little bow. 'I never expected to see you here, madame; this is indeed a pleasure.' Then as I, at a loss, stammered something, his eyes fell on Rommel. They widened, and he turned on me a look half amazed, half quizzical, and wholly amused.

'So it *was* you?' he said. I did not reply, but he appeared to notice nothing odd in my demeanour. He laughed. 'Tell me, where have you hidden him – the little boy you stole?'

'I – I—'

He made a gesture. His dark eyes were alight with amusement. 'Figure to yourself, madame, what it was like at the *hôtel*, this morning! The cries, the tears—'

'Tears?' I repeated the word dully. I was not taking this in. All my attention was on the trivial task of folding the notes very neatly, and putting them back into my bag.

'We – ell, perhaps not tears.' He grimaced slightly. 'There is no love lost there, *hein*? But *you*' – his eyes were dancing – '*you* the criminal! Tell me, why did you do it? He was unhappy, the little one? Did he tell you, perhaps—?'

'No, no. I didn't—'

'You haven't been caught yet, anyway?' He chuckled. '*Bon*. You caused a lot of trouble, you know, but it was *fort amusant*, just the same. I thought I was going to have to miss the end of it; I had to leave to-day for Nice, and I was *désolé* that I should never know what happened. And now, by the purest chance, I pull in here' – he gestured to the pumps – 'and here you are, with the evidence of the crime, red-fingered . . . or is it red-handed?'

But I was not listening. My eyes had followed his gesture, and for the moment my whole world was filled with what they saw.

The mechanic was just screwing the cap back into the petrol-tank of Paul Véry's car. And what a car! Long, low, and open, with *power* written along every gleaming line of her, the Mercedes-Benz lay along the garage-front like a liner at a fishing-jetty. From where I stood she looked about thirty feet long.

'Monsieur Véry—' It stirred in me, that crazy little hope that wouldn't die. My heart began to thud.

At something in my face his expression changed. The amusement dropped like a peeled-off mask. His eyes scanned me. 'I am sorry. I shouldn't have jested about it. You are in trouble.'

'Yes. Great trouble.' I came close to him and put out a hand that was not steady. 'You're going to Nice, you say . . . could you, *would* you, take me with you part of the way?'

'But of course. The boy—?'

'It's to do with the boy,' I said shakily. 'I know where he's gone. Please understand – it's terribly important to hurry; let me explain as we go. I – it's so urgent—'

His hand closed over mine, for a brief, reassuring moment. 'Don't worry, *ma belle*; we shall hurry. That car – it is difficult, with her, to do anything else.'

Two minutes later, with Rommel safely tied in the back seat, the Mercedes flicked through the traffic in the Canebière, and turned her nose to the east.

CHAPTER TWENTY-THREE

Tyger, Tyger——

BLAKE

Almost at once, it seemed, the glare and rattle of the Marseilles streets thinned around us, and we were threading the tree-lined suburbs, whose ever-sparser street-lamps and high shuttered houses flickered past in a gathering darkness. If there was a speed-limit here, Paul Véry ignored it. He drove fast, cutting dangerously through the remaining knots of traffic in a manner that made me at one moment feel glad of the speed we were making, and at another wonder if he reckoned the risks he took. If we should be stopped by the police ... for the Mercedes made no secret of her speed, it did not need the klaxon blaring at the crossing to advertise her coming: on a rising snarl she swept through the last of the thinning streets, and roared down the tunnel of her own undimmed lights, racing like a homing tiger for the forests of the night.

The gleaming tram-lines of Marseilles vanished from under our wheels: the lights of the last house flickered through its cypresses and were gone; and we were in the open country. A wind had risen. The wind of our own speed beat against us, whining along the great bonnet and clawing at the wind-screen, but I could tell from the drift of the high clouds against the starlight that the upper air, too, was alive. The moon had vanished, swallowed by those same clouds, and we raced through a darkness lit only by faint stars, save where the car's great lights flooded our road for what seemed half a racing mile ahead. And down that roaring wedge of light she went, gathering speed, peeling the flying night off over her shoulder as a comet peels the cloud. Along that rushing road the pines, the palisaded poplars, the cloudy olives, blurred themselves for an instant at the edge of vision, and were gone. The night itself was a blur, a roar of movement, nothing but a dark wind; the streaming stars were no more than a foam in our wake.

The road whipped wickedly under us like a snake. The world swung in a sickening lurch as the tyres screamed at a bend. Then we were straight again, tearing hell-bent down our long tunnel of light.

Paul Véry glanced at me with a little smile. 'Is this fast enough for you?'

'No,' I said.

In the glow of the dashboard I saw him look momentarily disconcerted, and I realized that, in taking so literally my demand for speed, he had expected me to be scared. Even at that moment I could feel a wry twinge of amusement at the idea that anyone who had lived with Johnny could ever be afraid of speed again: this bat-out-of-hell flight through the roaring darkness had been Johnny's normal way of driving home. But then, Johnny had been – Johnny: I admitted to myself, on a second thought, that I had had several qualms to-night already as we had bullied our way out of Marseilles. I had been in this kind of car too often not to know just what she could do with half-a-second off the chain.

'Nevertheless,' said Paul Véry, decelerating, 'it is as fast as is safe.' He, too, then, had felt that moment at the bend when the tiger had nearly got away from him.

'I'm sorry,' I said. 'I was worrying. I'm watching all the time for their tail-light, and I spoke without thinking. I'm most terribly grateful to you for taking me at all.'

'It's a pleasure.' He accompanied the formal words with a smile so delightful that, in spite of my heart-aching fear and apprehension, I smiled back. I found myself watching him as he leaned back in his seat, and settled the car down to a steady sixty-five, his eyes narrowed on the extreme arrow-tip of light ahead. In its reflected glow his face was a handsome mask of concentration.

The road tore towards us. Once my heart jumped and fluttered in my throat as a red light appeared in the blackness ahead, but it was only a small car, stationary, with a couple in it, a man and a girl. I sank back in my seat, and the blood seemed to seep back from my tingling finger-tips and slowly start to feed my heart again.

Paul Véry had glanced sideways at me, and now he spoke.

'That is not the tail-light you are looking for, I take it?'

'No.' I smiled a little uncertainly at him. 'I suppose you must be wondering what it's all about?'

His gaze was back on the road. 'But naturally. You talk of urgency, and you are anxious and afraid. Who would not wonder, madame? Believe me, I am eager to help . . . but there is not the least need to tell me your affairs if you would rather not.'

'You're very good. I – I told you it was something to do with the boy David.'

'*Eh bien?*'

'I *didn't* take him away, you know. But I do know where he is now. That's where I'm going.'

His hands moved a little, as if with surprise, on the steering-wheel, and the car gave a wicked swerve. He cursed it under his breath.

'Sorry,' I said. 'I didn't mean to startle you. But the rest of my story's a good deal more startling than that. I told no more than the truth when I said I was in trouble. I am: desperate trouble.' My voice wavered as the spectre of that desperation once more gibbered at me out of the dark. 'Life-and-death trouble,' I said, on a little sob.

'And you need help – badly.' It was almost a question, spoken very softly, without looking at me. There was a curious lilt to his voice, and I turned my head to look at him, the sob caught in my throat. Help . . . of course I needed help. Up to this moment, stupid with weariness and dazed by my terror for Richard, I had thought of Paul Véry only as a miraculous means of my reaching the little road beyond Aiguebelle. Further than that I had not gone. But now . . . the miracle was complete: I and Rommel were alone no longer, we had an ally, and our immediate objective was apparent. André was ahead of us, with Richard and David, and he was alone on the job. It was by no means probable that Jean, also, was before us: he would have had little, if any, start of us, and, at the rate we were going, we would almost certainly by now have caught any car going at a more normal speed.

André was alone, and there were two of us – and Rommel.

My heart lifted, and I turned gratefully to my companion. He was smiling; he looked extremely handsome, and also, I realized, entirely formidable.

'And where are "they" taking this little boy, *hein*? And who are "they"?' The strange note was back in his voice, and all at once I knew it for what it was. It was enjoyment. He sounded amused, excited, and not at all apprehensive. He had, of course, no idea yet of the real danger of the situation: it was the unusualness of it, the lady-in-distress touch, the mad speed through the dark – all this must be appealing to some sense of adventure in him. But I knew, too, as I looked at him as it were with new eyes, that no threat of danger to come would damp that enjoyment.

I found myself heartened by his demeanour, the lift of excitement, almost gaiety, in his voice and look. It was catching, and it was certainly, to anyone in my desperate plight, heartening, to be suddenly given an ally at once so eager and so redoubtable.

And redoubtable was by no means too strong a word. There was about him an impression of force, of energy leashed in only precariously . . . the whole personality of the man was, at such close quarters, almost overwhelming. I had, I realized, failed to estimate Monsieur Paul Véry. It was not only the headlong speed of the car that snatched at my breath as I began the explanation that was his due.

'It's a long story, and a nasty one,' I said quickly, 'and I mayn't have time to tell it all to you before things happen. But the main thing is that David, whose real name is David Byron, is going to be murdered to-night, along with his father, if we can't do something to prevent it.'

He shot me a startled look. 'But—'

'I know!' I cried. 'It sounds fantastic! But listen: I'll try to tell you a little about it. . . .'

I began, stumbling a little in my haste, to tell him what I knew about Kramer and Richard and Loraine. He listened in silence, but when at length I came to Marsden's part in the affair, he interrupted me with an exclamation that sounded amused.

'Monsieur Marsden? *That* one? The rest, yes; I will believe it because you tell me so, and because I think you really are in bad trouble. But *this* I cannot think, that the good Monsieur Marsden is a murderer. Besides, he is English.'

'He *says* he's English,' I said sharply. 'But I tell you he *is* her husband, and he's in Kramer's pay. You've *got* to believe me. The good Monsieur Marsden, as you call him, is on his way at this moment to murder both Richard and David Byron, unless we can do something to stop him!'

I could see his face in the dim light. He was smiling a little still, but his brows were drawn with bewilderment.

'*Mais, ma belle—*'

So I was to be spared none of the nightmare. The ordeal by unbelief was to be part of it. . . . and in my own bewildered terror I must try and sort out the affair's lunatic logic, so that this man might believe and help me. I clutched my shaking hands together, and fought to marshal my knowledge. I remember that the only clear thought in my head was a wish that Paul Véry would stop calling me '*ma belle*'.

'Listen, monsieur,' I said carefully, 'I am telling you no more than the truth, as I know it. There is no time to go back to the beginning. I can only tell you what is happening now, to-night, and beg that you will believe me. I'm not quite sure of this man Kramer's reasons for employing Loraine and Marsden to do murder for him, but I *think* it's because of something that happened during the War, Richard and a friend of his witnessed a – an atrocity, I suppose one would call it – in which Kramer was concerned.'

'That does not matter.' He spoke all of a sudden with sharp impatience. 'I have said that I will believe you. All this talk of the War – there is no time. Tell me now what you think this man plans to do – what *you* plan to do, now, to-night.'

The relief was so sharp, so intense, that the darkness blurred round me, and I shut my eyes and pressed the palms of my hands against them. I felt the car slow down, and took my hands away, to find that we were threading a decorous enough way between walls and houses. A festoon of street lamps swung up into the darkness, a lighted tram rattled out of a side-street, and suddenly we were plunged into a brilliance of neon-lights and cafés and the impatient blare of traffic.

'Toulon,' said Paul Véry. 'Go on. Tell me your plan.'

'Very well,' I said. 'Here it is, without trimmings. Somewhere along this road is a village called Aiguebelle. A little way beyond it, on the left, there is a group of parasol pines, and opposite them a lane branches right-handed off the road, along the cliff top. There, unless we overtake it on the road, a van will be waiting, in the charge of a man called André. In that van are Richard and David Byron, unconscious and, I believe, tied up. André has orders to wait there for the others, then they're going to stage an accident. Kramer's bringing Rich – Byron's own car, and Loraine's with him. But Marsden left before them. And at the rate we've been travelling, he's hardly had a chance to overtake us, but he won't be so very far behind.' I drew in my breath. 'He'll hurry a bit, of course,' I added, 'as André's alone on the job, and a bit of a fool into the bargain.'

I stopped. There was a pause, filled with the rushing wind. The town was behind us, and once again we were plunging down our lighted tunnel into the lonely night. I did not look at Paul Véry: I had pleaded my cause abominably, I knew, but weariness, bewilderment, and agony of mind were my excuse. I bit my lip, and waited.

His reaction, when it came, was unexpected. I heard him give a long-drawn whistle of stupefaction, then he swore softly, and laughed. But even as I opened my mouth to speak he moved one hand off the wheel to drop it lightly over mine.

'Forgive me, I did not mean to laugh . . . but you seem to be so deep in the confidence of this murderer. How do you know all this?'

I slid my hand from under his, and began to fumble in my bag for a cigarette. At least he was not alarmed, I reflected. I said: 'Does that matter now? You said we'd got to think of what to do.'

'Yes indeed.' He removed his hand at that, and reached in a pocket to produce a flat silver case. He handed it to me without looking at me. He seemed all at once to withdraw into his own thoughts; it was as if he had forgotten me, forgotten all but the immediate problem of action. When he spoke, his voice was abstracted, and he used his own language for the first time.

'Why did you not . . . light me one too, will you, *ma belle?* . . . why did you not go to the police?'

I answered in the same tongue: 'I hadn't time.' I took a cigarette from the case, and bent low behind the wind-screen, shielding my face from the draught as I flicked my lighter.

'And the dog . . . how did you come by the dog?'

The lighter went out, and I had to flick it two or three times to relight it. I huddled lower in the car, making a little draught-proof cave, and tried again. I did not reply, but he hardly appeared to notice; he was talking almost to himself, still in that preoccupied, almost absent voice.

'And the man Marsden; why should you be so certain that the man Marsden is the husband of Loraine?'

The lighter flared, and burned steadily. I lit the cigarette, and handed it up to him out of my cave. I fumbled in the open case on my knee for another. 'Does it matter?' I said again. 'Have you by any chance got a gun?'

'As it happens, I have,' said Paul Véry, and I could tell by his voice that he was smiling again. 'But tell me, how do you come to be in Marseilles anyway? And what is your connection with this Byron?'

I held the lighter to my cigarette, and drew at the flame. Then I froze, crouched there under the dash-board of the car, while the flame of the lighter, illuminating my tiny cave of blackness, flickered over the open lid of Paul Véry's cigarette-case.

There was an inscription there, beautifully tooled in the silver. It was only his name, and a date.

It read:

> *Jean-Paul.*
> *A jamais,*
>
>   *L.*   17.8.42

The lighter went out. Above me in the darkness, his voice said, ever so slightly mocking: 'Don't worry about it any more, *ma belle.* It'll be all right, I'll see to that. And you trust me, don't you?'

That phrase, softly spoken in French in the darkness . . . the voice of the Rocher des Doms; the voice I had heard less than an hour ago in

Kramer's office. . . . And, like another echo behind it, too late, whispered the ghost-voice of Louise: '*Paul Véry . . . something to do with antiques. . . .*'

'You do trust me, don't you?' repeated Jean, smiling into the darkness above me.

CHAPTER TWENTY-FOUR

Who rides the tiger cannot dismount

CHINESE PROVERB

It was cold. The Mediterranean night-wind, pine-scented, sea-scented, sang past my cheek in a warm dark tide, but I was shivering as I hugged myself deep into my coat and fought down the rising hysteria of hopelessness.

Fool that I was! I had heard Loraine's husband – I still thought of him as Paul Véry – go for his car. In the time it had taken me to escape from Kramer's yard and run as far as the garage he could just have got his car out and driven across to fill her up. In spite of his connection with the Tistet-Védène, in spite (I told myself savagely) of his now obvious eligibility for the rôle of Loraine's husband, I had not tumbled to it. I had run to him in thankfulness, like a fool, putting our last pitiful little chance straight into his hands. Murderer's hands.

The lights of Hyères swam up in front of us; they swooped by, and were engulfed in our dark wake. I huddled deeper into my seat, and stole a glance at him. Now that I knew . . . oh, yes, now that I knew, it was plain to see, the glint of amusement below the insolent lids, the arrogant tilt of the chin, the whole formidable confidence of the man. And I was aware again, sharply, of the impression of excitement that I had received before: somehow, it was there, banked and blazing, under the smoothly handsome exterior: the faint gleam of sweat over his cheek-bones betrayed it, the nostrils that flared to a quicker breathing above a rigid upper lip, the hands, too tight upon the wheel. Murderer's hands.

The dim road hurtled towards us. A village, a huddle of houses, flickered by like ghosts. Ahead two eyes gleamed: they stared, then darted like fireflies as the rabbit turned to run. Paul Véry gave a little laugh, and deliberately thrust down his foot. I heard the rabbit squeal as we hit it: behind me Rommel whined, sharply. Paul Véry laughed once more.

'Frightened?' The question came again; he must have heard me make some sound. This time I could honestly give him the satisfaction he wanted.

'Yes. Do we have to go as fast as this?'

He smiled at the tremor in my voice, but, to my surprise, slackened the car's headlong speed.

'And did you have to do that?' I said.

'Do what?'

'Kill that wretched rabbit.'

He laughed again, a charming, gay little laugh. He looked extraordinarily handsome. 'You don't like killing?'

'Of course not.' I hoped there was nothing in my voice but an austere disapproval, nothing of the cold creeping terror that was shaking me.

The car slowed still further. The speedometer, under its masked light, showed a decorous fifty as Paul Véry took a hand off the wheel and dropped it over mine. The contact, warm, vital, and wholly mocking, sent a new shock through me: it was as if the man were giving off tangible waves of excitement.

'Do you?' I asked, knowing the answer.

'If something gets in the way, *ma belle*, it's asking to be killed, isn't it?' Warm and strong, his hand tightened over mine. The car's speed dropped further, and he turned his head to smile down at me. 'Not afraid any more?'

I said 'No,' coolly enough, but I drew on my cigarette as if for succour, and my lips were unsteady. For I knew now what I was in for. I would have to be killed along with Richard and David; that much was obvious. Like the rabbit, I had got in the way. I knew, too, that Paul Véry was a real killer, who enjoyed the act of killing, and that this mad ride through the dark towards his dreadful objective had touched in him some ghastly stop of pure excitement. And my presence was the final titillation. Darkness, speed, danger, murder ... and a girl. Nothing was to be missing from Mr. Véry's white night.

The Mercedes sang down to thirty, twenty-five, twenty ... We were crawling at ten miles an hour down a sloping black tunnel of trees, and Paul Véry had thrown away his cigarette; his arm had slid round my shoulders and his handsome face was bent close to mine. I leaned back against the arm but it was like a bar of steel. At my involuntary movement of resistance it tightened brutally and I saw something begin to blaze in the eyes above me.

I suppose real terror is mercifully paralysing. I shut my eyes as he pulled me to him, only vaguely wondering if he would kill me here, or send me over the cliff with Richard. I even found myself wishing that he would watch the road when he was driving.

His rapid breathing was hot on my cheek. His voice said with something ruffling its deep velvet caress: '*Ma belle* ...' I felt his mouth searching for mine, and jerked my head away. He said again, on a note of surprised reproach: '*Ma belle* ...'

And even as I wondered half hysterically why a victim should be expected to want to kiss her murderer, the cobwebs of terror blew aside for one moment, and I remembered that he still had no idea that I knew him for what he was. His pained reproach held no hint of mockery:

passion had left no room for that. He was simply so damned handsome that no woman had ever refused him a kiss before.

My knowledge was my only weapon: it was a pitiful enough tool, a despicable tool if you like, but it was all I had. I didn't hesitate a second. I opened my eyes, and smiled Delilah-wise into his. 'It's only . . . do *please* watch the road,' I whispered.

I heard his little soft laugh of triumph as he turned his head away to glance at the road. I relaxed against his shoulder, and his arm tightened round me as the Mercedes drew to a sliding halt at the side of the road.

I threw away my cigarette with my free hand.

'Oh damn!'

The car slid to a stop.

'What's the matter, *chérie?*'

'My bag,' I said crossly. 'It went overboard when I threw my cigarette out.' I sat up and made as if to pull away from him.

He pulled the handbrake on with a sharp movement, and turned to prevent me, taking me in both arms and drawing me back towards him. 'Does it matter?' It was the brown velvet voice, irresistibly caressing, flatteringly urgent. He had forgotten to switch the engine off.

I hung back, pouting like a chorus starlet: 'Silly! Of course it matters! Get it for me, there's a dear.'

'Later,' he said, his voice roughening. His mouth came down on mine, and I sighed tremulously, and slid my arms round his neck. I began to wonder how soon we might expect Kramer in the Bentley. . . .

It seemed an age, a ghastly crawling age, before he relaxed his embrace a little and spoke again: 'Trembling, *ma belle?*'

I managed a breathless little laugh, which became half genuine as I saw the satisfied vanity in his face. It never occurred to him to doubt my surrender. I hastened to make him even surer of me.

'Paul.'

'*Chérie?*'

'You like me?'

'A silly question, *ma belle!*'

You're telling me, I thought. I said: 'Even looking the way I do now?'

He laughed complacently. 'Any way, madame. Tell me – what is Richard Byron to you?'

He must have felt me jump in his arms, but he put it down to startled recollection. 'Oh!' I cried. 'How *dreadful* of me! I'd actually forgotten!' I tried to push him away. 'Monsieur Véry, hadn't we better go on? I can't imagine what I was thinking about!'

'Can't you?' He was laughing again, and I had to control a sharp impulse to strike him across his beautiful complacent mouth. 'Answer me, *ma belle*. This Richard Byron—'

'I don't know Richard Byron,' I said quickly. 'It's the little boy I care about, little David – let's go on, Monsieur Véry!'

'You called me Paul a minute ago.'

'Paul, then. If we're not in time—'

'There is plenty of time.' He pulled me close again, and I went as if in spite of myself. I knew he had no intention of going on yet. I was afraid of pushing my hand and making him suspicious. I relaxed against him for another long, agonizing minute, while I strained my ears for the sound of Kramer's car, and the darkness pressed in around us. The silence seemed thick and heavy under the trees. Only by the faintest quivering of her body did the Mercedes betray that her engine still ran. Paul Véry either did not care, or he was too preoccupied to notice. I wondered just how long it would be before things got beyond me, and guessed that it would not be very long now. Would I be strangled, like Tony, or—

I gave another long sigh, and drew away. 'We must go,' I said huskily. 'The little boy, Paul, *chéri* – we mustn't forget him. I'd never forgive myself if anything happened to him because we'd—' I stopped and put up a hand to his cheek. 'Let's go on, Paul.'

He was as taut as a wire, and breathing fast. There was a queer look in his eyes, a kind of cold blaze that was uncanny, a blank look that I knew, suddenly, was the look of the killer. His hands moved, blindly. Things would be beyond me any moment now.

I pushed his hands away gently. 'Please!' I said. 'Get me my bag and then we'll go.'

He didn't move, but sat there still with his eyes on me.

I smiled at him. 'All right, handsome,' I said. 'We don't go. But get it for me anyway. I feel a fright and I want my mirror.'

I leaned forward quickly and kissed him, as earnest of good intentions, then reached across him and opened the door. He hesitated, then with a little shrug he got out of the car. *Humour the victim; she'll come quietly. . . .*

I had dropped the bag before the car stopped, and I judged it to be about twenty yards back.

He walked back up the road, peering at the dark verge.

I counted his steps, and put my hand on the handbrake, releasing the ratchet. I held it there, waiting.

Five, six, seven . . . he paused and I thought he glanced back.

'Can't you find it?' I called. 'Shall I come?'

'It's all right.' He moved on slowly.

Eight, nine. . . .

I reached a foot over to the left and threw out the clutch. We were on a slope; I eased the gear-lever into second.

Ten, eleven. . . .

'Here it is,' he said, and stooped to pick it up.

In a flash I was in the driver's seat. I shoved the brake off, opened the throttle with a roar, and let in the clutch. Behind me, I heard a shout and a curse. The Mercedes jerked forward sharply – too sharply. For a moment I feared I would stall her, and threw out the clutch again. Then she caught hold as a race-horse takes the bit, and we were away.

But my moment of fumbling with the unfamiliar controls had cost me dear enough.

As I swung her out to the crown of the road and changed up, I heard his hoarse breathing and the thud of feet, and felt the lurch as he flung himself on to the running-board of the car.

'*Rommel!*' I screamed above the rising snarl of the engine. '*Get him, Rommel!*'

I heard the dog give an excited bark, but there was no movement of attack. After all, the dog had seen me kissing the man only a few seconds before. Then I remembered that Paul Véry had a gun, and called, for the dog's sake, even more urgently: '*Down, Rommel!*' and heard Paul Véry's ugly little breathless laugh.

The Mercedes gathered speed with a roar. The man was cursing behind me as he clung to the rear door. We plunged out of the tunnel of trees, and went up a hill with the sickening swoop of a swing. Ahead of us, once more, our great floodlights made a funnel into the dark, and we hurtled down their narrowing glare.

In control now, my hands on the wheel, I felt suddenly, beautifully, icily cold. The needle began to creep over to the right of the dial. We slashed through a tiny village. The name Euzès swam up for a second into the light, and vanished, while I knitted my brows and tried to remember the map.

The Mercedes roared on, and out of the corner of my eye I saw Paul Véry, clinging like a remora, give a heave of his muscles and lift a leg to climb inboard. I waited till the leg was just about to slide over the door, then I gave the wheel a jerk that sent the car across the road in a sickening, screeching swerve.

I heard him scream, saw him lurch outwards, but somehow he managed to retain his grip. He clung there, huddled together, yelling God knew what blasphemies at me.

I gave him a moment or so, and then I did it again. The tyres tore at the road, and I listened indifferently enough. If I had a burst, it would be just too bad, but unless I could get rid of Paul Véry and his gun, then I might just as well die this way as any other. I drove my foot down and dragged at the wheel again. The rear wheels skidded savagely, and the car bucked like a mad stallion. The lights careened dizzily across the night, and the darkness swung in a great arc round us. For a moment I thought I had done it too violently, and had lost control. Paul Véry was yelling again, and I heard the frightened dog give a sharp howl as he was flung down. The car, rocking madly, lunged forward again at the same wicked pace. The beam swung ahead, swung and steadied like a search-light. Two fir-trees flickered by like ghosts, and then the lights met – nothing.

The road ahead had switched sharp left. I saw the verge of it leap towards our wheels, and beyond it a yard of dusty ground where thin grass waved spectral antennae against an immensity of darkness. Stars and wind, and a strange shifting luminous abyss of darkness. The edge of the sea.

This time I skidded the Mercedes in earnest. The wheel kicked like a live thing, and the dust mushroomed up behind us in an atomic cloud. We only missed hitting a rock with our off-front wheel because both off-side wheels were a foot from the ground.

Then we were round. There was blood on my bottom lip, but I was feeling good.

Then I realized that the left-handed swerve had helped Paul Véry to heave himself inboard at last. Cursing, half sobbing, he flung himself into the car, and, almost before I knew what had happened, he had scrambled into the front seat and was crouched beside me, thrusting a shaking hand into the pocket of his coat.

CHAPTER TWENTY-FIVE

In this heedless fury
He may show violence to cross himself.
I'll follow the event . . .

TOURNEUR

'Come on, you—,' he said, in an ugly voice. 'Pull her up, or you'll get it! I warned you I carried a gun!'

I didn't even glance at him. The second turning past Aiguebelle, I was thinking . . . by the big parasol pines. . . .

'In the belly,' said Paul Véry, and added a filthy word.

I laughed. I was as cool as lake-water, and, for the moment, no more ruffled. The feel of that lovely car under my hands, in all her power and splendour, was to me like the feel of a sword in the hand of a man who has been fighting unarmed. The Mercedes was my weapon now, and by God! I would use her. I knew just how frightened Paul Véry was: I had watched it all, the gradual stretching of his nerves . . . the savage excitement of his murderous assignment, the acute pleasure of baiting me, the speed, the anticipation of the final thrill . . . and then, this. The man's nerves were rasped naked. I had realized, watching him driving, that he was more than half afraid of his own speed. The delicious excitement of frightening himself, of terrifying me, had been half the thrill. No first-rate driver – I could hear Johnny telling me yet again – no first-rate driver is ever excited at speed. Driving, he would add, is just a job, and you can't afford to let your brain revv up along with your engine. Then he would give that little smile of his, and the hedges would accelerate past us into a long grey blur. *When you let excitement in,* Johnny would add, in a lecture-room sort of voice, *fear will follow.*

And fear was in the car with us now. I could hear it raw in his voice. I could smell the sweat of it.

And I had in my hands the weapon to break him with. If I could smash his nerve completely before we reached the parasol pines . . . if I could get that gun away from him. . . .

So I laughed, and drove my lovely shining sword slashing through the night.

'Put the thing away,' I said contemptuously. 'If you shoot me, what d'you suppose would happen to the car – and you?'

I heard his breath hiss, and thought for a moment that he was far enough gone to shoot without thinking. But he didn't. He merely cursed again, and moved up to me until I could feel something hard pressing against my body through my coat. It was shaking a little.

'I mean it,' he said hoarsely. 'I'll do you, you—! Pull in, I tell you, or I'll blow a hole in your guts and take the chance of stopping the car myself!'

We were on a long straight stretch of road. I drove my right foot hard down, and the Mercedes tore up the straight with a rising scream. The needle swung hard to the right and held there.

'Some chance,' I said derisively, 'but go ahead. It's Kramer's car, after all; and he's a fool to lend it you when he must know you're a lousy driver.'

The gun wavered. I heard him let out a quivering breath. 'If you tickle me with that thing at this speed,' I added, 'I can't answer for the consequences.'

The gun withdrew. Ahead, the road curved, and I let my foot up a bit. Above the roar of the overdrive I heard him begin to curse again . . . 'If I'd guessed you knew, you—, if I'd guessed—' he said between his teeth, and told me what he would have liked to do to me. He was speaking in French, and gutter-French at that, so I missed a good deal of it, but I had to stop it somehow, before it took my mind off the road.

I cut across the stream of filth. 'But it was obvious that I knew, monsieur.'

That shook him. 'How?'

My voice dripped contempt like an icicle. 'Do you really imagine that I'd have let you maul me about like that because I *liked* it? My dear Monsieur Véry, as a lover you'd hardly even pass the first test—'

Then he lurched at me. In lashing his precious vanity, I had gone too far. I thought he was going to shoot me and damn the consequences, but instead he lunged savagely at the wheel. I thought he had it, and that we would all go over the cliff; but he missed his grab, and fell against me, clawing at my legs.

I jerked the wheel, stamped on the brake, and sent the rear of the car round again in a left-handed skid. He was flung away from me against the side of the car.

'Keep your hands off me, please,' I told him, rather breathlessly, and straightened the Mercedes up.

He did not answer. He stayed slumped against the right-hand door of the car, breathing noisily through his throat. Poor Rommel, behind us, was whining with fear. I began to wonder just how much more assault and battery the tyres would stand.

And at that moment we roared by a fork in the road.

The first fork to the right. Not far to go. For the first time I glanced briefly at Paul Véry, and experienced a sense of shock at what I saw.

He, at least, had had as much assault and battery as his nerves could take. Gone was the immaculate Frenchman of the Tistet-Védène, gone the velvet-voiced Don Juan of the Mediterranean night; in their place huddled a man with twitching hands and a face shining with sweat. Nothing, not even fear, could strip Paul Véry of his extraordinary good looks, but, somehow, they had cheapened in front of my eyes: the man who sat there, staring in fascinated horror at the hurtling road, might have been brought up in any Paris gutter.

Formidable no longer. The power and competence that had seemed the very essence of the man had vanished: defeat – defeat by a woman – had knocked the props from under him. But he was still dangerous. The menace had not disappeared, it had only changed in quality. I was facing, instead of a powerful and relentless executioner, a mean and unpredictable thug.

What was more, I thought, a stupid thug. Only a stupid man, knowing how much I knew, would have talked to me as he had, taken the risks that he had taken, all for a moment's self-gratification. The significance of his final exchange with Kramer suddenly struck me: only a conceited fool would have forgotten, or pretended to forget, such information at such a moment. Paul Véry was a tool, and, up to a point, a good tool. But shake him out of his master's grip, and he was lost.

These speculations, flashing through my mind in the brief moment before I turned back to watch the road, effectively silenced any further attempts on my part to bait Paul Véry. In deliberately trying to crack his nerve, I had been running a far graver risk than I had known. He was, actually, quite stupid enough, in a moment of blind rage, to have shot me as I drove. The last incident had proved it, when, maddened by my mockery, he had flung himself at the wheel. If, at that moment, he had had his gun in his hand . . .

My heart gave a jerk in my breast, then seemed to tip over, sickeningly, and spill chilled blood down all my veins, so that even my fingers tingled. *If he had had his gun.*

Clearly, in imagination, I heard his voice again, as I had heard it in Kramer's office. '*Throw me my coat.*' Would he have spoken so carelessly if there had been a gun in the pocket? I remembered him standing, dark and handsome in his well-fitting suit, by the petrol pumps in Marseilles. No bulging pocket had spoiled the fit of that coat. . . .

I flashed a look at him as I lifted my foot a little. His eyes were fixed on the road.

I drew my left hand softly off the wheel, and, with a breath that was a prayer, felt down beside me. There was a pocket on the car door. I slipped my hand into it.

Cold, deadly, and infinitely comforting, the gun slid into my grasp.

And at that moment, like great grey clouds billowing in the furthermost tip of our beam of light, I saw the parasol pines.

CHAPTER TWENTY-SIX

We will die, all three

SHAKESPEARE

Like a flash, I cut out the headlights, but Paul Véry had seen them. I saw him stiffen, and shoot his neck out like a bird of prey.

There was only one thing to do. I must drive straight on past the turning, ditch my companion some way beyond, and then return to deal with André alone. It seems odd that it never occurred to me to shoot Paul Véry – though perhaps not; I had never handled a gun in my life.

'Listen to me,' I said rapidly. We were nearly there. The pines stood back from the road, making a great grove like a tent. 'I've got—'

But I was too late. Even as I spoke the first of the great trees loomed over the car, shutting out the stars, and our dimmed lights had picked out the shape of a van, parked on the beaten dust a little way ahead, and, beside the van, the figure of a man. André, who was a bit of a fool, had not parked out of sight.

Paul Very let out a yell: '*André! Ici Jean! Au secours!*'

I switched the headlights full on, and trod on the accelerator. The beam of light shot out, catching the man who ran forward under the cover of the pines.

It was Marsden. He had a gun in his hand.

'*A moi! André!*' yelled Paul Véry. He was standing, leaning forward, half out of the car.

Marsden had reached the edge of the road. Was in the road. I put a fist down on the klaxon, and my foot hard down on the boards, and, with a little sob of pure terror, I drove that ton or so of murderous, screaming metal straight at him.

I saw him jump; at least, I think I did, but the next few seconds were just a terrifying blur. I remember Marsden's face, white in the roaring light; his mouth was a gaping hole; he was yelling. There was a scarlet stab of flame: another. Then the car hit something, and the whole world heeled over in a rocketing, exploding skid. The Mercedes seemed to rear straight up in the air, and her headlights raked a dizzy arc of sky. Then they went out, and darkness stamped down on us as a man stamps on a beetle. Clinging to that crazily kicking wheel, blinded, half-stunned, wholly automatic, I fought the car. For a moment I thought I had her, then she swept into a bucketing turn. The night split, wheeled, hung suspended for a million years, then shattered into splinters of flame. Then silence, broken only by the tinkle of falling glass.

There was a shout, a thud of feet running. The door of the Mercedes was wrenched open, and hands seized me out of the darkness.

There was a roaring in my ears. The night, the stars, were spiralling down an enormous, narrowing funnel. Somewhere, far down the gyroscope, I heard a rough exclamation, then another shout – voices, urgent, sharp with something that might have been fear. Hands moved over me, patting, searching. Someone had hold of my head, and was forcing liquid between my teeth.

I choked, gasped, stirred, and the gyrating universe whirred slowly to a standstill, re-focusing itself around me. The stars steadied themselves, and hung, only faintly tremulous, in a still pall of sky. There were two men beside the car. One was holding me; the other bent over me in the darkness, peering down. His face blurred palely in front of me; it was Marsden. I was conscious, first of all, of a tremendous wave of pure relief; I hadn't killed him after all. Then I began to struggle feebly against the arms that held me.

'I've got a gun,' I said firmly.

Amazingly, somebody laughed, and the arms tightened.

'Lie still, you little fire-eater. Haven't you done enough for one night?'

I turned my head and blinked stupidly.

'*Richard!* But – but you're tied up in the van. I was going to rescue you.'

He laughed again, a little shakenly. 'Yes, I know, my darling. But there's no need to run over the police in the process.'

'*Police?*'

Marsden was grinning down at me. 'Strictly unofficial, madam. But Scotland Yard in person!'

'I – I'm awfully sorry,' I said feebly. 'I thought you were André. One of *them*, anyway. And you shot at me, didn't you?'

'We both did,' said Marsden ruefully. 'I knew it was Kramer's car, and I thought he'd seen me and was getting away.'

'But he was yelling for help.'

'My French isn't all that good,' said Marsden simply, 'and I couldn't really hear him anyway. There wasn't a great deal of time to think, you know.'

Richard spoke. 'Can you move all right, Charity? You'd better get out of the car. It's in a rather uncertain position, to say the least.'

I sat up out of his arms and felt my limbs gingerly.

'I think I'm all right.' With their assistance I climbed out of the Mercedes. Now that my eyes were accustomed to the darkness I could see quite clearly in the starlight. The car had skidded clean off the main road, and had ended up some yards down the track on the right, facing the way I had come. She was standing, decorously enough, on the seaward verge of the track, and for a moment I could not see what Richard meant. Then I saw. The night swayed perilously, and I was glad of the support of Richard's arm. The edge of the little road was the edge of the cliffs. A yard beyond the near-wheels of the car, the ground dropped sheer to the sea, three hundred feet below.

'I – I had some luck, didn't I?' I said shakily. 'What did we hit?'

'Nothing. Marsden got one of your front tyres. You turned round twice and skated backwards down here. The car's not even dented – except for a headlamp. I did that.'

I pushed my hair back from my forehead, and took a deep breath of the sweet night air. Things had steadied round me, and I felt a good deal more normal. Richard and Marsden were gently urging me across the road and under cover of the trees.

'It sounds like some very pretty shooting,' I said, then memory flooded back. 'David!' I cried. 'Where's David?'

'He's all right; he's still asleep. He's safe in a ditch a hundred yards or so away; we moved him from the danger zone.'

'And – and Paul Véry?'

'Alive,' said Marsden grimly. 'He's unconscious, and of course I don't know how badly he may be hurt. I haven't looked yet. He didn't look too good. Byron got him out of the car; he's lying behind it. I'll go back and have a look at him in a minute.'

'Right,' said Richard, 'but we'd better let Charity put us in the picture quickly, in case things start to move again. What were you doing in Kramer's car with that man? And where's Kramer? Marsden said Kramer was going to follow the van out.

'Kramer's coming,' I said. 'He and Loraine are following in your car. It was to be sent over the cliff with you and David in it, Richard.'

'My car, eh?' His voice was hard. 'We might have thought of that, Marsden. And I suppose that thug I laid out just now is Loraine's real husband?'

'Yes.'

'The man who murdered Tony and hit David . . .' His expression was ugly, but it changed as we reached the shelter of the trees and he spoke to me again: 'Are you sure you're all right?' He made me sit down behind an enormous double-trunked tree, with the van between me and the road.

'Yes, perfectly. Don't worry about me. Go and – oh!' My hand flew to my mouth. 'Rommel!' I said aghast.

'What?' Richard's voice was blank.

'Rommel, the dog. He was in the back of the car. I'll never forgive myself if he's hurt.'

'There wasn't any dog in the back of the car.'

'But there must have been—'

'I assure you there wasn't.'

I was on my feet, steadying myself by the trunk of one of the trees.

'He must have been thrown out. He'll be lying around somewhere. Perhaps he's hurt—'

His hand steadied me. We'll look presently. Now sit down again. Have some more brandy.'

'No, thank you.'

'Come on; do as you're told.'

I obeyed him. 'You seem to spend a lot of time forcing spirits down my throat, Richard.'

He corked the flask and put it down beside me. 'You seem a lot more worried about this dog than you do about friend Paul.'

'It's David's dog. Besides, Paul Véry ran over a rabbit,' I added, as if that explained everything.

'What—' began Richard, then checked himself and spoke rapidly: 'Now listen. Only Kramer and Loraine are coming in my car?'

'As far as I know.'

'How far behind you?'

'I don't know. He had to go to your garage first to get the car.'

'I see . . . well, that wasn't very far. You came fast, I take it?'

'Pretty fast, yes. We did stop once on the road; that wasted about five minutes, I'd say.'

'Did you indeed? What for?'

'A spot of love-making,' I said levelly.

'I – see.' He was silent for a moment. 'Of course. That was when you changed places, I suppose?'

'Yes. But Richard, tell me what's happened? This man Marsden—'

'Later. Listen; as things have turned out, we've every chance of winning. They'll stop when they see the van and the Mercedes, and we're two men armed, with surprise on our side. It'll be all right in a very short time, you'll see.'

'What are you going to do?'

He gave a little laugh. 'I've no idea. No doubt inspiration will come in the moment of crisis.'

'Where's Mr. Marsden?'

'Gone to take a look at our friend Paul . . . *listen, is that a car?*'

We froze, straining our ears through the myriad noises of the night's silence. I became conscious of the whispering of the sea; not the breathing, bell-tolling, ebbing-and-flowing sorrow of the northern tides I knew, but the long, murmurous *hush-hush* of the land-bound waters. And above us sang the pines.

'No,' I said presently in a low voice. 'I can't hear a car.'

He stayed for a while with his head cocked to listen, then he relaxed, and I saw the faint gleam of a gun as he turned it over in his hand.

'There was a gun in the car,' I said quickly. 'I had it on my knee when we skidded. If we can find it that makes three of us—'

'No.' His voice was flat. 'Indeed it doesn't. You'll stay behind the lines, lady – in the trenches, in fact.' I saw his arm lift, and point inland. 'About forty yards back of these trees there's a rocky bank, with a dry gully beyond it. David's there. You'll wait with him, please.'

I opened my mouth to protest, but at that moment Marsden interrupted us, looming suddenly out of the darkness.

'He's still unconscious,' he said in a rapid undertone, 'but nothing seems to be broken. We'll bring him over here, to be on the safe side, and tie him up in the van. We don't want to take the risk that they'll see him lying there, and be warned before they stop that there's something wrong. Is there any rope left?'

'I doubt it.' Richard was on his feet, and the two of them were moving about the van. 'I think we used all there was.'

I felt an absurd desire to laugh. 'On André?'

'Mmm?' Marsden's voice was muffled. He seemed to be investigating a tool-box. 'André? Who's he?'

'The driver of the van.'

'Oh. Yes. He's tied up in there. He's all right.'

Richard spoke softly from inside the van: 'Nothing here. Charity, is there a belt on your coat?'

'No.'

'Oh hell.' He landed beside me, soft-footed on the pine-needles. 'This is beginning to have all the elements of farce, isn't it? Too many villains, and nothing to tie them up with. And for the life of me I daren't give you my trouser-belt.'

'I doubt if he'll give much trouble,' said Marsden, 'but I'd rather be sure. There may be a rope in the boot of the car. Coming, Byron? We'll go and get him.'

'O.K.,' said Richard. 'Charity, if you hear a car, get back to that gully and stay with David till we come for you.'

'Yes, Richard,' I said meekly.

But Marsden was made of sterner stuff. 'I found a gun in the Mercedes. Perhaps she—'

'No,' said Richard once more, finally. 'Both you and I have had a pot at her to-night, and Kramer might be luckier.'

'Beautifully put,' I said, and Marsden laughed.

'Let's go.'

They had barely taken two paces when I was on my feet, backed against my tree, all my brittle self-confidence in fragments.

'There it is!' I said hoarsely. 'Listen!'

Through the ghostly song of the pines, through the secret breathing of the sea, we heard it, faint but unmistakable; the throb of an engine.

'Blast!' said Marsden softly.

'And coming at a wicked pace,' said Richard, and listened a moment longer. My heart was beating to suffocation. 'That's my car all right, damn him . . . Charity, please.'

'I'm going.' My voice, like my body, was shaking. I had to push myself away from the solid comfort of the pine-tree's bole. I was vaguely aware of the two men, moving like shadows in the cover of the van. I ran away from the road, through the trees. The Bentley's engine cut through the silence in a rising drone, urgent, *crescendo.* I was free of the pines, and dodging through head-high scrub. In front loomed a dark mass that might be the rocky bank. The Bentley was coming fast, her engine snarling on a wasp-note of anger ... I reached the foot of the rocky bank, and stopped. I could not go on. I suppose it was delayed shock, or something, but I know that I was stuck there, shaking and sweating and cold as ice, staring back through the leaves and the pine-trunks, towards the road. ·

I saw the glare of the Bentley's lights, cutting along the darkness of the cliff-top. The sound of her engine swelled suddenly as she rounded the curve half a mile away. The parasol pines soared again like great thunderhead clouds in the moving light.

The headlamps went out, and the Bentley swooped towards us in the little glow of her side-lights, confident, menacing – the tiger coming in to kill. He had seen the parasol pines; I heard his brakes grip momentarily as he swept into the last stretch of road. Any minute now he would see the van, and stop. The Bentley's snarl deepened. She was on us, moving fast. She was swinging right-handed into the track.

Then the night was ripped, unbelievably, by the roar of another engine. The Mercedes.

I don't remember moving at all, but I must have run towards the road like a mad thing. I only knew that Paul Véry had come round; had somehow got into the Mercedes, and was giving his warning.

I saw the Bentley veer into the track on the cliff-top, I heard the shriek of her brakes. I saw the Mercedes, roaring like a bomber, leap forward, then lurch on to her burst front tyre, and plunge broadside on across the road.

The Bentley never had a chance.

There was a yell, a dreadful scream, and then the cars met in a sickening crash of rending metal and shrieking tyres. Some hideous freak of chance knocked the Bentley's switch as she struck, so that, for one everlasting moment, as the two cars locked in a rearing tower of metal, her headlights shot skywards like great jets of flame. The cars hung there, black against the black sky, locked on the very brink of that awful cliff, then the beam swung over in a great flashing arc, and the locked cars dropped like a plummet down the shaft of a lift, straight into the sea.

And after that last appalling impact, silence, broken hideously by echo after echo of the sound, as the disturbed sea washed and broke, washed and broke, against the cliff below. For an age, it seemed, the agitated waves beat their terrible reiteration on the rock, till, spent at last, they sank and smoothed themselves to their old whispering.

The last clouds shifted, parted, broke under the wind, and the moonlight fell, infinitely pure, infinitely gentle, to whiten the moving water.

CHAPTER TWENTY-SEVEN

O most delicate fiend!
Who is't can read a woman?

SHAKESPEARE

David was still asleep. I had gone to find him, leaving the two men looking for a way down the cliff. They had driven the van across the road on to the track, switched on its lights, and turned it to face the sea. There was not a chance in a million, Marsden said, that any of the three in the cars was still alive, but we could hardly leave the place without attempting to find out.

With a shudder, I left them to it, and made my way back through the trees to look for David. As I emerged at the top of the rocky bank, I found that I could see my way plainly in the moonlight. Below me, in sharply shadowed monochrome, lay the gully; under a jut of rock and leafage, a darker shadow stirred. I scrambled down hurriedly, to be met by a shapeless shade that whined a little and wriggled with a somewhat subdued delight.

'Rommel!' I went down on my knees in the dust and hugged him. 'Oh Rommel! Did I nearly kill you, poor boy?'

Rommel lavished me with generous but damp forgiveness, and then ran, with a yelp of excitement, into the shelter of the rock. I followed.

David lay curled up, wrapped in a coat. He looked very young and touching, and the sweep of his dark lashes over his cheek was so like Richard's that I felt a sudden rush of some emotion stronger than any I had ever felt before. I knelt down again, beside him, and felt his hands; they were cold. I put a hand to his cheek, and was horrified to feel it wet to the touch, as if with sweat, but immediately Rommel, feverishly licking the other cheek, provided the clue. I pushed him off.

'It was very clever of you to find him,' I told him, 'but wait a minute, will you?'

I gathered David up close to me, and began to rub the cold hands, Rommel, pressing close with quivering body, watched eagerly.

And presently the dark lashes stirred, and lifted. He stared at me blankly, and his hands moved a little under mine.

'Hullo, David,' I said.

The wide gaze flickered. 'Mrs. – Selborne?'

'Yes. How d'you feel?'

'Pretty foul.' He moved his head gingerly, and blinked up at the moonlit bank with the great pines billowing beyond. 'Where am I?'

'Some way east of Marseilles. But don't worry. Everything's all right now.'

His eyes were on me again, with a look in them I couldn't quite fathom. I felt him move away from me a little. 'I remember now . . . Marseilles. How did you get here?'

I understood then. I reached out a hand and took hold of his. 'David, I tell you it's all right. I'm *not* one of them; you can trust me. I followed you out here – Rommel and I did, that is—'

'Rommel?'

He turned at that, and his eye fell for the first time on the dog, who, belly to earth, shivering with delight in every hair, was waiting to be noticed.

'He found you all by himself,' I said. 'Tracked you down.'

'Oh, *Rommel!*' said the boy, and burst into tears, with his head buried deep in the dog's fur, and his arms round its neck. I let him cry out his fright and loneliness and distrust, while Rommel administered comfort, but presently the sobs changed to hiccups, and a voice said uncompromisingly from Rommel's neck: 'I feel beastly sick.'

'I'm not surprised,' I said. 'It'll do you good. Don't mind me. . . .'

Some short time later, after a nasty little interlude, he came back and sat down beside me. I put my coat round him, and held him close. I was wondering how on earth to begin telling him about Richard.

'You'd better have a drop of this.'

'What is it?'

It was Richard's flask. 'Brandy.'

'Oh!' He was palpably pleased. '*Real* brandy? . . . ugh, it's horrible!'

'I know, but it's fine when it gets a bit further down. Have some more.'

'No, thanks. I feel all right, only hungry.'

'Great heavens!'

'What are we doing here anyway?' he demanded. 'What happened? I want to *know*. Are we—?'

'One thing at a time. We're waiting here for – for transport back to Marseilles.'

He spoke quickly, apprehensively: 'Marseilles? That shop? I don't want—'

'Not to the shop,' I said reassuringly. 'That's all over. The owner of that place has been dealt with. Will you tell me what happened there, or don't you want to talk about it?'

'I hardly remember. I took the bracelet in, and he looked at it, and then asked me where I got it. He looked so queerly at me that I thought he guessed I'd pinched it, and so I made up a few lies. He seemed all right then, and asked me into the office. He went to a drawer; I thought he was getting the money. But he turned round with a towel or something in his hand. I – I don't really remember what happened then.'

'Chloroform, I think.' The smell was still there very faintly, sweet and horrible. Kramer must have recognized him at once, I thought. Probably Loraine had rung up as soon as he was missing, and told her employer about the bracelet. My arm tightened round him. 'What on earth made you choose *that* shop, of all the shops in France?'

'Well, I had no money,' said David, 'and that beastly bracelet was all I could find. I thought Marseilles was the only place hereabouts where I could sell a thing like that and no questions asked, so I hitch-hiked here. It took *ages*. I took the bracelet into two or three places, but they wouldn't buy it. In the end one chap told me to go to that shop. He said the man was a dealer in silver and he'd probably take it.' He gave a little shudder, and burrowed his head against my shoulder.

'What were you planning to do after you'd got the money?'

'Eat.' The answer was prompt and emphatic.

I looked down at him. 'You poor wretch! D'you mean to tell me you've had nothing all day?'

'I had lunch with some lorry-drivers, but nothing since then.'

'Oh dear! And I had some chocolate in my bag, but I lost it. The only consolation is that you'd have been a lot sicker if you'd been chloroformed on top of a good meal. I dare say it won't be very long before you'll get something.' I lifted my head to listen, but there was no sound except the sighing of the pines. 'And after you'd eaten, David, what were you going to do then?'

'I was going back to Nîmes to look for Daddy.'

I was startled, and showed it. 'To look for *your father?*'

He gave me a slightly shamefaced look. 'Yes. It was really because you went away from the hotel that I decided to go.'

'I don't get it.'

'That day in Nîmes – you remember? – when we ran away from my father, and I told you I was afraid of him. . . . Well, it wasn't true.'

I began to sort out my ideas all over again. 'You never really thought he was mad? You weren't ever really afraid of him at all?'

David said, with scorn: 'Of course not. Afraid of *him?* I'd never be afraid of him as long as I lived!'

I said, helplessly: 'Then for heaven's sake explain! I can't get this straight. You *said* you didn't want to meet him; you *said* it was a matter of life and death, and you said he was mad. And you did look afraid; you looked scared stiff. Now, what's it all about?'

'I was afraid,' he said sombrely, 'terribly afraid, but *for* him, not *of* him. I'll try and tell you. . . . Shall I just begin at the beginning?'

'Please.'

He began to talk, in a clear little voice completely empty of emotion. It was a queer experience to hear the same beastly story of the night of murder and treachery, so soon retold in the voice of a child. It differed from Richard's in nothing but point of view.

'. . . And when I heard he'd been acquitted, I knew he would come down to Deepings straight away. But he didn't. I waited and waited, and then the police telephoned Mrs. Hutchings – that's the housekeeper – that Daddy'd had an accident, and was badly hurt. He'd been taken to hospital, they said. Of course I wanted to go and see him, but they said he was still unconscious, and I must wait. Then, quite late, *she* came.'

The pitch of his voice never changed, but suddenly, shockingly, I was aware of the cold hatred underneath it. Then, as he went on, I began to realize that David's story was more terrible, even, than Richard's.

'She came to my room. I wasn't asleep, of course. She told me she'd been to the hospital. She broke it ever so gently, you know, but – she told me Daddy had died. What did you say?'

'Nothing. Go on. *She told you your father was dead?*'

'She did. She also told me it was no use going to the hospital; she said I'd not be able to see him, because he'd been too badly burned. Of course,' said David, his mouth half buried somewhere near Rommel's right ear, 'I wasn't exactly *thinking* straight, you know. I didn't really want to go away with her, but I couldn't stick Deepings just then, and anyway, what could I do? Daddy was dead, and she was my step-mother, and I more or less thought I had to do as she said. There's not much you can do if you're only a boy, and besides, I'd not had much practice in thinking things out for myself, *then*. I have now.'

'I know that,' I said bitterly.

David went on: 'She'd taken a flat up near the Bois, and we lived there. She was quite decent to me, as I thought, and I was so dashed unhappy anyway that I didn't care what happened. I suppose I just moped around the place. I found Rommel one day in the Bois, with a can tied to his tail. After that it was better.'

I said, a little grimly: 'What happened next?'

'About three weeks ago, she told me Daddy was still alive.'

'How on earth did she explain away her lie about his death?'

'She told me she'd done it for my sake.' The grey eyes lifted to mine for a moment: they were quite expressionless. 'She said that, according to the reports she'd had from the doctors and the police, Daddy had tried to commit suicide.'

'David!'

'Yes. She implied, of course, that he *had* done that awful murder, and that it had been preying on his mind. Oh,' said David, with a large gesture, 'she spared me all she could. She said that he'd been going queerer and queerer for some time, and that he must have killed Uncle Tony – *and* knocked me down – in a sort of blackout. She prescribed it to – is that the word?'

'Ascribed.'

'Oh. She ascribed it to his terrible experiences during the War. Why did you laugh?'

'There's a certain irony in that,' I said, 'but it doesn't matter.'

'Well,' said David, 'that was her story. He was batty, and he was dangerous, so she'd removed me from the trouble zone.'

'Did you believe it?'

'No, I knew he wasn't mad; I knew he hadn't killed Uncle Tony; and of course I knew he hadn't hit me. I also knew for certain that he hadn't meant to crash his car and commit suicide, because he'd rung me up from London as soon as he got out of Court, and told me he was coming straight down.'

'Did you tell her that?'

'No.' He looked at me. 'I can't quite explain it, Mrs. Selborne, but I began to get more and more strongly the feeling that I ought to keep things to myself. There was something so – well, sort of queer and *wrong* about the whole set-up. Some of the things she said, the way she looked at me sometimes – the very fact that she'd taken me away with her when I was certain she disliked me anyway – oh! lots of things seemed odd. And now all this talk about father: I was certain that she didn't think he was mad, either. And of course nothing could excuse the lie she'd told about his death.' He paused.

'Why didn't you write to your father? Surely that—'

'It was the first thing I thought of, of course. But there was a catch in it, Mrs. Selborne. There were two chaps in the flat below – she said they were her cousins – and they were with us all the time. I never got a minute to myself. I couldn't have got a letter to him without them knowing, and reading it. What's more, she seemed to *want* me to write to him, and that was quite enough, at the time, to make me think twice about it.'

'She wanted you to ask him to come and see you?'

'Exactly.' His tone was a quaint echo of Richard's. 'She said she couldn't possibly let me go back to England till we saw how he was, and she suggested I write and ask him to come to France. She'd have read the letter; there was no question of my being able to tell him what the set-up was, and ask him what had really happened at his end. She went on and on about my writing to invite him, and in such a funny way that I got suspicious again, and just refused. I pretended that I'd believed her story about his being mad, and that I was frightened to see him.' He gave a dry little chuckle. 'Gosh! she was furious, being hoist in her own juice like that. Is that right? It sounds a bit odd.'

'I rather think you mean stewing with her own petard. But let it pass. I get it. She wrote to him herself in the end, you know.'

He shot me another look. 'Yes, I did know. I telephoned him one night.'

'You did? But—'

'He wasn't there. I – I was pretty disappointed. I managed to sneak down one night and phone from the cousins' flat while they were with *her*. Mrs. Hutchings answered. She said Daddy'd had a letter marked *Paris* that morning, and he'd left straight away. I said how was he, and she told me he was all right, but just worried to death, and only just out of hospital anyway. . . . The cousins caught me on the way up from the phone. I spun them a lie, but they didn't believe me, and after that I was never left alone. Next morning we all went to Lyons, and then, stage by stage, down here. It puzzled me no end, till I began to think they wanted Daddy down here, instead of in Paris. And I could only think that it was still something to do with that murder, and that they'd harm him.'

'A trap,' I said, 'with you as bait.'

'Exactly,' he said again. 'So I wasn't going to get into touch with Daddy just to lure him in; I wanted to be quite sure, first, that it was safe. The queer thing was that the cousins left us at Montélimar, and when we were in Avignon, she let me go round alone. . . .'

'She didn't,' I said, thinking of Paul Véry. 'Someone else had taken over. You were accompanied all the time.'

'*Was* I? Then I was right to run away in Nîmes?'

'Very probably.'

He spoke slowly, in an unconscious echo of his father's own bewilderment: 'It was pretty awful, not knowing what to do – not knowing whether people were enemies, or just ordinary people. It was as if' – he gave a little shiver – 'as if everything was upside down.' He shivered again.

'It's over now,' I said firmly. 'If you're cold, come under my coat again.'

'I'm not, really. I want to know what's happened, and how you know all this. I say, do we *have* to stay here, Mrs. Selborne? This "transport" you mentioned—'

'Is here now,' I said, and got to my feet. I could hear footsteps scrambling up the further side of the bank. David jumped up, looking a little scared, and Rommel bristled.

'Who—?'

Richard swung himself down the slope, and stood there in the moonlight, looking at his son. He hesitated a little, then put out a hand.

There was a rush of feet past me, and David hurtled into the moonlight like an arrow going into the gold. I saw his father's arms close round him, and the dark heads close together.

I went quickly past them, and Marsden's hand reached down to help me up the bank.

I looked a query at him.

He shook his head. 'Not a sign,' he said quietly.

We walked through the trees, towards the road where the van stood waiting, her nose towards Marseilles.

CHAPTER TWENTY-EIGHT

Two loves have I . . .

SHAKESPEARE

I woke to bright sunlight and a most delectable smell of coffee. Swimming up through the billows of a deep and dreamless sleep, I found myself blinking drowsily at the white walls and red-tiled floor of a room that was vaguely familiar. The sun blazed in bright bars through a closed shutter: the other had swung open, letting in a flood of gold. From outside the cries and clangs of the city rose musically, as if muted by the light.

The door had opened softly, letting in the lovely coffee smell that had roused me. I turned my head, then sat up, full awake.

'Louise!'

Immaculate as ever, she was standing just inside the door, looking speculatively at me across a loaded tray.

'So you are awake? Or did I disturb you? I thought it was high time—'

'Oh, Louise, how nice to see you! How did it happen? And what *is* the time?'

She set the tray on my knees, and went to open the shutter. 'High noon, my child.'

'Good Lord, is it really?' I poured coffee. 'When did you get here?'

'About an hour and a half ago. I got the first train.' She added, reasonably: 'You said you were in a jam, and I knew you hadn't any clothes with you.'

'My *dear*,' I said gratefully, 'don't tell me you've brought my clothes! I knew you were the most wonderful woman in the world.'

She laughed. 'No one can face a crisis unless they're suitably clad. How do you feel?'

'Fine – I think.' I stretched a few muscles gingerly, and was relieved. 'A bit stiff, and a bruise here or there, but otherwise' – I smiled at her – 'on top of the world.'

'Mmmm. . . .' Louise eyed me as she pulled an unsteady-looking wicker chair to the bedside. 'Ye-es. Your ghastly village seems to have been a pretty exciting place after all. What happened to you?'

I chuckled through a bite of *croissant*, aware of a miraculous spring-time lift of the heart, a champagne-tingling of the blood: the nightmare had gone; this fresh sun of morning rose on a different world where the last gossamer rag of fear and uncertainty must shrink and vanish in the superfluity of light. I said: 'I was – translated.'

'Yes. You look it. I suppose you met the Wolf of Orange?'

'In person,' I said happily.

'I thought so.' Her tone was bland. 'He rang up about half an hour ago. If you're feeling fit, we are to meet him for lunch at the Hôtel de la Garde. On the terrace, at one-fifteen. And now,' said Louise, settling herself in the wicker chair and regarding me placidly, 'I am dying by inches of curiosity, and I want to be told every single thing that has happened, including why this Richard Byron who is David Bristol's father and who I thought was a murderer anyway should be ringing you up in Marseilles and asking you to lunch, and why he should feel it necessary to inform me that neither he nor Mr. Marsden was in jail as yet and that Rommel had bitten André in the seat of the pants and that I was to let you sleep late and then take you some coffee and see you took a taxi to lunch as if' – finished Louise on a faintly accusing note – 'he had known you all your life instead of – how long?'

I said, in simple surprise: 'Three days . . . off and on.'

'And rather more off than on, at that,' said Louise, 'A dictatorial gentleman, I'd have said, at a guess.'

'He is a bit.' I stirred my coffee absorbedly.

'And you like it,' she accused me.

'I'm – well, I got used to it, you know. Johnny—'

'I know. No wonder you keep getting married and I don't,' said Louise, without rancour.

I coloured, and laughed a little. 'He hasn't asked me, as it happens.'

She merely raised a beautifully groomed eyebrow and handed me a cigarette.

'Well, come along, my girl. Tell me all about it.'

'It's a long story—'

'We've got an hour before we meet the Wolf. Go on: begin at the beginning, go on to the end, and then stop.'

'– and an utterly fantastic one.'

'I am all ears,' said Louise contentedly, and leaned back in her chair.

So I told her, lying back on the pillows in my little hotel room at the Belle Auberge, with the peaceful sunlight slanting across the coverlet, and the smoke from our cigarettes winding in placid spirals between us. I told her everything just as it had happened, and, like Paul Véry, she listened silently, only staring at me with a kind of shocked disbelief.

'We – ell,' she said at length, on a long note of amazement. 'What an extraordinary tale! Not, of course, that I believe a word of it, only—'

'You'd better ask the others,' I told her. 'Mr. Marsden said—'

Louise sat up. 'Yes! Now *that* I don't follow at all. What the dickens is John Marsden doing in this *galère* at all?'

It was my turn to raise an eyebrow. 'John?'

'After you left for Les Boos,' she said calmly, 'we got acquainted.'

'Well I'll be dashed,' I said. 'If I'd known that I'd have stopped suspecting him at once.'

'On the principle that all my men friends turn out to be Boy Scouts or curates on holiday,' agreed Louise. 'It certainly shook me to hear he's a great detective. Marsden of the C.I.D. Well, well. And he's very nice, even if he does read poetry. Go on. Did he tell you how he got to this awful place on the cliff?'

'Yes. He made it sound awfully simple. Apparently he was helping at first, this spring, in the investigation of Tony Baxter's murder. Richard, it turns out, had actually met him a couple of times, but didn't remember the name when I described Marsden to him. Well, Marsden was taken off to work on another big case, but he was interested in the Baxter murder, and the man in charge of it, Inspector Brooke, wasn't at all satisfied with the way the case finished. He came at length to believe, himself, that Richard hadn't done it; the murderer, therefore, must be still at large, possibly active, and the motive undiscovered. Richard's so-called car-accident shook him a good bit. Richard was safe in hospital, but Brooke began to wonder about Loraine, and to worry quite a lot about David.'

'Good for him.'

'Yes indeed. Well, Marsden was due for leave, and offered to do a spot of unofficial guardianship. He has friends at the Sûreté, and they said right, go ahead, so he came over to France to locate David.'

'Well, well,' said Louise. 'Then that's why he disappeared from the Tistet-Védène when David did.'

'Quite. I'd noticed him hanging round where David was, and imputed sinister motives to him. Well, to cut it short, he managed, with a good deal of difficulty, to get on to David's tail south to Marseilles. Apparently it took the poor child nearly all day to get here, as he felt obliged to hide at sight of every car, and the lorries were slow, and few and far between. But he got here, with Marsden faint but pursuing, and eventually landed in Kramer's beastly little shop.'

I glanced at my watch. 'I must get up soon. . . . Well, poor David was chloroformed – pretty heavily, too – while Marsden skulked about outside not knowing what had happened. I imagine that Kramer got busy on the telephone, then, to Avignon, and told Loraine to get onto the next train. Paul Véry must have left long before—'

'He did,' said Louise. 'He took his car out soon after lunch, ostensibly to look for David. The American couple did the same, and so did those two Germans. But Paul Véry didn't come back for dinner.'

'I've no doubt he did look for David,' I said, 'and probably passed him hiding in a ditch. He must either have telephoned Kramer later, and heard of David's capture, or have driven straight down here for orders; at any rate, Marsden says, he got here a good hour or so before Loraine. I saw him myself in the office when she landed in a taxi. Marsden was still hanging about waiting for David to leave the shop, when Paul Véry arrived, and turned into the garage opposite, just as if he'd lived there all his life. Marsden recognized him, and began to wonder just what was going on, so, when Paul Véry walked into the shop, and straight through into the office, Marsden, like me, found his way through to the back, and listened under the window. It must have been just about then,' I said meditatively, 'that Richard and I were sitting talking about four streets away. . . .'

'There seems to have been quite a procession into Kramer's parlour,' remarked Louise.

'Yes indeed.' I shuddered. 'Well, Marsden heard quite a bit under his window. He could tell that there were at least three men – Kramer and Jean-Paul and André – in the office, so, even when he learned what had happened to David, he couldn't do very much about it. His French was just good enough for him to realize they were planning to move David's body, so he didn't dare risk losing track of him by going to the police. He simply stuck around and hoped for a chance to grab David.'

'Poor John,' said Louise.

'He said it was hell,' I told her. 'He waited and waited, and they talked and talked, and then the door opened, and Richard walked in.'

'That must have been quite a moment.'

'Mustn't it? Richard of course, remembers nothing but the sight of David lying on a sofa. He started for him, and the three of them set on him straight away. Marsden, under the window, didn't see a thing, but he heard Richard say "David!" in English, and then the hullabaloo. Then Kramer said something about "putting them both in the van", so Marsden slipped across to the garage. He says he imagined they'd all three go with the van, and since his one thought was not to be left behind, he got inside it and hid under some sacks. But they dumped Richard and David in, locked the door on them, and Kramer told André to get out to that place on the coast, park under cover, and wait for him. Then he and Paul Véry went back to wait for Loraine. Marsden was furious. If he hadn't been locked in, he could have dealt with André then and there, and driven Richard and David straight off to the police-station. But he was stuck, so he lay low, untied Richard, and set about bringing him round.'

Louise sighed with satisfaction. 'So when poor André stopped the van and went to get the bodies—'

'Exactly. They knocked him cold, tied him up, and took his gun. They even took his coat to wrap David in. On the whole,' I said, 'I'm a little sorry for André. Kramer said he was a bit of a fool.'

Louise laughed. 'And now Rommel's bit him. Poor André.'

I pushed back the coverlet and got out of bed. 'Poor Rommel, you mean. He's had a lot to bear. David left him outside the shop, and the poor dog must have waited for centuries. He found his way round to the back streets in the end, and that's where I picked him up. Did you say something about bringing me some clothes?'

'They're in my room. I'll get them; I didn't want to wake you before.' She smiled at me as she rose. 'What a good thing I brought your very nicest dress!'

'*Not* the Mexican print?' I said gratefully. 'Dear Louise, you shall be my bridesmaid *again*.'

'Not on your life,' said Louise. 'It's unlucky, and anyway, I'm too old. I'll wait and be godmother.'

'You're a little premature,' I said.

'So I should hope,' said Louise, making for the door. She turned, and her sleek brows mocked me again. 'So are you, aren't you?'

'I?'

'Yes. He hasn't even asked you.'

The door shut gently behind her.

As I lifted my dress from the case Louise had brought, I saw the silver photograph-frame underneath. Johnny's eyes smiled up at me.

I picked up the photograph, and was looking down at the pictured face, when the fading bruise on my wrist caught, as it were, at the edge of my vision.

I smiled back at Johnny. Then I held my wrist very lightly against my cheek. Any hesitations I had had, all the doubts that my intellect had been placing in front of my heart, seemed, with the rest of the nightmare adventure, to resolve themselves and fade away. Past and future dovetailed into this moment, and together made the pattern of my life. I would never again miss Johnny, with that deep dull aching, as if part of me had been wrenched away, and the scar left wincing with the cold; but, paradoxically enough, now that I was whole again, Johnny was nearer to me than he had ever been since the last time that we had been together, the night before he went away. I was whole again, and Johnny was there for ever, part of me always. Because I had found Richard, I would never lose Johnny. Whatever I knew of life and loving had been Johnny's gift, and without it Richard and I would be the poorer. We were both his debtors, now and for ever.

I lifted Johnny's photograph and kissed it. It was the last time I should ever do so. Then I laid it gently back in the case, and picked up my dress again.

A short time later I opened my door, called Louise, and went out into the sunshine to meet Richard.

CHAPTER TWENTY-NINE

O frabjous day!

CARROLL

The terrace of the Hôtel de la Garde almost overhangs the edge of the sea. It is wide, and flagged with white stone, with beautifully formal little orange-trees in pots to give it shade, and a breeze straight off the Mediterranean to cool it. The bright little boats bob, scarlet and green and white, just below your table, and the *bouillabaisse* is wonderful.

We were a gay enough party. Richard and Marsden had spent the greater part of the night and morning with the police, and both looked tired, but about the former I noticed something I had not seen in him before; he was relaxed. The last of the strain had been lifted, and though his eyes were weary, they were clear, and his mouth had lost its hardness. As for David, he was in tearing spirits, and kept us all laughing until coffee and cigarettes came round.

Marsden got out his pipe and settled back in his chair with a long sigh of satisfaction. He, too, looked as if some strain were lifted, but with him it was rather a slackening of concentration, a putting, so to speak, of his intelligence into carpet slippers for a while. He had come off duty.

His blue eyes studied me over the match-flame as he held it to his pipe. At last this was going nicely.

'If I may say so, Mrs. Selborne,' he said, 'you've come out of this affair looking remarkably fit. How do you feel to-day?'

'Fine, thank you,' I said. 'Nothing to show but a few bruises.' I caught Richard's rueful grin, and smiled back. 'How restful it is, isn't it, now that everybody knows whose side they're on?'

'It certainly is,' agreed Marsden. He cocked an eye at Louise. 'I take it you've put Louise in the picture?'

'She told me the whole story,' said Louise, 'except for the most important thing – the reason for it all. That was just guesswork. Have you found out anything further about *why* Kramer employed those two to do the murders?'

'Our guesswork was right,' said Richard. 'The police searched Kramer's premises this morning, and there's evidence galore. The whole thing is clear enough now.'

'Tell us, please,' I said.

'I'll try.' He flicked the ash from his cigarette into the sea, then stared thoughtfully at the tip of it for a moment, before he spoke.

'We were right,' he said, looking at me. 'It all began on that beastly January day in 1944, when Tony Baxter and I, on our way to a prison camp, were witnesses to Kramer's murder of Emmanuel Bernstein – and, incidentally, to his connection with the mass-murder of the Jews.' He glanced at Louise. 'Did Charity tell you about that?'

'Yes. What a beastly affair! I don't wonder you lost your temper and blew up.'

Richard's eyes met mine. 'I do, sometimes,' he admitted. 'It's a fault I have. But this time Tony did as well. I'm glad of that, because if I'd been solely responsible for attracting Kramer's notice I'd feel a very heavy burden of guilt for Tony's death. As it is' – his face darkened for an instant, but he resumed in a normal tone: 'Well, you know what happened; we were eventually permitted to go, but Kramer had occasion to remember us, and his memory was excellent.'

He paused. 'That wouldn't have mattered at all, of course, if it hadn't been for the next connection between us: both Kramer and I were in the same line of business, the trade in antiques, and both, as it happens, particularly interested in old silver. When the War finished, and the Nuremburg witch-hunt started, Kramer somehow or other managed to disappear. He got out of Germany, and appeared in France as an Austrian refugee, one Karel Werfel. He had managed to salt away a pleasant little fortune in money and loot, and before long he was doing very nicely, with his headquarters in Paris, and branches in Lyons and Marseilles. I should mention here, perhaps, something that we found out this morning. Loraine was his' – his gaze fell on David, wide-eyed and absorbed – 'Loraine was with Kramer for a time immediately after the War.' Richard's voice was sombre, tinged with a kind of pity. 'She had a bad record; she was suspected of collaboration, and of having a hand in the murder of two French officers. Kramer helped her to avoid the consequences, but kept the proof himself and used it to gain a hold over her.'

He stubbed out his cigarette. 'By the time Tony and I appeared again on his horizon, Max Kramer had a lot to lose. He had this perfectly genuine and lucrative business, but he also had other business, even more lucrative, and highly criminal, for which the antique trade was a cloak. His real headquarters for that was here, in Marseilles. I'm not quite sure just what rackets he was concerned in, but at the moment the Marseilles police are having a fine old time rounding up some of the people whose names were in Kramer's safe. There hardly seems to be any pie he didn't have a finger in – smuggling, dope-running, and so forth, but the most important thing that came to light when his premises were searched is definite evidence that he's been mixed up in some of these underground movements to upset the present German government and bring back the National Socialists.'

'You mean those gangs of Neo-Hitlerites? Were-wolves, or whatever they called themselves?' asked Louise.

'Something like that.' It was Marsden who answered her. 'His genuine business, with its wide trade contracts, and the necessity for a good deal of foreign travel, made an excellent mask for the centre of a widish organization. The police think now that Kramer – or Werfel – was at the back of a good deal of organized thuggery, sabotage, and what-have-you in Germany and Northern France shortly after the end of the War. Go on, Byron.'

'Well, into this comfortable and prosperous picture,' resumed Richard, 'came, suddenly, Tony and myself. There was a big sale in Paris, for the disposal of the Lemaire collection of silver, and naturally I was there. Kramer, apparently, was there too, and must have seen us, though neither of us noticed him. But he made enquiries, and discovered that I was in the same line of country as himself, and had, in fact, opened an office in Paris. We were bound to meet. And if Tony or I recognized him, well' – his gesture was eloquent – 'even if he escaped a war crimes tribunal, there would be enquiries, and he couldn't afford the least investigation. It would be the end of Karel Werfel....'

'It was a pretty frightful coincidence, wasn't it.' said Louise, 'that David should have gone to *Kramer's* shop to sell the bracelet?'

'Frightful,' agreed Richard, 'but not so much of a coincidence, if you think it over. The thread that runs through the whole story, after all, is the antique-business: if Kramer and I hadn't happened to be in the same line of country, we would probably never have met after the War – and certainly the danger of our meeting more than once would have been slight. But we were both interested in the same thing, and would in all likelihood be thrown together again and again: and *that* Kramer dared not risk. Yes, the whole *raison d'être* of the affair, you might say, was "old silver", and the bracelet would almost inevitably act as a link. I bought it for Loraine; Loraine brought it – and David and me – down into Kramer's country: once David tried to sell such a thing hereabouts it was almost certain to come to Kramer's notice pretty soon. And that's what happened; David was advised to take it to him to get an opinion on its value. No, the coincidence lies in the fact that I saw the thing in the shop-window when I did; but that was just Kramer's luck. I was supposed to be got into his den sooner or later, it just happened to be sooner.'

'Paul Véry,' I said, as he stopped. 'Where did he come in?'

'He had a criminal record as long as your arm,' said Marsden cheerfully, 'and half a dozen aliases. Kramer had enough tucked away in his safe to send Paul Véry to Devil's Island for several lifers.'

'He must have promised to hand the papers over to Loraine and Paul after Richard was safely out of the way,' I said. 'I heard him tell them they'd be free of him once the job was over.'

'Was she really Paul Véry's wife?' asked Louise.

'Indubitably. They were married in 1942, then he was posted missing the following year. She picked up with Kramer in the autumn of 1945. When Paul Véry turned up again he appears to have accepted the situation (to some extent, I imagine, under pressure), and stayed on to work for Kramer. He seems to have taken a pretty – what shall I say? – liberal view of his wife's activities. When Kramer saw Byron and Baxter at the Lemaire sale, and decided they would have to be eliminated, he picked Paul Véry for the job.'

'Greatly helped,' said Richard bitterly, 'by the fool Byron, who, seeing Loraine at the sale, began to show signs of interest that made it easy for the precious trio to commit the first murder.'

'If you hadn't "married" her and taken her to Deepings,' said Marsden, 'they'd have managed some other way.'

'I dare say,' said Richard, 'but you can't say I didn't help. At least it's a comfort of a sort to know she was never legally my wife.... It was Paul Véry, of course, who killed Tony and knocked David out. It was Paul Véry who tried to ram my car. And when the attempt at double murder failed, they took David to France. I doubt if they had a plan worked out at all, but David was an obvious trump card.'

'I don't quite see why, you know,' said David.

'Don't you?' said his father. 'Loraine knew very well that I'd never willingly see her again. Kramer wanted me over here, but if she'd tried to get me to see her I'd either have ignored her or put my lawyers on to it. But you' – he flicked David's cheek with a casual finger – 'I can't afford to let you go. You're a rebate on my income-tax.'

'Talking of income-tax,' I said, 'your insurance company—'

'Oh God, yes,' said Richard. 'Two cars in four months! I know. I'm going to have a gay time explaining when I get back. . . . Anyway, that's the story. You know the rest. They planned to get me down here, where there were better facilities for disposing of me, and, heaven knows, their plan might have worked, if they hadn't left two important things out of their reckoning.'

'What two things?' demanded David.

Richard said soberly, looking at Marsden: 'The integrity and human-kindness of the English police, for one. I shan't forget it, Marsden, and neither will David. I'll write to Brooke tonight. We're deeply in your debt.'

Marsden looked acutely uncomfortable, and muttered something, then turned and began to tap out his pipe on the balustrade between the table and the sea.

'And the second thing?' asked David.

Richard smiled at me suddenly, so that my heart turned a silly somersault in my breast.

'The spanner in the works,' he said, and laughed.

'The what, Daddy?'

'Chance, my dear David, in the shape of Charity.'

David looked from him to me, and back again. 'Charity?'

I said: 'It's my name, David,' and blushed like a fool.

'Oh, I see.' His bright gaze rested on me for a speculative moment, then returned to his father, but all he said was: 'I thought you meant that stuff in the Bible about *Charity suffereth long and is kind.*'

'That, too,' said Richard, and laughed again.

'Your father exaggerates,' I told David. 'The only thing I did of real practical value was to find Rommel, and then I nearly killed him.'

'Your idea of practical value,' said Richard drily, 'is a distorted one, to say the least. That ill-favoured mongrel—'

David shot up in his chair. '*Mongrel?* He's not! Anyone can *see* he's well-bred! Can't they?' He appealed to Marsden, who grinned.

'Let us say that a good deal has gone into his breeding,' he said tactfully. 'I'm sure he's highly intelligent.'

'Of course he is!' David was emphatic. 'Look how he found me! Why, he's practically *police-trained!*'

Richard said dampingly: 'I suppose that means you've trained him to sleep on your bed?'

'The police,' began Marsden, 'don't as a rule—'

But David hadn't heard him. He was eyeing his father with some caution. 'As a matter of fact, I have.'

'And a very good habit too,' I said promptly. 'He can keep the – the mice away.'

Across David's look of gratification, Richard's eyes met mine.

'I – see,' he said. 'Collusion. Conspiracy against me in my own home. I seem to be letting myself in for—'

'*Daddy!*' David's eyes were round. He looked at me. 'Mrs. Selborne! Are you going to marry Daddy?'

'Yes,' I said.

David got to his feet. 'I'm terribly glad,' he said simply, and kissed me.

Above the general babel of question and congratulation the smooth voice of the *maître d'hôtel* insinuated at Richard's ear: 'Champagne for m'sieur?' They didn't miss much at the Hôtel de la Garde. Then the magnificent bottle arrived, all gold-foil and sparkling ice and bowing attendant acolytes, and Marsden, on his feet, was making a very creditable speech, unaware of – or unconcerned by – the broad smiles and palpable interest of the people at the other tables. Behind him the blue sea danced, diamond-spangled, and in his uplifted glass a million bubbles winked and glittered.

'. . . The only correct ending,' he was saying, 'to adventure. *So they lived happily ever after*. I give you the toast: Richard and Charity!'

He sat down among quite a small storm of clapping and general laughter.

'When's it to be?' he asked me.

Richard took a folded paper from his breast-pocket. 'In ten days' time,' he said. 'That's the very soonest you can do it in France. I made enquiries this morning when I got the licence.'

I heard Louise murmur: 'Dictatorial . . .' just beside me, and then David demanded:

'But when did all this *happen*?'

Richard was laughing at me across his glass of champagne, with devils in his eyes. I said: 'Actually, it hasn't happened. I mean, he hasn't asked me to marry him at all.'

'Hasn't *asked* you—'

Richard said: 'Will you marry me?'

'Yes,' I said.

David grabbed his glass again. 'Well, then,' he said, in briskly practical tones, 'that's settled, isn't it? All in front of witnesses, too. He'll not find that easy to wriggle out of, Mrs. Selborne. I'll see he gets held to it. And now may I have some more champagne?'

'It seems to me,' I said austerely, 'that you've had quite enough.'

He grinned at me. 'It was a very nice proposal,' he admitted. 'No words wasted, no beating about the bush. . . .' He reached for the champagne-bottle.

'No!' said Richard firmly, as I moved the bottle beyond David's reach.

'Collusion!' said David bitterly. 'Conspiracy! I can see—'

'I've had a lot of practice,' I told him, 'and I'm a very managing woman.'

Richard was grinning. 'Did Johnny always do as he was told?'

'Always,' I said composedly.

Louise laughed. 'Some day,' she told him, 'I'll tell you the truth about that.' She got to her feet, and smiled at the others, who had risen too.

'Well, thank you for my lunch and the champagne. Don't let me keep you from the police and the other joys in store. Will they want David? No? Then perhaps he could spend the afternoon with me?'

'Thanks very much,' said Richard. 'If the dog'll be in the way—'

'On the contrary,' said Louise, 'I wouldn't dream of leaving the dog behind. What do you suggest I do with the pair of them?'

Richard's hand slipped under my arm as we all turned to make our way out of the restaurant.

'Most people,' he said gravely, 'begin their sightseeing in Marseilles with a trip to the Château d'If.'

CHAPTER THIRTY

EPILOGUE

Upon the Islands Fortunate we fall,
Not faint Canaries but Ambrosiall.

DONNE

It was late the following afternoon, and the sun slanted a deepening gold through the boughs that arched the avenue where Richard and I were walking. The columns of the planes were warm in their delicate arabesques of silver and isabel and soft russet-red. Over our heads the leaves, deepening already towards the sere time, danced a little to the straying wind, and then hung still.

'At least,' said Richard, 'we have nine days to get to know each other in before it's too late. Are you sure you don't mind being rushed into it like this?'

'Quite sure.'

'The least I can do is to leave it to you to choose a place for a honeymoon.'

I said: 'The Isles of Gold.'

'Where's that? Ultima Thule?'

'Not quite. It's another name for Porquerolles. You sail from Hyères.'

'Wonderful. We'll have a fortnight there – and perhaps Corsica, too. The Dexters say David can stay as long as he likes and we can pick him up—'

'Oh, Richard, look!' I cried.

We were passing a shop window, and, backed against a neutral screen of porridge-grey, a single picture on a little easel was standing.

Richard turned and glimpsed it. He stopped.

'Oh,' was all he said, but it was said on a long note of discovery.

The picture was small, but against the flat background of the screen the colours in it glowed like jewels, so placed that they vibrated one against the other, until you could have sworn the boy in the picture smiled. He was standing against a shadowed ground of leaves and rock, very straight, with his dark head high, and a gallant look to him.

'It's David!' I said.

'It *is* David,' said Richard. 'See the sling in his hand? He's just setting off to face Goliath and the Philistines.'

'It's the first time I saw him,' I said, and gazed down at the pictured face, so young, and with that look I remembered so well of the grave acceptance of a burden too heavy for his shoulders. David, alone among his enemies, had faced them with just this same gaiety and temper that was written in the bearing of the young champion of Israel.

'May I have it for a wedding-present?' I asked.

'You certainly may. What a glorious bit of painting! And the man who painted that meant it with every stroke of the brush. Young Israel, up against the enemy ... I wonder—'

He broke off suddenly as he leaned forward to peer at the narrow strip of brass along the base of the frame.

At the look in his face I cried out: 'Richard, what is it?'

'Look for yourself,' he said.

I peered through the plate glass. In tiny letters on the brass I made out the legend:

LE JEUNE DAVID

and below this the name of the artist:

EMMANUEL BERNSTEIN

And so it ended, where it had begun, with the little Jewish painter whose death had been so late, but so amply avenged. And, ten days later, with *The Boy David* carefully boxed in the back of the Riley, my husband and I set our faces to the South, and the Isles of Gold.

TEWART MARY STEWART MARY STEWART MARY
STEWART MARY STEWART MARY STEWART MARY
TEWART MARY STEWART MARY STEWART MARY
STEWART MARY STEWART MARY STEWART MARY
TEWART MARY STEWART MARY STEWART MARY
STEWART MARY STEWART MARY STEWART MARY
TEWART MARY STEWART MARY STEWART MARY
STEWART MARY STEWART MARY STEWART MARY
TEWART MARY STEWART MARY STEWART MARY
STEWART MARY STEWART MARY STEWART MARY
TEWART MARY STEWART MARY STEWART MARY
STEWART MARY STEWART MARY STEWART MARY
TEWART MARY STEWART MARY STEWART MARY
STEWART MARY STEWART MARY STEWART MARY
TEWART MARY STEWART MARY STEWART MARY
STEWART MARY STEWART MARY STEWART MARY
TEWART MARY STEWART MARY STEWART MARY
STEWART MARY STEWART MARY STEWART MARY
TEWART MARY STEWART MARY STEWART MARY
STEWART MARY STEWART MARY STEWART MARY
TEWART MARY STEWART MARY STEWART MARY
STEWART MARY STEWART MARY STEWART MARY
TEWART MARY STEWART MARY STEWART MARY
STEWART MARY STEWART MARY STEWART MARY
TEWART MARY STEWART MARY STEWART MARY
STEWART MARY STEWART MARY STEWART MARY
TEWART MARY STEWART MARY STEWART MARY
STEWART MARY STEWART MARY STEWART MARY
TEWART MARY STEWART MARY STEWART MARY
STEWART MARY STEWART MARY STEWART MARY
TEWART MARY STEWART MARY STEWART MARY
STEWART MARY STEWART MARY STEWART MARY
TEWART MARY STEWART MARY STEWART MARY
STEWART MARY STEWART MARY STEWART MARY
TEWART MARY STEWART MARY STEWART MARY
STEWART MARY STEWART MARY STEWART MARY
TEWART MARY STEWART MARY STEWART MARY
STEWART MARY STEWART MARY STEWART MARY